DEATH'S END

CIXIN LIU is China's leading Science Fiction writer.
He has won the China Galaxy Science Fiction Award
nine times, the Nebula (Xingyun) award twice, and
was the first translated author to win the Hugo award.
Before becoming a writer, he was a computer engineer
in a power plant in Yangquan.

Translator KEN LIU is the winner of the Nebula,
Hugo, Locus, World Fantasy, Sidewise, and Science
Fiction & Fantasy Translation Awards. He is the
author of the epic series The Dandelion Dynasty, as
well as short story collections *The Paper Menagerie*
and *The Hidden Girl*.

BY CIXIN LIU

THE THREE-BODY TRILOGY

The Three-Body Problem

The Dark Forest

Death's End

Ball Lightning

The Supernova Era

Of Ants and Dinosaurs

SHORT STORY COLLECTIONS

The Wandering Earth

Hold Up the Sky

DEATH'S END

CIXIN 刘慈欣 LIU

TRANSLATED BY KEN LIU

HEAD ZEUS

An Ad Astra Book

Originally published as 死神永生 in 2010 by Chongqing Publishing Group in Chongqing, China. First published in the United States of America in 2016 by Tom Doherty Associates LLC, a Tor book

First published in the UK in 2016 by Head of Zeus Ltd
This paperback edition first published in the UK in 2017
by Head of Zeus Ltd

19

A CIP catalogue record for this book is available from the British Library.

ISBN (PB): 9781784971656
ISBN (E): 9781784971625

Typeset by Adrian McLaughlin

Printed and bound in Great Britain by
CPI Group (UK) Ltd, Croydon CR0 4YY

Head of Zeus Ltd
5–8 Hardwick Street
London EC1R 4RG
WWW.HEADOFZEUS.COM

A BRIEF NOTE FROM THE TRANSLATOR

Chinese and Korean names in this text are rendered with surnames first and given names last, in accordance with the customs of these cultures. For example, in the name "Yun Tianming," YUN is the surname and TIANMING is the given name.

CHARACTERS FROM *THE THREE-BODY PROBLEM* AND *THE DARK FOREST*

(Chinese names are written with surname first.)

Ye Wenjie	Physicist whose family was persecuted during the Cultural Revolution. She initiated contact with the Trisolarans and precipitated the Trisolar Crisis.
Yang Dong	Physicist; daughter of Ye Wenjie.
Ding Yi	Theoretical physicist and the first human to make contact with the Trisolaran droplets; Yang Dong's boyfriend.

Zhang Beihai	Officer in the Asian Fleet who hijacked *Natural Selection* during the Doomsday Battle, thus preserving a flicker of hope for humanity during their darkest hour. Possibly one of the first officers to understand the nature of dark battles.
Secretary General Say	UN secretary general during the Trisolar Crisis.
Manuel Rey Diaz	Wallfacer; he proposed the giant hydrogen bomb plan as a defense against the Trisolarans.
Luo Ji	Wallfacer; discoverer of the dark forest theory; creator of dark forest deterrence.

TABLE OF ERAS

Common Era	Present–201X C.E.
Crisis Era	201X–2208
Deterrence Era	2208–2270
Post-Deterrence Era	2270–2272
Broadcast Era	2272–2332
Bunker Era	2333–2400
Galaxy Era	2273–unknown
Black Domain Era for DX3906 System	2687–18906416
Timeline for Universe 647	18906416–...

DEATH'S
END

EXCERPT FROM THE PREFACE TO
A PAST OUTSIDE OF TIME

I suppose this ought to be called *history*; but since all I can rely on is my memory, it lacks the rigor of history.

It's not even accurate to call it the *past*, for the events related in these pages didn't occur in the past, aren't taking place now, and will not happen in the future.

I don't want to record the details. Only a frame, for a history or an account of the past. The details that have been preserved are already abundant. Sealed in floating bottles, they will hopefully reach the new universe and endure there.

So I've written only a frame; someday, the frame may make it easier to fill in all the specifics. Of course, that task won't fall to us. I just hope such a day will come for someone.

I regret that day didn't exist in the past, doesn't exist in the present, and will not exist in the future.

I move the sun to the west, and as the angle of the light shifts, the dewdrops on the seedlings in the field glisten like countless eyes suddenly popping open. I dim the sun so that dusk arrives earlier; then I stare at the silhouette of myself on the distant horizon, in front of the setting sun.

I wave at the silhouette; the silhouette waves back. Looking at the shadow of myself, I feel young again.

This is a lovely time, just right for remembering.

PART I

MAY 1453, C.E.
THE DEATH OF THE MAGICIAN

Pausing to collect himself, Constantine XI pushed away the pile of city-defense maps in front of him, pulled his purple robe tighter, and waited.

His sense of time was very accurate: The tremor came the moment he expected it, a powerful, violent quake that seemed to originate from deep within the earth. The vibrating silver candelabra hummed, and a wisp of dust that had sat on top of the Great Palace for perhaps a thousand years fell down and drifted into the candle flames, where the motes exploded in tiny sparks.

Every three hours—the time it took the Ottomans to reload one of the monstrous bombards designed by the engineer Orban—twelve-hundred-pound stone balls battered the walls of Constantinople. These were the world's strongest walls: first built by Theodosius II during the fifth century, they had been continually reinforced and expanded, and were the main reason that the Byzantine court had survived so many powerful enemies.

But the giant stone balls now gouged openings into the walls with each strike, like the bite of an invisible giant. The emperor could imagine the scene: While the debris from the explosion filled the air, countless soldiers and citizens rushed onto the fresh wound in the walls like a swarm of brave ants under a sky full of dust. They filled in the break with whatever was at hand: bits and pieces taken

from other buildings in the city, flaxen-cloth bags of earth, expensive Arabic carpets.... He could even imagine the cloud of dust, steeped in the light of the setting sun, drifting slowly toward Constantinople like a golden shroud.

During the five weeks the city had been under siege, these tremors had come seven times a day, spaced as regularly as the strokes of some colossal clock. This was the time and rhythm of another world, the time of heathens. Compared to these tremors, the ringing of the double-headed eagle copper clock in the corner that represented the time of Christendom seemed feeble.

The tremors subsided. After a while and with an effort, Emperor Constantine pulled his thoughts back to the reality before him. He gestured to let the guard know that he was ready for his visitor.

Phrantzes, one of the emperor's most-trusted ministers, came in with a slender, frail figure trailing close behind.

"This is Helena." Phrantzes stepped aside, revealing the woman.

The emperor looked at her. The noblewomen of Constantinople tended to favor clothes bedecked with elaborate decorative elements, while the commoners wore plain, shapeless white garments that draped to the ankles. But this Helena seemed a combination of both. Instead of a tunic embroidered with gold thread, she wore a commoner's white dress, but over it she draped a luxurious cloak; however, instead of the purple and red reserved for the nobility, the cloak was dyed yellow. Her face was enchanting and sensual, bringing to mind a flower that would rather rot in adoration than fade in solitude.

A prostitute, probably one who did rather well for herself.

Her body trembled. She kept her eyes lowered, but the emperor noticed that they held a feverish glow, hinting at an excitement and zeal rare for her class.

"You claim the powers of magic?" the emperor asked.

He wanted to conclude this audience as quickly as possible. Phrantzes was usually meticulous. Of the approximately eight thousand soldiers defending Constantinople now, only a small number came from the standing army, and about two thousand

were Genoese mercenaries. Phrantzes had been responsible for recruiting the rest, a few at a time, from the city's inhabitants. Though the emperor wasn't particularly interested in his latest idea, the capable minister's standing demanded that he at least be given a chance.

"Yes, I can kill the sultan." Helena's quiet voice quivered like silk strands in a breeze.

Five days earlier, standing in front of the palace, Helena had demanded to see the emperor. When guards tried to push her away, she presented a small package that stunned the guards. They weren't sure what she was showing them, but they knew it was not something she should have possessed. Instead of being brought to the emperor, she had been held and interrogated about how she had acquired the item. Her confession had been confirmed, and she was then brought to Phrantzes.

Phrantzes now took out the small bundle, unwrapped the flax cloth, and placed the contents on the emperor's desk.

The emperor's gaze was as stupefied as those of the soldiers five days ago. But unlike them, he knew immediately what he was looking at.

More than nine centuries earlier, during the reign of Justinian the Great, master craftsmen had cast two chalices out of pure gold, studded with gems and glowing with a beauty that seized the soul. The two chalices were identical save for the arrangement and shapes of the gems. One of the two was kept by successive Byzantine emperors, and the other one had been sealed along with other treasures into a secret chamber in the foundation of Hagia Sophia in 537 C.E., when the great church was rebuilt.

The glow of the chalice in the Great Palace that the emperor was familiar with had dulled with the passage of time, but the one in front of him now looked so bright it could have been cast only yesterday.

No one had believed Helena's confession at first, thinking that she had probably stolen the chalice from one of her rich patrons. Although many knew of the secret chamber under the great church,

few knew its exact location. Moreover, the secret chamber was nestled among the giant stones deep in the foundation, and there were no doors or tunnels leading to it. It should have been impossible to enter the chamber without a massive engineering effort.

Four days ago, however, the emperor had ordered the precious artifacts of the city collected in case of Constantinople's fall. It was really a desperate measure, as he understood very well that the Turks had cut off all routes leading to the city, and there would be nowhere for him to escape with the treasures.

It had taken thirty laborers working nonstop for three days to enter the secret chamber, whose walls were formed from stones as massive as those in the Great Pyramid of Cheops. In the middle of the chamber was a massive stone sarcophagus sealed shut with twelve thick, crisscrossing iron hoops. It took most of another day to saw through the iron hoops before five laborers, under the gaze of many guards, finally managed to lift the cover off the sarcophagus.

The onlookers were amazed not by the treasures and sacred objects that had been hidden for almost a thousand years, but by the bunch of grapes placed on top, still fresh.

Helena had claimed to have left a bunch of grapes in the sarcophagus five days ago, and as she had declared, half of the grapes had been eaten, with only seven left on the stem.

The workers compared the treasures they recovered against the listing found on the inside of the cover of the stone sarcophagus; everything was accounted for except the chalice. If the chalice hadn't already been found with Helena, and without her testimony, everyone present would have been put to death even if they all swore that the secret chamber and the sarcophagus appeared intact.

"How did you retrieve this?" the emperor asked.

Helena's body trembled even harder. Apparently, her magic did not make her feel safe. She stared at the emperor with terror-filled eyes, and squeezed out an answer. "Those places ... I see them ... I see them as ..." She struggled to find the right word. "... open.... "

"Can you demonstrate for me? Take out something from inside a sealed container."

8

Helena shook her head, dread stilling her tongue; she looked to Phrantzes for help.

Phrantzes spoke up. "She says that she can only practice her magic in a specific place. But she can't reveal the location, and no one must be allowed to follow her. Otherwise the magic will lose its power forever."

Helena nodded vigorously.

"In Europe, you would already have been burned at a stake," the emperor said.

Helena collapsed to the ground and hugged herself. Her small figure looked like a child's.

"Do you know how to kill?" the emperor pressed.

But Helena only trembled. After repeated urgings from Phrantzes, she finally nodded.

"Fine," the emperor said to Phrantzes. "Test her."

Phrantzes led Helena down a long flight of stairs. Torches in sconces along the way cast dim circles of light. Under every torch stood two armed soldiers whose armor reflected the light onto the walls in lively, flickering patterns.

Finally, the two arrived at a dark cellar. Helena pulled her cloak tighter around her. This was where the palace stored ice for use during the summers.

The cellar held no ice now. A prisoner squatted under the torch in the corner; an Anatolian officer, based on the way he was dressed. His fierce eyes, like a wolf's, glared at Phrantzes and Helena through the iron bars.

"You see him?" Phrantzes asked.

Helena nodded.

Phrantzes handed her a sheepskin bag. "You may leave now. Return with his head before dawn."

Helena took out a scimitar from the bag, glinting in the torchlight like a crescent moon. She handed it back to Phrantzes. "I don't need this."

9

Then she ascended the stairs, her footfalls making no sound. As she passed through the circles of light cast by the torches, she seemed to change shape—sometimes a woman, sometimes a cat—until her figure disappeared.

Phrantzes turned to one of the officers: "Increase the security around here." He pointed to the prisoner. "Keep him under constant observation."

After the officer left, Phrantzes waved his hand, and a man emerged from the darkness, draped in the black robes of a friar.

"Don't get too close," Phrantzes said. "It's all right if you lose her, but do not under any circumstances let her discover you."

The friar nodded and ascended the stairs as silently as Helena had.

That night, Constantine slept no better than he had since the siege of Constantinople began: The jolts from the heavy bombards woke him each time, just as he was about to fall asleep. Before dawn, he went into his study, where he found Phrantzes waiting for him.

He had already forgotten about the witch. Unlike his father, Manuel II, and elder brother, John VIII, Constantine was practical and understood that those who put all their faith in miracles tended to meet with untimely ends.

Phrantzes beckoned at the door, and Helena entered noiselessly. She looked as frightened as the last time the emperor had seen her, and her hand shook as she lifted the sheepskin bag.

As soon as Constantine saw the bag, he knew that he had wasted his time. The bag was flat, and no blood seeped from it. It clearly didn't contain the prisoner's head.

But the expression on Phrantzes's face wasn't one of disappointment. Rather, he looked distracted, confused, as though he was walking while dreaming.

"She hasn't retrieved what we wanted, has she?" the emperor asked.

Phrantzes took the bag from Helena, placed it on the emperor's

desk, and opened it. He stared at the emperor as though he was looking at a ghost. "She almost did."

The emperor looked inside the bag. Something grayish and soft was nestled on the bottom, like old mutton suet. Phrantzes moved the candelabra closer.

"It's the brain of that Anatolian."

"She cut open his skull?" Constantine glanced at Helena. She trembled in her cloak like a frightened mouse.

"No, the corpse of the prisoner appeared intact. I had twenty men observe him, five men per watch, keeping him in their sight from different angles. The guards at the cellar door were also on extra alert; not even a mosquito could have entered the space." Phrantzes paused, as though stricken by his own memories.

The emperor nodded at him to continue.

"Two hours after she left, the prisoner went into sudden convulsions and fell down dead. Among the observers at the scene were an experienced Greek doctor and veterans of many battles— none could recall anyone dying in this particular manner. An hour later, she returned and showed them this bag. The Greek doctor then cut open the corpse's skull. It was empty."

Constantine observed the brain in the bag: It was complete, showing no signs of damage. The fragile organ must have been retrieved with great care. Constantine focused on Helena's fingers grasping the lapels of her cloak. He imagined the slender fingers reaching forward, picking a mushroom nestled in the grass, picking a fresh blossom from the tip of a branch....

The emperor lifted his gaze up toward the wall, as though observing something rising over the horizon beyond. The palace shook with another pounding from the gigantic bombards, but, for the first time, the emperor did not feel the tremors.

If there really are miracles, now is the time for them to manifest.

Constantinople was in desperate straits, but not all hope was lost. After five weeks of bloody warfare, the enemy had also suffered heavy casualties. In some places, the Turkish bodies were piled as high as the walls, and the attackers were as exhausted as the

defenders. A few days ago, a brave fleet from Genoa had broken through the blockade of the Bosporus and entered the Golden Horn, bringing precious supplies and aid. Everyone believed that they were the vanguard of more support from the rest of Christendom.

Morale was low among the Ottoman camps. Most commanders secretly wanted to accept the truce terms offered by the Byzantine court and retreat. The only reason the Ottomans had not yet retreated was because of a single man.

He was fluent in Latin, knowledgeable about the arts and sciences, skilled in warfare; he had not hesitated to drown his brother in a bathtub to secure his own path to the throne; he had decapitated a beautiful slave girl in front of his troops to demonstrate that he could not be tempted by women.... Sultan Mehmed II was the axle around which the wheels of the Ottoman war machine revolved. If he broke, the machine would fall apart.

Perhaps a miracle truly has *manifested.*

"Why do you want to do this?" the emperor asked. He continued to stare at the wall.

"I want to be remembered." Helena had been waiting for this question.

Constantine nodded. Money or treasure held no allure for this woman; there was no vault or lock that could keep her from what she desired. Still, a prostitute wanted honor.

"You are a descendant of the Crusaders?"

"Yes." She paused, and carefully added, "Not the fourth."

The emperor placed his hand on Helena's head, and she knelt.

"Go, child. If you kill Mehmed II, you will be the savior of Constantinople, and be remembered as a saint forever. A holy woman of the Holy City."

At dusk, Phrantzes led Helena onto the walls near the Gate of St. Romanus.

On the ground near the walls, the sands had turned black with

the blood of the dying; corpses were strewn all over as though they had rained down from the sky. A bit farther away, white smoke from the giant cannons drifted over the battlefield, incongruously light and graceful. Beyond them, the Ottoman camps spread as far as the eye could see, banners as dense as a forest flapping in the moist sea breeze under the lead-gray sky.

In the other direction, Ottoman warships covered the Bosporus like a field of black iron nails securing the blue surface of the sea.

Helena closed her eyes. *This is my battlefield; this is my war.*

Legends from her childhood, stories of her ancestors recounted by her father, surfaced in her mind: In Europe, on the other side of the Bosporus, there was a village in Provence. One day, a cloud descended on the village, and an army of children walked out of the cloud, red crosses glowing brightly from their armor and an angel leading them. Her ancestor, a man from the village, had answered their call and sailed across the Mediterranean to fight for God in the Holy Land. He had risen through the ranks and become a Templar Knight. Later, he had come to Constantinople and met a beautiful woman, a holy warrior; they had fallen in love and given birth to this glorious family....

Later, when she was older, she had found out the truth. The basic frame of the story was true: Her ancestor had indeed been a member of the Children's Crusade. It was right after the plague had swept through the villages, and he had joined in the hope of filling his belly. When the man had gotten off the boat, he found himself in Egypt, where he and more than ten thousand other children were sold as slaves. After many years of bondage, he escaped and drifted to Constantinople, where he did indeed meet a woman warrior, a holy knight. However, her fate wasn't much better than his. The Byzantine Empire had been hoping for the elite troops of Christendom to fight off the infidels. Instead, they received an army of frail women as poor as beggars. The Byzantine court refused to supply these "holy warriors," and the women knights became prostitutes.

For more than a hundred years, Helena's "glorious" family had

barely eked out a living. By her father's time, the family's poverty had grown even more acute. A hungry Helena picked up the trade practiced by her own illustrious ancestor, but when her father found out, he had beaten her, telling her that he would kill her if he ever caught her again ... unless she took her clients back home so that he could negotiate a better price and keep the money "for her."

Helena left home and began to live and ply her trade on her own. She had been to Jerusalem and Trabzon, and even visited Venice. She was no longer hungry, and she dressed in beautiful clothes. But she knew that she was no different from a blade of grass growing in the mud by the road: indistinguishable from the muck, as travelers trampled over her.

And then, God granted Helena a miracle.

Even then, she didn't model herself after Joan of Arc, another woman who had been divinely inspired. What had the Maid of Orléans received from God? Only a sword. But God had given Helena something that would make her into the holiest woman besides Mary....

"Look, that's the camp of *el-Fātiḥ*, the Conqueror." Phrantzes pointed away from the Gate of St. Romanus.

Helena glanced over and nodded.

Phrantzes handed her another sheepskin bag. "Inside are three portraits of him from different angles and in different clothing. I've also given you a knife—you'll need it. We need his entire head, not just the brain. It's best if you wait until after nightfall. He won't be in his tent during the day."

Helena accepted the bag. "You remember my warning."

"Of course."

Don't follow me. Don't enter the place where I must go. Otherwise the magic will stop working, forever.

The spy who had followed her last time, in the guise of a friar, had told Phrantzes that Helena had been very careful, turning and looping back on her own path multiple times until she arrived in the Blachernae quarter, the part of the city where bombardment from the Turkish cannons was heaviest.

14

The spy had watched as Helena entered the ruins of a minaret that had once been part of a mosque. When Constantine had given the order to destroy the mosques in the city, this particular tower had been left alone because, during the last plague, a few diseased men had run inside and died, and no one wanted to get too close. After the siege began, a stray cannonball had blown away the top half of the minaret.

Following Phrantzes's admonition, the spy had not entered the minaret. But he had questioned two soldiers who had entered it before it had been struck by the stray missile. They told the spy that they had intended to set up a watch station on top of the structure but gave up after realizing it wasn't tall enough. They told the spy that there was nothing inside except a few bodies that had rotted until they were practically skeletons.

This time, Phrantzes didn't send anyone to follow Helena. He watched as she made her way through the soldiers thronging the top of the walls. Among the dirt-and-blood-encrusted armor of the soldiers, her bright cloak stood out. But the exhausted soldiers paid her no attention. She descended from the walls, and, without making an obvious effort to throw off anyone who might be following her, headed for the Blachernae quarter.

Night fell.

Constantine stared at the drying water stain on the floor, a metaphor for his vanishing hope.

The stain had been left by a dozen spies. Last Monday, dressed in the uniforms and turbans of the Ottoman forces, they had sneaked through the blockade in a tiny sailboat to welcome the European fleet that was supposed to be on its way to relieve the siege of Constantinople. But all they saw was the empty Aegean Sea, without even a shadow of the rumored fleet. The disappointed spies had carried out their duty and made their way back through the blockade to bring the emperor the terrible news.

Constantine finally understood that the promised aid from

Europe was nothing more than a dream. The kings of Christendom had coldly decided to abandon Constantinople to the infidels, after this holy city had withstood the tides of Mohammedans for so many centuries.

Anxious cries from outside filled his ears. A guard came and reported a lunar eclipse: a terrible portent. It was said that Constantinople would never fall as long as the moon shone.

Through the narrow slit of the window, Constantine observed the moon disappearing in shadow, as though entering a grave in the sky. He knew, without knowing exactly why, that Helena would never return, and he would never see the head of his enemy.

A day passed; then a night. There was no news of Helena.

Phrantzes and his men stopped in front of the minaret in the Blachernae quarter and dismounted from their horses.

Everyone was stunned.

Under the cold, white light of the newly risen moon, the minaret appeared complete: Its sharp tip pointed into the starry sky.

The spy swore that the last time he had been here, the minaret's top was missing. Several other officers and soldiers, familiar with the area, corroborated his testimony.

But Phrantzes gazed at the spy in cold fury. No matter how many witnesses testified to the contrary, he must certainly be lying: The complete minaret was ironclad proof. However, Phrantzes had no time to mete out punishment; now that the city was about to fall, no one would escape the punishment of the Conqueror.

A soldier off to the side knew that the missing top of the minaret hadn't been destroyed by a cannonball. He had found the top half of the minaret missing one morning two weeks ago. There had been no cannon fire the previous night, and he had recalled that there was no debris on the ground around the minaret. The two soldiers who had been with him that morning had both died in battle. However, seeing the look on Phrantzes's face, he decided to keep quiet about it.

Phrantzes and his men entered the bottom of the minaret. Even the spy who Phrantzes was sure had lied came along. They saw remnants of the corpses of plague victims that had been scattered around the ruin by feral dogs, but there were no signs of anyone living.

They ascended the stairs. In the flickering torchlight on the second story, they saw Helena curled under a window. She appeared to be asleep, but her half-closed eyes reflected the light from the torches. Her clothes were torn and dirty and her hair unkempt; a few bloody scratch marks crossed her face, perhaps self-inflicted.

Phrantzes looked around. This was the top of the minaret, an empty, cone-shaped space. He noted the thick layer of dust covering everything, but there were few marks in the dust, as though Helena, like them, had arrived only recently.

She awoke, and, scrabbling at the walls with her hands, stood up. Moonlight falling through the window turned the messy hair around her face into a silvery halo. She stared, wide-eyed, and seemed to return to the present only with effort. But she then closed her eyes again, as though trying to linger inside a dream.

"What are you doing here?!" Phrantzes shouted at her.

"I ... I can't go *there*."

"Where?"

With her eyes still half closed, as if to savor her memory like a child holding on to a favorite toy that she would not give up, she answered, "There's so much space there. So comfortable ..." She opened her eyes and looked around in terror. "But here, it's like the inside of a coffin, whether I'm inside the minaret or outside. I have to go *there*!"

"What about your mission?"

"Wait!" Helena crossed herself. "Wait!"

Phrantzes pointed outside the window. "It's too late for waiting."

Waves of noise cascaded over them. If one listened carefully, two sources could be distinguished.

One source was from outside the city. Mehmed II had decided to launch the final assault on Constantinople tomorrow. At this

moment, the young sultan was riding through the Ottoman camps, promising his soldiers that all he wanted was Constantinople itself—the treasure and women of Constantinople would belong to his army, and after the fall of the city, the soldiers would have three days to loot everything they desired. All the soldiers cheered at the sultan's promise, and the sound of trumpets and drums added to their glee. This joyous din, mixed with the smoke and sparks rising from fires in front of the camps, covered Constantinople like an oppressive tide of death.

The noise coming from inside Constantinople, on the other hand, was lugubrious and subdued. All the citizens had paraded through the city and gathered at Hagia Sophia to attend a final Mass. This was a scene that had never occurred and would never occur again in the history of Christianity: Accompanied by solemn hymns, under the light of dim candles, the Byzantine emperor, the Patriarch of Constantinople, Orthodox Christians of the East and Catholics from Italy, soldiers in full armor, merchants and sailors from Venice and Genoa, and multitudes of ordinary citizens all gathered in front of God to prepare for the final battle of their lives.

Phrantzes knew that his plan had failed. Perhaps Helena was nothing but a skilled fraud, and she possessed no magic at all— he preferred that possibility by far. But there was another, more dangerous alternative: She did possess magic, and she had already gone to Mehmed II, who had given her a new mission.

After all, what could the Byzantine Empire, teetering on the brink of ruin, offer her? The emperor's promise to make her into a saint was unlikely to be fulfilled: Neither Constantinople nor Rome was likely to declare a witch and a whore a saint. Indeed, she had likely returned with two new targets in mind: Constantine, and himself.

Hadn't Orban, the Hungarian engineer, already been an example of this? He had come to Constantine first with plans for his giant cannons, but the emperor had no money to pay his salary, let alone finance the construction of such monstrous engines. He had then gone to Mehmed II, and the daily bombardments had served as a constant reminder of his betrayal.

Phrantzes looked over at the spy, who immediately unsheathed his sword and stabbed at Helena's chest. The sword pierced her body and got stuck in a crack in the wall behind her. The spy tried to pull the sword out, but it wouldn't budge. Helena rested her hands on the sword's hilt. The spy let go of the weapon, unwilling to touch her hands.

Phrantzes left with his men.

Throughout her execution, Helena never made any noise. Gradually, her head drooped, and the silvery halo formed by her tresses fell away from the beam of moonlight and faded into darkness. The moon's glow lit a small patch of ground in the dark interior of the minaret, where a stream of blood flowed like a slender, black snake.

In the moments that preceded the great battle, noises from both inside and outside the city stopped. The Eastern Roman Empire welcomed its last dawn on this Earth, at the intersection of Europe and Asia, of land and sea.

On the second story of the minaret, the woman magician died, pinned to the wall. She was perhaps the only real magician in the entire history of the human race. Unfortunately, ten hours earlier, the age of magic, brief as it was, had also come to an end.

The age of magic began at four o'clock on the afternoon of May 3, 1453, when the high-dimensional fragment first intersected with the Earth. It ended at nine o'clock on the evening of May 28, 1453, when the fragment left the Earth behind. After twenty-five days and five hours, the world returned to its normal orbit.

On the evening of May 29, Constantinople fell.

As the bloody slaughter of the day was coming to its inevitable end, Constantine, faced with the swarming Ottoman masses, shouted, "The city is fallen and I am still alive." Then he tore off his imperial robe and unsheathed his sword to meet the oncoming hordes. His silvery armor glinted for a moment like a piece of metallic foil tossed into a tub of dark red sulfuric acid, and then vanished.

The historical significance of the fall of Constantinople would not be apparent for many years. For most, the obvious association

was that it marked the final gasp of the Roman Empire. Byzantium was a thousand-year rut behind the wheels of Ancient Rome, and though it enjoyed splendor for a time, it finally evaporated like a water stain under the bright sun. Once, ancient Romans had whistled in their grand, magnificent baths, thinking that their empire, like the granite that made up the walls of the pools in which they floated, would last forever.

No banquet was eternal. Everything had an end. Everything.

CRISIS ERA, YEAR 1
THE OPTION FOR LIFE

Yang Dong wanted to save herself, but she knew there was little hope.

She stood on the balcony of the control center's top floor, surveying the stopped particle accelerator. From her perch, she could take in the entire twenty-kilometer circumference of the collider. Contrary to usual practice, the ring for the collider wasn't an underground tunnel, but enclosed within an aboveground concrete tube. The facility looked like a giant full stop mark in the setting sun.[1]

What sentence does it end? Hopefully only the end of physics.

Once, Yang Dong had held a basic belief: Life and the world were perhaps ugly, but at the limits of the micro and macro scales, everything was harmonious and beautiful. The world of our everyday life was only froth floating on the perfect ocean of deep reality. But now, it appeared that the everyday world was a beautiful shell: The micro realities it enclosed and the macro realities that enclosed it were far more ugly and chaotic than the shell itself.

Too frightening.

It would have been better if she could just stop thinking about such things. She could choose a career that had nothing to do with

1 *Translator's Note:* The Chinese full stop punctuation mark looks like this: ◦

physics, get married, have children, and live a peaceful, contented life like countless others. Of course, for her, such a life would be only half a life.

Something else also bothered Yang Dong: her mother, Ye Wenjie. By accident, she'd discovered on her mother's computer some heavily encrypted messages that she had received. This aroused an intense curiosity in Yang.

Like many elderly people, Yang's mother wasn't familiar with the details of the web and her own computer, so she had only deleted the decrypted documents instead of digitally shredding them. She didn't realize that even if she had reformatted the hard drive, the data would still have been easily recoverable.

For the first time in her life, Yang Dong kept a secret from her mother, and recovered the information in the deleted documents. It took her several days to read through the recovered information, during which she learned a shocking amount about the world of Trisolaris and the secret shared by the extraterrestrials and her mother.

Yang Dong was utterly stunned. The mother she had depended on for most of her life turned out to be someone she didn't know at all, someone she couldn't even have believed existed in this world. She didn't dare to confront her mother, never would, because the moment she asked about it, her mother's transformation in her mind would be complete, irrevocable. It was better to pretend that her mother was still the person she had always known and continue life as before. Of course, for Yang, such a life would be only half a life.

Was it really so bad to live only half a life? As far as she could see, a considerable number of the people around her lived only half lives. As long as one was good at forgetting and adjusting, half a life could be lived in contentment, even happiness.

But between the end of physics and her mother's secret, Yang had lost two such half lives, which added up to a whole life. What did she have left?

Yang Dong leaned against the banister and stared at the abyss beneath her, terrified as well as enticed. She felt the banister shake

as it bore more of her weight, and she stepped back as though shocked by electricity. She dared not stay here any longer. She turned to walk back into the terminal room.

This was where the center kept the terminals for the super-computer used to analyze the data generated by the collider. A few days ago, all of the terminals had been shut down, but now a few were lit. This gave Yang Dong a bit of comfort, but she knew that they no longer had anything to do with the particle accelerator—other projects had taken over the supercomputer.

There was only one young man in the room, who stood up as Yang Dong came in. He wore glasses with thick, bright green frames, a distinct look. Yang explained that she was here only to retrieve a few personal items, but after Green Glasses heard her name, he became enthusiastic and explained the program running on the terminals to her.

It was a mathematical model of the Earth. Unlike similar projects in the past, this model combined factors from biology, geology, astronomy, atmospheric and oceanic sciences, and other fields of study to simulate the evolution of the Earth's surface from past to future.

Green Glasses directed her attention to a few large-screen displays. These did not show scrolling columns of numbers or crawling curves on a chart; instead, they showed bright, colorful pictures, as though one were viewing the continents and oceans from high above. Green Glasses manipulated the mouse and zoomed in on a few places to show close-up views of a river or a copse of trees.

Yang Dong felt the breath of nature seeping into this place that had once been dominated by abstract numbers and theories. She felt as if she were being released from confinement.

After the explanation from Green Glasses, Yang Dong retrieved her things, politely said good-bye, and turned to leave. She could feel Green Glasses staring at her back, but she was used to men behaving this way, so instead of being annoyed, she felt comforted, as if by sunlight in winter. She was seized by a sudden desire to communicate with others.

She turned to face Green Glasses. "Do you believe in God?"

Yang Dong was shocked by her own question. But considering the model displayed on the terminals, the question wasn't entirely out of place.

Green Glasses was similarly stunned. After a while, he managed to close his mouth and ask, carefully, "What kind of 'God' do you mean?"

"Just God." That overwhelming sensation of exhaustion had returned. She had no patience to explain more.

"I don't."

Yang pointed to the large screens. "But the physical parameters governing the existence of life are utterly unforgiving. Take liquid water as an example: It can exist only within a narrow range of temperatures. Viewing the universe as a whole, this becomes even more apparent: If the parameters of the big bang had been different by even one million billionth, we would have no heavy elements and thus no life. Isn't this clear evidence for intelligent design?"

Green Glasses shook his head. "I don't know enough about the big bang to comment, but you're wrong about the environment on Earth. The Earth gave birth to life, but life also changed the Earth. The current environment on our planet is the result of interactions between the two." He grabbed the mouse and started clicking. "Let's do a simulation."

He brought up a configuration panel on one of the large screens, a window filled with dense fields of numbers. He unchecked a checkbox near the top, and all the fields became grayed out. "Let's uncheck the option for 'life' and observe how the Earth would have evolved without it. I'll adjust the simulation to be coarse-grained so as not to waste too much time in computation."

Yang Dong glanced over at another terminal and saw that the supercomputer was operating at full capacity. A machine like that consumed as much electricity as a small city, but she didn't tell Green Glasses to stop.

A newly formed planet appeared on the large screen. Its surface was still red-hot, like a piece of charcoal fresh out of the furnace.

Time passed at the rate of geological eras, and the planet gradually cooled. The color and patterns on the surface slowly shifted in a hypnotic manner. A few minutes later, an orange planet appeared on the screen, indicating the end of the simulation run.

"The computations were done at the coarsest level; to do it with more precision would require over a month." Green Glasses moved the mouse and zoomed in on the surface of the planet. The view swept over a broad desert, over a cluster of strangely shaped, towering mountain peaks, over a circular depression like an impact crater.

"What are we looking at?" Yang Dong asked.

"Earth. Without life, this is what the surface of the planet would look like now."

"But ... where are the oceans?"

"There are no oceans. No rivers either. The entire surface is dry."

"You're saying that without life, liquid water would not exist on Earth?"

"The reality would probably be even more shocking. Remember, this is only a coarse simulation, but at least you can see how much of an impact life had in the present state of the Earth."

"But—"

"Do you think life is nothing but a fragile, thin, soft shell clinging to the surface of this planet?"

"Isn't it?"

"Only if you neglect the power of time. If a colony of ants continue to move clods the size of grains of rice, they could remove all of Mount Tai in a billion years. As long as you give it enough time, life is stronger than metal and stone, more powerful than typhoons and volcanoes."

"But the formation of mountains depends on geologic forces!"

"Not necessarily. Life may not be able to uplift mountains, but it can change the distribution of mountain ranges. Let's say there are three mountains, two of which are covered by vegetation. The one that is nude would soon be flattened by erosion. 'Soon' here means on the order of millions of years, a blink of an eye in geological terms."

"Then how did the oceans disappear?"

"We'd have to examine the records of the simulation, which would be a lot of work. However, I can give you an educated guess: plants, animals, and bacteria all have had important roles in the present composition of our atmosphere. Without life, the atmosphere would be very different. It's possible that such an atmosphere would not be able to shield the surface of the Earth against solar winds and ultraviolet rays, and the oceans would evaporate. Soon, greenhouse effects would turn the Earth's atmosphere into a copy of Venus's, and then water vapor would be lost to space over time. After several billion years, the Earth would be dry."

Yang Dong said no more as she stared at that yellow husk of a planet.

"Thus, the Earth that we live on now is a home constructed by life for itself. It has nothing to do with God." Green Glasses held out his arms in mock embrace of the large screen, clearly pleased with his own oration.

Yang Dong was not really in the mood to discuss such matters, but the moment Green Glasses unchecked the option for life in the configuration panel, a thought had flashed into her mind.

She asked the next terrifying question: "What about the universe?"

"The universe?"

"If we use a similar mathematical model to simulate the entire universe, and uncheck the option for life at the beginning, what would the resulting universe look like?"

Green Glasses thought for a moment. "It would look the same. When I talked about the effects of life on the environment, it was limited to the Earth. But if we're talking about the universe, life is exceedingly rare, and its impact on the evolution of the universe can be ignored."

Yang Dong held her tongue. She said good-bye again and struggled to put on an appreciative smile. She left the building and stared up at the star-studded night sky.

From her mother's secret documents, she knew that life was not so rare in the universe. In fact, the universe was downright crowded.

How much has the universe been changed by life?

A wave of terror threatened to overwhelm her.

She knew that she could no longer save herself. She tried to stop thinking, to turn her mind into empty darkness, but a new question stubbornly refused to leave her alone: *Is Nature really natural?*

CRISIS ERA, YEAR 4
YUN TIANMING

After Dr. Zhang's regular checkup on Yun Tianming, he left a newspaper with him, saying that since Tianming had been in the hospital for so long, he should be aware of what was happening in the world. There was a TV in Tianming's room, so he was puzzled, wondering if perhaps the doctor had something else in mind.

Tianming read the newspaper and came to the following conclusion: Compared to the time before he was hospitalized, news about Trisolaris and the Earth-Trisolaris Organization (ETO) no longer dominated everything. There were at least some articles that had nothing to do with the crisis. Humanity's tendency to focus on the here and now reasserted itself, and concern for events that would not take place for four centuries gave way to thoughts about life in the present.

This wasn't surprising. He tried to remember what was happening four hundred years ago: China was under the Ming Dynasty, and he thought—he wasn't sure—that Nurhaci had just founded the empire that would end up replacing the Ming, after slaughtering millions. The Dark Ages had just ended in the West; the steam engine wouldn't make its appearance for another hundred-plus years; and, as for electricity, one would have to wait three hundred years. If anyone at the time had worried about life four hundred years later, they'd be a laughingstock.

It was as ridiculous to worry about the future as to lament the past.

As for Tianming himself, based on the way his condition was developing, he wouldn't even need to worry about next year.

But one item of news attracted his attention. It was on the front page:

The Special Session of the Third Standing Committee of the
National People's Congress Passes Euthanasia Law

Tianming was confused. The special legislative session had been called to deal with the Trisolar Crisis, but this law seemed to have nothing to do with the crisis.

Why did Dr. Zhang want me to see this news?

A fit of coughing forced him to put down the newspaper and try to get some sleep.

The next day, the TV also showed some interviews and reports about the euthanasia law, but there didn't seem to be a lot of public interest.

Tianming had trouble sleeping that night: He coughed; he struggled to breathe; he felt weak and nauseous from the chemo. The patient who had the bed next to his sat on the edge of Tianming's bed and held the oxygen tube for him. His surname was Li, and everyone called him "Lao Li," *Old Li.*

Lao Li looked around to be sure that the other two patients who shared the room with them were asleep, and then said, "Tianming, I'm going to leave early."

"You've been discharged?"

"No. It's that law."

Tianming sat up. "But why? Your children are so solicitous and caring—"

"That is exactly why I've decided to do this. If this drags out much longer, they'd have to sell their houses. What for? In the end, there's no cure. I have to be responsible for my children and their children."

29

Lao Li sighed, lightly patted Tianming's arm, and returned to his own bed.

Staring at the shadows cast against the window curtain by swaying trees, Tianming gradually fell asleep. For the first time since his illness, he had a peaceful dream.

He sat on a small origami boat drifting over placid water, oarless. The sky was a misty, dark gray. There was a cool drizzle, but the rain apparently did not reach the surface of the water, which remained as smooth as a mirror. The water, also gray, merged with the sky in every direction. There was no horizon, no shore....

When Tianming awoke in the morning, he was baffled by how, in his dream, he was so certain that *there,* it would always be drizzling, the surface would always be smooth, and the sky always a misty, dark gray.

The hospital was about to conduct the procedure Lao Li had asked for.

It took a great deal of internal discussion before the news outlets settled on the verb "to conduct." "To execute" was clearly inappropriate; "to carry out" sounded wrong as well; "to complete" seemed to suggest that death was already certain, which was not exactly accurate, either.

Dr. Zhang asked Tianming whether he felt strong enough to attend Lao Li's euthanasia ceremony. The doctor hurried to add that since this was the first instance of euthanasia in the city, it would be better to have representatives from various interest groups present, including someone representing other patients. No other meaning was intended.

But Tianming couldn't help feeling that the request did contain some hidden message. Still, since Dr. Zhang had always taken good care of him, he agreed.

Afterwards, he suddenly realized that Dr. Zhang's face and name seemed familiar—did he know the doctor before his hospital-ization?—he couldn't recall exactly how. The fact that he hadn't had

this feeling of recognition earlier was because their interactions had been limited to discussions of his condition and treatment. The way a doctor acted and spoke while performing his job was different from when he spoke as just another person.

None of Lao Li's family members were present for the procedure. He had kept his decision from them and requested that the city's Civil Affairs Bureau—not the hospital—inform his family after the procedure was complete. The new law permitted him to conduct his affairs in this manner.

Many reporters showed up, but most were kept away from the scene. The euthanasia room was adapted from a room in the hospital's emergency department. A one-way mirror made up one of the walls so that observers could see what was happening inside the room, but the patient would not be able to see them.

Tianming pushed his way through the crowd of observers until he was standing in front of the one-way glass window. As soon as he saw the interior of the euthanasia room, Tianming was seized by a wave of fear and disgust. He wanted to throw up.

Whoever was responsible for decorating this room had made quite an effort: There were new, pretty curtains on the windows, fresh flowers in vases, and numerous pink paper hearts on the walls. But their well-intentioned attempt to humanize the situation had achieved the exact opposite: The frightful pall cast by death was mixed with an eerie cheerfulness, as though they were trying to turn a tomb into a nuptial chamber.

Lao Li was lying on the bed in the middle of the room, and he appeared to be at peace. Tianming realized that they had never properly said good-bye, and his heart grew heavy. Two notaries were inside, finishing up the legal part of the procedure. After Lao Li signed the documents, the notaries came out.

Another man went inside to explain the specific steps of the procedure to Lao Li. The man was dressed in a white coat, though it was unclear whether he was really a doctor. The man first pointed to the large screen at the foot of the bed and asked Lao Li whether he could read everything on it. Lao Li nodded. Then the man asked

Lao Li to try to use the mouse next to the bed to click the buttons on the screen, and explained that if he found the operation too difficult, other input methods were available. Lao Li tried the mouse and indicated that it worked fine.

Tianming recalled that Lao Li had once told him that he had never used a computer. When he needed cash, he had to go queue up at the counter at the bank. This must be the first time in Lao Li's life that he used a mouse.

The man in the white coat then told Lao Li that a question was going to be displayed on the screen, and the same question would be asked five times. Each time the question was displayed, there would be six buttons underneath, numbered from zero to five. If Lao Li wished to answer in the affirmative, he had to click on the specific numbered button indicated in the on-screen instructions, which would change randomly each time the question was asked. If Lao Li wished to answer in the negative, he just had to press zero, and the procedure would stop immediately. There would be no "Yes" or "No" button.

The reason for the complicated procedure, the man explained, was to avoid a situation where the patient simply continued to press the same button over and over without thinking about his answers each time.

A nurse went inside and secured a needle into Lao Li's left arm. The tube behind the needle was connected to an automatic injector about the size of a notebook computer. The man in the white coat took out a sealed package, unwrapped layers of protective film, and revealed a small glass vial filled with a yellowish liquid.

Carefully, he filled the injector with the contents of the vial, and left with the nurse.

Only Lao Li was left in the room.

The screen displayed the question, and a soft, gentle female voice read it aloud:

Do you wish to terminate your life? For yes, select 3. For no, select 0.

Lao Li selected 3.

> Do you wish to terminate your life? For yes, select 5. For no, select 0.

Lao Li selected 5.
The process repeated twice more. And then:

> Do you wish to terminate your life? This is your last prompt. For yes, select 4. For no, select 0.

A surge of sorrow made Tianming dizzy, and he almost fainted. Even when his mother died, he didn't feel such extreme pain and anger. He wanted to scream at Lao Li to select 0, to break the glass window, to suffocate that voice.

But Lao Li selected 4.

Noiselessly, the injector came to life. Tianming could see the column of yellowish liquid in the glass tube shorten and then disappear. Lao Li never moved. He closed his eyes and went to sleep.

The crowd around Tianming dissipated, but he remained where he was, his hand pressed against the glass. He wasn't looking at the lifeless body lying within. His eyes were open, but he wasn't looking at all.

"There was no pain." Dr. Zhang's voice was so low that it sounded like the buzzing of a mosquito. Tianming felt a hand land on his left shoulder. "It's a combination of a massive dose of barbitone, muscle relaxant, and potassium chloride. The barbitone takes effect first and puts the patient into a deep sleep, the muscle relaxant stops his breathing, and the potassium chloride stops the heart. The whole process takes no more than twenty, thirty seconds."

After a while, Dr. Zhang's hand left Tianming's shoulder, and Tianming heard his departing footsteps. Tianming never turned around.

He suddenly remembered how he knew the doctor. "Doctor,"

Tianming called out softly. The footsteps stopped. Tianming still didn't turn around. "You know my sister, don't you?"

The reply came after a long pause. "Yes. We were high school classmates. When you were little, I remember seeing you a couple of times."

Mechanically, Tianming left the main building of the hospital. Everything was clear now. Dr. Zhang was working for his sister; his sister wanted him dead. No, wanted him to "conduct the procedure."

Although Tianming often recalled the happy childhood he had shared with his sister, they had grown apart as they grew up. There was no overt conflict between them, and neither had hurt the other. But they had come to see each other as completely different kinds of people, and each felt that the other held them in contempt.

His sister was shrewd but not smart, and she had married a man who was the same way. They were not successful in their careers, and even with grown children, the couple couldn't afford to buy a home. Since her husband's parents had no room for them, the family had ended up living with Tianming's father.

Tianming, on the other hand, was a loner. In career and personal life, he wasn't any more successful than his sister. He had always lived by himself in dormitories that belonged to his employer, and left the responsibility for taking care of his frail father entirely to his sister.

Tianming suddenly understood his sister's thinking. The medical insurance was insufficient to cover the expenses for his hospitalization, and the longer it went on, the bigger the bill grew. Their father had been paying for it out of his life savings, but he had never offered to use that same money to help Tianming's sister and her family to buy a house—a clear case of favoritism. From his sister's point of view, their father was spending money that should be hers. Besides, the money was being wasted on treatments that could only prolong, but not cure, the illness. If Tianming chose euthanasia, his sister's inheritance would be preserved, and he would suffer less.

The sky was filled with misty, gray clouds, just like in his dream. Looking up at this endless grayness, Tianming let out a long sigh.

All right. If you want me to die, I'll die.

He thought of "The Judgment" by Franz Kafka, in which a father curses his son and sentences him to death. The son agrees, as easily as someone agreeing to take out the trash or to shut the door, and leaves the house, runs through the streets onto the bridge, and leaps over the balustrade to his death. Later, Kafka told his biographer that as he wrote the scene, he was thinking of "a violent ejaculation."

Tianming now understood Kafka, the man with the bowler hat and briefcase, the man who walked silently through Prague's dim streets more than a hundred years ago, the man who was as alone as he was.

Someone was waiting for Tianming when he returned to his hospital room: Hu Wen, a college classmate.

Wen was the closest thing to a friend from Tianming's college days, but what they had wasn't friendship, exactly. Wen was one of those people who got along with everyone and who knew everyone's name; but even for him, Tianming was in the most peripheral ring of his social network. They had had no contact since graduation.

Wen didn't bring a bouquet or anything similar; instead, he brought a cardboard box full of canned beverages.

After a brief, awkward exchange of greetings, Wen asked a question that surprised Tianming. "Do you remember the outing back when we were first years? That first time we all went out as a group?"

Of course Tianming remembered. That was the first time Cheng Xin had ever sat next to him, had ever spoken to him.

If she hadn't taken the initiative, he doubted if he ever would have gotten the courage to speak to her for the rest of their four years in college. At the outing, he had sat by himself, staring at the broad expanse of the Miyun Reservoir outside Beijing. She had sat down next to him and begun talking.

While they talked, she tossed pebbles into the reservoir. Their conversation meandered over usual topics for classmates who were becoming acquainted for the first time, but Tianming could still recall every word. Later, Cheng Xin had made a little origami boat out of a sheet of paper and deposited it on the water. A breeze carried the boat away slowly until it turned into a tiny dot in the distance....

That most lovely day of his time in college held a golden glow in his mind. In reality, the weather that day hadn't been ideal: There was a drizzle, and the surface of the reservoir was filled with ripples, and the pebbles they tossed felt wet in the hand. But from that day on, Tianming fell in love with drizzly days, fell in love with the smell of damp ground and wet pebbles, and from time to time he made origami boats and placed them on his nightstand.

With a start, he wondered if the world in his peaceful dream had been born from this memory.

But Wen wanted to talk about what had happened later in the outing—events that did not make much of an impression on Tianming. However, with prompts from Wen, Tianming managed to recall those faded memories.

A few of Cheng Xin's friends had come by and called her away. Wen then sat down next to Tianming.

Don't be too pleased with yourself. She's nice to everyone.

Of course Tianming knew that. But then Wen saw the bottle of mineral water in Tianming's hand and the conversation shifted.

What in the world are you drinking?!

The water in the bottle was a green color, and bits of grass and leaves floated in it.

I crumpled some weeds and added them to the water. It's the most organic drink.

He was in a good mood and so he was more loquacious than usual.

Someday I may start a company to produce this drink. It will surely be popular.

It must taste awful.

36

Do you think cigarettes and liquor really taste that good? Even Coca-Cola probably tasted medicinal the first time you tried it. Anything addictive is like that.

"Buddy, that conversation changed my life!" Wen said. He opened the cardboard box and took out a can. The outside was deep green, and on it was a picture of a grassland. The trademark was "Green Tempest."

Wen pulled the tab and handed the can to Tianming. Tianming took a sip: fragrant, herbal, with a trace of bitterness. He closed his eyes and was back at the shore of the drizzly reservoir, and Cheng Xin was next to him....

"This is a special version. The mass market recipe is sweeter," Wen said.

"Does it sell well?"

"Sells great! The main hurdle now is cost. You might think grass is cheap, but until I can scale up, it's more expensive than fruits or nuts. Also, to make it safe, the ingredients have to be detoxified and processed, a complicated procedure. The prospects are fantastic, though. Lots of investors are interested, and Huiyuan Juice wants to buy my company. Fuck them."

Tianming stared at Wen, not knowing what to say. Wen had graduated as an aerospace engineer, but now he had turned into a beverage entrepreneur. He was someone who did things, who got things done. Life belonged to people like that. But people like Tianming could only watch life pass them by, abandoned and left behind.

"I owe you," Wen said. He handed three credit cards and a slip of paper to Tianming, looked around, leaned in, and whispered, "There's three million yuan in the account. The password is on the note."

"I never applied for a patent or anything like that," Tianming said.

"But it's your idea. Without you, there would be no Green Tempest. If you agree, we'll just call it even, at least legally. But as a matter of our friendship, I'll always owe you."

"You don't owe me anything, legally or otherwise."

"You have to accept it. I know you need money."

Tianming said no more. For him, the sum was astronomical, but he wasn't excited. Money wasn't going to save him.

Still, hope was a stubborn creature. After Hu Wen left, Tianming asked for a consultation with a doctor. He didn't want Dr. Zhang; instead, after much effort, he got the assistant director of the hospital, a famous oncologist.

"If money were no issue, would there be a cure for me?"

The old doctor brought up Tianming's case file on his computer, and after a while, he shook his head.

"The cancer has spread from your lungs throughout your body. Surgery is pointless; all you have are chemo and radiation, conservative techniques. Even with money ...

"Young man, remember the saying: A physician can only cure diseases meant to be cured; the Buddha can only save those meant to be saved."

The last bit of hope died in Tianming, and his heart was at peace. That afternoon, he filled out an application for euthanasia.

He handed the application to his attending physician, Dr. Zhang. Zhang seemed to suffer some internal, moral conflict, and did not meet Tianming's gaze. He did say to Tianming that he might as well stop the chemo sessions; there was no point for him to continue to suffer.

The only matter that Tianming still had to take care of was deciding how to spend the money from Wen. The "right" thing to do would have been to give it to his father, and then let him distribute it to the rest of the family. But that was the same as handing the money to his sister, and Tianming didn't want to do that. He was already going to die, just as she wanted; he didn't feel he owed her any more.

He tried to see if he had any unfulfilled dreams. It would be nice to take a trip around the world on some luxury cruise ship ... but his body wasn't up for it, and he didn't have much time left. That was too bad. He would have liked to lie on a sun-drenched deck

and review his life as he gazed at the hypnotic sea. Or he could step onto the shores of some strange country on a drizzly day, sit next to a little lake and toss wet pebbles onto a surface full of ripples....

Once again, he was thinking of Cheng Xin. These days, he thought of her more and more.

That night, Tianming saw a news report on TV:

> The twelfth session of the UN Planetary Defense Council has adopted Resolution 479, initiating the Stars Our Destination Project. A committee formed from the UN Development Program, the UN Committee on Natural Resources, and UNESCO is authorized to implement the project immediately.
>
> The official Chinese website for the Stars Our Destination Project begins operation this afternoon. According to an official at the UNDP resident representative office in Beijing, the Project will accept bids from individuals and enterprises, but will not consider bids from nongovernmental organizations....

Tianming got up and told his nurse that he wanted to take a walk. But as it was already after lights out, the nurse refused to let him leave. He returned to his dark room, pulled open the curtains, and lifted the window. The new patient in Lao Li's old bed grumbled.

Tianming looked out. The lights of the city cast a haze over the night sky, but it was still possible to pick out a few silvery specks.

He knew what he wanted to do with his money: He was going to buy Cheng Xin a star.

EXCERPT FROM
A PAST OUTSIDE OF TIME
INFANTILISM AT THE START
OF THE CRISIS

Many of the events during the first twenty years of the Crisis Era were incomprehensible to those who came before and those who came after; historians summarized them under the heading of "Crisis Infantilism."

It was commonly thought that Infantilism was a response to an unprecedented threat to the entirety of civilization. That might have been true for individuals, but it was too simple an explanation when applied to humanity as a whole.

The Trisolar Crisis's impact on society was far deeper than people had imagined at first. To give some imperfect analogies: In terms of biology, it was equivalent to the moment when the ancestors of mammals climbed from the ocean onto land; in terms of religion, it was akin to when Adam and Eve were banished from Eden; in terms of history and sociology ... there are no suitable analogies, even imperfect ones. Compared to the Trisolar Crisis, everything heretofore experienced by human civilization was nothing. The Crisis shook the very foundation of culture, politics, religion, and economics. Although the impact reached the deepest core of civilization, its influence manifested most quickly at the

surface. The root cause for Crisis Infantilism may well be found in the interaction between these manifestations and the tremendous inertia of human society's inherent conservatism.

The classic examples of Crisis Infantilism were the Wallfacer Project and the Stars Our Destination Project, both international efforts within the framework of the United Nations—initiatives that soon became incomprehensible to anyone from outside that period. The Wallfacer Project changed history, and its influence so permeated the course of civilization that it must be discussed in another chapter. The same elements that led to the birth of the grand Wallfacer Project simultaneously conceived the Stars Our Destination Project. That project, on the other hand, quickly faded away after launch and was never heard from again.

There were two main motivations for the Stars Our Destination Project: first, to increase the power of the UN at the beginning of the Crisis; second, the genesis and popularity of Escapism.

The Trisolar Crisis was the first time that all of humanity faced a common enemy, and it was only natural that many placed their hopes in the UN. Even conservatives agreed that the UN ought to be completely reformed and given more power and more resources. Radicals and idealists pushed for an Earth Union and for making the UN into a world government.

Smaller countries, in particular, favored elevating the status of the UN because they saw the Crisis as an opportunity to get more technological and economic aid. The great powers, on the other hand, responded to this coolly. In actuality, the great powers all invested heavily in space defense after the Crisis. In part, this was because they realized that contribution to space defense would become the foundation for national strength and political status in future international relations; it was also because they had always wanted to invest in such large-scale basic research, but the domestic demands of their citizenry and constraints imposed by international politics had made such efforts impractical in the past. In a sense, the Trisolar Crisis provided the leaders of the great powers with an opportunity similar to the opportunity given to Kennedy by the

Cold War—similar, but a couple of orders of magnitude greater. While all the great powers were reluctant to place their efforts under the aegis of the United Nations, due to the rising tide of calls for true globalization, they were forced to cede to the UN some symbolic, political commitments that they had no intention of honoring. The common space defense system advocated by the UN, for example, received little substantive support from the great powers.

In the history of the early Crisis Era, UN Secretary General Say was a key figure. She believed that the time for a new UN had arrived and advocated transforming the institution from what was little more than a meeting place for the great powers and an international forum, into an independent political body with the power to genuinely direct the construction of the Solar System's defenses.

To achieve this goal, the UN needed sufficient resources, a requirement that appeared impossible to meet given the realities of international relations. The Stars Our Destination Project was an attempt by Say to acquire such resources for the UN. No matter the results, the very attempt was a testament to her political intelligence and imagination.

The basis for the project lay in the Space Convention, which was a product of pre-Crisis politics. Based on the principles enacted in the Law of the Sea Convention and the Antarctic Treaty, the Space Convention was negotiated and drafted over a long period of time. But the pre-Crisis Space Convention was limited to resources within the Kuiper Belt; the Trisolar Crisis forced the nations of the world to set their sights farther out.

Since humans had not even been able to set foot on Mars, any discussion of outer space was meaningless, at least prior to the expiration date of the Space Convention fifty years after it was drafted. But the great powers viewed the Convention as the perfect venue for political theater and amended it with provisions regarding resources outside the Solar System. The amendment provided that the development of natural resources outside the Kuiper Belt, and other economic activities regarding them, had to take place under the auspices of the United Nations. The amendment went into

excruciating detail to define "natural resources," but, basically, the phrase referred to resources not already occupied by nonhuman civilizations. This treaty also offered the first international law definition for "civilization." Historically, this document was referred to as the Crisis Amendment.

The second motivation for the Stars Our Destination Project was Escapism. At the time, the Escapist movement was still in its early stages, and its consequences were not yet apparent, such that many still considered it a valid choice for humanity in crisis. Under such conditions, other stars, especially stars with their own planets, became valuable.

The initial resolution proposing the Stars Our Destination Project would have the UN auction off the rights to certain stars and their planets. The intended bidders were states, businesses, NGOs, and individuals, and the proceeds from the auction would be used to fund the UN's basic research into a Solar System defense system. Secretary General Say explained that the universe had an abundance of stars. There were more than three hundred thousand stars within one hundred light-years of the Solar System, and more than ten million within one thousand light-years. A conservative estimate suggested that at least one-tenth of these stars had planets. Auctioning off a small proportion of these would not affect the future of space development much.

This unusual UN resolution attracted wide interest and attention. The permanent members of the Planetary Defense Council (PDC) mulled it over, but each decided that adopting it would not lead to adverse consequences in the foreseeable future. On the other hand, voting against it would incur a heavy cost under the prevailing international political climate. Still, debates and compromises followed, and the final version of the resolution that passed was limited to stars more than one hundred light-years away.

The project was halted almost as soon as it began for a simple reason: No one bought the stars. In total, only seventeen stars were auctioned off, and all at the minimum reserve price. The UN earned a grand total of only about forty million dollars.

None of the winning bidders ever revealed themselves. People speculated on why they spent so much money to buy a piece of useless paper—even if the paper was supposed to be a binding legal instrument. Maybe it felt cool to own another world, but what was the point when you could see but not touch it? Indeed, some of the stars were not even visible with the naked eye.

Say never thought of the project as a failure. She claimed that the results were just as she predicted. Fundamentally, the Stars Our Destination Project was a political proclamation by the UN.

The Stars Our Destination Project was quickly forgotten. It was a classic example of the irregular behavior of human society at the beginning of the Crisis.

CRISIS ERA, YEAR 4
YUN TIANMING

The day after making his decision to buy Cheng Xin a star, Yun Tianming called the number listed on the website for the Chinese office of the Stars Our Destination Project.

Then he called Hu Wen to get some basic information about Cheng Xin: contact address, national ID number, and so forth. He was prepared for any number of reactions from Wen in response to his request—sarcasm, pity, exclamation. Instead, after a long silence, all he heard was a soft sigh.

"No problem," Wen said. "But she's probably not in China right now."

"Just don't tell her I'm the one asking."

"Don't worry. I won't ask her directly."

The next day, Tianming got a text from Wen with all the information he had asked for, but nothing about Cheng Xin's employment. Wen explained that no one knew where Cheng Xin had gone after she left the Academy of Spaceflight Technology last year. Tianming saw that there were two mailing addresses for her: one in Shanghai and another in New York.

That afternoon, Tianming asked Dr. Zhang to give him permission to leave the hospital and run an errand. The doctor wanted to come with Tianming, but he insisted on going alone.

Tianming took a taxi and arrived at UNESCO's Beijing office.

After the Crisis, every UN office in Beijing had expanded rapidly, and UNESCO now took up most of an office building outside of the Fourth Ring Road.

A giant star map greeted Tianming as he entered the spacious office of the Stars Our Destination Project. Silver lines connected the stars in constellations against a pitch-black background. Tianming saw that the map was displayed on a high-definition screen, and a computer nearby allowed for zooming and searching. The office was empty except for a receptionist.

Tianming introduced himself, and the receptionist excitedly went away and returned with a blond woman.

"This is the director of UNESCO Beijing," the receptionist explained. "And also one of the people responsible for implementing the Stars Our Destination Project in the Asia-Pacific region."

The director appeared very pleased to see Tianming as well. She held Tianming's hand and told him, in fluent Chinese, that he was the first Chinese individual to express an interest in buying a star. She would have preferred a ceremony to generate as much media coverage as possible, but she refrained out of respect for his wish for privacy. She seemed quite sorry to lose out on a wonderful opportunity to publicize the project.

Don't worry, Tianming thought. *No other Chinese will be as dumb as me.*

A middle-aged, well-dressed man wearing glasses came in. The director introduced him as Dr. He, a researcher at the Beijing Observatory. The astronomer would help Tianming with the details of his purchase. After the director left, Dr. He asked Tianming to sit down, and called for tea to be served.

"Are you feeling all right?" he asked Tianming.

Tianming knew that he didn't exactly look healthy. But after stopping chemo—which had been like undergoing torture—he felt much better, almost as if he'd gotten a new lease on life. Ignoring Dr. He's question, he repeated the request he had already made on the phone.

"I want to buy a star as a gift. The title to the star should be

registered under the name of the recipient. I won't provide any personal information about myself, and I want my identity kept secret from her."

"No problem at all. Do you have an idea of what kind of star you want to buy?"

"As close to Earth as possible. One with planets. Ideally, Earthlike planets," Tianming said as he gazed at the star map.

Dr. He shook his head. "Based on the figure you gave me, that's impossible. The starting prices for stars meeting those criteria are much too high. You can only buy a star without planets, and it won't be very close. Let me tell you something: The amount of money you are offering is too low even for bare stars. But after your call yesterday, in consideration of the fact that you're the first person in China to express an interest, we decided to lower the starting bid on one of the stars to what you offered." He moved the mouse to magnify a region of the star map. "It's this one. Say yes and it's yours."

"How far away is it?"

"It's about two hundred eighty-six point five light-years from here."

"That's too far."

Dr. He laughed. "I can tell you're not completely ignorant about astronomy. Think about it: Does it really make a difference if it's two hundred eighty-six light-years or two hundred eighty-six billion light-years?"

Tianming thought about it. The astronomer was right. It made no difference.

"There's a very big advantage to this star," Dr. He said. "It's visible with the naked eye. In my opinion, aesthetics matters the most when you're buying a star. It's much better to possess a faraway star that you can see than a nearby star that you can't. It's much better to own a bare star that you can see than a star with planets that you can't. In the end, all we can do is look at it. Am I right?"

Tianming nodded. *Cheng Xin can see the star. That's good.*

"What's it called?"

"The star was first cataloged by Tycho Brahe hundreds of years ago, but it never acquired a common name. All it has is a number." Dr. He moved the mouse pointer over the glowing dot, and a string of letters and numbers appeared next to it: DX3906. Then, patiently, the astronomer explained to Tianming the meaning of the numbers and letters, the star's type, absolute and apparent magnitudes, location in the main sequence, and so on.

The paperwork for the purchase didn't take long. Two notaries worked with Dr. He to make sure everything was proper. Then the director appeared again, along with two officials from the UN Development Program and the UN Committee on Natural Resources. The receptionist brought a bottle of champagne and everyone celebrated.

The director declared that the title to DX3906 was now vested in Cheng Xin, and she presented Tianming with an expensive-looking black leather folder.

"Your star."

After the officials left, Dr. He turned to Tianming. "Don't answer me if you aren't comfortable, but I'm guessing you bought the star for a girl?"

Tianming hesitated for a moment, but then nodded.

"Lucky girl!" Dr. He sighed. "It's nice to be rich."

"Oh, please!" said the receptionist. She stuck her tongue out at Dr. He. "Rich? Even if you had thirty billion yuan, would you buy a star for your girlfriend? Ha! I haven't forgotten what you said two days ago."

Dr. He looked rather embarrassed. In fact, he was worried that she was going to blurt out his opinion of the Stars Our Destination Project: *This trick the UN is pulling was already tried by a bunch of scammers more than ten years ago. Back then they sold land on the moon and Mars. It would be a miracle if anyone falls for it again!*

Fortunately, the receptionist went on in a different vein. "This isn't just about money. It's about *romance*. Romance! Do you even understand?"

Throughout Tianming's purchasing process, the young woman had stolen glances at him from time to time, as though he were a figure from a fairy tale. Her expression had at first been curious, then awed and admiring. Finally, as the leather folder containing the deed to the star was handed over, her face filled with envy.

Dr. He tried to change the subject. "We'll send the formal documents to the recipient as soon as possible. Based on your instructions, we won't reveal any information about you. Well, even if we wanted to, we can't—look, I don't even know your name!" He stood up and looked out the window. It was already dark. "Next, I can bring you to see your star—sorry, I meant the star you bought for her."

"Can we see it from the top of the building?"

"No. There's too much light pollution inside the city. We have to go far into the suburbs. If you aren't feeling well, we can pick another day."

"Let's go now. I really want to see it."

They drove for more than two hours, until the glowing sea that was Beijing was far behind them. To avoid the lamps of passing cars, Dr. He drove off the road into a field. Then he turned off the headlights and they got out of the car. In the late-autumn sky, the stars were especially bright.

"You see the Big Dipper? Imagine a diagonal across the quadrilateral formed by the four stars, and extend it. That's right, in that direction. Can you see those three stars that form a flat triangle? Draw a line from the apex, perpendicular to the base, and keep extending it. Can you see it? Right there. That's your star—the star you gave her."

Tianming pointed to two stars in succession, but Dr. He said neither was right. "It's between those two, but a bit to the south. The apparent magnitude is five point five. Normally, you have to be trained to find it. But the weather tonight is ideal, so you should be able to see it. Try this: Don't look for it directly; move your gaze a bit to the side. Your peripheral vision tends to be more sensitive to faint light. After you find it, then you can move your gaze back...."

With Dr. He's help, Tianming finally saw DX3906. It was very faint, and he had to find it again it each time his attention wavered. Although people commonly thought of the stars as silvery, careful observation revealed that they each had different colors. DX3906 was dark red.

Dr. He promised to give him some materials to help Tianming find the star in different seasons. "You are lucky, as lucky as the girl who received your gift," said Dr. He.

"I don't think I'd call myself fortunate. I'm about to die."

Dr. He seemed unsurprised by this revelation. He lit a cigarette and smoked it in silence. After a while, he said, "Even so, I think you're blessed. Most people don't cast a glance at the universe beyond the world we live in until the day they die."

Tianming looked at Dr. He for a moment, then he looked back into the sky and found DX3906 easily. The smoke from Dr. He's cigarette drifted before his eyes, and the faint star flickered through the veil. *By the time she sees it, I'll be gone from this world.*

Of course, the star he saw and the star she would see were only an image from 286 years ago. The faint beam of light had to cross three centuries to meet their retinas. Another 286 years would have to pass before the light from the star at this moment would reach the Earth. By then, Cheng Xin would long have turned to dust.

What will her life be like? Maybe she'll remember that in the sea of stars, there's one that belongs to her.

This would be Tianming's last day.

He wanted to note something special about it, but there was nothing. He woke up at seven, as usual; a shaft of sunlight fell against its habitual spot on the wall; the weather was not great, but also not too bad; the sky was the same grayish blue; the oak tree in front of the window was bare (instead of, say, hanging on to a lone, symbolic leaf). Even his breakfast was the same.

This was a day like any other day in his life of twenty-eight years, eleven months, and six days.

Like Lao Li, Tianming didn't inform his family of his decision. He did try to write a note that could be given to his father after his procedure, but he gave up because he couldn't think of what to say.

At ten, he walked into the euthanasia room by himself, as calmly as if he were headed to his daily examination. He was the fourth person in the city to conduct the procedure, so there wasn't much media interest. Only five people were in the room: two notaries, a director, a nurse, and an executive from the hospital. Dr. Zhang wasn't there.

He could go in peace.

Pursuant to his request, the room was undecorated. All around him were the plain white walls of a normal hospital room. He felt comfortable.

He explained to the director that he was familiar with the procedure and did not need him. The director nodded and went to the other side of the glass wall. The notaries finished their business with him, then left him alone with the nurse. The nurse no longer showed the anxiety and fear that she had had to overcome the first time. As she pierced his vein with the needle, her motion was steady and gentle. Tianming felt a strange bond with the nurse: after all, she was the last person who would be with him in this world. He wished he knew who had delivered him when he was born twenty-nine years ago. That delivery doctor and this nurse belonged to the small number of people who had genuinely tried to help him during his life. He wanted to thank them.

"Thank you."

The nurse smiled at him and left, her footsteps as silent as a cat's.

Do you wish to terminate your life? For yes, select 5. For no, select 0.

He had been born to an intellectual family, but his parents lacked political savvy and social cunning, and they had not been successful in their lives. Though they did not live the life of elites,

they had insisted on giving Tianming an education they thought befit an elite. He was only permitted to read classic books and listen to classical music; the friends he tried to make had to be the kind that his parents deemed to be from cultured, refined families. They told Tianming that the people around them were vulgar, their concerns common. In contrast, their own tastes were far superior.

In primary school, Tianming had managed to make a few friends, but he never invited them home to play. He knew that his parents would not allow him to be friends with such "vulgar" children. By the time he was in middle school, his parents' intensified push for his elite education made him into a complete loner. That was also when his parents divorced, after his father met a young woman who sold insurance. His mother then married a wealthy general contractor.

Thus, both of his parents ended up with the kind of "vulgar" people they had told Tianming to stay away from, and finally realized that they had no moral authority to impose the kind of education they wanted on him. But what had already been done to Tianming was enough. He could not escape his upbringing, which was like a set of spring-loaded handcuffs: The more he struggled to free himself, the tighter they bound him. Throughout his high school years, he became more and more alone, more and more sensitive, grew further apart from others.

All his memories of his childhood and youth were gray.

He pressed 5.

Do you wish to terminate your life? For yes, select 2. For no, select 0.

He had imagined that college would be a frightening place: a new, strange environment; a new, strange crowd; more things for him to struggle to adjust to. And when he first entered college, everything pretty much matched his expectations.

Until he met Cheng Xin.

Tianming had been attracted to girls before, but not like this. He felt everything around him, which had been cold and strange,

become suffused with warm sunlight. At first, he didn't understand where the light had come from. It was like a sun seen through a heavy veil of clouds, only appearing to observers as a faint disk. It was only when it disappeared that people realized that it was the source of all light during the day. Tianming's sun disappeared at the start of the weeklong holiday around National Day, when Cheng Xin left school to visit home. Tianming felt everything around him grow dim and gray.

It was almost certain that more than one boy felt this way about Cheng Xin. But he didn't suffer the way other boys did, because he had no hope for his yearning. He knew that girls did not like his aloofness, his sensitivity. All he could do was to look at her from afar, bathing in the warm light she gave off, quietly appreciating the beauty of spring.

Initially, Cheng Xin gave Tianming the impression of being taciturn. Beautiful women were rarely reticent, but she wasn't an ice queen. She said little, but she listened, really listened. When she conversed with someone, her focused, calm gaze told the speaker that they were important to her.

Cheng Xin was different from the pretty girls who Tianming had gone to high school with. She didn't ignore his existence. Every time she saw him, she would smile and say hi. A few times, when classmates planned outings and parties, the organizers— intentionally or otherwise—forgot about Tianming. But Cheng Xin would find him and invite him. Later, she became the first among his classmates to call him just "Tianming," without using his surname. In their interactions—limited though they were—the deepest impression Cheng Xin left in Tianming's heart was the feeling that she was the only one who understood his vulnerabilities and seemed to care about the pain that he might suffer.

But Tianming never made more of it than what it was. It was just as Hu Wen said: Cheng Xin was nice to everyone.

One event in particular stood out in Tianming's mind: He and some classmates were hiking up a small mountain. Cheng Xin suddenly stopped, bent down, and picked up something from the

stone steps of the trail. Tianming saw that it was an ugly caterpillar, soft and moist, wriggling against her pale fingers. Another girl next to her cried out: *That's disgusting! Why are you touching it?* But Cheng Xin carefully deposited the caterpillar in the grass next to the trail. *It will get stepped on.*

In truth, Tianming had had very few conversations with Cheng Xin. In four years of college, he could remember talking with her one on one just a couple of times.

It was a cool, early summer night. Tianming had climbed to the deck on top of the library, his favorite place. Few students came here, and he could be alone with his thoughts. The night sky was clear after a summer rainstorm. Even the Milky Way, which normally wasn't visible, shone in the sky.

"It really looks like a road made of milk!"[2]

Tianming looked over at the speaker. A breeze stirred Cheng Xin's hair, reminding him of his dream. Then he and Cheng Xin gazed up at the galaxy together.

"So many stars. It looks like a fog," Tianming said.

Cheng Xin turned to him and pointed at the campus and city below them. "It's really beautiful down there, too. Remember, we live here, not in the faraway galaxy."

"But aren't we studying to be aerospace engineers? Our goal is to leave the Earth."

"That's so that we may make life here better, not abandon the planet."

Tianming understood that Cheng Xin had meant to gently point out his own aloofness and solitude. But he had no response. This was the closest he had ever been to her. Maybe it was his imagination, but he thought he could feel the warmth from her body. He wished the breeze would shift direction so a few strands of her hair would brush against his face.

2 *Translator's Note:* Some Anglophone readers may get the impression here that the Chinese name for our galaxy is also "Milky Way." It is not. The actual Chinese name for the galaxy is *Yinhe*, or "Silver River." All Chinese students, however, study English for years.

Four years of undergraduate life came to an end. Tianming failed to get into graduate school, but Cheng Xin easily got accepted into the graduate program at their university. She went home for the summer after graduation, but Tianming lingered on campus. His only goal was to see her again at the start of the new school year. Since he wasn't allowed to stay in the dorms, he rented a room nearby and tried to find a job in the city. He sent out countless copies of his résumé and went to interview after interview, but nothing resulted. Before he knew it, the summer was over.

Tianming returned to campus, but couldn't find Cheng Xin. He carefully made some inquiries, and found out that she and her advisor had gone to the school's graduate institute at the Academy of Spaceflight Technology in Shanghai, where she would finish her graduate studies. That was also the day Tianming finally found a job at a new company founded for civil aerospace technology transfer that desperately needed qualified engineers.

Just like that, Tianming's sun left him. With a wintery heart, he entered real life in society.

He pressed 2.

Do you wish to terminate your life? For yes, select 4. For no, select 0.

Right after he started working, he had been happy for a while. He discovered that, compared to his competitive peers in school, people in the business world were far more tolerant and easier to deal with. He even thought his days of being isolated and aloof were over. But after winding up on the losing end of a few office political maneuvers and bad deals, he understood the cruelties of the real world, and became nostalgic for campus life. Once again, he retreated into his shell and set himself apart from the crowd. Of course, the consequences for his career were disastrous. Even in a state-owned enterprise like his company, competition was intense. If you kept to yourself, you had no chance of advancement. Year after year, he fell farther and farther behind.

During that time, Tianming dated two women, but the relationships fizzled quickly. It wasn't that Cheng Xin already occupied his heart: For him, she would always be the sun behind a veil of clouds. All he wanted was to look at her, to feel her light and warmth. He dared not dream of taking a step toward her. He never even sought out news about her. He guessed, based on her intelligence, that she would go for a Ph.D., but he made no conjectures about her personal life. The main barrier between him and women was his own withdrawn personality. He struggled to build his own life, but it was too difficult.

Fundamentally, Tianming was not suited to live in society, nor out of it. He lacked the ability to thrive in society, but also the resources to ignore it. All he could do was hang on to the edge, suffering. He had no idea where he was headed in life.

But then, he saw the end of the road.

He pressed 4.

> Do you wish to terminate your life? For yes, select 1. For no, select 0.

By the time his lung cancer was discovered, it was already late stage. Maybe there had been an earlier misdiagnosis. Lung cancer was one of those cancers that spread fast in the body, so he didn't have much time left.

As he left the hospital, he wasn't scared. The only emotion he felt was loneliness. His alienation had been building up, but had been held back by an invisible dam. It was a kind of equilibrium that he could endure. But now, the dam had collapsed, and the weight of years of accumulated loneliness overwhelmed him like a dark ocean. He could not bear it.

He wanted to see Cheng Xin.

Without hesitation, he bought a plane ticket and flew to Shanghai that afternoon. By the time his taxi arrived at his destination, his fervor had cooled somewhat. He told himself that, as someone about to die, he shouldn't bother her. He wouldn't even let her know

of his presence. He just wanted to look at her once from afar, like a drowning man struggling to take one last breath before sinking down forever.

Standing in front of the gate to the Academy of Spaceflight Technology, he calmed down even more. He saw how irrational his own actions of the past few hours had been. Even if Cheng Xin had gone on to obtain a Ph.D., she would be finished with her studies by now, and she might not even be working here. He spoke to the guard in front of the door and found out that there were more than twenty thousand people working at the academy, and he had to know the exact department if he wanted to find someone. He had lost touch with his classmates, and had no more information to give the guard.

He felt weak and out of breath, and he sat down a little ways from the gate.

It was still possible that Cheng Xin did work here. It was almost the end of the workday, and if he waited here, he might see her.

The gate to the academy complex was very wide. Large golden characters engraved into the short black wall next to it gave the formal name for the place, which had expanded greatly since its early days. Wouldn't such a large complex have more than one entrance? With an effort, he got up and asked the guard again. Indeed, there were four more entrances.

Slowly, he walked back to his place, sat down, and waited. He had no other choice.

The odds were against him: Cheng Xin would still have to be working here after graduation; to be at the office, instead of away on business; to pick this door, as opposed to four others, when she got out of work.

This moment resembled the rest of his life: a dedicated watch for a slim, slim ray of hope.

It was the end of the workday. People began to depart the complex: some walking, some on bikes, some in cars. The stream of people and vehicles grew, and then shrank. After an hour, only a few stragglers remained.

Cheng Xin never passed.

He was certain that he would not have missed her, even if she drove. That meant that she was no longer working here, or maybe she hadn't come to work today, or maybe she had used another entrance.

The setting sun stretched out the shadows of buildings and trees, like numerous arms extended toward him in pity.

He remained where he was until it was completely dark. He didn't remember how he managed to hail a taxi to bring him to the airport, how he flew back to his city, how he returned to his company-owned single dormitory.

He felt he was already dead.

He pressed 1.

> Do you wish to terminate your life? This is your last prompt. For yes, select 3. For no, select 0.

What would he want as his epitaph? He wasn't even sure he would get a tomb. It was expensive to buy a burial plot near Beijing. Even if his father wanted to buy him one, his sister would probably disagree—she was still *alive*, and she didn't even own a home! Most likely, his ashes would be stored in a cubby in the wall at Babaoshan People's Cemetery. But if he were to have a tombstone, he would like it to say:

He came; he loved; he gave her a star; he left.

He pressed 3.

There was a commotion on the other side of the glass. Just as Tianming was pressing the mouse button, the door to the euthanasia room flew open and a group of people rushed in.

In the lead was the director, who dashed for the switch that would turn off the automatic injector. The hospital executive that followed him went and yanked the injector's power cord out of the wall. After them came the nurse, who pulled the tube attached to

the needle in Tianming's arm so hard that he winced from the sharp pain as the needle was jerked out.

Everyone gathered around the tube to examine it.

"That was close! None of the drugs went into him," someone said.

Then the nurse began to bandage up Tianming's bleeding left arm.

Only one person stood outside the door to the euthanasia room. But for Tianming, the whole world seemed brighter: Cheng Xin.

Tianming could feel the dampness on his chest—Cheng Xin's tears had soaked through his clothes.

When he first saw her, he thought she hadn't changed at all. But now he noticed that her hair was shorter—it no longer draped over her shoulders, but stopped at her neck. The ends curled prettily. He still didn't have the courage to reach out and touch the hair that he had long yearned for.

I'm really useless. But he felt like he was in heaven.

The silence seemed like the peace of paradise, and Tianming wanted that silence to last. *You can't save me,* he said to her in his mind. *I will listen to you and not seek euthanasia. But I'm going to end up in the same place anyway. I hope you take the star I gave you and find happiness.*

Cheng Xin seemed to hear this inner speech. She lifted her head. It was the first time their eyes were this close, closer than he had ever dared to dream. Her eyes, made even more beautiful by her tears, broke his heart.

But when she finally spoke, what she said was not at all what he expected.

"Tianming, did you know that the euthanasia law was passed specifically for you?"

CRISIS ERA, YEARS 1-4
CHENG XIN

The start of the Trisolar Crisis coincided with Cheng Xin's completion of her graduate studies, and she was selected to join the task force working on the design of the propulsion system for the next generation of Long March rockets. To others, this seemed like the perfect job: important and high profile.

But Cheng Xin had lost the enthusiasm for her chosen profession. Gradually, she had come to see chemical rockets as similar to the giant smokestacks of the early Industrial Age. Poets back then had praised those forests of smokestacks, thinking that they were the same as industrial civilization. People now praised rockets the same way, thinking they represented the Space Age. But if humanity relied on chemical rockets, they might never become a true spacefaring race.

The Trisolar Crisis simply highlighted this fact. Trying to build a Solar System defense system based on chemical rockets was pure lunacy. Cheng Xin had made an effort to keep her options open by picking some classes in nuclear propulsion. After the Crisis, all aspects of work within the aerospace system accelerated, and even the long-delayed first-generation space plane project was given the go-ahead. Her task force was also charged with designing the prototype for the engines that would be used by the plane in spaceflight. Professionally, Cheng Xin's future seemed bright:

Her abilities were recognized, and in China's aerospace system, most chief engineers began their careers in propulsion design. But since she believed chemical rocketry was yesterday's technology, she didn't think she would get very far in the long term. Heading in the wrong direction was worse than doing nothing at all, but her job demanded her complete focus and attention. She was deeply frustrated.

Then came an opportunity for her to leave chemical rockets behind. The United Nations began to create all sorts of agencies related to planetary defense. Unlike UN agencies from the past, these new agencies reported directly to the PDC, and were staffed by experts from various nations. The Chinese aerospace system sent many people to these agencies. A high-level official offered Cheng Xin a new position: Aide to the director of the Technology Planning Center for the PDC Strategic Intelligence Agency. Humanity's intelligence-gathering work against the Trisolarans had so far focused on the ETO, but the PDC Strategic Intelligence Agency, or PIA, would focus their efforts directly on the Trisolaran Fleet and the home world of Trisolaris itself. They needed people with strong backgrounds in the technical aspects of aerospace technology.

Cheng Xin took the job without hesitation.

The PIA Headquarters was located in an old six-story building not far from the UN Headquarters. Dating from the end of the eighteenth century, the building was thick and well-built, like a solid block of granite. When Cheng Xin entered it for the first time after her trans-Pacific flight, she felt a chill, as though entering a castle. The place wasn't at all what she had expected from an intelligence agency for the whole world; it reminded her more of a place where byzantine plots were hatched through whispers.

The building was mostly empty; she was among the first to report for duty. In an office full of unassembled furniture and just-unsealed cardboard boxes, she met her boss, PIA's Technology Planning Center director.

Mikhail Vadimov was in his forties, muscular, tall, and spoke English with a heavy Russian accent. It took a few moments before Cheng Xin even realized that he was speaking English. He sat on a cardboard box and complained to her that he had worked in the aerospace industry for more than a dozen years and had no need for any technical assistance. Every country was eager to fill the PIA with its own people, but much less willing to give cold, hard cash. Then he seemed to realize that he was talking to a hopeful young woman who was growing rather dejected from his speech, and tried to comfort her by saying: "If this agency manages to make history—a big possibility, even if it probably won't be very good history—we two will be remembered as the first to show up!"

Cheng Xin was cheered by the fact that she and her boss had both worked in aerospace. She asked Vadimov what he had worked on. He carelessly mentioned a stint on the Buran spacecraft; then that he'd served as the executive chief designer for a certain cargo-carrying spaceship; but after that, his explanations turned vague. He claimed that he had done a couple of years in diplomacy, then entered "some department" that "did the same kinds of things we do now."

"It's best if you don't probe too much into the employment histories of your future colleagues, okay?" Vadimov said. "The chief is here also. His office is upstairs. You should swing by and say hi, but don't take up too much of his time."

As soon as Cheng Xin walked into the PIA chief's spacious office, she was greeted by the strong smell of cigar smoke. A large painting hung on the wall. A leaden sky and the dim, snow-covered ground took up most of the painting; in the distance, where the clouds met the snow, a few dark shapes lurked. A closer examination revealed them to be dirty buildings, most of them one-story clapboard houses mixed with a few European-style houses with two or three stories. Based on the shape of the river in the foreground and other hints in the geography, this was a portrait of New York at the beginning of the eighteenth century. The overwhelming impression given off by the painting was coldness, which Cheng Xin thought fit the person sitting under the painting rather well.

Next to the large painting was a smaller picture. The main subject in the painting was an ancient sword with a golden cross guard and a bright, shining blade, held in a hand enclosed in bronze gauntlets—only the forearm was shown. The hand was lifting the sword to pick up a wreath woven from red, white, and yellow flowers floating over the water. In contrast to the larger painting, this picture was bright and colorful, but it nonetheless radiated eeriness. Cheng Xin noticed that bloodstains covered the white flowers in the wreath.

PIA Chief Thomas Wade, an American, was far younger than Cheng Xin had expected—he looked younger than Vadimov. He was also more handsome, with very classical features. Later, she would conclude that the classical appearance came mostly from Wade's expressionless face, like a cold, lifeless statue transplanted out of the cold painting behind him. Wade didn't look busy—the desk in front of him was completely empty, with no sign of a computer or paper documents. He glanced up as she entered, but returned to contemplating the cigar in his hand almost right away.

Cheng Xin introduced herself and expressed her pleasure at having a chance to study from him, and continued until Wade lifted his eyes to look at her.

Cheng Xin thought she saw exhaustion and laziness in those eyes, but there was also something deeper, something sharp that made her uncomfortable. A smile appeared on Wade's face, like water seeping out of a crack in the frozen surface of a river; there was no real warmth, and it didn't relax her.

She tried to respond with a smile of her own, but the first words out of Wade's mouth froze her face and entire body. "Would you sell your mother to a whorehouse?" Cheng Xin shook her head no, but she wasn't even trying to respond to the question; she was terrified that she had not understood what he said. But Wade waved at her with his cigar. "Thanks. Go do what needs to get done."

After she told Vadimov what had happened, Vadimov laughed. "That's just a line that used to be popular in our ... trade. I heard it started back during the Second World War. Veterans would use

63

it as a joke on novices. The point is: Our profession is the only one on Earth where lies and betrayal are at the very heart of what we do. We have to be … flexible when it comes to commonly accepted ethical norms. PIA is formed from two groups of people: Some are technical experts like you; others are veterans of the various intelligence agencies in the world. These two groups have different ways of thinking and acting. It's a good thing that I'm familiar with both and can help you adjust to the other."

"But our enemy is Trisolaris. This is nothing like traditional intelligence."

"Some things are constant."

Over the next few days, other new PIA staff members reported for duty. Most of them came from countries that were permanent members of the PDC.

They were polite to each other, but there was no trust. The technical experts kept to themselves and acted as if they were on guard against theft every minute. The intelligence veterans were gregarious and friendly—but they were constantly on the lookout for something to steal.

It was just like Vadimov had predicted: These people were far more interested in spying on each other than gathering intelligence on Trisolaris.

Two days after Cheng Xin's arrival, PIA held its first all-hands meeting, even though not everyone had shown up yet. Other than PIA Chief Wade, there were three assistant chiefs: one from China, one from France, and one from the United Kingdom.

Assistant Chief Yu Weiming spoke first. Cheng Xin had no idea what kind of work he had done in China—and he had the sort of face that took multiple meetings to remember what he looked like. Fortunately, he didn't engage in the habit—common among Chinese bureaucrats—of giving long, meandering speeches. Though he was just repeating platitudes about the PIA's mission, at least he spoke succinctly.

Assistant Chief Yu said that he understood that everyone in the PIA was sent by their own country, and so they had dual loyalties. PIA didn't demand, and didn't even hope, that they would place their loyalty to the agency above their duties to their own nations. However, since the PIA's task was the protection of the entire human race, he hoped that everyone present would at least try to balance the two appropriately. Considering that the PIA was going to work directly against the Trisolaran threat, they ought to become the most united of the new agencies.

While Assistant Chief Yu was giving this speech, Cheng Xin noticed that Wade was kicking the table legs and slowly maneuvering his chair away from the conference table as though he didn't want to be there. Later, whenever anyone asked him to say a few words, he shook his head and refused.

Finally, after everyone who wanted to make a speech had done so, he spoke. Pointing at the pile of boxes and fresh office supplies in the meeting room, he said, "I'd like the rest of you to take care of these matters on your own." Apparently, he was referring to the administrative details of getting the agency up and running. "Please don't take up my time or theirs"—here he pointed at Vadimov and his staff. "I need everyone in the Technology Planning Center with experience in spaceflight engineering to stay. The rest of you are dismissed."

About a dozen people remained in the now much less crowded conference room. As soon as the heavy oak doors closed, Wade dropped his bomb. "The PIA must launch a spy probe at the Trisolaran Fleet."

The stunned staff members looked at each other. Cheng Xin was surprised as well. She had certainly hoped to get to substantive technical work quickly, but she hadn't expected such directness or speed. Considering that the PIA had just been formed and there were, as yet, no national or regional branches, it seemed ill-equipped to take on big projects. But the real shocker was the boldness of Wade's proposal: The technical challenges and other barriers seemed insurmountable.

"What are the specific requirements?" asked Vadimov. He was the only one who seemed to take Wade's announcement in stride.

"I've consulted with the delegates of the permanent members of the PDC in private, but the idea hasn't yet been formally presented. Based on what I know, the PDC members are most interested in one specific requirement—and this is something that they won't compromise on: The probe must achieve one percent of lightspeed. The permanent members of the PDC have different ideas about other parameters, but I'm sure they'll come to some compromise during formal discussions."

An expert from NASA spoke up. "Let me get this straight. Given those mission parameters, and supposing we only worry about acceleration and provide no way for the probe to decelerate, the probe will take two to three centuries to reach the Oort Cloud. There, it will intercept and examine the decelerating Trisolaran Fleet. Forgive me, but this seems a project better reserved for the future."

Wade shook his head. "With those sophons zipping about at lightspeed, spying on us constantly, and completely blocking all fundamental physics research, it's no longer certain that we'll make significant technological progress in the future. If humanity is doomed to crawl at a snail's pace through space, we'd better get started as soon as possible."

Cheng Xin suspected that Wade's plan was at least partly motivated by politics. The first effort by humanity to make active contact with an extraterrestrial civilization would enhance the PIA's status.

"But given the current state of spaceflight technology, it will take twenty, maybe thirty thousand years to reach the Oort Cloud. Even if we launch the probe right now, we won't have gotten very far from Earth's front door by the time the Trisolaran Fleet arrives in four hundred years."

"That is precisely why the probe must achieve one percent of lightspeed."

"You're talking about boosting our current maximum speed a hundredfold! That requires a brand-new form of propulsion. We can't achieve that kind of acceleration with current technology,

and there's no reason to expect a technical breakthrough within the foreseeable future. This proposal is fundamentally impossible."

Wade slammed his fist down on the table. "You forget that we now have resources! Before, spaceflight was merely a luxury, but now it's an absolute necessity. We can ask for resources that far exceed what was imaginable before. We can throw resources at this problem until the laws of physics bend. Rely on brute force if you have to, but we must accelerate the probe to one percent of lightspeed!"

Vadimov instinctively looked around the room. Wade glanced at him. "Don't worry. There are no reporters or outsiders anywhere near here."

Vadimov laughed. "Please don't take offense. But saying we want to throw resources at the problem until the laws of physics bend is going to make our agency the laughingstock of the world. Please don't repeat it in front of the PDC."

"I already know you're all laughing at me."

Everyone held their tongue. The staff just wanted the meeting to be over. Wade looked at everyone in turn, then returned his gaze to Cheng Xin. "No, not everyone. She's not laughing." He pointed at her. "Cheng, what do you think?"

Under Wade's keen gaze, Cheng Xin felt as if he were pointing a sword at her, not a finger. She looked around helplessly. Who was *she* to talk?

"We need to implement MD here," said Wade.

Cheng Xin was even more baffled. MD? McDonald's? Doctor of medicine?

"But you're Chinese! How can you not know MD?"

Cheng Xin looked at the other five Chinese in the room; they looked just as confused.

"During the Korean War, the Americans discovered that even common Chinese soldiers taken as prisoners seemed to know a lot about their own field strategies. It turned out that your commanders had presented the battle plans to the troops for mass discussion, hoping thereby to find ways to improve them. Of course, if you

become Trisolaran prisoners of war in the future, we don't want you to know *that* much."

A few of those present laughed. Cheng Xin finally understood that MD meant "military democracy." The others in the conference room enthusiastically supported Wade's proposal. Of course, these elite experts didn't expect a mere technical aide to have any brilliant ideas, but they were mostly men, and they thought that by giving her a chance to talk, they would have a perfect excuse to appreciate her physical attributes. Cheng Xin had always made an effort to dress conservatively, but this sort of harassment was something she had to deal with constantly.

Cheng Xin began: "I do have an idea—"

"An idea for bending the laws of physics?" The speaker was an older Frenchwoman named Camille, a highly respected and experienced consultant from the European Space Agency. She looked at Cheng Xin contemptuously, as though she didn't belong in the room.

"Well, more like getting *around* the laws of physics." Cheng Xin smiled at Camille politely. "The most promising resource at our disposal is the stockpile of nuclear weapons from around the world. Without some technical breakthrough, these represent the most powerful sources of energy we can launch into space. Imagine a spaceship or probe equipped with a radiation sail, similar to a solar sail: a thin film capable of being propelled by radiation. If we set off nuclear bombs behind the sail periodically—"

A few titters. Camille laughed the loudest. "My dear, you have sketched for us a scene out of a cartoon. Your spaceship is filled with a pile of nuclear bombs, and there's a giant sail. On the ship is a hero who bears more than a passing resemblance to Arnold Schwarzenegger. He tosses the bombs behind the ship, where they explode to push the ship forward. Oh, it's *so* cool!" As the rest of the staff joined in the mirth, she continued. "You may want to review your homework from freshman year in college and tell me: one, how many nuclear bombs your ship will have to carry; and, two, with that kind of thrust-to-weight ratio, what sort of acceleration you can achieve."

"She didn't manage to bend the laws of physics, but she did fulfill the other aspect of the chief's demand," another consulting expert said. "I'm just sorry to see such a pretty girl fall under the spell of brute force." The wave of laughter reached a crescendo.

"The bombs will not be on the ship," Cheng Xin replied calmly. The laughter ceased abruptly; it was as if she had put her hand on the surface of a struck cymbal. "The probe itself will be a tiny core equipped with sensors attached to a large sail, but the total mass will be light as a feather. It will be easy to propel it with the radiation from extravehicular nuclear detonations."

The conference room became very quiet. Everyone was trying to think where the bombs would be. While the others were mocking Cheng Xin, Wade's mien had remained chilly and unmoved. But now, that smile, like water seeping from a crack in the ice, gradually reappeared on his face.

Cheng Xin retrieved a stack of paper cups from the drinking water dispenser behind her and laid them out on the conference table in a line. "We can use traditional chemical rockets to launch the nuclear bombs in advance, and distribute them along the first segment of the probe's route." She took a pencil and moved its tip along the line, from one cup to the next. "As the probe passes each bomb, we detonate it right behind the sail, accelerating it faster and faster."

The men now moved their gazes away from Cheng Xin's body. They were finally willing to take her proposal seriously. Only Camille continued to stare at her, as though at a stranger.

"We can call this technique 'en-route propulsion.' This initial segment is the acceleration leg, and it takes up only a tiny fraction of the overall course. As a very rough estimate, if we use one thousand nuclear bombs, they can be distributed along a path of about five astronomical units stretching from the Earth to Jupiter's orbit. Or we could even compress it further and distribute the bombs within Mars's orbit. That's definitely achievable with our current technology."

The silence was broken by a few whispers. Gradually, the voices grew louder and more excited, like a drizzle turning into a rainstorm.

"You didn't just come up with this idea, did you?" asked Wade. He had been listening to the discussion intently.

Cheng Xin smiled at him. "It's based on an old idea in aerospace circles. Stanislaw Ulam first proposed something like it back in 1946. It's called nuclear pulse propulsion."

"Dr. Cheng," Camille said, "we all know about nuclear pulse propulsion. But those previous proposals all required the fuel to be carried aboard the ship. The idea of distributing the fuel along the spacecraft's route is indeed your invention. At least, I've never heard the suggestion before."

The discussion grew heated. The assembled experts tore into the idea like a pack of hungry wolves presented with a piece of fresh meat.

Wade slammed the table again. "Enough! Don't get bogged down on details right now. We're not evaluating feasibility; rather, we're trying to figure out if it's worthwhile to study the idea's feasibility. Focus on big-picture barriers."

After a brief silence, Vadimov said, "The best thing about this proposal is that it's easy to get started."

Everyone immediately caught on to Vadimov's meaning. The first step in Cheng Xin's plan involved launching a large number of nuclear bombs into orbit around the Earth. Not only did humanity possess such technology, the bombs were already on launch vehicles: the ICBMs in service could easily be repurposed for this use. American Peacekeepers, Russian Topols, and Chinese Dongfengs could all directly launch their payloads into near-Earth orbits. Even intermediate-range ballistic missiles, if retrofitted with booster rockets, could do the job. Compared to the post-Crisis nuclear disarmament plans that required destroying the missiles, this plan would be far cheaper.

"Excellent. For now, let's pause our discussion of Cheng Xin's en-route propulsion idea. Any other proposals?" Wade looked around the room.

A few seemed to want to speak up, but finally decided to remain quiet. None of them thought their own ideas could compete with

Cheng Xin's. Eventually, everyone's eyes focused on her again, but this time, the meaning was completely different.

"We'll meet twice more to brainstorm and see if we can come up with a few more options. But we might as well get started on the feasibility study for en-route propulsion. We'll need a code name."

"Since the probe's velocity would go up a level each time a bomb explodes, it's a bit like climbing a flight of stairs," Vadimov said. "I suggest we call it the Staircase Program. Besides the requirement of a final velocity exceeding one percent of lightspeed, another parameter to keep in mind is the mass of the probe."

"A radiation sail can be made very thin and light. Based on the current state of material sciences, we can make a sail of about fifty square kilometers and limit the mass to about fifty kilograms. That should be big enough." The speaker was a Russian expert who had once directed a failed solar sail experiment.

"Then the key will be the mass of the probe itself."

Everyone's eyes turned to another man in the room, the chief designer of the Cassini-Huygens probe.

"If we include some basic sensors and take into account the necessary antenna and radioisotope power source to transmit information back from the Oort Cloud, about two to three thousand kilograms ought to do it."

"No!" Vadimov shook his head. "It has to be like Cheng Xin said: light as a feather."

"If we stick with the most basic sensors, maybe one thousand kilograms would be enough. I can't guarantee that's going to succeed—you're giving me almost nothing to work with."

"You're going to have to make it work," said Wade. "Including the sail, the entire probe cannot exceed one metric ton in mass. We'll devote the strength of the entire human race to propel one thousand kilograms. Let's hope that's light enough."

During the next week, Cheng Xin slept only on airplanes. As part of a task force led by Vadimov, she shuttled back and forth between

the space agencies of the US, China, Russia, and Europe to coordinate the feasibility study of the Staircase Program. During that week, Cheng Xin got to travel to more places than she had in her life up to that point, but she didn't get to do any sightseeing except through the windows of cars and conference rooms.

At first, they had thought they could get all the space agencies to do a combined feasibility study, but that turned out to be an impossible political exercise. In the end, each space agency performed an independent analysis. The advantage of this approach was that the four studies could be compared to get a more accurate result, but it also meant that the PIA had to do a lot more work. Cheng Xin worked harder on this project than anything in her professional career—it was her baby, after all.

The four feasibility studies quickly reached preliminary conclusions, which were very similar to each other. The good news was that the area of the radiation sail could be shrunk to twenty-five square kilometers, and with even more advanced materials, the mass of the sail could be reduced to twenty kilograms.

Then came some very bad news: In order to reach the required speed of 1 percent of lightspeed, the mass for the entire probe assembly had to be reduced by 80 percent—to only 200 kilograms. Subtracting the mass reserved for the sail left only 180 kilograms for sensors and communication devices.

Wade's expression didn't change. "Don't be sad. I have even worse news: At the last session of the PDC, the resolution proposing the Staircase Program was voted down."

Of the seven permanent members of the PDC, four voted no. Their reasons were surprisingly similar. In contrast to the technical staff of the PIA with background in spaceflight, the delegates were not interested in the propulsion technology. They objected that the probe's intelligence value was too limited—in the words of the American representative, "practically nil."

This was because the proposed probe had no way to decelerate. Even taking into account the fact that the Trisolaran Fleet would be decelerating, the probe and the fleet would pass by each other at a

relative speed of around 5 percent of lightspeed (assuming the probe wasn't captured by the fleet). The window for gathering intelligence would be extremely small. Since the small mass of the probe made active sensors such as radar impractical, the probe was limited to passive sensing, mainly of electromagnetic signals. Given the advanced state of Trisolaran technology, it was almost certain that the enemy would not be using electromagnetic radiation, but media such as neutrinos or gravitational waves—techniques beyond the current state of human technology.

Moreover, due to the presence of sophons, the plan for sending a probe would be completely transparent to the enemy, making its chances of successfully gathering any valuable intelligence nonexistent. Considering the enormous investment required to implement such a plan, the benefits were too minuscule. Most of the plan's value was purely symbolic, and the great powers were simply insufficiently interested. The other three permanent members of the PDC voted yes only because they were interested in the propulsion technology.

"And the PDC is right," said Wade.

Everyone silently mourned the Staircase Program. Cheng Xin was the most disappointed, but she comforted herself that as a young person with no record of achievements, having gotten this far on her first original idea wasn't too bad. Certainly, she had exceeded her own expectations.

"Ms. Cheng, you look unhappy," Wade said. "Apparently you think we're going to back off from the Staircase Program."

Everyone now stared at Wade, speechless.

"We're *not* going to stop." Wade stood up and paced around the conference room. "From now on, whether it's the Staircase Program or any other plan, you do not stop until *I* tell you to stop. Understand?" He dropped his habitual indifferent tone and screamed like a crazed wild animal. "We're going to advance! Advance! We'll stop at nothing to advance!"

Wade was standing right behind Cheng Xin. She felt as if a volcano had erupted behind her, and she cringed and almost screamed herself.

"What's our next step?" asked Vadimov.

"We're going to send a person."

Wade had resumed his calm, emotionless voice. Still in shock at his explosion, it took a while before those in the room understood what Wade meant. He wasn't talking about sending someone to the PDC, but out of the Solar System. He was proposing sending a live scout to the bleak, frigid Oort Cloud one light-year away to spy on the Trisolaran Fleet.

Wade kicked the leg of the conference table and sent his chair flying backwards so that he could sit behind everyone as they continued to discuss. But no one spoke. It was a repeat of the meeting a week ago when he had first brought up the idea of sending a probe to the Trisolaran Fleet. Everyone tried to chew over his words and unravel the riddle. Shortly, they came to see that the idea wasn't as ridiculous as it seemed at first.

Hibernation was a relatively mature technology. A person could complete the voyage in suspended animation. Assuming the person weighed 70 kilograms, that left 110 kilograms for the hibernation equipment and the hull—which would resemble a coffin. But what then? Two centuries later, when the probe met the Trisolaran Fleet, how would they wake this person up, and what could he or she do?

These thoughts revolved inside the heads of everyone present, but no one spoke up. But Wade seemed to be reading everyone's minds.

"We need to send a representative of humanity into the heart of the enemy," he said.

"This would require the Trisolaran Fleet to capture the probe," Vadimov said. "And to keep our spy."

"This is very likely." Wade looked up. "Isn't it?" Those inside the conference understood that he was speaking to the sophons hovering around them like ghosts. Four light-years away, on that distant world, other invisible beings were also "attending" their meeting. The presence of the sophons was something that people tended to forget. When they remembered it, besides fright, they also felt a kind of insignificance, as though they were a swarm of ants

under the magnifying glass of some playful, cruel child. It was very difficult to maintain confidence when one realized that whatever plans one came up with would be known by the enemy long before they were even explained to the supervisor. Humanity had to struggle to adjust to this kind of warfare, in which they were completely transparent to the enemy.

But now, Wade seemed to have changed the situation slightly. In his scenario, the enemy's knowledge of the plan was an advantage. The Trisolarans would know every detail about the trajectory of the probe, and could easily intercept it. Even though the sophons allowed the Trisolarans to learn about humanity, surely they would still be interested in capturing a live specimen for up-close study.

In traditional intelligence warfare, sending a spy whose identity was known to the enemy was a meaningless gesture. But this war was different. Sending a representative of humanity into the Trisolaran Fleet was, by itself, a valiant gesture, and it made no difference that the Trisolarans would know the individual's identity ahead of time. The PIA didn't even need to figure out what the spy had to do once he or she got there: As long as the person could be safely and successfully inserted into the fleet, the possibilities were endless. Given that the Trisolarans were transparent in thought and vulnerable to stratagems, Wade's idea became even more attractive.

We need to send a representative of humanity into the heart of the enemy.

EXCERPT FROM
A PAST OUTSIDE OF TIME
HIBERNATION: MAN WALKS FOR THE FIRST TIME THROUGH TIME

A new technology can transform society, but when the technology is in its infancy, very few people can see its full potential. For example, when the computer was first invented, it was merely a tool for increasing efficiency, and some thought five computers would be enough for the entire world. Artificial hibernation was the same. Before it was a reality, people just thought it would provide an opportunity for patients with terminal illnesses to seek a cure in the future. If they thought further, it would appear to be useful for interstellar voyages. But as soon as it became real, if one examined it through the lens of sociology, one could see that it would completely change the face of human civilization.

All this was based on a single idea: *Tomorrow will be better.*

This was a relatively new faith, a product of the last few centuries before the Crisis. Previously, such an idea of progress would have been laughable. Medieval Europe was materially impoverished compared to the Classical Rome of a thousand years earlier, and was more intellectually repressed. In China, the lives of the people were worse during the Wei, Jin, and Southern and Northern Dynasties compared to the earlier Han Dynasty, and the

Yuan and Ming Dynasties were much worse than the earlier Tang and Song Dynasties. But after the Industrial Revolution, progress became a constant feature of society, and humanity's faith in the future grew stronger.

This faith reached its apex on the eve of the Trisolar Crisis. The Cold War had been over for some time, and though problems such as environmental degradation persisted, they were merely unpleasant. The material comforts of life improved at a rapid pace, and the trend seemed to accelerate. If one surveyed people about visions of the future, they might give different answers for how things would be in ten years, but few would doubt that in another hundred years, humanity would be living in paradise. It was easy to believe such a thing: They could just compare their own lives with the lives of their ancestors a hundred years earlier!

If hibernation were possible, why would you linger in the present?

When examined from the perspective of sociology, the bio-technology breakthrough of human cloning was far less complicated than hibernation. Cloning raised moral questions, but they mostly troubled those with a moral view influenced by Christianity. The troubles brought about by hibernation, on the other hand, were practical, and affected the entire human race. Once the technology was successfully commercialized, those who could afford it would use it to skip to paradise, while the rest of humanity would have to stay behind in the comparatively depressing present to construct that paradise for them. But even more worrisome was the greatest lure provided by the future: the end of death.

As modern biology advanced apace, people began to believe that death's end would be achievable in one or two more centuries. If so, those who chose hibernation were taking the first steps on the staircase to life everlasting. For the first time in history, Death itself was no longer fair. The consequences were unimaginable.

The situation was akin to the dire conditions of post-Crisis Escapism. Later, historians would call it Early Escapism or Time Escapism. Thus, even pre-Crisis, governments around the world

suppressed hibernation technology more zealously than cloning technology.

But the Trisolar Crisis changed everything. In a single night, the paradise of the future turned into a hell on Earth. Even for terminal patients, the future no longer appealed: By the time they woke up, perhaps the world would be bathed in a sea of fire, and they wouldn't even be able to find an aspirin.

Thus, after the Crisis, hibernation was allowed to develop without constraints. Soon, the technology became commercially viable, and the human race possessed the first tool that allowed them to traverse large swaths of time.

CRISIS ERA, YEARS 1-4
CHENG XIN

Cheng Xin went to Sanya on Hainan Island to research hibernation.

This tropical island seemed an incongruous site for the largest hibernation research center, which was operated by the Chinese Academy of Medical Sciences. While it was the middle of winter on the mainland, spring ruled here.

The hibernation center was a white building hidden behind lush vegetation. About a dozen test subjects inside engaged in experimental, short-term hibernation. So far, no one had been put into hibernation with the intent of crossing the centuries.

Cheng Xin first asked whether it was possible to shrink the equipment necessary to support hibernation down to one hundred kilograms.

The director of the research center laughed. "One hundred kilograms? You'd be lucky getting it down to one hundred metric tons!"

The director was exaggerating, but only slightly. He showed Cheng Xin around the center, and Cheng Xin learned that artificial hibernation didn't exactly match its public image. For one thing, it didn't involve ultra-low temperatures. The procedure replaced the blood in the body with an antifreeze cryoprotectant, then brought the body temperature down to minus-fifty-degrees Celsius. Relying on an external cardiopulmonary bypass system,

the body's organs maintained an extremely low level of biological activity. "It's like standby mode on a computer," said the director. The entire system—hibernation tank, life-support system, cooling equipment—weighed about three metric tons.

As Cheng Xin discussed possible ways to miniaturize the hibernation setup with the center's technical staff, she was startled by a realization: If the body's temperature must be maintained around minus-fifty-degrees Celsius, then in the frigid conditions of outer space, the hibernation chamber needed to be heated, not cooled. In the long journey through trans-Neptunian space in particular, outside temperature would be close to absolute zero. In contrast, minus-fifty-degrees Celsius was like the inside of a furnace. Considering that the journey would take one to two centuries, the most practicable solution was radioisotope heating. The director's claim of one hundred metric tons was thus not too far from the truth.

Cheng Xin returned to PIA Headquarters and gave her report. After synthesizing all relevant research results, the staff again sank into depression. But this time, they gazed at Wade with hope.

"What are you all looking at? I'm not God!" Wade surveyed the conference room. "Why do you think your countries sent you here? To collect a paycheck and to give me bad news? I don't have a solution. Finding a solution is your job!" He kicked the leg of the conference table, and his chair slid back farther than ever. Ignoring the conference room's non-smoking rule, he lit up a cigar.

The attendees turned their attention back to the new hibernation experts in the room. None of them said anything, but they made no effort to disguise the anger and frustration of professionals faced with ignorant zealots who were asking for the impossible.

"Maybe ..." Cheng Xin looked around hesitantly. She was still unused to MD.

"Advance! We stop at nothing to advance!" Wade spewed smoke at her along with the words.

"Maybe ... we don't need to send a live person."

The rest of the team looked at her, looked at each other, and

then turned to the hibernation experts. They shook their heads, uncertain what Cheng Xin meant.

"We could flash-freeze a person to minus-two-hundred-degrees Celsius or below, then launch the body. We wouldn't need life support or heating systems, and the capsule holding the body could be made very small and light. The total mass should not exceed one hundred and ten kilograms. For us, such a body is a corpse, but that may not be the case for Trisolarans."

"Very good," Wade said, and nodded at her. This was the first time he had praised one of his staff since she had known him.

One of the hibernation experts said, "You're talking about cryo-preservation, not hibernation. The biggest barrier to reanimating a flash-frozen body is preventing cell damage from ice crystals during the thawing process. It's like what happens to frozen tofu: When you defrost it, it turns into a sponge. Oh, I guess most of you haven't had frozen tofu." The expert, who was Chinese, smiled at the confused Western faces around him. "Now, maybe the Trisolarans know techniques to prevent such damage. Perhaps they can restore the body to normal temperature within an extremely short period of time: a millisecond, or even a microsecond. We don't know how to do such a thing, at least not without vaporizing the body in the process."

Cheng Xin wasn't paying much attention to this discussion. Instead, she was focused on one thing: Who would this minus-two-hundred-degree corpsicle that would be shot into deep space be? She was trying her hardest to advance without regard for consequences, but she couldn't help but shudder at the thought.

The latest version of the Staircase Program was brought back to the current PDC session for a vote. Private discussions between Wade and the delegates of the various nations called for optimism. Since the plan, as modified, would represent the first direct contact between humanity and an extraterrestrial civilization, its meaning was qualitatively different from merely sending a probe. Moreover,

the person sent to the Trisolarans could be said to represent a ticking bomb implanted in the heart of the enemy. By skillfully using humanity's absolute superiority in tricks and ruses, he or she could change the course of the entire war.

Since the special session of the General Assembly was going to announce the Wallfacer Project to the world tonight, the PDC session was delayed by more than an hour. PIA personnel waited in the lobby outside the General Assembly Hall. During previous PDC sessions, only Wade and Vadimov were allowed to attend, while others had to remain outside, waiting to be summoned if their specific area of technical expertise was needed. But this time, Wade asked Cheng Xin to accompany him and Vadimov to the PDC session itself, a high honor for a lowly technical aide.

After the General Assembly finished its announcement, Cheng Xin and the others watched as a man surrounded by a swarm of reporters passed through the lobby and left the building through another exit—clearly one of the just-revealed Wallfacers. Since everyone from the PIA was focused on the Staircase Program, most weren't interested in the Wallfacers, and only a couple of them left the building to catch a glimpse of the man. Thus, when the famous assassination attempt of Luo Ji occurred, no one from the PIA heard the gunshot; they only saw the sudden commotion through the glass doors. Cheng Xin and the others ran outside and were immediately blinded by the bright searchlights from helicopters hovering overhead.

"Oh my God, one of the Wallfacers has been killed!" One of her colleagues ran over. "I heard that he was shot several times. In the head!"

"Who are the Wallfacers?" asked Wade. His tone indicated no particular interest.

"I'm not too sure either. I think three of them are from the pool of well-known candidates. But this fourth one, the one who was shot, was one of your people." He pointed at Cheng Xin. "But no one had heard of him. He's just some guy."

"In this extraordinary time, no one is 'just some guy,'" Wade

said. "Any random person could suddenly be handed a heavy responsibility, and anyone important could be replaced at any time." He looked at Cheng Xin and Mikhail Vadimov in turn. Then a PDC secretary called him aside.

"He's threatening me," Vadimov whispered to Cheng Xin. "He threw a fit yesterday and told me that you could easily replace me."

"Mikhail, I—"

Vadimov held up his hand to stop her. The bright searchlight from one of the helicopters shone through his palm and revealed the blood under his skin. "He wasn't joking. Our agency does not need to follow normal HR procedures. You're steady, calm, hardworking, and also creative; you display a sense of responsibility far above your official position. This is a rare combination of qualities in someone your age. Xin, really, I'm glad that you could replace me—but you *can't* do *quite* what I can do." He looked around at the chaos surrounding them. "You won't sell your mother to a whorehouse. You're still a child, when it comes to that aspect of our profession. My fervent hope is that you will always remain so."

Camille marched over to them holding a stack of paper. Cheng Xin guessed that it was the interim report on the feasibility of the Staircase Program. Camille held up the document for a few seconds, but instead of handing it over to either of them, she slammed it against the ground.

"Fuck them all!" Camille screamed. Even with the helicopters thundering overhead, a few onlookers turned to stare. "Fucking pigs don't know how to do anything except fuck around down here in the mud."

"Who are you talking about?" asked Vadimov.

"Everyone! The human race! Half a century ago, we walked on the moon. But now, we have nothing, can't change anything!"

Cheng Xin bent down and picked up the document. Indeed, it was the interim feasibility report. She and Vadimov flipped through it, but it was highly technical and difficult to skim. Wade had also returned to their circle—the PDC secretary had informed him that the session would begin in fifteen minutes.

Camille calmed down a bit in the presence of the PIA chief. "NASA has conducted two small tests of nuclear pulse propulsion in space, and you can read the results in the report. Basically, our proposed spacecraft is still too heavy to reach the required speed. They calculate the entire assembly needs to be one-twentieth its proposed mass. One-twentieth! That's ten kilograms!

"But wait, they also sent us some *good* news. The sail, it turns out, can be reduced to under ten kilograms. They took pity on us and told us that we can have an effective payload of half a kilogram. But that is the absolute limit, because any increase in the payload will require thicker cables for attachment to the sail. Every additional gram in the payload means three more grams of cables. Thus, we're stuck with zero point five kilograms. Haha, it's just like our angel predicted: light as a feather!"

Wade smiled. "We should ask Monnier, my mother's kitten, to go. Though, even she would have to lose half of her weight."

Whenever others were happily absorbed by their work, Wade appeared gloomy; when others were forlorn, he became relaxed and jokey. Initially, Cheng Xin had attributed this quirk to part of his leadership style. But Vadimov told her that she didn't know how to read people. Wade's behavior had nothing to do with his leadership style or rallying the troops—he just enjoyed watching others lose hope, even if he himself was among those who ought to be in despair. He took pleasure in the desperation of others. Cheng Xin had been surprised that Vadimov, who always tried to speak of others generously, held such an opinion of Wade. But right now, it did look as though Wade took pleasure in watching the three of them suffer.

Cheng Xin felt weak. Days of exhaustion hit her at once, and she sank to the lawn.

"Get up," said Wade.

For the first time, Cheng Xin refused to obey an order from him. She remained on the ground. "I'm tired." Her voice was wooden.

"You, and you," Wade said, pointing to Camille and Cheng Xin. "You're not allowed to lose control like this in the future. You must advance, stop at nothing to advance!"

"There's no way forward," said Vadimov. "We have to give up."

"The reason you think there's no path forward is because you don't know how to disregard the consequences."

"What about the PDC session? Cancel it?"

"No, we should proceed as though nothing has happened. But we can't prepare new documents, so we have to orally present the new plan."

"What new plan? A five-hundred-gram cat?"

"Of course not."

Vadimov's and Camille's eyes brightened. Cheng Xin also seemed to have recovered her strength. She stood up.

Accompanied by military escort vehicles and helicopters, an ambulance departed with the Fourth Wallfacer. Against the lights of New York City, Wade's figure appeared as a black ghost, his eyes glinting with a cold light.

"We'll send only a brain," he said.

EXCERPT FROM
A PAST OUTSIDE OF TIME
THE STAIRCASE PROGRAM

In fourteenth-century China, during the Ming Dynasty, the Chinese navy invented a weapon called Huolong Chu Shui, literally meaning "fiery dragon issuing from water." This was a multistage gunpowder rocket similar in principle to antiship missiles of the Common Era. The missile itself (Huolong) was augmented with booster rockets. When launched, the booster rockets propelled the missile toward the enemy ship by flying just above the surface of the water. As the booster rockets burnt out, they ignited a cluster of smaller rocket arrows stored inside the missile, and these would shoot out the front, causing massive damage to enemy ships.

Ancient warfare also saw the use of repeating crossbows, which prefigured Common Era machine guns. These appeared in both the West and the East, and Chinese versions have been discovered in tombs dating from the fourth century B.C.

Both of these weapon systems were attempts to utilize primitive technology in novel ways that demonstrated a power incongruous for their time period.

Looking back, the Staircase Program implemented at the beginning of the Crisis Era was a similar advance. Using only the primitive technology available at the time, it managed to boost a small probe

to 1 percent of lightspeed. This achievement should have been impossible without technology that would not appear for another one and a half centuries.

At the time of the Staircase Program, humans had already successfully launched a few spacecraft outside the Solar System and had managed to land probes on Neptunian satellites. Thus, the requisite technology to distribute nuclear bombs along the acceleration leg of the probe's course was relatively mature. But controlling the flight path of the probe to pass by each bomb, and detonating each at the precise moment, posed great technical challenges.

Every bomb had to detonate just as the radiation sail passed it. The distance from each bomb to the sail at the moment of the explosion ranged from three thousand to ten thousand meters, depending on the bomb's yield. As the probe's velocity increased, the timing needed to be more precise. However, even as the sail's speed reached 1 percent of lightspeed, the margin for error remained above the nanosecond range, well achievable by the technology of the time.

The probe itself contained no engine. Its direction was entirely determined by the relative positions of the detonating bombs. Each bomb along the route was equipped with small positional thrusters. As the sail passed each bomb, the distance between them was only a few hundred meters. By adjusting this distance, it was possible to alter the angle between the sail and the propulsive force generated by the nuclear explosion, and thus control the direction of flight.

The radiation sail was a thin film, and the only way to carry the payload was to drag it behind in a capsule. The entire probe thus resembled a giant parachute—except that the parachute flew "upwards." To avoid damage to the payload from the nuclear explosions occurring three to ten kilometers behind the sail, the cables connecting the sail to the payload had to be very long: about five hundred kilometers. An ablative layer protected the payload capsule itself. As the nuclear bombs exploded, the ablative material gradually vaporized, cooling the capsule as well as lowering the total mass.

The cables were made from a nanomaterial called "Flying Blade." Only about a tenth of the thickness of a strand of spider silk, the cables were invisible to the naked eye. Eight grams of the material could be stretched into a cable one hundred kilometers long, yet it was strong enough to securely pull the payload capsule during acceleration, and would not break from the massive radiation generated by the nuclear explosions.

Of course, Huolong Chu Shui was not, in fact, equivalent to a two-stage rocket, and the repeating crossbow was not the same as a machine gun. Similarly, the Staircase Program could not bring about a new Space Age. It was only a desperate attempt that drew upon everything humanity's primitive level of technology could offer.

CRISIS ERA, YEARS 1-4
CHENG XIN

The mass launch of Peacekeeper missiles had been in process for over half an hour. Trails from six missiles merged together, and, lit up by the moon, resembled a silvery road that reached into heaven.

Every five minutes, another fiery ball ascended this silvery road into the sky. Shadows cast by trees and people swept along the ground like the second hands of clocks. This first launch would involve thirty missiles, sending three hundred nuclear warheads with yields ranging from five hundred kilotons to 2.5 megatons into orbit.

At the same time, in Russia and China, Topol and Dongfeng missiles were also rising into the sky. The scene resembled a doomsday scenario, but Cheng Xin could tell by the curvature of the rocket trails that these were orbital launches instead of intercontinental strikes. These devices, which could have killed billions, would never return to the surface of the Earth. They would pool their enormous power to accelerate a feather to 1 percent of the speed of light.

Cheng Xin's eyes filled with hot tears. Each ascending rocket lit them up like bright, glistening pools. She told herself again and again that no matter what happened next, it was worth it to have pushed the Staircase Program this far.

But the two men beside her, Vadimov and Wade, seemed unmoved by the spectacular scene playing out before them. They didn't even bother looking up; instead, they smoked and conversed

in low voices. Cheng Xin knew very well what they were discussing: who would be chosen for the Staircase Program.

The last session of the PDC marked the first time a resolution had been passed based on a proposal that wasn't even written down. And Cheng Xin got to witness the debating skills of Wade, usually a man of few words. He argued that if we assumed the Trisolarans were capable of reviving a body in deep freeze, then it made sense to assume they were also capable of reviving a bare brain in similar condition and conversing with it through an external interface. Surely such a task was trivial for a civilization capable of unfolding a proton into two dimensions and etching circuits over the resulting surface. In some sense, a brain was no different from the whole person: It possessed the person's thoughts, personality, and memories. And it most definitely possessed the person's capacity for stratagems. If successful, the brain would still be a ticking bomb in the heart of the enemy.

Although the PDC members did not fully agree that a brain was the same as a whole person, they lacked better choices, especially since their interest in the Staircase Program was largely based on the technology for accelerating the probe to 1 percent of lightspeed. In the end, the resolution passed with five yeses and two abstentions.

Once the Staircase Program was approved, the problem of who should be sent came to the forefront. Cheng Xin lacked the courage to even imagine such a person. Even if his or her brain could be captured by the Trisolarans and revived, life afterwards—if such an existence could be called life—would be one interminable nightmare. Every time she thought about this, her heart felt squeezed by a hand chilled to minus-two-hundred-degrees Celsius.

The other leaders and implementers of the Staircase Program did not suffer her pangs of guilt. If PIA were a national intelligence agency, this matter would have been resolved long ago. However, since PIA was only a joint intelligence committee formed by the permanent member nations of the PDC, after the Staircase Program was revealed to the international community, the issue became extremely sensitive.

The key problem was this: Before launch, the subject would have to be killed.

After the initial panic of the Crisis subsided, a mainstream consensus gradually dominated international politics: It was important to prevent the Crisis from being leveraged as a tool to destroy democracy. PIA personnel were instructed by their respective nations to be extra careful during the process of selecting potential Staircase Program subjects and not commit political errors that would embarrass their countries.

Once again, Wade came up with a unique solution to the difficulty: advocating, through the PDC and then the UN, the passage of euthanasia laws in as many countries as possible. But even he wasn't confident that this plan would work.

Of the seven permanent members of the PDC, three quickly passed euthanasia laws. But these laws all clearly provided that euthanasia was only available to those suffering terminal illnesses. This was not ideal for the Staircase Program, but it seemed the outer boundary of political acceptability.

Thus, candidates for the Staircase Program had to be chosen from the population of terminally ill patients.

The thunderous noises and bright lights in the sky faded. The missile launches had come to an end. Wade and a few other PDC observers got into their cars and left, leaving only Vadimov and Cheng Xin.

"Why don't we take a look at your star?" he said.

Four days ago, Cheng Xin had received the deed to DX3906. She was utterly surprised and fell into a delirium of joy. For a whole day, she kept on repeating to herself: *Someone gave me a star; someone gave me a star; someone gave me a star....*

When she went to see Chief Wade to give a status report, her happiness was so palpable that Wade asked her what the matter was with her. She showed him the deed.

"A useless piece of paper," he said, and handed it back to her.

"If you're smart, you should drop the price and resell it right away. Otherwise you'll end up with nothing."

But Cheng Xin wasn't bothered by his cynicism—she had already known what he was going to say. She knew very little about Wade except his work history: service in the CIA, then deputy secretary of Homeland Security, and finally here. As for his personal life, other than the fact that he had a mother and his mother had a kitten, she knew nothing. No one else did, either. She didn't even know where he lived. He was like a machine: When he wasn't working, he was shut down somewhere unknown.

She couldn't help but bring up the star to Vadimov, who enthusiastically congratulated her. "Every girl in the world must be jealous," he said. "Including all living women and dead princesses. You're certainly the first woman in the history of humankind to be given a star." For a woman, was there any greater happiness than to be given a star by someone who loved her?

"But who *is* he?" Cheng Xin muttered.

"Shouldn't be hard to guess. He must be rich, for one thing. He just spent a few million on a symbolic gift."

Cheng Xin shook her head. She'd had many admirers and suitors, but none of them were *that* wealthy.

"He's also a cultured soul. Stands apart from the crowd." Vadimov sighed. "And he just made a romantic gesture that I'd call fucking ridiculous if I read it in a book or saw it in a movie."

Cheng Xin sighed as well. A much younger Cheng Xin had once indulged in rose-tinted fantasies that the Cheng Xin of the present would mock. This real star that appeared out of nowhere, however, far exceeded those romantic dreams.

She was certain that she knew no man like that.

Maybe it was a secret admirer from afar who, on impulse, decided to use a tiny part of his vast wealth to indulge in a bit of whimsy, to satisfy some desire she would never understand. Even so, she was grateful.

That night, Cheng Xin climbed onto the top of One World Trade Center, eager to see her new star. She had carefully reviewed the

materials that accompanied the deed explaining how to find it. But the sky in New York was overcast. The next day and the day after were the same. The clouds formed a giant teasing hand that covered her gift, refusing to let go. But Cheng Xin wasn't disappointed; she knew she had received a gift that couldn't be taken away. DX3906 was in this universe, and it might even outlast the Earth and the Sun. She would see it, one day.

She stood on the balcony of her apartment at night, gazing up at the sky and imagining her star. The lights of the city below cast a dim yellow glow against the cloud cover, but she imagined her star giving the clouds a rosy glow.

In her dream, she flew over the star's surface. It was a rose-colored sphere, but instead of scorching flames, she felt the coolness of a spring breeze. Below her was the clear water of an ocean, through which she could see swaying, rose-colored clouds of algae....

After she woke up, she laughed at herself. As an aerospace professional, even in her dreams she couldn't forget that DX3906 had no planets.

On the fourth day after she received the star, Cheng Xin and a few other PIA employees flew to Cape Canaveral to attend the launch ceremony for the first batch of missiles. Achieving orbit required taking advantage of the Earth's spin, and the ICBMs had been moved here from their original deployment bases.

The trails left behind by the missiles gradually faded against the clear night sky. Cheng Xin and Vadimov reviewed the observation guide for her star. Both had had some training in astronomy, and soon they were looking at the approximate location. But neither could see it.

Vadimov took out two pairs of military-issue binoculars. With them, it was easy to see DX3906. After that, even without the binoculars, they could find the star. Cheng Xin stared at the faint red dot, mesmerized, struggling to comprehend the unimaginable distance between them, struggling to translate the distance into terms that could be grasped by the human mind.

"If you put my brain on the Staircase Program probe and launched it at the star, it would take thirty thousand years to get there."

Cheng Xin heard no response. When she turned around, she saw that Vadimov was no longer looking at the star with her, but leaning against the car and looking at nothing. She could see that his face was troubled.

"What's wrong?"

Vadimov was silent for some time. "I've been avoiding my duty."

"What are you talking about?"

"I'm the best candidate for the Staircase Program."

After a momentary shock, Cheng Xin realized that Vadimov was right: He had extensive experience in spaceflight, diplomacy, and intelligence; he was steady and mature.... Even if they were able to expand the pool of candidates to include healthy individuals, Vadimov would still be the best choice.

"But you're healthy."

"Sure. But I'm still running from my responsibility."

"Have you been pressured?" Cheng Xin was thinking of Wade.

"No, but I know what I must do; I just haven't done it. I got married three years ago, and my daughter just turned one. I'm not afraid to die, but my family matters to me. I don't want them to see me turned into something worse than a corpse."

"You *don't* have to do this. Neither the PIA nor your government has ordered you to do this, and they can't!"

"Yes, but I wanted to tell you ... in the end, I'm the best candidate."

"Mikhail, humankind isn't just some abstraction. To love humanity, you must start by loving individual persons, by fulfilling your responsibility to those you love. It would be absurd to blame yourself for it."

"Thank you, Cheng Xin. You deserve your gift." Vadimov looked up at Cheng Xin's star. "I would love to give my wife and daughter a star."

A bright point of light appeared in the sky, then another. Their glow cast shadows on the ground. They were testing nuclear pulse propulsion in space.

The process of selecting a subject for the Staircase Program was fully underway, but the effort imposed little direct pressure on Cheng Xin. She was asked to perform some basic tasks such as examining candidates' knowledge of spaceflight, a primary requirement. Since the pool of candidates was limited to terminally ill patients, it was almost impossible to find someone with the requisite expertise. The PIA intensified efforts to identify more candidates through every available channel.

One of Cheng Xin's college classmates came to New York to visit her. The talk turned to what had happened to others in their class, and her friend mentioned Yun Tianming. She had heard from Hu Wen that Tianming was in the late stages of lung cancer and didn't have much time left. Right away, Cheng Xin went to Assistant Chief Yu to suggest Tianming as a candidate.

For the rest of her life, Cheng Xin would remember that moment. Every time, she had to admit to herself that she just didn't think much about Tianming as a person.

Cheng Xin needed to return to China for business. Since she was Tianming's classmate, Assistant Chief Yu asked her to represent the PIA and discuss the matter with Tianming. She agreed, still not thinking much of it.

After hearing Cheng Xin's story, Tianming slowly sat up on the bed. Cheng Xin asked him to lie down, but he said he wanted to be by himself for a while.

Cheng Xin closed the door lightly behind her. Tianming began to laugh hysterically.

What a fucking idiot I am! Did I think that because I gave her a star out of love, she would return that love? Did I think that she had flown across the Pacific to save me with her saintly tears? What kind of fairy tale have I been telling myself?

No, Cheng Xin had come to ask him to die.

He made another logical deduction that made him laugh even harder, until it was hard to breathe. Based on Cheng Xin's timing, she could not know that he had already chosen euthanasia. In other words, if Tianming hadn't already chosen this path, she would try to convince him to take it. Maybe she would even entice him, or pressure him, until he agreed.

Euthanasia meant "good death," but there was nothing good about the fate she had in mind for him.

His sister had wanted him to die because she thought money was being wasted. He could understand that—and he believed that she genuinely wanted him to die in peace. Cheng Xin, on the other hand, wanted him to suffer in eternity. Tianming was terrified of space. Like everyone who studied spaceflight for a living, he understood space's sinister nature better than the general public. Hell was not on Earth, but in heaven.

Cheng Xin wanted a part of him, the part that carried his soul, to wander forever in that frigid, endless, lightless abyss.

Actually, that would be the best outcome.

If the Trisolarans were to really capture his brain as Cheng Xin wished, then his true nightmare would begin. Aliens who shared nothing with humanity would attach sensors to his brain and begin tests involving the senses. They would be most interested in the sensation of pain, of course, and so, by turn, he would experience hunger, thirst, whipping, burning, suffocation, electric shocks, medieval torture techniques, death by a thousand cuts....

Then they would search his memory to identify what forms of suffering he feared the most. They would discover a torture technique he had once read in a history book—first, the victim was whipped until not an inch of his skin remained intact; then the victim's body was tightly wrapped in bandages; and after the victim had stopped bleeding, the bandages would be torn off, ripping open all the wounds at once—then send signals replicating such torture into his brain. The victim in his history book couldn't live for long in those conditions, but Tianming's brain would not be able to die. The most that could happen was that his brain

could shut down from shock. In the eyes of Trisolarans, it would resemble a computer locking up. They'd just restart his brain and run another experiment, driven by curiosity, or merely the desire for entertainment....

He would have no escape. Without hands or body, he would have no way to commit suicide. His brain would resemble a battery, recharged again and again with pain.

There would be no end.

He howled with laughter.

Cheng Xin opened the door. "Tianming, what's wrong?"

He choked off his laugh and turned still as a corpse.

"Tianming, on behalf of the UN-PDC Strategic Intelligence Agency, I ask you whether you're willing to shoulder your responsibility as a member of the human race and accept this mission. This is entirely voluntary. You are free to say no."

He gazed at her face, at her solemn but eager expression. She was fighting for humanity, for Earth.... But what was wrong with the scene all around him? The light of the setting sun coming through the window fell against the wall like a pool of blood; the lonesome oak tree outside the window appeared as skeletal arms rising out of the grave....

The hint of a smile—an agonized, melancholic smile—appeared at the corners of his mouth. Gradually, the smile spread to the rest of his face.

"Of course. I accept," he said.

CRISIS ERA, YEARS 5-7
THE STAIRCASE PROGRAM

Mikhail Vadimov died. While crossing the Harlem River on I-95, his car slammed through the guardrails on the Alexander Hamilton Bridge and plunged into the water below. It took more than a day before the car could be retrieved. An autopsy revealed that Vadimov had been suffering from leukemia; the accident was the result of retinal hemorrhages.

Cheng Xin mourned Vadimov, who had cared for her like a big brother and helped her adjust to life in a foreign country. She missed his generosity most of all. Though Cheng Xin had attracted notice with her intelligence and seemed to shine brighter than Vadimov—despite the fact that she was supposed to be his aide—he had never shown any jealousy. He had always encouraged her to display her brilliance on bigger and bigger stages.

Within the PIA, there were two types of reaction to Vadimov's death. Most of the technical staff, like Cheng Xin, grieved for their boss. The intelligence specialists, on the other hand, appeared more displeased by the fact that Vadimov's body had not been retrieved in time, rendering his brain unusable.

Gradually, a suspicion grew in Cheng Xin's mind. It seemed like too much of a coincidence. She shuddered the first time the idea surfaced in her mind—it was too frightening, too despicable to be endured.

She consulted medical specialists and learned that it was possible to intentionally induce leukemia. All you had to do was to place the victim in an environment with sufficient radiation. But getting the timing and dosage right was no trivial matter. Too little would not induce the illness in time, but too much would kill the victim with radiation sickness, possibly damaging the brain. Timing-wise, based on the advanced state of Vadimov's illness, the scheme against him would have to have begun right around the time the PDC started to promote euthanasia laws around the world. If there was a killer, he was extremely skilled.

Secretly, Cheng Xin swept Vadimov's office and apartment with a Geiger counter, but discovered nothing unusual. She saw the picture of Vadimov's family he kept under his pillow: His wife was a ballerina eleven years younger than him, and their little daughter ... Cheng Xin wiped her eyes.

Vadimov had once told Cheng Xin that, superstitiously, he never left family photos on desks or nightstands. Doing so seemed to him to expose them to danger. He kept the pictures hidden and only took them out when he wanted to look at them.

Every time Cheng Xin thought of Vadimov, she also thought of Yun Tianming. Tianming and six other candidates had been moved to a secret base near PIA Headquarters to undergo a final series of tests, after which one of them would be picked.

Since meeting Tianming back in China, Cheng Xin's heart had grown heavier over time, until she sank into a depression. She recalled the first time they met. It was just after the start of their first semester in college, and all the aerospace engineering students took turns introducing themselves. She saw Tianming sitting by himself in a corner. From the moment she saw him, she understood his vulnerability and loneliness. She had met other boys who were isolated and forlorn, but she had never felt like this: as though she had stolen into his heart and could see his secrets.

Cheng Xin liked confident, optimistic boys, boys who were like sunlight, warming themselves as well as the girls with them. Tianming was the very opposite of her type. But she always had

a desire to take care of him. In their interactions she was careful, fearful of hurting him, even if unintentionally. She had never been so protective of other boys.

When her friend had come to New York and Tianming's name came up, Cheng Xin discovered that although she had tucked him away in a distant corner of her memory, his image was surprisingly clear when she recalled him.

One night, Cheng Xin had another nightmare. She was again at her star, but the red sea algae had turned black. Then the star collapsed into a black hole, a lightless absence in the universe. Around the black hole, a tiny, glowing object moved. Trapped by the gravity of the black hole, the object would never be able to escape: It was a frozen brain.

Cheng Xin woke up and looked at the glow of New York's lights against her curtain. She understood what she had done.

From one perspective, she had simply passed along the PIA's request; he could have said no. She had recommended him because she was trying to protect the Earth and its civilization, and his life had almost reached its end—had she not arrived in time, he would be dead. In a way, she had saved him!

She had done nothing that she ought to be ashamed of, nothing that should trouble her conscience.

But she also understood that this was how someone could sell their mother to a whorehouse.

Cheng Xin thought about hibernation. The technology was mature enough that some people—mostly terminally ill patients seeking a cure in the future—had already entered the long sleep. Tianming had a chance. Given his social status, it would be hard for him to afford hibernation, but she could help him. It was a possibility, an opportunity that she had taken from him.

The next day, Cheng Xin went to see Wade.

As usual, Wade stared at his lit cigar in his office. She rarely saw him perform the tasks that she associated with conventional administration: making phone calls, reading documents, attending meetings, and so forth. She didn't know when, if ever, Wade did

these things. All she could see was him sitting, deep in thought, always deep in thought.

Cheng Xin explained that she thought Candidate #5 was unsuitable. She wanted to withdraw her recommendation and ask that the man be removed from consideration.

"Why? He has scored the best in our tests."

Wade's comment stunned Cheng Xin and chilled her heart. One of the first tests they conducted was to put each candidate under a special form of general anesthesia that caused the person to lose feeling in all parts of the body and sensory organs but remain conscious. The experience was intended to simulate the conditions of a brain existing independent of the body. Then the examiners assessed the candidate's psychological ability to adapt to alien conditions. Of course, since the test designers knew nothing about conditions within the Trisolaran Fleet, they had to fill out their simulation with guesses. Overall, the test was quite harsh.

"But he has only an undergraduate degree," Cheng Xin said.

"You certainly have more degrees," said Wade. "But if we used your brain for this mission, it would, without a doubt, be one of the worst brains we could have chosen."

"He's a loner! I've never seen anyone so withdrawn. He doesn't have any ability to adjust and adapt to the conditions around him."

"That is precisely Candidate #5's best quality! You're talking about human society. Someone who feels comfortable with this environment has also learned to rely on it. Once one is cut off from the rest of humanity and finds oneself in a strange environment, one is very likely to suffer a fatal breakdown. You're a perfect example of what I'm talking about."

Cheng Xin had to admit that Wade's logic was sound. She probably would suffer a breakdown from the simulation alone.

She certainly knew that she had no clout to get the top administrator of the PIA to give up on a candidate for the Staircase Program. But she didn't want to give up. She steeled herself. She would say whatever was necessary to save Tianming.

"He's made no meaningful attachments in life. He has no sense

of responsibility to humanity, or love." After saying this, Cheng Xin wondered if there was some truth to it.

"Oh, there is definitely something on Earth he's attached to."

Wade's gaze remained on the cigar, but Cheng Xin could feel his attention being deflected from the cigar's lit tip onto her, carrying with it some of the flame's heat. To her relief, Wade abruptly changed the subject.

"Another excellent quality of Candidate #5 is his creativity. This makes up for his lack of technical knowledge. Did you know that an idea of his made one of your classmates into a billionaire?"

Cheng Xin had indeed seen this in Tianming's background file—so she did know someone really rich, after all. But she didn't believe for a minute that Hu Wen was the one who had given her the star. The very idea was ridiculous. If he liked her, he would buy her a fancy car or a diamond necklace, not a star.

"I had thought none of the candidates were anywhere near being suitable, and I was running out of ideas. But you've reaffirmed my faith in #5. Thank you."

Wade finally lifted his eyes to look at Cheng Xin with his cold, predatory smile. As before, he seemed to take pleasure in her despair and pain.

But Cheng Xin didn't lose all hope.

She was attending the Oath of Allegiance Ceremony for Staircase Program candidates. According to the Space Convention, as amended post-Crisis, any person using resources of the Earth to leave the Solar System for economic development, emigration, scientific research, or other purposes must first take an oath pledging loyalty to humanity. Everyone had thought this provision would not be invoked until far in the future.

The ceremony took place in the UN General Assembly Hall. Unlike the session announcing the Wallfacer Project a few months ago, this ceremony was closed to the public. Besides the seven Staircase Program candidates, the only attendees were Secretary

General Say, the PDC rotating chair, and a few observers—including Cheng Xin and other members of the PIA working on the Staircase Program—who filled the first two rows of seats.

The ceremony didn't take long. In turn, each candidate put his or her hand on the UN flag held up by Secretary General Say and recited the required oath to be "loyal to the human race for all time, and to never perform any act that harms humanity's well-being."

Four candidates were lined up before Yun Tianming—two Americans, a Russian, and a British man—and two more stood behind him: another American, and another Chinese. All the candidates looked sickly, and two had to use wheelchairs. But all looked to be in good spirits—not unlike oil lamps giving off a final burst of light before burning out.

Cheng Xin looked at Tianming. Since the last time she had seen him, he looked thinner and more pallid, but appeared very calm. He didn't look back in her direction.

The first four candidates' oaths went off without a hitch. One of the Americans, a physicist in his fifties with pancreatic cancer, struggled up from his wheelchair and climbed onto the rostrum by himself. The candidates' voices echoed in the empty hall, frail but full of dedication. The only interruption in the routine was the British man asking whether he would be allowed to take his oath on a Bible. His request was granted.

It was Tianming's turn. Though Cheng Xin was an atheist, at that moment she wished she could grab the Bible from that man and pray to it: *Tianming, please take the oath, please! I know you're a responsible man. You'll be faithful to the human race. Like Wade said, there are things here that you cannot bear to part with....*

She watched as Tianming mounted the dais, watched as he walked in front of Secretary General Say, and then squeezed her eyes shut.

She didn't hear him repeat the oath.

Tianming picked up the blue UN flag from Say and lightly draped it on the lectern next to him.

"I will not take the oath. In this world, I feel like a stranger.

I've never experienced much joy or happiness, and didn't receive much love. Of course, these can all be attributed to my faults—"

His tone was placid, as though he was reviewing his own life. Cheng Xin, sitting below the dais, began to tremble as though waiting for an apocalyptic judgment.

"—but I will not take this oath. I do not affirm any responsibility to the human race."

"Then why have you agreed to be in the Staircase Program?" asked Say. Her voice was gentle, as were her eyes on Tianming.

"I want to see another world. As for whether I'll be faithful to humanity, it will depend on what kind of civilization I see among the Trisolarans."

Say nodded. "Your oath is entirely voluntary. You may go. Next candidate, please."

Cheng Xin shook as though she had fallen into an ice cellar. She bit her bottom lip and forced herself not to cry.

Tianming had passed the final test.

Wade, who was sitting in the front row, turned around to look at Cheng Xin. He took delight in even more despair and pain. His eyes seemed to speak to Cheng Xin.

Now you see what he's made of.

But … what if he's telling the truth?

If even we believe him, the enemy will believe him, too.

Wade turned back to the rostrum, then seemed to remember something vital, and glanced back at Cheng Xin again.

This is a fun game, isn't it?

Tianming's unexpected refusal seemed to change the atmosphere in the hall. The last candidate, a forty-three-year-old HIV-positive American NASA engineer named Joyner, also refused to take the oath. She explained that she had not wanted to be here, but she had felt compelled to come because she believed that if she refused, her friends and family would despise her and leave her to die alone. No one knew if she was telling the truth or if Tianming had inspired her.

The next night, Joyner's condition suddenly deteriorated. An

infection that turned into pneumonia caused her to stop breathing, and she died before dawn. The medical staff did not have enough time to remove her brain for flash freezing, and it was unusable.

Tianming was chosen to carry out the mission of the Staircase Program.

The moment had arrived. Cheng Xin was informed that Tianming's condition had suddenly deteriorated. They needed to remove his brain right away. The procedure would be conducted at Westchester Medical Center.

Cheng Xin hesitated outside the hospital. She didn't dare enter, but she couldn't bear to leave. All she could do was to suffer. Wade, who had come with her, walked ahead toward the hospital entrance alone. He stopped, turned around, and admired her pain. Then, satisfied, he delivered the final blow.

"Oh, I have another surprise for you: He gave you the star."

Cheng Xin stood frozen. Everything seemed to transform around her. What she had seen before were mere shadows; only now did life's true colors reveal themselves. The tidal wave of emotion made her stumble, as if the ground had disappeared.

She rushed into the hospital and dashed through the long, winding hallways until two guards outside the neurosurgery area stopped her. She struggled against them, but they held fast. She fumbled for her ID, waved it at them, and then continued her mad run toward the operating room. The crowd outside, surprised, parted for her. She slammed through the doors with glowing red lights over them.

She was too late.

A group of men and women in white coats turned around. The body had already been removed from the room. In the middle was a workbench, on top of which sat a cylindrical stainless steel insulating container, about a meter tall. It had just been sealed, and the white fog produced by the liquid helium still hadn't completely dissipated. Slowly, the white fog rolled down the surface of the

container, flowed across the workbench, cascaded over the edge like a miniature waterfall, and pooled on the floor, where it finally broke apart. In the fog, the container appeared otherworldly.

Cheng Xin threw herself at the workbench. Her motion broke up the white fog, and she felt herself enveloped in a pocket of cold air that dissipated in a moment. It was as if she had briefly touched what she was seeking before losing it to another time, another place, forever.

Prostrate in front of the container of liquid helium, Cheng Xin sobbed. Her sorrow filled the operating room, overflowed the hospital building, flooded New York City. Above her, the sorrow became a lake, then an ocean. At its bottom, she felt close to drowning.

She didn't know how much time passed before she felt the hand placed against her shoulders. Maybe the hand had been there for a long time, and maybe the owner of the hand had been speaking for a long time, as well.

"There is hope." It was the voice of an old man, gentle and slow. "There is hope."

Still wracked by sobs, Cheng Xin could not catch her breath, but what the voice said next got her attention.

"Think! If they can revive that brain, what would be the ideal container for it?"

The voice did not offer empty platitudes, but a concrete idea.

She lifted her head, and through tear-blurred eyes, she recognized the white-haired old man: the world's foremost brain surgeon, affiliated with Harvard Medical School. He had been the lead surgeon during the operation.

"It would be the body that had carried this brain in the first place. Every cell in the brain contains all the genetic information necessary to reconstruct his body. They could clone him and implant the brain, and in this way, he would be whole again."

Cheng Xin stared at the stainless steel container. Tears rolled down her face, but she didn't care. Then she recovered and stunned everyone: "What is he going to eat?"

She sprinted out of the room, in as much of a rush as when she had barged in.

The next day, Cheng Xin returned to Wade's office and deposited an envelope on his desk. She looked as pale as some terminally ill patients.

"I request that these seeds be included in the Staircase capsule."

Wade opened the envelope and emptied its contents onto the desk: more than a dozen small packets. He ticked through them with interest: "Wheat, corn, potatoes, and these are ... some vegetables, right? Hmmm, is this chili pepper?"

Cheng Xin nodded. "One of his favorites."

Wade put all the packets back into the envelope and pushed it across the desk. "No."

"Why? These weigh only eighteen grams in total."

"We must make every effort to remove even point one eight grams of excess mass."

"Just pretend his brain is eighteen grams heavier!"

"But it's *not*, is it? Adding this weight would lead to a slower final cruising speed for the spacecraft, and delay the encounter with the Trisolaran Fleet by many years." That cold smirk again appeared on Wade's face. "Besides, he's just a brain now—no mouth, no stomach. What would be the point? Don't believe that fairy tale about cloning. They'll just put the brain in a nice incubator and keep it alive."

Cheng Xin wanted to rip the cigar out of Wade's hand and put it out against his face. But she controlled herself. "I will bypass you and make the request to those with more authority."

"It won't work. Then?"

"Then I'll resign."

"I won't allow it. You're still useful to the PIA."

Cheng Xin laughed bitterly. "You can't stop me. You've never been my real boss."

"You will not do anything I don't allow."

Cheng Xin turned around and started to walk away.

"The Staircase Program needs to send someone who knows Yun Tianming to the future."

Cheng Xin stopped.

"However, that person must be a member of the PIA and under my command. Are you interested? Or do you want to hand in your resignation now?"

Cheng Xin continued walking, but her stride slowed down. Finally, she stopped a second time. Wade's voice came again. "You'd better be sure about your choice this time."

"I agree to go to the future," Cheng Xin said. She leaned against the doorframe for support. She didn't turn around.

The only time Cheng Xin got to see the Staircase spacecraft was when its radiation sail unfolded in orbit. The giant sail, twenty-five square kilometers in area, briefly reflected sunlight onto the Earth. Cheng Xin was already in Shanghai, and she saw an orange-red glowing spot appear in the pitch-black sky, gradually fading. Five minutes later, it was gone, like an eye that materialized out of nowhere to look at the Earth and then slowly shut its eyelid. The craft's journey as it accelerated out of the Solar System was not visible to the naked eye.

Cheng Xin was comforted by the fact that the seeds did accompany Tianming—not her seeds, exactly, but seeds that had been carefully selected by the space agricultural department.

The giant sail's mass was 9.3 kilograms. Four five-hundred-kilometer cables connected it to the space capsule, whose diameter was only forty-five centimeters. A layer of ablative material covered the capsule, making its launch mass 850 grams. After the acceleration leg, the capsule mass would be reduced to 510 grams.

The acceleration leg stretched from the Earth to the orbit of Jupiter. A total of 1,004 nuclear bombs were distributed along the route, two-thirds of which were fission bombs, the rest fusion. They were like a row of mines that the Staircase craft triggered as it

passed by. Numerous probes were also distributed along the route to monitor the craft's heading and speed and coordinate minute adjustments to the positions of the remaining bombs. Like the pulses of a heart, successive nuclear detonations lit up the space behind the sail with blinding glows, and a storm of radiation propelled this feather forward. By the time the spacecraft approached Jupiter's orbit and the 997th nuclear bomb exploded, monitoring probes showed that it had achieved 1 percent of lightspeed.

That was when the accident occurred. Analysis of the frequency spectrum of the light reflected from the radiation sail showed that the sail had begun to curl, possibly because one of the towing cables had broken. However, the 998th nuclear bomb detonated before adjustments could be made, and the craft deviated from the projected course. As the sail continued to curl, its radar profile rapidly shrank, and it disappeared from the monitoring system. Without precise parameters for its trajectory, it would never be found again.

As time passed, the spacecraft's trajectory would deviate farther and farther from the projection. Hopes that it would intercept the Trisolaran Fleet diminished. Based on its approximate final heading, it should pass by another star in six thousand years and depart the Milky Way in five million years.

At least the Staircase Program was a half success. For the first time, a man-made object had been accelerated to quasi-relativistic speeds.

There was no real reason to send Cheng Xin to the future anymore, but the PIA still asked her to enter suspended animation. Her mission now was to act as a liaison to the Staircase Program in the future. If this pioneering effort was to be helpful to humanity's spaceflight efforts in two centuries, someone who understood it deeply had to be there to explain the dead data and interpret the mute documents. Of course, perhaps the real reason for sending her was only one of vanity, a wish that the Staircase Program would not be forgotten by the future. Other large contemporary engineering projects had made similar efforts to send liaisons to the future for similar reasons.

If the future wished to pass judgment on our struggles, then at least it was now possible to send someone to the future to explain the misunderstandings brought about by the passage of time.

As Cheng Xin's consciousness faded in the cold, she held on to a ray of comfort: Like Tianming, she would drift through an endless abyss for centuries.

PART II

DETERRENCE ERA, YEAR 12
BRONZE AGE

It was now possible to see the Earth with the naked eye from the view window of *Bronze Age*. As the ship decelerated, those who weren't on duty came to the open space at the stern to observe the Earth through the wide portholes.

At this distance, the Earth still resembled a star, but it was possible to see a pale blue in its glow. The final deceleration stage had begun, and as the stellar drive came online, the crew, who had been floating in zero gravity, drifted toward the portholes like leaves falling in autumn, and finally landed against the broad sheets of glass. The artificial gravity generated by deceleration gradually increased until it reached 1G. The portholes now formed the floor, and the people lying down felt the weight like the embrace of Mother Earth ahead of them. Excitement echoed around the chamber.

"We're home!"

"Can you believe it?"

"I'll get to see my kids again."

"We can have kids!"

When *Bronze Age* left the Solar System, the law had dictated that no one could be born on the ship unless someone died.

"She said she'd wait for me."

"If you'll have her! You're now a hero of the human race; you'll have a flock of pretty girls after you."

"Oh, I haven't seen flocks of birds in *ages*!"

"Doesn't everything we've been through seem like a dream?"

"I feel like I'm dreaming now."

"I'm utterly terrified of space."

"Me too. I'm retiring as soon as we get back. I'm going to buy a farm and spend the rest of my life on solid ground."

It had been fourteen years since the complete destruction of the Earth's combined fleet. The survivors, after engaging in separate internecine battles of darkness, cut off all contact with the home planet. However, for a year and a half thereafter, *Bronze Age* continued to receive transmissions from Earth, most of which were surface radio communications, but which also included some transmissions intended for space.

And then, at the beginning of November in Year 208 of the Crisis Era, all radio transmissions from Earth ceased. Every frequency fell silent, as though the Earth was a lamp that had been suddenly shut off.

EXCERPT FROM
A PAST OUTSIDE OF TIME
NYCTOHYLOPHOBIA

When humanity finally learned that the universe was a dark forest in which everyone hunted everyone else, the child who had once cried out for contact by the bright campfire put out the fire and shivered in the darkness. Even a spark terrified him.

During the first few days, even mobile phone use was forbidden, and antennas around the world were forcibly shut down. Such a move, which would have once caused riots in the streets, was widely supported by the populace.

Gradually, as reason was restored, so were the mobile networks, but severe restrictions regarding electromagnetic radiation were put in place. All radio communications had to operate at minimum power, and any violators risked being tried for crimes against humanity.

Most people surely understood that these reactions were excessive and meaningless. The peak of the Earth's projection of electromagnetic signals into space had occurred during the age of analog signals, when television and radio transmission towers operated at high power levels. But as digital communication became prevalent, most information was transmitted via wires and optical cables, and even radio transmissions for digital signals required

far less power than analog signals. The amount of electromagnetic radiation spilling into space from the Earth had fallen so much that some pre-Crisis scholars had fretted that the Earth would become impossible to discover by friendly aliens.

Electromagnetic waves are, moreover, the most primitive and least power-efficient method of transmitting information in the universe. Radio waves attenuate and degrade rapidly in the vastness of space, and most electromagnetic signals spilling from the Earth could not be received beyond two light-years. Only something like the transmission by Ye Wenjie, which relied on the power of the sun as an antenna, could be intercepted by listeners among the stars.

As humanity's technology advanced, two far more efficient methods of signaling became available: neutrinos and gravitational waves. The latter was the main method of deterrence that humanity later deployed against Trisolaris.

The dark forest theory had a profound impact on human civilization. That child sitting by the ashes of the campfire turned from optimism to isolation and paranoia, a loner in the universe.

DETERRENCE ERA, YEAR 12
BRONZE AGE

Most of the crew aboard *Bronze Age* attributed the sudden cessation of all signals from the Earth to the complete conquest of the Solar System by Trisolaris. *Bronze Age* accelerated and headed for a star with terrestrial planets twenty-six light-years away.

But ten days later, *Bronze Age* received a radio transmission from Fleet Command. The transmission had been sent simultaneously to *Bronze Age* and *Blue Space,* which was at the other end of the Solar System. The transmission gave a brief account of what had happened on Earth and notified them of the successful creation of a deterrence system to defend against Trisolaris. The two ships were ordered to return to Earth immediately. Moreover, Earth had taken great risks to send out this message to the lost ships; it would not be repeated.

At first, *Bronze Age* dared not trust this message—wasn't it possible that it was a trap set by those who had conquered the Solar System? The warship stopped accelerating and repeatedly queried Earth for confirmation. No reply ever came, as Earth maintained radio silence.

Just as *Bronze Age* was about to begin accelerating away from home again, the unimaginable happened: A sophon unfolded into low dimensions on the ship, establishing a quantum communication channel with Earth. Finally, the crew received confirmation of all that had occurred.

The crew found that, as some of the only survivors of the holocaust suffered by the combined space forces of Earth, they were now heroes of the human race. The whole world awaited their return with bated breath. Fleet Command awarded all members of the crew with the highest military honors.

Bronze Age began its return voyage. It was currently in outer space, about twenty-three hundred AU from the Earth, far beyond the Kuiper Belt but still some distance from the Oort Cloud. As it was cruising near maximum speed, deceleration consumed most of its fusion fuel. Its journey toward the Earth had to be conducted at a low cruising speed, and took eleven years.

As they finally neared Earth, a small white dot appeared ahead of them and quickly grew. It was *Gravity,* the warship that had been dispatched to welcome *Bronze Age*.

Gravity was the first stellar-class warship built after the Doomsday Battle. Deterrence-Era spaceships were no longer constructed along fixed body plans. Rather, most large spaceships were constructed out of multiple modules that could be assembled into various configurations. But *Gravity* was an exception. It was a white cylinder, so regular that it seemed unreal, like a basic shape dropped into space by mathematical modeling software, a platonic ideal rather than reality.

If the crew of *Bronze Age* had seen the gravitational wave antennas on the Earth, they would have recognized *Gravity* as an almost perfect replica of them. Indeed, the entire hull of *Gravity* was a large gravitational wave antenna. Like its twins on the Earth's surface, the ship was capable of broadcasting gravitational wave messages toward all corners of the universe at a moment's notice. These gravitational wave antennas on Earth and in space comprised humanity's dark forest deterrence system against Trisolaris.

After another day of coasting, *Bronze Age,* escorted by *Gravity,* entered geosynchronous orbit and slowly sailed into the orbital spaceport. *Bronze Age*'s crew could see dense crowds filling the broad expanse of the habitat sector of the spaceport like the opening

ceremony of the Olympics or the Hajj in Mecca. The warship drifted through a colorful snowstorm of bouquets. The crew looked through the crowd for their loved ones. Everyone seemed to have tears in their eyes, crying out in joy.

With a final tremor, *Bronze Age* came to a complete stop. The captain gave a status report to Fleet Command and declared his intent to leave a skeleton crew behind on the ship. Fleet Command replied that the priority was to quickly reunite all members of the crew with their loved ones. There was no need to leave anyone behind on the ship. Another captain from the fleet boarded the ship with a small duty team who greeted everyone they encountered with tearful embraces.

It was unclear from the duty team's uniforms which of the three space fleets they belonged to, but they explained to those aboard the ship that the new Solar System Fleet was a single, unified force, and all those who had been part of the Doomsday Battle—including all the men and women aboard *Bronze Age*—would be key figures in the new fleet.

"In our lifetimes, we will conquer Trisolaris and open up a second solar system for human colonization!" the fleet captain said.

Someone replied that they found space too terrifying and they would rather remain on the Earth. The fleet captain said that was perfectly acceptable. As heroes of humanity, they were free to choose their own paths in life. However, after a bit of R&R, they might change their minds. He, for one, hoped to see this famed warship in action again.

The crew of *Bronze Age* began to disembark. Everyone entered the habitable region of the spaceport through a long passageway. Open space stretched around the crew. In contrast to the air on the ship, the air here smelled fresh and sweet, like after a rainstorm. Against the background of the spinning blue globe that was the Earth, the joyous shouts of the welcoming crowd filled the expansive area.

Per a request from the fleet captain, the captain of *Bronze Age* conducted a roll call. At the fleet captain's insistence, the roll call

was repeated, to confirm that every member of the crew had disembarked and was present and accounted for.

Then there was silence.

Although the celebrating crowd around them continued to dance and wave their arms, they made no sound. All that anyone from *Bronze Age* could hear was the fleet captain's voice. His face still bore a kind smile, but in that eerie silence, his voice sounded as sharp as the edge of a sword.

"You're hereby informed that you have been dishonorably discharged. You are no longer members of the Solar System Fleet. But the stain you have brought upon the fleet can never be erased! You will never see your loved ones again, because they have no wish to see you. Your parents are ashamed of you, and most of your spouses have long ago divorced you. Even though society has not discriminated against your children, they spent the past decade growing up in the shadow of your disgrace. They despise you!

"You are hereby transferred to Fleet International's justice system."

The fleet captain left with his team. Simultaneously, the celebratory crowd disappeared and was replaced by darkness. A few roving spotlights revealed the ranks of fully armed military police surrounding the crew of *Bronze Age*. Standing on platforms around the broad square, they aimed their guns at the crew.

Some members of the crew turned around and saw that the bouquets of flowers floating around *Bronze Age* were real, not holographic mirages. But now they made the warship seem like a giant coffin about to be buried.

Power to the magnetic boots worn by the crew was cut off, and they floated up in free fall, like a bunch of helpless target dummies.

A cold voice spoke to them from somewhere. "All armed crew members must immediately relinquish your weapons. If you do not cooperate, we cannot guarantee your safety. You're under arrest for murder in the first degree and crimes against humanity."

DETERRENCE ERA,
YEAR 13
TRIAL

The *Bronze Age* case was tried by a Solar System Fleet court-martial. Although Fleet International's main facilities were located near the orbit of Mars, the asteroid belt, and the orbit of Jupiter, due to the intense interest in the case from Earth International, the trial was held at the fleet base in geosynchronous orbit.

To accommodate the numerous observers from Earth, the base spun to generate artificial gravity. Outside the broad windows of the courtroom, blue Earth, bright Sun, and the silvery brilliance of the stars appeared in succession, a cosmic metaphor for the contest of values. The trial lasted a month under these shifting lights and shadows. Excerpts from the trial transcript follow.

Neil Scott, male, 45, captain, commanding officer of *Bronze Age*

JUDGE: Let's return to the events leading up to the decision to attack *Quantum*.

SCOTT: I repeat: The attack was my decision and I gave the order. I didn't discuss it ahead of time with any other officer aboard *Bronze Age*.

JUDGE: You've been consistently trying to claim all responsibility. However, this is not, in fact, a wise course of action for either you or those you're trying to protect.

PROSECUTION: We have already confirmed that a vote by the full crew was taken prior to the attack.

SCOTT: As I've explained, of the one thousand seven hundred and seventy-five crew members, only fifty-nine supported an attack. The vote was not the cause or basis for my decision to attack.

JUDGE: Can you produce a list of those fifty-nine names?

SCOTT: The vote was conducted anonymously over the ship's internal network. You can examine the cruise and battle logs to confirm this.

PROSECUTION: More lies. We have ample evidence that the vote was not anonymous. Moreover, the result was nothing like your description. You falsified the logs afterwards.

JUDGE: We need you to produce the true record of the vote.

SCOTT: I don't have what you want. The result I recited is the truth.

JUDGE: Mr. Neil Scott, let me remind you: If you continue to obstruct this tribunal's investigation, you will harm the innocent members of your crew. Some members did vote against the attack, but without the evidence that only you can provide, we cannot exonerate them, and must declare all officers, non-commissioned officers, and enlisted men and women of *Bronze Age* guilty as charged.

SCOTT: What are you talking about? Are you a real judge? Is this a real court of law? What about the presumption of innocence?

JUDGE: The presumption of innocence does not apply to crimes against humanity. This is a principle of international law established at the start of the Crisis Era. It's intended to ensure that traitors against humankind do not escape punishment.

SCOTT: We're not traitors against humanity! Where were you when we fought for Earth?

PROSECUTION: You are absolutely traitors! While the ETO from two centuries ago only betrayed the interests of humanity, today, you betray our most basic moral principles, a far worse crime.

SCOTT: *[silence]*

JUDGE: I want you to understand the consequences of fabricating evidence. At the commencement of this trial, you read a statement on behalf of all the accused expressing your remorse over the deaths of the one thousand eight hundred and forty-seven men and women aboard *Quantum*. It is now time to show that remorse.

SCOTT: *[after a long silence]* All right. I will produce the true results. You can recover the vote tally from an encrypted entry in the logs aboard *Bronze Age*.

PROSECUTION: We will work on recovering those immediately. Can you give me an estimate of how many voted to attack *Quantum*?

SCOTT: One thousand six hundred and seventy. That's ninety-four percent of the crew.

JUDGE: Order! Order in the court! I must remind members of the public to maintain silence during the proceedings.

SCOTT: But it wouldn't have mattered. Even if less than fifty percent had voted yes, I would have attacked anyway. The final decision was mine.

PROSECUTION: Nice try. But *Bronze Age* was not like the newer ships at the other end of the Solar System, such as *Natural Selection*. Your ship's AI systems were primitive. Without the cooperation of those under your command, you could not have carried out the attack alone.

Sebastian Schneider, male, 31, lieutenant commander, in charge of targeting systems and attack patterns aboard *Bronze Age*

PROSECUTION: Other than the captain, you're the only officer with the system authorization to prevent or terminate an attack.

SCHNEIDER: Correct.

JUDGE: And you didn't.

SCHNEIDER: I did not.

JUDGE: What went through your mind at that time?

SCHNEIDER: At that moment—not the moment of the attack, but the moment when I realized that *Bronze Age* would never return home, when the ship would be my entire world—I changed. There was no process; I was simply transformed from head to toe. It was like the legendary mental seal.

JUDGE: Do you really think that's a possibility? That your ship was equipped with mental seals?

SCHNEIDER: Of course not. I was talking metaphorically. Space itself is a kind of mental seal.... In that moment, I gave up my individual self. My existence would be meaningful only if the collective survived.... I can't explain it better than that. I don't expect you to understand, Your Honor. Even if you boarded *Bronze Age* and sailed twenty thousand AU from the Solar System, or even farther, you still wouldn't understand.

JUDGE: Why?

SCHNEIDER: Because you'd know that you could come back! Your soul would have remained on Earth. Only if the space behind the ship turned into a bottomless abyss—only if the Sun, the Earth, and everything else were swallowed by emptiness—would you have a chance of understanding the transformation that I went through.

I'm from California. In 1967, under the old calendar, a high school teacher in my hometown, Ron Jones, did something interesting—please don't interrupt me. Thank you.

In order to help his students understand Nazism and totalitarianism, he tried to create a simulation of a totalitarian society with his students. It took only five days for him to succeed and his class to become a miniature fascist state. Every student willingly gave up the self and freedom, became one with the supreme collective, and pursued the collective's goals with religious zeal. In the end, this teaching experiment that began as a harmless game almost spun out of control. The Germans made a film based on Jones's experiment, and Jones himself wrote a book about it: *The Third Wave*. When those of us aboard *Bronze Age* found out that we were doomed to wander space forever,

we formed a totalitarian state as well. Do you know how long it took?

Five minutes.

That's right. Five minutes into the all-hands meeting, the fundamental values of this totalitarian society had received the support of the vast majority of the crew. So, let me tell you, when humans are lost in space, it takes only five minutes to reach totalitarianism.

Boris Rovinski, male, 36, commander, executive officer of *Bronze Age*

JUDGE: You led the first boarding party onto *Quantum* after the attack?

ROVINSKI: Yes.

JUDGE: Were there any survivors?

ROVINSKI: None.

JUDGE: Can you describe the scene?

ROVINSKI: The individuals aboard died from the infrasonic waves generated by *Quantum*'s hull as it was struck by the electro-magnetic pulses of the H-bomb detonation. The bodies were well preserved, showing no external signs of damage.

JUDGE: What did you do with the bodies?

ROVINSKI: We built a monument to them, like *Blue Space* did.

JUDGE: You mean, you left the bodies in the monument?

ROVINSKI: No. I doubt that the monument built by *Blue Space* had any bodies in it, either.

JUDGE: You haven't answered my question. I asked what you did with the bodies.

ROVINSKI: We refilled the food stores on *Bronze Age* with them.

JUDGE: All of them?

ROVINSKI: All of them.

JUDGE: Who made the decision to turn the bodies into food?

ROVINSKI: I ... really can't remember. It seemed a completely natural thing to do at the time. I was responsible for logistics

and support aboard the ship, and I directed the storage and distribution of the bodies.

JUDGE: How were the bodies consumed?

ROVINSKI: Nothing special was done. They were mixed up with the vegetables and meats in the bio-recycling system and then cooked.

JUDGE: Who ate this food?

ROVINSKI: Everyone. Everyone onboard *Bronze Age* had to eat in one of the four mess halls, and there was only one source of food.

JUDGE: Did they know what they were eating?

ROVINSKI: Of course.

JUDGE: How did they react?

ROVINSKI: I'm sure a few were uncomfortable with it. But there was no protest. Oh, I do recall eating in the officer's mess hall once and hearing someone say, "Thank you, Carol Joiner."

JUDGE: What did he mean?

ROVINSKI: Carol Joiner was the communications officer aboard *Quantum*. He was eating a part of her.

JUDGE: How could he know that?

ROVINSKI: We were all fitted with a tracking and identification capsule about the size of a grain of rice. It was implanted under the skin of the left arm. Sometimes the cooking process didn't remove it. I'm sure he just found it on his plate and used his communicator to read it.

JUDGE: Order! Order in the courtroom! Please remove those who have fainted. Mr. Rovinski, surely you must have understood that you were violating the most fundamental laws that make us human?

ROVINSKI: We were constrained by other morals that you don't understand. During the Doomsday Battle, *Bronze Age* had to exceed its designed acceleration parameters. The power systems were overloaded, and the life support systems lost power for almost two hours, leading to massive damage throughout. The repairs had to be conducted slowly. Meanwhile, the hibernation systems were also affected, and only about five hundred people could be accommodated. Since more than one thousand

people had to eat, if we didn't introduce additional food sources, half of the population would have starved to death.

Even without these constraints, considering the interminable voyage that lay in front of us, to abandon so much precious protein in space would have been truly unconscionable....

I'm not trying to defend myself, and I'm not trying to defend anyone else on *Bronze Age*. Now that I've recovered the thinking patterns of humans anchored to the Earth, it is very difficult for me to speak these words. Very difficult.

Final statement made by Captain Neil Scott

I don't have much to say except a warning.

Life reached an evolutionary milestone when it climbed onto land from the ocean, but those first fish that climbed onto land ceased to be fish.

Similarly, when humans truly enter space and are freed from the Earth, they cease to be human. So, to all of you I say this: When you think about heading into outer space without looking back, please reconsider. The cost you must pay is far greater than you could imagine.

In the end, Captain Neil Scott and six other senior officers were convicted of murder and crimes against humanity and sentenced to life imprisonment. Of the remaining 1,768 members of the crew, only 138 were declared innocent. The rest received sentences ranging from twenty to three hundred years.

The Fleet International prison was located in the asteroid belt, between the orbits of Mars and Jupiter. Thus, the prisoners had to leave Earth again. Although *Bronze Age* had reached geo-synchronous orbit, the prisoners were doomed never to travel the

last thirty thousand kilometers of their 350-billion-kilometer voyage home.

As the prisoner transport ship accelerated, they once again drifted and fell against the portholes at the stern, like fallen leaves doomed to never reach the root of the tree. They looked outward as the blue globe that had haunted their dreams shrank and, once again, became just another star.

Before departing the fleet base, former Commander Rovinski, former Lieutenant Commander Schneider, and about a dozen other officers returned under guard to *Bronze Age* for the last time to assist with some details of the handover of the ship to her new crew.

For more than a decade, this ship had been their entire world. They had carefully decorated the inside with holograms of grasslands, forests, and oceans; cultivated real gardens; and built fishing ponds and water fountains, turning the ship into a real home. But now, all that was gone. All traces of their existence on the ship had been wiped away. *Bronze Age* was once again just a cold stellar warship.

Everyone they encountered in the halls looked at them coldly or simply ignored them. When they saluted, they made sure their eyes did not waver, to make it clear to the prisoners that the salute was for the military police escorting them only.

Schneider was brought to a spherical cabin to discuss technical details of the ship's targeting system with three officers. The three officers treated Schneider like a computer. They asked him questions in an emotionless voice and waited for his answers. There was not a hint of politeness, and not a single wasted word.

It took only an hour to complete the session. Schneider tapped the floating control interface a few times, as though closing some windows out of habit. All of a sudden, he kicked the spherical wall of the cabin hard, and propelled himself to the other end of the chamber. Simultaneously, the walls shifted and divided the cabin into two halves. The three officers and the military policeman were trapped in one half, and Schneider was alone in the other.

Schneider brought up a floating window. He tapped on it, his fingers a blur. It was the control interface for the communications

system. Schneider brought the ship's high-powered interstellar communications antenna online.

A faint *pop*. A small hole appeared in the cabin wall, and the cabin was filled with white smoke. The barrel of the military policeman's gun poked through the hole and aimed at Schneider.

"This is your last warning. Stop what you're doing immediately and open the door."

"*Blue Space,* this is *Bronze Age.*" Schneider's voice was quiet. He knew how far his message could travel had nothing to do with how loudly he spoke.

A laser beam shot through Schneider's chest. Red steam from vaporized blood erupted from the hole. Surrounded by a red fog made of his own blood, Schneider croaked out his last words:

"Don't come back. This is no longer your home!"

Blue Space had always responded to Earth's entreaties with more hesitation and suspicion than *Bronze Age* had, so they had only been decelerating slowly. Thus, by the time they received *Bronze Age*'s warning, they were still heading away from the Solar System.

After Schneider's warning, *Blue Space* instantly shifted from decelerating to accelerating full speed ahead.

When Earth received the intelligence report from the sophons of Trisolaris, the two civilizations had a shared enemy for the first time in history.

Earth and Trisolaris were comforted by the fact that *Blue Space* didn't currently possess the ability to engage in dark forest deterrence against the two worlds. Even if it tried to broadcast the locations of the two solar systems to the universe at full power, it would be almost impossible for anyone to hear it. To reach Barnard's Star, the nearest star that *Blue Space* could use as a superantenna to repeat Ye Wenjie's feat, would take three hundred years. However, it hadn't shifted its course toward Barnard's Star. Instead, it was still heading toward NH558J2, which it wouldn't reach for two thousand more years.

Gravity, as the only Solar System ship capable of interstellar flight, immediately began to pursue *Blue Space.* Trisolaris brought up the idea of sending a speedy droplet—formally, it was called a strong-interaction space probe—to pursue and destroy *Blue Space.* But Earth unequivocally refused. From humanity's perspective, *Blue Space* should be dealt with as a matter of internal affairs. The Doomsday Battle was humanity's greatest wound, and after more than a decade, the pain had not lessened one whit. Permitting another droplet attack on humans was absolutely politically unacceptable. Even though the crew of *Blue Space* had become aliens in the minds of most people, only humanity should bring them to justice.

Out of consideration for the ample time that remained before *Blue Space* could become a threat, Trisolaris acquiesced. However, Trisolaris emphasized that, since *Gravity* possessed the ability to broadcast via gravitational waves, its security was a matter of life and death for Trisolaris. Therefore, droplets would be sent as escorts, but would also ensure an overwhelming advantage against *Blue Space.*

Thus, *Gravity* cruised in formation with two droplets a few thousand meters away. The contrast between the sizes of the two ship types couldn't be greater. If one pulled back far enough to see the entirety of *Gravity,* the droplets would be invisible. And if one pulled close enough to a droplet to observe it, its smooth surface would clearly reflect an image of *Gravity.*

Gravity was built about a decade after *Blue Space.* Other than the gravitational wave antenna, it was not significantly more advanced. Its propulsion systems, for example, were only slightly more powerful than *Blue Space*'s. *Gravity*'s confidence in the success of their hunt was due to their overwhelming advantage in fuel reserves.

Even so, based on the ships' current velocities and accelerations, it would take fifty years for *Gravity* to catch *Blue Space.*

DETERRENCE ERA, YEAR 61
THE SWORDHOLDER

Cheng Xin gazed up at her star from the top of a giant tree. It was why she had been awakened.

During the brief life of the Stars Our Destination Project, a total of fifteen individuals were granted ownership of seventeen stars. Other than Cheng Xin, the other fourteen owners were lost to history, and no legal heirs could be located. The Great Ravine acted like a giant sieve, and too many did not make it through. Now, Cheng Xin was the only one who held legal title to a star.

Though humanity still hadn't begun to reach for any star beyond the Solar System, the rapid pace of technological progress meant that stars within three hundred light-years of the Earth were no longer of mere symbolic value. DX3906, Cheng Xin's star, turned out to have planets after all. Of the two planets discovered so far, one seemed very similar to Earth based on its mass, orbit, and a spectrum analysis of its atmosphere. As a result, its value rose to stratospheric heights. To everyone's surprise, they discovered that this star already had an owner.

The UN and the Solar System Fleet wanted to reclaim DX3906, but this couldn't be done legally unless the owner agreed to transfer the title. Thus Cheng Xin was awakened from her slumber after 264 years of hibernation.

The first thing she found out after emerging from hibernation was this: As she had expected, there was no news whatsoever about the Staircase Program. The Trisolarans had not intercepted the probe, and they had no idea of its whereabouts. The Staircase Program had been forgotten by history, and Tianming's brain was lost in the vastness of space. But this man, this man who had merged into nothingness, had left a real, solid world for his beloved, a world composed of a star and two planets.

A Ph.D. in astronomy named 艾 AA[3] had discovered the planets around DX3906. As part of her dissertation, AA had developed a new technique that used one star as a gravitational lens through which to observe another.

To Cheng Xin, AA resembled a vivacious bird fluttering around her nonstop. AA told Cheng Xin that she was familiar with people like her, who had come from the past—known as "Common Era people" after the old calendar—since her own dissertation advisor was a physicist from back then. Her knowledge of Common Era people was why she had been appointed as Cheng Xin's liaison from the UN Space Development Agency as her first job after her doctorate.

The request from the UN and the fleet to sell the star back to them put Cheng Xin in an awkward position. She felt guilty possessing a whole world, but the idea of selling a gift that had been given to her out of pure love made her ill. She suggested that she could give up all claim of ownership over DX3906 and keep the deed only as a memento, but she was told that was unacceptable. By law, the authorities could not accept such valuable real estate without compensating the original owner, so they insisted on buying it. Cheng Xin refused.

After much reflection, she came up with a new proposal: She would sell the two planets, but retain ownership of the star. At the same time, she would sign a covenant with the UN and the

3 *Translator's Note:* This is a name written in a mix of Chinese characters and English letters. The "艾" is the surname and is pronounced "Ai."

fleet granting humanity the right to use the energy produced by the star. The legal experts eventually concluded that this proposal was acceptable.

AA told Cheng Xin that since she was only selling the planets, the amount of compensation offered by the UN was much lower. But it was still an astronomical sum, and she would need to form a company to manage it properly.

"Would you like me to help you run this company?" AA asked.

Cheng Xin agreed, and AA immediately called the UN Space Development Agency to resign.

"I'm working for you now," she said, "so let me speak for a minute about your interests. Are you nuts?! Of all the choices available to you, you picked the *worst*! You could have sold the star along with the planets, and you would have become one of the richest people in the universe! Alternatively, you could have refused to sell, and kept the entire solar system for yourself. The law's protection of private property is absolute, and no one could have taken it away from you. And then you could have entered hibernation and woken up only when it's possible to fly to DX3906. Then you could go there! All that space! The ocean, the continents . . . you can do whatever you want, of course, but you should take me with you—"

"I've already made my decision," Cheng Xin said. "There's almost three centuries separating us. I don't expect us to understand each other right away."

"Fine." AA sighed. "But you should reevaluate your conception of duty and conscience. Duty drove you to give up the planets, and conscience made you keep the star, but duty again made you give up the star's energy output. You're one of those people from the past, like my dissertation advisor, torn by conflict between two ideals. But, in our age, conscience and duty are not ideals: an excess of either is seen as a mental illness called social-pressure personality disorder. You should seek treatment."

———

Even with the glow from the lights of the city below, Cheng Xin easily found DX3906. Compared to the twenty-first century, the air was far clearer. She turned from the night sky to the reality around her: She and AA stood like two ants on top of a glowing Christmas tree, and all around them stood a forest of Christmas trees. Buildings full of lights hung from branches like leaves. But this giant city was built on top of the earth, not below it. Thanks to the peace of the Deterrence Era, humanity's second cave-dwelling phase had come to an end.

They walked along the bough toward the tip. Each branch of the tree was a busy avenue full of floating translucent windows filled with information. They made the street look like a varicolored river. From time to time, a window or two left the traffic in the road and followed them for a while, and drifted back into the current when AA and Cheng Xin showed no interest. All the buildings on this branch-street hung below. Since this was the highest branch, the starry sky was right above them. If they had been walking along one of the lower branches, they would be surrounded by the bright buildings hanging from the branch above, and they would have felt like tiny insects flying through a dream forest, in which every leaf and fruit sparkled and dazzled.

Cheng Xin looked at the pedestrians along the street: a woman, two women, a group of women, another woman, three women—all of them were women, all beautiful. Dressed in pretty, luminous clothes, they seemed like the nymphs of this magical forest. Once in a while, they passed some older individuals, also women, their beauty undiminished by age. As they reached the end of the branch and surveyed the sea of lights below them, Cheng Xin asked the question that had been puzzling her for days. "What happened to the men?" In the few days since she had been awakened, she had not seen a single man.

"What do you mean? They're everywhere." AA pointed at the people around them. "Over there: See the man leaning against the balustrade? And there are three over there. And two walking toward us."

Cheng Xin stared. The individuals AA indicated had smooth, lovely faces; long hair that draped over their shoulders; slender, soft bodies—as if their bones were made of bananas. Their movements were graceful and gentle, and their voices, carried to her by the breeze, were sweet and tender.... Back in her century, these people would have been considered ultra-feminine.

Understanding dawned on her after a moment. The trend had been obvious even earlier. The decade of the 1980s was probably the last time when masculinity, as traditionally defined, was considered an ideal. After that, society and fashion preferred men who displayed traditionally feminine qualities. She recalled the Asian male pop stars of her own time who she had thought looked like pretty girls at first glance. The Great Ravine interrupted this tendency in the evolution of human society, but half a century of peace and ease brought about by the Deterrence Era accelerated the trend.

"It's true that Common Era people usually have trouble telling men and women apart at first," AA said. "But I'll teach you a trick. Pay attention to the way they look at you. A classical beauty like you is very attractive to them."

Cheng Xin looked at her, a bit flustered.

"No, no!" AA laughed. "I really am a woman, and I don't like you that way. But, honestly, I can't see what's attractive about the men of your era. Rude, savage, dirty—it's like they hadn't fully evolved. You'll adjust to and enjoy this age of beauty."

Close to three centuries ago, when Cheng Xin had been preparing for hibernation, she had imagined all kinds of difficulties she would face in the future, but this was something she was unprepared for. She imagined what it would be like to live the rest of her life in this feminine world ... and her mood turned melancholic. She looked up and searched for her star.

"You're thinking of him again, aren't you?" AA grabbed her by the shoulders. "Even if he hadn't gone into space and had spent the rest of his life with you, the grandchildren of your grandchildren would be dead by now. This is a new age; a new life. Forget about the past!"

Cheng Xin tried to think as AA suggested and forced herself to return to the present. She had only been here for a few days, and had just grasped the broadest outline of the history of the past three centuries. The strategic balance between the humans and the Trisolarans as a result of dark forest deterrence had shocked her the most.

A thought popped into her mind. *A world dedicated to femininity ... but what does that mean for deterrence?*

Cheng Xin and AA walked back along the bough. Again, a few informational windows drifted along with them, and this time, one drew Cheng Xin's attention. The window showed a man, clearly a man from the past: haggard, gaunt, messy hair, standing next to a black tombstone. The man and the tombstone were in shadows, but his eyes seemed to glow brightly with the reflected light of a distant dawn. A line of text appeared on the bottom of the screen:

Back during his time, a killer would be sentenced to death.

Cheng Xin thought the man's face looked familiar, but before she could look more closely, the image had disappeared. In his place appeared a middle-aged woman—well, at least Cheng Xin thought she was a woman. Wearing formal, non-glowing clothes that reminded Cheng Xin of a politician's, she was in the middle of giving a speech. The text earlier had been a part of the subtitles for her speech.

The window seemed to notice Cheng Xin's interest. It expanded and began to play the audio accompanying the video. The politician's voice was lovely and sweet, as though the words were strung together by strands of blown sugar. But the content of the speech was terrifying.

"Why the death penalty? Answer: because he killed. But that is only one correct answer.

"Another correct answer would be: because he killed too few. Killing one person was murder; killing a few or dozens was more murder; so killing thousands or tens of thousands ought to

be punished by putting the murderer to death a thousand times. What about more than that? A few hundred thousand? The death penalty, right? Yet, those of you who know some history are starting to hesitate.

"What if he killed millions? I can guarantee you such a person would not be considered a murderer. Indeed, such a person may not even be thought to have broken any law. If you don't believe me, just study history! Anyone who has killed millions is deemed a 'great' man, a hero.

"And if that person destroyed a whole world and killed every life on it—he would be hailed as a savior!"

"They're talking about Luo Ji," said AA. "They want to put him on trial."

"Why?"

"It's complicated. But basically, it's because of that world, the world whose location he broadcast to the universe, causing it to be destroyed. We don't know if there was life on that world—it's a possibility. So they're charging him with suspected mundicide, the most serious crime under our laws."

"Hey, you must be Cheng Xin!"

The voice shocked Cheng Xin. It had come from the floating window in front of her. The politician in it gazed at Cheng Xin, joy and surprise on her face, as though she were seeing an old friend. "You're the woman who owns that faraway world! Like a ray of hope, you've brought the beauty of your time to us. As the only human being ever to possess an entire world, you will also save this world. All of us have faith in you. Oh, sorry, I should introduce myself—"

AA kicked the window and shut it off. Cheng Xin was utterly amazed by the technology level of this age. She had no idea how her own image had been transmitted to the speaker, and no idea how the speaker was then able to pick her out of the billions who were watching her speech.

AA rushed in front of Cheng Xin and walked backwards as they talked. "Would you have destroyed a world to create this

form of deterrence? And, more importantly, if the enemy weren't deterred, would you press the button to ensure the destruction of two worlds?"

"This is a meaningless question. I would never put myself in that position."

AA stopped and grabbed Cheng Xin by the shoulders. She stared into her eyes. "Really? You wouldn't?"

"Of course not. Being put in such a position is the most terrifying fate I can think of. Far worse than death."

She couldn't understand why AA seemed so earnest, but AA nodded. "That puts me at ease.... Why don't we talk more tomorrow? You're tired and should get more rest. It takes a week to completely recover from hibernation."

The next morning, Cheng Xin got a call from AA.

AA showed up on the screen looking excited. "I'm going to surprise you and take you somewhere cool. Come on up. The car is at the top of the tree."

Cheng Xin went up and saw a flying car with its door open. She got in but didn't see AA. The door slid shut noiselessly and the seat molded itself around her, holding her tight like a hand. Gently, the car took off, merging into the streaming traffic of the forest-city.

It was still early, and shafts of sunlight, almost parallel to the ground, flickered through the car as it passed through the forest. Gradually, the giant trees thinned out and, finally, disappeared. Under the blue sky, Cheng Xin saw only grassland and woodland, an intoxicating green mosaic.

After the start of the Deterrence Era, most heavy industries had moved into orbit, and the Earth's natural ecology recovered. The surface of the Earth now looked more like it did in pre–Industrial Revolution times. Due to a drop in population and further industrialization of food production, much of the arable land was allowed to lie fallow and return to nature. The Earth was transforming into a giant park.

This beautiful world seemed unreal to Cheng Xin. Though awakened from hibernation, she felt as though she were in a dream.

Half an hour later, the car landed and the door slid open automatically. Cheng Xin got out, and the car rose into the air and left. After the turbulence from the propellers subsided, silence reigned over everything, pierced by occasional birdsong from far away. Cheng Xin looked around and found herself in the midst of a group of abandoned buildings. They looked like residential buildings from the Common Era. The bottom half of every building was covered in ivy.

The sight of the past covered by the green life of a new era gave Cheng Xin the sense of reality that she had been missing.

She called for AA, but a man's voice responded. "Hello."

She turned and saw a man standing on an ivy-covered second-story balcony. He wasn't like the soft, beautiful men of this time, but like the men of the past. Cheng Xin seemed to be dreaming again, a continuation of her nightmare from the Common Era.

It was Thomas Wade. He wore a black leather jacket, but he looked a bit older. Perhaps he had gone into hibernation after Cheng Xin, or perhaps he had awakened before her, or both.

Cheng Xin's eyes were focused on Wade's right hand. The hand, covered by a black leather glove, held an old Common-Era gun that was pointing at Cheng Xin.

"The bullet in here was designed to be shot underwater," said Wade. "It's supposed to last a long time. But it's been more than two hundred and seventy years. Who knows if it will work?" That familiar smile, the one he wore when he was taking delight in the despair of others, appeared on his face.

A flash. An explosion. Cheng Xin felt a hard punch against her left shoulder and the force slammed her against the broken wall behind her. The thick ivy muffled much of the noise from the gunshot. Distant birds continued to chitter.

"I can't use a modern gun," said Wade. "Every shot is automatically recorded in the public security databases now." His tone

was as serene as it had been when he used to discuss routine tasks with her.

"Why?" Cheng Xin didn't feel pain. Her left shoulder felt numb, as if it didn't belong to her.

"I want to be the Swordholder. You are my competitor, and you're going to win. I don't harbor any ill will toward you. Whether you believe me or not, I feel terrible at this moment."

"Did you kill Vadimov?" she asked. Blood seeped from the corner of her mouth.

"Yes. The Staircase Program needed him. And now, my new plan does not need you. Both of you are very good, but you're in the way. I have to advance, advance without regard for consequences."

Another shot. The bullet went through the left side of Cheng Xin's abdomen. She still didn't feel pain, but the spreading numbness made her unable to keep standing. She slid down against the wall, leaving a bright trail of blood on the ivy behind her.

Wade pulled the trigger again. Finally, the passage of nearly three centuries caught up with the gun, and it made no sound. Wade racked the slide to clear the dud out of the chamber. Once again, he pointed the gun at Cheng Xin.

His right arm exploded. A puff of white smoke rose into the air, and Wade's right forearm was gone. Burnt bits of bone and flesh splattered into the green leaves around him, but the gun, undamaged, fell to the foot of the building. Wade didn't move. He took a look at the stump of his right arm and then looked up. A police car was diving toward him.

As the police car approached the ground, several armed police officers jumped out and landed in the thick grass waving in the turbulence thrown up by the propellers. They looked like slender, nimble women.

The last one to jump out of the car was AA. Cheng Xin's vision was blurring, but she could see AA's tearful face and hear her sobbing explanation.

"... faked my call ..."

A fierce wave of pain seized her, and she lost consciousness.

When Cheng Xin woke up, she found herself in a flying car. A film clung to her and wrapped her tightly. She couldn't feel pain, couldn't even feel the presence of her body. Her consciousness began to fade again. In a faint voice that no one but herself could hear, she asked, "What is a Swordholder?"

EXCERPT FROM
A PAST OUTSIDE OF TIME
THE GHOST OF THE WALLFACERS:
THE SWORDHOLDER

Without a doubt, Luo Ji's creation of dark forest deterrence against Trisolaris was a great achievement, but the Wallfacer Project that led to it was judged a ridiculous, childish act. Humanity, like a child entering society for the first time, had lashed out at the sinister universe with terror and confusion. Once Luo Ji had transferred control of the deterrence system to the UN and the Solar System Fleet, everyone thought the Wallfacer Project, a legendary bit of history, was over.

People turned their attention to deterrence itself, and a new field of study was born: deterrence game theory.

The main elements of deterrence are these: the deterrer and the deteree (in dark forest deterrence, humanity and Trisolaris); the threat (broadcasting the location of Trisolaris so as to ensure the destruction of both worlds); the controller (the person or organization holding the broadcast switch); and the goal (forcing Trisolaris to abandon its invasion plan and to share technology with humanity).

When the deterrent is the complete destruction of both the deterrer and the deteree, the system is said to be in a state of ultimate deterrence.

Compared to other types of deterrence, ultimate deterrence is distinguished by the fact that, should deterrence fail, carrying out the threat would be of no benefit to the deterrer.

Thus, the key to the success of ultimate deterrence is the belief by the deteree that the threat will almost certainly be carried out if the deteree thwarts the deterrer's goals. This probability, or degree of deterrence, is an important parameter in deterrence game theory. The degree of deterrence must exceed 80 percent for the deterrer to succeed.

But people soon discovered a discouraging fact: If the authority to carry out the threat in dark forest deterrence is held by humanity as a whole, then the degree of deterrence is close to zero.

Asking humanity to take an action that would destroy two worlds is difficult: The decision would violate deeply held moral principles and values. The particular conditions of dark forest deterrence made the task even harder. Should deterrence fail, humanity would survive for at least one more generation. In a sense, everyone alive would be unaffected. But in the event of deterrence failing, carrying out the threat and broadcasting would mean that destruction could come at any moment, a far worse result than not carrying out the threat. Thus, if deterrence failed, the reaction of humankind as a whole could be easily predicted.

But an individual's reaction could not be predicted.

The success of dark forest deterrence was founded on the unpredictability of Luo Ji as an individual. If deterrence failed, his actions would be guided by his own personality and psychology. Even if he acted rationally, his own interests might not match humanity's interests perfectly. At the beginning of the Deterrence Era, both worlds carefully analyzed Luo Ji's personality and built up detailed mathematical models. Human and Trisolaran deterrence game theorists reached remarkably similar conclusions: Depending on his mental state at the moment deterrence failed, Luo Ji's degree of deterrence hovered between 91.9 percent and 98.4 percent. Trisolaris would not gamble with such odds.

Of course, such careful analysis wasn't possible immediately

after the creation of dark forest deterrence. But humanity quickly reached this conclusion intuitively, and the UN and the Solar System Fleet handed the authority to activate the deterrence system back to Luo Ji like a hot potato. The entire process from Luo Ji turning over the authority to getting it back took a total of eighteen hours. Yet that would have been long enough for droplets to destroy the ring of nuclear bombs surrounding the Sun and deprive humanity of the ability to broadcast their locations. The Trisolarans' failure to do so was widely considered their greatest strategic blunder during the war, and humanity, covered in cold sweat, let out a held breath.

Since then, the power to activate the dark forest deterrence system had always been vested in Luo Ji. His hand first held the detonation switch for the circumsolar ring of nuclear bombs, and then the switch for the gravitational wave broadcast.

Dark forest deterrence hung over two worlds like the Sword of Damocles, and Luo Ji was the single hair from a horse's tail that held up the sword. Thus, he came to be called the Swordholder.

The Wallfacer Project did not fade into history after all. Humanity could not escape the Wallfacers' ghost.

Although the Wallfacer Project was an unprecedented anomaly in the history of humankind, both dark forest deterrence and the Swordholder had precursors. The mutual assured destruction practiced by NATO and the Warsaw Pact during the Cold War was an example of ultimate deterrence. In 1974, The Soviet Union initiated the Perimeter System (Russian Система «Периметр»), or "Dead Hand." This was intended to guarantee that the Soviet Union possessed a viable second-strike capability in the event that an American-led first strike eliminated the Soviet government and high-level military command centers. The system relied on a monitoring system that gathered evidence of nuclear explosions within the Soviet Union; all the data was transmitted to a central computer that interpreted the data and decided whether to launch the Soviet Union's nuclear arsenal.

The heart of the system was a secret control chamber hidden

deep underground. If the system determined that a counterstrike must be launched, an operator on duty would initiate it.

In 2009, an officer who had been on duty in the room decades earlier told a reporter that at the time, he was a twenty-five-year-old junior lieutenant, freshly graduated from Frunze Military Academy. If the system determined that a strike was necessary, he was the last check before the complete destruction of the world. At that moment, all of the Soviet Union and Eastern Europe would likely be a sea of flames, and all of his loved ones above ground almost certainly dead. If he pushed the button, North America would also turn into hell on Earth in half an hour, and the following nuclear winter would doom all of humanity. He would hold the fate of human civilization in his hand.

Later, he was asked this question many times: If that moment had really arrived, would you have pushed the button?

The first Swordholder in history answered: *I don't know.*

Humanity hoped that dark forest deterrence would have a happy ending, like the mutually assured destruction of the twentieth century.

Time passed in this strange balance. Deterrence had been in effect for sixty years, and Luo Ji, who was now over a hundred, still held the switch to initiate the broadcast. His image among the populace had also gradually changed.

Hawks who wished to take the hard line against Trisolaris did not like him. Near the beginning of the Deterrence Era, they advocated imposing more severe conditions on the Trisolarans, with the goal of completely disarming Trisolaris. Some of their proposals were absurd. For instance, one idea was the "naked resettlement" program, which would have demanded that all Trisolarans dehydrate and allow themselves to be transported by cargo ships to the Oort Cloud, where they would be picked up by human spaceships and brought to the Solar System to be stored in dehydratories on Mars or the moon. Thereafter, if the Trisolarans satisfied certain conditions, they would be rehydrated in small batches.

The doves, similarly, did not like Luo Ji. Their primary

concern was whether the star 187J3X1, whose location had been broadcast by Luo Ji, had possessed planets that harbored life and civilization. No astronomer from the two worlds could definitively answer this question: It was impossible to prove the affirmative or the negative. But it was certain that Luo Ji could be suspected of having committed mundicide. The doves believed that in order for humanity and Trisolaris to peacefully coexist, the foundation must be universal "human" rights—in other words, the recognition that all civilized beings in the universe had inviolable, fundamental rights. To make such an ideal into reality, Luo Ji must be tried.

Luo Ji ignored them all. He held the switch to the gravitational wave broadcast system and silently stood at the Swordholder post for half a century.

Humanity came to realize that all policies with respect to the Trisolarans had to take the Swordholder into account. Without his approval, no human policy had any effect on Trisolaris. Thus, the Swordholder became a powerful dictator, much like the Wallfacers had.

As time passed, Luo Ji slowly came to be seen as an irrational monster and a mundicidal despot.

People realized that the Deterrence Era was a strange time. On the one hand, human society had reached unprecedented heights of civilization: Human rights and democracy reigned supreme everywhere. On the other hand, the entire system existed within the shadow of a dictator. Experts believed that although science and technology usually contributed to the elimination of totalitarianism, when crises threatened the existence of civilization, science and technology could also give birth to new totalitarianism. In traditional totalitarian states, the dictator could only enact his control through other people, which led to low efficiency and uncertainty. Thus, there had never been a 100 percent effective totalitarian society in human history. But technology provided the possibility for such a super-totalitarianism, and both the Wallfacers and the Swordholder were concerning examples. The combination of supertechnology and a supercrisis could throw humankind back into the dark ages.

But most people also agreed that deterrence remained necessary. After the sophons unblocked the progress of human technology and the Trisolarans began transferring their knowledge to humans, human science had advanced by leaps and bounds. However, compared to Trisolaris, Earth was still behind by at least two or three technology ages. Decommissioning the deterrence system was to be considered only when the two worlds were approximately equal in technology.

There was one more choice: turning over control of the deterrence system to artificial intelligence. This was a choice that had been evaluated seriously, and much effort was expended in researching its feasibility. Its biggest advantage was a very high degree of deterrence. But ultimately, it wasn't adopted. Handing over the fate of two worlds to machines was a terrifying idea. Experiments showed that AIs tended not to make correct decisions when faced with the complex conditions of deterrence—unsurprising, since correct judgment required more than logical reasoning. Moreover, changing from a dictatorship-by-man to a dictatorship-by-machine wouldn't have made people feel any better, and was politically worse. Finally, sophons could interfere with AI reasoning. Though no example of such interference had been discovered, the mere possibility made the choice inconceivable.

A compromise was to change the Swordholder. Even without the above considerations, Luo Ji was a centenarian. His thinking and psychological state were becoming more unreliable, and people were growing uneasy that the fate of both worlds rested in his hands.

DETERRENCE ERA, YEAR 61
THE SWORDHOLDER

Cheng Xin's recovery proceeded apace. The doctors told her that even if all ten seven-millimeter bullets in the gun had struck her, and even if her heart had been shattered, modern medicine was capable of reviving her and fixing her up good as new—though it would have been a different matter if her brain had been hit.

The police told her that the last murder case in the world had occurred twenty-eight years ago, and this city hadn't had a murder case in almost forty years. The police were out of practice when it came to the prevention and detection of murder, and that was why Wade had almost succeeded. Another candidate for the Swordholder position had warned the police. But Wade's competitor had presented no proof, only a suspicion of Wade's intent based on a sensitivity that this era lacked. The police, dubious of the accusation, wasted a lot of time. Only after discovering that Wade had faked a call from AA did they take action.

Many people came to visit Cheng Xin at the hospital: officials from the government, the UN, and the Solar System Fleet; members of the public; and, of course, AA and her friends. By now, Cheng Xin could easily tell the sexes apart, and she was growing used to modern men's completely feminized appearance, perceiving in them an elegance that the men of her era lacked. Still, they were not attractive to her.

The world no longer seemed so strange, and Cheng Xin yearned to know it better, but she was stuck in her hospital room.

One day, AA came and played a holographic movie for her. The movie, named *A Fairy Tale of Yangtze,* had won Best Picture at that year's Oscars. It was based on a song composed in *busuanzi* verse form by the Song Dynasty poet Li Zhiyi:

> *You live at one end of the Yangtze, and I the other.*
> *I think of you each day, beloved, though we cannot meet.*
> *We drink from the same river....*

The film was set in some unspecified ancient golden age, and told the story of a pair of lovers, one who lived at the source of the Yangtze, and the other at its mouth. The pair was kept apart for the entire film; they never got to see each other, not even in an imaginary scene. But their love was portrayed with utter sorrow and pathos. The cinematography was also wonderful: The elegance and refinement of the lower Yangtze Delta and the vigor and strength of the Tibetan Plateau contrasted and complemented each other, forming an intoxicating mix for Cheng Xin. The film lacked the heavy-handedness of the commercial films of her own era. Instead, the story flowed as naturally as the Yangtze itself, and absorbed Cheng Xin effortlessly.

I'm at one end of the River of Time, Cheng Xin thought, *but the other end is now empty....*

The movie stimulated Cheng Xin's interest in the culture of her new era. Once she recovered enough to walk, AA brought her to art shows and concerts. Cheng Xin could clearly remember going to Factory 798[4] and the Shanghai Biennale to see strange pieces of contemporary "art," and it was hard for her to imagine how much art had evolved in the three centuries she was asleep. But the paintings she saw at the art show were all realistic—beautiful

4 *Translator's Note*: A famous artistic community in Beijing housed in abandoned military factory buildings. Artists began to congregate there in the 1990s.

colors enlivened with vitality and feeling. She felt each painting was like a heart, beating gently between the beauty of nature and human nature. As for the music, she thought everything she heard sounded like classical symphonies, reminding her of the Yangtze in the movie: imposing and forceful, but also calm and soothing. She stared at the flowing river until it seemed that the water had ceased moving, and it was she that was moving toward the source, a long, long way....

The art and culture of this age were nothing like what she had imagined, but it wasn't simply a matter of a return to classical style, either. It was more of a spiraling sublimation of post-postmodernism, built upon a new aesthetic foundation. For instance, *A Fairy Tale of Yangtze* contained profound metaphors for the universe and space and time. But Cheng Xin was most impressed by the disappearance of the gloomy despair and bizarre noise so prevalent in the postmodern culture and art of the twenty-first century. In their place was an unprecedented warm serenity and optimism.

"I love your era," said Cheng Xin. "I'm surprised."

"You'd be even more surprised if you knew the artists behind these films, paintings, and music. They're all Trisolarans from four light-years away." AA laughed uproariously as she observed Cheng Xin's stunned gape.

EXCERPT FROM
A PAST OUTSIDE OF TIME
CULTURAL REFLECTION

After the creation of deterrence, the World Academy of Sciences—
an international organization at the same level as the UN—was
founded to receive and digest the scientific and technical information
transmitted to Earth from Trisolaris.

People first predicted that Trisolaris would only provide
knowledge to Earth in sporadic, disconnected fragments after
much pressure, and sprinkle deliberate falsehoods and misleading
ideas into what little they chose to share, so the scientists of Earth
would have to sift through them carefully for nuggets of truth.
But Trisolaris defied those expectations. Within a brief period
of time, they systematically transmitted an enormous amount of
knowledge. The treasure trove mainly consisted of basic scientific
information, including mathematics, physics, cosmology, molecular
biology of Trisolaran life forms, and so on. Every subject was a
complete system.

There was so much knowledge, in fact, that it completely over-
whelmed the scientific community on Earth. Trisolaris then provided
ongoing guidance for the study and absorption of this knowledge.
For a while, the whole world resembled a giant university. After
the sophons ended their interference with the particle accelerators,

Earth scientists were able to experimentally verify the core ideas of Trisolaran physics, giving humanity confidence in the veracity of these revelations. The Trisolarans even complained multiple times that humanity was absorbing the new knowledge too slowly. The aliens seemed eager for Earth to catch up to Trisolaris in scientific understanding—at least in the basic sciences.

Faced with such a puzzling response, humans came up with multiple explanations. The most plausible theory posited that the Trisolarans understood the advantage of the accelerating pace of human scientific development and wanted to gain access to new knowledge through us. Earth was treated as a knowledge battery: After it was charged fully with Trisolaran knowledge, it would provide more power.

The Trisolarans explained their own actions this way: Their generous gift of knowledge was done out of respect for Earth civilization. They claimed that Trisolaris had received even more benefits from Earth. Human culture gave Trisolaris new eyes, allowed Trisolarans to see deeper meanings in life and civilization and appreciate the beauty of nature and human nature in ways they had not understood. Human culture was widely disseminated on Trisolaris, and was rapidly and profoundly transforming Trisolaran society, leading to multiple revolutions in half a century and changing the social structure and political system on Trisolaris to be more similar to Earth's. Human values were accepted and respected in that distant world, and all Trisolarans were in love with human culture.

At the beginning, humans were skeptical of these claims, but the incredible wave of cultural reflection that followed seemed to prove them true.

After the tenth year of the Deterrence Era, besides additional scientific information, Trisolaris began to transmit cultural and artistic products done in imitation of human models: films, novels, poetry, music, paintings, and so on. Surprisingly, the imitations were not at all awkward or childish; right away, the Trisolarans produced sophisticated, high-quality art. Scholars called this

phenomenon cultural reflection. Human civilization now possessed a mirror in the universe, through which humanity gained a new understanding of itself through a novel perspective. In the following ten years, Trisolaran reflection culture became popular on Earth, and began to displace the decadent native human culture that had lost its vitality. Reflection culture became the new source for scholars seeking new cultural and aesthetic ideas.

These days, without being explicitly told, it was very hard to tell if a film or novel was authored by a human or a Trisolaran. The characters in Trisolaran artistic creations were all human, and they were set on Earth, with no trace of alienness. This seemed a powerful confirmation of the acceptance of Earth culture by Trisolaris. At the same time, Trisolaris itself remained shrouded in mystery, with almost no details about the world itself being transmitted. The Trisolarans explained this by saying that their own crude native culture was not ready to be shown to humans. Given the vast gap in biology and natural environment between the two worlds, such displays might erect unexpected barriers in the valuable exchange that was already taking place.

Humanity was glad to see everything developing in a positive direction. A ray of sunlight lit up this corner of the dark forest.

DETERRENCE ERA, YEAR 61
THE SWORDHOLDER

On the day of Cheng Xin's discharge, AA told her that Sophon wanted to meet her.

Cheng Xin understood that AA wasn't referring to the subatomic particles endowed with intelligence sent by Trisolaris, but to a woman, a robot woman developed by the most advanced human AI and bionics technology. She was controlled by the sophons and acted as the Trisolaran ambassador to Earth. Her appearance facilitated a more natural interchange between the two worlds than having sophons manifest themselves by unfolding in lower dimensions.

Sophon lived on a giant tree at the edge of the city. Viewed from the flying car, the leaves on the tree were sparse, as though it were late autumn. Sophon lived on the branch at the top, where a single leaf hung, an elegant dwelling made of bamboo and surrounded by a white cloud. The day was cloudless, and it was clear that Sophon's house generated the white mist.

Cheng Xin and AA walked along the branch until they reached the tip. The road was lined with smooth pebbles, and they saw lush lawns on both sides. They descended a spiraling staircase to reach the door of the house itself, where Sophon welcomed them. The gorgeous Japanese kimono on her petite figure resembled a layer of blooming flowers, but when Cheng Xin saw her face, the flowers seemed to lose color. Cheng Xin could not imagine a more perfect

beauty, a beauty animated by a lively soul. She smiled, and it was as though a breeze stirred a pond in spring and the gentle sunlight broke into a thousand softly undulating fragments. Slowly, Sophon bowed to them, and Cheng Xin felt her entire figure illustrated the Chinese character 柔, or *soft,* in both shape and meaning.

"Welcome, welcome! I wanted to pay a visit to your honored abode, but then I wouldn't be able to properly entertain you with the Way of Tea. Please accept my humble apologies. I am so delighted to see you." Sophon bowed again. Her voice was as gentle and soft as her body, barely audible, but it possessed an irresistible charm, as if all other voices had to pause and step aside when she spoke.

The pair followed Sophon into the yard. The tiny white flowers in her bun quivered, and she turned around to smile at them from time to time. Cheng Xin had completely forgotten that she was an alien invader, that she was controlled by a powerful world four light-years away. All she saw was a lovely woman, distinguished by her overwhelming femininity, like a concentrated pigment pellet that could turn a whole lake pink.

Bamboo groves lined both sides of the trail through the yard. A white fog hung among the bamboo, which reached about waist-high and undulated. They crossed a little wooden bridge over a trickling spring, and Sophon stepped to the side, bowed, and showed them into the parlor. The parlor was decorated in a pure Eastern style, full of sunlight and wide openings in the four walls so that the space resembled a pavilion. They could see the blue sky and white clouds outside. The clouds were generated by the house itself and dissipated into tendrils. A small *ukiyo-e* Japanese woodblock print hung on the wall, along with a fan decorated with a Chinese-brush-painting landscape. The whole place exuded an air of simple elegance.

Sophon waited until Cheng Xin and AA were sitting cross-legged on the tatami mats, then sat herself down gracefully. Methodically, she laid out the implements for the tea ceremony in front of her.

"You're going to have to be patient," AA whispered in Cheng Xin's ear. "It'll be two hours before you get to drink any tea."

Sophon retrieved a spotless white cloth from her kimono and began wiping the equally spotless implements. First, she carefully, slowly wiped each and every tea scoop, delicate spoons with long handles carved from single pieces of bamboo. Then she wiped each and every white porcelain and yellow copper tea bowl. With a bamboo ladle, she transferred the clear spring water from a ceramic container to a teapot and placed it above a refined copper brazier to boil. Then she scooped powdered green tea from the tea caddy into the tea bowls, brushing them with a bamboo tea whisk in a circular motion....

She performed each step in a deliberate, slow manner, even repeating some of the steps. Just wiping the tea ceremony implements took nearly twenty minutes. Clearly, Sophon executed these actions not for their results, but for their ceremonial significance.

But Cheng Xin didn't feel bored. Sophon's graceful, gentle movements had a hypnotic, mesmerizing effect on her. From time to time, a light breeze wafted through the room, and Sophon's pale arms seemed to move not of their own accord, but to drift with the breeze. Her hands, smooth as jade, seemed to be caressing not implements for making tea, but something softer, lighter, more cloudlike ... like *time*. Yes, she was caressing time. Time turned malleable and meandered slowly, like the fog that drifted through the bamboo groves. This was another time. Here, the history of blood and fire had disappeared, and the world of everyday concerns retreated somewhere far away. All that was left were clouds, the bamboo grove, and the fragrance of tea. They had achieved *wa kei sei jaku*—harmony, respect, purity, and tranquility, the four principles of the Way of Tea.

After an unknown amount of time, the tea was ready. Following another series of complicated ceremonial procedures, Sophon finally handed the bowls of tea to Cheng Xin and AA. Cheng Xin took a sip of the lush, green drink. A fragrant, bitter sensation suffused her body, and her mind seemed to clear.

"When all of us women are together, the world is so beautiful." Sophon's voice was still slow and mild, barely audible. "But our world is also very fragile. All of us women must take care to

protect it." Then she bowed deeply, and her voice grew excited. "Thank you for your care in advance! Thank you!"

Cheng Xin understood very well what was meant but not said, as well as the true significance of the tea ceremony.

The next meeting pulled Cheng Xin back into the complex reality around her.

The day after Cheng Xin visited Sophon, six Common Era men came to see her. These were the candidates competing to succeed Luo Ji in the Swordholder position. They were between thirty-four and sixty-eight years old. Compared to the beginning of the Deterrence Era, fewer Common Era individuals were emerging from hibernation, but they still formed a stratum of society on their own. All of them had some difficulty reintegrating into modern society. Most men from the Common Era tried to, consciously or otherwise, feminize their appearance and personality to adjust to the new feminine society. But the six men in front of Cheng Xin all stubbornly held on to their outdated masculine appearance and personality. If Cheng Xin had met them a few days ago, she would have found them comforting, but now, she felt only a sense of oppression.

She could see no sunlight in their eyes; their expressions appeared as masks that disguised their true feelings. Cheng Xin felt that she was facing a city wall built from six cold, hard rocks. The wall, roughened and toughened by the passing years, chilled her with its heaviness, and seemed to hint at death and bloodshed.

Cheng Xin first thanked the candidate who had warned the police. In this she was sincere—he had saved her life, after all. The forty-eight-year-old man was named Bi Yunfeng, and he had once been a designer for the world's largest particle collider. Like Cheng Xin, he was sent as a liaison to the future in the hope that the particle collider would be restarted once humankind broke through the lock placed on them by the sophons. Unfortunately, none of the particle accelerators built during his time had survived to the Deterrence Era.

"I hope I haven't made a mistake," he said. Perhaps he was trying to be funny, but Cheng Xin and the others didn't laugh.

"We're here to persuade you to not compete for the Swordholder position." Another man got right to the point. His name was Cao Bin, and he was thirty-four, the youngest of the candidates. At the start of the Trisolar Crisis, he had been a physicist, a colleague of the famous Ding Yi. After the truth of the sophons' lock on fundamental research was revealed, he was disappointed by the thought that physics had turned into a mathematical game divorced from experimental basis, and entered hibernation to wait for the lock to be released.

"If I do declare my candidacy, do you think I will win?" asked Cheng Xin. She had been pondering this question nonstop since her return from Sophon's home. She could barely sleep.

"If you do, it's almost certain that you will win," Ivan Antonov said. The handsome Russian was the next youngest of the candidates, at forty-three years old. He had an impressive résumé: Once the youngest vice-admiral in the Russian Navy, he later became the deputy commander of the Baltic Fleet. He had entered hibernation because of a terminal illness.

"Do I possess a lot of deterrent force?" asked Cheng Xin, smiling.

"You are not without qualifications. You once served in the PIA. During the last few centuries, that agency has actively gathered an enormous amount of intelligence about Trisolaris. Before the Doomsday Battle, it had even warned the human fleets about the imminent droplet attack, though the warning was ignored. Nowadays, the PIA is seen as a legendary organization, and this will give you points. In addition, you're the only human to possess another world, which makes you able to save this world.... Never mind that the leap in logic is suspect; that's how the public thinks—"

"Let me get to the point," a bald man interrupted Antonov. He was named A. J. Hopkins—or at least that's what he called himself. His identity had been completely lost by the time he emerged from hibernation, and he refused to divulge any information about himself, not even bothering to make it up. This made it difficult for

him to become a citizen of the new world—though his mysterious past also helped make him a competitive candidate. He and Antonov were considered to possess the most deterrent force. "In the eyes of the public, the ideal Swordholder looks like this: He should terrify the Trisolarans without terrifying the people of Earth. Since such a combination cannot exist, the people will lean toward someone who doesn't terrify them. You don't frighten them because you're a woman, and a woman who seems angelic in their eyes, at that. These sissies are more naïve than even the children of our time; all they can see are superficial qualities.... Look, they all think everything is developing wonderfully, and we are on the cusp of achieving universal peace and love. Deterrence is no longer so important, so they want someone with a gentler hand holding the sword."

"Isn't it true, though?" Cheng Xin asked. Hopkins's contemptuous tone annoyed her.

The six men didn't answer her, but they exchanged glances with each other. Their gazes now looked even darker and colder. Standing in their midst, Cheng Xin felt as if she were on the bottom of a well. She shivered.

"Child, you're not suited to be the Swordholder." At sixty-eight, the speaker was the oldest of the candidates. Before hibernation, he had been South Korea's vice minister of foreign affairs. "You have no political experience, you are young, you lack the judgment to evaluate situations correctly, and you don't possess the requisite psychological qualities to be the Swordholder. All you have is kindness and a sense of responsibility."

The last candidate, an experienced attorney, now spoke up. "I don't think you really want to be the Swordholder. You must know what kind of sacrifices are required."

This last speech silenced Cheng Xin. She had just learned what Luo Ji had endured during the Deterrence Era.

After the six candidates departed, AA said to Cheng Xin, "I don't think what the Swordholder goes through can be called living.

It's worse than being in hell. Why would these Common Era men want that?"

"To be able to determine the fate of all of humanity and another race with a single finger is very attractive to some men from that era. Some devote their entire lives to pursue such power. They become obsessed with it."

"Um, are you obsessed, too?"

Cheng Xin said nothing. Things were no longer simple.

"It's hard to imagine a man so dark, so crazy, so perverted." AA meant Wade.

"He's not the most dangerous."

This was true. Wade did not hide his viciousness deeply. The layers and layers of disguises that people of the Common Era wore to hide their real intentions and feelings were unimaginable to AA and contemporary humans. Who knew what was hidden behind the cold, expressionless masks worn by the six men? Who knew whether one of them might be another Ye Wenjie or Zhang Beihai? More terrifyingly, whether all of them were?

The beautiful world revealed its fragility to Cheng Xin, like a lovely soap bubble floating through a bramble bush: A single touch was enough to destroy everything.

A week later, Cheng Xin came to the UN Headquarters to attend the handover ceremony for the two planets in the DX3906 system.

Afterwards, the PDC chair spoke with her. On behalf of the UN and the Solar System Fleet, he asked her to declare her candidacy for the Swordholder. He explained that there was uncertainty about the six existing candidates. For any of them to be elected would lead to mass panic, as a considerable portion of the population believed each of the candidates to be a tremendous danger and threat. The consequences of electing any of them were unpredictable. In addition, all of the candidates distrusted Trisolaris and exhibited aggressive tendencies toward it. If one of them were elected, the second Swordholder might collaborate with the hardliners on

Earth and in Fleet International to impose harsher policies toward Trisolaris and demand more concessions from them. Such a move might terminate the developing peace and scientific and cultural exchange between the two worlds, leading to disaster....

But Cheng Xin could prevent all of this.

After humanity ended its second cave-dwelling stage, the UN Headquarters moved back to its old address. Cheng Xin was familiar with it: The exterior of the Secretariat Building looked the same as three centuries ago, and even the sculptures on the plaza in front were perfectly preserved, as was the lawn. Cheng Xin stood and recalled that tumultuous night 270 years ago: the announcement of the Wallfacer Project; Luo Ji's shooting; the chaotic crowd under the swaying spotlights; her hair blowing about in the turbulence from the helicopters; the ambulance departing with flashing red lights and shrill sirens ... everything was as clear as yesterday. Wade stood with his back against the lights of New York City, and uttered the line that had transformed her life: "We'll send only a brain."

Without that statement, everything that was happening now would have nothing to do with her. She would be a common woman and would have died more than two centuries ago. Everything about her would have disappeared without a trace upstream in time's long river. If she had been fortunate, her tenth-generation descendants would now be waiting for the selection of the second Swordholder.

But she was alive. She faced the crowd on the plaza. A hologram of her image floated above them like a colorful cloud. A young mother came up to Cheng Xin and handed her baby, only a few months old, to her. The baby giggled at her, and she held him close, touching her face to his smooth baby cheeks. Her heart melted, and she felt as if she were holding a whole world, a new world as lovely and fragile as the baby in her arms.

"Look, she's like Saint Mary, the mother of Jesus!" the young mother called out to the crowd. She turned back to Cheng Xin and put her hands together. Tears flowed from her eyes. "Oh, beautiful, kind Madonna, protect this world! Do not let those bloodthirsty and savage men destroy all the beauty here."

The crowd cried out in joy. The baby in Cheng Xin's arms, startled, began to cry. She held the baby tighter.

Do I have another choice?

The answer came to her, brooking no doubt.

No. None at all.

There were three reasons.

First, being declared a savior was just like being pushed under the guillotine: There was no choice involved. This had happened to Luo Ji, and now it was happening to her.

Second, the young mother and the soft, warm bundle in Cheng Xin's arms made her realize something. She understood for the first time her own feelings toward this new world: maternal instinct. She had never experienced such a feeling during the Common Era. Subconsciously, she saw everyone in the new world as her child, and she could not bear to see them come to harm. Before, she had mistakenly thought of it as a sense of responsibility. But, no, maternal instinct was not subject to rationalization; she could not escape it.

The third fact stood in front of her like an unscalable wall. Even if the first two reasons did not exist, this wall would remain: Yun Tianming.

This situation was a hell, a bottomless abyss, the same as the abyss Yun Tianming had plunged into for her sake. She could not back off now. She had to accept karma. It was her turn.

Cheng Xin's childhood had been full of her mother's love, but only her mother's love. She had asked her mother where her father was. Unlike some other single mothers, her mother responded calmly. She said she didn't know, and then, after a sigh, added that she wished she did. Cheng Xin had also asked her where she had come from, and her mother had told her she was found.

This wasn't a lie. Cheng Xin really had been found. Her mother had never married, but one night, while on a date with her boyfriend at the time, she saw a three-month-old baby abandoned on a park bench, along with a bottle of milk, a thousand yuan, and a slip of paper with the baby girl's birthday. Her mother and the boyfriend

had intended to bring the baby to the police, who would have turned the baby over to the city's civil affairs department, who would have sent her to an orphanage.

Instead, her mother decided that she wanted to bring the baby home and go to the police in the morning. Perhaps it was the experience of being a mother for a night, or some other reason, but the next morning, she found that she couldn't send the child away. Every time she thought of parting from the young life, her heart ached, and so she decided to become the child's mother.

The boyfriend left her because of this. During the following decade, she dated four or five other men, but all of them ended up leaving her because of Cheng Xin. Later, Cheng Xin found out that none of the men had explicitly objected to her mother's decision to keep her, but if any of them ever showed a trace of impatience or lack of understanding, her mother broke up with him. She refused to let any harm come to Cheng Xin.

When she was little, Cheng Xin never thought her family was incomplete. Instead, she thought it just the way it should be: a small world made up of mother and daughter. The small world possessed so much love and joy that she even suspected that adding a father would be extraneous. Later, she did miss having a father's love—at first, only a vague sensation, but later a growing ache. And that was when her mother did find a father for her, a very kind man full of love and a sense of responsibility. He fell in love with Cheng Xin's mother in large part because of how much she loved Cheng Xin. And so a second sun appeared in Cheng Xin's life. She felt that her small world really was complete, and so her parents did not have another child.

Later, Cheng Xin left her parents to go to college. After that, her life was like a runaway horse that carried her farther and farther until, finally, not only did she have to part from them in space, but also time—she had to be sent to the future.

That night when she left her parents for the last time would be carved in her mind forever. She had lied to her parents and said that she'd be back the next day—she couldn't bear to say good-bye,

and so she had to leave without saying anything. But they seemed to know the truth.

Her mother had held her hand and said, "My darling, the three of us are together because of love...."

Cheng Xin spent that night standing in front of her parents' window. In her mind, the night breeze and the twinkling stars and everything else repeated her mother's last words.

Three centuries later, she was finally ready to do something for love.

"I will be a candidate for the Swordholder," she said to the young mother.

DETERRENCE ERA, YEAR 62
GRAVITY, IN THE VICINITY OF
THE OORT CLOUD

Gravity had been pursuing *Blue Space* for half a century.

It finally approached its target. Only three AU separated the hunter and the hunted. Compared to the 1.5 light-years that the two ships had traversed, this was mere inches.

A decade ago, *Gravity* had passed through the Oort Cloud. This region, about one light-year from the sun at the edge of the Solar System, was the birthplace of comets. *Blue Space* and *Gravity* were the first human spaceships to cross this border. The region didn't feel anything like a cloud, though. Once in a while, a frozen ball of dirt and ice—a tailless comet—passed tens of thousands or hundreds of thousands of kilometers away, invisible to the naked eye.

Once *Gravity* left the Oort Cloud behind, the ship entered true outer space. From here, the sun appeared as just another star behind the ship. It lost its reality and became like an illusion. In every direction, all one could see was a bottomless abyss, and the only objects whose existence could be ascertained by the senses were the droplets flying in formation with *Gravity*. The droplets flanked the ship at a distance of about five kilometers, just visible to the naked eye. Those aboard *Gravity* liked to gaze at the droplets with telescopes as a source of comfort in the endless emptiness.

Observing the droplets was, in a sense, just looking at themselves. The mirrorlike surface of the droplets reflected an image of *Gravity*. The dimensions were a bit distorted, but due to the perfect smoothness of the surface, the image was particularly clear. With sufficient magnification on their telescopes, the observers could even pick out the porthole, and themselves in it, in the reflection.

Most of the one hundred-plus officers and crew aboard *Gravity* didn't experience this solitude because they had spent the majority of the past fifty years in hibernation. During routine cruising, only about five to ten crew members needed to be on duty. As the crew rotated through hibernation, each person was usually on duty for three to five years.

The entire pursuit was a complex game of acceleration between *Gravity* and *Blue Space*. First of all, *Blue Space* couldn't just accelerate continuously, as doing so would cost it precious fuel and ultimately deprive it of mobility. Even if it managed to escape *Gravity*, it would be committing suicide in the endless empty desert of outer space if it exhausted its fuel. Although *Gravity* had more fuel onboard than *Blue Space*, it had constraints of its own. Since it needed to be prepared for a return voyage, its fuel reserves had to be divided into four equal parts: the acceleration away from the Solar System; the deceleration before its destination; the acceleration toward the Solar System; and the deceleration before arriving at the Earth. Thus, the portion available for acceleration during the pursuit amounted to only one-quarter of the fuel. Based on calculations of *Blue Space*'s previous maneuvers and intelligence gathered by the sophons, *Gravity* had an accurate idea of *Blue Space*'s fuel reserves, but the latter had no information about the former's stores. Thus, in this game, *Gravity* knew all the cards held by *Blue Space*, while *Blue Space* struggled in ignorance. During pursuit, *Gravity* consistently maintained a speed higher than *Blue Space*, but neither ship approached their maximum velocities. Moreover, twenty-five years after the start of the chase, *Blue Space* stopped accelerating, perhaps because it had used up all the fuel it dared.

During the half century of the hunt, *Gravity* repeatedly hailed *Blue Space,* explaining that running was meaningless. Even if the crew of *Blue Space* somehow escaped the hunters from Earth, the droplets would catch up and destroy them. But if they returned to Earth, they would receive a fair trial. They had the option to greatly shorten the pursuit by surrendering. But *Blue Space* ignored these entreaties.

A year previously, when *Gravity* and *Blue Space* were thirty AU apart, something not entirely unexpected occurred: *Gravity* and the two accompanying droplets entered a region of space where the sophons lost their quantum ties to home, terminating real-time communications with Earth. *Gravity* had to communicate with Earth through only neutrinos and radio. Transmissions from *Gravity* now took a year and three months to reach the Earth, and the ship had to wait an equally long time to receive a reply.

EXCERPT FROM
A PAST OUTSIDE OF TIME
MORE INDIRECT EVIDENCE FOR
THE DARK FOREST: SOPHON-BLIND
REGIONS

———

Near the beginning of the Crisis Era, as Trisolaris sent sophons toward the Earth, it also launched six sophons at near-lightspeed to explore other regions of the galaxy.

All of these sophons soon entered blind regions and lost contact with home. The longest-lasting one managed to get seven light-years away. Additional sophons launched later met with the same fate. The closest blind region, only about 1.3 light-years from Earth, was the one encountered by the sophons that accompanied *Gravity*.

Once the quantum entanglement between sophons was broken, it could not be restored. Any sophon entering a blind region was lost forever.

Trisolaris remained mystified by the kind of interference the sophons received: Perhaps it was a natural phenomenon, or perhaps it was "man"-made. Scientists from both Trisolaris and Earth leaned toward the latter explanation.

Before being blinded, the sophons were able to explore only two nearby stars with planets. Neither system exhibited signs of life or

civilization. But Earth and Trisolaris both came to the conclusion that their desolation was precisely why the sophons were allowed to approach.

Thus, even deep into the Deterrence Era, the universe at large remained hidden from the two worlds by a mysterious veil. The existence of these blind regions seemed to provide indirect proof for the dark forest nature of the universe: Something was preventing the cosmos from becoming transparent.

DETERRENCE ERA, YEAR 62
GRAVITY, IN THE VICINITY OF
THE OORT CLOUD

Losing the sophons was not fatal to *Gravity*'s mission, though it did make the job much harder. Before, the sophons could enter *Blue Space* at will and report on everything that was going on; now *Blue Space* appeared to *Gravity* as a sealed box. Moreover, the droplets lost real-time communications with Trisolaris and had to rely on the onboard AI. This led to unpredictable results.

The captain of *Gravity* decided that he could no longer afford to wait. He ordered *Gravity* to accelerate further.

As *Gravity* approached, *Blue Space* hailed the hunters for the first time, proposing a plan: *Blue Space* would load two-thirds of the crew—including the main suspects—onto pinnaces and send the pinnaces to *Gravity* if the remainder of the crew was allowed to continue their voyage into deep space aboard *Blue Space*. This way, a vanguard and seed for the human race would be preserved in space, keeping alive the hope for further exploration.

Gravity vehemently denied this request. The entire crew of *Blue Space* was suspected of murder, and all had to be tried. Space had transformed them until they were no longer members of the human race. Under no circumstances could they be allowed to "represent" humanity in space exploration.

Blue Space apparently realized the futility of running and of resisting. If only a human spaceship pursued them, then they at least stood a chance if they fought. But the two droplets changed the strategic calculus. Before them, *Blue Space* was nothing but a paper target, and there was no chance of escape. When the two ships were only fifteen AU apart, *Blue Space* announced its surrender and began to decelerate at maximum power. The distance between the two ships shrank rapidly, and it seemed that the long hunt was at last coming to an end.

Gravity's crew emerged from hibernation and readied the ship for combat. The vessel, once silent and deserted, was once again filled with people.

Those who had been awakened faced the prospect of both a target nearly at hand and the loss of real-time communications with Earth. This loss did not pull them spiritually closer to the crew of *Blue Space*. To the contrary, like a child who was separated from her parents, the crew distrusted the parentless wild children even more. Everyone wished to capture *Blue Space* as quickly as possible and return home. Even though both crews were in the cold vastness of space, voyaging in the same direction at approximately the same speed, the natures of their voyages were completely different. *Gravity* had a spiritual anchor, while *Blue Space* was adrift.

In the ninety-eighth hour after the crew's emergence from hibernation, Dr. West, *Gravity*'s psychiatrist, received his first patient. This visit from Commander Devon surprised the doctor. According to his records, Devon had the highest stability score of anyone aboard. Devon was in charge of the military police aboard *Gravity*, and it would be his responsibility to disarm *Blue Space* and arrest the crew once it was caught. *Gravity*'s male crew members belonged to the last generation from Earth who still looked masculine, and Devon had the most masculine appearance among them. He was sometimes even mistaken for a Common Era man. He had often

spoken out in favor of taking a hard line toward the suspects, suggesting that the death penalty ought to be revived.

"Doctor, I know that you'll keep my confidence," Devon said carefully. His tone was in marked contrast to his usual hard-edged style. "I know that what I'm about to say will sound funny."

"Commander, in my professional capacity, I wouldn't laugh at anyone."

"Yesterday, at approximately stellar time 436950, I left Conference Room Four and followed Passageway Seventeen back to my cabin. As I approached the Intelligence Center, a sublieutenant came toward me—or, at least, a man dressed in the uniform of a Space Force sublieutenant. At that time, except for crew members on duty, everyone should have been asleep. But I didn't think it was so strange to meet someone in the passageway. Except ..." Devon shook his head and his eyes lost focus, as though trying to recall a dream.

"What was wrong?"

"The man and I passed by each other. He saluted me, and I glanced at him...."

Devon stopped again, and the doctor nodded for him to continue.

"He was ... he was the commander of the marines from *Blue Space,* Lieutenant Commander Park Ui-gun."

"You mean *Blue Space,* our prey?" West's tone was calm, betraying no hint of surprise.

Devon didn't answer the question. "Doctor, you know that as part of my duties, I've been monitoring the interior of *Blue Space* through the real-time images transmitted by the sophons. I know the crew of that ship better than I know the crew here. I know what Lieutenant Commander Park Ui-gun looks like."

"Maybe it was someone from our ship who looks like him."

"No, there's no one—I know everyone onboard. Also ... after the salute, he passed by me without any expression. I stood there, stunned. But by the time I turned around, the passageway was empty."

"When did you wake up from hibernation?"

"Three years ago. I needed to keep an eye on the activities

172

onboard our target. Before that, I was also among those aboard who had stayed out of hibernation the longest."

"Then you must have experienced the moment when we entered the sophons' blind region."

"Of course."

"Before that, you spent so much of your time watching those aboard *Blue Space* that I think you probably felt as though you were on *Blue Space* rather than *Gravity*."

"Yes, Doctor. I did often feel that way."

"And then, the surveillance images were cut off. You couldn't see anything over there anymore. And you were tired.... Commander, it's simple. Trust me: This is normal. I suggest you get more rest. We have plenty of people now to do the work that needs to be done."

"Doctor, I'm a survivor of the Doomsday Battle. After my ship exploded, I was curled up in a life pod the size of your desk, drifting in the vicinity of Neptune's orbit. By the time I was rescued, I was close to death, but my mind was still sound, and I never suffered any delusions.... I believe what I saw." Devon got up and walked away. He turned around at the cabin door. "If I meet that bastard again—doesn't matter where—I'm going to kill him."

Some time after that, an accident happened in Ecological Area #3 —a nutrient tube ruptured. The tube was made of carbon fiber, and as it wasn't subject to pressure, the probability of a malfunction was very low. Ecological Engineer Ivantsov passed through the aeroponically grown plants, as dense as a rainforest, and saw that others had already shut off the valve leading to the ruptured tube and were cleaning up the yellow nutrient broth.

Ivantsov stopped dead when he saw the ruptured tube.

"This ... is caused by a micrometeoroid!"

Someone laughed. Ivantsov was an experienced and prudent engineer, and that made his outburst even funnier. All the ecological areas were buried in the center of the ship. Ecological Area #3 was tens of meters away from the nearest section of the exterior hull.

"I worked more than a decade in external maintenance and I know what a micrometeoroid strike looks like! Look, you can see the typical signs of high-temperature ablation around the edges of the rupture."

Ivantsov closely examined the inside of the tube; then he asked a technician to cut off a ring of material around the rupture and magnify it. The chatter died down as everyone stared at the 1000x image. There were tiny black particles, a few microns in diameter, embedded in the wall of the tube. The particles twinkled like unfriendly eyes in the magnified image. They all knew what they were looking at. The meteoroid must have been about one hundred microns in diameter. It had shattered as it went through the tube, its broken pieces winding up embedded in the wall opposite the breach.

As one, they looked up.

The ceiling above the ruptured tube looked smooth and undamaged. Furthermore, above the ceiling, tens, maybe hundreds more bulkheads of various thicknesses separated this place from space. An impact-breach in any of these bulkheads would have triggered a high-level alert.

But the micrometeoroid had to have come from space. Based on the condition of the rupture, the micrometeoroid had struck the tube at a relative velocity of thirty thousand meters per second. It would have been impossible to accelerate the projectile to such speed from within the ship, much less from within the ecological area.

"It's like a ghost," a sublieutenant named Ike muttered, and left. His choice of words was meaningful: About ten hours earlier, he had seen another, bigger ghost.

Ike had been trying to fall asleep in his cabin when he saw a round opening appear in the wall opposite his bed. It was about a meter across, and occupied the space where a Hawaiian landscape had hung. It was true that many of the bulkheads on the ship could shift and transform so that doors could appear anywhere, but a circular

opening like this was impossible. Moreover, the cabin walls of mid-level officers were made of metal and could not deform this way. A closer examination by Ike revealed that the edge of the opening was perfectly smooth and reflective, like a mirror.

Although the hole was strange, Ike was rather pleased by it. Sublieutenant Vera lived next door.

Verenskaya was the AI system engineer aboard *Gravity*. Ike had been trying to get the Russian beauty to go out with him, but she hadn't shown any interest. Ike still remembered his latest attempt two days ago.

He and Verenskaya had just gotten off duty. As usual, they walked back to the officers' quarters together, and as they reached Verenskaya's cabin, Ike tried to invite himself in. Verenskaya blocked her door.

"Come on, sweetheart," Ike said. "Let me in for a visit. It's not very neighborly to never invite me over. They'll think I'm not a real man."

Verenskaya looked askance at Ike. "Any real men on this ship would be too worried about our mission to think about getting into the pants of every woman around them."

"What's there to worry? After we catch those murderers, there will be no more danger. Happy times will be here!"

"They're not murderers! Without deterrence, *Blue Space* would be humankind's only hope. Yet we're now hunting them down, allied with the enemies of the human race. Don't you feel ashamed?"

"Um ... baby, if you feel this way ... how did you ..."

"How did I get to join this mission? Is that what you want to say? Why don't you go to the psychiatrist and the captain to report me? They'll put me in forced hibernation and kick me out of the fleet after we return. That's just my wish!" Verenskaya slammed the door in his face.

However, now Ike had a perfect excuse to enter Verenskaya's cabin. He unbuckled his weightlessness belt and sat up in his bed, but stopped when he saw that the bottom half of the round opening made the top of the cabinet against the wall disappear as well.

The edge of what remained of the cabinet was also perfectly smooth and reflective, like the edge of the opening itself. It was as if some invisible knife had cut through the cabinet and everything inside, including the stacks of folded clothes. The mirrorlike surface of the cross-section ran up against the edge of the round opening, and the whole reflective surface looked like a portion of the inside of a sphere.

Ike pushed against the bed and lifted off in the weightlessness. Looking through the opening, he almost screamed in fright. *This must be a nightmare!*

Through the hole, he could see that a part of Verenskaya's bed, pushed up against the cabin wall, had also disappeared. Verenskaya's lower legs had been cut off. Although the cross section of the bed and the legs were also smooth and reflective, as though covered by a layer of mercury, he could see Verenskaya's muscles and bones through it. But Verenskaya seemed all right. She was still in deep sleep, and her firm breasts slowly moved up and down as she breathed. Normally, Ike would have admired such a sight, but right now he only felt a supernatural fright. When he calmed down and looked closer, he saw that the cross-section of Verenskaya's legs and bed also formed a spherical surface that matched the round opening.

He was looking at a bubble-shaped space about a meter in diameter, which erased everything within its path.

Ike picked up a violin bow from the nightstand, and, with a trembling hand, poked it into the bubble. The part of the bow extended inside the bubble disappeared, but the bow hair remained taut. He pulled the bow back and saw that it was undamaged. But he was still glad that he hadn't tried to go through the hole—who knew if he would emerge from the other side unharmed?

Ike forced himself to be calm and tried to think of the most rational explanation for the eerie sight. Then he made what he thought was a wise decision: He put on his sleep cap and lay back down on the bed. He buckled his weightlessness belt back on and set the sleep cap for half an hour.

He woke up after half an hour, and the bubble was still there.

So he set the sleep cap for an hour. When he woke up this time, the bubble and the hole in the wall were gone. The Hawaiian landscape was back on the wall and everything was as it was before the incident.

But Ike was worried about Verenskaya. He dashed out of his cabin and stopped in front of Verenskaya's door. Instead of ringing the doorbell, he pounded on the door. His mind was filled with the terrifying vision of Verenskaya, close to death, lying on the bed with her legs cut off.

It took a while before the door opened, and a not-completely-awake Verenskaya demanded to know what he wanted.

"I came to see if you are ... all right." Ike's gaze shifted down, and he saw that Verenskaya's beautiful legs were perfect below the hem of her nightgown.

"Idiot!" Verenskaya slammed the door shut.

After returning to his cabin, Ike put his sleep cap on and set it for eight hours. As for what he had seen, the only wise thing to do was to shut up and say nothing. Due to *Gravity*'s special mission, the crew's psychological state—especially that of the officers—was subject to constant monitoring. There was a special psychological monitoring corps aboard, comprising more than a dozen crew members out of the full complement of just over a hundred. Some crew members had wondered whether *Gravity* was a stellar ship or a psychiatric hospital. And then there was also the annoying civilian psychiatrist West, who thought of everything in terms of mental disorders and illnesses and blockages, until one could come to the conclusion that he would subject a clogged toilet to psychiatric analysis. The mental screening process onboard *Gravity* was extremely strict, and even slight mental disorders would result in the sufferer being forced into hibernation. Ike was terrified of missing the upcoming historical encounter between the two ships. If that happened, when the ship returned to Earth in half a century, the girls back home would not see him as a hero.

But Ike did feel a slight diminution in his dislike for the psych corps and Dr. West. He had always thought of them as making

mountains out of molehills, but he had never imagined that people could suffer such realistic delusions.

Compared to Ike's minor delusion, Petty Officer Liu Xiaoming's supernatural encounter would be considered quite spectacular.

Liu was performing a routine exterior hull inspection. This involved piloting a small pinnace at a certain distance from *Gravity* and examining the hull for any abnormalities, such as evidence of meteor strikes. This was an ancient, outdated practice no longer strictly necessary and rarely performed. The ship was full of sensors that monitored the hull continuously; any problems would be detected right away. Also, the operation could only be done when *Gravity* was coasting instead of accelerating or decelerating. As the ship approached *Blue Space,* frequent acceleration and deceleration was necessary for adjustments. This was one of those rare windows when the ship was coasting again, and Petty Officer Liu was ordered to take advantage of the opportunity.

Liu piloted the pinnace out of the bay in the middle of the ship and smoothly glided away from *Gravity* until he was at a distance where he could see the whole ship. The giant hull was bathed in the light from the galaxy. Unlike when most of the crew was in hibernation, light spilled from all the portholes, making *Gravity* seem even more magnificent.

But Liu noticed something incredible: *Gravity* was shaped like a perfect cylinder, however, right now, its tail ended in an inclined plane! The ship was also much shorter than it should be—about 20 percent shorter, to be exact. A giant, invisible knife had cut off *Gravity*'s tail.

Liu shut his eyes, then opened them a few seconds later. The tail was still missing. He felt chilled to the bone. The giant ship before him was an organic whole. If the tail were suddenly gone, the power distribution systems would suffer a catastrophic failure, and the ship would shortly explode. But nothing of the sort was happening. The ship cruised along without trouble, as though suspended in

space. No alerts of any kind came from his earpiece or were shown on his screens.

He pressed the switch for the intercom and got ready to give a report, but shut off the channel before saying anything. He recalled the words of an old spacer who had been at the Doomsday Battle: "Your intuition is unreliable in space. If you must act based on intuition, count from one to one hundred first. At least count from one to ten."

He closed his eyes and began to count. When he got to ten, he opened his eyes. The tail was still missing. He closed his eyes and continued to count, his breath coming faster now, but he struggled to remember his training, and forced himself to calm down. He opened his eyes when he reached thirty, and this time he saw the complete *Gravity*. He closed his eyes again, sighed, and waited until his heartbeat slowed down.

He piloted the pinnace to the stern of the ship, where he could see the three giant nozzles of the fusion drive. The engine wasn't on, and the fusion reactor was kept at minimal power so that the nozzles only showed a faint red glow, reminding him of the clouds back on Earth at dusk.

Petty Officer Liu was glad that he hadn't made a report. An officer might get therapy, but an NCO like himself would be forced into hibernation. Like Ike, Liu Xiaoming didn't want to return to Earth a useless man.

Dr. West went to find Guan Yifan, a civilian scholar who worked in the observatory at the stern. Guan had a midship cabin assigned to him as living quarters, but he rarely went there. Most of the time, he remained in the observatory and asked the service robots to bring his meals. The crew referred to him as "the hermit at the stern."

The observatory was a tiny spherical cabin where Guan lived and worked. His appearance was disheveled, with an unshaven face and long hair, but he still looked relatively youthful. When West saw Guan, he was floating in the middle of the cabin, looking

restless: sweaty forehead, anxious eyes, his hand pulling at his collar as if he was unable to catch his breath.

"I already told you on the phone: I'm working and don't have time for a visit."

"It's precisely because your call betrayed signs of mental disorder that I came to see you."

"I'm not a member of the space force. As long as I'm no danger to the ship or the crew, you have no power over me."

"Fine. I'll leave." West turned around. "I just don't believe that someone with claustrophobia can work in here without trouble."

Guan called out for West to stop, but West ignored him. As he expected, Guan chased after him and stopped him. "How did you know that? I am indeed ... claustrophobic. I feel like I'm being packed into a narrow tube, or sometimes squeezed between two iron plates until I'm flat as a sheet...."

"Not surprising. Look at where you are." The doctor indicated the cabin—it resembled a tiny egg nestled in a nest of crisscrossing cables and pipes. "You research phenomena at the largest scale, but you stay in the smallest space. And how long have you been here? It's been four years since your last hibernation, hasn't it?"

"I'm not complaining. *Gravity*'s mission is bringing fugitives to justice, not scientific exploration. I'm grateful to have this space at all.... Look, my claustrophobia has nothing to do with this."

"Why don't we take a walk on Plaza One? It will help."

The doctor pulled Guan Yifan along, and the two drifted toward the bow of the ship. If the ship were accelerating, going from the stern of the ship to the bow would be equivalent to climbing up a one-kilometer well, but in the weightlessness of coasting, the trip was a lot easier. Plaza #1 was located at the bow of the cylindrical ship, under a semispherical, transparent dome. Standing there was like standing in space itself. Compared to the holographic projections of the star field on the walls of spherical cabins, this place induced an even stronger sense of the "desubstantiation effect."

"Desubstantiation effect" was a concept from astronautic psychology. Humans on Earth were surrounded by objects, and the

image of the world in their subconscious was thus material and substantial. But in deep space, away from the Solar System, the stars were only distant points of light and the galaxy was nothing more than a luminous mist. To the senses and the mind, the world lost its materiality, and empty space dominated. A space voyager's subconscious image of the world thus became desubstantiated. This mental model was the baseline in astronautic psychology. Mentally, the ship became the only material entity in the universe. At sublight speeds, the motion of the ship was undetectable, and the universe turned into one boundless, empty exhibition hall. Here, the stars were illusions, and the ship was the only object on display. This mental model brought with it a profound sense of loneliness, and it could cause the voyager to have subconscious delusions of being a "superobserver" toward the lone "object on display." This feeling of being completely exposed could lead to passivity and anxiety.

Thus, many of the negative psychological effects of deep-space flight were due to the extreme openness of the external environment. In West's extensive professional experience, it was extremely rare to develop claustrophobia the way Guan Yifan did. Even stranger to West was the fact that Guan did not seem relieved by the vast, open sky of Plaza #1; the restlessness caused by claustrophobia seemed to abate not one whit. This tended to support Guan's assertion that his claustrophobia had nothing to do with the narrow confines of his observatory. West grew even more interested in his case.

"Don't you feel better?"

"No, not at all. I feel trapped. Here, everything is so ... enclosed."

Guan glanced at the starry sky and then focused his gaze in the direction *Gravity* was heading. The doctor knew he was looking for *Blue Space*. The two ships were now only one hundred thousand kilometers apart, and coasting at approximately the same speed. At the scale of deep space, the two ships were practically flying in close formation. The leadership of both ships was in the process of negotiating the technical details of their docking. But *Blue Space* was still too far away to be seen with the naked eye. The droplets

were invisible as well. Based on the agreement made with Trisolaris half a century ago, the droplets had shifted to a position about three hundred thousand kilometers from both *Gravity* and *Blue Space*. The two ships and the droplets formed a narrow isosceles triangle.

Guan Yifan turned his gaze back to West. "Last night, I had a dream. I went somewhere, somewhere *really* open, open in a way that you can't even imagine. After I woke up, reality felt very enclosed and narrow, and that was how I came to be claustrophobic. It's like ... if, as soon as you were born, you were locked inside a small box, you wouldn't care because that was all you've known. But once you've been let out and they put you back in, it feels completely different."

"Tell me more about this place in your dream."

Guan gave the doctor a mysterious smile. "I will describe it to the other scientists on the ship, maybe even the scientists on *Blue Space*. But I won't tell you. I don't have anything against you, Doctor, but I can't stand the attitude shared by everyone in your profession: If you think someone has a mental disorder, you treat everything he says as merely the delusion of a diseased mind."

"But you just told me it was a dream."

Guan shook his head, struggling to remember. "I don't know if it was a dream; I don't know if I was awake. Sometimes, you can think you're waking from a dream, only to find yourself still dreaming; other times, you're awake, but it seems like you're dreaming."

"The second situation is extremely rare. If you experienced that, then it was almost certainly a symptom of some mental disorder. Oh, sorry, now you're unhappy with me again."

"No, no. I think we're actually very similar. We both have our targets of observation. You observe the deranged, and I observe the universe. Like you, I also have some criteria for evaluating whether the observed objects are sound: harmony and beauty, in the mathematical sense."

"Of course the objects you observe are sound."

"But you're wrong, Doctor." Guan pointed at the glowing Milky Way, but his gaze remained on West, as though showing him some

monster that had suddenly appeared out of nowhere. "Out there is a patient who may be mentally sound, but whose body suffers from paraplegia!"

"Why?"

Guan curled up and hugged his knees. The movement caused his body to slowly rotate in place. The magnificent Milky Way revolved around him, and he saw himself as the center of the universe.

"Because of the speed of light. The known universe is about sixteen billion light-years across, and it's still expanding. But the speed of light is only three hundred thousand kilometers per second, a snail's pace. This means that light can never go from one end of the universe to the other. Since nothing can move faster than the speed of light, it follows that no information and motive force can go from one end of the universe to the other. If the universe were a person, his neural signals couldn't cover his entire body; his brain would not know of the existence of his limbs, and his limbs would not know of the existence of the brain. Isn't that paraplegia? The image in my mind is even worse: The universe is but a corpse puffing up."

"Interesting, Dr. Guan, very interesting!"

"Other than the speed of light, three hundred thousand kilometers per second, there's another three-based symptom."

"What do you mean?"

"The three dimensions. In string theory, excepting time, the universe has ten dimensions. But only three are accessible at the macroscopic scale, and those three form our world. All the others are folded up in the quantum realm."

"I think string theory provides an explanation."

"Some think that it is only when two strings encounter each other and some qualities are canceled out that the dimensions are unfolded into the macroscopic, and dimensions above three will never have such chances for encountering each other.... I don't think much of this explanation. It is not mathematically beautiful. Like I said, this is the universe's three and three hundred thousand syndrome."

"What do you propose as the cause?"

Guan laughed uproariously and put his arm around the doctor's shoulders. "Great question! I don't think anyone has thought this far. I'm sure there's a root cause, and it might be the most horrifying truth that science is capable of revealing. But ... Doctor, who do you think I am? I'm nothing more than a tiny observer curled up in the tail of a spaceship, and only an assistant researcher at that." He released West's shoulders, and, facing the galaxy, let out a long sigh. "I've been in hibernation the longest of anyone aboard. When we left Earth, I was only twenty-six, and even now I'm only thirty-one. But in my eyes, the universe has already transformed from a source of beauty and faith into a bloating corpse. I feel old. The stars no longer hold any attraction for me. I want to go home."

Unlike Guan Yifan, West had been awake for much of the voyage. He always believed that to maintain the mental health of others, he needed to keep his own emotions under control. But something seemed to buffet his heart now, and as he reviewed his own half century of travels, his eyes moistened. "My friend, I'm old, too."

As if in response to their conversation, the battle alert klaxons blared, sounding like the entire sky full of stars was screaming. Warning information scrolled on floating windows that appeared above the plaza. The overlapping windows sprang up one after another and quickly covered the Milky Way like colorful clouds.

"Droplet attack!" West said to the confused Guan Yifan. "They're both accelerating. One is headed for *Blue Space,* the other for us!"

Guan looked around, instinctively searching for something to grab on to in case the ship accelerated. But there was nothing around. In the end, he held on to the doctor.

West held his hands. "There won't be enough time for any evasive maneuvers. We have only a few seconds left."

After a brief panic, both felt an unexpected sense of relief. They were glad that death would arrive so quickly that there wasn't even

time to be terrified. Perhaps their discussion about the universe was the best preparation for death.

They both thought of the same thing, but Guan spoke it aloud first. "Looks like neither of us needs to worry about our patients anymore."

DETERRENCE ERA, YEAR 62
NOVEMBER 28, 4:00 P.M. TO
4:17 P.M.: DETERRENCE CENTER

The high-speed elevator continued to descend, and the increasing layers of earth above seemed to put all their weight on Cheng Xin's heart.

Half a year ago, a joint session of the UN and the Solar System Fleet had elected Cheng Xin to succeed Luo Ji as the Swordholder and given her authority to control the gravitational wave deterrence system. She had received almost twice as many votes as the next candidate. She was now proceeding to the Deterrence Center in the Gobi Desert, where the deterrence authority handover ceremony was to take place.

The Deterrence Center was the deepest man-made structure ever, about forty-five kilometers beneath the surface. This location was already below the crust, past the Mohorovičić discontinuity, in the mantle of the Earth. The pressure and temperature here were both far higher than in the crust, and the stratum around her was made up mostly of solid, hard peridotite.

The elevator took almost twenty minutes to reach its terminus. Cheng Xin stepped out of the elevator and saw a black steel door. White text on the door gave the formal name for the Deterrence Center: Gravitational Wave Universal Broadcast System Control

Station Zero. The insignias of the UN and the Solar System Fleet were embossed on the door.

This ultra-deep structure was quite complex. It possessed its own independent air circulation system and was not directly connected with the atmosphere above the surface—otherwise, the high air pressure generated by a depth of forty-five kilometers would cause great discomfort to the occupant. It was also equipped with a powerful cooling system to withstand the high temperature of the mantle, nearly five hundred degrees Celsius.

All Cheng Xin could see, however, was emptiness. The lobby's walls could all apparently act as electronic displays, but they showed nothing but whiteness, as though the building wasn't in use yet. Half a century ago, when the Deterrence Center was designed, Luo Ji had been consulted, but he had only provided one piece of input:

As simple as a tomb.

The handover ceremony was a solemn occasion, but the bulk of it had been held on the surface forty-five kilometers above. There, all the leaders of Earth International and Fleet International, representing all of humanity, had gathered, and they watched as Cheng Xin entered the elevator. Only two people would oversee the final handover: the PDC chair and the chief of staff for the Solar System Fleet, representing the two institutions directly operating the deterrence system.

The PDC chair pointed at the empty lobby and explained to Cheng Xin that they would redecorate the place based on her ideas. If she wanted, she could have a lawn, plants, a fountain, and so forth. She could also choose to have a holographic simulation of scenes from the surface.

"We don't want you to live like him," said the chief of staff. Perhaps because of his military uniform, Cheng Xin saw in him traces of men of the past, and his words warmed her slightly. But the heavy weight on her heart, as heavy as the forty-five kilometers of earth above her, did not lessen.

EXCERPT FROM
A PAST OUTSIDE OF TIME
THE CHOICE OF THE SWORDHOLDER:
TEN MINUTES BETWEEN EXISTENCE
AND ANNIHILATION

The first dark forest deterrence system consisted of more than three thousand nuclear bombs wrapped in an oil film substance deployed in orbit around the sun. After detonation, the film would cause the sun to flicker and broadcast the location of Trisolaris to the universe. Although the system was grand, it was extremely unstable. After the droplets stopped blockading electromagnetic radiation from the sun, a transmission system based on using the sun as a superantenna was immediately put in place to supplement the nuclear bomb deterrence system.

Both of these systems relied on electromagnetic radiation, including visible light, as the broadcast medium. We now know that this is the most primitive technique for interstellar communication, equivalent to smoke signals in space. Since electromagnetic waves decay and become distorted rapidly, the broadcast range is limited.

At the time of the founding of deterrence, humankind already had a basic grasp of the technology for detecting gravitational waves and neutrinos, but they lacked the ability to modulate and

transmit. These were the very first technologies humans demanded from Trisolaris. Compared to quantum communications, these technologies were still primitive, since both gravitational waves and neutrinos were limited by the speed of light, but they were a whole level above electromagnetic waves.

Both of these means of transmission decayed relatively slowly and had very long broadcast ranges. Neutrinos, in particular, interacted with almost nothing else. Theoretically, a modulated beam of neutrinos could transmit information to the other end of the universe, and the accompanying decay and distortion would not affect the decoding of the information. But while neutrinos must be focused in a particular direction, gravitational waves were omnidirectional, thus gravitational waves became the main method of establishing dark forest deterrence.

The fundamental principle of gravitational wave transmission relied on the vibration of a long string of extremely dense matter. The ideal transmission antenna would involve a large number of black holes connected together to form a chain that generated gravitational waves as it vibrated. But even Trisolaris didn't possess such a level of technology, and humankind had to resort to constructing the vibrating string out of degenerate matter. The extremely dense degenerate matter packed an enormous mass into strings mere nanometers in diameter. A single string took up only a minuscule portion of the giant antenna, the bulk of which consisted of support and protection for the ultra-dense string. Thus, the total mass of the antenna wasn't extraordinarily large.

The degenerate matter forming the vibrating string was naturally found in white dwarves and neutron stars. Under typical conditions, this substance naturally decayed and turned into regular matter over time. Man-made vibrating strings typically had a half-life of around fifty years, beyond which the antennas lost their effectiveness. Thus, every half century, the antennas needed to be refreshed with new ones.

During the earliest stage of gravitational wave deterrence, the main strategic concern was with ensuring deterrence power. Plans

were made to build a hundred broadcasting stations scattered around the continents. But gravitational wave communication suffered from a flaw: The transmission equipment could not be miniaturized. The complex, gigantic antennas were extremely costly to manufacture, and in the end only twenty-three gravitational transmitters were built. But the focus on ensuring deterrence finally faded, due to another event.

During the Deterrence Era, the ETO gradually disappeared, but another kind of extremist organization sprang up. They believed in the cause of human supremacy, and advocated for the complete annihilation of Trisolaris. The "Sons of the Earth" was one of the largest of these organizations. In Year 6 of the Deterrence Era, more than three hundred "Sons of the Earth" attacked a gravitational wave broadcasting station located on Antarctica with the aim of seizing the transmitter. Equipped with advanced weapons such as mini-infrasonic nuclear bombs, and aided by members who had infiltrated the broadcasting station ahead of time, the attackers nearly succeeded. If the defending troops stationed at the site hadn't destroyed the antenna in time, the consequences would have been disastrous.

This incident terrified both worlds. People began to realize the great danger posed by gravitational wave transmitters. Simultaneously, Trisolaris pressured Earth until gravitational wave transmission technology was strictly controlled, and the twenty-three broadcasting stations were cut down to four. Three of the stations were terrestrial, located in Asia, North America, and Europe, and the last one was the spaceship *Gravity*.

All the transmitters relied on an active trigger, because the dead hand trigger technique used in the circumsolar nuclear bomb system was no longer necessary. Luo Ji had established deterrence by himself, but now, if the Swordholder were killed, others would be able to take over.

Initially, the gigantic gravitational wave antennas had to be built on the surface. As technology advanced, in Year 12 of the Deterrence Era, the three terrestrial antennas and their support

systems moved deep underground. Everyone understood, however, that burying the transmitters and the control center beneath the Earth's surface primarily guarded against a threat originating from humankind itself, but was meaningless against an attack by Trisolaris. For droplets constructed from strong-interaction material, tens of kilometers of rock were not much different from mere liquid, barely able to impede their progress.

After Earth established deterrence, the Trisolar invasion fleet veered away, as verified through observation. With that threat diminished, most people turned their focus to the whereabouts of the ten droplets that had already reached the Solar System. Trisolaris insisted that four of the droplets remain in the Solar System, justifying the decision by arguing that the gravitational wave transmitters could be seized by extremist factions within humankind, and Trisolaris should have the power to take steps to protect both worlds in the event of such an occurrence. Reluctantly, the Earth agreed, but required the four droplets to stay beyond the Kuiper Belt. Moreover, each droplet had to be accompanied by a human probe, so that the droplets' locations and orbits were known at all times. Thus, in the event of a droplet attack, the Earth would have about fifty hours of advance warning. Of these four droplets, two eventually followed *Gravity* to hunt *Blue Space,* and only two remained in the vicinity of the Kuiper Belt.

No one knew where the other six droplets had gone.

Trisolaris claimed that the six droplets had left the Solar System to rejoin the Trisolaran Fleet, but no one on Earth believed this.

Trisolarans were no longer creatures of transparent thought. During the past two centuries, they had learned a great deal about strategic thinking—lies, ruses, and tricks. This was perhaps the greatest benefit they gained from studying human culture.

Most people were convinced that the six droplets were hidden somewhere in the Solar System. But because the droplets were tiny, fast, and invisible to radar, they were extremely difficult to locate and track. Even by spreading oil films or using other advanced detection techniques, humans could only reliably detect droplets

if they approached within 1/10 AU of the Earth, or fifteen million kilometers. Outside this sphere, the droplets were free to roam undetected.

At maximum speed, a droplet could cross fifteen million kilometers in ten minutes.

This was all the time the Swordholder would have to make a decision if dark forest deterrence broke down.

DETERRENCE ERA, YEAR 62
NOVEMBER 28, 4:00 P.M. TO
4:17 P.M.: DETERRENCE CENTER

With a deep rumble, the meter-thick heavy steel door opened and Cheng Xin and the others walked into the heart of the dark forest deterrence system.

More emptiness and openness greeted Cheng Xin. This was a semicircular hall, with the curved wall facing her. The surface was translucent, resembling ice. The floor and ceiling were pure white. Cheng Xin's first thought was that she stood in front of an empty, iris-less eye, exuding a desolate sense of loss.

Then she saw Luo Ji.

Luo Ji sat cross-legged on the ground in the middle of the white hall, facing the curved wall. His long hair and beard, combed neatly, were also white, almost merging with the white wall. The whiteness everywhere contrasted strongly with his black Zhongshan suit.[5] Sitting there, he appeared as a stable upside-down T, a lonely anchor on a beach, immobile under the winds of time howling overhead

5 *Translator's Note:* This style of Chinese tunic suit is usually known in the West as the "Mao suit." I've chosen to use a literal translation of the Chinese term to avoid unintended connotations. Sun Zhongshan (or Sun Yat-Sen) was the founder of the Republic of China, the predecessor state to the People's Republic of China on the mainland.

and before the roaring waves of the ages, steadfastly waiting for a departed ship that would never return. In his right hand, he held a red ribbon, the hilt of his sword: the switch for the gravitational wave broadcast. His presence gave the empty eye of this room an iris. Though he was but a black dot, the desolate sense of loss was relieved, giving the eye a soul. Luo Ji sat facing the wall so that his own eyes were invisible, and he did not react to his visitors.

It was said that Master Batuo, the founder of Shaolin Monastery, had meditated in front of a wall for ten years until his shadow was carved into the stone. If so, Luo Ji could have inscribed his own shadow into this wall five times.

The PDC chair stopped Cheng Xin and the fleet chief of staff. "Still ten minutes until the handover," he whispered.

In the last ten minutes of his fifty-four-year career as the Swordholder, Luo Ji remained steadfast.

At the beginning of the Deterrence Era, Luo Ji had enjoyed a brief period of happiness. He had been reunited with his wife, Zhuang Yan, and daughter, Xia Xia, and relived the joy of two centuries ago. But within two years, Zhuang Yan took the child and left Luo Ji. There were many stories told about her reasons. A popular version went like this: While Luo Ji remained a savior in the eyes of the public, his image had already transformed in the minds of those he loved the most. Gradually, Zhuang Yan had come to realize that she was living with a man who had already annihilated one world and held the fate of two more in his hand. He was a strange monster who terrified her, and so she left with their child. Another popular story said that Luo Ji left them, instead, so that they could live a normal life. No one knew where Zhuang Yan and their child had gone—they were probably still alive, living tranquil, ordinary lives somewhere.

His family had left him at the time when gravitational wave transmitters took over the task of deterrence from the circumsolar ring of nuclear bombs. Thereafter, Luo Ji embarked on his long career as the Swordholder.

In this cosmic arena, Luo Ji faced not the fancy moves of Chinese sword fighting, resembling dance more than war; nor the flourishes

of Western sword fighting, designed to show off the wielder's skill; but the fatal blows of Japanese *kenjutsu*. Real Japanese sword fights often ended after a very brief struggle lasting no more than half a second to two seconds. By the time the swords had clashed but once, one side had already fallen in a pool of blood. But before this moment, the opponents stared at each other like statues, sometimes for as long as ten minutes. During this contest, the swordsman's weapon wasn't held by the hands, but by his heart. The heart-sword, transformed through the eyes into the gaze, stabbed into the depths of the enemy's soul. The real winner was determined during this process: In the silence suspended between the two swordsmen, the blades of their spirits parried and stabbed as soundless claps of thunder. Before a single blow was struck, victory, defeat, life, and death had already been decided.

Luo Ji stared at the white wall with just such an intense glare, aimed at a world four light-years away. He knew that the sophons could show his gaze to the enemy, and his gaze was endowed with the chill of the underworld and the heaviness of the rocks above him, endowed with the determination to sacrifice everything. The gaze made the enemy's heart palpitate and forced them to give up any ill-considered impulse.

There was always an end to the gaze of the swordsmen, a final moment of truth in the contest. For Luo Ji, one participant in this universal contest, the moment when the sword was swung for the first and last time might never arrive.

But it could also happen in the next second.

In this manner, Luo Ji and Trisolaris stared at each other for fifty-four years. Luo Ji had changed from a carefree, irresponsible man into a true Wallfacer, who faced his wall for more than half a century; the protector of Earth civilization who, for five decades, was ready to deal the fatal blow at a moment's notice.

Throughout this time, Luo Ji had remained silent, not uttering a single word. As a matter of fact, after a person ceased to speak for ten or fifteen years, he lost his powers of speech. He might still be able to understand language, but he would not be able to speak.

Luo Ji certainly could no longer speak; everything he had to say, he put into his gaze against the wall. He had turned himself into a deterrence machine, a mine ready to explode on contact at each and every moment during the long years of the past half century, maintaining the precarious balance of terror between two worlds.

"It is time to hand over the final authority for the gravitational wave universal broadcast system." The PDC chair broke the silence solemnly.

Luo Ji did not move from his pose. The fleet chief of staff walked over, intending to help him get up, but Luo lifted a hand to stop him. Cheng Xin noticed that the motion of his arm was strong, energetic, without a hint of the hesitation one might expect in a centenarian. Then, Luo Ji stood up by himself, his posture steady. Cheng Xin was surprised to see that Luo Ji did not push against the ground with his hands as he uncrossed his legs and stood up. Even most young men couldn't perform such a motion effortlessly.

"Mr. Luo, this is Cheng Xin, your successor. Please pass the switch to her."

Luo Ji stood tall and straight. He looked at the white wall, which he had stared at for more than half a century, for a few more seconds. Then he bowed slightly.

He was paying his respects to his enemy. To have stared at each other across an abyss of four light-years for half a century had bonded them by a link of destiny.

Then he turned to face Cheng Xin. The old and new Swordholders stood apart, silently. Their eyes met for only a moment, but in that moment, Cheng Xin felt a sharp ray of light sweeping across the dark night of her soul. In that gaze, she felt as light and thin as a sheet of paper, even transparent. She could not imagine what kind of enlightenment the old man in front of her had achieved after fifty-four years of facing the wall. She imagined his thoughts precipitating, becoming as dense and heavy as the crust above them or as ethereal as the blue sky above that. She had no way to know, not until and unless she herself had walked the same path. Other than a bottomless profundity, she could not read his gaze.

With both hands, Luo Ji handed over the switch. With both hands, Cheng Xin accepted this heaviest object in the history of the Earth. And so, the fulcrum upon which two worlds rested moved from a 101-year-old man to a 29-year-old woman.

The switch retained the warmth from Luo Ji's hand. It really did resemble the hilt of a sword. It had four buttons, three on the side and one at the end. To prevent accidental activation, the buttons required some strength to press, and they had to be pressed in a certain order.

Luo Ji backed up two steps and nodded at the three people in front of him. With steady, strong strides, he walked toward the door.

Cheng Xin noticed that, throughout the entire process, no one offered a word of thanks to Luo Ji for his fifty-four years of service. She didn't know if the PDC chair or the fleet chief of staff meant to say something, but she could not recall any of the rehearsals for the ceremony including plans for thanking the old Swordholder.

Humankind did not feel grateful to Luo Ji.

In the lobby, a few black-suited men stopped Luo Ji. One of them said, "Mr. Luo, on behalf of the Prosecution for the International Tribunal, we inform you that you have been accused of suspected mundicide. You are under arrest and will be investigated."

Luo Ji did not even spare them a glance as he continued to walk toward the elevator. The prosecutors stepped aside instinctively. Perhaps Luo Ji did not even notice them. The sharp light in his eyes had been extinguished, and in its place was a tranquility like the glow of a sunset. His three-century-long mission was finally over, and the heavy load of responsibility was off his shoulders. From now on, even if the feminized humankind saw him as a devil and a monster, they all had to admit that his victory was unsurpassed in the entire history of civilization.

The steel door had remained open, and Cheng Xin heard the words spoken in the lobby. She felt an impulse to rush over and thank Luo Ji but stopped herself. Dejectedly, she watched him disappear into the elevator.

The PDC chair and the fleet chief of staff left as well, saying nothing.

With a deep rumble, the steel door closed. Cheng Xin felt her previous life seep out of the narrowing crack in the door like water escaping from a funnel. When the door shut completely, a new Cheng Xin was born.

She looked at the red switch in her hand. It was already a part of her. She and it would be inseparable from now on. Even when she slept, she had to keep it by her pillow.

The white, semicircular hall was deathly silent, as though time was sealed in here and no longer flowed. It really did resemble a tomb. But this would be her entire world from now on. She decided that she had to give life to this place. She didn't want to be like Luo Ji. She wasn't a warrior, a duelist; she was a woman, and she needed to live here for a long time—perhaps a decade, perhaps half a century. Indeed, she had been preparing for this mission her whole life. Now that she stood at the starting point of her long journey, she felt calm.

But fate had other ideas. Her career as the Swordholder, a career she had been preparing for since her birth, lasted only fifteen minutes from the moment she accepted the red switch.

THE FINAL TEN MINUTES OF THE DETERRENCE ERA, YEAR 62 NOVEMBER 28, 4:17:34 P.M. TO 4:27:58 P.M.: DETERRENCE CENTER

The white wall turned bloody red, as though the hellish magma behind it had burned through. Highest alert. A line of white text appeared against the red background, each character a terrifying scream.

Incoming strong-interaction space probes detected.
Total number: 6.
One is headed toward the L1 Lagrangian point between the
Earth and the Sun.
The other 5 are headed for the Earth in a 1-2-2 formation.
Speed: 25,000 km/s. Estimated arrival time at the surface:
10 minutes.

Five floating numbers appeared next to Cheng Xin, glowing with a green light. These were holographic buttons: Pressing any of them would bring up a corresponding floating window displaying more detailed information gathered from the advance warning system sweeping the region of space within fifteen million kilometers out from the Earth. The Solar System Fleet General Staff analyzed the data and passed it on to the Swordholder.

Later, Earth would learn that the six droplets had been hiding just outside the fifteen-million-kilometer advance-warning zone. Three of them had relied on solar interference from the Sun to avoid detection, and the other three had disguised themselves in the orbiting space trash scattered in this region. Most of the space trash consisted of spent fuel from the early fusion reactors. Even without these measures, it would have been nearly impossible for the Earth to discover them outside the advance-warning zone because people had always assumed that the droplets were hiding in the asteroid belt, farther away.

The thunderclap that Luo Ji had been waiting for for half a century arrived within five minutes of his departure, and struck Cheng Xin.

Cheng Xin didn't bother pressing any of the holographic buttons. She didn't need any more information.

Right away, she understood the profundity of her error. In the depths of her subconscious, the vision she had held of the mission of the Swordholder had always been utterly, completely wrong. To be sure, she had always planned for the worst, or at least made an effort to do so. Guided by specialists from the PDC and the fleet, she had studied the deterrence system in detail and discussed various possible scenarios with strategists. She had imagined scenarios even worse than the current one.

But she had also committed a fatal error, an error that she did not and could not have realized. The error, however, was also the very reason she had been elected to be the second Swordholder.

In her subconscious, she had never truly accepted that the events facing her now were possible.

Average distance of incoming formation of strong-interaction space probes: approximately 14 million kilometers. The closest one is at 13.5 million kilometers. Estimated arrival time at the surface: nine minutes.

In Cheng Xin's subconscious, she was a protector, not a

destroyer; she was a woman, not a warrior. She was willing to use the rest of her life to maintain the balance between the two worlds, until the Earth grew stronger and stronger with Trisolaran science, until Trisolaris grew more and more civilized with Earth culture, until one day, a voice told her: *Put down that red switch and return to the surface. The world no longer needs dark forest deterrence, no longer needs a Swordholder.*

When she faced that distant world as the Swordholder, Cheng Xin, unlike Luo Ji, did not feel this was a life-or-death contest. She thought of it as a game of chess. She would sit tranquilly before the chessboard, thinking of all the openings, anticipating the opponent's attacks, and devising her own responses. She was ready to spend her life playing this game.

But her opponents hadn't bothered to move any pieces on the board. Instead, they had simply lifted the chessboard and smashed it at her head.

The moment Cheng Xin accepted the red switch from Luo Ji, the six droplets had begun accelerating at maximum power toward the Earth. The enemy did not waste a single second.

Average distance of incoming formation of strong-interaction space probes: approximately 13 million kilometers. The closest one is at 12 million kilometers. Estimated arrival time at the surface: eight minutes.

Blankness.

Average distance of incoming formation of strong-interaction space probes: approximately 11.5 million kilometers. The closest one is at 10.5 million kilometers. Estimated arrival time at the surface: seven minutes.

Blankness, nothing but blankness. In addition to the white hall and the white letters, everything else around her had also turned a blank white. Cheng Xin seemed to be suspended in a milky universe,

just like a bubble of milk sixteen billion light-years across. In this vast blankness, she found nothing to hold on to.

> Average distance of incoming formation of strong-interaction space probes: approximately 10 million kilometers. The closest one is at 9 million kilometers. Estimated arrival time at the surface: six minutes.

What was she supposed to do?

> Average distance of incoming formation of strong-interaction space probes: approximately 9 million kilometers. The closest one is at 7.5 million kilometers. Estimated arrival time at the surface: five minutes.

The blankness began to dissipate. The forty-five-kilometer-thick crust above her reasserted its presence: sedimentary time. The lowest stratum, or the layer immediately above the Deterrence Center, had probably been deposited four billion years ago. The Earth had been born only five hundred million years before that. The turbid ocean was in its infancy, and nonstop flashes of lightning struck its surface; the Sun was a fuzzy ball of light in a haze-veiled sky, casting a crimson reflection over the sea. At short intervals, other bright balls of light streaked across the sky, crashing into the sea and trailing long tails of fire; these meteor strikes caused tsunamis that propelled gigantic waves to smash onto continents still laced with rivers of lava, raising clouds of vapor generated by fire and water that dimmed the Sun. . . .

In contrast to this hellish but magnificent sight, the turbid water brewed a microscopic tale. Here, organic molecules were born from lightning flashes and cosmic rays, and they collided, fused, broke apart again—a long-lasting game played with building blocks for five hundred million years. Finally, a chain of organic molecules, trembling, split into two strands. The strands attracted other molecules around them until two identical

202

copies of the original were made, and these split apart again and replicated themselves.... In this game of building blocks, the probability of producing such a self-replicating chain of organic molecules was so minuscule that it was as if a tornado had picked up a pile of metallic trash and deposited it as a fully-assembled Mercedes-Benz.

But it happened, and so, a breathtaking history of 3.5 billion years had begun.

> Average distance of incoming formation of strong-interaction space probes: approximately 7.5 million kilometers. The closest one is at 6 million kilometers. Estimated arrival time at the surface: four minutes.

The Archean Eon was followed by the Proterozoic Eon, each billions of years; then the Paleozoic: the Cambrian's seventy million years, the Ordovician's sixty million years, the Silurian's forty million years, the Devonian's fifty million years, the Carboniferous's sixty-five million years, and the Permian's fifty-five million years; then the Mesozoic: the Triassic's thirty-five million years, the Jurassic's fifty-eight million years, and the Cretaceous's seventy million years; then the Cenozoic: the Tertiary's 64.5 million years and the Quaternary's 2.5 million years.

Then humanity appeared. Compared to the eons before, mankind's history was but the blink of an eye. Dynasties and eras exploded like fireworks; the bone club tossed into the air by an ape turned into a spaceship. Finally, this 3.5-billion-year-long road full of trials and tribulations stopped in front of a tiny human individual, a single person out of the one hundred billion people who had ever lived on the Earth, holding a red switch.

> Average distance of incoming formation of strong-interaction space probes: approximately 6 million kilometers. The closest one is at 4.5 million kilometers. Estimated arrival time at the surface: three minutes.

Four billion years were layered on top of Cheng Xin, suffocating her. Her subconscious tried to reach the surface, to catch a breath above it. In her subconscious, the surface was teeming with life, the most prominent form being the giant reptiles, including dinosaurs. Densely, they packed the ground, all the way to the horizon. Among the dinosaurs, between their legs and under their bellies, were the mammals, including humans. Still lower, under and between countless pairs of feet, were surging black currents of water: innumerable trilobites and ants.... In the sky, hundreds of billions of birds formed a dark, swirling vortex that blotted out the firmament, and giant pterodactyls could be seen among them from time to time....

Everything was deathly quiet. The eyes were the most terrifying: the eyes of dinosaurs; the eyes of trilobites and ants; the eyes of birds and butterflies; the eyes of bacteria.... The humans alone possessed one hundred billion pairs of eyes, equal to the number of stars in the Milky Way. Among them were the eyes of ordinary men and women, and the eyes of Da Vinci, Shakespeare, and Einstein.

Average distance of incoming formation of strong-interaction space probes: approximately 4.5 million kilometers. The closest one is at three million kilometers. Estimated arrival time at the surface: two minutes.

Two of the probes are headed for Asia, two others for North America. The last one is aimed at Europe.

Pressing the switch would end the progress of 3.5 billion years. Everything would disappear in the eternal night of the universe, as though none of it had ever existed.

That baby seemed to be back in her arms: soft, cuddly, warm, his face moist, smiling sweetly, calling her *mama*.

Average distance of incoming formation of strong-interaction space probes: approximately 3 million kilometers. The closest one is at 1.5 million kilometers, and it is rapidly

> decelerating. Estimated arrival time at the surface: one
> minute and thirty seconds.

"No—" Cheng Xin screamed, and threw the switch away. She watched it slide across the ground, as though watching a devil.

> Strong-interaction space probes approaching lunar orbit
> and continuing to decelerate. Extending their trajectories
> suggests that their targets are the gravitational wave
> broadcasting stations in North America, Europe, and Asia,
> and Gravitational Wave Universal Broadcast System
> Control Station Zero. Estimated impact on the surface:
> thirty seconds.

Like a strand of spider silk, these final moments stretched out endlessly. But Cheng Xin did not vacillate; she had already made up her mind. This wasn't a decision born of thought, but buried deep in her genes. These genes could be traced to four billion years ago, when the decision was first made. The subsequent billions of years only strengthened it. Right or wrong, she knew she had no other choice.

It was good that release was at hand.

A great jolt tumbled her to the ground: The droplets had penetrated the crust. She felt as though the solid rocks around her had vanished, and the Deterrence Center was on top of a giant drumhead. She closed her eyes and imagined the sight of a droplet passing through the crust like a fish swimming through water, waiting for the arrival at cosmic velocity of the perfectly smooth devil that would turn her and everything around her into molten lava.

But the quaking stopped after a few violent beats, like a drummer punctuating the end of the piece.

The red light on the screen faded, replaced by the white background from before. The room seemed brighter and more open. A few lines of black text appeared:

> North American gravitational wave transmitter destroyed.
>
> European gravitational wave transmitter destroyed.
>
> Asian gravitational wave transmitter destroyed.
>
> Solar radio-amplification function suppressed on all bands.

Silence once again reigned over everything, except the faint sound of water trickling somewhere. A pipe had burst during the quake.

Cheng Xin understood that the droplet attack on the Asian gravitational wave transmitter had caused the earthquake. That antenna was about twenty kilometers from here and was also deeply buried.

The droplets had not even bothered attacking the Swordholder.

The black text disappeared. After some moments of blankness, a last screen of text faded in:

> Gravitational wave universal broadcast system cannot be recovered. Dark forest deterrence has been terminated.

POST-DETERRENCE ERA, FIRST HOUR
A LOST WORLD

Cheng Xin rode the elevator to the surface. Exiting the elevator station, she saw the plaza where the deterrence handover ceremony had taken place an hour ago. All the attendees had left, and the place was empty save for the long shadows cast by the flagpoles. The flags of the UN and the Solar System Fleet hung from the two tallest poles, and behind them were the flags of the various nations. The flags continued to flap tranquilly in the light breeze. Beyond them was the endless Gobi Desert. A few twittering birds landed in a stand of tamarisk nearby. In the distance, she could see the rolling Qilian Mountains, the snow cover on a few peaks giving them a silvery highlight.

Everything seemed the same, but this world no longer belonged to humans.

Cheng Xin didn't know what to do. No one had contacted her after the end of deterrence. The Swordholder no longer existed, just like deterrence.

She walked forward aimlessly. When she exited the gates of the compound, two guards saluted her. She was terrified of facing people, but she saw nothing but curiosity in their eyes—they didn't yet know what had happened. Regulations permitted the Swordholder to come onto the surface for brief intervals, and they must have thought she had come up to investigate the quake. Cheng

Xin saw a few military officers standing next to a flying transport parked by the gate. They weren't even looking at her, merely in the direction she had come from. One of them pointed in that direction.

She turned around and saw the mushroom cloud on the horizon. Formed by the earth and dust thrown up from deep underground, it was very thick, appearing almost solid. It looked so out of place in the serene scene that it resembled a bad Photoshop job. A closer examination led Cheng Xin to imagine it as an ugly bust showing a strange expression in the setting sun. That was where the droplet had penetrated the Earth.

Someone called her name. She turned and saw 艾 AA running toward her. Dressed in a white jacket, her hair waving in the wind, she panted and told Cheng Xin that she had come to see her, but the sentries wouldn't let her in.

"I've brought some flowers for your new place," she said, pointing at her parked car. Then she turned to the mushroom cloud. "Is that a volcano? Did that cause the earthquake just now?"

Cheng Xin wanted to pull AA into her arms and cry, but she controlled herself. She wanted to delay the moment when this happy girl found out the truth, wanted to let the reverberations of the good times that had just ended linger a bit longer.

EXCERPT FROM
A PAST OUTSIDE OF TIME
REFLECTIONS ON THE FAILURE OF
DARK FOREST DETERRENCE

The most important factor in the failure of deterrence was, of course, electing the wrong Swordholder. This is a topic that will be addressed elsewhere in a dedicated chapter. For now, let's focus on the technical weaknesses in the system design that contributed to the failure.

After the failure, most people immediately pointed to the small number of gravitational wave transmitters as a cause, and blamed people from the early Deterrence Era for dismantling nineteen of the twenty-three completed transmitters. But this reaction represented a failure to grasp the substance of the problem. From data gathered during the droplet attack, a droplet needed slightly more than ten seconds on average to penetrate the crust and destroy a transmitter. Even if the planned one hundred transmitters had been completed and deployed, it wouldn't have taken long for droplets to destroy the entire system.

The key was that the system *could* be destroyed. Humankind had had a chance to build an indestructible gravitational wave universal broadcast system, but hadn't taken it.

The problem wasn't the number of transmitters, but where they were deployed.

Imagine if the twenty-three transmitters had not been built on or below the surface, but in space—that is, twenty-three spaceships like *Gravity*. Normally, the ships would be scattered around the Solar System. Even if the droplets had conducted a surprise attack, it would be difficult for them to destroy all of them. One or more of the ships would have time to escape into deep space.

This would have greatly increased the degree of deterrence for the whole system, in a way that would not have been dependent on the Swordholder. The Trisolarans would have known that they controlled insufficient forces within the Solar System to completely destroy the deterrence system, and would have behaved with far more restraint.

Regrettably, there was only one *Gravity*.

There were two reasons that more ships with transmitters weren't built: First, there was the "Sons of the Earth" attack on the transmitter in Antarctica. Spaceships were deemed even more vulnerable to threats from extremist humans than underground stations. Second, it was a matter of economics. Since gravitational wave antennas were immense, they had to serve as the hull of the ship itself. Thus, the antenna had to be constructed out of materials that met the requirements of spaceflight, which increased costs many times. *Gravity* itself cost almost the equivalent of the twenty-three ground-based transmitters added together. Moreover, the hull of the ship itself could not be refreshed; when the vibrating string made of degenerate matter that ran the length of the ship reached its fifty-year half-life limit, a completely new gravitational wave ship had to be built.

But the deeper root cause could only be found in the minds of humankind. Never explicitly stated, and perhaps not even con-sciously understood, a gravitational wave ship was too powerful—so powerful that it terrified its creator. If something—a droplet attack or something else—forced such ships to depart for deep space, and they could never return to the Solar System due to the presence of enemy threats, they would turn into copies of *Blue Space* and *Bronze Age,* or something even more horrific. Each

gravitational wave ship, with its no-longer-human crew, would also possess the power to broadcast to the universe (though limited by the half-life of the vibrating string), thus controlling the fate of humanity. A frightful instability would be permanently scattered among the stars.

At its root, this fear was a fear of dark forest deterrence itself. This was characteristic of ultimate deterrence: The deterrer and the deteree shared the same terror of deterrence itself.

POST-DETERRENCE ERA, FIRST HOUR
A LOST WORLD

Cheng Xin walked toward the officers and asked them to take her to the site of the eruption. A lieutenant colonel in charge of security for the compound immediately dispatched two cars: one to take her, the other to carry a few guards for security. Cheng Xin asked AA to stay and wait for her, but AA insisted on coming and got into the car.

The flying cars hovered barely above the ground and headed to the mushroom cloud at a low speed. AA asked the driver what was wrong, but he didn't know. The volcano had erupted twice, a few minutes apart. He thought it might be the first time in recorded history that a volcano had erupted within China's borders.

He couldn't have imagined that the "volcano" had once hidden the strategic fulcrum for the world: the gravitational wave antenna. The first eruption was caused by the impact of the droplet penetrating the crust. After destroying the antenna, it retraced its path and emerged from the ground, causing a second eruption. The eruptions were due to the droplet releasing its tremendous kinetic energy in the ground, not an outburst of material from the mantle, so they were very brief. The extremely high velocity of the droplet meant that it could not be observed by the naked eye as it penetrated or emerged from the ground.

Small smoking pits dotted the Gobi as it passed beneath the

212

car: mini-impact craters from the lava and heated rocks that had been thrown up by the eruption. As they proceeded, the pits grew denser, and a thick layer of smoke hovered over the Gobi, revealing burning stands of tamarisk here and there. Though few people lived out here they occasionally saw old buildings collapsed by the quake. The whole scene resembled a battlefield where the fighting had just finished.

The cloud had dissipated a bit by now and no longer looked like a mushroom—it was more like a head of unkempt hair whose tips were colored crimson by the setting sun. A security line stopped the cars as they approached, and they had to land. But Cheng Xin persisted, and the sentries let her through. The soldiers didn't know that the world had already fallen, and they still respected Cheng Xin's authority as the Swordholder. They did, however, stop AA, and no matter how she screamed and struggled, they would not let her pass.

The steady wind had already driven most of the dust away, but the smoke broke the light of the setting sun into a series of flickering shadows. Cheng Xin walked about a hundred meters through the shadows until she reached the edge of a giant crater. Shaped like a funnel, the crater was forty or fifty meters deep at the center. Thick clouds of white smoke still poured out of it, and the bottom of the crater gave off a dim red molten glow: a pool of lava.

Forty-five kilometers below, the gravitational wave antenna, a cylinder with a length of fifteen hundred meters and a diameter of fifty meters suspended in an underground cave with magnetic levitation, had been smashed into smithereens and swallowed by the red-hot lava.

This should have been her fate. It would have been the best ending for a Swordholder who had given up the power to deter.

The red glow at the bottom of the crater attracted Cheng Xin. Just one more step, and she would achieve the release that she desired. As waves of heat buffeted her face, she stared at the dim red pool, mesmerized, until peals of laughter from behind her shook her out of her musing.

213

She turned around. In the flickering sunlight filtered by the smoke, a slender figure approached her. She didn't recognize the newcomer until she was very close: Sophon.

Other than the pale, lovely face, the robot looked completely different from the last time Cheng Xin had seen her. She was dressed in desert camouflage, and her hair, once tied up in a neat bun decorated with flowers, had been cut in a short and efficient style. Around her neck was the black scarf of a ninja, and on her back was strapped a long katana. She looked valiant and heroic, but the extreme femininity that she exuded had not vanished completely: Her postures and movements were still soft and gentle like water, but now they were also suffused with a glamorous air of killing and death, like a pliant but fatal noose. Even the heat spilling from the crater could not dispel the chill she brought.

"You acted just as we anticipated," Sophon said, sneering. "Don't be too hard on yourself. The fact is that humankind chose you, and they chose this result. Out of all the members of the human race, you're the only innocent."

Cheng Xin's heart jumped. She didn't feel comforted, but she had to admit that this lovely devil had a power that penetrated her soul.

Cheng Xin saw AA approach. She had apparently found out or guessed what had really happened. AA's eyes burned with fury as she stared at Sophon; she picked up a rock from the ground with both hands and smashed the back of Sophon's skull with it. But Sophon turned around and brushed the rock away like a mosquito. AA cursed at Sophon using every profane word she could think of, and went for another rock. Sophon unsheathed the katana on her back, easily pushing off the pleading Cheng Xin with her other hand, and twirled the katana. It sliced through the air, faster than the blades of an electric fan, whining loudly. When she stopped, strands of AA's hair drifted down around her head. AA stood frozen in place, terrified, her shoulders hunched.

Cheng Xin remembered that she had seen Sophon's katana in that eastern leaf-house shrouded in fog and cloud. Back then, it,

and two shorter swords, had rested on a refined wooden stand next to the tea table, looking more decorative than deadly.

"Why?" Cheng Xin muttered, as if asking herself.

"Because the universe is not a fairy tale."

Rationally, Cheng Xin understood that, had the balance maintained by deterrence continued, the brighter future belonged to humankind, not Trisolaris. But in her subconscious, the universe remained a fairy tale, a fairy tale about love. Her biggest mistake was not looking at the problem from the perspective of the enemy.

From Sophon's gaze, Cheng Xin finally understood why she had been kept alive.

As the gravitational wave broadcast system had been destroyed and the sun's ability to amplify radio waves had been suppressed, a living Cheng Xin posed no threat. On the other hand, in the unlikely event that humans still possessed some other method of broadcasting to the universe unknown to Trisolaris, eliminating the Swordholder might cause others to activate the broadcast. As long as the Swordholder was alive, however, the probability of that happening was virtually nil: Others would have a reason and excuse to shirk their responsibility.

Instead of the deterrer, Cheng Xin had been turned into a safety shield. The enemy had seen through her completely.

She was a fairy tale.

"Don't celebrate too early," AA said to Sophon, having recovered some of her courage. "We still have the spaceship *Gravity*."

Sophon returned the katana to its sheath on her back in a single, smooth motion. "Foolish girl, *Gravity* has been destroyed. It happened an hour ago, when the handover occurred a light-year away. I regret that I can't show you the wreckage because the sophons are in a blind zone."

The Trisolarans had been planning and preparing for this moment for a long time. The exact time for the handover had been determined five months ago, before the sophons accompanying *Gravity* had entered the blind zone. The two droplets with *Gravity*

had already received the order to destroy the ship at the moment of the handover.

"I'm leaving," said Sophon. "Please convey to Dr. Luo Ji the deepest respect of all of Trisolaris. He was a powerful deterrer, a great warrior. Oh, and if you get the chance, also give Mr. Thomas Wade our regrets."

Cheng Xin looked up, surprised.

"In our personality studies, your degree of deterrence hovered around ten percent, like a worm wriggling on the ground. Luo Ji's degree of deterrence was always around ninety percent, like a fearsome cobra poised to strike. But Wade—" Sophon gazed at the setting sun behind the smoke, only a sliver of which now was above ground. Terror glinted from her eyes. She shook her head vigorously, as though trying to chase away a mirage in her mind. "He had no curve at all. No matter what the other environmental parameters were, his degree of deterrence stayed at one hundred percent! What a devil! If he had become the Swordholder, none of this would have been possible. This peace would have had to last. We've already waited sixty-two years, but we'd have had to keep on waiting, maybe for fifty more years, or even longer. And then Trisolaris would face an Earth equal to us in technology and power. We'd have to compromise.... However, we knew that humanity would choose you."

Sophon walked away, taking large strides. She paused some distance away and turned around, calling out to the silent Cheng Xin and AA. "Get ready to go to Australia, you pitiful bugs."

POST-DETERRENCE ERA, DAY 60
A LOST WORLD

On the thirty-eighth day after the end of deterrence, the Ringier-Fitzroy observation station at the outer rim of the asteroid belt discovered 415 new trails in the interstellar dust cloud near the Trisolaran star system. Apparently, Trisolaris had sent a second fleet toward the Solar System.

This second fleet had left Trisolaris five years ago, and passed through the dust cloud four years ago. This had been a huge risk on Trisolaris's part—if they couldn't destroy humanity's dark forest deterrence system within five years, the discovery of this fleet might have led to the activation of the deterrence broadcast. This meant that as long ago as five years, Trisolaris already had sensed the shifting mood toward dark forest deterrence among humanity and correctly predicted the kind of second Swordholder that would be elected.

History seemed to have been reset; a new cycle had begun.

The end of deterrence once again cast the future of humankind into darkness, but, just like in the first crisis over two centuries earlier, people did not connect this darkness with their individual fates. Based on analysis of the trails, the Second Trisolaran Fleet's velocity wasn't so different from that of the First Trisolaran Fleet. Even if they could accelerate more, the fleet wouldn't arrive at the Solar System for at least two or three centuries. Everyone alive

would be able to live out the remainder of their lives in peace. After the lessons taught by the Great Ravine, modern men and women would never again sacrifice the present for the future.

But this time, humanity wasn't so fortunate.

Three days after the Second Trisolaran Fleet left the interstellar cloud, the observation system detected 415 trails in the second interstellar cloud. These trails couldn't belong to a different fleet. The First Trisolaran Fleet had taken five years to go from the first dust cloud to the second, while the Second Trisolaran Fleet had taken only six days.

The Trisolarans had achieved lightspeed.

Analysis of the trails in the second interstellar dust cloud confirmed that they continued to extend through the cloud at lightspeed. At such high velocities, the trails left by the ships' impacts became particularly prominent.

Timing wise, it appeared that the fleet had entered lightspeed as soon as it exited the first dust cloud; there didn't appear to be a stage during which it accelerated.

If that was true, then the Second Trisolaran Fleet should have already or almost reached the Solar System. Using midsized telescopes, it was possible to see a patch of 415 bright lights about six thousand AU from the Earth. These were the lights generated by deceleration. Apparently the ships' propulsion systems were conventional. The fleet's velocity was now only 15 percent of the speed of light. This was evidently the fastest speed that still permitted safe deceleration before arriving at the Solar System. Based on the observed velocity and deceleration, the Second Trisolaran Fleet would arrive at the edge of the Solar System in one year.

This was a bit puzzling. It appeared as if the Trisolar ships were capable of entering and dropping out of lightspeed within an extremely short period of time, but they chose not to do so too close to the Trisolaran star system or the Solar System. After the fleet had left Trisolaris, the ships accelerated under conventional power for an entire year, until they were about six thousand AU from home, before entering lightspeed. Similarly, they dropped out of lightspeed

at the same distance from the Solar System and switched to conventional deceleration. This distance could be covered in a month at lightspeed, but the fleet chose to spend a year traversing it. The cruise of the Second Trisolaran Fleet would thus take two years longer than it would if the entire voyage were conducted at lightspeed.

Only one explanation for this curious decision came to mind: It was motivated by a desire not to harm either solar system during the process of entering and dropping out of lightspeed. The safe radius appeared to be two hundred times the distance from the Sun to Neptune. This suggested that the power generated by the drives was two orders of magnitude greater than a star, which seemed unimaginable.

EXCERPT FROM
A PAST OUTSIDE OF TIME
TECHNOLOGY EXPLOSION
ON TRISOLARIS

Exactly when the rate of Trisolaran technological progress had shifted from constant to explosive was a mystery. Some scholars believed that the acceleration began before the Crisis Era; others believed that the forward leap didn't happen until the Deterrence Era. There was, however, general consensus on the causes for the technology explosion.

First, Earth civilization had a tremendous impact on Trisolaran civilization—on this point, at least, the Trisolarans likely didn't lie. Since the arrival of the first sophon, the massive inflow of human culture profoundly changed Trisolaris, and some human values resonated with the Trisolarans. Trisolaran society broke down the barriers to scientific progress imposed by the extreme totalitarian political system that had been adopted as a reaction to the chaotic eras, encouraged freedom of thought, and began to respect the individual. These changes might have triggered ideological transformation movements akin to the Renaissance in that distant world, leading to leaps in scientific and technological progress. This must have been a glorious period in Trisolaran history, but the specific details were unknown.

A second possibility was only a guess: The exploratory sophon missions sent in other directions in the universe were not fruitless, as the Trisolarans claimed. Before being blinded, they might have found at least one other civilized world. If so, Trisolarans might have not only received technological knowledge from this other civilization, but also important information about the condition of the dark forest in the universe. If so, Trisolaris far surpassed the Earth in every domain of knowledge.

POST-DETERRENCE ERA, DAY 60
A LOST WORLD

For the first time since the end of deterrence, Sophon appeared. Still dressed in camouflage and wearing the katana on her back, she announced to the world that the Second Trisolaran Fleet would arrive in four years to complete the total conquest of the Solar System.

Trisolaran policy toward humanity had changed since the first crisis. Sophon announced that Trisolaris no longer intended to exterminate human civilization, but would create reservations for humans within the Solar System—specifically, they would let humanity live in Australia and on one-third of the surface of Mars. This preserved the basic living space needed for human civilization.

To prepare for the Trisolaran conquest in four years, Sophon declared that humanity must immediately begin to resettle. To accomplish the so-called "defanging" of humanity, and to prevent the reappearance of dark forest deterrence or similar threats in the future, humanity must be completely disarmed and resettle "naked." No heavy equipment or facilities would be permitted in the reservations, and the resettlement must be completed within one year.

Human habitats on Mars and in space could accommodate about three million individuals at most; thus, the main destination for resettlement was Australia.

But most people still held on to the illusion that they would have at least a generation of tranquil life. After Sophon's speech, no country responded, and no one actually emigrated.

Five days after this historical "Reservation Proclamation," one of the five droplets cruising within the Earth's atmosphere attacked three large cities in Asia, Europe, and North America. The purpose of the attacks wasn't to destroy the cities, but to instill terror. The droplet passed straight through the giant forests of these cities, colliding with all hanging buildings that happened to be in the way. The struck buildings burned and then fell several hundred meters, like overripe fruits. Over three hundred thousand people died in the worst disaster since the Doomsday Battle.

People finally understood that, to the droplets, the human world was as fragile as eggs under a poised rock. Cities and large-scale facilities were defenseless. If the Trisolarans wanted, they could lay waste to every city, until the surface of the Earth was one large ruin.

As a matter of fact, humans had been working toward overcoming this disadvantage. Humans understood early on that only strong-interaction materials (SIM) could be used to defend against droplets. Before the termination of deterrence, research facilities on Earth and in the fleet could already produce small quantities of such material in laboratories, though large-scale manufacturing and utilization would not be possible for years. If humanity had had another ten years, production of large amounts of SIM would have been a reality. Although the propulsion systems of the droplets would still have been far beyond human capabilities, at least conventional missiles could have been made out of SIM to destroy the droplets by sheer numerical advantage. Alternatively, SIM could have been used to construct defensive screens. Even if the droplets had dared to attack these shields, they would have become one-time-use shells.

Alas, none of these visions would ever come true now.

Sophon made another speech, in which she explained that Trisolaris had changed its policy of extermination of humanity out of love and respect for human civilization. It was inevitable that

resettlement of humanity to Australia would cause them to suffer somewhat for a period of time, but it would last only three to four years. After the arrival of the Trisolaran Fleet, the conquerors were capable of helping the four billion people in Australia live comfortably. Also, the conquerors would assist humanity in constructing additional habitats on Mars and in space. Five years after the arrival of the Trisolaran Fleet, humanity could begin to migrate in large numbers to Mars and space, a process projected to take fifteen years. By then, humanity would possess adequate living space, and the two civilizations would begin a life of peaceful coexistence.

But all of this depended on the successful accomplishment of the initial resettlement to Australia. If the relocation effort did not commence immediately, the droplets would continue to attack the cities. After the expiration of the one-year period, any humans found outside the reservations would be exterminated as invaders on Trisolaran territory. Of course, if humans left the cities and scattered across the continents, the five droplets alone would not be enough to locate and kill every single individual. But the Second Trisolaran Fleet arriving in four years would no doubt be able to.

"The glorious and resplendent civilization of Earth earned humanity this one chance at survival," said Sophon. "Please treasure it."

Thus began the Great Resettlement of all of humanity to Australia.

POST-DETERRENCE ERA, YEAR 2
AUSTRALIA

Cheng Xin stood in front of Elder Fraisse's house and surveyed the Great Victoria Desert shimmering in the heat. Simple, just-completed shelter-houses were packed densely, as far as the eye could see. Under the noonday sun, the plywood and sheet-metal constructions seemed both brand-new and fragile, like origami toys scattered across the sand.

When James Cook had discovered Australia five centuries ago, he could never have imagined that, one day, all of humanity would be gathered on this empty, vast continent.

Cheng Xin and 艾 AA had come to Australia with the earliest wave of forced migrants. Cheng Xin could have gone to a big city like Canberra or Sydney for a relatively comfortable life, but she had insisted on living as an ordinary migrant and gone to the interior resettlement zone in the deserts near Warburton, where conditions were the roughest. She was touched that AA, who could also have gone to a big city, insisted on accompanying her.

Life in the resettlement zone was difficult. Near the beginning, when few people were there, it was still tolerable. The harassment by other people was far harder to bear than the material deprivations. At first, Cheng Xin and AA had a shelter-house all to themselves. But as additional migrants came, more people were packed into the shelter-house, until eight women in total shared it. The other six

women had all been born during the paradise-like Deterrence Era. Here, for the first time in their lives, they encountered rationing of water and food, dead walls that did not come alive with information, rooms with no air-conditioning, public toilets and showers, bunk beds.... This was a society of absolute equality: Money had no use here, and everyone received exactly the same ration. They had only ever seen such austerity in historical films, and life in the resettlement zones felt like hell. Naturally, Cheng Xin became the target of their fury. Unprovoked, they would curse at her and accuse her of being a waste of space—after all, she had not been able to deter Trisolaris. Her worst sin had been giving up as soon as she received the warning: Had she activated the gravitational wave broadcast, the Trisolarans would have run away in terror, and at least humanity would enjoy a few more decades of happiness. Even if the broadcast led to the immediate destruction of the Earth, it would be better than the current conditions.

At the beginning, the abuse was merely verbal, but it soon turned physical, and they began to snatch Cheng Xin's rations away from her. AA did all she could to protect her friend. She fought the other women, sometimes several times a day. Once, she grabbed the meanest one by the hair and slammed her head against a bed-post until blood covered her face. Thereafter, they left her and Cheng Xin alone.

But the enmity directed at Cheng Xin wasn't limited to their roommates: The migrants in the shelter-houses nearby also came to harass her. Sometimes they threw stones at Cheng Xin's shelter-house; sometimes a mob surrounded the shelter-house and shouted curses at her.

Cheng Xin bore all the abuse with equanimity. Indeed, the abuse even comforted her. As the failed Swordholder, she felt she deserved worse.

This persisted until an old man named Fraisse came and invited her and AA to move into his place. Fraisse was an Aboriginal man, over eighty years of age but still hale and hearty, with a white beard on his black face. As a native, he had been temporarily allowed

226

to keep his own house. During the Common Era, he had been in charge of an organization for Aboriginal cultural preservation, and he had gone into hibernation at the beginning of the Crisis Era in order to continue his task in the future. When he awoke, he saw that his prediction had come true: The Australian Aboriginals and their culture were close to disappearing.

Fraisse's house, built back in the twenty-first century, was old but solid and had a nice copse of trees nearby. Once they moved there, Cheng Xin and AA's lives became much more stable. More importantly, the old man provided them with spiritual tranquility. He did not share the popular searing anger and bone-deep hatred toward the Trisolarans; indeed, he rarely talked about the crisis at all. All he said was, "Whatever people do, the gods remember."

True. Even *people* still remembered whatever people did. Five centuries ago, civilized men of Earth—most of whom had actually been criminals in Europe—stepped onto this continent and shot the Aboriginal peoples in the woods for sport. Later, even when they recognized that their quarries were men and women, not beasts, the slaughter continued. The Aboriginal peoples had lived in this vast land for tens of thousands of years. By the time the white men arrived, the native population was more than a half million, but that number soon diminished to thirty thousand refugees who had to escape to the desolate western deserts to survive....

When Sophon proclaimed the establishment of "reservations," people paid attention. It brought to mind the tragic fate of the native peoples of North America, another faraway continent where the arrival of civilized men of Earth brought sorrow.

When she first arrived at Fraisse's, AA was curious about everything in the old house. It resembled a museum of Aboriginal culture. Everywhere there were rock and bark paintings, musical instruments made of wooden slats and hollow logs, woven grass skirts, boomerangs, spears, and other such objects. AA was most interested in a few pots of paint made of white clay and red and yellow ocher. She knew right away what they were for, and, dipping a finger into the pots, started to paint her own face. Then she began

dancing in imitation of tribal dancers she had seen somewhere, making fearsome noises as she danced.

"This would have terrified those bitches living with us," she said.

Fraisse laughed and shook his head. He explained that AA wasn't imitating the Aboriginal peoples of Australia, but the Māori of New Zealand. Outsiders sometimes confused the two, but the Aboriginal peoples of Australia were gentle, while the Māori were fierce warriors. And, even so, she wasn't imitating the Māori dance correctly, and had failed to capture their spirit. Fraisse then painted his own face into an impressive mask and took off his shirt, revealing a dark chest and powerful muscles that seemed incongruous with his advanced age. He picked up a taiaha from the corner of the house and began to dance a real war haka.

Cheng Xin and AA were mesmerized. Fraisse's kind everyday demeanor disappeared, and he transformed into a threatening, awe-inspiring demon. His whole body seemed suffused with magnificent force. Every cry and foot stomp made the glass window panes quake in their frames, and the two women trembled. But it was his eyes that shocked them the most: Murderous chill and searing rage spewed from those wide-open orbs, combining the forces of typhoons and thunder in Oceania. His powerful gaze seemed to project earth-shattering shouts: "Do not run away! I will kill you! I will eat you!"

The haka over, Fraisse went back to his usual kind self. "For a Māori warrior, the key is to hold the enemy's gaze. He must defeat the enemy first with his eyes, then kill him with the taiaha." He came back and stood in front of Cheng Xin. "Child, you failed to hold the enemy's gaze." Then he patted her gently on the shoulder. "But, it's not your fault. Really not your fault."

The next day, Cheng Xin did something that surprised even herself: She went to see Wade.

Wade was sealing up the windows of a shelter-house with

composite boards so that it could be used as a warehouse. One of his sleeves was empty. In this age, it would have been easy for him to acquire a prosthesis indistinguishable from the real thing, but for some reason, he had refused.

Two other prisoners—clearly also Common Era men—whistled at Cheng Xin. But once they realized who Cheng Xin had come to see, they shut up and went back to their work without looking up.

As Cheng Xin approached Wade, she was a bit surprised to see that while he was serving his sentence in harsh conditions, he looked much better groomed than the last time they met. He was clean-shaven and his hair was combed neatly. Prisoners in this age no longer wore uniforms, but his white shirt was the cleanest here, even more so than the shirts worn by the guards. Holding a few nails between his lips, he took them out one at a time with his left hand and pounded them into the composite boards with precise, forceful blows from the hammer. He glanced at Cheng Xin without changing his indifferent expression and went on working.

Cheng Xin knew right away that he had not given up. His ambitions, ideals, treachery, and whatever else was hidden in his heart, unknown to her—he had given up none of it.

Cheng Xin extended a hand to Wade. He glanced at her again, put down the hammer, spat out the nails, and deposited them in her hand. Then she handed him the nails one by one as he pounded them in, until they were all gone.

"Leave," he said. He grabbed another handful of nails from the tool chest. He didn't hand them over to Cheng Xin and didn't put them in his mouth. Instead, he placed them on the ground next to his feet.

"I ... I just ..." Cheng Xin didn't know what to say.

"I'm telling you to leave Australia." Wade's lips barely moved as he whispered. His gaze remained on the composite board. Anyone a little distance away would think he was concentrating on his work. "Hurry, before the resettlement is complete."

Like he had many times three centuries ago, Wade had managed to stun Cheng Xin with a single sentence. Each time it was as if he

had tossed her a knotted ball of string that she must untangle layer by layer before she could understand the complex meaning hidden within. But this time, Wade's words made her shiver. She didn't even have the courage to begin to untangle his riddle.

"Go." Wade didn't give her a chance to ask questions. Then he turned to her and once again revealed his special smirk, like a crack in a frozen-over pond. "*Now* I'm telling you to get out of this house."

On the way back to Warburton, Cheng Xin saw the densely packed shelter-houses stretching to the horizon, saw the busy crowd laboring in the cracks between the shelter-houses. Suddenly, she felt her vision shift, as though she were watching everything from somewhere outside the world, and everything she saw turned into a writhing nest of ants. A nameless terror gripped her and the bright Australian sunlight seemed as cold as rain in winter.

Three months after the start of the Great Resettlement, more than a billion people had been relocated to Australia. Simultaneously, the governments of the nations of the world began to relocate to large Australian cities. The UN moved its headquarters to Sydney. Each government directed the resettlement of its own citizens, with the UN Resettlement Commission coordinating the efforts. In their new land, the migrants gathered into districts based on their nation of origin, and Australia became a miniature replica of the whole Earth. Other than the names of the largest cities, old place names were abandoned. Now "New York," "Tokyo," and "Shanghai" were nothing more than refugee camps full of basic shelter-houses.

No one had any experience in dealing with resettlement at such a large scale, either in the national governments or the UN, and many difficulties and dangers soon surfaced.

First, there was the problem of shelter. Leaders soon realized that even if all the construction materials in the world were shipped to Australia, and per capita space were limited to the dimensions of a bed, not even one-fifth of the final total population would have a roof over their heads. By the time five hundred million migrants

were in Australia, there was no more material for building shelter-houses. They had to resort to erecting large tents, each of which was the size of a stadium and capable of housing more than ten thousand. But under such poor living and sanitation conditions, epidemics were a constant threat.

There was also the shortage of food. The agricultural factories in Australia were far from sufficient to satisfy the needs of the population, and it was necessary to transport food from across the world. As the population on the continent increased, the distribution of food became more complex and subject to more delays.

But the greatest danger was the prospect of loss of social order. In the resettlement zones, the hyper-information society disappeared. Newcomers poked the walls, bedside stands, or even their own clothes until they realized that everything was dead, un-networked. Even basic communications could not be guaranteed. People could obtain news about the world only through very limited channels. For a population used to a super-networked world full of information, it was as if they had all gone blind. Modern governments lost all their techniques for mass communication and leadership, and were ignorant of how to maintain order in a massively overcrowded society.

Simultaneously, resettlement was also proceeding in space.

At the end of the Deterrence Era, about 1.5 million people were living in space. About half a million spacers belonged to Earth International, living in space stations and space cities orbiting the Earth and bases on the moon. The rest belonged to the Solar System Fleet and were distributed between bases on Mars and around Jupiter, as well as warships patrolling the Solar System.

The spacers who belonged to Earth International mostly lived below the orbit of the moon. They had no choice but to return to the Earth and migrate to Australia.

The rest moved to the Martian base, which Trisolaris had designated as the second human reservation.

After the Doomsday Battle, the Solar System Fleet had never returned to its former size. Even at the end of the Deterrence Era, the fleet had barely more than one hundred stellar-class warships. Though technology had continued to improve, the maximum speed of the ships never increased, as fusion propulsion had already been pushed to the limit. The overwhelming advantage the Trisolar ships held was not only their ability to reach lightspeed, but, more terrifyingly, their ability to leap into lightspeed without a prolonged process of acceleration. In order to reach even 15 percent of lightspeed, human ships had to accelerate for a year, taking into account fuel consumption rates and the need to reserve fuel for the return voyage. Compared to Trisolaran ships, Earth ships were slow as snails.

When deterrence was dismantled, the stellar-class warships of the Solar System Fleet had a chance to escape into deep space. If the hundred-plus ships had sped away from the Solar System in different directions at maximum power, the eight droplets in the Solar System could not have caught them all. But not a single ship chose to do so; all obeyed Sophon and returned to Mars orbit. The reason for their obedience was simple: Resettlement on Mars was not like settling in Australia on Earth. Within the sealed habitat of the Martian base, a population of one million could maintain a comfortable, civilized existence. The base had been designed to accommodate the long-term needs of such a population. This was, without a doubt, superior to wandering deep space for the rest of their lives.

Trisolaris remained very wary of the humans on Mars. The two droplets recalled from the Kuiper Belt spent most of their time patrolling the space above the Martian city. Unlike the resettlement process on the surface of the Earth, although the Solar System Fleet had essentially been disarmed, people living on Mars still had access to modern technology—required for maintaining the habitability of the city. But the people living on Mars dared not engage in any adventures such as building a gravitational wave transmitter. The sophons certainly would have detected a large-scale venture

like that, and people hadn't forgotten the terror of the Doomsday Battle. The Martian base was as fragile as an eggshell, and the depressurization caused by a single droplet impact would have meant complete disaster.

The space resettlement process was completed in three months. Other than the Martian base, there was no more human presence in space in the Solar System, save for empty cities and ships drifting in orbit around the Earth, Mars, Jupiter, and through the asteroid belt. They seemed to form a silent, metallic graveyard, where humankind's glory and dreams were buried.

From the safety of Fraisse's house, Cheng Xin could only find out the situation in the larger world through TV. One day, she saw a live broadcast from a food distribution center. The holographic broadcast made her feel as if she were right there. The technology required ultra-broadband connections and was reserved for extremely important news these days. Most news was broadcast via simple 2-D.

The distribution center was located in Carnegie, on the edge of the desert. A gigantic tent appeared in the holographic display, like a broken half of an egg dropped in the desert with people spilling out of it like albumen. The crowd was rushing out because a new shipment of food had just arrived. Two flying transports, small but powerful, dangled a huge cube of packed food in nets.

After the first transport gently set down its cargo, the crowd surged like a flood from a burst dam and quickly overwhelmed the food pile. The security barrier formed by a few dozen soldiers collapsed at once, and the few food distribution workers climbed back into the hovering transport in terror. The pile of food disappeared into the crowd like a snowball thrown into muddy waters.

The lens zoomed in. People were now snatching food from those who had grabbed it from the pile. The bags of food, like rice grains in a swarm of ants, were quickly torn apart, and the mob fought over whatever tumbled out. The second transport deposited another

pile in an empty space a bit farther away. This time, there were no soldiers to provide security at all, and the distribution workers didn't dare get out of the plane. The crowd swarmed this new pile like iron shavings toward a magnet and quickly covered it.

A figure in green, slender and supple, leapt out of the transport and gracefully landed on the food pile about a dozen meters below. The crowd stopped. They saw that the figure standing atop it was Sophon. She was still dressed in camouflage, and the black scarf around her neck flapped in the hot wind, highlighting her pale face.

"Form a line!" Sophon shouted.

The lens zoomed in again. Sophon's beautiful eyes glared at the crowd. Her voice was very loud and could be heard over the rumbling of the transport engines. But the crowd below only paused briefly before resuming their agitated motion. Those closest to the pile began to cut through the netting to get at the food bags inside. The crowd became more frenzied, and a few daring ones began to climb up the pile, ignoring Sophon.

"You useless things! Why aren't you out here keeping order?" Sophon lifted her face and shouted at the transport. In the open door of the transport stood a few shocked officials from the UN Resettlement Commission. "Where are your armies? Your police? What about the weapons we allowed you to bring here? Where is your *responsibility*?"

The chair of the Resettlement Commission stood at the door of the transport. He held on to the doorframe with one hand for support, and waved his other hand at Sophon, shaking his head helplessly.

Sophon unsheathed her katana. Moving faster than the eye could see, she swung it three times and sliced three of the men climbing up the pile into six pieces. The three killing strokes were exactly the same: beginning at the left shoulder and ending at the right hip. The six pieces fell, and the viscera spilled out midair to land with a shower of blood among the rest of the people. Amidst screams of terror, she leapt from the pile and landed with her sword swinging, quickly killing more than a dozen individuals around her. The refugees shied away from her as though a drop of detergent had

been deposited into the oil film over a dirty bowl, quickly clearing out a space around her. The bodies left behind in that empty space were also split from the left shoulder to the right hip, a method that guaranteed the maximum spilling of organs and blood.

Faced with so much gore and blood, many fainted. As Sophon walked forward, people hurried to back away. An invisible force field seemed to surround her, repelling the mob and keeping the space around her clear. She stopped after a few steps and the crowd froze.

"Form a line," Sophon said. Her voice was soft.

The chaotic mob quickly organized itself into a long, winding line, as though the people were enacting an array-sorting algorithm. The line extended to the gigantic tent and wound around it.

Sophon jumped back onto the pile and pointed at the line with her bloody katana. "The era for humanity's degenerate freedom is over. If you want to survive here, you must relearn collectivism and retrieve the dignity of your race!"

Cheng Xin couldn't sleep that night. Noiselessly, she stepped out of her room.

The hour was late, and she could see a flickering light on the steps of the porch: Fraisse was smoking. On his knees lay a didgeridoo, an Aboriginal instrument made from a thick, hollowed-out branch about a meter long. Every night, he played it for a while. The sound made by the didgeridoo was a deep, rich, rumbling whine, not like music, but more akin to the snores of the ground itself. Every night, AA and Cheng Xin fell asleep listening to it.

Cheng Xin sat down next to Fraisse. She liked being with the old man. His transcendence in the face of a miserable reality soothed the pain of her broken heart. He never watched TV and seemed to pay no attention to the events of the outside world. At night, he rarely returned to his room, but fell asleep leaning against the doorframe, waking up when the rising sun warmed his body. He did so even on stormy nights, saying that it was more comfortable than

sleeping in a bed. Once, he said that if the government bastards ever came to take away his house, he would not move to the resettlement zones; instead, he would go into the woods and build himself a shelter out of woven grass. AA said that with his advanced age, such a plan was not realistic, but he countered that if his ancestors could live that way, then so could he. As early as the fourth ice age, his ancestors had crossed the Pacific from Asia in canoes. That had been forty thousand years ago, when Greece and Egypt didn't even exist as ideas. Back in the twenty-first century, he had been a wealthy doctor, with his own clinic in Melbourne. After emerging from hibernation in the Deterrence Era, he had also lived the comfortable life of a modern man. But when the Great Resettlement began, something in his body seemed to awaken. He felt himself becoming a creature of the earth and the forest and realized that very few things were truly necessary for life. Sleeping in the open was fine—very comfortable, in fact.

Fraisse said he didn't know what kind of portent this was.

Cheng Xin gazed at the resettlement zone in the distance. This late at night, the lights were sparse, and the endless rows of shelter-houses gave off a rarely-seen tranquility. A strange feeling seized her, as though she were seeing another age of immigration, the Australia of five centuries ago. The people sleeping in those houses were rough cowboys and ranchers, and she could even smell the fragrance of hay and the odor of horse excrement. Cheng Xin told Fraisse of the odd sensation.

"It wasn't so crowded back then," said Fraisse. "They say that if a white man wanted to buy land from another white man, he needed only to pay the price of a box of whiskey, and then he would ride out with the sunrise and return at sunset. The area he circum-navigated would belong to him."

Cheng Xin's past impressions of Australia had come from that old film of the same name. In the film, the hero and heroine crossed the spectacular landscape of north Australia on a cattle drive. However, the film wasn't set during Australia's age of immigration, but during the Second World War—still the recent past when she

was a young woman, but now ancient history. She felt a pang of sorrow as she realized that Hugh Jackman and Nicole Kidman had both been dead for probably over two centuries. Then she thought about how Wade had resembled the movie's hero as he labored in the shelter-house.

Thinking of Wade, she repeated to Fraisse what the man had told her. She had been meaning to tell him, but had worried about disturbing his transcendent state of mind.

"I know the man," Fraisse said. "Child, I can tell you that you should listen to him. But leaving Australia is impossible. Don't worry about it. It's useless to ponder what cannot be done."

It was true. Leaving Australia now would be very difficult. Not only did the droplets keep watch, but Sophon had recruited her own naval force of humans. Any aircraft or surface ship leaving Australia that was found to harbor resettled individuals would be attacked immediately. In addition, as Sophon's deadline approached, few wanted to attempt to return to their home countries. Though conditions in Australia were harsh, staying here was better than going back to certain death. A few cases of small-scale smuggling happened here and there, but Cheng Xin was a public figure, and such a path was closed to her.

Cheng Xin did not concern herself with these details. No matter what happened, she wasn't going to leave.

Fraisse seemed to want to change the topic, but Cheng Xin's silence in the darkness demanded more from him. "I'm an orthopedist. You probably know that when a bone is broken, it heals stronger because a knot forms around the fracture. The body, when given an opportunity to make up for an absence, may do so excessively, and recover to the point where it has more of that quality than those who had never suffered such inadequacy." He pointed up at the sky. "Compared to humans, the Trisolarans once lacked something. Do you think they also overcompensated? To what extent? No one knows."

Cheng Xin was stunned by the idea. But Fraisse was not interested in continuing the discussion. He looked up at the star-

studded sky and began reciting poetry in a low voice. The poems spoke of dreams of long ago, of broken trust and shattered weapons, of the deaths of peoples and ways of life.

Cheng Xin was moved the same way she had been when Fraisse played the didgeridoo.

"That's the work of Jack Davis, an Aboriginal poet of the twentieth century."

The elder leaned against the doorframe and, after a few minutes, began to snore. Cheng Xin remained sitting under the stars—which did not deviate one whit from their usual course despite the upheaval in the world below—until dawn arrived in the east.

Six months after the commencement of the Great Resettlement, half of the world's population, or 2.1 billion people, had moved to Australia.

Buried crises began to come to the forefront. The Canberra Massacre, seven months after the commencement of resettlement, was just the beginning of a string of nightmares.

Sophon had demanded that humans resettle "naked." During the Deterrence Era, hardliners on Earth had also proposed a similar policy to deal with the eventual migration of Trisolarans to the Solar System. Other than construction materials and parts needed to build new agricultural factories, as well as medical equipment and other life necessities, the resettled population was not permitted to bring any heavy equipment for military or civilian use. The military forces dispatched by the various nations to the resettlement zones were only allowed the light weapons needed to maintain order. Humankind was to be completely disarmed.

But the Australian government was exempt—it was allowed to keep everything, including all the hardware for its army, navy, and air force. Thus, this country that had been on the periphery of international affairs since its birth became the hegemon of the world.

No one could find fault with the behavior of the Australian government near the beginning of the process. The government and

238

all Australians made every effort to help with the influx of migrants. But as the flood of refugees from around the world poured into Australia, attitudes in this country—which was once the only state to possess an entire continent—changed. Native Australians complained bitterly, and they elected a new government that took a hard-line position against the newcomers. Those in the new government quickly discovered that their advantage over the rest of the world was comparable to the advantage Trisolaris held over the Earth. Late-arriving migrants were resettled in the desolate interior, whereas rich, desirable locations such as coastal New South Wales were "reserved territories" for Australians only. Canberra and Sydney were classified as "reserved cities," where immigration was similarly prohibited. The only large city in which migrants were permitted to settle was Melbourne. The Australian government also turned dictatorial toward the rest of the world, treating itself as superior to the UN and other national governments.

Although newcomers were not allowed to settle in New South Wales, it was impossible to prevent them from going there as tourists. Many migrants swarmed to Sydney in order to assuage their intense longing for city life—even if they couldn't stay, wandering the streets of Sydney homeless felt better than living in the resettlement zones. Here, at least, they felt they were still in civilized society. Sydney soon became overcrowded, and the Australian government decided to forcibly remove all migrants and bar them from visiting there. The police and army clashed with refugees who tarried in the city, and there were casualties.

The Sydney Incident set off the pent-up rage of the resettled population against the Australian government, and more than one hundred million people entered New South Wales, heading for Sydney. Facing a sea of rioting humanity, the Australian Army abandoned their positions. Tens of millions flooded Sydney and looted it in the same manner a swarm of ants devours a fresh corpse, leaving behind only a bare skeleton. Sydney was left in flames and lawless, transformed into a forest of terror. Life there, for those who remained, became worse than in the resettlement zones.

Thereafter, the mob of refugees shifted their target to Canberra, about two hundred kilometers away. Since Canberra was the Australian capital, about half of the world's national governments had relocated there as well. Even the UN had just moved there from Sydney. To keep these governments safe, the army had no choice but to fire on the mob. More than half a million people were killed, most of whom didn't die at the hands of the Australian Army, but due to hunger, thirst, and the panicked stampede of a hundred million people. During the chaos that lasted more than ten days, tens of millions were completely cut off from food and potable water.

The society of resettled populations transformed in profound ways. People realized that, on this crowded, hungry continent, democracy was more terrifying than despotism. Everyone yearned for order and a strong government. The existing social order broke down. All the people cared about was that the government would bring them food, water, and enough space for a bed; nothing else mattered. Gradually, the society of the resettled succumbed to the seduction of totalitarianism, like the surface of a lake caught in a cold spell. Sophon's words after she killed those people at the food distribution center—"The era for humanity's degenerate freedom is over"—became a common slogan, and discarded dregs from the history of ideas, including fascism, crawled out of their tombs to the surface and became mainstream. The power of religions also recovered, and people gathered into different faiths and churches. Thus, theocracy, a zombie even more ancient than totalitarianism, reanimated itself.

War was the inevitable result of totalitarian politics. Conflicts between nations became more frequent. At first, the conflicts were over food and water, but they soon evolved to planned contests over living space. After the Canberra Massacre, the Australian armed forces became a powerful deterrent force within Resettlement International. At the request of the UN, the Australian Army began to maintain international order by force. Without them, an intra-Australia version of a world war would have erupted—and just as someone had predicted during the twentieth century, this one would

be fought with sticks and stones. By this time, the armies of the various nations—Australia excepted—couldn't even manage to equip their personnel with mêlée weapons. The most common weapons were sticks made out of metal frames used for construction, and even ancient swords from museums were put into service again.

In those dark days, countless people woke up in the mornings incredulous that this was their reality. Within half a year, human society had regressed so far that one foot was already in the Middle Ages.

The only thing that prevented individuals and society as a whole from total collapse was the approaching Second Trisolaran Fleet. By now, the fleet had crossed the Kuiper Belt. On clear nights, it was even sometimes possible to see the flames of the decelerating ships with the naked eye. Upon those 415 dim lights now hung the hope of all of humanity. All recalled Sophon's promise and dreamed that the arrival of the fleet would bring a comfortable, serene life for everyone on this continent. A demon of the past transformed into an angel of salvation, and their only spiritual support. People prayed for their advent.

As the resettlement process continued, cities on continents outside of Australia fell dark one by one, turning into empty, silent shells. It was like a luxurious restaurant turning out the lights after the last diner had left.

By the ninth month of the Great Resettlement, 3.4 billion people lived in Australia. As living conditions continued to deteriorate, the resettlement process had to be halted temporarily. The droplets again attacked cities outside of Australia, and Sophon renewed her threat: Upon the expiration of the one-year period, the extermination of all humans outside of the reservations would begin immediately. Australia now resembled a prison cart heading down a road to a place it would never return from: The cage was already close to bursting from the number of captives aboard, but seven hundred million more still had to be packed in.

Sophon gave some thought to the difficulties posed by further immigration and proposed a solution: New Zealand and other

nearby islands could be used as a buffer zone. Her suggestion worked, and during the next two and a half months, 630 million more refugees were moved into Australia via the buffer zone.

Finally, three days before the expiration of the deadline, the last three million refugees left New Zealand on boats and planes and headed for Australia.

The Great Resettlement was complete.

At this point, Australia held the vast majority of the human population: 4.16 billion people. Outside of Australia, there were about eight million more individuals. These were divided into three parts: one million on the Martian base, five million in the Earth Security Force, and about two million in the Earth Resistance Movement. A small number of individuals who couldn't be resettled for various reasons were scattered around the world, but their exact number was unknown.

Sophon had recruited the Earth Security Force to monitor the resettlement process. She promised those who joined that they would not have to migrate to Australia and could eventually live freely in the Trisolaris-conquered territories of the Earth. Many volunteered eagerly, and, according to the final tally, more than a billion people applied online. Of these, twenty million were offered interviews, and, in the end, five million were accepted into the ESF. These fortunate few paid no attention to the spittle and looks of disdain thrown their way by other humans—they knew that many of those who spat at them had submitted applications as well.

Some compared the Earth Security Force to the Earth-Trisolaris Organization from three centuries ago, but the two organizations were fundamentally different. The ETO was formed by warriors of faith, but the ESF recruits merely wanted to avoid resettlement and live in comfort.

The ESF was divided into three corps: Asian, European, and North American. They inherited all the military hardware the national armies were forced to leave behind during the resettlement.

At the beginning of the process, the ESF behaved with some restraint, only following Sophon's orders to supervise the progress of emigration in various countries and protect the basic infrastructure in cities and regions from looting and sabotage. But as difficulties in Australia intensified, the resettlement failed to progress at a rate satisfactory to Sophon. Due to her constant demands and threats, the ESF became more crazed, and resorted to large-scale violence to enforce the resettlement. During this time, the ESF killed almost a million people. Finally, after the clock ran out on the resettlement period, Sophon gave the order to exterminate all humans outside of the reservations. The ESF now turned into demons. Riding flying cars and armed with laser sniper rifles, they soared over empty cities and fields like falcons and swooped down to kill anyone they saw.

In contrast, the Earth Resistance Movement represented the best of humanity, refined from the furnace of this disaster. This movement consisted of so many loose local branches that the exact number couldn't be verified. In total, an estimated one and a half to two million individuals participated. Hidden in remote mountains and deep tunnels beneath the cities, they waged guerrilla war against the ESF and waited for a chance to fight the final war against the Trisolaran invaders after their anticipated arrival in four years. Compared to all other resistance movements in human history, the Earth Resistance Movement doubtless made the greatest sacrifice. Because Sophon and the droplets assisted the ESF, every mission by the Earth Resistance Movement was akin to suicide. The conditions under which they fought also prevented them from pooling their forces, which made it possible for the ESF to eliminate them one cell at a time.

The composition of the Earth Resistance Movement was complex, and included individuals from all strata of society. A large portion were people from the Common Era. The six other candidates for the Swordholder position were all commanders in the resistance. At the end of the resettlement period, three of them had died in action: only Bi Yunfeng, the particle accelerator engineer, Cao Bing,

the physicist, and Ivan Antonov, the former Russian vice-admiral, were left.

Every member of the resistance understood that they were engaged in a hopeless war. The moment the Second Trisolaran Fleet arrived would mark their complete annihilation. Hungry, dressed in rags, and hidden in caves in the mountains and sewers beneath cities, these warriors fought for the human race's final shred of dignity. Their existence was the only bright spot in this, the darkest period of humankind's history.

A series of booming rumbles awoke Cheng Xin at dawn. She hadn't slept well during the night due to the constant noise of newly arrived refugees outside. But she realized that it was no longer thunderstorm season, and, after the rumblings it grew quiet outside. She shivered, rolled out of bed, threw on her clothes, and came outside. She almost tripped over the sleeping figure of Fraisse at the door. He glanced up at her with sleepy eyes and then leaned back against the doorframe to continue his interrupted slumber.

It was barely light outside. Many people stood around anxiously looking toward the east and muttering amongst themselves. Cheng Xin followed the direction of their eyes and saw a thick column of black smoke on the horizon, as though the pale dawn had been ripped apart.

Cheng Xin eventually managed to learn from the others that, about an hour ago, the ESF had begun a series of aerial raids in Australia. Their main targets seemed to be electrical systems, harbors, and large-scale transportation equipment. The column of smoke came from a destroyed nuclear fusion power plant about five kilometers away. People looked up in fear and saw five white contrails extending across the blue-black sky: ESF bombers.

Cheng Xin went back into the house. AA was up as well and turned on the TV. But Cheng Xin didn't watch—she didn't need any more information. For almost a year now, she had been constantly praying that this moment would never come. Her nerves had turned

extremely sensitive, and the slightest hint would lead her to the right conclusion. Even as she had been awakened by the rumbling noises, she already knew what had happened.

Wade was right, again.

Cheng Xin found that she was prepared for this moment. Without thinking, she knew what she had to do. Telling AA that she needed to visit the city government, she took a bike—the most convenient mode of transportation in the resettlement zones. She also brought some food and water, knowing that she very likely would not be able to accomplish her task and would have to be on the road for a long time.

She wound through the crowded streets, heading for the city government. The various nations had transplanted their own administrative systems to the resettlement zones, and Cheng Xin's zone was composed of people resettled from a midsized city in northwestern China. The city government was located in a large tent about two kilometers away, and she could see the tent's white tip.

A large number of refugees had flooded in during the last two weeks in the final push of the resettlement process. There was no time to distribute them to zones that corresponded to their origins, so they were stashed wherever there was room. Cheng Xin's zone was thus filled with people from other cities, regions, provinces, and even non-Chinese. The seven hundred million refugees shoved into Australia during the last two months made the already-crowded resettlement zones even more unbearable.

On both sides of the road, possessions were piled everywhere. The new arrivals had nowhere to live and slept in the open. The earlier explosions had awakened them, and now they looked anxiously in the direction of the column of smoke. The dawn light cast a dim blue glow over everything, making the faces around her even paler. Once again, Cheng Xin experienced the eerie feeling of looking down upon an ant colony. As she pressed between the pale faces, her subconscious mind despaired that the sun would never rise again.

A wave of nausea and weakness seized her. She squeezed the brakes, stopped by the side of the road, and retched, bringing tears to her eyes. She dry heaved until her stomach settled. She heard a child crying nearby, and looking up, saw a mother huddled in a bunch of rags hugging her baby. Haggard, hair disheveled, she didn't move as the child clutched at her, but continued to gaze woodenly toward the east. The dawn lit her eyes, which reflected only loss and numbness.

Cheng Xin thought of another mother, pretty, healthy, and full of life, handing her baby to Cheng Xin in front of the UN building ... where were she and her child now?

As she approached the tent housing the city government, Cheng Xin was forced to get off her bike and squeeze through the dense crowd. This place was always crowded, but now, even more people had gathered to find out what had happened. Cheng Xin had to explain who she was to the sentry line blocking the entrance before being allowed through. The officer didn't know her and had to scan her ID card. When he confirmed her identity, his stare seared itself into Cheng Xin's memory.

Why did we pick you back then?

The inside of the city government tent brought back memories of the hyper-information age. Numerous holographic windows floated around the vast space, hovering over various officials and clerks. Many of them had apparently been up all night and looked exhausted, but they were still very busy. A large number of departments were packed in and jostled for space, reminding Cheng Xin of the trading floor on Wall Street back in the Common Era. The workers tapped or wrote inside the windows hovering in front of them, and then the windows automatically floated over to the next worker in the process. These glowing windows were like ghosts of an age that had just ended, and here was their final gathering place.

In a tiny office formed from composite partitions, Cheng Xin saw the mayor. He was very young, and his feminized, handsome face looked as exhausted as the others. He also looked a bit dazed

and adrift, as though the load he had been given was beyond the ability of his fragile generation to bear. A very large information window appeared on one of the walls, showing an image of some city. Most of the buildings in the window looked old and conventional, with only a few tree-buildings sprinkled among them—evidently this was a midsized city. Cheng Xin noticed that the image wasn't static: Flying cars crossed the air from time to time, and it seemed to also be early morning there. Cheng Xin realized that the display simulated the view out of an office window, so perhaps this was where the mayor had once lived and worked before the Great Resettlement.

He looked at Cheng Xin, and his eyes also seemed to say *Why did we pick you?* Still, he remained polite, and asked Cheng Xin how he could help her.

"I need to contact Sophon," she said.

The mayor shook his head, but her unexpected request had chased away some of his exhaustion. He looked serious. "That's not possible. First, this department is too low level to directly establish contact with her. Even the provincial government doesn't have such authority. No one knows where on Earth she is now. Also, communication with the outside world is extremely difficult now. We've just been cut off from the provincial government, and we're about to lose electricity here."

"Can you send me to Canberra?"

"I can't provide an aircraft, but I can dispatch a ground vehicle. However, that may end up being even slower than walking. Ms. Cheng, I strongly urge you to stay put. There's chaos everywhere right now, and it's very dangerous. The cities are being bombed—believe it or not, it's relatively peaceful here."

Since there was no wireless power system, flying cars were not usable in the resettlement zones. Only self-powered aircraft and ground vehicles were available, but the roads had become impassable.

———

As soon as Cheng Xin left the city government, she heard another explosion. A new column of smoke rose in another direction, and the crowd turned from merely anxious to genuinely agitated. She pushed her way through and found her bike. She would have to ride more than fifty kilometers to reach the provincial government and try to contact Sophon from there. If that didn't work, she'd try to get to Canberra.

No matter what, she would not give up.

The crowd quieted as an immense information window appeared over the city government, almost as wide as the tent itself. This was used only when the government needed to broadcast extremely important news. Since the electric voltage wasn't stable, the window flickered, but against the dim sky of early dawn, it showed images very clearly.

In the window was Canberra's Parliament House. Though it was completed in 1988, people still referred to it as the "new" Parliament House. From a distance, the building appeared as a bunker nestled against a hill, and on top of it was possibly the world's tallest flag mast. The mast, over eighty meters in height, was further elevated by four gigantic steel beams. They were meant to symbolize stability, but they now resembled the frame of a large tent. The UN flag flew from the building: The UN had moved its headquarters here after the Sydney Riots.

Cheng Xin felt a giant fist close around her heart. She knew that the day of the Last Judgment had arrived.

The view shifted to inside the House of Representatives, which was filled by all the leaders of Earth International and Fleet International. Sophon had called for an emergency session of the UN General Assembly.

Sophon stood at the dispatch box, still dressed in camouflage and a black scarf, but without the katana. There was no trace on her face of the glamorous cruelty that everyone had grown used to in the past year; instead, she appeared radiant in her beauty. She bowed to the assembled leaders of humanity, and Cheng Xin saw again the gentle hostess practicing the Way of Tea whom she had met two years ago.

"The Great Resettlement is over!" Sophon bowed again. "Thank you! I'm grateful to all of you. This is a tremendous accomplishment, comparable to the walk out of Africa by your ancestors tens of thousands of years ago. A new era for our two civilizations has begun!"

Everyone in the House of Representatives turned their head anxiously as something exploded outside. The four lighting beams hanging from the ceiling swayed, and all the shadows along with them, as though the building was about to collapse. But Sophon continued speaking: "Before the magnificent Trisolaran Fleet arrives to bring you a happy new life, everyone must endure a difficult period lasting three months. I hope humanity will perform as well as it did during the Great Resettlement.

"I proclaim now the complete severance of the Australian Reservation from the outside world. Seven strong-interaction space probes and the Earth Security Force will enforce an absolute blockade. Anyone attempting to leave Australia will be treated as an invader of Trisolaris and be exterminated without mercy!

"The defanging of Earth must proceed. During the next three months, the reservation must be kept in a state of subsistence agriculture. The use of any modern technology, including electricity, is strictly prohibited. As everyone present can see, the Earth Security Force is in the process of systematically eliminating all electricity-generating equipment in Australia."

People around Cheng Xin looked at each other in disbelief, hoping that someone else could help explain what Sophon had just said.

"This is genocide!" someone in the House of Representatives cried out. The shadows continued to sway, like corpses dangling from nooses.

It was indeed genocide.

The prospect of keeping 4.2 billion people alive in Australia was difficult, but not unimaginable. Even after the Great Resettlement, the population density in Australia was only fifty people per square kilometer, lower than the population density of pre-Resettlement Japan.

But the plan had been premised on highly efficient agricultural factories. During the resettlement process, large numbers of agricultural factories had been relocated to Australia, and many of them had been reassembled and put in operation. In these factories, genetically modified crops grew at rates orders of magnitude above traditional crops, but natural lighting was insufficient to power such growth, so ultrabright artificial lights had to be used. This required massive amounts of electricity.

Without electricity, the crops in the growth tanks of the factories, dependent on ultraviolet or X-ray light for photosynthesis, would rot in a couple of days.

The existing food reserve was enough to maintain 4.2 billion people only for one month.

"I don't understand your reaction," Sophon said to the man who had yelled *genocide*. Her confusion appeared genuine.

"What about food? Where are we going to get *food*?" someone else shouted. They were no longer terrified of Sophon. All that was left was despair.

Sophon scanned the hall, meeting the eyes of everyone present. "Food? Everyone, look around: You are surrounded by food, living food."

Her tone was serene, as though reminding humanity of a storehouse they had forgotten.

No one said anything. The long-planned process of annihilation had reached its final step. It was too late for words.

Sophon continued. "The coming struggle for survival will eliminate most of humanity. By the time the fleet arrives in three months, there should be about thirty to fifty million people left on this continent. These final victors will begin a free and civilized life in the reservation. The fire of Earth civilization will not go out, but it will continue in a reduced form, like the eternal flame at a tomb."

The Australian House of Representatives was modeled on the British House of Commons. The high seats of the public galleries were to the sides, and the benches for the Members of Parliament—where the leaders of the world now sat—were down in the pit in the

middle. Those sitting there now felt as if they were in a tomb that was about to be filled in.

"Mere existence is already the result of incredible luck. Such was the case on Earth in the past, and such has always been the case in this cruel universe. But at some point, humanity began to develop the illusion that they're *entitled* to life, that life can be taken for granted. This is the fundamental reason for your defeat. The flag of evolution will be raised once again on this world, and you will now fight for your survival. I hope everyone present will be among the fifty million survivors at the end. I hope that you will eat food, and not be eaten by food."

"*Ahhhhhhh*—" A woman in the crowd near Cheng Xin screamed, slicing apart the silence like a sharp blade. But a deathlike hush immediately swallowed her scream.

Cheng Xin felt the sky and earth tumble around her. She didn't realize she had fallen down. All she saw was the sky pushing the government tent and the holographic window away, filling her entire field of view, then the ground touched her back, as though it had stood up behind her. The dawn sky appeared as a dim ocean, and the crimson clouds, lit by the rising sun, floated over it in bloody patches. Then a black spot appeared in her vision, spreading quickly, like a sheet of paper set aflame by the candle underneath, until murky shadows covered everything.

She recovered from the loss of consciousness quickly. Her hands found the ground—soft sand—and, pushing off it, she sat up. She grabbed her left arm with her right hand to be sure that she was okay. But the world had disappeared. All was enveloped in gloom. Cheng Xin opened her eyes wide, but she could see nothing but more darkness. She had gone blind.

Noises assaulted her; she could not tell which were real and which were illusions: footsteps like a tide, screams, sobs, and indistinct, eerie cries like a gale passing through a dead forest.

Someone running crashed into her, and she fell. She struggled to sit up. Darkness, only darkness remained before her eyes, thick as pitch. She turned to face what she thought of as the east, but even in

her mind she couldn't see the rising sun. What rose there instead was a gigantic dark wheel, scattering black light across the world.

In this endless obscurity she seemed to see a pair of eyes. The black eyes melted into the murk, but she could feel their presence, could feel their gaze. Were these the eyes of Yun Tianming? She had fallen into the abyss, where she ought to meet him. She heard Tianming call her name. She tried to push the hallucinatory voice out of her mind, but it persisted. Finally, she was certain that the voice came from reality, as it was a feminized male voice that could only be from this era.

"Are you Dr. Cheng Xin?"

She nodded. Or, rather, felt herself nod. Her body seemed to move on its own.

"What happened to your eyes? Can you not see?"

"Who are you?"

"I'm the commander of a special team in the Earth Security Force. Sophon sent us to retrieve you from Australia."

"Where are you taking me?"

"Anywhere you want. She'll take care of you. Of course, she said that you have to be willing to go."

Cheng Xin noticed another sound. She thought it was another hallucination at first: the rumbling of a helicopter. Although humanity had learned anti-gravity technology, it consumed too much energy for practical use. Aircraft still mostly relied on traditional propellers. She felt gusts of wind, proof that a helicopter was hovering nearby.

"Can I talk to Sophon?"

An object was pushed into her hand—a mobile phone. She put the phone next to her ear and heard Sophon's voice.

"Hello, Swordholder."

"I've been looking for you."

"Why? Do you still think of yourself as the savior of the world?"

Cheng Xin shook her head slowly. "No. I've never thought of myself that way. I just want to save two people. Please?"

"Which two?"

"艾 AA and Fraisse."

"Ah, your chattering friend and that old Aboriginal? You wanted to find me just for this?"

Cheng Xin was surprised. Sophon had met AA, but how did she know who Fraisse was?

"Yes. Have the people you sent bring them away from Australia so that they can live freely."

"That's easy. What about you?"

"You don't need to be concerned about me."

"Can't you see what's happening?"

"I can't. I can't see a thing."

"You mean you've gone blind? Haven't you been eating properly?"

Cheng Xin, AA, and Fraisse had always been provided adequate rations during the last year, and Fraisse's house had never been taken away by the government. And once she and AA had moved in, no one had harassed her. Cheng Xin had always thought it was because the local government was protecting her, but now she realized that it was because Sophon had kept watch over her.

Cheng Xin understood that it was a group of aliens that controlled Sophon from four light-years away, but she, like other humans, always thought of Sophon as an individual, a woman. This woman, who was in the process of slaughtering 4.2 billion people, cared about her welfare.

"If you remain there, you'll be eaten by the others."

"I know." Cheng Xin's voice was calm.

Is that a sigh? "All right. A sophon will stay near you. If you change your mind or need some help, just speak. I'll hear you."

Cheng Xin said nothing. Not even thank you.

Someone grabbed her by the arm—the Earth Security Force commander. "I've been given the order to retrieve those two. It's best that you leave with us, Dr. Cheng. This place will turn into hell on Earth in no time."

Cheng Xin shook her head. "You know where they are? Good. Please go. Thank you."

She listened for the helicopter. The blindness seemed to make

her hearing especially acute, like a third eye. She heard the helicopter take off and then land about two kilometers away. A few minutes later, it lifted off again, and gradually flew away.

Cheng Xin closed her eyes, satisfied. Whether she kept them open or not, there was only darkness. Finally, her broken heart had found some peace, bathed in a pool of blood. The impenetrable shadows now became a kind of protection. Outside the darkness was more terror. What had manifested there made even coldness itself shiver, even darkness itself stumble.

The frenzy around her intensified: sounds of running, clashing, guns firing, cursing, screaming, dying, crying ... *Have they already started to eat people? It shouldn't happen so fast.* Cheng Xin believed that even in a month, when there would be no more food, most people would still refuse to eat other people.

That's why most people will die.

It was not important whether the fifty million that survived would still be considered human, or become something else. As a concept, "humanity" would disappear.

A single line could now encompass all of human history: We walked out of Africa; we walked for seventy thousand years; we came into Australia.

In Australia, humanity returned to its origin. But there would be no new voyage. This was the end.

A baby cried nearby. Cheng Xin wanted to wrap her arms around that new life. She recalled the baby she had held in front of the UN building: soft, warm, such a sweet smile. Maternal instinct broke Cheng Xin's heart. She was afraid that the baby would go hungry.

THE FINAL TEN MINUTES OF THE DETERRENCE ERA, YEAR 62 NOVEMBER 28, 4:17:34 P.M. TO 4:27:58 P.M.: *GRAVITY* AND *BLUE SPACE*, DEEP SPACE

When the klaxons announced the droplet attack, only one man aboard *Gravity* felt a sense of relief: James Hunter, the oldest on the crew. He was seventy-eight, and everyone called him Old Hunter.

Half a century ago, at Fleet Command in Jupiter's orbit, a twenty-seven-year-old Hunter had received his mission from the chief of staff.

"You will be the culinary controller aboard *Gravity*."

This position was just a glorified name for the ship's cook. But since AI programming did most of the cooking on a warship, the culinary controller was responsible only for operating the system. This meant, for the most part, inputting the menu for each meal and choosing the staples. Most culinary controllers were petty officers, but Hunter had just been promoted to the rank of captain; in fact, he was the youngest captain in the fleet. But Hunter wasn't surprised. He knew what he was really supposed to do.

"Your real mission is to guard the gravitational wave transmitter. If the senior officers aboard *Gravity* lose control of the ship, you

must destroy the transmitter. In unexpected situations, you may use whatever means you deem necessary to accomplish your goal."

Gravity's gravitational wave broadcasting system included the antenna and the controller. The antenna was the ship's hull, impossible to destroy, but disabling the controller was enough to stop transmission. Given the materials available on *Gravity* and *Blue Space,* it would be impossible to assemble a new controller.

Hunter knew that men similar to himself had served on nuclear submarines in ancient times. Back then, in the ballistic missile submarine fleets of both the Soviet Union and NATO, there were seamen and low-ranked officers serving in humble posts who also had such missions. If anyone had come close to seizing control of a submarine and the missiles it carried, these men would have emerged, unexpectedly, to take drastic action to stop such plots.

"You must pay attention to everything happening on the ship. Your mission requires you to monitor the situation during every duty cycle. Thus, you cannot hibernate."

"I don't know if I can live until I'm a hundred."

"You only need to live until you're eighty. By then, the degenerate matter vibrating string in the ship will have reached its half-life, *Gravity*'s gravitational wave transmission system will fail, and you'll have completed your mission. Thus, you just need to stay out of hibernation for the voyage out, but may return asleep. However, the mission will essentially require you to devote the rest of your life to it. You have the right to refuse."

"I accept."

The chief of staff asked a question that commanders in past eras would not have bothered with. "Why?"

"During the Doomsday Battle, I was a PIA intelligence analyst stationed aboard *Newton*. Before the droplet destroyed my ship, I escaped in a life pod. Though it was the smallest kind of life pod, it was capable of holding five. At the time, a group of my crewmates were headed toward me, and I was alone in my pod. But I released it—"

"I know about that. The court-martial results are unequivocal.

You did nothing wrong. Ten seconds after jettisoning your life pod, the ship exploded. You had no time to wait for anyone else."

"Yes. But … I still feel it would have been better if I had stayed with *Newton*."

"I understand how our failures haunt us with survivor's guilt. But this time, you have a chance to save billions."

The two were silent for a while. Outside the window of the space station, the Great Red Spot of Jupiter stared at them like a gigantic eye.

"Before I explain to you the details of your task, I want you to understand one thing: Your highest priority is preventing the system from falling into the wrong hands. When you cannot ascertain the degree of risk with confidence, you should err on the side of destroying the transmission system—even if you should turn out to be mistaken. When you do decide to act, don't worry about collateral damage. If necessary, destroying the entire ship would be acceptable."

Hunter was in the first duty cycle when *Gravity* left Earth. During those five years, he regularly took a certain kind of small blue pills. At the end of the duty cycle, when he was scheduled to go into hibernation, a physical revealed that he had cerebrovascular coagulation disorder, which was also called "no-hibernation disease." Patients with this rare condition suffered no ill effects in daily life, but could not enter hibernation because the awakening process would cause massive brain damage. It was the only medical condition discovered so far that could prevent someone from going into hibernation. When the diagnosis was confirmed, everyone around Hunter looked at him as though they were at his funeral.

Thus, throughout the whole voyage, Hunter had remained awake. Every time someone emerged from hibernation, they saw he had aged more. He told all the newly awakened the interesting things that had happened in the dozen or so years that had passed while they slept. The lowly cook became the most beloved figure on the ship, and he was popular with officers and enlisted men alike. Gradually, he turned into a symbol of the long voyage of *Gravity*.

No one suspected that this easygoing, generous man held the same rank as the captain and was also the only man other than the captain with the authority and ability to destroy the ship in the event of a crisis.

During the first thirty years of the journey, Hunter had several girlfriends. In this matter he held an advantage others did not possess: He could date women in different duty cycles, one after the other. But after a few decades, as Hunter became Old Hunter, the women, still young, treated him as only a friend with interesting stories.

During this half century, the only woman Old Hunter ever truly loved was Reiko Akihara. But most of that time, more than ten million AU separated them. This was because Sublieutenant Akihara was aboard *Blue Space,* where she was a navigator.

The hunt for *Blue Space* was the only undertaking where Earth and Trisolaris truly shared the same goal, because this lone ship heading into deep space was a threat to both worlds. During the Earth's attempt to lure back the two ships that had survived the dark battles, *Blue Space* had learned the dark forest nature of the universe. If *Blue Space* someday mastered the ability to broadcast to the universe, the consequences would be unimaginable. The hunt thus received the total cooperation of Trisolaris. Before entering the blind region, the sophons had provided *Gravity* with a real-time, continuous view of the interior of the prey.

Over the decades, Hunter was promoted from petty officer second class to petty officer first class, and then, as a special promotion, became a commissioned officer. Starting as an ensign, he was promoted all the way up to lieutenant. But even at the end, he never had the formal authorization to view the live feed of the interior of *Blue Space* transmitted by the sophons. However, he did possess the backdoor codes to all the ship's systems, and he often viewed a palm-sized version of the video feed in his own cabin.

He saw that *Blue Space* was a completely different society from *Gravity*. It was militaristic, authoritarian, and governed by strict codes of discipline. Everyone devoted their spiritual energy to the

collective. The first time he saw Reiko was two years after the start of the chase. He was instantly smitten by this East Asian beauty. He would watch her for hours every day, and sometimes even thought he knew her life better than he knew his own. But a year later, Reiko went into hibernation, and the next time she woke up for duty was thirty years later. She was still young, but Hunter was already near sixty.

On Christmas Eve, after a wild party, he returned to his cabin and brought up the live feed from *Blue Space*. The view began with a diagram of the complex overall structure of the ship. He tapped the location of the navigation center, and the view zoomed in to show Reiko on duty. She was looking at a large holographic star map, on which a bright red line traced the course of *Blue Space*. Behind it was a white line that almost coincided with the red line, indicating the path taken by *Gravity*. Hunter noticed that the white line deviated slightly from *Gravity*'s true course. Right now, the two ships were still a few thousand AU apart. At this distance, it was difficult to track a target as small as a spaceship with certainty. The white line probably only indicated their best guess, although the estimate of the distance between the two ships was pretty accurate.

Hunter zoomed in some more. Reiko suddenly turned to face him, and, with a smile that made his heart clench, said, "Merry Christmas!" Hunter knew that Reiko wasn't talking to him, but to all those hunting her ship. She was aware that she was being watched by sophons, though she couldn't see her pursuers. Regardless, this was one of the happiest moments of Hunter's life.

Because the crew aboard *Blue Space* was large, Reiko's duty cycle didn't last long. One year later, she entered hibernation again. Hunter looked forward to the day he would meet Reiko face-to-face, when *Gravity* finally caught up to *Blue Space*. Sadly, he knew that he would be almost eighty by the time that happened. He hoped he would get to tell her he loved her and then watch as she was taken away for trial.

For half a century, Hunter faithfully carried out his mission. He remained alert for any unusual conditions aboard the ship,

preparing in his mind action plans for various crises. But the mission didn't really put too much pressure on him. He knew that another form of insurance, utterly reliable, accompanied *Gravity*. Like many others, he often watched the droplets cruising at a distance from the portholes. But the droplets, in his eyes, held another meaning. If anything unusual occurred on *Gravity,* especially if there were signs of a mutiny or illegal attempts to seize control of the gravitational wave transmission system, he knew that the droplets would destroy this ship. They could move far faster than he—a droplet could accelerate from a few thousand meters away and reach a target in no more than five seconds.

Now, Hunter's mission was almost over. The degenerate matter vibrating string at the heart of the gravitational wave antenna, less than ten nanometers in diameter but running the entire length of the fifteen-hundred-meter hull, had almost reached its half-life. In another two months, the density of the string would fall below the minimum threshold for gravitational wave transmissions, and the system would fail completely. *Gravity* would turn from a broadcast station that posed a threat to two worlds to an ordinary stellar spaceship, and Hunter's work would be done. He would reveal his true identity at that time. He was curious whether he would face admiration or condemnation from his crewmates. In any case, he would stop taking those blue pills, and his cerebro-vascular coagulation disorder would disappear. He would enter hibernation and awaken on the Earth to live out the rest of his days in a new era. But he would hibernate only after seeing Reiko, which should happen soon.

But then the sophons fell blind. During the voyage, he had imagined hundreds of possible crises, and this was one of the worst possibilities. The loss of the sophons meant that the droplets and Trisolaris no longer knew everything happening aboard *Gravity*. If the unexpected happened, the droplets could not react in time. This made the situation far more dangerous, and Hunter felt the weight on his shoulders increase tenfold, as though he had only started his mission.

Hunter now paid even closer attention to happenings on the ship. The entire crew of *Gravity* had been awakened from hibernation, and that made monitoring difficult. But Hunter was the only member of the crew everyone was familiar with, and he was popular and had an abundance of social connections. Moreover, his easygoing manner and his insignificant post meant that most were not on guard in his presence. The enlisted men and junior officers, especially, told him things they wouldn't dare say to senior officers or the psych corps. This allowed Hunter to have a full grasp of the situation.

After the sophons were blinded, strange things began to happen all over the ship: An ecological area in the middle of the ship was struck by a micrometeoroid; more than one person claimed to have seen openings suddenly appear in bulkheads, accompanied by the disappearance of certain objects that reappeared later, undamaged....

Out of all these oddities, the experience of Commander Devon, head of the MP, made the deepest impression on Hunter. Devon was one of the senior officers on the ship. Normally Hunter did not interact with them much. But when he saw Devon seek out the psychiatrist—whom most people on the ship avoided—he grew alert. Over a bottle of vintage whiskey, he finally got Devon to spill the story of his strange encounter.

To be sure, other than the micrometeoroid strike, the most reasonable explanation for all the strange goings-on was that the crew was suffering from hallucinations. The loss of the sophons might have, in some unknown way, triggered a kind of mass mental disorder—at least that was how Dr. West and the psych corps explained it. Hunter's duty did not allow him to accept this explanation easily; but other than hallucinations or a mass mental disorder, the strange stories told by the crew seemed impossible. However, Hunter's mission was to respond to impossibilities that somehow became possible.

Despite the massive antenna, the controller unit for the gravitational wave transmitter took up little space. Situated in a

small spherical cabin at the stern, the controller was completely independent and not connected to the other parts of the ship. The spherical cabin was like a reinforced safe. No one aboard *Gravity* had the codes for entry, not even the captain. Only the Swordholder on Earth could activate the gravitational wave broadcast—in such an event, a beam of neutrinos would be transmitted to *Gravity* and switch on the transmitter. Right now, such a signal would take a year to arrive from the Earth.

But if *Gravity* were hijacked, the safety measures around the spherical cabin would not last long.

Hunter's watch had a special button. When pressed, it would trigger a heat bomb inside the spherical cabin, which would vaporize everything inside. His job was very simple: No matter what the crisis, as soon as he judged the risk to be in excess of a certain threshold, he would press the button and destroy the controller, rendering the gravitational wave transmitter inoperable.

In a sense, Hunter was an "Anti-Swordholder."

Hunter didn't put all his trust in the button on his watch and the heat bomb in the cabin, which he had never laid eyes on. Ideally, he wanted to keep watch outside the control cabin day and night, but of course that would draw suspicion, and his hidden identity was his biggest advantage. Still, he wanted to be as close to the control cabin as possible, so he tried to regularly visit the astronomical observatory, also located at the stern. Since the entire crew was out of hibernation, Hunter had assistants to take care of his culinary duties, which gave him plenty of time to himself. In addition, as Dr. Guan Yifan was the only civilian scientist aboard and thus not subject to military discipline, no one thought it strange that Hunter often went to Guan to share the liquor that he was able to obtain due to his position. Dr. Guan, in turn, enjoyed the drinks, and lectured Hunter on the "universe's three and three hundred thousand syndrome." Soon, Hunter spent most of his time in the observatory, separated from the gravitational wave transmission controller by only a short corridor about twenty meters long.

Hunter was on his way to the observatory again when he passed

Guan Yifan and Dr. West heading for the bow of the ship. He decided that he would take a peek at the control cabin. When he was about ten meters away, the klaxons for the droplet attack started blaring. Due to his rank, the information window appearing before him displayed very few details, but he knew that the droplets were, at this time, farther away from the ship than when they had flown in formation. He had about ten to twenty seconds until impact.

During these final moments, Old Hunter felt only relief and joy. No matter what happened next, he would have completed his mission. He looked forward not to death, but to his victory.

This was why, half a minute later, when the klaxons stopped, Hunter became the only one aboard who felt no relief from his extreme terror. The cessation of the alarm indicated, for him, great danger: In a situation of great uncertainty, the gravitational wave transmitter was still intact. Without hesitation, he pressed the button on his watch.

Nothing happened. Even though the control cabin was tightly sealed, he should have been able to feel the tremors from the detonation. A line of text appeared on his wristwatch display:

Failure: The self-destruct module has been dismantled.

Hunter wasn't even surprised. He had already intuitively anticipated that the worst had happened. He had been but a few seconds from relief, but the relief would never come.

Neither droplet struck their respective targets. Both brushed by *Gravity* or *Blue Space* at extremely close range—only a few tens of meters.

Three minutes after the attack alert was lifted, Joseph Morovich, captain of *Gravity,* finally managed to gather his senior staff at the combat center, in the middle of which was a giant situation map. No stars were shown against the dark expanse of space, only the positions of the two ships and the attack trajectories of the droplets.

The two long white trails appeared as straight lines, but the data indicated they were parabolas with very low curvature. As the two droplets accelerated toward their targets in the simulation, their headings began to drift. The changes were small, but cumulatively, they resulted in the droplets barely missing their targets. Many of the senior officers had participated in the Doomsday Battle, and their memory of the sharp turns the droplets were capable of executing while moving at extremely high velocities still brought heart-stopping terror. However, the trajectories on the display were completely different: It was as though some outside force perpendicular to the attack vectors of the droplets had steadily pushed them out of the way.

"Replay the recording," the captain ordered. "Visible light range."

The stars and the galaxy appeared. This was no longer a computer simulation. In one corner, flickering numbers showed the passage of time. Everyone relived the terror of a few minutes ago, when all they could do was wait for death because evasive maneuvers and defensive shots were all meaningless. Soon, the numbers stopped changing. The droplets had already swept past the ships, but because they were moving so fast, no one could see them.

The display shifted to slow-motion replay of the high-speed recording. Since the complete recording, over ten seconds long, would take a long time to play through, only the last few seconds were shown. The officers saw a droplet pass in front of the camera like a faint meteor across the sea of stars in the background. The recording was played again, and froze when the droplet was in the middle of the screen. The image zoomed in until the droplet took up most of the display.

Half a century of cruising in formation with the droplets made everyone familiar with their appearance, and what they saw now shocked them. The droplet on the display was still shaped like a teardrop, but its surface was no longer a perfectly smooth mirror. Instead, it was dim and coppery yellow, as though full of rust. It was as if a magician's spell of eternal youth had failed, and the marks left by three centuries of spaceflight had all appeared at once.

Instead of a shining spirit, the droplet had turned into an ancient artillery shell drifting through space. Communications with the Earth during the last few years had given these officers some basic insight into the principles of strong-interaction materials. They knew that the surface of a droplet was held in a force field generated by mechanisms inside. This force field counteracted the electromagnetic force between particles, allowing the strong nuclear force to spill out. Without the force field, strong-interaction material reverted to ordinary metal.

The droplets had died.

Next, they reviewed the post-attack data. The simulation showed that after the droplet brushed by *Gravity,* the mysterious perpendicular force making small heading changes vanished, and the droplet coasted along its final vector. But this only lasted a few seconds. Thereafter, the droplet began to decelerate. The combat analysis computer concluded that the force decelerating the droplet was equal in magnitude to the force that had changed its heading. The obvious conclusion was that the source of the force had shifted from pushing at the side of the droplet to pushing from the front.

Since the recording was made by high-magnification telescopic lens, it was possible to see the back of the departing droplet. The droplet turned ninety degrees so that it was perpendicular to its own direction of motion and continued to coast. Then it began to decelerate. The next scene seemed to be taken from a fairy tale— good thing Dr. West was also present, or else he would again declare the others to be suffering from hallucinations. A triangular object, about twice as long as the droplet, appeared in front of it. The staff immediately recognized it as a shuttle from *Blue Space*! In order to increase its propulsive power, multiple small fusion drives were attached to the hull of the shuttle. Although the nozzles of the drives all pointed away from the camera, it was still possible to see the glow they made as they operated under maximum output. The shuttle was pushing against the droplet to slow it down. And it was easy to deduce that it was also the source of the force that caused the droplets to deviate from their attack vectors.

After the shuttle's appearance, two human figures wearing space suits appeared on the other side of the droplet—the side closest to the camera. The deceleration caused the figures to stick to the surface of the droplet; one of them held some kind of instrument in his hands and appeared to be analyzing the droplet. In the past, droplets had seemed almost divine in the eyes of humankind, not belonging to this world and not approachable. The only people who had ever come close to touching a droplet had been vaporized in the Doomsday Battle. But now, the droplet had lost all its mystery. Without its mirrorlike sheen, it seemed ordinary, broken-down, older and less advanced than the shuttle and the astronauts—some antique or piece of trash collected by the latter. A few seconds later, the shuttle and the astronauts disappeared, and the dead droplet was once again alone in space. But it continued to decelerate, indicating that the shuttle was still there pushing against it, only now invisible.

"They know how to disable the droplets!" someone cried out.

Captain Morovich could think of only one thing. Like Hunter a few minutes ago, he didn't hesitate to push the button on his watch. The error message appeared in a red information window that appeared midair:

Failure: The self-destruct module has been dismantled.

The captain dashed out of the combat center and headed for the stern. The other officers followed.

The first person from *Gravity* to arrive at the gravitational wave transmission control room was Old Hunter. Though he had no authorization to enter the cabin, he wanted to try to break the link between the controller and the antenna. This would at least temporarily disable the transmission system until he figured out how to destroy the controller itself.

But someone was already there, examining the control cabin.

Hunter took out his sidearm and aimed it at the man. He wore

the uniform of a sublieutenant on *Gravity,* not the uniform dating from the Doomsday Battle that Hunter expected to see—the man had stolen it. Hunter recognized him from the back. "I knew Commander Devon was right."

Lieutenant Commander Park Ui-gun, head of the marines on *Blue Space,* turned around. He looked no older than thirty, but his face showed that he had endured experiences that no one aboard *Gravity* could imagine. He was slightly surprised. Perhaps he didn't expect anyone here so soon; perhaps he didn't expect to see Hunter. Yet, he remained calm. With both hands half raised, he said, "Please let me explain—"

Old Hunter wasn't interested in an explanation. He didn't want to know how this man had boarded *Gravity,* and didn't even want to know if he was a man or a ghost. Whatever the facts, the situation was too dangerous. All he wanted was to destroy the transmission controller unit. It was his only goal in life, and this man from *Blue Space* stood in the way. He squeezed the trigger.

The bullet struck Park in the chest, and the impact threw him against the cabin door. Hunter's gun was loaded with special bullets designed for use inside the ship: They wouldn't damage the bulkheads or other equipment, but they also weren't as deadly as laser beams. Some blood oozed out of the wound, but Park managed to stay erect in the weightlessness and reached into his bloody uniform for his own weapon. Hunter shot again, and there was a fresh wound in Park's chest. More blood oozed out, floating in the gravity-less air. Finally, Hunter took aim at Park's head, but he didn't get a chance for the third shot.

This was the scene that greeted Captain Morovich and the other officers when they arrived: Hunter's gun was floating far away from him. The old cook's body was stiff, his open eyes showing only white, his limbs twitching. Blood erupted forth from his mouth like a fountain, coagulating into spheres of various sizes drifting around him in a cloud. In the middle of the bloody, translucent spheres was a dark red object about the size of a fist, dragging two tubes behind it like tails.

Rhythmically, it pulsed in midair, and with every pulse, more blood was squeezed out of its two tubular tails. The object propelled itself forward like a crimson jellyfish swimming through the air.

It was Hunter's heart.

During the struggle a few moments earlier, Hunter had slammed his right hand against his chest, and then, desperately, torn open his clothes. Thus, his bare chest lay revealed, and everyone could see that the skin was perfect, with not a single scratch.

"He can be saved if we get him into surgery right away," Sublieutenant Park said with some difficulty, his voice very hoarse. Blood continued to spill from the two wounds in his chest. "Good thing that doctors don't need to open his chest to reattach his heart anymore.... Don't move! It's as easy for them to pluck out your heart or brain as it is for you to pick an apple dangling from a branch in front of you. *Gravity* has been captured."

Fully armed marines rushed in from another corridor. Most of them wore the dark blue lightweight space suits dating from before the Doomsday Battle—apparently they were all from *Blue Space*. All the marines were equipped with powerful laser assault rifles.

Captain Morovich nodded at his officers. Without speaking, they tossed their weapons away. *Blue Space* had ten times more people than *Gravity*, and just their detachment of marines numbered more than a hundred. They could easily control *Gravity*.

There was nothing beyond belief anymore. *Blue Space* had turned into a supernatural warship wielding magic. The crew of *Gravity* again experienced the shock they had last suffered during the Doomsday Battle.

More than fourteen hundred people floated in the middle of *Blue Space*'s spherical great hall. The largest portion, over twelve hundred, belonged to the crew of *Blue Space*. Sixty years ago, the officers and enlisted men of this ship had also lined up here to accept Zhang Beihai's command, and most of them were still here. Since only a few individuals needed to be awake and on duty

for regular cruising, the crew had aged only three to five years on average. They hadn't experienced the bulk of the intervening years, and the searing flames of the dark battles and the cold funerals held in space remained fresh in their minds. The remainder belonged to the one-hundred-strong crew of *Gravity*. The two crews—one large, one small, wearing distinct uniforms and suspicious of each other—gathered into two clusters far apart from each other.

Before the two crews, the senior officers of the two ships were mixed together. Captain Chu Yan of *Blue Space* drew the most attention. He was forty-three, but looked younger, and he was the model of the scholarly military officer. Refined and calm in his speech and mannerisms, he even gave off a hint of shyness. But on Earth, Chu Yan was already a figure of legend. During the dark battles, he was the one who had given the order to turn the interior of *Blue Space* into a vacuum, thereby preventing the crew from death in the infrasonic nuclear bomb attack. Even now, public opinion on Earth remained divided as to whether *Blue Space*'s actions during the dark battle should be classified as self-defense or murder. After the founding of dark forest deterrence, he was the one who had resisted the heavy pressure of majority opinion aboard and delayed *Blue Space*'s return, thus giving the ship sufficient time to escape after the warning from *Bronze Age*. There were many other rumors concerning Chu Yan. For instance, when *Natural Selection* had chosen to defect and escape the Doomsday Battle, he was the only captain to ask to give chase. Some claimed that he had a different purpose in mind, wanting to hijack *Blue Space* and escape along with *Natural Selection*. Of course, those were just rumors.

"Almost everyone from the two ships is gathered here," said Chu Yan. "Although much still divides us, we prefer to think of everyone as belonging to the same world, formed from *Blue Space* and *Gravity*. Before we plan the future of our world together, we need to take care of an urgent matter."

A large holographic display window appeared midair, showing somewhere in space where the stars were sparse. In the middle of the region was a faint white fog, and the fog was etched with several

hundred straight parallel lines, like brush bristles. The white lines had clearly been enhanced and stood out in the image. In the past two centuries, these "brushes" had become very familiar to people, and some brands even used them in their logos.

"These trails were observed eight days ago in the stellar dust cloud near Trisolaris. Please pay attention to the video."

Everyone stared at the image, and the trails could be seen to grow in the fog.

"How many times have you sped up the video?" an officer from *Gravity* asked.

"It's not sped up at all."

The crowd grew agitated, like a forest struck by a sudden rainstorm.

"By a rough estimate . . . these ships are moving at close to the speed of light," Captain Morovich of *Gravity* said. His voice was very tranquil. He had experienced too many incredible sights in the last two days.

"That's right. The Second Trisolaran Fleet is heading for Earth at lightspeed, and should arrive in four years." Chu Yan looked at *Gravity*'s crew with caring eyes, as though sorry that he had to deliver this news. "After you left, the Earth sank into a dream of universal peace and prosperity, and completely misjudged the situation. Trisolaris has been waiting patiently, and now they've finally seized their chance."

"How do we know this is authentic?" someone from *Gravity* called out.

"I can attest to it!" said Guan Yifan. Among the small gathering in front of the crews, he was the only one not in a military uniform. "My observatory had also detected the same trails. However, since I was focused on large-scale cosmological observations, I didn't pay much attention to them. But I've gone back and retrieved the recorded data. The Solar System, the Trisolaran system, and our ships form a scalene triangle. The side between the Solar System and the Trisolaran system is the longest. The side between the Solar System and us is the shortest. The side going from the Trisolaran

system to us is in between. In other words, we are closer to the Trisolaran system than the Solar System is to the Trisolaran system. About forty days from now, the Earth will also detect the trails we're seeing."

Chu Yan took over. "We believe that something has already taken place on the Earth. More specifically, it happened about five hours ago, when the droplets attacked our two ships. Based on information provided by *Gravity*, that was the scheduled time for the Swordholder to transfer his authority to his successor. This was the opportunity Trisolaris had been waiting for for half a century. The two droplets had clearly been given orders before entering the blind zone. This was a long-planned, coordinated attack.

"I must conclude that the peace brought by dark forest deterrence has been breached. There are only two possibilities: The gravitational wave universal broadcast has been initiated, or it hasn't."

Chu Yan tapped in the air and brought up Cheng Xin's picture on the holographic display. This picture of the new Swordholder had also just been obtained from *Gravity*. Cheng Xin stood in front of the UN Secretariat Building, holding a baby. Her picture had been blown up to be as large as the "brush" bristles, and the contrast between the two images couldn't be sharper. The basic color scheme of space was black and silver—the depth of space and the cold light of the stars. But Cheng Xin resembled a Madonna from the East. A warm, golden glow bathed her and the baby, giving all those present the feeling of being close to the sun, a sensation that they had missed for half a century.

"We believe the latter scenario is true," Chu Yan said.

"How did they pick such a person to be Swordholder?" someone from *Blue Space* asked.

Captain Morovich answered. "It's been sixty years since you left home, and fifty for us. Everything on Earth has changed. Deterrence made a comfortable cradle, and as humanity napped inside, it regressed from an adult to a child."

"Don't you know that there are no more men on Earth?" someone from *Gravity* shouted.

"Humans on Earth lost the ability to maintain dark forest deterrence," Chu Yan said. "We had planned to capture *Gravity* and re-establish dark forest deterrence. But we've just found out that due to decay in the antenna, the ability to broadcast gravitational waves will only last two more months. Believe me, this has been an incredible blow to all of us. We have only one choice: immediately activate the universal broadcast."

The crowd erupted. Next to the view of cold space showing the lightspeed trails of the Trisolaran Fleet, Cheng Xin gazed at them, full of love. The two images portrayed their two choices.

"Are you really willing to commit mundicide?" Captain Morovich demanded.

Chu Yan maintained his serenity against the chaos. Ignoring Captain Morovich, he spoke to the crowd. "For us, initiating the broadcast is meaningless. Neither the Earth nor Trisolaris can catch us now."

Everyone understood this. The sophons were permanently severed from home, and the droplets had been destroyed. Earth and Trisolaris thus had no way to trace them. In the vast, deep space beyond the Oort Cloud, even Trisolaran ships operating at light-speed would never be able to find two motes of dust.

"Then you're just seeking revenge!" an officer from *Gravity* said.

"Vengeance against Trisolaris *is* our right. They must pay for the crimes they've committed. In war, it is right and just to destroy one's enemies. If my deduction is correct, humankind's gravitational wave transmitters have all been destroyed, and the Earth is now under occupation. It's very likely that the genocide of the human race is underway.

"Activating the universal broadcast would give the Earth one last chance. If the location of the Solar System is revealed, it would no longer have any value to Trisolaris because it could be destroyed at any moment. This would force the Trisolarans to leave the Solar System, and their lightspeed fleet would have to turn away. We may be able to save the human race from immediate annihilation.

To give them more time, our broadcast will include only the location of Trisolaris."

"That's the same as revealing the Solar System! It's too close."

"We all know that, but hopefully this will give the Earth a little more time and allow more humans to escape. Whether they will choose to do so is up to them."

"You're talking about destroying two worlds!" said Captain Morovich. "And one of them is our mother. This decision is the Last Judgment. It cannot be made so lightly."

"I agree."

A holographic rectangular red button about a meter long appeared between the two existing information windows. Below it was a number: 0.

Chu Yan continued. "As I said earlier: together, we are one world. Everyone in this world is an ordinary person, but fate has put us into the position of making the last judgment about two worlds. This decision must be made, but a single person or even a few persons shouldn't make it. This will be the decision of the whole world through a referendum. All in favor of broadcasting the location of Trisolaris to the universe, please press this red button. All opposed or abstaining, do nothing.

"Right now, the total number of people aboard *Blue Space* and *Gravity,* including all present and those on duty, is one thousand four hundred and fifteen. If the ayes reach or exceed two-thirds of the total, nine hundred forty-four, the universal broadcast will begin immediately. Otherwise, we will never activate the broadcast and let the antenna decay and fail.

"Begin."

Chu Yan turned and pressed the giant red button hovering in air. The button flashed, and the number below it turned from 0 to 1. Next, the two vice-captains of *Blue Space* pressed the buttons in quick succession. The tally went up to 3. Then the other senior officers of *Blue Space,* followed by the junior officers and enlisted men, filed past the red button in a long line, pressing the button again and again.

As the red button flashed, the tally crept up. These were the final beats of the heart of history, the final steps taken toward the terminal point.

When the number reached 795, Guan Yifan pressed the button. He was the first person from *Gravity* to support the broadcast. After him, several more officers and enlisted men from *Gravity* also pressed the button.

Finally, the number reached 943, and a large line of text appeared above the button:

The next affirmative vote will activate the universal broadcast.

The next person to vote was an enlisted man. Many others were lined up behind him. He placed his hand above the button, but didn't push. He waited until the ensign behind him put his hand on his, and then more hands joined theirs in a thick stack.

"Please wait," Captain Morovich said. He drifted over and, as everyone watched, placed his hand atop the pile.

Then dozens of hands moved together, and the button flashed one more time.

Three hundred fifteen years had passed since that morning in the twentieth century when Ye Wenjie had pushed another red button.

The gravitational wave broadcast began. Everyone present felt a strong tremor. The feeling seemed to come not from without, but from within each body, as though every person had become a vibrating string. This instrument of death played for only twelve seconds before stopping, and then everything was silent.

Outside the ship, the thin membrane of space-time rippled with the gravitational waves, like a placid lake surface disturbed by a night breeze. The judgment of death for both worlds spread across the cosmos at the speed of light.

POST-DETERRENCE ERA, YEAR 2
THE MORNING AFTER THE GREAT
RESETTLEMENT, AUSTRALIA

The noises around her quieted down, and Cheng Xin could hear voices coming from the information window over the city government tent. She could tell one of the voices belonged to Sophon, in addition to two others. But she was too far away to make out exactly what they said. She thought their voices cast a spell because the noises around her faded and finally disappeared. The world seemed to be frozen.

Then a tsunami erupted around her, and Cheng Xin trembled. She had been blind for a while, and the images of the real world in her mind were being squeezed out bit by bit by illusions. The sudden bedlam made her feel as if the Pacific had risen up all around her and swallowed Australia.

It took a few seconds before she understood that the crowd was cheering. *What's there to cheer about? Has everyone gone mad?* The clamor did not subside, though it was eventually replaced by speech. So many were talking at once it was as if, after the continent had been flooded, a storm lashed the surface of the sea. She could not tell what anyone was saying in the tumult.

But she picked out "*Blue Space*" and "*Gravity*" more than once. Her hearing gradually recovered its acuity, and she noticed a

faint sound amidst the general commotion: footsteps in front of her. She felt someone stop there.

"Dr. Cheng Xin, what is wrong with your eyes? Can you not see?" Cheng Xin felt movements disturbing the air. Perhaps the man was waving his hands before her eyes. "The mayor sent me for you. We're going home, back to China."

"I don't have a home," Cheng Xin said. The word "home" stabbed into her heart like a knife, and her heart, numbed by extreme pain, nevertheless convulsed one more time. She thought of that winter night three centuries ago when she left her home, thought of the dawn that had greeted her outside her window.... Both of her parents had died before the Great Ravine. They could never have imagined where their daughter had ended up, tempest-tossed by time and fate.

"No. Everyone's getting ready to go home. We're all leaving Australia and going back to where we came from."

Cheng Xin whipped her head up. She still couldn't get used to this stubborn darkness before her wide-open eyes. She tried to make out something, anything. "What?"

"*Gravity* initiated the universal broadcast."

How is that possible?

"The location of Trisolaris has been exposed—which of course means the Solar System is exposed as well. The Trisolarans are running away. The Second Fleet has changed direction to head away from the Solar System. All the droplets are gone. Sophon was explaining that there's no more need to worry about them invading the Solar System. Like the Trisolaran system, this is now a place of death that everyone will want to escape from."

How!?

"We're going home. Sophon has ordered the Earth Security Force to make every effort to assist with the evacuation of Australia. The process will get faster over time, but moving all the refugees out of Australia will take three to six months. You can leave first. The mayor wants me to take you to the provincial government."

"Was it *Blue Space*?"

"No one knows the details, not even Sophon. But Trisolaris received the universal broadcast, and it was initiated a year ago, when deterrence failed."

"Can you let me be by myself for a while?"

"All right, Dr. Cheng. But you should be happy. They did what you needed to do."

The man stopped talking, but Cheng Xin could still feel his presence. The commotion around her gradually died down, and was followed by a rainstorm of footsteps. The footsteps grew sparse—everyone must be leaving the city government tent to take care of their own business. Cheng Xin felt the sea retreat around her, revealing solid land beneath. She stood in the middle of an empty continent, the sole survivor after the Flood. Her face felt a trace of warmth: The sun was rising.

POST-DETERRENCE ERA,
DAY 1-DAY 5
GRAVITY AND *BLUE SPACE*, DEEP
SPACE BEYOND THE OORT CLOUD

"It's possible to detect the warped points using the naked eye," Chu Yan said. "But the best way is to monitor the electromagnetic radiation. The emission from these points is very faint, but it has a distinct spectral signature. The regular sensors on our ships can detect and locate them. Typically, a volume of space as large as a ship in this region contains one to two warped points, but we once found twelve at once. Look, right now there are three."

Chu Yan, Morovich, and Guan Yifan were floating through a long corridor on *Blue Space*. In front of them drifted an information window showing a map of the interior of the ship. Three red dots flashed on the map, and the three of them were approaching one of these dots now.

"Right there!" Guan pointed straight ahead.

In the bulkhead in front of them was a circular hole about a meter in diameter. The edge was smooth, mirrorlike. Through the hole they could see tubes of various thicknesses. Several tubes had entire sections missing in the middle. In two of the thicker tubes, they could see liquid flowing. The liquid seemed to flow from one section, disappear, and then reappear in the corresponding section of the

tube on the other side. The missing sections were of different lengths, but overall seemed to describe a spherical space. Based on the shape of the missing sections, part of the invisible bubble protruded into the corridor. Morovich and Guan carefully avoided it.

Chu Yan carelessly extended a hand into the invisible bubble, and half of his arm disappeared. Standing to the side, Guan Yifan saw a clear cross section of his cut-off arm, like the cross sections of Vera's legs that had been seen by Sublieutenant Ike aboard the *Gravity*. Chu Yan pulled his arm back and showed the astonished Morovich and Guan that it was unharmed. Then he encouraged them to try it. The two carefully reached into the invisible bubble. They watched their hands, and then arms, vanish, but they felt nothing.

"Let's go in," said Chu Yan. Then he jumped into the bubble, as though diving into a pool. Morovich and Guan watched in consternation as Captain Chu disappeared from head to toe. The cross section of his body on the surface of the invisible bubble rapidly changed shape, and the mirrorlike edge of the hole threw reflections onto the surrounding bulkheads like ripples.

As Morovich and Guan stared at each other, two hands and forearms emerged from the bubble and remained suspended in midair. Each hand grabbed hold of one of theirs, and they were pulled into fourth-dimensional space.

All who had experienced it agree that the sensation of being in four-dimensional space was indescribable. They would even say that it was the only thing encountered by humanity thus far that absolutely could not be captured by language.

People usually resorted to this analogy: Imagine a race of flat beings living inside a two-dimensional picture. No matter how rich or colorful the picture was, the flat people could only see the profile of the world around them. In their eyes, everything consisted of line segments of various lengths. Only when such a two-dimensional being was taken up out of the picture into three-dimensional space and looking down on the world could he see the entirety of the image.

This analogy simply expressed in some more detail the indescribability of experiencing four-dimensional space.

A person looking back upon the three-dimensional world from four-dimensional space for the first time realized this right away: He had never *seen* the world while he was in it. If the three-dimensional world were likened to a picture, all he had seen before was just a narrow view from the side: a line. Only from four-dimensional space could he see the picture as a whole. He would describe it this way: Nothing blocked whatever was placed behind it. Even the interiors of sealed spaces were laid open. This seemed a simple change, but when the world was displayed this way, the visual effect was utterly stunning. When all barriers and concealments were stripped away, and everything was exposed, the amount of information entering the viewer's eyes was hundreds of millions times greater than when he was in three-dimensional space. The brain could not even process so much information right away.

In Morovich and Guan's eyes, *Blue Space* was a magnificent, immense painting that had just been unrolled. They could see all the way to the stern, and all the way to the bow; they could see the inside of every cabin and every sealed container in the ship; they could see the liquid flowing through the maze of tubes, and the fiery ball of fusion in the reactor at the stern.... Of course, the rules of perspective remained in operation, and objects far away appeared indistinct, but everything was *visible*.

Given this description, those who had never experienced four-dimensional space might get the wrong impression that they were seeing everything "through" the hull. But no, they were not seeing "through" anything. Everything was laid out in the open, just like when we look at a circle drawn on a piece of paper, we can see the inside of the circle without looking "through" anything. This kind of openness extended to every level, and the hardest part was describing how it applied to solid objects. One could see the interior of solids, such as the bulkheads or a piece of metal or a rock—one could see all the cross sections at once! Morovich and Guan were drowning in a sea of information—all the details of the universe

were gathered around them and fighting for their attention in vivid colors.

Morovich and Guan had to learn to deal with an entirely novel visual phenomenon: unlimited details. In three-dimensional space, the human visual system dealt with limited details. No matter how complicated the environment or the object, the visible elements were limited. Given enough time, it was always possible to take in most of the details one by one. But when one viewed the three-dimensional world from four-dimensional space, all concealed and hidden details were revealed simultaneously, since three-dimensional objects were laid open at every level. Take a sealed container as an example: One could see not only what was inside, but also the interiors of the objects inside. This boundless disclosure and exposure led to the unlimited details on display.

Everything in the ship lay exposed before Morovich and Guan, but even when observing some specific object, such as a cup or a pen, they saw infinite details, and the information received by their visual systems was incalculable. Even a lifetime would not be enough to take in the shape of any one of these objects in four-dimensional space. When an object was revealed at all levels in four-dimensional space, it created in the viewer a vertigo-inducing sensation of depth, like a set of Russian nesting dolls that went on without end. Bounded in a nutshell but counting oneself a king of infinite space was no longer merely a metaphor.

Morovich and Guan looked at each other, then looked at Chu Yan to the side. They saw bodies revealed at every level with the details displayed in parallel: They could see bones, organs, the marrow inside the bones, the blood flowing through the ventricles and atria of the heart, the openings and closings of the mitral and tricuspid valves. When gazing at each other, they could see clearly the interior structure of the lenses of the eyes....

The phrase "in parallel" might also lead to misunderstanding. The physical locations of the parts of the body had not been shifted around: The skin still enclosed the organs and the bones, and the familiar shape of each person in three-dimensional space

persisted—but it was now merely one detail among an infinity of details, visible at the same time, in parallel.

"Be careful of where you move your hands," Chu Yan said. "You might poke an internal organ—yours or someone else's—by mistake. But as long as you don't use too much force, even contact won't be a big deal. You'll feel a bit of pain or nausea, and of course there's the risk of infections. Also, don't touch or move things unless you know exactly what they are. Everything on the ship is now naked: You might be touching a live wire or heated steam, or even integrated circuits, and cause system malfunctions. Overall, you're like gods in the three-dimensional world, but you have to get used to being in four-dimensional space before you can use your powers effectively."

Morovich and Guan quickly learned how to avoid touching inner organs. By moving in a certain direction, they could grasp someone's hand instead of the bones inside the hand. To touch the bones or organs required exertion in *another* direction—a direction that didn't exist in three-dimensional space.

Next, Morovich and Guan discovered something else that excited them: They could see the stars in every direction. They could see the bright glow of the Milky Way extending through the universal eternal night. They knew that they were still inside the ship—none of them wore space suits, and all breathed the air on the ship—but in the fourth dimension, they were exposed to space. All three veteran spacers had performed countless spacewalks, but they had never felt so utterly intimate with space. During spacewalks, they were at least enclosed by space suits, but now, nothing stood between space and them. The ship that revealed infinite details did not shield them from space. In the fourth dimension, the ship lay in parallel with all of space.

The brain that had been adapted from birth to sense and feel three-dimensional space could not handle the infinite information generated by countless details, and initially, information overload threatened to shut down processing. But the brain soon grew used to the four-dimensional environment, and without conscious

thought it learned to ignore most details, leaving only the frames around objects.

After the initial vertigo, Morovich and Guan experienced another, even greater shock. Once their attention was no longer completely absorbed by the inexhaustible details of the environment around them, they sensed space itself, or sensed the fourth dimension. Later, people would call this feeling "high-dimensional spatial sense." For those who had experienced it, high-dimensional spatial sense was hard to convey in words. They often tried to explain it this way: Concepts like "vastness" or "boundlessness" in three-dimensional space were replicated an infinite number of times in four-dimensional space in a direction that did not exist in three-dimensional space. They often resorted to the analogy of two mirrors facing each other: In either mirror one could see a boundless multitude of replicated mirrors, a hall of mirrors that extended into infinity. In this analogy, each mirror in the hall was a three-dimensional space. In other words, the vastness that one experienced in three-dimensional space was but a cross-section of the vastness of four-dimensional space. The difficulty of describing high-dimensional spatial sense lay in the fact that for observers situated in four-dimensional space, the space they could see was empty and uniform, but there was a *depth* to it that could not be captured by language. This *depth* was not a matter of distance: It was bound up in every point in space. Guan Yifan's exclamation later became a classic quote:

"A bottomless abyss exists in every inch."

The experience of high-dimensional spatial sense was a spiritual baptism. In one moment, concepts like *freedom, openness, profundity,* and *infinity* all gained brand-new meanings.

Chu Yan said, "We should return. The warped points remain stable for only a brief period of time before drifting away or disappearing. To find a new warped point requires moving in four-dimensional space. That's a dangerous undertaking for novices like you."

"How does one find a warped point in four-dimensional space?" Morovich asked.

"Simple. A warped point is usually spherical. Light is refracted inside the sphere, and objects inside are distorted, causing a visual break in the image of the objects. Of course, this is just an optical effect in four-dimensional space, not a real change in the shapes of the objects. Look over there—"

Chu Yan pointed in the direction they had come from. Morovich and Guan saw those tubes again, which now also lay open so that all the liquids flowing through them could be seen clearly. Inside the spherical region, the tubes were curved and distorted, and the sphere appeared like a drop of dew hanging on a spiderweb. This was different from how the region had appeared in three-dimensional space. There, the warped point didn't refract light, and so appeared completely invisible. Its presence could only be made known via the disappearance of objects that had entered four-dimensional space inside the bubble.

"If you come here again, you must wear space suits. Novices can't always tell locations accurately, and finding a new warped point for the return trip might result in landing outside the ship in three-dimensional space."

Chu Yan indicated that the other two should follow, and entered the dewdrop-like bubble. In an instant they were back inside the three-dimensional world, back in the corridor inside the ship, in exactly the place where, ten minutes ago, they had entered four-dimensional space. In fact, they had never left—the space they were in had just gained an extra dimension. The round opening in the bulkhead was still there, and they could still see the "broken" tubes inside.

But to Morovich and Guan, the world no longer seemed familiar. They now experienced the three-dimensional world as narrow and smothering. Guan dealt with it slightly better—he had at least experienced four-dimensional space once before, in a semiconscious state. But Morovich was feeling claustrophobic, as though he was being suffocated.

"This is normal. You'll get used to it after a few times." Chu Yan laughed. "The two of you now know what real vastness means.

Even if you put on space suits and go take a walk in space now, you'll feel confined."

"How did all this happen?" Morovich tore open his collar and gasped.

"We entered a region of space where space has four dimensions. That's it. We call this region a four-dimensional fragment."

"But we're in three-dimensional space now!"

"Four-dimensional space contains three-dimensional space, just as three-dimensional space contains two-dimensional space. To make another analogy: We're located inside a three-dimensional sheet of paper in four-dimensional space."

"Let me propose a model," said Guan excitedly. "The entirety of our three-dimensional space is a large, thin sheet of paper, sixteen billion light-years across. Somewhere on this sheet of paper is a tiny, four-dimensional soap bubble."

"Perfect, Dr. Guan!" Chu Yan clapped Guan's shoulder, making him tumble in weightlessness. "I've been trying to come up with a good analogy, and you hit it in one try. This is why we need a cosmologist! You're exactly right. We were on this three-dimensional sheet of paper, crawling over the surface. Then we came into the soap bubble. From a warped point, we can manage to leave the surface of the paper and entered the space inside the bubble."

"Though we were in four-dimensional space just now, our bodies remained three-dimensional," Morovich said.

"That's right. We were flat, three-dimensional people drifting in four-dimensional space. It's not clear how our bodies are able to survive in four-dimensional space, given that the physical laws are likely different. There are many such mysteries."

"What exactly are warped points?"

"The three-dimensional sheet of paper is not completely flat everywhere. Some places are warped, reaching into the fourth dimension. That's what a warped point is: a tunnel from lower dimensions into higher dimensions. We can get into four-dimensional space by jumping into them."

"Are there many warped points?"

"Oh yes. They're everywhere. *Blue Space* was able to discover their secret earlier because we have more people aboard, and so there were many more opportunities to encounter warped points. *Gravity,* besides having fewer people, also had a much stricter psychological monitoring regime—even those who encountered warped points dared not discuss them."

"Are all warped points this small?"

"No. Some are much bigger. There's one mystery we've never been able to solve: We once observed that the rear third of *Gravity* had warped into four-dimensional space, and stayed there for several minutes. How could you have not noticed anything odd?"

"Well, the last third of the ship usually had no crew. Oh, wait, he was there." Morovich turned to Guan Yifan. "You must have experienced that. I think I heard about it from Dr. West."

"I was only half awake. Later, that idiot convinced me that I was only hallucinating."

"It's not possible to look into the fourth dimension from three-dimensional space. But it *is* possible to be in four-dimensional space and see everything happening in three-dimensional space and to affect things in it. We were able to lay an ambush against the droplets from four-dimensional space. No matter how powerful the strong-interaction probes were, they were still three-dimensional objects. In a sense, three-dimensionality is synonymous with fragility. Viewed from four-dimensional space, it was an unrolled painting, defenseless. We approached it from the fourth dimension, and, without understanding its principles of operation, sabotaged its internal mechanisms—completely exposed—at random.

"Is Trisolaris aware of the existence of the four-dimensional fragment?"

"We think not."

"The soap bubble—uh, four-dimensional fragment—how big is it?"

"Talking about the size of four-dimensional space from three-dimensional space is kind of meaningless. We can only discuss how big the projection of the fragment is in three dimensions. Based on

preliminary investigation, we think the three-dimensional projection is spherical. If that's true, based on the data collected so far, its radius is between forty to fifty AU."

"About the size of the Solar System."

The round opening in the bulkhead next to the three of them began to move slowly and to shrink. When it was just over ten meters from them, the opening disappeared completely. But the information window floating near them indicated that two more warped points had appeared aboard *Blue Space*.

"How could a four-dimensional fragment appear in three-dimensional space?" Guan Yifan muttered to himself.

"No one knows. Doctor, this is your puzzle to solve."

After the discovery of the four-dimensional fragment, *Blue Space* had explored and studied the space inside extensively. The addition of *Gravity* brought more advanced equipment and techniques, so the crews could conduct more comprehensive and in-depth exploration.

In three-dimensional space, this region appeared very empty and showed no irregularities. Much of the exploration had to be conducted in four-dimensional space. Since releasing probes into four-dimensional space was no trivial matter, most of the research was conducted by inserting a telescope into the fragment through a warped point. Manipulating a three-dimensional instrument in four dimensions required some practice, and a period of adjustment, but once the scientists got the hang of it, they immediately made shocking discoveries.

Through the telescope, they discovered a ring-shaped object. Since it was impossible to determine its distance from the ship, it was also impossible to estimate its size. The best guess was that its three-dimensional diameter was between eighty to one hundred kilometers, and the band of the ring was about twenty kilometers thick. The whole thing resembled a giant wedding band spinning in space. Complex patterns resembling circuitry could be discerned on the surface of the band. Based on the evidence, it seemed reasonable to conclude that the ring had been constructed by intelligent beings.

This was the first time humanity had observed another civilization outside of the Earth and Trisolaris.

But the most shocking thing was that the "Ring" was sealed. It existed in four-dimensional space, but didn't reveal its interior as a three-dimensional object would have. Since its inside was concealed, that meant it was a true four-dimensional object. This was also the first true four-dimensional object detected by humanity since entering four-dimensional space.

People initially feared an attack, but the surface of the Ring showed no signs of any activity. They also detected no emission of any electromagnetic, neutrino, or gravitational wave signals. Other than a slow, stately revolving motion, the Ring showed no acceleration. The working theory was that this was a ruin, perhaps a long-abandoned space city or spaceship.

Further observations revealed more unknown objects in the depths of four-dimensional space. They were all sealed four-dimensional objects of different sizes and shapes, and many seemed to be artifacts fashioned by intelligence: pyramids, crosses, polyhedral frames, and so on. Other objects were irregular forms composed from simpler shapes, also clearly not natural. More than a dozen of these objects had shapes that could be discerned by telescope, though farther away were many more objects that appeared only as point sources. In total, about a hundred such objects were found. Like the Ring, none of them showed signs of activity, and they emitted no detectable signals.

Guan Yifan proposed to Captain Chu the plan of piloting a pinnace to the Ring and studying it up close. If possible, he wanted to enter the Ring. The captain denied this proposal unequivocally. Navigating through four-dimensional space was fraught with risks. To precisely fix one's location required four coordinates, but equipment brought from three-dimensional space could only determine three coordinates. This meant three-dimensional explorers could not determine the location of any object in four-dimensional space with precision. An explorer could not ascertain the location or distance of the Ring using instrumentation or visual

observation, so it would be possible to collide with the Ring at any moment.

Similarly, locating a warped point to return to three-dimensional space would be very difficult. Since the coordinate in one of the four directions could not be determined, when a warped point was found, all that was known was its direction, not its distance from the observer. The crew of the pinnace could use a warped point to return to three-dimensional space and, to their surprise, find themselves far away from *Blue Space*.

Finally, most of the radio waves linking *Blue Space* and the pinnace would spill into the fourth dimension, leading to far faster decay of signal strength and causing communication difficulties.

After that, *Blue Space* and *Gravity* suffered six micrometeoroid strikes in one day. A 140-nanometer micrometeoroid struck and completely destroyed the magnetic levitation controller of *Blue Space*'s fusion reactor core. This was a key system aboard the ship. The fusion reactor core could reach temperatures as high as a million degrees, which would vaporize any material it came in contact with. A magnetic field kept it centered within the reaction chamber. If the controller failed, the superheated reactor core could escape from the magnetic field and instantly destroy the ship. Fortunately, the backup unit kicked in immediately and shut off the reactor—which was operating at minimal power—and averted catastrophe.

As the two ships sailed deeper into the four-dimensional fragment, the density of micrometeoroid strikes increased, and even larger meteoroids, visible to the naked eye, passed near the ships. Their velocity relative to the ships was several times the third cosmic velocity. In three-dimensional space, the critical parts of the ships were wrapped in layers of protection, but here, they lay exposed to the fourth dimension, completely defenseless.

Chu Yan decided that the two ships should retreat from the four-dimensional fragment. The fragment as a whole was moving away from the Solar System, heading in the same direction as the ships' course; thus, although *Blue Space* and *Gravity* were sailing

away from the Solar System at a high speed, their velocity relative to the fragment was small, and they had only slowly caught up to the fragment. They weren't deep within the fragment and should be able to decelerate and leave it easily.

Guan Yifan raged against this decision. "The greatest mystery in the universe is right in front of us. The answers to all our cosmological questions may be found here. How can we leave?"

"Are you talking about the three and three hundred thousand syndrome? The fragment did remind me of it."

"Even if you focus only on the practical, we can probably recover unimaginable knowledge and artifacts from that ring-shaped ruin."

"Such gains are only meaningful if we survive this ordeal. Right now, both of our ships could be annihilated any moment."

Guan sighed and shook his head. "Fine. But before you leave, let me ride a pinnace to explore the Ring. Give me a chance. You spoke of survival, but perhaps our future survival depends on what I can discover here!"

"We can consider sending a drone."

"In a four-dimensional world, only a live observer can understand what is seen. You know this better than I."

After a brief discussion, the senior staff of both ships approved Guan's proposal. Guan Yifan, Lieutenant Zhuo Wen, and Dr. West made up the exploratory team. Lieutenant Zhuo was the science officer aboard *Blue Space* and had comparatively extensive experience navigating in four dimensions. Dr. West, on the other hand, simply insisted that he come; the request was ultimately approved because he had studied Trisolaran language before the voyage.

Prior to this, the longest voyage in four-dimensional space had been the attack on the droplets and *Gravity*. During the attack, a pinnace had sailed through four-dimensional space to approach *Gravity*, and then three people, including Lieutenant Commander Park Ui-gun, had entered *Gravity* via a warped point to reconnoiter.

Thereafter, more than sixty marines had boarded *Gravity* in three separate waves. The attack on the droplets had relied on smaller shuttles. But this voyage of discovery to the Ring would be far longer.

The pinnace entered four-dimensional space from a warped point between the two ships. At the tail of the pinnace, the small fusion reactor's core turned from dim red to a faint blue as its power level increased. This flame, together with the balls of fire in the reactors of the two larger ships, illuminated this world of infinity times infinity. *Blue Space* and *Gravity* quickly receded, and as the pinnace sailed deeper into four-dimensional space, the high-dimensional spatial sensation intensified. Although Dr. West had already been to four-dimensional space twice, he exclaimed, "How grand is the spirit that can grasp such a world!"

Lieutenant Zhuo piloted the pinnace using voice commands or by moving the cursor with his gaze—it was a good idea to avoid using hands and risking contact with some sensitive piece of equipment that now lay exposed in four dimensions. To the naked eye, the Ring was still but a barely visible dot, but Zhuo cautiously kept the pinnace flying at a very low speed. Due to the extra unmeasurable dimension, visual judgments of distance were completely unreliable. The Ring might be as far away as an astronomical unit or as close as the pinnace's bow.

After three hours, the pinnace had already exceeded the previous record of distance sailed from the ships in four-dimensional space. The Ring remained but a dot. Lieutenant Zhuo grew even more cautious and was prepared to decelerate at full power and to change the heading at a moment's notice. Guan Yifan grew impatient and asked Zhuo to fly faster. Just then, West cried out in surprise.

The Ring turned into a real ring—it just happened. One moment, it was still a dot; the next moment, it was a ring the size of a coin. There was no gradual process of change at all.

"You've got to remember that we're basically blind in the fourth dimension," Lieutenant Zhuo said. He decreased their speed again.

Two more hours passed. If they were still in three-dimensional

space, they would have sailed about two hundred thousand kilometers.

All of a sudden, the coin-sized Ring turned into a gigantic structure. Lieutenant Zhuo banked sharply and barely managed to avoid collision. The pinnace passed through the Ring like an arch in space. The pinnace decelerated, turned around, and came to a stop a short distance from the Ring.

This was the first time humans had come close to a four-dimensional object. Similar to high-dimensional spatial sense, they felt the magnificence of high-dimensional materiality. The Ring was completely sealed, and they could not look inside the band, but they could feel an immense sense of depth and of containment. What they were seeing wasn't just a Ring, but an infinity of Rings all stacked together in concealment. This sensation of four-dimensionality impressed itself upon the soul, and gave the observers the experience of seeing the mountain contained in a mustard seed described in Buddhist parables.

From up close, the surface of the Ring appeared very different from images taken by the telescope. Instead of a golden yellow light, it gave off a dark copper glow. Those faint etched lines that had looked like circuitry were really lines left by micrometeoroids striking its surface. There was still no evidence of any activity, and it didn't emit light or other radiation. Looking at the ancient surface of the Ring, all three felt a sense of familiarity. They recalled the destroyed droplets, and then tried to imagine the immense four-dimensional Ring with a mirrorlike smooth surface—it would have been a breathtaking sight.

Following the preestablished plan, Lieutenant Zhuo transmitted a message to the Ring via medium-frequency radio waves. This was a simple bitmap, a bit array that could be interpreted as six lines of dots that formed a sequence of prime numbers: 2, 3, 5, 7, 11, 13.

They weren't expecting any answers, but an answer arrived immediately, so fast that they couldn't believe their eyes. The information window hovering in the middle of the pinnace cabin displayed a simple bitmap similar to the one they had sent. It also

consisted of six lines portraying the next six prime numbers: 17, 19, 23, 29, 31, 37.

The original plan had intended the hailing message as an experiment; there was no preparation for how to develop further communications. While the three in the pinnace debated what to do, the Ring sent a second bitmap to the pinnace: 1, 3, 5, 7, 11, 13, 1, 4, 2, 1, 5, 9.

Then a third bitmap: 1, 3, 5, 7, 11, 13, 16, 6, 10, 10, 4, 7.

A fourth: 1, 3, 5, 7, 11, 13, 19, 5, 1, 15, 4, 8.

A fifth: 1, 3, 5, 7, 11, 13, 7, 2, 16, 4, 1, 14.

The bitmaps came one after another. The first six numbers in each consisted of the six prime numbers sent by the pinnace as a greeting. As for the next six numbers in each series, both Lieutenant Zhuo and Dr. West turned to Guan Yifan, the scientist. The cosmologist stared at the scrolling numbers in the floating window and shrugged.

"I can't see any pattern."

"Then let's suppose that there is no pattern." West pointed at the window. "The first six numbers were sent by us, so it's possible that they mean 'you.' The next six numbers in the transmissions show no recognizable pattern, so maybe they mean 'all'—'everything about you.'"

"They—or it—want to know everything about us?"

"Or at least a linguistic sample. It wants to decode it, study it, and then communicate with us further."

"Then we should send it the Rosetta System."

"We have to ask for authorization."

The Rosetta System was a database developed to teach Earth languages to Trisolarans. The database included about two million characters' worth of documents concerning the natural and human histories of Earth with numerous videos and images. There was also software to draw connections between the linguistic symbols and the images so that an alien civilization could decode and study Earth languages.

The mother ship authorized the request from the exploration

team. But the pinnace didn't have the Rosetta System in its onboard computer memory, and due to the extremely tenuous communication link between the pinnace and the mother ship, it was impossible to transmit such a large volume of data. The only solution was to have the mother ship beam the information directly at the Ring. This couldn't be done via radio, but luckily, *Gravity* was equipped with a neutrino communication system. They weren't sure if the Ring could receive neutrino signals, however.

Three minutes after *Gravity* transmitted the Rosetta System via a neutrino beam to the Ring, the pinnace received a new series of bitmaps from the Ring. The first one was a perfect square of sixty-four dots arranged eight by eight; the second bitmap was missing one dot in a corner, leaving sixty-three; the third bitmap was missing two, leaving sixty-two....

"It's a countdown, or a progress bar," said West. "I think this is to show that it has received the Rosetta System and is in the process of decoding it. We should wait."

"Why sixty-four dots?"

"It's a reasonably big number if you're in base two. It's like how we use one hundred for lots of things in base ten."

Lieutenant Zhuo and Guan were both glad to have West with them. The psychologist did seem to have some skills when it came to establishing communications with unknown intelligences.

When the countdown reached fifty-seven, something exciting happened: The next number didn't come in the form of a bitmap of dots. The Ring transmitted the Arabic number 56.

"Wow, fast learner," Guan said.

The number kept on decreasing by one every ten seconds or so. A few minutes later, the number reached 0. The last message consisted of four Chinese characters:

I am a tomb.

The Rosetta System was written in a language that mixed English with Chinese. It would make sense that the Ring would

use the same language to communicate with them. It just happened that this message consisted entirely of Chinese characters. Guan Yifan typed a question into the floating window, and began the conversation between humanity and the Ring.

Whose tomb is this?
The tomb of those who created it.
Is this a spaceship?
It used to be a spaceship. But now it's dead, and so it's a tomb.
Who are you? Who is conversing with us?
I am the tomb. It is the tomb speaking to you. I'm dead.
You mean you're a ship whose crew died? In other words, you're the control system for the ship?

(There was no reply to this.)

We can see many other objects in this region of space. Are they also tombs?
Most of them are tombs. The others will be tombs soon. I don't know them all.
Are you from far away? Or have you always been here?
I'm from far away; they're also from far away, from different places far away.
Where?

(There was no answer.)

Did you build this four-dimensional fragment?
You told me that you came from the sea. Did you build the sea?
Are you saying that for you, or at least for your creators, this four-dimensional space is like the sea for us?
More like a puddle. The sea has gone dry.
Why are so many ships, or tombs, gathered in such a small space?
When the sea is drying, the fish have to gather into a puddle.

> The puddle is also drying, and all the fish are going to disappear.
>
> Are all the fish here?
>
> The fish responsible for drying the sea are not here.
>
> We're sorry. What you said is really hard to understand.
>
> The fish who dried the sea went onto land before they did this. They moved from one dark forest to another dark forest.

The last sentence was like a thunderclap. The three inside the pinnace cabin and everyone in the distant two mother ships hearing the exchange via a faint link all shuddered.

> Dark forest ... what do you mean?
>
> The same thing you mean.
>
> Are you going to attack us?
>
> I'm a tomb; I'm dead; I won't attack anyone. There is no dark forest state between spaces of different dimensions. The lower-dimensional space cannot threaten the higher-dimensional space, and the resources of the lower-dimensional space are of no use to the higher-dimensional space. But the dark forest exists everywhere between those sharing the same dimensions.
>
> Can you give us any suggestions?
>
> Leave this puddle immediately. You are thin pictures. You're fragile. If you stay in the puddle, you'll turn into tombs in no time.... Wait, there seem to be fish on your pinnace.

Guan sat there, stunned for a few seconds, and then realized that the pinnace really did have some fish. He always carried an ecological sphere with him, about the size of a fist. Inside the glass sphere was water, a tiny fish, and some seaweed; together, everything formed a carefully designed miniature enclosed ecosystem. This was Guan's favorite possession, so he had taken it with him on this adventure. If he couldn't return, this would have accompanied him into the afterlife.

I like fish. Can I have it?

How do we give it to you?

Toss it over.

The three put on the helmets for their space suits and opened the pinnace's hatch. Guan lifted the ecological sphere to his eyes. Carefully, since he was in four-dimensional space, he held the sphere by its three-dimensional edge, and gave it a final glance. From this four-dimensional perspective, every detail in the sphere was revealed, and this tiny world of life seemed even more rich, varied, and colorful. Guan swung his arm and tossed the sphere in the direction of the Ring. He watched as the small, transparent sphere disappeared in space. Then he closed the hatch and continued the conversation.

Is this the only puddle in the universe?

There was no answer. After that, the Ring remained silent and responded no more to attempts at communication.

Gravity informed them that more micrometeoroids had struck *Blue Space*. An increasing number of drifting objects, including some small-scale four-dimensional objects, possibly debris from ships or other artifacts, surrounded both ships. Captain Chu ordered their immediate return. The plan to board the Ring had to be scrapped.

Since they now knew their distance from the mother ship, the return trip could be covered twice as fast. In two hours, they were back in the vicinity of *Blue Space,* and successfully located a warped point to return home.

The explorers were treated as heroes and given a celebratory welcome—even if their discoveries appeared to yield no practical applications for the future of the two ships.

Captain Chu asked, "Dr. Guan, what do you think is the answer to the last question you asked the Ring?"

"I go back to the analogy I made before. The probability that we

managed to stumble into the only soap bubble with a diameter of forty to fifty astronomical units on the surface of a sheet of paper sixteen billion light-years across is so minuscule that it might as well be zero. I'm certain that there are other soap bubbles, probably many more."

"Do you think we'll encounter more in the future?"

"I think there's an even more interesting question: Have we encountered them before? Think about the Earth: It's been careening through space for several billion years. Is it not possible that it had entered a four-dimensional fragment in the past?"

"That would have been an astonishing sight. I find it hard to imagine that humanity had experienced it.... But I wonder if dinosaurs could have located warped points ..."

"Why are there bubbles at all? Why are there so many four-dimensional fragments in three-dimensional space?"

"It's a great mystery."

"Captain, I think it's likely a dark secret."

Blue Space and *Gravity* began to back out of the fragment. As the ships accelerated, gravity pulled them toward the ships' sterns. Guan Yifan and the science officers from both ships tried to cram as much research about the fragment as possible into the next few days and spent almost all their time in four-dimensional space. This was only in part due to the requirements of their research—they also found the confinement and claustrophobia of being in three-dimensional space unbearable.

On the fifth day after beginning acceleration, all those in four-dimensional space found themselves back in three-dimensional space in a flash without having passed through a warped point. The electromagnetic sensors on the two ships indicated that there were no more warped points aboard either ship.

Blue Space and *Gravity* were outside the fragment.

This surprised them. Based on their calculations, they should still be cruising through the fragment for another twenty hours.

Their early exit was probably due to one of two reasons: one, the fragment had sped up in a direction opposite to the ships' current heading. Two, the fragment was shrinking. The crews believed reason number two was more likely. Other than the data, they also remembered the answer from the Ring:

When the sea is drying, the fish have to gather into a puddle. The puddle is also drying, and all the fish are going to disappear.

The two ships stopped accelerating and began to decelerate at full power. Finally, they stopped at the vicinity of the boundary of the four-dimensional fragment, where it was safe.

The edge of the four-dimensional fragment was invisible. The space before them was empty, placid like the surface of a deep pool. The sea of stars that was the Milky Way shone brightly, giving no hint that a great secret was hidden close by.

But soon they did notice a strange and spectacular sight: From time to time, luminous lines appeared in the space before them. Those lines were very thin, and very straight on first appearance. They seemed to have no thickness to the naked eye, and stretched in length between five thousand and thirty thousand kilometers. The lines appeared suddenly. At first, they gave off a blue glow. Then the color gradually shifted to red, and the straight lines curved and broke into many pieces, until they finally vanished. Observation showed that these lines manifested at the edge of the fragment, as though a giant pen constantly marked out the boundary.

They launched an unmanned probe toward the region of space where the lines appeared, and by luck, the probe managed to observe one of the lines when it flashed into existence at close range. The probe was about a hundred kilometers away, rushing toward the line at full speed. By the time it arrived, the line had curled, broken up, and disappeared. The probe detected massive quantities of hydrogen and helium in the vicinity, and also some dust from heavy elements, mainly iron and silicon.

After analyzing the data, Guan and the science officers concluded that the lines were created by four-dimensional matter entering three-dimensional space. As the fragment shrank, four-dimensional matter dropped into three-dimensional space and decayed instantly. Although these bits of matter took up very little volume in four-dimensional space, their decay into three dimensions flattened the fourth dimension, causing their volume to increase greatly and expand into the form of straight lines. By their calculations, a few tens of grams of four-dimensional matter could form a line stretching almost ten thousand kilometers in three dimensions.

Based on the rate at which the boundary of the fragment was receding, in twenty days or so, the Ring would also enter three-dimensional space. The two ships decided to wait to observe such a wonder of the universe—they had plenty of time, after all. Using the glowing decay-lines as markers, the two ships cautiously proceeded, maintaining the same speed as the receding edge of the fragment.

During the next dozen or so days, Guan Yifan was absorbed in deep thought and calculations, and the science officers engaged in vigorous debates. Finally, they reached the consensus that, based on current theoretical physics, they could not do too much theoretical analysis of the four-dimensional fragment. But the theories that had been developed in the past three centuries could at least make some predictions that were confirmed by observations: A higher dimension existing in macro form decayed toward lower dimensions as inevitably as water fell over a cliff. The decay of four-dimensional space into three dimensions was the root cause of the fragment's shrinking.

But the lost dimension wasn't truly lost: It simply curled up from the macroscopic to the microscopic and became one of the seven dimensions folded up within the quantum realm.

They could again see the Ring with the naked eye. The existence of this self-declared tomb would soon end in three-dimensional space.

Both *Blue Space* and *Gravity* stopped advancing and backed off three hundred thousand kilometers. As the Ring entered

three-dimensional space, the decay process would release tremendous amounts of energy—this was why the lines that appeared earlier had given off so much light.

Twenty-two days later, the edge of the fragment receded past the Ring. The moment the Ring entered three-dimensional space, the universe seemed to be cut in half. The cut surface glowed with a blinding light, as though a star had been pulled into a line in an instant. From the spaceships it was impossible to see the end points, but it was as if God had held a T-square against the plan for the universe and sketched a line straight across from left to right. Careful observation by instruments revealed that the line was close to one AU in length, or about 130 million kilometers, almost long enough to connect the Earth with the Sun. In contrast to other lines that had been observed, this one had a thickness that was visible even from several hundred thousand kilometers away. The light emitted by the line turned from a hot bluish-white to a merely warm red, and then gradually dimmed. The line itself also became twisted and loose, breaking into a belt of dust. It no longer glowed by itself, but seemed suffused with the light of the stars, a serene silver. Observers from both ships shared a strange impression: The dust belt resembled the Milky Way in the background. What had happened seemed to be the flash of a giant camera that took a picture of the galaxy. Afterwards, the photograph slowly developed in space.

Guan felt a trace of sorrow in the face of such a majestic sight. He was thinking of the ecological sphere he had given to the Ring. It wasn't able to enjoy the gift for long. As it decayed into three-dimensional space, the Ring's internal four-dimensional structures were annihilated instantaneously. Those other dead or dying ships within the fragment would not be able to escape a similar fate in the end. In this vast universe, they could only persist for a time in the tiny four-dimensional corner.

A vast and dark secret.

Blue Space and *Gravity* sent out many probes to the dust belt. Other than scientific investigation, they also wanted to see if they could gather some useful resources. The Ring had decayed into

common elements in three-dimensional space: mostly hydrogen and helium. These could be collected as fuel for nuclear fusion. However, since these elements existed mostly in the form of gas in the dust belt, they dissipated quickly, and in the end very little was collected. There were also some heavy elements, however, and they were able to gather some useful metals.

The two ships now had to consider their own future. A temporary council formed of the crews of both *Blue Space* and *Gravity* announced that everyone could pick between continuing the journey with the two ships or returning to the Solar System.

An independent hibernation ark would be constructed and powered by one of the seven fusion reactors on the two ships. Anyone wishing to go home would board this ark and return to the Solar System after a voyage of thirty-five years. The two ships would inform the Earth of the hibernation ark's course via a neutrino transmission so that the Earth could dispatch ships to meet it upon arrival. In order to prevent Trisolaris from locating *Blue Space* and *Gravity* based on this transmission, the neutrino transmission would only be made after the hibernation ark had already been on its way for some time. If the Earth could send out ships to assist the ark with deceleration before its arrival, more of the ark's fuel could be spent for acceleration and shorten the voyage to between ten and twenty years.

Assuming the Earth and the Solar System still existed by then.

Only about two hundred people chose to return. The rest didn't want to go back to that world doomed to destruction; they would rather stay with *Blue Space* and *Gravity* and continue into the unknown depths of space.

A month later, the hibernation ark and the two ships both embarked on their new voyages. The hibernation ark headed for the Solar System, while *Blue Space* and *Gravity* planned to divert around the four-dimensional fragment and then aim for a new target star system.

The luminous glow from the fusion reactors lit up the already sparse dust belt and cast it in a golden-red hue, like a warm sunset on Earth. Everyone, whether homeward bound or heading far away, felt hot tears filling their eyes. The beautiful space sunset quickly faded, and the eternal night fell over everything.

The two seeds of human civilization continued to drift into the depths of the starry sea. Whatever fate held in store for them, at least they were starting again.

PART III

BROADCAST ERA, YEAR 7
CHENG XIN

艾 AA told Cheng Xin that her eyes were even prettier and brighter than before, and perhaps she wasn't lying. Cheng Xin had been mildly myopic before, but now she saw everything with extreme clarity, as though the world had been given a fresh coat of paint.

Six years had passed since their return from Australia, but the trials of the Great Resettlement and the intervening years seemed to have left no mark on AA. She was like a fresh, resilient plant that allowed the hardships of the past to roll off her smooth leaves. During these six years, Cheng Xin's company had developed rapidly under AA's management and become one of the prominent players in near-orbit space construction. But AA didn't look like a powerful CEO; instead, she retained the look of a lively, fun young woman. Of course, that was not unusual in this age.

The six years hadn't touched Cheng Xin either—she had spent them in hibernation. After their return from Australia, her blindness had been examined and diagnosed. It had started out as psychosomatic—the result of extreme emotional distress—but later developed into a detached retina followed by necrosis. The recommended treatment was to produce cloned retinas suitable for transplant out of stem cells developed from her DNA, but the process would take five years. Cheng Xin spending five years in

complete darkness in her extremely depressed state would have led to total breakdown, and so the doctors allowed her to hibernate.

The world had indeed been refreshed. After receiving news of the gravitational wave universal broadcast, the whole world celebrated. *Blue Space* and *Gravity* became salvation ships out of myths, and the two crews became superheroes worshipped by all. The charge that *Blue Space* had committed suspected murder during the dark battles was withdrawn, and replaced with the affirmation that it had acted in justified self-defense after being attacked. Simultaneously, members of the Earth Resistance Movement who had persisted in a hopeless struggle during the Great Resettlement were also hailed as heroes. When those resistance fighters dressed in rags appeared before the public, everyone felt hot tears in their eyes. *Blue Space, Gravity,* and the Resistance became symbols of the grandness of the human spirit, and countless worshippers seemed to think that they themselves had also always possessed such spirit.

Retaliation against the Earth Security Force followed. Objectively speaking, the good done by the ESF far exceeded that done by the Resistance. The ESF had been able to protect the big cities and other basic infrastructure. Although they had done so for the benefit of Trisolaran civilization, their efforts allowed the world to recover economically after the Great Resettlement with minimal delay. During the post-resettlement evacuation of Australia, Australia almost plunged into total chaos multiple times due to the lack of food and electricity, and it was the ESF that maintained order and kept supplies flowing, making it possible to complete the evacuation in four months. During that extraordinary, tumultuous time, if this well-equipped armed force had not been present, the results would have been unimaginably tragic. But none of these accomplishments were taken into account by the tribunals sitting in judgment over them. All ESF members were tried, and half were convicted of crimes against humanity. During the Great Resettlement, many nations revived capital punishment, and this persisted even after the return from Australia. During these five years, many former ESF members were executed, even though

many among the cheering crowd had also submitted applications to the ESF.

Eventually, peace returned, and people began to rebuild their lives. As the cities and industrial infrastructure remained intact, recovery was rapid. Within two years, the cities had eliminated the scars from the chaotic times and recovered their pre-resettlement prosperity. Everyone resolved to enjoy life.

This tranquility was premised on this fact: When Luo Ji had conducted his dark forest experiment, 157 years had passed between when he first broadcast the coordinates of 187J3X1 to the universe and when that star was destroyed. That was equivalent to the life span of a modern human. To be sure, birthrates declined to their lowest levels in recorded history because no one wanted to bring a child into a world doomed to die. But most believed that they would be able to live out the rest of their days in peace and happiness.

The gravitational wave broadcast was far stronger than the Sun-amplified radio broadcast employed by Luo Ji, but humanity soon found refuge in a new way to comfort themselves: questioning the validity of dark forest theory itself.

EXCERPT FROM
A PAST OUTSIDE OF TIME
DELUSIONS OF
COSMIC PERSECUTION:
THE LAST ATTEMPT TO INVALIDATE
DARK FOREST THEORY

For sixty-some years—the entirety of the Deterrence Era—dark forest theory formed the backdrop to human history. But scholars had always questioned it, and until the start of the Broadcast Era, there had never been any scientific proof for its validity. The existing few pieces of evidence all lacked rigorous scientific foundation.

The first piece of evidence: Luo Ji's dark forest experiment that led to the destruction of 187J3X1 and its planetary system. The supposition that the system had been destroyed by some extraterrestrial intelligence had always been controversial. The astronomical community had always voiced the loudest objections. There were two main views: One camp believed that the object observed striking the star at lightspeed was insufficient to destroy the star. The death of 187J3X1 was thus likely the result of a natural supernova. Since there was incomplete predestruction data for this star, it was impossible to say definitively whether the star possessed the requisite conditions for going supernova. Considering

the long time that elapsed between Luo Ji's broadcast and the star's explosion, there was a high probability that the event was indeed natural. A second camp conceded that a lightspeed object did kill the star, but the "photoid" might very well be a natural phenomenon in the galaxy. Although to date no second photoid had been detected, there had been observations of massive objects being accelerated to extremely high speeds by naturally occurring forces. For instance, a supermassive black hole near the center of the galaxy was perfectly capable of accelerating some small object to near the speed of light. In fact, the center of the galaxy might produce a large number of such projectiles, but due to their small size, they were rarely seen.

The second piece of evidence: the terror Trisolaris showed for dark forest deterrence. This was, to date, the most convincing proof for dark forest theory, but humanity knew nothing of the Trisolarans' own process of derivation and the evidence they relied on; so, scientifically speaking, it was insufficient to constitute direct proof. It was possible that Trisolaris submitted to a state of deterrence balance with humanity for some other unknown reason, and finally gave up the conquest of the Solar System. Many hypotheses were proposed to explain this unknown reason, and although none were absolutely convincing, none could be conclusively disproven, either. Some scholars proposed a new theory of "delusions of cosmic persecution," which argued that the Trisolarans also had no proof of the validity of dark forest theory. However, due to the extremely harsh environment they had evolved in, the Trisolarans suffered a mass persecution complex against cosmic society. This persecution delusion was similar to Medieval religions on the Earth, and was merely a faith held by a majority of Trisolarans.

The third piece of evidence: the confirmation of dark forest theory given by the four-dimensional Ring. Clearly, the Ring had obtained the words "dark forest" from the Rosetta System, specifically the section discussing human history. This phrase appeared often in historical records dating from the Deterrence Era, and it was not surprising that the Ring would use it. However, in the dialogue between the Ring and the exploration team, the

section where the concept was invoked was very brief and its exact meaning ambiguous. It was not enough to conclude that the Ring really understood the meaning of the words it used.

Since the Deterrence Era, the study of dark forest theory had developed into its own subject. Other than theoretical research, scholars also conducted large numbers of astronomical observations and built numerous mathematical models. But for most scholars, the theory remained a hypothesis that could be neither confirmed nor disproven. Dark forest theory's true believers were the politicians and the public, and members of the public mostly chose to believe or disbelieve based on their own situations. After the commencement of the Broadcast Era, more and more people leaned toward treating dark forest theory as merely a delusion of cosmic persecution.

BROADCAST ERA, YEAR 7
CHENG XIN

After the dust settled, humanity turned its attention from the universal broadcast to reflecting on the end of the Deterrence Era. A veritable flood of accusations and denunciations against the Swordholder began to appear. If Cheng Xin had activated the broadcast at the start of the droplet attack, then, at a minimum, the disaster of the Great Resettlement could have been avoided. Most of the negative public opinion, however, was concentrated on the process of choosing the Swordholder.

The election had been a complicated process—public opinion had turned into political pressure exerted on the UN and Fleet International. The public vigorously debated who was ultimately responsible, but almost no one suggested that it was the result dictated by the herd mentality of all involved. Public opinion was relatively forgiving to Cheng Xin herself. Her positive public image provided some measure of protection, and her suffering as an ordinary person during the Great Resettlement gained her some sympathy. Most people tended to think she was also a victim.

Overall, the Swordholder's decision to capitulate made history take a long detour, but didn't change its overall direction. In the end, the universal broadcast had been initiated, and so the debate over that period of history eventually subsided. Cheng Xin gradually

faded from the public consciousness. After all, the most important thing was to enjoy life.

But for Cheng Xin, life had turned into an endless torture. Although her eyes could see again, her heart remained in darkness, sunken in a sea of depression. Although her internal pain was no longer searing and heart-rending, there also was no end in sight. Suffering and depression seemed to suffuse every cell in her body, and she could no longer recall the presence of sunlight in her life. She spoke to no one, did not seek out news about the outside world, and paid no attention even to her growing company. Although AA cared about Cheng Xin, she was busy and could spend little time with Cheng Xin. Fraisse was the only one who provided the support Cheng Xin needed.

During the dark period at the end of the Great Resettlement, Fraisse and AA had been taken out of Australia together. He lived in Shanghai for a while but didn't wait for the evacuation to complete before returning to his house near Warburton. After Australia returned to normalcy, he donated his house to the government to be used as an Aboriginal cultural museum. He, on the other hand, went into the woods and built a small tent, and really took up the primitive life of his ancestors. Though he lived in the open, his physical health seemed to improve. The only modern convenience he possessed was a mobile phone, which he used to call Cheng Xin a few times a day.

These conversations consisted of a few simple sentences:

"Child, the sun is rising here."

"Child, the sunset is lovely here."

"Child, I spent the day picking up debris from the shelter-houses. I'd like to see the desert return to how it was before."

"Child, it's raining. Do you remember the smell of humid air in the desert?"

There was a two-hour time difference between Australia and China, and gradually, Cheng Xin grew used to the daily rhythms of Fraisse's life. Every time she heard the old man's voice, she imagined herself also living in that distant forest surrounded by desert, sheltered under a tranquility that kept the rest of the world at bay.

One night, the telephone roused Cheng Xin from her slumber. She saw that the caller was Fraisse. It was 1:14 A.M. in China, and 3:14 in Australia. Fraisse knew that Cheng Xin suffered from severe insomnia, and without a sleep-aid machine, she could only manage two to three hours of rest a night. Unless it was an emergency, he would never be disturbing her at a time like this.

He sounded anxious. "Child, go out and look up in the sky."

Cheng Xin could already tell something unusual was happening. In her uneasy sleep, she had been gripped by a nightmare. The dream was a familiar one: A gigantic tomb stood in the middle of a plain covered by the darkness of night. A bluish glow spilled from within the tomb and illuminated the ground nearby....

Just that kind of blue light could be seen outside.

She went onto the balcony and saw a blue star in the sky, brighter than all the other stars. Its fixed position distinguished it from the man-made structures orbiting in near-Earth orbit. It was a star outside the Solar System. Its brightness was still intensifying, and even overpowered the lights of the city around her, casting shadows against the ground. About two minutes later, the brightness reached a peak and was brighter even than a full moon. It was no longer possible to look at it directly, and the color of the light shifted to a harsh white, illuminating the city as though it were daytime.

Cheng Xin recognized the star. For almost three centuries, humans had looked at it more than at any other spot in the heavens.

Someone screamed in the leaf-building nearby, and there was the sound of something crashing to the floor.

The star now began to fade. From white it gradually dimmed to red, and about half an hour later, it went out.

Cheng Xin hadn't brought the phone with her, but the floating communication window had followed her. She could still hear Fraisse's voice, which had recovered its usual serenity and transcendence. "Child, don't be afraid. What will happen, will happen."

A lovely dream had ended: Dark forest theory had received its final confirmation with the annihilation of Trisolaris.

EXCERPT FROM
A PAST OUTSIDE OF TIME
A NEW MODEL FOR THE
DARK FOREST

Trisolaris was shattered three years and ten months after the start of the Broadcast Era. No one had expected the attack to come so soon after the gravitational wave broadcast.

Since Trisolaris had always been under intense surveillance, plenty of data was captured concerning its extinction. The attack on the Trisolaran system was identical to the attack on Luo Ji's 187J3X1: A small object traveling near the speed of light struck one of the three stars in the system and destroyed it through its relativistically amplified mass. At the time, Trisolaris had just started to revolve around the star, and the stellar explosion annihilated the planet.

When it made the gravitational wave broadcast, *Gravity* was about three light-years from Trisolaris. Taking into account the lightspeed propagation of gravitational waves, the photoid must have been launched from a point that was even closer to Trisolaris than *Gravity*—and the launch must have been practically instantaneous after receiving the coordinates. Observations confirmed this: The trail of the photoid traversing the interstellar dust cloud near Trisolaris was clearly recorded, but there were no

other solar systems within this zone of space—the only conclusion was that the photoid had been launched from a spacecraft.

The old model for dark forest theory had always assumed planetary systems around stars as the foundation. People simply assumed that attacks on systems whose coordinates had been exposed must come from other planetary systems. But once the possibility of attacks from spacecraft entered the scene, the situation became far more complex. While the locations of stars were relatively well known, humans had no information at all concerning spacecraft made by other intelligences—save for the Trisolaran Fleet. How many extraterrestrial spaceships were there? How densely were they deployed in space? How fast did they fly? What were their headings? There were no answers to these questions.

The possible sources of dark forest attacks could no longer be predicted, and the attacks might come much faster than previously imagined. Other than the surviving stars of the Trisolaran system, the nearest star was six light-years from the Solar System. But the ghostlike alien spaceships could be, at that moment, passing next to the Sun. Death, once only a figure on the horizon, now loomed before our eyes.

BROADCAST ERA, YEAR 7
SOPHON

For the first time, humanity witnessed the extinction of a civilization, and realized such a fate might befall Earth at any moment. The threat of Trisolaris, a crisis that had lasted close to three centuries, dissipated overnight, yet what took its place was an even crueler universe.

However, the anticipated mass hysteria did not occur. Faced with the catastrophe four light-years away, human society became strangely quiet. Everyone seemed to be waiting, but at a loss as to what they were waiting for.

Ever since the Great Ravine, although history had taken multiple big turns, humanity, as a whole, had always lived in a society that was highly democratic, with ample welfare. For two centuries, the human race had held on to a subconscious consensus: No matter how bad things got, *someone* would step in to take care of them. This faith had almost collapsed during the disastrous Great Resettlement, but on that darkest of mornings six years ago, a miracle had nonetheless taken place.

They were waiting for another miracle.

On the third day after witnessing the destruction of Trisolaris, Sophon invited Cheng Xin and Luo Ji to tea. She said that she had no ulterior motives. They were old friends, after all, and she missed them.

The UN and Fleet International were intensely interested in the meeting. The expectant, lost attitude prevalent in society posed a terrible danger. Human society was as fragile as a sand castle on the beach, prone to collapse with a passing gale. The leaders wanted the two former Swordholders to gather some information from Sophon that would reassure the people. In an emergency session of the PDC convened for this purpose, someone even hinted to Cheng Xin and Luo Ji that even if they couldn't get such intelligence from Sophon, perhaps it was acceptable to manufacture some.

After the universal broadcast of six years ago, Sophon had retreated from public life. Once in a while, she might appear in public, but only to serve as an expressionless speaking tube for Trisolaris. She had remained in that elegant dwelling hanging from a tree branch, though most of the time she was probably in standby mode.

Cheng Xin met Luo Ji on the bough leading to Sophon's house. Luo Ji had spent the Great Resettlement with the Resistance. Although he did not directly participate or lead any operations, he remained the spiritual center of the resistance fighters. The Earth Security Force and the droplets had made every effort to seek him out and kill him, but somehow, he had managed to evade them. Not even the sophons could locate him.

To Cheng Xin's eyes, Luo Ji appeared to have retained his upright, cold demeanor. Other than the fact that his hair and beard appeared even whiter in the breeze, the past seven years seemed to have left no mark on him. But then, without speaking, he smiled at her, and the gesture made her feel warm. Luo Ji reminded Cheng Xin of Fraisse. Though the two were completely different, they both brought with them some mountainlike strength from the Common Era, and gave Cheng Xin the sense that they could be relied on in this strange new time. Wade, the Common Era man who was as evil and vicious as a wolf and who had almost killed her, also had it—so she found herself relying even on him. It was an odd feeling.

Sophon welcomed them in front of her house. Once again, she was dressed in a splendid kimono, and she wore fresh flowers in her bun. That vicious ninja dressed in camouflage had disappeared

completely, and she was once again a woman who resembled a bubbling spring nestled among flowers.

"Welcome, welcome! I wanted to pay a visit to your honored abode, but then I wouldn't be able to properly entertain you with the Way of Tea. Please accept my humble apologies. I am so delighted to see you." Sophon bowed to them, and her words were as gentle and soft as the first time Cheng Xin had met her. She led the two through the bamboo grove in her yard, across the little wooden bridge over the trickling spring, and into the pavilionlike parlor. Then the three sat down on tatami mats, and Sophon began to set out the implements for the Way of Tea. Time passed tranquilly, and clouds rolled and unfurled across the blue sky outside.

A complex mix of feelings flooded Cheng Xin's heart as she watched Sophon's graceful movements.

Yes, she (or they?) could have succeeded in wiping them out, and had almost succeeded several times. But each time, humanity had snatched victory from the jaws of defeat through tenaciousness, cunning, and luck. After a three-century-long march, all Sophon had managed was to see her home annihilated in a sea of flames.

Sophon had known of the destruction of Trisolaris four years ago. Three days earlier, after the light from the explosion had reached the Earth, she had given a brief speech to the public. She recounted the death of Trisolaris in simple words, and made no denunciation or judgment of the cause—the gravitational wave broadcast initiated by two human ships. Many suspected that four years ago, when Trisolaris had been wiped out, those who had controlled her from four light-years away had perished in the fiery flames, but her current controllers were more likely on the spaceships of the Trisolaran Fleet. During the speech, Sophon's tone and expression had been calm. This wasn't the same as the woodenness she had shown when she had merely acted as a speaking tube, but a manifestation of her controllers' soul and spirit, a dignity and nobility in the face of annihilation that humanity could not hope to equal. People now felt an unprecedented awe toward this civilization that had lost its home world.

The limited information provided by Sophon and the Earth's own observations drew a rough picture of Trisolaris's destruction.

At the time of the catastrophe, Trisolaris was in a stable era, orbiting around one of the three stars in the system at a distance of about 0.6 AU. The photoid struck the star and tore a hole through the photosphere and the convection zone. The hole was about fifty thousand kilometers in diameter, wide enough for four Earths laid side by side. Whether as a result of a deliberate choice by the attacker or coincidence, the photoid struck the star at a point along the line where the star intersected Trisolaris's ecliptic plane. Viewed from the surface of Trisolaris, an extremely bright spot appeared on the surface of the sun. Like a furnace with its door open, the powerful radiation generated by the core of the sun shot through the hole; passed through the convection zone, the photosphere, and the chromosphere; and struck the planet directly. All life outdoors on the hemisphere exposed to the radiation was burnt to a crisp within a few seconds.

Next, material from the core of the sun erupted from the hole, forming a fifty-thousand-kilometer-thick fiery plume. The spewed material was tens of millions of degrees in temperature, and while some of the material fell back onto the surface of the sun under the influence of gravity, the remainder reached escape velocity and shot into space. Viewed from Trisolaris, a brilliant tree of fire grew from the surface of the sun. About four hours later, the ejected solar material reached 0.6 AU from the surface of the sun, and the tip of the flaming tree intersected the orbit of Trisolaris. After another two hours, the orbiting planet reached the tip of the fire tree and continued to pass through the ejected solar material for about thirty minutes. During this time, the planet might as well be moving through the interior of the sun—even after the journey through space, the spewed material was still at a blazing temperature of tens of thousands of degrees. By the time Trisolaris emerged from the fire tree, it glowed with a dim red light. The entire surface had liquefied, and an ocean of lava covered the planet. Behind the planet was a long white trail through space—steam from the boiled-off

ocean. The solar wind stretched the trail out, making the planet appear as a long-tailed comet.

All signs of life on Trisolaris had been cleansed away, but only the fuse of the catastrophe had been lit.

The ejected solar material caused drag against the planet. After passing through the material, Trisolaris slowed down, and its orbit fell lower toward the star. The fire tree acted like a claw extended from the sun, pulling Trisolaris down with each revolution. After about ten more revolutions, Trisolaris would fall into the sun itself, and the cosmic football game played between three suns would come to its end. But this sun wouldn't survive long enough to see itself emerge as the victor.

The solar eruption also lowered the pressure inside the sun, temporarily slowing down the fusion within the core. The sun dimmed rapidly until it was but a hazy outline. The giant fiery tree growing from the surface, in contrast, appeared even more striking, more brilliant, like a sharp scratch made against the inky black film of the universe. The diminished fusion meant that the core radiation no longer exerted sufficient pressure against the weight of the solar shell, and the sun began to collapse. The dim shell fell into the core, triggering a final explosion.

This was the sight witnessed by humankind three days ago on Earth.

The solar explosion destroyed everything within the planetary system: The vast majority of spaceships and space habitats trying to escape were vaporized. Only a few extremely fortunate ships that happened to be behind the two other suns, which acted as shields, were safe.

Thereafter, the remaining two suns formed a stable double-star system, but no life would witness the regular sunrises and sunsets. The cinders of the exploded star and the incinerated Trisolaris formed two vast accretion discs around the two suns, like two gray graveyards.

"How many escaped?" Cheng Xin asked softly.

"Counting the Trisolaran Fleets far from home, no more than

one-thousandth of the entire population." Sophon's reply was even softer than Cheng Xin's query. She was focused on the Way of Tea, and did not raise her head.

Cheng Xin had much more to say, words from one woman to another, but she was a member of the human race, and the chasm that now divided her from Sophon could not be crossed. She resorted to the questions the leaders had wanted her to ask. The conversation that followed would come to be known as the Conversation of the Way of Tea, which would profoundly change the subsequent progress of history.

"How much longer do we have?" Cheng Xin asked.

"We can't tell. The attack could come at any moment. But probabilistically, you should have a bit more time: maybe as long as one to two centuries, like your last experiment." Sophon glanced at Luo Ji and then sat up straight, her face expressionless.

"But—"

"Trisolaris was in a different situation from the Solar System. First, the broadcast only included the coordinates of Trisolaris. To discover the existence of Earth based on this requires examining the record of communications between the two worlds from three centuries ago. That will definitely happen, but it will take time. More important, from a distance, the Trisolaran system appears far more dangerous than the Solar System."

Cheng Xin looked at Luo Ji in shock, but the latter showed no reaction. She asked, "Why?"

Sophon shook her head determinedly. "We can never explain this to you."

Cheng Xin returned to the planned questions. "The two attacks we've seen both used photoids striking the stars. Is this a common attack method? Will the future attack on the Solar System be similar?"

"Dark forest attacks all share two qualities: one, they're casual; two, they're economical."

"Elaborate, please."

"These attacks are not part of some interstellar war, but a matter of conveniently eliminating possible threats. By 'casual,' what I

mean is that the only basis for the attack is the exposure of the target's location. There will be no reconnaissance or exploration conducted against the target beforehand. For a supercivilization, such exploration is more expensive than a blind strike. By 'economical,' what I mean is that the attack will employ the least expensive method: using a small, worthless projectile to trigger the destructive potential already present in the target star system."

"The energy within the stars."

Sophon nodded. "That is what we've seen so far."

"Any possible defenses?"

Sophon smiled and shook her head. She spoke patiently, as though to a naïve child. "The whole universe is in darkness, but we remain lit. We're a tiny bird tied to a branch in the dark forest, with a spotlight trained on us. The attack could come from any direction, at any time."

"But based on the two attacks we've seen, there may be a way to engage in passive defenses. Even some Trisolaran ships survived in the home star system behind the other suns."

"Please believe me. Humankind has no chance of surviving a strike. Your only choice is to try to escape."

"Become refugees among the stars? But we cannot manage to get even one-thousandth of our population away."

"That's still better than complete annihilation."

Not by our values, Cheng Xin thought, though she said nothing.

"Let's talk no more of this. Please don't ask more questions. I've told you everything I can. I asked my friends here for tea." Sophon bowed to the two, and then presented two bowls of green tea.

Cheng Xin had many more questions on her list. She was anxious as she accepted the tea, but she knew that asking more questions would be useless.

Luo Ji, who had said nothing so far, seemed relaxed. He appeared familiar with the Way of Tea, and holding up his bowl in the palm of his left hand, he rotated it three times with his right hand before taking a drink. He drank slowly, letting time pass in silence, not finishing until the clouds outside the window were colored a golden

324

yellow by the setting sun. He set down the bowl slowly, and said his first words. "May I ask some questions, then?"

Luo Ji's respect among the Trisolarans had been shown through Sophon's attitude. Cheng Xin noticed right away that while Sophon was gentle and friendly with her, she was awed by Luo Ji. Whenever she faced Luo Ji, her eyes revealed her feelings, and she always sat farther away from Luo Ji than Cheng Xin, and bowed to him slower and deeper.

In response to Luo Ji's question, Sophon bowed again. "Please wait." She lowered her eyes and sat still, as though deep in thought. Cheng Xin knew that several light-years away, on the ships of the Trisolaran Fleet, Sophon's controllers were engaged in an urgent debate. About two minutes later, she opened her eyes.

"Honored Luo Ji, you may ask one question. I can only affirm, deny, or tell you I don't know."

Luo Ji set down the tea bowl again. But Sophon raised her hand, asking him to wait. "This is a gesture of respect from our world to you. My answer will be true, even if the answer could cause harm to Trisolarans. But you have only one question, and my answer must be from those three choices. Please consider it carefully before you speak."

Cheng Xin gazed at Luo Ji anxiously, but the latter didn't pause at all. In a decisive tone, he said, "I've considered it. Here's my question: If Trisolaris showed certain signs of being dangerous when observed from a distance, does there exist some sign that can be shown to the universe to indicate that a civilization is harmless and will not threaten anyone else, thus avoiding a dark forest strike? Can Earth civilization broadcast such a 'safety notice,' if you will, to the universe?"

Sophon did not answer for a long time. Again, she sat still, pondering with her eyes lowered. Cheng Xin felt time flow more slowly than ever. With every passing second, her hope diminished, and she was certain that Sophon's answer was going to be *no* or *I don't know*. But abruptly, Sophon looked up at Luo Ji with clear eyes—before then, she had never even dared to meet his gaze directly—and answered without any doubt:

"Yes."

"How?" Cheng Xin couldn't help herself.

Sophon looked away from Luo Ji, shook her head, and refilled their tea bowls. "I can tell you nothing more. Really. I can never tell you anything again."

The Conversation of the Way of Tea gave the tiniest bit of hope for the expectant mass of humanity: It was possible to broadcast a safety notice to the cosmos to avoid dark forest strikes.

EXCERPT FROM
A PAST OUTSIDE OF TIME
THE COSMIC SAFETY NOTICE:
A LONELY PERFORMANCE ART

After the conversation between Sophon, Cheng Xin, and Luo Ji was publicized, everyone began to ponder the problem of how to broadcast a safety notice. Countless proposals flooded in, sent by sources as august as the World Academy of Sciences and as humble as elementary schools. It was perhaps the first time in the history of humanity that the entire species focused their mental energy on the same practical problem.

The more they thought about it, the more the safety notice turned into a riddle.

All the proposals could be divided into two broad categories: the declaratory camp and the self-mutilation camp.

The declaratory camp's basic conception, as can be intuited from the name, was a broadcast to the universe proclaiming the harmlessness of Earth civilization. Their main efforts were directed at how to express such a message. But in the eyes of most, their premise seemed foolish. No matter how well crafted the message, who in this heartless universe would believe it? The fundamental requirement for a safety notice was that the countless civilizations in the universe would trust it.

The self-mutilation camp represented the majority view. They theorized that the safety notice had to represent the truth, which implied that the notice required both "talking" and "doing." And of the two, "doing" was the key. Humanity had to pay a price for living in the dark forest and transform Earth civilization into a truly safe civilization—in other words, Earth civilization had to mutilate itself to eliminate its potential to threaten others.

Most of the self-mutilation plans focused on technology and advocated humanity to retreat from the space age and the information age and found a low-technology society—perhaps a society reliant on electricity and the internal combustion engine, such as at the end of the nineteenth century, or even an agrarian society. Considering the rapid decline in global population, these plans were feasible. In that case, the safety notice would be nothing more than an announcement that the Earth possessed a low level of technology.

More extreme ideas emerging from the self-mutilation camp proposed intellectual disablement. Using drugs or other neuromanipulation techniques, humans could lower their own intelligence. Moreover, such lowered intelligence could be fixed via genetic manipulation in future generations. As a result, a low-technology society would result naturally. Most people were revolted by the notion, but it remained in wide circulation. According to the proponents, the safety notice was equivalent to public disclosure of humanity's low intelligence.

There were other ideas as well. For instance, the self-deterrence camp advocated building a system that, once activated, would be beyond human control. The system would monitor humanity for any behavior incongruent with its self-proclaimed safe nature and initiate the destruction of the world upon detection.

This was a feast for the imagination. Countless plans competed for attention: some subtle, some strange, yet others as sinister and terrifying as cults.

But none of these plans captured the essence of the safety notice. As Sophon pointed out, a key characteristic of dark forest strikes

was their casual nature. The attacker did not bother to conduct close-range surveillance of the target. All these plans engaged in performance art with no audience. No matter how faithful the act, no one would see it except the performer. Even under the most optimistic conditions—suppose some civilizations, like doting parents, cared to observe Earth civilization up close, perhaps even devoting long-term monitoring equipment to the Solar System similar to the sophons, they would still make up only a minuscule portion of the large number of civilizations in the universe. In the eyes of the vast majority of civilizations, the sun was but a dim dot many, many light-years away, showing no distinguishing details at all. This was the fundamental mathematical reality of the cosmic dark forest.

Once, when humankind had been far more naïve, some scientists had believed that it was possible to detect the presence of distant civilizations by astronomical observation: for instance, the absorption spectral signatures of oxygen, carbon dioxide, and water vapor in exoplanetary atmospheres, or electromagnetic emissions. They even came up with whimsical notions like searching for signs of Dyson spheres. But we found ourselves in a universe in which every civilization endeavored to hide itself. If no signs of intelligence could be detected in a solar system from far away, it was possible that it really was desolate, but it was also possible that the civilization there had truly matured.

A safety notice was in reality a universal broadcast as well, and it had to ensure that all listeners would trust its message.

Take a distant star, a barely visible dot. Anyone casually glancing at it would say: Oh, that star is safe; that star will not threaten us. That was what a cosmic safety notice had to accomplish.

Utterly impossible.

Another mystery that no one seemed able to solve: Why wouldn't Sophon tell humanity how to broadcast such a safety notice?

It was understandable that the survivors of Trisolaran civiliz-ation would no longer transfer technology to humanity. After the gravitational wave broadcast, both worlds faced enmity from

the entire galaxy, even the entire universe. They were no longer each other's greatest threats, and the Trisolarans had no time to spare for the Earth. As the Trisolaran Fleet sailed farther away, the connection between the two civilizations grew ever more tenuous. But there was one fact that neither Trisolarans nor humankind could forget: Everything that had happened started with Trisolaris. They were the ones who had initiated the invasion of the Solar System; who had attempted, but failed, to commit genocide. If the Earth managed to make great leaps in technology, revenge was inevitable. Humans were likely to come after whatever new home the surviving Trisolarans found among the stars, and they might complete their revenge before the Earth was destroyed in a dark forest strike.

But a safety notice was different: If such a notice could make the whole universe believe the Earth was harmless, then, by definition, the Earth would be harmless toward the Trisolarans. Wasn't this just what they wanted?

BROADCAST ERA, YEAR 7
SOPHON

Although there were no clues for how to send out a true safety notice, and any serious research only confirmed the impossibility of such an endeavor, the public's yearning for the notice could not be stopped. Although most people understood that none of the existing proposals would work, attempts to implement them never ceased.

A European NGO tried to build an extremely powerful antenna that would take advantage of the Sun's amplification ability to broadcast their draft version of such a notice. The police stopped them in time. The six droplets in the Solar System had left six years ago, and there were no more blocks on the Sun's amplification function, but such a transmission would have been extremely dangerous and exposed the Earth's location even sooner.

Another organization named Green Saviors had several million members. They advocated humanity's return to an agrarian existence, thereby proclaiming their safety to the universe. About twenty thousand of their members moved to Australia. On this sparsely populated continent where the Great Resettlement was but a memory, they planned to create a model society. The agrarian lives of these Green Saviors were continuously broadcast to the rest of the world. In this age, it was no longer possible to find traditional farming implements, and so the tools they used had to be custom-made with funds from their sponsors. There wasn't much arable

land in Australia, and all of it was devoted to high-end, expensive foods, and so the settlers had to open up new land in desolate areas designated by the government.

It took only one week before these pioneers stopped collective farming. It wasn't because the Green Saviors were lazy—their enthusiasm alone could have sustained them through some period of diligence—rather, it was because the bodies of modern humans had changed considerably from the past. They were more flexible and agile compared to past generations, but were no longer adapted to boring, repetitive physical labor. And opening up wastelands, even in agrarian times, was an extremely physically demanding task. After the leaders of the Green Saviors suitably expressed their respect for their farming ancestors, the movement dissolved, and the idea of a model agrarian society was abandoned.

Perverted ideas about the safety notice also led to vicious acts of terrorism. Some "anti-intellect" organizations were formed to put into practice the proposal to lower human intelligence. One of these planned to add large quantities of "neural suppressors" to the water supply of New York City, which would have caused permanent brain damage. Fortunately, the plot was uncovered in time and no harm was done, though NYC's water supply was out of commission for a few hours. Of course, without exception, these "anti-intellect" organizations wanted to maintain the intelligence of their own members, arguing that they had the responsibility to be the last of the intelligent people so that they could complete the creation of a society of low-intelligence humans and direct its operation.

Faced with the omnipresent threat of death and the lure of a different state of existence, religion once again took center stage in social life.

Historically, the discovery of the dark forest state of the universe was a giant blow to most major religions, especially Christianity. In fact, the damage to religion was evident even early on during the Crisis Era. When Trisolaran civilization was discovered, Christians had to wrestle with the fact that the aliens were not in the Garden

332

of Eden, and God never mentioned them in Genesis. For more than a century, churches and theologians struggled to complete a new interpretation of the Bible and of accepted doctrines—and just when they had almost succeeded in patching up the faith, the monster that was the dark forest appeared. People had to accept the knowledge that many, many intelligent civilizations existed in the universe, and if each civilization had an Adam and an Eve, then the population of Eden must have been about the same as the current population of Earth.

But during the disastrous Great Resettlement, religions revived themselves. A new belief now became popular: In the past seventy years, humanity twice came to the brink of utter annihilation, but each time, they escaped miraculously. The two miracles, the creation of dark forest deterrence and the initiation of the universal gravitational wave broadcast, shared many characteristics: They both happened under the direction of a small number of individuals; their occurrence depended on a series of improbable coincidences (such as the fact that *Gravity, Blue Space,* and the droplets all entered the four-dimensional fragment simultaneously) ... All these were clearly signs from some deity. At the time of both crises, the faithful had engaged in mass prayer sessions in public. It was precisely such fervent demonstrations of faith that finally led to divine salvation—though just which god was responsible was a topic of endless debate.

And so the Earth turned into a giant church, a planet of prayer. Everyone prayed with unprecedented faith for another act of salvation. The Vatican led numerous globe-wide Masses, and people prayed everywhere in small groups or individually. Before meals and sleep, they all prayed for the same thing: *Lord, please give us a hint; guide us to express our goodwill to the stars; let the cosmos know that we're harmless.*

A cosmopolitan space church was built in near-Earth orbit. Though it was called a church, there was no physical building other than a gigantic cross. The two beams making up the cross were twenty kilometers and forty kilometers long, respectively,

and glowed so bright that the cross was visible from the Earth at night. The faithful would drift below it in space suits in worship, and as many as tens of thousands sometimes participated. Drifting along with them were countless giant candles capable of burning in vacuum, and the candles competed with the stars in brilliance. Viewed from the surface, the candles and the worshipping congregation seemed like a cloud of glowing space dust. And each night, innumerable individuals on the surface prayed to the cross among the stars.

Even Trisolaran civilization became the object of worship. Historically, Trisolaran civilization's image changed continuously in the eyes of humankind. At the beginning of the Crisis Era, they were powerful, evil alien invaders, but were also deified by the ETO. Later, Trisolaris gradually changed from devils and gods to *people*. With the creation of dark forest deterrence, Trisolaris's position in the eyes of humanity reached its nadir, and Trisolarans became uncivilized savages living at the pleasure of humankind. After deterrence failed, the Trisolarans revealed themselves to be genocidal conquerors. However, after the universal broadcast was initiated—and especially after the destruction of Trisolaris— Trisolarans turned into victims who deserved sympathy from humans, fellow refugees in the same boat.

After finding out about the concept of a safety notice, humans initially reacted to the news unanimously: a vociferous demand that Sophon divulge the method to broadcast a safety notice accompanied by the warning that she not commit mundicide by withholding such information. Yet soon people realized that rage and denunciations were useless against a civilization that had mastered technology far beyond humanity's knowledge and was moving farther and farther away in interstellar space. It would be far better to ask nicely, which then turned into begging. Gradually, as humans begged and begged in a cultural environment of waxing religiosity, the image of the Trisolarans transformed again. Since they possessed the secret of broadcasting the safety notice, they were angels of salvation sent by God. The only reason that humanity had not yet received such

salvation was due to insufficient expression of their faith. And so the pleas directed at Sophon turned into prayers, and the Trisolarans once again became gods. Sophon's abode became a holy place, and every day, large numbers of the faithful gathered below the giant tree. At its peak, the congregation was a group several times larger than that of pilgrims in Mecca, forming an endless sea. Sophon's house hung in the air about four hundred meters above the crowd. From the surface it appeared tiny, hidden from time to time by the cloud it generated. Occasionally, Sophon would appear—the crowd couldn't see any details, but they could see her kimono as a tiny flower in the cloud. These moments were few and far between, and they became sacred. Adherents of every faith in the crowd expressed their piety in various ways: some prayed more fervently, some cheered, some cried and poured out their hearts, some knelt, some threw themselves down and touched their foreheads to the ground. On these occasions, Sophon bowed slightly to the mass of humanity below and then quietly retreated into her house.

"Even if salvation were to arrive now, it would be meaningless," said Bi Yunfeng. "We have no shred of dignity left." He had once been one of the candidates for the Swordholder position, as well as the commander of the Earth Resistance Movement's branch in Asia.

There were still many sensible people like him pursuing in-depth research on the safety notice in all areas of study. The explorers worked tirelessly, trying to find a method built on a solid scientific foundation. But all avenues of research seemed to lead to one inescapable conclusion: If there really were a way to release a safety notice, it would require a brand-new kind of technology. The technology must far exceed the current level of science on Earth and was unknown to humankind.

Like a moody child, human society's attitude toward *Blue Space,* which had already vanished in the depths of space, transformed again. From an angel of salvation, this ship again turned into a ship of darkness, a ship of devils. It had hijacked *Gravity* and cast a sinful spell of destruction on two worlds. Its crimes were unforgivable. It was Satan in the flesh. Sophon's worshippers also

pleaded for the Trisolaran Fleet to find and destroy the two ships, to safeguard justice and the dignity of the Lord. As with their other prayers, Sophon did not respond.

Simultaneously, Cheng Xin's image in the public consciousness slowly changed as well. She was no longer a Swordholder unqualified for the position; she was again a great woman. People dug up an ancient story, Ivan Turgenev's "Threshold," and used it to describe her. Like the young Russian girl in that story, Cheng Xin had stepped over the threshold that no others dared to approach. Then, at the crucial moment, she had shouldered an unimaginable burden and accepted the endless humiliation that would be her lot in the days to come by refusing to send out the signal of death to the cosmos. People did not linger on the consequences of her failure to deter; instead, they focused on her love for humanity, the love that had caused so much pain that she had gone blind.

At a deeper level, the public's feeling for Cheng Xin was a reaction to her subconscious maternal love. In this family-less age, mother's love was a rare thing. The welfare state that seemed like heaven satiated the children's need for the love of a mother. But now, humanity was exposed to the cruel, cold universe, where Death's scythe may fall at a moment's notice. The baby that was human civilization had been abandoned in a sinister, terrifying dark forest; it cried, hoping for a mother's touch. Cheng Xin was the perfect target for this yearning, mother's love incarnate. As the public's feelings for Cheng Xin gradually melded with the thickening atmosphere of religiosity, her image as the Saint Mary of a new era once again gained prominence.

For Cheng Xin, this cut off the last of her will to live.

Life had long ago become a burden and torture for Cheng Xin. She had chosen to remain alive because she didn't want to avoid what she needed to bear—her continued existence was the fairest punishment for her great error, and she accepted it. But now, she had turned into a dangerous cultural symbol. The growing cult centered on her was adding to the fog that already trapped a lost humanity. To vanish forever would be her last act of responsibility.

Cheng Xin found the decision to be easy—effortless, really. She was like someone who had long ago planned to go on a long journey: finally, she had been relieved of her daily grind, and she was ready to pack lightly and set off.

She took out a tiny bottle: the medication for short-term hibernation. There was only one capsule left inside. It was the same drug she had used to hibernate for six years, but without an external cardiopulmonary bypass system to maintain life, it was fatal.

Cheng Xin's mind was as transparent and empty as space: there was no memory, no sensation. The surface of her consciousness was smooth as a mirror, the setting sun of her life reflected in it, as natural as any dusk.... It was right and proper. If a world could turn to dust in the snap of a finger, then the end of a person's life should be as placid and indifferent as a dewdrop rolling off the end of a blade of grass.

Just as Cheng Xin picked up the capsule in her hand, her phone rang. It was Fraisse.

"Child, the moon is very lovely tonight. I just saw a kangaroo. I guess the refugees hadn't eaten them all."

Fraisse never used the video function of his phone, as though he thought his words would be more vivid than any image. Although she knew he couldn't see her, Cheng Xin smiled. "That's wonderful, Fraisse. Thank you."

"Child, everything is going to get better." Fraisse hung up.

He shouldn't have noticed anything different. Their conversations were all this brief.

艾 AA had come that morning as well, excitedly telling Cheng Xin that her company had won the bid on another large project: building an even bigger cross in geosynchronous orbit.

Cheng Xin realized that she still had two friends. In this brief, nightmarish period of history, she had only these two real friends. If she ended her life now, how would they feel? Her transparent, empty heart tightened and cramped up, as though squeezed by numerous hands. The placid surface of the lake in her mind shattered, and the reflected sunlight burned like fire. Seven years

337

ago, she hadn't been able to press that red button in front of all of humanity; now, thinking of her two friends, she could not swallow this capsule that would bring her relief. She saw again her boundless weakness. She was nothing.

A moment ago, the river in front of her had been frozen solid, and she could have easily walked to the other shore. But now, the surface had melted, and she would have to wade through the black, icy water. This was going to be a long process of torture, but she trusted herself to walk to the other shore. Perhaps she would hesitate and struggle until the next morning, but she would swallow that capsule in the end. She had no other choice.

The phone rang again. It was Sophon. She invited Cheng Xin and Luo Ji to tea again. She was going to tell them good-bye for the last time.

Slowly, Cheng Xin put the capsule back in the bottle. She would make this appointment. This meant she had enough time to wade across the river of pain.

The next morning, Cheng Xin and Luo Ji returned to Sophon's aerial abode. They saw a gigantic crowd gathered a few hundred meters below it. Sophon had announced to the world last night that she was going to leave, and the crowd of worshippers was several times larger than typical. Instead of the usual prayers and pleas, the congregation was silent, as though waiting for something.

In front of the door to her house, Sophon welcomed them the same way.

This time, the Way of Tea was conducted in silence. They all knew that everything that needed to be said between the two worlds had already been said.

Cheng Xin and Luo Ji could both feel the presence of the people below. The expectant crowd was like a giant noise-absorbing carpet that deepened the silence in the parlor. It was almost oppressive, as if the clouds outside the window had grown more solid. But Sophon's movements remained gentle and graceful, making no

noise even when the implements came in contact with porcelain. Sophon seemed to be using her grace and elegance to counteract the heavy air. More than an hour passed, but Cheng Xin and Luo Ji did not feel the flow of time.

Sophon presented a bowl of tea to Luo Ji with both hands. "I'm leaving. I hope the two of you will take care and be well." Then she presented Cheng Xin with her bowl. "The universe is grand, but life is grander. Perhaps fate will direct us to meet again."

Cheng Xin sipped the tea quietly. She closed her eyes to concentrate on the taste. The clear bitterness seemed to suffuse her body, as though she had drunk cold starlight. She drank slowly, but finally, she was done.

Cheng Xin and Luo Ji got up to say farewell for the last time. Sophon accompanied them all the way up onto the branch. They saw that the white clouds generated by Sophon's house had disappeared for the first time in memory. Below them, the sea of expectant people still waited in silence.

"Before we say good-bye, I'm going to finish my last mission. It's a message." Sophon bowed deeply to both of them. Then she straightened up and looked at Cheng Xin.

"Yun Tianming would like to see you."

EXCERPT FROM
A PAST OUTSIDE OF TIME
THE LONG STAIRCASE

Near the beginning of the Crisis Era, before the Great Ravine had extinguished humanity's enthusiasm, the nations of the Earth had banded together and accomplished a series of great deeds for the defense of the Solar System. These gigantic engineering projects had all reached or breached the limits of the most advanced technology of the time. Some of them, such as the space elevator, the test of the stellar-class nuclear bombs on Mercury, the breakthroughs in controlled nuclear fusion, and so on, had been recorded by history. These projects built a solid foundation for the technological leap after the Great Ravine.

But the Staircase Project wasn't one of them; it had been forgotten even before the Great Ravine. In the eyes of historians, the Staircase Project was a typical result of the ill-thought-out impulsiveness that marked the beginning of the Crisis Era, a hastily conducted, poorly planned adventure. In addition to the complete failure to accomplish its objectives, it left nothing of technological value. The space technology that eventually developed took a completely different direction.

No one could have predicted that nearly three centuries later,

the Staircase Project would bring a ray of hope to an Earth mired in despair.

It would probably forever remain a mystery how the Trisolarans managed to intercept and capture the probe carrying Yun Tianming's brain.

One of the cables holding the sail to the Staircase probe had broken near the orbit of Jupiter. The craft had deviated from its planned path, and the Earth, deprived of its flight parameters, lost it to the endless depths of space. If the Trisolarans had been able to intercept it later, they must have had its flight parameters after the cable broke; otherwise, even the advanced Trisolaran technology would have been incapable of locating such a small object in the vastness of space outside the Solar System. The most likely explanation was that the sophons had followed the Staircase Project probe, at least through its acceleration leg, to gather its final flight parameters. But it seemed unlikely that the sophons had followed the craft for the remainder of its long journey. The craft had passed through the Kuiper Belt and the Oort Cloud. In these regions, it could have decelerated or been pushed off course by interstellar dust. It appeared that none of these things happened, because Trisolarans wouldn't have been able to get updated parameters. Thus, the successful interception of the probe required some measure of luck.

It was virtually certain that a ship from the First Trisolaran Fleet was responsible for capturing the probe—most likely the one ship that had never decelerated. At the time, it had been sent way ahead of the rest of the fleet so that it could arrive in the Solar System a century and a half before the other ships—but, due to its extremely high velocity, it couldn't have decelerated in time, and would have had to pass straight through the Solar System. The goal of this ship was still a mystery. After the creation of dark forest deterrence, this ship, along with the rest of the First Trisolaran Fleet, had turned away from the Solar System. The Earth had never ascertained its precise flight parameters, but if it had turned in the same general direction as the rest of the First Fleet, then it was possible that

it encountered the Staircase probe. Of course, even so, the two crafts were still at great distances from each other; without precise parameters for the probe's trajectory, the Trisolaran ship couldn't have located it.

A rough estimate—the only estimate possible given the lack of more information—would place the moment of interception between thirty and fifty years ago, but not before the Deterrence Era.

It was understandable that the Trisolaran Fleet would attempt to capture the Staircase probe. Until the very end, direct contact between the Trisolarans and humans was limited to the droplets. They would have been interested in a live human specimen.

Yun Tianming was now aboard the First Trisolaran Fleet. Most of the ships in the fleet were headed in the direction of Sirius. His exact condition was unknown: Perhaps his brain was kept alive by itself; or perhaps it had been implanted in a cloned body. But people were far more interested in a different question:

Was Yun Tianming still working for the interests of humanity?

This was a reasonable worry. The fact that Yun Tianming's request to see Cheng Xin had been approved showed that he had already integrated into Trisolaran society, and perhaps even possessed some social status there.

The next question was even more troubling: Had he participated in recent history? Did the events of the past century between the two worlds have anything to do with him?

Still, Yun Tianming had appeared at the exact moment when Earth civilization seemed to be bereft of hope. When the news became public, people's first reaction was that their prayers had been answered: The angel of salvation had finally arrived.

BROADCAST ERA, YEAR 7
YUN TIANMING

Viewed through the portholes in the elevator, Cheng Xin's entire world consisted of an eighty-centimeter-thick guide rail. The guide rail extended endlessly both above and below her, shrinking into invisibility in each direction. She had been riding for an hour already and was more than a thousand kilometers above sea level, outside the atmosphere. The Earth below her was in the shadow of night, and the continents were mere hazy outlines with no substance. The space above her was inky blackness, and the terminal station, thirty thousand kilometers away, was invisible. One felt as though the guide rail pointed to a road from which there was no return.

Although she was an aerospace engineer from the Common Era, Cheng Xin had never been in space until this day, three centuries later. It no longer required special training to ride any space vehicles, but in consideration for her lack of experience, the technical support staff suggested that she ascend in the space elevator. Since the entirety of the ride was conducted at the same speed, there would be no hypergravity. And the gravity inside the elevator car now wasn't noticeably lower—gravity would diminish gradually, until she achieved complete weightlessness at the terminal station in geosynchronous orbit. At this altitude, one would experience weightlessness only when orbiting the Earth, not when going up in a space elevator. Occasionally, Cheng Xin saw tiny dots

sweep past in the distance—probably from satellites coasting at first cosmic velocity.

The guide rail's surface was very smooth, and it was almost impossible to see motion. The elevator car seemed to be sitting still on the rail. In reality, her velocity was fifteen hundred kilometers per hour, equivalent to a supersonic jet. Reaching geosynchronous orbit would take about twenty hours, which made this a very slow journey in the context of space. Cheng Xin recalled a conversation during college where Tianming had pointed out that in principle, it was perfectly possible to achieve spaceflight at low speeds. As long as one maintained an ever-upward speed, one could go into space going as slow as a car or even walking. One could even walk up to the orbit of the moon in this manner, though it would be impossible to step onto the moon—by then, the relative velocity of the moon with respect to the climber would be more than three thousand kilometers per hour, and if one were to attempt to remain at rest with respect to the moon, the result would once again be high-speed astronautics. Cheng Xin clearly recalled that he had said at the end that it would be an amazing sight to be in the vicinity of the moon's orbit and watch the gigantic satellite sweep overhead. She was now experiencing the low-speed spaceflight he had imagined.

The elevator car was shaped like a capsule, but divided into four decks. She was in the top deck, and those who accompanied her were in the lower three decks. No one came up to bother her. She was in the luxurious business-class cabin, like a room in a five-star hotel. There was a comfortable bed and a shower, but the suite was small, about the size of a college dorm room.

She was always thinking about her time in college these days, thinking about Tianming.

At this altitude, the Earth's umbral cone was narrower, and the Sun thus became visible. Everything outside was submerged in the powerful, bright light, and the portholes automatically adjusted to decrease their transparency. Cheng Xin lay on the sofa and watched the guide rail above her through the porthole overhead. The endless straight line seemed to descend directly from the Milky Way.

She wanted to see signs of motion against the guide rail, or at least to imagine it. The sight was hypnotic, and eventually she fell asleep.

She heard someone call her name softly, a man's voice. She saw that she was in a college dorm sleeping in the bottom bunk of a bunk bed. But the room was otherwise empty. A streak of light moved across the wall, like streetlights inside a moving car. She looked outside the window and saw that, behind the familiar Chinese parasol tree, the Sun swept across the sky rapidly, rising and setting every few seconds. Even when the Sun was up, however, the sky behind it remained inky black, and the stars shone along with the Sun. The voice continued to call her name. She wanted to get up to look around, but found her body floating up from the bed. Books, cups, her notebook computer, and other objects floated around her....

Cheng Xin woke up with a start, and found herself truly floating in air, hovering a small distance above the sofa. She reached out to pull herself back onto the sofa, but inadvertently pushed herself away. She rose until she was next to the porthole in the ceiling, where she turned around weightlessly and pushed against the glass, successfully sending herself back to the sofa. Everything looked the same in the cabin, except that the weightlessness released some of the settled dust motes, and they sparkled in the sunlight.

She saw that an official from the PDC had come up from the cabin below. It was probably he who had been calling her name earlier. He stared at her, astonished. "Dr. Cheng, I understand this is the first time you've been in space?" he asked. After Cheng Xin nodded, he smiled and shook his head. "But you look like an old spacer."

Cheng Xin herself felt surprised as well. This first experience of weightlessness did not cause her discomfort or anxiety. She felt relaxed, and there was no dizziness or nausea. It was as if she naturally belonged here, belonged to space.

"We're almost there," the official said, pointing up.

Cheng Xin looked up. She saw the guide rail again, but now she could tell they were moving by its surface—a sign that they were

slowing down. At the end of the rail, the geosynchronous terminal station was coming into view. It was formed of multiple concentric rings connected together by five radial spokes. The original terminal station was just a small part in the center. The concentric rings were later additions, with the outer rings being newer. The entire structure slowly rotated in place.

Cheng Xin also saw other space buildings appear around her. The dense cluster of buildings in this region was the result of engineers taking advantage of proximity to the space elevator terminal station for transportation of construction materials. The buildings were of different shapes and appeared from the distance as a bunch of intricate toys—only when one swept past at close range could their immensity be felt. Cheng Xin knew that one of these housed the headquarters of the Halo Group, her space construction company. AA was working in it right now, but she couldn't tell which building it was.

The elevator car passed through a massive frame. The dense struts in the frame made the sunlight flicker. By the time the car emerged from the other end of the frame, the terminal station took up most of the view, and the Milky Way twinkled only from the space between the concentric rings. The immense structure pressed down, and as the car entered the station, everything dimmed as though the car was entering a tunnel. A few minutes later, bright lights illuminated the outside: The car was in the terminal hall. The hall spun around the car, and for the first time Cheng Xin felt dizzy. But as the car detached from the guide rail, it was clamped by the platform. After a slight jolt, the car began to spin along with the station, and everything around her seemed to be still again.

Cheng Xin, accompanied by four others, emerged into the circular hall from the car. As their car was the only one at the platform, the hall seemed very empty. Cheng Xin felt a sense of familiarity right away: Although information windows floated everywhere, the main structure of the hall was built from metallic materials that were rare in this age, mainly stainless steel and lead alloys. She could see the marks left by the passage of years everywhere,

and she felt herself situated in an old train station instead of in space. The elevator she had ridden was the first space elevator ever built, and this terminal station, completed in Year 15 of the Crisis Era, had been in continuous operation for more than two centuries, even through the Great Ravine. Cheng Xin noticed the guardrails crisscrossing the hall, installed to help people move around in weightlessness. The guardrails were mainly made of stainless steel, though some were made from copper. Observing their surfaces, bearing the marks of countless hands through more than two centuries of service, Cheng Xin was reminded of the deep ruts left in front of ancient city doors.

The rails were leftovers from an earlier age, since everyone now relied on individual tiny thrusters which could be worn on the belt or over the shoulders. They generated enough thrust to propel people around in weightlessness, controlled by a handheld remote. Cheng Xin's companions tried to give her a first lesson in space—how to use the weightless thrusters. But Cheng Xin preferred to navigate around by grabbing on to the guardrails. As they arrived at the exit to the main hall, Cheng Xin paused to admire a few propaganda posters on the wall. These were ancient, and most of them dealt with the construction of the Solar System defense system. In one of the posters, a soldier's figure filled most of the image. He was dressed in a uniform unfamiliar to Cheng Xin, and his fiery eyes stared at the viewer. Below him was a line of large text: *The Earth needs you!* Next to it was an even larger poster in which people of all races and nationalities stood, arms linked, to form a dense wall. Behind them, the blue flag of the UN took up most of the picture. The text on the poster read: *Let us build a new Great Wall for the Solar System with our flesh!* Although Cheng Xin was interested in the posters, they didn't feel familiar. They seemed to harken back to an older style, reminding people of an age before she had even been born.

"These were from the beginning of the Great Ravine," one of the PDC officials traveling with her said.

That had been a brief, despotic age, when the whole world had

been militarized before everything, from faith to life, collapsed.... But why had these posters been kept until now? To remember, or to forget?

Cheng Xin and the others exited the main hall into a long corridor, whose cross section was also circular. The corridor extended ahead of her for some distance, and she couldn't see to the end. She knew that this was one of the five radial spokes of the station. At first, they moved in total weightlessness, but soon, "gravity" appeared, in the form of centrifugal force. At first, the force was very weak, but it was enough to induce a sense of up and down: the corridor suddenly turned into a deep well, and instead of floating, they were falling. Cheng Xin felt dizzy, but many guardrails protruded from the wall of the "well." If she felt she was falling too fast, she could decelerate by grabbing on to one of the rails.

They passed the intersection between the spoke and the first ring. Cheng Xin looked to the right and left, and saw that the ground rose up on both sides, as though she were at the bottom of a valley. Over the entrances to the ring on both sides were red-glowing signs: *First Ring, Gravity 0.15G*. The wall of the curved corridor of the ring was punctuated by multiple doors, which opened and closed from time to time. Cheng Xin saw many pedestrians. They stood on the floor of the ring due to the microgravity, but they still moved by leaping ahead with the aid of the weightless thrusters.

After passing through the first ring, the weight increased further, and free-falling was no longer safe. Escalators appeared on the wall of the "well," one going up and one going down. Cheng Xin observed the passengers riding up and saw that they were dressed casually, indistinguishable from Earth dwellers. The wall of the well had many information windows of different sizes, and more than a few of them were broadcasting the image of Cheng Xin stepping onto the space elevator more than twenty hours ago. But at the moment, Cheng Xin's four escorts surrounded her, and she was also wearing her wide-framed sunglasses. No one recognized her.

As they descended, they passed through seven more concentric rings. As the diameter of each successive ring grew, the curvature

of the corridors to the sides became less noticeable. Cheng Xin felt as though she was passing through strata of history. Each ring used different construction material from the rings before it, and looked newer. Each ring's method of construction and decorative style formed a time capsule of an age: the repressive militaristic uniformity of the Great Ravine; the optimism and romanticism of the latter half of the Crisis Era; the hedonistic freedom and indolence of the Deterrence Era. Before the fourth ring, the cabins in the rings were integrated into the structure of the rings, but starting with the fifth ring, the rings only provided construction spaces, and the buildings in the rings were planned and constructed later as additional fixtures, showing a rich variety of styles. As Cheng Xin descended through the rings, signs of this being a space station gradually faded, and the environment resembled daily life on the surface more. By the time they reached the eighth ring, the outermost ring of the station, the construction style and scenery were indistinguishable from a small city on the surface. The corridor looked like a bustling pedestrian promenade. Add to that the standard gravity of 1G, and Cheng Xin could almost forget that she was in space, thirty-four thousand kilometers above the Earth.

But the city scene soon disappeared, as a small motor vehicle brought them to a place where they could see space again. The entrance to the flat hall was marked with "Port A225," and a few dozen small spacecraft of various designs parked on the smooth, plazalike floor. One side of the hall was completely open to space and the stars spinning around the station. Not too far away from them, a bright light started to glow, illuminating the whole port. Gradually, the light turned from orange to pure blue, and the spaceship that had turned on its engines lifted off the floor, accelerated, and shot into space from the open side of the port. Cheng Xin was witnessing a technological miracle that had become commonplace for others, but she couldn't figure out how it was possible to maintain atmosphere and pressure in space without the area being completely enclosed.

They passed by the rows of spacecraft until they arrived at a

small open space at the end of the port. There, a small spaceship—a dinghy, really—sat by itself. Next to it stood a group of people who had apparently been waiting for her. The Milky Way slowly swept by the open side of the port, and its light cast long shadows from the dinghy and those standing next to it, turning the open space into a giant clock, over which the roving shadows acted as hands.

The group next to the dinghy consisted of the special team convened by the PDC and the fleet for this encounter. Cheng Xin knew most of the members—they had attended the Swordholder handover ceremony seven years ago. The two team heads were the rotating chair of the PDC and the chief of staff for the fleet. The rotating chair was new, but the fleet chief was the same person as before. These seven years, the longest in the history of the human race had left indelible marks on their faces. No one said anything as they silently shook hands and silently remembered.

Cheng Xin examined the dinghy before her. Short-range spacecraft now came in a variety of shapes, but the streamlined profile popular in the imagination of past generations was absent. This dinghy had the most common shape: a sphere. It was so regular that Cheng Xin couldn't even tell where the thruster was. The dinghy was about the size of an old medium-sized bus. It had only a serial number and no name. This common vehicle was going to carry her to the meeting with Yun Tianming.

The meeting was to take place at the point where the Earth's and the Sun's gravities balanced each other: a Lagrangian point about 1.5 million kilometers away. The sophons would facilitate the meeting with their real-time link with the First Trisolaran Fleet. There would be both voice and video.

Why conduct the meeting in space? In an age where neutrino communication was possible, being in space wasn't much more isolated than being on the surface of the Earth. Sophon had explained the request as symbolic: The meeting should occur in an isolated environment to show that it was independent of both worlds. The Lagrangian point was chosen to allow Cheng Xin's position to be relatively stable. Also, it was the long-held custom

among Trisolarans to conduct meetings at points of balance between celestial bodies.

That much Cheng Xin already knew, but now she was told something much more important.

The fleet chief brought Cheng Xin into the dinghy. There wasn't much room inside, just enough for four people. As soon as the two of them sat down, half of the spherical hull—the part facing them—became transparent, so that they seemed to be sitting inside the helmet of a gigantic space suit. This type of dinghy was chosen in part for its open field of view.

Modern spacecraft no longer had physical controls—the controls were holographic projections—thus, the interior of the hull was completely empty. If a Common Era person came here for the first time, he or she would think this was an empty shell with nothing inside. But Cheng Xin immediately noticed three unusual objects, clearly new additions. These were three circles attached to the hull above the transparent part, colored green, yellow, and red, reminding her of traffic lights from the past. The fleet chief explained:

"These three lights are controlled by Sophon. Your meeting will be monitored throughout by the Trisolarans. As long as they believe the contents of your conversation are acceptable, the green light will stay on. If they wish to warn you about topics verging on the unacceptable, the yellow light will be lit."

The fleet chief paused, and only after a long while, as though he had to prepare himself, did he explain the red light.

"If they think you're being given information you may not receive, the red light will be lit."

He turned around and pointed to the nontransparent part of the hull. Cheng Xin saw a small metallic attachment resembling a weight used on an ancient balance.

"This bomb is controlled by Sophon. It will detonate three seconds after the red light turns on."

"What will be destroyed?" Cheng Xin asked. She wasn't thinking of herself.

"Just our side of the meeting. You don't need to worry about

351

Tianming's safety. Sophon has made it clear that even if the red light is lit, only this dinghy will explode; Tianming will not be harmed in any way.

"The red light may be lit during your conversation. However, even if the meeting completes successfully, the Trisolarans may decide, upon review of the conversation record, to turn on the red light. I'm going to tell you the most important part now—" The fleet chief paused again.

Cheng Xin's gaze remained placid. She nodded at him, encouraging him to continue.

"You must remember that the lights will not be used as a traffic light. They may not warn you before deciding that you've stepped over the line. The green light may change to a red light immediately, without going through the yellow light."

"All right. I understand." Cheng Xin's voice was soft, like a passing breeze.

"Other than the contents of the conversation, Sophon may also light the red light if she discovers recording equipment on the dinghy or some means of transmitting your conversation outside the dinghy. You may rest easy on this point. We've examined this dinghy repeatedly for recording devices, and we've eliminated all communications equipment. The navigation system isn't even capable of keeping a log. Your entire journey will be directed by the shipboard AI system, which will not communicate with the outside world prior to your return. Dr. Cheng, please think through what I've said to be sure you understand the implications."

"If I don't return, then you get nothing."

"I'm glad you see. This is what we want to emphasize. Do as they say, and only talk about private matters between the two of you. Do not mention other topics, not even through hints or metaphors. At all times, remember that if you don't return, Earth gets absolutely nothing."

"But if I do as you say and return, Earth will still get nothing. That is not what I want."

The fleet chief looked at Cheng Xin, but not directly, only at

352

her reflection on the transparent hull. Her image was superimposed against the universe, and her lovely eyes serenely reflected the stars. He seemed to see her as the center of the universe, the stars revolving around her. Once again, he forced himself to not dissuade her from taking a risk.

Instead, he pointed behind him. "This is a miniature hydrogen bomb. Under the old measurement system you're familiar with, its yield is about five kilotons. If ... it really has to happen, everything will end in a flash. You will not feel it."

Cheng Xin smiled at the fleet chief. "Thank you. I understand."

Five hours later, the dinghy began its journey. The hypergravity of 3G pressed Cheng Xin against the seat—this was the limit on the acceleration an individual without special training could bear. In a window that showed what was behind her, she saw the immense hull of the terminal station reflecting the fire from her dinghy's drive. The tiny dinghy appeared as a spark flying out of a furnace, but the terminal station rapidly shrank, and soon turned into a tiny dot. Only the Earth itself, still imposing, took up half the sky.

The special team had told Cheng Xin again and again that the flight itself would be routine, no more special than the airplane rides she used to take. The distance between the terminal station and the Lagrangian point was about 1.5 million kilometers, or one hundredth of an astronomical unit. This was considered an extremely short spaceflight, and the craft she rode in was well suited for such brief trips. Cheng Xin recalled that three centuries ago, one of the things that had lured her into aerospace engineering was a great accomplishment by humankind during the twentieth century: fifteen men had managed to step onto the moon. Their voyage had only been a fifth as long as the journey she was about to undertake.

Ten minutes later, Cheng Xin got to see a sunrise in space. The Sun slowly rose over the curved edge of the Earth. From such distance, the waves over the Pacific were invisible, and the ocean was like a mirror reflecting sunlight. The clouds appeared as soapy

foam over the mirror. From this vantage point, the Sun appeared much smaller than the Earth, like a shining golden egg being birthed by this dark blue world. By the time the Sun had completely emerged from the curved horizon, the side of the Earth facing the Sun turned into a giant crescent. The crescent was so bright that the rest of the Earth merged into dark shadow, and the Sun and the crescent seemed to form a giant symbol hovering in space. Cheng Xin thought of the mark as symbolizing rebirth.

She knew that this could very well be her last sunrise. In the upcoming meeting, even if she and Tianming faithfully followed the rules around their conversation, there was a possibility that the distant Trisolarans would not permit her to live, and she wasn't interested in following the rules at all. But she thought everything was perfect; she had no regrets.

As the dinghy progressed, the lit portion of the Earth expanded. Cheng Xin saw the outlines of the continents, and easily picked out Australia. It resembled a dry leaf floating in the Pacific. The continent was emerging from the shadow, and the terminator was right in the middle of the continent. It was morning in Warburton, and she thought of the desert sunrise seen by Fraisse from the edge of the wood.

Her dinghy swept over the Earth. By the time the curved horizon had finally disappeared over the edge of the viewport, acceleration stopped. As the hypergravity disappeared, Cheng Xin felt as though a pair of arms hugging her tightly had relaxed. The dinghy coasted toward the Sun, and the light from the Sun overwhelmed all the stars. The transparent hull adjusted and dimmed until the Sun was a disc whose brightness was no longer blinding. Cheng Xin reached out to adjust it even more, until the Sun resembled the full moon. She still had six more hours to travel. She drifted in weightlessness, drifted in the moonlight-like sun.

Five hours later, the dinghy turned 180 degrees and the engine came to life for deceleration. As the dinghy turned, Cheng Xin saw the

Sun gradually move away, and then the stars and the Milky Way swept past her vision like a long scroll. By the time the dinghy stopped, the Earth was once again at the center of her view. It now looked about as big as the moon from the surface of the Earth, and the immensity it had displayed a few hours ago was gone. Now it looked fragile, like a fetus floating in blue amniotic fluid about to emerge from the warm womb and be exposed to the frigidity and darkness of space.

With the engine turned on, gravity returned to embrace Cheng Xin. The deceleration lasted about half an hour before the drive started to pulse for precision position maneuvers. Finally, gravity disappeared again, and everything became quiet.

This was the Lagrangian point. Here, the dinghy was a satellite of the Sun, orbiting in synch with the Earth.

Cheng Xin glanced at her watch. The voyage had been planned very well. She still had ten minutes before the meeting. The space around her was empty, and she struggled to empty her mind as well. She was preparing herself for the task of memorization: The only thing that could retain anything from the meeting was her brain. She had to turn herself into an emotionless audio and video recorder so that during the next two hours she could remember as much as possible of what she saw and heard.

She imagined the corner of space she happened to be in. Here, the Sun's gravity overcame the Earth's, reaching balance, so this place held an extra measure of emptiness compared to other spots in space. She was in this emptiness of zero, a lonely, independent presence that had no connections to any other part of the cosmos.... In this way, she managed to drive her complicated emotions out of her consciousness, until she achieved the blank, transcendent state she wanted.

Not too far ahead of the dinghy, a sophon began to unfold into lower-dimensional space. Cheng Xin saw a sphere about three or four meters in diameter appear a few meters in front of the dinghy. The sphere blocked the Earth and took up most of her view. The surface of the sphere was perfectly reflective, and Cheng Xin could

clearly see the reflection of her dinghy and herself. She wasn't sure if the sophon had been lurking inside the dinghy or if it had just arrived.

The reflection on the surface of the sphere disappeared as the sphere turned translucent, like a ball of ice. At times, Cheng Xin thought it resembled a hole dug in space. Next, countless snowflake-like bright spots floated up from deep within the sphere, forming a flickering pattern on the surface. Cheng Xin recognized that this was just white noise, like the random snow seen on a television screen when there was no reception.

The white noise lasted about three minutes, and then a scene from several light-years away took its place. It was crystal clear, with no signs of distortion or interference.

Cheng Xin had entertained countless guesses as to what she would see. Maybe she would only have voice and text; maybe she would see a brain floating in nutrient fluid; maybe she would see Yun Tianming whole. Though she believed that this last possibility was practically impossible, she tried to imagine the environment Tianming would be living in. She thought of innumerable scenarios, but none was like what she actually saw.

A golden field of wheat bathed in sunlight.

The field was about a tenth of an acre. The crop looked to be doing well, and it was time for the harvest. The soil appeared a bit eerie: pure black, and the particles sparkled in the sunlight like innumerable stars. A common shovel was stuck into the black soil next to the field of wheat. It looked perfectly ordinary, and even the handle appeared to be made of wood. A straw hat woven from wheat stalks hung from the top of the shovel—it looked old and well used, and loose stalks stuck out of the worn rim. Behind the wheat field was another field planted with something green, probably vegetables. A breeze passed through, and the wheat rippled.

Above this dark-soiled scene was an alien sky—a dome, to be exact, formed of a knotty mess of intertwined pipes, some thick, some thin, all of which were leaden gray in color. Among the

thousands of pipes, two or three glowed red. The light from them was very bright, making them appear as incandescent filaments. The exposed portions of these pipes illuminated the fields and apparently provided the source of energy for the crops. Each illuminated pipe only shone briefly before dimming, to be replaced by another pipe that lit up elsewhere. At each moment, two or three pipes were on. The shifting lights caused the shadows in the field to shift constantly as well, as though the sun were weaving in and out of clouds.

Cheng Xin was taken aback by the chaotic arrangement of the pipes. It wasn't the result of carelessness; on the contrary, to create this kind of utter chaos required great effort and design. The arrangement seemed to find even the hint of a pattern to be taboo. This suggested an aesthetic utterly at odds with human values: Patterns were ugly, but the lack of order was beautiful. Those glowing pipes gave the entire knotty mess a kind of liveliness, like sunlight glanced through clouds. Cheng Xin even wondered whether the arrangement was meant to be an artistic representation of the sun and clouds. But the next moment, she felt the arrangement evoking a giant model of the human brain, and the flickering, glowing pipes represented the formation of each neural feedback loop....

Rationally, she had to reject these fantasies. A far more likely explanation was that the entire system was nothing more than a heat dissipation device, and the farm fields below only took advantage of the lights as a side effect. Going by appearance alone, and without understanding its operation, Cheng Xin intuited that the system showed a kind of engineering ideal that could not be understood by humanity. She felt mystified, but also mesmerized.

A man walked toward her from deep within the wheat field. *Tianming.*

He wore a silver jacket, made out of some kind of reflective film. It looked as old as his straw hat, but was otherwise unremarkable. Cheng Xin couldn't see his pants due to all the wheat, but they were likely made of the same material. As he came closer, Cheng Xin

357

got a better look at his face. He looked young, about the same age as when they had parted three centuries ago. But his physique looked more fit, and his face was tanned. He wasn't gazing in Cheng Xin's direction; instead, he pulled off an ear of wheat, rubbed it in his fingers, blew away the husk, and then tossed the grains into his mouth. He emerged from the field still chewing. Just when Cheng Xin wondered whether Tianming knew she was there, he looked up, smiled, and waved at her.

"Hello, Cheng Xin!" he said. In his eyes was pure joy, a very natural kind of joy, like a farm boy working in the fields greeting a girl from the same village who had come back from the city. The three centuries that had passed did not seem to matter, and neither did the several light-years separating them. They had always been together. Cheng Xin had never imagined this. Tianming's gaze caressed her like a gentle pair of hands, and her high-strung nerves relaxed slightly.

The green light above the viewport came on.

"Hello!" Cheng Xin said. A wave of emotion that had traversed three centuries surged deep within her consciousness, like a volcano preparing to erupt. But she decisively blocked off all emotional outlets, and silently repeated to herself: *Memorize, just memorize, memorize everything.* "Can you see me?"

"Yes." Tianming smiled and nodded, and tossed another grain of wheat into his mouth.

"What are you doing?"

Tianming seemed taken aback by the question. He waved at the field. "Farming."

"For yourself?"

"Of course. How else would I get to eat?"

The Tianming in Cheng Xin's memory looked different. During the Staircase Project, he was a haggard, weak, terminal patient; before then, he was a solitary, alienated college student. But though the Tianming of the past had sealed his heart to the outside world, he had also exposed his state in life—it was possible to tell, at a glance, what his basic story was. The Tianming of the present

358

revealed only maturity. One couldn't read his story at all, though he certainly had stories, stories that probably offered more twists, strange events, and spectacular sights than ten *Odysseys*. Three centuries of drifting alone in the depths of space, an unimaginable life among aliens, the countless tribulations and trials endured in body and spirit—none of these had left any mark on his body. All that was left was maturity, a sunlit maturity, like the swaying stalks of golden wheat behind him.

Tianming was a victor in life.

"Thank you for the seeds you sent," Tianming said. His tone was sincere. "I planted them all. Generation after generation, they've done well. I couldn't get the cucumbers to grow though—they're tough."

Cheng Xin chewed over Tianming's words. *How does he know that I sent him the seeds? Did they tell him? Or ...*

"I thought you would have to grow them using aeroculture and aquaculture. I never thought there would be soil on a spaceship."

Tianming bent down and picked up a handful of black soil, letting the particles seep out from between his fingers. The soil sparkled as it fell. "This is made from meteoroids. Soil like this—"

The green light went off and the yellow light went on.

Apparently, Tianming could see the warning as well. He stopped, smiled, and raised a hand. The expression and gesture were clearly intended for those listening in. The yellow light went off and the green light went on again.

"How long has it been?" Cheng Xin asked. She deliberately asked an ambiguous question that could be interpreted many ways: how long he'd been planting; or how long his brain had been implanted in a cloned body; or how long ago the Staircase probe had been captured; or something else. She wanted to leave him plenty of room to pass on information.

"A long time."

Tianming's answer was even more ambiguous. He looked as calm as before, but the yellow light must have terrified him. He didn't want Cheng Xin to be hurt.

"At first I knew nothing about farming," said Tianming. "I wanted to learn by watching others. But, as you know, there are no real farmers anymore, so I had to figure it out myself. I learned slowly, so it's a good thing that I don't eat much."

Cheng Xin's earlier guess had been confirmed. What Tianming was really saying was very clear: If the Earth still had real farmers, he would have been able to observe them. In other words, he could see the information gathered by the sophons on Earth! This at least showed that Tianming had a close relationship with Trisolaran society.

"The wheat looks really good. Is it time for the harvest?"

"Yes. This has been a good year."

"A good year?"

"Oh, if the engines are operating at high power, then I have a good year, otherwise—"

The yellow light came on.

Another guess had been confirmed. The mess of pipes in the ceiling really was some kind of cooling system for the engines. Their light came from the antimatter propulsion system on the ship.

"All right, let's talk about something else." Cheng Xin smiled. "You want to know what I've been up to? After you left—"

"I know everything. I've always been with you."

Tianming's tone was steady and calm, but Cheng Xin's heart quaked. Yes, he had always been with her, observing her life through the sophons. He must have seen how she had become the Swordholder, how she had thrown away that red switch in the last moments of the Deterrence Era, how she had endured in Australia, how she had lost her sight from extreme pain, until, finally, how she had picked up that tiny capsule.... He had gone through all these trials with her. It was easy to imagine that when he had seen her struggle through her hell from several light-years away, he must have suffered even more pain. If she had known earlier that this man who loved her had crossed the light-years to keep watch over her, she would have been comforted. But Cheng Xin had thought Tianming lost forever in the vastness of space, and most of the time, she had never believed that he still existed.

"If I had known ..." Cheng Xin muttered, as if to herself.

"You couldn't have." Tianming shook his head.

The emotions Cheng Xin had pushed deep down surged again. She forced herself to not cry.

"Then ... what about your experience? Can you tell me anything?" Cheng Xin asked. This was a naked attempt at gathering intelligence. But she had to take a step.

"Hmmm, let me think ..." Tianming pondered.

The yellow light came up. Tianming hadn't even said anything. This was a serious warning.

Tianming shook his head resolutely. "I can't tell you anything. Absolutely nothing."

Cheng Xin said nothing. She knew that as far as her mission was concerned, she had done all she could. All she could do now was to wait and see what Tianming wanted to do.

"We can't talk like this," said Tianming, and sighed. Then, with his eyes, he said more: *for your sake.*

Yes, it was too dangerous. The yellow light had gone on three times already.

Cheng Xin sighed in her heart. Tianming had given up. Her mission would be unfulfilled. But there was no other choice. She understood.

Once they had set aside the mission, this space that contained them, a few light-years across, became their secret world. Indeed, between the two of them, they needed no language; their eyes were able to say everything they needed. Now that she was no longer so focused on the mission, Cheng Xin could feel even more meaning in Tianming's gaze. She was brought back to her college days, when Tianming had looked at her often in this way. He had been discreet, but her girlish instincts had felt him. Now, his gaze was infused with his maturity, and the sunlight crossed light-years to submerge her in warmth and happiness.

Cheng Xin wanted this silence to last forever, but Tianming spoke again. "Cheng Xin, do you remember how we used to spend our time when we were little?"

Cheng Xin shook her head. The question was unexpected and incomprehensible. *When we were little?* But she successfully hid her surprise.

"So many nights, we'd call each other and chat before going to bed. We made up stories and told them to each other. You always made up better stories. How many stories did we tell each other? At least a hundred?"

"Yes, I think so. A lot." Cheng Xin used to be unable to lie, but she was surprised to find herself performing well.

"Do you remember any of those stories?"

"Not many. I've moved far away from childhood."

"But it's not so far away from me. During these years, I've told those stories—yours and mine—again and again."

"To yourself?"

"No, not to myself. I came here, and I felt the need to give this world something. But what? After much thinking, I decided that I could bring childhood to this world, and so I told them our stories. The children here love them. I even put out a collection, *Fairy Tales from Earth,* which was very popular. This book belongs to both of us—I didn't plagiarize you; all the stories you told me still have your name in the byline. So you're a famous author here."

Based on the still very limited knowledge humans had of the Trisolarans, sex among them involved the two partners melding their bodies into one. Thereafter, the combined body would split into three to five new lives. These were their descendants, and the "children" referred to by Tianming. But these individuals inherited part of their parents' memories, and were relatively mature at birth, which differentiated them from human children. Trisolarans really didn't have childhood. Both Trisolaran and human scholars believed that this biological difference was one of the root causes of the great differences between their cultures and societies.

Cheng Xin became anxious again. She knew now that Tianming had not given up, and the key moment was here. She had to do something, but she had to be very, very careful. Smiling, she said,

"Although we can't talk about anything else, surely we can talk about those stories. Those belong only to us."

"The stories I made up or the ones you made up?"

"Tell the ones I made up. Bring me back to my childhood." Cheng Xin did not hesitate at all. Even she was surprised at how quickly she had caught on to Tianming's plan.

"All right. Then let's not talk about anything else. Just the stories. Your stories." Tianming spread his hands and looked up, clearly addressing those monitoring the conversation. His meaning was clear: *You shouldn't object to this, right? Everything is safe.* Then he turned to Cheng Xin. "We have about an hour. Which story? Hmmm ... how about 'The New Royal Painter'?"

And so, Tianming began to tell the story. His voice was deep and soothing, as though he was chanting an ancient song. Cheng Xin tried hard to memorize, but she was gradually absorbed by the story. Much time passed as Tianming spun his fairy tale. He told three stories, all connected to each other: "The New Royal Painter," "The Glutton's Sea," and "Prince Deep Water." After he finished the last story, the sophon put up a countdown, indicating that they had only one minute left.

The moment of parting was at hand.

Cheng Xin awakened from the dream of the fairy tales. Something struck her heart hard, and it was almost unbearable. She said, "The universe is grand, but life is grander. We're certain to meet again." Only when she was done did she realize she had almost repeated Sophon's farewell.

"Then let's pick a spot to meet, somewhere other than the Earth, somewhere in the Milky Way."

"How about at the star you gave me? Our star." Cheng Xin didn't even need to think.

"All right. At our star!"

As they gazed at each other across the light-years, the countdown reached zero, and the image disappeared, returning to the snow of white noise. Then the unfolded sophon turned purely reflective again.

The green light went off. Now none of the lights were on.

Cheng Xin understood that she was now on the precipice of death. On a ship in the First Trisolaran Fleet several light-years away, the conversation between her and Tianming was being replayed and examined. The red light of death could go on at any moment, and there would be no warning yellow light.

Against the unfolded spherical surface of the sophon, Cheng Xin saw the reflection of her own dinghy and herself. The half of her dinghy facing the sophon was completely transparent, like an intricate locket dangling from a necklace, and she herself was a picture placed in the locket. She was dressed in a snow-white lightweight space suit, and she appeared pure, youthful, beautiful. She was surprised by her own eyes: clear, placid, showing nothing of the surging waves inside her. She felt comforted as she imagined this lovely locket hanging on Tianming's heart.

After an unknown amount of time had passed, the sophon disappeared. The red light did not come on. The space outside looked the same as before: The blue Earth appeared again in the distance, and behind it the Sun. They were witness to all.

She felt hypergravity again. The dinghy's thruster was accelerating, and she was going home.

During the few hours of the return voyage, Cheng Xin adjusted the dinghy's hull so that it was completely solid. She sealed herself in and turned herself into a memorization machine. Again and again, she repeated Tianming's words and his stories. The acceleration stopped; the dinghy coasted; the thruster turned around; the dinghy decelerated—she didn't notice any of it. Finally, after a series of tremors, the door opened, and the terminal station port's light spilled in.

Two of the officials who had accompanied her to the station met her. Their faces were impassive. After a simple greeting, they brought Cheng Xin across the port to a sealed door.

"Dr. Cheng, you need to rest. Don't dwell on the past. We never held much hope that you'd get anything of use," the PDC official said. And then he gestured for Cheng Xin to enter the sealed door that had just opened.

Cheng Xin had thought this was the exit to the port, but she found herself in an extremely small room. All the walls were made of some dark metal. After the door closed behind her, she couldn't even see the seams. This was not a place of rest. It was simply furnished, with a small desk and a chair. On top of the desk was a microphone. Microphones were rarely seen in this age, and only used for high-fidelity recording. The air in the room had an acrid smell, almost sulfuric, and her skin felt itchy—the air was clearly heavy with static electricity.

The room was filled with people: All the members of the special team were here. As soon as the two officials who had received her entered, their expressions changed. They now looked as anxious and concerned as the rest.

"This is a blind zone for the sophons," someone said to Cheng Xin. Only then did she realize that humans had finally achieved the technology to shield themselves from the ever-present listeners, though it was only possible within extremely confined spaces like this one.

The fleet chief said, "Please recite the entirety of your conversation. Don't omit any details that you can recall. Every word may be important."

Then the members of the special team left the room one by one. The last to depart was an engineer who explained to Cheng Xin that the walls of the sophon-free room were all electrified, and she should be careful to not touch them.

Only Cheng Xin was left. She sat down at the desk and began to record everything she could remember. An hour and ten minutes later, she was done. She drank a bit of water and milk, took a brief break, and began to record a second time, then a third. When she was ready to record for the fourth time, she was asked to recount the events backwards, with the latest events first. The fifth recording was done under the guidance of a team of psychologists. They used some drug to keep her in a semi-hypnotized state, and she didn't even know what she said. Before she knew it, more than six hours had passed.

After she had finished the last recounting, the special team filled the room again. They embraced Cheng Xin and shook her hand. Hot tears flowed, and they told her she had accomplished a heroic deed. But Cheng Xin remained numb, like a memorization machine.

Only when she had returned to the comfortable cabin in the space elevator did the memorization machine in her brain shut off. She became a person again. Extreme exhaustion and waves of emotion overwhelmed her, and as she faced the approaching blue sphere of the Earth, she began to cry. Only one voice echoed in her mind:

Our star. Our star ...

At that moment, on the surface more than thirty thousand kilometers below, Sophon's house went up in flames. The robot that had been Sophon's avatar was burnt up as well. Before this, she had proclaimed to the world that all the sophons in the Solar System would be withdrawn.

People only half-believed Sophon. It was likely that only the robot was gone, but a few sophons remained on the Earth and in the Solar System. But it was also possible that she was telling the truth. Sophons were precious resources. What remained of Trisolaran civilization was in a fleet of spaceships, and they wouldn't be able to construct any new sophons for a long, long time. Besides, keeping watch over the Solar System and the Earth no longer had much meaning. If the fleet entered a blind region for the sophons, they might lose the sophons in the Solar System forever.

If the last situation occurred, then the Trisolarans and humanity would lose all contact, and once again become cosmic strangers. A three-century-long history of warfare and resentment would turn into so much ephemera in the universe. Even if they were to meet again because of fate—as Sophon had predicted—it would be in the distant future. But neither world knew if they had a future.

BROADCAST ERA, YEAR 7
YUN TIANMING'S
FAIRY TALES

The first meeting of the Intelligence Decipherment Committee (IDC) was also conducted in a sophon-free room. Although most people now favored the view that the sophons were gone, and the Solar System and the Earth were now "clean," they still took this precaution. Their main concern was that if the sophons were still present, they might endanger Yun Tianming.

The conversation between Tianming and Cheng Xin was publicized, but the real intelligence given by Tianming, the content of the three fairy tales, was kept in absolute secrecy. For a transparent, modern society, keeping such important information secret was a difficult task for both the UN and Fleet International. But the nations of the world soon reached consensus on this point: If the fairy tales were revealed, the world would be swept up by the enthusiasm of trying to decipher them, thereby exposing Tianming. The safety of Tianming wasn't just important for him individually, he, to date, the only person embedded in an alien society. His position was irreplaceable for humanity's future survival.

The secret decipherment of Tianming's message was another sign of the UN's authority and operational capabilities; it was another step on the way to a world government.

This sophon-free room was larger than the one Cheng Xin had used on the terminal station, though it wasn't by any means spacious for a conference room. The force field necessary to keep sophons out could enclose only a limited volume.

About thirty people were in attendance. Other than Cheng Xin, two other Common Era individuals were also present: the particle-accelerator engineer Bi Yunfeng and the physicist Cao Bin—both former candidates for the Swordholder position.

Everyone wore high-voltage protective suits because the metallic walls of the sophon-free room were electrified. In particular, everyone was required to wear protective gloves, lest someone tap a wall out of habit, in an attempt to summon an information window. No electronics could function within the force field, thus the room had no information windows at all. To help the force field stay evenly distributed, equipment within the room was reduced to a minimum. Only chairs were provided, and there was no table. Since the protective suits were requisitioned from electrical engineers, the meeting within the metallic room resembled an ancient pre-shift gathering on a factory floor.

No one complained about the crowded, rough conditions, or the acrid smell in the air and the tingling on the skin brought about by the electrified air. After living for nearly three centuries under the constant surveillance of the sophons, being free of the alien voyeurs brought a sudden, fresh sense of relief. The ability to shield space from sophons had been developed soon after the Great Resettlement. It was rumored that those who had entered the very first sophon-free room came down with something called "screen syndrome": They talked incessantly as if they were drunk, and bared all their secrets to their companions. A reporter described the condition this way: "In this narrow slice of heaven, the people opened their hearts. Our gazes were no longer veiled."

The IDC was a combined effort by Fleet International and the UN PDC to decipher Yun Tianming's message. It oversaw the work of twenty-five working groups focusing on different subjects and

areas of expertise. The attendees at this meeting were not experts or scientists, but the IDC committee members, who were also the leaders of the working groups.

The IDC chair first thanked Yun Tianming and Cheng Xin on behalf of Fleet International and the UN. He called Tianming the bravest warrior in the history of the human race. He was the first human to successfully survive in an alien world. Alone, deep in the heart of the enemy, situated in an unimaginable environment, he fought on and brought hope to an Earth in crisis. Cheng Xin, on the other hand, had successfully retrieved the intelligence from Tianming through a combination of wits and guts.

In a soft voice, Cheng Xin requested a chance to speak. She stood up and surveyed all those present. "All this is the result of the Staircase Project. This endeavor cannot be separated from a particular man. Three centuries ago, his steadfastness, decisive leadership, and peerless creativity allowed the Staircase Project to overcome multiple difficulties and become reality. The man I'm talking about is Thomas Wade, chief of the PDC Strategic Intelligence Agency. I think we should thank him as well."

The conference room sank into silence. No one seconded Cheng Xin's suggestion. For most people, Wade was the very symbol of the darkness in Common Era human nature, the very antithesis of the lovely woman—who had almost been killed by Wade—standing in front of them. They shivered just thinking about him.

The chair—he happened to also be the PIA's current chief, a successor to Wade's position, though they were divided by three centuries—said nothing in response to Cheng Xin's proposal. He simply continued down the agenda for the meeting. "The committee has established a basic principle and hope for the decipherment process. We believe the message is unlikely to contain any concrete technical information, but will more likely point out the correct direction for research. It may contain the guide to the correct theoretical framework for unknown technologies such as lightspeed spaceflight or the cosmic safety notice. If we can get that far, it will bring tremendous hope to humanity.

"In total, we gathered two pieces of intelligence: the conversation between Dr. Cheng and Yun Tianming, and the three stories he told. Preliminary analysis points to the important information being hidden entirely within the three stories. We won't be paying much attention to the conversation in the future, but I will summarize what we've gleaned from it here.

"First, we know that in order to send this message, Yun Tianming had to do a lot of preparatory work. He created over a hundred fairy tales, and mixed in three containing secret intelligence. He told these stories and published them over a long period of time to familiarize the Trisolarans with them—no easy task. If the Trisolarans hadn't discovered the secrets contained within them during that process, they'll likely continue to treat these stories as harmless in the future. But even so, he tried to place yet another layer of protection around the stories."

The chair turned to Cheng Xin. "I want to ask a question. Did you really know each other as kids, as Tianming said?"

Cheng Xin shook her head. "No. We met only in college. He and I did come from the same city, but we didn't go to the same primary or secondary schools."

"That bastard! His lie could have killed Cheng Xin!" yelled AA, who was sitting next to Cheng Xin. The others gave her angry looks. She wasn't a member of the IDC, and was allowed to attend only at Cheng Xin's insistence as her assistant. AA had once been an accomplished astronomer, but because her CV wasn't very long, the others looked down on her. They all thought Cheng Xin ought to have someone more qualified to be her technical aide, and even Cheng Xin herself sometimes forgot that AA was a scientist.

A PIA officer said, "He didn't take a great risk with the lie. Their childhoods predated the Crisis Era, before the sophons had even arrived on the Earth. And back then they couldn't have been targets of sophon surveillance."

"But they could check records from the Common Era."

"It's not so easy to get records of two children from before

370

the Crisis Era. Even if they somehow managed to check the household registration records or school records and found out that they hadn't gone to the same elementary school or middle school, they still couldn't rule out the possibility that they did know each other. And there's something else you aren't thinking of." The PIA officer didn't bother hiding his contempt for AA's lack of professional experience. "Tianming could direct the sophons. He must have checked the records already."

The chair continued. "The risk had to be taken. By attributing the three stories to Cheng Xin, he further convinced the enemy that these tales were innocuous. During the hour it took to tell the stories, the yellow light never came on. We also found out that by the time Tianming finished telling the last story, the deadline set by Sophon had already elapsed. The Trisolarans had, as a gesture of compassion, extended the encounter by six minutes so that Tianming could finish his story. This confirms that they really thought the stories harmless. Tianming credited her for a specific reason: to show us that the three stories contained important intelligence.

"There's not much else that we could get out of the conversation. We do all agree that Tianming's final words are very important." The chair waved his right hand in the air out of habit, in an attempt to invoke an information window. After noticing that there was no response, he went on awkwardly. "'Then let's pick a spot to meet, somewhere other than the Earth, somewhere in the Milky Way.' He meant two things by this: One, he was hinting that he would never be able to return to the Solar System. Two—" The chair paused, and waved his hand again, as if trying to dispel something. "It's not important. Let's just go on."

The air in the room grew heavier. Everyone knew what the chair was going to say: *Yun Tianming had very little faith that the Earth would survive.*

A document with a blue cover was distributed to the attendees. In this age, it was very rare to see paper documents. There was only a serial number, no title.

"The document can only be read in here. Do not bring it outside this room, and do not record it in any way. For most of you, this will be your first time reading it. Let's begin."

The room quieted. Everyone started to read these three fairy tales that might save human civilization.

THE FIRST TALE OF
YUN TIANMING
"THE NEW ROYAL PAINTER"

A long time ago, there was a kingdom called the Storyless Kingdom.

This kingdom had no stories. For a kingdom, not having any stories was a good thing. The people of such a kingdom were the happiest. Stories meant twists and catastrophes.

The Storyless Kingdom had a wise king, a kind queen, a group of just, capable ministers, and hardworking, honest common people. Life in the kingdom was as placid as a mirror: Yesterday was like today, and today is like tomorrow; last year was like this year, and this year is like next year. There were never any stories.

Until the princes and the princess grew up.

The king had two sons: Prince Deep Water and Prince Ice Sand. He also had a daughter: Princess Dewdrop.

As a child, Prince Deep Water had gone to Tomb Island in the middle of the Glutton's Sea and never returned. As for why, that's a story for later.

Prince Ice Sand grew up by the side of the king and queen, and they worried about him a great deal. The child was smart, but from a young age, he showed a cruel streak. He directed the servants to collect small animals from outside the palace, and he pretended he was the emperor of the animals. His "subjects" were his slaves,

and if they disobeyed him even a little, he ordered them beheaded. Often, at the end of one of his play sessions, all the animals were dead, and he stood in a pool of blood, laughing hysterically....

As he grew older, the prince became more restrained. He was a man of few words, and his gaze was somber. But the king knew that the wolf had only hidden his teeth, and in Prince Ice Sand's heart was a hibernating poisonous snake, waiting for the right moment to emerge. Ultimately, the king decided to not make him the crown prince, instead designating Princess Dewdrop the heir apparent. The Storyless Kingdom would eventually have a queen regnant.

If the good character the king and queen passed on to their children was a fixed quantity, then Princess Dewdrop must have inherited the portion Prince Ice Sand lacked. She was smart, kind, and beautiful beyond measure. When she walked about during the day, the sun dimmed its light, shamed by the comparison; when she took a stroll at night, the moon opened its eyes wide to get a better look; when she spoke, the birds stopped twittering to listen; and when she traipsed over barren ground, flowers bloomed. The people loved the thought of having her as their queen, and the ministers were certain to dedicate themselves to helping her. Even Prince Ice Sand voiced no objections, though his gaze became even more somber and cold.

And so, story came to the Storyless Kingdom.

The king made his announcement about the new plan of succession on his sixtieth birthday. On that night, the kingdom celebrated: Fireworks turned the sky into a splendid garden, and the brilliant lights everywhere transformed the palace into a crystalline, magical place. There was laughter and joyful conversation everywhere, and wine flowed like rivers....

Everyone was happy, and even Prince Ice Sand's cold heart seemed to have melted. Contrary to his typical moody silence, he humbly wished his father a happy birthday, and expressed his desire that the king live as long as the sun, bathing the kingdom with his light. He also declared his support for the king's decision, saying that Dewdrop really was better suited to be the monarch than he.

He congratulated his little sister and said he hoped that she would learn more of the skills for ruling a kingdom from their father so that she could discharge her future duties well. His sincerity and generosity moved everyone present.

"My son, I'm greatly pleased to see you like this," the king said, and caressed the prince's head. "I want it to be like this moment, always."

A minister suggested that a large painting of the scene should be made and hung in the palace to help remember this night.

The king shook his head. "The royal painter is old. The world is shrouded by a fog in his eyes, and his hands tremble so much that he can no longer capture the joy in our faces."

"I was just about to get to that." Prince Ice Sand bowed deeply. "Father, allow me to present you with a new painter."

The prince turned and nodded, and the new painter came in. He was an older boy, about fourteen or fifteen years of age. Wrapped in a friar's gray hooded mantle, he resembled a terrified mouse among the bejeweled guests standing in the splendor of the palace. As he approached, he huddled and compressed his already-thin body to be even smaller, as though he were trying to avoid invisible brambles all around him.

The king was a bit disappointed by the sight. "He's so young! Does he have enough skill?"

The prince bowed again. "Father, this is Needle-Eye, from He'ershingenmosiken. He's the best student of the great painter Master Ethereal. He began studying with the master at the age of five, and after ten years, has learned everything the great man can teach him. He is as sensitive to the colors and shapes of the world as we are to a red-hot branding iron. This sensitivity is then fixed and expressed by his paintbrush. Other than Master Ethereal himself, there is none with such skill in the world." The prince turned to Needle-Eye. "As the royal painter, you may look at the king directly without a breach in etiquette."

Needle-Eye looked up at the king, and then lowered his eyes again.

The king was surprised. "Child, your gaze is as piercing as a sword unsheathed next to a roaring fire. It's at odds with your youth."

Needle-Eye spoke for the first time. "Your Majesty, dread sovereign, please excuse a lowly painter if he has given offense. My eyes are a painter's eyes. A painter must paint first in the heart. I have already drawn in my heart an image of you, and of your dignity and wisdom. These I will transfer to the painting."

"You may also look at the queen," the prince said.

Needle-Eye looked at the queen, then lowered his eyes. "Your Majesty, most honored queen, please forgive a lowly painter's breach of decorum. I have already drawn in my heart an image of you, and of your nobility and elegance. These I will transfer to the painting."

"Look at the princess, the future queen regnant. You must paint her as well."

Needle-Eye took even less time to look at the princess. After the briefest of glances, he lowered his head and said, "Your Royal Highness, beloved princess of the people, please condone my lapse in courtly habits. Your beauty pains me like the midday sun, and I will, for the first time, feel the inadequacy of my paintbrush. But I have already drawn in my heart an image of you, and of your nonpareil loveliness. These I will transfer to the painting."

Then the prince asked Needle-Eye to look at each minister. He did, resting his gaze only briefly on each face. He lowered his eyes. "Your Honors, please excuse a lowly painter's offenses. I have already drawn in my heart an image of you, and of your talents and intellects. These I will transfer to the painting."

The celebration continued, and Prince Ice Sand pulled Needle-Eye into a corner. In a whisper, he asked, "Have you memorized all of them?"

Needle-Eye kept his head low, his face entirely hidden within the shadow of his hood. The cape appeared empty, containing only shadows and no substance. "Yes, my king."

"Everything?"

"Everything, my king. I can now paint a picture of each strand of hair on their bodies and head, and it will be an exact replica of the original."

The celebration ended after midnight. The lights in the palace went out, one after another. It was the darkest hour before dawn: The moon had already set, and dark clouds, like a curtain, veiled the sky from west to east. The earth was submerged in ink. A chill wind blew through, and birds shivered in their nests, while terrified flowers folded their petals together.

Like ghosts, two horses emerged from the palace and sped west. The riders were Needle-Eye and Prince Ice Sand. They came to an underground bunker a few miles from the palace. It seemed sunken into the deepest sea of night: dank, gloomy, like the belly of a cold-blooded beast in deep slumber. Their two shadows swayed and flickered in torchlight, and their bodies were but two dark spots at the end of the long shadows. Needle-Eye took a scroll out of a canvas bag and unrolled it: a painting, about as long as a man was tall. It was the portrait of an old man. White hair and beard surrounded his face like silver flames, and his piercing gaze was very similar to Needle-Eye's, though endowed with more depth. The portrait showed off the skill of the painter—lifelike, with every detail captured.

"My king, this is—was—my teacher, Master Ethereal."

The prince nodded. "Excellent. It was a smart decision to paint him first."

"Yes, I had to, so that he would not paint me first." With great care, Needle-Eye hung the portrait on the damp wall. "All right, now I can get to work on the new pictures for you."

From a corner of the bunker, Needle-Eye retrieved a roll of something snowy white. "My king, this is a section of the trunk of a snow-wave tree of He'ershingenmosiken. When the tree reaches a hundred years of age, the trunk can be unrolled like paper— the perfect medium for painting. My magic is only effective when

377

I paint on snow-wave paper." He placed the roll on a stone table, unrolled a section, and pressed it under an obsidian slab. Then he took a sharp knife and cut the paper against the edge of the slab. When he lifted off the slab, the section of cut paper was pressed flat against the table. The pure white surface seemed to glow by itself.

The painter retrieved his implements from the canvas bag and laid them out. "My king, look at these brushes, made from the ear tufts of the wolves found in He'ershingenmosiken. The paints are also from there: The red is made from the blood of giant bats; the black is the ink of squids caught in the deep sea; the blue and the yellow are extracted from meteorites.... All the paints must be mixed with the tears of a species of giant bird called the moon-blanket bird—"

"Just get on with it," the prince said.

"Of course, of course. Who should I paint first?"

"The king."

Needle-Eye picked up his brush. He worked casually, a dab here, a streak there. Gradually, various colors appeared on the paper, but no shape could be discerned. It was as if the paper had been laid out in a multicolored rain, and drops of all hues continuously fell onto the paper. Over time, the paper was filled with colors— a chaotic swirl, like a garden trampled by rampaging horses. The brush continued to glide through this maze of colors, as though the painter's hand no longer guided it, but it was leading the painter's hand. Puzzled, the prince watched from the side. He wanted to ask questions, but the movements of the colors emerging and gathering had a hypnotic effect, and he was mesmerized.

Then, in a moment, as though a rippling surface suddenly froze, all the random spots connected to each other, and all the colors had meaning. Shapes appeared, and quickly turned crystal clear.

The prince saw a portrait of the king. The king was dressed like he had been earlier at the palace: a golden crown on his head and a magnificent ceremonial robe draped over his body. But the expression on his face was different: There was no longer dignity and wisdom in his eyes. Instead, a complex mixture of emotions

could be detected: awakening from a dream, confusion, shock, sorrow ... and behind them all was a terror that couldn't be fully expressed, as though his closest companion was attacking him with a sword.

"The portrait of the king is finished," said Needle-Eye.

"Very good." The prince nodded at the portrait. The torches reflected in his irises, as though his soul burned in deep wells.

Miles away in the palace, the king disappeared from his bedchamber. In his bed, held up by posts carved into the shapes of four gods, the blankets still retained his body heat, and the sheets still retained the impression of his weight. But of his body, there was no trace.

The prince picked up the finished painting and threw it on the floor. "I will have this mounted and framed and hang it on the wall here. I'll come here from time to time to look at it. Paint the queen next."

Needle-Eye flattened another sheet of snow-wave paper with the obsidian slab, and began to paint the queen's portrait. This time, the prince did not stand to the side to observe, but paced around in the bunker. The empty space echoed with his repetitive footsteps. This time, the painting was done in only half the time it took to do the first.

"My king, the portrait of the queen is finished."

"Very good."

In the palace, the queen disappeared from her bedchamber. In her bed, held up by posts carved into the shapes of four angels, the blankets still retained her body heat, and the sheets still retained the impression of her weight. But of her body, there was no trace.

In the garden outside the palace, a hound seemed to detect something and barked loudly a few times. But the sounds were instantaneously swallowed up by the boundless darkness, and it

fell silent in fear. Trembling as it shrank into seclusion, it melded with the night.

"Is the princess next?" asked Needle-Eye.

"No, paint the ministers first. They are more dangerous. Of course, paint only those ministers who are loyal to my father. Do you remember them?"

"Of course, I remember everything. I can paint a picture of each strand of hair on their bodies and head—"

"Just do it. Hurry. You must finish before sunrise."

"That will not be a problem, my king. Before dawn, I will paint a portrait of each minister loyal to the old king, and the princess."

Needle-Eye flattened several sheets of snow-wave paper and began to paint like mad. Every time he finished a portrait, the subject disappeared from his or her bed. As the night flew by, the enemies of Prince Ice Sand turned one by one into pictures on the wall of the bunker.

Princess Dewdrop was awakened by insistent, loud knocks. No one had ever dared to knock on her door like this before. She got up and came to the door, which had just been opened by Auntie Wide.

Auntie Wide had been Dewdrop's wet nurse, and then cared for her as she grew up. The princess felt closer to her than even her own mother, the queen. Auntie Wide stared at the captain of the palace guards outside the door, whose armor still gave off the chill air of the night.

"Have you gone mad? How dare you wake the princess! She hasn't been sleeping well the last few nights."

The captain ignored Auntie Wide. He bowed slightly to Dewdrop. "Princess, someone wants to see you." Then he stepped aside, revealing an old man.

The old man's white hair and beard surrounded his face like silver flames. His gaze was both sharp and deep. This was the

man who had been in the first portrait shown to the prince by Needle-Eye. His face and cape were caked with grime, his boots were covered in mud, and he carried a large canvas bag on his back; clearly, he had been on a long journey.

But, oddly, he was holding up an umbrella. Stranger still was the fashion in which he held it: The umbrella spun nonstop in his hand. A closer examination of the umbrella revealed his reason: The pole and the canopy were both pure black, and at the tip of each rib was a small sphere made of some translucent, weighty stone. The stretchers for the ribs within the umbrella were all broken and could not hold the canopy up. Only by spinning the umbrella continuously to make the stones fly up could the canopy be kept open.

"How can you allow random strangers in here? And such a strange old man at that," said Auntie Wide.

"The sentries stopped him, of course, but he said"—the captain of the guards gave an anxious look to the princess—"that the king is already gone."

"What are you talking about? You *are* mad!" Auntie Wide shouted.

But the princess said nothing. Her hands clutched at the front of her nightgown.

"But the king really has disappeared, as has the queen. My men said that both bedchambers were empty."

The princess cried out and held on to Auntie Wide for support.

The old man spoke. "Your Royal Highness, please let me explain."

"Master, please come in," the princess said. Then she turned to the captain. "Guard this door."

Still spinning the umbrella, the old man bowed to the princess, as though respecting her for her calmness in the face of a crisis.

"Why are you spinning that umbrella like some clown?" Auntie Wide asked.

"I must keep this umbrella open lest I disappear like the king and the queen."

"Then come in with the umbrella," the princess said. Auntie Wide opened the door more so that the old man could come in with the spinning umbrella.

Once inside, the man set down the canvas bag on his back and let out an exhausted sigh. But the umbrella never stopped moving in his hand, and the small stone balls along the rim of the canopy flickered in the candlelight, casting bright spots along the walls like racing stars.

"I am Ethereal, a painter from He'ershingenmosiken. The new royal painter, Needle-Eye, is—was—my student."

"I've met him," said the princess.

"Did he look at you?" Ethereal asked, anxious.

"Yes, of course."

"Terrible news, Princess. Terrible!" Ethereal sighed. "He is a devil. With his devilish art, he paints people into pictures."

"That's a lot of wasted breath," said Auntie Wide. "Isn't the job of a painter to paint people into pictures?"

"You misunderstand me," said Ethereal. "After he paints a portrait, the subject is gone. A live person turns into a dead picture."

"Then we must dispatch men to kill him right away."

The captain poked his head into the room. "I've sent all the guards. We can't find him. I wanted to find the minister of war and ask him to mobilize the capital garrison. But Master Ethereal said that the minister of war is probably already gone as well."

Ethereal shook his head. "More soldiers won't be of any use. Prince Ice Sand and Needle-Eye are certainly no longer anywhere near the palace. Needle-Eye could be painting anywhere in the world and still kill everyone here."

"Did you say Prince Ice Sand?" asked Auntie Wide.

"Yes. The prince wants to wield Needle-Eye as a weapon and eliminate the king and all those loyal to him, so that he can become the king."

Ethereal saw that the princess, Auntie Wide, and the captain of the guards were not surprised by this revelation.

"We have to worry about the matter at hand! Needle-Eye could

be painting the princess any second—he might already be doing it right now." Auntie Wide wrapped her arms around the princess, as if she could keep her safe.

Ethereal continued. "Only I can stop Needle-Eye. He's already painted me, but this umbrella can ensure that I don't disappear. If I paint him, he'll be gone."

"Then start painting!" said Auntie Wide. "I'll hold up the umbrella for you."

Ethereal shook his head again. "No. The magic only works if I paint on snow-wave paper. But the paper I have with me hasn't been flattened, and cannot be used for painting."

Auntie Wide opened the master painter's canvas bag and retrieved a section of a snow-wave tree. The bark had already been peeled off, revealing the paper roll underneath. Auntie Wide and the princess unrolled a section, and the white paper seemed to brighten the room. They tried to flatten the paper on the floor, but no matter how much they pressed, as soon as they let go, the paper rolled back up.

The painter said, "It won't work. Only a slate made from the obsidian of He'ershingenmosiken can flatten snow-wave paper. That type of obsidian is very rare, and I only had one slab, which Needle-Eye stole from me."

"There's really nothing else that will flatten this?"

"No. Only the obsidian from He'ershingenmosiken will do the job. I was hoping to get the obsidian slab back from Needle-Eye."

"He'ershingenmosiken? Obsidian?" Auntie Wide slapped her forehead. "I have an iron that I use for pressing the princess's best formal gowns. It was made in He'ershingenmosiken, and it's obsidian!"

"That might work!"

Auntie Wide dashed out of the room and returned soon with a shiny black iron. She and the princess once again unrolled a section of the snow-wave scroll, and she pressed the iron against a corner for a few seconds. She lifted the iron, and the corner remained flat.

"Hold the umbrella for me, please, and I'll flatten the paper,"

Ethereal said to Auntie Wide. As he handed the umbrella over, he said, "Keep it spinning! If it ever falls closed, I'll disappear." He watched until Auntie Wide was spinning the umbrella overhead to his satisfaction. Then he squatted and began to flatten the paper, one small section at a time.

"Can't you fix the stretchers for the ribs?" asked the princess as she stared at the spinning umbrella.

"The umbrella did have stretchers." The painter continued to press the paper as he answered. "This umbrella has an unusual history. In the past, other painters of He'ershingenmosiken also had Needle-Eye's and my skill. Besides people, they were also able to capture animals and plants. One day, an abyss dragon came to our land. The dragon was black in color, and it could fly as well as swim in the deep sea. Three painters painted it, but it continued to fly and swim. Then, the painters pooled their money and hired a magic warrior, who finally managed to slay the dragon with a fire sword. The struggle was so fierce that the ocean near He'ershingenmosiken boiled. Most of the abyss dragon's body was burnt to charcoal, but I was able to collect some body parts out of the ashes to make this umbrella. The canopy is made from the dragon's wing membranes, and the pole, handle, and ribs were all made from the dragon's bones. The stones you see at the tips of the ribs were taken from the ashes of the dragon's kidneys. The umbrella has the power to protect the user from being painted into a picture.

"Later, the stretchers broke, and I tried to repair it with bamboo stretchers, but found the umbrella's magic disappeared. I took the bamboo out, and the magic returned. Then I tried to hold the canopy up with my hand, and that didn't work either. Apparently, no foreign material of any kind could be used in the umbrella. But I don't have any more dragon bones, and this is the only way to keep the umbrella open...."

The clock in the corner of the room sounded. Ethereal looked up and saw it was almost sunrise. He looked down and saw that only about a palm's width of the snow-wave paper lay flat on the floor, not enough for a painting. He dropped the iron and sighed.

"There's no time. It will take too long for me to paint my portrait of Needle-Eye, but he could be done with his painting of the princess at any moment. You two." He pointed at Auntie Wide and the captain. "Has Needle-Eye seen you?"

"I'm sure he hasn't seen me," said Auntie Wide.

"I saw him from a distance when he came into the palace," said the captain. "But I'm sure he didn't see me."

"Good." Ethereal stood up. "Please accompany the princess to the Glutton's Sea, and find Prince Deep Water on Tomb Island."

"But ... even if we get to the Glutton's Sea, we can't get onto Tomb Island. You know that the sea has—"

"Cross that bridge when you get to it. This is the only way. By dawn, all the ministers loyal to the king will have been painted into pictures, and Prince Ice Sand will have control of the capital garrison and the palace guards. He will seize the throne, and only Prince Deep Water can stop him."

"If Prince Deep Water returns to the palace, won't Needle-Eye paint him into a picture as well?" asked the princess.

"Don't worry. Needle-Eye will not be able to paint Prince Deep Water. The prince is the only person in the kingdom who cannot be painted by Needle-Eye. Luckily, I only taught Needle-Eye how to paint in the Western style, but never taught him Eastern painting."

The princess and the other two weren't sure what the master painter was talking about, but Ethereal didn't elaborate. He went on. "You must bring Deep Water back to the palace and kill Needle-Eye. Then you must find the painting of the princess and burn it. It's the only way to keep her safe."

"What if we can find the paintings of the king and the queen—"

"Your Royal Highness, it's too late. They're gone. They're now only paintings. If you find them, don't burn them. Keep them for memory."

Grief crushed Princess Dewdrop, and she fell to the floor sobbing.

"Princess, now is not the time for sorrow. If you want to avenge your father and mother, you had better be on your way." The old

master turned to Auntie Wide and the captain. "Remember, until you locate and destroy the princess's portrait, you must keep the umbrella open over her. She can't be without its protection, not even for a second." He took the umbrella from Auntie Wide's hands, and kept spinning it. "Don't spin it too slowly, because it will fall closed; but don't spin it too fast, because the umbrella is old, and it may fall apart. The umbrella is alive, in a sense. If you spin it too slow, it will cry out like a bird. Listen—" He slowed down the spinning until the stones at the rim of the canopy began to droop, and the umbrella emitted a nightingale-like sound. The slower he spun it, the louder the noise. The old master sped up the spinning. "If you spin it too fast, it will ring like a bell. Like this—" The old master spun the umbrella even faster, and the umbrella began to sound like a wind chime, but faster and louder. "All right. Now protect the princess." He handed the umbrella back to Auntie Wide.

"Master Ethereal, let's leave together," Princess Dewdrop said, looking up with tear-filled eyes.

"No. The dragon umbrella is only able to protect one person. If two individuals who have been painted by Needle-Eye try to use it together, they'll both die a terrible death: Half of each person will be painted into the picture, and the other half will remain under the umbrella.... Now raise the umbrella over the princess and go! Each moment you delay increases the danger. Needle-Eye may finish the picture any moment now!"

Auntie Wide kept spinning the umbrella over the old master. She looked at the princess, then back to the painter, hesitating.

"I taught that vile spawn how to paint. Death is what I deserve. What are you waiting for? Do you want to see the princess disappear before your eyes?"

Auntie Wide shivered. She moved the umbrella over the princess.

The old painter stroked his beard and smiled. "It's all right. I've painted all my life. To be turned into a painting is not a bad way to go. I trust my student's technique. The portrait will be excellent...."

As he spoke, his body slowly became transparent, then faded away like a wisp of fog.

Princess Dewdrop stared at the empty space where the painter had been and muttered, "Let's go. To the Glutton's Sea."

Auntie Wide said to the captain, "Can you keep the umbrella up for a while? I need to go pack."

The captain took over. "Hurry! Prince Ice Sand's men are everywhere. We'll have trouble getting away after daylight."

"But I have to pack! The princess has never been away. I've got to take her traveling cloak and boots, and lots of clothes, and her water, and ... also the bath soap from He'ershingenmosiken—she can't sleep if she doesn't bathe with it...." Auntie Wide continued to mutter as she left.

Half an hour later, by the faint glow of dawn, a light carriage left the palace from a side door. The captain drove. In the carriage were the princess and Auntie Wide, who held up the spinning umbrella. They were all dressed as commoners, and the carriage soon disappeared in the fog.

In that distant underground bunker, Needle-Eye had just completed the portrait of Princess Dewdrop.

"This is the most beautiful portrait I've ever painted," he said to Prince Ice Sand.

THE SECOND TALE OF
YUN TIANMING
"THE GLUTTON'S SEA"

Once they were outside the palace, the captain drove the horses as fast as they would go. All three were anxious. In the brightening darkness, they felt danger looming in every shadowy copse and field they passed. After the sky brightened even more, the carriage came to the top of a hill, where the captain stopped so they could look back along the road. The kingdom spread out below the hill, and the road was like a straight line that divided the world in half. At the end of the line was the palace, looking like a pile of toy blocks forgotten on the horizon. No one was chasing after them; apparently Prince Ice Sand thought the princess no longer existed because she had been captured by Needle-Eye's brush.

They continued in a more relaxed manner. As the sky continued to brighten and illuminate everything around them, the world resembled a picture being painted. At first, there were only vague outlines and hazy colors; later, the outlines became more defined, the colors richer and more vivid. The moment just before the sun rose was when the painting became complete.

The princess, who had always lived in the palace, had never seen such large patches of vibrant colors: the green of forests, grassland, and fields, the bright red and brilliant yellow of wildflowers,

the silver of the sky reflected in lakes and ponds, the snowy white of flocks of sheep … As the sun rose, it was as if the painter of this world-picture scattered a handful of gold dust boldly over the surface of the painting.

"It's so lovely outside," said the princess. "It's as if we're already in the picture."

"That's true," said Auntie Wide, spinning the umbrella. "But you're alive in *this* picture. In the other picture, you're already dead."

The princess was reminded of her departed parents. She forced herself to not cry. She understood that she was no longer a young girl, but a queen with duties she had to bear.

They talked about Prince Deep Water.

"Why was he exiled to Tomb Island?" asked the princess.

"They say he's a monster," said the captain.

"Prince Deep Water is no monster!" said Auntie Wide.

"They say he's a giant."

"He's no giant. I held him when he was a baby. I know."

"When we get to the sea, you'll see. Many others have seen him. He really is a giant."

"Even if he's a giant, he's still the prince," said the princess. "Why was he exiled to the island?"

"He wasn't exiled. When he was little, he took a boat to Tomb Island to fish. But that was when the glutton fish appeared in the sea. He couldn't come back, so he had to grow up on the island."

Now that it was light out, the road gradually filled with more pedestrians and carriages. Since the princess had rarely set foot outside the palace in the past, people did not recognize her. She was also wearing a veil so that only her eyes showed, but anyone who saw her still exclaimed at her beauty. The people also admired the handsome young carriage driver and chuckled at the sight of the silly old mother holding up the umbrella for her pretty daughter— and what a strange way to keep the umbrella up! It was a bright, sunny day, and everyone thought it was a parasol.

It was noon, and the captain shot two hares with his bow. The three ate by the side of the road in an open space between some trees. Princess Dewdrop caressed the soft grass next to her, inhaled the fragrance of herbs and wildflowers, watched the sunlight dappling the ground, and listened to the birds singing in the woods and some distant shepherd playing his flute—she was curious and delighted by this new world.

But Auntie Wide sighed. "Oh, Princess, I'm so sorry you have to be away from the palace, suffering."

"I think being outside is better than being in the palace."

"Silly girl, how can out here be better than the palace? You don't know what it's like out here. Right now, it's spring. But in winter, it's cold, and in summer, it's hot. There are gales, and rainstorms, and all kinds of different people out here—"

"I never knew anything about the outside before. In the palace, I studied music, painting, poetry, mathematics, and two languages that no one speaks anymore. But no one told me what was outside. How am I supposed to govern this kingdom?"

"Princess, your ministers will help you."

"The ministers who would have helped me have all been painted into pictures.... I still think the outside is better."

A day's journey lay between the palace and the sea. But the princess's party avoided the major roads and towns, so they didn't reach the sea until midnight.

Dewdrop had never seen such a wide, open sky full of stars, and for the first time she felt how *dark* and *silent* the night could be. The torch on the carriage could only illuminate a small patch around her, and the world beyond was black velvet. The horses' hoofbeats seemed loud enough to shake the stars from the sky. The princess pulled on the captain's arm and asked him to stop.

"Listen! What is that? It sounds like a giant breathing."

"It's the sound of the sea, Princess."

They went on a bit farther, and the princess could see vague shapes on both sides—giant bananas?

"What are these?"

The captain stopped, hopped down, and took the torch close to one of the objects. "Princess, you should recognize these."

"Boats?"

"Yes, boats."

"Why are the boats ... on land?"

"Because the sea has glutton fish."

The light from the captain's torch revealed a long-abandoned boat. The sand buried half of it, and the exposed part seemed like the skeleton of some beast.

"Look over there!" The princess pointed ahead. "A big white snake!"

"Don't be scared, Princess. That's not a snake, but the surf. We've reached the sea."

The princess and Auntie Wide, who kept the umbrella over her, climbed down from the carriage. She had only seen the sea in pictures before, and those painted seas were blue waves under a blue sky. But the sea she saw now was a black ocean at night, filled with the grandness and mystery of starlight, like another sky in liquid form. The princess advanced toward the sea, as if compelled by some force. The captain and Auntie Wide stopped her.

"It's dangerous to get too close," said the captain.

"I don't think the water is very deep. Will I drown?"

"The glutton fish will tear you apart and eat you!" said Auntie Wide.

The captain picked up a loose plank lying nearby and walked ahead, tossing it into the sea. The plank bobbed over the water a few times before a black shadow surfaced and headed for it. Since most of the shadowy creature was underwater, it was hard to tell how large it was. The scales on its body flickered in the torchlight. Then, three or four more shadows surfaced and also swam for the plank. The shadows fought over the plank, and as the water splashed, the sound of sharp teeth sawing through and crunching

the wood could be heard. In a few moments, the shadows and the plank all disappeared.

"They could make short work of even a large ship," said the captain.

"Where's Tomb Island?" asked Auntie Wide.

"In that direction." The captain pointed at the horizon. "But we can't see it now. We'll have to wait until daylight."

They camped on the beach. Auntie Wide handed the spinning umbrella to the captain and retrieved a small wooden basin from the carriage.

"Princess, I'm afraid you won't be able to bathe tonight. But at least you can wash your face."

The captain handed the umbrella back to Auntie Wide and took the basin to go find water. His figure disappeared in the night.

"What a good young man." Auntie Wide yawned.

The captain returned with a basin full of fresh water. Auntie Wide took out the princess's bath soap and touched it to the water. With a pop, the surface of the water became full of foam, and some of the foam spilled out the sides.

The captain stared at the soap foam. He turned to Auntie Wide. "May I see the soap?"

Auntie Wide carefully handed over the pure white bath soap. "Hold on tight! It's lighter than a feather. If you let go, it will float away."

The captain hefted the soap; it seemed to have no weight at all, like holding a white shadow. "This really is from He'ershingen-mosiken! I'm amazed we still have any."

"I think only two bars are left in the entire palace—no, the entire kingdom. I saved one from years back for the princess. Anything from He'ershingenmosiken is superior, but fewer and fewer of these objects are left." Auntie Wide took back the bath soap and carefully packed it away.

As she watched the white foam, the princess recalled her life in the palace for the first time since the start of the journey. Every night, in her elegant, ornate bathing suite, the bathing pool was

covered by foam just like this. In the light of the various lamps, the bubbles sometimes looked pure white like a cloud pulled from the sky, sometimes iridescent, like a pile of jewels. As she soaked among the bubbles, she felt her body turn soft as noodles, felt herself melt *into* the bubbles. It felt so comfortable that she didn't want to move anymore, so that the servant girls had to lift her out, dry her, and then carry her to the bed to sleep. The wonderful feeling lasted until the next morning.

After the princess washed her face with the He'ershingenmosiken bath soap, her face felt relaxed and soft, but her body remained tired and stiff. After a quick supper, she lay down on the beach—she tried lying on a blanket first, then realized that it was more comfortable to sleep on the sand directly. The sand retained some of the heat of the day, and made her feel as though she were being held in a warm, giant palm. The rhythmic surf was like a lullaby, and she soon fell asleep.

After an unknown amount of time, Princess Dewdrop was awakened by a ringing bell. The sound came from the black umbrella spinning overhead. Auntie Wide was asleep next to her, and the umbrella-spinner was the captain of the guards. The torches had already been extinguished, and night covered all like black velvet. The captain appeared as a cutout against the starry sky, and only his armor reflected the starlight, while his hair swayed with the wind. The umbrella spun steadily in his hand, a tiny dome that blocked out half the sky. She couldn't see his eyes, but could feel them and innumerable twinkling stars gazing at her.

"Sorry, Princess. I spun a bit too fast," whispered the captain.

"What time is it?"

"After midnight."

"We seem to be farther away from the sea."

"It's low tide. Tomorrow morning, the water will come back."

"Have you been taking turns with the umbrella?"

"Yes. Auntie Wide did it for the whole day. I'll relieve her by doing it a bit longer tonight."

"But you drove all day. Let me do it. You get some rest."

Princess Dewdrop was a bit surprised by her own words. As far as she could remember, this was the first time she had ever thought about the needs of others.

"No, Princess. Your hands are smooth and delicate; spinning the umbrella will give you blisters. Let me keep on doing this."

"What is your name?"

Though they'd traveled together for a whole day, she hadn't thought to ask for his name until now. Before, she would have thought this perfectly normal. But now she felt a bit guilty.

"I'm called Long-Sail."

"Sail?" The princess looked around. They were camped by the side of a large boat on the beach, which shielded them from the wind. Unlike the other boats stranded on the beach, this one still had its mast, like a sword pointing at the stars. "Isn't a sail the cloth hung on the long stick?"

"Yes. That's called a mast. The sail hangs from it so that the wind can push the boat."

"Sails are so white on the sea. Very pretty."

"Only in pictures. Real sails are not so white."

"I believe you are from He'ershingenmosiken?"

"That's right. My father was an architect in He'ershingenmosiken. He brought our whole family here when I was little."

"Do you ever think about going home—I mean, to He'ershingenmosiken?"

"Not really. I was so young when I left that I don't remember much of it. And even if I do remember, it's useless. I can never leave the Storyless Kingdom."

The waves crashed against the beach some distance away, as though repeating Long-Sail's words again and again: *can never leave; can never leave* ...

"Tell me some stories about the outside world. I don't know anything," said the princess.

"You don't need to know. You are the princess of the Storyless Kingdom, and it's natural that the kingdom has no stories for you. As a matter of fact, no one outside the palace tells their children

any stories either. But my parents were different. They were from He'ershingenmosiken, and so they did tell me some stories."

"My father told me that long ago, the Storyless Kingdom had stories, too."

"That's true.... Princess, do you know that the kingdom is surrounded by the sea? The palace is at the center of the kingdom. No matter which direction you pick, you'll end up eventually at the shore. The Storyless Kingdom is a big island."

"Of course. I knew that."

"In the past, the sea around the kingdom wasn't called the Glutton's Sea. Back then, there were no glutton fish, and ships plied the waters freely. Every day, countless ships passed between the Storyless Kingdom and He'ershingenmosiken—well, back then, this was called the Storyful Kingdom, and life was very different."

"Oh?"

"Life was full of stories, and filled with changes and surprises. There were several big bustling cities in the kingdom, and the palace wasn't surrounded by forests and fields, but by a flourishing capital. Everywhere in the cities you could find the valuable goods and the singular tools and utensils of He'ershingenmosiken. And the goods of the Storyless Kingdom—oh, I mean the Storyful Kingdom— flowed to He'ershingenmosiken over the sea without cease. People's lives were unpredictable, like riding a fast horse through the mountains: One moment you'd be atop a peak, and the next moment you'd have fallen into a ravine. There was opportunity and danger: A poor person could become rich overnight, and a wealthy person could also lose everything in a moment. Upon awakening, no one knew what was going to happen that day, or who they were going to meet. Life was stimulating and astonishing.

"But one day, a merchant ship from He'ershingenmosiken brought a stock of rare small fish in cast-iron barrels. The fish was only about as long as a finger, black in color, and looked perfectly ordinary. The merchant performed for the public in the markets: He stuck a sword into the iron barrel, and after an ear-piercing series of grinding noises, pulled the sword out to show that it had been bitten

into a saw. The fish were called glutton fish, a freshwater species found in dark pools deep in the caves of He'ershingenmosiken.

"The glutton fish sold very well in the kingdom. Although the fish's teeth were tiny, they were as hard as diamonds and could be used as drill heads. Their fins were also very sharp, and could be made into arrowheads or small knives. Thus, more and more glutton fish were shipped from He'ershingenmosiken to this kingdom. Once, a typhoon caused one of these transport ships to capsize near the coast, and more than twenty barrels of glutton fish were lost at sea.

"It turned out that the glutton fish thrived in the ocean, and grew to be as long as a man, far larger than their freshwater form. Also, they bred quickly, and their population exploded. They began to eat everything that floated on the surface. Ships and boats that weren't dragged onto the shore in time were chewed into pieces. When glutton fish surrounded a ship, they chewed huge holes through the bottom. But the ship didn't even have time to sink before it was chewed into nothing, as though it had melted. The schools of glutton fish swam around the kingdom and quickly formed a barrier in the sea.

"And so the glutton fish laid siege to the Storyful Kingdom, and the shore became a land of death. There were no more ships and sails, and the kingdom was sealed off, with all connections to He'ershingenmosiken and the larger world cut off. It reverted to a self-sufficient agrarian land. The bustling cities disappeared and turned into small towns and ranches. Life became calm and dull, with no more changes, no more stimulation and surprises. Yesterday was like today, and today is like tomorrow. The people gradually grew used to this and stopped yearning for a different life. Their memories of the past, like the exotic goods from He'ershingenmosiken, grew fewer with each passing day. People even deliberately tried to forget the past, and also the present. All in all, they no longer wanted stories, so they patterned their life into a storyless one. And so the Storyful Kingdom became the Storyless Kingdom."

Princess Dewdrop was mesmerized by the story. Only long after Long-Sail had stopped did she ask, "Are there still glutton fish everywhere in the sea?"

"No. They live only around the coast of the Storyless Kingdom. Those with good eyes can sometimes see distant seabirds floating on the surface of the ocean hunting for food. There are no glutton fish there. The ocean is immense and boundless."

"So, there are other places in the world in addition to the Storyless Kingdom and He'ershingenmosiken?"

"Princess, do you really think the world consists of only these two places?"

"That's what the royal tutor taught me when I was little."

"He doesn't even believe that lie himself. The world is very, very large. The ocean has no edge, and holds innumerable islands. Some are smaller than the kingdom, others larger. There are even continents."

"What are continents?"

"Land that is as vast as the sea. Even on a fast horse, you wouldn't be able to go from one end to the other after many months."

"As large as all that?" The princess sighed. Then, abruptly, she asked, "Can you see me?"

"I can only see your eyes. There are stars in them."

"Then you must be able to see my yearning. I want to ride a sailboat across the sea, and go to faraway places."

"Impossible. We can never leave the Storyless Kingdom, Princess, never ever.... If you're afraid of the dark, let's light the torches."

"All right."

The torches were lit. Princess Dewdrop looked at Captain Long-Sail, but noticed that he was looking elsewhere.

"What are you looking at?" the princess asked softly.

"There, Princess—look over there."

Long-Sail was pointing at a small clump of grass in the sand. A few small droplets glistened in the torchlight on the grass blades.

"Those are called dewdrops," said Long-Sail.

"Ah, like me. Do they look like me?"

"They do. You're all beautiful, like crystals."

"When it's daytime, they'll be even prettier in the sun."

The captain sighed deeply. He did it without making any noise, but the princess felt it.

"What's wrong?"

"Dewdrops will evaporate and disappear in the sun."

The princess nodded. Her eyes dimmed. "Then they're even more like me. If this umbrella closes, I will disappear. I will be the dewdrop in the sun."

"I will not let you disappear."

"You and I both know that we cannot get to Tomb Island, and we can't bring Prince Deep Water back."

"If so, I'll just hold the umbrella up for you forever."

THE THIRD TALE OF YUN TIANMING
"PRINCE DEEP WATER"

The next time Princess Dewdrop awakened, it was light out. The sea had turned from black to blue, but the princess still thought it looked completely different from pictures she had seen. The vastness that had been hidden by night now lay bare. Under the morning sun, the surface of the sea was completely empty. But in the princess's imagination, the glutton fish didn't cause this emptiness; rather, the sea was empty for her, just as her suites in the palace were empty, waiting for her. The yearning she had spoken of to Long-Sail during the night now became more intense. She imagined a white sail belonging to her appearing on the sea, drifting away with the wind until it disappeared.

Auntie Wide now held the umbrella up for her. The captain called for them from the beach ahead. When they came to his side, he pointed to the ocean. "Look, that's Tomb Island."

What the princess saw first wasn't the island, but the giant standing on the island. It was clearly Prince Deep Water. He stood on the island like a lonesome mountain: his skin bronzed by the sun, his muscles rippling and bulging like folds of rock, his hair drifting in the wind like trees near the peak. He looked like Ice Sand, but wasn't gloomy or dismal; rather, his gaze and expression all gave the viewer the feeling that he was open like the sea. The sun hadn't completely risen yet, but the giant's head was already bathed in the

golden light, as though he were on fire. He shaded his eyes with a huge hand, and for a moment, the princess thought her gaze met his, and she cried out:

"Big brother! I'm Dewdrop, your little sister! I'm your baby sister Dewdrop! We're here!"

The giant gave no indication that he heard. His gaze swept past where they stood and moved elsewhere. Then he put his hand down, shook his head thoughtfully, and turned away.

"Why isn't he paying attention to us?" asked the anxious princess.

"Who would notice three ants in the distance?" The captain turned to Auntie Wide. "I told you Prince Deep Water is a giant."

"But when I held him he really was just a tiny baby! How did he get so big? But it's a good thing he's a giant. No one can stop him. He can punish those evildoers and retrieve the princess's portrait."

"We still have to let him know what's happened first," said the captain.

"We must go over there! Let's go to Tomb Island!" The princess clutched at Long-Sail.

"We can't. In all these years, no one has been able to get on Tomb Island. And no one there can come here."

"Is there really no way?" Tears escaped the princess's eyes. "We came here to look for him! You must know what to do."

Watching the tearful princess, Long-Sail seemed helpless. "I really don't know of a way. Coming here was the right decision, because you had to get away from the palace—otherwise you'd just be waiting to die. But I knew from the start that we wouldn't be able to get to Tomb Island. Maybe ... we can send him a message by messenger pigeon."

"Great idea! Let's go find a messenger pigeon right away."

"But what good would it do? Even if he got the message, he still wouldn't be able to come here. He might be a giant, but even he would be torn apart by the glutton fish in the sea.... Let's have breakfast before we decide what to do. I'll go prepare."

"Oh no, my basin!" Auntie Wide cried out. It was high tide,

and the rising waves had reached the wooden basin the princess had used the night before to wash her face. The basin had already floated some distance into the sea. It was upside down, and the soapy water inside had thrown white foam across a patch of the sea. They could see a few glutton fish swimming toward the basin, their sharp fins cutting through the surface like knives. The basin was going to turn into woodchips in their teeth in a second.

But something incredible happened: The glutton fish didn't get to the basin. As soon as they reached the foam, they stopped swimming and floated to the surface. The fierce fish seemed to lose their drive, and became listless. A few slowly swung their tails back and forth—not to swim, but to display their relaxation. Others even decided to float with their white bellies up.

The three observed the sight in silence, stunned. Then the princess said, "I ... think I know how they feel. You're so comfortable in the foam that it's like you've gone boneless. They don't want to move."

Auntie Wide said, "The bath soap from He'ershingenmosiken really is wonderful. Too bad there are only two bars left."

"Even in He'ershingenmosiken, this kind of soap is very precious," said Captain Long-Sail. "Do you know how it is made? There's a magical forest in He'ershingenmosiken made up of thousand-year-old bubble trees, all very tall. Normally, there's nothing special about the bubble trees, but whenever there's a strong wind, soap bubbles come out of the trees. The stronger the wind, the more bubbles emerge. The He'ershingenmosiken bath soap is made from those bubbles, but collecting the bubbles is no easy matter. The bubbles drift very fast in the wind, and since they are transparent, it's very hard to see them. Only if someone were running as fast as the bubbles, such that they're at rest relative to the bubbles, would they be able to see them. This is possible only by riding the fastest horses, of which there are no more than ten in all of He'ershingenmosiken. Whenever the bubble trees begin to blow bubbles, the soap-makers ride these horses to chase after the wind and try to collect the bubbles with a thin gauze net. The bubbles

come in different sizes, but even the largest bubble, once it's in the net, will burst and end up smaller than the eye could see. Hundreds of thousands of such bubbles have to be collected—sometimes millions—to make one bar of soap.

"But once the soap is in the water, each bubble from the bubble tree turns into millions of new bubbles. This is why this kind of bath soap generates so much foam. The bubbles have no weight, which is why pure, authentic He'ershingenmosiken bath soap also has no weight. It's the lightest substance in the world, but extremely precious. The bars that Auntie Wide has were probably given as gifts by the He'ershingenmosiken ambassador at the king's coronation. After that—"

Long-Sail abruptly stopped talking and stared at the sea, deep in thought. The few glutton fish continued to float lazily in the white foam. In front of them was the wooden basin, undamaged.

"I think there may be a way to get to Tomb Island!" Long-Sail pointed to the basin. "What if that's a little boat?"

"Absolutely not!" said Auntie Wide. "How can the princess take such a risk?"

"I wasn't talking about the princess."

The princess could tell by his determined gaze that the captain had already made up his mind.

"If you go alone, how can you make Prince Deep Water believe you?" The princess's excited face was flushed. "I'll go, too. I have to!"

"Even if you get to the island, how can you prove you are who you say you are?" The captain looked meaningfully at the commoner's garb on the princess.

Auntie Wide said nothing. She knew there was a way.

"My brother and I can prove our relationship by testing our blood," said the princess.

"Even so, the princess cannot go. It's too frightening!" But Auntie Wide's tone was no longer so nonnegotiable.

"Do you think I'm going to be safe staying here?" The princess pointed to the spinning black umbrella in Auntie Wide's hand. "We'll attract too much attention, and Ice Sand is going to follow

us here. If I remain here, Ice Sand's army will catch me even if I don't end up in a painting. I'll be safer on Tomb Island."

And so they decided to go for it.

The captain found the smallest boat on the beach and used the horses to drag it to where the waves could just lick it. He couldn't find a working sail, but was able to retrieve a pair of old oars from other ships. He had the princess and Auntie Wide, who held the umbrella, board the boat first. Then he skewered the bar of He'ershingenmosiken bath soap with his sword and handed the sword to the princess.

"As soon as the boat is in the water, stick the soap in."

The princess nodded.

He pushed the boat into the sea and waded until the water had risen to his waist before jumping into the boat himself. He rowed with all his strength, and the boat headed for Tomb Island.

The black fins of the glutton fish began to appear around them and to approach. The princess sat at the stern, and submerged the soap on the sword into the water. Foam instantly swelled out of the sea until the bubbles were as high as a man before spreading out in the wake of the ship. As the glutton fish swam into the bubbles, they began to drift, as though they were enjoying the incomparable sensation of cozying up on a soft, white, plush blanket. This was the first time the princess had been able to get such a close look at the glutton fish: Except for their white bellies, they were entirely black, like machines made of steel and iron—and now they were lazy and docile in the foam.

The boat proceeded over the serene sea, dragging a long foamy wake like a wisp of cloud fallen to the sea. Innumerable glutton fish approached from both sides and swam into the foam like pilgrims congregating at a river of clouds. Once in a while, a few glutton fish approached from the front of the boat and managed to get a few bites in on the bottom—one even managed to bite off a chunk of the oar in the captain's hand. But soon, even these fish were lured away by the foam behind the boat, and not much damage was done. As the princess took in the pure white

cloud-river of bubbles behind the boat and the intoxicated multitude of glutton fish, she was reminded of Heaven as described by the priests.

The shore receded and the boat approached Tomb Island.

Auntie Wide cried out, "Look! Prince Deep Water seems to be growing shorter."

The princess looked. Auntie Wide was right. The prince was still a giant, but he was clearly smaller than he had been when seen from the shore. He still stood with his back to them and looked out in another direction.

The princess pulled her gaze back to Long-Sail, who was propelling the boat. He looked even more the embodiment of strength: his muscles bulging everywhere, the two oars in his hands swinging rhythmically like a pair of wings, pushing the boat ahead steadily. The man seemed born for the sea; his movements were freer and more confident than when he had been on land.

"The prince sees us!" Auntie Wide called out. On Tomb Island, Prince Deep Water turned in their direction. One of his hands pointed at them, and his eyes gave a look of surprise. His mouth moved as though shouting something. It was no wonder that he was surprised. Theirs was the only boat on this sea of death, the farther back it was from the boat, the wider the foamy wake grew. From his vantage point, the sea seemed to suddenly be inhabited by a long-tailed comet.

They soon realized that the prince wasn't shouting at them. A few normal-sized individuals appeared at the prince's feet. At this distance, the men looked tiny, and their faces couldn't be clearly seen. But they were all looking in the direction of the boat, and a few waved.

Tomb Island had once been uninhabited. Twenty years ago, when Deep Water had gone to the island for fishing, he had brought with him a palace guardian, a royal tutor, and a few guards and servants. As soon as they came onto the island, schools of glutton fish came into the nearby shallows and sealed off the way home.

The princess and the others noticed that the prince looked

shorter still. The closer they approached the island, the shorter the prince grew.

The boat was almost at the island. They could see eight or so normal-height people, most of them dressed in rough clothing made of canvas. like the prince himself. Two of them wore ceremonial robes from the palace, though they were very old and worn. Most also had swords. They ran onto the beach, leaving the prince behind them. By now he looked only about twice as tall as the others, no longer a giant.

The captain rowed harder and the boat dashed forward. The waves pushed the boat like a giant's hands, and the hull jolted as the bottom came to rest against the sand, almost toppling the princess out. The people onshore hesitated, apparently worried about the glutton fish, but four of them did come forward into the water to help stabilize the boat and support the princess as she disembarked.

"Careful! The princess has to be under the umbrella," Auntie Wide shouted. She was now very skilled with the umbrella, and managed to keep it spinning above the princess even with only one hand.

The welcoming party did not bother to disguise their surprise. They looked from the spinning black umbrella to the wake of the ship: The white foam from the He'ershingenmosiken bath soap and the countless floating glutton fish formed a speckled path of black and white across the sea, connecting the kingdom with Tomb Island.

Prince Deep Water came forward. Now he looked no taller than an ordinary man—in fact, he was shorter than two of his followers. He smiled at the newcomers like a kindhearted fisherman, but the princess could see shades of their father in his movements. With eyes full of hot tears, she called out, "Brother! I'm your sister, Dewdrop."

"You do look like my sister." The prince smiled and held out his arms for her. But a few of his guards stopped the princess and separated the newcomers from the prince. Some had unsheathed their swords and watched the captain with suspicion. Long-Sail ignored them, but he picked up the sword the princess had dropped to examine it. In order to put the prince's jittery guards at ease,

he held the sword by the tip. He saw that the trip to Tomb Island had consumed only about one-third of the He'ershingenmosiken bath soap skewered on the sword.

"You must prove the princess's identity," an old man said. His uniform, though worn and patched, was still neat. His face showed the trials of many years, but his beard was neatly trimmed. Even on this desolate island, he had clearly tried to maintain the dignity of his position as an official of the palace.

"Don't you recognize me?" Auntie Wide said. "You're Guardian Shaded-Forest, and that, over there, is Royal Tutor Open-Field."

Both of them nodded. Open-Field said, "Auntie Wide, you're looking hale and hearty, despite the years."

"And you two have aged, as well." Auntie Wide wiped her eyes with her free hand.

Guardian Shaded-Forest kept his expression grim. "It's been twenty years, and we have no idea what has happened back home. We must request that the princess prove her identity." He turned to the princess. "Are you willing to have your blood tested?"

The princess nodded.

"I don't think this is necessary," said the prince. "I know she's my sister."

"Your Royal Highness," said the guardian. "This must be done."

Someone brought over two tiny daggers and handed one each to Guardian Shaded-Forest and Royal Tutor Open-Field. Unlike the rusty swords worn by the prince's men, these daggers still gleamed like new. The princess held out a hand, and Shaded-Forest lightly pricked her index finger with the dagger and picked up a drop of blood with the tip of the dagger. Open-Field did the same with the prince. Then Shaded-Forest took both daggers and carefully touched the drops of blood together. The red blood instantly turned blue.

"She is indeed Princess Dewdrop," the guardian said solemnly. Then, together with the royal tutor, they both bowed to the princess. The prince's other followers also knelt on one knee. Then they stood up and backed away, giving the royal siblings a chance to embrace.

"I held you when you were little," said the prince. "Back then, you were only about this big."

A sobbing princess told the prince all that had happened in the Storyless Kingdom. The prince held her hand and listened without interrupting. His face, marked by the tribulations of twenty years, but still youthful, remained calm and steady throughout.

Everyone gathered around the prince and the princess to listen to the story, but Captain Long-Sail engaged in some odd antics. He ran some distance away on the beach to look at the prince, and then came back, before dashing away again. Finally, Aunt Wide pulled him aside.

"I told you: Prince Deep Water is not a giant," whispered Auntie Wide.

"He *is* and he *isn't*," whispered the captain. "When you look at a regular person, the farther away he is, the smaller he appears in our eyes, right? But the prince is not like this. No matter how far away he is, he looks the same size in our eyes. This is why from far away he appears to be a giant."

Auntie Wide nodded. "I've noticed the same thing."

After the princess finished her story, Prince Deep Water simply said, "Let's go back."

They took two boats. The prince joined the princess's party on the small boat; the other eight took a larger boat, the same one that had carried the prince and his followers to Tomb Island twenty years ago. The larger boat leaked, but was safe enough for a short trip. They took care to retrace the wake of the princess's boat. Although the foam had dissipated somewhat, the glutton fish remained adrift without moving much. Once in a while, one of the boats or oars would strike a floating glutton fish, but the fish only wriggled lazily out of the way without a more strenuous response. The big boat's sail was still somewhat functional, and so it sailed in front, opening up a path through the floating schools of glutton fish for the small boat.

"I think it's best if you dip the soap back into the sea for insurance. What if they wake up?" Auntie Wide nervously surveyed the drifting mass of glutton fish.

"They've remained awake—they're not moving much because they're too comfortable. We don't have much of the soap left, and I don't want to waste any. I won't be bathing with it in the future, either."

Someone in the big boat ahead called out, "The army!"

A detachment of cavalry appeared on the shores of the kingdom. They rushed onto the beach like a dark tide. The armor and weapons of the mounted warriors gleamed in the sun.

"Keep on going," said Prince Deep Water.

"They're here to kill us!" Blood drained from the princess's face.

"Don't be afraid," said the prince, and lightly patted her hand.

Dewdrop looked at her older brother. She knew now that he was even better suited to the throne than she.

As the wind was at their backs, the return trip took much less time despite the floating glutton fish bumping into the boats along the way. As both boats came onto the beach, the cavalry surrounded them like a solid wall. Both the princess and Auntie Wide were terrified, but Captain Long-Sail, who was more experienced, relaxed a bit. He saw that the soldiers all kept their swords sheathed and their lances vertical. More important, he noticed the eyes of the men: They wore heavy armor so that only their eyes were visible, but the eyes were focused beyond the fugitives at the foamy path over the sea filled with glutton fish. Long-Sail saw only awe in those eyes.

An officer dismounted and jogged over to the beached boats. The people on the boats disembarked, and the prince's followers unsheathed their swords and stepped between the officer and the prince and princess.

"This is Prince Deep Water and Princess Dewdrop. Watch your words and acts!" Guardian Shaded-Forest shouted at the officer.

The officer knelt down on one knee and bowed his head. "We know. But our orders are to pursue and kill the princess."

"Princess Dewdrop is the heir to the throne by law! But Ice Sand is a traitor, guilty of regicide and patricide! How can you follow his orders?"

"We know this as well, which is why we will not carry out this order. But Prince Ice Sand ascended to the throne yesterday afternoon. We ... are uncertain whose orders we should obey."

Shaded-Forest was about to say more, but Prince Deep Water stepped forward and stopped him. The prince turned to the officer. "Why don't the princess and I return to the palace with you? We'll confront Ice Sand there and resolve this once and for all."

The newly crowned King Ice Sand was celebrating in the most luxurious hall in the palace with those ministers who had sworn fealty to him, when messengers arrived to report that Prince Deep Water and Princess Dewdrop were speeding toward the palace at the head of an army. They would arrive in an hour. The hall instantly became silent.

"Deep Water? How did he cross the sea? Did he grow wings?" Ice Sand muttered to himself, but his face didn't show the terror and surprise evident on others'. "Don't worry. The army will not obey those two, unless I'm dead.... Needle-Eye!"

Needle-Eye emerged from the shadows. He was still dressed in his gray cloak, and appeared even frailer than before.

"Take snow-wave paper and your brushes and ride toward Deep Water. When you see him, paint him. It will be easy. You won't need to get too close. As soon as he appears over the horizon, you'll get a good look at him."

"Yes, my king." Needle-Eye departed noiselessly like a rat.

"As for Dewdrop, what can a mere girl do? I'll tear that umbrella away from her." Ice Sand lifted his flagon.

The celebratory feast ended in a subdued atmosphere. The ministers left with worried expressions, and only Ice Sand remained in the empty hall.

After an unknown amount of time, Ice Sand saw Needle-Eye return. Ice Sand's heart sped up—it wasn't because Needle-Eye's hands were empty, and it wasn't because of Needle-Eye's appearance: He looked as sensitive and careful as before. Rather, it was because

Ice Sand heard Needle-Eye's footsteps. Before, the painter had always moved in complete silence, like a squirrel gliding across the floor, but now, Ice Sand heard the echoes of his loud steps, like a heartbeat that couldn't be suppressed.

"I saw Prince Deep Water," said Needle-Eye, his eyes lowered. "But I couldn't paint him."

"Did he have wings?" Ice Sand's voice was chilly.

"Even if he did, I could still capture him. I could paint each feather in his wing and make it lifelike. But, my king, the truth is more frightening than if he had sprouted wings: He does not obey the laws of perspective."

"What is perspective?"

"The principles of perspective dictate that objects farther away appear smaller than those up close. I am a painter trained in Western traditions, and Western painting follows the rules of perspective. I cannot paint him."

"Are there schools of painting that do not follow the rules of perspective?"

"Indeed. My king, look at those Eastern paintings." Needle-Eye pointed to a brush-painting landscape scroll hanging on one of the walls in the hall. The scroll showed an elegant, ethereal landscape where the negative space, the emptiness, resembled water and fog. The style contrasted sharply with the colorful, solid oil paintings nearby. "You can tell that the scroll does not obey the laws of perspective. But I never studied Eastern painting. Master Ethereal refused to teach me—perhaps he had foreseen today."

"You may leave." Ice Sand's face was impassive.

"Of course. Deep Water will arrive at the palace soon. He will kill me, and he will kill you. But I won't wait helplessly for death. I will take my own life by painting a masterpiece with it." Needle-Eye left, again moving noiselessly.

Ice Sand summoned his guards. "Bring me my sword."

Dense hoofbeats came into the hall from the outside: at first barely audible, then growing to resemble a thunderstorm. The sounds abruptly ceased right outside the palace.

Ice Sand stood up and exited the hall with his sword. He saw that Deep Water was ascending the stairs in front of the palace, and Dewdrop was behind him, with Auntie Wide next to her, holding up the umbrella. In the plaza below the stairs, the army stood in dense array. The soldiers waited quietly, not clearly showing their support for either side. When Ice Sand saw Deep Water for the first time, he seemed twice as tall as an ordinary man. But as he came closer, he seemed to shrink to a more normal size.

Ice Sand's thoughts returned in a flash to his childhood more than twenty years ago. He had known that the glutton fish were amassing around Tomb Island, but he nonetheless lured Deep Water to go fishing there. Back then, their father had been in the grip of some disease, and he told Deep Water that Tomb Island was the home to a special kind of fish whose liver oil could cure the king's illness. Deep Water, normally so careful, believed him, and, as Ice Sand had wanted, left without coming back. That had always been one of Ice Sand's proudest plots, and no one in the kingdom knew the truth.

Ice Sand's thoughts returned to the present. Deep Water was now on the dais at the top of the stairs, before the door to the palace. He looked as tall as a regular person.

"My brother," said Ice Sand. "I'm glad to see you and Dewdrop. But you must understand that this is my kingdom, and I am the king. You must immediately pledge fealty to me."

One of Deep Water's hands was on the grip of his rusty sword, and the other hand pointed at Ice Sand. "You have committed unforgivable crimes."

Ice Sand chuckled. "Needle-Eye may not be able to paint you, but I can pierce your heart." He unsheathed his sword.

Ice Sand and Deep Water were equally skilled swordsmen, but since Deep Water didn't obey the laws of perspective, it was very hard for Ice Sand to judge accurately how far away his opponent was. The fight quickly came to an end when Deep Water's sword stabbed through Ice Sand's chest. Ice Sand tumbled down the stairs and left a long trail of blood on the stone steps.

411

The army cheered and declared their fealty to Prince Deep Water and Princess Dewdrop.

While Deep Water and Ice Sand struggled, Captain Long-Sail had been searching for Needle-Eye in the palace. Someone informed him that the painter had gone to his own studio, which was in a distant corner of the palace. The captain saw that only one sentry stood at the door. He had served under Long-Sail.

"He came here an hour ago," said the sentry. "He's been inside since."

The captain broke down the door and stepped in.

The studio was windowless. The candles on the two silver candelabras had mostly burnt out, and the studio was as dim as an underground bunker. The place was empty.

But Long-Sail saw a painting on the easel. It had just been completed, and the paint wasn't even dry: a self-portrait of Needle-Eye. The painting truly was a masterpiece. It was like a window to another world, and Needle-Eye stood there gazing at this world. Although an uplifted corner of the snow-white paper showed that this was but a painting, the captain felt compelled to avoid the piercing gaze of the man in the painting.

Long-Sail looked around and saw other portraits hanging on the wall: the king, the queen, and the ministers loyal to them. He saw the painting of Princess Dewdrop, and the beautiful princess in the painting seemed to make this dim studio as bright as heaven. The eyes in the picture seized his soul, and he felt himself growing intoxicated. But in the end, Long-Sail came to his senses. He took down the painting, tossed away the frame, and lit the rolled-up scroll with one of the candles.

Just as the flames consumed the painting, the door to the studio opened and the real Princess Dewdrop came in. She was still dressed in the garb of a commoner, and she held up the spinning black umbrella by herself.

"Where's Auntie Wide?"

"I told her to stay outside; I have some things I want to say … just to you."

"Your portrait is gone." Long-Sail pointed to the still-glowing ashes on the ground. "You don't need the umbrella anymore."

The princess slowed down the spinning, and the umbrella began to cry like a nightingale. As the canopy fell, the cries grew louder and faster, until they resembled the screams of jackdaws—the final warning before the advent of Death. Then the umbrella closed and the stone spheres at the rim collided together in a series of sharp snaps.

The princess was unharmed.

The captain looked at the princess and let out a long sigh of relief. He turned to the ashes. "It's too bad. The portrait was lovely, and I would have liked you to see it. But I dared not delay ... it was really, really beautiful."

"Prettier than me?"

"It was you."

The princess retrieved the two bars of He'ershingenmosiken bath soap. She let go, and the weightless, white bars floated in the air like feathers.

"I'm going to leave the kingdom and sail the seas. Will you come with me?" asked the princess.

"What? But Prince Deep Water already announced that your coronation is tomorrow. He pledged to aid you with all his heart."

The princess shook her head. "My brother is more suited to be king than I. And if he hadn't been imprisoned on Tomb Island, he ought to have inherited the throne. When he's the king, he can stand somewhere high in the palace, and the entire kingdom can see him. But I don't want to be a queen. I like the outside more than the palace. I don't want to live the rest of my life in the Storyless Kingdom. I want to go where there are stories."

"That life is full of danger and hardship."

"I'm not afraid." The princess's eyes glowed with the spark of life in the candlelight. Long-Sail felt everything around him growing brighter again.

"I'm not afraid, either. Princess, I will follow you to the end of the sea, to the end of the world."

"Then we'll be the last two to leave the kingdom." The princess reached out and grabbed the two floating bars of soap.

"We'll take a sailboat."

"Yes, with snow-white sails."

The next morning, on a beach somewhere in the kingdom, people saw a white sail appear in the sea. Behind the sail was a long wake of cloudlike foam. It headed away from the kingdom by the light of the rising sun.

Thereafter, no one in the kingdom knew what happened to Princess Dewdrop and Long-Sail. As a matter of fact, the kingdom never received any information of the outside world. The princess had taken away the last bars of He'ershingenmosiken bath soap, and no one could break through the barriers formed by the schools of glutton fish. But no one complained. The people were used to their serene lives. After this story, there were never any other stories in the Storyless Kingdom.

But sometimes, late at night, some would tell stories that were not stories: imagined lives of Princess Dewdrop and Long-Sail. Everyone imagined different things, but all agreed that they journeyed to many exotic, mysterious kingdoms, including continents as vast as the sea. They lived ever after in wandering and trekking, and no matter where they went, they were happily together.

BROADCAST ERA, YEAR 7
YUN TIANMING'S FAIRY TALES

In the sophon-free room, those who had finished reading began to talk amongst themselves, though most were still absorbed in the world of the Storyless Kingdom, the sea, the princess and the princes. Some remained deep in thought; some stared at the document, as though hoping to glean more meaning from the cover.

"That princess is a lot like you," said AA to Cheng Xin.

"Try to focus on the serious business here ... and am I really that delicate?! I would have held up the umbrella myself." Cheng Xin was the only one who didn't bother reading the document. The stories were seared into her memory. She had, of course, wondered many times if Princess Dewdrop was modeled in some measure on herself. But the captain of the guards didn't resemble Yun Tianming.

Does he think I'm going to sail away somehow? With another man?

Once the chair noticed that everyone present had finished reading, he asked for opinions—mainly suggested directions for next steps to be taken by the various working groups under the IDC.

The committee member representing the literary analysis group asked to speak first. This group had been a last-minute addition, composed mainly of writers and scholars of Common Era literature. It was thought that there might be a minuscule chance—unlikely though it was—that they could be of use.

The speaker was a writer of children's stories. "I know that from now on, my group is unlikely to make any useful contributions. But I wanted to say a few words first." He lifted the blue-covered document. "I'm sorry to say that I don't believe this message can ever be deciphered."

"Why do you say that?" asked the chair.

"To be clear, we're trying to ascertain the strategic direction of humanity's struggles for the future. If this message really exists, no matter what it is, it must have a concrete meaning. We can't take vague, ambiguous information and turn it into strategic directions. But vagueness and ambiguity are at the heart of literary expression. Out of security considerations, I'm sure the true meaning behind these three stories is buried very deeply, and this makes the interpretations even more vague and ambiguous. The difficulty we are facing isn't that we can't get anything useful out of these three stories, but that there are too many plausible interpretations, and we can't be certain of any of them.

"Let me say something else that's not directly relevant here. As a writer, I want to express my respect for the author. As fairy tales, these are very good."

The next day, the IDC's work of deciphering Yun Tianming's message began in earnest. Very soon, everyone came to appreciate the warning by the children's story writer.

The three tales of Yun Tianming were rich in metaphors and symbolism; every detail could be interpreted in multiple ways, and each interpretation could find some support, but it was impossible to tell which one was the message intended by the author, and thus it was impossible to take any interpretation as strategic intelligence.

For instance, the idea of painting people into pictures was, by consensus, a rather obvious metaphor. But experts in different fields could not agree on a single interpretation. Some believed that the paintings were a reference to the digitization trend in the modern world, and thus this detail in the story suggested that humans

416

should also be digitized as a way to avoid dark forest strikes. Scholars who held this view also noted that those who had been painted into the paintings were no longer able to harm those in the real world, and so digitizing humanity was perhaps a way to promulgate the cosmic safety notice.

But another camp held that the paintings were intended to suggest special dimensions. The real world and the world of the paintings were of different dimensionalities, and when a person was painted, that person disappeared from three-dimensional space. This brought to mind the experiences of *Blue Space* and *Gravity* in the four-dimensional fragment, and so perhaps Tianming had intended to suggest that humanity could use four-dimensional space as a refuge, or broadcast the cosmic safety notice in some manner through four-dimensional space. Some scholars pointed to Prince Deep Water's violations of the rules of perspective as further evidence that the author meant four-dimensional space.

As another example, what was the meaning of the glutton fish? Some focused on their large numbers, their habit of remaining hidden, and their fierce, aggressive tendency, and reached the conclusion that they symbolized cosmic civilization as a whole in the dark forest state. The soap that allowed the glutton fish to feel so comfortable as to forget to attack represented some unknown principles behind the cosmic safety notice. Others, however, reached the opposite conclusion: They believed that the glutton fish represented intelligent machines that must be built by humankind. These machines would be small in size and capable of self-replication. Once released into space, the machines would use the matter found in the Kuiper Belt or the Oort Cloud to self-replicate in large numbers until they formed an intelligent barrier around the Solar System. The barrier could have multiple functions, e.g., intercepting photoids headed for the Sun, or altering the appearance of the Solar System from a distance in a manner that would achieve the goal of a cosmic safety notice.

This explanation, dubbed the Shoaling Interpretation, was given more attention than other competing interpretations. Compared

to the other hypotheses, the Shoaling Interpretation offered a relatively clear technical framework and became one of the first interpretations to be treated as an in-depth research topic by the World Academy of Sciences. But the IDC never put too much hope in the Shoaling Interpretation—although the idea seemed technically feasible, further study revealed that it would take tens of thousands of years for the self-replicating "shoals of fish" to form a barrier around the Solar System. Moreover, the limited functionality of AI machines meant that the protective and safety notice functions of the barrier were at best impractical visions. Ultimately, the Shoaling Interpretation had to be abandoned.

Countless competing interpretations were also offered for the spinning umbrella, the mysterious snow-wave paper and obsidian slab, the He'ershingenmosiken bath soap ...

Just like the writer of children's literature had said, all these explanations seemed justifiable, but it was impossible to ascertain which one was really meant.

It was not the case, however, that all the contents of the three stories were so vague and ambiguous. The IDC experts were certain that at least one detail in the story offered a concrete piece of intelligence, and was perhaps the key to unlocking the secrets of Yun Tianming's message.

They referred to the strange place name in the stories: *He'ershingenmosiken.*

Tianming had told Cheng Xin his stories in Chinese. People noticed that most of the place names and names of the characters had clear meanings in Chinese: the Storyless Kingdom, the Glutton's Sea, Tomb Island, Princess Dewdrop, Prince Ice Sand, Prince Deep Water, Needle-Eye, Master Ethereal, Captain Long-Sail, Auntie Wide, etc. However, mixed in was also this other name that appeared to be a phonetic transcription of the name of a foreign place. Not only was it strange phonetically for Chinese, it was also really long. The name also appeared repeatedly in the story in a way that clearly suggested something out of the ordinary: Needle-Eye and Master Ethereal had come from He'ershingenmosiken; the

snow-wave paper they used also came from He'ershingenmosiken; the obsidian slab and iron used for pressing the paper were also of He'ershingenmosiken; Captain Long-Sail had been born in He'ershingenmosiken; the bath soap of He'ershingenmosiken; the glutton fish of He'ershingenmosiken.... The author seemed to be repeatedly emphasizing the importance of this name, but there was no detailed description of He'ershingenmosiken at all. Was it another large island like the Storyless Kingdom? A continent? An archipelago?

Experts weren't even sure what language the name came from. When Yun Tianming had left on the Staircase probe, his English proficiency wasn't great, and he didn't know a third language— but it was possible that he had learned another language later. The name didn't resemble English, and it wasn't even clear if the name belonged to some Romance language. Of course the name couldn't be Trisolaran, since the Trisolaran language wasn't spoken or expressed by sounds.

Scholars tried to spell the name in all the world's known languages, to seek help from all fields, to search for it on the web and in all kinds of specialized databases, but nothing came of these efforts. Before this name, the most brilliant minds of humanity in various fields of study stood helpless.

The leaders of the various teams asked Cheng Xin: Was she sure she had remembered the pronunciation of the name correctly? Cheng Xin was unequivocal: She had noticed right away how strange the name sounded, and paid special attention to memorize it correctly. The name also appeared repeatedly in the story, and it was impossible that she had gotten it wrong.

The IDC's analysis made no progress. Such difficulties were not entirely unexpected: If humans could easily decipher Yun Tianming's stories for strategic intelligence, then so could the Trisolarans. The real intelligence information must be hidden deep. The experts in the various teams were exhausted, and the static electricity and

acrid odor in the sophon-free room made them irritable. Each team was divided into multiple factions who argued over competing interpretations without reaching consensus.

As the decipherment effort reached an impasse, doubts began to creep into the hearts of those in the IDC. Did the three stories really contain meaningful strategic intelligence? The suspicion was mainly directed at Yun Tianming himself. After all, he had only an undergraduate degree dating back to the Common Era, which meant that he had less knowledge than a contemporary middle school student. In his pre-mission life, he had mostly worked on routine, entry-level tasks, without any experience in conducting advanced scientific research or reasoning about novel fundamental scientific theories. Of course, after he was captured and cloned, he had plenty of opportunity for study, but the experts were doubtful whether he could understand the supertechnology of the Trisolarans, especially the basic theories that supported such technology.

Even worse, as the days went on, some unavoidable complexities began to creep into the IDC. At first, everyone strove to solve the riddle for the future of humanity as a whole. But later, various political forces and interest groups began to make themselves felt: Fleet International, the UN, the various nation states, multinational corporations, religions, and so on. All of these groups tried to interpret the stories according to their own political aims and self-interest, and treated the work of interpretation as just another opportunity to disseminate propaganda about their brand of politics. The stories turned into empty baskets capable of carrying any goods. The work of the IDC changed, and the debates between the various factions became politicized and utilitarian, which lowered morale.

But the lack of progress by the IDC also had a positive effect: It forced people to give up the illusion of a miracle. In actuality, the public had long ago stopped believing in the miracle, since they didn't even know of the existence of Yun Tianming's message. The political pressure exerted by the populace forced Fleet International and the UN to shift their attention from Yun Tianming's message

to searching for ways to preserve Earth civilization based on known technologies.

Viewed at the scale of the cosmos, the destruction of Trisolaris had occurred right next door, giving humans a chance to observe in detail the complete process of the extinction of a star and to gather massive amounts of data. Since the star that was destroyed was very similar to the Sun in terms of mass and position in the main sequence, humanity could potentially create a precise mathematical model of the catastrophic failure of the Sun in the event of a dark forest strike. As a matter of fact, this research had begun in earnest as soon as those on Earth had witnessed the end of Trisolaris. The direct result of research in this direction was the Bunker Project, which took the place of Yun Tianming's message as the focus of international attention.

EXCERPT FROM
A PAST OUTSIDE OF TIME
THE BUNKER PROJECT: AN ARK
FOR EARTH CIVILIZATION

I. Projected timeframe from exposure of Earth's coordinates to dark forest strike against the planet: optimistic scenario, one hundred to one hundred fifty years. Average scenario: fifty to eighty years. Pessimistic scenario: ten to thirty years. Plans for the survival of the human race used seventy years as a benchmark.

II. Total number of individuals who would need to be saved: Based on the rate of decrease in world population, the number would be six hundred to eight hundred million in seventy years.

III. Projected course of the anticipated dark forest strike: Using data from the destruction of Trisolaris's star, a mathematical model of the explosion of what would happen to the Sun if struck in the same way was constructed. Simulations based on the model showed that if the Sun were struck by a photoid, all terrestrial planets within the orbit of Mars would be destroyed. Immediately after the strike, Mercury and Venus would be vaporized. The Earth would retain some of its mass and keep a spherical form, but a

five-hundred-kilometer surface layer, including all of the crust and part of the mantle, would be stripped away. Mars would lose a layer about one hundred kilometers thick. Later, all the remaining terrestrial planets would lose velocity due to the material released by the solar explosion and crash into the surviving core of the Sun.

The model indicated that the destructive force of the solar explosion—including radiation and impact from solar material—would be inversely proportional to the square of the distance from the Sun. That is, the destructive force would diminish rapidly for objects far enough from the Sun. This would allow the Jovian planets to survive the explosion.

During the initial phase of the strike, the surface of Jupiter would be greatly disturbed, but its overall structure would be undamaged, including its satellites. The surfaces of Saturn, Uranus, and Neptune would also be disturbed without deeper damage. The dissipating ejected solar material would slow the orbits of the planets down to some degree, but later, as the solar material formed into a spiraling nebula, the angular velocity of its spin would match that of the Jovian planets and not degrade the orbits of those planets further.

The four gas giants, Jupiter, Saturn, Uranus, and Neptune, would survive a dark forest strike relatively unscathed. This prediction was the fundamental premise for the Bunker Project.

IV. Abandoned plans for the survival of the human race

1. Stellar Escape Plan: technically impossible. Humanity could not gain large-scale stellar navigation capabilities within the timeframe required. No more than one-thousandth of the overall population could fit into stellar escape arks. Moreover, it was highly unlikely that such arks would be able to locate and reach habitable exoplanets prior to fuel exhaustion and permanent breakdowns in long-term life support and ecological cycling systems.

As any plan along these lines could ensure the survival

of only an extremely small portion of the total population, it violated the fundamental values and moral principles of the human race. Politically, it was also unfeasible, as it could lead to massive social upheaval and the total collapse of society.

2. Long-distance Avoidance Plan: extremely low feasibility. This plan would involve constructing a human habitat at sufficient distance from the Sun to avoid its explosive destructive power. Based on the model and projected development of engineering techniques for hardening space cities in the foreseeable future, the minimum safe distance would be sixty AU from the Sun, which is beyond the Kuiper Belt. At that distance, few resources would be available in space for constructing a space city. Similarly, the lack of resources meant that even if such a city were built, it would be almost impossible to maintain for human occupation.

V. The Bunker Project: the four gas giants could be used as barriers to avoid the solar explosion from a dark forest strike. In the shade of the four planets, away from the sun, sufficient space habitats would be constructed to house the entirety of the human population. These space cities would be located next to the planets, but would not be their satellites. Instead, they would orbit the Sun in synchrony with the planets, staying within their shadows. The plan called for a total of fifty space cities, each of which was capable of housing about fifteen million individuals. Specifically, twenty cities would be shielded by Jupiter, twenty by Saturn, six by Uranus, and four by Neptune.

VI. Technical challenges facing the Bunker Project: The technology required by this plan had all been mastered by humanity. Fleet International possessed extensive experience constructing space cities, and there was already a sizable base around Jupiter. There were some technical challenges that could be overcome within the required timeframe, such as

how to regulate the positions of the space cities. Since the space cities would not be satellites of the gas giants, but would have to stay in close proximity of the planets, they would fall toward the planets, unless propulsion systems were installed to counteract gravity and maintain their distance from them. Initially, the plan called for the space cities to be positioned at the L2 Lagrangian points, such that the space cities' orbital periods would match their respective gas giants' without needing to expend much energy. However, it was later discovered that the L2 Lagrangian points would be too far away from the gas giants to provide sufficient protection.

VII. **The survival of the human race in the Solar System after a dark forest strike:** After the destruction of the Sun, the space cities would rely on nuclear fusion as their energy source. By then, the Solar System would appear as a spiral nebula, and the scattered solar material would provide an inexhaustible supply of easily collectable fusion material. It should also be possible to gather more fusion fuel from the remaining core of the Sun, sufficient to ensure humanity's long-term energy needs. Every space city could be equipped with its own artificial sun that would generate an amount of energy equivalent to the amount that had reached the surface of the Earth before the strike. From an energy efficiency point of view, the energy supply available to humans would actually be orders of magnitude higher than the pre-strike period because the space cities would consume fusion fuel at only one-billion-billionth the rate of the Sun. In that sense, the extinction of the Sun would be an improvement, because it would stop the extremely wasteful consumption of fusion material in the Solar System.

Once the nebula had stabilized somewhat after the dark forest strike, all the space cities could leave their barrier planets and find more suitable locations within the Solar System. It might be advisable for them to depart from the ecliptic plane so that they could avoid disturbance from the nebula while

being able to dip into it for resources. Since the solar explosion would destroy the terrestrial planets, the mineral resources of the Solar System would be scattered in the nebula, making them easier to collect. This would make it possible for more space cities to be constructed. The only projected resource limitation on the number of space cities was water, but there was a 160-kilometer-deep ocean covering Europa, providing a source of water greater in volume than the Earth's oceans, and capable of supplying a thousand space cities with individual populations ranging from ten to twenty million. More water could also be obtained from the nebula itself.

Thus, the post-strike Solar System nebula was capable of supporting over ten billion people in comfort, leaving human civilization plenty of room for development.

VIII. Impact on international relations from the Bunker Project: It was an unprecedented plan for the entire human race to construct a new world. The greatest barrier standing in its way wasn't technical, but a matter of international politics. The public was worried that the Bunker Project would exhaust the Earth's resources and reverse global progress in social welfare, politics, and economics, perhaps even leading to a second Great Ravine. But Fleet International and the UN were in agreement that such danger could be avoided. The Bunker Project was to be engineered entirely with resources from the Solar System outside the Earth, mainly from the satellites of the four Jovian planets and the rings of Saturn, Uranus, and Neptune. There should be no drain on Earth resources or its economy. In fact, once development of space resources reached a certain stage, the project might even enhance the Earth's economy.

IX. Overall program for the Bunker Project: It would take twenty years to build the industrial infrastructure for extracting and exploiting resources from the gas giants, and sixty years to construct the space cities. The two stages would overlap by ten years.

X. The possibility of a second dark forest strike: The results of the first dark forest strike should convince most distant observers that the Solar System was lifeless. Simultaneously, as a result of the destruction of the Sun, the Solar System would no longer contain an energy source capable of supporting an economical attack from a distance. Thus, the possibility of a second dark forest strike seemed minute. The conditions of 187J3X1 after its destruction also provided support for this view.

BROADCAST ERA, YEAR 7
YUN TIANMING'S FAIRY TALES

As preparations for the Bunker Project got underway, Yun Tianming faded from the public consciousness. The IDC continued to work on deciphering the message, but it was only treated as one of the PDC's many projects. The hope for retrieving important strategic intelligence from the stories diminished daily. Some members of the IDC even connected the Bunker Project with Yun Tianming's fairy tales and came up with several interpretations that pointed to that as the right plan. For instance, the umbrella was naturally read as a hint at some defensive structure. Someone pointed out that the stone spheres at the rim of the canopy could symbolize the Jovian planets, but there were only four planets within the Solar System capable of acting as barriers. Tianming's stories did not mention the number of ribs in the canopy, but, rationally, four ribs for an umbrella seemed rather low. Of course, not many people really believed this interpretation, but in some sense, Tianming's stories had now acquired a status akin to the Bible. Without realizing it, people were no longer searching for real strategic intelligence, but reassurance that they were already on the right course.

Then came the unexpected breakthrough in interpreting the stories.

One day, 艾 AA came to see Cheng Xin. She had long ceased to accompany Cheng Xin to the IDC meetings, but devoted all her energy to the pursuit of involving the Halo Group in the Bunker Project. Building a new world outside the orbit of Jupiter represented a limitless opportunity for a space construction company. And wasn't it fortuitous that the company was named the Halo Group when the "halos" of the Jovian planets would provide much of the resources for constructing the space cities?

"I want a bar of bath soap," said AA.

Cheng Xin ignored her. Her eyes didn't leave the e-book in front of her, and she asked AA a question about fusion physics. After her awakening, she had devoted herself to the study of modern science. Common Era spaceflight technologies had all disappeared by this point, and even a tiny shuttlecraft now relied on nuclear fusion propulsion. Cheng Xin had to begin with basic physics, but she made rapid progress. As a matter of fact, the gap of years didn't impose too high a barrier in her studies: Most of the shifts in fundamental theory had occurred only after the start of the Deterrence Era. With some diligence, most scientists and engineers from the Common Era could once again adapt to their chosen professions.

AA turned off Cheng Xin's book. "Give me bath soap!"

"I don't have any. You understand that actual bath soap doesn't have the magic of those fairy tales, right?" What Cheng Xin really meant was for AA to stop acting so childish.

"I know. But I like bubbles. I want to take a bubble bath like the princess!"

Modern baths had nothing to do with bubbles. Soap and other similar toiletries had disappeared more than a century ago. Contemporary bathing practices involved two methods: supersonic waves and cleaning agents. Cleaning agents were nanorobots invisible to the naked eye. One could use them with or without water. They cleaned skin and other surfaces instantaneously.

Cheng Xin had to go with AA to shop for bath soap. Whenever she had been depressed in the past, AA often dragged her out like this to cheer her up.

Faced with the giant forest that was the city, they pondered their choices and decided in the end that the most likely place to find bath soap was a museum. They succeeded in their quest in a city history museum's exhibit hall dedicated to the daily necessities of Common Era life: home appliances, clothing, furniture, etc. These objects were well preserved, and some even looked brand new. Mentally, Cheng Xin couldn't accept that these were artifacts from centuries ago; to her, they seemed to be from just yesterday. Although so much had happened since she was first awakened, this new age still felt like a dream to her. Her spirit had stubbornly been living in the past.

The bath soap was in a display case along with other cleaning products such as laundry detergent. Cheng Xin stared at the translucent bar and saw the familiar eagle logo carved into the soap: product of the Nice Group. It was pure white, just like the soap in the story.

The museum director initially claimed that the bath soap was a precious artifact and not for sale, but then he proceeded to name an outrageous price.

"That's enough money to build a small factory for cleaning products," said Cheng Xin to AA.

"So? I've been working for you for years as the CEO. You should give me a present. And who knows? Maybe it will appreciate in value in the future."

And so they bought the bath soap. Cheng Xin had suggested that if AA really wanted a bubble bath, then it would be better to buy the bottle of bubble bath liquid. But AA insisted on the soap because the princess used soap. After the bar of bath soap was carefully retrieved from the display case, Cheng Xin held it and noticed that, despite the passage of more than two centuries, the soap still gave off a faint fragrance.

After returning home, AA ripped off the packaging and went into the bathroom with the soap. Then came the sound of the tub being filled.

Cheng Xin knocked on the door. "I suggest you don't bathe

with it. The soap is alkaline. Since you've never used it, your skin might be damaged."

AA didn't respond. A long time later, after the water stopped, the bathroom door opened. Cheng Xin saw that AA was still dressed. Waving a white sheet of paper at Cheng Xin, AA asked, "Do you know how to make an origami boat?"

"I suppose this is also a lost art?" asked Cheng Xin as she took the paper.

"Obviously. We hardly see paper now."

Cheng Xin sat down and began to fold. Her thoughts returned to that drizzly afternoon in college. She and Tianming sat by the reservoir and watched as the tiny paper boat she made drifted away on the water covered by mist and rain. Then she thought about the white sail at the end of Tianming's stories....

AA picked up the canopied paper boat and admired it. Then she indicated that Cheng Xin should follow her into the bathroom. With a pocketknife, she cut off a tiny corner from the bar of soap, poked a hole in the stern of the boat, and stuck the soap fragment into the hole. After giving Cheng Xin a mysterious smile, she deposited the boat into the calm water in the bathtub.

The boat began to move by itself, sailing from one edge of the tub to the other.

Cheng Xin understood right away. As the soap dissolved in the water, it lowered the surface tension of the water behind the boat. But as the tension in the water in front of the boat remained unchanged, it pulled the boat forward.

A bolt of lightning seemed to illuminate Cheng Xin's thoughts. In her eyes, the serene surface of the water in the tub turned into the darkness of space, and the white paper boat sailed across this endless sea at the speed of light....

Then Cheng Xin remembered something else: Tianming's safety.

The string of her thought stopped vibrating immediately, as though a hand had been placed against it. Cheng Xin forced herself to look away from the boat, maintaining, as much as possible, a look of boredom and disinterest. The boat had now reached the

431

other edge of the tub and stopped. She picked it out of the tub, shook off the water, and dropped it on the washstand. She almost tossed the boat into the toilet to flush it away, but thought that might appear excessive. She made up her mind, however, to not put the boat in water again.

Danger.

Though Cheng Xin also leaned to the view that no sophons were present in the Solar System, it was better to be cautious.

Cheng Xin and AA locked gazes. They each saw in the eyes of the other the same thing: the excitement of enlightenment dancing within. Cheng Xin looked away. "I don't have time to waste on silly games. If you want a bubble bath, go for it." She left the bathroom.

AA followed. They poured themselves two glasses of wine and began to chat about random topics. First, they discussed the future of the Halo Group in the Bunker Project. Then they recalled their college lives in different centuries. Then they talked about life in the present. AA asked Cheng Xin why she had not found a man she liked after living in the new age for so long, and Cheng Xin replied that she couldn't live a regular life, not yet. Then she pointed out that AA's problem was that she dated too many men—of course she was welcome to bring her boyfriends to visit Cheng Xin, but it was best to bring only one at a time. They also discussed the fashions and tastes of the women of their respective eras, their similarities and differences. . . .

Language was merely the vehicle through which they expressed their excitement. They dared not stop, lest the silence rob them of their hidden joy. Finally, in a break in the meandering conversation that would not be noticed by a listener, Cheng Xin said, "Curvature—"

She finished her sentence with her eyes: *propulsion?*

AA nodded. Her eyes said, *Yes, curvature propulsion!*

EXCERPT FROM
A PAST OUTSIDE OF TIME
MOTION THROUGH
BENDING SPACE

Space wasn't flat, but curved. If one imagined the universe as a large, thin membrane, the surface would be shaped like a bowl. The entire membrane might even be an enclosed bubble. Though at the local scale, the membrane seemed flat, the curvature of space was omnipresent.

During the Common Era, many ambitious ideas for spaceflight were proposed. One of them involved folding space. The idea was to imagine an increase in the curvature of space and fold it like a sheet of paper so that two spots tens of millions of light-years apart could touch each other. Strictly speaking, this wasn't a plan for spaceflight, but "space-dragging." It didn't involve navigating to the destination, but pulling the destination over to you by bending space.

Only God could have carried out such a plan—and once the limitations of basic theory were taken into account, perhaps not even God.

Later, there was a more moderate and localized proposal for taking advantage of curved space for navigation. Supposing a spaceship could somehow iron flat the space behind it and decrease

its curvature, the more curved space in front of it would pull it forward. This was the idea of curvature propulsion.

Unlike folding space, curvature propulsion couldn't get a spaceship to its destination instantaneously, but it would be possible to drive it asymptotically to the speed of light.

Until Yun Tianming's message had been correctly interpreted, curvature propulsion remained a dream, like hundreds of other proposals for lightspeed spaceflight. No one knew whether it was possible at either a theory or practice level.

BROADCAST ERA, YEAR 7
YUN TIANMING'S FAIRY TALES

A jubilant AA said to Cheng Xin, "Before the Deterrence Era, clothes with animated images were popular. Back then, everyone looked like blinking Christmas trees, but now, only children dress like that. Classical looks are in vogue again."

But AA's eyes were saying something else entirely. Her eyes dimmed. *This interpretation looks very good, but it's still impossible to be certain. We can never get confirmation.*

Cheng Xin said, "I'm most surprised that precious metals and gems no longer exist! Gold is now a common metal, and both of our drinking glasses are made of diamonds.... Did you know that where—er, when—I come from, owning a tiny diamond—like this big—would have been an unattainable dream for most girls."

Her eyes were saying, *No, AA, this time it's different. We can be sure.*

"Well, at least you had cheap aluminum. Before the invention of electrolysis, aluminum was a precious metal as well. I've heard that some kings even had crowns made of aluminum."

How can we be sure?

Cheng Xin couldn't express what she wanted with only her eyes. IDC had once offered to build her a sophon-free room in her apartment. That would have involved a large amount of noisy equipment, so she had turned them down. Now she regretted that decision.

"Snow-wave paper," she whispered.

AA's eyes lit up again. The flame of excitement burned even brighter than before.

> *"There's really nothing else that will flatten this?"*
>
> *"No. Only the obsidian from He'ershingenmosiken will do the job. I was hoping to get the obsidian slab back from Needle-Eye."*

> *The clock in the corner of the room sounded. Ethereal looked up and saw it was almost sunrise. He looked down and saw that only about a palm's width of the snow-wave paper lay flat on the floor, not enough for a painting. He dropped the iron and sighed.*

A scroll was a rolled-up sheet of paper with curvature; a section was pulled out and ironed flat, decreasing the curvature.

This was clearly a hint for the difference in space in front of and behind a ship driven by curvature propulsion. It couldn't mean anything else.

"Let's go," said Cheng Xin as she got up.

"Yes," AA said. They needed to get to the nearest sophon-free room.

Two days later, the IDC chair announced at a committee meeting that the heads of all the working groups had unanimously endorsed the curvature propulsion interpretation.

Yun Tianming was telling the Earth that the Trisolaran ships used space curvature drives.

This was an extremely important piece of strategic intelligence. Out of all the possible paths for researching lightspeed spaceflight, curvature propulsion was confirmed to be feasible. Like a beacon in dark night, this indicated the right direction for further development of human spaceflight technology.

Equally important was the fact that the interpretation provided the model for how Tianming had hidden his message in the three stories. He employed two basic methods: dual-layer metaphors and two-dimensional metaphors.

The dual-layer metaphors in the stories did not directly point to the real meaning, but to something far simpler. The tenor of this first metaphor became the vehicle for a second metaphor, which pointed to the real intelligence. In the current example, the princess's boat, the He'ershingenmosiken soap, and the Glutton's Sea formed a metaphor for a paper boat driven by soap. The paper boat, in turn, pointed to curvature propulsion. Previous attempts at decipherment had failed largely due to people's habitual belief that the stories only involved a single layer of metaphors to hide the real message.

The two-dimensional metaphors were a technique used to resolve the ambiguities introduced by literary devices employed in conveying strategic intelligence. After a dual-layer metaphor, a single-layer supporting metaphor was added to confirm the meaning of the dual-layer metaphor. In the current example, the curved snow-wave paper and the ironing required to flatten it served as a metaphor for curved space, confirming the interpretation of the soap-driven boat. If one viewed the stories as a two-dimensional plane, the dual-layer metaphor only provided one coordinate; the supporting single-layer metaphor provided a second coordinate that fixed the interpretation on the plane. Thus, this single-layer metaphor was also called the bearing coordinate. Viewed by itself, the bearing coordinate seemed meaningless, but once combined with the dual-layer metaphor, it resolved the inherent ambiguities in literary language.

"A subtle and sophisticated system," a PIA specialist said admiringly.

All the committee members congratulated Cheng Xin and AA. AA, who had always been looked down on, saw her status greatly elevated among the committee members.

Cheng Xin's eyes moistened. She was thinking of Tianming, of

the man who struggled alone in the long night of outer space and an eerie, sinister alien society. To convey his important message to the human race, he must have racked his brain until he had devised such a metaphorical system, and then spent ages in his lonely existence to create over a hundred fairy tales and carefully disguise the intelligence report in three of those stories. Three centuries ago, he had given Cheng Xin a star; now, he brought hope to the human race.

Thereafter, steady progress was made in deciphering the message. Other than the discovery of the metaphorical system, the effort was also aided by another guess that was commonly accepted, though unconfirmed: While the first part of the message to be successfully deciphered involved escape from the Solar System, the rest of the message likely had to do with the safety notice.

The interpreters soon realized that compared to the first bit of intelligence, the rest of the information hidden in the three stories was far more complex.

At the next IDC meeting, the chair produced a custom-made umbrella that looked just like the one in the fairy tales. The black umbrella had eight ribs, and at the end of each was a small stone sphere. In this era, umbrellas were no longer in common use. To avoid the rain, modern people used something called a rainshield, a device about the size of a flashlight that protected the user by blowing air up to form an invisible canopy. People certainly knew about umbrellas and saw them in movies, but few had experience with the real thing. Curious, they played with the chair's umbrella, and noticed that, just like in the stories, the canopy could be kept open by spinning. Spinning faster or slower resulted in corresponding alarm sounds.

"This is really tiring," someone complained as he spun the umbrella.

Everyone gained new respect for the princess's wet nurse, who'd managed to spin the umbrella nonstop for a whole day.

AA took over the umbrella. Her hands weren't as strong, and the canopy began to fall. They all heard the warning birdsong.

Cheng Xin had kept her eyes on the umbrella since the chair had opened it. Now she cried out to AA, "Don't stop!"

AA spun faster, and the birdsong stopped.

"Faster," said Cheng Xin.

AA put all her strength into spinning, and the wind chime began to play. Then Cheng Xin asked her to slow down, until the birdsong appeared. This went back and forth a few times.

"This is not an umbrella at all!" said Cheng Xin. "But I know what it is now."

Bi Yunfeng, who stood to the side, nodded. "Me too." Then he turned to Cao Bin. "Probably only the three of us can recognize this object."

"Yes," said an excited Cao. "But even in our time, this was rarely seen."

Some of the attendees looked at these three individuals from the past; others looked at the umbrella. All were puzzled, but also expectant.

"It's a centrifugal governor," said Cheng Xin. "For steam engines."

"What's that? Some kind of control circuit?"

Bi Yunfeng shook his head. "The world wasn't electrified back when this was invented."

Cao Bin explained. "This was a device from the eighteenth century for regulating the speed of a steam engine. It's made of two or four lever arms equipped with spherical masses at the ends and a central spindle with a sleeve—it looks just like this umbrella, except with fewer ribs. The steam engine's operation rotates the spindle. When it spins too fast, the metal balls lift the lever arms due to centrifugal force, which pulls up on the sleeve and reduces the aperture of the throttle valve connected to the sleeve, thereby reducing the fluid entering the cylinder and the engine's speed. Conversely, when it spins too slowly, the lever arms fall due to the weight of the metal balls—like an umbrella closing—and the sleeve is pushed down, increasing the aperture of the throttle valve and the speed of the engine.... This was one of the earliest industrial automatic control systems."

Thus was the first level of the dual-layer metaphor in the umbrella decoded. But unlike the soap-propelled boat, the centrifugal

governor didn't seem to clearly point to anything. This second-layer metaphor could be interpreted in multiple ways, with two possibilities deemed most likely: negative-feedback automatic control and constant speed.

The interpreters began to look for the corresponding bearing coordinate for this dual-layer metaphor. Soon, they fixed on Prince Deep Water. The prince's height didn't change in the observers' eyes regardless of distance. This could also be interpreted in multiple ways, with two possibilities being most obvious: a method of information transmission where the signal strength did not decay due to distance, or a physical quantity that remained constant regardless of the frame of reference used.

Taken together with the metaphorical meanings of the umbrella, the true meaning instantly emerged: a constant speed that did not change with the frame of reference.

Clearly, it referred to the speed of light.

Unexpectedly, the interpreters found yet another bearing coordinate for the metaphor of the umbrella.

> The He'ershingenmosiken bath soap is made from those
> bubbles, but collecting the bubbles is no easy matter.
> The bubbles drift very fast in the wind.... Only if
> someone were running as fast as the bubbles, such that
> they're at rest relative to the bubbles, would they be able
> to see them. This is possible only by riding the fastest
> horses.... The soap-makers ride these horses to chase
> after the wind and try to collect the bubbles with a thin
> gauze net.... The bubbles have no weight, which is why
> pure, authentic He'ershingenmosiken soap also has no
> weight. It's the lightest substance in the world....

The fastest; with no weight, or massless—this was a clear, single-layer metaphor for light.

Everything indicated that the umbrella stood in for light, but capturing the bubbles from the bubble tree had two possible

interpretations: collecting the power of light or lowering the speed of light.

Most interpreters didn't think the first interpretation had much to do with humanity's strategic goals, so most of the focus was on the second interpretation.

Although they still couldn't tell the exact meaning of the message, the interpreters debated the second interpretation, concentrating on the connection between lowering the speed of light and the cosmic safety notice.

"Suppose that we could lower the speed of light in the Solar System. That is, within the Kuiper Belt or Neptune's orbit, we could produce an effect observable from a distance—at cosmic scales."

This thought excited everyone.

"Suppose we reduced the speed of light by ten percent within the Solar System—would that make a cosmic observer think we're safer?"

"Undoubtedly. If humans possessed lightspeed spaceships, it would take them longer to emerge from the Solar System. But it wouldn't mean *that* much."

"To really indicate to the universe that we're safe, a reduction by ten percent is insufficient. We may have to reduce the speed of light to ten percent of its original value, or maybe even one percent. Observers would see that we've surrounded ourselves in a buffer zone that made certain that our ships would take a long time to emerge from the Solar System. This should increase their feelings of safety."

"But by that reasoning, lowering the speed of light to one-tenth of one percent would be insufficient. Think about it: Even at three hundred kilometers per second, it still wouldn't take that long to get out of the Solar System. Also, if humans were capable of modifying a physical constant within a region of space with a radius of fifty astronomical units, then this would be tantamount to a declaration that humans possessed very advanced technology. Instead of a cosmic safety notice, it would be a cosmic danger warning!"

From the dual-layer metaphor of the umbrella and the bearing

coordinates provided by Prince Deep Water and the bubble tree, the interpreters were able to ascertain the general tenor of their import, but not the specific strategic intelligence. The metaphor was no longer two-dimensional but three-dimensional. Some started to guess at the existence of yet another bearing coordinate, and the interpreters searched exhaustively through the stories, but they turned up nothing.

Just then, the mysterious name He'ershingenmosiken was finally deciphered.

A linguistic working group was added by the IDC specifically to deal with He'ershingenmosiken. A historical linguist and philologist, Palermo, had been added to the group because his expertise differed from the others'. Instead of focusing on one language family, he was familiar with the ancient languages of many linguistic families. But even Palermo could offer no insight on this strange name. That he succeeded was due to an unexpected stroke of good luck, and had little to do with his professional expertise.

One morning, after Palermo woke up, his girlfriend, a blond Scandinavian, asked him whether he'd ever been to her homeland.

"Norway? No, never."

"Then why were you mumbling those two place names in your dream?"

"What names?"

"Helseggen and Mosken."

The names sounded vaguely familiar to Palermo. Since his girlfriend had nothing to do with the IDC, it was a little eerie to hear those sounds coming from her. "You mean *He'ershingenmosiken*?"

"Yes, though you're running them together and not saying them quite right."

"I'm saying the name of a single place. It's a Chinese transliteration—so the sounds are approximate. If you break the syllables into arbitrary groups, they probably sound like the names of many places in different languages."

442

"But both of these places are in Norway."

"A coincidence, that's all."

"Let me tell you, the average Norwegian isn't likely to know those places either. They are ancient names, no longer used. I know of them only because my specialty is Norwegian history. Both are in Nordland County."

"My dear, that's still just a coincidence. You can break that string of syllables anywhere."

"Oh please, stop teasing! You must have known that Helseggen is the name of a mountain, and Mosken is a tiny island in the Lofoten archipelago."

"I really didn't. Look, there's a phenomenon in linguistics where a listener who doesn't know the language will arbitrarily divide a series of syllables into groupings almost subconsciously. That's what's happening here."

Palermo had encountered such arbitrary divisions numerous times during his work for the IDC, so he didn't take his girlfriend's "discovery" seriously. But what she said next changed everything.

"Fine, let me point out one more thing: Helseggen is located right next to the sea. You can see Mosken from the top—it's the closest isle to Helseggen!"

Two days later, Cheng Xin stood on Mosken Island and looked over the sea at the craggy cliffs of Helseggen. The cliffs were black, and because the sky was overcast, the sea appeared black as well. Only a white line of surf appeared at the foot of the cliffs. Before coming here, Cheng Xin had heard that although this location was within the Arctic Circle, warm sea currents made the climate relatively mild. However, the wind coming off the sea still chilled her.

The steep, craggy Lofoten Islands were carved by glaciers, and formed a 160-kilometer-long barrier between the North Sea and deep Vestfjorden, like a wall that divided the Arctic Ocean from the Scandinavian Peninsula. The currents between the islands were strong and rapid. In the past, few people had inhabited the islands,

and most were seasonal fishermen. Now that seafood mainly came from aquaculture, open-sea fishing had virtually disappeared. The islands had again grown desolate, and probably resembled how they had looked during the time of the Vikings.

Mosken was only a tiny isle in the archipelago, and Helseggen was a nameless mountain—these names had changed at the end of the Crisis Era.

Faced with the forlorn desolation at the world's end, Cheng Xin nonetheless felt serenity in her heart. Not long ago, she had thought her own life had reached its terminus, but now there were many reasons to continue living. She saw a sliver of blue revealed at the edge of the leaden sky, and the sun peeked out of the opening for a few minutes, instantaneously changing this cold world. It reminded her of a line from Tianming's stories: ... *as if the painter of this world-picture scattered a handful of gold dust boldly over the surface of the painting.* This was her life now, hope hidden in despair, warmth felt through frost.

AA had come with her, as well as a few IDC experts, including Bi Yunfeng, Cao Bin, and Palermo the linguist.

Mosken's only inhabitant was an old man named Jason. He was more than eighty years of age and had come from the Common Era. His square face showed the marks left by the years and reminded Cheng Xin of Fraisse. When he was asked if there was anything special in the vicinity of Helseggen and Mosken, Jason pointed to the western edge of the island.

"Of course. Look there."

They saw a white lighthouse. Although it was only dusk, the lighthouse was already lit and blinked rhythmically.

"What's that for?" asked AA.

"Ha! Children these days ..." Jason shook his head. "It's an ancient navigation aid. Back during the Common Era, I was an engineer responsible for designing lighthouses and beacon lights. As a matter of fact, many lighthouses remained in use until the Crisis Era, though they're all gone by now. I built this lighthouse here so that kids would know that such a thing existed once."

The IDC members were all interested in the lighthouse. It reminded them of the centrifugal governor for steam engines, another ancient technology that had disappeared. But a brief investigation showed that this couldn't be what they were looking for. The lighthouse had been constructed recently and utilized modern building materials that were strong and light. It had taken only half a month to complete. Jason was also certain that historically, Mosken did not have a lighthouse. Thus, based on timing alone, the lighthouse had nothing to do with Tianming's hidden message.

"Anything else interesting or special around here?" someone asked.

Jason shrugged at the cold sky and sea. "What could be here? I don't like this bleak and dreary place, but they wouldn't let me build a lighthouse anywhere else."

So everyone decided to go to Helseggen and take a look around. Just as they were about to get into the helicopter, AA suddenly had the idea to go over on Jason's tiny boat.

"Sure thing, but the waves are powerful today, child. You'll get seasick," Jason said.

AA pointed to the mountain across the strait. "This is a really short ride."

Jason shook his head. "I can't sail straight across. Not today. We have to go the long way around."

"Why?"

"The maelstrom, of course. It will swallow up any boat."

Cheng Xin's party looked at each other and then turned to Jason as one. Someone asked, "I thought you said there was nothing special here."

"The Mosskstraumen is nothing special for us locals. It's just part of the sea. You can often see it there."

"Where?"

"Right there. You may not be able to see it, but you can hear it."

They quieted, and did hear a rumbling from the sea, like thousands of horses stampeding in the distance.

The helicopter could take them to investigate the maelstrom, but Cheng Xin wanted to go over on a boat, and the others agreed. Jason's boat, the only one available on the island, could seat five or six safely. Cheng Xin, AA, Bi Yunfeng, Cao Bin, and Palermo got onto the boat while the others took the helicopter.

The boat left Mosken Island, bumping over the waves. The wind over the open sea was stronger and colder, and salty spray struck their faces without cease. The surface of the sea was a dark gray, and appeared eerie and mysterious in the dimming light. The rumbling grew louder, but they still couldn't see the great whirlpool.

"Oh, I remember now!" Cao Bin shouted.

Cheng Xin also remembered. She had thought that perhaps Tianming had found out something new about this place through the sophons, but the real answer was far simpler.

"Edgar Allan Poe," said Cheng Xin.

"What? Who?" asked AA.

"A nineteenth-century writer."

Jason said, "Right. Poe wrote a story about Mosken—'A Descent into the Maelstrom.' I read it when I was younger. It's very exaggerated. I remember him writing that the surface of the whirlpool formed a forty-five-degree angle. That's absurd."

Written narrative literature had disappeared more than a century ago. "Literature" and "authors" still existed, but narratives were constructed with digital images. Classical written novels and stories were now treated as ancient artifacts. The Great Ravine had caused the loss of the works of many ancient writers, including Poe.

The rumbling grew even louder. "Where's the whirlpool?" someone asked.

Jason pointed at the sea surface. "The maelstrom is lower than the surface here. Look at that line: you have to cross it to see the Mokstraumen." The passengers saw a fluctuating band of waves whose frothy tips formed a long, white arc that extended into the distance.

"Then let's cross it!" Bi Yunfeng said.

Jason glared at him. "That's a line separating life from death. A boat that crosses cannot return."

"How long could a boat circle around the inside of the whirlpool before being pulled under?"

"Forty minutes to an hour."

"Then we should be fine. The helicopter will save us in time."

"But my boat—"

"We'll compensate you."

"Cheaper than a bar of soap," AA interjected. Jason didn't know what she was talking about.

Carefully, Jason aimed the boat at the band of waves and navigated through. The boat swayed from side to side violently and then stabilized. Some invisible force seemed to seize it, and the boat began to glide along in the same direction as the waves as if riding on rails.

"The maelstrom has caught us," Jason cried out. "My God, this is the first time I've been this close!"

The Moskstraumen revealed itself below them as though they stood on top of a mountain. The monstrous funnel-shaped depression was about a kilometer in diameter. The slanting sides were indeed not as steep as the forty-five degrees mentioned by Poe, but they were at least thirty degrees. The surface of the vortex was smooth as a solid. Since the boat was only at the edge of the whirlpool, the spin wasn't very fast. But as they got closer to the center, the spin would become faster. At the tiny hole down in the center, the speed of the churning sea was highest, and the bone-shattering rumbling came from there. The rumbling expressed a mad power capable of grinding everything into pieces and sucking them out of existence.

"I refuse to believe we can't force our way out," said AA. She shouted at Jason, "Follow a straight line at maximum power!"

Jason did as she asked. The boat was electrically powered, and the quiet engine sounded like a mosquito in the rumbling of the whirlpool. The boat approached the wave band at the edge of the maelstrom and appeared to come close to leaving, but then lost

momentum and turned away from the froth, like a tossed pebble that passed the apex of its trajectory. They tried a few more times, but each time, they slid back down farther into the maelstrom.

"Now you see: this is the gate of hell. No normal boat can return," said Jason.

By now, the boat was so deep down in the whirlpool that the frothy waves at the rim were no longer visible. Behind them was the mountain formed of seawater, and they could only see the slow-moving top of the mountain at the other side of the whirlpool. Everyone felt the terror of being at the mercy of an irresistible force. Only the helicopter hovering overhead gave them any measure of comfort.

"Let's have supper," said Jason. The sun had not yet set behind the clouds, but since it was the Arctic summer, it was already after 9 P.M. Jason took a large cod out of the hold and explained that it had been freshly caught. Then he took out three bottles of wine, placed the fish on a large iron platter, and poured a bottle of wine over the fish. With a lighter, he set the fish on fire, explaining that this was the local method of preparation. Five minutes later, he began to pull pieces off of the still-burning fish and eat them. The passengers imitated him, enjoying the fish, wine, and the magnificence of the maelstrom.

"Child, I recognize you," Jason said to Cheng Xin. "You were the Swordholder. I'm sure you and your people came here for some important mission, but you must keep your cool. We can't avoid the apocalypse, so we must enjoy the present."

"I doubt you could keep your cool if that helicopter weren't there," said AA.

"Ha, kid, I would. I surely would. Back in the Common Era, I was only forty when I found out I had a terminal illness. But I wasn't afraid, and I never even planned to go into hibernation. It was only after I went into shock that the doctors put me into hibernation. By the time I woke up, it was already the Deterrence Era. I thought I had been given a new life, but that turned out to be just an illusion. Death only backed off a little ways to wait for me on the road ahead. . . .

448

"The night I finished building the lighthouse, I took my boat out to the sea to look at it from a distance. And all of a sudden I had a thought: Death is the only lighthouse that is always lit. No matter where you sail, ultimately, you must turn toward it. Everything fades in the world, but Death endures."

It had been twenty minutes since they entered the whirlpool, and the boat had slid about a third of the way down toward the bottom. The boat became more slanted, but due to centrifugal force, the passengers weren't sliding toward the portside. The wall of water filled their field of view, and they could no longer see the top, even on the other side of the whirlpool. Everyone avoided looking up at the sky because, in the maelstrom, the boat moved along with the spinning wall of water, and it was almost impossible to feel the motion—the boat seemed to adhere to the side of a watery basin. But if they looked up, the motion instantly became evident. The cloud-filled sky spun overhead faster and faster, making them dizzy. Since the centrifugal force was stronger lower in the vortex, the water wall below the boat became even smoother and felt more solid, like ice. The rumbling from the eye of the maelstrom overwhelmed every other sound, and conversation was no longer possible. The Sun in the west peeked out of cracks in the cloud cover, and a ray of golden light shone into the swirling vortex. But the light couldn't reach the maw at the bottom, and only illuminated a small part of the wall of water, making the bottom appear even more dark and menacing by contrast. Mist and fog swirled out of the eye at the center, forming a rainbow in the ray of sunlight that arced grandly across the rotating abyss.

"I remember Poe describing a rainbow in the maelstrom as well. I think it was even in moonlight. He called it a bridge between Time and Eternity." Jason was shouting, but no one could hear what he was saying.

The helicopter came to their rescue. Hovering about two or three meters above the boat, it dangled a rope ladder so that everyone in the boat could climb out. Then the empty boat drifted away and continued to circle the monstrous vortex. The unfinished cod on the boat still glowed with the remnants of a blue flame.

The helicopter hovered above the maw of the maelstrom, and as everyone looked down at the spinning funnel, they soon felt nauseated and dizzy. Someone entered directions into the navigation system for the helicopter to spin, matching the whirlpool's rotation below. This way, the whirlpool appeared still, but the world outside—sky, sea, and mountains—began to spin around them. The maelstrom seemed to become the center of the world, and the observer's nausea wasn't reduced in the slightest. AA vomited up all the fish she had eaten.

As she gazed at the whirlpool below, another whirlpool appeared in Cheng Xin's mind: It was made up of a hundred billion silver stars spinning in the sea that was the universe, taking 250 million years to complete one rotation—it was the Milky Way. The Earth was not even as big as a mote of dust in this whirlpool, and the Moskstraumen was but another mote of dust on the Earth-dust.

Half an hour later, the boat fell into the eye and disappeared abruptly. Amidst the unchanging rumbling, they seemed to detect the sound of the boat being ground apart.

The helicopter dropped Jason off at Mosken, and Cheng Xin promised to compensate him with a new boat as soon as possible. Then they said farewell and the helicopter headed for Oslo, the nearest city with a sophon-free room.

Everyone remained deep in thought through the voyage, not even conversing with their eyes.

The Moskstraumen's meaning was so obvious that no thought was required.

But the question remained: What did lowering the speed of light have to do with black holes? What did black holes have to do with the cosmic safety notice?

A black hole couldn't change the speed of light; all it could do was to change the wavelength.

Lowering the speed of light in vacuum to one-tenth, one-hundredth, or even one-thousandth of its natural speed would mean thirty thousand kilometers per second, three thousand kilometers

per second, and three hundred kilometers per second, respectively. It was hard to tell how black holes would be involved.

There was a threshold here that had to be crossed—hard to do for normal patterns of thinking, but not so for this group, among the most brilliant minds humanity had to offer. Cao Bin, in particular, was good at unconventional ideas. As a physicist who had crossed three centuries, he knew something else: Back during the Common Era, a research group had successfully reduced the speed of light through a medium in a lab to seventeen meters per second, slower than someone riding a bike. Of course, this was not the same as lowering the speed of light through vacuum, but at least it made what he imagined next seem not so crazy.

What if the speed of light were reduced even further, to thirty kilometers per second? Would that involve black holes? It still seemed essentially the same process as before ... wait!

"Sixteen point seven!" Cao Bin shouted. The fire in his eyes quickly set the other eyes around him ablaze.

The third cosmic velocity of the Solar System was 16.7 kilometers per second. A spacecraft from the Earth could not leave the Solar System without exceeding this limit.

It was the same with light.

If the speed of light through vacuum in the Solar System were reduced to below 16.7 kilometers per second, light would no longer be able to escape the gravity of the Sun, and the Solar System would become a black hole. This was an inescapable consequence of the derivation of the Schwarzschild radius of an object, even if the object was the Solar System. More precisely, the necessary speed limit would be even lower if a larger Schwarzschild radius were desired.

Since nothing could exceed the speed of light, if light couldn't leave the Solar System's event horizon, nothing else could either. The Solar System would be hermetically sealed off from the rest of the universe.

And therefore completely safe—as far as the rest of the universe was concerned.

How would a distant observer see the Solar System black hole created by lowering the speed of light? There were two possibilities: for technologically primitive observers, the Solar System would simply disappear; and, for technologically advanced observers, they should be able to detect the black hole, but instantly understand that the system was safe.

Take a distant star, a barely visible dot. Anyone casually glancing at it would say: Oh, that star is safe; that star will not threaten us.

This was the cosmic safety notice. The impossible was possible, after all.

The interpreters thought of the Glutton's Sea, thought of the Storyless Kingdom sealed off from the rest of the universe by the sea. This additional bearing coordinate really wasn't necessary—they already understood.

Later, people would call a black hole formed by lowering the speed of light a "black domain." Compared to black holes where the speed of light was unaltered, a reduced-lightspeed black hole had a much larger Schwarzschild radius. The interior was not a space-time singularity, but a fairly open region.

The helicopter continued above the clouds. It was now after 11 P.M., and the sun slowly set in the west, leaving only a slice visible. In the golden light of the midnight sun, everyone tried to imagine life in a world where light moved just below 16.7 kilometers per second, tried to imagine the creeping light of such a sunset.

By now, most of the puzzle pieces in Yun Tianming's stories had fallen into place. But one piece remained: the paintings of Needle-Eye. The interpreters couldn't figure out the dual-layer metaphor or find any bearing coordinates. Some thought that the paintings might be another bearing coordinate for the Moskstraumen, symbolizing the event horizon of the black domain. They reasoned that from an outside observer's perspective, anything entering the black domain would be forever fixed at the event horizon, which resembled

being painted into a picture. But most interpreters disagreed. The meaning of the Moskstraumen was very clear, and Tianming had used the Glutton's Sea to act as a bearing coordinate. There was no need for another.

Ultimately, this last piece of the puzzle could not be deciphered. Like the missing arms of *Venus de Milo,* the paintings of Needle-Eye remained mysterious. But as this detail formed the foundation for all three stories and described an elegant ruthlessness, an exquisite cruelty, and a beautiful death, it must have hinted at a great secret of life and death.

EXCERPT FROM
A PAST OUTSIDE OF TIME
THREE PATHS OF SURVIVAL FOR
EARTH CIVILIZATION

I. The Bunker Project: This was the plan with the most hope for success, because it was based entirely on known technologies and involved no theoretical unknowns. In some sense, the Bunker Project could be viewed as a natural continuation of the development of the human race. Even without the threat of a dark forest strike, it was time for humanity to begin colonizing the rest of the Solar System. The Bunker Project just made the effort more focused and the goals clearer.

This was also a plan devised entirely by the Earth itself; it had not been described in the message from Yun Tianming.

II. The Black Domain Plan: This involved transforming the Solar System into a reduced-lightspeed black hole to broadcast a cosmic safety notice. Out of all the choices, this was the most technically challenging. Within a region of space fifty AU (or 7.5 billion kilometers) in radius, a physical constant had to be altered. This was dubbed God's Engineering Project. The theoretical unknowns were immense.

But if the Black Domain Plan were to succeed, it would

provide the most protection for Earth civilization. Setting aside its effect as a cosmic safety notice, the black domain itself would act as a highly effective protective barrier. Any external missile, such as a photoid, would be traveling at a very high velocity to produce the necessary destructive power, and would thus enter the black domain with a speed far in excess of the modified speed of light inside. Under the theory of relativity, such an object would have to proceed at the (new, low) speed of light as soon as it crossed the barrier, and its excess kinetic energy would be converted to mass. The first part of the object entering the black domain would suddenly slow down and acquire a much larger mass, while the rest of the object, still moving at the unaltered speed of light, would run into the first part, thereby destroying the entire missile with the impact. Calculations showed that even objects made of strong-interaction materials such as droplets would be completely shattered at the boundary of the black domain. Thus, a black domain was also dubbed "the cosmic safe."

There was yet another advantage to the Black Domain Plan: Out of all three choices, it was the only plan that allowed humanity to continue to live on the familiar surface of the Earth and avoid an exile in space.

But Earth civilization would pay a heavy price. The Solar System would be completely divided from the rest of the universe, equivalent to humanity shrinking their universe from 16 billion light-years across to one hundred AU. Moreover, it was impossible to know what life in such a world would be like. It was certain that electronic and quantum computers would have to operate at extremely low speeds, so humanity might regress to a low-technology society. This would be an even more absolute seal than the technology seal imposed by the sophons. Besides being a cosmic safety notice, the Black Domain Plan was also a form of technological self-mutilation. Humans would never be able to escape from this reduced-lightspeed trap.

III. Lightspeed Spaceflight Plan: Although the theoretical foundation for curvature propulsion was unknown, it was clearly easier than the Black Domain Plan.

Lightspeed spaceflight could not, however, provide any security for Earth civilization. It was only good for escape into the stars. Of all three plans, this involved the most unknowns. Even if it succeeded, members of the human race who escaped into the vast emptiness of space faced unpredictable dangers. Also, the dangers of escapism meant that the plan faced numerous political barriers and traps.

Yet a portion of humanity was certain to be obsessed with lightspeed spaceflight for reasons other than survival.

For people of the Broadcast Era, the only smart choice was to carry out all three plans simultaneously.

BROADCAST ERA, YEAR 8
FATE'S CHOICE

Cheng Xin came to the headquarters of the Halo Group.

This was her first time here. She had never participated in its operation because, subconsciously, she never thought of the enormous wealth as truly hers, or Yun Tianming's. They possessed that star, but the wealth generated by the star belonged to society.

But now, perhaps, the Halo Group could help her realize her dream.

The corporate headquarters occupied an entire giant tree. Interestingly, all the buildings on the tree were transparent. Moreover, as the refractive index in the construction material was close to that of the air, all internal structures were visible. One could see employees moving inside as well as countless information windows. The hanging buildings resembled transparent ant farms with colorful ants milling about inside.

Inside the large conference room at the tip of the tree, Cheng Xin got to meet most of the high-level executives of the Halo Group. They were all young, smart, and vivacious. Most of them had never met Cheng Xin before, and they did not disguise their awe and adoration.

After the meeting, when only Cheng Xin and AA remained in the large, empty room, they began to talk about the future of the company. The message from Yun Tianming and the deciphering

457

progress remained secrets from the public. To protect Tianming, Fleet International and the UN planned to release the results gradually to the public and to make them appear as the fruits of research on Earth. Some deliberate false research results would also be mixed in to further conceal the real origin of the information.

Cheng Xin had gotten used to the transparent floor and no longer felt so acrophobic. A few large information windows drifted in the conference room, displaying live video feeds from a few of the Halo Group's construction projects in Earth orbit, one of which was the giant cross in geosynchronous orbit. After Tianming's reappearance, the public's hopes for a miracle gradually faded, and with the initiation of the Bunker Project, the religious fervor dimmed. The church stopped investing in the giant cross, and it was abandoned. Now it was in the process of being dismantled so that only a giant "l" remained—a rather meaningful sight.

"I don't like 'black domain,'" said AA. "It would be more appropriate to call it 'black tomb,' a tomb we dig for ourselves."

Cheng Xin looked at the city below through the transparent floor. "I don't think of it that way. During the era I was from, the Earth was completely separated from the rest of the universe. Everyone lived on the surface, and very rarely did they glance up at the stars. People had lived that way for five thousand years, and you can't just say that wasn't a good life. Even now, the Solar System is basically separated from the rest of the universe. The only people who are in deep space are the thousand or so people on those two spaceships."

"But I feel that if we separate ourselves from the stars, dreams will die."

"Not at all. In ancient times there was happiness and joy as well, and they had no fewer dreams than we. Also, even inside a black domain, we would still see the stars, only ... who knows what that would look like.... Personally, I don't like 'black domain' either."

"I know you don't."

"I like lightspeed ships."

"We all like lightspeed ships. The Halo Group should build lightspeed ships!"

"I thought you weren't going to agree," Cheng Xin said. "This requires heavy investment in basic research."

"You think I'm just a capitalist? Well, you're not wrong. I am, and so are the members of the board of directors. We want to maximize profits. But that doesn't conflict with lightspeed spaceships. Politically, the government will devote the most resources into the Bunker Project and the black domain, but lightspeed ships will be left to entrepreneurs.... We should put our efforts into the Bunker Project, and then use some of the profits to research lightspeed ships."

"Here's my thinking, AA: Curvature propulsion and the black domain probably share some fundamental theories. We can wait for the government and the World Academy of Sciences to complete that part of the research, then develop it toward curvature propulsion."

"All right. We should start a Halo Group Academy of Sciences, too, and recruit scientists. Many of them have dreamed about lightspeed spaceflight, but they can't find such opportunities in national or international projects—"

AA was interrupted by a sudden surge of new information windows. Windows of all sizes appeared in every direction like a colorful avalanche, quickly burying the few original information windows showing feeds from the Halo Group's projects. A "window avalanche" like this usually indicated the sudden occurrence of some important event, but the flood of information often caused people to be overwhelmed, unable to find out what actually happened. Such was the case with AA and Cheng Xin. They saw that most of the windows were filled with complex text and animated figures, and only those windows that showed pure images could be taken in at a glance. In one of the windows, Cheng Xin saw a few faces looking upwards, then the lens zoomed in until a frightened pair of eyes filled the frame, accompanied by a cacophony of screams....

A new window came to the forefront showing AA's secretary. She stared at AA and Cheng Xin, her face full of terror and shock.

"A warning! An attack!" she shouted.

"Any specifics?" AA asked.

"They activated the first observation unit in the Solar System advance warning system and found a photoid right away!"

"In what direction? How far?"

"I don't know. I don't know anything. All I know—"

"Is this an official warning?" Cheng Xin asked calmly.

"I don't think so. But it's in all the media. I'm sure it's real! Let's get to the spaceport and run for our lives!" The secretary disappeared from the window.

Cheng Xin and AA passed through the dense congeries of information windows and arrived at the transparent wall of the conference room. They saw that panic had already seized the city below them. A massive increase in the number of flying cars outside resulted in chaos, and every vehicle tried to force itself through the jam at high speed. One of the cars struck a giant tree building and erupted into a fireball. Soon, fire and columns of smoke appeared in two other locations in the city....

AA picked out a few information windows and perused them carefully. Cheng Xin, on the other hand, tried to get in touch with the members of the IDC. Most of their phones were busy, and Cheng Xin managed to talk to only two committee members. One of them, like AA and Cheng Xin, knew nothing. The other, a PDC official, told Cheng Xin that he could confirm that Observation Unit #1 in the Solar System advance warning system had noticed some significant anomaly, but he didn't know the specifics. He also confirmed that Fleet International and the UN had not issued a formal dark forest strike alarm, but he wasn't optimistic.

"There are two possibilities for why no alarm has been issued: One, nothing has happened. Two, the photoid is too close and an alarm would be useless."

AA was only able to obtain one piece of specific information from her reading: The photoid was coming along the ecliptic plane. There were conflicting reports concerning its exact direction and distance from the Sun, and estimates of when the photoid would strike the sun diverged wildly: Some claimed that the world had another month; others said only a few hours.

"We should go to *Halo*," AA said.

"Is there enough time?"

Halo was a corporate spaceship that belonged to the Halo Group. Right now, it was parked at the company's geosynchronous base. If the alarm was real, their only hope now was to ride the ship to Jupiter and hide out behind the gas giant before the photoid struck. As Jupiter was in opposition, and therefore as close to the Earth as it could be, it would take twenty-five to thirty days for the ship to fly from the Earth to Jupiter, which was just under the upper end of the range of estimates for when the photoid would strike. But this estimate seemed highly unreliable: The advance warning system was still being constructed, and couldn't have given such an early alert.

"We have to do something instead of waiting here to die!" AA said. She dragged Cheng Xin out of the conference room and onto the parking lot at the top of the tree. They ducked into a flying car, but AA seemed to remember something and got out again. A few minutes later, she returned with an oblong object that resembled a violin case. She opened the case, took out what was inside, and carried it with her into the car, leaving the case behind.

Cheng Xin looked at what was in AA's hand and recognized the implement: a rifle, though adapted to shoot laser bolts instead of bullets.

"Why are you bringing this?" Cheng Xin asked.

"The spaceport is sure to be filled with people—who knows what's going to happen?" AA tossed the rifle onto the backseat and started the flying car.

Every city had a spaceport to service various small space vessels —rather like ancient airports.

The flying car merged into a mighty aerial stream of traffic. All the countless cars in the stream, like a swarm of locusts, were headed for the spaceport. They cast a flowing shadow along the ground, as though the city's blood was seeping out.

Ahead, a dozen or so white lines rose into the blue sky, trails left by spaceships. They rose straight up and then turned east

and disappeared in the depths of the firmament. New white lines continuously shot up from the ground and extended into air, each line headed by a fireball that was brighter even than the sun: the flame from the fusion drives of the ships.

On an information window inside the car, Cheng Xin saw a live video feed taken from near-Earth orbit. Countless rising white lines appeared against the tan background of the continent and extended upward. They grew more numerous, denser, as though the Earth was growing white hair. The fireballs at the ends of the white lines were like fireflies drifting into space. This was the greatest collective escape into space in human history.

Their car arrived above the spaceport. About a hundred space-craft were arrayed below, and more were being moved out of the giant hangar in the distance. Space planes had long since fallen out of use, and modern shuttles all took off vertically. Unlike the oddly shaped spacecraft Cheng Xin had seen at the port in the space elevator terminal station, these shuttles all had streamlined profiles, with three or four tail fins. They were now erected helter-skelter in the parking lot of the spaceport, like a forest of steel.

AA had called ahead to the hangar to move one of the Halo Group's shuttles onto the lot. She quickly picked out the shuttle from the air and landed their car next to it.

Cheng Xin looked at the shuttles around her. They were of different sizes: The smaller ones were only about a few meters tall, looking like giant versions of artillery shells. It was hard to imagine that such tiny crafts could escape the Earth's gravity well. There were also larger vessels, some as big as ancient airliners. The Halo Group's shuttle was medium-small in size, about ten meters tall, covered with a reflective metallic surface reminiscent of the droplets. The shuttle was parked on a wheeled launch frame so that it could be dragged to the launch point at a moment's notice. They would ride this shuttle to reach *Halo* in orbit.

A loud rumbling came from the launch area, strangely reminding Cheng Xin of the noise made by the Moskstraumen. The ground quaked and her legs felt numb. A great bright glow appeared in the

launch area, and a shuttle rose into the air on a ball of flame, adding yet another column of smoke to the sky. A great billowing cloud of white fog flowed toward them, bringing with it a strange burning smell. The fog wasn't generated by the engine of the shuttle, but by the boiled water from the coolant pool below the launch pad. As the launch area and the ships disappeared in the sweltering, muggy steam, people became even more agitated and anxious.

AA and Cheng Xin climbed up a slender set of stairs to board the shuttle. As the fog dissipated, Cheng Xin saw a crowd of children gathered not too far away. They appeared to be elementary school students under the age of ten, dressed in their school uniforms. A young teacher stood with them. Her long hair was buffeted by gusts of wind and she looked around helplessly.

"Can we wait a bit?" Cheng Xin asked.

AA looked over at the children and understood what Cheng Xin wanted. "All right. Go. We have to wait for our turn to get to the launch pad. It will be a while."

In principle, shuttles could take off from any flat part of the ground. However, to prevent ground damage from the ultrahigh-temperature plasma generated by the fusion drive, the shuttles used a launch pad. The launch pad was equipped with a coolant pool and diversion channels to safely redirect the plasma.

The teacher saw Cheng Xin walking over, and came up and grabbed her. "This shuttle is yours, isn't it? Please, please save the children." Her bangs stuck to her forehead, and tears and condensed fog wetted her face. She stared at Cheng Xin intently, as if hoping to seize her with her gaze. The children came over as well, and looked expectantly at Cheng Xin. "They're here for space camp, and they were scheduled to go up in orbit. But after the alert was issued, they refused to take us and sent others up in our place."

"Where's your ship?" AA asked as she walked over.

"It's gone. Please, please!"

"Let's bring them," Cheng Xin said to AA.

AA looked at Cheng Xin for a few seconds. *There are billions of people on the Earth. Do you think you can save them all?*

Cheng Xin's gaze did not waver.

AA shook her head. "We can only bring three more."

"But our shuttle's capacity is eighteen!"

"*Halo* can only seat five under maximum acceleration because it's equipped with only five deep-sea-state capsules. Anyone not in a deep-sea state is going to be crushed into a meat pie."

The answer surprised Cheng Xin. The deep-sea acceleration fluid was only necessary for stellar spaceships. But she had always thought *Halo* was a planetary ship and wasn't capable of voyaging beyond the Solar System.

"All right. Then bring three!" The teacher let go of Cheng Xin and grabbed on to AA, terrified of losing this one chance.

"You pick three, then," said AA.

The teacher let go of AA and stared at her, even more terrified than before. "How am I supposed to pick? How ..." She looked around, not daring to meet the eyes of the children. She looked to be in utter pain, as if the gazes of the children burned her.

"Fine. I'll pick," AA said. She turned to the children and smiled. "Everyone, listen up. I'm going to ask three questions. Whoever gives the right answers first gets to come with us." She ignored the stunned looks from the teacher and Cheng Xin, and held up a finger. "First question: Say we have a light which is off. After one minute, it blinks. Half a minute later, it blinks again. Fifteen seconds later, it blinks a third time. It keeps on going like this, blinking at intervals that are half of the immediately preceding interval. I want to know how many times it will have blinked by the two-minute mark."

"A hundred!" one of the children blurted out.

AA shook her head. "Wrong."

"A thousand!"

"No. Think carefully."

After a long pause, a timid voice spoke up. The speaker was a gentle and quiet little girl and it was hard to hear her with all the noise. "An infinite number of times."

"Come here," AA said, pointing at the little girl. When she walked over, AA guided her to stand behind herself. "Second

question: Say we have a rope whose thickness is uneven. To burn it from one end to the other takes an hour. How do you use this rope to track the passage of fifteen minutes? Remember, the thickness is uneven!"

This time, no child spoke up in a hurry, and they all fell into deep thought. Soon, a boy raised his hand. "Fold the rope end to end, and then burn it from both ends at the same time."

AA nodded. "Come over." She pulled the boy behind her to stand with the girl. "Third question: eighty-two, fifty, twenty-six. What's the next number?"

"Ten!" a girl shouted.

AA gave her a thumb up. "Well done. Come over." Then she nodded at Cheng Xin, took the three children, and headed for the shuttle.

Cheng Xin followed them to the stairs for boarding the shuttle. She looked back. The remaining children and their teacher looked at her as if at a sun that would never rise again. Tears blurred the scene in front of her, and as she climbed up, she could still feel the gazes of despair behind her, like ten thousand arrows piercing her heart. She had felt like this before, during the last moments of her brief career as the Swordholder, and also in Australia when Sophon had announced the plan for exterminating the human race. It was a pain worse than death.

The cabin inside the shuttle was spacious; eighteen seats were arranged in two columns. Since the cabin was vertical, like a well, everyone had to climb a ladder to get to the seats. Cheng Xin experienced the same feeling she had when inside the spherical spacecraft she took to meet Tianming—the shuttle seemed to be a shell only, and she couldn't see where there was space for the engine and the control systems. She thought back to the chemical rockets of the Common Era, each as big as a skyscraper, but the effective payload was only a tiny capsule near the top.

She couldn't see any control surfaces inside the shuttle, and only a few information windows drifted by. The shuttle's AI seemed to recognize AA. As soon as she entered, the windows gathered

around her. They moved with her while she went around securing the children's and Cheng Xin's seat belts.

"Don't look at me like that. I gave them a chance. Competition is necessary for survival," AA whispered to Cheng Xin.

"Auntie, are they going to die on the surface?" the boy asked.

"Everyone is going to die. It's just a matter of when." AA sat down next to Cheng Xin. She didn't buckle her seat belt, but continued to examine the information windows. "Damn it. There are still twenty-nine launches ahead of us."

The spaceport had a total of eight launch pads. After each launch, the pad had to cool for ten minutes before the next use because the coolant pools needed to be replenished with fresh water.

The wait shouldn't have mattered much to their survival. The flight to Jupiter would take a month. If the dark forest strike happened before they arrived, it really made no difference if they were on the ground or in space. However, the problem now was that any delay might cause them to not be able to take off at all.

Society had already descended into pandemonium. Driven by the instinct for survival, the more than ten million inhabitants of the city swarmed toward the spaceport. The shuttles, like passenger aircraft during ancient times, could only carry away a small number of people in a short period of time. Possessing a private space vessel was like owning a private airplane, an unattainable dream for most of the population. Even with the space elevator, no more than one percent of the population could reach near-Earth orbit within a week. Those who could finally make the voyage to Jupiter would be one-tenth of that one percent.

There were no portholes on the shuttle, but a few information windows showed the scene outside. They saw dark masses flooding into the parking area. Crowds surrounded every vessel, screaming with their fists raised, hoping to squeeze onto one of them. At the same time, outside the spaceport, some flying cars that had landed took off again. The cars were all empty, and their owners piloted them by remote control in an attempt to stop any more space launches. More and more flying cars gathered in the air, forming

a dark, hovering barrier above the launch pads. Very soon, no one would be able to leave.

Cheng Xin minimized the information window and turned around to comfort the three children seated behind her. AA screamed. Cheng Xin turned around and saw a window that had been maximized to fill the entire cabin. In the window, a blinding fireball had appeared in the forest of shuttles.

Someone had begun to launch while surrounded by people in the parking lot!

The plasma emitted by the nuclear fusion drive was tens of times hotter than the emissions of ancient chemical rockets. When launched from a flat surface, the plasma would melt the crust instantaneously and spill out in every direction. No one could survive within a thirty-meter radius. The video feed in the window showed many black dots scattering from the fireball. One of the dots struck a nearby shuttle and left a black mark: a burnt-up body. Several other shuttles around the one that took off toppled, probably because their launch frames had been melted.

The crowd quieted. They looked up and saw the shuttle that had probably killed dozens of people lifting off from the parking lot, rumbling, dragging its white trail until it was high in the air, then turning east. They seemed unable to believe their eyes. A few seconds later, yet another shuttle took off from the parking lot, even closer to them. The rumbling, flames, and waves of superheated air threw the stunned crowd into complete panic. Then a third, a fourth ... the shuttles in the parking lot took off one after another. Amidst the fiery balls of flame, burnt remains of bodies flew through the air, turning the parking lot into a crematorium.

AA watched the horrifying scene and bit her bottom lip. Then she waved the window away and began to type on another small window.

"What are you doing?" Cheng Xin asked.

"We're taking off."

"No."

"Look." AA tossed another small window at Cheng Xin, which showed the few shuttles around them. A cooling loop was located just above the tail nozzle of each vehicle. The loops were used to dissipate the heat from the fusion reactors. Cheng Xin saw that the loops of all the surrounding shuttles had begun to glow with a dim red light, indicating that their reactors had been turned on in preparation for liftoff.

"We'd better launch before they do," said AA. If any of these shuttles took off, the plasma would probably melt the launch frames of the rest of the shuttles, causing them to topple onto the molten ground.

"No. Stop." Cheng Xin's voice was calm, but unwavering. She had experienced even worse catastrophes, and she would face this one with serenity.

"Why?" AA's voice was equally calm.

"Because there are people around."

AA stopped typing and turned to face Cheng Xin. "Soon, you, me, the crowd, and the Earth itself will all turn into tiny fragments. Can you tell which ones are honorable and which ones despicable in that mess?"

"Our values still hold, at least for now. I'm the president of the Halo Group. This shuttle belongs to the Halo Group, and you're the company's employee. I have the authority to make this decision."

AA stared at Cheng Xin for a few moments, then she nodded and closed the control window. She also turned off all the other information windows, thus isolating the cabin from the mad, noisy world outside.

"Thank you," said Cheng Xin.

AA said nothing. But then she jumped up, as if suddenly remembering something. She picked up the laser rifle from one of the empty seats and climbed down the ladder. "Keep your seat belts on. The shuttle might fall over any moment."

"What are you going to do?" Cheng Xin asked.

"If we can't leave, they can't leave either. Fuck them."

AA opened the cabin door, went out, and immediately closed the

door and locked it to prevent anyone from trying to force their way in. Then she climbed down the stairs and began to shoot at the tail fin of the nearest shuttle. Smoke rose up from the tail fin, leaving behind a tiny hole about the size of a finger. That was enough. The self-monitoring system within the shuttle would discover the damage to the tail fin and the AI would refuse to initiate the launch sequence. This was a safety measure that couldn't be overridden by those inside. The cooling ring around the shuttle began to fade, indicating a reactor shutdown. AA turned around in a circle and shot a hole through the tail fins of each of the eight shuttles around them. As the crowd was in total panic, no one noticed what she was doing amidst the waves of heat and smoke and dust.

The door of one of the other shuttles opened, and an elegantly dressed woman climbed down. She walked around the tail of the shuttle and soon discovered the hole. She began to cry hysterically, then rolled around on the ground. She tried to head-butt the launch frame, but no one paid any attention to her. All the crowd cared about was the door to her shuttle, which had been left open. They surged up the stairs and tried to squeeze into the shuttle that could no longer fly.

AA climbed back up the stairs and pushed Cheng Xin, who had poked her head out, back in. Then she followed and shut the door behind her. She began to vomit.

"It smells like ... barbeque out there," AA finally said after the heaves subsided.

"Are we going to die?" asked one of the girls, poking her head into the aisle from the seat above them.

"We're going to witness a magnificent sight of the cosmos," AA said, a mysterious expression on her face.

"What sight?"

"It's the most impressive thing ever. The Sun is going to turn into a giant firework."

"And then?"

"Then ... nothing. What can there be when there's nothing?" AA climbed up and patted the three children on their heads in turn.

She wasn't going to lie to them. If they could answer her questions, surely they were smart enough to understand the situation.

Again, AA and Cheng Xin sat down next to each other. Cheng Xin put a hand over AA's hand. "I'm sorry."

AA smiled back. It was a smile Cheng Xin was familiar with. In her eyes, AA had always seemed young, less worn down by the darkness of the world that Cheng Xin had experienced. She felt more mature in front of AA, but also powerless.

"Don't worry about it. It's all just busywork anyway. In the end, the result is going to be the same. At least now we can relax." AA exhaled.

If *Halo* really were a stellar ship, then it would be able to get to Jupiter much faster than she had expected. Although the distance between the Earth and Jupiter wasn't long enough for it to reach maximum acceleration, the whole journey should take only about two weeks.

AA seemed to sense what Cheng Xin was thinking. "Even if the advance warning system had been completely operational, we'd get at most a day's warning.... But now that I've thought about it some, I think it's likely a false alarm."

Cheng Xin wasn't sure if that was why AA had submitted to her authority earlier so easily.

AA's theory was quickly proven. The PDC official who was also a member of the IDC called Cheng Xin to let her know that Fleet International and the UN had issued a joint statement that the alarm was false. No signs of a dark forest strike had been detected. AA opened a few information windows, and most of them were broadcasting the announcement from Fleet International and the UN. Outside, the unauthorized launches had ceased. It was still chaotic, but at least the situation wouldn't deteriorate further.

Once the outside had calmed down a bit, Cheng Xin and AA exited the shuttle. The scene that greeted them was like a battlefield. Burnt bodies lay everywhere, charcoal-black, a few still on fire. Many of the shuttles lay on the ground while others leaned against each other. In total, nine shuttles had taken off from the parking

lot, and their trails were still clearly visible in the sky, like sliced-open wounds. The crowd was no longer frantic. Some sat on the still-hot ground, some stood in place, stunned, some wandered around aimlessly—and everyone seemed uncertain whether they were experiencing reality or a nightmare. The police had arrived to maintain order, and rescue operations were underway.

"The next warning may be real," AA said to Cheng Xin. "You should come with me to the back of Jupiter. The Halo Group will build a space city for the Bunker Project."

Instead of answering her, Cheng Xin asked, "What is going on with *Halo*?"

"We're not talking about the original ship with that name, but a new miniature stellar spaceship. It can seat twenty during planetary voyages, and five for stellar flight. The board of directors agreed to build it for you, and you can use it as a mobile office at Jupiter."

The difference between a planetary spaceship and a stellar spaceship was like the difference between a ferryboat with a single oar plying a river and an oceangoing container ship with a tonnage measured in tens of thousands. Of course, in spaceships, the difference wasn't merely a matter of volume—there were small stellar spaceships, too. Compared to planetary ships, stellar ships had more advanced propulsion systems, were equipped with ecological cycling systems, and every subsystem had three or four backups. If Cheng Xin really rode the new *Halo* into the shadow of Jupiter, the ship would be able to maintain her for the rest of her life, no matter what happened.

Cheng Xin shook her head. "You should go. Take *Halo*. I don't participate in the day-to-day operations of the company, and it's fine for me to stay on the Earth."

"You just don't want to be one of the few to survive."

"I'm here with billions of people. No matter what happens, if it happens to several billion at the same time, it won't be frightening."

"I'm worried about you," AA said, and grabbed Cheng Xin by both shoulders. "I'm not worried that you'll die along with a few billion others, but that you'll experience things worse than death."

"I've been through that already."

"If you continue to pursue the dream of lightspeed spaceflight, you'll encounter more such experiences. Can you really endure them?"

The false alarm was the largest social disturbance since the Great Resettlement. Although brief in duration and limited in the damage caused, it left an indelible mark in the psyche of the world.

Most of the thousands of spaceports across the world had shuttles that took off while surrounded by crowds, and more than ten thousand people died in the flames of fusion drives. Armed conflicts also took place at the base stations of space elevators. Unlike at the spaceports, the fights at the space elevators involved nations. Some countries attempted to occupy the international elevator's base station in tropical waters, and only the timely confirmation that the attack alarm was false prevented full-scale warfare. In orbits around Earth, and even on Mars, groups of people fought over spaceships.

In addition to the degenerates who were willing to kill to ensure their own survival, the public discovered something else that disgusted them during the course of the false alarm: tens of small stellar spaceships and near-stellar spaceships were discovered to be in secret construction in geosynchronous orbit and on the dark side of the moon. Near-stellar spaceships possessed the ecological cycling systems of stellar ships, but were only equipped with propulsion systems for interplanetary flight. Some of these luxurious yachts belonged to large companies, and others to extremely wealthy individuals. All the crafts were small, and could only maintain a few people with their ecological cycling systems. They had only one purpose: long-term seclusion behind the giant planets.

The advance warning system that was still being constructed could only provide a warning window of about twenty-four hours. If a dark forest strike really arrived, there wasn't enough time for any spacecraft to go from the Earth to Jupiter, the nearest barrier

planet. In actuality, the Earth dangled over a sea of death. Rationally, everyone understood this, and the ugly fights that broke out during the false alarm were nothing more than meaningless mass madness driven by a survival instinct that overwhelmed rational thinking. Currently, about fifty thousand individuals resided at Jupiter—most of them were space force personnel at the Jupiter base, along with some staff doing preparatory work for the Bunker Project. They had plenty of justification for being at Jupiter, and the public did not begrudge them their place. But once these secret stellar ships were completed, their wealthy owners would be able to hide in the shadow of Jupiter indefinitely.

Legally—at least right now—there was no international or national prohibition against the construction of stellar ships by organizations or individuals, and hiding out behind the gas giants wasn't the same as Escapism. However, the inequality here was seen as the greatest in human history: inequality before death.

Historically, inequality mainly manifested itself in areas like economics or social status, but death basically treated everyone the same. To be sure, such equality wasn't absolute: For instance, access to medical care wasn't evenly distributed; the wealthy fared better in natural disasters than the poor; soldiers and civilians had different rates of survival in war; and so on. But never before had a situation like this presented itself: less than one-ten-thousandth of the population could go into safe hiding, leaving billions on Earth to die.

Even in ancient times, such manifest inequality would have been intolerable, let alone now.

This led directly to international skepticism about the plan for lightspeed ships.

Although spaceships hiding permanently behind Jupiter or Saturn could survive a dark forest strike, life on those ships would not be enviable. No matter how comfortable the ecological cycling systems made the shipboard environment, the occupants would be living in the cold, desolate regions of the outer Solar System in isolation. But as observations of the Second Trisolaran Fleet

revealed, spacecraft powered by curvature propulsion could achieve lightspeed almost instantaneously. A lightspeed ship could go from the Earth to Jupiter in less than an hour, and the advance warning system would be more than sufficient. Powerful and wealthy individuals who possessed lightspeed ships could thus live in comfort on the Earth and then escape at the last minute, without regard for the billions left behind. This was a prospect society simply could not tolerate. The terrifying sights from the false alarm remained fresh in the public's mind, and most people agreed that the appearance of lightspeed ships would lead to world-wide chaos. Thus, the plan for developing lightspeed ships faced unprecedented resistance.

The false alarm was the result of the explosive amplifying effects of a hyper-information society when fed sensitive news. Its source was an anomaly detected by the first observation unit of the advance warning system. The anomaly was real, though it had nothing to do with photoids.

EXCERPT FROM
A PAST OUTSIDE OF TIME
SPACE SENTRIES:
THE SOLAR SYSTEM
ADVANCE WARNING SYSTEM

The Earth had observed photoids only twice in the past: the destruction of 187J3X1 and of the Trisolaran system. Knowledge about the phenomenon was thus limited. All that was known was that a photoid moved at close to the speed of light, but there was no data concerning its volume, rest mass, or relativistic mass as it approached the speed of light. A photoid was certainly the most primitive weapon capable of attacking a star, since it relied only on the enormous kinetic energy generated by its high relativistic mass to damage the target. Once a civilization possessed the technology to accelerate an object to near the speed of light, a "bullet" with very little mass possessed immense destructive power. This was indeed "economical."

The most valuable data concerning photoids was obtained right before the annihilation of the Trisolaran system. Scientists were able to make an important discovery: Due to a photoid's ultrahigh velocity, powerful radiation ranging from visible light to gamma rays was emitted as it collided with the few atoms scattered in space

and interstellar dust. The radiation had distinctive characteristics. Since the photoids were extremely small, direct observation of them was impossible. But the characteristic radiation could be detected.

At first blush, it seemed impossible to give advance warning for photoids, because they moved at close to the speed of light. This meant that they moved almost as fast as the radiation they generated, and reached their target almost simultaneously. In other words, the observer was outside the event's light cone.

But reality was a bit more complicated. Any object with rest mass could not achieve lightspeed. Although a photoid's speed approached lightspeed, it was still slightly slower than true lightspeed. This difference meant that the radiation from the photoid moved just a bit faster than the photoid itself. If the photoid had to travel a long distance, this difference was magnified. Also, a photoid's trajectory to the target wasn't an absolute straight line. Since it wasn't massless, it couldn't avoid the gravitational attractions of nearby celestial bodies, and its path typically ended up being slightly curved. The curvature was much greater than the curvature of light through the same gravitational field. For the photoid to strike the target, its trajectory had to take this effect into account. This meant that the path traveled by the photoid was longer than the path taken by its radiation.

For these two reasons, the radiation from the photoid would reach the Solar System before the photoid itself. The twenty-four-hour estimated warning period was calculated based on the maximum distance at which photoid emissions could be observed. By the time the radiation reached the Earth, the photoid itself would still be about 180 AU away.

But that was merely the ideal scenario. If the photoid were launched from a nearby spaceship, there would be almost no warning—like what had happened to Trisolaris.

Thirty-five observation units were planned for the Solar System advance warning system. These would monitor the sky in every direction for photoid emissions.

BROADCAST ERA, YEAR 8
FATE'S CHOICE

Two days before the false alarm; Observation Unit #1

Observation Unit #1 was in fact just the Ringier-Fitzroy Station from the end of the Crisis Era. More than seventy years ago, it was this observation station that had first discovered the strong-interaction space probes—the droplets. The station was still located on the outer edge of the asteroid belt, but all its equipment had been updated. Take the visible light telescope, for instance: The lenses were even bigger, and the first lens's diameter had increased from twelve hundred meters to two thousand meters, big enough for a small town to fit on it. These gigantic lenses were made from materials taken directly from the asteroid belt. The first one was a medium-sized lens five hundred meters in diameter. After that was finished, it was used to focus sunlight on asteroids so that the melted rock could be made into pure glass and then formed into additional lenses. In total, six lenses floated in a ten-kilometer-long column in space, far apart from each other. The observation station itself was located at the end of the column of lenses, and could only hold a crew of two.

The crew was still made up of a scientist and a military officer. The officer was responsible for monitoring photoid emissions, while

the scientist conducted astronomical and cosmological research. Thus, the tradition of fighting for observation time begun three centuries ago by General Fitzroy and Dr. Ringier continued.

After this, the largest telescope in history, had completed its shakedown tests and successfully taken its first image—a star forty-seven light-years away—Widnall, the astronomer on the crew, was as excited as if he'd just had a son. Laymen did not understand that previous telescopes could only amplify the luminosity of stars outside the Solar System, not reveal any shapes. No matter how powerful the telescopes were, the stars always showed up as tiny point sources, only incrementally brighter than images taken by lesser telescopes. But now, in the view of this ultrapowerful telescope, a star showed up as a disk for the first time. Though it was small, like a Ping-Pong ball seen from tens of meters away, and one couldn't see any details in the disk, this was still an epochal moment in the history of the ancient science of visible-light astronomy.

"The cataracts have been removed from the eyes of astronomy!" said Widnall dramatically, wiping his eyes.

But Sublieutenant Vasilenko wasn't impressed. "I think you need to remember our role here: We are sentries. In the old days, we'd be perched atop a wooden watchtower on the frontier, a desolate desert or snowfield around us. Standing erect in the frigid breeze, we'd be gazing in the direction of the enemy. As soon as we saw tanks coming up the horizon, or men on horses, we'd make a call or light smoke signals to inform the homeland that the enemy invasion had begun. . . . You need to get into that mental space. Don't think of yourself as being in an observatory."

Widnall's eyes temporarily left the terminal showing the image from the telescope and looked out the porthole of the station. He could see a few irregularly shaped rocks drifting at some distance: fragments of asteroids left from the glass-making operation. They spun slowly in the cold sunlight and seemed to emphasize the desolation of space. The scene did seem to evoke a sense of the "mental space" the sublieutenant described.

Widnall said, "If we really discover a photoid, it would be better

to not issue a warning at all. It's useless, anyway. To die suddenly without even knowing what hit you is actually a rather fortunate fate. But you'd rather torture a few billion people for twenty-four hours. I think that's akin to a crime against humanity."

"By that logic, you and I would be the most unfortunate people in the world since we would know about our fate the longest."

The observation station received new orders from Fleet Command to adjust the telescope and observe the remnants of the Trisolaran system. Widnall didn't argue with Vasilenko this time, because he was very interested in that ruined world as well.

The floating lenses began to move around and adjust their positions, the plasma thrusters at the rims of the lenses emitting blue flames. Only now did the lenses in the distance reveal themselves, the blue flames marking out the overall shape of the telescope. The ten-kilometer-long group of lenses slowly turned, stopping when the telescope was pointed in the direction of the Trisolaran system. Then the lenses shifted up and down the axis to focus. Finally, most of the flames went out, with only a few fireflies flickering now and then as the lenses engaged in precision focus adjustments.

In the unprocessed view of the telescope, the Trisolaran system looked very ordinary, just a small patch of white against the background of space, like a feather. But after the image had been processed and magnified, it appeared as a magnificent nebula that took up the entire screen. It had been seven years since the explosion of the star, so what they were seeing now was the scene three years after the explosion. Under the influence of gravity and the exploded star's angular momentum, the nebula had turned from sharp radiating rays into a soft blur of clouds, which was then flattened by the centrifugal force of the spin into a spiral. Above the nebula, the two remaining stars could be seen. One of them showed up as a disk, while the other one, more distant, remained a point of light distinguished only by its motion against the background stars.

The two stars that survived the catastrophe achieved the dream of generations on Trisolaris and formed a stable double-star system, but no life would enjoy their light, as the entire system was now

uninhabitable. It was now apparent that the dark forest strike had destroyed only one star out of the three, not only because of economics, but also to achieve a more sinister goal: As long as the system still retained one or two stars, the material in the nebula would be constantly absorbed by the stars, generating powerful radiation in the process. The Trisolaran system was now a radiation furnace, a domain of death for life and civilization. It was the powerful radiation that caused the nebula itself to glow and appear so clear and bright on the telescope.

"I'm reminded of the clouds viewed from atop Mount Emei," said Vasilenko. "That's a mountain in China. Viewing the moon from the peak is an exquisite sight. The night I was there, the peak floated in a boundless sea of clouds, turned pure silver by the moon above. It looked a lot like this."

Seeing this silvery graveyard more than forty trillion kilometers away made Widnall wax philosophical. "From a scientific perspective, 'destroy' isn't really accurate. Nothing has disappeared. All the matter that used to be there is still there, and so is all the angular momentum. It's only the arrangement of matter that has changed, like a deck of cards being reshuffled. But life is like a straight flush: Once you shuffle, it's gone."

Widnall examined the image some more and made an important discovery.

"What is *that*?!" He pointed at a spot in the image some distance from the nebula. By scale, it was about thirty AU from the nebula center.

Vasilenko stared at the spot. He lacked the trained eye of an astronomer, and couldn't see anything unusual at first. But eventually, he saw a vague circular outline against the pitch-black background, like a soap bubble in space.

"It's very large. The diameter is about ... ten astronomical units. Is it dust?"

"Absolutely not. Dust doesn't look anything like that."

"You've never seen it before?"

"No one could have seen it. Whatever it is, it's transparent, with

a very faint border. The largest telescopes in the past wouldn't have been able to detect it."

Widnall zoomed out a bit to get a better sense of the position of the strange new object with respect to the double stars, and to try to observe the spin of the nebula. On the screen, the nebula again turned into a small patch of white against the black abyss of space.

About six thousand AU from the Trisolaran system, he found another "soap bubble." This one was much bigger than the first, with a diameter of about fifty AU, spacious enough to contain the Trisolaran system or the Solar System.

"My God!" Vasilenko cried out. "Do you know where that is?"

Widnall stared at the screen for a while and said, tentatively, "That's where the Second Trisolaran Fleet went into lightspeed, isn't it?"

"Exactly."

"You're certain?"

"My old job was to observe this part of space. I know it better than the palm of my hand."

The conclusion was inescapable: Ships using curvature propulsion left behind trails as they accelerated to lightspeed. The trails apparently did not fade with time, but expanded and altered the nature of the space around them.

The first, smaller bubble was inside the Trisolaran system. There were several possible explanations for its existence. Perhaps the Trisolarans did not know initially that curvature propulsion would leave behind such trails, and the bubble was an accident created during engine tests or test flights; or perhaps they did know about the trails, but left them within the star system by mistake. But it was certain that they wanted to avoid purposefully leaving such trails. Eleven years ago, the Second Trisolaran Fleet had cruised for a full year using conventional means, and only when they were six thousand AU from their home world did they engage the curvature engines to enter lightspeed. The purpose was to start the trails as far from the home world as possible, though by that time it was already too late.

At the time, the behavior of the Second Trisolaran Fleet had puzzled people. The most convincing explanation was that they were trying to avoid ill effects on the home world caused by 415 ships entering lightspeed. However, it was clear now that they were trying to avoid exposing the location of Trisolaris by the trails of curvature propulsion. The Second Trisolaran Fleet had exited lightspeed when it was still six thousand AU from the Solar System for the same reason.

Widnall and Vasilenko stared at each other, and they could each see the terror building in the other's eyes. They had reached the same conclusion.

"We have to report this right away," said Widnall.

"But it's not time yet for our scheduled report. A report now would be treated as an alarm."

"This *is* an alarm! We have to tell people not to expose us."

"That's a bit of a stretch. We've just begun researching light-speed ships. It would be impressive if we managed to build one in half a century."

"But what if an initial test generates such a trail? Maybe they're already conducting such trials somewhere in the Solar System!"

And so this information was transmitted to Fleet Command with an alarm-level neutrino beam, then passed on to the PDC. There, it was leaked and mistaken as a photoid attack alarm, which caused the global panic two days later.

The curvature trails were left behind when ships entered lightspeed, just as a rocket launching from the ground left burn marks on the launch pad. Once the ship was at lightspeed, it continued to coast by inertia, and left no more trails. It was a reasonable conjecture that dropping out of lightspeed would leave behind similar marks. It was still unknown how long such trails would persist in space. A guess was that the trails represented some kind of distortion in space due to curvature propulsion, and might last a long time—maybe even forever.

It was reasonable to conclude that Sophon had claimed Trisolaris appeared more dangerous than the Solar System when

observed from a distance because of the ten-AU-diameter curvature propulsion trail left behind within the Trisolaran system, which is what caused the dark forest strike against Trisolaris to come so quickly. The trail and the broadcast of Trisolaris's location mutually provided confirmation and made the danger value of the Trisolaran system skyrocket.

During the following month, Observation Unit #1 discovered six more curvature propulsion trails in different parts of space. All of these were approximately spherical, though their sizes varied widely, ranging from fifteen to two hundred AU. One of these bubbles was only six thousand AU from the Solar System, apparently the mark left by the Second Trisolaran Fleet as it dropped out of lightspeed. The directions and distances of the other trails, however, seemed to indicate that they had nothing to do with the Second Trisolaran Fleet. It appeared that curvature propulsion trails were common in the universe.

After *Blue Space* and *Gravity*'s discovery inside the four-dimensional space fragment, this provided yet more direct evidence that large numbers of highly intelligent civilizations existed in the cosmos.

One of the trails was only 1.4 light-years from the Sun, close to the Oort Cloud. A spaceship had apparently lingered there and then left by entering lightspeed. No one knew when this had happened.

The discovery of the curvature propulsion trail finally eliminated lightspeed space flight, already facing mounting skepticism, from consideration as a viable plan. Fleet International and the UN quickly enacted legislation prohibiting any further research and development of curvature propulsion, and the nation states followed suit. This was the most severe legal restriction against a technology since the nuclear nonproliferation treaties of three centuries ago.

Humanity now had only two choices left: the Bunker Project and the Black Domain Plan.

EXCERPT FROM
A PAST OUTSIDE OF TIME
TERROR OF THE ENDLESS NIGHT

Superficially, research and development of lightspeed spaceflight died for obvious reasons: to avoid advance exposure of the existence of Earth civilization by the trails generated from curvature propulsion, and to prevent increasing the Solar System's danger value in the eyes of observers elsewhere in the cosmos, either of which might have led to an earlier dark forest strike. But there were deeper reasons, too.

From the Common Era to the end of the Crisis Era, humanity looked at the stars with hope. But the first few steps they took toward the stars resulted in failure and pain. The tragic Doomsday Battle revealed the extent of humanity's fragility in the cosmos, and the internecine warfare of the Battle of Darkness had injured the human spirit in equal measure. Later events, such as the judgment of *Bronze Age* and the hijacking of *Gravity* by *Blue Space,* resulting in the universal broadcast, all deepened these wounds and elevated the pain to the level of philosophy.

As a matter of fact, most of the general public was relatively uninvested in the quest for lightspeed spaceships. They believed that even if such ships could be built within their lifetimes, they would have no chance of making use of them.

They cared far more about the Bunker Project, which seemed the most practical path to survival. To be sure, they also cared for the Black Domain Plan, because three centuries of horror had infused them with a strong desire for a serene life, and the Black Domain Plan promised just such a life. Although people were disappointed at the prospect of being sealed off from the rest of the universe, the Solar System itself was large enough that the disappointment was tolerable. The reason they were more interested in the Bunker Project than the Black Domain Plan was because even laypeople could see the extreme technical challenges of slowing down lightspeed, and generally agreed that it was unlikely for mere Man to complete God's Engineering Project.

On the other hand, both staunch opponents and fervent supporters of lightspeed spaceships belonged to the elite classes of society.

The faction in support of researching lightspeed spaceflight believed that the ultimate security of the human race required expansion into the Milky Way and settlement among the stars. In this unfeeling cosmos, only outward-facing civilizations had a chance of survival, and isolationism ultimately led to annihilation. Those who held such views generally did not oppose the Bunker Project, but passionately despised the Black Domain Plan, viewing it as an attempt to dig humankind's own grave. Even though they conceded that a black domain would guarantee the long-term survival of the human race, they saw such life as death for the civilization.

The faction opposed to researching lightspeed vessels felt this way for political reasons. They believed that human civilization had suffered many trials before reaching a nearly ideal democratic society, but once humanity headed for space, it would inevitably regress socially. Space was like a distorting mirror that magnified the dark side of humanity to the maximum. A line from one of the Bronze Age defendants, Sebastian Schneider, became their slogan:

> When humans are lost in space, it takes only five minutes
> to reach totalitarianism.

For a democratic, civilized Earth to scatter innumerable seeds of totalitarianism among the Milky Way was a prospect that these people found intolerable.

The child that was human civilization had opened the door to her home and glanced outside. The endless night terrified her so much that she shuddered against the expansive and profound darkness, and shut the door firmly.

BROADCAST ERA, YEAR 8
SUN-EARTH LAGRANGIAN POINT

Cheng Xin once again returned to the point in space where the Sun's and the Earth's gravities balanced each other out. A year had passed since the meeting with Yun Tianming, and she was far more relaxed for this trip. She was here as a volunteer for the Bunker Project simulation test.

Fleet International and the UN conducted this simulation jointly. Its goal was to test the effectiveness of the giant planets as barriers in the event of a solar explosion.

A supersized hydrogen bomb would play the role of the exploding sun. The power of nuclear bombs was no longer measured in TNT-equivalents, but this bomb's yield would be approximately three hundred megatons. In order to more realistically simulate the physical conditions of a solar explosion, the hydrogen bomb was wrapped in a thick shell to mimic the solar material that would be thrown off by the explosion. The eight planets were modeled with fragments of asteroids. Of these, the four asteroids modeling terrestrial planets were around ten meters in diameter; the ones modeling the gas giants were far bigger, each around one hundred meters in diameter. The eight fragments were positioned around the hydrogen bomb at distances that replicated the relative distances of the planets, so that the entire system resembled a miniature Solar System. "Mercury," which was closest, was about four kilometers from the "Sun," and

"Neptune," which was farthest, was about three hundred kilometers away. The test was conducted at the Lagrangian point to minimize the effects of the Sun's and the planets' gravities so that the system could remain stable for some time.

Scientifically, this experiment wasn't really necessary. Computer modeling based on existing data was more than adequate to produce results that could be trusted. Even if physical tests had to be done, they could have taken place in a laboratory. Though the scale would have to be smaller, careful design would have yielded considerable precision. As a science experiment, this large-scale simulation in space was clumsy to the point of being idiotic.

But the experimenters who had envisioned, designed, and implemented the simulation understood that the ultimate goal of this trial wasn't science. It was actually an expensive propaganda effort to stabilize international faith in the Bunker Project. The trial had to be direct and visually impactful, so that it could be broadcast to the world.

After the total rejection of any further research into lightspeed spaceflight, conditions on Earth resembled the beginning of the Crisis Era. Back then, global defense against the Trisolaran invasion expended effort in two areas: one was the mainstream plan of constructing the Solar System's defenses, and the other was the Wallfacer Project. Now, humankind's mainstream survival plan was the Bunker Project, and the Black Domain Plan, like the Wallfacer Project, was a gamble filled with unknowns. The plans were carried out in parallel, but since only theoretical research was possible on black domains, limited resources were committed. The Bunker Project, on the other hand, extensively impacted all of human society, and great effort had to be expended to secure the public's support.

It would have been sufficient to leave monitoring equipment behind the rocky fragments, in order to test the shielding effects of the "gas giants," or perhaps animal subjects. But in order to ensure a sensational reaction, the organizers decided that live human subjects were necessary, and so a global effort was undertaken to recruit volunteers.

艾 AA was the one who suggested Cheng Xin send in an application. AA believed that this was an excellent opportunity to do some free marketing to burnish the Halo Group's public image in preparation for entry into the Bunker Project. She and Cheng Xin also both understood that the trial had been planned carefully. It might look unsettling, but there was basically no danger.

Cheng Xin's spacecraft stopped in the shadow of the fragment representing Jupiter. This irregular asteroid was shaped like a potato. It was about 110 meters long, with an average width of around seventy meters. Over a period of two months, the asteroid had been pushed from its home in the asteroid belt to here. During its voyage, some artistic engineer who had too much time on his hands had painted it with colorful bands similar to the ones on the real Jupiter, including the Great Red Spot. Overall, however, the painted asteroid did not resemble Jupiter, but some space monster with a Cyclopean red eye.

As on her last voyage, Cheng Xin's spacecraft flew against the brilliant sun, but once it entered the shadow of the asteroid, everything darkened immediately, because there was no air in space to scatter the sunlight. The Sun on the other side of the asteroid might as well not have existed. Cheng Xin felt she was at the foot of a cliff at midnight.

Even without the barrier of the asteroid, it would have been impossible to see the hydrogen bomb simulating the Sun fifty kilometers away. But in the other direction, she could see the simulated "Saturn." By scale, it was just about a hundred kilometers from the "Sun" and fifty kilometers from "Jupiter." It was about the same size as this asteroid fragment, and, illuminated by the real Sun, stood out against the backdrop of space so that Cheng Xin could just tell its shape. She could also see "Uranus" about two hundred kilometers away, though that was just a shiny dot, hard to tell apart from the stars. The rest of the "planets" were invisible.

Along with Cheng Xin's dinghy, about nineteen other space vessels were parked behind "Jupiter." Together, these simulated the twenty planned Jovian space cities. The spaceships were lined up

in three rows behind the asteroid, and Cheng Xin was in the front-most row, about ten meters from the asteroid. More than a hundred volunteers were seated in the ships. Originally, AA had planned to come with Cheng Xin, but company business kept her away. Thus, Cheng Xin's dinghy might be the only one sheltered behind "Jupiter" with a lone passenger.

They could see the bright blue Earth about 1.5 million kilometers away. More than three billion people there were watching a live broadcast of the trial.

The countdown indicated that about ten minutes remained before the start of the detonation. The communications channels quieted. Abruptly, a man's voice spoke up.

"Hello. I'm next to you."

Cheng Xin shuddered as she recognized the voice. Her dinghy was at one end of the five vessels in the first row. Looking to her right, she saw a spherical dinghy very similar to the one she had ridden in a year ago parked right next to hers. Almost half the hull was transparent, and she could see five passengers inside. Thomas Wade was sitting on the side closest to her, and waved at her. Cheng Xin was able to recognize him right away because, unlike the other four passengers, he wasn't wearing a lightweight space suit; instead, he wore only his black leather jacket, as if to show his contempt for space. His sleeve remained empty, indicating that he still had not gotten a prosthetic hand.

"Let's dock so I can come over," Wade said. Without waiting for Cheng Xin to agree, he initiated the docking sequence. The dinghy he was in started its maneuvering thrusters and slowly approached Cheng Xin's dinghy. Reluctantly, Cheng Xin initiated the docking procedure as well. After a slight tremor, the two ships were connected, and both sets of cabin doors slid open noiselessly. As the pressure between the two ships equalized, Cheng Xin's ears popped.

Wade floated over. He couldn't have had much experience in space, but like Cheng Xin, he moved as though he was born to it. Though he had only one hand, his movements in weightlessness

were steady and firm, as though gravity still worked on him. The interior of the cabin was dim. Sunlight, reflected from the Earth, was deflected again by the asteroid into the dinghy. In this obscure light, Cheng Xin looked Wade over and found him not much changed by the intervening eight years. He still looked pretty much the same as he had in Australia.

"What are you doing here?" Cheng Xin asked, trying to keep her voice cool. But she always seemed to have trouble maintaining her composure in front of this man. After what she had gone through the last few years, everything in her heart had been polished until it was as smooth as the asteroid in front of her, but Wade remained a singular sharp corner.

"I finished my sentence a month ago." Wade took half of a cigar from his jacket pocket—though he couldn't light it here. "It was reduced. A murderer, out in eleven years—I know that's not fair ... to you."

"We all have to follow the law. There's nothing unfair about that."

"Follow the law in everything? Including lightspeed propulsion?"

Just like before, Wade got straight to the point without wasting any time. Cheng Xin didn't answer.

"Why do you want lightspeed ships?" Wade asked. He turned and stared at Cheng Xin brazenly.

"Because that is the only choice that makes humankind grand," Cheng Xin said. She met his gaze fearlessly.

Wade nodded and took the cigar out of his mouth. "Very good. You're grand."

Cheng Xin looked at him, her eyes asking the unspoken question.

"You know what is right, and you have the courage and sense of duty to do it. This makes you extraordinary."

"But?" Cheng Xin prompted.

"But, you don't have the skill or the will to complete this task. We share the same ideal. I also want to see lightspeed ships built."

"What are you trying to say?"

"Give it to me."

"Give what to you?"

491

"Everything you own. Your company, your wealth, your authority, your position—and if possible, your reputation and glory. I will use them all to build lightspeed ships, for your ideals, and for the grandness of the human spirit."

The thrusters of the dinghy came on again. Although the asteroid generated little gravity, it was still enough to make the dinghy fall toward it slowly. The thrusters pushed the dinghy away from the rock until it returned to its assigned location. The plasma nozzle illuminated the surface of the asteroid fragment, and the red spot painted on it looked like a suddenly opened eye. Cheng Xin's heart tensed, whether due to this eye or Wade's words. Wade stared back at the giant eye, his gaze sharp and cold, with a hint of mockery.

Cheng Xin said nothing. She couldn't think of anything to say.

"Don't make the same mistake a second time," Wade said. Each word struck Cheng Xin's heart like a heavy hammer.

It was time: The hydrogen bomb exploded. Without the obstruction of an atmosphere, nearly all of its energy was released in the form of radiation. In the live feed taken from about four hundred kilometers away, a fireball appeared next to the Sun. Soon, the brightness and size of the fireball exceeded the Sun itself, and the camera's filters quickly dimmed the light. If someone were to gaze at it directly from this distance, he or she would be blinded permanently. By the time the fireball reached maximum brightness, there was nothing in the camera's view but pure whiteness. The flame seemed ready to swallow the entire universe.

Sheltered in the shadow of the giant rock, Cheng Xin and Wade did not witness this sight. The live broadcast feed was shut off within the cabin, but they could see "Saturn" behind them increase in brightness abruptly. Next, the molten lava generated on the side of "Jupiter" facing the "Sun" flew around them. The lava glowed red as it dripped away from the edge of the asteroid, but after it flew some distance away, the reflected light from the nuclear detonation exceeded its inherent red glow, and the thin dribbles of lava turned into brilliant fireworks. The view from the dinghy resembled the view from the top of a silvery waterfall tumbling down toward

the Earth. By now, the four smaller asteroid fragments simulating the terrestrial planets had been incinerated, and the four larger asteroid fragments simulating the gas giants behaved as four scoops of ice cream being heated on one side by a blowtorch. The side facing the detonation melted and turned into a smooth hemisphere, and every "planet" dripped a silvery tail of lava. More than ten seconds after the radiation reached "Jupiter," the simulated stellar material, consisting of pieces of the exploded shell of the hydrogen bomb, struck the massive asteroid fragment, causing it to quake and drift slowly away from the "Sun." The dinghy's thrusters activated and maintained distance from the fragment.

The fireball persisted for about thirty seconds before going out. Space seemed like a hall where the light had suddenly been shut off. The real Sun, about one AU away, appeared dim. As the fireball disappeared, the light emitted by the red-glowing half of the asteroid fragment became visible. Initially, the light was very bright, as though the rock were on fire, but the frigidity of space quickly chilled it to a dim red glow. The solidified lava at the rim of the fragment formed a circle of long stalactites.

The fifty spaceships sheltered behind the four giant asteroid fragments were unharmed.

The live feed arrived at the Earth five seconds later, and the world erupted into cheers. Hope for the future exploded everywhere like the hydrogen bomb. The goal of the Bunker Project simulation test had been achieved.

"Don't make the same mistake twice," Wade repeated, as though all that had just happened was nothing more than noise that had briefly interrupted their conversation.

Cheng Xin stared at the dinghy Wade had come from. The four men in space suits had been looking in this direction the entire time, oblivious to the magnificent sight that had just taken place. Cheng Xin knew that tens of thousands of people had volunteered for the test, and only famous or important people had been selected. Although Wade had just gotten out of prison, he already had powerful followers—those four men, at least—and the dinghy probably

also belonged to him. Even eleven years ago, when he had competed for the Swordholder position, he had had many loyal followers, and even more supporters. It was rumored that he had founded a secret organization, which had perhaps survived. He was like a piece of nuclear fuel. Even when it was sealed up in a lead container, one could feel its power and threat.

"Let me think about it," said Cheng Xin.

"Of course you need to think about it." Wade nodded at Cheng Xin, then left noiselessly as he drifted back to his own ship. The cabin door closed, and the two ships separated.

In the direction of the Earth, the cooled lava bits drifted languidly against the starry background like a field of dust. Cheng Xin felt the tension in her heart give way, and she herself felt like a mote of dust drifting through the cosmos.

On the way back, when the dinghy was within three hundred thousand kilometers of the Earth so that there was essentially no delay in communications, Cheng Xin called AA and told her about the meeting with Wade.

"Do as he said," AA said without hesitation. "Give him everything he asked for."

"You …" Cheng Xin stared at AA in the information window, astonished. She had imagined AA would be the biggest obstacle.

"He's right. You don't have the capacity for this. The attempt will ruin you! But he can get it done. This bastard, devil, murderer, careerist, political hooligan, technophilic madman … he can get it done. He has the will and skill for this, so let him! It's hell, so step aside for him to jump in."

"What about you?"

AA smiled. "I would never work under him, of course. Ever since they proscribed lightspeed ships, I've grown afraid, too. I will take what I deserve and go do something I enjoy. I hope you do, too."

———

Two days later, in the transparent conference hall at the top of the Halo Group headquarters, Cheng Xin met with Wade.

"I can give you everything you want," Cheng Xin said.

"Then you'll go into hibernation," Wade said. "Because your presence may affect our task."

Cheng Xin nodded. "Yes. That is my plan."

"We'll awaken you on the day we achieve success, which will be your success as well. On that day, if lightspeed ships are still against the law, we'll accept all responsibility. If such ships are welcomed by the world, the honor will belong to you.... It will be at least half a century, or even longer. We'll be old, but you'll still be young."

"I have one condition."

"Speak."

"If this project ever has the potential to harm the human race, you must awaken me. The final decision is mine, and I have the right to take back all the authority I give you."

"I can't accept that."

"Then we have nothing to discuss. I'll give you nothing."

"Cheng Xin, you must know what path we'll be taking. Sometimes, one must—"

"Forget it. We'll go our separate ways."

Wade stared at Cheng Xin. In his eyes were feelings rarely seen in him: hesitation, even helplessness. It was as unexpected to see these things in him as it was to see water in fire. "Let me think about it."

He turned and walked over to one of the transparent walls and gazed at the metropolitan forest outside. On that night three centuries ago at the plaza in front of the UN, Cheng Xin had also seen the back of this black figure against the lights of New York City.

About two minutes later, Wade turned around. Still standing at the transparent wall, he looked at Cheng Xin from across the room. "All right. I accept."

Cheng Xin remembered that three centuries ago, after turning around, he had said, "We'll send only a brain." Those words had changed the course of history.

"I don't have many means to enforce our deal. I can only trust your promise."

That smile, like a crack in the ice, spread across Wade's face. "You are perfectly aware that if I break my promise, it will actually be a blessing for you. But unfortunately, I will keep my promise."

Wade walked back and straightened his leather jacket, which only caused more wrinkles to appear. He stood in front of Cheng Xin and solemnly said, "I promise that if, during the process of researching lightspeed spaceflight, we discover anything that may harm the human race, regardless of the form of the danger, we'll awaken you. You'll have the final say and can take back all of my authority."

After hearing about the meeting with Wade, AA said to Cheng Xin, "Then I'll need to go into hibernation with you. We have to be prepared to take back the Halo Group at a moment's notice."

"You believe he'll keep his promise?" asked Cheng Xin.

AA stared straight ahead, as though looking at a ghost Wade. "I do. I think the devil will do as he says. But just like he said, that's not necessarily a good thing for you. You could have saved yourself, Cheng Xin, but in the end, you didn't."

Ten days later, Thomas Wade became the president of the Halo Group and took over all operations.

Cheng Xin and AA entered hibernation. Their consciousnesses gradually faded in the cold. It felt as though they had been drifting for a long time in a river. Exhausted, they climbed onto the shore, stopped, and watched the river continue to flow before their eyes, watched as the familiar water flowed into the distance.

While they stepped briefly outside the river of time, the story of humanity went on.

PART IV

PART IV

BUNKER ERA, YEAR 11
BUNKER WORLD

#37813, your hibernation is at an end. You have been in
hibernation for 62 years, 8 months, 21 days, and 13 hours.
Your remaining hibernation allotment is 238 years, 3 months,
9 days. This is Asia Hibernation Center #1, Bunker Era, Year
11, May 9, 2:17 P.M.

The small information window hovered in front of the just-awakened
Cheng Xin for no more than a minute before disappearing. She
looked at the smooth metallic ceiling. Out of habit, she stared
at a certain spot in the ceiling. During the age she last entered
hibernation, doing so would have caused the ceiling to recognize
her gaze and bring up an information window. But the ceiling didn't
respond. Although she still didn't have the strength to turn her
head, she was able to see part of the room: All the walls were made
of metal and there were no information windows. The air remained
empty as well, with no holographic displays. The metal in the wall
looked familiar: stainless steel or aluminum alloy, no decorations.

A nurse appeared in her field of view. She was very young and
didn't look at Cheng Xin. Instead, the nurse busied herself around
her bed, probably disconnecting the medical equipment attached
to her body. Cheng Xin's body couldn't sense what the nurse was

doing, but something about the nurse seemed familiar to her—her uniform. During the last age Cheng Xin was awake, people wore self-cleaning clothes that always looked brand new, but this nurse's white uniform showed signs of wear. Although it was still clean, she could see signs of it being old, signs of the passage of time.

The ceiling began to move. Cheng Xin's bed was being pushed out of the awakening room. She was astonished to find that the nurse was pushing the bed—the bed actually needed someone to push it to move.

The hallway was made of empty metallic walls as well. Other than some ceiling lights, there were no other decorations. The lights looked ordinary enough, and Cheng Xin saw that the frame around one of the lights was loose and dangled from the ceiling. Between the frame and the ceiling she saw ... wires.

Cheng Xin struggled to recall the information window she had seen upon first awakening, but she couldn't be certain it had really been there. It now seemed a hallucination.

There were many pedestrians in the hallway, and no one paid attention to Cheng Xin. She concentrated on the clothes people wore. A few were medical personnel in white uniforms, and the rest wore simple, plain clothing that resembled work overalls. Cheng Xin had the impression that many people here seemed to be from the Common Era, but soon realized that she was wrong. The Common Era was a long time ago, and the human race had changed eras four times already. It was impossible for so many Common Era people to be around.

Her impression was due to the fact that she saw some men who looked like the men she was used to.

The men who had disappeared during the Deterrence Era had returned. This was another age capable of producing men.

Everyone seemed to be in a hurry. This seemed to be another swing of the pendulum: the leisure and comfort of the last age had disappeared, and it was once again a harried society. In this age, most people no longer belonged to the leisure class, but had to work for a living.

Cheng Xin's bed was pushed into a small room. "Number 37813 awakened without irregularities," the nurse called out. "She's in recovery room twenty-eight." Then the nurse left and closed the door. Cheng Xin noticed that she had to pull the door shut.

She was left alone in the room. For a long time, no one came to check on her, a situation in total contrast to the previous two awakenings she had experienced, when she had received a great deal of attention and care. She was certain of two things: First, in this age, hibernation and awakening were common events. Second, not many people knew that she had awakened.

After Cheng Xin recovered some motor control, she moved her head and saw the window. She remembered the world before she had gone into hibernation: The hibernation center had been a giant tree at the edge of the city, and she had been in one of the leaves near the top, from where she could see the grand city-forest. But now, outside this window, she could only see a few ordinary buildings erected on the ground, all of them the same shape and design. Based on the sunlight glinting off them, they were constructed of metal as well. The buildings gave her the feeling of having returned to the Common Era.

She suddenly wondered if she had just awakened from a long dream. The Deterrence Era, the Broadcast Era—they were all dreams. Although the memories were clear, they seemed too surreal, fantastic. Perhaps she had never leapt across time on three occasions, but had been in the Common Era all along?

A holographic display window appeared next to her bed, removing her doubts. The window contained only a few simple buttons that could be used to call for the doctor and the nurse. The place seemed very familiar with the hibernation recovery process: The window had appeared just as Cheng Xin recovered the ability to lift her hand. But it was only a small window; the hyperinformation society where information windows filled every surface was gone.

Unlike the previous two awakenings, Cheng Xin recovered very quickly. By the time it was dark out, she was already able to get out of bed and walk about a bit. She found that the center provided

only the simplest services. A doctor came in once to give her a cursory examination and then left; she had to do everything else by herself. She had to bathe herself while she still felt weak all over. As for meals, if she hadn't asked for them through that tiny holographic display, she might never have gotten to eat. Cheng Xin wasn't annoyed by this lack of solicitousness, as she had never completely adjusted to that excessively generous era where every person's every need was taken care of. She was still a Common Era woman at heart, and she felt at home here.

The next morning, a visitor came to see her. She recognized Cao Bin right away. This physicist had once been the youngest Sword-holder candidate, but now he was much older, and a few strands of white appeared in his hair. Cheng Xin was certain, though, that he had not aged by sixty-two years.

"Mr. Thomas Wade asked me to come and get you."

"What happened?" Cheng Xin's heart sank as she recalled the conditions for her awakening.

"We'll talk about it after we get there." Cao Bin paused, and then added, "I'll take you around this new world before then so that you can make the right decision based on facts."

Cheng Xin glanced at the undistinguished buildings outside the window; she didn't feel the world was new.

"What happened to you? You weren't awake these last sixty years," Cheng Xin asked.

"I went into hibernation at about the same time you did. Seventeen years later, the circumsolar particle accelerator was operational, and I was awakened to research basic theory. That took fifteen years. Later, the research work turned to technical applications, and I was no longer needed, so I went back into hibernation until two years ago."

"How's the curvature propulsion project going?"

"There have been some developments.... We'll talk about it later." Cao Bin clearly didn't relish the topic.

Cheng Xin looked outside again. A breeze passed by, and a small tree in front of the window rustled. A cloud seemed to pass overhead,

and the glint given off by the metallic buildings dimmed. How could such a commonplace world have anything to do with light-speed spaceships?

Cao Bin followed Cheng Xin's gaze and laughed. "You must feel the same as when I first awakened—rather disappointed in this era, aren't you? ... If you are up to it, let's go outside and take a look."

Half an hour later, Cheng Xin, dressed in a white outfit appropriate for this era, came onto a balcony of the hibernation center with Cao Bin. The city spread out before her, and Cheng Xin was again struck by the feeling that time had flowed backwards. After she had awakened for the first time during the Deterrence Era, the impact of seeing the giant forest-city for the first time was indescribable. After that, she never thought she would again see a cityscape so familiar: The plan for the city was very regular, as though all the buildings had been erected at once. The buildings themselves were monotonous and uniform, as though designed solely for utility with no consideration for architectural aesthetics. All of them were rectangular with no surface decorations, and all sported the same metallic gray exterior—reminding her strangely of the aluminum lunch boxes of her youth. The buildings were neatly and densely arranged as far as she could see. At the horizon, the ground rose up like the side of a mountain, and the city extended onto the mountainside.

"Where is this?" Cheng Xin asked.

"Hmm, why is it overcast again? We can't see the other side." Cao Bin didn't answer her question, but shook his head at the sky in disappointment, as though the weather had something to do with Cheng Xin's understanding of this new world. But soon, she saw how strange the sky was.

The sun was below the clouds.

The clouds began to dissipate, revealing a large opening. Through the opening, Cheng Xin did not see a blue sky; instead, she saw ... more ground.

The ground in the sky was studded with the buildings of a city very similar to the city around her, except she was now looking

"down"—or "up"—at it. This must have been the "other side" Cao Bin referred to. Cheng Xin realized that the rising "mountainside" in the distance wasn't a mountain at all, but continued to rise until it connected with the "sky." The world was a giant cylinder, and she was standing on the inside of it.

"This is Space City Asia I, in the shadow of Jupiter," Cao Bin said.

The new world that had seemed so common a moment ago now stunned her. Cheng Xin felt that she had finally, truly awakened.

In the afternoon, Cao Bin brought Cheng Xin on a trip to the gateway terminal at the northern end of the city.

By custom, the central axis of the space city was treated as oriented north-south. They got on a bus outside the hibernation center—this was a real bus that moved along the ground; probably running on electricity, but it looked indistinguishable from an ancient city bus. The bus was crowded, and Cheng Xin and Cao Bin took the last two seats at the back so that additional passengers had to stand. Cheng Xin thought back to the last time she had taken a bus—even during the Common Era, she had long ceased riding crowded public transportation.

The bus moved slowly, so she could take in the view leisurely. Everything now held a new meaning for her. She saw swaths of buildings sweep past the window, interspersed with green parks and pools; she saw two schools with exercise yards painted in blue; she saw brown soil covering the ground on the sides of the road, looking no different from soil on Earth. Broad-leafed trees resembling Chinese parasol trees lined the road, and advertising billboards appeared from time to time—Cheng Xin didn't recognize most of the products or brands, but the style of the ads was familiar.

The main difference from a Common Era city was that the entire world seemed to be constructed out of metal. The buildings were metallic, and the inside of the bus seemed to be mostly metal as well. She saw no plastic, and no composites either.

Cheng Xin paid the most attention to the other passengers on the bus. Across the aisle sat two men, one of whom dozed with a black briefcase on his lap, while the other wore yellow work overalls with black oil stains. Next to the man's feet was a tool bag, and some instrument Cheng Xin did not recognize poked out of it: It resembled an ancient power drill, but was translucent. The man's face showed the exhaustion and numbness of someone who performed physical labor. The last time Cheng Xin had seen such an expression was on the faces of migrant laborers in Common Era cities. In front of her sat a young couple. The man whispered something in the woman's ear, and the woman giggled from time to time while spooning something pink out of a paper cup—ice cream, since Cheng Xin picked up the sweet fragrance of cream, no different from her memory of more than three centuries ago. Two middle-aged women stood in the aisle—they were of a type familiar to Cheng Xin: The drudgery of everyday life had ground away their glamour, and they no longer took care with their appearance or were fashionable. Women like that had disappeared during the Deterrence Era or the Broadcast Era. Back then, women always had smooth, delicate skin, and no matter how old they were, they looked beautiful and refined, appropriate for their age. Cheng Xin eavesdropped on their conversation:

"You got it wrong. The morning market and the evening market have similar prices. Don't be lazy. Go to the wholesale market on the west side."

"They don't have enough, and they won't sell at wholesale prices anyway."

"You have to go later, after seven or so. The vegetable vendors will be gone, and they'll sell at wholesale prices."

She overheard snippets of other conversations in the bus as well.

"The city government is different from the atmospheric system, much more complicated. When you get there, pay attention to the office politics. Don't get too close to anyone at first, but don't hold yourself apart either." ... "It's not right to charge separately for the heat; that should have been included in the electric bill." ...

"If they had subbed for that fool earlier they wouldn't have lost so badly." ... "Don't be so disappointed. I've been here since the city was built, and how much do you think I make every year?" ... "That fish is no longer fresh. Don't even think about steaming it." ... "The other day, when they had to make an orbital adjustment, Park Four's water spilled again and flooded a large area." ... "If she doesn't like him, he should just give up. All that effort is just going to be wasted." ... "That can't be authentic. I don't even think it's a high-quality imitation. Are you kidding me? At that price?" ...

Cheng Xin's heart felt warm and content. Ever since she had awakened for the first time during the Deterrence Era, she had been searching for this feeling. She had thought she'd never find it. She absorbed the conversations around her as though slaking a thirst, and didn't pay much attention to Cao Bin's narration of the city.

Space City Asia I was one of the earliest to be built as part of the Bunker Project. It was a regular cylinder that simulated gravity with the centrifugal force generated by spinning. With a length of thirty kilometers and a diameter of seven kilometers, its usable interior surface area was 659 square kilometers, about half the size of ancient Beijing. Once, about twenty million inhabitants had lived here, but after the completion of newer cities, the population had decreased to about nine million, so that it was no longer so crowded....

Cheng Xin saw another sun appear in the sky before her. Cao Bin explained that there were a total of three artificial suns in the space city, all of them floating along the central axis, each separated by about ten kilometers. These produced energy by nuclear fusion, and brightened and dimmed on a twenty-four-hour cycle.

Cheng Xin felt a series of jolts. The bus was already at a stop, and the tremors seemed to originate from deep within the ground. She felt a force pushing against her back, but the bus remained unmoving. Outside the window, she could see the shadows cast by the trees and buildings suddenly shift to a new angle as the artificial suns abruptly shifted positions. But soon, the suns moved back into

place. Cheng Xin saw that none of the passengers seemed surprised by this.

"The space city was adjusting its position," said Cao Bin.

The bus arrived at the last stop after about thirty minutes. After getting off the bus, she saw that the everyday scenes that had so intoxicated her disappeared. In front of her was an enormous wall whose immense size made her gasp. It was as though she was standing at the end of the world—and indeed, she *was*. This was the "northernmost" point in the city, a large circular disk eight kilometers in diameter. She couldn't see the entire disk from where she stood, but she could tell that the ground rose up on both sides of her. The top of the disk—the other side of the city—was about as high as the peak of Mount Everest. Many radial spokes converged from the rim of the disk to the center, four kilometers above. Each spoke was an elevator shaft, and the center was the space city's gateway.

Before entering the elevator, Cheng Xin cast a lingering glance back at this city that already seemed so familiar. From here, all three suns were visible in a row toward the other end of the city. It was dusk, and the suns dimmed, turning from a blinding orange-white to a gentle red, bathing the city in a warm golden glow. Cheng Xin saw a few girls in white school uniforms chatting and laughing on a lawn not too far away, their hair wafting in the breeze and drenched in the golden glow of the evening sun.

The interior of the elevator car was very spacious, like a large hall. The side facing the city was transparent, turning the car into an observation deck. Every seat was equipped with seat belts because, as the elevator rose, gravity quickly diminished. As they looked outside, the ground sank lower, while the "sky," another ground, grew clearer. By the time the elevator reached the center of the circle, gravity had completely disappeared, as well as the sensation of "up" and "down" when looking outside. Since this was the axis around which the city spun, the ground surrounded them in every direction. Here, the view of the city was at its most magnificent.

The three suns had dimmed to the level of moonlight, and their colors shifted to silver. Viewed from here, the three suns—or moons—were stacked on top of each other. All the clouds were concentrated in the gravity-free zone, forming an axis of white mist extending through the center of the city to the other end. The "southern" end, forty-five kilometers away, could be seen clearly. Cao Bin told Cheng Xin that that was where the city's thrusters were located. The lights of the city had just come on. In Cheng Xin's eyes, a sea of lights surrounded her and extended into the distance. She seemed to be looking down a giant well whose wall was covered with a brilliant carpet.

Cheng Xin casually locked her gaze on a certain spot in the city, and found the arrangement of buildings there very similar to the residential district of her home back in the Common Era. She imagined a certain ordinary apartment building in that area and a certain window on the second floor: Through blue curtains, a gentle light seeped, and behind the curtain, her mom and dad waited for her....

She could not hold back her tears.

Ever since awakening for the first time during the Deterrence Era, Cheng Xin had never been able to integrate into the new eras, always feeling like a stranger from another time. But she could never have imagined that she would once again feel at home more than half a century later, here behind Jupiter, more than eight hundred million kilometers from the Earth. It was as if everything that she had been familiar with from more than three centuries ago had been picked up by a pair of invisible hands, rolled up like a giant painting, and then placed here as a new world slowly spinning around her.

Cheng Xin and Cao Bin entered a weightless corridor. This was a tube in which people moved by pulling themselves along handholds on cables. The passengers riding up from all the elevators along the rim gathered here to exit the city, and the corridor was filled with streaming crowds. A row of information windows appeared around the circular wall of the corridor, and the animated images in the

windows were mostly news and ads. But the windows were few in number and neatly arranged, unlike the chaotic profusion of information windows in the previous era.

Cheng Xin had long since noticed that the overwhelming hyperinformation age had apparently ended. Information appeared in this world in a restrained, directed manner. Was this the result of changes in the Bunker World's political and economic systems?

Emerging from the corridor, Cheng Xin first noticed the stars spinning overhead. The spin was very rapid and made her dizzy. The view around her opened up dramatically. They were standing on a circular plaza with a diameter of eight kilometers "atop" the space city. This was the city's spaceport, and many spacecraft were parked here. Most of the vessels were shaped not too differently from those Cheng Xin had seen over sixty years ago, though these were generally smaller. Many were about the size of ancient automobiles. Cheng Xin noticed that the flames at the nozzles of the spaceships as they took off were far dimmer than what she remembered from more than half a century ago. The glow was a dark blue and no longer so blinding. This probably meant that the miniature fusion engines were much more efficient.

Cheng Xin saw an eye-catching red-glowing circle all around the exit, with a radius of about a hundred meters. She quickly understood its meaning: The space city was spinning, and, outside the circle, the centrifugal force became very strong. Moving out-side the warning circle meant a dramatic increase in centrifugal force, and vessels parked out there had to be anchored, while pedestrians needed to wear magnetic shoes lest they be thrown out.

It was very cold here. Only when a nearby vessel took off did the engine's heat bring a brief feeling of warmth. Cheng Xin shuddered—not just from the cold, but because she realized that she was completely exposed to space! But the air around her and the air pressure were real, and she could feel cold breezes. It appeared that the technology to contain an atmosphere in a nonenclosed area had

advanced even further, to the point where an atmosphere could be maintained in completely open space.

Cao Bin saw her shock and said, "Oh, right now we can only maintain an atmosphere about ten meters thick above 'ground.'" He hadn't been in this world for too long, either, but he was already jaded by the technology that seemed like magic to Cheng Xin. He wanted to show her far more impressive sights.

Against the background of the spinning stars, Cheng Xin saw the Bunker World.

From here, most of the space cities behind Jupiter could be seen. She saw twenty-two cities (including the one she stood on), and there were four more blocked by the city they stood on. All twenty-six cities (six more than planned) were hiding in the shadow of Jupiter. They were loosely lined up in four rows, and reminded Cheng Xin of the spaceships lined up behind the giant rock in space more than sixty years ago. To one side of Asia I was North America I and Oceania I, and to the other side was Asia III. Only about fifty kilometers separated Asia I from its neighbors on either side, and Cheng Xin could feel their immensity, like two planets. The next row of four cities was 150 kilometers away, and it was difficult to tell their size visually. The most distant space cities were about one thousand kilometers away, and looked like delicate toys from here.

Cheng Xin thought of the space cities as a school of tiny fish hovering in place behind a giant rock to avoid the torrents in the river.

North America I, closest to Asia I, was a pure sphere. It and the cylindrical Asia I represented the two extremes of space city design. Most of the other space cities were football-shaped, though the ratios of major to minor axes were different in each. A few other space cities took on unusual shapes: a wheel with spokes, a spindle, etc.

Behind the other three gas giants were three more space city clusters, consisting of a total of thirty-eight space cities. Twenty-six were behind Saturn, four behind Uranus, and eight more behind Neptune. Those space cities were in safer locations, though the environs were even more desolate.

One of the space cities in front suddenly emitted a blue light. It was as though a small blue sun appeared in space, casting long shadows of the people and spaceships on the plaza. Cao Bin told Cheng Xin that this was because the space city's thrusters had been activated to adjust its position. The space cities revolved around the Sun in parallel with Jupiter, just outside its orbit. Jupiter's gravity gradually pulled the cities closer, and the cities had to constantly adjust their positions with thrusters. This operation required a great deal of energy. Once, the suggestion had been floated to turn the cities into Jupiter's satellites that would only shift into new orbits around the Sun after the issuance of a dark forest strike warning. But until the advance warning system had been further refined and proven to be reliable, no space city wanted to take the risk.

"Lucky you! Now you get to see a sight that happens only once every three days." Cao Bin pointed into space. Cheng Xin saw a tiny white dot in the distance, gradually growing bigger. Soon, it was a white sphere as big as a Ping-Pong ball.

"Europa?"

"That's right. We're very close to its orbit right now. Watch your footing and don't be scared."

Cheng Xin tried to figure out what Cao meant. She had always thought of celestial bodies as moving slowly, almost imperceptibly— as they did in most Earth-based observations. But then she remembered that the space city was not a Jovian satellite but remained stationary relative to it. Europa, on the other hand, was a satellite that moved very fast. She remembered its speed was about fourteen kilometers per second. If the space city was very close to Europa's orbit, then ...

The white sphere expanded rapidly—so fast that it seemed unreal. Europa soon took up most of the sky, and turned from a Ping-Pong ball into a giant planet. The sensation of "up" and "down" switched in an instant, and Cheng Xin felt as if Asia I were falling toward that white world. Next, the three-thousand-kilometer-diameter moon swept overhead so that for an instant, it took up the entire sky. The space city was skimming over the icy

oceans of Europa, and Cheng Xin could clearly see the crisscrossing lines in that frozen landscape, like lines in a giant palm print. The air, disturbed by the passage of Europa, whipped around her, and Cheng Xin felt an invisible force dragging her from left to right—if she weren't wearing magnetic shoes, she was sure she'd be pulled off the ground. Whatever was nearby that hadn't been secured to the ground flew up, and a few cables attached to spaceships also drifted into the air. A terrifying rumbling came from below her—it was the immense frame of the space city reacting to the rapidly shifting gravity field of Europa. It took only about three minutes for Europa to hurtle past Asia I, and then it was on the other side of the city and began to shrink rapidly. The eight space cities in the two front-most rows all activated their thrusters to adjust their positions after the disturbance caused by Europa. Eight fireballs lit up the sky.

"How ... how close was that?" Cheng Xin asked in an unsteady voice.

"The closest approach, like you experienced just now, was a hundred and fifty kilometers, basically brushing right by us. We don't really have a choice. Jupiter has thirteen moons, and it's impossible for the space cities to avoid them all. Europa's orbit is inclined only slightly from the equator, and so it's very close to these cities here. It's the main source of water for the Jovian cities, and we've built a lot of industry on it. But when the dark forest strike comes, all of it will have to be sacrificed. After the solar explosion, all of the Jovian moons' orbits will shift dramatically. Maneuvering the space cities to avoid them at that time will be a very complicated operation."

Cao Bin found the dinghy he had taken to come here. It was tiny, shaped and sized like an ancient automobile, capable of seating only two. Cheng Xin instinctively felt unsafe going into space in such a tiny vehicle, even though she knew her fear wasn't reasonable. Cao Bin told the AI to go to North America I, and the dinghy took off.

Cheng Xin saw the ground receding quickly, and the dinghy flew along at a tangent to the spinning city. Soon, the eight-kilometer-diameter plaza came into view, followed by the entirety

of Asia I. Behind the cylinder was a vast expanse of dark yellow. Only when the edge of this yellow expanse appeared did Cheng Xin realize that she was looking at Jupiter. Here, in the shadow of the gas giant, everything was cold and dark, and the Sun seemed to not exist at all. Only the phosphorescence of the planet's liquid helium and hydrogen, diffused through the thick atmosphere, formed patches of hazy light roving about like eyeballs behind the closed eyelids of a dreamer. The immensity of Jupiter astonished Cheng Xin. From here, she could only see a small portion of its rim, and the rim's curvature was minuscule. The planet was a dark barrier that blocked out everything, and once again gave Cheng Xin the feeling of standing at a giant wall at the end of the world.

In the following three days, Cao Bin took Cheng Xin to visit four more space cities.

The first was North America I, the closest city to Asia I. The main advantage of its spherical construction was that a single artificial sun at the center was sufficient to illuminate the entire city, but the disadvantage of such a design was obvious as well: The gravity changed depending on one's latitude. The equator had the most gravity, which decreased as you went up in latitude. The polar regions were weightless. Inhabitants in the different regions had to adjust to life under various gravity conditions.

Unlike Asia I, small spacecraft could enter the city directly from the gateway at the north pole. Once the dinghy was inside, the entire world spun around it, and the dinghy had to match the city's spin before landing. Cheng Xin and Cao Bin rode a high-speed rail to go to low-latitude regions, and the train moved far faster than the bus in Asia I. Cheng Xin saw that the buildings here were denser and taller, looking like a metropolis. At the high-latitude, low-gravity regions especially, the buildings' heights were limited only by the volume of the sphere. Near the polar regions, some buildings were as tall as ten kilometers, looking like long thorns extending up from the ground toward the sun.

North America I had been completed early on. With a radius of twenty kilometers and twenty million inhabitants, it was the largest city by population. It acted as the prosperous commercial center for all the Jovian cities.

Here, Cheng Xin got to see a splendid sight that was absent from Asia I: the equatorial ring-ocean. As a matter of fact, most space cities had ring-oceans of various widths, and Asia I was rather unique in lacking one. In spherical or football-shaped cities, the equator was the lowest point in the city's simulated gravity, and all the city's water naturally collected there, forming a sparkling, undulating belt for the city. Standing on the shore, one could see the ocean rising on both sides and dividing the "sky" behind the sun. Cheng Xin and Cao Bin took a fast boat and navigated around the sea—a journey of some sixty kilometers. The water in the sea came from Europa, clear, cold, and reflecting rippling light onto the skyscrapers on both sides. The dikes along the edge of the sea closest to Jupiter were higher, to avoid the water spilling out when the city accelerated during position adjustments. Even so, when the city had to engage in unexpected maneuvers, small-scale flooding would occur from time to time.

Next, Cao Bin took Cheng Xin to Europe IV, which sported a typical football-shaped design. Its distinguishing characteristic was the lack of a common artificial sun. Every district had its own miniature fusion sun, and the tiny suns hovered about two hundred to three hundred meters high to provide illumination. The advantage of this approach was that the weightless axis could be more efficiently utilized. The axis of Europe IV was taken up by the longest—or tallest—building among all the space cities. It was forty kilometers long and connected the north and south poles of the football. Since the interior of the building was weightless, it was mainly used as a spaceport and commercial entertainment district.

Europe IV had the smallest population of all the cities, only 4.5 million. It was the wealthiest city of the Bunker World. The

exquisite houses illuminated by miniature suns amazed Cheng Xin. Each house came with its own swimming pool, and a few had wide lawns. Tiny white sails dotted the serene equatorial sea, and people sat on the shore, fishing leisurely. She saw a yacht sail by slowly, and it looked as luxurious as any yacht on ancient Earth. There was a cocktail party being held aboard the yacht with live musicians.... She was astonished that such life could be transplanted into the shadow of Jupiter, eight hundred million kilometers from the Earth.

Pacific I, on the other hand, was the antithesis of Europe IV. This was the very first city completed by the Bunker Project, and like North America I, it was a sphere. Unlike all the other Jovian cities, it did orbit Jupiter as a satellite.

Millions of construction workers had lived in Pacific I during the early years of the Bunker Project. As the project progressed, it was used to warehouse construction materials. Later, as the numerous flaws of this early-phase experimental space city became apparent, it was abandoned. But, after the resettlement to the Bunker World had been completed, people began to live here again, and finally formed a city of their own, with a city government and police force. However, the authorities only maintained the most basic public infrastructure, and society was left basically to run on its own. Pacific I was the only city to which people were free to immigrate without a residential permit. Most of the population consisted of unemployed and homeless wanderers, poor people who had lost social security for various reasons, and bohemian artists. Later, it became the base for extremist political organizations.

Pacific I had no city thrusters, and there was no artificial sun inside. It also didn't spin, so the interior was completely weightless.

After entering the city, Cheng Xin saw a fairy-tale world. It was as if a broken-down but once prosperous city had lost gravity abruptly, so that everything floated in the air. Pacific I was a city in permanent night, and each building maintained illumination with a nuclear battery. Thus, the interior was filled with glowing,

floating lights. Most of the buildings in the city were simple shacks built from abandoned construction materials. Since there was no "up" or "down," most of the shacks were cube-shaped, with windows (which also acted as doors) on all six sides. Some were shaped as spheres, which had the advantage of being more resilient, as the drifting buildings inevitably collided against each other.

There was no notion of land ownership in Pacific I because all the buildings drifted around with no permanent location. In principle, each resident had the right to use any space in the city. The city had a large number of homeless individuals who didn't even possess a shack. All of their possessions were kept in a large net sling to prevent them from scattering everywhere, and the owners drifted along with the net slings. Transportation within the city was simple: There were no cars or weightless cables or personal thrusters. The residents moved around by pushing and kicking off buildings and drifting. Since the buildings were densely packed inside the city, one could navigate anywhere that way, but this method of locomotion required great skill. As Cheng Xin observed the residents flitting around the dense clusters of floating buildings, she was reminded of gibbons swinging easily from branch to branch.

Cheng Xin and Cao Bin drifted close to a group of homeless men gathered around an open fire. Such a fire would have been prohibited in any other city. The fuel seemed to be some kind of flammable construction material. Due to the weightlessness, the flames did not rise up, but formed a ball of fire floating in place. The way they drank was also special. They tossed alcohol out of bottles, forming liquid spheres in the air. Then the men, dressed in rags and with unshaven faces, drifted along with them, capturing the spheres with their mouths and swallowing. One of the drunken men vomited, and the vomit rushing out of his mouth propelled him back, sending him tumbling in midair....

Cheng Xin and Cao Bin came to a market. All the goods floated in the air, forming a heterogeneous mess illuminated by a few drifting lights, with customers and vendors drifting among the hovering objects. In this chaos, it seemed hard to tell what belonged

to whom, but if a customer examined something closely, a vendor would drift over to haggle. The goods offered for sale included clothing, electronics, food and liquor, nuclear batteries of various capacities, small arms, and so on. There were also exotic antiques on sale. In one place, a few metallic fragments were offered at very high prices. The vendor claimed that it was debris gathered from the outer Solar System from warships destroyed during the Doomsday Battle—it was impossible to tell if he was telling the truth.

Cheng Xin was surprised to find a vendor who sold antique books. She flipped through a few—these books were not ancient for her. All the books drifted in a cloud, and many had their pages spread open like a flock of white-winged birds in the light.... Cheng Xin saw a small wooden box drift in front of her, marked as cigars. She caught it, and immediately a young boy kicked his way over and swore up and down that these were authentic ancient Havana cigars that had been preserved for close to two hundred years. Since they had dried out a bit, he was willing to let them go at a low price that she would not be able to find anywhere else in the Solar System. He even opened the box to let Cheng Xin see what she was getting. She agreed and bought them.

Cao Bin took Cheng Xin to the edge of the city—the inside face of the spherical hull. There were no buildings attached to the hull, and there was no soil—everything was left as bare as the day the city was constructed. It was impossible to tell the curvature in a small area, and they seemed to be standing on a large, flat plaza. Above them, the dense buildings of the city floated, and flickering lights projected onto the "plaza." Cheng Xin saw that the hull was marked with all kinds of graffiti, stretching as far as she could see. These pictures were vibrant, wild, unrestrained, wanton and full of energy. In the shifting, uncertain light, they seemed to come alive, as though they were dreams deposited from the city above.

Cao Bin didn't bring Cheng Xin deeper into the city. According to him, the center of the city was chaotic and rather violent. Gangs fought each other, and a few years ago, one of the gang fights had managed to rupture the hull, causing a massive decompression

incident. Later, the gangs seemed to come to some kind of unspoken agreement, and settled their disputes in the center of the city, away from the hull.

Cao Bin also told Cheng Xin that the Federation Government had devoted enormous resources to build a social welfare system here in Pacific I. The six million or so inhabitants here were mostly unemployed, but at least they could get the basic necessities for life.

"What will happen here in the event of a dark forest strike?"

"Only annihilation. This city has no thrusters, and even if it did have them, it would be impossible to move it into the shadow of Jupiter and keep it there. Look—" He pointed to the drifting buildings. "If the city accelerated, everything would smash through the hull. Then the city would be like a bag with a hole in the bottom. If we receive a dark forest strike alert, the only thing that can be done is to evacuate the population to the other cities."

As they left the floating city in eternal night, Cheng Xin gazed at it through the porthole of the dinghy. This was a city of poverty and homelessness, but it also possessed its own rich life, like a weightless version of the famous Song Dynasty painting, *Along the River During the Qingming Festival*.

She understood that compared to the last era, the Bunker World was not at all an ideal society. The migration to the rim of the Solar System had caused some toxic social conditions, long eliminated by progress, to reemerge. This wasn't exactly regression, but a kind of spiraling ascent, a necessary condition for the exploration and settlement of new frontiers.

After they left Pacific I, Cao Bin brought Cheng Xin to see a few more space cities with unusual designs. One of them, fairly close to Pacific I, was a wheel with spokes, not unlike a larger version of the space elevator terminal station that Cheng Xin had visited more than sixty years ago.

Cheng Xin was a bit puzzled by the designs of the cities. As a matter of engineering, the wheel seemed ideal. It was far easier to

construct than the large, hollow shells used by the other cities, and when completed, a wheel was stronger and better able to survive disasters, as well as being easier to expand.

Cao Bin's succinct reply to Cheng Xin's query was "world-sense."

"What?"

"The sensation of being inside a world. A space city has to have ample interior volume and wide-open views so that the residents can feel they are living inside a world. Although the usable interior surface area isn't too different from a hollow-shell design, in a wheel design, people always know that they are living inside a narrow tube or a series of such tubes."

There were some other cities with even stranger designs. Most of these were industrial or agricultural centers with no permanent residents. For instance, there was a city called Resource I. Its length was 120 kilometers, but the diameter was only three kilometers, like a thin stick. It did not spin around the long axis, but rather, tumbled about its center, end over end. The city's interior was divided into levels, and the gravity at each level differed dramatically. Only a few levels were suitable for living, while the rest were devoted to various industries adapted to the different gravities. According to Cao Bin, near Saturn and Uranus, there were cities formed by combining two or more stick-shaped cities into crosses or stars.

The earliest city clusters of the Bunker Project were built near Jupiter and Saturn. Later, as cities were built near Uranus and Neptune, some new city-design concepts emerged. The most important idea was city docking. In those two clusters at the edge of the Solar System, every city was equipped with one or more standardized docks so that cities could be interconnected. Docking multiplied the space available for inhabitants and created even better world-sense, greatly encouraging economic development. In addition, after docking, the atmospheres and ecological systems of the various cities merged, and that helped to stabilize their operation and maintenance.

Currently, most cities docked along their axis of spin. This way, after docking, the cities could continue to spin as before without

changing the distribution of gravity. There were proposals for parallel or perpendicular docking as well, which would allow the combined cities to expand in multiple directions, as opposed to only along the axis of spin. But the spin of such combinations would dramatically change the interior distribution of gravity, and these proposals had not been tested so far.

The biggest combined city so far was located at Neptune, where four of the eight cities were docked together along their axis of spin, forming a two-hundred-kilometer-long combined city. When necessary—such as when a dark forest strike alert was issued—the combined city could be quickly taken apart to increase the mobility of each city. People hoped that, one day, all the cities in each cluster could be combined into one, so that humanity would live in four complete worlds.

In total, behind Jupiter, Saturn, Uranus, and Neptune, there were sixty-four large space cities and nearly a hundred medium and small cities, plus numerous space stations. Nine hundred million people lived in the Bunker World.

This was almost the entirety of the human race. Even before the arrival of the dark forest strike, Earth civilization had battened down the hatches.

Every space city was politically equivalent to a state. The four city clusters together formed the Solar System Federation, and the original UN had evolved into the Federation Government. Most of the Earth's major ancient civilizations had passed through a city-state stage—and now, city-states had reemerged at the rim of the Solar System.

The Earth was now barely inhabited. Only about five million people remained there. These were individuals who did not wish to leave their home and who had no fear of the prospect of Death at any moment. Many brave men and women living in the Bunker World also traveled to Earth as tourists, though each journey meant gambling with their lives. As time passed, the anticipated dark forest strike loomed larger, and people gradually adapted to life in the Bunker World. Their yearning for their homeland lessened as

they busied themselves in their new homes, and fewer and fewer now visited the Earth. The public no longer cared much about news from the home world, and were only vaguely aware that Nature was enjoying a resurgence. Forests and grasslands covered every continent, and those who stayed behind had to carry guns to defend against wild beasts when they went out, but it was rumored that they lived like kings, each with a vast estate and personal forests and lakes. The entire Earth was now only a single city in the Solar System Federation.

Cheng Xin and Cao Bin's small dinghy was now at the outer edge of the Jovian cities. Before the immense, dark Jupiter, these cities appeared so small, so alone, like a few shacks at the foot of a gigantic cliff. From a distance, faint candlelight spilled out of them. Though tiny, they were the only hints of warmth, of home, in this endless frigidity and desolation, the goal of all weary travelers. Cheng Xin's mind churned up a short poem she had read in middle school, a composition by a long-forgotten Chinese poet of the Republican era:

> The sun has set.
> Mountain, tree, rock, river—
> All the grand buildings are buried in shadows.
> People light their lamps with great interest,
> Delighting in all they can see,
> Hoping to find what they wish.[6]

6 *Translator's Note:* The poem is by Xu Yunuo (1894–1958), a modern Chinese poet most prominently associated with the May Fourth Movement.

BUNKER ERA, YEAR 11
LIGHTSPEED II

The final destination of Cheng Xin and Cao Bin was Halo City, a medium space city. Medium cities were space cities whose interior areas were below two hundred square kilometers but above fifty square kilometers. Typically, these cities were mixed within formations of large cities, but two of the medium cities, Halo City and Lightspeed II, were situated far from the Jovian city cluster, almost outside the protection of Jupiter's shadow.

Before arriving at Halo City, the dinghy passed by Lightspeed II. Cao Bin told Cheng Xin that Lightspeed II used to be a science city and was one of the two research centers studying how to lower the speed of light to achieve the black domain state, but it had been abandoned. Cheng Xin was very interested and wanted to stop for a visit. Reluctantly, Cao Bin turned the dinghy in that direction.

"Why don't we just take a look from the outside?" Cao Bin said. "It's best not to go in."

"Is it dangerous?"

"Yes."

"But we went inside Pacific I, which was also dangerous."

"It's not the same. There's no one inside Lightspeed II. It's a ... ghost city. At least, that's what everyone says."

As the dinghy approached, Cheng Xin realized that the city really was in ruins. It didn't spin, and the exterior appeared broken

and cracked. In some places, the skin of the city had been ripped open, revealing the structural frame underneath. As she surveyed the giant ruin illuminated by the searchlights of the dinghy, Cheng Xin felt awe as well as terror. She thought of the ruin as a beached whale. It had lain there for eons, until all that was left was cracked skin and bones, and life had long ago drained away. She seemed to be looking at something even older than the Acropolis of Athens, with even more secrets.

They slowly approached a large crack, several times as wide as the body of their dinghy. The beams in the structural frame were also bent and twisted, opening up a way to the interior. The beam of the searchlight shone in so that Cheng Xin could see the distant "ground," which was completely bare. After the dinghy descended a short distance into the interior of the space city, it stopped and swept the searchlight about them. Cheng Xin saw that the "ground" was bare in every direction. Not only were there no buildings, there wasn't anything at all to indicate that people had once lived here. The crisscrossing beams forming the frame for the city were visible on the "ground."

"Is it just an empty shell?" Cheng Xin asked.

"No."

Cao Bin looked at Cheng Xin for a few seconds, as if assessing her courage. Then he reached out and shut off the searchlights.

At first, all Cheng Xin could see was darkness. Starlight spilled in from the crack in front, as though she was gazing up at the sky through a broken roof. Eventually, her eyes adjusted to the dark, and she realized that the interior of the ruined space city wasn't entirely dark, but was illuminated with a faint, flickering blue light. Cheng Xin shivered. She forced herself to calm down and looked for the source. The blue glow came from the center of the interior of the space city.

The light source blinked without pattern, like a twitching eye. The empty ground was filled with strange shadows, like a desolate wasteland illuminated by flashes of lightning on the horizon at night.

"The light is caused by space dust falling into the black hole," Cao Bin said, pointing in the direction of the light source. He was trying to relieve some of Cheng Xin's terror.

"There's a black hole over there?"

"Yes. It's about … no more than five kilometers from here. A microscopic black hole with a Schwarzschild radius of twenty nanometers and a mass equivalent to Leda, the Jovian moon."

In this phosphorescent blue glow, Cao Bin told Cheng Xin the story of Lightspeed II and 高 Way.[7]

The research into lowering the speed of light through vacuum began at about the same time as the Bunker Project. As the Black Domain Plan was the second path for human survival, the international community devoted enormous resources to it, and the Bunker Project even built a large space city as a research center devoted to the subject—that would be Lightspeed I, located in the Saturn cluster. But sixty years of extensive research yielded no breakthroughs, and not even much advancement in theoretical foundation.

Lowering the speed of light through a medium wasn't particularly difficult. As early as 2008 C.E., researchers had succeeded in lowering the speed of light through a medium to an incredible seventeen meters per second in a laboratory setting. But this was fundamentally different from lowering the speed of light through vacuum. The former only required causing the atoms in the medium to absorb and re-emit the photons—light continued to travel at its usual speed between atoms. This wasn't useful for the Black Domain Plan.

The speed of light through vacuum was one of the fundamental constants of the universe. Altering it was equivalent to altering the laws of physics. Thus, lowering the speed of light required breakthroughs in fundamental physics—and considerable serendipity.

7 *Translator's Note:* Like "艾 AA," "高 Way" is a mixed Chinese-English name ("高" is the surname and pronounced "Gao").

After sixty years, the only substantive result of basic research was the creation of the circumsolar particle accelerator. This, in turn, led to the success of the largest project under the Black Domain Plan: the Black Hole Project.

Scientists had tried all kinds of extreme physical techniques in their efforts to alter the speed of light. Once, the strongest artificial magnetic field had been used. But the best way to influence light in vacuum was through a gravity field. Since it was extremely difficult to generate a local gravity field in a laboratory setting, the only path forward seemed to be a black hole. The circumsolar particle accelerator was capable of creating microscopic black holes.

The head of the Black Hole Project was 高 Way. Cao Bin had worked with him for a few years. He could not hide his complex feelings about the man as he described him to Cheng Xin.

"The man suffered from severe autism—no, I'm not talking about some kind of lonely genius choosing to isolate himself, but a real mental condition. He was extremely closed off and had trouble communicating with anyone, and he had never even touched a woman. His extraordinary professional success would only be possible in this age, but despite his accomplishments, most of his supervisors and colleagues thought of him as merely a high-powered intelligence battery. He was tortured by his illness and tried to change himself, and in this, he was different from other geniuses.

"Starting from, oh, I think the eighth year of the Broadcast Era, he dedicated himself to the theoretical study of lowering the speed of light. Over time, I think he began to develop a strange identification between the speed of light and his own personality—if he could change the speed of light, then it was the same as changing himself.

"But the speed of light through vacuum really was the most stable thing in the cosmos. Research into lowering the speed of light resembled torturing light without regard for consequences. People tried to do everything with light: strike it, twist it, break it, dissect it, stretch it, crush it, even destroy it—but the result was, at most, a change in its frequency in vacuum. But the speed of light remained unchanged, like an unscalable wall. After all these

decades, theoreticians and experimenters alike were in despair. There was a saying: If there really were a Creator, the only thing He welded shut in all Creation was the speed of light.

"For 高 Way, the despair had yet another layer. By the time I went into hibernation, he was almost fifty. He had still never been with a woman, and he thought of his own fate as being as resistant as the speed of light; he became even more withdrawn and solitary.

"The Black Hole Project began in Year 1 of the Bunker Era and lasted eleven years. The planners did not invest much hope in it. Both theoretical calculations and astronomical observations had indicated that even black holes could not change the speed of light. These demons of the universe could only use their gravity fields to change the path of light and its frequency, not affecting the speed of light through vacuum one iota. However, to continue the research for the Black Domain Plan, it was necessary to create experimental conditions with superpowerful gravity fields, which depended on black holes. In addition, since a black domain is in essence a large-scale reduced-lightspeed black hole, perhaps close-range observation of a microscopic regular-lightspeed black hole would yield unexpected insights.

"The circumsolar particle accelerator was capable of producing microscopic black holes rapidly, but these tiny black holes also evaporated very quickly. To produce a stable black hole, a microscopic black hole was guided out of the accelerator as soon as it was produced, and then injected into Leda.

"Leda was Jupiter's smallest moon, with a mean radius of only eight kilometers. It was nothing more than a large rock. Before making the black hole, they had lowered the moon from its high orbit and turned it into a body orbiting the Sun in parallel with Jupiter, like the city cluster. However, unlike the city cluster, it was located at the Sun-Jupiter L2 Lagrangian point, which is where we are now. This allowed it to maintain a stable distance from Jupiter without having to constantly adjust its position. At the time, this was the most massive body humans had managed to move through space until then.

"After the microscopic black hole was injected into Leda, it began to absorb mass and rapidly grow. At the same time, the intense radiation generated by material falling into the black hole melted the surrounding rock. Soon, the eight-kilometer-radius Leda melted entirely, and the potato-shaped rock turned into a red-glowing ball of lava. The lava ball shrank slowly, but glowed brighter and brighter, until it finally disappeared with a blinding flash. Observation showed that other than a small amount of material ejected by the radiation, most of the mass of Leda had been absorbed by the black hole. The black hole remained stable, and its Schwarzschild radius, or event horizon radius, had grown from the size of a fundamental particle to twenty-one nanometers.

"They constructed a space city around the black hole—that's Lightspeed II. The black hole was suspended in the middle of the space city, which was empty, didn't spin, and whose interior was a vacuum connected to space. It was, in essence, a giant container for the black hole. Personnel and equipment could be brought into the city to study the black hole.

"The research continued for many years. This was the first time that humans could study a black hole specimen in laboratory conditions, and many discoveries were made that helped with the development of theoretical physics and fundamental cosmology. But none of these results helped with the task of lowering the speed of light in vacuum.

"Six years after the commencement of studies on the black hole specimen, 高 Way died. According to the official account of the World Academy of Sciences, he was accidentally 'sucked into the black hole' during an experiment.

"Anyone with some basic scientific background knows that the probability that Gao was 'sucked' into the black hole was practically nonexistent. The reason that black holes are traps from which even light cannot escape isn't because their overall gravitational power is overwhelming—though a large black hole formed by the collapse of a star does possess immense overall gravity—but due to the density of their gravitational fields. From a distance, the total gravity of a

black hole is no different from the gravity of a quantity of normal matter of equivalent mass. If the Sun collapsed into a black hole, the Earth and the other planets would still continue on in their orbits without being sucked in. It's only when you got very close to the black hole that its gravity displayed strange behavior.

"Inside Lightspeed II, there was a protective net around the black hole with a radius of five thousand meters. Research personnel were forbidden to enter. Since the radius of Leda was originally only eight thousand meters, the black hole's gravity at this distance was not much greater than the gravity on the surface of the original Leda. It's not a very powerful pull—a person standing there was essentially weightless, and could easily escape using the thrusters on their space suit. Thus, Gao couldn't have been 'sucked' in.

"Ever since the stable black hole specimen was obtained, 高 Way was infatuated with it. After struggling against the speed of light for so many years and not being able to alter even a single one of the many digits in this constant that came close to three hundred thousand, Gao was agitated and filled with a sense of failure. As the constancy of the speed of light was one of the fundamental laws of nature, he had come to despise the laws of nature, as well as being afraid of them. But now, in front of his eyes, was something that had compressed Leda into twenty-one nanometers. Within its event horizon, in that space-time singularity, known laws of nature had no effect.

"高 Way often hung against the protective net and stared for hours at the black hole five kilometers away. He watched its luminescence—like we're doing now—and sometimes claimed that the black hole was talking to him, that he could decipher the message of its flickering light.

"No one saw the process of Gao's disappearance, and if there was a recording, it's never been released. He was one of the Black Hole Project's principal physicists, and he had the password to open the protective net. I'm certain that he went in and drifted toward the black hole until he was too close to return.... He probably wanted to get a close-up look at the object of his infatuation, or perhaps

he wanted to enter into that singularity where the laws of nature no longer mattered, so that he could escape all this.

"What happened after 高 Way was sucked in was almost too strange to describe. Scientists observed the black hole via remote-controlled microscopes, and discovered that at the black hole's event horizon—that's the surface of that tiny sphere with a diameter of twenty-one nanometers—there was the figure of a person. It was 高 Way passing through the event horizon.

"Under general relativity, a distant observer would see a clock near the event horizon slow down, and the process of 高 Way falling toward the event horizon would also slow down and stretch into infinity.

"But within 高 Way's own frame of reference, he had already passed through the event horizon.

"Even more oddly, the figure's proportions were normal. Perhaps it was because the black hole was so small, but tidal forces did not seem to be at work. He had been compressed into the nanometer range, but space there was also extremely curved. More than one physicist believed that the body structure of 高 Way wasn't harmed at the event horizon. In other words, he's probably still alive at this moment.

"And thus the life insurance company refused to pay out, although 高 Way had passed through the event horizon in his frame of reference, and should now be dead. But the insurance contract was made within the frame of reference of our world, and from this perspective, it is impossible to prove that 高 Way is dead. It's not even possible to begin the settlement process. Insurance claims settlement can only occur after the conclusion of an accident, but as 高 Way is still falling toward the black hole, the accident isn't over, and will never be over.

"A woman then sued the World Academy of Sciences and demanded that the academy cease all further research on this black hole specimen. By that point, distant observation was unlikely to yield any further results. In order to be useful, future research would have to manipulate the black hole in some way, such as

sending experimental objects into the black hole, which would generate massive amounts of radiation, and might disturb space-time in the vicinity of the event horizon. If 高 Way were still alive, these experiments might endanger his life. The woman didn't win her suit, but for a variety of reasons, research on this black hole stopped, and Lightspeed II was abandoned. Now we can only wait for this black hole to evaporate, which is estimated to take another half century.

"However, we now know that at least one woman did love 高 Way, though he never knew it. Later, that woman still came here regularly and tried to send radio or neutrino messages at the black hole. She even wrote her love in big letters and posted it against the protective net, hoping that the falling 高 Way could see it. But based on his own frame of reference, he had already passed through the event horizon into the singularity.... It's a complicated matter."

Cheng Xin stared at the blue phosphorescence far away in the darkness. She now knew that there was a man there, a man who was falling forever, at the event horizon where time stopped. Such a man was still alive when viewed from this world, but had already died in his own world.... So many strange fates, and so many unimaginable lives....

Cheng Xin now felt the flickering black hole was really sending out a message, even more like someone blinking. She pulled her gaze back, feeling as empty in her heart as this ruin in space. Softly, she said to Cao Bin, "Let's go to Halo City."

BUNKER ERA, YEAR 11
HALO CITY

As they approached Halo City, Cheng Xin and Cao Bin's dinghy encountered the Federation Fleet's blockade line. More than twenty stellar-class warships surrounded Halo City, and the blockade had lasted two weeks already.

The stellar-class ships were immense, but next to the space city they appeared as tiny skiffs around a giant ocean liner. The Federation Fleet had sent the bulk of their ships to enforce this blockade of Halo City.

After the two Trisolaran Fleets had disappeared in the depths of space and the Trisolarans lost all contact with humankind, the extraterrestrial threats facing humanity took on an entirely new form. Fleet International, which had been formed to combat the Trisolaran invasion, lost its reason for existence and gradually diminished in relevance until it was finally dissolved. The Solar System Fleet that had belonged to Fleet International became the property of the Solar System Federation. This was the first time in human history where a unified world government controlled the majority of humanity's armed forces. Since it was no longer necessary to maintain a large space force, the fleet's size was drastically reduced. After the commencement of the Bunker Project, most of the then-extant hundred-plus stellar-class warships were converted for civilian use. After they were disarmed and their

ecological cycling systems removed, they became interplanetary industrial transports for the Bunker Project. Only about thirty stellar-class warships remained in service. Over the last sixty-plus years, no new warships had been built because large warships were extremely expensive. It took the same amount of investment to build two or three stellar-class warships as it did to build a large space city. Moreover, there was no need for new warships. Most of the Federation Fleet's efforts were devoted to building the advance warning system.

The dinghy stopped advancing as it received the blockade order. A military patrol boat sailed toward it. It was very small, and from a distance Cheng Xin could only see the glow from its thrusters—its hull could be seen only once it got closer. When the patrol boat docked with the dinghy, Cheng Xin had a chance to look at the uniformed men inside it. Their military uniforms were very different from those of the last era and seemed to hearken to the styling of an earlier age. The uniforms had fewer space-based characteristics and looked more like the uniforms of old Earth-based armies.

The man who drifted over after the two vessels docked was middle-aged and dressed in a suit. Even in weightlessness, he moved gracefully and calmly, not appearing ill at ease at all in the cramped space that was meant only for two.

"Good day. I'm Blair, special envoy of the Federation president. I'm about to try, for the last time, to negotiate with Halo City's city government. I could have talked to you from my ship, but out of respect for Common Era customs, I decided to come here in person."

Cheng Xin noticed that even the politicians of this age had changed. The assertive and outspoken mannerisms of the last era had been replaced by prudence, restraint, and politeness.

"The Federation Government has announced a total blockade of Halo City, and no one is permitted to enter or leave. However, we know that the passenger here is Dr. Cheng Xin." The envoy nodded at her. "We give you permission to pass and will assist your entrance into Halo City. We hope that you will use your influence

to persuade the city government to cease their deranged, illegal resistance, and prevent the situation from deteriorating further. I am expressing the wishes of the Federation president."

The special envoy waved his hand and opened up an information window. The Federation president appeared in the window. In the office behind him were the flags of the various cities of the Bunker World, none of which were familiar to Cheng Xin. Nation states had disappeared along with their flags. The president was an ordinary-looking man of Asian descent. His face looked tired, and after nodding a greeting at Cheng Xin, he said, "Envoy Blair is right. This is the will of the Federation Government. Mr. Wade said that the final decision rests with you, an assertion that we do not fully believe. But we wish you the best of success. I'm glad to see you still looking so young. Although, for this matter, perhaps you're too young."

After the president disappeared from the window, Blair said to Cheng Xin, "I know that you already have some understanding of the situation, but I'd still like to give you an overall explanation. I'll strive to be objective and fair."

Cheng Xin noticed that both the envoy and the president spoke only to her, ignoring Cao Bin's presence, indicating by this omission the deep enmity they felt toward him. As a matter of fact, Cao Bin had already explained the situation to her in detail, and the envoy's account wasn't too different.

After Thomas Wade took over the Halo Group, the company became a key contractor in the Bunker Project. Within eight years, it had grown tenfold and become one of the largest economic entities in the world. Wade himself was not an extraordinary entrepreneur; indeed, he was not even as skilled as 艾 AA at managing the company's operations. The company's growth was the result of the new management team he put in place. He personally did not participate in the running of the company and had little interest in it, but much of the profit generated by the company was taken by him and reinvested in the development of lightspeed spaceflight.

As soon as the Bunker Project began, the Halo Group constructed Halo City as a research center. The Sun-Jupiter L2 Lagrangian point was chosen as the ideal space to set up Halo City in order to eliminate the need for city thrusters and the consumption of resources for position maintenance. Halo City was the only space science city outside the jurisdiction of the Federation Government. While Halo City was being constructed, Wade also began the construction of the circumsolar particle accelerator, a project that was dubbed "The Great Wall of the Solar System" because it enclosed the Sun in a ring.

For half a century, the Halo Group devoted itself to basic research for lightspeed spaceflight. Ever since the Deterrence Era, large companies had often engaged in basic research. In the new economic system, basic research could generate enormous profits. Thus, the behavior of the Halo Group wasn't too unusual. The Halo Group's ultimate goal of constructing lightspeed spaceships was an open secret, but as long as it stuck to basic research, the Federation Government could not accuse it of violating the law. However, the government continued to be suspicious of the Halo Group, and investigated it multiple times. For half a century, the relationship between the company and the government was basically cordial. Since lightspeed ships and the Black Domain Plan called for much of the same basic research, the Halo Group and the World Academy of Sciences maintained a good collaborative working relationship. For instance, the Academy's Black Hole Project used the Halo Group's circumsolar particle accelerator to produce its black hole specimen.

However, six years ago, the Halo Group had suddenly announced its plan to develop curvature propulsion ships. Such open defiance caused an uproar in the international community. Thereafter, conflict between the Halo Group and the Federation Government never ceased. After multiple rounds of negotiations, the Halo Group promised that when the curvature propulsion drive was ready for trials, the testing site would be at least five hundred AU from the Sun so as to avoid exposing the location of Earth

civilization with the trails. But the Federation Government felt that the very development of lightspeed ships was a gross violation of the laws and constitution of the Federation. The danger of lightspeed ships lay not only in the trails, but also in upsetting the new social stability in the Bunker World, a prospect that could not be tolerated. A resolution was passed to authorize the government takeover of Halo City and the circumsolar particle accelerator, and to put a complete stop to the Halo Group's theoretical research and technical development in curvature propulsion. Thereafter, the Halo Group's behavior would be subjected to close monitoring.

In response, the Halo Group declared independence from the Solar System Federation. Thus, the conflict between the Halo Group and the Federation escalated yet further.

The international community did not take the Halo Group's declaration of independence too seriously. As a matter of fact, after the commencement of the Bunker Era, conflicts between individual space cities and the Federation Government were not infrequent. For instance, two space cities in the distant city clusters near Uranus and Neptune, Africa II and Indian Ocean I, had declared independence in the past, but nothing had ultimately come of those efforts. Although the Federation Fleet was nowhere near the size it had been in the past, it was still an overwhelming force if applied against individual space cities. By law, space cities were not allowed to possess their own independent armed forces—they could only have limited national guards who had no capacity for space warfare at all. The economy of the Bunker World was also highly integrated such that no individual space city could survive a blockade longer than two months.

"On this point, I can't understand Wade either," said Cao Bin. "He's a man with foresight, and mindful of the big picture, and he never takes a step without having thought through the consequences. So why declare independence? It seems idiotic to provide the Federation Government with an excuse to take over Halo City by force."

The envoy had already left, and the dinghy, now occupied only by Cheng Xin and Cao Bin, continued on course to Halo City. A ring-shaped structure appeared in space ahead, and Cao Bin ordered the dinghy to approach it and decelerate. The smooth metallic surface of the ring reflected the stars as long streaks and distorted the image of the dinghy, bringing to mind the Ring that *Blue Space* and *Gravity* had encountered in four-dimensional space. The dinghy stopped and hovered next to the ring. Cheng Xin estimated that the ring's diameter was about two hundred meters across, and the band about fifty meters thick.

"You're looking at the circumsolar particle accelerator," Cao Bin said, his tone awed.

"It's ... rather small."

"Oh, sorry; I wasn't clear. This is but one of the coils in the particle accelerator. There are thirty-two hundred coils like this, each about one point five million kilometers apart, forming a large circle around the Sun in the vicinity of Jupiter's orbit. Particles pass through the center of these coils, where they're accelerated by the force field generated by the coil toward the next coil, where they're accelerated again.... A particle might travel around the Sun multiple times during the process."

When Cao Bin had spoken to Cheng Xin about the circumsolar particle accelerator in the past, she had always pictured it as a giant doughnut hanging in space. But in reality, to build a solid "Great Wall" around the Sun, even within the orbit of Mercury, would have been an impossible feat approaching the level of God's Engineering Project. Cheng Xin finally realized that while an enclosed tubular ring was necessary for terrestrial particle accelerators to maintain vacuum, it was not necessary in the vacuum of space. The particles being accelerated could simply fly through space, being accelerated by one coil after another. Cheng Xin couldn't help turning to look past the coil for the next one.

"The next coil is one point five million kilometers away, four or five times the distance from the Earth to the moon. You can't see it," Cao Bin said. "This is a supercollider capable of accelerating a

particle to the energy level of the big bang. Ships are not allowed anywhere near the orbit of the accelerator. A few years ago, a lost freighter drifted into the orbit by mistake and was hit by a beam of accelerated particles. The ultrahigh-energy particles struck the ship and produced high-energy secondary showers that vaporized the ship and its cargo of millions of tons of mineral ore in an instant."

Cao Bin also told Cheng Xin that the circumsolar particle accelerator's chief designer was Bi Yunfeng. Of the past sixty-plus years, he had spent thirty-five of them working on this project and hibernated for the rest. He had been awakened last year, but was much older than Cao Bin now.

"The old man's lucky, though. He had worked on a terrestrial accelerator back during the Common Era, and now, three centuries later, he got to build a circumsolar particle accelerator. I'd call that a successful career, wouldn't you? But he's a bit of an extremist, and a fanatic supporter of Halo City independence."

While the public and the politicians opposed lightspeed ships, many scientists supported the effort. Halo City became a holy site for scientists who yearned for lightspeed spaceflight and attracted many excellent researchers. Even scientists working within the Federation scientific establishment often collaborated with Halo City—openly or in secret. This caused Halo City to be on the cutting edge in many areas of basic research.

The dinghy left the coil and continued its voyage. Halo City was straight ahead. This space city was built along the rarely seen wheel plan. The structure provided strength but had little interior volume, lacking "world-sense." It was said that the inhabitants of Halo City did not need world-sense, because for them, the world was the entire universe.

The dinghy entered the axis of the giant wheel, where Cheng Xin and Cao Bin had to enter the city through an eight-kilometer spoke. This was one of the least convenient aspects of a wheel plan. Cheng Xin was reminded of her experience more than sixty years ago at the terminal station of the space elevator, and she thought about

the great hall that reminded her of an old train station. But the feeling here was different. Halo City was more than ten times larger than that terminal station, and the interior was rather spacious and didn't look run-down.

On the escalator of the spoke, gravity gradually set in. By the time it reached 1G, they were in the city proper. The science city was made up of three parts: the Halo Academy of Sciences, the Halo Academy of Engineering, and the Control Center for the circumsolar particle accelerator. The city was in fact a ring-shaped tunnel thirty-some kilometers in length. Although it wasn't nearly as open or spacious as the large, hollow shells of other cities, one didn't feel claustrophobic, either.

Cheng Xin didn't see any motor vehicles in the city at first. Most residents got around on bicycles, many of which were parked on the side of the road for anyone to use. But a small convertible motor vehicle came to pick up Cheng Xin and Cao Bin.

Since the simulated gravity in the ring pulled toward the outer rim, the city was built along that surface. A holographic image of blue sky with white clouds was projected onto the inner rim, which made up some for the lack of world-sense. A flock of twittering birds flitted overhead, and Cheng Xin noticed that they were not holograms, but real. Here, Cheng Xin felt a sense of comfort that she had not experienced in the other space cities. There were plenty of trees and lawns everywhere. None of the buildings was very tall. Those belonging to the Academy of Sciences were painted white, while those belonging to the Academy of Engineering were painted blue, but each building was unique. The delicate buildings were half-hidden by the green plants, and made her feel as though she were on a college campus.

Cheng Xin saw an interesting sight on her drive. There was a ruin like an ancient Greek temple. On a stone platform stood a few broken Greek columns covered with climbing ivy. In the middle of the columns was a fountain shooting a column of limpid water merrily into the sunlight. A few casually dressed men and women were leaning against the columns or lying on the lawn next to the

fountain, lazing about comfortably. They seemed not to care that the city was under siege by the Federation Fleet.

A few statues were scattered on the lawn next to the ruin. Cheng Xin's attention was drawn to one of the statues: A gauntleted hand was picking wreaths woven with stars out of a pool with a sword, and flowing water dripped from the wreaths continuously. This sight triggered something deep in Cheng Xin's memory, but she couldn't recall where exactly she had seen it before. She gazed at the statue from the motorcar until it disappeared.

The car stopped in front of a blue building. It was a laboratory marked with a sign: "Academy of Engineering, Basic Technology 021." Cheng Xin saw Wade and Bi Yunfeng on the lawn in front of the laboratory.

Wade had never entered hibernation since taking over the Halo Group, and was now 110 years old. He kept his hair and beard short, but both were now white as snow. He didn't use a cane, and his stride was steady, but his back was a bit bent, and one of his sleeves still hung empty. In the moment they locked gazes, Cheng Xin understood that time had not defeated this man. What was at his core had not been worn away by the passing years, but had only become more prominent—like a rock revealed after the snow and ice had melted away.

Bi Yunfeng should be much younger than Wade, but he looked older. He was very excited to see Cheng Xin and seemed eager to show her something.

"Hello, little girl," Wade said. "I'm now three times your age." His smile still couldn't make Cheng Xin warm, but it no longer felt as cold as ice water.

Cheng Xin faced these two old men with mixed feelings. They had struggled for their ideals for more than sixty years and were now near the end of their lives' journeys. She, on the other hand, had gone through so many trials after awakening for the first time during the Deterrence Era—but in reality, she had spent no more than four years out of hibernation. She was now 33, still a young woman in this era where average life expectancy was 150.

Cheng Xin greeted the two, and then no one wasted time by saying more. Wade led Cheng Xin into the laboratory with Bi Yunfeng and Cao Bin following. They entered a spacious, windowless hall. The familiar acrid odor of static told Cheng Xin they were in a sophon-free room. After more than sixty years, people still could not be sure that the sophons had left the Solar System, and maybe they'd never be sure. The hall must have been filled with instruments and equipment not long ago, but now all the lab equipment was scattered in a chaotic pile next to the walls, as though it had been moved away in a hurry to clear out the center. In the middle of the hall was a single machine. The surrounding chaos and the emptiness in the center displayed an irrepressible excitement, as though a team of treasure hunters had suddenly found a priceless artifact, tossed their tools to the side, and carefully moved their prize to the center of the open space.

The machine's complex structure reminded Cheng Xin of a tokamak from the Common Era, but miniaturized. The bulk of the machine consisted of a sphere bisected horizontally by a flat black metallic plane that extended several meters over the edge of the sphere. The plane, holding up the sphere at about waist-height, also served as a lab bench with sturdy legs. The surface of the bench was mostly empty save for a few tools and manipulators attached to telescoping arms.

The metal hemisphere below the bench was studded with tubes of various thicknesses, all aimed at the invisible center of the sphere, causing the machine to look like a naval mine studded with Hertz horns. Apparently, the arrangement was designed to concentrate some kind of energy at the center.

The hemisphere above the bench, in contrast, was made of transparent glass. The two hemispheres together formed a whole divided by the metal plane, contrasting simple transparency with complex opacity.

Looking down through the glass dome, Cheng Xin could see a small rectangular metallic platform whose sides measured only a few centimeters, about the size of a pack of cigarettes, and whose surface

was smooth and reflective like a mirror. The platform under the glass dome was like a tiny, delicate stage; and the complicated mechanism below the plane the orchestra that would accompany the performance, though it was unimaginable what that performance would be.

"Let's allow a physical part of you to experience this grand moment," Wade said. Bi Yunfeng lifted the glass dome as Wade walked over to Cheng Xin and held up a pair of scissors. Cheng Xin tensed, but did not shy away. Carefully, assisted by a tool on the platform, Wade lifted a strand of her hair and cut off a small section at the end. He held the hair clipping with the tool, examined it, and concluded it was still too long. He cut the clipping in half so that the remaining piece was only about two or three millimeters long, almost invisible. Wade walked over to the side of the opened glass dome and carefully placed the hair on the smooth metal platform. Although Wade was over a hundred years of age and had only one hand, his movements were precise and steady, showing no tremors.

"Come, watch carefully," Wade said.

Cheng Xin leaned down to look through the glass dome. She could see her hair resting against the smooth stage. There was a red line down the middle of the stage, and the hair was on one side of it.

Wade nodded at Bi Yunfeng, who opened a control window in the air and activated the machine. Cheng Xin looked down and saw that a few tubes connected to the machine began to glow red, reminding her of the glimpse she had caught of the inside of the Trisolaran spaceship. She heard a rumbling but didn't feel any heat. She returned her gaze to the small platform and felt some invisible disturbance spread out from the platform, brushing across her face like a light breeze. She couldn't be sure it wasn't just an illusion.

She saw that her hair had moved to the other side of the red line, but she hadn't seen it move.

After another series of rumblings, the machine stopped.

"What did you see?" Wade asked.

"You spent half a century to move a three-millimeter section of hair two centimeters," said Cheng Xin.

"It was curvature propulsion," Wade said.

"If we used the same technique to continue to accelerate the hair, it would be moving at lightspeed in about ten meters," Bi Yunfeng said. "Of course we can't achieve this now, and we dare not try it here. If we did, this bit of hair, moving at lightspeed, would destroy Halo City."

Cheng Xin pondered the strand of hair that had been moved two centimeters by curving space. "You are saying that you've invented gunpowder and managed to make a firecracker, but the ultimate goal is to make a space rocket. A thousand years may separate those two achievements."

"Your analogy is flawed," Bi Yunfeng said. "We have invented the equation relating energy to mass, and we've discovered the principle of radioactivity. The ultimate goal is to make the atom bomb. Only a few decades divide those two achievements."

"In fifty years, we should be able to construct curvature propulsion spaceships capable of lightspeed flight. This will require massive amounts of technical testing and development work. We have to lay our cards on the table now so that the government can back off and give us the environment necessary to carry out these tasks."

"But your current approach will make you lose everything."

"Everything depends on your decision," Wade said. "You must think that we're helpless against the power of that fleet out there. Not so." He gestured at the door. "Come in."

A group of forty or fifty armed men filed in and soon filled the hall. They were all young men dressed in black space camouflage, and their presence seemed to make the hall dimmer. They wore military-issue lightweight space suits that seemed no different from ordinary military uniforms, but they could enter space as soon as they put on helmets and life-support backpacks. Cheng Xin was astonished, however, to see the weapons they carried: rifles, from the Common Era. Perhaps they were newly made, but the design was ancient and entirely mechanical, with manual bolts and triggers. The ammunition they carried confirmed this: Everyone wore two crossed bandoliers filled with glistening yellow cartridges.

To see these men in this age was akin to seeing a group of men armed with bows and swords during the Common Era. This was not to say that the fighters did not appear visually intimidating. Cheng Xin felt the presence of the past not only because of their ancient weapons, but also their appearance. They displayed a trained esprit de corps: they were uniform not only in dress and equipment, but also in their spirit. The men appeared tough and strong, with muscles bulging beneath their thin space suits. The gazes and expressions on their bold, angular faces were very similar: an indifferent, metallic grimness that viewed life as cheap as grass.

"This is our city self-defense force." Wade waved at the assembled men. "They are all we have to protect Halo City and the ideal of the lightspeed ship. You can see almost all of them here—there are a few more outside, but the total is no more than a hundred. As for their equipment—" Wade took a rifle from one of the soldiers and pulled the bolt. "You can trust your eyes: ancient weapons constructed of modern materials. The bullets do not rely on gunpowder as the propellant and have much better range and precision compared to genuine ancient weapons. In space, these rifles can hit a ship from two thousand kilometers away, but fundamentally, they're primitive weapons. You must think this ridiculous, and I would, too, except for one thing." He returned the rifle to the soldier and pulled one of the cartridges from his bandolier. "As I said, the cartridges are basically of ancient design, but the bullets are new. So new, in fact, that they might as well come from the future. The bullet is a superconducting container and the interior is a pure vacuum. A magnetic field suspends a small ball in the middle to prevent it from contacting the bullet's body. The ball is made of antimatter."

Bi Yunfeng's voice was filled with pride. "The circumsolar particle accelerator was not only used for basic research experiments, but also to produce antimatter. In the last four years, we've used it to make antimatter practically the entire time. We now possess fifteen thousand bullets of this design."

The primitive-seeming cartridge held in Wade's hand now caused Cheng Xin to suffer chills. She now worried about the reliability of the containment magnetic field within that superconducting bullet: a single malfunction would be enough to cause the complete destruction of Halo City in a brilliant flash. She looked at the golden bandoliers hanging over the chests of every soldier: These were the chains of the god of Death. A single bandolier possessed enough power to destroy the entire Bunker World.

Wade continued, "We don't even have to go into space to attack. We just have to wait until the fleet approaches the city. We can shoot dozens or even hundreds of bullets at each of the twenty or so ships—a single hit is enough to destroy it. Although the tactic is primitive, it's effective and flexible. A single soldier with a gun is a fighting unit capable of threatening an entire warship. Also, we have agents in other space cities with handguns." He returned the cartridge to the soldier's bandolier. "We don't want war. During the final negotiations, we'll show our weapons to the Federation envoy and explain our tactics. We hope the Federation Government will weigh the costs of war and abandon their threat against Halo City. We're not asking for much, only to build a research center several hundred AU from the Sun devoted to curvature propulsion testing."

"But if we go to war, can you guarantee victory?" Cao Bin asked. He had not spoken so far. Unlike Bi Yunfeng, he apparently was not in favor of war.

"No," Wade answered calmly. "But neither can they. We can only try."

As soon as Cheng Xin saw the antimatter bullet in Wade's hand, she knew what she must do. She wasn't too worried about the Federation Fleet—she believed that they'd come up with ways to deal with this tactic. Her mind was focused on only one thing:

Also, we have agents in other space cities with handguns.

If war were to erupt, any of the guerrilla fighters hidden in the other space cities could casually shoot one of the antimatter bullets at the ground and the explosion of matter-antimatter annihilation would instantaneously tear apart the thin shell of the city and

incinerate everything within. Next, the spinning space city would break into fragments and millions would die.

Space cities were as fragile as eggs.

Wade had not explicitly said that he would attack the space cities, but he also hadn't said he wouldn't. She again saw Wade aiming a gun at her 133 years ago—an image which had been branded into her heart. She didn't know how cold a man would have to be to make such a decision, but the core of this man was the utter madness and coldness brought about by extreme rationality. She seemed to see again the young Wade from three centuries ago, screaming like a crazy beast: "Advance, advance without regard for consequences!"

Even if Wade did not want to attack the space cities, what if others on his force did?

As if confirming Cheng Xin's fear, a soldier spoke to her. "Dr. Cheng, please be assured that we will fight to the end."

Another soldier spoke up. "We are not fighting for you, for Mr. Wade, or this city." He pointed upwards, and fire seemed to light up his eyes. "Do you know what they're trying to take away from here? Not the city or lightspeed ships, but the entire universe outside the Solar System! There are billions and billions of new worlds out there, but they won't let us go; they want to lock us and our descendants in this prison, a prison fifty astronomical units in radius called the Solar System. We are fighting for freedom, for a chance to live as free men in the universe. Our cause is the same as every ancient struggle for freedom. We will fight to the very last. I speak for everyone in the self-defense force."

The other soldiers nodded at Cheng Xin, their eyes grim and cold.

In the years to come, Cheng Xin would recall the soldier's words countless times. But at this moment, they did not move her. She felt the world going dark, and she was mired in terror. She felt as though she was again standing in front of the UN headquarters, holding that baby from more than 130 years ago. She felt the baby in her arms was facing a flock of hungry wolves, and she had to protect the child at all costs.

"Will you keep your promise?" she asked Wade.

Wade nodded. "Of course. Why else would I ask you to come here?"

"Then stop all preparation for war and cease all resistance. Turn over all antimatter bullets to the Federation Government. Order those agents you've sent to the other cities to do the same immediately!"

The soldiers gazed at Cheng Xin, as if trying to burn her to a crisp with their eyes. The power differential between the two sides was overwhelming. She was faced with a cold machine of war. Every man carried more than a hundred hydrogen bombs, and, led by a strong, mad leader, they formed a powerful black wheel capable of crushing all resistance. She was nothing more than a blade of grass in front of this giant wheel, not able to even slow down its progress. But she had to do what she could.

However, things did not develop as she expected. The gazes of the soldiers moved away from her one by one, turning to Wade. The suffocating pressure seemed to let up gradually, but she still had trouble breathing. Wade continued to look at the curvature propulsion platform under the glass dome holding up Cheng Xin's hair as though gazing at a sacred altar. Cheng Xin could imagine that Wade had once gathered his warriors around this altar to prophesy war.

"Why don't you think about it some more?" Wade said.

"There's no need." Cheng Xin's voice was like iron. "I have made my final decision. Cease all resistance, and turn over all antimatter in Halo City."

Wade lifted his head and looked at Cheng Xin with rarely seen helplessness and pleading. He spoke slowly. "If we lose our human nature, we lose much, but if we lose our bestial nature, we lose everything."

"I choose human nature," Cheng Xin said, looking around at everyone. "I believe you all will, as well."

Bi Yunfeng was about to speak, but Wade stopped him. His eyes dimmed. Something had gone out in them, extinguished forever.

The weight of years abruptly crushed him, and he appeared exhausted. He supported himself on the metal platform with his one hand and slowly sat down on a chair someone else brought over. Then he lifted his hand and pointed to the platform in front of him, keeping his eyes down. "Disarm. Leave all your ammunition here."

No one moved at first. But Cheng Xin felt something soften. That dark force was dissipating. The soldiers looked away from Wade and no longer focused on a single point. Finally, someone walked over and placed two bandoliers on the platform. Though his movements were gentle, the metallic sound made by the cartridges scraping against the platform caused Cheng Xin to shudder. The bandoliers lay still on the platform like two gold-colored snakes. A second man walked over and deposited his bandoliers, then more. The platform was soon covered by a golden pile. After all the cartridges had been collected, the metallic noises stopped, and everything became quiet again.

"Order all of our agents in the Bunker World to disarm and surrender to the Federation Government," Wade said. "The Halo City government will collaborate with the fleet to turn over the city. Do not take any drastic action."

"All right," someone answered. Deprived of their bandoliers, these men dressed in black space suits made the place even dimmer.

Wade gestured for the self-defense force to leave. They departed noiselessly, and the hall brightened as though a dark cloud had dissipated. Wade struggled to stand, walked around the pile of antimatter cartridges, and slowly opened the glass dome. He blew at the curvature propulsion platform and Cheng Xin's hair disappeared. He closed the dome, turned to Cheng Xin, and smiled. "You see, I've kept my promise, little girl."

After the Halo City Incident, the Federation Government did not immediately disclose the existence of antimatter weapons. The international community thought the event concluded as they had expected, and there wasn't much reaction. As the creator of the

circumsolar particle accelerator, the Halo Group enjoyed great prestige internationally, and public opinion was mostly forgiving of them, suggesting that there was no reason to pursue anyone legally, and Halo City should be allowed to self-govern again as soon as possible. As long as the Halo Group promised to never again engage in any research and development of curvature propulsion and submitted to Federation monitoring, it should be allowed to go on with its business.

But one week later, Federation Fleet Command revealed to the world the captured antimatter bullets. The pile of golden Death stunned everyone.

The Halo Group was declared an illegal organization, and the Federation Government confiscated all its property and took over the circumsolar particle accelerator. The Federation Fleet declared a long-term occupation of Halo City, and the Academies of Science and Engineering were dissolved. More than three hundred people, including Wade, the other leaders of the Halo Group, and the city self-defense force, were arrested.

In the subsequent trial in Federation court, Thomas Wade was convicted of crimes against humanity, war crimes, and violations of the laws prohibiting research into curvature propulsion. The sentence was death.

Cheng Xin went to a detention center located near the Supreme Federation Court in Earth I, the Solar System Federation's capital, to see Wade one last time. They looked at each other through a transparent barrier and said nothing. Cheng Xin saw that this old man, 110 years old, was as placid as the puddle at the bottom of a well that was about to dry out. There would be no more ripples.

Cheng Xin passed the box of cigars she had bought in Pacific I through an opening in the barrier. Wade opened the box, took out three of the ten cigars, and pushed the box back through the opening.

"I won't be able to use the rest," he said.

"Tell me more about yourself. Your work, your life. I want to tell those who would come later about you," Cheng Xin said.

Wade shook his head. "I am but one of the countless who have died and will die. What is there to tell?"

Cheng Xin knew that what divided them wasn't just this transparent barrier, but also the deepest chasm in this world, a chasm that could never be bridged.

"Do you have anything to say to me?" Cheng Xin asked. She was surprised that she wanted to hear his answer.

"Thank you for the cigars."

It took a long while before Cheng Xin understood that this was what Wade wanted to say to her. His last words. All his words.

They sat in silence, neither looking at the other. Time turned into a stagnant pool that drowned them. Then, the tremors of the space city adjusting its position returned Cheng Xin to reality. She stood up slowly and softly said good-bye.

Once she was outside the detention center, Cheng Xin picked out one of the cigars and borrowed a light from one of the guards. She took her first puff of a cigar in her life. Oddly, she didn't cough. She watched the white smoke rise in the sunlight of the capital, watched it dissipate in her tear-filled vision like the three centuries she and Wade had lived through.

Three days later, a powerful laser vaporized Thomas Wade in one-ten-thousandth of a second.

Cheng Xin returned to Asia I's hibernation center and awakened 艾 AA. They returned to the Earth.

They rode *Halo* back. After the Halo Group had been dissolved and its property confiscated, the Federation Government returned a small portion of the company's vast wealth to Cheng Xin. The amount was about equal to the value of the Halo Group at the time Wade took over. It was still a large sum, though minuscule when compared to the total wealth of the vanished company. *Halo* was part of the property returned to Cheng Xin—though this was the

third ship to bear that name. It was a small stellar yacht capable of seating up to three. The shipboard ecological cycling system was comfortable and refined, like a lovely small garden.

Cheng Xin and AA wandered over the barely inhabited continents of the Earth. They swept over endless forests, rode on trotting horses across grasslands, lingered over empty beaches. Most cities had become covered by forests and vines, leaving only small patches of civilization for the remaining residents. The total human population on the Earth was about what it was near the end of the Neolithic Age.

The longer they stayed on the Earth, the more all of civilization's history seemed a dream.

They returned to Australia. Only Canberra remained inhabited, and a tiny town government there called itself the Australian Federal Government. The Parliament House where Sophon had proclaimed the plan for the extermination of the human race was still there, but thick layers of vegetation sealed its doors, and vines climbed up the eighty-meter-tall flagpole. They found Fraisse's record in the government archives. He had lived until he was 150, but finally, time had defeated him. He had died more than ten years ago.

They went to Mosken Island. The lighthouse built by Jason was still there, but it was no longer lit. The region was completely uninhabited. They heard again the rumbling of the Mosktraumen, but all they could see was the empty sea in the light of the setting Sun.

Their future was equally empty.

AA said, "Why don't we go to the world after the strike, the world after the Sun is gone? Only then will we find a life of serenity."

Cheng Xin also wanted to go to that time, but not for a life of serenity. She had stopped a catastrophic war and she was becoming the target of the worship of millions. She could no longer live in this era. She wanted to see Earth civilization survive the dark forest strike and prosper after—it was the only hope that could comfort her heart. She imagined life in that post-strike nebula. There, she would find true tranquility, maybe even happiness. That would be the last harbor of her life's voyage.

She was only thirty-three.

Cheng Xin and AA rode *Halo* back to the Jovian city cluster and once again entered hibernation in Asia I. The contracted-for time was two hundred years, but they included a provision in the contract stating they should be awakened if a dark forest strike occurred before then.

And then they slept. Dreamless.

PART V

BUNKER ERA, YEAR 67
ORION ARM OF THE MILKY WAY

Examining the data was Singer's job; judging the sincerity of the coordinates was Singer's joy.

Singer understood that what he did wasn't important—it just filled in the pieces. But it had to be done, and the task was enjoyable.

Speaking of enjoyment, when this seed had departed from the home world, that world was still a place full of joy. But later, as the home world began to war against the fringe world, joy diminished. By now, more than ten thousand grains of time had passed. There wasn't much joy to speak of on the home world or in this seed. The happiness of the past was recorded in classical songs, and singing those songs was another of the few joys left.

Singer sang one of these classical songs as he reviewed the data.

> I see my love;
> I fly next to her;
> I present her with my gift,
> A small piece of solidified time.
> Lovely markings are carved into time
> As soft to the touch as the mud in shallow sea.

Singer did not complain much. Survival required so much thought and mental energy.

Entropy increased in the universe, and order decreased. The process was like the boundless wings of the giant balance bird pressing down upon all of existence. But low-entropy entities were different. The low-entropy entities decreased their entropy and increased their order, like columns of phosphorescence rising over the inky-dark sea. This was meaning, the highest meaning, higher than enjoyment. To maintain this meaning, low-entropy entities had to continue to exist.

As for any meaning higher than that, it was pointless to think about. Thinking about the subject led nowhere and was dangerous. It was even more pointless to think about the apex of the tower of meaning—maybe there wasn't an apex at all.

Back to the coordinates. Many sets of coordinates flitted across space, like the matrix insects flitting across the sky of the home world. Picking up coordinates was the job of the main core, which swallowed all the messages passing through space: medium membrane, long membrane, light membrane, and maybe one day even short membrane. The main core remembered the positions of all the stars. By matching the received data against various map projections and position schema, it could pick out the coordinates of the messages' origin. It was said that the main core could match position schema from five hundred million time grains ago. Singer never tried anything like that—it would be meaningless. In that distant age, the low-entropy clusters in space were rare and far apart, and had not evolved the hiding gene and the cleansing gene. But now—

Hide yourself well; cleanse well.

Out of all the coordinates, only some were sincere. Believing in insincere coordinates meant cleansing empty worlds. This was wasteful. And there were other harms besides. These empty worlds might be useful in the future. It was incomprehensible why anyone would send out insincere coordinates—they would get what they deserved someday.

Sincere coordinates followed certain patterns. For instance, a mass cluster of coordinates was usually insincere. But these patterns

556

were all only heuristics. Judging the sincerity of coordinates effectively required intuition. The main core on this seed was incapable of this task, and even the supercore back on the home world could not do it. This was one reason why low-entropy entities had no substitute.

Singer had this skill, this intuition, but it wasn't a gift or instinct; rather, it was something honed by the accumulated experience of tens of thousands of time grains. A set of coordinates seemed nothing more than a simple matrix in the eyes of the uninitiated, but to Singer, it was alive. Its every detail was expressive. For instance, how many reference points were taken? What was the method for marking the target star? And many other subtle details besides. The main core was able to provide some information, such as the historical records associated with this set of coordinates, the direction of the coordinate broadcast source, the broadcast time, and so forth. Together, these formed an organic whole, and what emerged in Singer's consciousness was a sense of the coordinate broadcaster himself. Singer's spirit crossed the chasm of space and time, resonated with the spirit of the broadcaster, and felt its terror and anxiety, along with other feelings unfamiliar to the home world, such as hatred, envy, greed, and so on. But for the most part, it was terror. Terror was what endowed a set of coordinates with sincerity. For all low-entropy entities, terror guaranteed existence.

Just then, Singer noticed a sincere set of coordinates near the course of the seed. The set of coordinates was broadcast by long membrane, and even Singer himself couldn't be sure what told him that the set of coordinates was sincere—intuition could not always be explained. He decided to cleanse it. He wasn't busy, and the task wasn't going to distract him from singing. Even if he got it wrong, it was not a big deal. Cleansing was not a precision task and didn't require absolute accuracy. It also wasn't urgent. He just had to get it done eventually. This was also why his position wasn't prestigious.

Singer took a mass dot out of the seed's magazine, then he turned to look for the star indicated by the set of coordinates. The main

core guided his gaze, like a spear sweeping through the starry sky. Singer grasped the mass dot with a force field feeler and prepared to flick it. But then he saw the location indicated by the set of coordinates and the feeler relaxed.

Of the three stars, one was missing. There was a white cloud of dust in its place, like the feces of an abyss whale.

It's already been cleansed. Nothing more to do.

Singer put the mass dot back into storage.

That was fast.

He activated a main core process to trace the source of the mass dot that had killed that star. This was a hopeless task with almost zero chance of success, but required by established procedure. The process soon terminated, and like every other time, yielded no results.

Singer soon understood why the cleansing had happened so fast. He saw a slow fog in the vicinity of that destroyed world. The slow fog was about half a structure length away from that world. Seen by itself, it wasn't apparent where the fog had come from, but when connected with the broadcast coordinates, it was obvious that the fog belonged to that world. The slow fog showed that the world was dangerous, which was why the cleansing had come so quickly. It appeared that there were other low-entropy entities with even sharper intuition than he; but that wasn't strange. It was as the Elder said: *In the cosmos, no matter how fast you are, someone will be faster; no matter how slow you are, someone will be slower.*

Every set of broadcast coordinates would eventually be cleansed; it was just a matter of sooner versus later. One low-entropy entity might think this set of coordinates insincere, but on the millions upon millions of low-entropy worlds there were billions upon billions tasked with cleansing—someone would think it sincere. All low-entropy entities possessed the cleansing gene, and cleansing was an instinct. Also, cleansing was a very simple thing. The cosmos was full of sources of potential power—one just had to trigger them to complete the task. It required so very little, and didn't even delay singing.

If Singer were patient, all sincere coordinates would eventually be cleansed by other, unknown low-entropy entities. But this was not a good thing for either the home world or the seed. Since Singer had received the set of coordinates and even glanced at the world pointed to by the coordinates, Singer had a connection to that world. It would be naïve to think of this connection as unidirectional. Recall the great law of reversible discovery: If you could see a low-entropy world, then that low-entropy world could also see you— it was only a matter of time. Thus, waiting for others to complete cleansing was dangerous.

The next task was to put this now-useless set of coordinates into the data bank called the tomb. This was also required by established procedure. Of course, all other information having to do with the location needed to go into the data bank as well, just as personal effects were buried with the body, as was the custom on the home world.

Among the "personal effects" was something that piqued Singer's interest. It was a record of the dead world's three communications with another location using medium membrane. Medium membrane was the least efficient communication membrane, also called primitive membrane. Most communications preferred long membrane, though it was said that even short membrane could be used to convey messages. If true, that would make the communicators akin to gods. But Singer liked primitive membrane. He thought primitive membrane possessed a simple beauty, symbolizing an age full of joy. He often turned primitive membrane messages into songs. He thought they sounded pretty, even if he didn't understand them. Understanding them wasn't necessary, however; other than coordinates, primitive membrane messages didn't have much useful information. It was enough to enjoy the music.

But this time, Singer was able to understand some of the message, because some parts carried a self-decoding system! Although Singer was only able to understand a little, grasp an outline, it was enough for him to see an incredible history.

First, the other location had broadcast a message via primitive

membrane. The low-entropy entities of that world clumsily plucked their star—Singer decided to call them the Star-Pluckers—like ancient bards of the home world plucking the strings of the rough country zither, to send out the message. It was this message that contained the self-decoding system.

Although the self-decoding system was primitive and clumsy, it was sufficient to allow Singer to see that a subsequent message sent out by the dead three-star world followed the same encoding scheme—apparently an answer to the first message sent by the Star-Pluckers! This was already nearly inconceivable, but after that, the Star-Pluckers responded again!

Interesting. Very interesting!

Singer had indeed heard of low-entropy worlds that possessed neither the hiding gene nor the hiding instinct, but this was the first time he had seen one. Of course, the three communications between these two would not reveal their absolute coordinates, but they did expose the distance between the two worlds. If the distance were fairly large, it wouldn't be a big deal either; but the distance was very short, only 416 structures—the two worlds were practically on top of each other. This meant that if one world's coordinates were exposed, the other would also be exposed—it was just a matter of time.

This was how the Star-Pluckers' coordinates were revealed.

Nine time grains after the first three communications, another record appeared: The Star-Pluckers plucked their star again to send out another broadcast ... a set of coordinates! The main core was certain that it was a set of coordinates. Singer looked for the star indicated by the coordinates and saw that it had also been cleansed, about thirty-five time grains ago.

Singer thought that perhaps he had been wrong. The Star-Pluckers must have possessed the hiding gene. They obviously had the cleansing gene, so it was impossible that they didn't also possess the hiding gene. But like most coordinate broadcasters, they didn't have the ability to cleanse on their own.

Interesting. Very interesting.

Why did whoever cleansed the dead three-star world not also cleanse the world of the Star-Pluckers? Many possibilities. Perhaps they hadn't noticed these three communications—primitive membrane messages often didn't get much attention. But given the millions upon millions of worlds out there, *someone* would have noticed—Singer was just one who did. Even without Singer, some other low-entropy entity would have noticed them; it was just a matter of time. Or perhaps they *had* noticed them, but decided that a low-entropy group that didn't possess the hiding gene wasn't much of a threat, and cleansing them was more trouble than it was worth.

But that would be a mistake, a terrible mistake! Broadly speaking, if low-entropy entities like these Star-Pluckers really didn't have the hiding gene, then they would not be afraid of exposing their own presence, and they would expand and attack without fear.

At least until they got killed.

However, as applied to this particular case, the situation was more complicated. The first three communications were followed nine time grains later by the coordinate broadcast. Then, sixty time grains after that, there was another long-membrane coordinate broadcast from somewhere else, pointing at the dead three-star world. The chain of events painted an uneasy picture, a picture that indicated danger. The cleansing against the dead three-star world had happened twelve time grains ago, so the Star-Pluckers must have realized that their own position had been revealed. Their only choice was to shroud themselves in slow fog so that they would appear perfectly safe and no one would bother them.

But they hadn't. Maybe they didn't have the ability? But more than sufficient time had passed from the time they could pluck their star to send out a primitive membrane message for them to possess this ability.

Perhaps they didn't want to shroud themselves.

If that was so, that made the Star-Pluckers very dangerous; far more dangerous than the dead world.

Hide yourself well; cleanse well.

Singer gazed at the world of the Star-Pluckers. It was an ordinary star that had at least a billion more time grains of life left. It possessed eight planets: four giant liquid planets and four solid ones. Singer's experience told him that the low-entropy entities who had sent out the primitive membrane broadcast lived on one of the solid planets.

Singer activated the process for the big eye—he rarely did this; he was exceeding his authority.

"What are you doing?" asked the seed's Elder. "The big eye is busy."

"I'd like to take a closer look at one of the low-entropy worlds."

"Your job doesn't require close-up examinations."

"I'm just curious."

"The big eye has to observe more important targets. There's no time for your curiosity. Go back to doing your job."

Singer didn't persist in his request. The cleansing agent had the lowest position on the seed. Everyone thought of him contemptuously, thought of his work as easy and trivial. But they forgot that coordinates that had been broadcast often indicated far more danger than the vast majority who kept themselves well hidden.

The only thing left was cleansing. Singer took a mass dot out of the magazine again, then realized that he couldn't use a mass dot to cleanse the Star-Pluckers. Their planetary system had a different structure than the dead world's system: it possessed blind corners. Using a mass dot might leave something behind, thereby wasting effort. He needed to use a dual-vector foil. However, Singer didn't have the authority to retrieve a dual-vector foil out of the magazine; he had to ask the Elder for approval.

"I need a dual-vector foil for cleansing."

"Permission granted," said the Elder.

The dual-vector foil drifted in front of Singer. It was sealed in its package, crystal clear. Although it was an ordinary object, Singer liked it a lot. He didn't like the expensive tools too much; they were too violent. He liked the unyielding tenderness displayed by the dual-vector foil, a kind of aesthetic that could turn death into a song.

Yet Singer felt a bit uneasy. "Why did you give it to me without so much as asking a question?"

"It's not like this is very costly."

"But if we make too much use of this—"

"It's being used everywhere in the cosmos."

"Yes, that is true. But in the past, we've always been restrained. Now—"

"Have you heard something?" The Elder began to riffle through Singer's thoughts, and Singer shuddered. Very quickly, the Elder found the rumor in Singer's mind. It wasn't a great sin—the rumor was an open secret on the seed.

It was a rumor about the war between the home world and the fringe world. Before, news about the war had been frequent, but then the reports stopped, indicating that the war wasn't going well, perhaps even heading into a crisis. But the home world couldn't coexist with the fringe world. The fringe world had to be destroyed, lest the home world be destroyed by it. If the war couldn't be won, then . . .

"Has the home world decided to transform into two dimensions?" Singer asked. Of course, the Elder already knew the question.

The Elder did not answer, which was also an answer.

If the rumor was true, then it was a great sorrow. Singer couldn't imagine such a life. On the tower of values, survival ranked above all. When survival was threatened, all low-entropy entities could only pick the lesser of two evils.

Singer removed these thoughts from his organ of cogitation. These were not thoughts he should have, and he was only going to be uselessly troubled by them. He tried to remember where he had stopped in his song. It took a while before he found his place. He continued to sing:

> *Lovely markings are carved into time*
> *As soft to the touch as the mud in shallow sea.*
> *She covers her body with time,*
> *And pulls me along to fly to the edge of existence.*

> *This is a spiritual flight:*
> *In our eyes, the stars appear as ghosts;*
> *In the eyes of the stars, we appear as ghosts.*

As he continued to sing, Singer picked up the dual-vector foil with a force field feeler and carelessly tossed it at the Star-Pluckers.

BUNKER ERA, YEAR 67
HALO

Cheng Xin awakened to find herself in weightlessness.

Hibernation wasn't like regular sleep. A hibernator didn't feel the passage of time. Throughout the entire process, one could only feel time during the hour spent entering hibernation and the hour emerging from it. No matter how much time passed during hibernation, subjectively, the hibernator only felt that he or she had slept no more than two hours. Thus, waking up always involved a sharp break, a feeling that the self had passed through a door in time and emerged into a new world.

Cheng Xin found herself in a white spherical space. She saw that 艾 AA was floating nearby, dressed in the same skintight hibernation suit. Her hair was wet and her limbs were spread out powerlessly; clearly, she had just been awakened as well. As their eyes met, Cheng Xin wanted to speak, but the numbness caused by the cold had still not left her, and she couldn't make any noise. AA shook her head, meaning that she was in the same state and didn't know anything.

Cheng Xin noticed that the space was filled with a golden light like the setting sun. The light came in through a circular window—a porthole. Outside the porthole, Cheng Xin could see only blurred streaks and swirling lines. The lines were arranged into parallel bands of blue and yellow, revealing a world covered by raging storms

and torrents, clearly the surface of Jupiter. Cheng Xin saw that the surface of Jupiter looked much brighter than she remembered.

Strangely, the wide, raging cloud band in the middle reminded her of the Yellow River. She knew, of course, that an eddy in this "Yellow River" was big enough to contain the Earth. Against this background, Cheng Xin saw an object. The main body of the object was a long column whose sections were of different diameters. Three short cylinders were perpendicularly attached to the main column at different locations. The entire assembly slowly rotated around the axis of the column. Cheng Xin decided that she was looking at a combined space city formed from eight separate space cities docked together.

She discovered another amazing fact as well: The place they were in stayed at rest relative to the combined space city, but Jupiter was slowly moving in the background. Based on the brightness of Jupiter, they were now on the side facing the Sun, and she could see the shadow of the combined space city against the gaseous surface of Jupiter. After a while, the Jovian terminator appeared, dividing Jupiter's day from night, and she saw the monstrous eye that was the Great Red Spot drifting into view. Everything confirmed the fact that both the place they were in and the combined space city were not in Jupiter's shadow and did not orbit the Sun in parallel with Jupiter; instead, they were Jupiter's satellites and revolved around the gas giant.

"Where are we?" Cheng Xin asked. She was finally able to speak in a hoarse voice, but she still couldn't move her body.

AA shook her head again. "No idea. I think we're on a spaceship."

They continued to drift in the golden glow of Jupiter, like a dreamscape.

"You're on *Halo*."

The voice came from an information window that had just popped up next to them. In the window was an old man with a head full of white hair. Cheng Xin recognized him as Cao Bin. Based on his age, she realized that she had leapt across another long stretch of years. Cao Bin told her that it was now May 19 of Year 67 of the

Bunker Era. She realized that fifty-six more years had passed since her last brief awakening.

She avoided life by staying outside of time, and she watched as others aged, seemingly in an instant. Her heart was filled with regret and guilt. She decided that no matter what happened from now on, this was her last hibernation.

Cao Bin told them that they were on the latest ship to bear the *Halo* name. It had been constructed only three years ago. After the Halo City Incident, more than half a century earlier, he and Bi Yunfeng had both been convicted, though both had served short sentences and then been released. Bi Yunfeng had died more than ten years earlier, and Cao Bin brought along his well wishes for her and AA. Cheng Xin's eyes moistened.

Cao Bin also told them that there were now fifty-two large space cities in the Jupiter cluster, most of which had been combined into bigger cities. What they could see was Jupiter Combination II. Since the advance warning system had been refined twenty years ago, all cities had decided to become Jovian satellites. Only after an alert was issued would the cities change orbit and go into hiding.

"Life in the cities is once again like being in paradise. It's too bad that you won't get to see it, because there's no time." Cao Bin paused. Cheng Xin and AA exchanged uneasy glances. They realized that he had been so loquacious until now because he was trying to delay this moment.

"Was there an attack alert?"

Cao Bin nodded. "Yes, there's been an alert. During the last half century, there were two false alarms, and each time, we almost awakened you. But this time it's real. Children—I'm already one hundred and twelve years of age, so I think I can call you that—the dark forest strike is finally here."

Cheng Xin's heart tensed. It wasn't because the attack had arrived—humanity had been preparing for this moment for more than a century. Rather, she sensed that something was wrong. She and AA had been awakened by contract. It would have taken at least four to five hours for them to recover to this stage, which meant that

the alert had been issued some time ago. But outside the porthole, Jupiter Combination II had not disassembled nor changed its orbit, but continued to drift as a Jovian satellite, as though nothing had happened. They turned to Cao Bin: The centenarian's expression was too placid, as though hiding utter despair.

"Where are you now?" AA asked.

"I'm at the advance warning center," Cao Bin said, and pointed behind him.

Cheng Xin saw a hall behind him that looked like a control center. Information windows filled almost every bit of space. The windows drifted around the hall, but new windows kept on popping open before them, only to be covered in turn by still newer windows—like the flood after a burst dam. But the people in the hall seemed to be doing nothing. Half of them were in military uniforms, but they all either stood leaning against a desk or sat still. Everyone had dull eyes, and all had the same ominous calm expression that was on Cao Bin's face.

It shouldn't be like this.

This didn't look like a world hunkered down inside a bunker, certain it could survive the attack. It looked more like three centuries ago—no, four centuries ago now—when the Trisolar Crisis had first developed. Back then, at the offices of the PIA and the PDC, Cheng Xin had seen this kind of atmosphere and expression everywhere: despair against some superpowerful force in the universe, a kind of numbness and indifference that said *We give up*.

Most of the people in the control center were quiet, but a few whispered to each other with somber faces. Cheng Xin saw a man sitting numbly. A cup had fallen over on the table in front of him, and a blue liquid spilled off the table onto his pants, but he ignored it. On the other side, in front of a large information window that seemed to show some complicated, evolving situation, a man in military uniform embraced a woman dressed as a civilian. The woman's face seemed wet....

"Why aren't we entering Jupiter's shadow?" AA pointed at the combined city outside the porthole.

"There's no point. The bunker is useless," Cao Bin said, lowering his eyes.

"How far is the photoid from the Sun?" Cheng Xin asked.

"There's no photoid."

"Then what have you found?"

Cao Bin gave a wretched laugh. "A slip of paper."

BUNKER ERA, YEAR 66
OUTSIDE THE SOLAR SYSTEM

A year before Cheng Xin's awakening, the advance warning system discovered an unknown flying object sweeping past the edge of the Oort Cloud at a speed close to lightspeed. At its closest approach, the object was only 1.3 light-years from the Sun. The object's volume was immense, and at its near-lightspeed velocity, the radiation generated by its impact with the scattered dust and atoms in space was intense. The advance warning system also observed the object making a small course change during flight to avoid a patch of interstellar dust, before resuming its previous course. It was most certainly an intelligent spaceship.

This was the first time that Solar System humans—as opposed to Galactic humans—had observed another extraterrestrial civilization besides the Trisolarans.

Due to lessons learned from the previous three false alarms, the Federation Government did not publicize this discovery. No more than a thousand people in the entire Bunker World knew about it. During the few days when the spaceship had been closest to the Solar System, these individuals lived in extreme anxiety and terror. In the few tens of space observation units comprising the advance warning system, in the advance warning center (a space city in the Jupiter cluster), in the battle center of Federation Fleet Command, and in the office of the president of the Solar System Federation,

people held their breaths and watched the spaceship's course like a trembling school of fish hiding at the bottom of a pond, waiting for the trawler to pass overhead. These individuals' terror developed to absurd levels later: They refused to use radio communications, walked noiselessly, and spoke only in whispers.... In reality, everyone understood that these gestures were meaningless, not the least because what the advance warning system observed had happened a year and four months ago. By now, the spaceship was already gone.

After the extraterrestrial spaceship moved farther away, these individuals did not relax. The advance warning system discovered something else that was worrisome. The strange spaceship did not shoot a photoid at the Sun, but did launch something else. This object was also shot at the Sun at lightspeed, but it produced none of the emissions associated with photoids and was completely invisible electromagnetically. The advance warning system only managed to discover it through gravitational waves. The object continuously emitted weak gravitational waves whose strength and frequency remained constant. The waves clearly carried no message, and were probably the result of some physical characteristic of the projectile. When the advance warning system initially discovered these gravitational waves, the source was thought to be the extraterrestrial spaceship. But they soon found that the source was separate from the spaceship, and it was approaching the Solar System at lightspeed.

Further analysis of the observation data revealed that the projectile wasn't aimed precisely at the Sun. According to its current trajectory, it would sweep past the Sun outside the orbit of Mars. If the intended target had been the Sun, this was a relatively gross error. This showed another way that the projectile was different from a photoid: The data gathered from the previous two photoid strikes all showed that after a photoid was launched, it followed a precise, straight trajectory to the target star (taking into account the motion of the star) and did not require any course correction. It could be surmised that a photoid was essentially a rock flying under inertia at lightspeed. Tracking the gravitational wave source showed that the projectile did not make any course corrections,

apparently indicating that its target was not the Sun. This provided some comfort for everyone involved.

When the projectile was about 150 AU from the Sun, the gravitational waves it emitted began to rapidly decrease in frequency. The advance warning system discovered that this was due to its deceleration. Within a few days, the projectile's velocity went from lightspeed to one-thousandth of lightspeed, and continued to decrease. Such low speed meant that it wasn't enough to threaten the Sun, which provided further comfort. In addition, at this speed, human spacecraft could keep up with it. In other words, it was possible to send out ships to intercept it.

Revelation and *Alaska* departed the Neptune city cluster and flew in formation to investigate the unknown projectile.

Both ships were equipped with gravitational wave reception systems and could form a positioning network to determine the location of the transmission source with precision at close range. Since the Broadcast Era, more ships had been built that could transmit and receive gravitational waves. But the design concepts used in these ships were very different from earlier antenna ships. One of the main innovations was separating the gravitational wave antenna from the ship itself so that they formed two independent units. The antenna could then be combined with different ships, and could be replaced after it failed due to decay. *Revelation* and *Alaska* were only medium-sized ships, but they had about the same total volumes as large ships because the gravitational wave antennas made up a large portion of their structures. The two ships resembled helium-filled airships of the Common Era: They looked immense, but the effective payload was just the small gondola hanging below the gasbags.

Ten days after the two ships left port, General Vasilenko and 白 Ice,[8] dressed in lightweight space suits and magnetic shoes, took a

8 *Translator's Note:* The surname "白" is pronounced "Bai."

stroll on the gravitational wave antenna of *Revelation*. They enjoyed doing this because there was much more space out here compared to the interior of the spaceship, and walking around the antenna made one feel like walking on solid earth. They were the leaders of the first exploratory team: Vasilenko was the commander while 白 Ice was in charge of technical matters.

Alexei Vasilenko had been an observer in the advance warning system during the Broadcast Era. Together with Widnall, he had discovered the trails of the Trisolaran lightspeed ships, which led to the first false alarm. After the incident, Sublieutenant Vasilenko was made one of the scapegoats and was dishonorably discharged. But he thought the punishment unjust and hoped that history would ultimately clear his name, and thus entered hibernation. As time passed, the discovery of the lightspeed trails grew in importance, and the damage from the first false alarm was gradually forgotten. Vasilenko awakened in Year 9 of the Bunker Era, was restored to his former rank, and by now had been promoted to vice admiral of the Solar Federation Space Force. However, he was close to eighty years of age. As he looked at 白 Ice strolling next to him, he thought how unfair life was: This man had been born eighty years before himself and came from the Crisis Era; yet, after hibernation, he was just over forty.

白 Ice's original name was Bai Aisi.[9] After awakening, he wanted to appear more integrated and not so behind the times, and chose a more common modern name that mixed English and Chinese elements. He had been a doctoral student under Ding Yi and had gone into hibernation near the end of the Crisis Era, awakening only twenty-two years ago. Usually, such a long leap across the years meant the hibernator would have trouble catching up to the new age, but theoretical physics was a special case. The sophon lock meant that Common Era physicists could still be considered professionally relevant during the Deterrence Era, and the creation

9 *Translator's Note:* This is the pinyin romanization of the original fully Chinese name: "白艾思."

573

of the circumsolar particle accelerator upended all the assumptions of fundamental theoretical physics, as though a deck of cards had been reshuffled.

Back during the Common Era, superstring theory had been thought of as advanced theory, the physics of the twenty-second century. The creation of the circumsolar particle accelerator allowed superstring theory to be confirmed via experiments. The result, however, was disastrous. Concepts that had to be rejected far outnumbered predictions that were confirmed. Many results that the Trisolarans had passed on were falsified. Based on the high level of technology the Trisolarans were later able to achieve, it was inconceivable that they had made such mistakes in fundamental theory. The only conclusion was that they had lied to humans even in the areas of basic theory.

白 Ice had proposed some theoretical models that were among the few confirmed by the circumsolar particle accelerator. By the time he awakened, physics had essentially been called back to the starting line. He quickly distinguished himself and won great honors, and after ten or so years, he was once again at the vanguard of the field.

"Look familiar?" Vasilenko gestured at everything around them.

"Indeed. But the self-confidence and arrogance of humanity are all gone," said 白 Ice.

This resonated with Vasilenko. He looked back along the ship's course. Neptune was only a tiny blue dot and the Sun a faint spot of light, incapable of even casting their shadows against the antenna surface. Where were the two thousand stellar-class warships that had formed a magnificent phalanx all those years ago? Now, there were just these two lonely ships with a complement of no more than a hundred crew. *Alaska* was about a hundred thousand kilometers away but not visible to them. That ship wasn't only acting as the other end of the positioning network, but also held another exploratory team organized the same as the team aboard *Revelation*. Fleet Command called the team aboard *Alaska* the backup, indicating that the brass had made ample preparations for the risk and danger inherent in this expedition. Here, at the cold,

desolate frontier of the Solar System, the antenna under their feet seemed a lonesome island in the universe. Vasilenko wanted to sigh, but thought better of it. He took something out of the pocket of his spacesuit and let it float between the two of them, spinning slowly.

"Check this out."

The object appeared to be a bone from some animal. In fact, it was a metallic machine component; the frigid light of the stars glinted against its smooth surface.

Vasilenko pointed at the spinning object. "About a hundred hours ago, we detected a patch of floating metallic debris next to the ship's course. A drone retrieved a few items, and this is one of them: a piece of the cooling system for a nuclear fusion reactor aboard a stellar-class warship from the end of the Crisis Era."

"It's from the Doomsday Battle?" asked an awed 白 Ice.

"Yes. We also found the armrest from a chair and a bulkhead fragment."

They had been passing through the vicinity of the ancient battlefield from nearly two centuries earlier. After the Bunker Project started, people often discovered remnants of ancient warships. Some were placed in museums while others were bought and sold through the black market. 白 Ice held the component and felt a chill pass through the glove of the space suit, straight into his marrow. He let it go, and the component continued to spin slowly, as though moved by some soul embedded within. 白 Ice moved his eyes away and gazed into the distance. All he could see was a bottomless, empty abyss. Two thousand warships and millions of dead bodies had been drifting in this patch of desolate space for nearly two centuries. The sacrificial blood of the dead had long ago sublimated from ice to gas and dissipated.

"The target of our exploration might be more dangerous than even the droplets this time," 白 Ice said.

"True. Back then, we already had some familiarity with the Trisolarans. But we know nothing about the world that created and sent this…. Dr. Bai, do you have any guesses as to what we will encounter?"

"Only a massive object can emit gravitational waves, so I guess that object must be large both in mass and volume, perhaps even a spaceship.... Well, in this business, the unexpected is to be expected."

The two ships of the expedition continued on their course for another week until the distance between them and the gravitational wave source was only about a million kilometers. The expedition decelerated until their velocity was zero, and began to accelerate toward the Sun. This way, by the time the projectile caught up to the expedition, they would fly in parallel. Most of the close-range exploration would be conducted by *Revelation*; *Alaska* would observe from a distance of about a hundred thousand kilometers.

The distance continued to shrink; the projectile was now only about ten thousand kilometers from *Revelation*. The gravitational wave emissions were very clear and could be used for precise positioning. But even from this distance, radar returned no echo and nothing could be seen in the visible light range. By the time the distance shrank to one thousand kilometers, they still couldn't see anything at the location of the gravitational wave source.

The crew of *Revelation* was close to panicking. Before departure, they had imagined all kinds of scenarios, but the idea of not being able to see their target when they were practically on top of it had never occurred to them. Vasilenko radioed the base at Neptune for instructions, and forty minutes later, received the order to approach the target until they were only 150 kilometers away.

Finally, the visible light detection systems noticed something: a small white dot at the gravitational wave source, visible even with a common telescope from the ship. *Revelation* sent out a drone to investigate. The drone flew at the target, the distance between them shrinking rapidly: five hundred kilometers, fifty kilometers, five hundred meters ... Finally, the drone stopped five meters from the target. The clear holographic video it transmitted allowed the

crew of both ships to see this extraterrestrial object that had been shot at the Sun.

A slip of paper.

There was really no better description. Formally, the object was called a rectangular membrane-like object: length: 8.5 cm; width: 5.2 cm; slightly bigger than a credit card. It was so thin that its thickness could not be measured. The surface was pure white, looking exactly like a slip of paper.

The members of the exploratory team were among the best officers and professionals in the world, and all had cool, rational minds. But instinct was more powerful. They had been prepared for giant, invasive objects. Some had guessed they would find a spaceship the size of Europa—a not unlikely possibility, given the strength of its gravitational wave emissions.

Faced with this paper slip—that was what they all called it—everyone heaved a sigh of relief. Rationally, they were still guarded. The object could certainly be a weapon that possessed enough power to destroy both spaceships. But it was impossible to believe that it could threaten the entire Solar System. By appearance, it was delicate, harmless, like a white feather floating in night air. People had long ceased to write letters on paper, but they were familiar with the concept from period films about the ancient world, and so the paper slip seemed almost romantic in their eyes.

Further investigation showed that the paper slip did not reflect electromagnetic radiation at any wavelength. The slip's white color wasn't reflected light, but light emitted by the object itself. All electromagnetic radiation, including visible light, simply passed through the slip, which was thus completely transparent. Images taken at close range showed the stars behind the slip, but due to interference from the white light it emitted and the dark background of space, it appeared as an opaque white from a distance. At least superficially, the object seemed harmless.

Maybe it really was a letter?

Since the drone had no appropriate collection tools, another drone with a mechanical arm and a sealable scoop had to be

dispatched to capture the slip. As the open scoop extended toward the slip at the end of the mechanical arm, the hearts of everyone on the two ships hung in their throats.

This was another scene that seemed familiar.

The scoop closed around the slip and the arm pulled back.

But the slip remained where it was.

The attempt was repeated several more times with the same result. The drone operators aboard *Revelation* tried to maneuver the mechanical arm to touch the slip. The arm passed right through the slip, and neither appeared damaged. The arm felt no resistance, and the slip didn't change its position. Finally, the operator directed the drone to approach the paper slowly, in an attempt to push it. As the hull of the drone came into contact with the slip, the slip disappeared inside the drone, and as the drone continued to move forward, the slip emerged from the stern, unchanged. During the process when the slip was inside the drone, its internal systems detected no anomalies.

By now, the expedition members understood that the paper slip was no ordinary object. It was like an illusion that did not interact with anything in the physical world. It was also like a tiny cosmic reference plane that maintained its position, unmovable. No contact was capable of shifting its position—or, more accurately, its set trajectory.

白 Ice decided to go investigate in person. Vasilenko insisted on coming with him. Having both leaders of the first exploratory team go together was a controversial proposition, and they had to wait forty minutes to receive approval from the base at Neptune. Their request was reluctantly granted, as Vasilenko would not back down, and there was also a backup team.

The two headed for the paper slip in a pinnace. As *Revelation* and its immense gravitational wave antenna shrank in the distance, 白 Ice thought he was leaving the only support in the universe, and his heart became fearful.

"Your advisor, Dr. Ding, must have felt the same way years ago," Vasilenko said. He appeared perfectly calm.

白 Ice agreed with the sentiment in silence. He did feel spiritually connected to the Ding Yi of two centuries ago. Both of them headed for a great unknown, toward equally unknown fates.

"Don't worry. This time, we can trust our intuition." Vasilenko patted 白 Ice on the shoulder, but 白 Ice did not feel much comfort.

The pinnace was now next to the paper slip. After checking their space suits, they opened the pinnace's hatch so that they were exposed to space. They fine-tuned the pinnace's position until the paper slip hung half a meter above their heads. The tiny white plane was perfectly smooth, and through it they saw the stars behind, confirming that it really was a glowing, transparent object. The white light it emitted made the stars behind it appear a bit blurred.

They lifted themselves up in the pinnace until their eyes were lined up with the edge of the plane. Just like the camera had shown, the paper had no thickness. From the side, it completely disappeared. Vasilenko extended a hand toward the paper, but 白 Ice caught him.

"What are you doing?" 白 Ice asked severely. His eyes said the rest. *Think about what happened to my teacher.*

"If it really is a letter, perhaps the message won't be released until an intelligent body makes direct contact with it." Vasilenko brushed off 白 Ice's hand.

Vasilenko touched the paper with his gloved hand. His hand passed through the paper and was not damaged. Vasilenko received no mental message, either. He again moved his hand through the paper and stopped, allowing the small white plane to divide his hand into two parts. Still, he felt nothing. The paper showed an outline of the cross section of the hand where the hand penetrated it: clearly, the sheet hadn't been broken, but passed through the hand unharmed. Vasilenko pulled his hand back, and the slip hung still as before—or, more accurately, continued to move toward the Solar System at the rate of two hundred kilometers per second.

白 Ice also tried to touch the slip, then pulled his hand back. "It's like a projection from another universe that has nothing to do with ours."

Vasilenko had more practical concerns. "If nothing can affect it, then we have no way to bring it to the ship for further analysis."

白 Ice laughed. "That's a simple problem to solve. Have you forgotten the story told by Francis Bacon? 'If the mountain will not come to Muhammad, then Muhammad must go to the mountain.'"

And so, *Revelation* slowly sailed toward the paper slip, made contact, and then allowed it to enter the ship. Even more slowly, it adjusted its position until the slip hung in the middle of the laboratory cabin. The only way to move the slip during study was to move the ship itself. This odd way to manipulate the research subject posed some challenges near the beginning, but luckily, *Revelation* was originally designed to investigate small space objects in the Kuiper Belt and possessed excellent maneuverability. The gravitational wave antenna was equipped with twelve high-precision thrusters. After the ship's AI grew used to the necessary adjustments, the manipulation became quick and precise. If the world could not affect the slip in any way, the only solution was to let the world surround the slip and move about it.

Thus, an odd sight came to be: The slip was located in the center of *Revelation,* but the ship had no dynamical connection to the slip. The two simply happened to occupy the same space as both moved toward the Solar System at the same velocity.

Inside the spaceship, due to the stronger background light, the transparency of the slip became more obvious. It now no longer resembled a slip of paper, but some transparent film that only indicated its presence by the faint light it emitted. People continued to refer to it as a paper slip, however. When the ambient light was very strong, it was sometimes possible to lose sight of it, so the researchers had to dim the lights in the laboratory to see the slip better.

The first thing the researchers tried to do was to ascertain the slip's mass. The only applicable method was to measure the gravity it generated. However, even at the highest precision level, the gravity meter showed nothing, suggesting that the slip's mass was extremely small, perhaps even zero. Based on the latter possibility,

some guessed that the object might be a photon or neutrino in macro form, but its geometric shape suggested that it was artificial.

No progress could be made on analysis of the slip because electromagnetic waves of all wavelengths passed through it without diffraction. Magnetic fields, no matter how strong, seemed to have no effect on it. The object appeared to have no internal structure.

Twenty hours later, the exploratory team still knew next to nothing about the slip. They were able to observe one thing, however: The intensity of the light and gravitational waves emitted by the slip was decreasing. This suggested that the light and gravitational waves it emitted were probably a form of evaporation. Since these two were the only indication of the existence of the slip, their disappearance would be the same as the disappearance of the slip itself.

The base informed the exploratory team that *Tomorrow*, a large science vessel, had left the Neptune city cluster and would meet the expedition in seven days' time. *Tomorrow* possessed more advanced investigative instruments, and could study the slip in more depth.

As they became more used to the slip, the crew on *Revelation* became less guarded and were no longer so careful about keeping a respectful distance from it. They knew that the object did not interact with the real world and emitted no harmful radiation. They touched it casually, allowing it to pass through their bodies. Someone even let the plane pass through his eyes and brain, asking a friend to take a picture of the sight.

白 Ice was enraged when he saw this. "Stop it! This is not some joke," he screamed. Having worked nonstop in the lab for more than twenty hours, he left the laboratory and returned to his own cabin.

白 Ice turned off the light in his cabin and tried to go to sleep. But in the darkness he felt uneasy; he imagined the paper slip would float into his cabin, glowing white, at any moment. So he turned on the light and drifted in the gentle light and memories.

———

One hundred and ninety-two years had passed since he said good-bye to his teacher for the last time.

It was dusk, and he and Ding Yi had come to the surface from the underground city and taken a car into the desert. Ding Yi liked to stroll and think in the desert, and even to hold his lectures there sometimes. His students hated the experience, but he explained his eccentric habit this way: "I like desolate places. Life is a distraction for physics."

The weather that day was good. There was no wind and no sandstorms, and the early spring air smelled fresh. The two of them, teacher and student, lay against a dune. The desert of Northern China was bathed in the light of the setting sun. Normally, Bai Aisi thought of these rolling dunes as a woman's body—possibly a comparison that had originated with Ding Yi himself—but now he thought of them as an exposed brain. In the golden dusk, the brain revealed its profusion of grooves and folds. He looked up at the sky. Today, the dusty air managed to let through a bit of long-missed blue, like a mind about to be enlightened.

Ding Yi said, "Aisi, I want to tell you a few things that you should not repeat to others. Even if I don't return, don't tell others. There's no special reason. I just don't want to be laughed at."

"Professor Ding, why not wait until you're back to tell me?"

Bai Aisi wasn't trying to comfort Ding Yi. He was sincere. He was still drunk with the ecstasy and vision of humanity's imminent great victory over the Trisolaran fleet, and he did not think Ding Yi's trip to the droplet would involve much danger.

"Answer a question first, please." Ding Yi ignored Bai Aisi's question and pointed at the desert lit by the westering sun. "Forget about the uncertainty principle for a minute and suppose everything is determinable. If you know the initial conditions, you can calculate and derive the conditions at any later point in time. Suppose an extraterrestrial scientist were given all data about the Earth several billion years ago. Do you think it could predict the existence of this desert solely through calculation?"

Bai Aisi pondered this. "No. This desert wasn't the result of

582

the Earth's natural evolution, but the result of man-made forces. The behavior of civilizations can't be grasped through the laws of physics."

"Very good. Then why do we and our colleagues all want to try to explain the conditions of today's cosmos, and to predict its future, solely through deductions based on the laws of physics?"

Ding Yi's words surprised Bai Aisi. The man had never revealed such thoughts in the past.

Bai Aisi said, "I think that's beyond physics. The goal of physics is to discover the fundamental laws of nature. Although the man-made desertification of the Earth could not be calculated directly from physics, it still follows laws. Universal laws are constant."

"Heh heh heh heh." Ding Yi's laugh was not joyous at all. As he recalled it later, Bai Aisi thought it was the most sinister laughter he had ever heard. There was a hint of masochistic pleasure, an excitement at seeing everything falling into the abyss, an attempt to use joy as a cover for terror, until terror itself became an indulgence. "Your last sentence! I've often comforted myself this way. I've always forced myself to believe that there's at least one table at this banquet filled with dishes that remain fucking untouched.... I tell myself that again and again. And I'm going to say it one more time before I die."

Bai Aisi thought Ding Yi's mind was elsewhere and that he talked as if he were dreaming. He didn't know what to say.

Ding Yi continued, "At the beginning of the crisis, when the sophons were interfering with the particle accelerators, a few people committed suicide. At the time, I thought what they did made no sense. Theoreticians should be excited by such experimental data! But now I understand. Those people knew more than I did. Take Yang Dong, for instance. She knew much more than I did, and thought further. She probably knew things we don't even know now. Do you think only sophons create illusions? Do you think the only illusions exist in the particle accelerator terminals? Do you think the rest of the universe is as pure as a virgin, waiting for us to explore? Too bad that she left with everything she knew."

"If she had talked with you more back then, perhaps she wouldn't have chosen to go."

"Perhaps I would have gone with her."

Ding Yi dug a pit in the sand and watched as the sand on the rim flowed back in like a waterfall. "If I don't come back, everything in my room is yours. I know that you've always liked those Common Era things I brought."

"That's true, especially those tobacco pipes.... But I don't think I'll get them."

"I hope you're right. I also have some money—"

"Please, Professor!"

"I want you to use it to pay for hibernation. The longer the better—of course, that's assuming you want to. I have two goals in mind: One, I want you to go look at the endgame for me—the endgame for physics. Two ... how do I say this? I don't want you to waste your life. After others have decided that physics actually exists, there will still be plenty of time for you to go do physics."

"That ... seems like something Yang Dong would say."

"Maybe it's not nonsense."

Bai Aisi noticed that the pit Ding Yi had dug in the desert was rapidly expanding. They stood up and backed away as the pit continued to grow, getting deeper as well as wider. Soon, the bottom disappeared in shadows. Sand flooded into the pit in torrents, and soon, the diameter of the pit was close to a hundred meters, and a nearby dune was swallowed up. Bai Aisi ran toward the car and got into the driver's seat; Ding Yi followed into the passenger seat. Bai Aisi noticed that the car was moving slowly toward the pit, dragged along by the sand underneath. He turned on the engine and the wheels began to turn, but the car continued to slide backwards.

Ding Yi laughed that sinister laugh again. "Heh heh heh heh ..."

Bai Aisi turned the electric motor to the highest setting and the wheels spun madly, throwing up sand everywhere. But the car still moved toward the pit like a plate pulled along on a tablecloth.

"Niagara Falls! Heh heh heh heh ..."

Bai Aisi looked back and saw a sight that made his blood curdle:

The pit now took up his entire field of vision. The whole desert was swallowed up by it, and the world was like a giant pit whose bottom was an abyss. At the rim, flowing sand poured in and formed a spectacular yellow sandfall. Ding Yi wasn't exactly right in his description: The Niagara Falls were minuscule compared to this sandfall of terror. The sandfall extended from the near edge of the pit all the way to the far edge on the horizon, forming an immense sandfall ring. The sand torrents rumbled as if the world itself were coming apart. The car continued to slide toward the pit, faster and faster. Bai Aisi floored the accelerator and leaned his weight into it, but there was no effect.

"You fool. Do you really think we can escape?" Ding Yi said while still laughing sinisterly. "Escape velocity! Why don't you calculate the escape velocity? Are you thinking with your butt? Heh heh heh heh ..."

The car tumbled over the rim and dropped in the sandfall. The sand raining down around them seemed to stop as everything plunged into the abyss. Bai Aisi screamed with utter terror, but he couldn't hear himself. All he heard was Ding Yi's wild laughter.

"Hahahahaha ... There's no table untouched at the dinner party, and there's no virgin untouched in the universe ... waheeheeheehee ... wahahahaha ..."

白 Ice woke from his nightmare and found himself covered in cold sweat. Around him, more droplets of sweat hung suspended in air. He floated for a while, his body stiff, and then dashed out of his cabin and headed for Vasilenko's cabin. It took a while before the door opened, as Vasilenko was also sleeping.

"General! Do not keep that thing, that thing they call a slip of paper, in the spaceship! No, I mean, don't allow *Revelation* to hover around it. We should leave immediately, and get as far away as possible!"

"What have you discovered?"

"Nothing. It's my intuition."

"You don't look so good. Exhaustion? I think you're worrying too much. That thing ... I don't think it's anything. There's nothing inside. It should be harmless."

白 Ice grabbed Vasilenko by the shoulders and gazed into his eyes. "Don't be arrogant!"

"What?"

"Don't be arrogant. Weakness and ignorance are not barriers to survival, but arrogance is. Remember the droplet!"

白 Ice's last sentence had an effect. Vasilenko stared at him in silence for a few seconds, then nodded slowly. "All right, Dr. Bai, I'll listen to you. *Revelation* will depart from the slip and back off one thousand kilometers. We'll leave just a pinnace to monitor it.... Maybe two thousand kilometers?"

白 Ice let Vasilenko go and wiped his forehead. "You decide. I suggest, the farther the better. I will write a formal report as soon as possible and let Command know of my theories." Stumbling, he drifted away.

Revelation left the slip. It passed through the ship's hull and was reexposed to space. Since the background was dark again, it once again appeared to be an opaque white slip of paper. *Revelation* pulled away from the slip until the two were about two thousand kilometers apart, then continued to sail in parallel, waiting for the arrival of *Tomorrow*. A pinnace with a crew of two stayed about ten meters from the slip to monitor it continuously.

The gravitational waves emitted by the paper slip continued to diminish, and its light gradually dimmed.

On *Revelation,* 白 Ice shut himself in the laboratory. Around him, he set up more than a dozen information windows, all connected to the ship's quantum computer, which was carrying out massive computations. The windows were packed with equations, curves, and matrices. Surrounded by the windows, 白 Ice was anxious and irritable, like a trapped animal.

Fifty hours after the separation from *Revelation,* the gravitational

wave emitted from the paper slip disappeared completely. The white light from it blinked twice and also went out. The slip of paper was gone.

"Has it evaporated?" Vasilenko asked.

"I don't think so. But we can't see it anymore." 白 Ice shook his head wearily and closed the information windows around him one by one.

After another hour during which no signs of the slip could be detected, Vasilenko ordered the pinnace to return to *Revelation*. But the two crew members on duty in the pinnace didn't acknowledge the order; the radio only transmitted a hurried conversation between them.

"Look out below! What's going on?"

"It's rising!"

"Don't touch it! Get out!!"

"My leg! Ahhh—"

After the scream, the monitoring terminal on *Revelation* showed one of the crew members leaving the pinnace and activating the thrusters on his space suit in an attempt to escape. They saw a bright light; the source was the bottom of the pinnace, which was melting! The pinnace looked like a scoop of ice cream dropped onto a scalding sheet of glass: The bottom was melting and spreading in every direction. The "glass" was invisible, and the plane's existence was indicated only by the spreading pool of melted pinnace material. The pool spread into an extremely thin sheet and emitted bewitching, colorful lights, like fireworks scattered through a sheet of glass.

The escaped crewman flew some distance but seemed to be pulled by gravity toward that plane marked by the melted pinnace. His feet touched the plane and immediately melted into a shiny puddle. The rest of his body also began to spread out on the plane, and he had time only for a scream that was abruptly cut off.

"All hands to hypergravitation seats! Full Ahead!"

As soon as he saw the escaping crewman's feet touch the invisible plane, Vasilenko gave the order. *Revelation* wasn't a stellar ship,

so when it engaged in Full Ahead acceleration, the crew did not need to enter into the protective deep-sea state. But the hypergravity was enough to sink everyone deep into their seats. Since the order was given in such a hurry, a few couldn't get to their seats in time and fell to the stern of the ship with injuries. *Revelation*'s exhaust nozzles emitted a plasma stream several kilometers long that pierced the dark night of space. Far in the distance, where the pinnace was still melting, they could see the phosphorescent glow like will-o'-the-wisps in the wilderness.

From the zoomed-in view on the monitoring terminal, they could see that only the very top part of the pinnace was left, and that too soon disappeared into the brilliant plane. The body of the dead crewman was also diffused into the plane, showing up as a gigantic, man-shaped glow. His body had been transformed into a slice on the plane without thickness. Though large in area, it had no volume.

"We're not moving," the pilot of *Revelation* said. He had trouble talking through the hypergravity. "The ship isn't accelerating."

"What are you babbling about?" Vasilenko wanted to shout, but the hypergravity turned it into a whisper.

It really did seem as if the pilot should have been wrong. Everyone on the ship was pressed against their seat by hypergravity, which indicated that the ship was in the process of extreme acceleration. It was visually impossible for a passenger to tell whether the ship was moving in space because all celestial bodies that could act as reference points were too far away, so they couldn't see parallax in a short time frame. However, the ship's navigation system could detect even tiny amounts of motion and acceleration; it couldn't be wrong.

Revelation was under hypergravity, but had no acceleration. Some force had nailed it to this point in space.

"There *is* acceleration," said 白 Ice weakly. "But the space in this region is flowing in the opposite direction, thus canceling out our motion."

"The space is flowing? Where to?"

"There, of course."

白 Ice couldn't lift his hand, which was now too heavy. But everyone knew where he meant. *Revelation* sank into a deathlike silence. Normally, hypergravity made people feel safe, as though they were escaping from danger under the embrace of some protective power. But now it seemed as oppressive and suffocating as a tomb.

"Open a channel to Command," 白 Ice said. "There's no time, so we'll treat this as our formal report."

"Channel open."

"General, you once said, 'I don't think it's anything. There's nothing inside.' You were right. That slip really wasn't anything, and contained nothing. It's only space, just like the space around us, which isn't anything and contains nothing. But there's a difference: It's two-dimensional. It's not a block, but a slice. A slice without thickness."

"Hadn't it evaporated?"

"The protective field around it evaporated. The force field acted like packaging that separated the two-dimensional space from the three-dimensional space. But now the two are in direct contact. Do you remember what *Blue Space* and *Gravity* saw?"

No one answered, but they all remembered: the four-dimensional space falling into three dimensions, like a waterfall off a cliff.

"Just as four-dimensional space collapses into three dimensions, three-dimensional space can collapse into two dimensions, with one dimension folding and curling into the quantum realm. The area of that slice of two-dimensional space—it only has area—will rapidly expand, causing more space to collapse.... We're now in space that is falling toward two dimensions, and ultimately, the entire Solar System will follow. In other words, the Solar System will turn into a painting with no thickness."

"Can we escape it?"

"Escaping this is like rowing a boat above a waterfall. Unless we exceed a certain escape velocity, we'll tumble over the cliff. It's like tossing a pebble up from the ground: No matter how high you throw the rock, it will eventually fall back down. The entire Solar

System is within the zone of collapse, and anyone trying to escape must reach escape velocity."

"What is the escape velocity?"

"I've computed it four separate times. Pretty sure I got it right."

"What is it?!"

Everyone aboard *Revelation* and *Alaska* held their breaths and listened to this final calculation as representatives of humanity.

白 Ice calmly announced his judgment. "Lightspeed."

The navigation system showed that *Revelation* was now moving in the opposite direction from its heading. It started by moving slowly toward the two-dimensional space, but gradually accelerated. The ship's drive was still powering Full Ahead. This would at least slow down the rate of the ship's fall and delay the inevitable.

On the plane two thousand kilometers away, the light emitted by the two-dimensionalized pinnace and crewmen had already gone out. Compared to collapsing from four dimensions to three, the fall from three dimensions to two gave off much less energy. Two two-dimensional structures were revealed clearly by the starlight. On the two-dimensionalized pinnace, it was possible to see the details of three-dimensional structures unfolded in two dimensions—the crew cabin, the fusion reactor, and so on—as well as the curled-up figure of the crewman in the cabin. In the figure of the other crewman, the bones and blood vessels could be clearly discerned, as well as all the body parts. During the process of falling into two dimensions, every point on a three-dimensional object was projected onto the plane in accordance with precise geometric principles, and so these two figures turned out to be the most complete and precise images of the original three-dimensional pinnace and people. All the internal structures were now laid out side by side in two dimensions with nothing hidden. The projection process, however, was very different from that used in engineering drawings, and so it was difficult to visually reimagine the shapes' original three-dimensional structure. The greatest difference from engineering drawings lay in the fact that the two-dimensional unfolding occurred at every scale: All the original three-dimensional

structures and details were laid out in parallel in two dimensions, and the result replicated, in some measure, the effect of viewing the three-dimensional world from four-dimensional space. This closely resembled drawings of fractals: No matter how much you zoomed in on a part of the image, it would get no less complex. However, fractals were theoretical concepts—actual representations were inevitably limited by the resolution, and after zooming in a number of times, the images lost their fractal nature. The complexity of the two-dimensionalized three-dimensional objects, on the other hand, was real: The resolution was at the level of fundamental particles. On the monitoring terminal of *Revelation,* the eye could only see a limited resolution, but the complexity and number of details already made the viewers dizzy. This was the universe's most complicated image; staring at it for too long would drive one mad.

Of course, the pinnace and the crewmen no longer possessed any thickness.

It was unclear how large the plane had spread by now; only those two images indicated its presence.

Revelation slid faster toward the plane, toward that abyss whose thickness was zero.

"Everyone, don't be sad. No one will be able to escape from the Solar System, not even a bacteria or virus. All of us will become a part of this grand picture." 白 Ice now looked calm and stoic.

"Stop accelerating," said Vasilenko. "What difference does a few minutes make? Let's at least breathe easier at the end."

Revelation's engine shut off. The plasma column at the stern of the ship disappeared, and the ship drifted, powerless, in space. In reality, the ship was still accelerating toward the two-dimensional patch of space, but since the ship moved along with the surrounding space, those inside could not feel any gravity from acceleration. They enjoyed the weightlessness and took deep breaths.

"You know what I'm thinking of? Needle-Eye's pictures from Yun Tianming's fairy tales," 白 Ice said.

Only a few people aboard *Revelation* knew about Yun Tianming's secret message. Now, in a flash, they all understood

the meaning of this detail in the stories. It was a simple metaphor, and there were no bearing coordinates because it was so direct. Yun must have thought he was taking a great risk to put such an obvious metaphor into his stories, yet he had to try because the message was so important.

He probably thought that with the knowledge of *Blue Space* and *Gravity*'s discoveries, humanity would understand the metaphor. Unfortunately, he had overestimated their ability to comprehend.

The inability to decipher this key piece of information led humanity to place all their hopes in the Bunker Project.

It was true that both dark forest strikes humans had witnessed involved photoids, but they ignored a salient fact: Those two target planetary systems were structured differently from the Solar System. The star known as 187J3X1 had three giant Jupiter-like planets, but they all orbited extremely close to their sun. Their average distance from the sun was but 3 percent of the distance from Jupiter to the Sun, even closer than Mercury's orbit. Since they almost brushed up against their sun, the solar explosion destroyed them completely, and they could not have been used as barriers. The Trisolaran system, on the other hand, had only one planet, Trisolaris.

The structure of the planetary system around a star was a characteristic observable from a distance. For a sufficiently advanced civilization, a quick glance was sufficient.

If humans could figure out the plan to use the gas giants as barriers, couldn't observers from such advanced civilizations do so, as well?

Weakness and ignorance are not barriers to survival, but arrogance is.

Revelation was now no more than a thousand kilometers from the plane; it fell faster and faster.

"Thank you, everyone, for doing your duty. Although we haven't been together long, we worked together well," Vasilenko said.

"I also thank every member of the human race," said 白 Ice. "Once, we lived together in the Solar System."

Revelation fell into the two-dimensional space. In a few seconds, it was flattened. Light akin to fireworks once again lit up the darkness of space. This was a vast two-dimensional image that could be clearly seen from *Alaska,* a hundred thousand kilometers away. It was possible to distinguish every individual on *Revelation*: They were laid out side by side, holding hands, every single cell in their body exposed to space in two dimensions.

They were the first to be painted into this grand painting of annihilation.

BUNKER ERA, YEAR 68
PLUTO

"Let's head back to the Earth," Cheng Xin said softly. This was the first idea that floated up through the chaos and darkness of her jumbled thoughts.

"The Earth is not a bad place to wait for the end. A falling leaf seeks to return to the root. But we hope *Halo* will go to Pluto," Cao Bin said.

"Pluto?"

"Pluto is at its apogee, rather far from the two-dimensional space. The Federation Government is about to issue a formal attack alert to the world, and many ships will be headed there. Although the final result will be the same, at least there will be more time left."

"How much longer?"

"The entire Solar System within the Kuiper Belt will collapse into two dimensions in eight to ten days."

"That's not long enough to be worth worrying about. Let's go back to Earth," said AA.

"The Federation Government would like to ask you to do something."

"What can we possibly do now?"

"Not anything important. There's nothing important now. But someone came up with the idea that theoretically, there might exist image-processing software that could process a two-

dimensionalized image of a three-dimensional object and re-create the three-dimensional object. We hope that in the distant future, some intelligent civilization might re-create a three-dimensional representation of our world from its two-dimensionalized image. Though it would be nothing more than a dead representation, at least human civilization would not be forgotten.

"The Earth Civilization Museum is on Pluto. A large portion of humanity's precious artifacts are stored there. The museum is buried under the surface, however, and we are concerned that during the process of falling into the plane, these artifacts would be mixed together with the strata of the crust and their structures would be damaged. We'd like to ask you to carry some of the artifacts away from Pluto on *Halo* and scatter them in space so that they can fall into two dimensions separately. This way, their structures would be preserved without harm in two dimensions. I guess this counts as a kind of rescue mission.... Of course, I admit that the idea is nearly science fiction, but doing something now is better than doing nothing.

"Also, Luo Ji is on Pluto. He wants to see you."

"Luo Ji? He's alive?!" AA cried out.

"Yes. He's almost two hundred."

"All right. Let's go to Pluto," Cheng Xin said. In the past, this would have been an extraordinary journey. But now, nothing mattered.

A pleasant male voice spoke up. "Do you wish to go to Pluto?"

"Who are you?" asked AA.

"I'm *Halo*, or *Halo*'s AI. Do you wish to go to Pluto?"

"Yes. What do we do?"

"You just have to confirm the request. There's no need to do anything. I will complete the voyage for you."

"Yes, we want to go to Pluto."

"Authorization confirmed. Processing. *Halo* will accelerate at 1G in three minutes. Please pay attention to the direction of gravity."

Cao Bin said, "Good. Better leave early. After the attack alert is issued, there might be total mayhem. Hopefully we'll get a chance

to talk again." He closed the window link before AA and Cheng Xin could say good-bye. At this moment, AA, Cheng Xin, and *Halo* were not his top priorities.

Outside the porthole, they could see a few blue reflections appearing on the shell of the combined city—reflections of *Halo*'s nozzle lights. Cheng Xin and AA fell to one side of the spherical hall and felt their bodies grow heavier. The acceleration soon reached 1G. After the two of them—still weak from hibernation—struggled up and looked outside the porthole again, they saw the entirety of Jupiter. It was still immense, and shrinking at too slow a rate to be perceived.

The ship's AI led AA and Cheng Xin on a tour of the ship to familiarize them with it. Like its predecessor, this new *Halo* was still a small stellar yacht with a maximum capacity of four. Most of the space on the ship was taken up by the ecological cycling system. By conventional measures, the ecological cycling system was extremely redundant—a volume of space that would have supported forty was used to provide for only four. The system was divided into four identical subsystems, linked together and acting as each other's backups. If any of the four failed accidentally, the other three could bring it back to life. *Halo*'s other distinguishing characteristic was the ability to land directly on a medium-sized solid planet. This was a rare design choice among stellar ships—similar ships typically used shuttles to carry landing parties onto planets. Directly descending into a planet's deep gravity well required the ship to have a very strong hull, which greatly increased the cost. Moreover, the need for atmospheric flight required a streamlined profile, which was also very rare among stellar ships. All of these design features meant that if *Halo* could find another Earthlike planet in outer space, it could act as a habitable base for the crew on the surface of the planet for a considerable amount of time. Maybe it was these characteristics of *Halo* that led to it being chosen for the artifact-rescuing mission to Pluto.

There were numerous other unusual features on the yacht. For instance, it had six small courtyards, each about twenty to thirty

square meters in size. Each courtyard automatically adjusted to the direction of gravity under acceleration, and, during coasting, spun independently within the ship to generate artificial gravity. Each courtyard displayed a different natural scene: a green lawn with a babbling brook running through the grass; a small copse with a spring in the middle; a beach with waves of clear water throwing up surf.... These scenes were small but exquisite, like a string of pearls made of the best parts of the Earth. On a small stellar spaceship, such a design was extremely luxurious.

Cheng Xin felt both distressed and sorry for *Halo*. Such a perfect little world was soon going to be turned into a slice without thickness. She tried to avoid thinking about those other grander things facing imminent destruction—annihilation covered the sky of her thoughts like a giant pair of black wings, and she dared not look directly up at it.

Two hours after departure, *Halo* received the formal dark forest attack alert issued by the Solar System Federation Government. The president, a beautiful woman who looked very young, made the announcement. She stood in front of the blue flag of the Federation and spoke without expression. Cheng Xin noticed that the blue flag resembled the ancient UN flag, though a diagram of the Sun replaced the diagram of the Earth. This most important document, marking the end of human history, was very short:

> Five hours ago, the advance warning system confirmed that a dark forest strike has been initiated against our world.
>
> The attack takes the form of a dimensional strike, which will collapse the space around the Solar System from three dimensions to two dimensions. The result will be the complete destruction of all life.
>
> The process is estimated to take eight to ten days. At this moment, the collapse is ongoing and the rate and extent of collapse are rapidly growing.
>
> We have confirmed that the escape velocity for the collapsing region is the speed of light.

An hour ago, the Federation Government and Parliament have passed a new resolution that repeals all laws regarding Escapism. However, the government wishes to remind all citizens that the escape velocity far exceeds the maximum velocity of all human space vehicles. The probability of a successful escape is zero.

The Federation Government, Parliament, the Supreme Court, and Federation Fleet will carry out their duties until the end.

AA and Cheng Xin didn't bother to watch more news. It was possible that, just like Cao Bin said, the Bunker World had approached paradise. They wanted to see what paradise looked like, but they didn't dare look. If everything was heading toward ruination, the more beautiful it all was, the more pain they would suffer. In any event, it was a paradise that was collapsing in the terror of death.

Halo stopped accelerating. Behind it, Jupiter became a small yellow dot. The next few days of the voyage were spent in the uninterrupted slumber produced by the sleep-aid machine. In this lonely voyage through the night before the end, just the unstoppable mad imaginings were enough to make anyone fall apart.

Halo's AI awakened AA and Cheng Xin from their dreamless sleep as the ship reached Pluto.

Out of the porthole and on the monitor they could see the entirety of Pluto. Their initial impression of the dwarf planet was one of darkness, like an eye that remained perpetually shut. This far from the Sun, the light was extremely dim. Only when *Halo* entered low orbit could they see the colors on the surface of the planet: Pluto's crust appeared to be made of patches of blue and black. The black was rocks—not necessarily black in color, but the light was too dim to tell otherwise. The blue was solidified nitrogen and methane. Two centuries ago, when Pluto had been near its perigee and inside Neptune's orbit, the surface would have looked

completely different. The ice cover would have partially melted and produced a thin atmosphere. From the distance, it would have appeared a deep yellow.

Halo continued to descend. On Earth, this would have involved a soul-stirring atmospheric reentry, but *Halo* continued to fly through the silent vacuum, decelerating by the power of its own thrusters. On the blue-black ground below, an attention-grabbing line of white text appeared:

EARTH CIVILIZATION

The text was written in the modern script that mixed Latin and Chinese elements. After it, there were a few more lines of smaller text repeating the same thing in different scripts. Cheng Xin noticed that none of them said "museum." The yacht was still about one hundred kilometers above the surface, which meant that the text was gigantic. Cheng Xin couldn't make an exact estimate of the size of the characters, but she was certain that these were the largest written characters ever produced by humankind, each big enough to contain a city. By the time *Halo* was only about ten thousand meters above the surface, one of the large characters took up the entire field of view. Finally, *Halo* touched down on the broad landing field, which was the topmost dot in the Chinese character *qiu* (球), a part of the word *Earth*.

With the guidance of the ship's AI, Cheng Xin and AA put on light space suits and exited *Halo* onto the surface of Pluto. Given the frigid surroundings, the heating systems in their space suits were operating at maximum power. The landing field was empty, white, and seemed to phosphoresce in the starlight. The numerous burn marks left on the ground indicated that many spacecraft had once landed and taken off here, but *Halo* was the only ship here now.

During the Bunker Era, Pluto was akin to Antarctica on ancient Earth. No one lived here permanently, and few came to visit.

In the sky, a black sphere moved rapidly among the stars. It was large, but the surface was shrouded in darkness: Charon,

Pluto's moon. Its mass was a tenth of Pluto's, and the two almost formed a double-planet system, revolving around a common center of mass.

Halo turned on its searchlights. Due to the lack of atmosphere, there wasn't a visible beam of light. It cast a circle of light on a distant rectangular object. This black monolith was the only protrusion above the white ground. It gave off an eerie sense of simplicity, as though it was an abstraction of the real world.

"That looks a bit familiar," Cheng Xin said.

"I don't know what it is, but I don't have a good feeling about it."

Cheng Xin and AA headed for the monolith. Pluto's gravity was only one-tenth of the Earth's, and so they proceeded by leaping. Along the way, they noticed a row of arrows pointing toward the monolith on the ground. Only when they reached the monolith did its immensity impress itself on their minds. When they looked up, it was as though a chunk had been taken out of the starry sky. They looked around and saw that there were rows of arrows coming from other directions, all pointing toward the monolith. At the foot of the monolith was another prominent protuberance: a metal wheel about a meter in diameter. To their surprise, they found the wheel to be hand-operated. Above the wheel was a diagram formed from white lines against the black surface of the monolith. Two curved arrows indicated the directions in which the wheel could be turned. Next to one of the arrows was a drawing of a half-open door, while the other bore a drawing of a shut door. Cheng Xin turned to survey the arrows on the ground pointing to the monolith. All the simple, clear, wordless instructions gave her a strange feeling, which AA voiced.

"These things ... I don't think they're intended for humans."

They turned the wheel clockwise. The wheel was stiff, but eventually a door opened in the surface of the monolith. Some gas escaped, and the water vapor within quickly deposited into ice crystals that glinted in the searchlight. They entered the door and saw another door facing them, also operated by a wheel. This time, there were simple written instructions above the wheel, informing

them that they were in an air lock and needed to close the first door before opening the second. This was unusual, since as early as the end of the Crisis Era, pressurized buildings could open their doors directly to vacuum without needing an air lock.

Cheng Xin and AA turned the wheel on the inside of the door they had entered to shut it. The searchlight was cut off. They were about to turn on the lights on their space suits to hold off the terror of darkness when they noticed a small lamp in the ceiling of the narrow air lock. This was the first sign they had seen of electricity. They began to turn the wheel to open the second door. Cheng Xin was certain that even if they hadn't closed the first door, they would still have been able to open the second. The only thing that prevented air from leaking was following the instructions. In this low-technology environment, there was no automatic mechanism to prevent errors.

The rush of air almost toppled them, and the rapidly warming temperature fogged their visors. But the space suits told them that the external air pressure and composition was breathable; they could open their helmets.

They saw a tunnel lit by a series of dim lamps heading into the earth. The dark walls of the tunnel swallowed up the dim light they emitted so that, between the cones of light, all was darkness. The floor of the tunnel was a smooth incline. Although the angle was steep, close to forty-five degrees, there were no stairs. This design was probably motivated by two considerations: There was no need for stairs in low gravity, or the path wasn't meant for humans.

"There's no elevator?" AA asked. She was frightened by the steep way down.

"An elevator might break down over time. This building was intended to last through geologic eons." The voice came from the other end of the tunnel, where an old man appeared. In the dim light, his long white hair and beard floated in the low gravity. They seemed to be giving off their own light.

"Are you Luo Ji?" AA shouted.

"Who else? Children, my legs don't work so well anymore,

so forgive me for not coming up to meet you. Come on down by yourselves."

Cheng Xin and AA descended the incline in leaps. Due to the low gravity, this wasn't a very dangerous maneuver. As they approached the old man, they saw that he was indeed Luo Ji. He wore a long white *changshan,* a Chinese-style robe, and leaned against a cane. His back was slightly bowed, but his voice was hale and loud.

At the bottom of the incline, Cheng Xin bowed deeply. "Honored Elder, hello."

"Haha, there's no need for that." Luo Ji waved his hands. "We used to be ... colleagues." He looked at Cheng Xin and in his eyes was a surprised delight that almost seemed incongruent with his age. "You're still so young. There was a time when I saw you only as the Swordholder, and then, gradually, you became a lovely young woman. Haha...."

In Cheng Xin's and AA's eyes, Luo Ji had also changed. The stately Swordholder was gone. They didn't know that the cynical, playful Luo Ji in front of them now was a return to the Luo Ji from four centuries ago, before he had become a Wallfacer. That Luo Ji had returned, as if awakening from hibernation, but the passage of time had moderated him, and filled him with more transcendence.

"Do you know what has happened?" AA asked.

"Of course, child." He pointed behind him with his cane. "Those idiots all left on spaceships. They knew that they ultimately couldn't escape, but they still tried to run. Foolish."

He meant the other workers in the Earth Civilization Museum.

"You and I have both busied ourselves for nothing," said Luo Ji to Cheng Xin.

It took Cheng Xin a bit of time before she understood what he meant, but the flood of emotions and memories was interrupted by Luo Ji's next words. "Forget it. *Carpe diem* has always been the right path. Of course there's not much *diem* now for *carpe,* but we need not look for trouble. Let's go. You don't need to help support me. You haven't even learned how to walk properly around here yet."

Given Luo Ji's advanced age of two hundred, the difficulty of

locomotion under such low gravity wasn't moving too slow, but too fast. The cane wasn't so much a support as a decelerator.

After a while, space opened up before them. Cheng Xin and AA realized that they were now in a much wider and bigger tunnel—a cavern, really. The ceiling was high above, but the space was still only lit by a dim row of lights. The cavern looked very long, and the other end was not visible.

"This is the main body of the museum," Luo Ji said.

"Where are the artifacts?"

"In the halls down at the other end. Those aren't so important. How long can they keep? Ten thousand years? A hundred thousand years? A million, at the most. Practically all of them will have turned to dust by then. But these—" Luo Ji pointed around them. "—were intended to be preserved for hundreds of millions of years. Why, do you still think this is a museum? No, no one visits here. This is not a place for visitors. All of this is but a tombstone—humankind's tombstone."

Cheng Xin looked around the empty, dim cavern and thought back to all she had seen. Indeed, everything was filled with hints of death.

"How did such an idea come up?" AA looked all around.

"You ask that because you're too young." Luo Ji pointed to Cheng Xin and himself. "During our time, people often planned for their own gravesites while they were still alive. Finding a graveyard for humanity isn't so easy, but erecting a tombstone is doable." He turned to Cheng Xin. "Do you remember Secretary General Say?"

Cheng Xin nodded. "Of course."

Four centuries ago, while she had worked for the PIA, Cheng Xin had met Say, the UN secretary general, a few times at various meetings. The last time was at a PIA briefing. Wade was there, too. On a big screen, Cheng Xin had given Say a PowerPoint presentation about the Staircase Project. Say had sat there quietly and listened to the whole thing without asking any questions. Afterwards, Say walked next to Cheng Xin, leaned in, and whispered, "We need more people to think like you."

"She was a true visionary. I've thought of her often through the years. Could she really have died almost four hundred years ago?" Luo Ji leaned on the cane with both hands and sighed. "She was the one who thought of this first. She wanted to do something so that humanity would leave behind a legacy that could be preserved for a long time after our civilization was gone. She planned an unmanned ship filled with cultural artifacts and information about us, but it was deemed a form of Escapism, and the project halted with her death. Three centuries later, after the Bunker Project began, people remembered it. That was a time when people worried that the world was going to end any moment. The new Federation Government decided to build a tombstone at the same time that the Bunker Project was built, but it was officially referred to as the Earth Civilization Museum so as not to be seen as a sign of pessimism. I was named the chair of the tombstone committee.

"At first, we engaged in a large research project to study how to preserve information across geologic eons. The initial benchmark was a billion years. Ha! A billion. Those idiots thought that would be easy—after all, if we could build the Bunker World, how difficult could this be? But they soon realized that modern quantum storage devices, while capable of storing a whole library in a grain of rice, could only preserve the information without loss for about two thousand years. After that, decay would make it impossible to decode. As a matter of fact, that only applied to the highest-quality storage devices. Two-thirds of more common varieties failed within five hundred years. This suddenly transformed the project from a detached, contemplative matter into an interesting practical problem. Five hundred years was real—you and I came from only four hundred years ago, right? So the government stopped all work on the museum and directed us to study how to back up important data about the modern world so that it could be read in five hundred years, heh heh.... Eventually, a special institute had to be set up to tackle the problem so that the rest of us could focus on the museum, or tombstone.

"Scientists realized that in terms of data longevity, storage devices from our time were better. They found some USB flash drives and hard drives from the Common Era and some still had recoverable data! Experiments showed that if these devices were of high quality, information was safe on them for about five thousand years. The optical disks from our era were especially resilient. When made from special metal, they could reliably preserve data for a hundred thousand years. But none of these were a match for printed material. Special ink printed on composite paper could be read in two hundred thousand years. But that was the limit. Our conventional data storage techniques could preserve information for two hundred thousand years, but we needed to get to a billion!

"We informed the government that, given current technology, preserving ten gigabytes of images and one gigabyte of text—that was the basic information requirement for the museum—for one billion years was impossible. They wouldn't believe us, and we had to show them the evidence. Finally, they agreed to lower the requirement to one hundred million years.

"But this was still an extremely difficult task. We looked for information that had survived for such a long time. Patterns drawn on prehistoric pottery survived about ten thousand years. Cave paintings in Europe were from about forty thousand years ago. If you count the markings made on stones back when our ancestors, the hominids, made the first tools as information, then the earliest instances occurred during the Pliocene, two point five million years ago. And we did indeed find information left one hundred million years ago, though it wasn't left by humans: dinosaur footprints.

"The research continued, but there was no progress. The other specialists had obviously reached conclusions, but they didn't want to speak up. I told them, 'Don't worry about it. Whatever conclusions you've reached, no matter how bizarre or outrageous, we must accept them if there are no alternatives.' I promised them that there was nothing that could be more bizarre and outrageous

than what I'd gone through, and I would not laugh at them. So they told me that, according to the most advanced theories and techniques in every field, based on extensive theoretical research and experimentation, through analysis and comparison of multiple proposals, they did find a way to preserve information for about one hundred million years. And they emphasized that this was the only method known to be practicable. Which is—" Luo Ji lifted the cane over his head, and as his white hair and beard danced in the air, he resembled Moses parting the Red Sea. Solemnly, he intoned, "—carving words into stone."

AA giggled. But Cheng Xin wasn't laughing. She was stunned.

"Carving words into stone." Luo Ji pointed at the walls of the cavern.

Cheng Xin walked to one of the walls. In the dim light, she saw that it was covered with dense, carved text, as well as images in relief. The wall was not the original rock, but seemed to have been infused with metal, or perhaps the surface had been coated with some durable titanium alloy or gold. Fundamentally, however, it was no different from carving words into stone. The carved text wasn't small: each character or letter was about a square centimeter. This was another feature intended to help with information longevity, as smaller text tended to be harder to preserve.

"Of course, this approach meant that the information storage capacity was greatly reduced, leaving us with less than one-ten-thousandth of the planned amount. But they had no choice but to accept this limitation," Luo Ji said.

"These lamps are really strange," said AA.

Cheng Xin looked at the lamp on the cave wall. First, she noticed its shape: an arm poking out of the wall holding a torch. She thought this was a familiar design, but clearly that wasn't what AA meant. The torch-shaped lamp seemed very clumsy. The size and structure resembled an ancient searchlight, but the light it emitted was very weak, about the same as an ancient twenty-watt incandescent light bulb. After passing through the thick lampshade, the light was not much brighter than a candle.

Luo Ji said, "Back that way is the machinery dedicated to providing electricity to this complex, like a power plant. This lamp is an amazing accomplishment. There's no filament or excitable gas inside, and I don't know what the luminous element is, but it can continue to glow for a hundred thousand years. The doors you came through should continue to be operable under normal conditions for five hundred thousand years. After that, the doors will deform and whoever wants to come in will have to break them down. By then, these lamps will have gone out more than four hundred thousand years earlier, and darkness will reign here. But that will be but the start of the journey of a hundred million years."

Cheng Xin took off a space suit glove and caressed the characters carved into the cold stone. Then she leaned against the cave wall and stared woodenly at the lamps. She realized where she had seen this design: the Panthéon in Paris. A hand holding a torch just like the one on Rousseau's tomb. The faint yellow lights before her now didn't seem to be electric, but like tiny flames about to go out.

"You are not very talkative," Luo Ji said. His voice was suffused with a solicitousness that Cheng Xin had long missed.

"She's always been like that," said AA.

"Ah, I used to love to talk, and then I forgot how. But now I've learned again. I can't stop chattering, like a kid. I hope I'm not bothering you?"

Cheng Xin struggled to smile. "Not at all. It's just that ... looking at all this, I don't know what to say."

True. What was there to say? Civilization was like a mad dash that lasted five thousand years. Progress begot more progress; countless miracles gave birth to more miracles; humankind seemed to possess the power of gods; but in the end, the real power was wielded by time. Leaving behind a mark was tougher than creating a world. At the end of civilization, all they could do was the same thing they had done in the distant past, when humanity was but a babe:

Carving words into stone.

Cheng Xin examined the carvings on the wall carefully. They began with the relief carving of a man and a woman, perhaps an attempt to show future discoverers what humans looked like. But unlike the stiff bearing of the drawings of the man and woman on the metal plaque carried by the Pioneer probes during the Common Era, the two cave carvings were done with lively expressions and postures, evoking Adam and Eve.

Cheng Xin walked along the wall. After the man and the woman came some hieroglyphs and cuneiforms, probably copied from ancient artifacts—it was possible that some of them were not even intelligible to modern men and women, and if so, how would future extraterrestrial discoverers understand them? Going further, Cheng Xin saw Chinese poetry—or, at least, she could tell the carvings were poetry based on the arrangement of the characters. But she didn't recognize any of the characters; she could only tell they were in Great Seal Script.

"That's the *Classic of Poetry,* from a millennium before the time of Christ," Luo Ji said. "If you keep on walking, you'll see fragments of Classical Greek philosophy. To see letters and characters that you can read, you'll have to walk tens of meters."

Under the Greek letters, Cheng Xin saw another relief, which seemed to portray ancient scholars in simple robes debating in an agora surrounded by stone columns.

Cheng Xin had a strange idea. She turned back and looked near the beginning of the cave carvings, but didn't find what she was looking for.

"You are looking for a Rosetta Stone?" Luo Ji asked.

"Yes. Isn't there some system to help with interpretation?"

"Child, we're talking about carving in stone, not a computer. How can we possibly fit something like that here?"

AA looked at the cave wall and then stared at Luo Ji. "You're saying that we've carved things here that we don't even understand with the hope that someday, some extraterrestrial will be able to read them?"

True, to the extraterrestrial discoverers of the far future, the

human classics left on the walls here would probably resemble Linear A, Cretan hieroglyphics, and other ancient scripts that no one could read. Perhaps there was no realistic hope that anyone would. By the time the builders of this monument truly understood the power of time, they no longer believed that a vanished civilization could really leave behind any marks that would last through geologic eons. As Luo Ji had said, this wasn't a museum.

A museum was built for visitors; a tombstone was built for the builders.

The three continued onward, and Luo Ji's cane tapped along the ground rhythmically.

"I often stroll around here thinking my own crazy thoughts." Luo Ji paused and pointed at a relief carving of an ancient soldier in armor and wielding a spear. "This is about the conquests of Alexander the Great. If he had kept on going a bit farther east, he would have encountered the Qin at the end of the Warring States Period—what would have happened then? And how would history have changed?" They walked some more, and he pointed at the cave wall again. By now, the characters carved on the wall had turned from Small Seal Script to Clerical Script. "Ah, we've reached the Han Dynasty. From here to later, China completed two unifications. Are a unified territory and a unified system of thought good things for civilization as a whole? The Han Dynasty ended up endorsing Confucianism above all, but if the multiplicity of schools of thinking during the Spring and Autumn Period had continued, what would have happened later? How would the present be different?" He waved his cane around in a circle. "At every moment in history, you can find endless missed opportunities."

"Like life," said Cheng Xin softly.

"Oh, no no no." Luo Ji shook his head vigorously. "At least not for me. I don't think I've missed anything, haha." He looked at Cheng Xin. "Child, do you think you've missed out? Then don't let opportunities go by again in the future."

"There's no future now," said AA coldly. She wondered if Luo Ji was suffering from dementia.

They reached the end of the cave. Turning around to survey this underground tombstone, Luo Ji sighed. "We had designed this place to last a hundred million years, but it won't even survive a hundred."

"Who knows? Perhaps a flat two-dimensional civilization will be able to see all this," said AA.

"Interesting! I hope you're right.... Look, this is where the artifacts are kept. We have a total of three halls."

Cheng Xin and AA saw space open up before them once more. The room they were in didn't resemble an exhibit hall so much as a warehouse. All the artifacts were placed in identical metal boxes, and each box was labeled in detail.

Luo Ji tapped one of the nearby boxes with his cane. "As I said, these are not so important. Most of these objects have longevities shorter than fifty thousand years, though some of the statues can survive up to a million years. But I suggest you not move the statues: Though the gravity makes them easy to move, they take up too much space.... All right, pick whatever you like."

AA looked around excitedly. "I suggest we take paintings. We can forget about old classics and ancient manuscripts—no one will understand those." She walked in front of one of the metal boxes and pushed what looked like a button on top, but the box didn't open by itself, and there were no instructions. Cheng Xin walked over and struggled to lift the cover open. AA took out an oil painting.

"I guess paintings take up a lot of space, too," said AA.

Luo Ji picked up a set of work overalls from on top of another box and retrieved a small knife and screwdriver from the pockets. "The frame takes up a lot of space. You can take it off."

AA picked up the screwdriver, but before she could get started on the painting, Cheng Xin cried out. "No!" The painting was Van Gogh's *Starry Night*.

Cheng Xin's surprise wasn't just because the painting was valuable. She had seen it once before. Four centuries ago, right after she had started working at the PIA, she had visited New

York's Museum of Modern Art on a weekend and saw a few of Van Gogh's paintings. Van Gogh's representation of space had left a deep impression on her. In his subconscious, space seemed to have structure. Cheng Xin wasn't an expert in theoretical physics back then, but she knew that according to string theory, space, like material objects, was made up of many microscopic vibrating strings. Van Gogh had painted these strings: In his paintings, space—like mountains, wheat fields, houses, and trees—was filled with minute vibrations. *Starry Night* had left an indelible mark in her mind, and she was amazed to see it again four centuries later on Pluto.

"Get rid of the frame. That way, you can take more." Luo Ji waved his cane carelessly. "Do you think these objects are still worth a city's ransom? Now, even a city is worthless."

And so they pried away the frame that was perhaps five centuries old, but they kept the hard backing to avoid damaging the painting by bending the canvas. They continued to do the same to other oil paintings, and soon, empty frames littered the floor. Luo Ji came over and put his hand on a small painting.

"Would you leave this one for me?"

Cheng Xin and AA moved the painting aside and set it on top of a box next to the wall. They were surprised to see that it was the *Mona Lisa*.

Cheng Xin and AA continued to work at disassembling frames. AA whispered, "Clever old man. He kept the most expensive piece for himself."

"I don't think that's the reason."

"Maybe he once loved a girl named Mona Lisa?"

Luo Ji sat next to the *Mona Lisa* and caressed the ancient frame with one hand. He muttered, "I didn't know you were here. Otherwise I could have come to see you often."

Cheng Xin saw that he wasn't looking at the painting. His eyes stared ahead as if looking into the depths of time. Cheng Xin saw that his ancient eyes were filled with tears, and she wasn't sure if she was mistaken.

Inside the grand tomb under the surface of Pluto, lit by the dim lamps that could shine for a hundred thousand years, Mona Lisa's smile seemed to appear and disappear. The smile had puzzled humankind for nearly nine centuries, and it looked even more mysterious and eerie now, as though it meant everything and nothing, like the approaching Death.

BUNKER ERA, YEAR 68
THE TWO-DIMENSIONAL SOLAR
SYSTEM

Cheng Xin and AA carried the first batch of artifacts to the surface. Other than a dozen or so frameless paintings, they also carried two bronze ritual vessels from the Western Zhou Period and some ancient books. Under standard 1G gravity, they would not have been able to move all these, but with Pluto's weak gravity, it didn't require too much effort. Going through the air lock, they were careful to close the inner door first before opening the outer door, lest they and the artifacts be blown into the open by escaping air. As soon as they opened the outer door, the small amount of air inside the air lock turned into a flurry of ice crystals. Initially, they thought the ice crystals were illuminated by the searchlight on *Halo,* but after the flurry subsided, they realized that *Halo*'s searchlight had already shut off. Some source of light in space illuminated Pluto's surface, and *Halo* and the black monolith cast long shadows on the white ground. They looked up, and backed up two steps with shock.

A pair of giant eyes stared down at them from space.

Two glowing ovals hung in space, looking exactly like eyes. The "whites" were white or light yellow, and the "irises" were dark.

"That's Neptune, and the other one is Ura—oh, no, that's Saturn!" AA said.

Both gas giants had been two-dimensionalized. Uranus's orbit was outside Saturn's, but since Uranus was currently on the other side of the Sun, Saturn had fallen into the two-dimensional plane first. The giant planets ought to look like circles after collapsing, but due to the angle of view from Pluto, they appeared as ovals. The two-dimensional planets showed up as clear, concentric rings. Neptune consisted mainly of three rings: the outermost was blue, bright and vivid, like lashes and eye shadow—that was the atmosphere of hydrogen and helium. The middle ring was white—that was the twenty-thousand-kilometer mantle, which astronomers thought of as a water-ammonia ocean. The dark center was the core, formed of rocks and ice, with a mass equal to the entire Earth. Saturn's structure was similar, except it didn't have the outer blue ring.

Each large ring was composed of many smaller rings, full of detailed structures. As they examined the planets further, the two giant eyes now more resembled the rings of a newly felled tree. Around each two-dimensional planet were a dozen or so small circles—moons that had also been flattened. Around Saturn was another faint large circle—its rings. They could still find the Sun in the sky, a small disk emitting faint yellow light. Since the two planets were still on the other side of the sun, their area after collapsing into two dimensions was breathtaking.

Both planets had no thickness anymore.

In the light emitted by these two-dimensional planets, Cheng Xin and AA carried the artifacts across the white landing field toward *Halo*. The ship's smooth, streamlined body was like a fun-house mirror, and the reflections of the two-dimensional planets were stretched into long, flowing shapes. The yacht's profile naturally made people think of droplets, and evinced a comforting strength and lightness. On the way to Pluto, AA had told Cheng Xin that she thought *Halo*'s hull was probably made up in large part of strong-interaction materials.

As they approached, the door on the bottom of the ship slid open noiselessly. They carried the artifacts up the airstair and into the cabin, took off their helmets, and took a deep breath in their cozy

little world. Relief filled their hearts—without consciously being aware of it, they already thought of the yacht as *home*.

Cheng Xin asked the ship's AI whether it had received any transmissions from Neptune and Saturn. As soon as she made the request, information windows flooded forth like a colorful avalanche that threatened to bury them. The scene reminded them of the first false alarm of 118 years ago. Back then, most of the information had come from media reports, but now, the news media seemed to have disappeared. Most of the information windows contained no discernible images at all—some were blurred, others shook, and most showed meaningless close-ups. But a few of the windows were filled with patches of gorgeous color which, as they flowed and shifted, revealed complex, detailed structures. They probably showed the two-dimensional universe.

AA asked the AI to filter the images. The AI asked them what kind of information they wanted. Cheng Xin asked for information about the space cities. The flood of windows cleared and was replaced by about a dozen others arranged in order. One of the windows enlarged and moved before the others. The AI explained that this had been taken twelve hours ago at Europe VI in the Neptune cluster. The city had once been part of a combined city that had separated after the strike alert.

The image was stable, and the field of view wide. The camera was probably at one end of the city, and almost the entire city could be seen.

Electricity had gone out in Europe VI, and only a few searchlight beams projected unsteady circles of light onto the city's far side. The three artificial fusion suns along the city's axis had all turned into silvery moons, giving out only illumination, but no heat. This was a standard football-shaped city, but the buildings inside the city were very different from what Cheng Xin had seen half a century ago. The Bunker World had prospered, and the buildings inside the city were no longer monotonous and uniform. They were much taller, and each had a unique design. The tips of some of the skyscrapers almost touched the axis of the city. Buildings in the shapes of trees

reappeared as well, and they looked about as large as the ones that had been built on Earth, though the leaves hung more densely. It was possible to imagine the city's beauty and magnificence when lit up at night. But now, only cold moonlight illuminated it, and the tree-buildings cast wide shadows so that the rest of the city appeared as ruins nestled in the shade of a giant forest.

The city had stopped spinning and everything was weightless. Countless objects floated through the air—vehicles, miscellaneous goods, and even entire buildings.

A black belt of clouds appeared along the city's axis, connecting the two poles. The ship's AI outlined a rectangular region in the image and zoomed in, creating a new information window. Cheng Xin and AA were shocked to see that the black cloud was formed from people drifting in the middle of the city! Some of the weightless individuals had pulled together into a cluster; some had linked hands and formed a line; but most floated alone. Everyone wore helmets and clothes that covered all parts of their body— most likely space suits. Even during Cheng Xin's last time out of hibernation, it was hard to tell everyday clothes apart from space suits. Everyone seemed to have a pack for life-support systems— some wore it on their back, while others held it in their hands. But most people had their visors open, and it was possible to see a light breeze blowing through the city, indicating that the city still retained a breathable atmosphere. Many had congregated around the suns, perhaps hoping for more light as well as a bit of warmth, but the light emitted by the fusion suns was cold light. The silvery light shone through cracks in the people-cloud and turned into dappled shadows in the surrounding city.

According to the ship's AI, of the six million inhabitants of Europe VI, half had already left the city on space vehicles. Of the remaining three million, some had no way to get off the city, but most understood that any attempt at escape was hopeless. Even if some ships miraculously managed to escape the collapsing zone and reached outer space, most ships had no ecological cycling system to maintain life for long. Access to stellar ships that could survive

indefinitely in outer space was still a privilege of the very few. These people chose to wait for the end in a place they were familiar with.

The transmission wasn't muted, but Cheng Xin couldn't hear anything. The people-cloud and the city were both eerily quiet. Everyone looked in one direction. That part of the city looked no different from any other, filled with crisscrossing streets and row upon row of buildings. Everyone waited. In the watery, cold moonlight, people's faces appeared as white as ghosts. The sight reminded Cheng Xin of the bloody dawn in Australia 126 years ago. Like then, Cheng Xin felt as though she were looking down upon an ant colony, and the black people-cloud looked just like a drifting swarm of ants.

Someone in the people-cloud screamed. A glowing dot appeared at a spot on the city's equator, the same spot where everyone had been gazing. It was like a small opening in the roof of a dark house letting in the sunlight.

That was where Europe VI first came into contact with two-dimensional space.

The light grew rapidly and turned into a glowing oval. The light it emitted was sliced into many shafts by the tall buildings all around, and illuminated the people-cloud on the city's axis. The space city now resembled a giant ship whose bottom had been breached, sinking in a flat sea. The plane of the two-dimensional space rose like water, and everything that came into contact with the surface instantaneously turned into two dimensions. Clusters of buildings were cut, and their two-dimensional images spread out on the plane. Since the city's cross section was but a small portion of the entire flattened city, most of the two-dimensionalized buildings had expanded beyond the oval marked by the city's hull. On the rising, expanding plane, gorgeous colors and complicated structures flashed by and zoomed away in every direction, as though the plane was a lens through which one could see colorful beasts running. Because the city still possessed air, they could hear the sound of the three-dimensional world falling into two dimensions: a crisp, piercing series of crunches, as though the buildings and the

city itself were made of exquisitely carved glass and a giant roller was crushing everything.

As the plane continued to rise, the people-cloud began to spread out in the opposite direction, like a curtain being lifted by an invisible hand. The scene reminded Cheng Xin of a massive flock of millions of birds that she had seen once. The flock had seemed like a unified organism changing shape in the dusk sky.

Soon, the plane had swallowed one-third of the city, and it continued to flicker frantically as it rose irresistibly toward the axis. Some people had begun to fall into the plane by now. They either fell behind due to malfunctions in their space suit thrusters or they had given up on running. Like drops of colorful ink, they spread open on the plane in an instant, and each appeared as a unique figure in two dimensions. On one of the zoomed-in images shown by the AI, they saw a pair of lovers leaping into the plane while in an embrace. Even after the two had been flattened, it was possible to see the figures in an embrace lying side by side—their postures appeared odd, as though drawn by a clumsy child who did not understand the principles of perspective. Nearby there was a mother who lifted her baby overhead as she fell into the plane, all so that the baby would survive for an extra tenth of a second. The mother and child were also vividly portrayed in this giant painting. As the plane kept on rising, the rain of people falling on it became denser. Two-dimensional human figures flooded forth on the plane, most moving outside the boundary of the space city.

By the time the two-dimensional space approached the axis, most of the surviving population had landed against the city's far side. Half of the city was now gone, and as people looked "up" they could no longer see the familiar city on the other side, but only a chaotic, two-dimensional sky pressing down on the parts of Europe VI that remained in three dimensions. It was now no longer possible to escape from the main gateway at the north pole, so people congregated around the equator, where there were three emergency exits. The weightless crowd piled into mountains around the exits.

The two-dimensional space passed through the axis and swallowed up the three suns, but the light emitted by the two-dimensionalizing process made the world even brighter.

A low whistling sound began: The city was losing its air to space. The three emergency exits along the equator were wide open, each as large as a football field; outside them was the still-three-dimensional space.

The ship's AI pushed another information window to the front. This was a feed from space looking down at Europe VI. The two-dimensionalized portion of the space city spread across the invisible plane, making the rapidly sinking, still-three-dimensional portion look minuscule by comparison, like the back of a whale peering out of the vast ocean. Three clumps of black smoke rose out of the city and dissipated in space; the "smoke" was formed from the people blown out by the fierce winds of the decompressing space city. The lonely, three-dimensional island continued to sink and melt into the two-dimensional sea. In less than ten minutes, all of Europe VI had turned into a painting.

The painting of Europe VI was so vast that it was hard to estimate its exact area. It was a dead city, but perhaps it was more accurate to call it a 1:1 drawing of the city. The drawing reflected every detail of the city, down to every screw, every fiber, every mite, and even every bacterium. The precision of the drawing was at the level of the individual atom. Every atom in the original three-dimensional space was projected onto its corresponding place in two-dimensional space according to ironclad laws. The basic principles governing this drawing were that there could be no overlap and no hidden parts, and every single detail had to be laid out on the plane. Here, complexity was a substitute for grandeur. The drawing wasn't easy to interpret—it was possible to see the overall plan of the city and recognize some big structures, such as the giant trees, which still looked like trees even in two dimensions. But buildings looked very different after being flattened: it was almost impossible to deduce the original three-dimensional structure from the two-dimensional drawing by imagination alone. However,

it was certain that image-processing software equipped with the right mathematical model would be able to.

In the information window, it was also possible to see two other flattened space cities in the distance. The cities appeared as perfectly flat continents drifting in dark space, gazing at each other across the plane. But the camera—perhaps located on a drone—was also falling toward the plane, and soon the two-dimensional Europe VI filled the screen.

Close to a million people had escaped Europe VI via the emergency exits; now, caught by the three-dimensional space around them collapsing into two dimensions, they fell toward the plane like a swarm of ants caught in a waterfall. A majestic rain of people fell onto the plane, and the two-dimensional human figures in the city multiplied. Flattened persons took up a lot of area—though still minuscule compared to the vast two-dimensional buildings—and resembled tiny, barely man-shaped marks in the immense picture.

More objects appeared in three-dimensional space in the information window: the skiffs and dinghies that had left Europe VI earlier. Their fusion reactors were operating at maximum capacity, but they still fell inexorably toward the plane. For a moment, Cheng Xin thought the blue flame of the fusion drives penetrated that depthless plane, but the plasma had simply been two-dimensionalized. In those areas, the two-dimensional buildings were distorted and twisted by the two-dimensional flames. Next, the skiffs and dinghies became part of the giant drawing. Obeying the no-overlapping principle, the two-dimensionalized city expanded to give these new objects space, and the whole image resembled spreading ripples on the surface of a pond.

The camera continued to fall toward the plane. Cheng Xin stared at the approaching two-dimensional city, hoping to find signs of movement in the city. But no, other than the distortion caused by the plasma flames earlier, everything in the flat city was still. Similarly, the two-dimensional bodies did not move at all, and gave no signs of being alive.

This was a dead world. A dead picture.

The camera moved still closer to the plane, falling toward a two-dimensional body. The body's limbs soon filled the whole image, and then came the complicated patterns of muscle fibers and blood vessels. Perhaps it was just an illusion, but Cheng Xin seemed to see red, two-dimensional blood flowing through two-dimensional blood vessels. In a flash, the picture was gone.

Cheng Xin and AA began their second trip to retrieve more artifacts. They both felt the mission was likely to be meaningless. After observing the two-dimensionalized cities, they understood that the process preserved most of the information from the three-dimensional world. Any information loss would be at the atomic level. Due to the nonoverlapping principle used in projection, the flattened Pluto's crust wouldn't be commingled with the artifacts in the museum, and so the information in the artifacts should be preserved. But since they had accepted this mission, they would finish it. Like Cao Bin said, doing something was better than doing nothing.

They exited *Halo* and saw the two flattened planets still suspended overhead, but now they were much dimmer. This made the new long, glowing belt that appeared below the planets even more noticeable. The light belt went from one end of the sky to the other, like a necklace formed from numerous individual glowing spots.

"Is that the asteroid belt?" Cheng Xin asked.

"Yes. Mars will be next," said AA.

"Mars is on this side of the Sun right now."

The two fell silent. Without looking at the flattened asteroid belt, they walked toward the black monolith.

The Earth was next.

In the great hall of the museum, they saw that Luo Ji had already prepped a bunch of additional artifacts for them. Many of them were Chinese-brush-painting scrolls. AA unrolled one of them: *Along the River During the Qingming Festival*.

Cheng Xin and AA no longer had the initial awe and delight of seeing such precious works of art—compared to the grandeur of the

destruction in process outside, this was nothing more than an old painting. When future explorers arrived at the great painting that was the flattened Solar System, they would have trouble imagining that this twenty-four-centimeter-by-five-meter rectangle was once very special.

Cheng Xin and AA asked Luo Ji to come onto *Halo*. Luo Ji said he would like to see it, and went to look for a space suit.

As the three of them carried the artifacts out of the monolith, the sight of a flattening Earth greeted them.

The Earth was the first solid planet to collapse into two dimensions. Compared to Neptune and Saturn, the "tree rings" in the two-dimensionalized Earth were even more replete with fine details—the yellow mantle gradually shifted over to the deep red nickel-iron core—but the overall area was much smaller than the gas giants.

Unlike in their imagination, they couldn't see any hint of blue.

"What happened to our oceans?" Luo Ji asked.

"They should be near the outside ... But two-dimensionalized water is transparent, so we can't see it," AA said.

The three carried the artifacts to *Halo* in silence. They couldn't feel the grief yet, like one didn't immediately feel the pain of a fresh wound cut by a sharp knife.

But the flattened Earth did show her own wonders. At her outermost rim, a white ring gradually appeared. At first it was barely visible, but soon it stood out sharply against the black backdrop of space. The white ring was pure, flawless, but seemed uneven in its makeup, like it was formed from countless small white grains.

"That's our ocean!" Cheng Xin said.

"The water froze in two-dimensional space," said AA. "It's cold there."

"Oh—" Luo Ji wanted to stroke his beard, but the visor got in the way of his hand.

The three carried the boxes of artifacts onto *Halo*. Luo Ji seemed familiar with the ship's layout, heading for the ship's hold without instruction from Cheng Xin or AA. The ship's AI also recognized him, and accepted his orders. After they secured the artifacts, the

three returned to the yacht's living quarters. Luo Ji asked the AI for a cup of hot tea, and soon, a little robot that Cheng Xin and AA had never seen before brought it to him. Clearly, Luo Ji had some history with this ship that the two women did not know about. They were curious about the story, though more urgent matters had to be taken care of first.

Cheng Xin asked the AI to play some news from the Earth, but the AI said that it had received only a few transmissions from the planet, and the visual and audio content was essentially impossible to make sense of. They looked at the few open information windows and saw only blurred images taken by unmanned cameras. The AI added that it could provide the video taken by the spacecraft monitoring system near the Earth. A new, large window popped up and the flatted Earth filled the screen.

The three immediately thought the image looked unreal, even suspecting that the AI had synthesized the image to fool them.

"What in the world is this?" AA cried out.

"It's the Earth about seven hours ago. The camera is fifty astronomical units away, and angular magnification is four hundred and fifty times."

They looked more closely at the holographic video taken by the telescopic lens. The body of the flattened Earth appeared very clearly, and the "tree rings" were even denser than when observed with the naked eye. The collapse had probably already been completed, and the two-dimensional Earth was dimming. But what really shocked them was the frozen two-dimensional ocean—the white ring around the rim of the Earth. They could clearly make out the grains forming the ring: snowflakes! These were unimaginably large snowflakes, hexagonal in plan, but each with unique crystal branches—exquisite, lovely beyond words. To see snowflakes from fifty AU away was already extremely surreal, and these immense snowflakes were arranged side by side on the plane with no overlap, which further enhanced the feeling of unreality. They seemed to be purely artistic portrayals of snowflakes, powerfully decorative, turning the frozen two-dimensional sea into a piece of stage art.

"How big are the snowflakes?" AA asked.

"Most have diameters between four thousand and five thousand kilometers." The ship's AI, incapable of wonder, continued to speak in a serene tone.

"Bigger than the moon!" Cheng Xin said.

The AI opened a few other windows, and each showed a zoomed-in snowflake. In these images, the sense of scale was lost, and they seemed to be tiny spirits under a magnifying lens, each snowflake ready to turn into a tiny droplet as soon as it touched down on a palm.

"Oh—" Luo Ji stroked his beard again, and this time, succeeded.

"How are they formed?" AA asked.

"I don't know," the AI said. "I can't find any information about the crystallization of water at astronomical scales."

In three-dimensional space, snowflakes formed in accordance with the laws of ice-crystal growth. Theoretically, these laws did not restrict the size of snowflakes. The largest snowflake previously on record was thirty-eight centimeters in diameter.

No one knew the laws of ice crystal growth in two-dimensional space. Whatever they were, they permitted ice crystals in two dimensions to grow to five thousand kilometers.

"There's water on Neptune and Saturn, and ammonia can also form crystals. Why didn't we see large snowflakes there?" Cheng Xin asked.

The AI said it didn't know.

Luo Ji squinted his eyes and enjoyed the two-dimensional version of the Earth. "The ocean looks rather nice this way, don't you think? Only the Earth is worthy of such a lovely wreath."

"I really want to know what the forests look like, what the grasslands look like, what the ancient cities look like," Cheng Xin said slowly.

Grief finally struck them, and AA began to sob. Cheng Xin turned her eyes away from the snowflake ocean and made no sound as her eyes filled with tears. Luo Ji shook his head, sighed, and continued to sip his tea. Their grief was moderated to some extent

by the thought that the two-dimensional space would also be their home in the end.

They would attain their eternal rest alongside Mother Earth on that plane.

The three decided to begin their third cargo trip. They exited *Halo*, gazed up at the sky, and saw the three two-dimensional planets. Neptune, Saturn, and the Earth had grown even larger, and the asteroid belt was wider. This was no hallucination. They asked the AI about it.

"The navigation system has detected a split in the Solar System's navigational frame of reference. Frame of reference one continues as before. The navigational markers within this system—the Sun, Mercury, Mars, Jupiter, Uranus, Pluto, and some asteroids and Kuiper Belt objects—still satisfy the recognition criteria. Frame of reference two, however, has transformed dramatically. Neptune, Saturn, the Earth, and some asteroids have lost their characteristics as navigational markers. Frame of reference one is moving toward frame of reference two, which leads to the phenomenon you've observed."

In the sky in the other direction, many moving points of light appeared before the stars—the fleet of ships seeking to escape the Solar System. Some of the glowing blue lights dragged long tails behind them. Some of the ships swept by the three of them, fairly close. The bright lights of their engines operating at maximum capacity cast moving shadows of the three observers on the ground. None of the ships tried to land on Pluto.

But it was impossible to escape from the collapsing zone. *Halo*'s AI was trying to say this: The three-dimensional space of the Solar System was like a large carpet that was being pulled by invisible hands into a two-dimensional abyss. These ships were nothing more than worms on the carpet inching along—they couldn't extend their already limited allotment of time by much.

"Go ahead by yourselves," Luo Ji said. "Just take a few more

objects. I want to wait here. I don't want to miss it." Cheng Xin and AA understood what he meant by "it," but they had no desire to witness the scene.

After returning to the underground hall, Cheng Xin and AA, not in the mood to pick and choose, randomly gathered a collection of artifacts. Cheng Xin wanted to take along a Neanderthal skull, but AA tossed it aside.

"You'll have plenty of skulls on this picture," AA said.

Cheng Xin acknowledged that she was right. The earliest Neanderthals had lived no more than a few hundred thousand years ago. Optimistically, the flattened Solar System would not have visitors until a few hundred thousand years from now. In their eyes, Neanderthals and modern humans would appear to be the same species. Cheng Xin looked around at the other artifacts, and none excited her. For themselves in the present, and for those unimaginable observers in the far future, nothing here mattered as much as the world that was dying outside.

They took a last look at the dim hall and left with the artifacts. Mona Lisa watched them leave, smiling sinisterly and eerily.

On the surface, they saw that yet another two-dimensional planet had appeared in the sky: Mercury (Venus was on the other side of the Sun at this moment). It looked smaller than the two-dimensional Earth, but the light generated by its recent collapse into two dimensions made it very bright.

After they packed the artifacts in the hold, Cheng Xin and AA came out of *Halo*. Luo Ji, who was waiting outside, leaning on his cane, said, "All right. I think that's enough. It's meaningless to carry more, anyway."

The women agreed. They stood together with Luo Ji on the Plutonian ground and waited for the most magnificent scene of the play: the flattening of the Sun.

At this moment, Pluto was forty-five AU from the Sun. Earlier, since both Pluto and the Sun were in the same region of three-dimensional space, the distance between them hadn't changed. But when the Sun came into contact with the plane, it ceased to move,

while Pluto continued to fall toward it, along with the space around it, causing the distance between them to shrink rapidly.

When the Sun began to two-dimensionalize, the naked eye could only see that its brightness and size appeared to increase suddenly. The latter was due to the rapid expansion of the flattened portion of the Sun on the plane, but from a distance it appeared as though the Sun itself was growing. *Halo*'s AI projected a large information window outside the ship to show a holographic feed from a telescopic lens, but as Pluto pulled closer to the Sun, even the naked eye could see the grand spectacle of a star collapsing into two dimensions.

As soon as the Sun began to two-dimensionalize, a circle expanded on the plane. Soon, the planar Sun's diameter exceeded the diameter of the remaining part of the Sun. This process took only thirty seconds. Based on the mean solar radius of seven hundred thousand kilometers, the rim of the two-dimensional Sun grew at the rate of twenty thousand kilometers per second. The planar Sun continued to grow, forming a sea of fire on the plane, and the three-dimensional Sun sank slowly into this blood-red sea of fire.

Four centuries ago, Ye Wenjie had stood on the peak of Red Coast Base and watched such a sunset during the last moments of her life. Her heart had struggled to beat like a zither string about to break, and a black fog had begun to cloud her eyes. On the western horizon, the Sun that was falling into the sea of clouds seemed to melt, and the Sun's blood seeped into the clouds and the sky, creating a large crimson swath. She had called it humanity's sunset.

And now, the Sun really was melting, its blood seeping into the deadly plane. This was the last sunset.

In the distance, white fog rose from the ground outside the landing field. Pluto's solid nitrogen and ammonia sublimated, and the fresh, thin atmosphere began to scatter the sunlight. The sky no longer appeared pure black, but showed hints of purple.

While the three-dimensional Sun was setting, the two-dimensional Sun was rising. A flat star could still radiate its light inside the plane, so the two-dimensional Solar System received its

first sunlight. The sides of the four two-dimensional planets facing the sun—Neptune, Saturn, the Earth, and Mercury—all took on a golden glow, though the light only fell along a one-dimensional curved edge. The giant snowflakes that surrounded the Earth melted and turned into white vapor, which was blown by two-dimensional solar wind into two-dimensional space. Some of the vapor soaked up the golden sunlight and appeared as if the Earth had hair that drifted with the wind.

An hour later, the Sun had completely collapsed into two dimensions.

From Pluto, the Sun appeared as a giant oval. The two-dimensional planets were tiny fragments compared to it. Unlike the planets, the Sun did not display clear "tree rings" but was separated into three concentric sections around a core. The center was very bright, and no details could be seen—probably corresponding to the core of the original Sun. The wide ring outside the core probably corresponded to the original radiation zone—a boiling, two-dimensional, bright red ocean where countless cell-like structures rapidly formed, split, combined, and disappeared in a manner that seemed chaotic and agitated when viewed locally, but followed grand patterns and order when viewed as a whole. Outside that was the original Sun's convection zone. Like in the original Sun, currents of solar material transferred heat into space. But unlike the chaotic radiation zone, the new convection zone revealed clear structure, as many ring-shaped convection loops, similar in shape and size, arranged themselves side by side in neat order. The outermost layer was the solar atmosphere. Golden currents leapt away from the circular rim and formed a large number of two-dimensional prominences, resembling graceful dancers cavorting wantonly around the Sun. Some of the "dancers" even escaped the Sun and drifted far into the two-dimensional universe.

"Is the Sun still alive in two dimensions?" asked AA. She spoke for the hope of all three. They all wished for the Sun to continue to give light and heat to the planar Solar System, even if there was no more life in it.

But her hope was soon dashed.

The flattened Sun began to dim. The light from the core diminished rapidly and soon it was possible to see fine annular structures within. The radiation zone was also quieting, and the boiling calmed down, turning into a viscous peristalsis. The loops in the convection zone distorted, broke apart, and soon disappeared. The golden dancers around the rim of the Sun wilted like dried leaves and lost their vivaciousness. Now it was possible to tell that at least gravity continued to function in the two-dimensional universe. The dancing solar prominences lost the support of solar radiation and began to be dragged back to the edge of the Sun by its gravity. Finally, the dancers yielded to gravity and fell lethargically, until the Sun's atmosphere was no more than a thin, smooth ring wrapped around the Sun. As the Sun went out, the golden arcs at the edges of the planets also dimmed, and the Earth's two-dimensional hair, formed from the sublimated ocean, lost its golden glow.

Everything in the three-dimensional world died after collapsing into two dimensions. Nothing survived in a painting with no thickness.

Perhaps a two-dimensional universe could possess its own sun, planets, and life, but they would have to be created and operate under completely different principles.

While the three were focused on the flattening Sun, Venus and Mars collapsed into the plane as well. Compared to the Sun, however, the two-dimensionalization of these two terrestrial planets was rather unremarkable. The flattened Mars and Venus were very similar to the Earth in terms of their "tree ring" structure. There were many hollow areas near the rim of Mars, places in the Martian crust that contained water, suggesting that Mars had possessed far more water than people thought. After a while, the water also turned an opaque white, but no giant snowflakes appeared. There were giant snowflakes around the flattened Venus, but they weren't anywhere as numerous as the ones near the Earth, and the Venusian

snowflakes were yellow in hue, indicating that they were not water crystals. A while later, the asteroids on that side of the Sun were also flattened, completing the other half of the Solar System necklace.

Tiny snowflakes—three-dimensional ones—now fell from the light purple Plutonian sky. These were the nitrogen and ammonia that had sublimated in the burst of energy during the Sun's flattening, and which were now freezing into snow as the temperature plummeted following the Sun's extinguishment. The snow fell more heavily, and soon accumulated a thick layer over the monolith and *Halo*. Although there were no clouds, the heavy snow blurred Pluto's sky, and the two-dimensional Sun and the planets turned hazy behind a curtain of snow. The world looked smaller.

"Don't you feel at home?" AA lifted both hands and spun in the snow.

"I was just thinking the same thing," Cheng Xin said, and nodded. She had also thought of snow as something unique to the Earth, and the giant snowflakes around the flattened Earth had confirmed this feeling. The snow falling on this cold, dark world on the edge of the Solar System surprisingly provided her a trace of the warmth of home.

Luo Ji watched as AA and Cheng Xin tried to catch the snow. "Hey, you two! Don't even think about taking off your gloves!"

Cheng Xin did feel an impulse to take off her gloves and catch the snow with her bare hands. She wanted to feel the slight chill, and watch the crystalline snowflakes melt with her own body heat.... but of course she had enough presence of mind to not indulge the impulse. The nitrogen-ammonia snowflakes were at a temperature of minus-210-degrees Celsius. If she really took off her gloves, her hand would turn as fragile and hard as glass and the feeling of being on Earth would disappear instantaneously.

"There's no more home," Luo Ji said, shaking his head and leaning against his cane. "Home is now just a picture."

The nitrogen-ammonia snow didn't last long. The snowflakes thinned out and the purple haze from the nitrogen-ammonia atmosphere faded. The sky was once again perfectly transparent

and dark. They saw that the Sun and the planets had grown even bigger, indicating that Pluto had moved even closer to that two-dimensional abyss.

When the snow stopped, a bright glowing light appeared near the horizon. The intensity of the light grew rapidly, and soon overwhelmed the fading two-dimensional Sun. Although they couldn't see the details, they knew that it was Jupiter, the Solar System's largest planet, falling into the plane. Pluto spun slowly, and part of the flattened Solar System had fallen below the horizon, so they thought they wouldn't get to witness Jupiter's collapse, but it appeared that the rate of fall into two dimensions was accelerating.

They asked *Halo*'s AI to look for transmissions from Jupiter. Very few images and videos were being transmitted now, and most were indecipherable. Almost all of the messages they got were audio only. Every communication channel was filled with noise, mostly human voices, as though all the remaining space in the Solar System had been filled with a frenzied sea of people. The voices cried, screamed, sobbed, laughed hysterically ... and some even sang. The chaotic background noise made it impossible to tell what they were singing, only that it was many voices singing in harmony. The music was solemn, slow, like a hymn. Cheng Xin asked the AI whether it was possible to receive any official broadcasts from the Federation Government. The AI said that all official communications from the government had terminated when the Earth was flattened. The Federation Government couldn't fulfill the promise to carry out its duties until the end of the Solar System after all.

Ships trying to escape continued to stream by the vicinity of Pluto.

"Children, it's time to go," said Luo Ji.

"Let's go together," said Cheng Xin.

"What's the point?" Luo Ji shook his head and smiled. He pointed at the monolith with his cane. "I'm more comfortable over there."

"All right. We'll wait until Uranus is flattened so that we get to spend more time with you," AA said. There really didn't seem

to be any point in insisting. Even if Luo Ji got on *Halo*, it would only delay the inevitable by another hour. He didn't need that bit of time. Indeed, if Cheng Xin and AA didn't have a mission to carry out, they wouldn't care for that bit of time either.

"No. You must go now!" Luo Ji said. He struck the ground with his cane forcefully, which made him float up under the low gravity. "No one knows how much faster the collapse is happening now. Carry out your mission! We can stay in contact, and that's no different from being together."

Cheng Xin hesitated for a moment, then nodded. "All right. We'll leave. Stay in contact!"

"Of course." Luo Ji lifted his cane in farewell and turned to walk toward the monolith. With the light gravity, he almost floated over the snow on the ground and had to use the cane to slow himself. Cheng Xin and AA watched until the aged figure of this Wallfacer, Swordholder, and humanity's final grave keeper disappeared behind the door of the monolith.

Cheng Xin and AA went back inside *Halo*. The yacht took off right away, its thrusters tossing up snow everywhere. Soon, the ship achieved Pluto's escape velocity—just a hair above one kilometer per second—and reached orbit. From the porthole and the monitor they could see that swaths of white now joined the blue and black patches of the Plutonian surface. The giant words "Earth Civilization," written in multiple scripts and languages, had been covered by the snow and were almost illegible. *Halo* passed through the gap between Pluto and Charon as though flying through a canyon, the two celestial bodies were so close.

In this "canyon" there were now many other moving stars— the escaping spaceships. They all moved far faster than *Halo*. One ship swept past *Halo* at a distance of no more than a hundred kilometers, and the glow from its nozzles lit up Charon's smooth surface. They could clearly see its triangular hull and the nearly ten-kilometer-long blue flame shooting out of its nozzles.

The AI explained, "That's *Mycenae,* a midsized planetary ship without an ecological cycling system. After leaving the Solar

System, a passenger would not last five years, even if all the ship's supplies were used to sustain only them."

The AI didn't know that *Mycenae* would not be able to leave the Solar System. Like all the other escaping ships, it would continue to exist for no more than three hours in three-dimensional space.

Halo flew out of the Pluto-Charon canyon and left the two dark worlds for open space. They saw the entirety of the two-dimensionalized Sun and Jupiter, whose flattening process was almost over. Now, except for Uranus, the vast majority of the Solar System had fallen into the plane.

"Oh, heavens! Starry sky!" AA cried out.

Cheng Xin knew that she was referring to Van Gogh's painting. True, the universe really did look like the painting. The painting in her memory was almost a perfect copy of the two-dimensional Solar System before her eyes. Giant planets filled space, the areas of the planets seeming to exceed even the gaps between them. But the immensity of the planets did not give them any sense of substantiality. Rather, they looked like whirlpools in space-time. In the universe, every part of space flowed, churned, trembled between madness and horror like fiery flames that emitted only frost. The Sun and the planets and all substance and existence seemed to be only hallucinations produced by the turbulence of space-time.

Cheng Xin now recalled the strange feeling she had experienced each time she had looked at Van Gogh's painting. Everything else in the painting—the trees that seemed to be on fire, and the village and mountains at night—showed perspective and depth, but the starry sky above had no three-dimensionality at all, like a painting hanging in space.

Because the starry night was two-dimensional.

How could Van Gogh have painted such a thing in 1889? Did he, having suffered a second breakdown, truly leap across five centuries and see the sight before them using only his spirit and delirious consciousness? Or, maybe it was the opposite: He had seen the future, and the sight of this Last Judgment had caused his breakdown and eventual suicide.

"Children, is everything all right? What are you going to do next?" Luo Ji appeared in a pop-up window. He had taken off his space suit, and his white hair and beard floated in the low gravity like in water. Behind him was the tunnel that had been intended to last a hundred million years.

"Hello! We're going to toss the artifacts into space," AA said. "But we want to keep *Starry Night*."

"I think you should hold on to them all. Don't toss any. Take them and leave."

Cheng Xin and AA looked at each other. "Go where?" AA asked.

"Anywhere you like. You can go to any place in the Milky Way. In your lifetimes, you could probably get to the Andromeda Galaxy. *Halo* is capable of lightspeed flight. It is equipped with the world's only curvature propulsion drive."

Utter shock. AA and Cheng Xin couldn't speak.

"I was a part of the group of scientists who worked on curvature propulsion in secret," said Luo Ji. "After Wade died, those who had worked at Halo City didn't give up. After those who had been imprisoned were released, they built another secret research base, and your Halo Group was revived and developed enough to keep it going. Do you know where the base was? Mercury, another place in the Solar System where few set foot. Four centuries ago, another Wallfacer, Manuel Rey Diaz, used giant hydrogen bombs to blast a crater there. The base was built in that crater, and its construction took over thirty years. The whole base was covered with a dome. They claimed that it was a research institute to study solar activity."

A bright shaft of light pierced the porthole. AA and Cheng Xin ignored it, but the ship's AI explained that Uranus had also undergone "state change," meaning that it had also collapsed into two dimensions. By now, nothing stood between them and Pluto.

"Thirty-five years after Wade's death, the research into curvature propulsion picked up at the Mercury base. They continued from the point where they were able to move a two-millimeter segment of your hair two centimeters. The research continued for half a

century—though they were interrupted a few times for various reasons—and they gradually moved from theoretical research to technological development. During the last stages of the development process, they had to perform experiments on large-scale curvature propulsion. This was a problem for the Mercury base because the base's resources were limited, and an experiment would produce massive trails, which would expose the Mercury base's true goals. In reality, based on the comings and goings at the base for more than fifty years, it was inconceivable that the Federation Government had no clue what the Mercury base was really up to, but due to the small scale of the experiments and the fact that all the research was done under cover of other projects, the government had tolerated the base's activities. Large-scale experiments, however, required the government's cooperation. We sought it out, and the collaboration went very well."

"Did they repeal the laws proscribing lightspeed ships?" Cheng Xin asked.

"No, not at all. The government collaborated with us because ..." Luo Ji tapped his cane against the ground and hesitated. "Let's not get into that for now. A few years ago, we completed three curvature engines and conducted three unmanned tests. Engine Number One entered lightspeed about one hundred and fifty astronomical units from the Sun, and returned here after flying at lightspeed for a while. For the engine itself, the experiment lasted only ten minutes or so, but for us, it was three years before the engine returned. The second test involved Engines Number Two and Number Three simultaneously. Right now, both of them are outside the Oort Cloud, and should return to the Solar System in six years.

"Engine Number One, which has already been tested, is installed in *Halo*."

"But how could they have sent Cheng Xin and I alone?" AA shouted. "There should at least be two men with us."

Luo Ji shook his head. "There was no time. The collaboration between the Halo Group and the Federation Government occurred in secret. Very few people knew of the existence of the curvature

635

engines, and even fewer knew where the only engine left in the Solar System was installed. And it was too dangerous. Who knows what people are capable of when the end is nigh? Everyone would fight over *Halo,* and maybe nothing would be left afterward. And so we had to get *Halo* away from the Bunker World before releasing news of the dark forest strike to the public. There really wasn't any time left. Cao Bin sent *Halo* to Pluto because he wanted you to take me with you. He should have just had *Halo* enter lightspeed at Jupiter."

"Why didn't you come with us?" AA shouted.

"I've lived long enough. Even if I get onto the ship, I won't live much longer. I'd rather stay here as a grave keeper."

"We can come back for you!" Cheng Xin said.

"Don't you dare! There's no time!"

The three-dimensional space they were in accelerated toward the two-dimensional plane. The two-dimensional Sun, which had now completely extinguished and appeared as a vast, dark red, dead sea, took up most of the view from *Halo.* Cheng Xin and AA noticed that the plane was not completely flat, but undulating! A long wave slowly rolled across the plane. It was a similar wave in three-dimensional space that had allowed *Blue Space* and *Gravity* to find warp points to enter four-dimensional space. Even in places where there were no two-dimensional objects in the plane, the rippling wave was apparent. The waves were a visualization of two-dimensional space in three dimensions that occurred only when the two-dimensional space was large enough.

On *Halo* itself, the space-time distortion produced by the accelerated fall had started to become apparent as space was stretched in the direction of the fall. Cheng Xin noticed that the circular portholes now appeared as ovals, and the slender AA now looked short and squat. But Cheng Xin and AA felt no discomfort, and the ship's systems were operating normally.

"Return to Pluto!" Cheng Xin ordered the AI. Then she turned to Luo Ji's window. "We're going to come back. There's time— Uranus is still being flattened."

The AI replied stiffly, "Among all authorized users in communication range, Luo Ji has the highest authorization level. Only he can order *Halo* to return to Pluto."

Luo Ji smiled before the tunnel. "If I wanted to go, I would have gotten on the ship with you earlier. I'm too old for voyages far from home. Do not worry about me, children. Like I said, I don't think I've missed anything. Prepare for curvature propulsion!"

Luo Ji's last words were directed at the ship's AI.

"Course parameters?" asked the AI.

"Continue along the current heading. I don't know where you want to go, and I don't think you know, either. If you do think of a destination, just point it out on the star map. The ship is capable of automatic navigation to most stars within fifty thousand light-years."

"Affirmative," said the AI. "Initiating curvature propulsion in thirty seconds."

"Do we need to be immersed in deep-sea fluid?" AA asked—though rationally, she knew that under conventional propulsion, such acceleration would compress her into a pancake no matter what kind of fluid she was immersed in.

"You don't need any kind of preparation. This propulsion method relies on manipulating space, so there's no hypergravity. Curvature propulsion drive online. System is operating within normal parameters. Local space curvature: twenty-three point eight. Forward curvature ratio: three point forty-one to one. *Halo* will enter lightspeed in sixty-four minutes, eighteen seconds."

For Cheng Xin and AA, the AI's announcement was like a Full Stop order, because everything suddenly quieted down. They understood that the silence was due to the nuclear fusion engine being shut off, but the humming produced by the fusion reactor and the thrusters disappeared without being replaced by any other noise. It was hard to believe that some other engine had been started.

But signs of curvature propulsion did appear. The distortion in space gradually disappeared: The portholes returned to being circles, and AA looked slender again. Looking through the

portholes, they could still see other escaping ships passing by *Halo,* but they now passed far more slowly.

The ship's AI began to play some of the messages passing between the escaping ships—perhaps because the messages concerned *Halo.*

"Look at that ship! How is it able to accelerate so fast?" a woman screamed.

"Oh! The people inside must have been crushed into meat pies," a man said.

Another man spoke up. "You idiots. The ship itself would be crushed under that kind of acceleration. But look at it: It's perfectly fine. That's not a fusion drive, but something entirely different."

"Curvature propulsion? A lightspeed ship? That's a lightspeed ship!"

"The rumors were true, then. They were building secret lightspeed ships so that they could escape...."

"Aaahhhhh ..."

"Hey, any ships ahead? Stop that ship! Crash into it. No one should live if we all have to die!"

"They can reach escape velocity! They can run away and live! Ahhhh! I want the lightspeed ship! Stop them; stop them and kill everyone inside!"

Another scream—this one from AA inside the ship. "How can there be two Plutos?"

Cheng Xin turned to the information window AA was looking at. The window showed a view of Pluto taken by the ship's monitoring system. Although Pluto was some distance away, it was clear that both Pluto and Charon had been duplicated, and the twins were lined up side by side. Cheng Xin noticed that some of the flattened objects in the two-dimensional space had also been duplicated. The effect was like selecting a portion of a picture using image-processing software, cloning it, and then moving the clone a bit to the side.

"That's due to the fact that light slows down inside the trail left by *Halo,*" Luo Ji said. His image was growing distorted, but his voice still came through clearly. "Pluto is still moving. One of

the Plutos you are seeing is the result of slow light. Once Pluto has moved outside of *Halo*'s trail, light traveling at standard speed provides you with a second image. That's why you're seeing double."

"The light slows down?" Cheng Xin sensed a great secret was being revealed.

Luo Ji continued, "I understand that you figured out curvature propulsion from a small boat propelled by soap. Let me ask you: After the ship reached the other side of the bathtub, did you pull it back and try again?"

They hadn't. Due to the fear of sophons, Cheng Xin had tossed the paper boat aside. But it was easy to figure out what would have happened.

"The ship would not move, or at least it would only move slowly," Cheng Xin said. "After the first trip, the surface tension of the water in the tub had already been reduced."

"That's right. It's the same principle with lightspeed ships. The very structure of space itself is changed by the trail of a curvature-propelled ship. If a second curvature-propelled ship were placed inside the trail of the first, it would hardly move. Within the trails of lightspeed ships, one must use a more powerful curvature propulsion drive. It would still be possible to use curvature propulsion to achieve the highest speed possible within such a space, but the maximum velocity is much lower than the maximum velocity of the first ship. In other words, the speed of light through vacuum is lowered within the trail of lightspeed ships."

"How much lower?"

"Theoretically, it could be reduced to zero, but that's not achievable in reality. But if you adjust the curvature ratio of *Halo*'s engine to the maximum, you can lower the speed of light in its trail down to exactly what we've been looking for: sixteen point seven kilometers per second."

"Then you'd have ..." AA said, staring at Luo Ji.

The black domain, Cheng Xin thought.

"The black domain," Luo Ji said. "Of course, a single ship is

639

insufficient to produce a black domain containing an entire star and its planetary system. We calculated that it would take more than a thousand curvature propulsion ships to accomplish such a thing. If all these ships started near the Sun and spread out in every direction at lightspeed, the trails they produced would expand and connect to each other, forming a sphere that contained the entire Solar System. The speed of light within this sphere would be sixteen point seven kilometers per second—a reduced-lightspeed black hole, or a black domain."

"So the black domain can be a product of lightspeed ships. . . ."

In the cosmos, the trail of a curvature propulsion drive could be a sign of danger, as well as a safety announcement. A trail far away from a world was the former; a trail that shrouded a world the latter. It was like a noose, indicating danger and aggression when held in the hand, but safety when wrapped around the holder's own neck.

"Correct, but we found out about it too late. While studying curvature propulsion, the experimenters plowed ahead of the theoreticians. You should know that was Wade's style. Many experimental discoveries could not be explained by theory, but without a theoretical framework, some phenomena were simply ignored. During the earliest years of research—when their biggest achievement was moving your hair—the trails produced by curvature propulsion were thin and small, and hardly anyone paid any attention, even though there were plenty of signs of something strange going on: For instance, after the trail expanded, the low speed of light caused quantum integrated circuits in nearby computers to malfunction, but no one sought to investigate. Later, after the experiments grew in scale, people finally discovered the secret of lightspeed trails. It was because of this discovery that the Federation Government agreed to collaborate with us. They did, in fact, pour all the resources they could command into the development of lightspeed spaceships, but there just wasn't enough time." Luo Ji shook his head and sighed.

Cheng Xin said what he couldn't bring himself to say. "There were thirty-five years between the Halo City Incident and the

completion of the Mercury base. Thirty-five precious years were lost."

Luo Ji nodded. Cheng Xin thought the way he looked at her was no longer kind, but rather resembled the fires of the Last Judgment. His gaze seemed to say, *Child, look at what you've done.*

Cheng Xin now understood that of the three paths of survival presented to humanity—the Bunker Project, the Black Domain Plan, and lightspeed ships—only lightspeed ships were the right choice.

Yun Tianming had pointed this out, but she had blocked it.

If she hadn't stopped Wade, Halo City might have achieved independence. Even if the independence was short-lived, they could have discovered the effects of lightspeed trails and changed the government's attitude toward lightspeed ships. Humanity might have had time to construct a thousand lightspeed ships and build the black domain, to avoid this dimensional strike.

Humanity could have divided into two parts: those who wanted to fly to the stars, and those who wanted to stay within the black domain and live in tranquility. Each would have gotten what they wanted.

In the end, she had committed another grave error.

Twice, she had been placed in a position of authority second only to God, and both times she had pushed the world into the abyss in the name of love. This time, no one could fix her mistake for her.

She began to hate someone: Wade. She hated that he had kept his promise. Why? Out of his masculine pride, or for her? Cheng Xin understood that Wade did not know the effects of curvature propulsion trails. His goal in researching lightspeed ships was stated eloquently by that anonymous Halo City soldier: a fight for freedom, for a chance to live as free men in the cosmos, for the billions and billions of new worlds out there. She believed that if he had known that lightspeed spaceflight was the only path to life for humanity, he would not have kept his promise.

She could not shirk her responsibility. It didn't matter whether she really was second only to God—if she was in that position, she had to carry out her duty.

Not long ago on Pluto, Cheng Xin had experienced one of the most relaxed moments of her life. Indeed, it was easy to face the end of the world: All responsibilities were gone, as were all worries and anxieties. Life was as simple and pure as the moment when one first emerged from the mother's womb. Cheng Xin just had to wait in peace for her poetic, artistic end, for her moment to join the giant painting of the Solar System.

But now, everything had been turned upside down. Early cosmology had presented a paradox: If the universe was infinite, then every spot in the universe would feel the cumulative effects of the infinite gravity exerted by an infinity of celestial bodies. Cheng Xin really did feel an infinite gravity now. The power came from every corner of the universe, ruthlessly tearing at her soul. The horror of her last moments as the Swordholder 127 years ago resurfaced as four billion years of history pressed down on her and suffocated her. The sky was full of eyes staring at her: the eyes of dinosaurs, trilobites, ants, birds, butterflies, bacteria ... just the number of men and women who had lived on the Earth possessed a hundred billion pairs of eyes.

Cheng Xin saw AA's eyes, and understood the words in her gaze: *You've finally experienced something worse than death.*

Cheng Xin knew that she had no choice but to live on. She and AA were the last two survivors of human civilization. Her death would mean the death of half of all that was left of humanity. Living on was the appropriate punishment for her mistake.

But the course ahead was a blank. In her heart, space was no longer black, but colorless. What was the point of going anywhere?

"Where should we go?" Cheng Xin muttered.

"Go find them," Luo Ji said. His image was even more blurred and now only black and white.

His words illuminated Cheng Xin's dark thoughts like lightning. She and AA looked at each other and immediately understood who "them" meant.

Luo Ji continued, "They're still alive. The Bunker World received a gravitational wave transmission from them five years ago. It was

a short message, and didn't explain where they were. *Halo* will periodically hail them with gravitational waves. Maybe you'll find them; maybe they'll find you."

Luo Ji's black-and-white image disappeared as well, but they could still hear his voice. He said one last thing, "Ah, it's time for me to go into the picture. Safe travels, children."

The transmission from Pluto was cut off.

On the monitor, they could see Pluto light up and expand in two dimensions. The part of Pluto containing the museum was the first to touch the plane.

The Doppler effect of *Halo*'s speed was now visible. The light from the stars ahead shifted to bluish, while the light from the stars behind shifted to reddish. The color shift was apparent in the two-dimensional Solar System.

Outside, no other fleeing spaceships could be seen; *Halo* had passed them all. All the fleeing spaceships were now falling onto the two-dimensional space like drops of rain against glass.

Very few transmissions could now be received from the direction of the Solar System. Due to the Doppler effect, the brief bursts of voices sounded strange, like singing.

"We're very close! Are you behind us?" ... "Don't do this! No!" ... "There's no pain. I'm telling you, it'll be over in a flash." ... "You still don't believe me, after all this? Fine, don't believe me." ... "Yes, sweetie, we'll become very thin." ... "Come here! We should be together."

Cheng Xin and AA listened. The voices became fewer and fewer, and separated by longer gaps. After thirty minutes, they heard the last voice coming out of the Solar System:

"Ahhhhhhhhh—"

The voice was cut off. The giant painting called the Solar System was complete.

Halo continued to fall toward the plane. The speed it had already achieved was slowing down its fall, but the ship still hadn't achieved escape velocity. By now, *Halo* was the only man-made three-dimensional object in the Solar System, and Cheng Xin and

AA were the only people not in the painting. *Halo* was very close to the plane, and from this angle, looking at the two-dimensional Sun was like looking at the sea from shore: the dim, dark red surface stretched into the distance without bounds. The freshly flattened Pluto was now very large, and still expanded at a rate that was visible to the naked eye. Cheng Xin examined the exquisite "tree rings" of Pluto and tried to find traces of the museum, but she couldn't see anything—it was too small. The giant waterfall that was three-dimensional space tumbling into the flat plane seemed inexorable. Cheng Xin began to doubt whether the curvature propulsion engine really was capable of propelling the ship to lightspeed. She hoped for everything to be over.

But then, the ship's AI spoke.

"*Halo* will enter lightspeed in one hundred and eighty seconds. Please select a destination."

"We don't know where to go," said AA.

"You can select a destination after we've entered lightspeed. However, you won't subjectively be spending much time in lightspeed, and it's easy to overshoot your destination. It's best if you select it now."

"We don't know where to find them," Cheng Xin said. Their existence gave the future some light, but she still felt lost.

AA clutched Cheng Xin's hands. "Have you forgotten? Other than them, *he* also exists in the universe."

Yes, he still exists. Cheng Xin was overwhelmed by heartache. She had never yearned to see anyone as much as him.

"You have a date," AA said.

"Yes, we have a date," Cheng Xin repeated mechanically. The torrents of emotion left her numb.

"Then let's go to your star."

"Yes, let's go to our star!" Cheng Xin turned to the ship's AI. "Can you find DX3906? That was the assigned number back at the beginning of the Crisis Era."

"Yes. The star is now numbered S74390E2. Please confirm."

A large holographic star map appeared before them. It showed

everything within five hundred light-years of the Solar System. One of the stars glowed bright red, and a white arrow pointed at it. Cheng Xin was very familiar with it.

"That's the one. Let's go there."

"Course set and confirmed. *Halo* will enter lightspeed in fifty seconds."

The holographic star map disappeared. In fact, the ship's entire hull disappeared, and Cheng Xin and AA seemed to be floating in space itself. The AI had never employed this display mode before. In front of them was the starry sea that was the Milky Way, which was now pure blue, reminding them of the real sea. Behind them was the two-dimensional Solar System, suffused with a bloody red.

The universe shuddered and transformed. All the stars in front of them shot straight ahead, as though that half of the universe had transformed into a black bowl and all the stars were falling into the bottom. They clustered ahead of the ship and fused into a single glow, like a giant sapphire in which it was not possible to distinguish individual stars. From time to time, individual stars shot out of the sapphire and swept past the pure black space to fall behind the ship, changing color the whole way: from blue to green, then yellow, and turning red once they were behind the ship. Looking back from the ship, the two-dimensional Solar System and the stars fused into a red ball like a campfire at the end of the universe.

Halo flew at the speed of light toward the star that Yun Tianming had given Cheng Xin.

PART VI

GALAXY ERA, YEAR 409
OUR STAR

Halo shut off the curvature engine and coasted at lightspeed.

During the voyage, AA tried to comfort Cheng Xin, even though she knew this was a hopeless task.

"It's ridiculous for you to blame yourself for the destruction of the Solar System. Who do you think you are? Do you think if you stand on your hands, you've lifted the Earth? Even if you hadn't stopped Wade, the outcome of that war would have been hard to predict.

"Could Halo City really have achieved independence? Even Wade couldn't be certain of that. Could the Federation Government and Fleet really have been scared of a few antimatter bullets? Maybe Halo City could have destroyed a few warships, or even a space city, but ultimately, Halo City would have been exterminated by the Federation Fleet. And in that version of history, there would be no Mercury base, no second chance.

"Even if Halo City had managed to achieve independence, continued to research curvature propulsion, discovered the slowing effects of the trails, and finally collaborated with the Federation Government to build more than a thousand lightspeed ships in time, do you think people would have agreed to build the black domain? Remember how confident people were that the Bunker World would survive a dark forest strike—why would they have agreed to isolate themselves in the black domain?"

AA's words slid across Cheng Xin's thoughts like drops of water across a lily pad, leaving no trace. Cheng Xin's only thought was to find Yun Tianming and tell him everything. In her mind, a journey of 287 light-years would take a long time, but the ship's AI informed her that the trip would only take fifty-two hours in the ship's frame of reference. Everything felt unreal to Cheng Xin, as though she had already died and gone to another world.

Cheng Xin spent a long time gazing out of the portholes at space. She understood that each time a star leapt out of the blue cluster in front, swept past the ship, and joined the red cluster behind the ship, it meant that *Halo* had passed it. She counted the stars and watched as they turned from blue to red—the sight was hypnotic. Eventually, she fell asleep.

By the time Cheng Xin awakened, *Halo* was close to its destination. It turned 180 degrees and activated the curvature engine for deceleration—in fact, the ship was pushing against its own trail. As the ship decelerated, the blue and red clusters began to spread out like two clusters of exploding fireworks, and soon evolved into a sea of stars distributed evenly around the ship. The slowing down of the ship also gradually erased the red and blue shifts. Cheng Xin and AA saw that the Milky Way ahead of them still looked about the same, but behind them, none of the stars looked familiar. The Solar System was long gone.

"We're now two hundred eighty-six point five light-years from the Solar System," said the ship's AI.

"So two hundred eighty-six years has already passed back there?" AA asked. She looked as if she had just awakened from a dream.

"Yes, if you are using their frame of reference."

Cheng Xin sighed. For the Solar System in its current condition, was there a difference between 286 years and 2.86 million years? But she thought of something.

"When did the collapse into two dimensions stop?"

The question made AA speechless, as well. Right: When—if ever— did it stop? Was there an instruction within that small, packaged two-dimensional foil that would eventually stop it? Cheng Xin and

AA had no theoretical understanding of how three-dimensional space collapsed into two dimensions, but they instinctively thought the idea of an instruction embedded into two-dimensional space to halt its infinite expansion was too magical, the kind of magic that seemed impossible.

Would the collapse never stop?

It was best to not think about it too much.

The star called DX3906 was about the Sun's size. As *Halo* began decelerating, it still looked like an ordinary star, but by the time the curvature engine shut off, the star appeared as a disk whose light seemed redder than the Sun's.

Halo engaged the fusion reactor, and the silence on the ship was broken. The humming of the engine filled the ship, and every surface vibrated slightly. The ship's AI analyzed the data obtained by the monitoring system and confirmed the basic facts about this solar system: DX3906 had two planets, both of them solid. The one farther from the star was about the size of Mars, but it had no atmosphere and appeared gray in color—so Cheng Xin and AA decided to call it Planet Gray. The other planet, closer to the star, was about the size of the Earth, and its surface resembled the Earth's: an atmosphere containing oxygen and many signs of life, but without evidence of agriculture or industry. Since it was blue, like the Earth, they decided to call it Planet Blue.

AA was very happy that her research had been confirmed. More than four hundred years ago, she had discovered the star's planetary system. Before then, people had thought it was a bare star without any planets. Through that work, AA had gotten to know Cheng Xin. Without that coincidence, her life would have turned out completely differently. Fate was such an odd thing: Four centuries ago, when she had gazed at this distant world through the telescope, she could never have imagined that she'd come here one day.

"Were you able to see these two planets back then?" Cheng Xin asked.

"No. They were impossible to see in the visible light range. Maybe those telescopes from the Solar System advance warning

system could have seen them, but all I could do was deduce their existence through the data obtained via the solar gravitational lens.... I did theorize about the appearance of these two planets, and it looks like I was basically right."

Halo had taken only fifty-two hours (by the ship's frame of reference) to traverse the 286 light-years between the Solar System and the planetary system around DX3906, but it took eight full days to cross the sixty AU between the rim of the planetary system and Planet Blue at sub-light speeds. As *Halo* approached Planet Blue, Cheng Xin and AA discovered that its resemblance to the Earth was only superficial. The blue hue of this planet wasn't the result of an ocean, but the color of the vegetation covering the continents. Planet Blue's oceans were light yellow and took up only about a fifth of the planet's surface. Planet Blue was a cold world; about a third of its continental surface was covered by blue vegetation, with the rest shrouded in snow. Most of the ocean was frozen, and only small patches near the equator were in liquid form.

Halo entered orbit around Planet Blue and began its descent. But the ship's AI announced a new discovery. "An intelligent radio signal has been detected from the surface. It's a landing beacon using communication formats dating from the start of the Crisis Era. Would you like me to follow its instructions?"

Cheng Xin and AA looked at each other excitedly. "Yes!" Cheng Xin said. "Follow its instructions to land."

"Hypergravity will approach 4G. Please enter into secured landing positions. Landing sequence will be initiated once you're secure."

"Do you think it's him?" AA asked.

Cheng Xin shook her head. In her life, moments of happiness were only gaps between mass catastrophes. She was now afraid of happiness.

Cheng Xin and AA sat in hypergravity seats, and the seats closed around them like giant palms squeezing them tight. *Halo* decelerated and descended, entering Planet Blue's atmosphere after a series of powerful jolts. They could see the blue-and-white

continents swinging into view in the images captured by the ship's monitoring system.

Twenty minutes later, *Halo* landed near the equator. The ship's AI suggested that Cheng Xin and AA wait ten minutes before getting out of their seats, to give their bodies a chance to adjust to Planet Blue's gravity, which was similar to the Earth's. Out of the porthole and on the monitoring system terminals, they could see that the yacht had landed in the middle of a blue grassland. Not too far away, they could see rolling mountains covered by snow—the landing site was near the foot of the mountain range. The sky was a light yellow, like the ocean when viewed from space. A light red sun shone in the sky. It was noon on Planet Blue, but the sky and the sun's colors made it resemble dusk on the Earth.

Cheng Xin and AA didn't examine the environment around them too carefully. Their attention was taken up by another small vehicle parked near *Halo*. It was a tiny craft, about four to five meters tall, with a dark gray surface. The profile was streamlined, but the tail fins were tiny. It didn't seem to be an aircraft, but rather a ground-to-space shuttle.

A man stood next to the shuttle, dressed in a white jacket and dark-colored pants. The turbulence of *Halo*'s landing disturbed his hair.

"Is that him?" AA asked.

Cheng Xin shook her head. She knew right away that this wasn't Yun Tianming.

The man waded through the blue sea of grass toward *Halo*. He moved slowly, and his posture and movements showed some exhaustion. He didn't show any signs of surprise or excitement, as if the appearance of *Halo* was a perfectly normal occurrence. He stopped a few tens of meters away from the yacht and waited patiently in the grass.

"He's good-looking," said AA.

The man looked to be in his forties. He was East Asian in appearance, and he was indeed more handsome than Yun Tianming, with a broad forehead and wise but gentle eyes. His gaze made you believe he was always thinking, as if nothing in the universe,

653

including *Halo,* could surprise him, but only cause him to think more. He lifted his hands and moved them around his head, indicating a helmet. Then he shook his head and waved one hand, indicating that they didn't need space suits out there.

The ship's AI agreed. "Atmospheric composition: thirty-five percent oxygen, sixty-three percent nitrogen, two percent carbon dioxide, with trace amounts of inert gasses. Breathable. But the atmospheric pressure is only point five three of Earth standard. Do not engage in strenuous exercise."

"What is that biological entity standing next to the ship?" asked AA.

"Standard human being," the AI replied.

Cheng Xin and AA exited the ship. They hadn't adjusted to the gravity yet, and stumbled a bit as they walked. Outside, they breathed easily, not feeling the thinness of the air. A chill breeze blew at them and brought the fragrance of grass, refreshing them. The wide-open view showed the blue-and-white mountains and earth, the light yellow sky and red sun. The whole thing resembled a false-color photograph of the Earth. Other than the strange colors, everything looked familiar. Even the blades of grass looked just like the grass on the Earth, except for their blue hue. The man came to the foot of the stairs.

"Wait a minute. The stairs are too steep. I'll help you down." He climbed up the stairs easily and helped Cheng Xin down. "You should have rested longer before coming out. There's no urgency." Cheng Xin could hear an obvious Deterrence Era accent.

His hand felt warm and strong to Cheng Xin, and his broad body shielded her from the chill wind. She had the impulse to jump into this man's arms, the first man she had met after traveling more than two hundred light-years from the Solar System.

"Did you come from the Solar System?" the man asked.

"Yes." She leaned against the man and descended the stairs. She felt her trust for him grow, and put more of her weight on him.

"There's no more Solar System," AA said as she sat down at the top of the stairs.

"I know. Did anyone else escape?"

Cheng Xin was now on the ground. She sank her feet into the soft grass and sat down on the bottom step. "Probably not."

"Oh ..." The man nodded and climbed up again to help AA. "My name is Guan Yifan. I've been waiting for you here."

"How did you know we would come?" AA asked, allowing Yifan to hold her hand.

"We received your gravitational wave transmission."

"You're from *Blue Space*?"

"Ha! If you'd asked those who had just left that question, they'd think you very strange. *Blue Space* and *Gravity* are ancient history from more than four centuries ago. But I really am an ancient. I was a civilian astronomer aboard *Gravity*. I've been hibernating for four centuries, and only awakened five years ago."

"Where are *Blue Space* and *Gravity* now?" Cheng Xin struggled to stand, pulling herself up by the railing of the stairs. Yifan continued down with AA.

"In museums."

"Where are the museums?" AA asked. She put her arm around Yifan's shoulder so that Yifan was practically carrying her down.

"On World I and World IV."

"How many worlds are there?"

"Four. And two more are being opened up for settlement."

"Where are all these worlds?"

Guan Yifan gently deposited AA on the ground and laughed. "A word of advice: In the future, no matter who you meet—human or otherwise—don't ask for the location of their worlds. That's a basic bit of manners in the cosmos—like how it's impolite to ask a lady's age.... Nonetheless, let me ask you, how old are you now?"

"We're as old as we look," AA said, and sat down on the grass. "She's seven hundred and I'm five hundred."

"Dr. Cheng looks about the same as she did four centuries ago."

"You know her?" AA looked up at Guan Yifan.

"I had seen pictures in transmissions from Earth. Four centuries ago."

"How many people are on this planet?" Cheng Xin asked.

"Just the three of us."

"That must mean that your worlds are all better than this one," AA said.

"You mean the natural environment? Not at all. In some places, the air is barely breathable, even after a century of terraforming. This is one of the best planets we've seen for settlement. Although we welcome you here, Dr. Cheng Xin, we do not recognize your claim of title."

"I'd given that up a long time ago," Cheng Xin said. "So why haven't people settled here?"

"It's too dangerous. Outsiders come here often."

"Outsiders? Extraterrestrials?" AA asked.

"Yes. This is close to the center of the Orion Arm. Two busy shipping lanes flow through here."

"Then what are you doing here? Just waiting for us?"

"No. I came with an exploratory expedition. They've already left, but I stayed to wait for you."

About a dozen hours later, the three welcomed night on Planet Blue. There was no moon, but compared to the Earth, the stars here were far brighter. The Milky Way was like a sea of silver fire that cast their shadows on the ground. This place wasn't much closer to the center of the galaxy than the Solar System. However, the space between here and the Sun was filled with interstellar dust, making the Milky Way appear much dimmer from the Solar System.

In the bright starlight, they could see the grass around them moving. At first, Cheng Xin and AA thought it was an illusion produced by the wind, but then they realized that the grass underfoot was writhing as well, and making a rustling noise. Yifan told them that the blue grass really did move. The roots of the grass were also feet, and as the seasons changed, the grass migrated across the latitudes, mainly at night. As soon as AA heard that, she tossed away the stalks of grass she was playing with in her hands. Yifan explained that

the blades of grass really were plants, and relied on photosynthesis, possessing only a basic sense of touch. The other plants in this world were also capable of moving. He pointed to the mountains and they saw the forests moving in the starlight. The trees moved far faster than the grass, and resembled armies marching at night.

Yifan pointed at a spot in the sky where the stars were slightly less dense. "A few days ago we could see the Sun in that direction, much more clearly than you could see this star from the Earth. Of course, what we saw was the Sun of two hundred eighty-seven years ago. The Sun went out on the day the expedition left me here."

"The Sun is no longer emitting light, but its area is huge. Perhaps you can still see it through telescopes," AA said.

"No, you won't be able to see anything." Yifan shook his head and pointed at that patch of sky again. "Even if you go back there now, you wouldn't be able to see anything. That part of space is empty. The two-dimensional Sun and planets you saw were actually just the result of the release of energy when three-dimensional material collapsed into two dimensions. What you saw wasn't two-dimensional material, only the refraction of electromagnetic radiation at the interface between two-dimensional and three-dimensional space. After the energy was released, nothing would be visible. The two-dimensional Solar Space has no contact with three-dimensional space."

"How can that be?" Cheng Xin asked. "It's possible to see the three-dimensional world from four-dimensional space."

"True. I personally got to see three-dimensional space from four-dimensional space, but it's not possible to see the two-dimensional world from three dimensions. This is because three-dimensional space has thickness, meaning that there is a dimension that could stop and scatter the light from four-dimensional space, making it visible from four dimensions. But two-dimensional space has no thickness, so light from three-dimensional space passes through it without hindrance. The two-dimensional world is completely transparent and cannot be seen."

"There's no way at all?" AA asked.

"No. In theory, nothing allows it."

Cheng Xin and AA were silent for a while. The Solar System had disappeared completely. The only hope they had held out for the mother world was gone. But Guan Yifan did bring them a bit of comfort.

"There's only one way to detect the presence of the two-dimensional Solar System from three-dimensional space: gravity. The gravity of the Solar System still has an effect, so, in that empty space ought to be detectable as an invisible source of gravity."

Cheng Xin and AA looked at each other thoughtfully.

"Sounds like dark matter, doesn't it?" Yifan laughed. Then he changed the subject. "Why don't we talk about the date you came for?"

"You know Yun Tianming?" AA asked.

"No."

"What about the Trisolaran Fleet?" Cheng Xin asked.

"We don't know much. The First and Second Trisolaran Fleets never joined together. More than sixty years ago, there was a large-scale space battle near Taurus. It was brutal, and the resulting wreckage formed a new interstellar dust cloud. We know that one of the sides in the battle was the Second Trisolaran Fleet, but we don't know who they were fighting against. We also don't know how the battle ended."

"What happened to the First Trisolaran Fleet?" Cheng Xin asked. Her eyes flickered in the starlight.

"We haven't received any information about them.... In any event, you shouldn't stay here too long. This is not a safe place. Why don't you come with me to our world? The terraforming there is over, and life is getting better."

"I agree!" AA said. Then she held Cheng Xin by the arm. "Let's go with him. Even if you wait here for the rest of your life, you most likely won't hear anything. Life shouldn't be a lifetime of waiting."

Cheng Xin nodded silently. She knew that she was chasing a dream.

———

They decided to wait one more day on Planet Blue before departing.

Guan Yifan had a small spaceship waiting in synchronous orbit. The ship was tiny and didn't have a name, only a number. But Yifan called it *Hunter,* and explained that the name was to honor the memory of a friend who'd lived on *Gravity* more than four hundred years ago. *Hunter* was not equipped with an ecological cycling system, and for long voyages passengers had to enter hibernation. Although *Hunter* was only a few percent of *Halo*'s volume, it was also a lightspeed ship equipped with a curvature engine. They decided to have Yifan ride on *Halo* as well and control *Hunter* as a drone. Cheng Xin and AA didn't ask about the course they would take, and Yifan even refused to answer questions about the duration of the anticipated voyage. He was extremely cautious when it came to information about the location of human worlds.

For the day, the three took short hikes in the vicinity of *Halo*. This was a day of many firsts for Cheng Xin, AA, and all the Solar System humans who had disappeared along with the home world: the first trip to an extrasolar planetary system; the first steps on the surface of an exoplanet; the first voyage to a world with life outside the Solar System.

Compared with the Earth, the ecology of Planet Blue was relatively simple. Other than the mobile blue vegetation, there was not much life to be found, except for a few species of fish in the ocean. There were no complex animals on land, only simple insects. The world resembled a simplified Earth. It was possible for Earth plants to survive here, so humans could live here even without advanced technology.

Guan Yifan was filled with admiration for *Halo*'s design. He said that for Galactic humans, people who had made their home in the Milky Way, there was one quality about Solar System humans that they did not inherit and could not learn: enjoyment of life. He spent much time in the lovely courtyards, and indulged himself with holographic projections of grand sights from ancient Earth. He still looked as thoughtful as ever, but his eyes were moist.

During this time, 艾 AA cast Yifan frequent amorous glances.

The relationship between them gradually changed as the day went on. AA thought up all kinds of excuses to be close to Yifan, and listened intently while he spoke, nodding from time to time and smiling. She had never behaved like this in front of any other man. During the centuries Cheng Xin had known her, AA had countless lovers, often dating two or more at the same time, but Cheng Xin knew that AA had never really been in love. However, she was clearly smitten with this cosmologist from the Deterrence Era. Cheng Xin was happy to see this. AA deserved a happy new life in this new world.

As for Cheng Xin, she knew that she was spiritually dead. The only hope that had sustained her was finding Tianming, and now this hope seemed like an impossible dream. Truthfully, she had always known that a date made for four centuries later and 286 light-years away was an impossible dream. She would continue to keep her body alive, but it was just a matter of fulfilling her duty of preventing the death of half of the population to survive the destruction of Earth civilization.

Night fell again. They decided to sleep aboard *Halo* and leave in the morning.

At midnight, Guan Yifan was awakened by his wrist communicator. It was a call from *Hunter* in synchronous orbit. *Hunter* passed on the information gathered by the three small monitoring satellites left by the expedition—two of which orbited around Planet Blue and the last around Planet Gray. The alert had come from the one around Planet Gray.

Thirty-five minutes ago, five unidentified spacecraft had landed on Planet Gray. Twelve minutes later, the spacecraft had lifted off and disappeared without even entering planetary orbit. There was strong interference with the satellite, and the images it transmitted were blurry.

Yifan's expedition was responsible for seeking out and studying traces left in this planetary system by other civilizations. After receiving the alert from the satellite, he immediately decided to take the shuttle up to *Hunter* to investigate. Cheng Xin insisted

on coming with him. Yifan initially refused, but agreed after AA spoke to him.

"Let her come with you. She wants to know whether this has anything to do with Yun Tianming."

Before departure, Yifan reminded AA to not communicate with *Hunter* unless it was an emergency. No one knew what other extraterrestrial monitoring equipment might be lurking in this system, and any communication could expose them to danger.

In this lonely world of only three people, even a brief separation was an occasion for anxiety. AA hugged Cheng Xin and Guan Yifan and wished them a safe journey. Before stepping onto the shuttle, Cheng Xin looked back and saw AA waving at them, lit by the watery starlight. Blue grass surged around her, and the cold wind lifted her short hair and made ripples in the grass.

The shuttle took off. In the view from the monitoring system, Cheng Xin saw the grass lit up by the flame from the thruster, and the blue grass scattering in every direction. As the shuttle rose up, the bright patch on the ground quickly dimmed, and soon, the ground sank back into starlight.

An hour later, the shuttle docked with *Hunter* in synchronous orbit. *Hunter* was tetrahedral in shape, like a tiny pyramid. The inside was very cramped and bare, and most of the space was taken up by the hibernation chamber, which had a maximum capacity for four.

Like *Halo*, *Hunter* was equipped with both a curvature engine and a fusion engine. When traveling between planets within the same system, only the fusion engine was used, because the curvature engine would have caused the ship to overshoot the target with no time for deceleration. *Hunter* left orbit and headed for Planet Gray, which appeared as a small spot of light. Out of consideration for Cheng Xin, Guan Yifan initially limited the acceleration to 1.5G, but Cheng Xin told him not to worry about her and just make the trip faster. He increased the acceleration, the blue flame emitted by the nozzles doubled in length, and the hypergravity increased to 3G. At this point, all they could do was to sit in the embrace of

the acceleration seats. They were not able to move much, so Yifan switched the ship to surround-holographic display mode, and the ship's hull disappeared. Suspended in space, they watched Planet Blue recede. Cheng Xin imagined the 3G gravity as coming from Planet Blue so that space separated into up and down, and they were flying up toward the galaxy.

It was possible to speak under 3G without too much trouble, so they began to converse. Cheng Xin asked Yifan why he had hibernated for so long. He told her that he had no duties during the long voyage searching for habitable worlds. After the two ships discovered the habitable World I, much of life consisted of opening up the world for settlement and constructing the basics. The first settlement resembled a small town from agrarian times, and the rough conditions did not permit any kind of scientific research. The new world's government passed a resolution to let all scientists enter or remain in hibernation, to be awakened only when conditions permitted basic research. He was the only basic scientist aboard *Gravity*, although *Blue Space* had seven more. He was the last to be awakened of all the hibernators. Two centuries had passed since the day the two ships arrived at World I.

Cheng Xin was mesmerized by Yifan's account of the new human worlds. But she noticed that while he discussed Worlds I, II, and IV, nothing was said about III.

"I've never been there. No one else has, either. Well, it's more accurate to say that anyone who goes there cannot return. That world is sealed inside a light tomb."

"A light tomb?"

"It's a reduced-lightspeed black hole produced by the trails of lightspeed ships. Something happened on World III that caused them to think that their coordinates had been exposed. They had no choice but to turn their world into such a black hole."

"We call such a place a black domain."

"Ah, good name. As a matter of fact, the people of World III initially called it a light curtain, but outsiders referred to it as a light tomb."

"Like a shroud?"[10]

"That's right. Different people see things differently. The inhabitants of World III said it was a happy paradise—though I don't know if they still think that way. After the light tomb was completed, it was impossible for any message from that world to reach the outside. But I think people there are pretty happy. For some people, safety is the sine qua non for happiness."

Cheng Xin asked Yifan when the new world first produced lightspeed ships, and was told it was a century ago. Judging by this, her interpretation of Tianming's secret message had allowed Solar System humans to achieve this stage about two centuries ahead of Galactic humans. Even taking into account the time it took to open up the worlds for settlement, Tianming had accelerated progress by at least a century.

"He's a great man," Yifan said after hearing Cheng Xin's account.

But the civilization of the Solar System hadn't been able to seize this opportunity. Thirty-five precious years had been lost, probably due to her. Her heart no longer felt pain as she thought of this; all she felt was the numbness that indicated a dead heart.

Yifan said, "Lightspeed spaceflight was a tremendous milestone for humankind. It was like another Enlightenment, another Renaissance. Lightspeed flight fundamentally transformed human thinking and changed civilization and culture."

"I can see that. The moment I entered lightspeed, I felt myself change. I realized that I could, in my lifetime, leap across spacetime and reach the edge of the cosmos and the end of the universe. Things that used to seem only philosophical suddenly became concrete and practical."

"Yes. Things like the fate and goal of the universe used to be only ethereal concerns of philosophers, but now every ordinary person must consider them."

10 *Translator's Note:* This is a wordplay in Chinese. 幕 (*mu*), or "curtain," is a pun for 墓 (*mu*), or "tomb."

"Has anyone in the new world thought of going to the end of the universe?"

"Of course. Five ultimate spaceships have already been launched."

"Ultimate spaceships?"

"Some call them doomsday ships. These lightspeed ships have no destination at all. They turn their curvature engines to maximum and accelerate like crazy, infinitely approaching the speed of light. Their goal is to leap across time using relativity until they reach the heat death of the universe. By their calculations, ten years within their frame of reference would equal fifty billion years in ours. As a matter of fact, you don't even need to plan for it. If some malfunction occurs after a ship has accelerated to lightspeed, preventing the ship from decelerating, then you'd also reach the end of the universe within your lifetime."

"I pity Solar System humans," said Cheng Xin. "Even at the very end, most of them lived lives confined to a tiny portion of space-time, like those old men and women who never left their home villages during the Common Era. The universe remained a mystery to them until the end."

Yifan lifted his head to gaze at Cheng Xin. Under 3G, this was a very strenuous exercise. But he persisted for some time.

"You don't need to pity them. Really, let me tell you: don't. The reality of the universe is not something to envy."

"Why?"

Yifan lifted a hand and pointed at the stars of the galaxy. Then he let the 3G force pull his arm back to this chest.

"Darkness. Only darkness."

"You mean the dark forest state?"

Guan Yifan shook his head, a gesture that appeared to be a struggle in hypergravity. "For us, the dark forest state is all-important, but it's just a detail of the cosmos. If you think of the cosmos as a great battlefield, dark forest strikes are nothing more than snipers shooting at the careless—messengers, mess men, etc. In the grand scheme of the battle, they are nothing. You have not seen what a true interstellar war is like."

"Have you?"

"We've caught a few glimpses. But most things we know are just guesses.... Do you really want to know? The more you possess of this kind of knowledge, the less light remains in your heart."

"My heart is already completely dark. I want to know."

And so, more than six centuries after Luo Ji had fallen through ice into that lake, another dark veil hiding the truth about the universe was lifted before the gaze of one of the only survivors of Earth civilization.

Yifan asked, "Why don't you tell me what the most powerful weapon for a civilization possessing almost infinite technological prowess is? Don't think of this as a technical question. Think philosophy."

Cheng Xin pondered for a while and then struggled to shake her head. "I don't know."

"Your experiences should give you a hint."

What had she experienced? She had seen how a cruel attacker could lower the dimensions of space by one and destroy a solar system. *What are dimensions?*

"The universal laws of physics," Cheng Xin said.

"That's right. The universal laws of physics are the most terrifying weapons, and also the most effective defenses. Whether it's by the Milky Way or the Andromeda Galaxy, at the scale of the local galactic group or the Virgo Supercluster, those warring civilizations possessing godlike technology will not hesitate to use the universal laws of physics as weapons. There are many laws that can be manipulated into weapons, but most commonly, the focus is on spatial dimensions and the speed of light. Typically, lowering spatial dimensions is a technique for attack, and lowering the speed of light is a technique for defense. Thus, the dimensional strike on the Solar System was an advanced attack method. A dimensional strike is a sign of respect. In this universe, respect is not easy to earn. I guess you could consider it an honor for Earth civilization."

"I thought of something I wanted to ask you. When will the

collapse of space in the vicinity of the Solar System into two dimensions cease?"

"It will never cease."

Cheng Xin shuddered.

"You are scared? Do you think that in this galaxy, in this universe, only the Solar System is collapsing into two dimensions? Haha ..."

Guan Yifan's bitter laughter caused Cheng Xin's heart to seize up. She said, "What you're saying makes no sense. At least, it doesn't make sense to lower spatial dimensions as a weapon. In the long run, that's the sort of attack that would kill the attacker as well as the target. Eventually, the side that initiated attack would also see their own space fall into the two-dimensional abyss they created."

Nothing but silence. After a long while, Cheng Xin called out, "Dr. Guan?"

"You're too ... kind-hearted," Guan Yifan said softly.

"I don't understand—"

"There's a way for the attacker to avoid death. Think about it."

Cheng Xin pondered and then said, "I can't figure it out."

"I know you can't. Because you're too kind. It's very simple. The attacker must first transform themselves into life forms that can survive in a low-dimensional universe. For instance, a four-dimensional species can transform itself into three-dimensional creatures, or a three-dimensional species can transform itself into two-dimensional life. After the entire civilization has entered a lower dimension, they can initiate a dimensional strike against the enemy without concern for the consequences."

Cheng Xin was silent again.

"Are you reminded of anything?" Yifan asked.

Cheng Xin was thinking of more than four hundred years ago, when *Blue Space* and *Gravity* had stumbled into the four-dimensional fragment. Yifan had been a member of the small expedition that conversed with the Ring.

Did you build this four-dimensional fragment?

You told me that you came from the sea. Did you build the sea?

Are you saying that for you, or at least for your creators, this four-dimensional space is like the sea for us?

More like a puddle. The sea has gone dry.

Why are so many ships, or tombs, gathered in such a small space?

When the sea is drying, the fish have to gather into a puddle. The puddle is also drying, and all the fish are going to disappear.

Are all the fish here?

The fish responsible for drying the sea are not here.

We're sorry. What you said is really hard to understand.

The fish that dried out the sea went onto land before they did this. They moved from one dark forest to another dark forest.

"Is it worth it to pay such a price for victory in war?" Cheng Xin asked. She could not imagine how it was possible to live in a world of one fewer dimension. In two-dimensional space, the visible world consisted of a few line segments of different lengths. Could anyone who was born in three-dimensional space willingly live in a thin sheet of paper with no thickness? Living in three dimensions must be equally confining and unimaginable for those born to a four-dimensional world.

"It's better than death," said Yifan.

While Cheng Xin was still recovering from the shock, Yifan continued, "The speed of light is also frequently used as a weapon. I'm not talking about building light tombs—or, as you call them, black domains. Those are just defensive mechanisms employed by weak worms like us. The gods do not stoop so low. In war, it's possible to make reduced-lightspeed black holes to seal the enemy inside. But more commonly, the technique is used to construct the equivalents of pits and city walls. Some reduced-lightspeed belts

are large enough to traverse an entire arm of a galaxy. In places where the stars are dense, many reduced-lightspeed black holes can be connected together into chains that stretch for tens of millions of light-years. That's a Great Wall at the scale of the universe. Even the most powerful fleets, once trapped, would not be able to escape. Those barriers are very difficult to cross."

"What is the ultimate result of all this manipulation of space-time?"

"Dimensional strikes will eventually cause more and more of the universe to become two-dimensional, until one day the entire universe is two-dimensional. Similarly, the construction of fortifications will eventually cause all the reduced-lightspeed areas to connect, until the different lowered lightspeeds all average out: This new average will be the new c for the universe.

"At that time, any scientist from a baby civilization—like us—would think that the speed of light through vacuum is barely a dozen kilometers per second, and this is an ironclad universal constant, just like we now think the same of three hundred thousand kilometers per second.

"Of course, I've only brought up two examples. Other universal laws of physics have been used as weapons as well, though we don't know all of them. It's very possible that every law of physics has been weaponized. It's possible that in some parts of the universe, even ... Forget it, I don't even believe that."

"What were you going to say?"

"The foundation of mathematics."

Cheng Xin tried to imagine it, but it was simply impossible. "That's ... madness." Then she asked, "Will the universe turn into a war ruin? Or, maybe it's more accurate to ask: Will the laws of physics turn into war ruins?"

"Maybe they already are.... The physicists and cosmologists of the new world are focused on trying to recover the original appearance of the universe before the wars more than ten billion years ago. They've already constructed a fairly clear theoretical model describing the pre-war universe. That was a really lovely

time, when the universe itself was a Garden of Eden. Of course, the beauty could only be described mathematically. We can't picture it: Our brains don't have enough dimensions."

Cheng Xin thought back to the conversation with the Ring again.

Did you build this four-dimensional fragment?
You told me that you came from the sea. Did you
build the sea?

"You are saying that the universe of the Edenic Age was four-dimensional, and that the speed of light was much higher?"

"No, not at all. The universe of the Edenic Age was ten-dimensional. The speed of light back then wasn't only much higher —rather, it was close to infinity. Light back then was capable of action at a distance, and could go from one end of the cosmos to the other within a Planck time.... If you had been to four-dimensional space, you would have some vague hint of how beautiful that ten-dimensional Garden must have been."

"You're saying—"

"I'm not saying anything." Yifan seemed to have awakened from a dream. "We've only seen small hints; everything else is just guessing. You should treat it as a guess, just a dark myth we've made up."

But Cheng Xin continued to follow the course of the discussion taken so far. "—that during the wars after the Edenic Age, one dimension after another was imprisoned from the macroscopic into the microscopic, and the speed of light was reduced again and again...."

"As I said, I'm not saying anything, just guessing." Yifan's voice grew softer. "But no one knows if the truth is even darker than our guesses.... We are certain of only one thing: The universe is dying."

The ship stopped accelerating, and weightlessness returned. Before Cheng Xin's eyes, space and the stars appeared more and

more hallucinatory, more and more like a nightmare. Only the 3G hypergravity had brought some sense of solidity. She had welcomed the powerful embrace of those arms, an embrace that had provided some protection against the terror and frigidity of the dark myths of the universe. But now the hypergravity was gone, and only nightmare remained. The Milky Way appeared as a patch of ice hiding bloody remains, and DX3906 nearby appeared as a cremator burning over an abyss.

"Can you turn off the holographic display?" Cheng Xin asked.

Yifan turned it off, and Cheng Xin returned from the vastness of space to the cramped eggshell interior of the cabin. Here, she recovered a trace of the security she craved.

"I shouldn't have told you all that," Yifan said. His sorrow was sincere.

"I would have found out sooner or later," Cheng Xin said.

"Let me repeat: They are just guesses. There's no real scientific proof. Don't think about it too much. Focus on what's before your eyes; focus on the life you must live." Yifan put a hand over hers. "Even if what I told you is true, those events are measured at the scale of hundreds of millions of years. Come with me to our world, which is now also your world. Live out your life and stop skipping across the surface of time. As long as you live your life within a hundred thousand years and a thousand light-years, none of those things need concern you. That ought to be enough for anyone."

"Yes, it is enough, thank you." Cheng Xin held Yifan's hand.

Cheng Xin and Guan Yifan spent the rest of the journey in the forced slumber of the sleep-aid machine. The trip lasted four days. By the time they awakened in the hypergravity of deceleration, Planet Gray took up most of their field of view.

Planet Gray was a small planet. It visually resembled the moon, a barren rock, but instead of craters, much of Planet Gray's surface was taken up by desolate plains. *Hunter* entered orbit around Planet Gray. Due to the lack of an atmosphere, the orbit was very low.

The ship approached the coordinates provided by the monitoring satellite, where the five unidentified spacecraft had landed and then taken off. Yifan had planned to land the shuttle there and investigate the traces left by the spacecraft, but he and Cheng Xin had not anticipated that the mysterious visitors would leave behind such large signs that they were visible from space.

"What is *that*?" Cheng Xin cried out.

"Death lines." Yifan recognized them right away. "Don't get too close," he said to the AI.

He was referring to five black lines. One end of each line was connected to the surface of the planet, and the other end extended into space, like five black hairs growing out of Planet Gray. Each line stretched higher than *Hunter*'s orbit.

"What are they?"

"Trails left by curvature propulsion. Those lines are the result of extreme curvature manipulation. The speed of light within the trails is zero."

On the next orbit, Guan Yifan and Cheng Xin entered the shuttle and descended toward the surface. Due to the low orbit and the lack of an atmosphere, the descent was smooth and fast. The shuttle landed about three kilometers from the death lines.

They leapt across the surface under 0.2G. A thin layer of dust covered the surface of Planet Gray, along with gravel of various sizes. Due to the lack of atmospheric scattering of sunlight, shadows and lit areas were sharply delineated. When they were about a hundred meters from the death lines, Yifan waved Cheng Xin to a stop. Each death line was about twenty or thirty meters in diameter, and from here, they resembled death columns.

"These are probably the darkest things in the universe," Cheng Xin said. The death lines showed no details except an exceptional blackness showing the boundaries of the zero-lightspeed region, with no real surface. Looking up, the lines showed up clearly even against the dark backdrop of space.

"These are the deadest things in the universe as well," said Guan Yifan. "Zero-lightspeed means absolute, one hundred percent

death. Inside it, every fundamental particle, every quark is dead. There is no vibration. Even without a source of gravity inside, each death line is a black hole. A zero-gravity black hole. Anything that falls in cannot reemerge."

Yifan picked up a rock and tossed it toward one of the death lines. The rock disappeared inside the absolute darkness.

"Can your lightspeed ships produce death lines?" Cheng Xin asked.

"Far from it."

"So you've seen these before, then?"

"Yes, but only rarely."

Cheng Xin gazed up at the giant black columns reaching into space. They lifted up the domed sky and seemed to turn the universe into a Palace of Death. *Is this the ultimate end for everything?*

In the sky, Cheng Xin could see the end of the columns. She pointed in that direction. "So the ships entered lightspeed at the end?"

"That's right. These are only about a hundred kilometers high. We've seen columns even shorter than these, presumably left by ships that entered lightspeed almost instantaneously."

"Are these the most advanced lightspeed ships?"

"Maybe. But this is a rarely seen technique. Death lines are usually the products of Zero-Homers."

"Zero-Homers?"

"They're also called Resetters. Maybe they're a group of intelligent individuals, or a civilization, or a group of civilizations. We don't know exactly who they are, but we've confirmed their existence. The Zero-Homers want to reset the universe and return it to the Garden of Eden."

"How?"

"By moving the hour hand of the clock past twelve. Take spatial dimensions as an example. It's practically impossible to drag a universe in lower dimensions back into higher dimensions, so maybe it's better to work forward in the other direction. If the universe can be lowered into zero dimensions and then beyond,

the clock might be reset and everything returned to the beginning. The universe might possess ten macroscopic dimensions again."

"Zero dimensions! Have you seen such a thing done?"

"No. We've only witnessed two-dimensionalization. We've never even seen one-dimensionalization. But somewhere, some Zero-Homers must be trying. No one knows if they've ever succeeded. Comparatively, it's easier to lower the speed of light to zero, so we've seen more evidence of such attempts to lower the speed of light past zero and return it to infinity."

"Is that even theoretically possible?"

"We don't know. Maybe the Zero-Homers have theories that say yes, but I don't think so. Zero-lightspeed is an impassable wall. Zero-lightspeed is absolute death for all existence, the cessation of all motion. Under such conditions, the subjective cannot influence the objective in any way, so how can the 'hour hand' be shifted past it? I think the Zero-Homers are practicing a kind of religion, a kind of performance art."

Cheng Xin stared at the death lines, her terror mixed with awe. "If these are trails, why don't they spread?"

Guan Yifan clutched Cheng Xin's arm. "I was just getting to that. We've got to get out of here. Leave not just Planet Gray, but the entire system. This is a very dangerous place. Death lines are not like regular trails. Without disturbance, they'll stay like this, with a diameter equal to the effective surface of the curvature engine. But if they're disturbed, they'll spread very rapidly. A death line of this size can expand to cover a region the size of a solar system. Scientists call this phenomenon a death line rupture."

"Does a rupture make the speed of light zero in the entire region?"

"No, no. After rupture, it turns into a regular trail. The speed of light inside goes up as the trail dissipates over a wider region, but it will never be much more than a dozen meters per second. After these death lines expand, this entire system might turn into a reduced-lightspeed black hole, or a black domain.... Let's go."

Cheng Xin and Guan Yifan turned toward the shuttle and began to run and leap.

"What kind of disturbance makes them spread?" Cheng Xin asked. She turned to give the death lines another glance. Behind them, the five death lines cast long shadows that stretched across the plain to the horizon.

"We're not sure. Some theories suggest that the appearance of other curvature trails nearby would cause disturbance. We've confirmed that curvature trails within a short distance can influence each other."

"So, if *Halo* accelerates—"

"That's why we must get farther away using only the fusion engine before engaging the curvature engine. We've got to move … using your units of measurement … at least forty astronomical units away."

After the shuttle took off, Cheng Xin continued to stare at the receding death lines. She said, "The Zero-Homers give me a bit of hope."

Yifan said, "The universe contains multitudes. You can find any kind of 'people' and world. There are idealists like the Zero-Homers, pacifists, philanthropists, and even civilizations dedicated only to art and beauty. But they're not the mainstream; they cannot change the direction of the universe."

"It's just like the world of humans."

"At least the Zero-Homers' task will ultimately be completed by the cosmos itself."

"You mean the end of the universe?"

"That's right."

"But based on what I know, the universe will continue to expand, and become sparser and colder forever."

"That's the old cosmology you know, but we've disproved it. The amount of dark matter had been underestimated. The universe will stop expanding and then collapse under gravity, finally forming a singularity and initiating another big bang. Everything will return to zero, or home. And so Nature remains the final victor."

"Will the new universe have ten dimensions?"

"Who knows? There are infinite possibilities. That's a brand-new universe, and a brand-new life."

The trip back to Planet Blue was as uneventful as the trip to Planet Gray. Most of the time, Cheng Xin and Guan Yifan remained asleep under the sleep-aid machines. By the time they were awakened, *Hunter* was in orbit around Planet Blue. Looking down at the blue-and-white world, Cheng Xin almost thought she was home.

AA hailed them, and Yifan replied. "*Hunter* here. What's wrong?"

AA's voice was agitated. "I've called you multiple times, and the ship's AI refused to wake you!"

"I told you we have to maintain radio silence. What happened?"

"Yun Tianming is here!"

Cheng Xin was thunderstruck. The last traces of sleep left her, and even Yifan's jaw hung open.

"What?" Cheng Xin said softly.

"Yun Tianming is here! His ship landed three hours ago."

"Oh," Cheng Xin answered mechanically.

"He's still young, as young as you!"

"Really?" Cheng Xin's voice seemed to come from far away, even to herself.

"He brought a gift for you."

"He already gave me a gift. We're inside his gift now."

"That's nothing. Let me tell you, this is an awesome gift, and much bigger.... He's outside right now. Let me get him."

Yifan interrupted. "No. We're coming down right now. So much radio transmission is dangerous. I'm cutting it off."

Yifan and Cheng Xin stared at each other, and then laughed. "Are we really awake?" Cheng Xin asked.

Even if it was just a dream, Cheng Xin wanted to be dreaming for longer. She turned on the holographic display, and the starry sky no longer seemed so dark and cold—in fact, it seemed filled with a clear beauty like the sky after a fresh rain. Even the starlight

seemed to exude the fragrance of spring buds. It was the feeling of being reborn.

"Let's get into the shuttle and land," Yifan said.

Hunter initiated the shuttle separation sequence. Inside the cramped cabin, Yifan used an interface window to perform the final check prior to atmospheric reentry.

"How did he get here so fast?" Cheng Xin muttered, as if still dreaming.

Yifan was now completely calm. "This confirms our guess. The First Trisolaran Fleet founded a colony nearby, within a hundred light-years of here. They must have received the gravitational wave signal from *Halo*."

The shuttle separated from *Hunter*. They could see the tiny pyramid of *Hunter* recede on the monitoring system.

"What kind of gift is bigger than a sun and its planetary system?" Yifan asked, smiling.

An excited Cheng Xin shook her head.

The shuttle's fusion reactor activated, and the cooling ring outside began to glow red. The thrusters were preheating, and the control interface window showed that deceleration would begin in thirty seconds. The shuttle was about to descend rapidly as it entered Planet Blue's atmosphere.

Cheng Xin heard an abrupt noise, as though something had sliced across the shuttle from bow to stern. Sharp jolts followed. And then, she experienced an eerie moment—eerie, because she couldn't be sure it was just a moment. The moment seemed to be infinitely short but also infinitely long. She had a strange feeling of stepping across time but being situated outside of time.

Later, Yifan would explain to her that she had experienced a "time vacuum." The length of that moment could not be measured in time because, during that moment, time did not exist.

At the same time, she felt herself collapse, as though she was going to turn into a singularity. Meanwhile, the mass of her, Guan Yifan, and the shuttle approached infinity.

And then everything plunged into darkness. At first, Cheng Xin

thought something was wrong with her eyes. She couldn't believe the inside of the shuttle could be so dark, so dark that she couldn't see her fingers waving before her eyes. Cheng Xin called for Guan Yifan, but there was only silence in the space suit's earpiece.

Yifan felt around in the darkness until he grabbed Cheng Xin's head. She felt her own face touching his. She did not resist; she only felt comfort. Then she understood that Yifan was only trying to talk to her. The communications system inside the space suits had shut down, and the only way they could talk to each other was to press the visors of their helmets together so that their voices could be transmitted across.

"Don't be scared. Don't panic. Listen to me and don't move!" Cheng Xin heard Yifan's voice from the visor. She could tell from the vibrations that he was shouting, but what she heard was very faint, like a whisper. She felt his hand moving around in the dark until the inside of the cabin lit up. The light came from something held in his hand, a strip about the size of a cigarette. Cheng Xin knew it was some kind of chemical light source. *Halo* was equipped with similar emergency supplies. Bending it caused it to emit a cold light.

"Don't move. The space suits are no longer providing oxygen. Slow down your breathing. I'll repressurize the cabin now. It won't take long!" Yifan handed the glow stick to Cheng Xin, pulled open a storage unit next to his seat, and took out a metal bottle that resembled a small fire extinguisher. He twisted the bottle's opening, and a white gas rushed out of the bottle in raging torrents.

Cheng Xin's breath quickened. All she had left was the air remaining in her helmet, and the harder she inhaled, the more suffocated she felt. Her hand reached instinctively for the visor of her helmet, but Yifan stopped her in time. He embraced her again, this time to calm her down. She imagined that he was trying to rescue her from drowning. In the cold light, she saw his eyes, which seemed to be telling her that they were almost at the surface. Cheng Xin could feel the air pressure in the cabin rising, and just when she was about to pass out from lack of air, Yifan snapped her visor open, as well as his own. The two gulped air.

After she caught her breath, Cheng Xin examined the metal bottle. She noticed the pressure gauge near the neck of the bottle, an ancient analog dial with a swinging needle that was now pointing into the green zone.

Yifan said, "The oxygen from that won't last long, and the cabin is going to get very cold very fast. We need to change space suits." He pushed off from his seat and dragged out two metal boxes from the back of the cabin. He opened one and showed Cheng Xin the space suit inside.

Modern space suits—in the Solar System and here—were very lightweight. If one kept the suit unpressurized, left off the small life-support pack, and took off the helmet, a modern space suit was virtually indistinguishable from ordinary clothes. However, the space suits in the boxes were heavy and clumsy, resembling Common Era space suits.

They could now see their breaths. Cheng Xin took off her original space suit and felt the bone-chilling cold inside the cabin. The heavy space suit was difficult to put on, and Yifan had to help her. She felt like a child dependent on this man, a feeling that she had not experienced in a long time. Before Cheng Xin put on the helmet, Yifan explained the suit's features to her in detail—the oxygen dial, the pressurization toggle, the knob for temperature adjustment, the switches for communications and illumination, and so on. The space suit had no automatic systems, and everything required manual operation.

"There are no computer chips inside this suit at all. Right now, none of our computers—electronic or quantum—work anymore."

"Why?"

"The speed of light right now is less than twenty kilometers per second."

Yifan helped Cheng Xin put on her helmet. Her body was almost frozen. He turned on the oxygen and the heater in her suit, and she felt herself thawing out. Yifan now turned to put on his own suit. He worked fast, but it took some work between when he put on his helmet and the two suits could be connected for

communications. Neither was able to speak until their chilled bodies had recovered.

The suits were so heavy and clumsy that Cheng Xin could imagine how difficult it would be to move around in them under 1G. Her suit wasn't so much a suit as a house, the only place where she could find refuge. The light-emitting strip drifting in the cabin was dimming, so Yifan turned on the lamp on his own suit. Inside the cramped space, Cheng Xin thought they were like ancient miners trapped underground.

"What happened?" Cheng Xin asked.

Yifan floated up from his seat and struggled until he managed to open the screen over one of the portholes—the automatic controls for the porthole screens were also nonfunctional. He drifted to the other side of the cabin and repeated the operation with another porthole.

Cheng Xin looked at the transformed universe outside.

She saw two star clusters at the two ends of space: The cluster in front glowed blue and the cluster behind glowed red. Cheng Xin had seen a similar sight earlier when *Halo* was flying at lightspeed, but the two star clusters she saw now were not stable. Their shapes shifted abruptly like two balls of flame in fierce wind. Instead of stars leaping from the blue cluster into the red cluster from time to time, two light belts connected the two ends of the universe, only one of which was visible on each side of the ship.

The wider belt took up half the space on one side. Its two ends were not connected to the blue and red star clusters; instead, the belt ended in two round tips. Cheng Xin could tell that this "belt" was actually an extremely flattened oval—or perhaps a circle that had been stretched out. Colored patches of various sizes flitted across the wide belt: blue, white, and light yellow. Instinctively, Cheng Xin understood that she was looking at Planet Blue.

The light belt on the other side of the ship was thinner but brighter, and its surface showed no details. Unlike Planet Blue, this belt's length cycled rapidly between a bright line that connected the red and blue clusters, and a bright circle. The belt's periodic circular state told Cheng Xin that she was looking at the star DX3906.

"We're orbiting Planet Blue at lightspeed," said Guan Yifan. "Except the speed of light is now very slow."

The shuttle had been moving far faster, but as the speed of light was an absolute speed limit, the shuttle's velocity had been cut down to that.

"The death lines ruptured?"

"Yes. They spread out to cover the entire solar system. We're trapped here."

"Was it due to the disturbance from Tianming's ship?"

"Perhaps. He didn't know the death lines were here."

Cheng Xin didn't want to ask what their next step was, knowing that nothing more could be done. No computer could operate when the speed of light was below twenty kilometers per second. The shuttle's AI and control systems were all dead. Under such conditions, not even a light inside the spacecraft could be turned on—it was just a metal can with no electricity or power. *Hunter* was the same, also dead. Before falling into reduced lightspeed, the shuttle had not yet began decelerating, and so the small spaceship should be nearby—but it might as well be on the other side of the planet. Without the control systems, neither the shuttle nor *Hunter* could open their doors.

Cheng Xin thought about Yun Tianming and 艾 AA. They were both on the ground, and should be safe. But now there was no way for the two sides to communicate. She never even got to say hello to him.

Something light gently struck the visor of her helmet: the metal bottle. Cheng Xin looked at the ancient pressure gauge on it again, and touched her own space suit. Hope, once extinguished, lit up again like a firefly.

"You've been preparing for situations like this?" she asked.

"Yes." Yifan's voice sounded distorted in Cheng Xin's earpiece due to the use of ancient analog signals. "Not for ruptured death lines, of course, but we were prepared for accidentally drifting into the trails of lightspeed ships. The situations are similar: The reduced lightspeed stops everything.... Next, we need to start the neurons."

"What?"

"Neural computers. Computers that can operate under reduced lightspeed. The shuttle and *Hunter* both have two control systems, one of which is based on neural computers."

Cheng Xin was amazed that such machines existed.

"The key isn't the speed of light, but the system design. The transmission of chemical signals in the brain is even slower, only two or three meters per second—not much faster than us walking. Neural computers can still work because they imitate the highly parallel processing found in the brains of higher animals. All the chips are designed specifically to function under reduced-lightspeed conditions."

Yifan opened a metal bulkhead decorated with many dots connected in a complex web like the tentacles of an octopus. Inside was a small control panel with a flat display, as well as several switches and indicator lights. The whole assembly was built from components deemed obsolete by the end of the Crisis Era. He toggled a red switch and the screen lit up: text scrolling by. Cheng Xin could tell it was the boot sequence of some operating system.

"The parallel neural mode hasn't been started yet, so we have to load the operating system serially. You'll probably have a hard time believing how slow serial data transmission is under reduced lightspeed: look, the data rate is a few hundred bytes per second. Not even a kilobyte."

"Then the boot sequence will take a long time."

"That's right. But as the parallel mode gradually builds up, the loading will speed up. Still, it really will take a long time to complete the sequence." Yifan pointed to the progress indicator, a line of text on the bottom of the screen.

Remaining load time for boot module: 68 hours 43 minutes *[flickering]* seconds. Total remaining system load time: 297 hours 52 minutes *[flickering]* seconds.

"Twelve days!" Cheng Xin exclaimed. "What about *Hunter*?"

"Its systems will detect the reduced-lightspeed condition and automatically boot the neural computer. But it will take about as long to complete."

Twelve days. They could only get to the survival resources in the shuttle and on *Hunter* after twelve days. Until then, they had to rely on their primitive space suits. If the space suits were powered by nuclear batteries, the electricity should last long enough, but they didn't have enough oxygen.

"We have to hibernate," said Yifan.

"Do we have the equipment for hibernation on the shuttle?" As soon as she asked the question, Cheng Xin realized her error. Even if the shuttle had such equipment, it would be controlled by the computer, which was out of commission right now.

Yifan opened the storage unit from which he had taken the oxygen bottle earlier and took out a small box. He opened it to show Cheng Xin a few capsules. "These are drugs for short-term hibernation. Unlike regular hibernation, you won't need an external life-support system. Once you are in hibernation, your respiration will slow down to the point where you consume very little oxygen. One capsule is enough for fifteen days of hibernation."

Cheng Xin opened her visor and swallowed one of the pills. She watched as Yifan also took one. Then she looked outside the portholes.

Patches of color now moved so fast over Planet Blue—the broad belt that connected the blue and red ends of the lightspeed universe on one side of the ship—that they turned into a blur.

"Can you see the patterns on the belt repeating periodically?" Yifan wasn't looking outside at all. His eyes were half-closed as he strapped himself into the hypergravity seat.

"They're moving too fast."

"Try to follow the motion with your eyes."

Cheng Xin tried to match her moving gaze with the patterns flowing across the belt. For a moment, she could see the blue, white, and yellow patches, but they blurred almost immediately. "I can't," she said.

"That's all right. They're moving too fast. The pattern could be repeating several hundred times per second." Yifan sighed. Cheng Xin noticed his sorrow, despite his effort to hide it. And she knew why.

She understood that every time the pattern repeated on the broad belt, it meant that the shuttle had completed another orbit around Planet Blue at lightspeed. Even at reduced lightspeed, the demonic rules of the theory of special relativity still held. In the planet's frame of reference, time was passing tens of millions of times faster than in here, like blood seeping out of her heart.

A moment here; eons there.

Cheng Xin turned away from the porthole and strapped herself into the seat as well. Light flickered through the porthole on the other side. Outside, the sun of this world was alternately a bright line that connected the two ends of the universe, and a ball of light. It was dancing the mad dance of death.

"Cheng Xin." Yifan called for her softly. "It's possible that when we wake up, we'll find the screen telling us that an error has occurred."

Cheng Xin turned and smiled at him through the visor. "I'm not afraid."

"I know you're not afraid. I just want to tell you something in case we don't . . . I know about your experience as the Swordholder. I want to let you know that you didn't do anything wrong. Humanity chose you, which meant they chose to treat life and everything else with love, even if they had to pay a great price. You fulfilled the wish of the world, carried out their values, and executed their choice. You really didn't do anything wrong."

"Thank you," Cheng Xin said.

"I don't know what happened to you after that, but you still didn't do anything wrong. Love isn't wrong. A single individual cannot destroy a world. If that world was doomed, then it was the result of the efforts of everyone, including those living and those who had already died."

"Thank you," Cheng Xin said. Her eyes felt hot and wet.

"As for what will happen next, I'm not afraid either. When I was on *Gravity*, all those stars in the emptiness made me afraid and tired, and I wanted to stop thinking about the universe. But it was like a drug, and I couldn't stop. Well, now I can stop."

"That's good. You know something? The only thing I'm scared of is that you'll be afraid."

"I'm the same."

They held hands, and as the sun continued its mad dance, they gradually lost consciousness and stopped breathing.

ABOUT SEVENTEEN BILLION YEARS AFTER THE BEGINNING OF TIME
OUR STAR

It took a long time to wake up.

Cheng Xin recovered her awareness gradually. After her memory and sight came back, she knew right away that the neural computer had booted successfully. A soft light illuminated the inside of the cabin, and she could hear the machines humming reassuringly. The air was warm. The shuttle had been revived.

But Cheng Xin soon realized that the lights inside the cabin came from different fixtures than before—perhaps these were backups designed specifically for reduced-lightspeed use. There were no information windows in the air. It was possible that the reduced lightspeed meant such holographic displays were no longer operable. The interface of the neural computer was limited to that flat screen, which now resembled a color bitmap display from the Common Era.

Guan Yifan was drifting in front of the display, tapping on it with the fingers of a gloveless hand. He turned and smiled at Cheng Xin, made a hand gesture indicating that it was okay to drink, and then handed her a bottle of water.

"It's been sixteen days," he said.

The bottle felt warm. Cheng Xin saw that she wasn't wearing

gloves, either. She realized that although she was still wearing the primitive space suit, her helmet had been removed. The temperature and pressure inside the cabin were comfortable.

Since she had recovered enough to move her hands, Cheng Xin unstrapped herself and drifted next to Yifan to look at the screen with him, their space suits squeezed tightly side by side. Several windows were up on the screen, each showing rapidly scrolling numbers: diagnostics on the shuttle's various systems. Yifan told Cheng Xin that he had established contact with *Hunter,* whose neural computer had also apparently booted successfully.

Cheng Xin looked up and saw that the two portholes were still open. She drifted over. Guan Yifan dimmed the cabin lights so she could see through them without glare. They anticipated each other's needs now as though they were a single person.

At first, the universe didn't appear to have changed from what she had seen before: The ship continued to orbit around Planet Blue at reduced lightspeed; the two star clusters, blue and red, continued to change their shapes erratically at the two ends of the universe; the sun continued to dance madly between being a line and a circle; and color patches continued to whip across Planet Blue's surface. When Cheng Xin tried to match her gaze to the rapidly flowing surface of Planet Blue, she finally noticed something different: the blue and white patches had been replaced by purple ones.

Yifan pointed to the screen. "The propulsion system self-diagnosis is complete. Everything's basically working. We can decelerate out of lightspeed anytime."

"The fusion drive still works?" Cheng Xin asked. Before they entered hibernation, this question had weighed on her mind. She had not asked because she knew that she was likely to receive a disappointing answer, and she didn't want to give Yifan more to worry about.

"Of course not. With such a reduced lightspeed, nuclear fusion puts out too little power. We have to use the backup antimatter drive."

"Antimatter? But wouldn't the containment field be affected by the reduced lightspeed?"

"No problems there. The antimatter engine was designed specifically for reduced-lightspeed conditions. When we're on long expeditions like this, we equip all our spacecraft with reduced-lightspeed propulsion systems.... Our world puts a lot of effort into developing such technologies. The goal isn't to solve the problem of accidentally entering trails left by curvature propulsion; rather, it's because we have to plan for the possibility of having to conceal ourselves inside a light tomb, or a black domain."

Half an hour later, the shuttle and *Hunter* both activated their antimatter engines and began decelerating. Cheng Xin and Guan Yifan were pressed against their seats by the hypergravity, and the porthole screens rose to block out the outside. Violent jolts seized the shuttle, but gradually subsided. The deceleration process took less than twenty minutes. Then the engines shut off, and they were again weightless.

"We're out of lightspeed," Guan Yifan said. He pressed a button, and the screens over the two portholes retracted.

Through the portholes, Cheng Xin saw that the blue and red star clusters were gone, and the sun was now a normal sun. But the sight of Planet Blue in the porthole on the other side surprised her: Planet Blue was now "Planet Purple." Other than the ocean, which was still a light yellow, the rest of the planet was covered by purple—even the snow was gone. She was, however, most shocked by the appearance of space itself.

"What are those lines?" Cheng Xin cried out.

"I think they are ... stars." Yifan was as amazed as she.

All the stars in space had turned into thin lines of light. Cheng Xin was actually familiar with such a sight: She had seen plenty of long-exposure photographs taken of the starry sky from Earth. Due to the Earth's rotation, the stars in the pictures all became concentric arcs of approximately the same length. But now, the stars she saw were segments of different lengths and aligned every which way. The longest few lines, in fact, took up almost a third of the sky. These lines crossed each other at different angles and made space appear far more confusing and chaotic than before.

"I think they're stars," repeated Yifan. "A star's light must pass through two interfaces before getting to us: First, it must go through the interface between regular lightspeed and reduced lightspeed, and then through the event horizon of the black hole. That's why the stars look so strange to us now."

"We're inside the black domain?"

"That's right. We're inside the light tomb."

The DX3906 solar system was now a reduced-lightspeed black hole completely sealed off from the rest of the universe. The starry sky woven by the multitude of crisscrossing silver threads was a dream that could be seen but would never be achieved.

"Let's go down to the surface," Yifan said after a long silence.

The shuttle decelerated further and lowered its orbit. With a series of powerful jolts, it entered the atmosphere of the planet and descended toward the surface of this world in which the two of them were doomed to spend the rest of their lives.

The purple continents took up most of the view from the monitoring system. They were able to confirm that the purple was due to the color of the vegetation. The change in the sun's radiation had probably caused the plants on Planet Blue to change from blue to purple as they evolved to adapt to the new light.

As a matter of fact, the very existence of the sun puzzled Cheng Xin and Guan Yifan. Since $E = mc^2$, reduced-lightspeed nuclear fusion could produce only small amounts of energy. Perhaps the interior of the sun maintained normal lightspeed?

The shuttle's landing coordinates were set to the same spot from which it had taken off and left *Halo*. As they approached the surface, they saw a dense purple forest at the landing spot. Just when the shuttle was about to lift off again in search of a more open spot, the trees dashed away to escape the flames from the shuttle's thrusters. The shuttle then gently set itself down in the open space vacated by the fleeing trees.

The screen showed that the outside air was breathable. Compared to the last time they had been here, the oxygen content in the atmosphere was substantially higher. Moreover, the atmosphere

was denser, and the atmospheric pressure was one and a half times higher than at the last landing.

Cheng Xin and Guan Yifan exited the shuttle and once again stepped onto the surface of Planet Blue. Warm, moist air welcomed them, and a layer of soft, bouncy humus covered the ground. The soil around them was filled with numerous holes left by the roots of the trees that had gotten out of the way. Those trees now huddled around the clearing, their broad leaves rustling in the breeze, like a crowd of whispering giants gathered around them. The clearing was completely covered by their shade. Such dense vegetation made Planet Blue a completely different world than the one they had seen before.

Cheng Xin didn't like purple. She'd always thought of it as a sick, depressing color that reminded her of the lips of invalids whose hearts did not supply them with sufficient oxygen. Yet now she was surrounded by purple everywhere she looked, and she would have to spend the rest of her life in this purple world.

There was no sign of *Halo,* no sign of Yun Tianming's ship, no sign of any human presence.

Guan Yifan and Cheng Xin surveyed the landscape around them and realized that the geographical features were completely different from the last time. They clearly remembered that there had been rolling mountains nearby, but now the forest was growing over a plain. They went back to the shuttle to confirm that the coordinates were really correct—they were. Then they looked even more carefully all around them, but still found no trace of any prior human visit. The site resembled virgin land—it was as though their last visit had occurred on another planet in another space-time that had nothing to do with here.

Yifan returned to the shuttle and established a link with *Hunter,* which was still in near-ground orbit. *Hunter's* neural computer was very powerful, and its AI was capable of direct natural language communications. Under reduced-lightspeed conditions, the conversation from ground to space suffered a transmission delay of over ten seconds. After dropping out of lightspeed along with the

shuttle, *Hunter* had been scanning the surface of the planet from low orbit. By now, it had completed a survey of most of the land on Planet Blue, and it had discovered no trace of humans or signs of any other intelligent life.

Next, Cheng Xin and Guan Yifan had to turn to a task that terrified them but was absolutely necessary: determining how much time had elapsed in this frame of reference. There was a special technique for radiometric dating under reduced-lightspeed conditions: Some elements that did not decay under normal lightspeed decayed at different rates under reduced lightspeed, which could be used to precisely tell the passage of time. Given its scientific mission, the shuttle was equipped with a device for measuring atomic decay, but the instrument required a computer for processing. Yifan had to go to some trouble to connect the instrument to the neural computer on the shuttle. They directed the instrument to test the ten rock samples taken from different parts of the planet one after another so that the results could be compared. The assay required half an hour.

While waiting for the test results, Cheng Xin and Guan Yifan left the shuttle and waited in the clearing. Sunlight illuminated the clearing through gaps in the canopy. Many strange, small creatures flitted through: Some were insects with spinning rotors on top like helicopters; others were like tiny, transparent balloons that drifted through the air, giving off a rainbow sheen as they passed through shafts of sunlight; but none of them had wings.

"Maybe several tens of thousands of years have passed," Cheng Xin muttered.

"Or even longer," said Guan Yifan, looking deep into the woods. "In our current state, tens of thousands of years aren't very different from hundreds of thousands of years."

Then they said no more, but sat on the stairs outside the shuttle, leaning against each other and taking comfort in their heartbeats.

Half an hour later, they climbed back into the shuttle to face facts. The screen on the control panel showed the test results from the ten samples. Many elements had been tested and the charts were

complicated. All the samples yielded similar results. Underneath, the average of the results was listed simply:

Average atomic decay dating results (error range: 0.4%):
Stellar time periods lapsed: 6,177,906; Earth years lapsed:
18,903,729.

Cheng Xin counted the digits in the last number three times, turned around, and quietly exited the shuttle. She descended the stairs and returned to this purple world. Tall purple trees surrounded her, a beam of sunlight cast a tiny circle of brightness next to her feet, moist wind lifted her hair, living balloons drifted overhead, and almost nineteen million years followed her.

Yifan came to her. They locked gazes, and their souls embraced.

"Cheng Xin, we missed them."

More than eighteen million years after the DX3906 system turned into a reduced-lightspeed black hole, seventeen billion years after the birth of the universe, a man and a woman held each other tightly.

Cheng Xin sobbed her heart out over Yifan's shoulder. In her memories, she had cried like this only once before, when Tianming's brain had been taken out of his body. That was ... 18,903,729 years plus six centuries ago, and those six centuries were but a rounding error at such geologic timescales. This time, she cried not only for Tianming. She cried out of a sense of surrender. She finally understood how she was but a mote of dust in a grand wind, a small leaf drifting over a broad river. She surrendered completely and allowed the wind to pass through her, allowed the sunlight to pierce her soul.

Letting the past go, she allowed her growing esteem for Guan Yifan to take over her heart.

They sat on the yielding humus and continued to hold each other, letting time flow by. The dappled sunlight gently shifted around them as the planet continued to rotate. Sometimes Cheng Xin asked herself, *Has another ten million years passed by?*

A small, rational part of her mind strangely whispered to her that such a thing was possible: There really were worlds where one could step through a thousand years at will. Consider the death lines: If they ruptured and expanded just a bit, the speed of light within would rise from zero to an extremely small number, like the rate at which continents drifted over the ocean: a centimeter for every ten thousand years. In such a world, if you got up from your lover and walked a few steps away, you would be separated from him by ten million years.

They'd missed each other.

After they knew not how long, Yifan asked her softly, "What should we do?"

"I want to look more. There must be some sign."

"There really won't be anything. Eighteen million years will erase everything: Time is the cruelest force of all."

"Carving words into stone."

Yifan looked at Cheng Xin, confused.

"艾 AA would know to carve words into stone," Cheng Xin muttered.

"I don't understand...."

Cheng Xin didn't explain; instead, she grabbed Yifan by the shoulders: "Can you have *Hunter* do a deep scan of this area and see if there's anything under the surface?"

"What are you looking for?"

"Words. I want to see if there are words."

Yifan shook his head. "I understand your desire, but—"

"To better last through the eons, the words ought to be large."

Yifan nodded, but obviously only to appease her. They returned to the shuttle. Although this was a walk of only a few steps, they leaned against each other as if afraid time would divide them if they were physically separated. Yifan contacted *Hunter* and directed it to do a deep scan of the area within a circle centered on this coordinate with a radius of three kilometers. The depth of the scan was set to be between five and ten meters, focusing on human writing or other significant markings.

Hunter passed overhead fifteen minutes later and sent back the results about ten minutes after that: nothing.

Guan Yifan ordered the ship to do another scan at a depth range between ten and twenty meters. This took another hour, the bulk of which was spent waiting for the ship to pass overhead. Still nothing. At that depth there was no more soil, only bedrock.

Guan Yifan adjusted the scanning range to between twenty and thirty meters. "This is the last time," he said to Cheng Xin. "The sensors can't go deeper than that."

They waited for the ship to orbit Planet Blue another time. The sun was setting and the sky was full of lovely, fiery clouds, while the purple woods were limned with a golden glow.

This time, the shuttle's screen showed the images transmitted back by the ship. After processing by enhancement software, they could see a few fragments of white words embedded in the dark rock: "e," "liv," "a," "life," "you," "little," "side," "Go." The white color was to indicate that the words were carved into the bedrock; each character was about a meter square, and they were arranged into four rows. The words were twenty-three to twenty-eight meters below them, carved into a forty-degree incline.

> WE LIVED A HAPPY LIFE TOGETHER
> WE GIVE YOU A LITTLE
> SURVIVE THE COLLAPSE INSIDE
> GO TO THE NEW

Hunter's AI invoked the geological expert system to interpret the results. They found out that the giant characters had initially been carved into the surface of a large sedimentary rock formation on the side of a mountain. The original surface was about 130 square meters. Over the eons, the mountain on which the rock had been located sank, and that was how the carved rock ended up below them. More than four lines of text had been carved into it, but the lower portion of the rock had been broken up during the geological transformations and all the text there lost. The surviving

text was incomplete as well—the last three lines all had missing characters at the end.

Cheng Xin and Guan Yifan embraced again. They cried tears of joy at the news concerning 艾 AA and Yun Tianming, and shared the happiness that they had enjoyed more than one hundred eighty thousand centuries ago. Their despairing hearts grew peaceful.

"I wonder what their life here was like?" Cheng Xin asked, tears glistening in her eyes.

"Anything was possible," said Yifan.

"Did they have children?"

"Anything was possible. They could have even founded a civilization here."

Cheng Xin knew that was indeed possible. But even if that civilization had lasted ten million years, the eight million-plus years that had come after would have erased all traces of it.

Time really was the cruelest force of all.

Something strange interrupted their meditation: a rectangle limned by faint lines of light, about a man's height, hovered over the clearing like the dashed selection lines marked out by dragging a mouse. It moved through the air, but did not go far before returning to its original position. It was possible that it had been there all along, but the outline was so faint and thin that it was invisible during daytime. Whether it was made by a force field or actual substance, there was no doubt it was the creation of intelligence. The lines making up the rectangle seemed to evoke the line-shaped stars in the sky.

"Do you think this is the ... gift they left for us?" Cheng Xin asked.

"Seems hard to believe. How could it have survived more than eighteen million years?"

But he was wrong. The object had indeed survived eighteen million years. And, if necessary, it could survive until the end of the universe, because it existed outside of time.

The door remembered that, initially, it had been placed next to the rock carved with text, and it had a real metal frame. But the

metal had eroded away after only five hundred thousand years, though the object had always remained brand new. It had no fear of time because its own time had not yet started. It had been thirty meters underground, next to the carved rock, but it had detected the presence of humans and risen to the surface. During the process, it did not interact with the crust, moving like a ghost. It now confirmed that these two were indeed the ones it had been expecting.

"I think it looks like a door," Cheng Xin said.

Yifan picked up a small branch and tossed it at the rectangle. The branch passed through it and landed on the other side. They saw a luminescent flock of little balloon creatures drift over. A few passed through the rectangle and one even crossed the glowing outline.

Yifan reached out and touched the frame. The light and his finger passed through each other, and he felt nothing. Without even thinking, he extended his hand into the space outlined by the rectangle. Cheng Xin screamed. Yifan pulled his hand back, and everything looked unharmed.

"Your hand.... It didn't go through." Cheng Xin pointed to the other side of the rectangle.

Yifan tried again. His hand and forearm disappeared as they entered the plane of the rectangle and did not go through. From the other side, Cheng Xin saw the cross section of his forearm, like the surface of a window. All his bones, muscles, and blood vessels were clearly visible. He pulled his hand back and tried again with a branch. It went through the frame without problems. Right after, two insects with spinning rotors passed through the rectangle as well.

"It really is a door—a smart door that recognizes what's going through it," Yifan said.

"It allowed you in."

"Probably you, as well."

Cheng Xin gingerly tried, and her arm also disappeared in the "door." Yifan observed the cross section of her arm from the other side, and had a moment of déjà vu.

695

"Wait for me here," Yifan said. "I'll go investigate."

"We should go together," Cheng Xin said resolutely.

"No, you wait here."

Cheng Xin grabbed him by both shoulders and turned him to face her. She looked into his eyes. "Do you really want us to also be separated by eighteen million years?"

Yifan stared back into her eyes for a long moment, and finally nodded. "Perhaps we should bring some things with us."

Ten minutes later, they passed through the door, hand in hand.

OUTSIDE OF TIME
OUR UNIVERSE

Primordial darkness.

Cheng Xin and Guan Yifan were once again immersed in a time vacuum. The sensation was similar to when they had entered reduced lightspeed back in the shuttle. Time did not flow here, or maybe it was more accurate to say that time did not exist. They lost all sense of time, and experienced again that feeling of stepping across time, but existing outside of it.

Darkness disappeared; time began.

There is no appropriate expression in human language to express the moment at the start of time. To say that time began after they entered the door would be wrong because "after" required time. There was no time here, and thus no before or after. The time "after" they entered could have been shorter than a billion-billionth of a second, or longer than a billion billion years.

The sun brightened. It did so very gradually: At first it was just a disk, and then the light began to unveil the world. It was like a song that began as barely audible notes, then grew and grew into a mighty chorus. A circle of blue appeared around the sun, expanded, and turned into a blue sky. Under the blue sky, a pastoral scene slowly took shape. There was an unplanted field with black soil; next to it was an exquisite white house. There were also a few trees that brought a hint of the exotic with their broad, strangely

shaped leaves. As the sun continued to brighten, the peaceful scene appeared like a welcoming embrace.

"There are people here!" Guan Yifan pointed at the distance.

They could see the backs of two figures standing on the horizon: a man and a woman. The man had just put down his uplifted arm.

"That's us," said Cheng Xin.

In front of those two figures, they could see a distant white house and trees, exact duplicates of the ones nearby. They couldn't see what was at the feet of those figures due to the distance, but they could guess that it was another black field. At the end of the world was a duplicate of it, or maybe a projection.

Duplicates or projections of the world existed all around them. They looked to their sides and saw the same scene repeated. The two of them also existed in those worlds, but all they could see were the backs of those figures, who turned their heads away as Cheng Xin and Yifan turned to look at them. They looked behind them and saw the same thing—except now they were looking at the world from the other direction.

The entrance to the world had disappeared.

They followed a path of stepping-stones, and around them, the copies of themselves in the copies of their world walked along with them. The path was broken by a brook with no bridge over it, but the brook was so small that they could step over it. Only now did they realize that gravity was a standard 1G. They passed the copse of trees and came to the white house. The door was shut and the windows covered by blue curtains. Everything looked brand new, dustless—as a matter of fact, they were brand new, also, as time had just begun to flow.

In front of the house was a pile of simple, primitive farming tools: shovels, rakes, baskets, water pails, and so on. Although some of them were shaped a bit oddly, it was easy to tell their function by appearance. What most drew their attention, though, was a row of metal columns erected next to the farming tools. They were about the height of a person, and the smooth surfaces glinted in the sunlight. Each column had four metal attachments that

seemed to be folded limbs. The columns were probably robots in a resting state.

They decided to familiarize themselves with the environment before entering the house, and so they continued to walk past it. After a bit less than a kilometer, they reached the edge of the small world and faced the duplicate world before them. At first, they thought it was just a reflected image of their own world, though it was not mirrored. But after they were halfway there they decided that it couldn't be a reflection: Everything looked so real. They took a step forward and entered the duplicate world without any resistance. Looking around, Cheng Xin was struck with a hint of terror.

Everything looked the same as when they had first entered the world. They were in the same pastoral scene, with duplicates of the scene before them and to the sides, and in those copies, copies of them also existed. They turned around to look back, and they saw copies of themselves at the far end of the world they had just left, looking behind them.

Yifan let out a long sigh. "I don't think we need to go any farther. We'll never reach the end." He pointed up and then down. "I bet that without these barriers, we'd see the same scene above and below us as well."

"Do you know what this is?"

"Are you familiar with the work of Charles Misner?"

"Who was he?"

"A physicist of the Common Era. He was the one who first came up with this concept. The world we're in is actually very simple. It's a regular cube about a kilometer on each side. You can imagine it as a room with four walls and a ceiling as well as a floor. But the room is constructed such that the ceiling is also the floor, and each wall is the same as the opposite wall. In reality, it has only two walls. If you walk through one of the walls, you'll immediately reappear at the opposite wall, and the same is true of the floor and ceiling. Thus, this is a completely enclosed world in which the end is also the beginning. The images we see all around us are the result of

light returning to the starting point after crossing the world. We're still in the same world we started from, because this is the only world that exists. Every copy we see around us is just an image of this world."

"So this is . . ."

"Yes!" Yifan swept his arm around to indicate everything. "Yun Tianming once gave you a star, and now he's given you a universe. Cheng Xin, this is an entire universe. It might be small, but it's a complete universe."

Cheng Xin looked around, at a loss for words. Yifan sat down quietly on a ridge in the field and picked up a fistful of black earth, letting the soil slip from between his fingers. He sounded depressed. "He's quite a man to be able to give the woman he loved a star and a universe. But I can't give you anything."

Cheng Xin sat down as well and leaned on his shoulder. She laughed as she said, "You're the only man in this universe. I don't think you need to give me anything."

The feeling of being alone in the universe was soon shattered by the sound of a door opening. A figure in white came out of the house and walked toward them. The world was so small that it was possible to clearly see anyone at any distance. They saw that the newcomer was a woman dressed in a kimono. The kimono, decorated with tiny red flowers, was like a walking flower bush that brought the feeling of spring to the universe.

"Sophon!" Cheng Xin cried out.

"I know her," Yifan said. "She's the robot controlled by sophons."

They walked over to meet the woman under one of the trees. Cheng Xin saw that it really was Sophon: That unparalleled beauty remained unchanged.

Sophon bowed deeply to Cheng Xin and Guan Yifan. When she straightened, she smiled at Cheng Xin. "I said that the universe is grand, but life is grander. Fate has indeed directed us to meet again."

"I couldn't have imagined," Cheng Xin said. "I'm really glad to see you. Really." Sophon brought her to the past—more than

eighteen million years ago. But that wasn't really accurate, because they were now in another time stream altogether.

Sophon bowed again. "Welcome to Universe 647. I am its manager."

"The manager of the universe?" Yifan looked at Sophon, astounded. "What a grand title! For a cosmologist like me, that sounds like—"

"Oh no!" Sophon laughed and waved his remark away. "You are the true masters of Universe 647 and have full authority over everything here. I'm just here to serve you."

Sophon made a gesture indicating that they should follow her. They followed her to a refined parlor inside the house. The parlor was decorated in an Eastern style with a few calming brush paintings and calligraphy scrolls hung on the walls. Cheng Xin looked for artifacts taken from Pluto by *Halo* but didn't find any. After they sat down at an antique wooden desk, Sophon poured tea for them—without going through the complicated steps of the Way of Tea. The tea leaves seemed to be Longjing, and they stood up at the bottom of the cups like a tiny green forest, giving off a fresh fragrance.

To Cheng Xin and Guan Yifan, everything seemed to be a dream.

Sophon spoke. "This universe is a gift. Mr. Yun Tianming gave it to the both of you."

"I think it's meant for Cheng Xin," said Yifan.

"No. You're also one of the intended recipients. Your authorization was added to the recognition system later; otherwise you wouldn't have been allowed in. Mr. Yun hoped that you could hide in this tiny universe and avoid the collapse of the great universe— or the big crunch—and, after the next big bang, enter the new universe and see its Edenic Age. Right now, we exist in an independent timeline. Time is passing rapidly in the great universe, and you will certainly be able to see its end within your lifetimes. More specifically, I estimate that the great universe will collapse into a singularity after about ten years here."

"If a new big bang occurs, how will we know?" asked Yifan.

"We'll know. We can sense the conditions in the great universe through the supermembrane."

Sophon's words reminded Cheng Xin of what Yun Tianming and 艾 AA had carved into the rock. But Guan Yifan was reminded of something else. He noticed that Sophon spoke of the "Edenic Age" of the new universe. This was a term invented by the Galactic humans. Two possibilities presented themselves. One was that coincidentally, the Trisolarans had also picked this term. The second possibility was far more terrifying: the Trisolarans had already discovered the Galactic humans. Given how quickly Yun Tianming had arrived on Planet Blue, it was apparent that the First Trisolaran Fleet was very close to the worlds of humankind. And now, the Trisolaran civilization had developed to the point where they were capable of constructing small universes: This was a great threat to humanity.

Then he laughed.

"What are you laughing at?" Cheng Xin asked.

"Myself."

He found himself ridiculous. More than eighteen million years had passed since the day he'd departed World II to come to Planet Blue, and that was before they entered this small universe with its own time. By now, hundreds of millions of years must have passed in the great universe. He was worried about truly ancient history.

"Have you seen Yun Tianming?" Cheng Xin asked.

Sophon shook her head. "No. I've never met him."

"What about 艾 AA?"

"The last time I saw her was on Earth."

"Then how did you come to be here?"

"Universe 647 was a custom order. I've been here since its completion. Remember that I am fundamentally just a collection of digital bits, and many copies of me can be made."

"Did you know that Tianming brought this universe to Planet Blue?"

"I don't know what Planet Blue is. If it's a planet, then Mr. Yun couldn't have brought Universe 647 to it, because this is an independent

universe that does not exist within the great universe. He could only bring the entrance to the universe there."

"Why aren't Tianming and AA here?" Yifan asked. This was also the question Cheng Xin most wanted answered. She hadn't asked earlier because she was afraid of hearing an answer she didn't want to know.

Sophon shook her head again. "I don't know. The recognition system has always had Mr. Yun's authorization."

"Is anyone else's authorization in the system?"

"No. Only the three of you."

After a while, Cheng Xin said to Yifan, "AA always cared more than me about the world around her. I don't think she would have been interested in a new universe tens of billions of years later."

"I'm interested," said Yifan. "I really want to see what a new universe is like before it's distorted and tampered with by life and civilization. I think it must exhibit the highest degree of harmony and beauty."

Cheng Xin said, "I also want to go to the new universe. The singularity and the new big bang will erase all memories of our universe. I want to bring some memory of humanity there."

Sophon nodded solemnly at Cheng Xin. "That is a great task you've set yourself. There are others doing similar work, but you're the first human from the Solar System to do this."

"You've always had higher goals in life than I," Yifan whispered to Cheng Xin. She couldn't tell if he was joking or being serious.

Sophon stood up. "Welcome to your new life in Universe 647. Why don't we go outside and take a look around?"

Outside, the spring planting was in full swing. The columnar robots were all working the fields. Some used the rakes to level and smooth out the field—the soil was so loose already that it did not need to be plowed; some were planting seeds in the parts that had already been smoothed. The farming techniques they employed were primitive: There were no drag harrows, so the robots had to use small rakes to level the field a bit at a time; there were no planters, so the robots each carried a bag of seeds and buried the

seeds in the field one at a time. The entire scene invoked a sense of ancient simplicity. Here, robots seemed somehow more natural than real farmers.

Sophon explained, "We have only enough food stored here to last two years. After that, you'll need to rely on the food you grow. These seeds are descended from the seeds Cheng Xin sent along with Mr. Yun. Of course, they've all been genetically improved."

Yifan looked somewhat puzzled by the black soil. "I feel that soilless cultivation tanks would be more suitable here."

Cheng Xin said, "Anyone from the Earth has a kind of nostalgia for soil. Remember what Scarlett's father told her in *Gone With the Wind*? 'Why, land is the only thing in the world worth workin' for, worth fightin' for, worth dyin' for, because it's the only thing that lasts.'"

Yifan said, "The Solar System humans spilled their last drop of blood to stay with their land—well, save for two drops: you and AA. But what was the point? They didn't last, and neither did their land. Hundreds of millions of years have passed in the great universe, and do you think anyone still remembers them? This obsession with home and land; this permanent adolescence where you're no longer children but are afraid to leave home—this is the fundamental reason your race was annihilated. I am sorry if I've offended you, but it's the truth."

Cheng Xin smiled at the agitated Yifan. "You haven't offended me. What you said is true. We knew that, but we couldn't help it. You probably can't help it, either. Don't forget that you and all the crew of *Gravity* were prisoners before becoming Galactic humans."

"That is true." Guan Yifan lost some of his fire. "I've never thought of myself as a man qualified for space."

By the standards of space, there were not too many "qualified" men—and it was doubtful Cheng Xin would like any of them. She did think of one person who was probably qualified. His voice still echoed in her ears: *We're going to advance! Advance! We'll stop at nothing to advance!*

"Don't dwell on the past," Sophon said in her sweet voice. "Everything starts anew here."

A year passed in Universe 647.

The wheat had been harvested twice, and Cheng Xin and Guan Yifan had now watched twice as the green seedlings gradually turned into a sea of golden stalks. The vegetable fields next to the wheat had always remained green.

In this tiny world they were provided with all the other necessities of life. None of the objects had manufacturing marks or brand logos—Trisolarans made them—but they looked exactly like human products.

Cheng Xin and Guan Yifan sometimes went into the fields to work alongside the robots. Sometimes they strolled about the universe—as long as they were careful not to leave footprints, they could keep on walking indefinitely and experience the feeling of traversing countless worlds.

They spent most of their time in front of the computer, however. It was possible to invoke a terminal from anywhere in the small universe, but they didn't know where the CPU for the computer was located. The computer had a massive databank of text, image, and video from the Earth, most of which dated from before the Broadcast Era. The Trisolarans had clearly gathered the info as they studied humanity, and the material covered every field in the sciences and the humanities.

But even more information existed in the databank written in the Trisolaran language. This massive ocean of data was what interested them the most. Since they couldn't find any software on the computer for translating Trisolaran writing into human languages, they had to study the Trisolaran script itself. Sophon acted as their teacher, but they soon discovered that this was an extremely difficult endeavor because Trisolaran writing was purely ideographic; unlike human scripts, which were mostly phonetic, Trisolaran writing had no connection to their speech,

but expressed ideas directly. In the distant past, humans had also used ideographic scripts—such as some hieroglyphs—but most of these later disappeared.[11] Humans read by decoding speech made visible. However, the difficulty didn't last long. The more they persisted, the easier the learning process became. After struggling for two months, they found themselves making rapid progress. Compared to phonetic scripts, the biggest advantage of an ideographic script was how fast one could read—Cheng Xin and Guan Yifan read at least ten times as fast in Trisolaran as they did with human scripts.

They began to read the Trisolaran material in the databank—at first haltingly, and then faster. They had two initial goals in mind: First, they wanted to know how the Trisolarans had recorded the period of history between their civilization and Earth civilization. Second, they wanted to know how this mini-universe was constructed. For the latter, they understood that they would likely not achieve a specialist's level of understanding, but they wanted to at least understand it at the level of popular science. Sophon estimated that in order to achieve these two goals, they would need to spend one year to learn how to read Trisolaran better, then take another year to read in depth.

The fundamental principles underlying the small artificial universe seemed unimaginable to them; even the most basic mysteries puzzled them for the longest time. For instance, how could a complete ecological cycle function in a sealed space of only one cubic kilometer? What was the sun? What was its energy source? And most confounding: As a completely sealed system, where did the heat of the mini-universe go?

11 *Translator's Note:* Some Anglophone readers may raise an eyebrow at this assertion. The common description of Chinese characters—the script this novel was originally written in—as "ideograms" is inaccurate. The Chinese script is phonetic, like almost every other script still in use, though it still contains a few (very few) ideographic elements that have survived through the ages. An introduction to how Chinese characters really function may be found in John DeFrancis's *Chinese Language: Fact and Fantasy.*

They asked Sophon these questions. Some she could answer; for others, she referred them to materials in the computer.

They also cared about the answer to one question in particular: Could the mini-universe communicate with the great universe? Sophon told them that there was no way for the mini-universe to transmit any information to the greater universe, but it was possible for the mini-universe to receive broadcasts from the great universe. She explained that all the universes were bubbles above a supermembrane—this was a fundamental conceptual image from Trisolaran physics and cosmology, and she could explain it no further. The great universe had enough energy to propagate information across the supermembrane. However, this was difficult and required a great expenditure of energy—the great universe would have to convert a Milky Way's worth of matter into pure energy. As a matter of fact, the monitoring systems in Universe 647 often received messages from other great universes on the supermembrane. Some were natural phenomena; some were messages from intelligent beings that could not be decoded—but they had never received any message from the particular great universe they had come from.

Time flowed by day after day like the smooth, placid water in that little brook.

Cheng Xin began to write her memoir so that she could record the history she knew. She named the book *A Past Outside of Time*.

Sometimes, they also tried to imagine life in the new universe. Sophon told them that according to cosmological theories, the new universe was certain to possess more than four macro dimensions, perhaps even more than ten macro dimensions. After the birth of the new universe, Universe 647 could automatically construct an entrance to it and examine the interior conditions. If the new universe possessed more than four dimensions, the mini-universe's exit could be moved around until a suitable habitable location was found in the great universe. Simultaneously, their mini-universe could establish communications with the refugees of other Trisolaran mini-universes, or even with Galactic human

migrants. In the new universe, all the migrants coming from the old universe would practically be one race, and should be able to work together to construct a new world. Sophon emphasized that one characteristic greatly increased the probability of survival in a high-dimensional universe: Out of the many macro dimensions, it was likely that more than one dimension would belong to time.

"Multi-dimensional time?" Cheng Xin couldn't understand the concept at first.

"Even if time were only two-dimensional, it would be a plane instead of a line," Yifan explained. "There would be an infinite number of directions, and we could simultaneously make countless choices."

"And at least one of those choices would turn out to be right," added Sophon.

One night, after the second harvest, Cheng Xin woke up to find Yifan not beside her. She got up, went outside, and saw that the sun had already turned to the moon, and the little world was immersed in the watery, cool light. She saw Yifan sitting by the brook, his posture morose.

In this world of two, each of them had grown especially sensitive to the moods of the other. Cheng Xin had already known that something was troubling Yifan. Earlier, he had been sunny and upbeat. Until a few days ago, he had regularly shared his dream that, if they could find a peaceful life in the new great universe, perhaps their children could re-create the human race. But then he had abruptly changed, frequently going off by himself to ponder something, or to calculate something at a computer terminal.

Cheng Xin sat down next to Yifan, and he pulled her into his arms. The moonlit world was very quiet, and all they heard was the babbling brook. The moon revealed a field of ripe wheat; they'd have to start the harvest tomorrow.

"Loss of mass," Yifan said.

Cheng Xin said nothing. She watched the moonlight dancing in the brook, knowing that Yifan was going to explain.

"I've been reading Trisolaran cosmology, and came across a proof for the elegance of the mathematics behind the great universe we all came from. The design of the total mass in the universe was precise and perfect. The Trisolarans had proved that the total mass of the universe was just enough to allow the big crunch. If the total mass were reduced even slightly, the universe would turn from being closed to open, and expand indefinitely."

"But mass has been lost," Cheng Xin said. She understood right away what he was getting at.

"Yes. The Trisolarans have already constructed several hundred mini-universes. How many more have been constructed by other civilizations in the universe to escape the big crunch, or for some other purpose? Each of these mini-universes took away some matter from the great universe."

"We need to ask Sophon."

"I have. She told me that at the time of Universe 647's completion, the Trisolarans had not observed any influence from the loss of mass in the great universe. That universe was closed and was certain to eventually collapse."

"What about after Universe 647 was constructed?"

"She had no idea, of course. She also mentioned that there was a group of intelligent beings in the universe that resembled the Zero-Homers, but they called themselves the Returners. They advocated against the construction of mini-universes, and called for the mass in completed mini-universes to be returned to the great universe.... But she didn't know much else about them. All right, let's forget all this. We're not God."

"But we've long been called on to think about matters that belonged to the province of God."

They sat by the brook until the moon turned into the sun again.

Three days after the harvest, once all the wheat had been threshed and winnowed and stored away, Cheng Xin and Guan Yifan stood at the edge of the field and watched as the robots

plowed the field to prepare for the next planting. The granary was now full, so there was no room for more wheat. Before, they would have debated what to plant for the next season. But now, both of them were troubled and had no interest in the topic. Throughout the entire harvest and threshing process, they had stayed in the house and discussed possible futures. They realized that even their individual life choices affected the fate of the universe, or even the fates of multiple universes. They really felt like God. The weight of responsibility made it hard to breathe, and so they left the house.

They saw Sophon walking toward them along one of the field ridges. Sophon rarely disturbed them and only appeared when they needed her. This time, her walk was different—she was in a hurry and did not exhibit her typical grace and dignity. Her anxious expression was also something they had not seen before.

"We've received a supermembrane broadcast from the great universe!" Sophon brought up a window and enlarged it. To make the window easier to see, she also dimmed the sun.

A torrent of symbols scrolled up the screen—the bitmap from the supermembrane broadcast. The symbols were strange and indecipherable. Cheng Xin and Guan Yifan noticed that each row of symbols was different: They rolled past like the surface of a chaotic river.

"The broadcast has been going on for five minutes and is still continuing." Sophon pointed at the window. "In actuality, the message in the broadcast is very simple and brief, but it has lasted this long because it's in many languages. We've seen a hundred thousand languages already!"

"Is the broadcast aimed at all the mini-universes?" Cheng Xin asked.

"Absolutely. Who else would receive it? They expended so much energy that the message must be important."

"Have you seen Trisolaran or Earth languages?"

"No."

Cheng Xin and Guan Yifan realized that this message was a record of which species had survived in the great universe.

By now, tens of billions of years had passed in the great universe.

Regardless of the content of the broadcast, if a civilization's language was listed in the broadcast, it meant that the civilization still existed or had existed once and lasted so long that it had left an indelible mark in the great universe.

The river of symbols continued to flow up the screen: two hundred thousand languages, three hundred thousand, four hundred thousand ... a million. The number continued to go up.

There were no Trisolaran and no Earth languages.

"It doesn't matter," Cheng Xin said. "We know that we existed; we lived." She and Guan Yifan leaned against each other.

"Trisolaran!" Sophon cried out and pointed at the screen. By now, over 1.3 million languages had been broadcast, and one row, written in Trisolaran, flashed by. Cheng Xin and Guan Yifan couldn't catch it, but Sophon did.

"Earth!" Sophon cried out again a few seconds later.

After 1.57 million languages, the broadcast finished.

The window now showed only the message written in Trisolaran and Earth languages. Cheng Xin and Guan Yifan couldn't even read the message because tears blurred their eyes.

On the day of the universe's Last Judgment, two humans and a robot belonging to the Earth and Trisolaran civilizations embraced each other in ecstasy.

They knew that languages and scripts evolved very quickly. If the two civilizations had survived for a long time or even continued to exist now, their scripts were surely very different from what was being shown on the screen. But to allow those hiding in mini-universes to understand, they had to write in ancient scripts. Compared to the total number of civilizations that had lived in the great universe, 1.57 million was a tiny number.

In the eternal night of the Orion Arm of the Milky Way Galaxy, two civilizations had swept through like two shooting stars, and the universe had remembered their light.

After Cheng Xin and Guan Yifan calmed down, they read the message. The content of the message in both scripts was the same, and very simple:

Cheng Xin and Guan Yifan locked gazes. In each other's eyes, they saw the dark future for the great universe. In perpetual expansion, all the galaxies would move farther away from each other until none were visible from any other. By then, standing at any point in the universe, all one would see was darkness in every direction. The stars would go out one by one, and all celestial bodies would turn into thin dust clouds. Coldness and darkness would reign over all, and the universe would become a vast, empty tomb. All civilizations and all memories would be buried in that endless tomb for eternity. Death would be eternal.

The only way to prevent this future was to return the matter locked up in all the mini-universes constructed by all the civilizations. But such a decision meant that the mini-universes would not survive, and all the refugees in the mini-universes had to return to the great universe. That was the meaning of the name of the Returners' movement.

The two said everything they needed to say to each other with their eyes and made their decision wordlessly. But Cheng Xin still spoke aloud. "I want to go back. But if you want to stay here, I'll stay with you."

Yifan shook his head slowly. "I study a grand universe whose diameter is sixteen billion light-years. I don't want to spend the rest of my life in this universe that's only a kilometer in each direction. Let's go back."

"I must advise against that," said Sophon. "We can't precisely determine how fast time is passing in the great universe, but I can be certain that at least ten billion years have passed there since the time you came here. Planet Blue has long since vanished, and

712

the star Mr. Yun gave you was extinguished a long time ago. We know nothing of the conditions in the great universe, and it's possible that it's not even three-dimensional anymore."

"I thought you could move the exit of the mini-universe at lightspeed," Yifan said. "Can't you move it around to find a habitable location?"

"If you insist, I will try. But I still think staying here is the best choice. There are two possible futures if you remain: If the Returners succeed in their mission, the great universe will collapse into a singularity and lead to a new big bang so that we can go to the new universe. But if the Returners fail and the great universe dies, you can live out the rest of your lives in this mini-universe. This isn't too bad."

"If everyone in every mini-universe thinks that way," said Cheng Xin, "then they will have doomed the great universe."

Sophon gazed at Cheng Xin wordlessly. Given the speed of Sophon's thought, perhaps this period of time felt as long as several centuries to her. It was hard to imagine that software and algorithms could produce such a complex expression. Perhaps Sophon's AI software had brought up all the memories accumulated across almost twenty million years since she had met Cheng Xin. All these memories seemed to precipitate in her gaze: sorrow, admiration, surprise, reproach, regret ... so many complicated feelings mixed together.

"You're still living for your responsibility," Sophon said.

EXCERPT FROM
A PAST OUTSIDE OF TIME
THE STAIRS OF RESPONSIBILITY

All my life has been spent climbing up a flight of stairs made of responsibility.

When I was little, my only duty was to study hard and obey my parents.

Later, in high school and college, the responsibility to study hard continued, but there was also the added obligation to make myself useful rather than a drain on society.

By the time I started to work toward my doctorate, my responsibilities became more concrete. I needed to contribute to the development of chemical rockets, to build more powerful, more reliable rockets so that more materials and a few men and women could be sent into Earth orbit.

Later, I joined the PIA, and my responsibility was to send a probe into space a light-year away to meet the invading Trisolaran Fleet. This was a distance about ten billion times greater than the distance I had worked with as a rocket engineer.

And then, I received a star. During the new era, it brought me previously unimaginable responsibilities. I became the Swordholder, whose duty was to maintain dark forest deterrence. Looking back on it now, perhaps it was a bit of an exaggeration to claim that

I held the fate of humankind; but I really did control the direction of development for two civilizations.

Later, my responsibilities became more complicated: I wanted to endow humans with lightspeed wings, but I also had to thwart that goal to prevent a war.

I don't know how much those catastrophes and the final destruction of the Solar System had to do with me. Those are questions that could never be answered definitively. But I'm certain they had something to do with me, with my responsibilities.

And now, I've climbed to the apex of responsibility: I am responsible for the fate of the universe. Of course this responsibility doesn't belong only to me and Guan Yifan, but we own a share of the responsibility, a share of something that I never could have imagined.

I want to tell all those who believe in God that I am not the Chosen One. I also want to tell all the atheists that I am not a history-maker. I am but an ordinary person. Unfortunately, I have not been able to walk the ordinary person's path. My path is, in reality, the journey of a civilization.

And now we know that this is the journey that must be made by every civilization: awakening inside a cramped cradle, toddling out of it, taking flight, flying faster and farther, and, finally, merging with the fate of the universe as one.

The ultimate fate of all intelligent beings has always been to become as grand as their thoughts.

OUTSIDE OF TIME
OUR UNIVERSE

Through Universe 647's control system, Sophon managed to move the mini-universe's exit inside the great universe. The door moved quickly through the great universe, searching for a habitable world. The amount of information that the door could transmit to the mini-universe was very limited, and no images or videos were possible. All that could be sent back was a rough analysis of the environment. This was a number between negative ten and ten, indicating the habitability of the environment. Humans could survive only if the number were greater than zero.

The door jumped tens of thousands of times in the great universe. After three months, only once did they discover a habitable planet, with a rating of three. Sophon had to concede that this was probably the best result they could get.

"A rating of three indicates a dangerous and inhospitable world," Sophon warned.

"We're not afraid," said a resolute Cheng Xin. Yifan nodded. "Let's go there."

The door appeared in Universe 647. Like the door Cheng Xin and Guan Yifan had seen on Planet Blue, it was also a rectangle limned by glowing lines. But this door was much bigger, perhaps to make it easier to transport material through it. Initially, the door was not connected to the great universe, and anything could pass

through it without leaving the mini-universe. Sophon adjusted its parameters so that anything moving through it would disappear and reappear in the great universe.

Next, it was time to return matter from the mini-universe to the great universe.

Sophon had explained that the mini-universe had no matter of its own. All of its mass had come from material brought out of the great universe. Of the several hundred mini-universes constructed by the Trisolarans, Universe 647 was one of the smallest. In total, it required about five hundred thousand metric tons of matter from the great universe, which was about the carrying capacity of a large oil tanker. It was practically nothing at the scale of the universe.

They began with the soil. After the last harvest, the field had been left fallow. The robots used a wheelbarrow to cart the moist earth; at the door, two of the robots lifted the wheelbarrow to dump the soil through the door; and the soil disappeared. It happened very quickly. Three days later, all the soil in the mini-universe was gone. Even the trees around the house had been returned through the door.

With all the soil removed, they saw the metallic floor of the mini-universe. The floor was pieced together with smooth metal tiles that reflected the sun like a mirror. The robots took off the metal tiles one by one and sent them through the door as well.

Underneath the floor was a small spaceship. Although the ship was less than twenty meters long, it contained the most advanced technologies of the Trisolarans. Designed with human occupants in mind, it could seat three, and was equipped with both a nuclear fusion drive and a curvature drive. There was a miniature ecological cycling system aboard suitable for human needs as well as equipment for hibernation. Like *Halo,* it was capable of landing and taking off from planetary surfaces. It had a slender, streamlined profile, perhaps to make it easier to go through the mini-universe's door. It had been intended for the inhabitants of Universe 647 to enter the new great universe after the next big bang. It could serve as a living base for a considerable amount of time, until they found a suitable

location in the new universe. But now, they would use it to return to the old great universe.

As the rest of the metal floor tiles were removed, they also revealed more machinery beneath. These were the first objects Cheng Xin and Guan Yifan had seen in the mini-universe that bore obvious signs of being of Trisolaran origin. Like Cheng Xin had suspected, the design of these machines evinced an aesthetic completely different from human ideals. Cheng Xin and Guan Yifan couldn't even tell at first that they were looking at machinery; rather, the objects resembled strange sculptures or natural geologic formations. The robots began to disassemble the machinery and send the pieces through the door.

Cheng Xin and Sophon busied themselves in a room and wouldn't let Yifan in. They said that they were working on a "women's project" and would surprise him later.

After some machine under the floor was shut off, gravity disappeared from the mini-universe. The white house began to float in air.

The weightless robots disassembled the sky, which was a thin membrane capable of displaying a blue sky and white clouds. Finally, the remnants of the floor below the machinery were also disassembled and sent away.

The water in the mini-universe had evaporated and fog was everywhere. The sun shone from behind a veil of clouds and a spectacular rainbow appeared that crossed from one end of the universe to the other. Whatever liquid water was left in the mini-universe formed spheres of various sizes and drifted around the rainbow, reflecting and refracting sunlight.

Disassembling the machines also meant turning off the ecological cycling system. Cheng Xin and Yifan had to put on space suits.

Sophon adjusted the parameters in the door again to allow gas through. A low rumble shook the mini-universe, caused by air escaping through the door. Below the rainbow, the white fog cloud formed a great maelstrom around the door, like a view of a typhoon from space. And then, the whirling fog turned into a tornado, and

let out a high-pitched howl. The drifting balls of water were sucked into the twister, torn apart, and disappeared through the door. Countless small objects drifting in the air were also swallowed up by the cyclone. The sun, the house, the spaceship, and other large objects also drifted in the direction of the door, but robots equipped with thrusters quickly secured them back in place.

As the air thinned, the rainbow disappeared, and the fog dissipated. The air became more transparent, and gradually, the mini-universe's space appeared. Like space in the great universe, it was also dark and deep, but there were no stars. Only three objects floated in space: the sun, the house, and the spaceship, along with about a dozen weightless robots. In Cheng Xin's eyes, this simplified world resembled the naïve, clumsy pictures she had drawn in her childhood.

Cheng Xin and Guan Yifan activated the thrusters on their space suits and flew toward the depths of space. After a kilometer, they reached the end of the universe and, in a flash, found themselves back where they had started. They could see the projected images of every floating object repeated endlessly in every direction. Like two mirrors placed against each other, the images extended in rows into infinity.

The house was disassembled. The last room to be taken apart was the parlor decorated in an Eastern style in which Sophon had welcomed them. All the scrolls, the tea table, and the pieces of the house were sent out the door by the robots.

The sun finally went out. It was a metal sphere where one hemisphere, the part that had emitted light, was transparent. Three robots pushed it through the door. Only lamps now illuminated the mini-universe, and the vacuum that was space soon cooled. What was left of the water and air soon turned into ice fragments that sparkled in the lamplight.

Sophon directed the robots to line up and go through the door, one after the other.

Finally, only the slender ship was left in the mini-universe, along with three figures drifting near it.

Sophon held a metal box. This box would be left behind in the mini-universe, a message in a bottle for the new universe that would be born after the next big bang. The box contained a miniature computer whose quantum memory held all the information in the mini-universe's computer—this was practically the entire memory of the Trisolaran and Earth civilizations. After the birth of the new universe, the metal box would receive a signal from the door, and it would go through the door using its own tiny thrusters and enter the new universe. It would drift through the high-dimensional space of the new universe until the day it was picked up and read. At the same time, it would continuously broadcast its message using neutrinos—assuming the new universe also had neutrinos.

Cheng Xin and Guan Yifan believed that in the other mini-universes, at least those mini-universes that heeded that call of the Returners, the same things were being done. If the new universe were really born, it would contain many bottles containing messages drifting through it. It was believable that a considerable number of bottles contained storage mechanisms that held the memories and thoughts of every individual of that civilization, as well as their complete biological details—maybe the records would be sufficient for a new civilization in the new universe to revive that old civilization.

"Can we keep another five kilograms here?" Cheng Xin asked. She was on the other side of the ship and dressed in her space suit. In her hand, she held a glowing, transparent sphere. The sphere was about half a meter in diameter, and a few balls of water drifted inside it. Inside some of the water spheres were tiny fish, along with green algae. There were also two miniature drifting continents covered with green grass. The light came from the top of the transparent sphere, where there was a tiny glowing emitter, the sun of this miniature world. This was a completely sealed ecological sphere, the result of more than ten days of work by Cheng Xin and Sophon. As long as the tiny sun inside the sphere continued to give off light, this miniature ecological system would persist. As long as it remained here, Universe 647 would not be a lifeless, dark world.

"Of course," said Guan Yifan. "The great universe isn't going to fail to collapse because it misses five kilograms." He had another thought that he did not voice: Perhaps the great universe really would fail to collapse because it lacked a single atom's mass. The precision of Nature can sometimes exceed the imagination. For instance, life itself required the precise collaboration of various universal constants within a billion-billionth of a certain range. But Cheng Xin could still leave behind her ecological sphere. Out of all the countless mini-universes created by the countless civilizations, it was certain that some number of them would not heed the call of the Returners. Ultimately, the great universe was certain to lose at least a few hundred million tons of matter, or perhaps even a million billion billion tons.

Hopefully, the great universe could ignore such a loss.

Cheng Xin and Guan Yifan entered the spaceship, and Sophon came in last. She had long ceased wearing her magnificent kimono and turned once again into that lean and nimble warrior dressed in camouflage. She had all sorts of weapons and survival gear strapped to her body, the most prominent being the katana on her back.

"Don't worry," she said to her two human friends. "As long as I'm alive, no harm will come to you."

The fusion drive activated and the thrusters emitted a dim blue light. The spaceship slowly went through the door of the universe.

The message in a bottle and the ecological sphere were the only things left in the mini-universe. The bottle faded into the darkness so, in this one-cubic-kilometer universe, only the little sun inside the ecological sphere gave off any light. In this minuscule world of life, a few clear watery spheres drifted serenely in weightlessness. One tiny fish leapt out of a watery sphere and entered another, where it effortlessly swam between the green algae. On a blade of grass on one of the miniature continents, a drop of dew took off from the tip of the grass blade, rose spiraling into the air, and refracted a clear ray of sunlight into space.

TRANSLATOR'S POSTSCRIPT

I'm indebted to the following beta readers for their invaluable help during the translation process: Anatoly Belilovsky, John Chu, Elías Combarro, Rachel Cordasco, Derwin Mak, Alex Shvartsman, and Igor Teper. All translators should be so lucky.

I'm also thankful for special assistance from the following individuals: Wang Meizi, for advice on transliterated names; Anna Gustafsson Chen, for pointers on Scandinavian geography; and Emma Osborne, for tracking down books for me on the other side of the globe.

My heartfelt gratitude goes to David Brin for championing the Three-Body series and acting as a wonderful sounding board for me.

I continue to be awed by the genius of Liu Cixin every time I read another passage from this novel. Of the three books in the trilogy, this third one is my favorite. I've been very fortunate to get the chance to work on this book with Da Liu.

Finally, I want to thank the many individuals who played indispensable (though often underappreciated) roles in the epic tale of bringing Three-Body to the English-speaking world: Li Yun and Song Yajuan at China Educational Publications Import & Export Corporation Ltd., for seeing the potential of a global audience for the series and commissioning the translation; Joel Martinsen, who translated *The Dark Forest* and, by example, showed me how to handle some tricky parts in this book; Emily Jiang, Wang Meizi, and Chen Qiufan, for building the bridge that connected Tor Books to Liu Cixin; Joe Monti, for encouraging me to take on this

project in the first place; and the many wonderful individuals at Tor Books who worked so hard to make the vision of these books a reality. Among them are: Irene Gallo, Stephan Martinière, and Jamie Stafford-Hill, for extraordinary art direction, artwork, and cover design; Leah Withers and Diana Griffin, for an outstanding publicity campaign; Joe Bendel for his sales and marketing insight; Kevin Sweeney, Heather Saunders, Nathan Weaver, Karl Gold, and Megan Kiddoo, from Tor's production department; Christina MacDonald, who ensured that errors and bugs would not survive in the manuscript; Miriam Weinberg, for assisting with editorial matters; and most of all, Liz Gorinsky, who left an indelible mark on the text with her meticulous and insightful editorial touch, improving this translation in innumerable ways. I hope to continue to make beautiful books with them all in the future.

THE
DARK
FOREST

CIXIN LIU is China's leading Science Fiction writer. He has won the China Galaxy Science Fiction Award nine times, the Nebula (Xingyun) award twice, and was the first translated author to win the Hugo award. Before becoming a writer, he was a computer engineer in a power plant in Yangquan.

Translator JOEL MARTINSEN is also the translator (with Alice Xin Liu) of *The Problem With Me*, a collection of essays by Han Han. His translations of short fiction have appeared in *Pathlight*, *Chutzpah* and *Words Without Borders*. He lives in Beijing.

BY CIXIN LIU

THE THREE-BODY TRILOGY

The Three-Body Problem

The Dark Forest

Death's End

Ball Lightning

The Supernova Era

Of Ants and Dinosaurs

SHORT STORY COLLECTIONS

The Wandering Earth

Hold Up the Sky

THE
DARK
FOREST

CIXIN 刘慈欣 LIU

TRANSLATED BY JOEL MARTINSEN

HEAD
of ZEUS

An Ad Astra Book

Originally published as 黑暗森林 in 2008 by Chongqing Publishing Group in Chongqing, China. First published in the United States of America in 2015 by Tom Doherty Associates LLC, a Tor book

First published in the UK in 2015 by Head of Zeus Ltd
This paperback edition first published in 2016 by Head of Zeus Ltd

Translation by Joel Martinsen

25

A CIP catalogue record for this book is available from the British Library.

ISBN (PB): 9781784971618
ISBN (E): 9781784971588

Typeset by Adrian McLaughlin

Printed and bound in Great Britain by
CPI Group (UK) Ltd, Croydon CR0 4YY

Head of Zeus Ltd
5–8 Hardwick Street
London EC1R 4RG
WWW.HEADOFZEUS.COM

LIST OF CHARACTERS

ORGANIZATIONS

ETO	Earth-Trisolaris Organization
PDC	Planetary Defense Council
SFJC	Solar Fleet Joint Conference

CAST OF CHARACTERS

Chinese names are written with surname first.

Luo Ji	Astronomer and sociologist
Ye Wenjie	Astrophysicist
Mike Evans	ETO financial backer and key leader
Wu Yue	Captain in the PLA Navy
Zhang Beihai	Political commissar in the PLA Navy; Space Force officer
Chang Weisi	General in the PLA; Space Force commander
George Fitzroy	US general; coordinator at the Planetary Defense Council; military liaison to Hubble II project
Albert Ringier	Hubble II astronomer
Zhang Yuanchao	Recently retired chemical plant worker in Beijing
Yang Jinwen	Retired middle school teacher in Beijing
Miao Fuquan	Shanxi coal boss; neighbor to Zhang and Yang
Shi Qiang	PDC security department officer, nicknamed Da Shi

Shi Xiaoming	Shi Qiang's son
Kent	Liaison to the PDC
Secretary General Say	Secretary general of the UN
Frederick Tyler	Former US secretary of defense
Manuel Rey Diaz	Former president of Venezuela
Bill Hines	English neuroscientist; former president of the EU
Keiko Yamasuki	Neuroscientist; Hines's wife
Garanin	PDC rotating chair
Ding Yi	Theoretical physicist
Zhuang Yan	Graduate of the Central Academy of Fine Arts
Ben Jonathan	Fleet Joint Conference special commissioner
Dongfang Yanxu	Captain of *Natural Selection*
Major Xizi	Science officer of *Quantum*

PROLOGUE

The brown ant had already forgotten its home. To the twilight
Earth and the stars that were just coming out, the span of time
may have been negligible, but, for the ant, it was eons. In days now
forgotten, its world had been overturned. Soil had taken flight,
leaving a broad and deep chasm, and then soil had come crashing
down to fill it back in. At one end of the disturbed earth stood a
lone black formation. Such things happened frequently throughout
this vast domain, the soil flying away and returning, chasms open-
ing up and being filled, and rock formations appearing like visible
markers of each catastrophic change. Under the setting sun, the ant
and hundreds of its brethren had carried off the surviving queen to
establish a new empire. Its return visit was only a chance passing
while searching for food.

The ant arrived at the foot of the formation, sensing its indomi-
table presence with its feelers. Noting that the surface was hard
and slippery, yet still climbable, up it went, with no purpose in
mind but the random turbulence of its simple neural network.
Turbulence was everywhere, within every blade of grass, every
drop of dew on a leaf, every cloud in the sky, and every star beyond.
The turbulence was purposeless, but in huge quantities of purpose-
less turbulence, purpose took shape.

The ant sensed vibrations in the ground and knew from how
they intensified that another giant presence was approaching from
somewhere on the ground. Paying it no mind, the ant continued
its climb up the formation. At the right angle where the foot of the

formation met the ground, there was a spider web. This, the ant knew. It carefully detoured around the sticky hanging strands, passing by the spider lying in wait, its legs extended to feel for vibrations in the threads. Each knew of the other's presence but—as it had been for eons—there was no communication.

The vibrations crescendoed and then stopped. The giant being had reached the formation. It was far taller than the ant and blotted out most of the sky. The ant was not unfamiliar with beings of this sort. It knew that they were alive, that they frequently appeared in this region, and that their appearances were closely related to the swiftly disappearing chasms and multiplying formations.

The ant continued its climb, knowing that the beings were not a threat, with a few exceptions. Down below, the spider encountered one such exception when the being, which had evidently noticed its web reaching between the formation and the ground, whisked away the spider and web with the stems of a bundle of flowers it held in one limb, causing them to land broken in a pile of weeds. Then the being gently placed the flowers in front of the formation.

Then another vibration, weak but intensifying, told the ant that a second living being of the same sort was moving toward the formation. At the same time, the ant encountered a long trough, a depression in the surface of the formation with a rougher texture and different color: off-white. It followed the trough, for its roughness made for a far easier climb. At each end was a short, thinner trough: a horizontal base from which the main trough rose, and an upper trough that extended at an angle. By the time the ant climbed back out onto the slick black surface, it had gained an overall impression of the shape of the troughs: "I."

Then the height of the being in front of the formation was cut in half, so it was roughly even with the formation. Evidently it had dropped to its knees, revealing a patch of dim blue sky where the stars had begun to come out behind it. The being's eyes gazed at the top of the formation, causing the ant to hesitate momentarily while deciding whether it ought to intrude into his line of sight. Instead, it changed direction and started crawling parallel with the

2

ground, quickly reaching another trough and lingering in its rough depression as it savored the pleasant sensation of the crawl. The color was reminiscent of the eggs that surrounded its queen. With no hesitation, the ant followed the trough downward, and after a while, the layout become more complicated, a curve extended beneath a complete circle. It reminded the ant of the process of searching out scent information and eventually stumbling across the way home. A pattern was established in its neural network: "9."

Then the being kneeling before the formation made a sound, a series of sounds that far exceeded the ant's capacity to comprehend: "It's a wonder to be alive. If you don't understand that, how can you search for anything deeper?"

The being made a sound like a gust of wind blowing across the grass—a sigh—and then stood up.

The ant continued to crawl parallel to the ground and entered a third trough, one that was nearly vertical until it turned, like this: "7." The ant didn't like this shape. A sharp, sudden turn usually meant danger or battle.

The first being's voice had obscured the vibrations, so it was only now that the ant realized that the second being had reached the formation. Shorter and frailer, the second being had white hair that stood out against the dark blue background of the sky, bobbing silver in the wind, connected somehow to the increasing number of stars.

The first being stood up to welcome her. "Dr. Ye, is it?"

"You're . . . Xiao Luo?"[1]

"Luo Ji. I went to high school with Yang Dong. Why are you . . . here?"

"It's a nice place, and easy to get to by bus. Lately, I've been coming here to take walks fairly often."

"My condolences, Dr. Ye."

"That's all in the past. . . ."

1 *Translator's Note: Xiǎo* is a diminutive meaning "little" or "young" and is used before a surname when addressing children or to show affection.

Down on the formation, the ant wanted to turn toward the sky, but then discovered another trough ahead of it, identical to the "9"-shaped trough it had crawled through before the "7." So it continued horizontally through the "9," which it found better than both the "7" and the "1," although it could not say exactly why. Its aesthetic sense was primitive and single-celled. The indistinct pleasure it had felt upon crawling through the "9" intensified. A primitive, single-celled state of happiness. These two spiritual monocells, aesthetics and pleasure had never evolved. They had been the same a billion years ago, and would be the same a billion years hence.

"Xiao Luo, Dong Dong often spoke of you. She said you're in . . . astronomy?"

"I used to be. I teach college sociology now. At your school, actually, although you had already retired when I got there."

"Sociology? That's a pretty big leap."

"Yeah. Yang Dong always said my mind wasn't focused."

"She wasn't kidding when she said you're smart."

"Just clever. Nothing like your daughter's level. I just felt astronomy was an undrillable chunk of iron. Sociology is a plank of wood, and there's bound to be someplace thin enough to punch through. It's easier to get by."

In the hope of reaching another "9," the ant continued its horizontal advance, but the next thing it encountered was a perfectly straight horizontal like the first trough, except longer than the "1" and turned on its side. And no smaller troughs at the ends. A "–" shape.

"You shouldn't put it like that. It's a normal person's life. Not everyone can be Dong Dong."

"I really don't have that kind of ambition. I drift."

"I've got a suggestion. Why don't you study cosmic sociology?"

"Cosmic sociology?"

"A name chosen at random. Suppose a vast number of civilizations are distributed throughout the universe, on the order of the number of detectable stars. Lots and lots of them. Those

4

civilizations make up the body of a cosmic society. Cosmic sociology is the study of the nature of this supersociety."

The ant had not crawled very much farther along the formation. It had hoped, after crawling out of the "–" depression, to find a pleasurable "9," but instead it encountered a "2," with a comfortable initial curve but a sharp turn at the end that was as fearsome as that of the "7." The premonition of an uncertain future. The ant continued onward to the next trough, a closed shape: "o." The path seemed like part of a "9," but it was a trap. Life needed smoothness, but it also needed direction. One could not always be returning to the point of origin. This, the ant understood. Although there were still two more troughs up ahead, it had lost interest. It turned vertically again.

"But . . . ours is the only civilization we know of right now."

"Which is why no one's done it before. The opportunity is left to you."

"Fascinating, Dr. Ye. Please go on."

"My thinking is that this can link your two disciplines together. The mathematical structure of cosmic sociology is far clearer than that of human sociology."

"Why do you say that?"

Ye Wenjie pointed at the sky. Twilight still illuminated the west, and they could still count the stars that had come out, making it easy to remember how the firmament had looked a few moments ago: a vast expanse and a blue void, or a face without pupils, like a marble statue. Now, though the stars were few in number, the giant eyes had pupils. The void was filled. The universe had sight. The stars were tiny, just single twinkling points of silver that hinted at some unease on the part of its creator. The cosmic sculptor had felt compelled to dot pupils onto the universe, yet had a tremendous terror of granting it sight. This balance of fear and desire resulted in the tininess of the stars against the hugeness of space, a declaration of caution above all.

"See how the stars are points? The factors of chaos and randomness in the complex makeups of every civilized society in

the universe get filtered out by the distance, so those civilizations can act as reference points that are relatively easy to manipulate mathematically."

"But there's nothing concrete to study in your cosmic sociology, Dr. Ye. Surveys and experiments aren't really possible."

"That means your ultimate result will be purely theoretical. Like Euclidean geometry, you'll set up a few simple axioms at first, then derive an overall theoretic system using those axioms as a foundation."

"It's all fascinating, but what would the axioms of cosmic sociology be?"

"First: Survival is the primary need of civilization. Second: Civilization continuously grows and expands, but the total matter in the universe remains constant."

The ant had not gone far before it realized that there were other troughs above it, many of them, in a complicated maze structure. The ant was sensitive to shapes and was confident of being able to work it out, but the limited storage capacity of its tiny neural network meant it had to forget the shapes it had previously crawled through. It did not feel any regret at forgetting the "9," for constant forgetting was part of life. There were few things that it needed to remember forever, and those were etched by its genes into the storage area known as instinct.

Having cleared its memory, the ant entered the maze. After navigating its twists and turns, it established another pattern in its simple consciousness: the Chinese character 墓—*mu,* meaning "grave," although the character and its meaning were not known to the ant. Farther up was another combination of troughs—far simpler this time, but to continue its exploration the ant had no choice but to clear its memory and forget the *mu.* Then it entered a wonderful line-trough, a shape that reminded it of the abdomen of a recently deceased cricket it had discovered not long ago. It quickly made out the new structure: 之, *zhi,* the Chinese possessive modifier. Then, as it continued upward, it encountered two more trough combinations, the first of which consisted of two droplet-shaped

depressions and a cricket stomach: the character 冬—*dong,* meaning "winter." The top one was split into two parts, which together formed the character 杨—*yang,* meaning "poplar." This was the last shape the ant remembered, and the only one it retained from its entire journey. The interesting shapes it previously encountered had all been forgotten.

"Those two axioms are solid enough from a sociological perspective . . . but you rattled them off so quickly, like you'd already worked them out," Luo Ji said, a little surprised.

"I've been thinking about this for most of my life, but I've never spoken about it with anyone before. I don't know why, really. . . . One more thing: To derive a basic picture of cosmic sociology from these two axioms, you need two other important concepts: chains of suspicion, and the technological explosion."

"Interesting terms. Can you explain them?"

Ye Wenjie glanced at her watch. "There's no time. But you're clever enough to figure them out. Use those two axioms as a starting point for your discipline, and you might end up becoming the Euclid of cosmic sociology."

"I'm no Euclid. But I'll remember what you said and give it a whirl. I might come to you for guidance, though."

"I'm afraid there won't be that opportunity. . . . In that case, you might as well just forget I said anything. Either way, I've fulfilled my duty. Well, Xiao Luo, I've got to go."

"Take care, Professor."

Ye Wenjie went off through the twilight to her final meetup.

The ant continued its climb and reached a round basin on the rock face, whose slick surface bore an extremely complicated image. It knew that its tiny neural net had no way to store such a thing, but after determining the overall shape of the image, its primitive one-cell aesthetic was as sparked as it had been by the sense of the "9." And somehow it seemed to recognize part of the image, a pair of eyes. The ant was sensitive to eyes, because their gaze meant danger. Yet it felt no anxiety now, for it knew the eyes were lifeless. It had already forgotten that when the giant being

named Luo Ji knelt down in silence before the formation, he had been looking at those eyes. The ant climbed out of the basin and up onto the formation's peak. It felt no sense of towering above its surroundings, because it had no fear of falling. It had been blown off of places higher than this many times without any injury. Without the fear of heights, there can be no appreciation for the beauty of high places.

At the foot of the formation, the spider that Luo Ji had swept aside with the flowers was beginning to reconstruct its web. It drew a glistening strand from the rock face and swung itself like a pendulum to the ground. Three more swings and the skeleton of the web was complete. Ten thousand times the web could be destroyed, and ten thousand times the spider would rebuild it. There was neither annoyance nor despair, nor any delight, just as it had been for a billion years.

Luo Ji stood in silence for a while and then departed. When the vibrations in the ground had dissipated, the ant crawled a different way down the formation to hurry back to the nest and report on the location of a dead beetle. The stars had grown dense in the sky. When the ant passed the spider down at the foot of the formation, they felt each other's presence, but did not communicate.

As that distant world held its breath to listen, neither ant nor spider was aware that they, out of all life on Earth, were the sole witnesses to the birth of the axioms of cosmic civilization.

Somewhat earlier, in the dead of night, Mike Evans was standing on the bow of *Judgment Day* as the Pacific Ocean slipped past like a swath of satin beneath the heavens. Evans enjoyed talking with the distant world at times like these because the text the sophon displayed on his retinas stood out wonderfully against the night sea and sky.

This is our twenty-second real-time conversation. We have come across some difficulties in our communication.

"Yes, Lord. I've learned that you can't actually understand a significant amount of the reference materials on humanity we've given you."

Yes. You've explained the parts very clearly, but we are unable to understand the whole. Something is different.

"Just one thing?"

Yes. But it sometimes seems as if your world is missing something, other times that it has something extra, and we don't know which.

"What is the area of confusion?"

We've carefully studied your documents and have discovered that the key to understanding the problem lies in a pair of synonyms.

"Synonyms?"

There are many synonyms and near-synonyms in your languages. In the first language we received from you, Chinese, there were words that expressed the same meaning, like "cold" and "chill," "heavy" and "weighty," "long" and "far."

"What pair of synonyms created the obstacle to understanding you've just mentioned?"

"Think" and "say." We've just learned, to our surprise, that they are not, in fact, synonyms.

"They are not synonyms at all."

In our understanding, they ought to be. "Think" means using thought organs to conduct mental activity. "Say" means communicating the content of thoughts to a counterpart. The latter, in your world,

9

is accomplished through the modulation of vibrations in the air produced by the vocal cords. Are these definitions correct?

"They are. But doesn't this demonstrate that 'think' and 'say' aren't synonyms?"

In our understanding, this shows that they are synonyms.

"May I think about this for a moment?"

Very well. We both need to think about it.

For two minutes, Evans gazed in thought at the waves undulating beneath the starlight.
"My Lord, what are your organs of communication?"

We do not have organs of communication. Our brains can display our thoughts to the outside world, thereby achieving communication.

"Display thoughts? How is that done?"

The thoughts in our brains emit electromagnetic waves on all frequencies, including what is visible light to us. They can be displayed at a significant distance.

"So that means that to you, thinking is speaking?"

Hence they are synonyms.

"Oh . . . That is not the case for us, but even so, that shouldn't present an obstacle to understanding those documents."

True. In the areas of thought and communication, the differences between us are not large. We both have brains, and our brains produce intelligence through huge numbers of neural connections.

The only difference is that our brain waves are stronger and can be directly received by our counterparts, eliminating the need for communication organs. That's the only difference.

"No. I suspect a major difference might be getting lost. My Lord, let me think about it again."

Very well.

Evans left the bow and strolled along the deck. Over the gunwale, the Pacific rose and fell silently in the night. He imagined it as a thinking brain.

"My Lord, let me tell you a story. To prepare for it, you need to understand the following elements: wolf, child, grandmother, and a house in the forest."

These elements are all easy to understand, except for "grandmother." I know that this is a blood relation among humans, and usually means a woman of advanced age. But her actual kinship status requires more explanation.

"Lord, that is not important. All you need to know is that she and the children have a close relationship. She is one of the only people the children trust."

Understood.

"I'll make it simple. Grandmother had to go out, so she left the children in the house, telling them they must make sure the door is shut and not to open it to anyone but her. On the road, Grandmother met a wolf, which ate her, and then put on her clothing and assumed her appearance. Then it went to the house and came up to the door, and said to the children, 'I'm your grandmother. I've come back. Open the door for me.' The children looked through the crack in the door and saw what looked like

their grandmother, and so they opened the door, and the wolf came in the house and ate them. Do you understand this story, my Lord?"

Not the slightest bit.

"Then maybe I've guessed right."

First of all, the wolf wanted all along to enter the house and eat the children, correct?

"Correct."

It engaged in communication with the children, correct?

"Correct."

This is what's incomprehensible. In order to achieve its own aims, it shouldn't have communicated with the children.

"Why?"

Isn't it obvious? If there was communication between them, the children would have known that the wolf wanted to come in and eat them, and they wouldn't have opened the door.

Evans stayed silent for a while. "I understand, my Lord. I understand."

What do you understand? Isn't what I said obvious?

"Your thoughts are completely exposed to the outside world. You can't hide."

How can thoughts hide? Your ideas are confusing.

"I mean, your thoughts and memories are transparent to the outside world, like a book placed out in public, or a film projected in a plaza, or a fish in a clear fishbowl. Totally exposed. Readable at a glance. Er, maybe some of the elements I just mentioned are . . ."

I understand them all. But isn't all that perfectly natural?

Evans was silent again. "So that's it. . . . My Lord, when you communicate face-to-face, everything you communicate is true. It's impossible for you to cheat or lie, so you can't pursue complicated strategic thinking."

We can communicate over significant distances, not just face-to-face. The words "cheating" and "lying" are another two that we have had a hard time understanding.

"What sort of a society is it when thought is completely transparent? What sort of culture does it produce? What sort of politics? No scheming, no pretending."

What are "scheming" and "pretending"?

Evans said nothing.

Human communication organs are but an evolutionary deficiency, a necessary compensation for the fact that your brains can't emit strong thought waves. This is one of your biological weaknesses. Direct display of thought is a superior, more efficient form of communication.

"A deficiency? A weakness? No, my Lord, you are wrong. This time you are totally wrong."

Is that so? Let me think about it. It's a shame you can't see my thoughts.

This time the interruption was longer. When twenty minutes had passed and no more text had appeared, Evans strolled from bow to stern, watching a school of fish leaping out of the ocean, tracing an arc on the surface that glittered silver under the starlight. Several years ago, he had spent some time on a fishing boat in the South China Sea investigating the effect of overfishing on coastal life. The fishermen called this phenomenon "the passing of dragon soldiers." To Evans, they looked like text projected on the eye of the ocean. Then text appeared before his own eyes.

You are correct. Looking back at those documents, I understand them a little better.

"My Lord, there's a long road to travel before you arrive at a true understanding of human matters. I'm almost afraid that you'll never be able to."

Indeed, they are complicated. All I know now is why I didn't understand them before. You are right.

"My Lord, you need us."

I am afraid of you.

The conversation stopped. This was the last time that Evans received a message from Trisolaris. He stood at the stern watching the snow-white body of *Judgment Day* stretch off into the hazy night, like time slipping away.

PART I

THE WALLFACERS

YEAR 3, CRISIS ERA

Distance of the Trisolaran Fleet from the Solar System:
4.21 light-years

It looks so old. . . .

This was Wu Yue's first thought as he faced *Tang*, the massive ship under construction in front of him, bathed in the flickering of electric arcs. Of course, this impression was simply the result of countless inconsequential smudges on the manganese steel plates of the ship's nearly completed body, left behind by the advanced gas-shield welding used on the hull. He tried unsuccessfully to imagine how sturdy and new *Tang* would look with a fresh coat of gray paint.

Tang's fourth offshore fleet training session had just concluded. During that two-month session, *Tang*'s commanders, Wu Yue and Zhang Beihai, who was standing just beside Wu Yue, had occupied an uncomfortable role. Formations of destroyers, submarines, and supply ships were directed by battle group commanders, but *Tang* was still under construction in the dock, so the carrier's position was either occupied by the training ship *Zheng He* or simply left empty. During the sessions, Wu Yue often stared vacantly at an empty patch of sea where the surface of the water, disturbed by crisscrossing trails left by passing ships, undulated uneasily, much like his mood. *Would the empty spot ever be filled?* he asked himself more than once.

Looking now at the unfinished *Tang*, what he saw was not just age but the passage of time itself. It seemed like an ancient, giant,

discarded fortress, its mottled body a stone wall, the shower of welding sparks falling from the scaffolding like plants covering the stones . . . like it was less construction than archeology.

Afraid of pursuing these thoughts, Wu Yue turned his attention to Zhang Beihai next to him. "Is your father any better?" he asked.

Zhang Beihai gently shook his head. "No. He's just holding on."

"Ask for leave."

"I did when he first went to the hospital. Given the situation, I'll deal with it when the time comes."

Then they went silent. Every social interaction between the two of them was like this. Where work was concerned they had more to say, of course, but something always lay between them.

"Beihai, work isn't going to be like it was. Since we're sharing this position now, I think we ought to communicate more."

"We've communicated just fine in the past. Our superiors put us together on *Tang,* no doubt thanks to our successful cooperation aboard *Chang'an.*" Zhang Beihai laughed as he said this, but it was the sort of laugh that Wu Yue couldn't read. Zhang Beihai's eyes could easily read deep into the heart of everyone aboard the ship, be they captain or sailor. Wu Yue was entirely transparent to him. But Wu Yue could not read what was inside Zhang. He was certain that the man's smile came from within him, but had no hope of understanding him. Successful cooperation does not equate to successful understanding. There was no question that Zhang Beihai was the most capable political commissar on the ship, and he was forthright in his work, exploring every last issue with complete precision. But his internal world was a bottomless gray to Wu Yue, who always felt like Zhang Beihai was saying: *Just do it this way. This way's best, or most correct. But it's not what I really want.* It began as an indistinct feeling that grew increasingly obvious. Of course, whatever Zhang Beihai did was always the best or most correct, but Wu Yue had no idea what he actually wanted.

Wu Yue adhered to one article of faith: Command of a warship was a dangerous position, so the two commanders must understand each other's minds. This presented Wu Yue with a knotty

problem. At first, he thought that Zhang Beihai was somehow on guard, which offended Wu. In the tough post of captain of a destroyer, was anyone more forthright and guileless than he was? *What do I have worth guarding against?*

When Zhang Beihai's father had briefly been their superior officer, Wu Yue had spoken with him about his difficulties talking to his commissar. "Isn't it enough for the work to be done well? Why do you need to know how he thinks?" the general had said, gently, then added, perhaps involuntarily, "Actually, I don't know either."

"Let's get a closer look," Zhang Beihai said, pointing to *Tang* through the sparks. Then both their phones chirped at the same time: a text message recalling them back to their car. This usually meant an emergency, since secured communications equipment was only available in the vehicle. Wu Yue opened the car door and picked up the receiver. It was a call from an advisor at battle group HQ.

"Captain Wu, Fleet Command have issued you and Commissar Zhang emergency orders. The two of you are to report to General Staff immediately."

"General Staff? What about the fifth fleet training exercise? Half the battle group is at sea, and the rest of the ships will join them tomorrow."

"I'm not aware of that. The order is simple. Just that one command. You can look at the specifics when you get back."

The captain and commissar of the still-unlaunched *Tang* glanced at each other, then had one of the rare moments throughout the years where their thoughts aligned: *Looks like that patch of water will remain empty.*

Fort Greely, Alaska. Several fallow deer ambling along the snowy plain grew alert, sensing vibrations in the earth beneath the snow. Ahead of them, a white hemisphere opened. It had been placed there long ago, a giant egg half-buried beneath the ground, but the deer always felt it didn't belong to this frozen world. The egg split open and issued forth thick smoke and flames, then, with a roar,

it hatched a cylinder that accelerated upward, spurting flames from its bottom. The surrounding snowdrifts were thrown by the fire into the air, where they fell again as rain. When the cylinder gained enough height, the explosions that had terrified the deer were again replaced by peace. The cylinder vanished into the sky trailing a long white tail behind it, as if the snowscape was a giant ball of yarn from which a giant invisible hand had pulled a strand skyward.

"Damn it! Just a few more seconds and I'd have confirmed a launch interrupt!" said Target Screening Officer Raeder as he tossed aside his mouse. Raeder was thousands of kilometers away in the Nuclear Missile Defense Control Room at the NORAD Command Center, three hundred meters beneath Cheyenne Mountain near Colorado Springs.

"I figured it was nothing as soon as the system warning came up," Orbital Monitor Jones said, shaking his head.

"Then what's the system attacking?" asked General Fitzroy. Nuclear Missile Defense was just one of the duties of his new position, and he wasn't entirely familiar with it yet. Looking at the monitor-covered wall, the general attempted to locate the intuitive graphical displays they'd had at the NASA control center: a red line snaking across the world map, forming a sine wave atop the map's planar transformation. Novices found this inexplicable, but at least it let you know that something was shooting into space. But there was nothing so simple here. The lines on the screens were a complicated abstract jumble that was meaningless to him. Not to mention all the screens with swiftly scrolling numbers that had meaning only to the NMD duty officers.

"General, do you remember when they replaced the reflective film on the ISS multipurpose module last year? They lost the old film. That's what this was. It balls up and then unfurls in the solar wind."

"But . . . it ought to be included in the target screening database."

"It is. Here." Raeder brought up a page with his mouse. Below piles of complicated text, data, and forms, there was an inconspicuous photograph, probably taken with an Earth telescope,

of an irregular white patch against a black background. The strong reflection made it difficult to make out details.

"Major, since you've got this, why didn't you terminate the launch program?"

"The system ought to have searched the target database automatically. Human reaction times aren't quick enough. But data from the old system hasn't been reformatted for the new one, so it wasn't linked in with the recognition module," Raeder said. His tone was a little aggrieved, as if to say, *I've demonstrated my proficiency by managing to pull this up so quickly in a manual search when the NMD supercomputer couldn't, but I still have to put up with your clueless questions.*

"General, the order came to switch over to actual operational state after the NMD moved its intercept headings into space, but before software recalibration was completed," a duty officer said.

Fitzroy said nothing. The chatter of the control room annoyed him. Here in front of him was humanity's first planetary defense system, but it was nothing more than an existing NMD system whose intercepts had been redirected from various terrestrial continents and into space.

"I say we should take a photo for a memento!" Jones said. "This has got to be Earth's first strike at a common enemy."

"Cameras are prohibited," Raeder said coldly.

"Captain, what are you talking about?" Fitzroy said, angry all of a sudden. "The system didn't detect an enemy target at all. It's not a first strike."

After an uncomfortable silence, someone said, "The interceptors carry nuclear warheads."

"Yeah, one point five megatons. So what?"

"It's nearly dark outside. Given the target location, we ought to be able to see the flash!"

"You can see it on the monitor."

"It's more fun from outside," Raeder said.

Jones stood up nervously. "General, I . . . my shift's over."

"Mine too, General," Raeder said. This was just a courtesy.

Fitzroy was a high-level coordinator with the Planetary Defense Council and had no command over NORAD and the NMDs.

Fitzroy waved his hand: "I'm not your commanding officer. Do as you please. But let me remind all of you that in the future, we may be spending a lot of time working together."

Raeder and Jones headed topside at a run. After passing through the multi-ton antiradiation door, they were out on the peak of Cheyenne Mountain. It was dusk and the sky was clear, but they didn't see the flash of a nuclear blast in outer space.

"It should be right there," Jones said, gesturing skyward.

"Maybe we've missed it," Raeder said. He didn't look upward. Then, with an ironic smile, he said, "Do they really believe the sophon will unfold in lower dimensions?"

"Unlikely. It's intelligent. It won't give us that chance," Jones said.

"NMD's eyes are pointed upward. Is there really nothing to defend against on Earth? Even if the terrorist countries have all turned into saints, there's still the ETO, right?" He snorted. "And the PDC. Those military guys clearly want to chalk up a quick accomplishment. Fitzroy's one of them. Now they can declare that the first stage of the Planetary Defense System is complete, even though they've done practically nothing to the hardware. The system's sole purpose is to stop her from unfolding in lower dimensions near to Earth's orbit. The technology's even simpler than what's needed for intercepting guided missiles, because if the target really does appear, it'll cover an immense area. . . . Captain, that's why I've asked you up here. Why were you acting like a child, what with that first-strike photograph business? You've upset the general, you know. Can't you see he's a petty man?"

"But . . . wasn't that a compliment?"

"He's one of the best hype artists in the military. He's not going to announce at the press conference that this was a system error. Like the rest of them, he'll say it was a successful maneuver. Wait and see. That's how it's gonna be." As he was speaking, Raeder sat down and leaned back on the ground, looking up with a face full of yearning at the sky, where the stars had already emerged.

"You know, Jones, if the sophon really does unfold again, she'll give us a chance to destroy her. Wouldn't that be something!"

"What's the use? The fact is that they're streaming toward the Solar System right now. Who knows how many of them. . . . Hey, why did you say 'she' rather than 'it' or 'he'?"

The expression on Raeder's upturned face turned dreamy: "Yesterday, a Chinese colonel who just arrived at the center told me that in his language, she has the name of a Japanese woman, Tomoko."[2]

The day before, Zhang Yuanchao filed his retirement papers and left the chemical plant where he had worked for more than four decades. In the words of his neighbor Lao Yang,[3] today was the start of his second childhood. Lao Yang told him that sixty, like sixteen, was the best time in life, an age where the burdens of one's forties and fifties had been laid down, but the slowdown and illness of the seventies and eighties had not yet arrived. An age to enjoy life. Zhang Yuanchao's son and daughter-in-law had steady jobs, and although his son had married late, he would be holding a grandson before long. He and his wife wouldn't have been able to afford their current house except that they had been bought out when their old place had been demolished. They had been living in the new place for a year now. . . .

When Zhang Yuanchao thought about it, everything was completely satisfactory. He had to admit that as far as affairs of state were concerned, Lao Yang was right. Still, as he looked out from his eighth-story window at the clear sky over the city, he felt like there was no sunlight in his heart, much less a second childhood.

Lao Yang, first name Jinwen, was a retired middle school

2 *Translator's Note: Zhizi* (智子), literally "knowledge particle." The character for "particle" frequently appears in female given names in Japanese, where it is pronounced "ko."

3 *Translator's Note: Lǎo*, meaning "old," is often used before a surname of those older than the speaker to show respect or familiarity.

teacher who frequently advised Zhang Yuanchao that if he wanted to enjoy his waning years, he ought to be learning new things. For example: "The Internet. Even babies can learn it, so why don't you?" He even pointed out that Zhang Yuanchao's biggest failing was that he had absolutely no interest in the outside world: "Your old lady can at least brush aside her tears while sitting in front of the TV watching those trashy soaps. But you, you don't even watch TV. You should pay attention to national and world affairs. That's part of a full life." Zhang Yuanchao may have been an old Beijinger, but he didn't seem like one. A taxi driver could hold forth with cogent analyses of domestic and world situations, but even if Zhang Yuanchao knew the current president's name, he certainly didn't know the premier's. This was actually a point of pride for him. He lived the steady-going life of a commoner, he said, and couldn't be bothered to care about such irrelevant things. They had nothing to do with him, and ignoring them rid him of a significant number of headaches in life. Yang Jinwen paid attention to affairs of state and made a point of watching the evening news every day, arguing with online commenters till he was red in the face over national economic policy and the tide of international nuclear proliferation, but what had it gotten him? The government hadn't increased his pension by even a cent. He said, "You're being ridiculous. You think it's irrelevant? That it's got nothing to do with you? Listen, Lao Zhang. Every major national and international issue, every major national policy, and every UN resolution is connected to your life, through both direct and indirect channels. You think the US invasion of Venezuela is none of your concern? I say it's got more than a penny's worth of lasting implications for your pension." At the time, Zhang had merely laughed at Lao Yang's wonkish outburst. But now he knew that his neighbor was right.

Zhang Yuanchao rang Yang Jinwen's doorbell, and Yang answered, looking like he had just gotten back home. He seemed particularly relaxed. Zhang Yuanchao looked at him like a man in the desert who has encountered a fellow traveler and won't let him go.

"I was just looking for you. Where did you go off to?"

"I took a trip to the market. I saw your old lady shopping for food."

"Why is our building so empty? It's like a . . . mausoleum."

"It's not a holiday today. That's all." He laughed. "Your first day of retirement. That feeling is totally normal. At least you weren't a leader. They've got it worse when they retire. You'll soon get used to it. Come on, let's check out the neighborhood activity center and see what we can do for fun."

"No, no. It's not because I've retired. It's because . . . how should I put it? Because of the country, or rather, the world situation."

Yang Jinwen pointed at him and laughed. "The world situation? I never thought I'd hear those words come out of your mouth. . . ."

"That's right, I didn't use to care about the big issues, but they've gotten too huge. I never thought anything could get so big!"

"Lao Zhang, it's actually really funny, but I've started to come around to your way of thinking. I don't care about those irrelevant issues anymore. Believe it or not, I haven't watched the news in two weeks. I used to care about the big issues because people matter. We could have an effect on the outcome of current events. But no one has the power to overcome this. What's the point of troubling yourself about it?"

"But you can't simply not care. Humanity will be gone in four hundred years!"

"Hmph. You and I will be gone in forty-odd years."

"What about our descendants? They'll be wiped out."

"That doesn't concern me as much as it does you. My son in America is married but doesn't want children, so I don't really care. But the Zhang family will last another dozen generations, right? Isn't that enough?"

Zhang Yuanchao stared at Yang Jinwen for a few seconds, then looked at his watch. He turned on the television, where the news channel was airing the day's major stories:

> The AP reports that at 6:30 p.m. EST on the twenty-ninth, the
> US National Missile Defense System successfully completed

the test destruction of a lower-dimensional unfolded sophon in near-Earth orbit. This is the third test of an NMD intercept since targets were shifted to outer space. The latest target was the reflective film discarded from the International Space Station last October. A Planetary Defense Council spokesman said that the warhead-equipped interceptor successfully destroyed the three-thousand-square-meter target. This means that well before the sophon's three-dimensional unfolding reaches sufficient area, and before it presents a reflective surface that is a threat to human targets on the ground, the NMD system will be able to destroy it. . . .

"What pointlessness. A sophon's not going to unfold," Yang said as he reached for the remote in Zhang's hand. "Change the station. There might be a repeat of the European Cup semifinals. I fell asleep on the sofa last night. . . ."

"Watch it at home." Zhang Yuanchao gripped the remote and didn't let him have it. The news continued:

The physician at 301 Military Hospital in charge of the treatment of academician Jia Weilin confirmed that Jia's death was due to a hematological malignancy, also known as leukemia, the proximate cause of death being organ failure and loss of blood in the advanced stage of the disease. No abnormalities were present. Jia Weilin, a noted expert in superconductivity who made major contributions in the field of room-temperature superconductors, died on the tenth. Stories claiming that Jia died in a sophon strike are pure rumor. In a separate report, a spokesman for the Ministry of Health confirmed that several other deaths supposedly due to sophon strikes were in fact due to ordinary illnesses or accidents. The station spoke with noted physicist Ding Yi about the matter.

Reporter: What's your take on the emerging panic over the sophons?

Ding Yi: It's due to a lack of common knowledge about physics. Representatives of the government and the scientific community have explained this on numerous occasions: A sophon is just a microscopic particle which, despite possessing a high intelligence, has the potential for only a limited effect on the macroscopic world due to its microscopic scale. The primary threats they pose to humanity lie in their erroneous and random interference to high-energy physics experiments, and in the quantum entanglement network that monitors Earth. In its microscopic state, a sophon cannot kill, and it cannot engage in any other offensive attack. If a sophon wants to produce a larger effect on the macroscopic world, it can only do so in a lower-dimensional unfolded state. And even in that situation, its effects are highly limited, because a sophon unfolded in lower dimensions on a macroscopic scale is very weak. Now that humanity has established a defense system, sophons cannot do this without providing us with an excellent opportunity to destroy them. I believe that the mainstream media ought to do a better job of disseminating this scientific information to the public to rid it of a panic that has no basis in science.

Zhang Yuanchao heard someone enter the living room without knocking, calling "Lao Zhang" and "Master Zhang." He knew who it was from the footsteps he'd heard hammering up the staircase just before. Miao Fuquan, another neighbor on their floor, came in. A Shanxi coal boss who ran a fair number of mines in that province, Miao Fuquan was a few years younger than Zhang Yuanchao. He owned a larger home in another part of Beijing and used this apartment as a place to keep a mistress from Sichuan who was about the same age as his daughter. When he had first moved in, the Zhang and Yang families had basically ignored him save for an argument over the stuff he left strewn about the hallway, but they eventually discovered that although he was a little vulgar, he was

a decent, friendly man. Once building management had smoothed over a dispute or two, harmony was gradually established among the three families. Although Miao Fuquan said he had turned over his business affairs to his son, he was still a busy man and rarely spent any time at this "home," so the three-bedroom place was usually only occupied by the Sichuan woman.

"Lao Miao, you haven't been around for months. Where have you struck it rich this time?" asked Yang Jinwen.

Miao Fuquan casually picked up a glass, filled it halfway from the water dispenser, and gulped down the water. Then he wiped his mouth and said, "No one's getting rich. . . . There's trouble at the mine, and I've got to go clean it up. It's practically war time. The government really means it this time. The laws on wildcat mining never used to work, but the mines aren't going to be running for much longer now."

"Bad days are here," Yang Jinwen said, without taking his eyes from the game on television.

The man had been lying on the bed for several hours. The light shining through the basement window, the room's only source of illumination, was moonlight now, and the cool rays cast bright spots on the floor. In the shadows, everything looked like it was carved from gray stone, as if the entire room was a tomb.

No one ever knew the man's true name, but eventually, they called him the Second Wallbreaker.

The Second Wallbreaker had spent several hours looking back on his life. After confirming that there had been no omissions, he twisted the muscles of his numb body, reached under the pillow, and drew out a gun, which he slowly aimed at his temple. Just then, a sophon text appeared before his eyes.

Don't do that. We need you.

"Lord? Every night for a year I dreamt that you called, but the

28

dreams went away recently. I figured I'd stopped dreaming, but that doesn't seem to be the case now."

This is not a dream. I am in real-time communication with you.

The Wallbreaker gave a chilly laugh. "Good. It's over, then. There definitely aren't any dreams on the other side."

You require proof?

"Proof that there aren't dreams on that side?"

Proof that it's really me.

"Fine. Tell me something I don't know."

Your goldfish are dead.

"Hah! That doesn't matter. I'm about to meet them in a place where there's no darkness."

You should really take a look. This morning when you were distracted, you flicked away a half-smoked cigarette and it landed in the fishbowl. The nicotine that leached into the water was fatal to your fish.

The Second Wallbreaker opened his eyes, put down his gun, and rolled out of bed, his lethargy completely wiped away. He groped for the light and then went over to look at the fishbowl on the small table. Five dragon eye goldfish were floating in the water, their white bellies at the surface, and in their midst was a half-smoked cigarette.

I'll perform an additional confirmation. Evans once gave you an encrypted letter, but the encryption has changed. He died before he

was able to notify you of the new password, and you've never been able to read the letter. I'll tell you the password: CAMEL, the brand of cigarette you poisoned your fish with.

The Second Wallbreaker scrambled to retrieve his laptop, and as he waited for it to start up, tears streamed down his face. "Lord, my Lord, is it really you? Is it really you?" he choked out through his sobs. After the computer booted up, he opened the e-mail attachment in the Earth-Trisolaris Organization's proprietary dedicated reader. He entered the password into the popup box, and when the text was displayed he no longer had any mind to read it carefully. Throwing himself to his knees, he cried out, "Lord! It really is you, my Lord!" When he had calmed down, he raised his head and said, his eyes still wet, "We were never notified of the attack on the gathering the commander attended, or of the ambush at the Panama Canal. Why did you cast us aside?"

We were afraid of you.

"Is it because our thoughts aren't transparent? That doesn't matter, you know. All of the skills that you lack—deceit, trickery, disguise, and misdirection—we use in your service."

We don't know if that's true. Even supposing it is true, the fear remains. Your Bible mentions an animal called the snake. If a snake crawled up to you and said it would serve you, would your fear and disgust cease?

"If it told the truth, then I would overcome my disgust and fear and accept it."

That would be difficult.

"Of course. I know that you've already been bitten once by the snake. Once real-time notification became possible and you gave detailed answers to our questions, there was no reason for you to

30

tell us quite a bit of that information, such as how you received the first signal from humanity, and how the sophons are constructed. It was hard for us to understand: We were not communicating via transparent display of thoughts, so why not be more selective in the information you sent?"

That option did exist, but it doesn't cover up as much as you imagine it might. In fact, forms of communication do exist in our world that don't require displays of thought, particularly in the age of technology. But transparent thought has become a cultural and social custom. This might be hard for you to understand, just like it's hard for us to understand you.

"I can't imagine that deceit and scheming are totally absent in your world."

They exist, but they are far simpler than in yours. For example, in the wars on our world, opposing sides will adopt disguises, but an enemy who becomes suspicious about the disguise and inquires about it directly will usually obtain the truth.

"That's unbelievable."

You are equally unbelievable to us. You have a book on your bookshelf called *A Story of Three Kingdoms*.

"*Romance of the Three Kingdoms*.[4] You won't understand that."

I understand a small part, like how an ordinary person who has a hard time understanding a mathematics monograph can make out some

4 *Translator's Note:* A historical novel attributed to Luo Guanzhong (c. 1330–1400), *Romance of the Three Kingdoms* describes the contest between three regional powers from the waning days of the Eastern Han Dyansty (184) to the reunification of the empire under the Jin Dynasty (280). It is known for its iconic characters, battle scenes, and political intrigue.

of it through enormous mental effort, and by giving full play to the imagination.

"Indeed, that book lays out the highest levels of human schemes and strategy."

But our sophons can make everything in the human world transparent.

"Except for people's own minds."

Yes. The sophon can't read thoughts.

"You must know about the Wallfacer Project."

More than you do. It is about to be put into action. This is why we have come to you.

"What do you think of the project?"

The same feeling you get when you look at the snake.

"But the snake in the Bible helped humans gain knowledge. The Wallfacer Project will set up one or several mazes that will seem to you to be particularly tricky and treacherous. We can help you find your way out."

This difference in mental transparency gives us all the more resolve to wipe out humanity. Please help us wipe out humanity, and then we will wipe you out.

"My Lord, the way you express yourself is problematic. Clearly, it's determined by how you communicate through the display of transparent thoughts, but in our world, even if you express your true thoughts, you must do so in an appropriately euphemistic way. For example, although what you just said is in accord with the ideals

of ETO, its overly direct formulation might repel some of our members and cause unanticipated consequences. Of course, it may be that you'll never be able to learn to express yourself appropriately."

It is precisely the expression of deformed thoughts that makes the exchange of information in human society, particularly in human literature, so much like a twisted maze. As far as I am aware, ETO is on the brink of collapse.

"That's because you abandoned us. Those two strikes were fatal, and now, the Redemptionists have disintegrated and only the Adventists have maintained an organized existence. You're certainly aware of this, but the most fatal blow was a psychological one. Your abandonment means that the devotion of our members to our Lord is being tested. To maintain that devotion, ETO desperately needs our Lord's support."

We can't give you technology.

"That won't be necessary, so long as you go back to transmitting information to us through the sophons."

Naturally. But what ETO must do first is execute the critical order you just read. We issued it to Evans before his death, and he ordered you to execute it, but you never solved the encryption.

The Wallbreaker remembered the letter he had just decrypted on his computer and read it over carefully.

Simple enough to carry out, is it not?

"It's not too difficult. But is it truly that important?"

It used to be important. Now, because of humanity's Wallfacer Project, it is incredibly important.

"Why?"

The text did not show for a while.

Evans knew why, but evidently he didn't tell anyone. He was right. This is fortunate. Now, we don't need to tell you why.

The Wallbreaker was overjoyed. "My Lord, you have learned how to conceal! This is progress!"

Evans taught us much, but we are still at the very beginning, or in his words, only at the level of one of your five-year-old children. The order he gave you contains one of the strategies we can't learn.

"Do you mean this stipulation: 'To avoid attention, you must not reveal that it was done by ETO'? This . . . well, if the target is important, then this requirement is only natural."

To us it is a complicated plan.

"Fine. I will take care of it in accordance with Evans's wishes. My Lord, we will prove our devotion to you."

In one remote corner of the vast sea of information on the Internet, there was a remote corner, and in a remote corner of that remote corner, and then in a remote corner of a remote corner of a remote corner of that remote corner—that is, in the very depths of the most remote corner of all—a virtual world came back to life.

Under the strange, chilly dawn was no pyramid, UN building, or pendulum, just a broad and hard expanse of emptiness, like a giant slab of frozen metal.

King Wen of Zhou came over the horizon. Wearing tattered robes, he carried a tarnished bronze sword, and his face was as filthy and wrinkled as the pelt he was wrapped in. But there was energy in his eyes, and his pupils reflected the rising sun.

"Is anybody here?" he shouted. "Anyone?"

King Wen's voice was swallowed up immediately by the wilderness. He shouted for a while, and then sat wearily on the ground and accelerated the passage of time, watching the suns turn into shooting stars, and the shooting stars turn back into suns, and the suns of the Stable Eras sweep across the sky like clock pendulums, and the days and nights of the Chaotic Eras turn the world into a vast stage where the lighting was out of control. Time sped by, but nothing changed. It remained the eternal, metallic wasteland. The three stars danced in the heavens, and King Wen turned into a pillar of ice in the cold. Then a shooting star turned into a sun, and when that fiery giant disc passed overhead, the ice on his body melted and his body became a pillar of fire. Just before turning entirely to ash, he let out a long sigh, and then exited.

Thirty army, navy, and air force officers fixed their eyes on the insignia on the deep-red screen, a silver star shooting rays in four directions. The rays, in the shape of sharp swords, were flanked by the Chinese characters for eight and one.[5] It was the insignia of the Chinese Space Force.

General Chang Weisi motioned for everyone to be seated. Then, placing his cap squarely down upon the conference table, he said, "The ceremony formally establishing the space force will be held tomorrow morning, at which time you will be issued uniforms and pins. However, comrades, as of this moment we belong to the same branch of the military."

They looked at each other, noting that among the thirty people there were fifteen dressed in navy uniforms, nine in air force uniforms, and six in army uniforms. When they turned their attention back to General Chang, they had a hard time disguising their confusion.

5 *Translator's Note:* The insignia of the People's Liberation Army is a star inscribed with the characters eight and one.

With a smile, Chang Weisi said, "It's an odd ratio, isn't it? You can't use the scale of today's aerospace program to assess space forces of the future. Spaceships, when their day comes, will probably be even bigger and carry a larger crew than today's aircraft carriers. Future space warfare will be based on large-tonnage, high-endurance combat platforms, and engagements will resemble naval battles more than air combat, with a battlefield in three dimensions instead of two. So the military's space branch must be based upon the navy. I know, we all assumed that the foundation would be the air force, which means our naval comrades might be ill prepared. You've got to adapt as quickly as possible."

"Sir, we had no idea," Zhang Beihai said. Wu Yue sat ramrod straight and motionless beside him, but Zhang Beihai acutely sensed that something in his level eyes had been extinguished.

Chang Weisi nodded. "In fact, the navy's not all that far removed from space. Don't they call them 'space ships' rather than 'space planes'? That's because space and the ocean have long been linked together in the popular mind."

The mood of the room relaxed somewhat. He continued, "Comrades, at this moment, the thirty-one of us are all that makes up this new branch of the military. As for the future space fleet, basic research is being conducted in all scientific disciplines, with a particular focus on the space elevator, and on fusion engines for large-scale space ships. . . . But this isn't the work of the space force. Our duty is to establish a theoretical framework for space warfare. It's a daunting task, since we have zero knowledge of this type of warfare, but the future space fleet will be built atop this foundation. In its preliminary stage, then, the space force will be more like a military academy. The primary task of those of us seated here is to organize that academy, and then invite a sizeable group of scholars and researchers to join up."

Chang stood up and walked over to the insignia, where he addressed the assembled officers with words they would remember for the rest of their lives: "Comrades, the space force has a tough road ahead of it. Initial predictions see basic research taking at

least fifty years across all disciplines, with at least another hundred years before practical use of the technology required for large-scale space travel becomes possible. Then, after its initial construction, the space fleet will require another century and a half to achieve its planned scale. That means that full combat capacity will take the space force three centuries from its establishment. Comrades, I'm sure you all understand what that means. None of us sitting here will make it to space, much less have the chance to see our space fleet, and we may not even see a credible model of a space warship. The first generation of officers and crew won't be born until two centuries from now, and two and a half centuries from that, Earth's fleet will meet the alien invaders. Aboard those ships will be the fifteenth generation of our grandchildren."

The assembly fell into a prolonged silence. Ahead of them stretched the leaden road of time, terminating somewhere in the mists of the future, where all they could see were flickering flames and luster of blood. The brevity of a human lifespan tormented them as never before, and their hearts soared above the vault of time to join with their descendants and plunge into blood and fire in the icy cold of space, the eventual meeting place for the souls of all soldiers.

As usual, when Miao Fuquan returned, he asked Zhang Yuanchao and Yang Jinwen to have a drink at his place, where the Sichuan woman had laid out a sumptuous feast on the table. As they were drinking, Zhang Yuanchao brought up Miao Fuquan's visit to the Construction Bank that morning to withdraw some money.

"Haven't you heard?" Miao Fuquan said. "People were being trampled to death at the banks! There were people three deep on the floor at the counter."

"And your money?" asked Zhang Yuanchao.

"I was able to get some of it. The rest was frozen. It's criminal!"

"The hair you shed is worth more than the rest of us have altogether," said Zhang Yuanchao.

Yang Jinwen said, "The news said that when the social panic

37

eases a little, the government will gradually unfreeze accounts. Perhaps just a certain percentage at first, but the situation will eventually return to normal."

Zhang Yuanchao said, "I hope so. The government made a mistake in calling it a state of war so early on, putting people in a panic. Now people are only thinking of themselves. How many people are thinking about the defense of Earth four hundred years in the future?"

"That's not the biggest problem," Yang Jinwen said. "I said it before and I'll say it again, China's savings rate is an enormous land mine. Am I right? High savings, low social security. People's life savings are in the bank, and then everyone goes into mass hysteria at the slightest gust of wind."

Zhang Yuanchao asked, "So this wartime economy, what do you think it'll be like?"

"It's too sudden. I don't think anyone has a full mental picture of it yet, and the new economic policies are still being drafted. But one thing's certain: Tough days are ahead."

"Tough days, my ass. It's nothing people our age haven't seen before. It'll be like the sixties all over again, I expect," said Miao Fuquan.

"I just feel for the kids," said Zhang Yuanchao, and drained his glass.

Just then a news fanfare drew their attention to the television. A familiar sound these days, the music had the ability to make everyone drop what they were doing and pay attention. It was the bumper fanfare for a breaking news announcement, which were being broadcast more often than ever these days. The three old men remembered how this sort of news was frequently broadcast over radio and television prior to the 1980s, but during the long period of prosperity and tranquility that came afterward, it disappeared.

The broadcast began:

According to this station's correspondent at the UN Secretariat, a UN spokesperson at a just-concluded press conference announced that

a special session of the General Assembly will be convened in the near future to discuss the problem of Escapism. The special session will be co-facilitated by the permanent members of the Planetary Defense Council and will be aimed at pushing the international community to reach a consensus on Escapist attitudes and develop corresponding international laws.

Let's take a brief look back at the emergence and development of Escapism.

The doctrine of Escapism arose alongside the Trisolar Crisis. Its primary argument holds that given the locked state of humanity's advanced sciences, it does not make any sense to plan for a defense of Earth and the Solar System in four and a half centuries. Considering the extent to which human technology can develop over the next four centuries, a more realistic goal would be to construct starships to enable a small portion of the human race to flee to outer space, thereby avoiding the total extinction of human civilization.

Escapism has three possible destinations. Option one: a New World—that is, searching among the stars for a world where humanity can survive. Without question, this is the ideal, but it requires extremely high navigation speeds and the voyage will be long. Given the level that human technology can attain during the Crisis period, this option is unlikely to be realized. Option two: a Starship Civilization—that is, humanity will use their escape ships as a permanent abode, and human civilization will endure on an eternal voyage. This option faces the same difficulties as the New World, although it places a greater emphasis on the establishment of closed ecosystem technologies. A generation ship running a fully enclosed biosphere is far beyond humanity's current technical capabilities. Option three: Temporary Refuge. Once Trisolaris has completed settlement of the Solar System, there can be active exchanges between Trisolaran society and the humans that have fled to outer space. By pushing for a relaxation of policies toward residual humans in outer space, they will eventually be able to return to the Solar System and coexist on a smaller scale with the Trisolarans. Although Temporary Refuge is considered the most realistic plan, there are still too many variables.

Not long after the emergence of Escapism, news outlets worldwide reported that the United States and Russia, two leaders in space technology, had secretly started work on plans for fleeing into outer space. Although the governments of the two countries denied the existence of any plans, an uproar in the international community sparked a "socialized technology" movement. At the third special session, a host of developing countries demanded that the United States, Russia, Japan, China, and the European Union release their technology and provide all advanced technology, including aerospace technology, free of charge to the international community so that all nations of humanity would have an equal opportunity to face the Trisolar Crisis. The supporters of the socialized technology movement brought up a precedent: At the beginning of the century, several major European pharmaceutical companies exacted high license fees from African countries for the manufacture of state-of-the-art AIDS treatments, prompting high-profile litigation. Under pressure from public opinion and the rapid spread of the disease in Africa, the companies renounced their patent rights prior to trial. The ultimate crisis that Earth is now facing means that open technology is the unavoidable responsibility that advanced countries have to all humanity. The socialized technology movement found a unanimous response from developing countries and even won the support of some members of the EU, but all related initiatives were rejected at meetings of the UN-PDC. At the fifth special session of the UN General Assembly, a proposal by China and Russia of a "limited socialized technology" plan that advocated making technology open to all permanent members of the PDC was vetoed by the US and Britain. The US government said that no form of socialized technology was realistic, that it was a naïve idea, and that under the present circumstances US national security was a priority "second only to planetary defense." The failure of the limited socialized technology proposal caused a split among technological powers and led to the bankruptcy of the plan to establish a United Earth Space Force.

The implications of the frustrated socialized technology movement are far-reaching, and people have been made aware that even in the

40

face of the devastating Trisolar Crisis, the unity of the human race is still a distant dream.

The socialized technology movement was launched by the Escapists. Only when the international community reaches a consensus on Escapism will it be able to bridge the gap that has opened up between developed and developing nations, and between the developed countries themselves. This is the environment in which the UN special session is set to open.

"Oh, that reminds me," Miao Fuquan said. "The information I told you over the phone a few days ago is reliable."

"What's that?"

"The escape fund."

"Lao Miao, how can you believe that? You don't seem like an easy mark," Yang Jinwen said disapprovingly.

"No, no," Miao Fuquan said, lowering his voice and looking back and forth between the other two. "The young guy's name is Shi Xiaoming. I checked out his background through various channels, and his father Shi Qiang works for the PDC's security department! He used to be chief of a municipal antiterrorism squad, and now he's a key person in the PDC in charge of combatting the ETO. I've got a number here for his department. You can check it out for yourselves."

The other two looked at each other, and Yang Jinwen laughed as he picked up the bottle and poured himself another glass. "So what if it's true? Who cares if there's an escape fund? How can I afford it?"

"That's right. It's for you rich folks," Zhang Yuanchao slurred out.

Yang Jinwen suddenly grew excited: "And if it's really true, then the state's a pack of morons! If anyone's going to flee, it should be the cream of our descendants. Why the hell would you give it to anyone who can pay? What's the point of that?"

Miao Fuquan pointed at him and laughed. "Fine, Yang. Let's get to your real point. What you really want is for your descendants

to be the ones to go, right? Look at your son and daughter-in-law: Ph.D. scientists. Elites. So your grandsons and great-grandsons will most likely be elites too." He lifted his glass and nodded. "But if you think about it, everyone should be equal, right? There's no reason elites should get a, you know, free lunch, right?"

"What do you mean?"

"Everything has a cost. It's a law of nature. I'll spend to ensure a future for the Miaos. That's a law of nature, too!"

"Why is this something that can be bought? The duty of escaping is to extend human civilization. They'll naturally want the cream of civilization. Sending a bunch of rich dudes across the cosmos," he snorted. "What'll that do? Hmph."

The awkward smile on Miao Fuquan's face vanished, and he pointed a thick finger at Yang Jinwen. "I've always known you look down on me. No matter how rich I get, I'll just be a vulgar moneybags to you. Isn't that right?"

"Who do you think you are?" asked Yang Jinwen, fueled by the alcohol.

Miao Fuquan slapped the table and stood up. "Yang Jinwen, I'm not going to stand for your bile. I'm gonna—"

Then Zhang Yuanchao slammed the table with a noise three times louder, knocking over two of the cups and startling a yelp from the Sichuan woman. He pointed his finger at the other two in turn. "Fine. You're an elite, and you've got money. That leaves me. What the hell do I have? I'm just a poor man, so it serves me right that my line will be wiped out?" With obvious effort he restrained himself from kicking over the table, then turned and stormed out. Yang Jinwen followed him.

The Second Wallbreaker carefully put new goldfish into the bowl. Like Evans, he enjoyed isolation, but he needed the companionship of beings other than humans. He often spoke to the goldfish like he spoke to the Trisolarans, two forms of life whose long-term presence on Earth he was looking forward to.

42

Just then the sophon's text appeared on his retina.

I've recently been studying *A Story of Three Kingdoms*, and like you said, deceit and trickery are an art, just like the markings on a snake.

"My Lord, once again you bring up the snake."

The more beautiful the markings on a snake, the more fearsome it looks. We didn't use to care about humanity escaping, so long as they stopped existing in the Solar System, but now we have adjusted our plans and have decided to prevent humanity from fleeing. Letting an enemy whose thoughts are totally opaque flee into the cosmos is very dangerous.

"Do you have a specific plan in mind?"

The fleet has made adjustments to its Solar System deployment. It will detour in four directions at the Kuiper Belt[6] and encircle the Solar System.

"If humanity really flees, your fleet will be too late to do anything by the time they do."

That is true, so we require your assistance. The next mission of the ETO is to halt or delay humanity's escape plans.

The Wallbreaker smiled. "My Lord, you really don't have to worry about that at all. No large-scale flight of humanity will ever happen."

Even given the present, limited space for technological development, humanity might be able to build generation ships.

6 *Translator's Note:* The Kuiper Belt is a region extending from the orbit of Neptune, at roughly 30 AU, to roughly 50 AU, and is home to Pluto and two other dwarf planets, among other objects.

"The greatest obstacle to flight is not technology."

Then is it disputes among countries? This UN special session may resolve that problem, and if it can't, then developed countries are entirely capable of brushing aside the opposition of developing countries and forcing a plan through.

"The greatest obstacle to flight is not disputes among countries, either."

Then what is it?

"Disputes among people. The question of who goes and who stays behind."

That doesn't seem like a problem to us.

"We thought so at first, but it turns out to be an insurmountable obstacle."

Can you explain?

"You may be familiar with human history, but you will probably find this hard to comprehend: Who goes and who remains involves basic human values, values which in the past promoted progress in human society, but which, in the face of ultimate disaster, are a trap. Right now, the majority of humanity has not realized how deep this trap is. Lord, please believe my words. No human can escape this trap."

"Uncle Zhang, you don't have to decide now. You've asked all the necessary questions, and it's not a small amount of money, after all," Shi Xiaoming said to Zhang Yuanchao, his face a picture of serenity.

44

"It's not that. Is the plan for real? The TV says—"

"Don't you mind what the TV says. Two weeks ago the government spokesperson said that freezing accounts was impossible, but now look what's happened. . . . Think reasonably. You're an ordinary man, and you're thinking about the continuation of your family line. What about the president and the premier? Won't they be thinking about the continuation of the Chinese people? And the UN about the continuation of the human race? This UN special session is actually an international cooperative plan that will formally launch the Human Escape Plan. This is a pressing matter."

Lao Zhang slowly nodded. "It does seem that way when you think about it. But I still feel like escape is a long way off. Should I really be worrying about it?"

"Uncle Zhang, you misunderstand. Escape can't be all that far off. Do you think the escape ships will only take off three or four hundred years from now? If that were true, then the Trisolaran Fleet could catch them easily."

"Then when will the ships head out?"

"You're about to have a grandson, right?"

"Yes."

"Your grandson will see those ships take off."

"He'll be aboard one?"

"No, that's impossible. But his grandson could be."

"That's . . ." Zhang worked it out. "About seventy or eighty years."

"It'll be longer than that. The wartime government will tighten population controls and build delays into the birth restrictions, so it'll be forty years to a generation. The ships will take off in about one hundred twenty years."

"That's pretty quick. Can they be built in time?"

"Uncle Zhang, think back to what things were like one hundred twenty years ago. It was still the Qing Dynasty! It took over a month to go from Hangzhou to Beijing, and the emperor had to spend days cooped up in a sedan chair to get to his summer retreat. Now it's less than three days from Earth to the moon. Technology develops

45

fast, which means that the pace of development is always on the increase. If you add to that the fact that the whole world is pouring all its energy into space technology, then there's no question at all that spaceships can be created in about one hundred twenty years."

"Isn't space travel pretty dangerous?"

"That's true, but won't Earth be dangerous then, too? Look at how things are changing now. The country's main economic force is being used to establish a space fleet, which is not a commercial good and will not bring in one cent in profit. People's lives will only get worse. Add to that the sheer size of our base population, and simply having enough to eat becomes a problem. And then take a look at the international situation. Developing countries don't have the ability to escape, and developed countries have refused to socialize their technology. But the poorer and smaller countries won't give up. Aren't they threatening to pull out of the Non-Proliferation Treaty? And they may take more extreme actions in the future. Who knows—in a hundred and twenty years, before the alien fleet even arrives, the world might be engulfed in the flames of war! Who knows what sort of life your great-grandson's generation will lead. Besides, the escape ships aren't what you imagine. Comparing them to the Shenzhou spaceship and the ISS is ridiculous. The ships will be big, each of them a small city, and a complete ecosystem to boot. Just like a tiny Earth. Humanity can live on them forever without any outside supplies. And most importantly, there will be hibernation. We can do that now, even. The passengers on board will spend most of their time in hibernation, where a century feels like no more than a day, until they reach the new world or they reach an accord with the Trisolarans to return to the Solar System. Then they'll wake up. Isn't that a much better life than suffering back on Earth?"

Zhang Yuanchao thought this over in silence.

Shi Xiaoming went on. "Of course, to be completely honest with you, space travel is indeed a dangerous thing. No one knows what sort of hazards they might encounter in space. I know you're mostly doing this for the continuation of your Zhang lineage, but don't let it worry you . . ."

46

Zhang stared at him as if he had been pricked. "How can you young people say things like that? Why wouldn't I worry?"

"Let me finish, Uncle Zhang. I don't mean it like that. I just mean that even if you don't plan on sending your descendants to flee in spaceships, this fund is worth buying, guaranteed. Once it's available for the general public to buy, the price will soar. There are lots of rich people, you know, and there aren't many other avenues for investment, and hoarding is illegal. Besides, the more money you have, the more you think about preserving your line, wouldn't you say?"

"Right. I know that."

"Uncle Zhang, I'm being totally honest here. The escape fund is currently in a preliminary phase and has only a small number of special internal salespeople. It wasn't easy for me to get in on the quota. At any rate, when you've thought it over, give me a call, and I'll help you fill out the paperwork."

When Shi Xiaoming had gone, Lao Zhang stood on the balcony looking out at the sky, which hung a little hazily over the halo of the city, and said to himself, *My children, will your grandpa really send you someplace where night lasts forever?*

When King Wen of Zhou next set foot onto the desolation of *Three Body* world, a small sun was rising. Although it did not give much heat, it lit the wasteland quite clearly. The wasteland was completely empty.

"Is there anyone here? Anyone?"

Then his eyes lit up as he saw someone riding a galloping horse from the horizon. Recognizing him at a distance as Newton, he ran toward him, waving wildly. Newton soon reached his side, reined in his horse, and, after dismounting, hurriedly adjusted his wig.

"What are you shouting for? Who restarted this damned place?"

King Wen didn't answer his question, but took his hand and said urgently, "Comrade, my comrade, listen to me. The Lord has not abandoned us. Or, rather, Its abandonment was for a reason, and It will need us in the future. It . . ."

"I know that," Newton said, impatiently brushing aside King Wen's hand. "The sophons sent me a message too."

"So that means that the Lord sent a message to lots of us at the same time. Excellent. The organization's contact with the Lord won't ever be monopolized again."

"Does the organization still exist?" Newton wiped away sweat with a handkerchief.

"Of course it exists. The Redemptionists totally collapsed after the global strike, and the Survivors split off and developed into an independent force. Only the Adventists are left in the org now."

"The strike purified the org. This is a good thing."

"Since you're here, you must be an Adventist. But you seem to be out of the loop. Are you on your own?"

"My only contact is with one other comrade, and he didn't tell me anything but this Web address. I barely escaped the awful global strike with my life."

"Your escape instincts were ably demonstrated during the Qin Shi Huang era."

Newton looked around. "Is it safe?"

"Of course. We're at the bottom of a multilevel maze, and it's practically impossible to discover. Anyone who managed to storm their way in here wouldn't be able to trace user locations. For security reasons, after the strike, the org put every branch into isolation with mutual contact kept to a minimum. We need a place to meet, and a buffer area for new members. This is more secure than the real world."

"Have you noticed that attacks on the organization in the real world have slackened considerably?"

"They're clever. They know the org is the only means of obtaining intelligence on the Lord, as well as the only opportunity of getting their hands on the technology that the Lord passes to us, even though there's only a minute chance of that happening. That's the reason they'll let the org continue to exist to a certain extent, but I think they'll come to regret it."

"The Lord isn't so clever. It doesn't even comprehend the ability to be clever."

"So It needs us. The existence of the org is valuable, and all comrades should know of this as soon as possible."

Newton mounted his horse. "Very well. I've got to go. I'll stay longer once I've verified that it's really secure here."

"I guarantee to you that it's absolutely safe."

"If that's true, then there'll be more comrades gathering here next time. Good-bye." Saying this, Newton urged his horse off into the distance. By the time its hoofbeats had dissipated, the small sun had become a shooting star, and a cloak of darkness descended upon the world.

Luo Ji lay limp on the bed, watching the woman put on clothes after a shower through eyes still hazy from sleep. The sun, already high in the sky, shone through the curtains and turned her into a graceful projected silhouette, like a scene from a black-and-white movie he had forgotten the name of. But what he needed to remember now was her name. What was she called? Keep calm. First, her last name: If it was Zhang, then she would be Zhang Shan. Or was it Chen? Then, Chen Jingjing . . . no, those were previous women. He thought about looking at his phone, but it was still in his pocket and he had tossed his clothes on the carpet. Besides, they had only known each other for a little while and he hadn't entered her number into his phone yet. The important thing now was not to have it be like that one time he'd asked outright—the consequences had been disastrous. So he turned to the television, which she had turned on and muted. On the screen, seated around a large round table, the UN Security Council was in session—wait, it wasn't the Security Council anymore, but he couldn't remember its new name. He was really out of it.

"Turn it up," he said. His words sounded distant without a term of endearment, but he didn't care about that now.

"You really seem to be interested." She sat combing her hair but didn't adjust the sound.

Luo Ji reached over to the bedside table and picked up a lighter

49

and a cigarette and lit it as he stretched his bare feet out of his towel and wiggled his big toes in satisfaction.

"Look at you. You call yourself a scholar?" She watched his wriggling toes in the mirror.

"A young scholar," he added, "with few accomplishments. But that's because I don't put in the effort. I'm actually full of inspiration. Sometimes, what other people might spend a lifetime working on, I can figure out with a moment's thought. . . . Believe it or not, I was almost famous once."

"Because of that subculture stuff?"

"No, not that. It was another thing I was working on at the same time. I established cosmic sociology."

"What?"

"It's the sociology of aliens."

She snickered, then tossed her comb aside and began putting on her makeup.

"Don't you know about the celebrity tendency in academia? I could've been a star."

"Alien researchers are a dime a dozen these days."

"That's only after all this new crap came out," Luo Ji said as he pointed at the mute television, which was still showing the large table and the people seated round it. The segment was awfully long. Was it live? "Academics didn't use to study aliens. They sifted through piles of old paper and become celebrities that way. But later the public got tired of the cultural necrophilia of that old crew, and that's when I came along." He stretched his bare arms toward the ceiling. "Cosmic sociology, aliens, and lots of alien races. More of them than there are people on Earth, tens of billions! The producer of that *Lecture Room* television program talked about doing a series with me, but then it all actually happened, and then . . ." He swept a circle with a finger, and sighed.

She wasn't listening too closely to him, reading the subtitles on the television instead: " 'We reserve all options in regard to Escapism . . .' What does that mean?"

"Who's talking?"

"It looks like Karnoff."

"He's saying that Escapism needs to be treated as harshly as the ETO, and that a guided missile needs to be dropped on anyone making a Noah's Ark."

"That's kind of harsh."

"No," he said forcefully. "It's the wisest strategy. I came up with it long ago. And even if it doesn't come to that, no one's going to fly away, anyway. You ever read a book by Liang Xiaosheng called *Floating City*?"

"I haven't. It's pretty old, isn't it?"

"Right. I read it when I was a kid. Shanghai's about to fall into the ocean, and a group of people go house to house seizing life preservers and then destroying them en masse, for the sole purpose of making sure that no one would live if everyone couldn't. I remember in particular there was one little girl who took the group to the door of one house and cried out, 'They still have one!'"

"You're just the sort of asshole that always sees society as trash."

"Bullshit. The fundamental axiom of economics is the human mercenary instinct. Without that assumption, the entire field would collapse. There isn't any fundamental axiom for sociology yet, but it might be even darker than economics. The truth always picks up dust. A small number of people could fly off into space, but if we knew it would come to that, why would we have bothered in the first place?"

"Bothered with what?"

"Why would we have had the Renaissance? Why the Magna Carta? Why the French Revolution? If humanity had stayed divided into classes, kept in place by the law's iron rule, then when the time came, the ones who needed to leave would leave, and the ones who had to stay behind would stay. If this took place in the Ming or Qing Dynasties, then I'd leave, of course, and you'd stay behind. But that's not possible now."

"I wouldn't mind if you took off right now," she said.

Which was, in fact, the truth. They had reached a mutual parting of ways. He had been able to reach this point with all of his

previous lovers, never early or late. He was especially pleased with his control over the pace this time. He had known her for just one week, and the breakup proceeded smoothly, as elegantly as a rocket discarding its booster.

He backtracked to an earlier topic: "Hey, it wasn't my idea to establish cosmic sociology, you know. Do you want to know whose it was? You're the only one I'm going to tell, so don't get scared."

"Whatever. I can't believe most of what you say anyway, apart from one thing."

"Uh . . . forget it. What one thing?"

"Come on and get up. I'm hungry." She picked up his clothes from the carpet and threw them on the bed.

They ate breakfast in the main restaurant of the hotel. Most of the occupants of the tables around them looked serious, and at times they could catch snatches of conversation. Luo Ji didn't want to listen, but he was like a candle on a summer night. The words, like insects crowding around the flame, kept working their way into his head: Escapism, socialized technology, ETO, transformation to a wartime economy, equatorial base, charter amendment, PDC, near-Earth primary warning and defensive perimeter, independent integrated mode . . .

"Our age has gotten really dull, hasn't it?" Luo Ji said. He stopped cutting his egg and set down his fork.

She nodded. "I agree. I saw a game show question on TV yesterday that was really moronic. Hands on buzzers." She pointed a fork at Luo Ji in imitation of the host. "One hundred and twenty years before the doomsday, your thirteenth generation will be alive. True or false?"

Luo Ji picked up his fork again and shook his head. "It's not going to be any generation of mine." He folded his hands as if in prayer. "My grand family line will die out with me."

She gave a dismissive snort. "You asked me which of your lines I believe. That's the one. You've said it before. That's the sort of person you are."

So that's why she was leaving him? He didn't want to ask about

52

it for fear of complicating the issue, but she seemed to read his thoughts, and said, "I'm that sort of person too. It's really annoying to see certain things about yourself in other people."

"Particularly in a member of the opposite sex," Luo Ji said, nodding.

"But if you need to justify it, it's perfectly responsible behavior."

"What behavior? Not having kids? Of course it is." Luo Ji pointed his fork at the people around them discussing economic transformation. "You know what sort of lives their descendants will be living? They'll be spending their days slaving away in the shipyards—the spaceship yards—and then they'll line up at the canteen, bellies rumbling as they hold out their lunch pails waiting for that ladle of porridge . . . and when they're older, it'll be Uncle Sam Wants . . . no, Earth Wants You, and it's off to find glory in the army."

"It'll be better for the doomsday generation."

"Retiring to face doomsday. How miserable. And besides, that last generation's grandparents might not get enough to eat. Still, even *that* future's not going to come to pass. Just look at how stubborn the people of Earth are. I bet they resist till the end, at which point the real mystery is how they'll eventually die."

They left the hotel after their meal and emerged into the warm embrace of the morning sun. The air had a sweetness that was intoxicating.

"I've got to learn how to live. If I can't swing that, it'll be a damn shame," Luo Ji said as he watched the passing traffic.

"Neither of us is gonna learn," she said, her eyes searching for a taxi.

"Then . . ." Luo Ji looked inquiringly at her. Evidently there would be no need to remember her name.

"Good-bye." She nodded in his direction, and then they shook hands and shared a quick kiss.

"Maybe we'll meet again." He regretted this as soon as he said it. Everything had been fine up till this point, so why risk causing trouble? But his concern was unnecessary.

"I doubt it." She turned quickly as she spoke, sending the bag on her shoulder flying into the air, a detail that Luo Ji repeatedly called to mind afterward in an attempt to determine whether or not it had been deliberate. It was a distinctive LV bag, and he had seen her send it swinging while turning around many times before. But this time the bag swung straight at his face, and when he took a step backward to dodge it, he stumbled over the fire hydrant behind him and fell flat on his back.

That fall saved his life.

Meanwhile, the following was taking place on the street in front of them: Two cars collided head on, but before the noise of the impact had subsided, a Polo swerved to avoid the crash and came hurtling toward where the two of them were standing. Luo Ji's fall turned into a successful dodge. Only the front bumper of the Polo brushed one of his feet, the one that was still elevated, nudging his body into a ninety-degree turn on the ground so that he faced the back end of the car. He didn't hear the heavy thud of the other impact, but then he saw the woman's body soar over the top of the car and fall behind it on the road like a boneless rag doll. As it tumbled, the trail of blood it left behind on the ground seemed like it ought to mean something. As he stared at the bloody symbol, Luo Ji finally remembered her name.

Zhang Yuanchao's daughter-in-law was about to give birth. She had been moved into the delivery room while the rest of the family gathered in the waiting room outside, where a television was playing a video of mother and baby wellness information. It all gave him a feeling of warmth and humanity that he had never felt before, a lingering coziness of a past Golden Age being eroded by the ever worsening era of crisis.

Yang Jinwen came in. Zhang Yuanchao's first thought was that he was taking this opportunity to patch up their relationship, but Yang Jinwen's expression told him that wasn't the case. Without so much as a greeting, Yang Jinwen dragged him from the waiting

room into the hallway. "Did you really buy into the escape fund?" he asked.

Zhang Yuanchao ignored him and turned to go, as if to say, *That's none of your business.*

"Look at this," Yang Jinwen said, handing him a newspaper. "It's today's." The top headline stood out in black before his eyes:

Special UN Session Passes Resolution 117, Declares Escapism Illegal

Zhang Yuanchao carefully read through the start of the article underneath:

By an overwhelming majority, a special session of the United Nations General Assembly passed a resolution declaring Escapism a violation of international law. In strong language, the resolution condemned the division and turmoil that Escapism has created within human society, and described Escapism as a crime against humanity in the eyes of international law. The resolution called on member states to enact legislation as soon as possible to put a stop to Escapism.

In a statement, the Chinese delegate reiterated the stance of the Chinese government regarding Escapism and said that it firmly supports UN Resolution 117. He conveyed the Chinese government's pledge to take immediate action to establish and improve legislation, and to adopt effective measures to stop the spread of Escapism. He concluded by saying, "We must cherish the unity and solidarity of the international community in this time of crisis and uphold the principle, recognized by the international community, that all humanity has an equal right to survival. The Earth is the common home of its people, and we must not abandon her."

"Why . . . why are they doing this?" he stammered.

"Isn't it obvious? Put a little thought into it, and you'll realize that escape into the cosmos was never going to work. The critical question is who gets to leave, and who has to stay. This isn't

ordinary inequality. It's a question of survival, and no matter who gets to leave—elites, the rich, or ordinary people—so long as some people get left behind, it means the collapse of humanity's fundamental value system and ethical bottom line. Human rights and equality have deep roots. Inequality of survival is the worst sort of inequality, and the people and countries left behind will never just sit and wait for death while others have a way out. There will be increasingly extreme confrontations between the two sides until there's world chaos, and then no one goes! The UN resolution is quite wise. How much did you spend, Lao Zhang?"

Zhang Yuanchao scrambled for his phone. He called Shi Xiaoming's number, but it was unreachable. His legs threatened to give out, and he slid down the wall to sit on the ground. He had spent 400,000 yuan[7].

"Call the police! There's one thing that that Shi kid doesn't know: Lao Miao looked up his daddy's work unit. The scammer won't get away."

Zhang Yuanchao just sat there shaking his head. He said with a sigh, "Sure, we can find him, but the money's long gone. What'll I say to my family?"

There was the sound of crying, and then a nurse shouted, "Number nineteen. It's a boy!" Zhang Yuanchao bounded off into the waiting room as everything else suddenly became insignificant.

In the thirty minutes that he had been waiting, ten thousand new babies had come into the world, babies whose combined cries formed a tremendous chorus. Behind them was the Golden Age, the good times that began in the 1980s and ended with the Crisis. Ahead of them, humanity's arduous years were about to unfold.

All Luo Ji knew was that he was locked in a tiny basement room. The basement was deep, and he had felt the descent of the elevator (one of those rare old-style elevators with a manually operated

7 *Translator's Note:* Roughly equivalent to $65,000 in early 2015.

lever) even as the mechanism confirmed his sensations, counting backward to negative ten. Ten levels below ground! Once again he took stock of his small room. The twin bed, simple furnishings, and an ancient wooden writing desk gave the place the look of a guard room, not a prison cell. Clearly no one had been here for quite some time, and although the bedclothes were new, the rest of the furniture was covered in dust and gave off a dank, musty smell.

The door opened and a stocky middle-aged man entered. He nodded wearily at Luo Ji. "Dr. Luo, I'm here to keep you company, but since you've just come over I don't expect you're climbing the walls just yet."

Just come over. The phrase grated—surely "sent down" would have been more accurate. Luo Ji's heart sank. His guess had been confirmed, it seemed: Although the men who had brought him here had been polite, it was clear he had been arrested.

"Are you a policeman?"

The man nodded. "Used to be. Name's Shi Qiang." He sat down on the bed and pulled out a pack of cigarettes. *The smoke wouldn't have any place to dissipate in this sealed room,* Luo Ji thought, but he didn't dare say anything. As if reading his mind, Shi Qiang looked around and said, "There ought to be a ventilation fan." Then he pulled a cord next to the door, and a fan started humming. It was pretty rare to see a pull-cord switch. Luo Ji also noticed an obsolete red rotary phone lying in a corner, covered in dust. Shi Qiang handed him a cigarette, which he accepted after a moment's hesitation.

When they had lit their cigarettes, Shi Qiang said, "It's early yet. Shall we chat?"

"Ask away," Luo Ji said, head down as he exhaled a cloud of smoke.

"Ask what?" Shi Qiang said, looking at Luo Ji in surprise.

Luo Ji jumped up from the bed and tossed the cigarette aside. "How can you suspect me? You've got to know it was just a traffic accident! The two cars collided, and then she was hit by the one behind them as it tried to avoid the crash. It's plain as day." He held out his hands, at a loss for words.

Shi Qiang raised his head and looked at him, his tired eyes suddenly alert, as if an invisible malice, honed with practice, were hidden behind the smile he usually wore. "You said that, not me. My superiors don't want me to say anything more, and I don't know anything more. To think I was worried we wouldn't have anything to talk about. Come, sit down."

Luo Ji didn't sit down. He got in Shi Qiang's face and continued: "I'd only known her for a week. We met at a bar next to the university, and when the accident happened I couldn't even remember her name. Tell me, what could there possibly have been between us to lead your thoughts in that direction?"

"You couldn't even remember her name? No wonder you didn't care at all when she died. You're pretty much the same as another genius I know." He chuckled. "The wonderful life of Dr. Luo, meeting a new woman every time you turn around. And what women they are!"

"Is that a crime?"

"Of course not. I'm just jealous. I've got one rule in my work: Never make moral judgments. The guys I've got to deal with, they're the real deal. If I go and nag them, 'Look at what you've done! Think about your parents, and about society . . .' and so on, I might as well be slapping them across the face."

"I'd rather talk about her, Officer Shi. Do you really believe I killed her?"

"Look at you, bringing up the issue on your own. Saying you may have killed her, even. We're just having a casual chat. What's your hurry? You're new at this, that much is clear."

Luo Ji stared at Shi Qiang, and for a moment the hum of the fan was the only audible sound. Then he cackled and picked up his cigarette. "Luo, my man," Shi Qiang said. "Luo, my boy. Destiny's brought us together. You know, I've been involved in sixteen cases that ended in the death penalty. I personally escorted nine of them."

Luo Ji handed a cigarette to Shi Qiang. "I'm not going to let you escort me. So, if you'll be so good as to notify my lawyer."

"Excellent, my boy," Shi Qiang said, clapping Luo Ji on the

shoulder. "Decisiveness is a trait I admire." Then he drew up close to him and said, through a cloud of smoke, "You can come across all sorts of things, but what's happened to you is really . . ." He trailed off. "Actually, I'm here to help. You know how the joke goes: On the way to the execution ground, a condemned criminal complained that it was going to rain, and the executioner said, 'What have you got to worry about? We're the ones who've got to go back through it!' That's the attitude you and I ought to have for what comes next. Well, then. There's still some time before we get going. Might as well get some sleep."

"Get going?" Again, Luo Ji stared at Shi Qiang.

There was a knock at the door, and then a keen-eyed young man entered and dropped a suitcase on the ground. "Captain Shi, it's been moved ahead. We're leaving now."

Zhang Beihai gently pushed open the door to his father's hospital room. Half-reclining against a pillow on the bed, his father looked better than he had imagined. The golden rays of the setting sun that shone in through the window gave his face some color and made him look less like a man at death's door. Zhang Beihai set his hat on the coatrack by the door and took a seat beside his father's bed. He didn't ask about his condition, because the old soldier would give him a straight answer, and he didn't want a straight answer.

"Dad, I've joined the space force."

His father nodded but said nothing. For father and son, the silence conveyed more information than words. Growing up, his father had used silence rather than speech to educate him, and words were merely the punctuation between the silences. It was his silent father who had made him into the man he was today.

"Just like you thought, they're building the space fleet on a naval foundation. They believe space warfare will be closest in form and theory to naval warfare."

His father nodded. "Very good."

"So what should I do?"

I've finally asked it, Dad. The question I spent a sleepless night gathering the resolve to ask. I hesitated just now when I saw you, because I know it's the question that will disappoint you the most. I remember when I finished grad school and joined the fleet as a cadet lieutenant, you told me, "Beihai, you've got a long way to go. I say that because I can still easily understand you, and being understandable to me means that your mind is still too simple, not subtle enough. On the day I can no longer read you or figure you out, but you can easily understand me, that's when you'll finally have grown up." And then I grew up like you said, and you could no longer so easily understand your son. I know you must have felt at least some sorrow at that. But your son is indeed becoming the kind of person you'd hoped for, someone not particularly likeable, but capable of succeeding in the complicated and dangerous realm of the navy. For me to ask this question surely means that the training you've given me for three decades has failed at the crucial juncture. But Dad, tell me anyway. Your son is not as great as you imagine. Tell me, just this once.

"Think some more," his father said.

Fine, Dad. You've given me an answer. They've told me quite a lot, those three words, more than could be said in thirty thousand. Believe me, I'm listening to them with my whole heart, but I still need you to be clearer, because this is far too important.

"And after I've thought?" Zhang Beihai asked, gripping the bedsheet with both hands. His palms and forehead were laced with sweat.

Dad, forgive me. If I disappointed you the last time, then let me go further, go back to being a kid once more.

"Beihai, all I can say is to think long and hard first," his father replied.

Thank you, Dad. You've made it very clear, and I understand.

Zhang Beihai let go of the sheet and grasped his father's bony hand. "Dad, I'm not going to sea anymore. I'll come and see you all the time."

His father smiled but shook his head: "This isn't anything serious. Concentrate on your work."

They spoke for a while longer, first of family matters, and then about the establishment of the space force, with his father contributing lots of ideas of his own, including advice for Zhang Beihai's future work. They imagined the shape and size of space battleships, debated the weaponry of space warfare, and even whether Mahan's theory of sea power applied to space battles. . . .

But there was little significance in their conversation, just father and son taking a verbal stroll together. The significance was in the three lines their hearts exchanged:

"Think some more."

"And after I've thought?"

"Beihai, all I can say is to think long and hard first."

Zhang Beihai said good-bye to his father. As he was leaving the room, he turned back at the door to look at him, shrouded in shadow now that the light of the setting sun had departed. His eyes pierced the shadows and noticed one last scrap of illumination on the wall opposite. Although it was about to fade, this was the time when the setting sun was at its most beautiful. The last rays of sunlight shone, too, on the waves that rolled endlessly on the angry ocean and in shafts of light that pierced the jumbled clouds in the west and cast enormous golden bands on the water's surface like petals fallen from heaven. Beyond the petals, dark clouds loomed over a world black as night as a thunderstorm hung between heaven and earth like the curtain of the gods, and only periodic lightning lit the snowlike spray thrown up by the waves. In one golden band, a destroyer struggled to lift its prow from the trough, and then broke through the wall of the wave with a thunderous crash, the spray greedily absorbing the light like a giant roc stretching enormous glittering wings to the sky.

Zhang Beihai put on his cap, which bore the insignia of the Chinese Space Force. He said to himself, *Dad, we think alike. This is my good fortune. I won't bring you glory, but I'll give you rest.*

"Mr. Luo, please change into this," said the young man, who knelt down to open a suitcase upon entering the room. Though the man seemed entirely polite, Luo Ji couldn't shake a certain discomfort, like he had swallowed a fly. But when he saw the clothing the man took out, he realized that he wouldn't be wearing a convict's uniform: It looked like an ordinary brown jacket. He took it and inspected the thick material. Shi Qiang and the young man put on similar jackets in different colors.

"Put it on. It's comfortable and it breathes. Not like the old stuff we used to wear, which was sticky as hell," Shi Qiang said.

"Bulletproof," the young man said.

Who would want to kill me? Luo Ji thought as he changed jackets.

The three of them left the room and followed the corridor to the elevator. The ceiling was lined with rectangular metal ductwork and they passed several heavy, sealed doorways. Luo Ji noticed a faint slogan on one of the mottled walls. Only part of it was visible, but he knew the whole slogan: "Dig deep tunnels, keep vast stores of grain, don't seek hegemony."[8]

"Civil Air Defense?" he asked.

"Not the ordinary kind. Defense against the atom bomb, but it's obsolete now. Back in the day, you had to be someone special to get in here."

"So we're at . . . the Western Hills?" Luo Ji asked, but Shi Qiang and the young man did not reply. Luo Ji had heard stories about the secret command center. They entered the old-style elevator and began to ascend immediately, accompanied by a tremendous scraping. The operator was a People's Armed Police soldier armed with a submachine gun. This seemed to be his first time at this job, and he had to fiddle with the controls a bit before the elevator finally stopped at floor 1.

8 *Translator's Note:* Vast networks of tunnels were built in cities across China
 beginning in the late 1960s as defensive measures against enemy attack.
 This slogan, adapted from advice given to the founder of the Ming Dynasty,
 was promulgated as a directive from Mao Zedong in the *People's Daily*'s annual
 New Year's Editoral in January 1973.

Exiting the elevator, Luo Ji saw that they were in a large hall with a low ceiling, like an underground parking garage. A number of different cars were parked here, some of them with engines on, filling the air with noxious exhaust. People were standing beside the lines of cars or walking among them. With only one light in a distant corner turned on, the place was dim and the people dark shadows. Only when they passed the lamplight did Luo Ji see that they were fully armed soldiers. Some were shouting into radios, trying to be heard over the engine noise. Their voices sounded tense.

Shi Qiang led Luo Ji through the two lines of cars, with the young man close behind. The lamplight and red taillights shining though the gaps in the cars cast an ever-changing pattern of color on Shi Qiang's body and reminded Luo Ji of the dim bar where he had met the woman.

Shi Qiang led Luo Ji to one car, opened the door, and had him get in. The car was roomy, but the edges of its abnormally tiny windows revealed the thickness of the car's body. A reinforced vehicle with tinted glass in its small windows, probably as an antibomb measure. The car door was ajar, and Luo Ji could hear Shi Qiang and the young man talking.

"Captain Shi, they called just now to say they've been over the route. All guard positions have been set up."

"The route is too complicated. We've only been able to do a couple of quick runs through the whole thing. Not enough for comfort. And about the guard positions—it's like I said, you've got to think like them. If you were on their side, where would you be hiding? Consult with the experts from the People's Armed Police again. Hey, what's the plan for the handoff?"

"They didn't say."

Shi Qiang raised his voice. "Morons. They can't leave such an important part up in the air."

"Captain Shi, it looks like the brass want us to follow along the entire way."

"I can follow along my entire life, but since there's got to be a handoff once we're there, there needs to be a clear demarcation of

responsibilities. There's got to be a line. Anything that happens before it is on us, and afterward on them."

"They didn't say . . ." The young man sounded uncomfortable.

"Zheng, I know you've been feeling sorry for yourself since Chang Weisi got promoted. Hell, it's like we don't even exist to his former subordinates. But we should have some self-respect. Who the fuck are they? Have they been under fire, or have they ever fired at anyone? That crew used so many high-tech tricks in the last operation it was like a circus. They even brought out the airborne early warning system. But in the end, who did they use to find the meeting place? Us. That won us some cred. Zheng, it took a lot of convincing to get the lot of you over here, but I wonder if that might not end up causing you harm."

"Captain Shi, don't say that."

"It's a troubled world. Do you get that? Morality isn't what it used to be. Everyone foists their bad luck off onto other people, so you've got to be on your guard. . . . I'm going on like this because I'm worried about how long I'm going to last. I'm afraid that all of it's going to land in your lap."

"Captain Shi, you've really got to think about your illness. Didn't the higher-ups schedule you for hibernation?"

"I've got to get lots of things taken care of first. Family, work. And do you think I'm not worried about the lot of you here?"

"Don't worry about us. With your condition, you can't put it off. Your teeth were bleeding out again this morning."

"That's nothing. I've got good luck. You should know. Three of the guns I've been shot at with were duds."

The cars at one end of the hall were beginning to pull out. Shi Qiang got in and closed the door, and when the neighboring car started to move, their car followed. Shi Qiang pulled the curtains closed on either side, and the opaque divider between the back and front seats totally obscured Luo Ji's view of the outside. As they rode, Shi Qiang's radio chirped endlessly, but Luo Ji couldn't make out the comments Shi Qiang was replying to in clipped sentences.

When they had ridden a short way, Luo Ji said to Shi Qiang, "Things are more complicated than you said."

"That's right. Everything's complicated now," Shi Qiang said perfunctorily, his attention still focused on the radio. They spoke no more for the rest of the trip.

The ride was smooth and unbroken, and after about an hour they came to a stop.

When Shi Qiang got out of the car, he motioned to Luo Ji to wait inside, and then closed the door. Luo Ji heard a rumbling that seemed to come from above the vehicle. After a few minutes, Shi Qiang opened the door again and had Luo Ji get out, at which point he realized they were at an airport. The rumbling had turned thunderous. He looked up to see two helicopters hovering overhead, oriented in opposite directions like they were monitoring the open area. In front of him was a large aircraft that looked like a passenger plane, except that there was no insignia on any part he could see. An airstair stood in front of the car door, and Shi Qiang and Luo Ji took it up to the aircraft. When Luo Ji glanced back out the door after they entered, the first thing that caught his eye were the fighter jets lined up on a distant apron, which informed him that this wasn't a civilian airport. Closer in, he saw the cars from their convoy and the soldiers that had exited their vehicles in a ring around the plane. The sun was setting, casting a long shadow down the runway ahead of the plane, like a giant exclamation point.

Luo Ji and Shi Qiang entered the cabin. Three men in black suits welcomed them and took them past the forward cabin, which was totally empty but resembled a passenger plane with four rows of seats. In the middle cabin, Luo Ji saw a fairly spacious office, and another suite through whose half-open door he glimpsed a bedroom. The furnishings were unremarkable but neat and orderly, and apart from the green safety belts on the sofa and chairs you wouldn't have known you were on a plane. Luo Ji knew that there were very few charter planes of this kind in the country.

Two of the three men who led them in vanished through a door to the rear cabin, leaving behind the youngest one, who said,

"You can sit anywhere you like, but you need to buckle up, not just on takeoff and landing but throughout the entire flight. If you sleep, then buckle the sleep-belt too. Nothing that's not fixed in place can be left out in the open. Stay in your seat or bunk at all times, and if you must move about, please inform the captain first. This is an intercom button. There's one at every seat and every bunk. Hold it down to talk. If there's anything you need, please use it to call us at any time."

Luo Ji looked in confusion at Shi Qiang, who said, "The plane may execute some special maneuvers."

The man nodded. "Correct. Please let me know if you have any problems. Call me Xiao Zhang. I'll bring you dinner when we're in the air."

After Xiao Zhang left, Luo Ji and Shi Qiang sat on the sofa and fastened their seatbelts. Luo Ji looked about him. Apart from the round windows and the slightly curved walls they were set into, the room seemed so conventional and familiar that it felt a little strange to be wearing seatbelts in an ordinary office. But soon the noise and vibration of the engine reminded him he was aboard a plane taxiing down the runway, and a few minutes later the engine noise changed and the two of them were pressed back into the sofa. Then the ground vibrations disappeared and the office floor took on a slant. As the plane climbed, the sun, which had already dipped below the ground, returned through the window, just as the same sun had sent the day's final rays of sunlight into the hospital room of Zhang Beihai's father just ten minutes before.

By the time Luo Ji's plane reached the coast, Wu Yue and Zhang Beihai were once again looking over the unfinished *Tang*, ten thousand meters below. This was the closest he would ever get to the two soldiers.

As on their previous visit, *Tang*'s enormous frame was shrouded in the dim light of dusk. The showers of sparks on the hull didn't seem quite as plentiful, and the lamps illuminating the ship had

dimmed substantially. And this time, Wu Yue and Zhang Beihai no longer belonged to the navy.

"I heard the General Armaments Department has decided to terminate the *Tang* project," Zhang Beihai said.

"What's that got to do with us?" Wu Yue said coldly, his eyes sweeping from *Tang* to the last bits of sunset in the west.

"You've been in a bad mood since joining the space force."

"You should know the reason. You can always read my thoughts, sometimes more clearly than I can, and then you remind me what it is I'm really thinking about."

Zhang Beihai turned to Wu Yue. "You're depressed about joining what's inevitably a losing war. You're jealous of that final generation that will be young enough to fight in the space force at the end and be buried in the cosmos together with their fleet. Devoting a lifetime of effort to a hopeless endeavor is hard for you to accept."

"Do you have any advice?"

"No. Technofetishism and technological triumphalism are deeply rooted in your mind, and I learned long ago that I can't change you. I can only try to minimize the harm that sort of thinking can cause. Besides, I don't think it's impossible for humanity to win this war."

Wu Yue dropped his cold mask and met Zhang Beihai's gaze. "Beihai, you used to be a practical person. You opposed building *Tang,* and on multiple occasions, on the record, voiced doubts about building a blue-water navy, arguing that it was incompatible with our national strength. You believe that our naval forces ought to remain in coastal waters under the support and protection of shore-based firepower, an idea ridiculed as a turtle-shell strategy by the young hotheads, but you've persisted in it. . . . So where do you get your confidence in a space victory from now? Do you really believe that wooden boats can sink an aircraft carrier?"

"After independence, the newly founded navy used wooden boats to sink Nationalist destroyers. And even earlier, there were times when our army used cavalry to defeat tanks."

"You can't seriously think those miracles count as ordinary military theory."

"On this battlefield, terrestrial civilization won't need to follow commonplace, ordinary military theory." Zhang Beihai held up a finger. "One exception is sufficient."

Wu Yue shot him a mocking smile. "I'd like to hear how you'll achieve this exception."

"I don't know anything about space warfare, of course, but if you want to compare it to a wooden boat versus a carrier, then I think it's just a matter of having the courage to act and the confidence in a victory. A wooden boat could carry a small squad of divers who'll wait in the carrier's path. When the enemy draws near, they'll dive in and the boat will leave. Then when the carrier comes close, they'll attach a bomb to the bottom of the hull and sink the carrier. . . . Of course this would be exceedingly difficult, but it's not impossible."

Wu Yue nodded. "Not bad. People have tried it before. In the Second World War, the British did that as part of the effort to sink the *Tirpitz,* only they used a minisub. In the 1980s, during the Malvinas War, a few Argentine special forces soldiers took Italian limpet mines into Spain and attempted to blow up a British warship docked in the harbor at Gibraltar. You know what happened to them."

"But what we have is not just a small wooden boat. A one- or two-thousand-ton nuclear bomb can be made small enough for one or two divers to take underwater, and when it's attached to the underside of a carrier, it won't just sink it, it'll blow the whole carrier to smithereens."

"Sometimes you've got a fantastic imagination," Wu Yue said with a smile.

"I've got confidence in our victory." Zhang Beihai looked out at *Tang,* the distant shower of welding sparks reflected in his pupils like two small flames.

Wu Yue too looked out at *Tang,* and a new vision took hold of him: The ship was no longer a ruined ancient fortress but a

prehistoric cliff with a multitude of deep caves carved into it, and the scattered sparks were flickering firelight in those caves.

After takeoff and all through dinner, Luo Ji refrained from asking Shi Qiang anything about where they were headed, or what exactly had happened, reasoning that if Shi Qiang was going to tell him anything, he would already have come out with it. Once, he unbuckled his seatbelt and got up to look out the cabin window, even though he knew he would see nothing through the darkness, but Shi Qiang followed him and pulled down the window shade, saying that there was nothing to see out there.

"Why don't we chat for a while longer, and then go to sleep. What do you say?" asked Shi Qiang as he drew out a cigarette, then quickly put it back, remembering he was on a plane.

"Sleep? So this is a long flight?"

"Who cares? It's a plane with beds. I say we take advantage of them."

"You're only responsible for taking me to my destination, right?"

"What are you complaining for? We've still got to make the return trip!" Shi Qiang grinned broadly, as if immensely pleased with himself. Cutting humor seemed to give him pleasure. But then he turned more serious: "I don't know much more about your trip than you do. Besides, it's not yet time for me to tell you anything. Take it easy. There'll be someone at the handoff to explain things to you."

"I've been guessing for hours, but I've only come up with one possible explanation."

"Let me hear it, and let's see if it's the same as what I'm thinking."

"The woman who died was an ordinary person, so that means her social or family connections had to be something special." Luo Ji didn't know anything about her family, just like his previous lovers. He wasn't interested, and forgot whatever they told him.

"Who? Oh, that lover of yours? Put her out of your mind, since you don't care anyway. Or, if you want, why not compare her name and face to some famous figures?"

Luo Ji's mind flipped through comparisons, but nothing matched.

"Luo, my man, can you bluff?" Shi Qiang asked. Luo had noticed a pattern in how he addressed him. When he was joking, he called him "my boy," but when he was a little more serious, it was "my man."

"Do I need to bluff against someone?"

"Of course you do. . . . So how about I teach you how to bluff? Of course, I'm not a master of it either. My work is more along the lines of breaking scams. Here, I'll tell you a few tricks for the interrogation room. You might find it useful later to figure out what's going on. Naturally, these are just the most basic, common ones. It's hard to explain anything more complicated. We'll start with the gentlest one, which happens to be the simplest: The List. That means drawing up a whole list of questions connected to the case, and then asking them one by one and recording the subject's answers, and then starting over again from the top and recording those answers too. Questions can be asked repeatedly if necessary, and then you can compare the transcripts of the answers and find out if the subject is lying about something, since the answers will be different every time. The technique is simple, but don't look down your nose at it. No one who hasn't undergone training in counter-interrogation techniques will be able to pass it, so the most effective way of dealing with The List is simply to remain silent." Shi Qiang fiddled unconsciously with his cigarette as he spoke, but then put it away again.

"Ask them. It's a charter flight, so they ought to allow smoking," Luo Ji said.

Shi Qiang had grown excited while speaking and seemed a little put out at Luo Ji's interruption. It occurred to Luo Ji that he might be serious, or else he had an odd sense of humor. Shi Qiang pressed the red intercom button beside the sofa, and Xiao Zhang told him he could do what he liked. So the two of them lit up.

"The next technique is only half-gentle. You can reach the ashtray—it's fixed in place, you've just got to pull it up. Right. This technique is called Black and White. It requires the cooperation

of lots of people and is a little more complicated. First, the bad cops come out, at least two of them on most occasions, and they're really nasty to you. Some of them verbally and others physically, but they're all mean. There's a strategy to it: not just to make you afraid, but more importantly to make you feel alone, to make you feel like the whole world wants to consume you. Then the good cop comes out, just one, and he's got a kind face, and he stops the bad cops and tells them that you're a human being, that you've got rights, so how can they treat you that way? The bad cops tell him to beat it, that he's affecting their work. The good cop persists, and says, 'You can't do this!' The bad cops say, 'I always knew you didn't have the stones for this work. If you can't handle it, then get lost.' The good cop shields you with his body, and says. 'I'm going to protect his rights, and protect justice under the law!' The bad cops say, 'Tomorrow you're out of here, just you wait!' Then they leave in a huff. So it's just the two of you left, and the good cop wipes off your blood and sweat and tells you not to be afraid, and that you have the right to be silent! Then, as you can imagine, he becomes your one friend in the world, so when he draws you out, you aren't silent anymore. . . . This technique is most effective against intellectuals, but it differs from The List in that it loses its effect when you're aware of it."

He spoke animatedly and seemed about to take off his seatbelt and stand up. Luo Ji was seized by dread and despair and felt as if he had fallen into an ice pit. Noticing his discomfort, Shi Qiang stopped. "Well, then, let's not talk about interrogation, even if it might be useful to you. You can't take it in all at once. Besides, I was going to tell you how to trick people, so just remember this: Real shrewdness means not letting any shrewdness show. It's not like in the movies. The truly astute don't sit in the shadows all day striking a pose. They don't show off that they're using their brains. They look all carefree and innocent. Some of them are tacky and mawkish, others careless and unserious. What's critical is not to let others think you're a person of interest. Let them look down on you or dismiss you and they won't feel you're an obstacle. You're

just a broom in the corner. The pinnacle of this is to make them not notice you at all, as if you don't exist until the moment right before they die at your hands."

"Will I ever have the need or opportunity to become that sort of person?" Luo Ji broke in to ask.

"Like I said, I know no more about this than you do. But I've got a premonition that you need to become such a person. Luo, my man, you've got to!" Shi Qiang grew excited again and clapped him on the shoulder with enough force to make him wince.

Then they sat in silence watching the clouds of smoke curl upward to the ceiling, where they were sucked away into a crack.

"Screw it. Let's hit the sack," Shi Qiang said as he ground out his cigarette in the ashtray. He shook his head with a smile. "I've been going on like an idiot. When you think back on this, don't laugh at me."

In the bedroom, Luo Ji took off his bulletproof jacket and wrapped himself in the safety sleeping bag. Shi Qiang helped him tighten the straps holding it to the bed, and then set down a small vial on the bedside cabinet.

"Sleeping pills. Take them if you can't sleep. I asked for alcohol, but they said there isn't any."

Shi Qiang reminded Luo Ji that he should notify the captain before getting out of bed, then turned to leave.

"Officer Shi," Luo Ji called after him.

At the door, Shi Qiang half-turned back to look at him. "I'm not any sort of cop. The police aren't involved in this thing. Everyone calls me Da Shi."

"Well then, Da Shi, when we were talking just now, I noticed the first thing you said. Or, I guess, the first thing you said in reply to me. I said, 'the woman,' and you didn't realize for a moment who I was talking about. That means that she's not a major part of this case."

"You're one of the calmest people I've ever met."

"The calmness comes from cynicism. There's not much in the world that can make me care."

"Whatever it is, I've never seen someone who could stay calm

in a situation like this. Forget all that stuff I said before. I just like to kid around about things."

"You're just looking for something to hold my attention so that you can smoothly complete your mission."

"If I've set your imagination going, I apologize."

"What do you think I should think about now?"

"In my experience, any thinking is liable to go off the rails. You should just go to sleep."

Shi Qiang left. After he closed the door, the room was dark except for a small red lamp at the head of the bed. The ever-present background rumble of the engine was particularly conspicuous, as if the infinite night sky on the other side of the wall was emitting a deep hum.

Then Luo Ji felt that it wasn't an illusion, that the sound really was coming from some far-off place outside. He unbuckled the sleeping bag and crawled out, then pushed up the shade over the window by the bed. Outside, the moon was shining on a sea of clouds, a vast ocean of silver. Luo Ji realized that above the clouds were other things shining with a silver light, four ramrod-straight lines that caught the eye against the backdrop of the night sky. They were extending at the same speed as the plane, and their trailing ends faded out and blended into the night like four silver swords flying over the clouds. Luo Ji looked back at the tips and noticed that the silver lines were being drawn out by four objects with a metallic glint. Four fighter jets. It wasn't hard to guess that another four were on the other side of the plane.

Luo Ji pulled down the shade and burrowed back into the sleeping bag. He closed his eyes and willed his mind to relax. He didn't want to sleep, but to wake up from his dream.

In the dead of night, the space force work meeting was still in progress. Zhang Beihai pushed aside the notebook and documents that lay on the desk in front of him and stood up, scanning the tired faces of the officers before turning toward Chang Weisi.

"Commander, before we report on our work, I'd first like to share some of my own views. I believe that the military leadership has not paid sufficient attention to political and ideological work among the forces. For example, the political department is the last of the six established departments to present its report at this meeting."

Chang Weisi nodded. "I concur. The political commissars have not yet reported for duty, so it's fallen to me to oversee political work. Now that we've finally begun work in all areas, it's difficult to give it enough attention. For the bulk of the work, we'll have to rely on you and the others who are in charge of specifics."

"Commander, in my opinion, the present situation is dangerous." This remark drew the attention of several officers, and Zhang Beihai continued. "Please forgive me for speaking pointedly. For one thing, we've been in meetings all day and we're all tired, so no one will listen if I'm not blunt." A few people laughed, but the rest were still mired in their fatigue. "More importantly, I'm truly worried. The battle we are facing has a force disparity unprecedented in the history of human warfare, so I believe that for the indefinite future the greatest danger facing the space force is defeatism. Its threat can't be overstated. The spread of defeatism will not only result in an erosion of morale, but may lead to the total collapse of space-based military power."

Chang Weisi nodded again. "I agree. Defeatism is our greatest enemy at present. The military commission is acutely aware of this. It's why political and ideological work in the services will be critical. Once the basic units of the space force are in place, the work will become more complex."

Zhang Beihai flipped open his notebook. "The work report follows," he said, and began to read: "Since the establishment of the space force, our primary focus in political and ideological work among the troops has been to conduct a survey of the overall ideological status of officers and soldiers. Since the organization of this new branch is simple at the present time, with few members and few administrative levels, the survey was conducted through informal meetings and personal interaction, and a corresponding

forum was set up on the intranet. The results of the survey are worrying. Defeatist thinking is prevalent and spreading swiftly among the troops. The mentality of a sizeable proportion of our comrades consists of terror toward the enemy and a lack of confidence in the future of war.

"The source of this defeatism stems primarily from the worship of technology, and the underestimation or complete dismissal of the role of human initiative and the human spirit in war. It is a development and extension of techno-triumphalism and the 'weapons decide everything' theory that has cropped up in the armed forces in recent years. The trend is particularly pronounced among highly educated officers. Defeatism among the troops takes the following forms:

"One. Treating one's duty in the space force as an ordinary job: despite working with dedication and responsibility, lacking enthusiasm and sense of mission and doubting the ultimate significance of one's work.

"Two. Passive waiting: believing that the outcome of the war depends on scientists and engineers; believing that prior to breakthroughs in basic research and key technologies, the space force is just a pipe dream, and subsequent confusion about the importance of its present work; being satisfied simply with completing tasks related to establishing this military branch; lacking innovation.

"Three. Harboring unrealistic fantasies: requesting to use hibernation technology to leap four centuries into the future and take part in the Doomsday Battle directly. A number of younger comrades have already expressed this wish, and one has even submitted a formal application. On the surface, this is a positive state of mind, a desire to throw oneself onto the front lines, but it is essentially just another form of defeatism. Lacking confidence in victory and doubting the significance of our present work, a soldier's dignity becomes the only pillar sustaining work and life.

"Four. The opposite of the above: doubts about the dignity of the soldier, the belief that the military's traditional moral code is no longer suitable for the battlefield, and that fighting to the end

has no meaning; the belief that a soldier's dignity only exists when there is someone to see it, and when a battle ends in defeat and no humans are left in the universe, then this dignity loses its significance. Although only a minority hold this notion, the abrogation of the very worth of the space force is exceedingly harmful."

Here Zhang Beihai looked out at the assembly and saw that although his speech had attracted some interest, it still hadn't managed to shake the fatigue from the meeting hall. He was confident that what he had to say next would change the situation.

"I'll give you a specific example of a comrade who exhibits a typical form of defeatism. I am referring to Colonel Wu Yue." Zhang Beihai held out his hand in the direction of Wu Yue's seat at the conference table.

The tiredness of the room was swept away and the attendees pricked up their ears. Everyone looked nervously at Zhang Beihai and then at Wu Yue, who gazed placidly back, the picture of calmness.

"Wu Yue and I have worked together in the navy for quite some time and we know each other very well. He has a strong technology complex, and as a captain he is a technical type, or, if you want, an engineer. This in itself isn't a bad thing, but unfortunately, his military thinking is over-reliant on technology, and while he doesn't come out and say it, he subconsciously believes that technological advancement is the primary and perhaps sole determinant of combat effectiveness. He completely neglects the human role in battle, particularly in his lack of understanding of the unique advantages formed in our army by difficult historical conditions. When he learned of the Trisolar Crisis, he lost all confidence in the future, and once he joined the space force, this despair only became more pronounced. Comrade Wu Yue's defeatist sentiment is so heavy and ingrained that we have no hope of pulling him out of it. We must adopt strong measures as soon as possible to arrest the spread of defeatism in the troops, and therefore I believe that Comrade Wu Yue is no longer suitable for work in the space force."

All eyes were on Wu Yue, who was now looking at the space force emblem on his hat lying on the table. He remained calm as before.

Throughout the course of his speech, Zhang Beihai had not even glanced in Wu Yue's direction. He continued: "Commander, Comrade Wu Yue, and the rest of you, I ask for your understanding. I say this only out of concern for the present ideological state of the troops. Of course, I also hope to engage Wu Yue in face-to-face, frank, and open discussion."

Wu Yue raised a hand requesting permission to speak, and at a nod from Chang Weisi, he said, "What Comrade Zhang Beihai has said about my mental state is accurate, and I accept his conclusion: I am no longer fit to serve in the Space Force. I will abide by whatever the organization arranges."

The atmosphere turned tense. Several officers looked at the notebook in front of Zhang Beihai, wondering who else its contents might concern.

One senior colonel in the air force got up and said, "Comrade Zhang Beihai, this is an ordinary work meeting. You ought to go through the proper organizational channels instead of bringing up issues like this. Do you think it's appropriate to talk about this openly?"

His words were immediately echoed by many of the other officers.

Zhang Beihai said, "I know that my remarks violate organizational principles, and I am prepared to accept all responsibility. However, I do believe that I must, by whatever means, bring the seriousness of our current situation to your attention."

Chang Weisi raised a hand to prevent any other replies. "First, the sense of responsibility and urgency that Comrade Zhang Beihai has shown in his work must be commended. The existence of defeatism amongst the troops is a fact, and we must face it rationally. So long as a technology gap exists between our two sides, defeatism will not vanish. It is not a problem that can be solved through simple methods but will require long and painstaking work, as well as more interaction and discussion. However, I also agree with the suggestion proposed by the colonel: matters concerning personal ideology should be resolved primarily through communication and

exchange, and if a report is necessary, it should be made through the proper channels."

The officers let out a sigh of relief. At this meeting, at least, Zhang Beihai would not be mentioning their names.

Imagining the boundless night sky above the cloud layer, Luo Ji struggled to collect his thoughts. Involuntarily, his mind drifted to thoughts of the woman: her voice and laughing face appeared in the dimness, and a sorrow he had never felt before weighed upon his heart. This was followed closely by self-reproach, a disdain he had felt on countless prior occasions, but never so intensely. Why was she on his mind now? Up to this point, his only reaction to her death apart from fear and astonishment had been self-absolution, and only now that he knew her role in the situation was negligible did he spare her any of his precious sorrow. What sort of a person was he?

But what could be done? That's just the sort of person he was.

In his bed, the minute oscillations of the plane gave Luo Ji the feeling of being in a cradle. He had slept in a cradle as a baby, he remembered, and one day in his parents' basement he had seen, covered in dust under an old kid's bed, the rockers of a cradle. Now when he closed his eyes and imagined the couple rocking his cradle, he asked himself, *From the day you left that cradle, have you ever cared about anyone else besides those two people? Have you ever made even a small, permanent bit of room in your heart for anyone else?*

Yes, he had made room, once. Five years before, the golden light of love had inhabited his heart. But that had been an unreal experience.

Everything had started with Bai Rong, an author of young-adult novels. She wrote them in her spare time but had gained enough of a following to bring her more in royalties than she made in salary. Out of all the women he had met, he had spent the most time with Bai Rong, and had even reached the point of considering

marrying her. Their relationship was the ordinary sort, not particularly intense or unforgettable, but they felt it suited them to be relaxed and happy together. Despite a certain dread of marriage, they felt giving it a try was the responsible thing to do.

At Bai Rong's behest, he had read all of her work, and while he wouldn't say he appreciated it, it wasn't as torturous as the other works in the genre he had flipped through. She had an elegant style, and a mature lucidity that her peers lacked. But this style was not complemented by the novels' content. Reading them was like looking at dewdrops on the undergrowth: pure and transparent, but distinguished from each other only by the way the light reflected and refracted through them and how they rolled about on the leaves, fusing together where they met and separating when they fell, until they evaporated entirely within the space of a few minutes after sunrise. Every time he read one of her books, beneath the graceful style he was left with one question: What do these people live on if they spend twenty-four hours a day in love?

"That love you write about—do you think it exists in the real world?" he asked one day.

"I do."

"Something you've seen, or something you've experienced yourself?"

She squeezed his neck. "Either way, I'm telling you that it exists," she said cryptically into his ear.

Sometimes he would give her suggestions for the novels she was working on, or even help her revise them.

"It's like you're more talented than I am," she said once. "You're not revising plot, but character, and that's the hardest thing to do. Every time, you're adding the touches that make the characters most vivid. Your skill at creating literary figures is first rate."

"You've got to be kidding. My background's in astronomy."

"Wang Xiaobo[9] studied mathematics, remember."

9 *Translator's Note*: Wang Xiaobo (1952–1997) was an influential novelist, essayist, and screenwriter whose work became enormously popular after his untimely death.

On her birthday last year, she had asked him for a specific present: "Can you write a novel for me?"

"A whole novel?"

"Well, at least fifty thousand characters long."

"With you as the protagonist?"

"No. I saw a really interesting exhibition of paintings by male artists of the most beautiful women they could imagine. The protagonist of your novel should be the same. You can leave reality behind and create an angel based entirely on your dream of feminine perfection."

To this day he had no idea of the motivation for her request. Maybe she didn't know herself. Thinking back now, it seemed her mood at the time had been a mixture of craftiness and ambivalence.

So he began constructing a character. He first imagined her face, and then designed her clothes, and then thought of her environment and the people around her, and finally placed her in that environment and had her move about and speak, letting her live. But this soon turned tedious, and he told Bai Rong about the difficulties he had encountered: "She's like a puppet on a string. Every word and action arises from the design but lacks the spark of life."

She said, "Your approach is wrong. You're writing an essay rather than creating a literary figure. What a literary character does in ten minutes might be a reflection of ten years' experience. You can't be limited to the plot of a novel—you've got to imagine her entire life, and what actually gets put into words is just the tip of the iceberg."

So he followed her advice. He threw out everything he wanted to write and instead imagined the character's entire life and every detail of it. He imagined her nursing at her mother's breast, her tiny mouth sucking energetically and burbling with satisfaction; chasing a red balloon tumbling down the street but making it just one step before falling to the ground, wailing as she watched the balloon drift away without realizing that she had just taken her first step; walking in the rain and impulsively folding up her umbrella to feel the raindrops; her first day at elementary school, sitting alone in a strange classroom, unable to see her parents through the

windows or door, and nearly starting to cry, only to realize that her best friend from kindergarten was at a nearby desk, and crying in joy instead; her first night at college, lying on her dorm bunk and watching the shadows of trees thrown by streetlamps onto the ceiling. . . . He imagined every one of her favorite foods, the color and style of every item of clothing in her dresser, the decorations on her mobile phone, the books she read, the music on her media player, the Web sites she visited, the movies she liked; but never her makeup, because she didn't need makeup. . . . Like a creator outside of time, he wove the different stages of her life together and gradually came to discover the endless pleasure of creation.

One day at the library, he imagined her standing by a row of shelves, reading. He put her in his favorite outfit, so her petite form would stand out more vividly in his mind. Suddenly, she looked up from the book and over at him, and flashed him a smile.

He was taken aback: Had he told her to smile? The smile had already imprinted itself on his memory like a stain on ice, never to be wiped away.

The real turning point came the following night. The snow and wind picked up, temperatures plummeted, and he watched from the warmth of his dorm the bluster that blanketed the other sounds of the city, the buffeting of the snowflakes on the widow like the patter of sand. A huge carpet of snow covered everything outdoors. The city seemed to no longer exist, leaving the faculty dormitory standing on an infinite snowy plain. He went back to bed, but before he drifted off to sleep he had a sudden thought: If she were outside in this awful weather, she would be terribly cold. Then he reminded himself: It doesn't matter, she won't be outside unless you put her there. But this time his imagination failed, and she continued walking outside in the blizzard like a blade of grass that could blow away at any moment. She still wore that white coat and that red scarf, which was all he could make out, vaguely, through the swirling snow, like a tiny flame fighting against the storm.

It was impossible for him to sleep. He sat up in his bed, then threw on some clothes and sat on the sofa. He wondered if he should

have a smoke but, remembering that she detested the smell, instead made a cup of coffee and drank it slowly. He had to wait for her. The blizzard and the cold night weighed on his heart. This was the first time he had felt such heartache for someone, or such yearning.

As his mind was sputtering to life, she came quietly, her small frame wrapped in a layer of cold from the outdoors, but with a breath of spring amid the chilliness. The snowflakes in her hair quickly melted into gleaming droplets as she unwrapped her scarf and put her hands to her mouth to blow on them. He folded her hands in his to warm the icy softness, and she looked at him with excitement and asked the question he was about to ask her: "Are you okay?"

He could only nod dumbly. Then, as he helped her out of her coat, he said, "Come and get warm." He rubbed her soft shoulders and guided her to the fireplace.

"It's really warm. Wonderful . . ." She sat on the rug in front of the fireplace, laughing happily as she watched the firelight.

Damn it! What's wrong with me? he said to himself, in the middle of the empty room. Wouldn't it be enough to just come up with any fifty thousand words, print them on high-grade bond, Photoshop a gorgeous cover and flap, have it professionally bound, have it gift-wrapped, and then give it to Bai Rong on her birthday? Why had he fallen so deep into this trap? He was amazed to find that he had tears in his eyes. And then another realization: *A fireplace? When the hell did I get a fireplace? Why would I think of a fireplace?* But then he understood: What he wanted wasn't a fireplace, but the glow of the fire, for it is in firelight that a woman is most beautiful. He recalled how she had looked just then against the glow of the fire. . . .

No! Don't think about her. It will be a disaster! Go to sleep!

Contrary to his expectations, he did not dream of her the entire night. He slept well, imagining the single bed as a small boat floating on a rosy sea. When he awoke the next morning, he felt reborn, like he was a candle that had been covered in dust for years before being lit by that tiny flame in last night's snowstorm. He walked

excitedly down the road to the classroom building, and though the air was hazy after the snowfall, he felt like he could see a thousand miles. There was no snow on the poplar trees lining the road, their bare branches poking up toward the cold sky, but to him they were more alive than in springtime.

He took the podium, and just as he had hoped, there she was again, seated in the back of the amphitheater, the only one in an empty row, at a distance from the other students. Her pure white coat and red scarf were on the seat beside her, and she was wearing a beige turtleneck sweater. She did not have her head down, flipping pages in her textbook like the other students. Instead, she watched him, and flashed him another snowy-sunrise of a smile.

He grew nervous. His pulse increased, and he had to leave through a side door to stand on the balcony and calm himself in the cold air. The only other times he had been in a similar state were during his two doctoral thesis defenses. In his lecture he did his utmost to show off, and his extensive citations and impassioned language won a rare burst of applause from the auditorium. She didn't join in, but merely smiled at him and nodded.

After class, he walked side by side with her along the tree-lined avenue that offered no shade, listening to the crunch of her blue boots in the snow. The two lines of winter poplars listened in silence to their heartfelt conversation.

"You lecture quite well, but I didn't really understand."

"You're not in this major, are you?"

"No, I'm not."

"Do you often sit in on classes in other majors?"

"Only the past few days. I'll go into a lecture hall at random and sit for a while. I just graduated and will be leaving soon. I suddenly realized that it's great here, and I'm afraid of the outside. . . ."

Over the next three or four days, he spent the majority of his time with her, although to others, it looked as if he was spending most of his time alone, strolling on his own. It was quite easy to explain to Bai Rong: He was thinking about her birthday gift. And indeed, this was no lie.

On New Year's Eve, he bought a bottle of red wine, which he had never drunk before, returned to his dorm room, shut off the light, and lit some candles on the table next to the sofa. When all three candles were burning, she sat down wordlessly next to him.

"Oh, look," she exclaimed, pointing at the wine bottle with childlike excitement.

"What?"

"Look at it from here, where the candles shine through. The wine is lovely."

Shining through the wine, the candlelight was a deep, crystalline red, the stuff of dreams.

"Like a dead sun," he said.

"Don't think like that," she said, with a sincerity that melted his heart. "I think it's like . . . the eyes of twilight."

"Why not the eyes of dawn?"

"I like twilight better."

"Why?"

"When twilight fades, you can see the stars. When dawn fades, all that's left is . . ."

"All that's left is the harsh light of reality."

"Yes, that's right."

They spoke about everything, sharing a common language in even the most trivial of things, until the bottle that had contained the eyes of twilight had been emptied into his stomach.

He lay drowsily in bed and watched the candles still burning on the table. She had vanished from the candlelight, but he was not worried. So long as he was willing, she could reappear at any time.

Then there was a knock on the door. He knew the knock came from reality and had nothing to do with her, so he ignored it. The door opened and Bai Rong entered. When she turned on the light it was like switching on the gray of reality. She glanced at the table with the candles, then sat down at the head of his bed and sighed lightly. "It's still okay."

"What is?" He used a hand to block the harsh light.

"You haven't gotten to the point of leaving a glass for her, too."

He covered his eyes but said nothing. She pulled away his hands, and then, looking straight at him, asked, "She's alive, isn't she?"

He nodded and sat up. "Rong, I used to think that a character in a novel was controlled by her creator, that she would be whatever the author wanted her to be, and do whatever the author wanted her to do, like God does for us."

"Wrong!" she said, standing up and beginning to pace the room. "Now you realize you were wrong. This is the difference between an ordinary scribe and a literary writer. The highest level of literary creation is when the characters in a novel possess life in the mind of the writer. The writer is unable to control them, and might not even be able to predict the next action they will take. We can only follow them in wonder to observe and record the minute details of their lives like a voyeur. That's how a classic is made."

"So literature, it turns out, is a perverted endeavor."

"It was like that for Shakespeare and Balzac and Tolstoy, at least. The classic images they created were born from their mental wombs. But today's practitioners of literature have lost that creativity. Their minds give birth only to shattered fragments and freaks, whose brief lives are nothing but cryptic spasms devoid of reason. Then they sweep up these fragments into a bag they peddle under the label 'postmodern' or 'deconstructionist' or 'symbolism' or 'irrational.' "

"So you mean that I've become a writer of classic literature?"

"Hardly. Your mind is only gestating an image, and it's the easiest one of all. The minds of those classic authors gave birth to hundreds and thousands of figures. They formed the picture of an era, and that's something that only a superhuman can accomplish. But what you've done isn't easy. I didn't think you'd be able to do it."

"Have you ever done it?"

"Just once," she said simply, and dropped the subject. She grabbed his neck, and said, "Forget it. I don't want that birthday present anymore. Come back to a normal life, okay?"

"And if all this continues—what then?"

She studied him for a few seconds, then let go of him and shook

her head with a smile. "I knew it was too late." Picking up her bag from the bed, she left.

Then he heard people outside counting down, four, three, two, one. From the classroom building, which until then had been resounding with music, came peals of laughter. On the athletic field people lit fireworks. Looking at his watch, he saw that the final second of that year had just passed.

"It's a holiday tomorrow. Where should we go?" he asked. He lay on the bed, but knew his character had already appeared beside the nonexistent fireplace.

"You're not taking *her?*" she asked in all innocence, pointing toward the still-open door.

"No. Just the two of us. Where would you like to go?"

She drank in the dancing flames in the fireplace and said, "It's not important where we go. I think it's a wonderful feeling just being on a journey."

"Then we'll set out and see where we end up?"

"Excellent."

The next morning, he drove his Accord off campus and headed west, a direction he chose purely because it avoided the headaches of having to traverse the entire city. He felt for the first time the wonderful freedom of traveling with no destination in mind. As the buildings outside slowly thinned out and fields began to appear, he cracked his window to let the cold winter air in. He sensed her long hair catching the wind, and strands of it blew over to tickle his right temple.

"Look, mountains." She pointed off in the distance.

"Visibility is good today. Those are the Taihang Mountains. They run parallel to this road, and then bend around to form a block in the west, where the road goes into them. I'd say that right now we're—"

"No, no. Don't say where we are! Once we know where we are, then the world becomes as narrow as a map. When we don't know, the world feels unlimited."

"Okay. Then let's do our best to get lost." He turned onto an

emptier road, and before they had gone very far, turned a second time. On both sides of them were now endless fields where the snow had not yet melted completely, the snowy patches and snow-free ground roughly equal. No green anywhere, although the sunlight was brilliant.

"A classic northern scene," he said.

"This is the first time I've ever felt that land without the slightest bit of green could be beautiful."

"The green is buried in the fields and is waiting for springtime. The winter wheat will sprout while it's still very cold, then this will be a sea of green. Imagine, all this expanse . . ."

"It doesn't need green. It's beautiful right now. Look, doesn't the land look like a big milk cow asleep under the sun?"

"What?" He looked in surprise, first at her and then through the windows at the patchy snow on either side of the car. "Oh, there really is a resemblance! So, what's your favorite season?"

"Autumn."

"Why not spring?"

"Spring . . . has so many sensations squashed together. It gets tiring. Autumn is better."

He stopped the car and went out with her to the edge of the field to look at the magpies, which foraged on the ground until they got quite close, at which point they flew off to some trees in the distance. Then they went down a riverbed that was practically dried up, with only a thin stream of water flowing down the center. But it was a northern river all the same, and so they picked up small chilly smooth stones from the riverbed and pitched them in, watching the cloudy yellow water gush out of the holes they broke in the thin ice. They passed a small town and spent a while at the market there. She knelt down by a goldfish vendor, the fish in their glass bowls like liquid flames under the sun, and wouldn't leave. He bought her two and put them, water and all, in plastic bags on the backseat of the car. They entered a hamlet, but found nothing that felt like the countryside. The houses and compounds were brand new, cars were parked outside of many of the gates,

the cement roads were wide, and people were dressed no differently than in the cities—a few girls were even stylish. Even the dogs were the same long-haired, short-legged parasites found in the cities. More interesting was the large stage at the entrance to the village—they marveled at how such a small village could have such an immense stage. It was empty, so with some effort he climbed up and—looking down at his lone audience member—sang a verse from "*Tonkaya Ryabina*" about the slender hawthorn tree. At noon, they ate in another town, where the food was more or less the same as in the city, only the portions were about twice as large. After lunch, they sat drowsily in the warmth of the sun on a bench outside the town hall, and then drove onward with no direction in mind.

Before they knew it, the road had entered the mountains, which were plain and ordinary in shape and devoid of vegetation apart from withered grasses and vitex vines in the crevices of the gray rocks. Over the course of hundreds of millions of years, the mountains, weary of standing, had lain down, sunken into flatness amid time and sunlight, and turned anyone walking among them just as indolent. "The mountains here are like old villagers basking in the sun," she said, but they hadn't seen any of those old men in the villages they passed through; none more at ease than the mountains. More than once their car had been stopped by a flock of sheep crossing the road. Beside the road there at last appeared the kind of villages they had imagined, with cave houses and persimmon and walnut trees and stone-tiled low buildings, roofs piled high with stripped corn cob. Even the dogs were larger and more fierce.

They started and stopped as they went through the mountains, and before they knew it the entire afternoon was spent. The sun was setting, and the road had entered the shadows long ago. He drove along a dirt road pitted with potholes up onto a high ridge where the sun still shone, and they decided that this would be the terminus of their journey: They would watch the sun set and then head back. Her long hair blew in the light evening breeze, seemingly striving to seize hold of the last golden rays.

They had only just turned onto the highway when the car broke down. The rear axle had broken, meaning they had to call for help. A while later he was able to learn the name of the place from the driver of a small passing truck. He was comforted by the fact that his phone had a signal. When he gave his location to the person at the repair station, he was informed that the repair truck would take at least four or five hours to get there.

The mountain air chilled quickly after sunset. After their surroundings began to grow dusky, he collected some corn stalks from a nearby terraced field and started a fire.

"Nice and warm," she said, gazing into the fire, as happy as she had been that first night in front of the fireplace. Again he was transfixed by her appearance in the firelight, drowned in emotions he had never felt before, as if he was a bonfire himself and the only purpose of his existence was to give her warmth.

"Are there wolves?" she asked, looking around at the growing darkness.

"No. Northern China is still in the interior. It just looks desolate, but it's actually one of the most densely populated regions. Look at the road. A car drives past every two minutes, on average."

"I was hoping you'd say there were wolves," she said with a sweet smile, then looked off at the cloud of sparks flying off like stars into the night.

"Okay. There are wolves, but I'm right here."

They said nothing more, but sat silently before the fire, occasionally feeding it another bunch of straw.

Later—he didn't know how much later—his phone rang. Bai Rong.

"Are you with her?" she asked gently.

"No, I'm alone," he said as he looked up. He wasn't lying. He truly was by himself, next to a bonfire along a road in the Taihang Mountains. The firelight revealed stones around him, and overhead was only a starry sky.

"I know you're alone. But are you with her?"

He paused and softly said, "Yes," and when he looked beside

him, there she was, feeding straw into the fire and smiling at the flames that lit up the area where they sat.

"Now do you believe that the love I write about in my novels really exists?"

"Yes, I believe it."

When he said those four words, he immediately realized how great the distance between the two of them really was. They were silent for a long time, during which radio waves spun their gossamer strands through the mountains to sustain this final contact.

"You have one of your own, don't you?" he asked.

"Yes. For a long time."

"Where is he now?"

He could hear her laugh softly. "Where else would he be?"

He laughed too. "Yes, where else?"

"Well. Take it easy. Good-bye." Bai Rong hung up, snapping the thread that stretched across the night sky and leaving the people at the two ends a little saddened, but nothing more than that.

"It's too cold outdoors. Let's sleep in the car," he said to her.

She gently shook her head. "I want to be with you here. You like me by the fire, right?"

It was midnight by the time the repair truck arrived from Shijiazhuang. The repairmen were surprised to find him sitting beside a fire. "Sir, you've gotta be freezing. The engine's not busted. Wouldn't it be warmer to sit in the car with the heat turned on?"

After the car was repaired, Luo Ji dashed home through the night, out of the mountains and back onto the plain, reaching Shijiazhuang by dawn. It was already ten in the morning by the time he got back to Beijing.

Rather than returning to school, he drove straight to the psychologist.

"You may need a bit of adjustment, but it's nothing serious," the doctor said, after listening to his lengthy narrative.

"Nothing serious?" Luo Ji opened his bloodshot eyes wide. "I'm madly in love with a fictional person from a novel of my own creation. I've been with her, I've traveled with her, and I've even

90

broken up with my real-life girlfriend over her. Is that nothing serious to you?"

The doctor smiled tolerantly.

"Don't you get it? I've given my most profound love to an illusion!"

"Are you under the impression that the object of everyone else's love actually exists?"

"Is that even a question?"

"Sure. For the majority of people, what they love exists only in the imagination. The object of their love is not the man or woman of reality, but what he or she is like in their imagination. The person in reality is just a template used for the creation of this dream lover. Eventually, they find out the differences between their dream lover and the template. If they can get used to those differences, then they can be together. If not, they split up. It's as simple as that. You differ from the majority in one respect: You didn't need a template."

"So this isn't a sickness?"

"Only in the way your girlfriend pointed out: You've got natural literary talent. If you want to call that a sickness, go right ahead."

"But isn't imagining to this degree a little excessive?"

"There's nothing excessive about imagination. Especially where love is concerned."

"So what should I do? How can I forget about her?"

"It's impossible. You can't forget her, so don't make the effort. That will only lead to side effects, and maybe even mental disorders. Let nature take its course. Once more, for emphasis: Don't try to forget about her. It won't work. But as time passes, her influence on your life will decrease. And you're actually quite lucky. Whether or not she really exists, you're fortunate to be in love."

This was Luo Ji's most deeply felt romantic experience, a love that only comes around once in a man's life. After that, he took to an insouciant lifestyle, going where life took him, just like the day they had set out in the Accord. And like the psychologist had said, her influence in his life decreased. When he was with a real

woman, she didn't appear, and eventually she rarely appeared even when he was alone. But he knew that the most secluded part of his soul belonged to her, and she would be there for life. He even saw clearly the world she inhabited, a still snowscape where the sky was forever graced with silver stars and a crescent moon, the snow falling steadily. In the silence you could practically hear the snowflakes coming to rest on the ground like smooth white sugar. In her exquisite cabin in the snow, the Eve that Luo Ji had formed out of one of his mind's ribs sat before an ancient fireplace quietly watching the dancing flames.

Now that he was alone on this ominous plane flight, he wanted to have her companionship, to guess with her what lay at the journey's end. But she didn't appear. He could still see her in a far-off region of his soul, sitting silently before the fireplace, never feeling lonely, because she knew her world was within him.

Luo Ji reached out a hand to the medicine bottle by the bed with the thought of using a sleeping pill to force himself to sleep, but the instant his fingers touched the bottle it flew off the cabinet and up to the ceiling, as did the clothing that he had flung onto the chair. They remained on the ceiling for a couple seconds. He felt himself leave the bed, but since the sleeping bag was attached, he didn't fly away, and when the bottle landed, he fell heavily back into the bed. For a few seconds his body felt like it was being pressed down by a heavy object, and he couldn't move. The sudden weightlessness and hypergravitation made him dizzy, a condition that continued for less than ten seconds before everything returned to normal.

He heard the soft swish of footsteps on the carpet outside the door. A number of people were in motion, and then the door opened and Shi Qiang poked his head in. "Luo Ji, are you okay?"

When Luo Ji said he was fine, he closed the door without coming in. Outside, a dialogue continued in low voices.

"It looks like a misunderstanding during the escort change. Nothing to worry about."

"What did the higher-ups say on the call earlier?" That was Shi Qiang's voice.

"They said that the escort formation would require a midair refueling in half an hour, and that we shouldn't be alarmed."

"The plan doesn't mention this interruption, does it?"

"Not even close. In the chaos just now, seven of the escort planes jettisoned their secondary fuel tanks."

"Why all the jumpiness? Forget it. You should go back to sleep. Don't get too worked up."

"How are we supposed to sleep in a state like this?"

"Leave someone on watch. What good are you if you're tired out? They may try to keep us on high alert all the time, but I maintain my own opinion of security work: When you've thought of everything you should, and done everything you need to, then let whatever happens happen. There's nothing more anyone can do, you know? Don't psych yourselves out."

At the mention of "escort change," Luo Ji reached over, opened the cover to the window, and looked outside. There was still a sea of clouds in the night sky. The moon was inclining toward the horizon, and he could see the trails of the fighter formation, now with an additional six lines. He inspected the tiny aircraft heading up those trails and noticed that they were a different model than the four he'd seen earlier.

The bedroom door opened and Shi Qiang poked his torso in to say, "Luo, my man, just a small issue. Don't worry. Nothing else from now on. Go back to sleep."

"There's still time to sleep? How many hours have we been flying?"

"We've still got a few more hours. Go to sleep." He closed the door and left.

Luo Ji turned over in the bed and picked up the pill bottle. Shi had been thorough: It contained just one pill. He took it, looked at the small red light beneath the window, imagining it was the light of a fireplace, and drifted off to sleep.

When Shi Qiang woke Luo Ji up, he had been sleeping dream-free for more than six hours and was feeling pretty good.

"We're nearly there. Get up and get ready."

Luo Ji went to the washroom to wash up, and when he returned to the office for a simple breakfast, he became aware of the plane's descent. Ten minutes later, after a flight of fifteen hours, the charter plane was resting on the ground.

Shi Qiang had Luo Ji wait in the office and went out himself. He brought back a man with a European face who was tall and immaculately dressed, and who seemed like a high-level official. "Is this Dr. Luo?" the official ventured as he looked at him. Noticing Shi Qiang's difficulty with English, he repeated his question in Chinese.

"He's Luo Ji," answered Shi Qiang, and then briefly introduced the man to Luo Ji. "This is Mr. Kent. He's here to welcome you."

"I am honored," Kent said with a bow.

When they shook hands, Luo Ji sensed that the man was incredibly experienced. So much was hidden behind his decorum, but the gleam in his eyes betrayed the presence of secrets. Luo Ji was fascinated by the man's gaze, like a devil and an angel, like an atom bomb and an identical-size precious stone. . . . In the complex information conveyed by those eyes, Luo Ji could make out just one thing: This moment was immensely important to the man's whole life.

Kent turned to Shi Qiang. "You've done very well. Your segment was the most cleanly done. The others had a bit of trouble on their way over."

"We listened to our superiors. The principle we observed was to minimize the total number of stages," Shi Qiang said.

"Absolutely correct. In the present circumstances, minimizing the stages makes for maximum security. And now we'll follow the same principle and head straight for the conference hall."

"When does the session start?"

"In one hour."

"We've cut it that close?"

"The start of the session is set by the arrival of the final candidate."

"That's pretty good. Shall we hand off, then?"

"No. You are still responsible for the security of this one. Like I said before, you are the best."

Shi Qiang was silent for a second or two as he looked at Luo Ji. Then he nodded. "As we've been getting acquainted with the situation over the past few days, our people have run into quite a few obstacles."

"I guarantee that nothing of the sort will happen from now on. You have the full cooperation of the local police and military. Well then," Kent said, looking at the two men. "We can set off."

It was still nighttime, Luo Ji realized as he stepped through the door of the aircraft. Thinking back to their takeoff time, he had a pretty good idea of which general area of the globe they were in. The fog was thick, and the lights shone a dim yellow as events from their takeoff seemed to be replaying before their eyes: the patrol helicopters in the air, only dimly visible through the fog as shadows with glowing lights; the plane quickly surrounded by a ring of military vehicles and outward-facing soldiers; and several officers with radios clustered in a group discussing something and occasionally throwing a glance in the direction of the airstair. A buzzing from somewhere overhead set Luo Ji's scalp on fire, and even the imperturbable Mr. Kent covered his ears. Looking up, they could see an indistinct light flying low overhead: the escort formation, still circling above them, its exhaust tracing a large circle in the air that was hazily visible through the fog, as if a cosmic giant had tagged the Earth with chalk at this very spot.

The four of them boarded an obviously bulletproofed car waiting at the end of the airstair and sped off. The window curtains were drawn, but judging from the light that came in, Luo Ji knew that they were smack in the middle of a convoy. Silence reigned on the ride, a road to the ultimate unknown. Although it took only forty minutes, this part of the journey felt terribly long.

When Kent said they had arrived, Luo Ji could make out a shape through the curtains, backlit by the even light from the building to its rear that cast its silhouette onto the curtain. He could never mistake such a distinctive shape: a giant revolver with a knot tied

95

in its barrel. Luo Ji knew exactly where he was: the United Nations building in New York.

He was surrounded as soon as he got out by people who seemed like security personnel: they were tall, and many of them wore dark glasses despite the night. He couldn't make out his surroundings, but was pushed forward by the cluster, squeezed with such force that his feet practically left the ground, the scraping of footsteps the only sound that broke the silence. Just as the bizarre tension had pushed him almost to the breaking point, the men in front of him gave way. Light flashed before his eyes, and then the rest of them halted in their steps, leaving him, Shi Qiang, and Kent to continue forward. They were walking in a large quiet hall, empty but for a few black-clothed guards who spoke quietly into a handheld radio each time the three of them passed one of them. They crossed a hanging balcony in the direction of a stained-glass panel whose riot of colors and intricate lines described the distorted shapes of humans and animals. Turning left, they entered a small room. After the door closed, Kent and Shi Qiang exchanged a smile, and a look of relief came over them.

Luo Ji glanced around him and discovered that the room was fairly peculiar. The wall at one end was entirely covered by an abstract painting made up of yellow, white, blue, and black geometric shapes, which overlapped randomly and seemed suspended atop an ocean of pure blue. But the strangest thing was the large stone in the shape of a rectangular prism sitting right in the center of the room and illuminated by several weak lamps. A closer look revealed that the stone bore rust lines. The abstract painting and the stone were the only furnishings, and apart from them the room was empty.

"Dr. Luo, do you need to change clothes?" Kent asked in English.

"What's he saying?" Shi Qiang asked, and when Luo Ji translated, he shook his head firmly. "No, just wear this."

"But this is a formal occasion," Kent struggled out in Chinese.

"No," said Shi Qiang with another shake of his head.

"The hall is only open to national representatives, not the media. It should be fairly secure."

"I said no. If I've understood correctly, I'm in charge of his safety now."

Kent relented. "Very well. It's not a big issue."

"You really should give him a general explanation," Shi Qiang said, jerking his head in Luo Ji's direction.

"I'm not authorized to explain anything."

"Just say anything," Shi Qiang said with a laugh.

Kent turned toward Luo Ji, his dignified face suddenly tense, and subconsciously adjusted his tie. Luo Ji then realized that he had been avoiding looking directly at him. He also noticed that Shi Qiang seemed like a different person. The ever-present smirk was gone, replaced by a solemn expression, and he looked at Kent in a rare posture of attention. Then Luo Ji knew that everything Shi Qiang had said to him before was correct: He really had no idea of the purpose of the visit.

Kent said, "Dr. Luo, all I can tell you is this: You are about to take part in an important meeting at which there will be an important announcement. And at this meeting, you do not need to do anything."

Then they were silent. The room was completely quiet. Luo Ji could clearly hear the beating of his heart. This, he realized, was the Meditation Room. The centerpiece was a six-ton rock made of the purest raw iron, symbolizing timelessness and strength. It had been a gift from Sweden. But right now, far from wanting to meditate, he tried as hard as possible to think of nothing, convinced of what Shi had said: Any thinking is liable to go off the rails. He counted the shapes in the painting.

The door opened, and the head that poked in signaled to Kent, who then turned to Luo Ji and Shi Qiang: "Time to go in. No one knows Dr. Luo, so there won't be any disruption if he and I go in together."

Shi Qiang nodded, then waved a hand at Luo Ji with a smile: "I'll wait for you outside." It warmed his heart. Right then Shi Qiang was his sole spiritual support.

Then he followed Kent out of the Meditation Room and into the United Nations General Assembly Hall.

The hall was full and the people seated in it buzzed with conversation. He didn't attract attention at first when Kent led him up along the aisle, but heads began to turn once they got close to the front. Depositing him in an aisle seat in the fifth row, Kent went on ahead and sat down in the second row.

Luo Ji looked around him at the place he had seen countless times on television. Based on these glimpses, he had been wholly unable to appreciate the meaning the building's architects wanted to express. Straight ahead of him, the tall yellow wall inset with the UN insignia that served as a backdrop for the podium was tilted forward at an acute angle, like a cliff face that was liable to collapse at any time. The dome, built to resemble a starry sky, was structurally separate from the yellow wall and did nothing to stabilize it, acting instead as an immense weight bearing down from above, adding to the wall's instability and lending the whole environment the overpowering feeling of being ready to tumble down at any moment. Under the present circumstances, however, it seemed as if the eleven architects who had designed the building in the mid-twentieth century had wonderfully predicted humanity's present predicament.

Turning his attention away from the distant wall, he heard two people talking next to him. He couldn't make out their nationality, but they were speaking idiomatic English.

"Do you really believe in the decisive role of the individual in history?"

"Well, I think it's a question that can't be proven or disproven, unless we restart time, kill off a few great men, and see how history proceeds. Of course, you can't rule out the possibility that the course of history was determined by the rivers carved out and dammed up by those great figures."

"But there's another possibility: Those great figures of yours might be no more than swimmers in history's river. They may have left their names in history because of the world records they set

and the praise and renown they won, but they had no effect on the river's flow. . . . Ah, with things the way they are, what's the point of thinking about all that?"

"The problem is that throughout the entire decision-making process, no one thought about issues on this level. The countries are all tangled up in stuff like candidate equality and resource rights."

The hall grew quiet as Secretary General Say walked to the podium. The administration of this Filipino politician had straddled the pre- and postcrisis eras. If the vote had come just a little bit later, she never would have been elected, because a refined Asian lady didn't project the sense of power the world was looking for in the face of the Trisolar Crisis. Now her small frame seemed tiny and helpless against the sloping cliff wall. As she was ascending the podium, Kent stopped her and whispered something in her ear. She looked down, nodded, and then continued walking.

Luo Ji was certain that the secretary general had looked in the direction of his seat.

On the rostrum, she surveyed the assembly, and then said, "The nineteenth meeting of the Planetary Defense Council has arrived at the final item on its agenda: the disclosure of the Wallfacer candidates and the announcement of the start of the Wallfacer Project.

"Before we move on to that agenda item, I believe it is necessary to take a brief look back at the Wallfacer Project.

"At the start of the Trisolar Crisis, the permanent members of the former Security Council held emergency negotiations and conceived the Wallfacer Project.

"The countries took note of the following facts: After the first two sophons appeared, burgeoning evidence demonstrated that additional sophons were constantly reaching the Solar System and coming to Earth, a process that continues even now. Therefore, as far as the enemy is concerned, the Earth is a completely transparent world. To them, everything is an open book, one they can read at any time. Humanity has no secrets at all.

"The international community has recently launched a mainstream defense program which, in both overall strategic thinking

and the tiniest of technological and military details, is completely exposed to the enemy's eyes. Every meeting room, every file cabinet, the hard drives and memory of every computer—there is nowhere the sophons do not see. Every plan, program, and deployment, no matter the size, will be visible to the enemy command four light-years away the moment they take shape on the Earth. Human communication in any form will result in leaks.

"We should be aware of this one fact: Strategic and tactical tricks do not advance in proportion to technological progress. Precise intelligence has proven that the Trisolarans communicate through direct, open thoughts, making them highly deficient at tricks, camouflage, and deception, and giving human civilization a huge advantage over the enemy. This is one advantage we can't afford to lose. The founders of the Wallfacer Project believe that a number of other strategic plans should proceed in parallel to the mainstream defense program, and that these plans should be secret, not transparent to the enemy. A number of proposals were put forward, but ultimately only the Wallfacer Project is feasible.

"One correction to what I just said: Humanity still has secrets, in the inner world that each of us possesses. The sophons can understand human language, and they can read printed texts and information on every kind of computer storage media at ultrahigh speeds, but they can't read human thoughts. So long as we do not communicate with the outside world, every individual keeps things secret forever from the sophons. This is the basis of the Wallfacer Project.

"At its heart, the project consists of selecting a group of people to formulate and direct strategic plans. They will develop their plans entirely in their own minds, with no communication of any kind with the outside world. The true strategy of these plans, the necessary steps for completion, and the ultimate aims will remain hidden inside the brain. We shall call them the Wallfacers because that ancient Eastern name for meditators mirrors the unique characteristics of their work. As they direct the execution of their strategic plans, the thoughts and behaviors these Wallfacers present to the outside world will be entirely false, a carefully crafted

mélange of disguise, misdirection, and deception. The subject of this misdirection and deception will be the entire world, both enemy and ally, until a huge, bewildering maze of illusions is erected to make the enemy lose its judgment, and to delay as long as possible the moment it works out our true strategic intent.

"These Wallfacers will be granted extensive powers that will enable them to mobilize and exploit a portion of Earth's existing military resources. As they carry out their strategic plans, the Wallfacers need not make any explanation for their actions and commands, regardless of how incomprehensible their behavior may be. Monitoring and control of the Wallfacer activity will be undertaken by the UN Planetary Defense Council, the sole institution granted the authority to veto Wallfacer commands under the UN Wallfacer Act.

"To guarantee the continuity of the Wallfacer Project, the Wallfacers will take advantage of hibernation technology to bridge the centuries to the Doomsday Battle. When and under what circumstances they will awaken, and for how long, will be decided by the Wallfacers themselves. Over the next four centuries, the UN Wallfacer Act will exist under international law on a level equal to the UN Charter and will act in concert with the national laws to guarantee the execution of the Wallfacers' strategic plans.

"The Wallfacers are undertaking the most difficult mission in human history. They will truly be on their own, their souls closed off to the world, to the entire universe. Their only communication partner and sole spiritual support will be themselves. Shouldering this great responsibility, they will pass through the long years alone, so let me speak for all humanity and offer them our deepest respect.

"Now, on behalf of the United Nations, I will announce the final four Wallfacer candidates as chosen by the UN Planetary Defense Council."

Luo Ji, like the entire assembly, had been listening to the secretary general's speech with rapt attention, and he held his breath for the announcement of the list of names. He wanted to find out what sort of person would be tasked with this unimaginable mission.

His own fate was completely forgotten for the time being, because nothing that could happen to him would amount to more than a speck when measured against this historic moment.

"The First Wallfacer: Frederick Tyler."

When the secretary general uttered his name, Tyler stood up from his seat in the first row and walked with deliberate steps up to the rostrum, where he looked down at the assembly without expression. There was no applause as everyone sat in silence and stared at the First Wallfacer. Tyler's tall, thin body and square-framed glasses were well known across the world. The recently retired US secretary of defense, he had exerted a deep influence on his country's national strategy. His ideological focus was expressed in a book titled *The Truth of Technology,* in which he argued that small countries are the ultimate beneficiaries of technology, and that the unstinting efforts toward technological development on the part of larger countries was in fact paving the way for world dominance by the smaller ones. This was because technological progress rendered the population and resource advantages of larger countries unimportant, but provided small countries with leverage to move the world. One consequence of nuclear technology was that it allowed a country of just a few million people to pose a substantial threat to one with a hundred million, something that at one time had been practically impossible. One of his key points was that the advantages of a large country were only truly advantageous in low-technology eras and would ultimately be weakened by the swift pace of technological progress, which would meanwhile enhance the strategic weight of small countries. Some might experience a sudden rise, gaining world dominance like Spain and Portugal once did. There was no question that Tyler's thinking provided a theoretic foundation for the United States' global war on terror. But he was not just a strategist. He was also a man of action, and on multiple occasions had won popular acclaim for demonstrating courage and foresight in the face of major threats. Hence, as far as both the depth of his thinking and his leadership were concerned, Tyler made a worthy Wallfacer.

"The Second Wallfacer: Manuel Rey Diaz."

When this brown-skinned, stocky South American with a stubborn look in his eyes ascended the rostrum, Luo Ji was surprised: It was highly unusual for this man to even appear at the UN. But on second thought, it stood to reason. He even wondered why it hadn't already occurred to him. Rey Diaz was the current president of Venezuela, which, under his leadership, had aptly demonstrated Tyler's theory about the rise of small countries. He carried forward the Bolivarian Revolution instigated by Hugo Chavez: In a contemporary world ruled by capitalism and market economics, he promoted in Venezuela what Chavez called Socialism of the Twenty-First Century, founded on lessons drawn from the experience of the international socialist movements of the previous century. Surprisingly, he had achieved considerable success, boosting the country's power across the board and—for a time—turning Venezuela into a city on a hill, a symbol of equality, justice, and prosperity for the world. The other countries in South America followed suit, and socialism briefly caught fire on the continent. Rey Diaz inherited not only Chavez's socialist ideology but his strong anti-Americanism, which reminded the United States that its Latin American backyard could become a second Soviet Union if left unchecked. A rare opportunity presented by an accident and a misunderstanding gave the United States the excuse to launch a full-scale invasion of Venezuela that sought to overthrow the Rey Diaz government along the Iraq model. But with this war, the post–Cold War streak of victories by major western powers over small Third World countries had finally broken. When the US Army entered Venezuela, it discovered that the uniformed military was nowhere to be found. The entire army had been divided by squad into guerilla teams concealed among the people, and their sole combat objective was killing the enemy's vital forces. Rey Diaz's basic approach to warfare was built atop a single, clear idea: Modern high-tech weapons might be useful against point targets, but, for area targets, their performance is no better than conventional weapons and their cost and limited quantity make

them essentially nonfactors. He was a genius at low-cost, high-tech exploits. At the turn of the century, an Australian engineer had built a cruise missile for five thousand dollars with the aim of boosting vigilance against terrorists, but Rey Diaz's thousands of guerilla teams were armed with a total of two hundred thousand of them, mass produced for just three thousand dollars apiece. Although the missiles were made out of parts that were cheap and widely available on the market, they were fully equipped with a radar altimeter and GPS and could hit targets within a five-kilometer radius at an accuracy of within five meters. Their hit rate may have been less than 10 percent during the war, but they caused enormous destruction to the enemy. Other mass-produced high-tech gadgets, like proximity-fuse sniper rifle bullets, had a similarly brilliant track record during the war. During its short time in Venezuela, the US Army suffered casualties that approached Vietnam War levels, and it eventually had to withdraw. The defeat of the strong at the hands of the weak made Rey Diaz a hero for the twenty-first century.

"The Third Wallfacer: Bill Hines."

A debonair Englishman ascended the rostrum, a picture of refinement next to Tyler's coldness and Rey Diaz's stubbornness. He gave the assembly a graceful salute. He, too, was well known to the world, although he lacked the aura of the other two men. Hines's life was split into two entirely distinct stages. As a scientist, he was the only person in history to be nominated for the Nobel Prize in two sciences simultaneously for the same discovery. During research conducted with the neuroscientist Keiko Yamasuki, he discovered that brain activity for thoughts and memories operated on the quantum level rather than on the molecular level as previously believed. This discovery pushed brain mechanisms downward to the microstate of matter, rendering all prior research nothing more than superficial attempts that merely skimmed the surface of neuroscience. This discovery also demonstrated that the animal brain's capacity to process information was several orders of magnitude higher than previously imagined, which lent credence to long-held speculation that the brain had a holographic

structure. Hines was nominated for Nobel Prizes in both Physics and Physiology or Medicine for the discovery. Although his work was too radical for him to win either award, Keiko Yamasuki—who by this time was his wife—won the prize in Physiology or Medicine that year for her application of the theory to the treatment of amnesia and mental illness.

In the second stage of his life, he was a politician and served as president of the EU for two years. Hines was recognized as a prudent and experienced politician, but his term in office was not marked by many challenges that tested his political skills. The nature of the EU's work at the time, which was largely transactional coordination, meant that his qualifications to face a major crisis stacked up rather poorly compared to the other two men. Still, the choice of Hines evidently took into account both his scientific and political credentials, a perfect combination that was quite rare indeed.

Seated in the very last row of the hall, Keiko Yamasuki, the world authority in neuroscience, gazed lovingly down at her husband on the rostrum.

The assembly remained silent as all waited for the announcement of the final Wallfacer. The first three, Tyler, Rey Diaz, and Hines, represented balance and compromise among the political powers of the United States, Europe, and the Third World, so there was considerable interest in the final selection. As he watched Say turn back to the paper in the folder, world-famous names flashed through Luo Ji's mind. The final Wallfacer would be one of them. He looked ahead four rows and surveyed the backs of the first-row occupants. That's where the first three Wallfacers had been before they ascended the rostrum, but from behind he couldn't make out whether any of the people he had in mind were seated there. Still, the Fourth Wallfacer would definitely be there.

Say slowly raised her right hand, and he watched as it pointed to a spot not in the first row.

She was pointing at him.

"The Fourth Wallfacer: Luo Ji."

"It's my Hubble!" shouted Albert Ringier, clapping his palms together. The tears brimming in his eyes reflected the distant blazing ball of fire that rumbled for a few seconds before passing on. He and the cheering crowd of astronomers and physicists behind him ought to have been watching the launch from a VIP platform closer in, but a damn NASA official said they lacked proper qualifications for access, because the object being sent heavenward did not belong to them. Then the official had turned back to the group of uniformed, ramrod-straight generals and, groveling like a dog, had led them past the sentry post to the viewing platform. Ringier and his colleagues were forced to remain at this far-off spot where, in the previous century, a countdown clock had been built across a lake from the launch site. It was open to the public, but on this late night, there were no other observers apart from scientists.

Viewed from this distance, the blastoff looked like a spedup sunrise. The floodlights did not follow the rocket as it lifted off, leaving its massive body indistinct except for the spurting flames. From its hiding place in the dark of night, the world burst forth into a magnificent light show, and golden waves whipped up on the inky black surface of the lake as if the flames had ignited the water itself. They watched the rocket ascend. When it passed through the clouds, it turned half the sky the kind of red only found in dreams before it disappeared into the Florida sky, the brief dawn once again swallowed up by the night.

The Hubble II Space Telescope was a second-generation model, its diameter enlarged to 21 meters from its predecessor's 4.27 meters, which enhanced its observational capability by a factor of fifty. It used a compound lens technology consisting of lens components manufactured on the ground and assembled in orbit. To put the whole lens into space required eleven launches, and this was the final one. The assembly of Hubble II in the vicinity of the International Space Station was nearing completion. In two months, it would be able to turn its gaze to the depths of the universe.

"You pack of thieves! You've stolen another thing of beauty," Ringier said to the tall man beside him, the only one in the group

unaffected by the sight before them. George Fitzroy had seen too many of the launches, and spent the entire process leaning against the countdown clock smoking a cigarette. He had become the military's representative after Hubble II's requisition, but since he wore civilian clothes most of the time, Ringier didn't know his rank and never called him sir. Calling a thief by his name worked just fine.

"Doctor, in wartime the military has the right to requisition all civilian equipment. Besides, you people didn't grind a single lens component or design a single screw of the Hubble II. You're just there to enjoy its success, so it's not your place to complain." Fitzroy yawned, as if it was tiring work dealing with this pack of nerds.

"But without us, it wouldn't have any reason to exist! Civilian equipment? It can see the edge of the universe, but you shortsighted types only want to use it to look at the nearest star!"

"Like I've said before, this is wartime. A war to defend all humanity. Even if you've forgotten that you're an American, you at least remember you're human, right?"

Ringier groaned and nodded, then shook his head with a sigh. "But what do you want Hubble II to see? You've got to be aware that it won't be able to see the Trisolaran planet."

Fitzroy said with a sigh, "It's worse than that. The public thinks that it will be able to see the Trisolaran Fleet."

"Great," Ringier said. Though his face was indistinct in the darkness, Fitzroy could sense the schadenfreude in Ringier's expression, which made Fitzroy as uncomfortable as the acrid odor that now wafted over from the launch platform and filled the air.

"Doctor, you ought to know the consequences."

"If the public has placed its hope in Hubble II, then they probably won't believe the enemy really exists until they have seen the Trisolaran Fleet with their own eyes."

"And you find this acceptable?"

"You've explained it to the public, right?"

"Of course we've explained it! We've held four press conferences, and I've repeatedly explained that although Hubble II is orders of magnitude more powerful than the largest telescopes currently

available, there's no way it can detect the Trisolaran Fleet. It's too small! Detecting a planet in another star system from our Solar System is like detecting a mosquito on a lamp on the East Coast from the West Coast, but the Trisolaran Fleet is only as big as the bacteria on one of that mosquito's legs. How much clearer can I be?"

"That's pretty clear."

"But what else can we do? The public will believe whatever it wants. I've been in this job for a while now, and I haven't seen any major space project that they haven't misinterpreted."

"I said long ago that the military has lost all credibility as far as space projects are concerned."

"But they're willing to believe you. Don't they call you a second Carl Sagan? You've made a mint off those popular cosmology books of yours. Give us a hand. That's what the military wants, and now I'm formally passing on their request."

"Is this a private negotiation of terms?"

"There aren't any terms! It's your duty as an American. As a citizen of Earth."

"Assign me a bit more observational time. I don't need much. Bump me up to twenty percent, okay?"

"You're doing quite well at twelve point five percent right now, and no one can say if those allotments can be guaranteed in the future." Fitzroy waved a hand in the direction of the launch pad, where the dissipating smoke left by the rocket smeared a dirty patch across the night sky. Illuminated by the launch pad lights, it looked like a milk stain on a pair of jeans. The odor had grown more unpleasant. The rocket's first stage was fueled by liquid oxygen and liquid hydrogen and shouldn't have had that odor, so something nearby had probably been burnt by the stream of flames diverted by the launch pad. Fitzroy said, "I'm telling you, all of this is definitely going to get worse."

Luo Ji felt the weight of the slanted cliff face pressing down on him, and for a moment he was paralyzed. The hall was totally silent,

until a voice behind him said softly, "Dr. Luo, if you please." He stood up stiffly and walked with mechanical steps to the rostrum. On the short journey, it was like he had returned to a child's sense of helplessness and wanted someone to hold his hand and guide him forward. But no one extended a hand. He ascended the platform and stood next to Hines, then turned to face the assembly and the hundreds of pairs of eyes focused on him, eyes that represented six billion people from more than two hundred countries on Earth.

As for what went on during the rest of the session, Luo Ji had absolutely no idea. All he knew was that after standing there for a while, he was led off to a seat in the middle of the first row alongside the other three Wallfacers. In a haze, he had missed the historic moment of the announcement of the launch of the Wallfacer Project.

Some time later, when the session seemed to have ended and people, including the three Wallfacers sitting to Luo Ji's left, had begun to disperse, a man, perhaps Kent, whispered something into his ear before leaving. Then the hall was empty except for the secretary general, still standing on the rostrum, her petite figure in far-off opposition to his against the sloping cliff.

"Dr. Luo, I imagine you have some questions." Say's gentle feminine voice echoed in the empty hall like a spirit descending from the heavens.

"Has there been some mistake?" Luo Ji said. His voice, sounding similarly ethereal, didn't feel like his own.

From the rostrum, Say gave a laugh that clearly meant, *Do you really think that's possible?*

"Why me?" he asked.

"You need to find your own answer to that," she said.

"I'm just an ordinary man."

"In the face of this crisis, we are all ordinary people. But we all have our own responsibilities."

"No one solicited my opinion in advance. I was totally in the dark about this."

Say laughed again. "Doesn't your name mean 'logic' in Chinese?"

"That's right."

"Then you should be able to work out that it would have been impossible to solicit the opinions of the people undertaking this mission before it was handed to them."

"I refuse," he said firmly, without even thinking over what Say had just said.

"You may."

The swiftness of this reply, right on the heels of his refusal, left him at a loss for a moment. After a few seconds of silence, he said, "I reject the position of Wallfacer, I reject all the powers granted it, and I will not undertake any responsibility you force upon me."

"You may."

The simple, immediate reply to his statement, light as a dragonfly touching on the water, shut down his brain's ability to think and made his mind a total blank.

"So am I free to leave?" was all he could ask.

"You may, Dr. Luo. You are free to do anything."

Luo Ji turned and walked out past the rows of empty seats. The ease with which he was able to discard the Wallfacer identity and its responsibilities did not give him the slightest shred of comfort or release. Filling his mind now was an absurd sense of unreality, as if all of this was part of some postmodern play devoid of all logic.

He looked back at the exit and saw Say watching him from the rostrum. She seemed small and helpless against the cliff, but when she saw him looking back, she nodded and smiled at him.

He continued onward, past the Foucault Pendulum at the entrance that showed the rotation of the Earth, and ran into Shi Qiang, Kent, and a group of black-suited security personnel who looked inquiringly at him. In their eyes he saw a new respect and awe. Even Shi Qiang and Kent, who had always behaved naturally toward him, made no attempt to mask their expressions. Luo Ji passed through their midst, saying nothing. He walked through the bare lobby, occupied as on his arrival only by black-clothed guards. As before, whenever he passed one, they spoke softly into a radio. When he came to the exit, Shi Qiang and Kent stopped him.

"It may be dangerous outside. Do you need security?" Shi Qiang asked.

"No, I don't. Get out of my way," Luo Ji said, keeping his eyes straight ahead.

"Very well. We can only do as you tell us," Shi Qiang said as he moved aside. Kent did the same. Luo Ji went out the door.

The cool air hit him in the face. It was still nighttime, but the outside was clearly lit by the bright lamps. The delegates to the special session had driven off, and the few people left in the plaza were tourists or locals. The historic meeting had not yet made the news, so no one recognized him, and his presence did not attract any attention.

And so Luo Ji the Wallfacer walked as if sleepwalking through absurd fantastic reality. In his trance, he had lost the capacity for rational thought and was unaware of where he came from, much less where he was going. Unwittingly, he walked onto the lawn and came to a statue. When his gaze passed over it, he noticed that it was of a man hammering a sword: *Let Us Beat Swords into Plowshares*. It had been a gift to the UN from the former Soviet Union, but to his mind the powerful composition formed by the hammer, the bulky man, and the sword being bent beneath him imbued the work with hints of violence.

And then the man with the hammer was smacking Luo Ji savagely in the chest with a fierce blow that sent him tumbling to the ground and knocked him out before he even hit the grass. But the shock passed quickly, and soon partial consciousness returned amid pain and dizziness. He had to shut his eyes against the blinding flashlights that were all around him. Then the rings of light receded and he could make out a circle of faces over him. In the black cloud of haze and agony he recognized Shi Qiang the moment he heard his voice:

"Do you need security protection? We can only do as you tell us!"

Luo Ji nodded weakly. Then everything happened in a flash. He felt himself lifted onto what seemed like a stretcher, and then the stretcher was hoisted up. He was surrounded by a tight clutch of people, as if he was in a narrow pit with walls formed by human bodies. The only thing visible out of the mouth of the pit was the

black night sky, and it was only from the motion of the legs of the people surrounding him that he could tell he was being carried. Soon the pit vanished, as did the sky above him, replaced by the lit ceiling panels of an ambulance. He tasted blood in his mouth and then emptied his stomach in a bout of nausea. Someone beside him caught his vomit—blood and what he had eaten on the plane—in a plastic bag with a practiced hand. After he vomited, someone strapped an oxygen mask to his face. When he could breathe easier he felt a little better, although his chest still hurt. He felt his clothes getting cut off at the chest, and imagined in a panic that fresh blood was spurting from a wound, but that didn't seem to be right, since no bandaging seemed to be taking place. He was covered in a blanket. Not long after that, the vehicle stopped. He was carried out, and the night sky and the lit ceilings of hospital corridors passed over him, then the ceiling of an emergency room, and then, moving slowly overhead, the glowing red slit of the CT scanner. Faces of doctors and nurses occasionally popped into view and caused him pain with their inspections and manipulation of his chest. Finally, when he could see the ceiling of the ward overhead, everything settled down.

"One broken rib and minor internal bleeding. It's not serious. You're not badly injured, but you need rest due to the bleeding," the bespectacled doctor looking down at him said.

This time Luo Ji didn't refuse sleeping pills, but took them with a nurse's help and quickly fell asleep. Two scenes alternated in his dreams: the rostrum of the UN assembly hall looming above him, and the man from *Let Us Beat Swords into Plowshares* swinging a hammer into him over and over. Later, he came to the quiet patch of snow deep in his heart and entered the simple, exquisite cabin. The Eve of his own creation stood up from the fireplace, her beautiful eyes brimming with tears. . . . Then he woke up and felt tears in his own eyes and a spot of wetness on the pillow. They had dimmed the lights for him, and since she didn't appear while he was awake, he fell back to sleep in the hope of returning to the cabin. But this time he slept without dreaming.

When he woke next, he knew that he had been asleep for a long time. He felt refreshed, and although there was still intermittent pain in his chest, he could believe now that his injuries weren't serious. When he tried to sit up, the blond nurse didn't stop him, but simply adjusted his pillow for him to lean on. After a while, Shi Qiang came in and sat down by his bed.

"How are you feeling? I've been shot three times while wearing a bulletproof vest. This shouldn't be anything serious," he said.

"Da Shi, you saved my life," Luo Ji said weakly.

Shi Qiang waved a hand. "This happened because we fell down on the job. We didn't take timely and effective protection measures. We have to do what you say. It's over now, though."

"And the other three?"

Shi Qiang knew immediately who he was referring to. "They're fine. They weren't as careless as you, walking out alone."

"Does the ETO want to kill us?"

"Probably. The assailant has been detained. It's a good thing we set up a snake-eye behind you."

"A what?"

"A precise radar system that can quickly determine the shooter's position from the path of the bullet. The assailant's identity has been confirmed. He's a professional guerilla in the ETO militia. We never imagined he would dare to attack in a downtown area like this. His actions were practically suicidal."

"I'd like to see him."

"Who? The assailant?"

Luo Ji nodded.

"Sure. But that's not within the scope of my authority. I'm only in charge of security protection. I'll put in a request." Having said this, Shi Qiang turned and left. He seemed more careful and cautious now, different from the lackadaisical image he used to project. Luo wasn't used to it.

Shi Qiang quickly returned and said, "You may, either here or somewhere else. The doctor says walking isn't an issue."

Luo Ji wanted to tell him that he'd like to change venues.

113

He even started to get up, but then the thought struck him that a sickly appearance better suited his purpose, so he lay back down again. "I'll see him here."

"They're on their way over, so you'll have to wait for a while. Why don't you have something to eat? It's been a day since you ate on the plane. I'll set it up." Then he went out again.

The assailant was brought in right after Luo Ji had finished eating. He had a handsome European face, but his most prominent feature was his slight smile, a smile that seemed so plastered on it never went away. He was not in cuffs, but when he entered, two people who looked like professional escorts sat down on chairs, and two others stood at the doorway. They were wearing badges that identified them as PDC officers.

He tried to look as close to death's door as possible, but the assailant saw through him. "Doctor, surely it's not as serious as all that?" He smiled as he said this, a different smile appearing over his permanent one like an ephemeral oil slick floating on water. "I'm very sorry."

"You're sorry for trying to kill me?" Luo Ji raised his head off the pillow to look at his attacker.

"Sorry I didn't kill you, sir. I thought you wouldn't be wearing a vest to a meeting like this. Never imagined you would be so scrupulous with protecting your life. Otherwise I'd have used armor-piercing bullets, or simply aimed for your head. Then I would have completed my mission, and you would be freed from yours, this unnatural mission no normal person can shoulder."

"I'm already free of it. I submitted my refusal to the secretary general, rejecting the Wallfacer position and all of its rights and responsibilities, and she agreed on behalf of the UN. Of course, you didn't know this when you were trying to kill me. The ETO wasted an assassin."

The smile on the assailant's face grew brighter, like a monitor whose brightness had been turned up. "You're a funny man."

"What do you mean? I'm telling you the honest truth. If you don't believe me—"

"I believe you, but you're still a funny man," the assailant said, the bright smile still on his face. It was a smile that Luo Ji noted in passing but that would soon be imprinted on his consciousness as if by liquid metal, marking him for life.

He shook his head and, with a sigh, lay back down on the bed. He did not speak.

The assailant said, "Doctor, I don't think we have much time. I presume you did not call me here purely to tell this infantile joke."

"I still don't understand what you mean."

"If that's the case, then your intelligence does not qualify you to be a Wallfacer, Dr. Luo Ji. You're not as logical as your name suggests. My life really has been wasted, it appears." The assailant looked at the two people standing on alert behind him and said, "Gentlemen, I think we can leave."

The two cast an inquiring glance at Luo Ji, who waved a hand at them, and then the assailant was led out.

Luo Ji sat up in bed and thought over the assailant's words. He had the odd feeling that something wasn't right, but he didn't know what it was. He got out of bed and took a couple of steps: no impediments apart from the dull pain in his chest. When he went to the door and looked out, the guards armed with rifles sitting beside it stood up immediately, and one of them spoke into the radio on his shoulder. Luo Ji saw a bright and clean hallway that was completely empty except for two more armed guards at the very end. He shut the door, went over to the window, and drew back the curtain. Looking down from this height he saw that guards armed to the teeth were posted all over the hospital entrance, and two green military vehicles were parked out front. Apart from the occasional white-clothed hospital staffer hurrying in or out, he saw no one else. Looking more carefully, he noticed that on the roof of the building opposite were two people surveying the surroundings through binoculars next to a sniper rifle, and he was instinctively certain that similar snipers were on the roof of his own building.

The guards weren't police. They looked like military. He called for Shi Qiang.

"The hospital is still under heavy security, correct?" he asked.

"Yes."

"And if I asked you to dismiss all of the security, what would happen?"

"We would do as you asked. But I advise you not to do so. It's dangerous at the moment."

"What department are you with? What are you in charge of?"

"I belong to the Planetary Defense Security Department, and I'm in charge of your safety."

"But I'm no longer a Wallfacer. I'm just an ordinary citizen, so even if my life is in danger, the duty ought to fall to the ordinary police. Why should I still enjoy this degree of protection from planetary defense security? And to have them dismissed or recalled if I so desire? Who gave me that power?"

Shi Qiang's face remained expressionless, like a rubber mask. "These are the orders we were given."

"Then . . . where's Kent?"

"Outside."

"Call him in!"

Kent came in shortly after Shi Qiang left. His manner had returned to the gracious demeanor of a UN official.

"Dr. Luo, I wanted to wait to see you until you had recovered."

"What are you doing now?"

"I'm your day-to-day liaison with the Planetary Defense Council."

"But I'm not a Wallfacer anymore!" Luo Ji shouted. Then he asked, "Has the media announced the Wallfacer Project?"

"To the entire world."

"And my refusing to be a Wallfacer?"

"It's in there too, of course."

"What did it say?"

"It was quite simple. 'After the conclusion of the UN special session, Luo Ji declared his refusal of the Wallfacer position and mission.'"

"Then what are you still doing here?"

"I'm in charge of your day-to-day liaisons."

Luo Ji looked at him blankly. Kent seemed to be wearing the same rubber mask as Shi. He was unreadable.

"If there's nothing else, then I'll be going. Rest well. Call for me at any time," Kent said, and then started to leave. Just as he stepped through the door, Luo Ji called for him to stop.

"I want to see the secretary general."

"The Planetary Defense Council is the specific agency in charge of the direction and execution of the Wallfacer Project. The supreme leader is the PDC's rotating chair. The UN secretary general exercises no direct leadership over the PDC."

Luo Ji thought this over. "I'd still like to see the secretary general. I ought to have that power."

"Very well. Wait one moment." Kent left the room, but soon returned and said, "The secretary general is waiting for you in her office. Shall we be off, then?"

All along the way to the secretary general's office on the thirty-fourth floor of the Secretariat Building, Luo Ji remained under security so tight he was practically shut up in a movable safe. The office was smaller than he had imagined, and simply furnished, with a fair bit of space taken up by a UN flag standing behind the desk. Say came around the desk to welcome him.

"Dr. Luo, I'd wanted to visit you in the hospital yesterday, but you see . . ." She gestured to the pile of papers on the desk, whose only personal touch was a finely crafted bamboo pencil holder.

"Ms. Say, I have come to reiterate the statement I made to you at the close of the meeting," he said.

Say nodded but said nothing.

"I want to go home. If I am in danger, please notify the New York Police Department and have them be responsible for my safety. I am just an ordinary citizen. I don't need PDC protection."

Say nodded again. "That certainly can be done, but I advise you to accept your current protection, because it is more specialized and reliable than the NYPD."

"Please answer me honestly. Am I still a Wallfacer?"

Say returned to her desk. Standing beside the UN flag, she

smiled slightly at Luo Ji. "What do you think?" Then she motioned for him to take a seat on the sofa.

The slight smile on Say's face was familiar. He had seen the same smile on the face of the young assailant, and in the future he would see it in the eyes and on the face of everyone he met. The smile would come to be called "the Wallfacer smile," and it would be as famous as the smile of the *Mona Lisa* or the grin of the Cheshire cat. Say's smile calmed him down at last, the first time he had been truly calm since before she had stood on the rostrum and announced to the world that he was a Wallfacer. He sat slowly down on the sofa, and by the time he got situated, he understood everything.

My god!

It took just an instant for Luo Ji to comprehend the true nature of his status as Wallfacer. Like Say had said, before the mission was handed down, the ones who would undertake it could not have been consulted. And once the Wallfacer mission and identity were granted, they could not be refused or abandoned. This impossibility was not due to any individual's coercion, but because cold logic, as determined by the project's very nature, meant that once someone became a Wallfacer, an invisible and impenetrable screen was immediately thrown up between them and ordinary people that made their every action significant. And that was what the smiles directed at Wallfacers meant:

How are we supposed to know whether or not you have already started work?

He now understood that the Wallfacers had a mission far weirder than any in history, its logic cold and twisted, yet unyielding as the chains that bound Prometheus. It was an unliftable curse impossible for the Wallfacers to break under their own strength. No matter how he struggled, the totality of everything would be greeted with the Wallfacer smile and imbued with the significance of the Wallfacer Project:

How are we supposed to know whether or not you are working?

His heart surged with a towering fury such as he had never before experienced. He wanted to shout hysterically, to inquire

after Say's mother and the UN's mother, to inquire after the mothers of all of the delegates at the special session and on the PDC, to inquire after the mothers of the entire human race, and finally to inquire after the nonexistent mothers of the Trisolarans. He wanted to jump up and down and smash things, to sweep aside the documents, globe, and bamboo pencil holder on Say's desk, and then tear the blue flag to shreds. . . . But in the end he understood where he was and who he was facing, controlled himself, and stood up, only to fall heavily back upon the sofa again.

"Why was I chosen?" Luo Ji began, hands covering his face. "Next to the three of them, I have no qualifications. I have no talent and no experience. I've never seen war, much less led a country. I'm not a successful scientist. I'm just a university professor who muddles through by throwing together crappy papers. I'm someone who lives for today. I don't want kids of my own, and I could care less about the continuation of human civilization. . . . Why was I picked?" By the end of this speech, he had jumped up from the sofa.

Say's smile vanished. "To tell you the truth, Dr. Luo, we're baffled by this too. And that's the reason you have access to the fewest resources out of all of the Wallfacers. Choosing you is the greatest gamble in history."

"But there's got to be a reason why I was chosen!"

"Yes, but only indirectly. No one knows the real reason. Like I said, you have to find your own answer."

"Then what about the indirect reason?"

"I'm sorry. I'm not authorized to tell you. But I do believe that you'll know when the time is right."

Luo Ji sensed that they had reached the end of their conversation, so he turned to leave, only realizing when he reached the door that he hadn't said good-bye. He turned around. Like in the assembly hall, Say nodded at him with a smile. Only this time, he knew the meaning behind that smile.

She said, "It's a pleasure to meet you again. But in the future, your work will be conducted within the framework of the PDC, so you will report directly to the PDC rotating chair."

"You don't have any confidence in me, do you?" Luo Ji asked.

"I said that choosing you was a huge gamble."

"Then you're right."

"Right to have gambled?"

"No. Right to have no confidence in me."

Again with no good-bye, he walked straight out of the office. Relapsing to the state he had been in just after being declared a Wallfacer, he walked aimlessly. At the end of the hallway, he entered an elevator and rode it down to the hall on the ground floor, then exited the Secretariat Building and came once more to the United Nations Plaza. He was surrounded by security guards the entire way, and though he pushed them impatiently a few times, they stuck to him like magnets and followed him wherever he went. It was daytime now, and Shi Qiang and Kent walked up to him in the sunny square and asked him to either go back inside or enter a vehicle as quickly as possible.

"I'm never going to see the sun again my entire life, am I?" he asked Shi Qiang.

"It's not that. They've cleared the vicinity, so it's relatively safe here. But there are lots of visitors who all recognize you. Crowds are hard to handle, and you probably don't want that either."

Luo Ji looked around him. At least for now, no one paid any attention to their small group. He headed toward the General Assembly Building and entered quickly for a second time. His goal was clear and he knew where he had to go. Past the empty balcony, he saw the colorful stained-glass panel. Turning right, he entered the Meditation Room, closing the door to keep Shi Qiang, Kent, and the guards outside.

When he saw the oblong slab of iron ore for a second time, his first instinct was to dash himself into it headfirst and put an end to everything. Instead he lay down on the stone's smooth surface, whose coolness drained off some of the irritation from his mind. With his body, he felt the hardness of the ore and, weirdly, thought

120

of a problem put forth by his high school physics teacher: How can you make a marble bed as soft as a Simmons mattress? The answer: Dig out a depression in that marble the exact size and shape of a human body. Then when you lie in that depression, the pressure will be evenly distributed and it would feel incredibly soft. He closed his eyes and imagined that the warmth of his body was melting the iron ore beneath him and forming that kind of depression. . . . Gradually, this calmed him. After a time, he opened his eyes and looked up at the bare ceiling.

The Meditation Room had been designed by Dag Hammarskjöld, second secretary general of the UN, who believed that the UN ought to have a place for meditation removed from the history-making decisions of the General Assembly Hall. Luo Ji didn't know whether any head of state or ambassador to the UN had actually meditated here, but surely when Hammarskjöld died in 1961 he never imagined that a Wallfacer like himself would be daydreaming here.

Luo Ji felt himself getting snared once again in a logical trap, and once again was convinced that he could not extricate himself.

So he turned his attention to the power in his hands. The least of all the Wallfacers, Say had said, but he would certainly be able to make use of a terrifying amount of resources. Most importantly, he didn't have to justify his use of them to anyone. In fact, an important part of his mandate was to act in such a way as to keep others guessing, and furthermore, to do as much as possible to engender misunderstandings. Never in human history had there been such a thing! Maybe the absolute monarchs of old had been able to do whatever they wished, but even they ultimately had to account for their actions.

If all I'm left with is this peculiar power, why not make use of it? Luo Ji thought to himself, and sat up. After a short time thinking it over, he decided what his next step would be.

He got off the hard bed of stone, opened the door, and asked to see the chair of the PDC.

The incumbent chair, a Russian named Garanin, was a burly, white-bearded old man. The chair's office was one floor below the

secretary general's. He was sending off a few visitors, half of them in uniform, when Luo Ji entered.

"Oh, Dr. Luo. I heard you had some minor problems, so I wasn't in a hurry to get in touch with you."

"What are the other three Wallfacers doing?"

"They're busy setting up general staff departments, a task I'd advise you to get on with immediately. I'll send some advisors to assist you in the initial stages."

"I don't need a general staff department."

"Oh? If you think it would be better that way. . . . If you do have the need, one can be set up at any time."

"May I have a pen and paper?"

"Of course."

Looking at the paper, Luo Ji asked, "Mr. Chair, have you ever had a dream?"

"What sort?"

"For instance, have you ever dreamt of living in some perfect place?"

Garanin shook his head with a wry smile. "I just flew in from London yesterday. I worked the entire trip, and when I arrived I slept less than two hours before I had to rush to work. When today's regular PDC meeting finishes, I'll have to fly overnight to Tokyo. . . . My whole life is rushing around, and I'm at home no more than three months out of the year. What's the point of that kind of dream for me?"

"In my dreams, I've got lots of those places. I've chosen the most beautiful." Luo Ji picked up the pencil and began sketching on the paper. "This isn't colored, so you've got to imagine it. See these snowcapped mountains here? They're steep like the swords of the gods or the tusks of the earth, and they shine a satiny silver against the blue sky. Utterly dazzling . . ."

"Ah," Garanin said, watching with careful attention. "That's a very cold place."

"Wrong! The land beneath the snowcaps must not be cold. It's a subtropical climate. This is important! In front of the mountains

122

there's a broad lake, and the water is even bluer than the sky, as blue as your wife's eyes. . . ."

"My wife's eyes are black."

"Well, the lake water is a blue so deep it looks black. That's even better. Surrounding the lake are swaths of forest and grasslands, but remember that there have to be both, not just one of the two. This is the place: snow peaks, a lake, forests, and grasslands. And everything is in its untouched, primeval state. When you see the place, you would imagine that man had never set foot on the Earth. Here, on the grass beside the lake, build a house. It doesn't need to be large, but it should be fully equipped for modern living. The style can be either classical or modern, but it should complement its natural surroundings. And the necessary facilities—fountains, a swimming pool—should be provided so that its master can live the comfortable life of the aristocracy."

"And who will its master be?"

"Myself."

"What are you going to do there?"

"Live out my days in peace."

Luo Ji waited for Garanin to say something rude, but the chair simply nodded gravely, and said, "After an audit by the commission, we will carry this out at once."

"You and your commission won't raise any questions about my motivation?"

Garanin shrugged. "The commission can question the Wallfacers in two areas: use of resources exceeding the set scope, and harm caused to human lives. Apart from these, all questions are in violation of the spirit of the Wallfacer Project. And truth be told, Tyler, Rey Diaz, and Hines have left me disappointed. Looking at their strategizing over the past two days, you can tell immediately what they are up to with their grand strategic plans. You're different from them. Your behavior is baffling. That's what a Wallfacer should be like."

"Do you really believe the place I described exists?"

Garanin smiled, winked, and made an "okay" sign. "The world

is big enough to have a place like that. Besides, to tell you the truth, I've seen it before."

"That's wonderful, truly. And make sure that I can live a comfortable aristocrat's life. This is part of the Wallfacer Project."

Garanin nodded gravely.

"Oh, and one other thing. When you find a suitable place, never tell me where it is."

No, you can't say where it is! Once I know where I am, then the world becomes as narrow as a map. When I don't know, the world feels unlimited.

Garanin nodded again, seemingly pleased this time. "Dr. Luo, you've got another trait that satisfies my notion of being a Wallfacer: Your project requires the smallest investment of the four, at least for the time being."

"If that's the case, then mine will never have the largest investment."

"Then you'll be a blessing to all my successors. Money is a real headache. . . . The specific departments in charge of executing this may consult with you on some details. The house, in particular, I think."

"Oh, the house," Luo Ji said. "I forgot one very important detail."

"Go on."

Luo Ji imitated Garanin's wink and smile. "It needs a fireplace."

After his father's funeral, Zhang Beihai went with Wu Yue one more time to the carrier dry dock, where construction on *Tang* had been suspended entirely. The welding sparks had vanished from the hull, and there were no signs of life anywhere on the giant ship lying in the noonday sun. The overarching impression it gave was one of the passage of time.

"It's dead," Zhang Beihai said.

"Your father was one of the wisest generals among the navy's top brass. If he were still with us, I might not have gotten so thoroughly stuck," Wu Yue said.

Zhang Beihai said, "Your defeatism is built on a rational basis, or at least it's your own reasoning, so I don't believe there's anyone who can truly cheer you up. I'm not here to apologize, Wu Yue. I know you don't hate me over this."

"I'd like to thank you, Beihai. You got me out."

"You can return to the navy. Working there should suit you quite well."

Wu Yue shook his head slowly. "I've submitted my discharge application. What would I do if I went back? Construction on new destroyers and frigates has stopped, and I no longer have any place in the fleet. Sit in an office in Fleet Command? Forget it. Besides, I'm not a good soldier at all. A soldier who's only willing to engage in a winnable war is unqualified to be one."

"Victory or defeat is not for us to see."

"But you have faith in victory, Beihai. I envy you, really, to the point of jealousy. Faith like yours is the height of happiness for a military man these days. You truly are your father's son."

"So do you have any plans?"

"No. I feel like my life is over." Wu Yue pointed at *Tang* in the distance. "Just like that, over before it even launched."

A low rumble came from the direction of the shipyard, and *Tang* slowly started to move. To vacate the dock, it had to take to the water ahead of schedule and be towed to another dock for demolition. When *Tang*'s sharp prow split the seawater, Zhang Beihai and Wu Yue sensed a trace of anger in the massive hull. Quickly, it entered the sea, tossing up huge waves that caused the other boats in the port to rock, as if paying tribute. *Tang* crept slowly forward in the water, quietly enjoying the sea's embrace. In its brief and aborted career, this giant ship had at least met the ocean once.

In the virtual *Three Body* world, it was the dead of night. Apart from scraps of starlight, all was immersed in an inky blackness, so that even the horizon was invisible, and the empty land and sky blended together in the dark.

"Administrator, start up a Stable Era. Can't you see we're holding a meeting?" shouted a voice.

The administrator's voice seemed to come from the sky itself. "I can't do that. The era is run randomly along the core model and can't be set externally."

Another voice in the darkness said, "Then increase the speed and find some stable daylight. It won't take too long."

The world flashed. Suns flew across the sky, and soon time returned to normal. One stable sun illuminated the world.

"Okay. I don't know how long this will last," the administrator said.

The sun shone in the wilderness on a group of people, some familiar faces among them: King Wen of Zhou, Newton, Von Neumann, Aristotle, Mozi, Confucius, and Einstein. Sparsely distributed, they faced Qin Shi Huang, who stood on a rock with a sword across his shoulders.

"I am not alone," he said. "This is the core leadership of seven speaking."

"You shouldn't be talking about a new leadership before it's been finalized," someone said, and a clamor rose among the rest.

"Enough," Qin Shi Huang said, struggling to raise the sword. "Setting aside the leadership controversy for the moment, we shall turn to more pressing matters. We all know of the launch of the Wallfacer Project, humanity's attempt to use closed-off, private strategic thinking to resist sophon surveillance. Since the Lord's transparent mind cannot possibly thread that labyrinth, humanity has regained its edge through this plan, and the four Wallfacers pose a threat to the Lord. In accordance with the resolution of the previous offline meeting, we must launch the Wallbreaker Project immediately."

At those last words, silence reigned, and no one voiced any objections.

Then Qin Shi Huang said, "We will appoint a Wallbreaker for each Wallfacer. Like the Wallfacers, the Wallbreakers will be authorized to tap all of the organization's resources, but their greatest

resource will be the sophons, which will render the Wallfacers' every action utterly exposed. The only secret will be their thoughts. The Wallbreakers' mission, then, is to analyze the Wallfacers' open and clandestine actions, with the help of the sophons, and decipher the true nature of their strategic aims as early as possible. The leadership will now appoint the Wallbreakers."

Qin Shi Huang extended the sword and, as if conferring knighthood, touched it to Von Neumann's shoulder. "You are the First Wallbreaker," he said. "You are Frederick Tyler's Wallbreaker."

Von Neumann knelt down and placed his left hand to his right shoulder in a salute. "I accept the mission."

Qin Shi Huang touched the sword to Mozi's shoulder. "You are the Second Wallbreaker. You are Manuel Rey Diaz's Wallbreaker."

Mozi did not kneel, but stood straight and nodded haughtily. "I will be the first to break a wall."

The sword touched Aristotle's shoulder. "You are the Third Wallbreaker. You are Bill Hines's Wallbreaker."

Aristotle did not kneel either, but shook his robe and said thoughtfully, "Yes, I'm the only one who can break his wall."

Qin Shi Huang returned the sword to his own shoulder and swept his gaze across the crowd. "Good. We now have Wallbreakers. You, like the Wallfacers, are the elite of the elite. The Lord be with you! Assisted by hibernation, you will start the long journey to the end of days together with the Wallfacers."

"I don't think hibernation is necessary," Aristotle said. "I can complete the Wallbreaker mission before we finish our normal lifespan."

Mozi nodded in agreement. "When I break the wall, I will face my Wallfacer in person, and I will savor how his spirit collapses in anguish and despair. Devoting the rest of my life to this is well worth it."

The final Wallbreaker likewise stated his intent to break their Wallfacers in person. Von Neumann said, "We will unmask the last traces of every secret that humanity harbors from the sophons. This is the final thing we can do for the Lord, for afterward there will be no reason for us to exist."

"What about Luo Ji's Wallbreaker?" someone asked.

The question seemed to touch something in Qin Shi Huang's mind. He planted the sword into the ground and fell deep in thought. The sun suddenly sped up its descent to the Earth, lengthening the shadows until they extended to the horizon. When it had set halfway, it abruptly changed direction and rose and fell a few times along the horizon, like the gleaming back of a whale cresting out of the black ocean, pulling the vast wilderness and the small group of people that made up this stark world back and forth between light and darkness.

"Luo Ji is his own Wallbreaker. He needs to find out what threat he poses to the Lord," Qin Shi Huang said.

"Do we know whether or not he is a threat?" someone asked.

"I don't know, but the Lord knows, and Evans knew. Evans taught the Lord how to keep this secret, and he's dead. We can't know."

"So of all the Wallfacers, is Luo Ji the greatest threat?" someone hesitantly asked.

"We don't know that either. Only one thing is clear," Qin Shi Huang said, looking up at the canopy of the sky as it changed from blue to black. "Out of the four Wallfacers, he is the only one in direct contest with the Lord."

Work meeting, Space Force Political Department

Chang Weisi stayed silent for a long while after opening the meeting, something he had never done before. He swept his eyes across the two rows of political officers at the conference table, then looked into the infinite distance while gently tapping his pencil on the tabletop, a light tapping that seemed to mark time for his thoughts. At last, he pulled himself out of his reverie.

"Comrades, by an order announced yesterday by the Central Military Commission, I am now serving as commander of the Political Department of the Armed Forces. I accepted the appointment one week ago, but only now that we are seated together do

I feel conflicted. I have suddenly realized that in front of me is the most beleaguered group of people in the space force, and now I am one of your number. I didn't realize this before, and for this I apologize to you." He opened the document in front of him. "This portion of the meeting will be off the record. Comrades, let us have a candid exchange of views. Let us be Trisolarans for once and open our thoughts to each other. This is crucial for our future work."

Chang Weisi's gaze lingered on the face of each officer for a second or two, but they remained silent. Then he stood up and paced along the table behind the row of seated officers.

"Our duty is to build in our forces the faith that we will be victorious in the future war. So, do we have that faith ourselves? Please raise your hands if you do. Remember, we are speaking our minds."

No one raised a hand. Nearly everyone was staring at the table. But Chang Weisi noticed one man's gaze was fixed straight ahead: Zhang Beihai.

He went on, "Do you believe that victory is possible? By possible, I mean not an accidental few tenths of a percent, but an actual, meaningful possibility."

Zhang Beihai raised a hand. His was the only hand raised.

"First let me thank all of you for your honesty," Chang Weisi said, and then turned to Zhang Beihai. "Excellent, Comrade Zhang. Tell us, on what do you base your confidence?"

Zhang Beihai stood up, but Chang Weisi motioned for him to sit down. "This is not a formal meeting," he said. "It's just a heart-to-heart chat."

Still standing at attention, Zhang Beihai said, "Commander, I can't answer your question sufficiently in just a few words, because building faith is a long and complicated process. First of all, I'd like to make note of the mistaken thinking among the troops at the present time. We all know that prior to the Trisolar Crisis, we had been advocating for the examination of the future of war from scientific and rational perspectives, and a powerful inertia has sustained this mentality to the present day. This is particularly

the case in the present space force, where it has been exacerbated by the influx of a large number of academics and scientists. If we use this mentality to contemplate an interstellar war four centuries in the future, we'll never be able to establish faith in a victory."

"What Comrade Zhang Beihai says is peculiar," a colonel said. "Is steadfast faith not built upon science and reason? No faith is solid that is not founded on objective fact."

"Then let's take another look at science and reason. Our own science and reason, remember. The Trisolarans' advanced development tells us that our science is no more than a child collecting shells on the beach who hasn't even seen the ocean of truth. The facts we see under the guidance of our science and reason may *not* be the true, objective facts. And since that's the case, we need to learn how to selectively ignore them. We should see how things change as they develop, and we shouldn't write off the future through technological determinism and mechanical materialism."

"Excellent," Chang Weisi said, and nodded at him to continue.

"We must establish faith in victory, a faith that is the foundation of military duty and dignity! When the Chinese military once faced a powerful enemy under extremely poor conditions, it established a firm faith in victory through a sense of responsibility to the people and the motherland. I believe that today, a sense of responsibility to the human race and to Earth civilization can encourage the same faith."

"But how are we supposed to go about specific ideological work?" asked an officer. "The space force is made up of complicated parts, which means that its ideology is complex. We've got our work cut out for us."

"I think that for the time being, at least, we should start with the mental condition of the troops," Zhang Beihai said. "Big picture: Last week I visited troops from the air force and naval air force that have just been brought under our branch, and I discovered that day-to-day training for these forces is incredibly slack. Small picture: Problems with military discipline are cropping up with increasing frequency. There was supposed to be a total switch

to summer uniforms, but lots of people in headquarters are still wearing their winter uniforms. This state of mind must be changed as quickly as possible. Look, the space force is turning into an academy of sciences. Of course, we can't deny that its present mission is that of an academy of military sciences, but we ought to be conscious that we are an army, and we're an army in a state of war!"

The conversation went on for a while longer, and then Chang Weisi returned to his seat. "Thank you. I hope that we will be able to continue having frank conversations. Now, let's move on to the contents of the formal meeting." As he spoke, he looked up and once again saw Zhang Beihai's steady gaze, which revealed a determination that warmed his heart a little.

Zhang Beihai, I know you have faith. With a father like that, it would be impossible for you not to. But things are definitely not as simple as you say. I don't know what you base your faith on, and I don't even know what else your faith encompasses. Just like your father. I admired him, but I have to admit that in the end I couldn't figure him out.

Chang Weisi flipped open the document in front of him. "Research on space warfare theory is in full swing at present, but one problem has already cropped up: The study of interplanetary warfare needs to be founded on a certain level of technological development, no doubt about it. But right now, basic research has only just begun, and technological breakthroughs will occur far in the future. This means our research has no support. Headquarters has revised the research plan in light of the circumstances, and has divided unified research on the theory of space warfare into three parts, to cater to the possible technological levels that the human world may reach in the future. Namely: a low-tech strategy, a mid-tech strategy, and a high-tech strategy.

"Work is currently in progress to define these three levels of technology, as well as to define a large number of index parameters in every major scientific discipline, but the core parameter will be the speed and range of a ten-kiloton-class spaceship."

"The Low-Tech Level: Spacecraft speed achieves fifty times the third cosmic velocity,[10] or roughly eight hundred kilometers per second. Spacecraft are not equipped with life support. Under these conditions, the craft has a combat radius limited to the inner Solar System. That is, within Neptune's orbit, or thirty AU from the sun.

"The Mid-Tech Level: Spacecraft speed achieves three hundred times the third cosmic velocity, or forty-eight hundred kilometers per second. Spacecraft are equipped with partial life support. Under these conditions, the combat radius of the craft extends beyond the Kuiper Belt, and includes all space within one thousand AU of the sun.

"The High-Tech Level: Spacecraft speed achieves one thousand times the third cosmic velocity, or sixteen thousand kilometers per second, which is five percent of the speed of light. Spacecraft are fully equipped with life support. Under these conditions, the combat radius extends to the Oort Cloud,[11] with preliminary interstellar navigation capabilities.

"Defeatism is the greatest threat to the armed forces in space, so political and ideological workers will shoulder an extremely important responsibility in the space force. Political departments in the military will participate fully in the study of space warfare theory to eradicate the stain of defeatism and guarantee the correct direction of research.

"Those of you present today will become members of a space warfare theory task force. Although there will be some overlap among members of the three branches, the research institutions are independent, and will tentatively be known as the Institute for Low-Tech Strategy, the Institute for Mid-Tech Strategy, and the

10 *Translator's Note:* First cosmic velocity is the initial velocity a body needs to achieve orbit, second cosmic velocity the amount needed to leave an object's gravitational pull, and third cosmic velocity the amount needed to leave the Solar System.

11 *Translator's Note:* The Oort Cloud is a collection of icy objects in a spherical distribution that surrounds the Solar System at a distance of 50,000 to 100,000 AU and is believed to be the source of long-period comets.

Institute for High-Tech Strategy. At today's meeting, I'd like to hear from each of you which one you would choose, as a reference for the Political Department's next round of work appointments. Let's share our selections."

Of the thirty-two political officers at the meeting, twenty-four selected low-tech and seven selected mid-tech. Just one officer chose high-tech: Zhang Beihai.

"Looks like Comrade Beihai wants to get into science fiction," someone said, to scattered laughter.

"My choice is the only hope for victory. That's the only level of technology that gives humanity any chance of building an effective defensive system for the Earth and Solar System," Zhang Beihai said.

"We haven't even mastered controlled nuclear fusion. Sending a ten-thousand-ton warship to five percent of the speed of light? Ten thousand times faster than the truck-sized spacecraft humanity has today? It's not even science fiction. It's fantasy!"

"But don't we have four more centuries? We've got to keep potential progress in mind."

"But progress in fundamental physics is impossible."

"We haven't even tapped one percent of the potential applications of existing theories," Zhang Beihai said. "My feeling is that the biggest problem right now is the technology sector's approach to research. They're wasting too much time and money on low-end technology. In propulsion, for example, there's no reason at all to work on the fission drive, but right now they're not only throwing huge amounts of R&D at it, they're even putting the same amount of effort into studying next-gen chemical propulsion! We should focus our resources on studying fusion engines, and move directly to the development of media-free fusion engines, leapfrogging media-based fusion. The same problem exists in other areas of research. Sealed ecosystems, for instance, are a necessary technology for interstellar spacecraft, one that is not particularly dependent on fundamental theory, but research in this area is very limited."

Chang Weisi said, "Comrade Zhang Beihai has posed at least one question worthy of attention: The military and scientific

communities are all busy starting their own work, but there is insufficient communication among them. Fortunately, both sides are aware of the situation and are organizing a joint conference, and the military and the scientific communities have each established special agencies to strengthen communication between the two sides and establish a fully interactive relationship between space strategy and scientific research. The next step is to dispatch military representatives to the various research areas and to involve a large group of scientists in studying the theory of space warfare. Again, we can't sit and wait for technological breakthroughs. We ought to form our own ideological strategy as soon as possible and then promote it in every field.

"Next, I'd like to talk about another layer of relationships: that between the space force and the Wallfacers."

"The Wallfacers?" someone asked in wonder. "Are they going to interfere in space force work?"

"There's no sign of that at the moment, although Tyler has proposed paying an inspection visit to the military. But we ought to realize that they do have that power, and any interference that does take place may have unanticipated effects. We need to be mentally prepared for it. When such a situation does occur, we should maintain a balance between the Wallfacer Project and mainstream defense."

After the meeting, Chang Weisi sat alone in the empty conference room smoking a cigarette. The smoke wafted into a beam of sunlight shining through the window and seemed to catch fire.

Whatever happens, at least it's begun, he thought to himself.

For the first time, Luo Ji felt that a dream had come true. He had imagined that Garanin was only boasting—of course he could find a stunning, untouched place, but it was certain to be quite different from the place in his imagination. But when he got off the helicopter, it was like he had stepped into a dream world: the distant snow peaks, the lake in front of him, the grassy plain and

forest beside the lake, all of it laid out exactly as he had sketched it for Garanin. And he hadn't dared permit himself to imagine such an immaculate environment. Everything seemed to have sprung out of a fairy tale. There was a slight sweetness to the fresh air, and even the sun seemed to be cautious, sending the softest and most exquisite part of its glow into this place. The most incredible thing was the small estate beside the lake and the villa at its heart. Kent, who was traveling with him, said the house was built in the mid-nineteenth century, but it looked older, and the passage of time had made it blend in with its environment.

"Don't be surprised. Sometimes people dream of places that really exist," Kent said.

"Does anyone live here?" Luo Ji asked.

"No one in a five-kilometer radius. Beyond that there are a few small villages."

Luo Ji guessed that the place might be in northern Europe, but he didn't ask.

Kent led him into the house. With his first glance at the spacious European-style living room, Luo Ji saw a fireplace, with fruitwood stacked neatly next to it that gave off a fresh fragrance.

"The former master of the house bids you welcome. He is proud to have a Wallfacer living here." Kent went on to tell him that the estate contained more than just the facilities he had requested: stables with ten horses, because the best way to get to the mountains was by walking and riding; a tennis court and a golf course; a wine cellar; and, on the lake, a motorboat and a few sailboats. Beneath its old exterior, the house had been fully modernized. Every room was equipped with a computer, broadband, and satellite television, and there was a digital projection room as well. In addition to all of this, Luo Ji had noticed a helipad when he arrived. It was clearly not built at the last minute.

"The man's got money."

"Not just money. He doesn't want to disclose his identity, but you would probably recognize his name if I told you. He donated the land to the UN, a far larger gift than Rockefeller's. Just so

you're clear, the land and all of the real estate on it belong to the UN. You only have right of residence. But you're not getting nothing. When the owner left, he said that he had taken away all of his personal belongings and that whatever is left is yours. These paintings alone must be worth quite a bit."

Kent took Luo Ji on a tour of every room in the house. He noticed that the original owner had good taste and had furnished every room with a sense of elegant tranquility. A considerable portion of the books in the library were old Latin editions. The paintings were mostly in the modernist style, but they did not seem out of place in rooms with a rich classical atmosphere. One thing in particular that struck him was the total absence of landscapes, the mark of a mature aesthetic sensibility: hanging landscape paintings in a house situated in the Garden of Eden would be as pointless as pouring a bucket of water into the ocean.

Returning to the living room, Luo Ji sat down on the deliciously comfortable chair in front of the fireplace. He stretched out his hand and brushed against an object, which he then picked up and inspected. A churchwarden pipe, the kind with a long, thin stem, used indoors by the leisure class. He looked toward the wall and its empty shelves and imagined what had been taken down.

Then Kent came in and introduced a few people: the house-keeper, cook, driver, groom, and boat master, all of whom had been in the previous owner's service. When they had gone, Kent introduced him to a lieutenant colonel in civvies, who was responsible for security. After he left, Luo Ji asked Kent where Shi Qiang was.

"He's handed over your security detail and has probably returned home."

"Let him take the place of that guy just now. I think he'll do a better job."

"I feel the same way, but he doesn't speak English. It would be hard for him to do his job."

"Then bring in Chinese guards to replace the ones here."

Kent agreed and left to make the call. Luo Ji also left the room and walked across the manicured lawn onto a pier leading out

into the middle of the lake. He held the railing at the end and gazed at the reflection of the snowcaps in the lake's mirror surface. Surrounded by sweet air and sunshine, he said to himself, "Compared to life today, what does the world four centuries from now matter?"

Screw the Wallfacer Project.

"How did that bastard get in?" the researcher at the terminal said softly.

"Wallfacers are naturally free to enter," his neighbor answered quietly.

"It's pretty dull, isn't it? I expect you're disappointed, Mr. President," Dr. Allen, director of the Los Alamos National Laboratory, said to Rey Diaz as he led him past the rows of computer terminals.

"I'm no longer president," Rey Diaz said severely, as he surveyed his surroundings.

"This is our nuclear weapons simulation center. Los Alamos has four of these centers, and Lawrence Livermore has three."

Two objects caught Rey Diaz's eye as being not entirely dull. They looked new, with large displays and consoles with lots of fine knobs. He headed over to take a closer look, but Allen pulled him back. "That's a game machine. The terminals here aren't for gaming, so we brought in two machines for relaxation."

Rey Diaz noticed another two not-entirely-dull objects. Transparent and structurally complicated, they contained a bubbling liquid. Again, he started over to take a look, and this time Allen shook his head with a smile and did not stop him. "That one's a humidifier. The climate is dry in New Mexico. The other one's just a coffee machine. Mike, pour Mr. Rey Diaz a cup of coffee. . . . No, wait, not from that. I'll brew you a cup of top-shelf roast in my office."

The only thing left for Rey Diaz to do was to examine the blownup black-and-white photographs hanging on the wall. He recognized the skinny man wearing a hat and smoking a pipe as

Oppenheimer, then Allen directed his attention back to the bland terminals.

"These displays are obsolete," Rey Diaz said.

"But behind them is the most powerful computer in the world, operating at thirty petaFLOPS."

An engineer came up to Allen. "Doctor, the AD4453OG is operational."

"Excellent."

The engineer lowered his voice. "We've suspended the output module," he said, and glanced at Rey Diaz.

"Run it," Allen said, then turned to Rey Diaz: "See, we've got nothing to hide from the Wallfacers."

Then Rey Diaz heard tearing sounds and saw the people at the terminals ripping paper apart. Assuming that they were destroying documents, he muttered, "Don't you even have a shredder?" But then he noticed that they were tearing up blank copy paper. Then someone shouted, "Over!" and everyone cheered and tossed the shredded paper into the air, making the cluttered floor even more like a garbage dump.

"This is a simulation center tradition. When the first atom bomb was exploded, Dr. Fermi tossed torn paper into the air, and according to the distance the pieces drifted in the shock wave, he was able to accurately compute the yield of the bomb. Now we do the same thing for every simulation we run."

Rey Diaz brushed the paper from his head and shoulders, and said, "You run nuclear tests every day, but to you it's as easy as playing a video game. It's not like that for us. We don't have super-computers. We've got to do real tests. . . . We do the same things, but the poor always end up being the nuisance."

"Mr. Rey Diaz, no one here is interested in politics."

Rey Diaz leaned in to take a closer look at the terminals, but saw only scrolling data and shifting curves. When he finally did locate some graphics, they were so abstract he couldn't make anything out. When he leaned toward another terminal, the physicist seated in front of it looked up and said, "Mr. President, if you're

looking for a mushroom cloud, it's not there."

"I'm not the president," Rey Diaz repeated, as he accepted the coffee Allen handed him.

Allen said, "Then we ought to talk about what we can do for you."

"Design a nuclear bomb."

"Of course. Los Alamos may be a multidisciplinary institution, but I suspected you wouldn't be here for any other reason. Can you give me any specifics? What type? What yield?"

"The PDC will send you the completed technical requirements before long, so I'll just brief you on the key points. Large yield, the largest possible. As large as you can make it. Two hundred megatons at an absolute minimum."

Allen stared at him for a moment, and then bent his head in thought. "That will require some time."

"Don't you have mathematical models?"

"Of course we do. We have models for everything from five-hundred-ton shells to large twenty-megaton bombs, from neutron bombs to EMP bombs, but the explosive yield you're asking for is far too large. It's more than ten times the world's largest thermo-nuclear device. It would have to have a totally different trigger and staging from a conventional nuclear weapon, and it might even require an entirely new structure. We don't have a model that fits."

They spoke some more about the general planning of various research projects, and when it came time to leave, Allen said, "Mr. Rey Diaz, I know you have the best physicists on your staff at the PDC. I assume they've told you about the applications of nuclear weapons to space warfare?"

"You're permitted to be redundant."

"Very well. In space warfare, nuclear bombs may be low-efficiency weapons, since nuclear explosions produce no shock wave in the vacuum of space and only negligible pressure from the light they generate, so they don't produce the mechanical impact found in explosions in the atmosphere. All their energy is released in the form of radiation and electromagnetic pulses, and, at least for humans, radiation and

EM shielding on spacecraft is a fairly mature technology."

"And if the target is directly hit?"

"That's a different thing altogether. In that case, heat will be a decisive factor, and the target may be melted or even vaporized. But one bomb of a few hundred million tons will probably be as big as a building, so I'm afraid it won't be easy to score a direct hit. . . . In fact, the mechanical impact of nuclear weapons doesn't measure up to kinetic weapons, their radiation is less intense than particle beam weapons, and their thermal destruction can't compare to gamma-ray lasers."

"But those weapons aren't combat ready. Nuclear bombs are humanity's most powerful mature weapons. And as for the performance issues you mention in space combat, ways can be found to improve them. Adding a medium to create a shock wave, for example, like putting ball bearings in a grenade."

"That's an intriguing idea. Your STEM background shows through."

"My studies were in nuclear energy, which is why I like nuclear bombs. I've got a good feeling about them."

Allen laughed. "I almost forgot: It's ridiculous to discuss issues like this with a Wallfacer."

The two men laughed, but Rey Diaz quickly grew serious and said, "Dr. Allen, like everyone else, you're treating the Wallfacer strategy as something mysterious. The most powerful combat-ready weapon available to mankind right now is the hydrogen bomb. Focusing on that is only natural, isn't it? I believe my approach is the correct one."

The two men stopped on the quiet path through the woods they had been walking along. Allen said, "Fermi and Oppenheimer walked down this road countless times. After Hiroshima and Nagasaki, most of the architects of the first generation of nuclear weapons spent the rest of their lives mired in depression. They would be gratified if they knew the mission that humanity's nuclear weapons are now facing."

"No matter how frightening they might be, weapons are a

good thing. . . . Just to let you know, the next time I come, I hope I won't see you throwing scrap paper around. We should make a tidy impression on the sophons."

Keiko Yamasuki woke up in the middle of the night to find herself alone, the sheets beside her cool. She got up, dressed, and went out the door. At first glance she saw her husband's shadow in the bamboo grove in the yard, as usual. They had homes in England and in Japan, but Hines preferred his Japanese home. He said that the moonlight of the East calmed his heart. There was no moon tonight. The bamboo and his kimono-clad figure lost their dimensionality and looked like paper cuttings hung beneath the stars.

Hines heard Keiko Yamasuki's footsteps but did not look back. Strangely, Keiko wore the same shoes in England as in Japan. Even in her hometown she never wore geta. But it was only here, never in England, that he could hear her footsteps.

"My love, you haven't slept properly for days," she said. Her voice was soft, but the summer insects stopped chirping and peace flooded like water over everything.

She heard her husband sigh. "Keiko, I can't do it. I can't think of anything. Really, I can't come up with anything at all."

"No one can. I say an ultimate victory plan doesn't exist." She took two steps forward but was still separated from Hines by a few stalks of bamboo. The grove was their place for contemplation, and the inspiration for most of their previous research had its source here. They rarely brought intimacy to this sacred place, but always addressed each other courteously, as befitted an atmosphere seemingly imbued with Eastern philosophy. "Bill, you should relax. Doing the best you can is enough."

He turned around, but in the darkness of the grove his face was indistinct. "How is that possible? Every step I take consumes a massive amount of resources."

"Then why not adopt this approach?" Keiko's answer came

swiftly. She had obviously been thinking about the question. "Choose a direction that, even if you're unsuccessful, will do something beneficial while it is being carried out."

"Keiko, that's exactly what I've been thinking about. Here's what I've decided to do: Even if I can't come up with a plan, I can help other people think of one."

"What other people? The other Wallfacers?"

"No, they're not much better off than I am. I mean our descendants. Keiko, have you ever considered this fact? The outcome of natural biological evolution requires at least twenty thousand years to manifest itself, but human civilization has just five thousand years of history, and modern technological civilization just two hundred. That means that the study of modern science today is being done by the brain of primitive man."

"You want to use technology to accelerate the brain's evolution?"

"We've been doing brain research, and we ought to put more effort into expanding it to a scale that can tackle a planetary defense system. If we work hard for a century or two, we might be able to increase human intelligence and allow the science of the future to break out of the sophons' prison."

"Intelligence is a vague term in our field. What in particular—"

"I mean intelligence in the broadest sense of the word. Not just the traditional meaning of logical reasoning, but learning ability, imagination, and innovation as well. And also the ability to accumulate common sense and experience while preserving intellectual vigor. And enhancing mental endurance, so that a brain can think continuously without fatigue. And we can even consider the possibility of eliminating sleep. And so forth."

"What will it take? Do you have even a rough idea?"

"No. Not yet. Perhaps the brain can be connected directly to a computer, which can use its computing power to amplify human intelligence. Or maybe we can achieve a direct interface between human brains and blend different people's thoughts. Or inherit memories. But whatever avenue we ultimately take to increase

human intelligence, we must first begin from a fundamental under-standing of the mechanisms of the human brain."

"And that's precisely our area of interest."

"We can continue in the same career as before. The difference will be that we can tap huge resources to do it!"

"Love, I'm truly happy. I'm ecstatic! There's just one thing. As a Wallfacer, don't you think this plan is a little . . ."

"A little indirect? Maybe. But think about it, Keiko. Human civilization ultimately comes down to humans themselves. If we start by elevating humans, doesn't that make this a far-reaching plan? Besides, what else can I do?"

"Bill, you're wonderful!"

"So think about this for a moment: If we turn neuroscience and thought research into a world engineering project, and can invest an inconceivably enormous amount of money in it, how long will we have to wait for success?"

"About a century, more or less."

"Let's be a little more pessimistic and say two centuries. Then the highly intelligent humans will still have two centuries left, and if they use one century to develop fundamental science and another to turn those theories into technology . . ."

"Even if it fails, we'll have done what we wanted to do."

"Keiko, come with me to the end of days," Hines murmured.

"Yes, Bill. We certainly have the time."

The insects in the grove seemed to have grown accustomed to their presence and resumed their musical chirping. When a soft wind blew through the bamboo and the stars in the night sky flashed through the gaps between the leaves, it was as if the insect chorus was issuing from those stars.

It was day three of the PDC's first Wallfacer Project Hearing. Rey Diaz and Hines had spoken about the first phase of their respective projects, which were put to preliminary discussion by representatives of the PDC permanent members.

Rey Diaz and Hines had both submitted their plans at the previous hearing, but Tyler had delayed his first disclosure until this session, leaving representatives particularly eager for details.

Tyler started with a brief introduction: "I need to establish an armed force in space that will supplement Earth's fleet but be under my command."

Just one sentence in, the hands of the other two Wallfacers shot up.

"Mr. Hines and I have been accused of overuse of resources in our plans," Rey Diaz broke in. "But this is absurd. Mr. Tyler wants to have his own space force!"

"I didn't say it was a space force," Tyler said calmly. "The intent is not to construct warships or large spaceships, but to establish a fleet of space fighters. They'll each be roughly the size of a conventional Earth-based fighter and will carry a single pilot. They'll be like mosquitoes in space, so I've dubbed this the 'mosquito swarm plan.' The formation needs to be at least equal to the size of the invading Trisolaran Fleet. A thousand ships."

"You would attack a Trisolaran warship with a mosquito? That's not even going to raise a welt," a hearing member said dismissively.

Tyler raised a finger. "Not if each of those mosquitoes is equipped with a hundred-megaton-class hydrogen bomb. So I'm going to need the latest superbomb technology. . . . Don't turn me down immediately, Mr. Rey Diaz. You can't turn me down, in fact. According to the principles of the Wallfacer Project, that technology isn't your proprietary property. Once it's been developed, I have the right to requisition it."

Rey Diaz glanced up at him. "My question is, do you intend to plagiarize my plan?"

Tyler smiled sardonically. "If a Wallfacer's plan can be copied, is he still a Wallfacer?"

"Mosquitoes can't fly very far," said Garanin, the PDC rotating chair. "These toy space fighters can only engage in combat within the orbit of Mars, I believe."

"Watch out. His next request might be for a space carrier," Hines said with a chuckle.

Tyler answered with aplomb. "That will be unnecessary. These space fighters can be networked to turn the entire squadron into a single entity, a mosquito group, that acts as a space carrier and is propelled by an external engine or by the engines of a small portion of its member fighters. At cruising speed, the group will possess the long-range space navigation capabilities of large spacecraft. Once it reaches the battlefield, the huge entity will disassemble and go into battle as a fleet of independent fighters."

"Your mosquito group will take years to reach the defensive zone at the perimeter of the Solar System. A fighter pilot can't spend such a long journey in a cockpit that doesn't even permit them to stand up. Will there even be room for supplies in such a small craft?" someone asked.

"Hibernation," Tyler said. "They'll have to hibernate. My plan relies on the realization of two technologies: miniaturized super-bombs and miniaturized hibernation units."

"Hibernating for a few years in a metal coffin, then waking up, only to launch a suicide attack. Clearly, the job of a mosquito pilot is not one to be envied," Hines said.

Tyler's enthusiasm disappeared, and he remained silent for a moment. Then he nodded. "Yes. Finding pilots is the hardest part of the mosquito swarm plan."

Details of Tyler's plan were distributed to the members of the hearing, but there was no interest in discussion. The chair declared the hearing adjourned.

"Luo Ji still hasn't arrived?" asked the annoyed US representative.

"He won't be coming," said Garanin. "He declared that his seclusion and nonparticipation in the PDC hearing is part of his plan."

At this, the attendees whispered among themselves. Some of them seemed annoyed, while others flashed cryptic smiles.

"He's a deadbeat, a waste!" Rey Diaz said.

"Then what are *you*?" Tyler asked rudely, even though his

mosquito swarm plan relied on Rey Diaz's super hydrogen bomb technology.

Hines said, "I'd rather express my regard for Dr. Luo. He knows himself and knows his own abilities, so he doesn't want a pointless waste of resources." He turned graciously to Rey Diaz. "I think Mr. Rey Diaz should learn something from him."

Everyone could see that Tyler and Hines were not defending Luo Ji, but that their enmity toward Rey Diaz was far deeper by comparison.

Garanin rapped the gavel on the table. "First of all, Wallfacer Rey Diaz has spoken out of order. I remind you to show respect to the other Wallfacers. Similarly, I remind Wallfacers Hines and Tyler that your words are also inappropriate for this meeting."

Hines said, "Mr. Chair, what Wallfacer Rey Diaz has demonstrated in his plan is nothing but the crudeness of a soldier. Following in the footsteps of Iran and North Korea, his country fell under UN sanctions because of its nuclear weapons program, and this has given him a twisted complex for the bomb. There is essentially no difference between Mr. Tyler's mosquito swarm program and Rey Diaz's giant hydrogen bomb plan. Both are disappointments. The two straightforward plans will have their strategic intent exposed right from the start. Neither exhibits the canniness that's the strategic advantage of the Wallfacer Project."

Tyler shot back, "Mr. Hines, your plan is like some sort of naïve daydream."

When the hearing ended, the Wallfacers went to the Meditation Room, their favorite place in UN Headquarters. It now seemed to them that this room designed for silence was built especially for Wallfacers. Gathered there, they waited in silence, each of them feeling that they would never be able to exchange thoughts until the final war came. The slab of iron ore lay silently in their midst, as if absorbing and collecting their thoughts and silently bearing witness.

Hines said softly, "Have you heard about the Wallbreakers?"

Tyler nodded. "The ETO just announced it on their public Web site, and it's been verified by the CIA."

The Wallfacers lapsed into silence again, each one conjuring in his mind an image of his own Wallbreaker. It was an image that would appear countless times in their nightmares, for the day a Wallbreaker actually appeared would likely spell the end of that Wallfacer.

When Shi Xiaoming saw his father enter, he edged toward the corner, but Shi Qiang simply sat down quietly next to him.

"Don't be afraid. I won't hit you or curse at you this time. I don't have the energy." He brought out a pack of cigarettes, took out two, and offered one to his son. Shi Xiaoming hesitated before accepting it. They lit up and smoked for a while in silence. Then Shi Qiang said, "I've got a mission. I'll be leaving the country soon."

"What about your illness?" Shi Xiaoming looked up through the smoke and gave his father a worried look.

"Let's talk about you first."

Shi Xiaoming's expression turned pleading. "Dad, there's going to be a heavy sentence for this—"

"Any other crime, and I'd be able to work it out for you, but that's not how this is going to work. Ming, we're both adults. We need to be responsible for our actions."

Shi Xiaoming bowed his head in despair and took a silent draw on his cigarette.

Shi Qiang said, "I'm half to blame. I never had any concern for you when you were growing up. I came home late every night, so tired I'd just have a drink and then go to bed. I never went to a parents' meeting at school, and I never had a good talk with you about anything. . . . It's the same thing again: We have to be responsible for our own actions."

Tears in his eyes, Shi Xiaoming ground the cigarette back and forth repeatedly on the edge of the bed, like he was extinguishing the latter half of his life.

"Prison is like a criminal training course. Forget about reform when you go in, just don't get mixed up with the other prisoners.

And learn how to protect yourself a little. Take these—" Shi Qiang placed a plastic bag on the bed. Inside were two cartons of ordinary Yun Yan cigarettes. "And if you need anything else, your mother will send it to you."

Shi Qiang went to the door, then turned and said to his son, "Ming, you may still meet your dad again. You'll probably be older than me at that point, and then you'll understand what's in my heart right now."

Through the small window in the door, Shi Xiaoming watched his father exit the detention center. From the back, he looked quite old.

In an era where anxiety had taken hold of everything, Luo Ji was now the world's most laid-back man. He strolled beside the lake, took a boat out into the water, had the chef turn the mushrooms he picked and the fish he caught into tasty delicacies, browsed through the library's rich collection, and when he tired of that, went outside and golfed with the guards. He rode on horseback through the grassland and on the forest path in the direction of the snow peak, but he never reached the foot of the mountain. Oftentimes, he would sit on a bench on the lakeside and look at the mountain's reflection in the water, doing and thinking nothing as an entire day passed unknowingly.

He was alone during this time, with no connection to the outside world. Kent was in the manor, too, but he had his own small office and rarely bothered him. Luo Ji had only spoken once to the officer in charge of security, to ask that the security detail not trail along behind him, and if they absolutely had to, to make sure that he could not see them.

He felt like the boat in the water, floating quietly with its sail furled, ignorant of where it was moored and not caring where it floated. Now and then when he thought about his former life, he was surprised to discover that in the short space of a few days, he could no longer recognize it. This state satisfied him.

He was particularly interested in the wine cellar. He knew that the dust-covered bottles lying horizontally on the racks held nothing but the best. He drank in the living room, he drank in the library, and sometimes he drank on the boat; but never too much, just enough to keep him in that perfect, half-drunk, half-sober state, and then he would take out that long-stemmed pipe left by the previous owner and puff away.

Even when it rained and the living room grew chilly, Luo Ji never had the fireplace lit. He knew it wasn't yet time.

He never went online here, but he sometimes watched television, skipping over the news and watching programs that had nothing to do with current events or even the present day. This sort of content was still possible to find, although it was growing increasingly rare in the last ebbs of the Golden Age.

Late one night, he got carried away by a bottle of cognac that, from the label, was thirty-five years old. Wielding the remote, he skipped past the several news stations on the high-definition television, but one English-language news item caught his eye. It concerned the salvage of a mid-seventeenth-century wreck, a clipper that had sailed from Rotterdam to Faridabad and had sunk off Cape Horn. Among the objects that divers had retrieved from the wreck was a small, sealed cask of fine wine that experts speculated was still drinkable. Not only that, but after three centuries in storage at the bottom of the ocean, its taste would be unparalleled. Luo Ji recorded most of the program, and then called for Kent.

"I want that cask. Buy it for me," he said.

Kent went to make a call. Two hours later he told Luo Ji that the price of the cask was astonishingly high: Bidding would start at three hundred thousand euros.

"That amount is nothing to the Wallfacer Project. Buy it. It's part of the plan."

And thus, the Wallfacer Project produced a second idiom after the "Wallfacer smile." Anything that was clearly absurd but which had to be done anyway was called "part of the Wallfacer plan," or simply, "part of the plan."

Two days later, the cask, its aged surface covered in shells, was placed in the villa's living room. Luo Ji took out a tap with a twist drill specially made for wooden casks, which he found in the cellar, and carefully drilled it into the side to pour out the first glass. The liquid was a tempting emerald green. He sniffed it, and then put the glass to his lips.

"Doctor, is this part of the plan too?" Kent asked softly.

"That's right. It's part of the plan." Luo Ji was about to drink, but seeing the people present in the room, he said, "All of you, out."

Kent and the rest of them did not move.

"Sending you out is part of the plan too. Out!" He glared at them. Kent gently shook his head and led the others out.

Luo Ji took a sip. Although he did his utmost to convince himself that the flavor was heavenly, in the end he did not have the guts to take a second sip. But that one sip didn't let him go unscathed. That night he was sick out both ends until he spat up bile the color of the wine and his body was so weak he couldn't get out of bed. Later, after doctors and experts opened the cask lid, they found that it had a rather large brass label on the inside wall, as was the custom in those days. Over time there had been some sort of reaction between the normally peacefully coexisting copper and the wine, and some sort of substance had dissolved into the wine. . . . When the cask was carried off, Luo Ji could see the schadenfreude on Kent's face.

Deeply exhausted, he lay in bed watching his IV drip, and an intense loneliness seized him. He knew that his recent leisure was merely the weightlessness of tumbling into the abyss of loneliness, and now he had reached the bottom. But he had anticipated this moment, and he had been prepared. He was waiting for someone, and then the next step of the plan would begin. He was waiting for Da Shi.

Tyler stood holding an umbrella against the Kagoshima drizzle. Behind him, two meters away, stood defense chief Koichi Inoue, whose umbrella remained unopened. The past two days he had

maintained the same separation from Tyler, both physically and mentally. They were at the Chiran Peace Museum for Kamikaze Pilots, and in front of them was a statue of a special attack unit next to a white plane, call sign 502. A light layer of rain painted the surface of the statue and the aircraft and made them deceptively lifelike.

"Isn't there any room for discussion of my proposal?" Tyler asked.

"I strongly advise you not to speak of this to the media. It will cause trouble." Koichi Inoue's words were as icy as the rain.

"Is it still that sensitive, even today?"

"What's sensitive isn't the history, but your proposal to restore the kamikaze special attack units. Why don't you do it in the US or some other place? Are the Japanese people the only ones in the world who can die out of duty?"

Tyler closed up his umbrella and drew closer to Koichi Inoue, who—although he didn't recoil—seemed to have a force field surrounding him that prevented Tyler from getting close. "I've never said that the future kamikaze forces would be made up only of Japanese members. It's an international force, but since it originated in your great country, isn't it only natural to revive it here?"

"In interplanetary war, does this mode of attack really have any significance? You should realize that victories for those special attack units were limited, and they didn't turn the tide of battle."

"Commander, sir, the space force I have established is a fleet of fighters equipped with super hydrogen bombs."

"Why do you need humans? Can't computer-controlled fighters get close enough to attack?"

This question seemed to give Tyler the opportunity he was waiting for, and he grew excited. "That's exactly the problem! Today's computers are unable to replace human brains, and advancements in fundamental theory would be necessary for quantum and other next-gen computers. But that's been locked up by the sophons. So four centuries from now, computing intelligence will still be limited, and human-controlled weapons will be indispensable. . . . To tell you the truth, reviving the kamikaze squads only has moral

significance now, because it will be ten generations before any of them go to their death. But establishing that spirit and faith means starting now!"

Koichi Inoue turned around to face Tyler for the first time. His wet hair was plastered against his forehead and the raindrops on his face looked like tears. "That approach violates the basic moral principles of modern society: Human lives come first, and the state and the government can't require any individual to take up a death mission. I seem to remember a line Yang Wenli said in *Legend of the Galactic Heroes*:[12] 'In this war lies the fate of the country, but what does it matter next to individual rights and freedoms? All of you just do your best.'"

Tyler sighed. "You know what? You have thrown away your most precious resource." Then he snapped open his umbrella and turned and walked angrily away. When he reached the gate of the memorial, he looked back and saw Koichi Inoue still standing in the rain before the statue.

As Tyler walked in the sea breeze, his mind returned to a sentence from a suicide note from a kamikaze pilot to his mother that he had seen in the exhibit:

Mom, I'm going to be a firefly.

"It's worse than I imagined," Allen said to Rey Diaz. They were standing next to a black obelisk made of lava rock, the monument marking ground zero of humankind's first atom bomb.

"Is its structure really that different?" Rey Diaz asked.

"Totally different from today's nuclear bombs. Constructing its mathematical model might be more than a hundred times more complicated than today's bombs. This is an enormous under-taking."

"What do I need to do?"

"Cosmo's on your staff, right? Get him to come to my lab."

12 *Translator's Note:* Yang Wenli is one of the protagonists of *Legend of the Galactic Heroes*, a series of Japanese science fiction novels launched in 1982 by Yoshiki Tanaka, and followed by manga and anime adaptations.

"William Cosmo?"

"Yes."

"But he's . . . he's . . ."

"An astrophysicist. An authority on stars."

"What's he going to do?"

"That's what I'm gonna tell you. To your mind, a nuclear bomb is detonated and then explodes, but the actual process is more like burning. The greater the yield, the longer the combustion. A twenty-megaton nuclear explosion, for example, has a fireball that can last for over twenty seconds. The superbomb we're designing is two hundred megatons, and its fireball will burn for several minutes. Think about that. What will it look like?"

"A small sun."

"Correct! Its fusion structure is very like that of a star, and it reproduces stellar evolution over a very abbreviated period. So the mathematical model we need to construct is essentially the model of a star."

White sands stretched out in front of them. In the moments just before dawn, the details of the dark desert couldn't be made out. As they gazed at the scenery, they were involuntarily reminded of the basic setting of *Three Body*.

"I'm very excited, Mr. Rey Diaz. Please forgive me for our lack of enthusiasm at the start. Looking at the project now, the significance far exceeds the construction of a superbomb itself. Do you know what we're doing? We're creating a virtual star!"

Rey Diaz shook his head in disapproval. "What does that have to do with the defense of Earth?"

"Don't be limited by planetary defense. Me and my colleagues in the lab are scientists, after all. Besides, this thing is not without practical significance. So long as you input the appropriate parameters, the star could be a model for our sun. Think about it. It's always useful to have the sun in your computer memory. It's the biggest presence that's close to us in the cosmos, but we could take more advantage of it. The model may have many more discoveries lying in wait."

Rey Diaz said, "One previous use of the sun is what brought humanity to the brink, and brought you and me to this place."

"But new discoveries might bring humanity back. So today, I've invited you here to watch the sunrise."

The rising sun was now just peeking its head over the horizon. The desert in front of them came into focus like a developing photograph, and Rey Diaz could see that this place, once blasted by the fires of hell, was now covered in sparse undergrowth.

"I am become death, the destroyer of worlds," Allen exclaimed.

"What?" Rey Diaz whipped his head around, as if someone had shot him from behind.

"Oppenheimer said that when he watched the first nuclear explosion. I think it's a quote from the Bhagavad Gita."

The wheel in the east expanded rapidly, casting light across the Earth like a golden web. The same sun was there on that morning when Ye Wenjie had tuned the Red Shore antenna, and even before that, the same sun had shone upon the dust settling after the first bomb blast. Australopithecus a million years ago and the dinosaurs a hundred million years ago had turned their dull eyes upon this very sun, and even earlier than that, the hazy light that penetrated the surface of the primeval ocean and was felt by the first living cell was emitted by this same sun.

Allen went on, "And then a man called Bainbridge followed up Oppenheimer's statement with something completely nonpoetic: 'Now we are all sons of bitches.'"

"What are you talking about?" Rey Diaz said. Watching the rising sun, his breathing became ragged.

"I'm thanking you, Mr. Rey Diaz, because from now on we're not sons of bitches."

In the east, the sun rose in overarching solemnity, as if declaring to the world, "Everything is as fleeting as a shadow before me."

"What's the matter, Mr. Rey Diaz?" Allen saw that Rey Diaz had fallen into a crouch, one hand on the ground, and was convulsing in dry heaves. His face had turned pale and was covered in a cold sweat, and he had no strength to move his hand from the

clump of thorns it was pressing on.

"Go, go to the car," he said weakly. He turned his head in the direction opposite the sun, and he raised his other hand to block the sunlight. He was unable to get up. Allen tried to assist but couldn't budge his stocky body. "Drive the car over. . . ." Rey Diaz wheezed out, while pulling his hand back to cover his eyes. When Allen drove over to him, he had fallen to the ground. With difficulty, Allen helped him into the backseat. "Sunglasses. I need sunglasses. . . ." He half-reclined into the backseat, his hands clawing at the air. Allen handed Rey Diaz a pair of sunglasses he found on the dashboard. After he put them on his breathing grew smoother. "I'm all right. Let's get out of here. Quickly," he said feebly.

"What on earth happened? What's wrong?"

"It might be the sun."

"Uh . . . when did you start having this sort of reaction?"

"Just now."

The peculiar phobia for the sun that afflicted Rey Diaz pushed him to the edge of mental and physical breakdown whenever he saw it and kept him confined indoors from then on.

"Was the flight very long? You look like you don't have any energy," was the first thing Luo Ji said after Shi Qiang arrived.

"Yeah. You'll never find a plane as comfortable as that one we were on," Shi Qiang said as he appraised his surroundings.

"Not bad, eh?"

"It's awful," Shi Qiang said, shaking his head. "Woods on three sides, so it's easy to hide close to the house. And there's a lake. With the shore this close to the house, it would be difficult to defend against divers coming from the woods on the other side. But the surrounding grassland is pretty good, and provides some open space."

"Can't you be any more romantic?"

"I'm here to work, my boy."

"It's romantic work I'm thinking of." Luo Ji led Shi Qiang into

the living room. He surveyed it, but did not seem much impressed by the luxury and elegance. Luo Ji poured him a drink in a crystal goblet, but Shi Qiang turned it down with a wave of his hand.

"It's thirty-year-old aged brandy."

"I can't drink right now. . . . Tell me of this romantic work of yours."

Luo Ji sipped his brandy and sat down next to him. "Da Shi, I'm asking you to do me a favor. In your old job, did you ever have to look across the entire country for a particular person, or even around the world?"

"Yes."

"Were you good at it?"

"At finding people? Of course."

"Great. Help me find a person. A woman in her early twenties. This is part of the plan."

"Nationality? Name? Address?"

"None. The possibility that she even exists in the world is low."

Shi Qiang looked at him, and after a few seconds said, "You dreamed her?"

Luo Ji nodded. "Daydreams, too."

Shi Qiang nodded, too, then said something Luo Ji had not expected him to say. "Okay."

"What?"

"Okay, so long as you know what she looks like."

"She's, well, she's Asian, so let's say Chinese." As Luo Ji spoke, he took out a paper and pencil. "Her face is like this. Her nose, like this. And her mouth . . . geez, I can't draw. And her eyes . . . damn it, how can I draw her eyes? Do you have one of those things, a piece of software that will let you pull up a face and then adjust the eyes and nose and so on according to the eyewitness's description to come up with an accurate depiction of the person the witness saw?"

"Sure. I've got one right here on my laptop."

"Then get it out and let's draw!"

Shi Qiang stretched out on the sofa and situated himself comfortably. "Not necessary. You don't need to draw her. Just keep

talking. Put aside her appearance, and first talk about what sort of person she is."

Something in Luo Ji's mind caught fire, and he stood up and began to pace restlessly in front of the fireplace. "She . . . how should I put it? She came into this world like a lily growing out of a rubbish heap, so . . . so pure and delicate, and nothing around her can contaminate her. But it can all harm her. Yes, everything around her can hurt her! Your first reaction when you see her is to protect her. No, to care for her, to let her know that you are willing to pay any price to shield her from the harm of a crude and savage reality. She . . . she's so . . . ah, I've got a clumsy tongue. I can't say anything clearly."

"It's always like that," Shi Qiang said with a laugh. His laugh, which had seemed crude and silly the first time Luo Ji heard it, felt full of wisdom now, and it soothed him. "But you've been clear enough."

"Okay. Well, I'll go on, then. She . . . but what am I saying? No matter what I say, I can't express what she's like in my heart." He grew irritated, and seemed to want to tear out his heart to show to Shi Qiang.

Shi Qiang calmed him with a wave. "Forget it. Just talk about what happens when the two of you are together. The more detailed the better."

Luo Ji's eyes widened in amazement. "How did you know about the two of us?"

Shi Qiang laughed again. Then he looked around. "There wouldn't happen to be any cigars in this place, would there?"

"Yes, there are!" Luo Ji grabbed an elegant wooden box from the mantel, took out a thick Davidoff, and used an even more elegant guillotine-style cigar cutter to slice off the end. Then he passed it to Shi Qiang, and lit it for him with a cedar strip specially designed for cigars.

Shi Qiang took a puff and nodded his head, pleased. "Go on."

Luo Ji overcame his earlier language barrier and grew garrulous. He described how she had come alive for the first time in

the library, how she appeared in his classroom during a lecture, how the two of them had met in front of the imaginary fireplace in his dormitory, the beauty of the firelight shining onto her face through the bottle of wine like the eyes of twilight. He recalled with pleasure their road trip, describing every last detail: the fields after the snow, the town and village under the blue sky, the mountains like old villagers basking in the sun, and the evening and bonfire at the foot of the mountain. . . .

After he finished, Shi Qiang stubbed out his cigar. "Well, that's about enough. I'll guess a few things about the girl, and you see if I'm right."

"Great!"

"Education: She's got at least a bachelor's, but less than a doctorate."

Luo Ji nodded. "Yes, yes. She's knowledgeable, but not to the point where it calcifies her. It only makes her more sensitive to life and to the world."

"She was probably born into a highly educated family and lived a life that wasn't too rich but more affluent than most families. Growing up she enjoyed her parents' love, but she had little contact with the community, particularly the lower rungs of society."

"Right, absolutely right! She never told me about her family circumstances, or actually anything about herself, but I think that ought to be the case."

"Now, if any of the following speculations are wrong, let me know. She likes to wear—how would you put it—simple, elegant clothing, a little plainer than other women her age." Luo Ji nodded dumbly, over and over. "But there's always something white, like a shirt or a collar, that contrasts sharply with the dark colors of the rest of the outfit."

"Da Shi, you're . . ." Luo Ji said, admiration in his eyes, as he watched Shi Qiang speak.

Brushing him aside, Shi Qiang went on, "Finally, she's not tall, one hundred and sixty centimeters or so, and her body is . . . well, I guess you could say slender, as if a gust of wind could blow her

away, so she doesn't seem so short. . . . I can come up with more, of course. Not far off, is it?"

Luo Ji was ready to fall on his knees before Shi Qiang. "Da Shi, I throw myself on the ground before you. You're the reincarnation of Sherlock Holmes!"

Shi Qiang stood up. "Now I'll sketch her on the computer."

That night, he brought the computer to Luo Ji. When the woman's portrait appeared onscreen, Luo Ji stared, not moving a muscle, like he had been struck by a curse. Shi Qiang had evidently expected this, and retrieved another cigar from the mantel, clipped it with the guillotine, lit it, and began to smoke. When he had taken a few puffs, he came back to find Luo Ji still staring at the screen.

"Tell me what's off and I'll adjust it for you."

With difficulty, Luo Ji tore his gaze from the screen, stood up, and walked to the window, where he watched the moonlight shining on the distant snow peak. He murmured, dreamlike, "Nothing."

"I thought so," Shi Qiang said, and closed the computer.

Still gazing into the distance, Luo Ji uttered a phrase that others had used to evaluate Shi Qiang: "Da Shi, you're a devil."

Shi Qiang sat down on the sofa, exhausted. "There's nothing supernatural about it. We're both men."

Luo Ji turned to him. "But every man's dream lover is quite different!"

"Dream lovers are basically the same for men of a certain type."

"Still, getting it so close should be impossible!"

"Remember, you told me a lot of stuff."

Luo Ji walked over to the computer and opened it up again. "Send me a copy." Then, as Shi Qiang worked on copying the image, he asked, "Can you find her?"

"All I can say now is that it's quite likely. But I can't rule out not finding her."

"What?" Luo Ji's hands stopped their movements and he turned to look at Shi Qiang in astonishment.

"With this sort of thing, how can you guarantee one hundred percent success?"

"No, that's not what I mean. The total opposite, in fact. I thought you would say that it's practically impossible, but you wouldn't rule out a random, one-ten-thousandth of a percent chance of finding her. And if you had said that, I'd have been satisfied." He turned back to the picture on the screen, and murmured again, "Can such a person really exist in the world?"

Shi Qiang smiled scornfully. "Dr. Luo, how many people have you seen?"

"Not as many as you, of course, but I know that there's no perfect person in the world, much less a perfect woman."

"Like you said earlier, I'm often able to find a particular individual out of tens of thousands, and I can tell you from the experience of most of my life that there are all kinds of people out there. All kinds, my boy. Perfect people, perfect women. You just haven't met them."

"That's the first time I've heard anyone say that."

"It's because someone who's perfect in your mind isn't necessarily perfect in the minds of others. This girl of your dreams—to me, she's got obvious, well, imperfections. So there's a good chance of finding her."

"But directors can search for an ideal actor out of tens of thousands of people and not find them in the end."

"Those directors can't match our professional search capabilities. We're not just looking at tens of thousands, or even hundreds of thousands or millions of people. The tools and techniques we use are more sophisticated than any director's. The computers at the police analysis center, say, can find a match out of upwards of a hundred million faces in just half a day. . . . The only catch is that this is beyond the scope of my duties, so I'll need to report to the higher authorities first. If they approve and assign the task to me, then of course I'll do my best."

"Tell them that it's an important part of the Wallfacer Project and must be taken seriously."

Shi Qiang chuckled opaquely and then took his leave.

———

"What? The PDC needs to find him . . . ?" Kent groped for the Chinese term. "A dream lover? The guy's been indulged too much. I'm sorry. I can't pass along your request."

"Then you are in violation of the Wallfacer Project principle: No matter how incomprehensible a Wallfacer's order is, it must be reported and executed. Any veto belongs to the PDC."

"But we can't use society's resources to allow a person like him to live the life of an emperor! Mr. Shi, we haven't been working together long, but I really respect you. You're an experienced and insightful man, so tell me the truth. Do you really think Luo Ji is carrying out the Wallfacer Project?"

Shi Qiang shook his head. "I don't know." He raised a hand to stop Kent from arguing. "However, sir, that's just my ignorance, not the opinion of our superiors. This is the biggest difference between you and me: I'm just someone who faithfully carries out orders. You, you're someone who always has to ask why."

"Is that wrong?"

"It's not about right or wrong. If everyone had to be clear about why before they executed an order, then the world would have plunged into chaos long ago. Mr. Kent, you do outrank me, but when you get down to it, we're both people who carry out orders. We ought to understand that some things aren't for people like us to think over. It's enough to do our duty. If you can't do that, then I'm afraid you'll have a rough time."

"I'm already having a rough time! We just wasted gobs of money buying that sunken wine. I just think . . . look, does he look like a Wallfacer at all?"

"What should a Wallfacer look like?"

Kent was speechless for a moment.

"Even if there were a template for a Wallfacer, Luo Ji is not entirely inconsistent with it."

"What?" asked Kent, a little taken aback. "You're not saying that you see a certain amount of quality in him?"

"That I am."

"Well, damn it, what do you see?"

Shi Qiang clapped a hand to Kent's shoulder. "You, for example. If the Wallfacer mantle descended upon you, you would be an opportunistic hedonist just like him."

"I'd have broken down long before now."

"That's right. But Luo Ji's carefree. Nothing bothers him. Kent, old fellow, do you think what he's doing is easy? Open-mindedness, is what this is, and anyone who wants to do great things needs to be open-minded. Someone like you won't accomplish great things."

"But he's so . . . I mean . . . if he's just carefree like that, how does it relate to the Wallfacer Project?"

"I've been explaining it all this time and you still don't get it? I said that I don't know. How do you know that what the guy's doing right now isn't part of the plan? Once again, this isn't something for you or I to judge. Taking a step back, even if we're correct in what we think,"—Shi Qiang drew close to Kent and lowered his voice—"some things require time."

Kent stared at Shi Qiang for a long moment, and at last shook his head, unsure whether or not he understood that last sentence. "Fine. I'll make the report. But can you let me see that dream lover of his first?"

When he saw the woman on the screen, Kent's old face grew gentle for an instant. He rubbed his jaw and said, "Oh . . . my god. I don't believe for a moment that anyone like that exists, but I hope you find her soon."

"Colonel, do you find it a little abrupt for me to inspect the political and ideological work of your military in my capacity?" Tyler said when he met Zhang Beihai.

"No, Mr. Tyler. There's precedent for it. Rumsfeld once visited the Central Military Commission's Party School when I was studying there." Zhang Beihai lacked the curiosity, caution, and distance that Tyler had observed in the other officers. He appeared sincere, and that made the conversation easier.

"You've got good English. You must be from the navy."

"That's right. The US Space Force drew an even larger proportion from the navy than we did."

"That venerable old branch of the services would never have imagined that its warships would be sailing into space. . . . I'll be frank. When General Chang Weisi introduced you as the finest political cadre in the space force, I thought you would be army, because the army is the soul of your military."

Zhang Beihai clearly did not agree, but he laughed graciously. "The same soul is found throughout the different branches of the military. In every country's nascent space force, the military culture bears the imprint of its various branches."

"I'm quite interested in your political and ideological work. I was hoping I could do some in-depth investigation."

"Not a problem at all. My superiors have instructed me to hold nothing back, within the scope of my work."

"Thank you!" Tyler hesitated before going on. "My purpose in this trip is to obtain an answer. I'd like to ask you first."

"Of course. Go ahead."

"Colonel, do you believe that we can restore the spirit of armies of the past?"

"What do you mean by 'past'?"

"A wide range of time, from perhaps ancient Greece through the Second World War. What's key is the spiritual commonalities I mentioned: duty and honor above all, and, in time of need, to unhesitatingly lay down one's life. You may have noticed that after the Second World War, this spirit vanished from the military in democratic and authoritarian countries alike."

"The army is drawn from society, so it would mean that the past spirit you speak of would need to be restored throughout society."

"Our views agree on this point."

"But, Mr. Tyler, that is impossible."

"Why? We have four hundred years. In the past, human society used exactly that amount of time to evolve from the era of

collective heroism to one of individualism, so why can't we use the same amount of time to evolve back?"

Zhang Beihai considered this for a moment, then said, "This is a profound question, but I think that society has grown up and can never return to its childhood. In the four hundred years that led to the formation of modern society, we see no cultural or mental preparation for this sort of crisis."

"Then from what do you draw your confidence? As far as I'm aware, you are a committed triumphalist. How will a space fleet brimming with defeatism face a powerful enemy?"

"Didn't you just say we have four hundred years? If we can't go backward, then we must move resolutely forward."

Zhang Beihai's answer was opaque. Tyler obtained nothing else from the ensuing conversation but a feeling that the man's thoughts went deeper than a brief visit could reveal.

Tyler passed a sentry as he left the space force headquarters. When their eyes met, the sentry greeted him with a shy smile. It was something he hadn't seen in other countries' militaries, whose sentries stared intently straight ahead. Looking at the young man's face, Tyler once again repeated that line to himself:

Mom, I'm going to be a firefly.

It began to rain that evening for the first time since Luo Ji had arrived at the estate, and the living room was quite cold. He sat beside the unlit fireplace and listened to the rain outside, feeling that the house was located on a lonely island in the middle of a dark ocean. He wrapped himself in the boundless solitude. With Shi Qiang gone, he had been restlessly waiting, and this lonely wait was itself a kind of happiness. Then he heard a car pull up to the porch and caught snatches of conversation. The soft, gentle voice of a woman saying "Thank you" and "Good-bye" jolted him like an electric shock.

Two years ago, he had heard the same sound day and night in his dreams. The ethereal sound, a wisp of gossamer floating

164

through the blue sky, brought a fleeting sunshine to the gloomy evening.

Then there was a light knock at the door. He sat stiffly in place and only after a long while did he finally open his mouth and say, "Come in." The door opened. A slender figure floated in on a breath of rain. The sole light in the living room was a floor lamp with an old-fashioned lampshade that cast a circle of illumination beside the fireplace but lit the rest of the room only dimly. Luo Ji couldn't make out her face, but noticed that she wore white trousers and a dark jacket that stood in stark contrast to her white collar and made him think of lilies.

"Hello, Mr. Luo," she said.

"Hello," he said, standing up. "Is it cold outside?"

"Not in the car." Although he couldn't see her clearly, he knew she was smiling. "But here"—she looked around her—"here it's a little cold. . . . Er, I'm Zhuang Yan, Mr. Luo."

"Hello, Zhuang Yan. Let's light the fireplace."

And so Luo Ji knelt down and put some of the neatly stacked fruitwood into the fireplace. He said, "Have you ever seen one before? Here, come have a seat."

She came over and sat on the sofa, still in the shadows. "Oh . . . only in the movies."

Luo Ji struck a match and lit the fire-starter under the wood pile. The flame stretched like it was alive, and the woman gradually took shape in its soft golden glow. Luo Ji gripped tightly to the match with two fingers as it burnt down. He needed the pain to tell him this wasn't a dream. It was like he had ignited the sun, which now shone on a dreamworld-turned-reality. Outside, the sun could remain forever hidden by clouds and night, so long as his world had her and the firelight in it.

Da Shi, you really are a devil. Where did you find her? How the hell were you able to find her?

Luo Ji looked away, back into the fire, and tears came unbidden to his eyes. This made him a little scared to look at her, until he realized there was no reason to hide—she would probably think it was the

165

smoke that made him cry. He rubbed his tears away with a hand.

"It's really warm, and nice . . ." she said with a smile as she watched the flames.

Her words and her smile made Luo Ji's heart tremble.

"Why is it like this?" She looked up and glanced around the dim living room a second time.

"It's not the same as you imagined?"

"It's not the same."

"It's not . . ." He thought about her name. "It's not 'dignified' enough for you?"

She smiled at him. "My name is the 'yan' that means color, not dignity."

"Oh, I see. Perhaps you think there ought to be lots of maps, and a large screen, and clusters of uniformed generals, and I'd be here pointing at things with a stick?"

"That's it exactly, Mr. Luo." Delighted, her smile blossomed like a rose in bloom.

Luo Ji stood up. "You must be tired from the journey. Have some tea." He hesitated. "Or would you care for some wine? It'll ward off the cold."

She nodded. "Okay." She accepted the goblet with a quiet "Thank you," and took a small sip.

Looking at her innocently holding the wineglass stirred the most delicate parts of his mind. She drank when invited. She trusted the world and had no wariness about it at all. Yes, everything in the world was lying in wait to hurt her, except here. She needed to be cared for here. This was her castle.

He sat down and looked at her, and then said, as calmly as he could, "What did they tell you before you came?"

"That I'd be coming to work, of course." She flashed him that innocent smile that dashed his heart to pieces. "Mr. Luo, what will I be working on?"

"What did you study?"

"Traditional painting, at the Central Academy of Fine Arts."

"Ah. Have you graduated?"

"Yes. I just graduated, and have been looking for work while I prepare for grad school."

Luo Ji considered this for a while, but he couldn't come up with anything for her to do. "Well, as for work, we'll talk about that tomorrow. You must be tired. First you must sleep well. . . . Do you like it here?"

"I don't know. There was a lot of fog when I came from the airport, and then it got dark, so I couldn't see anything. . . . Mr. Luo, where is this?"

"I don't know either."

She nodded and chuckled to herself, clearly not believing him.

"I really don't know where we are. The land looks like Scandinavia. I could call and ask right now." He reached for the phone next to the sofa.

"No, don't, Mr. Luo. It's nice not knowing."

"Why?"

"Once you know, the world turns narrow."

My god, he exclaimed to himself.

All of a sudden, she exclaimed, "Mr. Luo, look at how lovely the wine is in the firelight."

The wine, soaked in the light of the fire, shone with a glistening crimson found only in dreams.

"What do you think it looks like?" he asked nervously.

"Well, I think it looks like eyes."

"The eyes of twilight, no?"

"The eyes of twilight? That's a marvelous way to put it, Mr. Luo."

"Dawn or twilight? You prefer twilight, do you?"

"That's right. How did you know? I love painting the twilight." Her eyes shone crystalline in the firelight, as if asking, *What's wrong with that?*

The next morning, after the rain had cleared, Luo Ji felt as if God had washed out this Garden of Eden to prepare for Zhuang Yan's arrival. When she saw its true appearance for the first time, what Luo Ji heard was not the squeals and fussing and exclamations that young women like her usually made. No, in the face of

167

such a magnificent vista, she fell into an awed and breathless state and was unable to speak even one word of praise. He could tell that she was far more sensitive to natural beauty than other women.

"So you really like to paint?" he asked.

She stared speechless at the distant snow peak, and it was some time before she recovered her senses. "Oh, yes. But if I'd grown up here, I probably wouldn't."

"Why's that?"

"I've imagined lots of wonderful places, and when I paint them it's like I've been there. But this place has everything from my dreams and imagination, so what would a painting do?"

"That's true. When the beauty in your imagination becomes reality, it's really . . ." He trailed off, and glanced at Zhuang Yan against the sunrise, the angel who had stepped out of his dream. The happiness in his heart rippled like the waves on the lake sparkling in the light. The UN and the PDC never imagined that this would be a consequence of the Wallfacer Project. If he died now, he wouldn't care.

"Mr. Luo, if it rained so much yesterday, why hasn't the snow on that mountain been washed away?" she asked.

"The rain fell below the snowline. That mountain has snow year-round. The climate here is very different from back in China."

"Have you been to the mountain?"

"No. I haven't been here very long." He noticed that the girl's eyes never left the mountain. "Do you like snowcaps?"

She nodded.

"Then let's go."

"Really? When?" she exclaimed in excitement.

"We can set off now. There's a simple roadway that runs to the foot of the mountain, and if we go now, we can be back by evening."

"What about work?" Zhuang Yan tore her eyes from the mountain and looked at Luo Ji.

"Work can be set aside for now. You just arrived," he said perfunctorily.

"Well . . ." She tilted her head, giving his heart a jolt. The naïve

expression was one he had seen on her countless times before. "Mr. Luo, I've got to know what it is I'm doing."

He looked into the distance and thought for a few seconds, then said with finality, "I'll tell you when we've reached the mountain."

"Great! Then we should be off, shouldn't we?"

"Right. It's easier if we take the boat to the other side of the lake and then drive from there."

They walked to the end of the pier. Luo Ji noted that the wind was favorable, so they could take the sailboat. The direction would change at night so they would be able to catch it again coming back. He took her by the hand to help her into the boat. It was the first time he had touched her, and her hands were exactly like the ones he had first clasped on that winter night in his imagination, so soft and cool. She was pleasantly surprised when he raised the white spinnaker. When the boat left the pier, she plunged a hand into the water.

"The lake water is very cold," he said.

"But it's so clean and clear!"

Like your eyes, he said to himself. "Why do you like snowcaps?"

"I like traditional painting."

"What's that got to do with snowcaps?"

"Mr. Luo, are you aware of the difference between traditional painting and oil painting? Oil paintings are brimming with rich colors. A master once said that in oil painting, white is as precious as gold. But it's different with traditional painting. There's lots and lots of blank space, and blank space forms the painting's eyes. The scenery is just the border for that blank space. Look at that snowy peak. Doesn't it look like the blank space in a traditional painting?"

This was the most she had ever said to him. She lectured the Wallfacer, pouring out words and turning him into an ignorant schoolboy, without any sense of being out of line.

You're like the blank space in a traditional painting: pure, but to a mature appreciation, infinitely appealing, he thought as he looked at her.

The boat docked at a pier on the opposite shore, where an

open-top Jeep was parked next to the trees. The driver who had parked it there was gone.

"Is this a military car? I saw troops around when I arrived, and had to go past three sentry points," she said as they got into the car.

"That doesn't matter. They won't bother us," he said, starting the engine.

The road passing through the forest was narrow and rough, but the car drove smoothly on it. In the forest, where the morning mist had not yet lifted, the sun penetrated the tall pines with shafts of light, and even through the engine sound they could hear the calls of birds in the trees. A sweet breeze whipped up Zhuang Yan's hair and tossed it about on Luo Ji's face, and the itching made him think of the winter road trip two years ago.

Everything about their surroundings was completely remote from Mount Taihang and the snowy northern China plains, but his dreams from that trip were so seamlessly connected to today's reality that he found it hard to believe that it was actually happening to him.

He turned to look at Zhuang Yan and found her looking back at him. She had been for a long time, it seemed. The look in her eyes was one of slight curiosity mixed with goodwill and innocence. Sunbeams flickered over her face and body. When she saw Luo Ji looking at her, she did not turn away.

"Mr. Luo, do you really have the ability to defeat the aliens?" she asked.

He was completely overcome by her childlike nature. The question was one that no one but her would ever ask a Wallfacer, and they had known each other so briefly.

"Zhuang Yan, the core meaning of the Wallfacer Project is to encapsulate humanity's real strategy in the mind of one person, the only place in the world that's safe from sophon spying. They had to choose a few people, but that doesn't mean those people are supermen. Superman doesn't exist."

"But why were you chosen?"

That question was even more abrupt and outrageous than the previous one, but it sounded natural coming from Zhuang Yan's

170

lips, because in her transparent heart, every sunbeam was transmitted and refracted with crystalline clarity.

Luo Ji slowed the car to a stop. She looked at him in surprise as he stared straight ahead at the patches of sun on the roadway.

"Wallfacers are the most untrustworthy people in history. The world's greatest liars."

"That's your duty."

He nodded. "But, Zhuang Yan, I'm going to tell you the truth. Please believe me."

She nodded. "Mr. Luo, please continue. I believe you."

He was silent for a long while, increasing the weight of the words he then uttered. "I don't know why I was chosen." He turned to her. "I'm just an ordinary man."

She nodded again. "It must be very hard."

Those words and Zhuang Yan's look of innocence again brought tears to his eyes. It was the first time he had received such an acknowledgement since becoming a Wallfacer. The girl's eyes were his paradise, and in that clear gaze he saw no trace of the expression that everyone else directed at the Wallfacers. Her smile was paradise for him, too. It wasn't the Wallfacer smile, but a pure, innocent smile, like a sun-drenched dewdrop falling softly into the driest part of his soul.

"It'll be hard, but I'd like to make it easier. . . . That's all. Here endeth the truth. We now return to the Wallfacer state," he said, as he restarted the engine.

They drove on in silence, until the trees grew sparse and the deep blue sky emerged overhead.

"Mr. Luo, look at that eagle!" Zhuang Yan shouted.

"And that over there looks like deer!" He pointed, fast enough to distract her attention, because he knew that the object in the sky wasn't an eagle but a circling sentry drone. This reminded him of Shi Qiang. He took out his phone and dialed.

Shi Qiang answered. "Hey, brother Luo. So now you remember me, eh? First, tell me: How's Yan Yan doing?"

"Fine. Excellent. Wonderful. Thank you!"

"That's good. So it turns out I've completed my final mission."

"Final mission? Where are you?"

"Back home. I'm getting ready for hibernation."

"What?"

"I've got leukemia. I'm going to the future to cure it."

Luo Ji slammed his foot down on the brakes and stopped short. Zhuang Yan yelped. He looked at her in concern, but, seeing that nothing was wrong, he resumed talking to Shi Qiang.

"Er . . . when did this happen?"

"I got irradiated on a previous mission and then got ill last year."

"My god! I didn't delay you, did I?"

"With this sort of thing, delay isn't relevant. Who knows what medicine will be like in the future?"

"I'm truly sorry, Da Shi."

"Oh, it doesn't matter. It's all part of the job. I didn't bother you about it because I figured we would be able to meet again sometime. But I'd like to tell you something in case we can't."

"Please."

After a lengthy silence, Shi Qiang said, " 'Three things are unfilial, and having no issue is the greatest.'[13] Brother Luo, the lineage of the Shi family four hundred years from now is in your hands."

The call disconnected. Luo Ji looked up at the sky, where the drone had disappeared. The empty blue wash of the sky was his heart.

"You were talking to Uncle Shi?" Zhuang Yan asked.

"Yes. Did you meet him?"

"I met him. He's a nice man. The day I left he accidentally broke the skin on his hand and it wouldn't stop bleeding. It was pretty scary."

"Oh . . . Did he say anything to you?"

"He said you were doing the most important thing in the world, and he asked me to help you."

13 *Translator's Note:* This famous quote about filial piety appears in *Mencius*, a collection of conversations and anecdotes related to the Confucian philosopher of the same name, who lived in the late fourth century BC.

Now the forest had entirely disappeared, leaving only grassland between them and the mountain. In silver and green, the composition of the world had turned simple and pure, and, to Luo Ji's mind, more and more like the girl sitting beside him. He noticed a hint of melancholy in her eyes, and he became aware that she was sighing softly.

"Yan Yan, what's wrong?" he asked. It was the first time he had called her that, but he thought, *If Da Shi can call her that, why can't I?*

"It's such a beautiful world, but when you think about how someday there may be no one here to see it, it's quite sad."

"Won't the aliens be here?"

"I don't think they appreciate beauty."

"Why?"

"My dad said that people who are sensitive to beauty are good by nature, and if they're not good, then they can't appreciate beauty."

"Yan Yan, their approach to humans is a rational choice. It's the responsible thing to do for the survival of their species, and has nothing to do with good or evil."

"That's the first I've heard of it. Mr. Luo, you're going to see them, aren't you?"

"Perhaps."

"If they're really like you say, and you defeat them in the Doomsday Battle, then, well, could you . . ." She tilted her head to look at him, and hesitated.

He was about to say that the possibility of that was practically nil, but he controlled himself, and said, "Could I what?"

"Why do you have to drive them out into space to die? Give them a plot of land, and let them coexist with us? Wouldn't that be wonderful?"

Luo Ji dealt silently with his emotions for a moment, then pointed up to the sky and said, "Yan Yan, I'm not the only one who heard what you just said."

Zhuang Yan looked up nervously. "Oh, right. There must be tons of sophons around us."

"It might have been the Trisolar High Consul himself who heard you."

"And you're all laughing at me, aren't you?"

"No. Yan Yan, do you know what I'm thinking right now?" He had a strong impulse to take hold of her slender left hand, which was lying next to the steering wheel, but he controlled himself. "I'm thinking that the person who might actually have a chance of saving the world is you."

"Me?" She burst out laughing.

"You, except that you're not enough. Or, rather, there aren't enough people like you. If a third of humanity was like you, then Trisolaris might negotiate with us about the possibility of coexisting on the world. But now . . ." He let out a long sigh.

Zhuang Yan flashed a helpless smile. "Mr. Luo, it hasn't been easy for me. Going out into the world after graduation, I was like a fish swimming into the sea, where the water was muddy and I couldn't see anything at all. I wanted to swim to clearer waters, but all that swimming got tiring. . . ."

I wish I could help you swim to those waters, he said to himself.

The road began to climb the mountain, and as the altitude increased, the vegetation grew sparse, exposing the naked black rock. For one stretch of road, they seemed to be driving on the surface of the moon. But soon they crossed the snowline and were surrounded by white, and a crisp chill filled the air. He grabbed down jackets from the travel bag in the backseat, and they put them on and continued ahead.

Before long they reached a roadblock, a conspicuous sign in the middle of the road that warned, DANGER: AVALANCHE SEASON. ROAD AHEAD CLOSED. So they got out of the car and walked to the snow at the roadside.

The sun had started its descent, casting shadows around them on the snowy slope. The pure snow was pale blue in color, almost weakly fluorescent. The jagged peaks in the distance were still lit and shone silver in all directions, a light that seemed to issue from

the snow itself, as if it was this mountain and not the sun that had been illuminating the world all along.

"Okay, now the painting's entirely blank," he said, sweeping his hands about him.

Zhang Yan drank in the white world around her. "Mr. Luo, I actually did do a painting like this once. From a distance, it was a white sheet of paper, almost entirely blank, but closer in you would see fine reeds in the lower left corner, and in the upper right the traces of a disappearing bird. In the blank center, two infinitesimally tiny people. . . . It's the painting I'm proudest of."

"I can imagine it. It must be magnificent. . . . So, Zhuang Yan, now that we're in this blank world, are you interested in learning about your job?"

She nodded, but looked anxious.

"You know about the Wallfacer Project, and you know that its success relies on its incomprehensibility. At its highest level, no one on Earth or Trisolaris, apart from the Wallfacer himself, understands it. So, Zhuang Yan, no matter how inexplicable you find your work, it definitely has meaning. Don't try to understand it. Just do it as best you can."

She nodded nervously. "Yes, I understand." Then she laughed and shook her head. "I mean, I get it."

Looking at her amid the snow, the whiteness lost all dimension, and the world faded around her, leaving her its only presence. Two years before, when the literary image he had created had come to life in his imagination, he had tasted love. Now, in the blank space of this grand natural painting, he understood love's ultimate mystery.

"Zhuang Yan, your work is to make yourself happy."

Her eyes widened.

"You must become the happiest woman on Earth. This is part of the Wallfacer plan."

The light of the peak that illuminated their world was reflected in her eyes, and complex feelings drifted across the purity of her

gaze. The snowy peak absorbed all sound from the outside world, and he waited patiently in the silence, until finally she said, in a voice that seemed to come from a great distance, "Then . . . what should I do?"

Luo Ji grew animated. "Whatever you want to! Tomorrow, or when we go back tonight, you can go wherever you want and do whatever you wish, and live life as you please. As a Wallfacer, I can help you realize all of it."

"But I . . ." She looked at him helplessly. "Mr. Luo, I . . . I don't need anything."

"That's not possible. Everyone needs something! Aren't young people always chasing after something?"

"Have I ever chased after anything?" She slowly shook her head. "No, I don't think so."

"Ah, yes. A carefree young woman like you might not need to. But you've got to have a dream, at least. You like painting, so have you ever thought of having an individual exhibition at the world's largest gallery or art museum?"

She laughed, as if Luo Ji had turned into a foolish child. "Mr. Luo, I paint for myself. I've never thought about that stuff."

"Well then. You must have dreamed of love," he said without hesitation. "You've got the means now, so why not go find it?"

The sunset was draining its light from the snowy peak. Zhuang Yan's eyes darkened, and her expression softened. She said gently, "Mr. Luo, that's not something you can go in search of."

"True." He calmed himself down and nodded. "Then, how about this: Don't think long term, just think about tomorrow. Tomorrow, you know? Where do you want to go tomorrow? What do you want to do? What will make you happy tomorrow? You're able to come up with something, surely."

She thought earnestly for a while, and finally said, hesitantly, "If I tell you, can you really make it happen?"

"Of course. Tell me."

"Then, Mr. Luo, can you take me to the Louvre?"

———

176

When Tyler removed the blindfold, his eyes weren't adjusted to the light and he had to squint. Despite the bright lights affixed to the rock walls of this mountain cave, it was dark here—quite dark, in fact—because the light was absorbed by the walls. He smelled antiseptic, and noticed the cave was set up like a field hospital, with lots of open aluminum cases containing neatly packed drugs, as well as oxygen tanks, small UV disinfectant cabinets, mobile shadowless operating lamps, and several portable medical devices that looked like X-ray machines and defibrillators. It looked like it had just been unpacked and could be re-boxed at any time. Tyler saw two assault rifles hanging on a rock wall, but their similarity in color to the rock behind made them easy to miss. A stony-faced man and woman walked past him. They weren't in white lab coats, but they were definitely a doctor and a nurse.

The bed, near the cave entrance, was a sea of white: the curtains behind it, the old man under the bedsheets, the old man's long beard, the scarf around his head, and even his face—all white. The light in that area was more like candlelight, obscuring some of the whiteness and casting a weak golden sheen across the remainder, turning the place into a classical oil painting of a saint.

Tyler spat inwardly. "Damn it to hell. How did it come to this?"

As he walked over to the bed, he tried to overcome the pain in his hip and inner thigh by adopting a stately, steady pace. He stopped at the bedside, before the man that he and his government had dreamed of finding for so many years. He could hardly believe he was real. He looked at the old man's pale face, and it was like the media always said: This was the kindliest face in the world.

Man truly was a peculiar animal.

"I'm honored to meet you," Tyler said with a slight bow.

"As am I," the old man said politely. He didn't move, but while his voice was reed-thin, it could render power inert but never snap, like spider silk. The old man gestured to the end of the bed, and Tyler sat down gingerly, not knowing whether or not it was intended as kindness. There was no chair, after all. The old man said, "You must be tired. Was it your first time on a mule?"

"Ah, no. I rode one when I visited the Grand Canyon." Although his legs hadn't hurt so much back then. "Are you doing well?"

The old man slowly shook his head. "Surely you can see that I don't have long to live." A playful light suddenly entered his deep eyes. "You're about the least likely person to want me to die of illness. I am truly sorry."

The irony in this last sentence pricked Tyler, but it was the truth. One of his greatest fears had once been that the man would die of illness or old age. The secretary of defense had prayed on many an occasion that an American cruise missile or Special Forces bullet would drop on the man's head before he died of natural causes, even if it happened just a minute before death. Natural death would be the man's greatest triumph, and mark the failure of the war on terror. Even now, the man was edging close to glory. There had been opportunities, of course: Once a Predator drone had snapped his picture in the courtyard of a mosque in the mountains of northern Afghanistan. Simply crashing the drone into him would have made history, not to mention the fact that it had been carrying Hellfire missiles that day. But the young officer on duty lacked the courage to make a unilateral decision once he made the positive ID. Instead, he had reported it up the command chain, and when they checked again the target was gone. Tyler, roused from his bed, had erupted in anger and shattered a precious piece of Chinese porcelain he had at home.

Tyler wanted to avoid the awkward subject, so he brought out his briefcase and set it on the bed. "I have a small gift for you," he said, opening the case. He took out a set of hardcover books. "This is the latest Arabic version."

With effort, the old man reached out a hand as thin as kindling and plucked out the bottommost volume. "Ah, I've only read the first trilogy. I had someone buy the others, but I never had the time to read them, and then I lost them. . . . Excellent, thank you. I like them very much."

"There's a legend that says you named your organization after these novels."[14]

The old man set the book gently to one side and smiled. "Let it stay a legend. You have your wealth and technology. Legends are all we have."

Tyler picked up the book the old man had set down, and faced him like a pastor holding a Bible. "I've come to make you into Seldon."

The same playful light returned to the old man's eyes. "Oh? What do I need to do?"

"Let your organization be preserved."

"Preserved until when?"

"Until four centuries from now. Until the Doomsday Battle."

"And you think that's possible?"

"Yes, if it continues to develop. Let its soul and spirit permeate the space force so that your organization will be part of it forever."

"And you value that so highly because?" The sarcasm in the old man's voice grew stronger.

"Because it's one of the few armed forces available to humanity that uses lives as a weapon. You know, fundamental science has been frozen by the sophons, and this imposes corresponding limitations on advances in computer science and artificial intelligence. In the Doomsday Battle, space fighters will still be piloted by humans, and that requires an army who possesses that spirit. Ball lightning requires a close-range attack."

"What else have you brought with you besides those books?"

Tyler stood up excitedly from the bed. "That depends on what you need. So long as you can ensure the preservation of your organization, I can give you anything."

The old man motioned for Tyler to sit down. "I sympathize with you. After so many years, you still don't know what our needs truly are."

"You can tell me."

14 *Translator's Note:* "Al-Qaeda" is translated into Chinese rather than transliterated, and is known as *Jīdì*, the same term used for the title of Asimov's *Foundation* novels.

"Weapons? Money? No, no. What we need is far more precious. The organization doesn't exist because of Seldon's ambitious goals. You can't get a sane, rational person to believe in and die for that. It exists because it possesses something, something that's its air and blood, and without which the organization would wither away immediately."

"What's that?"

"Hatred."

Tyler was silent.

"On the one hand, thanks to our common enemy, our hatred of the West has faded. On the other, the human race that the Trisolarans want to wipe out includes the hated West, so to us, perishing together would be a joy. So we don't hate the Trisolarans." The old man spread his hands. "You see, hatred is a treasure more precious than gold or diamonds, and a weapon keener than any in the world, but now it's gone. It's not yours to give back. So the organization, like me, does not have long to live."

Tyler remained silent.

"As for Seldon, I'd say his plan is an impossible one."

Tyler let out a sigh and sat back down on the bed. "You mean you've read the ending?"

The old man raised an eyebrow in surprise. "No, I haven't read it. That's just what I think. What? Does the Seldon Plan fail in the book? The author is an exceptional man, if that's the case. I'd imagined he wrote a happy ending, may Allah protect him."

"Asimov's been dead for many years."

"Ah, the wise always die young. May he find heaven, whichever one it is. . . ."

For most of the way back, Tyler was not blindfolded, giving him the opportunity to see the steep, barren mountains of Afghanistan. The young man who led his mule even trusted him enough to leave his assault rifle hanging from the saddle, right next to Tyler's hand.

"Have you killed anyone with that gun?" he asked.

The young man didn't understand, but an older, unarmed man

riding next to them answered for him. "No. There hasn't been any fighting for a long time."

The young man looked up questioningly at Tyler. He had no beard on his childlike face, and his eyes were as clear as the blue sky of western Asia.

Mom, I'm going to be a firefly.

At the Fourth PDC Wallfacer Hearing, Tyler appeared fatigued from his long journey as he submitted revisions to his mosquito swarm plan. "I want every fighter in the mosquito fleet to be equipped with two control systems: a pilot-operated mode and a drone mode. Switching to drone mode will allow me to control all of the fighters in the fleet."

"You're very hands-on." Hines snickered.

"I'll be able to instruct the fleet to form a mosquito group and voyage to the battle zone, then tell it to disassemble and reenter formation. When it engages the enemy fleet, I will command the weapons module on each fighter to select its own target and attack automatically. I'd imagine that even with the lockdown on the fundamentals of physics, current AI technology will develop enough in the next three centuries to permit that."

"Do you mean that you plan to hibernate until the Doomsday Battle, and then directly engage the Trisolaran Fleet?"

"Do I have a choice? You know I've just been to Japan, China, and Afghanistan and didn't find what I'm looking for there."

"And you paid someone a visit," the US representative said.

"That's right. I saw him. But . . ." Tyler gave a long, dejected sigh. "Nothing. I'll keep trying to establish a force of dedicated space fighters, but if I can't, then I'll have to guide them into the final attack myself."

No one spoke. Where the Doomsday Battle was concerned, people usually chose to be silent.

Tyler continued, "I have another supplement to the mosquito swarm plan. I want to conduct my own studies, of certain bodies

in the solar system, in areas of my choosing. These bodies include Europa, Ceres, and several comets."

"How is this related to the space fighter fleet?" someone asked.

"Do I need to answer that?" Tyler asked, looking at the rotating chair.

No one spoke. Of course he didn't have to answer.

"Finally, I have a recommendation. The PDC and every nation on Earth should scale back their attacks on the ETO."

Rey Diaz jumped out of his chair. "Mr. Tyler, even if you claim that this is part of the plan, I strongly oppose this outrageous proposal!"

Tyler shook his head. "This is not part of the plan. It's totally unconnected to the Wallfacer Project. The reason for my suggestion is obvious: If we persist in our attacks on the ETO, in two or three years we may wipe it out, and we will lose the only direct channel for communication between Earth and Trisolaris. We'll have lost the most important source of enemy intelligence. I'm sure you understand what the consequences would be."

Hines said, "I agree. But this proposal shouldn't be made by a Wallfacer. The three of us are a unit in the minds of the public, so please keep *our* reputation in mind."

The hearing ended in unresolved arguments, but an agreement was reached for the PDC to conduct further study of the three revisions to Tyler's plan and put them to a vote at the next hearing.

Tyler remained seated until he was the last one in the assembly hall. He was exhausted and drowsy after his lengthy travels, and as he looked around the empty room, he suddenly realized a risk he had overlooked: He needed to find a doctor or a psychologist, and a specialist in sleep medicine.

He had to find someone to stop him from talking in his sleep.

Luo Ji and Zhuang Yan walked toward the main entrance of the Louvre at ten p.m. Kent had advised them to visit at night to facilitate more convenient security.

The first thing they saw was the glass pyramid, shielded from the nighttime din of Paris by the U-shaped palace building, and standing quietly under the watery moonlight as if it were made of silver.

"Mr. Luo, don't you get the feeling that it flew in from outer space?" Zhuang Yan asked, pointing to the pyramid.

"Everyone has that feeling," Luo Ji said.

"At first it feels a little out of place, but the more you look at it, the more it seems to be an integral part of the place."

The meeting of two vastly different worlds, Luo Ji thought, but did not say.

Then the whole pyramid lit up, turning from moonlit silver to a brilliant gold. At the same time the fountains came on in the surrounding pools, sending tall columns of water and light skyward. Zhuang Yan glanced at Luo Ji in alarm, unsettled by the Louvre's awakening at their arrival. Accompanied by water sounds, they made their way down the pyramid into the Hall Napoléon, and then into the palace.

Their first destination was the largest exhibition hall. It was two hundred meters long and softly lit, and their footsteps echoed down the emptiness. Luo Ji quickly realized that it was only his footsteps echoing, for Zhuang Yan walked lightly on catlike steps, like a child in a fairy tale who enters a magic castle and is afraid of waking what slumbers there. He slowed his pace—not for the artwork, which didn't interest him at all, but to let the distance between them grow and allow him to appreciate her among this world of art, gazing upon the beauty of this Eastern woman along with the full-figured Greek gods, angels, and the Blessed Virgin in the surrounding classical oil paintings. Like the glass pyramid in the courtyard, she soon blended into the environment and became part of the sacred realm of art. Without her, this place would be missing something. In a reverie or a dream or a vision, he let time pass by quietly.

After a time, Zhuang Yan finally remembered Luo Ji's presence and flashed a smile back at him. His heart quaked at what felt to

him like a bolt of light sent to the mortal realm from a painting of Mount Olympus.

"I've heard that with a trained eye, it would take you a whole year to see all of the pieces here," he said.

"I know," was her simple reply, but her eyes said, *What should I do?* Then she turned her attention to the paintings. In all this time she had seen only five of them.

"It doesn't matter, Yan Yan. I can look at them with you every night for a year." The words slipped out.

She turned to look at him, visibly excited. "Really?"

"Really."

"Well . . . Mr. Luo, have you ever been here before?"

"No. But I went to the Centre Pompidou when I came to Paris three years ago. At first I thought you would be more interested in going there."

She shook her head. "I don't like modern art."

"Then, all this—" He glanced around at the gods, angels, and Blessed Virgin. "You don't think it's too old?"

"I don't like it too old. I just like the paintings of the Renaissance."

"Those are pretty old, too."

"But they don't feel old to me. Those painters were the first to discover human beauty, and they painted God as a pleasing person. Looking at these works, you can sense their joy in painting, the same joy I felt when I first saw the lake and the snow peak."

"That's good, but the humanistic spirit pioneered by the Renaissance masters has become a stumbling block."

"You mean, in the Trisolar Crisis?"

"Yes. You must have seen what's been happening lately. Four centuries from now, the post-disaster world might return to the Middle Ages, with humanity once again subjected to extreme repression."

"And art will enter a long winter's night, right?"

Looking at her innocent eyes, he smiled wryly to himself. *Silly kid, you talk about art, but if humanity does manage to survive, regressing to a primitive society would be a small price to pay.* But he said, "When that time comes, there may be a second Renaissance,

and you could rediscover forgotten beauty and paint it."

She smiled a smile tinged with sadness, clearly understanding the meaning behind Luo Ji's consoling words. "I'm just thinking: After doomsday, what will happen to these paintings and artworks?"

"You're worried about that?" he asked. When she mentioned doomsday, his heart ached, but if his last attempt at comfort had failed, he was confident that he would succeed this time. So he took her hand and said, "Come on, let's go to the Asian Art exhibit."

Before the pyramid lobby was built, the Louvre was a giant maze. Getting to any particular gallery meant a long and winding detour. But now you could go directly from the Hall Napoléon beneath the pyramid to any point in the museum. Luo Ji and Zhuang Yan returned to the entrance hall, followed the signs leading to the Arts of Africa, Asia, Oceania, and the Americas, and wound up in an entirely different world from the galleries of classical European paintings.

Luo Ji pointed out the sculptures, paintings, and old documents from Asia and Africa, and said, "These were taken by an advanced civilization from a backward one. Some were looted, others were stolen or defrauded, but look at them now: They're all well preserved. Even during the Second World War, these objects were transferred to a safe place." They stood before a Dunhuang mural sealed in a glass case. "Think about how much turmoil and war that land of ours has seen since the time Abbot Wang gave these to the Frenchman.[15] If the murals were left there, can you be certain they would have been this well preserved?"

"But will the Trisolarans preserve humanity's cultural heritage? They have no regard for us at all."

15 *Translator's Note:* Dunhuang, an oasis on the Silk Road in what is now Gansu province, was home to spectacularly decorated Buddhist grottoes inhabited from the fourth to fourteenth centuries. In 1900, Wang Yuanlu, a Taoist abbot at Dunhuang's Mogao Caves, discovered a sealed-up Library Cave containing a cache of ancient documents that he subsequently sold to Hungarian-British archeologist Aurel Stein and French sinologist Paul Pelliot.

"Because they said we're bugs? But that's not what that means. Yan Yan, do you know what the greatest expression of regard for a race or civilization is?"

"No, what?"

"Annihilation. That's the highest respect a civilization can receive. They would only feel threatened by a civilization they truly respect."

They passed silently through the twenty-four galleries housing Asian art, walking through the distant past while imagining a gloomy future. Without realizing it, they reached the Egyptian Antiquities gallery.

"Do you know who I'm thinking of here?" Luo Ji stood beside a glass case containing the golden mask of a mummified pharaoh and tried out a lighter topic of conversation. "Sophie Marceau."

"Because of *Belphegor, Phantom of the Louvre,* right? Sophie Marceau is gorgeous. She's got Eastern looks, too."

For some reason, right or wrong, Luo Ji sensed traces of jealousy and offense in her voice.

"Yan Yan, she's not as beautiful as you. That's the truth." He also wanted to say, *One might be able to find her beauty among these works of art, but yours eclipses them,* but he didn't want to come off as sarcastic. The hint of a shy smile flitted across her face like a cloud, the first time he had seen this smile he remembered from his dreams.

"Let's go back to the oil paintings," she said softly.

They returned to the Hall Napoléon, but forgot which entrance to use. The most visible signs pointed to the three jewels of the palace: the *Mona Lisa,* Venus de Milo, and Winged Victory.

"Let's see the *Mona Lisa,*" he suggested.

As they headed in that direction, she said, "Our teacher said that after he visited the Louvre, he was a little disgusted with the *Mona Lisa* and Venus de Milo."

"Why was that?"

"Because tourists come for those two objects but have no interest in less famous but equally great works of art."

"I'm one of the great uncultured."

They arrived at the mysterious smile, which was behind a thick wall of protective glass and much smaller than Luo Ji had imagined. Even Zhuang Yan didn't seem particularly excited.

"Seeing her reminds me of all of you," she said, pointing at the figure in the painting.

"All of us?"

"The Wallfacers, of course."

"What's she got to do with the Wallfacers?"

"Well, I wonder—and this is just speculation, so don't laugh—I wonder whether we could find a form of communication that only humans can comprehend, but which the sophons never will. That way, humanity can be free of sophon monitoring."

Luo Ji looked at her for several seconds, and then stared at the *Mona Lisa*. "I get what you mean. Her smile is something that the sophons and the Trisolarans will never understand."

"That's right. Human expressions, and people's eyes in particular, are subtle and complex. A gaze or a smile can transmit so much information! And only humans can understand that information. Only humans have that sensitivity."

"True. One of the biggest problems in artificial intelligence is identifying facial and eye expressions. Some experts even say that computers may never be able to read the eyes."

"So is it possible to create a language of expressions and then speak with the face and the eyes?"

Luo Ji thought this over seriously, then shook his head with a smile. He pointed at the *Mona Lisa*. "We can't even read *her* expression. When I stare at her, the meaning of her smile changes every second and never repeats itself."

Zhuang Yan jumped up and down excitedly, like a child. "But that means that facial expressions really can convey complex information!"

"And if the information is: 'The spacecraft have left Earth, destination Jupiter'? How would you convey that using facial expressions?"

"When primitive man began to speak, surely it was only to

convey simple meanings. It may even have been less complex than birdcalls. Language gradually grew in complexity after that."

"Well, let's try to convey a simple meaning through facial expressions."

"Okay!" She nodded her head excitedly. "Here, let's each think of a message, and then exchange them."

Luo Ji paused for a moment. "I've thought of mine."

Zhuang Yan thought for a much longer time, and then nodded. "Then let's begin."

They stared at each other, but held that pose for less than half a minute before they burst out laughing at practically the same instant.

"My message was, 'Tonight I'd like to invite you to have supper on the Champs-Élysées,'" he said.

She doubled over with laughter. "Mine was, 'You . . . need to shave!'"

"These are grave matters concerning the fate of humanity, so we ought to remain serious," Luo Ji said, holding in his laughter.

"This time, no laughing allowed!" she said, as serious as a child redefining the rules of a game.

They stood back to back, each thinking of a message, and then turned around and locked eyes once again. Luo Ji felt the urge to laugh and strove to suppress it, but the task soon became much easier, for Zhuang Yan's clear eyes had begun to pluck at his heartstrings again.

And so it was that the Wallfacer and the young woman stood, gazes locked, in front of the smile of *Mona Lisa* in the Louvre in the dead of night.

The dam in Luo Ji's soul had sprung a tiny leak, and this trickle eroded it, expanding the tiny fissure into a turbulent stream. He grew afraid and strove to patch the crack in the dam, but was unable to. A collapse was inevitable.

Then he felt like he was standing on a towering cliff top, and the girl's eyes were the vast abyss beneath, covered in a pure white sea of clouds. But the sun shone down from all directions and turned the clouds into a brilliance of color that surged endlessly. He felt

himself sliding downward, a very slow slide, but one he could not arrest under his own power. In a panic, he shook his limbs to try to find a place to hold on. But beneath his body was nothing but slick ice. His slide accelerated, until, finally, with a burst of vertigo, he began to fall into the abyss. In an instant, the joy of falling reached the upper limit of pain.

The *Mona Lisa* was deforming. The walls were deforming, melting like ice as the Louvre collapsed, its stones turning to red-hot magma as they fell. When the magma passed over their bodies, it felt cool as a clear spring. They fell with the Louvre, passing through a melted Europe toward the center of the Earth, and when they reached it, the world around them exploded in a shower of gorgeous cosmic fireworks. Then the sparks extinguished, and in the twinkling of an eye, space became crystal clear. The stars wove crystal beams into a giant silver blanket, and the planets vibrated, emitting beautiful music. The starfield grew dense like a surging tide. The universe contracted and collapsed, until at last everything was annihilated in the creative light of love.

"We need to observe Trisolaris right now!" General Fitzroy said to Dr. Ringier. They were in the control room of the Hubble II Space Telescope, a week after its assembly was completed.

"General, I'm afraid that's not possible."

"I have the feeling that the observations in progress right now are actually private work that you astronomers are doing on the side."

"I'd have done my own work if it were possible, but Hubble II is still in the testing phase."

"You're working for the military. Carrying out orders is all you need to do."

"No one here is military apart from you. We're following NASA's testing plan."

The general's tone softened. "Doctor, can't you just use Trisolaris as a test target?"

"Test targets have been carefully selected according to distance

and brightness classes, and the test plan has been formulated to be maximally economical, so that the telescope completes all tests after just one rotation. In order to observe Trisolaris now, we would need to rotate through an angle of nearly thirty degrees and back, and spinning this bad boy uses up propellant. We're saving the military money, General."

"Let's have a look at how you're saving it, then. I just found this on your computer," Fitzroy said as he brought a hand out from behind his back. He held a printout of a photograph, an overhead shot of a group of people looking upward excitedly. They were recognizably the crew from this very control room, Ringier in their midst, along with three women in sexy poses who might have been the girlfriends of some in the group. The location of the photo was evidently the roof of the control room building, and the photo was very clear, as if it had been shot from ten or twenty meters above. Where it differed from an ordinary photograph was in the complicated numbers overlaid atop it. "Doctor, you're stand-ing on the highest point of the building. It doesn't have a rocker arm like a movie set, does it? You're telling me that rotating Hubble II thirty degrees costs money. Well, how much does it cost to rotate it three hundred sixty degrees? Besides, that ten-million-dollar investment wasn't made so you could snap photos of you and your girlfriends from space. Should I add that sum to your bill?"

"General, your order must of course be carried out," Ringier said hastily, and the engineers immediately went to work.

Coordinate data was quickly called up from the target database. In space, the enormous cylinder, over twenty meters in diameter and more than a hundred meters long, slowly started to turn, pan-ning across the starfield displayed on the screen in the control room.

"This is what the telescope sees?" asked the general.

"No, this is just the image returned by the positioning system. The telescope returns still photos that need to be processed before they're viewable."

Five minutes later, the panning stopped. The control system reported that positioning had been achieved, and after another five

minutes, Ringier said, "Good. Now return to the test position."

In surprise, Fitzroy asked, "What? Is it done?"

"Yes. Now the images are being processed."

"Can't you take a few more?"

"General, we've captured two hundred ten images at multiple focal lengths." At that moment the first observation image finished processing, and Ringier pointed to the screen. "Look, General. There's the enemy world you want to see so badly."

Fitzroy saw nothing but a group of three halos against a dark background. They were diffuse, like streetlights through fog. These were the three stars that would decide the fate of two civilizations.

"So we really can't see the planet." Fitzroy couldn't hide his disappointment.

"Of course we can't. Even when the hundred-meter Hubble III is finished, we'll only be able to observe Trisolaris at a very few set positions, and we'll only be able to make it out as a dot, with no detail at all."

"But there's something else here, Doctor. What do you think this is?" asked one of the engineers, pointing to a spot close to the three halos.

Fitzroy leaned in but saw nothing. It was so faint that only an expert could catch it.

"It's got a diameter larger than a star," an engineer said.

After enlarging the area several times, the thing covered the entire screen.

"It's a brush!" shouted the general in alarm.

The layman always comes up with better names than the expert, which is why when experts name things they, too, work from an outsider's perspective. And thus "brush" became the figure's name, because the general's description was accurate: It was a cosmic brush. Or, to be more precise, a set of cosmic bristles without a handle. Of course, you could also see it as hair standing on end.

"It must be a scratch in the coating! I mentioned in the feasibility study that a pasteup lens would cause problems," Ringier said, shaking his head.

"All the coatings have been through stringent testing. A scratch of this sort wouldn't happen. And it's not generated by any other lens flaw, either. We've already returned tens of thousands of test images, and it's never come up before," said an expert from Zeiss, the lens's manufacturer.

A hush fell over the control room. They all gathered to stare up at the image on the screen until it got so crowded that some of them called up the image on other terminals. Fitzroy sensed the change in the room's atmosphere: People who had grown lazy from the fatigue of lengthy tests were anxious now, like they had been hit by a curse that rooted everything in place but their eyes, which grew ever brighter.

"God!" exclaimed several people at the same time.

The frozen formation abruptly turned into excited activity. The snatches of dialogue Fitzroy picked up were a bit too technical for him.

"Any dust around the target's position? Check it—"

"No need. I completed that item. Observing the absorption of the background stellar radial movement, there's an absorption peak at two hundred millimeters. It may be a carbon microparticle, F-class density."

"Any opinions on the effect of high-speed impact?"

"The wake diffuses along the impact axis, but the diffusion scope . . . Do we have a model of that?"

"Yes. One moment. . . . Here it is. Impact speed?"

"A hundred times third cosmic velocity."

"Is it already that high?"

"That's a conservative figure. . . . For the impact cross section, use . . . Right, that's right. That's just about it. Just a rough estimate."

With the experts busy, Ringier stood next to Fitzroy. "General, can you try your best to count the bristles in the brush?"

The general nodded, and then bent over a terminal and began counting.

The computer needed four or five minutes to complete every

calculation, but there were a number of errors, so it was half an hour before the results were ready.

"The wake diffuses the dust to a maximum diameter of two hundred forty thousand kilometers, or twice the size of Jupiter," the astronomer running the mathematical model said.

"That makes sense," Ringier said. He raised his arms and looked up at the ceiling, as if looking through it to the heavens. "And that confirms it." There was a tremble to his voice, and then, as if to himself, he said, "So it's been confirmed. Nothing wrong with that."

Silence fell over the control room again, heavy and oppressive this time. Fitzroy wanted to ask a question, but at the sight of the solemn, bowed heads, he couldn't open his mouth. After a while, he heard gentle sobs and saw a young man trying to hide his tears.

"Knock it off, Harris. You're not the only skeptic here. It's hard for everyone," someone said.

The young man, Harris, lifted his teary eyes and said, "I know skepticism is just a way to comfort myself, but I wanted to live out my life in comfort. God, now I'm not even lucky enough for that."

Silence returned.

At last Ringier remembered Fitzroy. "General, let me explain. The three stars are surrounded by interstellar dust. Previously, a number of bodies moving at high speed crossed that dust, and their high-speed impact with the dust left behind a wake. The wake continued to expand and has now reached a diameter twice that of the planet Jupiter. There are only subtle differences between the wake and the surrounding dust, so they are undetectable at close range. Only here, four light-years away, are they observable."

"I've counted the bristles. There are about a thousand," General Fitzroy said.

"Of course. That number confirms our intelligence reports. General, we're looking at the Trisolaran Fleet."

Hubble II's discovery, the final confirmation of the reality of the

Trisolaran invasion, extinguished the last of humanity's fantasies. The descent of a new round of despair, panic, and confusion ushered the human race into life under the Trisolar Crisis. Then the hard times began. With a rocky change of direction, the vehicle of time veered off along a new track.

The only constant in a world of tremendous change is the swift passage of time. Five years passed like a blur.

PART II

THE SPELL

YEAR 8, CRISIS ERA

Distance of the Trisolaran Fleet from the Solar System:
4.20 light-years

Tyler had been jumpy lately. Despite the setbacks, the mosquito swarm plan eventually won PDC approval. Development of the space fighters began, but progress was slow due to a lack of advanced technologies. Humanity continued to improve on the technology of its stone age axes and clubs, inventing chemically propelled rockets. Tyler's supplemental project, the study of Europa, Ceres, and various comets, was odd enough that some people suspected that he had come up with it purely to add a sense of mystery to the overly direct main plan. However, since it could be incorporated into the mainstream defense program, he was allowed to start working on that as well.

So Tyler had to wait. He went home and, for the first time in his five years as a Wallfacer, led the life of a normal person.

The Wallfacers were subject to increasing scrutiny from the community. Whether they had asked for the role or not, they had been set up in the eyes of the masses as messiah figures. Accordingly, a Wallfacer cult sprang up. No matter how many explanations the UN and PDC issued, legends of their supernatural abilities circulated widely and grew increasingly fanciful. In science fiction movies, they were shown as superheroes, and, in the eyes of many, they were the sole hope for humanity. This gave the Wallfacers an enormous amount of popular and political

capital that guaranteed things would go smoothly when they tapped huge amounts of resources.

Luo Ji was the exception. He remained in seclusion, never showing his face. No one knew where he was or what he was doing.

One day, Tyler had a visitor. Like the other Wallfacers, his home was under heavy guard, and all visitors had to pass stringent background checks. But when he first saw the visitor in the living room, he knew that the man would pass through easily, because it was obvious at a glance that he posed no threat to anyone. On this hot day he wore a wrinkled suit, a similarly wrinkled tie, and, more annoyingly, the sort of bowler hat no one wore anymore. He evidently wanted to present a more formal appearance for his visit, since he had probably never attended a formal occasion before. Pale and emaciated, he looked malnourished. His glasses sat heavily on his skinny, pale face, his neck hardly seemed able to support the weight of his head, and his suit looked practically empty, as if it was hanging on a rack. As a politician, Tyler saw at a glance that he belonged to one of those mean social classes whose poverty was more spiritual than material, like Gogol's petty bureaucrats who, despite their lowly social station, still worry about preserving that status and spend their whole lives engaged in uncreative, exhausting random tasks that they carry out exactingly. In everything they do, they fear making mistakes; with everyone they meet, they fear causing displeasure; and they dare not take the slightest glance through the glass ceiling to a higher plane of society. Tyler detested those people. They were utterly dispensable, and when he thought about how they made up the majority of the world that he wanted to save, it left a bad taste in his mouth.

The man walked gingerly through the living room door, but did not dare venture further. He seemed afraid of marking the carpet with the dirty soles of his shoes. He took off his hat and looked at the master of the house through his thick glasses as he bowed repeatedly. Tyler made up his mind to send him off as soon as he spoke his first sentence, for even if what the man had to say was important to him, to Tyler it was meaningless.

In a frail voice, the pitiful man uttered his first sentence. It struck Tyler like a bolt of lightning and so dazed him that he practically sat down on the ground. Every word was like a thunderclap.

"Wallfacer Frederick Tyler, I am your Wallbreaker."

"Who would have thought we'd one day be facing a battle map like this," Chang Weisi exclaimed as he looked at a one-to-one-trillion-scale chart of the Solar System displayed on a monitor large enough to be a movie screen. It was almost entirely dark, except for the tiny spot of yellow in the center that was the sun. The chart radius reached the middle of the Kuiper Belt. When it was displayed in its entirety, it was like looking down on the Solar System from a distance of fifty AU above the ecliptic plane. The chart accurately marked the orbits of planets and satellites, as well as the conditions of known asteroids, and it could display a precise sectional layout of the Solar System for any point in the next millennium. Now that positional markings for celestial bodies had been turned off, the chart display was bright enough that you could make out Jupiter if you looked closely enough. It was just an indistinct, tiny bright spot, but from this distance the other seven major planets were invisible.

"Yes, we are facing major changes," Zhang Beihai said. The military had just completed a meeting to assess its first space map, and now only the two of them remained in the spacious war room.

"Commander, I wonder if you noticed the eyes of our comrades when they saw this map," he said.

"Of course I noticed. It's understandable. They would have imagined a space map to be like what you find in popular science books. A couple of colored billiard balls rotating around a fireball. It's only when they're faced with one drawn to an accurate scale that they come to an appreciation of the vastness of the Solar System. And, whether they're air force or navy, the furthest their air and water craft can go doesn't even amount to one pixel on the big screen."

"It seems that looking at the battlefield of the future did not inspire a stitch of confidence or passion for battle in our comrades."

"And now we're back to defeatism."

"Commander, I don't want to talk about the reality of defeatism today. That's a subject for a formal meeting. What I'd like to discuss is . . . well . . ." He faltered, and smiled, a rare thing for someone who was usually so outspoken.

Chang Weisi turned away from the map and smiled back at him. "Seems you've got something highly unorthodox to say."

"Yes. Or something unprecedented, at least. I'm making a recommendation."

"Proceed. Get right down to the topic. Of course, you don't need encouragement for that."

"Yes, Commander. Over the past five years, little progress has been made in basic planetary defense and space travel research. The preliminary technology in those two programs—controlled nuclear fusion and the space elevator—are still at square one, with no hope in sight, and there are all kinds of problems with higher-thrust chemical rockets. If things continue in this vein, then I fear a space fleet, even at the low-tech level, will remain science fiction forever."

"You chose high-tech, Comrade Beihai. You ought to be well aware of the rules of scientific research."

"Of course I'm aware of them. Research is a process of leaping forward, and qualitative change is only produced by long-term quantitative accumulation. Breakthroughs in theory and technology are mostly achieved in concentrated bursts. . . . Still, Commander, how many people understand the problem like I do? It's very likely that in ten or twenty or fifty years, or even a century, we still won't have any major breakthroughs in any scientific or technical field, and at that point, how far will defeatist thinking have developed? What spiritual and mental state will have taken hold in the space force? Commander, am I really taking this too far?"

"Beihai, what I most admire about you is that you always keep the long term in mind as you work. It's a rare thing among political cadres in this military. Please go on."

"Well, I can only speak from the scope of my own work. Working under the above assumptions, what sort of difficulties and pressures will be faced by our future comrades engaged in political and ideological work in the space force?"

"A grimmer question is, how many ideologically qualified political cadres will be left in the forces?" added Chang Weisi. "To contain defeatism, we first need to have a firm faith in victory ourselves. But this is certain to be more difficult in your hypothetical future."

"That's where my worry lies, Commander. When that time comes, political work in the space force won't be up to the task."

"Your recommendation?"

"Send reinforcements!"

Chang Weisi looked at Zhang Beihai for a few seconds, then turned back to the big screen. He moved the cursor and enlarged the sun until their epaulets reflected the sunlight.

"Commander, what I mean is . . ."

He raised a hand. "I know what you mean." Then he pulled back until the entire map was displayed, plunging the war room back into gloom, and then brought the sun forward again . . . and again and again as he thought, until at last he said, "Has it ever occurred to you that if political and ideological work in the space force is a complex and difficult task right now, it will considerably weaken today's work to hibernate the most outstanding political officers and send them to the future?"

"I realize that, Commander. I'm just voicing a personal suggestion. Big-picture thinking is, of course, up to my superiors."

Chang Weisi stood up and turned on the lights, illuminating the war room. "No, Comrade Beihai, this is a job for you now. Drop everything else. Starting tomorrow, you will focus on the Space Force Political Department, do some research into the other branches, and draft a preliminary report for the Central Military Commission as soon as possible."

The sun was setting behind the mountains when Tyler arrived. Exiting the car, he faced a vision of paradise: the softest light of the day shining on the snow peaks, the lake, and the forest, and Luo Ji and his family enjoying the otherworldly evening in the grass on the lakeshore. What first caught his eye was the mother, so young-looking, like an older sister to the one-year-old child. From a distance it was hard to make her out, but as he drew closer, his attention shifted to the child. If he hadn't seen it with his own eyes, he wouldn't have believed that such an adorable little being actually existed. Like a stem cell of beauty, the embryonic state of all that is beautiful. Mother and child were drawing on a large sheet of white paper as Luo Ji stood off to one side watching with interest as he had in the Louvre, gazing from a distance at his beloved, now a mother. Moving closer still, Tyler saw in his eyes an infinite bliss, a happiness that seemed to permeate everything between mountain and lake in this Garden of Eden. . . .

Having just arrived from the grim outside world made the scene before his eyes feel unreal. He had been married twice but was now single, and the joys of family had meant little to him in his pursuit of a man's glory. Now, for the first time ever, he felt he had lived an empty life.

Luo Ji, captivated by his wife and child, only noticed Tyler when he had gotten quite close. Due to the psychological barriers erected by their common situation, there had been no personal contact between Wallfacers up to this point. But having spoken with him on the phone, Luo Ji showed no surprise at Tyler's arrival, and met him with polite warmth.

"Madam, please excuse the interruption," Tyler said with a slight bow to Zhuang Yan, who had come over with the child.

"Welcome, Mr. Tyler. We seldom have guests, so we are pleased that you could come." Her English was strained, but her voice retained a childlike softness and she still had that cool spring of a smile, which stroked his weary soul like an angel's hands. "This is our daughter, Xia Xia."

He wanted to hug the child, but was afraid of losing control

of his feelings, so he simply said, "Seeing you two angels is worth the trip."

"We'll let you talk. I'll go and prepare dinner," she said as she smiled at the two men.

"No, that's not necessary. I just want to have a brief chat with Dr. Luo. I won't take up too much time."

Zhuang Yan warmly insisted that he stay for dinner, then left with the child.

Luo Ji motioned for Tyler to sit on a white chair in the grass. When he sat down, his whole body went limp, as if his tendons had been removed. He was a traveler who had at last reached his destination after a long voyage. "Doctor, it seems like you've been lost to the world for the past two years," Tyler said.

"Yes." Luo Ji remained standing. He swept a hand about him. "This is my everything."

"You are truly a smart man, and at least from one perspective, a more responsible man than me."

"What do you mean by that?" Luo Ji asked, with a puzzled smile.

"At least you haven't wasted resources. . . . So she doesn't watch TV either? I mean, your angel."

"Her? I don't know. She's always with Xia Xia these days, so I don't think she watches much."

"Then you really don't know what's happened out there over the past few days?"

"What happened? You don't look well. Are you tired? What can I get you to drink?"

"Anything," Tyler said, watching the last golden rays of the setting sun on the lake dazedly. "Four days ago, my Wallbreaker appeared."

Luo Ji stopped pouring the wine, and after a moment's silence, said, "So soon?"

Tyler nodded heavily. "That's the first thing I said to him, too."

"So soon?" Tyler said to the Wallbreaker. He tried to keep his voice calm but it ended up sounding feeble.

"I'd like to have come sooner, but I thought I'd collect more comprehensive evidence, so I'm late. I am sorry," the Wallbreaker said. He stood behind Tyler like a servant and spoke slowly, with a servant's humility. His final sentence even contained a meticulousness and thoughtfulness, the understanding that an executioner shows to his victim.

Then a suffocating silence took hold. At last Tyler screwed up the courage to look at the Wallbreaker, who then asked respectfully, "Sir, shall I go on?"

Tyler nodded but averted his gaze. He sat down on the sofa and did his best to calm down.

"Thank you, sir." The Wallbreaker bowed again, his hat still in hand. "First, I'll briefly describe the plan you've shown to the outside world: Using a fleet of nimble space fighters carrying hundred-megaton-class superbombs, your fighters will assist Earth's fleet by executing a suicide strike on the Trisolaris Fleet. Perhaps I've oversimplified, but that's basically it, right?"

"There's no point in discussing this with you," Tyler said. He had been considering whether to terminate the conversation. The moment the Wallbreaker revealed himself, Tyler's intuition as a politician and strategist informed him that the other man was the victor, but at this point he would be lucky if his mind had not been laid entirely bare.

"If that's the case, sir, then I don't have to go on, and you can arrest me. But you surely must know that regardless of what happens, your true strategy, and all of the evidence used to prove my hypothesis, will make the news across the world tomorrow, or maybe even tonight. At the cost of the rest of my life I stand before you today, and I hope that you will value my sacrifice."

"You may continue," Tyler said with a wave of his hand.

"Thank you, sir. I am truly honored, and I will not use up too much time." The Wallbreaker bowed again. A humble respect so rarely seen among modern people seemed to be in his blood, able to manifest at any time, like a noose gradually tightening around Tyler's neck. "Then, sir, was my rendition of your strategy just now correct?"

"It was."

"It was not," the Wallbreaker said. "Sir, pardon my saying it, but it was not correct."

"Why?"

"Given humanity's technological capabilities, the most powerful weapons we are likely to possess in the future are super hydrogen bombs. In a spacebattle environment, the bombs must be detonated in direct contact with their target to be capable of destroying enemy ships. Space fighters are nimble and can be deployed in large numbers, so sending the fighter fleet in for swarmlike suicide strikes is undoubtedly the best option. Your plan is eminently reasonable. All of your behavior, including trips to Japan, China, and even the mountains of Afghanistan in search of space kamikaze pilots with a spirit of self-sacrifice, and your plan to put the mosquito fleet under your direct control once that search failed, was also entirely reasonable."

"What's wrong with that?" Tyler asked, sitting up on the sofa.

"Nothing's wrong with that. But that's just the strategy you presented to the outside." The Wallbreaker bent down, drew near to Tyler's ear, and continued speaking in a soft voice. "Your true strategy had small alterations. For quite a long time, you had me stumped. It was agonizing for me, and I nearly gave up."

Tyler realized that he had a death grip on a sofa handle, and tried to relax.

"But then you gave me the key to unlock the whole puzzle. It was such a good fit that for a moment I doubted my good fortune. You know what I'm referring to: Your study of several bodies in the solar system, Europa, Ceres, and the comets. What do they have in common? Water. They all possess water, and in large quantities! On their own, Europa and Ceres have more water than in all of the oceans on Earth. . . .

"Rabies sufferers fear the water and can go into spasms at the mere mention of the word. I imagine you have similar feelings right now."

The Wallbreaker drew close to Tyler and spoke directly into his

ear. His breath was not the least bit warm, but felt like a ghostly wind flavored with the grave. "Water," he whispered, as if talking in his sleep. "Water . . ."

Tyler remained silent, his face like a statue's.

"Is there any need for me to continue?" the Wallbreaker asked, standing up.

"No," Tyler said in a low voice.

"But I'll continue anyway," the Wallbreaker said, almost gleefully. "I'll leave historians with a complete record, even if history won't endure for much longer. And an explanation for the Lord as well, of course. Not everyone has the keen intellect of the two of us, able to grasp the whole from the merest part. Particularly the Lord, who may not even understand a complete explanation." He raised up a hand, as if to acknowledge the Trisolaran listeners, and laughed. "Forgive me."

Tyler's features slackened, and then his bones seemed to melt. He slumped into the sofa. He was finished, and his spirit no longer inhabited his body.

"Now then. Setting aside the water, let's talk about the mosquito swarm. Its first attack target will not be the Trisolaran invaders, but Earth's own space force. This hypothesis is a bit of a reach based on the barest of signs, but I maintain that it is correct. You went around the world seeking to establish a kamikaze force for humanity, but your efforts failed. You anticipated this, but from this failure you were able to obtain two things you desired. One was total despair in humanity—this, you have achieved fully. The second I'll discuss in a moment."

The blade fell.

"After traveling the world you became utterly disillusioned with modern humanity's dedication. You also became convinced that Earth's space force did not stand a chance of defeating Trisolaris via standard combat. You therefore hatched a strategy even more extreme. In my opinion, this is a very faint hope, and an immense risk. Nevertheless, the principles of the Wallfacer Project dictate that in this war, the safest bet is to take a risk.

"Of course, this was only the beginning. Your betrayal of humanity would be a long process, but you had time on your side. In the following months and years, you were prepared to engineer events that would add to the wall you erected between yourself and the human race. Your despair would gradually grow and your sorrow intensify, and you would leave the human world further and further behind, growing closer and closer to the ETO and Trisolaris. In fact, you took your first steps on this road when you urged mercy for the ETO at the PDC hearing not long ago. That wasn't just for show, though. You truly need them to endure. You need members of the ETO to pilot your space fighters in the Doomsday Battle. It is a matter of time and patience, but you would succeed, because the ETO also needs you. It needs your assistance, and the resources you possess. It wouldn't be difficult to turn over the mosquito fleet to the ETO, so long as it was kept a secret from the outside world. And if it were discovered, you could claim that it was all part of the plan."

Tyler did not seem to be listening to the Wallbreaker. He sat on his sofa with his eyes half-closed, looking fatigued, as if he had already given up and was beginning to relax.

"Very well. Let's talk about the water now. In the Doomsday Battle, the ETO-controlled mosquito fleet would likely launch a sneak attack on Earth's fleet and then flee to the Lord's fleet. Because they had just demonstrated their disloyalty to Earth, Trisolaris might be willing to let them join the fleet, but the Lord would not be so fast to accept the turncoat army. A sufficiently meaningful gift would be required to win them over. What would the Lord need that the Solar System possesses? Water. On their four-century voyage, most of the water in the Trisolaran Fleet would be used up. As they approached the Solar System, dehydrated Trisolarans on board would need to be rehydrated. Since the water used for this would become part of their bodies, clean water would certainly be preferred to the stale water that had been recycled innumerable times on the ship. The mosquito fleet would offer the Lord an iceberg formed out of huge quantities of water

obtained from Europa, Ceres, and the comets. I'm not certain of the specifics—I expect you don't know right now either—but let's say tens of thousands of tons.

"This giant chunk of ice would be propelled by the mosquito group. The mosquito fleet would likely draw very close to the Lord's fleet when presenting the gift, at which point the second consequence of the failure of your attempt to build a kamikaze force would be put to use. That failure prompted your very logical request for independent control of the entire mosquito fleet. When Earth's fleet draws close to the Lord's fleet, you would take over control of the fighters from the ETO pilots and switch them to drone mode, ordering the fighters to strike their chosen targets. The superbombs would be detonated at point-blank range, annihilating all of the Lord's ships."

The Wallbreaker straightened up and, leaving Tyler's side, approached the floor-to-ceiling windows that overlooked the garden. The hellish wind he had blown into Tyler's ear dissipated, but not before the chill had penetrated his body.

"An outstanding plan. That's not a lie. But certain oversights are inexplicable. Why were you so eager to pursue the study of water-bearing heavenly bodies? The technology to extract and transport water in quantity does not exist right now, and engineering-side R&D could take years or even decades. Even if you felt you had to start right away, why not toss in a few targets that don't contain water—the moons of Mars, for instance? If you had done so, although it wouldn't have prevented me from eventually exposing your plan, it would have vastly increased the difficulty. How could a great strategist such as yourself overlook such simple tricks? On the other hand, I do recognize the pressure you are under."

The Wallbreaker placed a gentle hand on Tyler's shoulder, and Tyler felt a flash of tenderness, as of an executioner for his victim. He was even a little moved.

"Don't beat yourself up. You did well enough, really. I hope history remembers you." The Wallbreaker removed his hand, a flush

of restored energy on his formerly wan and sickly face. He stretched out his arms. "Well, Mr. Tyler, I'm done. Call your people."

Tyler, his eyes still shut, said without energy, "You may leave."

When the Wallbreaker opened the door, Tyler croaked out a final question: "If what you say is true, so what?"

The Wallbreaker turned back toward him. "So nothing. Mr. Tyler, regardless of whether or not I've broken your plan, the Lord does not care."

Luo Ji was rendered speechless for a long while after hearing Tyler's account.

When an ordinary person spoke with one of them, they would always be thinking, *He's a Wallfacer, his words can't be trusted*, and those suggestions would present a barrier to communication. But when two Wallfacers spoke with each other, the suggestions that existed in both minds cross-multiplied those communication barriers. Such an exchange, in fact, rendered anything either side said meaningless, so that communication itself lost all significance. This was why there had been no private interaction between Wallfacers.

"How do you evaluate the Wallbreaker's analysis?" Luo Ji asked to break the silence, even though he knew there was no point to the question.

"He guessed right," Tyler said.

Luo Ji wanted to say something, but what? What could be said? They were both Wallfacers.

"That was my true strategy," Tyler went on. He evidently had a strong desire to speak and didn't care whether or not his listener believed him. "Of course, it's still in the preliminary stages. The technology alone is quite difficult, although I expected a gradual resolution to all of the theoretic and technical issues over the course of four centuries. But judging from the enemy's attitude toward the plan, it wouldn't make any difference. They don't care, and that's the height of contempt."

"And that was . . . ?" Luo Ji felt like a machine for meaningless dialogue.

"The day after the Wallbreaker's visit, a complete analysis of my strategy was posted online. The material ran into the millions of words, most of it obtained through sophon monitoring, and it caused a sensation. The day before yesterday, the PDC called a hearing on the issue, at which it resolved the following: 'Wallfacer Plans may not contain anything that poses a threat to human life.' If my plan actually existed, then its execution would be a crime against humanity. It must be stopped, and its Wallfacer punished by law. Notice how they invoke crimes against humanity, a term that's being thrown around more than ever these days? But the resolution concluded by saying, 'According to the basic principles of the Wallfacer Project, the evidence available to the outside world may just be a part of the Wallfacer's strategy of deception and cannot be used to prove that the Wallfacer has actually developed and is executing this plan.' So I won't be charged."

"I'd thought as much," Luo Ji said.

"But at the hearing, I declared that the Wallbreaker's analysis was correct, and that my strategy was indeed the mosquito swarm. I asked to be tried in accordance with national and international law."

"I can imagine their reaction."

"The PDC's rotating chair and all the permanent member representatives looked at me with that Wallfacer smile on their face, and the chair declared the meeting adjourned. Those bastards!"

"I know the feeling."

"I had a total breakdown. I fled out of the hall and into the square outside, shouting, 'I am Wallfacer Frederick Tyler! My Wallbreaker exposed my strategy! He was right! I'm going to attack the Earth fleet with the mosquito swarm! I'm anti-human! I'm a devil! Punish me and kill me!'"

"That was a meaningless act, Mr. Tyler."

"What I hate the most is the expression people have when they look at me. A crowd of people surrounded me in the square, their eyes revealing the fantasies of children, the reverence of the

210

middle-aged, and the concern of the elderly. All of their eyes said, 'Look, he's a Wallfacer. He's at work, but he's the only one in the world who knows what he's doing. See what a great job he's doing? He's pretending so well. How will the enemy know what his real strategy is? That great, great, great strategy that only he knows and that will be the salvation of the world . . .' Complete and utter crap! Those idiots!"

At last Luo Ji decided to remain silent, and merely smiled word-lessly at Tyler.

As Tyler stared at him, a thin smile wavered on his pale face and then developed into full-blown hysterical laughter. "Ha! You're smiling the Wallfacer smile! A smile from one Wallfacer to another! You think I'm at work. You believe I'm acting the part, and you think I'll save the world!" He cackled again. "How did we end up in such a hilarious situation?"

"This is a vicious cycle we'll never be free of, Mr. Tyler," Luo Ji said, and sighed softly.

Tyler's laughter stopped abruptly. "Never be free? No, Dr. Luo, there's a way out. There really is a way, and I'm here today to tell it to you."

"You need a break. Rest here for a few days," Luo Ji said.

Tyler nodded slowly. "Yeah, I need a break. We're the only ones who understand each other's pain, Doctor. That's why I've come." He looked up. The sun had set a while ago, and the Garden of Eden had grown indistinct in the twilight. "This is paradise. Can I go for a walk alone by the lake?"

"You may do whatever you like here. Take it easy, and I'll call you to dinner in a while."

Tyler walked down to the lake, leaving Luo Ji to sit down, sunken in heavy thoughts.

For five years, he had bathed in an ocean of happiness. The birth of his Xia Xia in particular had made him forget everything about the outside world. The love of his wife and child blended together and intoxicated his soul, and, in this gentle home isolated from the rest of the world, he had fallen deeper and deeper into an

illusion: Perhaps the outside world really was something akin to a quantum state, and did not exist unless he observed it.

But it was a state that could no longer endure now that the abominable outside world had burst into his Garden of Eden to confuse and frighten him. His thoughts shifted to Tyler, whose last words still resounded in his ears. Was it really possible for Wallfacers to break free of the vicious cycle, to shatter the iron shackles of logic . . . ?

He jerked to his senses and ran toward the lake. He wanted to shout, but was afraid of scaring Zhuang Yan and Xia Xia, so he just ran as fast as he could through the quiet twilight, the swish of his feet against the grass on the hillside the only sound. But into this rhythm a soft *crack* inserted itself.

The sound of a gunshot from the lake.

Luo Ji returned home late that evening after the child was sound asleep. Zhuang Yan asked softly, "Did Mr. Tyler leave?"

"Yes. He's gone," he said wearily.

"He seemed worse off than you."

"Yes. That's because he didn't take an easy path. . . . Yan, have you watched TV recently?"

"No. I . . ." She paused, and Luo Ji knew what she was thinking. With the outside world growing more serious by the day, and the gap widening between life here and life outside, the difference made her uneasy. "Is our life really part of the Wallfacer plan?" she asked, looking at him with that same innocent face.

"Of course. What is there to doubt?"

"But can we truly be happy when all humanity is unhappy?"

"My love, your responsibility when all of humanity is unhappy is to make yourself happy. With Xia Xia, your happiness gains a point, and the Wallfacer plan gains a point toward its success."

Zhuang Yan stared silently at him. The language of facial expressions she had envisioned in front of the *Mona Lisa* five years ago seemed to have been partially realized between her and Luo Ji. More and more, he could read her mind through her eyes, and what he read now was, *How can I believe that?*

Luo Ji pondered this for a long time, and finally said, "Yan, everything has an ending. The sun and the universe will die one day, so why should humanity believe that it ought to be immortal? Listen, this world is paranoid. Fighting a hopeless war is a fool's errand, so look at the Trisolar Crisis from a different perspective and leave your cares behind. Not just the ones involving the crisis, but everything else from before that. Use the time that's left to enjoy life. Four hundred years! Or, if we refuse the Doomsday Battle, then nearly five hundred. That's a fair amount of time. Humanity used the same period to go from the Renaissance to the information age, and in the same space could create a carefree, comfortable life. Five idyllic centuries without needing to worry about the distant future, where the sole responsibility is to enjoy life. How wonderful. . . ."

He realized that he had spoken unwisely. Claiming that the happiness of her and the child were part of the plan added another layer of protection to her life by making her happiness into a responsibility. This was the only way to ensure that she maintained a balanced mind in the face of the cruel world. He could never resist her eternally innocent eyes, so he didn't dare look at her when she questioned him. But now, because of the Tyler factor, he had involuntarily told the truth.

"When you say that, are you being a Wallfacer?" she asked.

"Yes, of course I am," he said, to fix the situation.

But her eyes said, *You really did seem to believe that!*

UN Planetary Defense Council,
Wallfacer Project Hearing #89

At the start of the hearing, the rotating chair spoke to strongly urge that Luo Ji be required to attend the next hearing, arguing that refusal to participate was not part of the Wallfacer plan because the PDC's supervisory authority over the Wallfacers trumped the Wallfacers' own strategic plans. The proposal was unanimously adopted by all permanent member representatives, and with the

emergence of the first Wallbreaker and the suicide of Wallfacer Tyler in mind, the other two Wallfacers attending the meeting heard the unspoken implications of the chairman's words.

Hines spoke first. His neuroscience-based plan was still in its infancy, but he described the equipment he was envisioning as a basis for further research. He called it the Resolving Imager. Based on computed tomography and nuclear magnetic resonance, it operated by scanning in all cross sections of the brain at once, which required cross sectional accuracy on the scale of the internal structure of brain cells and neurons. This would bring the number of simultaneous CT scans to several million, to be synthesized by computer into a digital model of the brain. Other technical requirements were even greater: The scan needed to be conducted at a rate of twenty-four frames per second to produce a dynamic synthetic model that could capture all brain activity at a neuron-level resolution, making it possible to precisely observe thought activity in the brain, or even replay all neural activity throughout the thinking process.

Then Rey Diaz described the progress of his plan. After five years of research, the digital star model for super-high-yield nuclear weapons had been completed and was now being thoroughly debugged.

Next, the PDC scientific advisory panel presented a report on its feasibility study of the two Wallfacers' plans.

The advisory panel felt that although there were in theory no obstacles to Hines's Resolving Imager, the technical difficulties far exceeded current conditions, and modern CT scanning was about as far from RI technology as black-and-white film was from modern high-definition cameras. Data processing presented the biggest technical hurdle to the RI device, because scanning and modeling an object the size of the human brain with neuron-level precision required power that was unavailable to modern computers.

The obstacle to Rey Diaz's stellar bomb was the same: present computing power was insufficient. After inspecting the calculations required by the completed portion of the model, the panel's expert group felt that the most powerful of today's computers

would take twenty years to model a hundredth of a second of the fusion process. Since the model would need to be run repeatedly in the course of research, practical application was an impossibility.

The panel's chief computer scientist said, "Right now, computer technology based on traditional integrated circuits and Von Neumann architecture is nearing the limit of its technological development. Moore's law is going to collapse. Of course, we can still squeeze out the last few drops of lemonade from these traditional electronic and technological lemons. In our opinion, even given the present deceleration in supercomputer progress, the computing power required by the two plans is still achievable. It just requires time. Optimistically, twenty to thirty years. Those goals, if they are reached, will represent the peak of human computing technology, and any further progress will be difficult. With frontier physics under sophon lockdown, the next-gen and quantum computers that we once dreamed of are now very unlikely to be realized."

"We've reached the wall that the sophons have erected across our scientific road," the chair said.

"Then there's nothing that we can do for twenty years," Hines said.

"Twenty years is the most optimistic estimate. As a scientist, you ought to know what cutting-edge research is like."

"Then the only thing to do is hibernate and wait the arrival of capable computers," Rey Diaz said.

"I've decided to hibernate, too," Hines said.

"If that's the case, then I will ask the two of you to greet my successor in twenty years," the chair said with a smile.

The mood of the hearing relaxed. Now that the two Wallfacers had decided to enter hibernation, the hearing's participants sighed with relief. The emergence of the first Wallbreaker and his Wallfacer's suicide had dealt a heavy blow to the entire project. Tyler's suicide in particular had been a foolish act. If he had lived, people would still be in doubt about whether the mosquito swarm had really been his plan. His death was tantamount to a final confirmation of the existence of the terrible plan. He had vaulted out of the vicious

cycle at the cost of his life, prompting increasing murmurs of criticism of the Wallfacer Project among the international community. Public opinion demanded further restrictions on Wallfacer power, but the very nature of the Wallfacer Project meant that too many restrictions would make it difficult for the Wallfacers to conduct their strategic deceptions, rendering the entire project meaningless. The Wallfacer Project possessed a leadership structure that human society had never before seen, and it required time to adjust and adapt to it. It was clear that the hibernation of the two Wallfacers would provide a buffer period for that to take place.

A few days later, in a top-secret underground structure, Rey Diaz and Hines entered hibernation.

Luo Ji found himself in an ominous dream. He dreamt he was walking the halls of the Louvre. It was a dream he had never had before, because the past five years of bliss had given him no cause to dream of previous joys. In this dream, he was alone with the loneliness that had been absent for five years. His every footstep reverberated through the palace halls, and something seemed to leave him with every reverberation, until at last he dared not take another step. In front of him was the *Mona Lisa*. She no longer smiled, but looked on him with compassion in her eyes. When his footsteps stopped, the sound of the outdoor fountains trickled in and gradually grew louder, at which point he awoke to find that the sound was coming from the real world. It was raining.

Luo Ji reached out to hold his beloved's hand, and discovered that his dream had become a reality.

Zhuang Yan was gone.

He rolled out of bed and entered the nursery, where a lamp was softly glowing, but Xia Xia wasn't there. On the little bed, tidily made up, was one of Zhuang Yan's paintings, a favorite of both of theirs. It was practically blank, and from a distance it looked like a sheet of paper. Closer in, you could see fine reeds in the lower left, and in the upper right the traces of a vanishing goose. In the blank

center were two infinitesimally tiny people. But now, a graceful line of text had been added to it:

My love, we're waiting for you at doomsday.

It was bound to happen sooner or later. Could such a dream life last forever? *It was bound to happen, so don't worry. You're mentally prepared for it,* Luo Ji told himself, but a wave of dizziness came over him. As he picked up the painting and went toward the living room, his legs quavered and he felt as if he was floating.

The living room was empty, but the embers in the fireplace glowed a hazy red that made everything look like melting ice. The rain continued outside. It was to the same sound of rain that she had walked out of his dreams five years ago, and now she had returned to them, taking their child with her.

He picked up the phone to call Kent, but then he heard soft footsteps outside. A woman's footsteps, but not Zhuang Yan's. Even so, he tossed the phone down and went outside.

Luo Ji immediately recognized the slender figure standing on the porch in the rain, even though he could only see a silhouette.

"Hello, Dr. Luo," Secretary General Say said.

"Hello . . . Where are my wife and child?"

"They're waiting for you at doomsday," she said, repeating the words in the painting.

"Why?"

"This is a PDC resolution, to let you work and fulfill your Wallfacer responsibilities. No harm will come to them, and children are better suited to hibernation than adults."

"You've kidnapped them! That's criminal!"

"We did not kidnap anyone."

Luo Ji's heart quaked at the implications of Say's statement, and he pushed them out of his mind rather than face that reality. "I said that having them here was part of the plan!"

"But after a thorough investigation, the PDC decided that it was not part of the plan, and so took steps to prompt you to get to work."

"Even if it's not kidnapping, you took away my child without my consent, and that's against the law." When he realized who he

was including in "you," his heart quaked again and he leaned back feebly against the pillar behind him.

"True, but it is well within acceptability. Do not forget, Dr. Luo, that this and all of the resources you have tapped do not fall under existing legal frameworks, so the UN's actions in the present time of crisis can be justified under the law."

"Are you still working on behalf of the UN?"

"Yes."

"You were reelected?"

"Yes."

He wanted to change the subject to avoid facing the cold facts, but he failed. *What will I do without them? What will I do without them?* his heart asked over and over. Finally it slipped out of his mouth as he slid down the pillar to the ground. It felt like everything was collapsing around him, turning to magma from the top down, except that this time the magma was burning and pooled inside his heart.

"They're still here, Dr. Luo. They're waiting for you safe and sound in the future. You've always been a sober person, and you must become even more sober now. If not for all humanity, then for your family." Say looked down at the ground, where Luo Ji sat beside the column on the brink of a breakdown.

Then a gust of wind blew rain onto the porch. Its refreshing chill and Say's words managed to cool the fire raging in Luo Ji's heart to an extent.

"This was your plan from the beginning, wasn't it?"

"Yes, but this step was taken only when there was no other choice."

"So she was . . . When she came, was she really a woman who did traditional painting?"

"Yes."

"From the Central Academy of Fine Arts?"

"Yes."

"Then was she . . ."

"Everything you saw was the real her. Everything you knew

about her was true. Everything that made her *her*: Her past life, her family, her personality, and her mind."

"You mean she really was that kind of woman?"

"Yes. Do you really think she could have faked it for five years? That's how she really was. Innocent and gentle, like an angel. She didn't fake anything, including her love for you, which was very real."

"Then how could she carry out such a cruel deception? To never let anything slip for five years?"

"How do you know she never let anything slip? Her soul was shrouded in melancholy from the first time you saw her on that rainy night five years ago. She didn't hide it. That melancholy stayed with her for five years like an ever-present background music that never stopped the whole time, and that's why you didn't notice."

Now he understood. When he first saw her, what had it been that had touched the softest place in his heart? That made him feel like the entire world was an injury to her? That made him willing to protect her with his life? It was that gentle sadness concealed within her clear, innocent eyes—a sadness that, like the light in the fireplace, shone gently through her beauty. It was indeed an imperceptible background music that had quietly permeated his subconscious and pulled him step by step into the abyss of love.

"I can't find them, can I?" he asked.

"That's right. Like I said, this is a PDC resolution."

"Then I'll go with them to doomsday."

"You may."

Luo Ji had imagined he would be turned down, but—just as when he had given up his Wallfacer status—there was practically no space between his statement and Say's reply. He knew that things weren't as easy as that. He asked, "Is there a problem?"

"No. This time it really is fine. You know, since the birth of the Wallfacer Project there has always been dissent within the international community. Out of their own interests, most countries have supported some of the Wallfacers while opposing others, so there was always going to be a side that wants to be rid of you.

Now that the first Wallbreaker is out and Tyler has failed, forces opposed to the project have grown more powerful and have driven its supporters to a stalemate. If at this point you proposed going directly to doomsday, it would be a compromise plan acceptable to both sides. But, Dr. Luo, are you truly willing to do that while humanity is fighting for survival?"

"You politicians sound off about humanity at the drop of a hat, but I can't see humanity. I can only see individuals. I'm just one individual, an ordinary person, and I can't take on the responsibility of saving all of humanity. I just want to live my own life."

"Very well. But Zhuang Yan and Xia Xia are two of those individuals. Don't you want to fulfill your responsibility to them? Even if she hurt you, I can see you still love her. And there's the child, too. From the moment Hubble II finally confirmed the Trisolaran invasion, one thing has been certain: Humanity will fight to the end. When your beloved and your child awaken in four centuries, doomsday and the flames of war will be upon them, but by that time you'll have lost your Wallfacer status and will be powerless to protect them. They will only be able to share a hellish existence with you while you await the final annihilation of the world. Is that what you want? Is that the life you want to give your wife and child?"

Luo Ji said nothing.

"If you won't think of anything else, then just imagine that Doomsday Battle four centuries from now, and the look in their eyes when they see you! What sort of a person will they see? A man who abandoned the woman he loves most, together with all of humanity? A man unwilling to save all of the world's children? A man who wouldn't even save his own child? Are you, as a man, capable of withstanding their gaze?"

Luo Ji bent his head in silence. The sound of the nighttime rain falling on grass and lake was like myriad entreaties from another time and space.

"Do you really believe that I can change all of that?" Luo Ji asked, raising his head.

"Why not try? Of all the Wallfacers, you may have the greatest hope of success. I've come today to tell you that."

"Go on, then. Why?"

"Because out of all of humanity, you are the only person that Trisolaris wants dead."

Leaning against the pillar, Luo Ji stared at Say, but saw nothing. He struggled to remember.

Say went on. "That car crash was meant for you. It just accidentally hit your girlfriend."

"But that really was an accident. That car changed direction because two other cars collided."

"They had been planning that for a long time."

"But I was just an ordinary person back then, with no special protection. It would've been simple to kill me. Why go to such lengths?"

"To make the murder look like an accident, so as not to attract any attention. They almost succeeded. There were fifty-one traffic accidents that killed five people in the city that day. But a scout hidden within the ETO provided an intelligence report confirming that the ETO had orchestrated the attempt on your life. And what's most frightening is this: The order came from Trisolaris itself, conveyed to Evans through the sophons. To this date, that is the only assassination they've ever ordered."

"Me? Trisolaris wants to kill me? For what reason?" Again, Luo Ji felt displaced from himself.

"I don't know. No one knows, now. Evans may have known, but he's dead. He was evidently the one who added the requirement to the assassination order that it not attract attention. That only reinforces your importance."

"Importance?" Luo Ji shook his head with a wry smile. "Look at me. Do I really look like someone with superpowers?"

"You don't have superpowers, so don't let your thoughts go in that direction. It'll only lead you astray," Say said, gesturing emphatically. "You had no special powers in your prior research, be they supernatural abilities or extraordinary technical skills within the known laws of nature. Or, at least, none that we have

been able to discover. That Evans required that the assassination not attract attention demonstrates this point as well, because it proves that your ability can be acquired by others."

"Why didn't you tell me?"

"We were afraid of influencing whatever it is you have. Too many unknowns. We felt it best to let things ride."

"I'd once had a notion to work on cosmic sociology, because . . ." Then a small voice deep within him said, *You're a Wallfacer!* This was the first time he had heard that voice. He also heard another nonexistent sound: the buzzing of the sophons as they flew about him. He even thought he saw a few blurry, firefly-like points of light. So for the first time, he acted like a Wallfacer and swallowed his words, saying only, "Is that relevant?"

Say shook her head. "Probably not. As far as we are aware, that's just the topic of a research application that never actually went forward, much less obtained any results. Besides, even if you had done the research, we wouldn't expect you to come up with results any more valuable than any other researcher."

"And why is that?"

"Dr. Luo, we're speaking frankly here. As I understand it, you're a failure of a scholar. You perform research not out of any thirst for exploration, nor out of a sense of duty and mission, but simply as a way to make a living."

"Isn't that the way things are these days?"

"There's nothing wrong with that, of course, but you exhibit all kinds of behaviors unbecoming a serious and dedicated scholar. Your research is utilitarian, your techniques opportunistic, you seek out sensationalism, and you have a history of embezzling funding. Character-wise, you're cynical and irresponsible, and you harbor a mocking attitude toward a scholar's vocation. . . . We're actually well aware of the fact that you don't care about the fate of the human race."

"And that's why you would stoop to such despicable means to coerce me. You've despised me all along, haven't you?"

"Under normal circumstances, a man like you would never be

tasked with such an important duty, but there is this one overriding detail: Trisolaris is afraid of you. Be your own Wallbreaker. Find out why."

When Say finished, she stepped off the porch, got into the waiting car, and disappeared into the rainy mist.

Standing there, Luo Ji lost his sense of time. Gradually, the rain stopped and the wind picked up, blowing the night sky free of clouds, revealing the snow peaks, and letting the bright round moon bathe the world in silvery light.

Before going back inside, Luo Ji took one last look at the silver Garden of Eden, and his heart said to Zhuang Yan and Xia Xia, *My love, wait for me at doomsday.*

Standing in the giant shadow cast by the space plane *High Frontier* and looking up at its massive body, Zhang Beihai was involuntarily reminded of the carrier *Tang,* now long dismantled, and even wondered if the hull of *High Frontier* could contain a few steel plates from *Tang.* Over the course of more than thirty reentries, the burning heat had left scorch marks on the body of the space plane, and it really did look the way *Tang* had when it was under construction. The body had the same sense of age, but the two cylindrical booster rockets beneath the wings were new, making it resemble repairs to ancient architecture in Europe: The newness of the patches stood in stark contrast to the coloring of the original building, reminding visitors that those parts were modern additions. But if the boosters were removed, *High Frontier* would look like a big old transport plane.

The space plane was a very new thing, one of the few breakthroughs in aerospace technology over the last five years, and quite possibly the last generation of chemically propelled spacecraft. The concept had been proposed the previous century as a replacement for the space shuttle that could take off from a runway like an ordinary plane and fly conventionally to the top layer of the atmosphere, at which point the rockets would be turned on for

spaceflight and it would enter orbit. *High Frontier* was the fourth such space plane in operation, and many more were under construction. They would, in the near future, take on the task of building the space elevator.

"I once imagined that we would never get the chance to go to space in our lifetime," Zhang Beihai said to Chang Weisi, who had come to see him off. He and twenty other space force officers, all of them members of the three strategic institutes, would take *High Frontier* to the ISS.

"Are there naval officers who've never been to sea?" Chang Weisi said, smiling.

"Of course there are. Lots of them. Some people in the navy sought exactly that. But I'm not that sort of person."

"Beihai, be aware of one thing: The active-duty astronauts are still air force personnel, so you are the first representatives of the space force to go into space."

"It's a shame there's no specific mission."

"Experience is the mission. A space strategist ought to have a consciousness of space. This wasn't feasible before the space plane, since sending up one person cost tens of millions, but it's much cheaper now. We'll try to put more strategists into space soon, since we're the space force, after all. Right now we're more like a college of bullshit, and that just won't do."

Then the boarding call was issued, and the officers began climbing the airstair to the plane. They wore uniforms but not space suits, and looked no different than if they were taking standard air travel. It was a sign of progress, demonstrating that going to space was a little more normal than it had been. From the uniforms, Zhang Beihai noticed that there were people from other departments boarding the plane as well.

"Ah, Beihai, there's another important thing," Chang Weisi said as Beihai was about to pick up his carryon. "The CMC has studied the report we submitted on sending political cadres to the future as reinforcements, and the brass feel that conditions are still premature."

Zhang Beihai squinted, as if warding against a glare, though

they were still in the space plane's shadow. "Commander, my feeling is that we ought to keep the entire four-century period in mind when making plans, and to be clear about what's urgent and what's important. . . . But please be assured that I won't say that in any formal setting. I know very well that our superiors are considering the bigger picture."

"The higher-ups have affirmed your long-term thinking and commend you for it. The document stresses one point: The plan to send reinforcements to the future has not been denied. Research and planning will continue, but present conditions are still premature for execution. I feel—and this is of course my personal opinion—that we need additional qualified political cadres in our ranks to lessen the current work pressures before we can consider it."

"Commander, surely you are aware of what 'qualified' means in the context of the Space Force Political Department, and what the basic requirements are. Qualified people are becoming increasingly rare."

"But we've got to look forward. If there are breakthroughs in the two key technologies of phase one, the space elevator and controlled fusion—and there's hope of this in our lifetimes—then things will be better. . . . Okay then. Off with you."

Zhang Beihai saluted him and then stepped onto the stairs. His first feeling upon entering the cabin was that it wasn't much different than a civilian airliner, except the seats were wider, having been designed to accommodate space suits. During the first flights of the space plane, all passengers had to wear space suits as a precaution, but there was no need for that now.

He had a window seat, and the seat immediately next to his was also occupied. A civilian, judging from his clothing. Zhang Beihai nodded to him in greeting before turning his attention to fastening the seat's complicated safety belt.

There was no countdown. *High Frontier* started its air engines and began taxiing. Because of its weight, it spent longer on the ground during takeoff than an ordinary plane, but at last it lifted ponderously off the ground and embarked on its voyage into space.

"This is the thirty-eighth flight of the space plane *High Frontier*. The aviation phase has started and will last approximately thirty minutes. Please do not unfasten your safety belts," said a voice over the intercom.

As he watched the ground recede through the cabin window, Zhang Beihai's thoughts turned to the past. During training to become a carrier captain, he had completed naval aviation pilot training and had passed the level three fighter pilot exam. On his first solo trip he had watched Earth recede like this and suddenly discovered that he loved the sky even more deeply than the ocean. Now, his longing was for the space beyond the sky.

He was a man destined to fly high and fly far.

"Not much different from civil aviation, you think?"

He turned to see the speaker sitting in the next seat, and recognized him at last. "You must be Dr. Ding Yi. I've been wanting to meet you."

"But it's going to get rough in just a little bit," the man said, ignoring Zhang Beihai's salutation. He went on, "The first time, I didn't take off my glasses after the aviation phase, and they crushed my nose with the weight of a brick. The second time I took them off, but then they flew off after gravity went away. It wasn't easy for the guy to find them for me in the air filter in the plane's tail."

"I thought you went up on the space shuttle the first time. On TV, that didn't look like a very nice trip," Zhang Beihai said with a grin.

"Oh, I'm talking about taking the space plane. If we count the shuttle, then this is my fourth time. On the shuttle, they took away my glasses before takeoff."

"Why are you going to the station this time? You've just been put in charge of a controlled fusion project. The third branch, isn't it?"

Four branches had been set up for the controlled fusion project, each pursuing a different direction of research.

Restrained by the safety belt, Ding Yi lifted a hand to point at Zhang Beihai. "You study controlled fusion and you can't go to space? You sound the same as those guys. The ultimate goal of

our research is spaceship engines, and the real power held by the aerospace industry today remains to a large degree in the hands of the people who used to make chemical rocket engines. They're saying now that we're just supposed to devote ourselves to controlled fusion on the ground, and that we basically have no say in the general plan of the space fleet."

"Dr. Ding, your views are identical to mine." Zhang Beihai loosened his safety belt and leaned over. "For a space fleet, space travel is an entirely different concept from chemical rocketry. Even the space elevator is different from today's aerospace techniques. But right now the aerospace industry of the past still holds too much power. Its people are ideologically ossified and legalistic, and if things continue, there will be all kinds of trouble."

"There's nothing to be done. At least they've managed to come up with this in the course of five years." He pointed around him. "And this gives them the capital to squeeze out outsiders."

The cabin intercom started up. "Please take care: We are approaching an altitude of twenty thousand meters. Due to the thin atmosphere we will now be flying through, there may be sharp drops in altitude that will produce momentary weightlessness. Please do not panic. Again, please keep your safety belts fastened."

Ding Yi said, "But our trip to the station this time is unrelated to the controlled fusion project. It's to recover those cosmic ray catchers. That's some expensive stuff."

"The space-based high-energy physics research project has been stopped?" asked Zhang Beihai, retightening his safety belt.

"It's stopped. Knowing that there's no need to waste effort in the future counts as a kind of success."

"The sophons won."

"That's right. So humanity only has a few reserves of theory remaining: classical physics, quantum mechanics, and a still-embryonic string theory. How far their applications can be pushed is up to fate."

High Frontier continued to climb, its aviation engines rumbling under the strain as if it were struggling up a tall mountain, but

there were no sudden drops. The space plane was now approaching thirty thousand meters, the limit of aviation. Looking out, Zhang Beihai saw that the blue of the sky was fading as it got dark, even though the sun became even more dazzling.

"Our current flight altitude is thirty-one thousand meters. The aviation phase is complete and the spaceflight phase is about to begin. Please adjust your seats according to the illustration onscreen to minimize the discomfort of hypergravitation."

Then Zhang Beihai felt the plane rise gently, as if it had discarded a burden.

"Aircraft engine assembly separated. Aerospace engine ignition countdown: ten, nine, eight . . ."

"For them, this is the real launch. Enjoy," Ding Yi said, and closed his eyes.

When the countdown reached zero, there was a huge roar, as if the entire sky outside was shouting, and then hypergravity came like a giant, slowly tightening fist. With effort, Zhang Beihai twisted his head to look out the window. He was unable to see the flames spurting from the engine, but a wide swath of the rarefied air of the sky outside was painted red, as if *High Frontier* was floating through a sunset.

Five minutes later, the boosters detached, and after another five minutes of acceleration, the main engine cut off. *High Frontier* had entered orbit.

The giant hand of hypergravity suddenly let go and Zhang Beihai's body bounced back from the depths of his seat. Although the restraint of his safety belt kept him from floating away, to his senses he and the *High Frontier* were no longer parts of the same whole. The gravity that had once bonded them together was gone, and he and the plane were now flying in parallel paths through space. Out the window were the brightest stars he had ever seen in his life. Later, when the space plane adjusted its attitude, the sun streamed in through the windows and myriad points of light danced in its beams: dust particles that had weightlessly taken to the air. As the plane gradually rotated, he saw the Earth.

From this low orbital position he couldn't see the entire sphere, only the arc of the horizon, but he could clearly make out the shapes of the continents.

Then the starfield, that long-awaited sight, finally came into view, and he said in his heart, *Dad, I've taken the first step.*

For five years, General Fitzroy had felt like a Wallfacer in the actual sense of the word, in that the wall he faced was the big screen with the image of the stars between Earth and Trisolaris. At first glance it was entirely black, but closer inspection of the screen revealed points of starlight. He had grown so well acquainted with those stars that when he had attempted to sketch their position on a piece of paper at a dull meeting the previous day and compared it to the actual photo afterward, he was basically correct. The three stars of Trisolaris lying inconspicuously at the center looked like a single star in the standard view, but every time he magnified them he found that their positions had changed. This chaotic cosmic dance so fascinated him that he forgot what he was looking for in the first place. The brush that had been observed five years ago had gradually faded away, and no second brush had appeared. The Trisolaran Fleet left a visible wake only when it passed through interstellar dust clouds. Earth's astronomers had verified through observations of the absorption of background starlight that during the fleet's four-century-long voyage through space, it would pass through five of them. People dubbed these "snow patches" after the way that passersby left tracks on snowy ground.

If the Trisolaran Fleet had maintained a constant acceleration over the past five years, it would pass the second snow patch today.

Fitzroy arrived at the Hubble II Space Telescope Control Center early. Ringier laughed when he saw him. "General, why do you remind me of a child who wants another present so soon after Christmas?"

"Didn't you say that they would cross the snow patch today?"

"That's right, but the Trisolaran Fleet has only traveled 0.22 light-years, so it's still four light-years away. Light reflected from

its passage through the snow won't reach Earth for another four years."

"Oh, I'm sorry. I forgot about that," Fitzroy said with an embarrassed shake of his head. "I really wanted to see them again. This time, we'll be able to measure their speed and acceleration at the time of passage, and that's very important."

"I'm sorry. We're outside the light cone."

"What's that?"

"It's what physicists call the cone shape that light describes as it emanates along the time axis. It's impossible for people outside the cone to comprehend events taking place inside the cone. Think about it: Information about who-knows-how-many major events in the universe is flying toward us right now at the speed of light. Some of it has been traveling for hundreds of millions of years, but we're still outside the light cones of those events."

"Fate lies within the light cone."

Ringier considered this, then gave him an appreciative nod. "General, that's an excellent analogy! But sophons outside the light cone can see events on the inside."

"So the sophons have changed fate," Fitzroy said with feeling, and turned back to an image-processing terminal. Five years before, the young engineer Harris had started to cry at the sight of the brush, and afterward had suffered from depression so severe that he became practically useless at his job and was let go. No one knew where he had ended up.

Fortunately, there weren't many people like him.

Temperatures were cooling rapidly these days, and it had started to snow, causing the green to gradually disappear from the surrounding area and a thin layer of ice to freeze on the surface of the lake. Nature lost its bright coloring, like a color photograph turned black-and-white. Warm weather here had always been short-lived, but to Luo Ji, the Garden of Eden felt like it had lost its aura since the departure of his wife and child.

Winter was a season for thinking.

When Luo Ji began to think, he was surprised to find that his thoughts were already in progress. He remembered back to middle school and a lesson a teacher had taught him for language arts exams: First, take a look at the final essay question, then start the exam from the top, so that as you work on the exam, your subconscious will be thinking over the essay question, like a background process in a computer. Now he knew that from the moment he became a Wallfacer, his thinking had started up and had never stopped. The entire process was subconscious and he had never been aware of it.

He quickly retraced the steps his thoughts had already completed.

He was now certain that everything about his current situation stemmed from his chance encounter with Ye Wenjie nine years ago. Afterward, he had never spoken of the meeting with anyone for fear of causing unnecessary trouble for himself, but with Ye Wenjie gone, the meeting was a secret known only to him and Trisolaris. In those days, only two sophons had reached Earth, but he could be certain that on that evening, they had been there by Yang Dong's grave, listening to their every word. And the fluctuation in their quantum formation that instantly crossed the space of four light-years meant that Trisolaris had also been listening.

But what had Ye Wenjie said?

Secretary General Say had been wrong about one thing. Luo Ji's never-begun research into cosmic sociology *was* quite likely the immediate reason why Trisolaris wanted to kill him. Of course, Say didn't know that the project had been Ye Wenjie's suggestion, and although it had just seemed to Luo Ji like an excellent opportunity to make scholarship entertaining, he had been looking for just such an opportunity. Prior to the Trisolar Crisis, the study of alien civilization was indeed a sensational project that would have garnered easy media attention.

The aborted research project wasn't important in and of itself. What mattered was the instruction that Ye Wenjie had given him, so that's where Luo Ji's mind was stuck.

Over and over again he recalled her words: *Suppose a vast number of civilizations are distributed throughout the universe, on the order of the number of detectable stars. Lots and lots of them. The mathematical structure of cosmic sociology is far clearer than that of human sociology.*

The factors of chaos and randomness in the complex makeups of every civilized society in the universe get filtered out by the immense distance, so those civilizations can act as reference points that are relatively easy to manipulate mathematically.

First: Survival is the primary need of civilization. Second: Civilization continuously grows and expands, but the total matter in the universe remains constant.

One more thing: To derive a basic picture of cosmic sociology from these two axioms, you need two other important concepts: chains of suspicion and the technological explosion. I'm afraid there won't be that opportunity. . . . Well, you might as well just forget I said anything. Either way, I've fulfilled my duty.

He had returned countless times to these words, analyzing each sentence from every angle and chewing over every word. The component words had been strung into a set of prayer beads, and like a pious monk he stroked them time and again; and unstrung them, scattered them, and restrung them in different orders until a layer of each had been worn away.

Try as he might, he couldn't extract the clue from those words, the clue that made him the only person that Trisolaris wanted to destroy.

During his lengthy contemplation he strolled aimlessly. He walked along the desolate lakeside, walked through the wind as it grew ever colder, oftentimes completing a circuit of the lake unawares. Twice he even walked to the foot of the snow peak, where the patch of exposed rock that looked like a moonscape was blanketed with snow, becoming one with the snowcap ahead of him. Only then did his mood leave the track of his thoughts, Zhang Yan's eyes appearing before his own in the boundless blank white of the natural painting. But he was now able to keep his mood in check and continue turning himself into a thinking machine.

A month went by without him knowing it, and then winter came in full force. But he still conducted his lengthy thought process outside, sharpening his mind on the cold.

By this time, most of the prayer beads had been worn faint, except for twenty-one of them. These ones seemed only to get newer the more he polished them, and now emitted a faint light:

Survival is the primary need of civilization.

Civilization continuously grows and expands, but the total matter in the universe remains constant.

He fixated on these two sentences, the axioms Ye Wenjie had proposed for cosmic civilization. Although he did not know their ultimate secret, his long meditation told him that the answer lay within them.

But it was too simple a clue. What could he and the human race gain from two self-evident rules?

Don't dismiss simplicity. Simple means solid. The entire mansion of mathematics was erected on a foundation of this kind of irreducibly simple, yet logically rock-solid, axiom.

With this in mind, he looked around him. All that surrounded him was huddled up against the icy cold of winter, but most of the world still teemed with life. It was a living world brimming with a complex profusion of oceans, land, and sky as vast as the foggy sea, but all of it ran according to a rule even simpler than the axioms of cosmic civilization: survival of the fittest.

Luo Ji now saw his problem: Where Darwin had taken the boundless living world and made a rule to sum it up, Luo Ji had to use the rules he knew to uncover a picture of cosmic civilization. It was the opposite road to Darwin's, but a more difficult one.

So he began sleeping in the daytime and thinking at night. Whenever the perils of his mental roadway terrified him, he found comfort in the stars overhead. Like Ye Wenjie had said, the distance hid the complex structure of each star, making them just a collection of points in space with a clear mathematical configuration. It was a thinker's paradise, his paradise. To Luo Ji, at least, it felt like the world in front of him was far clearer and more concise than Darwin's.

But this simple world held a perplexing riddle: The entire galaxy was a vast empty desert, but a highly intelligent civilization had appeared on the star nearest to us. In this mystery, his thoughts found an entry point.

Gradually, the two concepts Ye Wenjie had left unexplained came into focus: chains of suspicion and the technology explosion.

The weather that day was colder than usual, and from Luo Ji's vantage point on the lakeshore, the cold seemed to make the stars into an even purer silver lattice against the black sky, solemnly displaying for him their clear mathematical configuration. All of a sudden, he found himself in a state that was entirely new. In his perception, the entire universe froze, all motion stopped, and everything from stars down to atoms entered a state of rest, with the stars just countless cold, dimensionless points reflecting the cold light of an outside world. . . . Everything was at rest, waiting for his final awakening.

The distant bark of a dog brought him back to reality. Probably a service canine belonging to the security forces.

Luo Ji was beside himself with excitement. Although he hadn't actually glimpsed that final mystery, he had clearly felt its presence just now.

He collected his thoughts and tried to reenter that state, but was unsuccessful. Though the stars remained the same, the world around him interfered with his thinking. All was shrouded in darkness, but he could make out the distant snowcap, the lakeside forest and grassland, and the house behind him, and through the house's half-open door he could see the dark glow of the fire. . . . Next to the simple clarity of the stars, everything in the vicinity represented a complexity and chaos that mathematics would be forever unable to grasp, so he attempted to remove them from his perception.

He walked out onto the frozen lake—cautiously, at first, but when he found that the icy surface seemed solid, he walked and slid ahead more quickly, until he reached a point where he could no longer make out the lakeshore through the night around him. Now he was surrounded on all sides by smooth ice. This distanced

him somewhat from earthly complexity and chaos, and by imagining that the icy plane extended infinitely in every direction, he obtained a simple, flat world; a cold, planar mental platform. Cares vanished, and soon his perception reentered that state of rest, where the stars were waiting for him. . . .

Then, with a crunch, the ice beneath Luo Ji's feet broke and his body plunged straight into the water.

At the precise instant the icy water covered Luo Ji's head, he saw the stillness of the stars shatter. The starfield curled up into a vortex and scattered into turbulent, chaotic waves of silver. The biting cold, like crystal lightning, shot into the fog of his consciousness, illuminating everything. He continued to sink. The turbulent stars overhead shrank into a fuzzy halo at the break in the ice above his head, leaving nothing but cold and inky blackness surrounding him, as if he wasn't sinking into ice water, but had jumped into the blackness of space.

In the dead, lonely, cold blackness, he saw the truth of the universe.

He surfaced quickly. His head surged out of the water and he spat out a mouthful. He tried crawling onto the ice at the edge of the hole but could only bring his body up halfway before the ice collapsed again. He crawled and collapsed, forging a path through the ice, but progress was slow and his stamina began to give out from the cold. He didn't know whether the security team would notice anything unusual on the lake before he drowned or froze to death. Stripping off his soaked down jacket to lessen the burden on his movement, he had the idea that if he spread out the jacket on the ice, it might distribute the pressure and allow him to crawl onto it. He did so, and then, with just enough energy left for one last attempt, he used every last ounce of strength to crawl onto the down jacket at the edge of the ice. This time the ice didn't collapse, and at last his entire body was lying on top of it. He crept carefully ahead, daring to stand up only after putting a fair distance between him and the hole. Then he saw flashlights waving on the shore and heard shouts.

He stood on the ice, his teeth chattering in the cold, a cold that

seemed to come not from the lake water or icy wind, but from a direct transmission from outer space. He kept his head down, knowing that from this moment on, the stars were not like they once were. He didn't dare look up. As Rey Diaz feared the sun, Luo Ji had acquired a severe phobia of the stars. He bowed his head, and through chattering teeth, said to himself:

"Wallfacer Luo Ji, I am your Wallbreaker."

"Your hair's turned white over the years," Luo Ji said to Kent.

"For many years to come, at least, it's not going to get any whiter," Kent said, laughing. In Luo Ji's presence, he had always worn a courteous, studied face. This was the first time Luo Ji had seen him with such a sincere smile. In his eyes, he saw the words that remained unspoken: *You've finally begun to work.*

"I need someplace safer," he said.

"Not a problem, Dr. Luo. Any particular requests?"

"Nothing apart from safety. It must be absolutely secure."

"Doctor, an absolutely safe place does not exist, but we can come very close. I'll have to warn you, though, these places are always underground. And as for comfort . . ."

"Disregard comfort. However, it'd be best if it's in China."

"Not a problem. I'll take care of it immediately."

When Kent was about to leave, Luo Ji stopped him. Pointing out the window at the Garden of Eden, which was now completely blanketed in snow, he said, "Can you tell me the name of this place? I'm going to miss it."

Luo Ji traveled more than ten hours under tight security before reaching his destination. When he exited the car, he knew immediately where he was: It was here, in the broad, squat hall that looked like an underground parking garage, that he had embarked on his fantastic new life five years before. Now, after five years of dreams alternating with nightmares, he had returned to the starting point.

Greeting him was a man named Zhang Xiang, the same young man who—along with Shi Qiang—had sent him off five years ago, and who now was in charge of security. He had aged considerably in five years and now looked like a middle-aged man.

The elevator was still operated by an armed soldier—not the one from back then, of course, but Luo Ji still felt a certain warmth in his heart. The old-style elevator had been swapped for one that was completely automated and did not require an operator, so the soldier merely pressed the "10" button and the elevator started its descent.

The underground structure had clearly undergone a recent renovation: The ventilation ducts in the hallways had been hidden, the walls coated with moisture-proof tile, and all traces of the civil air defense slogans had disappeared.

Luo Ji's living quarters took up the whole of the tenth basement floor. While it was no match in comfort for the house he had just left, it was equipped with comprehensive communications and computer equipment, along with a conference room set up with a remote video conferencing system, giving the place the feel of a command center.

The administrator made a particular point of showing Luo Ji a set of light switches in the room, each of which bore a small picture of the sun. The administrator called them "sun lamps" and said they needed to be turned on for no fewer than five hours a day. Originally intended as labor-safety products for mine workers, they could simulate sunlight, including UV rays, as supplementary daylight for people spending long periods underground.

The next day, as Luo Ji had requested, the astronomer Albert Ringier visited the tenth basement.

When he saw him, Luo Ji said, "You were the first to observe the flight path of the Trisolaran Fleet?"

Ringier looked a little unhappy to hear this. "I've repeatedly issued statements to reporters, but they insist on forcing this honor on my head. It should be credited to General Fitzroy. He was the one who demanded that Hubble II observe Trisolaris during

237

testing. Otherwise we might have missed the chance, since the wake in the interstellar dust would have faded."

"What I'd like to talk to you about isn't connected to that. I did a bit of astronomy once, but not in much depth, and I'm no longer familiar with the subject. My first question is this: If, in the universe, there exists another observer apart from Trisolaris, has Earth's position been revealed to them?"

"No."

"You're sure of that?"

"Yes."

"But Earth has exchanged communication with Trisolaris."

"That low-frequency communication would reveal only the general direction of Earth and Trisolaris in the Milky Way Galaxy, and the distance between the two worlds. That is, if there's a third-party recipient, the communication would make it possible for them to know of the existence of two civilized worlds 4.22 light-years apart in the Orion Arm of the Milky Way, but they would still be ignorant of the precise position of those two worlds. In fact, determining each other's position through this kind of exchange is only feasible for stars in close proximity, like the sun and the stars of Trisolaris. For a slightly more distant third-party observer, however, even if we communicate directly with them, we wouldn't be able to determine each other's position."

"Why is that?"

"Marking the position of a star for another observer in the universe is hardly as easy as people imagine. Here's an analogy: You're taking a plane through the Sahara Desert and a grain of sand below you shouts 'Here I am!' You hear the shout, but can you fix a location for that grain of sand from the plane? There are nearly two hundred billion stars in the Milky Way. It's practically a desert of stars."

Luo Ji nodded in apparent relief. "I understand. So that's it, then."

"What is?" Ringier asked in confusion.

Luo Ji didn't answer, but asked instead, "Using our present

level of technology, is there a way to indicate the position of a star in the universe?"

"Yes, by using directed very high frequency electromagnetic waves, equal to or higher in frequency than visible light, and then harnessing stellar power to transmit information. In simple terms, you'd make the star flash, like a cosmic lighthouse."

"This far exceeds our present technical capabilities."

"Oh, I'm sorry. I overlooked your precondition. At our present technical capabilities, it would be fairly difficult to show a star's position to the far reaches of the universe. There's still a way, but interpreting the positional information requires a level of technology far beyond that of humanity, and even, I believe, beyond that of Trisolaris."

"Tell me about that approach."

"The key information is the relative position of stars. If you specify a region of space in the Milky Way that contains a sufficient number of stars—perhaps a few dozen would be sufficient—their relative arrangement in three-dimensional space would be totally unique, like a fingerprint."

"I'm starting to understand. We send out a message containing the position of the star we wish to point out, relative to the surrounding stars, and the recipient compares the data to its star map to determine the star's location."

"Right. But things aren't that simple. The recipient must possess a three-dimensional model of the entire galaxy that precisely indicates the relative position of every one of a hundred billion stars. Then, after receiving our message, they would have to search through that enormous database to find an area of space that matches the pattern of positions we sent out."

"No, it's not simple at all. It's like recording the relative position of every grain of sand in the desert."

"Even harder than that. The Milky Way, unlike the desert, is in motion, and the relative positions of its stars are constantly changing. The later the position information is received, the greater the error caused by these changes. This means the database has to be

able to predict the changes in position of each of those hundred billion stars. In theory, it's not a problem, but to actually do it . . . God . . ."

"Would it be hard for us to send that positional information?"

"No, because we would only need to have a position pattern for a limited number of stars. And now that I've had time to think about it, given the average stellar density of the outer arm of the galaxy, a position pattern with no more than thirty stars should be sufficient. That's a small amount of information."

"Good. Now I'll ask a third question: Outside the Solar System, there are other stars with planets. You've discovered several hundred, right?"

"More than a thousand to date."

"And the closest to the sun?"

"244J2E1, sixteen light-years from the sun."

"As I remember it, the serial numbers are set like this: the prefix digits represent the order of discovery; the letters J, E, and X stand for Jupiter-type planets, Earth-type planets, and other planets, respectively; and the digits following the letter indicate the number of that type of planet in the system."

"That's right. 244J2E1 is a star with three planets, two of them Jupiter-type and one Earth-type."

Luo Ji thought for a moment, then shook his head. "That's too close. How about a little farther, like . . . around fifty light-years?"

"187J3X1, 49.5 light-years from the sun."

"That one's fine. Can you draw up a position pattern for that star?"

"Of course I can."

"How long would it take? Would you need help?"

"I can do it here if there's a computer with Internet. For a pattern of, say, thirty stars, I can give it to you tonight."

"What time is it now? It's not nighttime already?"

"I'd say it's probably morning, Dr. Luo."

Ringier went to the computer room next door, and Luo Ji called in Kent and Zhang Xiang. He first explained to Kent that

he wanted the PDC to hold the next Wallfacer hearing as soon as possible.

Kent said, "There are lots of PDC meetings these days. Once you've submitted the application, you'll probably only have to wait a few days."

"Then I'll have to wait. But I'd really like it as soon as possible. Also, I have a request: to attend the hearing here via video rather than go to the UN."

Kent looked reluctant. "Dr. Luo, don't you think that's a little inappropriate? For such a high-level international meeting . . . It's a question of respect for the participants."

"It's part of the plan. All those bizarre requests I made in the past were fulfilled, but this one's over the line?"

"You know . . ." Kent faltered.

"I know that a Wallfacer's status isn't like it once was, but I insist on this." When he continued, it was in a softer voice, even though he knew that the sophons hanging in the vicinity could still hear. "There are two possibilities now: One, if everything is like it used to be, I wouldn't mind going to the UN. But there's another possibility: I may be in a very dangerous situation, and I can't take that risk."

Then he said to Zhang Xiang, "That's why I've brought you here. We may become a target for a concentrated enemy attack, so security must be strengthened."

"Don't worry, Dr. Luo. We're located two hundred meters below ground. The area above us is under lockdown, an antimissile system has been deployed, and a state-of-the-art subterranean warning system has been installed to detect the digging of a tunnel from any direction. I guarantee to you that our security is foolproof."

When the two men left, Luo Ji took a walk down the hallway, his thoughts turning involuntarily to the Garden of Eden (he knew its name now, but still called it that in his heart) and its lake and snow peak. He knew that it was quite likely he would spend the rest of his life underground.

He looked around at the sunlamps in the hallway ceiling. The light they emitted was nothing like the sun.

Two meteors moved slowly across the starfield. All was dark on the ground, and the distant horizon blended into one with the night sky. A burst of whispers sounded through the dark, although the speakers remained unseen, as if the voices themselves were invisible creatures floating in the darkness.

With a clink, a small flame appeared in the darkness, its dim light revealing three faces: Qin Shi Huang, Aristotle, and Von Neumann. The flame came from a lighter in Aristotle's hand. When a few torches were extended, he lit one, which then passed fire among the others to form a shaky light in the wilderness and illuminate a group of people drawn from every era. Their whispers continued.

Qin Shi Huang leapt up on a stone and brandished his sword, and the crowd fell silent.

"The Lord has issued a new command: Destroy Wallfacer Luo Ji," he said.

"We too have received this command. This is the second assassination order that the Lord has issued for Luo Ji," Mozi said.

"But it will be difficult to kill him now," someone said.

"Difficult? It's impossible!"

"If Evans hadn't added that condition to the first assassination order, he would have been dead five years ago."

"Perhaps Evans was right to do so. After all, we don't know his reasons. Luo Ji was lucky to escape a second time in the UN Plaza."

Qin Shi Huang stopped the debate with a wave of his sword. "Shall we talk instead about what to do?"

"There's nothing we can do. Who can even get anywhere near a bunker two hundred meters deep, much less get inside? It's guarded too tightly."

"Shall we consider nuclear weapons?"

"The place is an antinuke bunker from the Cold War, damn it."

"The only viable option is sending someone to infiltrate security."

"Can that be done? We've had years. Has there ever been a successful infiltration?"

"Infiltrate his kitchen!" This prompted some laughter.

"Cut the crap. The Lord ought to tell us the truth, and maybe we can come up with a better option."

Qin Shi Huang answered the last speaker: "I also made that request, but the Lord said the truth was the most important secret in the universe and could not be revealed. The Lord spoke of it with Evans under the impression that humanity already knew but later learned otherwise."

"Then ask the Lord to transfer technology!"

Many other voices echoed this. Qin Shi Huang said, "This was another request I made. To my surprise, the Lord uncharacteristically did not reject it entirely."

A commotion took hold of the crowd, but Qin Shi Huang's next words quieted the excitement: "But once the Lord learned the location of the target, the request was swiftly rejected. It said that as far as the target's location was concerned, any technology It could transfer to us would be ineffective."

"Is he really that important?" Von Neumann asked, unable to conceal a note of jealousy in his voice. As the first successful Wallbreaker, he had risen rapidly in the organization.

"The Lord is afraid of him."

Einstein said, "I have thought this over for a long time, and I believe that the Lord's fear of Luo Ji has only one possible reason: He is the mouthpiece of certain power."

Qin Shi Huang shut down further discussion of the subject: "Don't get into that. Instead, let's think of how to fulfill the Lord's command."

"It can't be done."

"It really can't be done. It's a mission that can't be completed."

Qin Shi Huang clanged his sword on the rock beneath his feet. "This mission is crucial. The Lord may really be under threat.

Besides, if we complete it, the organization will be greatly elevated in the Lord's eyes! Gathered here are the elite of every sphere throughout the world, so how can we fail to think of something? Go back and think it over, and send your plans here to me through other channels. We've got to get on this!"

The torches burned out in succession and darkness swallowed everything. But the whispering went on.

The PDC Wallfacer Project Hearing did not convene for two weeks. After Tyler's failure and the hibernation of the other two Wallfacers, the PDC's main priority and attention had turned to mainstream defense.

Luo Ji and Kent awaited the start of the meeting in the video-conference room. The conference video connection had been made, and the big screen displayed the PDC auditorium, where the circular table familiar from the Security Council days was still completely empty. Luo Ji had arrived early as something of an apology for not attending in person.

While they waited, he chatted with Kent and asked him how he was managing. Kent said that he had lived in China for three years when he was younger, so he was quite accustomed to it and was doing well. At any rate, he didn't have to spend all day underground like Luo Ji, and his rusty Chinese had recently regained its fluency.

"You sound like you have a cold," Luo Ji said.

"I've just caught the bed flu," he replied.

"Bird flu?" Luo Ji said in alarm.

"No. Bed flu. That's what the media's calling it. It started going around in a nearby city a week ago. It's infectious, but symptoms are light. There's no fever, just a runny nose, and some patients get a sore throat. There's no need for medication, and it goes away on its own in three days or so after a little bed rest."

"The flu is usually more serious than that."

"Not this time. A lot of soldiers and staff here have already been infected. Haven't you noticed that they replaced the caretaker?

She caught the bed flu too, but was afraid of giving it to you. But as your liaison, I can't be replaced for the time being."

Onscreen the national delegates had begun to enter the auditorium. They sat down and started talking in low voices, as if they hadn't noticed Luo Ji's presence. The incumbent rotating chair of the PDC opened the meeting, saying, "Wallfacer Luo Ji, the Wallfacer Act was amended at the special session of the UN General Assembly that just adjourned. You've seen it?"

"Yes," he answered.

"Then you must have noticed that the Act strengthens the examinations and restrictions on Wallfacer resource allocation. I hope that the plan you will submit to the hearing today will comply with the Act's requirements."

"Mr. Chair," Luo Ji said, "the other three Wallfacers have allocated an enormous amount of resources to the execution of their own strategic plans. To limit my plan's resources in this way is unfair."

"Resource allocation privileges depend on the plan itself, and you must be aware that the other three Wallfacer plans are not in conflict with mainstream defense. In other words, the research and engineering they are conducting would have been carried out even without the Wallfacer Project. I hope that your strategic plan is also of this nature."

"I'm sorry to say that my plan is not of this nature. It has absolutely nothing to do with mainstream defense."

"Then I'm sorry, too. Under the new Act, the resources you can allocate to this plan are very limited."

"Even under the old plan, I couldn't allocate all that much. However, this isn't a problem, Mr. Chair. My strategic plan consumes practically no resources at all."

"Just like your previous plans?"

The chair's remark prompted snickers from several participants.

"Even less than in the past. Like I said, it consumes practically no resources at all," he said simply.

"Then let's have a look," the chair said, nodding.

"The specifics of the plan will be introduced by Dr. Albert

245

Ringier, although I presume you all received the corresponding file. To sum up, using the radio wave magnification capabilities of the sun, a message will be sent into the cosmos containing three simple images, along with additional information to demonstrate that these images have been sent by an intelligence as opposed to occurring naturally. The images are included in the file."

The sound of rustling paper filled the auditorium as the attendees located the three sheets. The images were also displayed on the screen. They were quite simple. Each consisted of black dots, seemingly scattered at random, but they all noticed that each image contained one conspicuously larger dot that was marked with an arrow.

"What is it?" asked the US representative, who, like the rest of the attendees, was inspecting the images carefully.

"Wallfacer Luo Ji, according to the basic principles of the Wallfacer Project, you do not need to answer that question," the chair said.

"It's a spell," he said.

The rustling and murmuring in the auditorium stopped abruptly. Everyone looked up in the same direction, so that Luo Ji now knew the location of the screen displaying his feed.

"What?" asked the chair, with narrowed eyes.

"He said it's a spell," someone seated at the circular table said loudly.

"A spell against whom?"

Luo Ji answered, "Against the planets of star 187J3X1. Of course, it could also work directly against the star itself."

"What effect will it have?"

"That's unknown right now. But one thing is certain: The effect of the spell will be catastrophic."

"Er, is there a chance these planets have life?"

"I consulted repeatedly with the astronomical community on that point. From present observational data, the answer is no," Luo Ji said, narrowing his eyes like the chair had. He prayed silently, *May they be right.*

"After the spell is sent out, how long will it take to work?"

"The star is around fifty light-years from the sun, so the spell will be complete in fifty years at the earliest. But we won't be able to observe its effects for one hundred years. This is just the earliest estimate, however. The actual time it takes might stretch out much farther."

After a moment of silence in the auditorium, the US representative was the first to move, tossing the three sheets and their printed black dots onto the table. "Excellent. We finally have a god."

"A god hiding in a cellar," added the UK representative, to peals of laughter.

"More like a sorcerer," sniffed the representative of Japan, which had never been admitted to the Security Council, but had been accepted immediately once the PDC was established.

"Dr. Luo, you have succeeded in making your plan weird and baffling, at least," said Garanin, the Russian representative who had held the rotating chair on several occasions during Luo Ji's five years as a Wallfacer.

The chair banged the gavel, silencing the commotion in the auditorium. "Wallfacer Luo Ji, I have a question for you. Given that this is a spell, why don't you direct it at the enemy's world?"

Luo Ji said, "This is a proof of concept. Its actual implementation will wait for the Doomsday Battle."

"Can't Trisolaris be used as the test target?"

Luo Ji shook his head with finality. "Absolutely not. It's too close. It's close enough that the effects of the spell might reach us. That's why I rejected any planetary star system within fifty light-years."

"One final question: Over the next hundred or more years, what do you plan on doing?"

"You'll be free of me. Hibernation. Wake me when the effects of the spell on 187J3X1 are detected."

As he was preparing for hibernation, Luo Ji came down with the bed flu. His initial symptoms were no different from everyone else, just a runny nose and a slight throat inflammation, and neither he

nor anyone else paid it any attention. But two days later his condition worsened and he began to run a fever. The doctor found this abnormal and took a blood sample back to the city for analysis.

Luo Ji spent the night in a fevered torpor, haunted endlessly by restless dreams in which the stars in the night sky swirled and danced like grains of sand on the skin of a drum. He was even aware of the gravitational interaction between these stars: It wasn't three-body motion, but the 200-billion-body motion of all of the stars in the galaxy! Then the swirling stars clustered into an enormous vortex, and in that mad spiral the vortex transformed again into a giant serpent formed from the congealed silver of every star, which drilled into his brain with a roar. . . .

At around four in the morning, Zhang Xiang was awakened by his phone. It was a call from the Planetary Defense Council Security Department leadership who, in severe tones, demanded that he report immediately on Luo Ji's condition, and ordered the base to be put under a state of emergency. A team of experts was on its way over.

As soon as he hung up the phone, it rang again, this time with a call from the doctor in the tenth basement, who reported that the patient's condition had sharply deteriorated and he was now in a state of shock. Zhang Xiang descended the elevator at once, and the panicked doctor and nurse informed him that Luo Ji had begun spitting up blood in the middle of the night and then had gone unconscious. Zhang Xiang saw Luo Ji lying on the bed with a pale face, purple lips, and practically no signs of life in his body.

The team, consisting of experts from the Chinese Center for Disease Control and Prevention, doctors from the general hospital of the PLA, and an entire research team from the Academy of Military Medical Sciences soon arrived.

As they observed Luo Ji's condition, one expert from the AMMS took Zhang Xiang and Kent outside and described the situation to them. "This flu came to our attention a while ago. We felt that its origin and characteristics were highly abnormal, and it's clear now that it's a genetic weapon, a genetic guided missile."

"A guided missile?"

"It's a genetically altered virus that is highly infectious, but only causes mild flu symptoms in most people. However, the virus has a recognition ability which allows it to identify the genetic characteristics of a particular individual. Once the target has been infected, it creates deadly toxins in his blood. We now know who the target is."

Zhang Xiang and Kent glanced at each other, first in incredulity and then in despair. Zhang Xiang blanched and bowed his head. "I accept full responsibility."

The researcher, a senior colonel, said, "Director Zhang, you can't say that. There's no defense against this. Although we had begun to suspect something odd about the virus, we never even considered this possibility. The concept of genetic weapons first appeared in the last century, but no one believed that anyone would actually produce one. And although this one's imperfect, it truly is a frightening tool for assassination. All you need to do is spread the virus in the target's general vicinity. Or, rather, you don't even need to know where the target is: You could just spread it across the globe, and because the virus causes little to no illness in ordinary people, it will spread quickly and would probably strike its target in the end."

"No, I accept full responsibility," Zhang said, covering his eyes. "If Captain Shi was here, this wouldn't have happened." He dropped his hand and his eyes shone with tears. "The last thing he said to me before hibernation was to warn me of what you said about no defense. He said, 'Xiao Zhang, in this job of ours we need to sleep with one eye open. There's no certainty of success, and some things we can't defend against.'"

"So what do we do next?" Kent asked.

"The virus has penetrated deep. The patient's liver and cardio-pulmonary functions have failed, and modern medicine is helpless. Hibernate him as soon as possible."

After a long while, when Luo Ji recovered a little of the consciousness that had totally disappeared, he had sensations of cold,

a cold that seemed to emanate from within his body and diffuse outward like light to freeze the entire world. He saw a snow-white patch in which there first was nothing but infinite white. Then a small black dot appeared at its very center, and he could gradually make out a familiar figure, Zhuang Yan, holding their child. He walked with difficulty through a snowy wilderness so empty that it lost all dimension. She was wrapped in a red scarf, the same one she had worn seven years ago on the snowy night he first saw her. The child, red-faced from the cold, waved two small hands at him from her mother's embrace, and shouted something that he couldn't hear. He wanted to chase them through the snow, but the young mother and child vanished, as if dissolved into snow. Then he himself vanished, and the snowy white world shrank into a thin silver thread, which in the unbounded darkness was all that remained of his consciousness. It was the thread of time, a thin, motionless strand that extended infinitely in both directions. His soul, strung on this thread, was gently sliding off at a constant speed into the unknowable future.

Two days later, a stream of high-power radio waves was sent off from Earth toward the sun, penetrating the convection zone and reaching the energy mirror in the radiation zone, where its reflection, magnified hundreds of millions of times, carried Wallfacer Luo Ji's spell into the cosmos at the speed of light.

YEAR 12, CRISIS ERA

Distance of the Trisolaran Fleet from the Solar System:
4.18 light-years

Another brush had appeared in space. The Trisolaran Fleet had crossed the second patch of interstellar dust, and because Hubble II had been closely monitoring the area, the fleet's wake was captured as soon as it appeared. This time, it looked nothing like a brush. Rather, it resembled a patch of grass that had just begun to sprout in the dark abyss of space. Those thousand blades of grass grew with a speed that was perceptible to the naked eye, and they were much clearer than the wake had been nine years before, due to nine years of acceleration that had greatly increased the fleet's speed and had made its impact on the interstellar dust more dramatic.

"General, look closely here. What can you see?" Ringier said to Fitzroy as he pointed to the magnified image on the screen.

"There still seem to be about a thousand."

"No, look closer."

Fitzroy looked carefully for a long moment, then pointed to the middle of the brush. "It looks like . . . one, two, three, four . . . ten bristles are longer than the others. They're extended out."

"Right. Those ten wakes are quite weak. They're only visible after image enhancement."

Fitzroy turned to Ringier, wearing the same expression he had when the Trisolaran Fleet had been discovered a decade earlier. "Doctor, does this mean that those ten warships are accelerating?"

"All of them are accelerating. But those ten show a greater acceleration. But they're not ten warships. The number of wakes has increased by ten, to one thousand and ten. An analysis of the morphology of those ten wakes shows that they are far smaller than the warships behind them: about one ten-thousandth the size, or about the size of a truck. But due to their high speed, they still produce detectable wakes."

"So small. Are they probes?"

"Yes, they must be probes."

This was another of Hubble II's shocking discoveries: Humanity would make contact with Trisolaran entities ahead of schedule, even if they were just ten small probes.

"When will they reach the Solar System?" Fitzroy asked nervously.

"We can't say for certain. It depends on the acceleration, but they will definitely arrive before the fleet. A conservative estimate would be half a century earlier. The fleet acceleration is evidently at a maximum, but for some reason we don't understand, they want to reach the Solar System as quickly as possible, so they launched probes that can accelerate even faster."

"If they have sophons, then what's the need for probes?" one engineer asked.

This question made them all stop and think, but Ringier soon broke the silence. "Forget it. This isn't something we can figure out."

"No," Fitzroy said, raising a hand. "We can figure out at least a part of it. . . . We're looking at events from four years ago. Can you determine the exact date that the fleet launched the probes?"

"We're fortunate that the fleet launched them on the snow . . . I mean, in the dust . . . allowing us to pinpoint the time from our observations of the intersection of the probe wakes and the fleet tracks." Then Ringier told him the date.

Fitzroy was speechless for a moment, then lit a cigarette and sat down to smoke. After a while, he said, "Doctor, you're not politicians. Just like I couldn't make out those ten longer bristles, you can't tell that this is a crucial fact."

"What's so special about that date?" Ringier asked, uncertainly.

"On that day four years ago, I attended the PDC Wallfacer Hearing, at which Luo Ji proposed using the sun to send a spell out into the universe."

The scientists and engineers glanced at each other.

Fitzroy went on, "And it was right around that time that Trisolaris issued a second command to the ETO calling for Luo Ji's elimination."

"Him? Is he really that important?"

"You think he was first a sentimental playboy and then a pretentious sham sorcerer? Of course. We thought so too. Everyone did, except for Trisolaris."

"Well . . . what do *you* think he is, General?"

"Doctor, do you believe in God?"

The suddenness of the question left Ringier momentarily speechless. ". . . God? That's got a variety of meanings on multiple levels today, and I don't know which you—"

"I believe, not because I have any proof, but because it's relatively safe: If there really is a God, then it's right to believe in him. If there isn't, then we don't have anything to lose."

The general's words prompted laughter, and Ringier said, "The second half is untrue. There is something to lose, at least as far as science is concerned. . . . Still, so what if God exists? What's he got to do with what's right in front of us?"

"If God really exists, then he may have a mouthpiece in the mortal world."

They all stared at him for ages before they understood the implication of his words. Then one astronomer said, "General, what are you talking about? God wouldn't choose a mouthpiece from an atheist nation."

Fitzroy ground out his cigarette end and spread out his hands. "When you have eliminated the impossible, whatever remains, no matter how improbable, must be the truth. Can you think of a better explanation?"

Ringier mused, "If by 'God' you mean a force of justice in the universe that transcends everything—"

253

Fitzroy stopped him with a raised hand, as if the divine power of what they had just learned would be reduced if it were stated outright. "So believe, all of you. You can now start believing." And then he made the sign of the cross.

The trial run of *Tianti III* was airing on television. Construction on three space elevators had begun five years ago, and since *Tianti I* and *Tianti II* had been put into operation at the start of the year, the test of *Tianti III* did not cause much of a commotion. All space elevators were currently being built with just a single primary rail, giving them a far smaller carrying capacity than the four-rail models still under design, but this was already an altogether different world from the age of chemical rockets. Setting aside construction, the cost of going into space by elevator was substantially lower than by civilian aircraft. This in turn had led to an increase in the number of bodies in motion in Earth's night sky: These were humanity's large-scale orbiting structures.

Tianti III was the only space elevator based on the ocean. Its base was located on the Equator on an artificial floating island in the Pacific Ocean that could navigate at sea under its own nuclear power, which meant that the elevator's position on the Equator could be adjusted if necessary. The floating island was a real-life version of the Propeller Island Jules Verne had described, and so it had been dubbed "Verne Island." The ocean wasn't even visible on the television, which was showing a shot of a metal, pyramid-shaped base surrounded by a steel city, and— at the bottom of the rail—the cylindrical transport cabin that was ready to launch. From this distance, the guide rail extending into space was invisible due to its sixty-centimeter diameter, although at times you could catch a glint of reflected light from the setting sun.

Three old men, Zhang Yuanchao and his two old neighbors, Yang Jinwen and Miao Fuquan, were watching this on television. All of them were now past seventy, and while no one would call

them doddering, they were now definitely old. For them, recalling the past and looking toward the future were both burdens, and since they were powerless to do anything about the present, their only option was to live out their waning years without thinking about anything in this unusual era.

Zhang Yuanchao's son Zhang Weiming led his grandson Zhang Yan through the door. He was carrying a paper sack, and said, "Dad, I've picked up your ration card and your first batch of grain tickets." Then he took out a pack of colorful tickets from the bag and gave them to his father.

"Ah, just like in the old days," Yang Jinwen said, as he watched from the side.

"It's come back. It always comes back," Zhang Yuanchao murmured emotionally to himself, as he took the tickets.

"Is that money?" asked Yan Yan, looking at the bits of paper.

Zhang Yuanchao said to his grandson, "It's not money, child. But, from now on, if you want to buy nonquota grain, like bread or cake, or want to eat at a restaurant, you'll need to use these along with money."

"This is a little different from the old days," Zhang Weiming said, taking out an IC card. "This is a ration card."

"How much is on it?"

"I get twenty-one and a half kilos, or forty-three *jin*. You and Xiaohong get thirty-seven *jin*, and Yan Yan gets twenty-one *jin*."

"About the same as back then," the elder man said.

"That should be enough for a month," Yang Jinwen said.

Zhang Weiming shook his head. "Mr. Yang, you lived through those days. Don't you remember? It might be fine now, but very soon there'll be fewer nonstaples, and you'll need numbers to buy vegetables and meat. So this paltry bit of grain really won't be enough to eat!"

"It's not that serious," Miao Fuquan said with a wave of his hand. "We've been through times like these a few decades ago. We won't starve. Drop it, and watch TV."

255

"Oh, and industrial coupons[16] may be coming soon, too," Zhang Yuanchao said, putting the grain tickets and ration card on the table and turning his attention to the television.

On the screen, the cylindrical cabin was rising from the base. It ascended quickly and accelerated rapidly, then disappeared into the evening sky. Because the guide rail was invisible, it looked like it was ascending on its own. The cabin could reach a maximum speed of five hundred kilometers per hour, but even at that speed it would take sixty-eight hours to reach the space elevator's terminus in geostationary orbit. The scene cut to a downward-facing camera installed beneath the cabin. Here, the sixty-centimeter rail occupied the larger part of the screen. Its slick surface made motion practically undetectable, except for the fleeting scale markings that showed the camera's upward velocity. The rail quickly tapered into nothing as it extended downward, but it pointed at a spot far below where Verne Island, now visible in total, seemed like a giant platter suspended from the lower end of the rail.

Something occurred to Yang Jinwen. "I'll show you two a real rarity," he said, as he got up and walked somewhat less nimbly out the door, perhaps to his own home. He soon returned with a thin slice of something about the size of a cigarette box and laid it on the table. Zhang Yuanchao picked it up and looked at it: The object was gray, translucent, and very lightweight, like a fingernail. "This is the material *Tianti* is made out of!" Yang Jinwen said.

"Great. Your son stole strategic materials from the public sector," Miao Fuquan said, pointing at the slice.

"It's just a leftover scrap. He said that when *Tianti* was under construction, thousands upon thousands of tons of this stuff was shot into space, and it was made into the guide rail there and then hung back down from orbit again. . . . Soon, space travel will be

16 *Translator's Note:* China instituted a ration system for grain and cooking oil in the early 1950s, and expanded it in 1961 to include goods ranging from shoes and scissors to home appliances and electronics. With the transition from planned economy to market economy in the 1980s, use of the ration system declined, and it was terminated in the early 1990s.

popularized. I've asked my son to hook me up with business in that area."

"You want to go to space?" asked Zhang Yuanchao, surprised.

"It's not such a big deal. I've heard there's not even hypergravity when you go up. It's just like taking a long-distance sleeper train," Miao Fuquan said dismissively. In the many years he had been unable to operate his mines, his family had gone into decline. He had sold off his villa four years ago, leaving this as his only residence. Yang Jinwen, whose son worked on the space elevator project, had in a single bound become the wealthiest of the three, and this sometimes made old Miao jealous.

"I'm not going to space," Yang Jinwen said, looking up, and when he saw that Weiming had taken the boy to another room, he went on. "But my remains will. Hey, you two fellows don't have any taboos about talking about this, do you?"

"What's taboo about it? Still, why do you want to put your remains up there?" Zhang Yuanchao asked.

"You know there's an electromagnetic launcher at the end of *Tianti*. When it's time, my casket will be fired off at the third cosmic velocity and will fly out of the Solar System. It's called a cosmic burial, you know. After I die, I don't want to stay on an alien-occupied Earth. It's a form of Escapism, I guess."

"And if the aliens are defeated?"

"That's practically impossible. Still, if it really happens, it's no great loss. I get to roam the universe!"

Zhang Yuanchao shook his head. "You intellectuals with your weird ideas. They're pointless. The fallen leaf returns to the root. I'm going to be buried in the yellow soil of the Earth."

"Aren't you afraid that the Trisolarans will dig up your grave?"

At this, Miao Fuquan, who had been silent, suddenly grew excited. He motioned for the others to draw closer, and lowered his voice, as if afraid that the sophons would hear: "Don't tell anyone, but I've thought of something. I have lots of empty mines in Shanxi. . . ."

"You want to be buried there?"

"No, no. They're all small pit mines. How deep can they be? But in several places they're connected to major state-owned mines, and by following their abandoned works, you can get all the way down to four hundred meters below ground. Is that deep enough for you? Then we blast the shaft wall. I don't think the Trisolarans will be able to dig down there."

"Sheesh. If Earthlings can dig that far, why can't the Trisolarans? They'll find a tombstone and just keep digging down."

Looking at Zhang Yuanchao, Miao Fuquan was unable to hold back his laughter. "Lao Zhang, have you gone stupid?" Seeing him still at a loss, he pointed to Yang Jinwen, who had grown bored with their conversation and was watching the television broadcast again. "Let an educated man tell it to you."

Yang Jinwen chuckled. "Lao Zhang, what do you want a tombstone for? Tombstones are meant for people to see. By then, there won't be any people left."

All along the way to the Third Nuclear Fusion Test Base, Zhang Beihai's car drove through deep snow. But as he neared the base, the snow melted entirely, the road turned muddy, and the cold air turned warm and humid, like a breath of springtime. On the slopes lining the road he noticed patches of peach flowers blooming, unseasonable in this harsh winter. He drove on toward the white building in the valley ahead, a structure that was merely the entrance for the majority of the base, which was underground. Then he noticed someone on the hillside picking peach flowers. Looking closer, he saw it was the very person he had come to see, and he stopped his car.

"Dr. Ding!" he called to him. When Ding Yi came over to the car carrying a bunch of flowers, he laughed and asked, "Who are those flowers for?"

"They're for myself, of course. They're flowers that have bloomed from fusion heat." He practically beamed under the influence of the brightly colored flowers. Evidently he was still

in the throes of excitement at the breakthrough that had just been achieved.

"It's pretty wasteful, letting all this heat disperse." Zhang Beihai got out of the car, took off his sunglasses, and took stock of the mini-spring. He couldn't see his breath, and he could feel the heat of the ground even through the soles of his shoes.

"There's no money or time to build a power plant. But that doesn't matter. From now on, energy is not something that Earth needs to conserve."

Zhang Beihai pointed at the flowers in Ding Yi's hands. "Dr. Ding, I really was hoping that you had gotten distracted. This breakthrough would have happened later without you."

"Without me here, it would've happened even earlier. There are over a thousand researchers at the base. I just pointed them in the right direction. I've felt for a long time that the tokamak approach[17] is a dead end. Given the right approach, a breakthrough was a certainty. Me, I'm a theoretician. I don't get experimentation. My blind pointing probably only delayed the progress of research."

"Can't you postpone the announcement of your results? I'm being serious here. And I'm also informally conveying the wish of Space Command."

"How could we postpone it? The media has been actively tracking the progress of all three fusion test bases."

Zhang Beihai nodded and let out a sigh. "That's bad news."

"I know a few of the reasons, but why don't you tell me why."

"If controlled nuclear fusion is achieved, spacecraft research will begin immediately. Doctor, you know about the two current research forks: media-propelled spacecraft and non-media radiation-drive spacecraft. Two opposing factions have formed around these two directions of research: the aerospace faction advocates research into media-propelled spacecraft, while the space force is pushing

17 *Translator's Note:* In a tokamak, plasma is confined to a torus shape by a toroidal electromagnetic field surrounding the torus and a current induced in the plasma itself. Developed by Soviet scientists in the 1950s, they produced better results than other plasma containment devices.

radiation-drive spacecraft. The projects will consume enormous resources, and if the two directions can't progress simultaneously on equal footing, then one direction must take the mainstream."

"The fusion people and I are in favor of the radiation drive. For my part, I feel that it's the only plan that enables interstellar cosmic voyages. Of course, I'll grant that Aerospace has its logic, too. Media-propelled spacecraft are actually a variant of chemical rockets that use fusion energy, so the prospects are a little safer for that line of research."

"But there's nothing safe in the space war of the future! As you said, media-propelled spacecraft are just huge rockets. They have to devote two-thirds of their carrying capacity to their propulsion media, and it's consumed very quickly. That type of spacecraft requires planetary bases in order to navigate through the Solar System. We do that, and we would be reenacting the tragedy of the Sino-Japanese War, with the Solar System as Weihaiwei."[18]

"That's a keen analogy," Ding Yi said, raising his bouquet at Zhang Beihai.

"It's a fact. A navy's front line defenses ought to be at the enemy's ports. We can't do that, of course, but our defensive line ought to be pushed out as far as the Oort Cloud, and we should ensure that the fleet possesses sufficient flanking capabilities in the vast reaches outside the Solar System. This is the foundation of space force strategy."

"Internally, Aerospace isn't entirely monolithic," Ding Yi said. "It's the old guard left over from the chemical rocket era that's pushing for media spacecraft, but forces from other disciplines have entered the sector. Take the people on our fusion system. They're mostly pushing for radiation spacecraft. These two forces are evenly matched, and all that's needed is three or four people in

18 *Translator's Note:* The Battle of Weihaiwei was the last major battle of the First Sino-Japanese War. In February 1895, the ships of the Beiyang Fleet, the Qing Dynasty's northern navy, were anchored in the harbor at Weihaiwei, Shandong province, their home base, for safety from the advancing Imperial Japanese Navy. When Japanese land forces seized shore fortifications, the Chinese fleet was forced to surrender.

key positions to break the equilibrium. Their opinions will decide the ultimate course of action. But those three or four key people are, I'm afraid, all part of the old guard."

"This is the most critical decision in the entire master strategy. If it's a misstep, the space fleet will be built atop a mistaken foundation, and we might waste a century or two. And by that time, I'm afraid there will be no way to change direction."

"But you and I aren't in a position to fix it."

After lunching with Ding Yi, Zhang Beihai left the fusion base. Before he had driven very far, the moist ground was again covered with wet snow that glowed white under the sun. As the air temperature plummeted, his heart also chilled.

He was in dire need of a spacecraft capable of interstellar travel. If other roads led nowhere, then just one was left. No matter how dangerous it might be, it had to be taken.

When Zhang Beihai entered the home of the meteorite collector, situated in a courtyard house in the depths of a *hutong* alleyway, he noticed that the old, dimly lit home was like a miniature geological museum. Each of its four walls was lined with glass cases in which professional lights shone on rock after unremarkable rock. The owner, in his fifties, hale in spirit and complexion, sat at a workbench examining a small stone with a magnifying lens, and he greeted the visitor warmly when he saw him. He was, Zhang Beihai noticed immediately, one of those fortunate people who inhabited a beloved world of his own. No matter what changes befell the larger world, he could always immerse himself in his own and find contentment.

In the old-fashioned atmosphere unique to old houses, Zhang Beihai was reminded that he and his comrades were fighting for the survival of the human race, while the majority of people were still clinging to their existing lives. This gave him a sense of warmth and peace of mind.

The completion of the space elevator and the breakthrough in controlled fusion technology were two enormous encouragements

to the world, and eased defeatist sentiment to a considerable extent. But sober leaders were aware that this was only the beginning: If the construction of the space fleet was analogous to naval fleets, then humanity had just now arrived at the seashore, carrying tools. Not even the shipbuilding dockyards had been built yet. Apart from the construction of the main spacecraft body, research into space weapons and recirculating ecosystems, as well as the construction of space ports, represented an unprecedented technological frontier for humanity. Just getting the foundations in place might take a century.

Human society faced another challenge aside from the terrifying abyss: The construction of a space defense system would consume an enormous amount of resources, and this consumption would likely drag the quality of life back a century, which meant that the greatest challenge to the human spirit was still to come. With that in mind, the military leadership had decided to begin implementing the plan to use political cadres from the space force as future reinforcements. As the initial proponent of the plan, Zhang Beihai had been named commander of the Special Contingent of Future Reinforcements. Upon accepting the mission, he proposed that all of the officers in the special contingent ought to undergo at least a year of space-based training and work before entering hibernation in order to provide them with the necessary preparations for their future work in the space force. "The brass won't want their political commissars to be landlubbers," he said to Chang Weisi. This request was swiftly approved, and one month later, he and the first special contingent of thirty comrades went to space.

"You're a soldier?" the collector asked as he served tea. After receiving a nod, he went on: "Soldiers these days aren't much like soldiers used to be, but you, I could tell at a glance."

"You were a soldier once too," Zhang Beihai said.

"Good eye. I spent most of my life serving in the General Staff Department's Surveying and Mapping Bureau."

"How did you get interested in meteors?" Zhang Beihai asked as he looked appreciatively at the rich collection.

"Over a decade ago I went with a survey team to Antarctica in

search of meteorites buried beneath the snow, and I got hooked. They come from outside of Earth, from distant space, so naturally they've got that attraction. Whenever I pick one up, it's like I'm going to a new and alien world."

Zhang Beihai shook his head with a smile. "That's just a feeling. The Earth itself is formed out of aggregated interstellar matter, so it's basically just a giant meteorite. The stone beneath our feet is meteorite. This teacup I'm holding is meteorite. Besides, they say that the water on Earth was brought here by comets, so"—he raised the teacup—"what's contained in this cup is meteorite, too. There's nothing particularly special about what you have."

The collector pointed at him and laughed. "You're sharp. You've already started to bargain. . . . Still, I trust my feelings."

The collector couldn't resist taking Zhang Beihai on a tour, and he even opened a safe to show him the treasure of his house: a Martian achondrite the size of a fingernail. He had him view the small round pits on the meteorite's surface and said that they might be microbial fossils. "Five years ago, Robert Haag wanted to buy her for a thousand times the price of gold, but I didn't agree."

"How many of these did you collect on your own?" asked Zhang Beihai, pointing around the room.

"Only a small part. The majority were bought from the private sector or traded from the community. . . . So, let's hear it. What sort do you want?"

"Nothing too valuable. It should be high density, shouldn't break easily under impact, and should be easily workable."

"I see. You want to engrave it."

He nodded. "You could say that. It would be great if I could use a lathe."

"Then an iron meteorite," the collector said as he opened a glass case and took out a dark-colored stone the size of a walnut. "This one. It's composed mainly of iron and nickel, with cobalt, phosphorus, silicon, sulfur, and copper. You want dense? This one's eight grams to the cubic centimeter. It's easily workable, and highly metallic, so the lathe won't be a problem."

"Good. It's just a little too small."

The collector took out another piece the size of an apple.

"Do you have anything even bigger?"

The collector looked at him and said, "This stuff's not sold by weight. The big ones are expensive."

"Well, do you have three the size of this one?"

The collector brought out three iron meteorites of roughly the same size and began to lay the groundwork for his asking price: "Iron meteorites are not very common. They represent just five percent of all meteorites, and these three are fine specimens. See here—this one's an octahedrite. Look at the crisscross pattern on the surface. They're called Widmanstätten patterns. And here's a nickel-rich ataxite. These parallel lines are called Neumann lines. This piece contains kamacite, and this one is taenite, a mineral not found on Earth. This piece is one I found in the desert using a metal detector, and it was like fishing a needle out of the ocean. The car got stuck in the sand and the drive shaft snapped. I almost died."

"Name your price."

"On the international market, a specimen of this size and grade would have a price of about twenty USD per gram. So how's this: sixty thousand yuan per piece, or three for one hundred eighty thousand?"[19]

Zhang Beihai took out his phone. "Tell me your account number. I'll pay right away."

The collector said nothing for quite some time. When Zhang Beihai looked up, he gave a slightly embarrassed laugh. "Actually, I was ready for you to counter-offer."

"No. I accept."

"Look. Now that space travel is for everyone, the market price has dropped somewhat even though it's not as easy to get meteorites in space as it is on the ground. These, well, they're worth—"

Zhang Beihai cut him off decisively. "No. That's the price. Treat it as a sign of respect for their recipients."

19 *Translator's Note:* Roughly $10,000 per piece, or a total of $30,000.

After leaving the collector's house, Zhang Beihai took the meteorites to a modeling workshop in a research institute belonging to the space force. Work had let out and the workshop, which contained a state-of-the-art CNC mill, was empty. First, he used the mill to slice the three meteorites into cylinders of equal diameter, about the thickness of a pencil lead, and then cut them into small segments of equal length. He worked very carefully, trying to minimize waste as much as possible, and ended up with thirty-six small meteorite rods. When this was done, he carefully collected the cutting debris, removed the special blade he had selected for cutting the stone from the machine, and then left the workshop.

The remainder of the work he conducted in a secret basement. He set thirty-six 7.62 mm pistol cartridges on the table before him and removed each projectile in turn. If they had been old-style brass cartridges, this would have required a lot of effort, but two years ago the entire military had updated its standard guns to use caseless ammunition, whose projectile was glued directly to the propellant and was easy to detach. Next, he used a special adhesive to affix a meteorite rod onto each propellant. The adhesive, originally developed to repair the skin of space capsules, ensured that the bond would not fail in the extreme hot and cold temperatures of space. In the end he had thirty-six meteorite bullets.

He inserted four meteorite bullets into a magazine, which he then loaded into a P224 pistol and fired at a sack in the corner. The gunshot was deafening in the narrow basement room and left behind a strong scent of gunpowder.

He carefully examined the four holes in the sack, noting that they were small, which meant that the meteorite had not shattered upon firing. He opened the sack and withdrew a large hunk of fresh beef, and with a knife carefully extracted the meteorite that had penetrated it. The four meteorite rods had shattered completely, leaving a small pile of rubble that he poured onto his palm. It showed practically no sign of having been worked. This outcome satisfied him.

The sack that held the beef was made out of materials used in space suits. To make the simulation even more realistic, it had

been arranged in layers that sandwiched insulation sponges, plastic tubing, and other material.

He carefully packed up the remaining thirty-two meteorite bullets and exited the basement, heading off to make preparations for his visit to space.

Zhang Beihai hung in space five kilometers out from Yellow River Station, a wheel-shaped space station that lay three hundred kilometers above the space elevator terminus as a counterweight. It was the largest structure humanity had ever constructed in space and it could house over a thousand long-term residents.

The region of space within a five-hundred-kilometer radius of the space elevator was home to other space facilities, all of them much smaller than Yellow River Station and scattered about like the nomadic tents that dotted the prairie during the opening of the American West. These formed the prelude of humanity's large-scale entrance into space. The shipyards that had just commenced construction were the largest yet and would eventually cover an area ten times greater than Yellow River Station, but right now, all that had been put up was scaffolding that looked like the skeleton of a leviathan. Zhang Beihai had come from Base 1, a separate space station eighty kilometers away and just one-fifth the size of Yellow River Station, the space force's base in geostationary orbit. He had been living and working with the other members of the first Special Contingent of Future Reinforcements for three months now and had only been back to Earth once.

At Base 1, he had been waiting for an opportunity, and now an opportunity presented itself: the aerospace faction was holding a high-level work conference on Yellow River Station, and all three of his targets for elimination would be attending. Once Yellow River Station went into operation, Aerospace had held quite a few meetings there, as if to make up for the regrettable fact that most of the people in the aerospace sector had never gotten the chance to go to space.

Before leaving Base 1, Zhang Beihai had dropped his space

suit's positioning unit in his own cabin so the surveillance system would not be aware that he had left the base and there would be no record of his movements. Using the thrusters on his suit, he flew eighty kilometers through space to the position he had selected. Then he waited.

The meeting was over, but he was waiting for the participants to come out and take a group photo.

It was a tradition for all meeting participants to take a group photo in space. Usually, the photograph would be taken against the sun, because that was the only way to get a clear shot of the space station. Since every person in the group shot had to turn their helmet visors to transparent to expose their face during the photo, they would have to keep their eyes shut against the sun's intense rays if they faced it, not to mention the fact that the inside of their helmets would get intolerably hot. So the best time for a group shot was when the sun was just about to rise or fall over the horizon of the Earth. In geosynchronous orbit, one sunrise and one sunset took place every twenty-four hours, although the night was very short. Zhang Beihai was waiting for the sun to set.

He knew that Yellow River Station's surveillance system was able to detect his presence, but that wouldn't attract any attention. As the point of origin for space development, the region was littered with construction materials both unused and abandoned, as well as an even greater quantity of garbage. Much of this floating material was roughly the size of a human. Moreover, the space elevator and the surrounding facilities had a relationship like a metropolis and its surrounding villages, with the supplies for the latter coming entirely from the former, so traffic between them was quite busy. As people became used to the environment of space, they gradually adopted the habit of crossing solo. Using space suits as a sort of space bicycle with thrusters that could push them to speeds of up to five hundred kilometers per hour was the easiest means of travel within a few hundred kilometers of the space elevator. By this point, people were flying between the space elevator and the surrounding stations all the time.

But right now, Zhang Beihai knew the surrounding space was empty. Apart from the Earth (which was visible as a complete sphere from geosynchronous orbit) and the sun, about to dip below its edge, everything in all directions was a pitch-black abyss, and the myriad stars were shining dust that was powerless to alter the emptiness of the universe. He knew that his suit's life-support system would only hold up for twelve hours, and before that time ran out he had to make it eighty kilometers back to Base 1, now just a shapeless point far off in the distance of the abyss of space. The base itself would not survive very long, either, if it left the umbilical cord of the space elevator. But now, as he floated in the vast void, he felt like his contact with the blue world down below had been cut off. He was an independent presence in the universe, unattached to any world, dangling in the cosmos, no ground beneath his feet and surrounded by empty space on all sides, with no origin or destination, like the Earth, the sun, and the Milky Way. He simply existed, and he liked this feeling.

He even sensed that his father's departed spirit might share this very same feeling.

The sun made contact with the edge of the Earth.

Zhang Beihai raised one hand. The glove of his suit held a telescopic sight which he used to observe one of Yellow River Station's exits, ten kilometers distant. On the large, curved-metal exterior wall, the round air lock door was still sealed.

He turned his head toward the sun, which had now set halfway and looked like a glittering ring atop the Earth.

Looking back through the scope at the station, this time he saw that the beacon light next to the exit had turned from red to green, indicating that the air inside the air lock had been emptied. Immediately afterward, the hatch slid open and a group of figures wearing white space suits filed out. There were about thirty of them. As they flew off in a group, the shadow they cast on the outer wall of Yellow River Station expanded.

They had to fly a considerable distance to fit the entire station into frame, but before long they slowed down and began their

weightless lineup under the photographer's direction. By now the sun had sunk by two-thirds. The remainder looked like a luminous object inlaid into the Earth above a smooth sea mirror that was half blue and half orange-red, its top covered by sun-soaked clouds that looked like pink feathers.

As the light dropped in intensity, the people in the distant group photo began to turn their visors transparent, revealing the faces in the helmets. Zhang Beihai increased his scope's focal length and quickly found his targets. Just as he had expected, due to their rank, they were in the center of the front row.

He released the scope, leaving it suspended in front of him, and with his left hand he twisted the metal retaining ring of his right glove to detach it. Now that his right hand was wearing just a thin cloth glove, he immediately felt the minus-one-hundred-degree temperature of space, so to avoid a quick freeze he turned his body to an angle that let the weak sunlight shine on his hand. He extended the hand into a side pocket of his suit and withdrew a pistol and two magazines. Then, with his left hand, he grasped the floating scope and affixed it to the pistol. The scope had been a rifle sight that he had modified with a magnetic attachment so it could be used on a pistol.

The vast majority of firearms on Earth could shoot in space. The vacuum was not a problem, because the bullet's propellant contained its own oxidizer, but you did need to worry about the temperature of space: Both extremes differed greatly from atmospheric temperatures and had the potential to affect the gun and ammunition, so he was afraid to leave the pistol and magazines exposed for too long. To shorten that time, over the past three months he had drilled repeatedly in taking out the gun, mounting the sight, and changing magazines.

He started to aim, and captured his first target in the cross hairs of the scope.

In Earth's atmosphere, even the most sophisticated sniper rifles couldn't hit a target at a distance of five kilometers, but an ordinary pistol could in space. The bullets moved in a zero-gravity

vacuum, free of any outside interference, so as long as their aim was true, they would follow an extremely stable trajectory directly to the target. Zero air resistance, meanwhile, meant that the bullets would not decelerate during flight and would strike the target with the initial muzzle velocity, ensuring a lethal blow from a distance.

He pulled the trigger. The pistol fired in silence, but he saw the muzzle flash and felt the recoil. He fired ten rounds at the first target, then quickly replaced the magazine and fired another ten rounds at the second target. Replacing the magazine again, he fired the last ten rounds at the third target. Thirty muzzle flashes. If anyone in the direction of Yellow River Station had been paying attention, they would have seen a firefly against the dark backdrop of space.

Now the thirty meteorites were speeding toward their targets. The Type 2010 pistol had a muzzle velocity of five hundred meters per second, so they would take around ten seconds to cross the distance, during which Zhang Beihai could only pray that his targets did not change position. This hope wasn't groundless, because the two back rows had not yet gotten situated for the group photo, and even when they were all situated, the photographer had to wait until the mist sprayed out by the space suit thrusters dissipated, so the leaders in the front row had to wait. But since the targets were, after all, floating in space and weightless, they could easily drift, causing the bullets to not only miss their targets but possibly hurt innocents.

Innocent? The three people he was about to kill were innocent, too. In the years before the Trisolar Crisis, they had made what, looking back now, seemed like particularly meager investments, and had crept carefully over the thin ice toward the dawn of the space age. That experience had imprisoned their thinking. They had to be destroyed for the sake of interstellar-capable spacecraft. Their deaths could be viewed as their final contribution to the cause of humanity's endeavors in space.

As a matter of fact, Zhang Beihai had deliberately sent a few bullets wide of the mark in the hope of hitting people other than his targets. Ideally he would only wound them, but if he happened

to kill an extra person or two, that didn't matter. That would only serve to reduce any potential suspicion.

He lifted the empty gun and looked soberly through the scope. He was prepared for failure. In that eventuality, he would dispassionately begin the search for a second opportunity.

Time passed second by second, and at last there were signs that a target had been hit. Zhang Beihai did not see the hole in the space suit, but a white gas spurted out. Immediately afterward, an even larger burst of white steam erupted from between the first and second rows, perhaps because the bullet had passed out the target's back and penetrated his thruster pack. He was confident of the bullets' power: When the meteorite projectiles struck their targets with practically no decrease in speed, it would be like being shot at gunpoint. Cracks suddenly appeared across the helmet visor of one target, rendering it opaque, but he could still see the blood that splashed up on the inside before mixing with leaking gases and spraying out of the bullet hole, where it quickly froze into snowflake-like crystals. His observations soon confirmed that five people, including the three targets, had been hit, and each target had been struck at least five times.

Through their visors he saw everyone in the crowd screaming in terror, and from the shape of their lips he knew that their words included the ones he was expecting:

"Meteor shower!"

Everyone in the photo group turned their thrusters to full power and sped back to the station, trailing tails of white mist behind them, and then they were through the round hatch and back inside Yellow River Station. Zhang Beihai saw that the five who had been hit were dragged back with them.

He activated his own thruster pack and accelerated toward Base 1. His heart was now as cold and calm as the empty space around him. He knew that the death of the three key aerospace figures did not guarantee that the non-media radiation drive would become the mainstream of spacecraft research, but he had done all he could. No matter what happened next, as far as the watchful eyes of his father in the beyond were concerned, he could now relax.

At practically the same time as Zhang Beihai was returning to Base 1, back on Earth's Internet, a group of people hastily assembled in the wilderness of the virtual *Three Body* world to discuss what had just happened.

"This time, the information transmitted via sophon was very thorough, or we wouldn't have believed he actually did it," Qin Shi Huang said as he waved the sword about him in his uneasiness. "Look at what he did, and then look at our three attempts on Luo Ji." He sighed. "Sometimes we're just too nerdy. We don't have that kind of cool competency."

"Are we just going to sit by and let him do this?" Einstein asked.

"In accordance with the Lord's intentions, that's all we can do. The man is an extremely stubborn holdout and a triumphalist, and the Lord doesn't want us to interfere unnecessarily with that type of human. Our attention must be focused on Escapism. The Lord believes that defeatism is more dangerous than triumphalism," Newton said.

"If we are to work sincerely and seriously in the service of the Lord, we can't wholly believe the Lord's strategy. After all, it's just the counsel of a child," Mozi said.

Qin Shi Huang knocked his sword on the ground. "Nevertheless, nonintervention is correct as far as this matter is concerned. Let them turn their development in the direction of radiation-drive spacecraft. With physics under sophon lockdown, that will be a technological peak that's practically unsurpassable. Not to mention a bottomless abyss into which humanity will pour all of their time and energy and end up with nothing."

"We are agreed on this point. But I believe this man is critical. He's dangerous," Von Neumann said.

"Precisely!" Aristotle said, nodding repeatedly. "We used to think he was a pure soldier, but is this the behavior of a soldier who acts in accordance with strict discipline and rules?"

"He is indeed dangerous. His faith is rock-solid, he's farsighted

and dispassionately ruthless, and he acts with calm resolve. Ordinarily he's precise and serious, but when there's a need he can go outside the lines and take extraordinary action," Confucius said with a sigh. "Just like the First Emperor said, this is the sort of person we lack."

"He won't be hard to deal with. All we have to do is denounce his murders," Newton said.

"It's not that simple!" Qin Shi Huang said, flipping a sleeve at him. "It's all your fault. You've been using the information you receive from the sophons to sow discord in the space force and the UN, so how did this happen? Denunciation would be an honor, or even a symbol of loyalty!"

"And we don't have any conclusive evidence," Mozi said. "His plans were thorough. The bullets shattered when they hit, so any autopsy would retrieve only authentic meteorites from the bodies of the dead and wounded. Everyone is going to think they died in a meteor shower. The truth is so bizarre that no one would believe it."

"It's a good thing he's going to reinforce the future. At least he won't be making trouble for us for a while."

Einstein let out a long sigh. "Gone. Everyone's gone. Some of us should go to the future too."

Although they said they would meet again, everyone knew in their hearts that this was a final farewell.

When the Special Contingent of Future Reinforcements headed to the hibernation center, Chang Weisi and a number of other senior space force generals came to the airport to see them off. He handed a letter to Zhang Beihai.

"This letter is for my future successor. In it, I explain your circumstances and strongly recommend you to the future Space Command. You'll awaken no sooner than fifty years in the future, possibly longer than that, at which time you may be faced with a more challenging work environment. You'll have to adapt to the future first, even as you preserve the spirit of the soldiers of our

time. You must be cognizant of our working methods today, and know which are obsolete and which should be carried on. This may turn out to be your greatest advantage in the future."

Zhang Beihai said, "Commander, for the first time I feel a bit of regret that I'm an atheist. Otherwise, we'd have the hope of meeting again at some other time and place."

Chang Weisi was a little taken aback at this sentiment coming from the ordinarily sober man, and the words resonated in the hearts of everyone else. But, as soldiers, they kept the beating of their hearts deeply hidden.

"I'm gratified that we've been able to meet in this lifetime. Be sure to greet our future comrades for us," Chang Weisi said.

After a final salute, the special contingent boarded the plane.

Chang Weisi's eyes did not leave Zhang Beihai's back for a moment. A steadfast soldier was leaving, and there might never be another like him. Where did his firm faith come from? The question had always lain hidden in the depths of his mind, and sometimes it even prompted a bit of jealousy. A soldier with faith in victory was fortunate. In the Doomsday Battle, those lucky people would be few and far between. As Zhang Beihai's tall frame disappeared inside the cabin door, Chang Weisi had to admit that, up to the very end, he had never really understood him.

The plane took off, carrying those who would perhaps have the chance to see humanity's final outcome, then disappeared behind thin, pale clouds. It was a bleak winter's day. The sun that shone listlessly behind a shroud of gray clouds and the chilly wind that blew across the empty airport gave the air the feel of solidified crystal, conjuring up the sense that the springtime might never really arrive. Chang Weisi tightened the collar of his army coat. He turned fifty-four years old today, and in the dreary winter wind he saw his own end, and the end of the human race.

YEAR 20, CRISIS ERA

Distance of the Trisolaran Fleet from the Solar System:
4.15 light-years

Rey Diaz and Hines were awakened from hibernation at the same time to the news that the technology they awaited had appeared.

"So soon?!" they exclaimed upon learning that just eight years had passed.

They were informed that due to unprecedented investment, technology had progressed with amazing speed over the past few years. But not everything was optimistic. Humanity was simply making a final sprint across the distance between them and the sophon barrier, so the progress they were making was purely technological. Cutting-edge physics remained stopped up like a pool of stagnant water, and the reservoir of theory was being drained. Technological progress would begin to decelerate and eventually come to a complete halt. But, for the time being at least, no one knew when the end of technology would arrive.

On feet that were still stiff from hibernation, Hines walked into a stadium-like structure whose interior was shrouded in a white fog, although it felt dry to him. He couldn't identify what it was. A soft moonlight glow illuminated the fog, which was fairly sparse at the height of a person but grew dense enough up above that the roof was obscured. Through the fog, he saw a petite figure whom

he recognized at once as his wife. When he ran to her through the fog, it was like chasing a phantom, except that in the end they came together in an embrace.

"I'm sorry, love. I've aged eight years," Keiko Yamasuki said.

"Even so, you're still a year younger than me," he said as he looked her over. Time seemed to have left no mark on her body, but she looked pale and weak in the fog's watery moonlight. In the fog and moonlight, she reminded him of that night in the bamboo grove in their yard in Japan. "Didn't we agree that you would enter hibernation two years after me? Why have you waited all this time?"

"I wanted to work on preparations for our post-hibernation work, but there was too much to do, so that's what I've been doing," she said as she brushed a strand of hair from her forehead.

"Was it hard?"

"It was very hard. Six next-gen supercomputer research projects were launched not long after you went into hibernation. Three of them employed traditional architecture, one used non–Von Neumann architecture, and the other two were quantum and bio-molecular computing projects. But two years later, the lead scientists of those six projects told me that the computing power we desired was impossible. The quantum computing project was the first to be terminated, because it failed to find sufficient support in current theoretic physics: Research had run into the sophon barrier. Next, the biomolecular project was discontinued. They said it was only a fantasy. The last to end was the non–Von Neumann computer. Its architecture was actually a simulation of the human brain, but they said it was a shapeless egg that would never turn into a chicken. Only the three traditional architecture projects were still ongoing, but for a long time there was never any progress."

"So that's it. . . . I ought to have been with you the whole time."

"It would have been no use. You only would have wasted eight years. It was only recently, during a period of time when we were totally discouraged, that we came up with the crazy idea of simulating the human brain in a practically barbaric way."

"And what was that?"

"To put the previous software simulation into hardware by using a microprocessor to simulate one neuron, letting all the microprocessors interact, and allowing for dynamic changes to the connection model."

Hines thought about this for a few seconds, then realized what she meant. "Do you mean manufacturing a hundred billion microprocessors?"

She nodded.

"That's . . . that's practically the sum total of all the micro-processors that have been manufactured in human history!"

"I didn't run the numbers, but it's probably more than that."

"Even if you really had all those chips, how long would it take to connect them all together?"

Keiko Yamasuki smiled wearily. "I knew it wasn't workable. It was just a desperate idea. But we really thought about doing it back then, and making as many as we could." She pointed around her. "This here is one of the thirty virtual brain assembly shops we had planned. But it's the only one that got built."

"I really should have been here with you," Hines repeated with more emotion.

"Fortunately we still got the computer we wanted. Its performance is ten thousand times better than when you entered hibernation."

"Traditional architecture?"

"Traditional architecture. A few more drops squeezed out of the lemon of Moore's law. It astonished the computing commu-nity—but this time, my love, we've really come to the end."

A peerless computer. If humanity failed, it would never be equaled, Hines thought, but did not say it out loud.

"With this computer, research on the Resolving Imager became much easier." Then she suddenly asked, "Love, do you have any idea of what a hundred billion looks like?" When he shook his head, she smiled and stretched out her hands around her. "Look. This is a hundred billion."

"What?" At a loss for words, Hines looked at the white fog around him.

"We're in the middle of the supercomputer's holographic display," she said as she manipulated a gadget hanging at her chest. He noticed a scroll wheel on it, and thought it might be something like a mouse.

As she adjusted it, he felt a change in the surrounding fog. It thickened in what was clearly a magnification of a particular region. Then he noticed that it was made up of an uncountable number of tiny glowing particles, and these particles were emitting the moonlike illumination rather than scattering light from an outside source. As the magnification continued, the particles became shining stars, but instead of seeing the starry sky over Earth, it was like he was situated at the heart of the Milky Way, where the stars were dense and left practically no room for darkness.

"Every star is a neuron," she said. Their bodies were plated in silver by the ocean formed from a hundred billion stars.

As the hologram continued to enlarge, he noticed innumerable thin tentacles extending radially from every star to form intricate connections, wiping out the starfield and situating him inside an infinitely large network structure.

The image enlarged further, and every star began to exhibit a structure that was familiar to him from electron microscopy, that of brain cells and synapses.

She pressed the mouse and the image returned instantly to the white fog state. "This is a full view of the structure of the brain captured using the Resolving Imager scanning three million cross sections simultaneously. Of course, what we're seeing now is the processed image—for the convenience of observation, the distance between neurons has been magnified by four or five orders of magnitude so it looks like we vaporized a brain. However, the topology of the connections between them has been preserved. Now, let's take a look at a dynamic view. . . ."

Disturbances appeared in the fog, glittering points in the mist that looked like a pinch of gunpowder sprinkled onto a flame. Keiko Yamasuki enlarged the image until it resembled a starfield, and Hines saw the surging of startide in a brain-universe, the

disturbances in the ocean of stars appearing in different forms at different locations: some like streams, others like vortexes, and others like the sweeping tides, all of it instantly mutable and giving rise to stunning pictures of self-organization within the teeming chaos. Then the image changed again to resemble a network, and he saw myriad nerve signals busily passing messages along thin synapses, like flashing pearls within the flow of an intricate network of pipes. . . .

"Whose brain is this?" he asked in wonder.

"Mine," she said, looking lovingly at him. "When this thought picture was taken, I was thinking of you."

Please note: When the light turns green, the sixth batch of test propositions will appear. If the proposition is true, press the right-hand button. If the proposition is false, press the left-hand button.

Proposition 1: Coal is black.
Proposition 2: $1 + 1 = 2$.
Proposition 3: The temperature in winter is lower than in summer.
Proposition 4: Men are generally shorter than women.
Proposition 5: A straight line is the shortest distance between two points.
Proposition 6: The moon is brighter than the sun.

The statements were displayed in succession on the small screen in front of the test subject. Each proposition was displayed for four seconds, and the subject pressed the left-hand or right-hand buttons according to his own judgment. His head was encased in a metal cover that allowed the Resolving Imager to capture a holographic view of his brain, which the computer would process into a dynamic neural network model for analysis.

In this, the initial stage of Hines's research project, the subject

engaged in only the simplest of critical thinking, and the test propositions had concise and clear answers. During such simple thoughts, the operation of the cerebral neural network was relatively easy to identify and provided a starting point for a more in-depth study of the nature of thought.

The research teams led by Hines and Keiko Yamasuki had made some progress. They discovered that critical thinking was not produced in any specific location in the cerebral neural network but used a particular mode of nerve impulse transmission, and that with the powerful computer's assistance, this model could be retrieved and located from among the vast network of neurons using a method quite similar to the star positioning the astronomer Ringier had provided to Luo Ji. Unlike finding a particular position pattern in a starfield, in the universe of the brain the pattern was dynamic and was only identifiable by its mathematical characteristics. It was a little like looking for a small whirlpool in an expansive ocean, which meant that the computing power it required was many orders of magnitude greater than that of the starfield and was only feasible on this latest machine.

Hines and his wife strolled through the cloud map of the brain in the holographic display. Every time a point of critical thinking was identified in the subject's brain, the computer would indicate its position on the image with a flashing red light. This was actually just a way to provide a more intuitive feast for the eyes and was not strictly required by the study. The important thing was the analysis of the internal structure of nerve impulse transmission at the point of thought, for there lay hidden the mysteries of the essence of the mind.

Just then the research team's medical director came in and said that Subject 104 was experiencing problems.

When the Resolving Imager had just been developed, scanning such a huge quantity of cross sections generated powerful radiation that was fatal to any life being scanned, but successive improvements had brought the radiation below the danger line, and a large number of tests had demonstrated that so long as filming was kept

below a set length of time, the Resolving Imager would not cause any damage to the brain.

"He seems to have caught hydrophobia," the medical director said, as they hurried toward the medical center.

Hines and Keiko Yamasuki stopped in their tracks in surprise. Hines stared at the medical director: "Hydrophobia? Did he somehow get rabies?"

The medical director raised a hand and tried to sort out his thoughts: "Oh, I'm sorry. That wasn't accurate. He doesn't have any physical problems, and his brain and other organs have not been damaged at all. It's just that he's afraid of the water, like someone with rabies. He refuses to drink, and he won't even eat moist food. It's an entirely psychological effect. He just believes that water is toxic."

"Persecutory delusion?" Keiko Yamasuki asked.

The medical director waved a hand. "No, no. He doesn't think that anyone put poison in the water. He just believes the water itself is toxic."

Again, Hines and his wife stopped still, and the medical director shook his head helplessly. "But psychologically, he's completely normal in every other way. . . . I can't explain it. You've got to see it for yourselves."

Subject 104 was a volunteer college student who had come to earn some pocket money. Before they entered the patient's room, the director told Hines and his wife, "He hasn't had a drink in two days. If this continues, he'll become severely dehydrated and we'll have to hydrate him by force." Standing at the door he pointed to a microwave oven, and said, "You see that? He wants bread and other food baked completely dry before he'll eat it."

Hines and his wife entered the patient's room. Subject 104 looked at them with fear in his eyes. His lips were cracked and his hair disheveled, but otherwise he looked entirely normal. He tugged at Hines's sleeve and said in a hoarse voice, "Dr. Hines, they want to kill me. I don't know why." Then he pointed a finger at a glass of water sitting on the cabinet next to the head of the bed. "They want me to drink water."

Hines looked at the glass of clear water, certain that the subject did not have rabies, because true hydrophobia would cause spasms of terror at the mere sight of it. The sound of running water would induce madness, and there might even be an intense fear response if others simply talked about it.

"From his eyes and speech, he ought to be in a normal psychological state," Keiko Yamasuki said to Hines in Japanese. She had a degree in psychology.

"Do you really believe that water is toxic?" Hines asked.

"Is there any question? Just like the sun has light and the air has oxygen. You can't deny this basic fact, can you?"

Hines leaned on his shoulder and said, "Young man, life was born in the water and can't exist without it. Your own body is seventy percent water."

Subject 104's eyes darkened, and he slumped back in bed, clutching his head. "That's right. This question tortures me. It's the most incredible thing in the universe."

"Let me see Subject 104's experiment record," Hines said to the medical director after they left the patient's room. When they reached the director's office, Keiko Yamasuki said, "Look at the test propositions first."

The test propositions displayed on the computer screen one by one:

Proposition 1: Cats have a total of three legs.
Proposition 2: Rocks are not living.
Proposition 3: The sun is shaped like a triangle.
Proposition 4: Iron is heavier than cotton of the same volume.
Proposition 5: Water is toxic.

"Stop," Hines said, pointing to Proposition 5.

"His answer was 'false,'" the director said.

"Look at all parameters and operations following the answer to Proposition 5."

The records indicated that once Proposition 5 was answered,

the Resolving Imager increased the strength of its scan of the critical thinking point in the subject's cerebral neural network. To improve the accuracy of the scan of this area, the intensity of the radiation and the magnetic field were increased in this small region. Hines and Keiko Yamasuki carefully examined the long list of recorded parameters on the screen.

"Has this enhanced scan been done to other subjects and on other propositions?" Hines asked.

The director said, "Because the effect of the enhanced scan was not particularly good, it was canceled after four tries due to fears of excessive localized radiation. The previous three . . ." He consulted the computer, and then said, "were all benign true propositions."

"We should use the same scanning parameters and repeat the experiment for Proposition 5," Keiko Yamasuki said.

"But . . . who will do it?" asked the director.

"I will," Hines said.

Water is toxic.

Proposition 5 appeared in black text on a white background. Hines pressed the left "False" button, but he felt nothing apart from a slight sensation of heat produced by the intensive scanning at the back of his head.

He exited the Resolving Imager lab and sat down at a table, as a crowd, which included Keiko Yamasuki, watched. On the table stood a glass of clear water. He picked up the glass and slowly drew it to his lips and took a sip. His movements were relaxed and he wore an expression of quiet calm. Everyone began to sigh with relief, but then they noticed that his throat wasn't moving to swallow the water. The muscles of his face stiffened and then twitched slightly upward, and into his eyes came the same fear Subject 104 exhibited, as if his spirit was fighting with some powerful, shapeless force. Finally he spat out all of the water in his mouth and knelt down to vomit, but nothing came out. His face turned purple.

Hugging Hines to her, Keiko Yamasuki clapped him on the back with one hand.

When he had recovered his senses, he held out a hand: "Give me some paper towels," he said. He took them and carefully wiped off the droplets of water that had splashed on his shoes.

"Do you really believe that water is toxic, love?" Yamasuki asked, tears in her eyes. Prior to the experiment she had asked him repeatedly to replace the proposition with a false one that was entirely harmless, but he had refused.

He nodded. "I do." He looked up at the crowd, helplessness and confusion in his eyes. "I do. I really do."

"Let me repeat your words," she said, clapping him on the shoulder. "Life was born in the water and can't exist without it. Your own body is seventy percent water!"

Hines bowed his head and looked at the water stains on the floor. Then he shook his head. "That's right, dear. This question tortures me. It's the most incredible thing in the universe."

Three years after the breakthrough in controlled nuclear fusion, new and unusual heavenly bodies had taken their place in the Earth's night sky, up to five of them now simultaneously visible in one hemisphere. The bodies changed dramatically in luminance, outshining Venus at their brightest, and often blinked rapidly. Sometimes one of them would suddenly erupt with a rapid increase in brightness, then go out after two or three seconds. They were fusion reactors undergoing tests in geosynchronous orbit.

Non-media radioactive propulsion had won out as the research path for future spacecraft. This type of propulsion required high-powered reactors that could only be tested in space, leading to these glowing reactors thirty thousand kilometers out in space known as nuclear stars. Every time a nuclear star erupted, it represented a disastrous defeat. But contrary to what most people believed, nuclear star eruptions were not explosions in the nuclear reactor, but the exposure of the core when the outer

hull of the reactor melted from the heat produced by fusion. The fusion core was like a small sun, and because it melted Earth's most heat-tolerant materials as if they were wax, it had to be contained by an electromagnetic field. These restraints frequently failed.

On the balcony of the top floor of Space Command, Chang Weisi and Hines had just witnessed one such eruption. Its moon-like glow cast its shadows onto the wall before disappearing. Hines was the second Wallfacer that Chang Weisi had met, after Tyler.

"The third time this month," Chang Weisi said.

Hines looked out at the now-darkened night sky. "The power of these reactors only reaches one percent of what's needed for future spacecraft engines, and they don't operate stably. And even *if* the required reactors were developed, engine technology will be even more difficult. We're sure to encounter the sophon block there."

"That's true. The sophons are blocking our every path," Chang Weisi said as he looked off into the distance. The sea of lights in the city seemed even more brilliant now that the light in the sky had disappeared.

"A glimmer of hope fades as soon as it is born, and one day it will be destroyed forever. It's like you said: The sophons block our every path."

Chang Weisi said, with a laugh, "Dr. Hines, you're not here to talk defeatism with me, are you?"

"That's precisely what I want to talk about. The resurgence of defeatism is different this time. It's based on the drastically reduced living conditions in the general population and has an even greater impact in the military."

Chang Weisi looked back from the distance but said nothing.

"I understand your difficulties, General, and I'd like to help you."

Chang Weisi looked at Hines in silence for a few seconds, his expression unreadable to the other man. Then, without replying to his offer, he said, "The evolution of the human brain needs twenty thousand to two hundred thousand years to achieve noticeable changes, but human civilization has a history of just five thousand years. So what we're using right now is the brain of primitive

man. . . . Doctor, I really applaud your unique ideas, and perhaps this is where the real answer lies."

"Thank you. All of us are basically Flintstones."

"But is it really possible to use technology to enhance mental ability?"

This got Hines excited. "General, you're not so primitive, at least compared to others! I notice you said 'mental ability' rather than 'intelligence.' The former is much broader than the latter. To overcome defeatism, for example, we can't simply rely on intelligence. Given the sophon block, the higher your intelligence, the more trouble you have establishing a faith in victory."

"So give me an answer. Is it possible?"

Hines shook his head. "How much do you know about my and Keiko Yamasuki's work before the Trisolar Crisis?"

"Not too much. I believe it was: The essence of thought is not on the molecular level but is carried out on the quantum level. I wonder, does that imply—"

"It implies that the sophons are waiting for me. Just like we're waiting for them," Hines said pointing at the sky. "But right now, our research is still quite a ways from our goal. Still, we've come up with an unexpected by-product."

Chang Weisi smiled and nodded, showing cautious interest.

"I won't talk about the details. Basically, we discovered the mind's mechanism for making judgments in the cerebral neural network, as well as the ability to have a decisive impact on them. If we compare the process by which a human mind makes judgments to a computer's process, there's the input of external data, calculation, and then the final outcome. What we're able to do is omit the calculation step of the process and directly produce an outcome. When a certain piece of information enters the brain, it exerts an influence on a particular part of the neural network, and we can cause the brain to render a judgment—to believe that the information is genuine—without even thinking about it."

"Has this already been achieved?" Chang Weisi asked softly.

"Yes. It started with a chance discovery, which we subjected

to in-depth research, and now we've done it. We call it the 'mental seal.'"

"And if the judgment—or if you will, faith—is at odds with reality?"

"Then the faith will eventually be overturned. But the process will be quite painful, because the judgment produced in the mind by the mental seal is particularly stubborn. Once, this had me convinced that water was toxic, and it was only after two months of psychotherapy that I was able to drink unimpeded. That process is . . . not something I want to remember. But the toxicity of water is an extremely clear false proposition. Other beliefs may not be. Like the existence of God, or whether humanity will be victorious in war. These don't have a clearly determined answer, and in the normal course of establishing these beliefs, the mind is slightly tilted in a certain direction by all sorts of choices. If the belief is established by the mental seal, it will be rock-solid and absolutely unshakeable."

"That is truly a great achievement." Chang Weisi grew serious. "I mean, for neuroscience. But in the real world, Dr. Hines, you have created a truly troublesome thing. Really. The most troublesome thing in history."

"You don't want to use this thing, the mental seal, to create a space force possessing an unshakeable faith in victory? In the military, you have political commissars and we have chaplains. The mental seal is just a technological means of accomplishing their work more efficiently."

"Political and ideological work establishes faith through rational, scientific thinking."

"But is it possible to establish faith in a victory in this war on the basis of rational, scientific thought?"

"If not, Doctor, we'd rather have a space force that lacks faith in victory yet retains independent thought."

"Apart from this one belief, the rest of the mind would of course be entirely autonomous. We would just be performing a tiny intervention in the mind, using technology to leapfrog thought

to implant a conclusion—just one alone—into the mind."

"But one is enough. Technology is now capable of modifying thoughts just like modifying a computer program. After the modifications, are people still people, or are they automatons?"

"You must have read *A Clockwork Orange*."

"It's a profound book."

"General, your attitude is what I expected," Hines said with a sigh. "I'll continue my efforts in this area, the efforts a Wallfacer must exert."

At the next PDC Wallfacer Project Hearing, Hines's introduction of his mental seal triggered rare emotion in the assembly. The US representative's concise evaluation expressed the feeling of the majority of the attendees: "With their extraordinary talent, Dr. Hines and Dr. Yamasuki have opened up a great door into darkness for humanity."

The French representative left his seat in his excitement. "Which is more tragic for humanity: the loss of the ability and right to think freely, or defeat in this war?"

"Of course the latter is more tragic!" Hines retorted, standing up. "Because under the first condition, humanity at least has the chance of regaining independent thought!"

"I have doubts about that. If this thing really does get used . . . Look at all you Wallfacers," the Russian representative said, raising his hands toward the ceiling. "Tyler wanted to deprive people of their lives, and you want to deprive them of their minds. What are you trying to do?"

His words caused a commotion.

The UK representative said, "Today we are merely proposing a motion, but I believe that the governments of all countries will be unanimous in banning this thing. Regardless of what happens, nothing is more evil than thought control."

Hines said, "Why is it that everyone gets so sensitive at the mention of thought control? From commercial advertising to

Hollywood culture, thought control is everywhere in modern society. You are, to use a Chinese phrase, mocking people for retreating a hundred paces when you've retreated fifty yourselves."

The US representative said, "Dr. Hines, you haven't gone just one hundred paces. You've walked up to the threshold of darkness and are threatening the very foundations of modern society."

Another commotion swept through the assembly, and Hines knew that now was the time to seize control of the situation. He raised his voice and said, "Learn from the little boy!"

Sure enough, there was a lull in the noise after his utterance. "What little boy?" asked the rotating chair.

"I think we're all familiar with this story: In a forest, a little boy got his leg caught under a fallen tree. He was alone at the time, and his leg was bleeding uncontrollably. It would have killed him, except that he made a decision that would shame every one of you delegates: He took up his saw and sawed off the leg that was pinned, then climbed into a car and found a hospital. He saved his own life."

Hines saw with satisfaction that no one in the meeting room had attempted to interrupt him, at least. He went on. "Humanity is now facing a life-and-death problem. The life or death of our species and civilization as a whole. In these circumstances, how can we not give up a few things?"

Two light thumps sounded. The chair was banging the gavel, even though there wasn't much noise in the assembly. The attendees were reminded that the German man had maintained an unusual silence during the course of the hearing. In a gentle voice, the chair said, "First of all, I hope that each of you can take a good look at the current situation. Investment in building a space defense system is constantly increasing, and the world economy is experiencing a sharp recession during this time of transition. The prediction that the standard of living will retreat a century may come to pass in the not-too-distant future. Meanwhile, space defense–related scientific research is running up against the sophon block, and technological progress is slowing. This will trigger a new wave of

defeatism in the international community, and this time, it may cause the total collapse of the Solar System Defense Program."

The chair's words calmed the assembly completely. After a silence of nearly half a minute, he continued. "Like each of you, when I learned of the existence of the mental seal, I felt the kind of fear and loathing I'd get from seeing a poisonous snake. But the most rational approach to take right now is to calm down and seriously consider it. When the devil does actually appear, the best option is calmness and rationality. At this hearing, we are simply putting forward a votable motion."

Hines saw a thread of hope. "Mr. Chair, Representatives, since my initial proposal is unable to be put to an assembly vote, maybe we all can take a step back."

"No matter how many steps back you take, thought control is absolutely unacceptable," the French representative said, but in a slightly softer tone than before.

"And if it weren't thought control? Perhaps something in between control and freedom?"

"The mental seal equals thought control," the Japanese representative said.

"Not so. In thought control, there must be a controller and a subject. If someone voluntarily places a seal in their own mind, then tell me, where is the control in that?"

The assembly fell silent again. Feeling that success was near, Hines went on, "I propose that the mental seal be opened up, like a public facility. It would have but one proposition: belief in a victory in the war. Anyone willing to gain that faith through the use of the seal could, totally voluntarily, take advantage of the facility. Of course, all of this would be conducted under strict supervision."

The assembly opened up a discussion and added to Hines's basic proposal a fair number of new restrictions on the use of the mental seal. The most crucial of these was the one limiting its use to the space forces, because it was relatively easy for people to accept the idea of uniform thinking in the military. The hearing continued for nearly eight hours, the longest ever, and eventually formulated

a motion to be voted on at the next meeting, and which the permanent member states would take back to their own governments.

"Shouldn't we come up with a name for this facility?" asked the US representative.

"How about calling it the Faith Relief Center?" the UK representative said. The British humor of the odd name drew a burst of laughter.

"Take out 'relief,' and call it the Faith Center," Hines said, in all earnestness.

At the gate to the Faith Center stood a reduced-scale replica of the Statue of Liberty. Its purpose was unknown—perhaps it was an attempt to use "liberty" to dilute the feeling of "control"—but the most notable thing about the statue was the altered poem on its base:

> *Give me your hopeless souls,*
> *Your fearful crowds that thirst for victory,*
> *The dazed refuse of your treacherous shoals.*
> *Send these, the downcast, wand'ring ones to me,*
> *For lo, my lamp of golden faith consoles.*

The golden faith of the poem was prominently inscribed in many different languages on a black granite stone called the Faith Monument that stood beside the statue:

In the war of resistance against the invasion from Trisolaris, humanity will be victorious. The enemy invading the Solar System will be destroyed. Earth will endure in the cosmos for ten thousand generations.

The Faith Center had been open for three days, during which time Hines and Keiko Yamasuki had been waiting in the majestic foyer. The smallish building erected near the United Nations Plaza had

become the latest tourist attraction, with people constantly coming up to take photos of the Statue of Liberty and the Faith Monument, but no one had entered. They all seemed to be maintaining a cautious distance.

"Do you get the feeling we're running a struggling mom-and-pop store?" she said.

"My dear, one day this will be a sacred place," Hines said solemnly.

On the afternoon of the third day, someone finally walked into the Faith Center. The bald, melancholy-looking, middle-aged man walked unsteadily and smelt of alcohol when he approached. "I've come to get faith," he slurred out.

"The Faith Center is only open to members of national space forces. Please show your ID," Keiko Yamasuki said while bowing. She seemed to Hines like a polite waitress at the Tokyo Plaza Hotel.

The man fished out his ID. "I'm a space force member. Civilian personnel. Is that okay?"

After inspecting the ID, Hines nodded. "Mr. Wilson, do you want to do it now?"

"That would be great," he said, and nodded. "The . . . the thing you call a belief proposition. I've written it here. I want to believe this." He pulled a neatly folded piece of paper from his breast pocket.

Keiko Yamasuki wanted to explain that according to the PDC resolution, the mental seal was only permitted to operate on one proposition, the one written on the monument at the gate. It had to be done exactly as written, and any alteration was prohibited. But Hines gently stopped her. He wanted to take a look at the proposition the man had submitted first. Unfolding the paper, he read what was written on it:

Katherine loves me. She has never and will never have an affair!

Keiko Yamasuki stifled a laugh, but Hines angrily crumpled up the paper and tossed it in the drunken man's face. "Get the hell out!"

After Wilson left, another man passed the Faith Monument,

the boundary beyond which ordinary tourists maintained their distance. As the man paced behind the monument, he soon came to Hines's attention. Hines called Keiko Yamasuki over and said, "Look at him. He must be a soldier!"

"He looks mentally and physically exhausted," she said.

"But he's a soldier. Believe me," he said. He was about to go out and talk to the man when he saw him heading up the steps. The man looked about Wilson's age and, though his Asian features were handsome, it was like Keiko Yamasuki had said: He seemed a little melancholy, but in a different way from the previous hardluck case. His melancholy looked lighter, but also deeper, as if it had been with him for years.

"My name is Wu Yue. I'd like to get belief," the visitor said. Hines noticed how he referred to "belief" instead of "faith."

Keiko Yamasuki bowed and repeated her earlier line: "The Faith Center is only open to members of every country's space force. Please show your ID."

Wu Yue did not move, but he said, "Sixteen years ago, I spent a month serving in the space force, and then I retired."

"You served for one month? Well, if you don't mind my asking, what was your reason for retiring?" Hines asked.

"I'm a defeatist. My superiors and I felt that I was no longer suited to work in the space force."

"Defeatism is a common mentality. You're evidently just an honest defeatist, and stated your own ideas forthrightly. Your colleagues who continued serving may have harbored an even stronger defeatist complex, but they just kept it hidden," Keiko Yamasuki said.

"Maybe. But I've been lost all these years."

"Because you left the service?"

Wu Yue shook his head. "No. I was born into a family of scholars, and the education I received made me treat humanity as a single unit, even after I became a soldier. I always felt that a soldier's highest honor would be to fight for the entire human race. This opportunity came, but it was a war that we were destined to lose."

Hines was about to say something, but was interrupted by Keiko Yamasuki. "Permit me to ask a question. How old are you?"

"Fifty-one."

"If you are really able to return to the space force after obtaining faith in victory, don't you think that at your age it's a little late to start up in the service again?"

Hines could see that she didn't have the heart to refuse him directly. No doubt this deeply melancholy man was very attractive to a woman's eyes. But this didn't worry him, because the man was obviously so consumed by his despair that nothing else had any meaning for him.

Wu Yue shook his head. "You misunderstand. I don't want to gain faith in victory. I'm just looking for peace for my soul."

Hines wanted to speak, but again Keiko Yamasuki stopped him.

Wu Yue went on. "I met my present wife when I was studying at the naval academy in Annapolis. She was a fervent Christian and faced the future with a calmness that made me jealous. She said that God had everything planned out, from the past to the future. We children of the Lord did not need to understand his plans. We just needed to firmly believe that this plan was the most reasonable one in the universe, and then live peacefully according to the Lord's will."

"So you mean that you've come to gain a belief in God?"

Wu Yue nodded. "I've written out my belief proposition. Please have a look." He reached into his shirt pocket as he spoke.

Again Keiko Yamasuki stopped Hines from saying anything. She said to Wu Yue, "If that's the case, then just go and believe. There's no need to resort to such extreme, technological means."

The former space force captain showed a trace of a wry smile. "I grew up under a materialist education. I'm a staunch atheist. Do you think gaining this belief would be easy for me?"

"Absolutely not!" Hines said, getting out in front of Keiko Yamasuki. He decided to clear things up as quickly as he could. "You ought to know that according to the UN resolution, the mental seal can only operate on one proposition." As he spoke, he took out a large, exquisitely fashioned red card case and opened it up for

Wu Yue to see. There, on the black velvet lining, in letters engraved in gold, was the victory oath from the Faith Monument. He said, "This is a faith book." He took out a set of cases in different colors. "These are faith books in different languages. Mr. Wu, let me tell you how stringent the supervision is for use of the mental seal. To guarantee safe and reliable operation, the proposition is not put up on a display but is given to the volunteer to read from this primitive faith book. As a reflection of the voluntary principle, the specific procedure is completed by the volunteer. He opens up this faith book, then presses the Start button on the mental seal device. Prior to actually performing the procedure, the system will give three confirmation opportunities. Before each procedure, the faith book is inspected by a panel of ten special commissioners from the members of the UN Human Rights Commission and the permanent member states of the PDC. During the operation of the mental seal device, the ten-member panel will be on site to strictly supervise the entire affair. So, sir, your request can't be fulfilled. Forget about your proposition for religious belief. Changing even one word in the faith book is a crime."

"Then I'm sorry to have troubled you," Wu Yue said, nodding. He appeared to have anticipated this outcome. As he turned to walk out, he appeared lonely and old from the back.

"The rest of his life will be hard," Keiko Yamasuki said softly, with a voice full of tenderness.

"Sir!" Hines called, stopping Wu Yue just outside the door. He ran out to where the light of the setting sun was reflecting like fire off the Faith Monument and the glass-walled UN building in the distance. He squinted his eyes against the flames and said, "You might not believe me, but I nearly did the exact opposite."

Wu Yue looked puzzled. Hines looked back and, seeing that Keiko Yamasuki had not followed him, took out a piece of paper from his pocket and opened it for Wu Yue. "This is the mental seal I wanted to apply to myself. I was hesitant, of course, and in the end didn't do it." The bold text on the paper read:

God is dead.

"Why?" asked Wu Yue, raising his head.

"Isn't it obvious? Isn't God dead? Screw the Lord's plan. Screw his mild yoke!"

Wu Yue looked at Hines in silence for a moment, then turned and walked down the steps.

When Wu Yue walked into the shadow cast by the Faith Monument, Hines called after him, "Sir, I wish I could disguise my contempt for you, but I can't."

The next day, the people Hines and Keiko Yamasuki were waiting for finally started to arrive. In the bright sunshine that morning, four people walked in, three men with European faces and one woman with Asian features. Young, standing straight and tall, and walking at a steady pace, they looked confident and mature. But Hines and Keiko Yamasuki saw in their eyes something familiar, the same melancholy confusion that had been in Wu Yue's.

They set their documents neatly down on the reception desk, and their leader said solemnly, "We're space force officers, and we've come to get faith in victory."

The mental seal process was quite fast. After the faith books were passed among the ten members of the oversight panel, each of whom carefully checked the contents, they signed their names to the notary certificate. Then, under their supervision, the first volunteer received the faith book and sat down in front of the mental seal scanner. In front of him was a small platform on which he placed the book, and which had a red button in the lower right-hand corner. When he opened the faith book, a voice asked, "Are you certain that you want to obtain a faith in this proposition? If so, please press the button. If not, please leave the scanning area."

The question was repeated three times, and each time it was asked, the button glowed red. A positioning apparatus slowly contracted to fix the volunteer's head in place, and then the voice said, "The mental seal procedure is ready to start. Please read the proposition silently and then press the button."

When the button was pressed, it turned green, and after about half a minute, it went out. The voice said, "The mental seal

procedure is complete." The positioning apparatus separated, and then the volunteer got up and left.

After all four officers completed the procedure and returned to the foyer, Keiko Yamasuki carefully looked them over, confirming almost immediately that her perception of their improved moods was not just her imagination. The melancholy and confusion had disappeared from the four pairs of eyes, which now were serene as water.

"How do you feel?" she asked, smiling.

"Excellent," one young officer said, returning her smile. "How it ought to be."

When they left, the Asian woman turned around and added, "Doctor, I really feel great. Thank you."

At that moment, the future was certain, at least in the minds of those four young people.

From that day forward, members of the space force came without pause to obtain faith—at first mostly on their own, but eventually in larger groups. They wore civilian clothes at first, but later most of them wore military uniforms. If more than five people came at a time, the supervisory panel convened a review meeting to verify that no one had been coerced.

One week later, more than a hundred space force members had obtained faith in victory through the mental seal. They ranged in rank from private to senior colonel, the highest rank permitted by national space forces to use the mental seal.

That night, in the moonlight at the Faith Monument, Hines said to Keiko Yamasuki, "Dear, we need to go."

"To the future?"

"That's right. We're not any better than other scientists in the study of the mind, and we've accomplished everything we needed to. We have pushed forward the wheel of history, so now let's go to the future and wait for it."

"How far?"

"Very far, Keiko. Very far. To the day when the Trisolaran probes reach the Solar System."

"Before we do that, let's go back to that house in Tokyo for a while. After all, this age is going to be buried forever."

"Of course, dear. I miss it too."

Six months later, as Keiko Yamasuki sank into the deepening cold and was about to enter hibernation, the cold froze and filtered out the riot of noise in her mind. This brought the thread of her focused thoughts into sharp relief in the lonely darkness, like the moment ten years before when Luo Ji plunged into the icy lake. All of a sudden, her hazy thoughts became unusually clear, like the chilly sky in the dead of winter.

She wanted to shout for the hibernation to stop, but it was too late. The ultra-low temperatures had seeped into her body and she had lost the ability to produce sound.

The operators and doctors noticed that just as she was entering hibernation, her eyes suddenly opened a crack, revealing an expression full of horror and despair. If the cold hadn't frozen her eyelids, her eyes would have been wide open. But this was just a normal reflex during the process that had been seen on previous hibernators, so they paid it no mind.

The UN PDC Wallfacer Project Hearing deliberated the stellar hydrogen bomb test.

The giant breakthrough in computing technology meant that computers were at last capable of handling the theoretical stellar model of a nuclear explosion developed over the past decade, and the manufacture of large-yield stellar hydrogen bombs could begin forthwith. The projected yield of the first bomb was the equivalent of 350 megatons of TNT, or seven times more powerful than the largest hydrogen bomb ever manufactured by humanity. It was impossible for this superbomb to be tested in the atmosphere, and a detonation in an underground shaft of the depth previously used would eject the surrounding rock into the air, so testing on Earth

would require digging an ultra-deep shaft. But even detonating in an ultra-deep shaft would cause powerful shock waves to spread across the world and might have an unanticipated effect on a broad range of geological structures, possibly touching off disasters including earthquakes and tsunamis. Therefore, the stellar hydrogen bomb could only be tested in space. Yet it was impossible in high orbit, because at that distance, the electromagnetic pulse the bomb generated would have a catastrophic effect on Earth's telecommunications and power systems. The ideal test location, then, was on the back side of the moon. However, Rey Diaz chose differently.

"I've decided to conduct the tests on Mercury," he said.

This proposal surprised the representatives in attendance, and they voiced questions about the meaning of the plan.

"According to the basic principles of the Wallfacer plan, I do not have to explain," he answered icily. "The tests should be conducted underground. We need to dig ultra-deep shafts on Mercury."

The Russian representative said, "We can consider tests on the surface of Mercury, but underground tests are too expensive. Digging deep shafts there could cost a hundred times what a similar engineering project would cost on Earth. Besides, the effects of a nuclear bomb on the environment of Mercury would tell us nothing useful."

"Even a surface test on Mercury is impossible!" the US representative said. "To date, Rey Diaz has consumed the most resources of all of the Wallfacers. The time has come to stop him!" This sentiment was echoed by representatives from the UK, France, and Germany.

Rey Diaz said with a laugh, "Even if I used as few resources as Dr. Luo, you'd still be keen to veto my plan." He turned to the rotating chair. "I would ask the chair and each representative to remember that out of all the strategies proposed by the Wallfacers, my plan is most closely in harmony with mainstream defense, to the point that you could view it as part of the mainstream. In absolute numbers the consumption of resources might look large, but a considerable portion of that overlaps the mainstream. Therefore—"

The UK representative cut him off. "You still ought to explain why you need to conduct underground tests on Mercury. Unless you're just doing it to spend money. We can't find any explanation for it."

"Mr. Chair, Representatives," Rey Diaz countered calmly, "you may have noticed that the PDC no longer has even the barest respect for Wallfacers or for the Wallfacer principle. If we have to explain every detail of our plans, then how is the Wallfacer Project meaningful?" One by one, he turned his scorching gaze on every representative, forcing them to turn away.

He went on, "Even so, I am willing to offer an explanation of the issue just raised. The goal of conducting deep underground tests on Mercury is to blast out a large cave on the planet to serve as a future Mercury base. This is clearly the most economical way of conducting an engineering project of this kind."

His words stirred up whispers, and one representative asked, "Wallfacer Rey Diaz, do you mean you want to use Mercury as the launch base for stellar hydrogen bombs?"

With confidence, Rey Diaz answered, "Yes. Current strategic theory in mainstream defense holds that emphasis should be placed on the outer planets, and so the inner planets, which are not believed to be defensively significant, have not been given sufficient attention. The Mercury base I have planned is intended to mend this weak link in mainstream defense."

"He's afraid of the sun, but he wants to go to the planet closest to it. Isn't that a little strange?" the US representative said. There was a bit of laughter, followed by a warning from the chair.

"It doesn't matter, Mr. Chair. I've grown accustomed to this lack of respect. I was used to it even before I became a Wallfacer," Rey Diaz said with a wave of his hand. "But all of you should respect the facts at hand. When the outer planets and Earth have fallen, the Mercury base will be the last bastion of humanity. Backed by the sun and situated amid the cover of radiation, it will be the most rugged of positions."

"Wallfacer Rey Diaz, does this mean that your plan's entire significance lies in a last stand when humanity's situation is already

hopeless? This is quite consistent with your character," the French representative said.

"Gentlemen, we can't simply refuse to consider the final resistance," Rey Diaz said gravely.

"Very well, Wallfacer Rey Diaz," the chair said. "Now, would you be able to tell us, in your overall deployment scenario, how many stellar hydrogen bombs you'll need, all told?"

"The more the better. Manufacture as many as the Earth has capacity to produce. The specific number depends on the yield that hydrogen bombs will be able to achieve in the future, but according to current figures, the first batch in the deployment plan requires at least a million."

Laughter shook the auditorium at Rey Diaz's words.

"Evidently Wallfacer Rey Diaz doesn't just want to make a small sun. He wants to make a small galaxy!" the US representative said loudly. Then he leaned toward Rey Diaz. "Do you really think that the ocean's protium, deuterium, and tritium were prepared just for you? Because of your perverted affection for the bomb, the Earth should be turned into a bomb workshop?"

By this point Rey Diaz was the only one in the assembly with a straight face. He waited quietly until the clamor he had sparked died down, and then said, one word at a time, "This is the ultimate war of the human race, so the number I ask for is not at all large. But I did anticipate today's outcome. Nevertheless, I will work hard. I will build bombs. I will build as many as I can, I tell you. I will work hard and I won't stop."

In response, the representatives of the US, UK, and France put forth a joint proposal, P269, to terminate the strategic plan of Wallfacer Rey Diaz.

Only two colors were visible on the surface of Mercury: black and gold. The black was the planet's land, and its low reflectance meant that even under close illumination from the fierce sun, it remained a sheet of black. The gold was the sun, which occupied

a considerable portion of the sky. In its broad wheel you could clearly see the surging of its fiery seas and the sunspots drifting by like black clouds, and, at its edges, the graceful dance of solar prominences.

And on this hard chunk of rock suspended atop the sun's fiery sea, humanity was planting another small sun.

With the completion of the space elevator, humanity had begun the large-scale exploration of the other planets in the Solar System. Manned spacecraft landings on Mars and the moons of Jupiter had not caused much of a stir because people knew that the purpose of these expeditions was much clearer and more practical than in the past: They were purely intended to establish bases for the defense of the Solar System. These voyages, which relied mainly on chemical-propulsion rockets and spacecraft, were merely the tiniest of steps toward that goal. Initial explorations focused primarily on the outer planets, but as the study of space strategy deepened, neglecting the strategic value of the inner planets was increasingly called into question. Hence the exploration of Venus and Mercury was stepped up, and so it was that the PDC narrowly passed Rey Diaz's plan to test the stellar hydrogen bomb on Mercury.

Excavating the shaft through the rock of Mercury was the first large-scale engineering project humanity had undertaken on another planet in the Solar System. Because construction could only take place during Mercury's night, in stretches of eighty-eight Earth days, the project would take three years to complete. However, in the end it only reached one-third of the projected depth, due to the discovery of an unusually hard layer farther down, a mixture of metal and rock. Continued excavation would be much slower and far more costly. Ultimately, it was decided to terminate the project. If tests were carried out at the present depth, the surrounding rock would most certainly be ejected by the blast and would form a crater, making it basically a watered-down atmospheric test. And because of the interference from the surrounding crust, it would be far harder to observe the test's outcome than with a purely atmospheric test. But Rey Diaz thought that if a cover were fitted onto

this crater, it could still serve as a base, and insisted on conducting the test underground at the current depth.

The test was carried out at dawn. Sunrise on Mercury was a process that took over ten hours, and a faint light had just appeared on the horizon. When the detonation countdown reached zero, rings of ripples centered on ground zero spread outward, and the ground on Mercury seemed momentarily to become soft as satin. Then, at the blast site, a mountain slowly rose like the back of a waking giant. When the peak had risen to around three thousand meters, the entire mountain exploded, sending billions of tons of mud and rock flying into the air in a towering display of rage by the ground toward the sky. And alongside the surging ground came the radiant light of the underground nuclear fireball, which shone on the rock and earth flying through the air to cause a grand spectacle of fireworks in the black Mercury sky. The fireball lasted for five minutes, as chunks of rock fell to the ground amid a nuclear glow, before it went out.

Ten hours after the conclusion of the blast, observers noticed that a ring had appeared around Mercury. This was due to the considerable amount of rock that had achieved cosmic velocity in the violent explosion and had turned into myriad satellites of various sizes. They spread out evenly in orbit, making Mercury the first ringed terrestrial planet. The ring was thin, and as it sparkled in the harsh light of the sun, it looked almost like someone had taken a highlighter to the planet.

Another proportion of the rocks achieved escape velocity and left Mercury behind entirely, becoming satellites of the sun in their own right and forming an extremely sparse asteroid belt in Mercury's orbit.

Rey Diaz lived underground not out of any concern for security, but because of his heliophobia. The claustrophobic environment, far removed from the sunshine, made him feel a little more comfortable. He watched the live broadcast of the Mercury test from the basement where he lived. It wasn't actually live, since the

images took about seven minutes to reach Earth. When the blast on Mercury had concluded and the rock rain was still falling in the post-fireball darkness, he received a telephone call from the rotating chair of the PDC, who said that the tremendous power of the stellar hydrogen bombs had made a deep impression on the PDC leadership, and that the permanent member states had requested that the next Wallfacer hearing be held as soon as possible to discuss the bombs' manufacture and deployment. The chair said that although the number of bombs Rey Diaz had requested was an impossibility, the major powers were indeed interested in the production of this weapon.

Over ten hours after the conclusion of the Mercury test, as he was watching Mercury's new ring sparkling on the television, a guard's voice came over the intercom to tell him that his psychiatrist had arrived for an appointment.

"I never asked for any psychiatrist. Send him away!" He felt exasperated, like he had suffered some great indignity.

"Don't be like that, Mr. Rey Diaz," said another, calmer voice, evidently the visitor's. "I can let you see the sun . . ."

"Get the hell out," he shouted, but then immediately changed his mind. "No. Seize that idiot and find out where he came from."

". . . because I know the cause of your condition," the voice continued, still calm. "Mr. Rey Diaz, please believe me. You and I are the only ones in the world who know."

At this, Rey Diaz suddenly grew alert, and said, "Let him in." He stared at the ceiling for a few seconds through haggard eyes, then got up slowly and picked up a tie from the cluttered sofa, only to toss it back again. He walked over to the mirror, straightened his collar, and combed his hair with his hands, like he was preparing for a solemn event.

He knew that it was indeed a solemn event.

The visitor was a handsome middle-aged man who walked in but did not introduce himself. He frowned slightly at the room's heavy odor of cigars and alcohol, then simply stood there calmly as Rey Diaz looked him over.

"Why do I have the feeling I've seen you before?" he said, as he looked at the visitor.

"That's not strange, Mr. Rey Diaz. Everyone says I look like Superman, from the old movies."

"Do you really believe you're Superman?" Rey Diaz said. He sat down on the sofa, picked up a cigar, bit off the end, and began to light it.

"That question shows that you already know what kind of man I am. I'm not Superman, Mr. Rey Diaz. Nor are you." As he spoke, the younger man took a step forward. Rey Diaz found that the man was standing directly in front of him, peering down at him through the cloud of smoke he had just exhaled. So he stood up.

The visitor said, "Wallfacer Manuel Rey Diaz, I am your Wallbreaker."

Gloomily, Rey Diaz nodded.

"May I sit down?" the Wallbreaker asked.

"You may not," Rey Diaz said, slowly blowing smoke in the other man's face.

"Don't be depressed," the Wallbreaker said with a considerate smile.

"I'm not," Rey Diaz said, his voice cold and hard like stone.

The Wallbreaker walked over to the wall and flipped a switch. Somewhere, ventilator fans started humming.

"Don't mess with things around here," Rey Diaz warned.

"You need a little fresh air. And, more than that, you need sun. I'm quite familiar with this room, Wallfacer Rey Diaz. In the images sent by the sophons I have often watched you pace back and forth like a caged beast. No one in the world has stared at you for as long as I have, and on those days, believe me, it wasn't any easier for me."

The Wallbreaker looked straight at Rey Diaz, whose expression was as blank as an ice sculpture, and then he went on. "Compared to Frederick Tyler, you are a brilliant strategist. A competent Wallfacer. Please trust that this is not flattery. I must admit that for quite some time, for nearly a decade, you had me fooled. Your

mania for the superbomb, such an inefficient weapon in a space battle, successfully concealed your own strategic direction, and for a long while I couldn't find any clue to crack your true strategy. I struggled in the maze that you laid down, and at one point almost despaired." The Wallbreaker looked up at the ceiling, overcome by the memory of those difficult times. "Later, I thought of checking out information from before you became a Wallbreaker, but this wasn't easy, because the sophons were unable to help. You know, in those days, only a limited number of sophons had reached Earth, and as a South American head of state you had not attracted their attention. So I had to resort to conventional means to gather materials. This took three years. In those materials, one man stood out: William Cosmo. You met him in secret on three occasions. The sophons did not record the content of your conversations, so I will never know, but for the head of a small, undeveloped country to meet three times with a Western astrophysicist is highly unusual. We now know that at that time you had already been preparing to become a Wallfacer.

"No doubt what interested you was the fruit of Dr. Cosmo's research. How those results first came to your attention I am not clear on at this time, but you had a background in engineering, and you had the successful experience of your socialism-loving predecessor, who had equal enthusiasm for a nation ruled by engineers. This was a major reason why you became his successor. So you ought to have had the capability and sensitivity to notice the potential significance of Cosmo's research.

"Once the Trisolar Crisis began, Dr. Cosmo's research team worked on studying the atmosphere of the Trisolaran stellar system. They speculated that the atmosphere had been produced by a former planet that had collided with a star. As it collided, it broke apart the outer layers, its photosphere and troposphere, causing the stellar matter inside to be ejected into space and form a surrounding atmosphere. Due to the total irregularity of the system's motion, there are times when the stars pass each other quite closely, and at those times, one star's atmosphere is dispersed by the gravity of the other star, only to be replenished by eruptions on the stellar

surface. These aren't constant eruptions, more like volcanoes that experience sudden outbreaks. This is the reason for the continual contraction and expansion of the stars' atmosphere. To prove this hypothesis, Cosmo searched the universe to find another star with an atmosphere that was ejected following a collision with a planet. In the third year of the Crisis Era, he succeeded.

"Dr. Cosmo's team discovered planetary system 275E1, about eighty-four light-years from the Solar System. Hubble II had not gone into operation at that time, so they used the wobble method. By observing and calculating the wobble frequency and light mask, they learned that the planet was quite close to its parent star. At first, this discovery did not attract too much attention because the astronomy community had by then discovered more than two hundred planetary systems, but further observations revealed a shocking fact: The distance between planet and star was continually shrinking, and the rate of shrinkage was accelerating. This meant that humanity would, for the first time, observe a planet falling into a star. One year later—or, rather, eighty-four years prior to observation—it happened. Observational conditions at the time meant that the collision could only be determined based on the gravitational wobble and the periodic light mask. But then something wondrous happened: A spiral of matter appeared around the star, and this spiral flow continued to expand. It looked like a mainspring slowly unwinding with the star as its center. Cosmo and his colleagues realized that the material flow had been ejected from the planet's crash point. The chunk of rock had crashed through the shell of that distant sun and ejected its stellar matter into space, where, due to the star's own rotation, it formed a spiral.

"There were several key pieces of data here, sir. The star is a yellow G2 class with an absolute magnitude of 4.3 and a diameter of 1.2 million kilometers. Quite similar to our sun. The planet was about four percent of the mass of Earth, or a little smaller than Mercury, and the spiral cloud of material produced from the collision had a radius of up to three AU, more than the distance between our sun and the asteroid belt.

"And it was in this discovery that I found the crack with which to break open your real strategic plan. Now, as your Wallbreaker, I will explain your grand strategy.

"Supposing that you are ultimately able to obtain those million or more stellar hydrogen bombs, you will, as you promised to the PDC, stockpile them all on Mercury. If the bombs are detonated in the rock of Mercury, they'll be like a turbo-engine decelerating the planet. Eventually its speed will no longer be able to keep it in low orbit and it will fall into the sun. Next, what happened on 275E1 eighty-four light-years away is reenacted here: Mercury punctures the sun's convective shell and ejects a huge amount of stellar matter from its radiation layer into space at high speed; which, as the sun rotates, forms a spiral atmosphere similar to that in 275E1. The sun differs from the Trisolaran system in that, as a lone star, it will never cross paths with another star, and therefore its atmosphere will continue to increase uninhibited until it becomes even thicker than the atmosphere of those stars. This was also confirmed by observations of 275E1. When the spiral flow of ejected matter expands outward from the sun like an unwound mainspring, its thickness eventually passes Mars's orbit, at which point a magnificent chain reaction begins.

"First, three terrestrial planets—Venus, Earth, and Mars—pass through the sun's spiraling atmosphere, losing speed due to the atmospheric friction and turning into three giant meteors that eventually crash into the sun. But well before this happens, the Earth's atmosphere is stripped away by the intense friction of the solar matter. The oceans evaporate, and the lost atmosphere and evaporated oceans turn the Earth into a giant comet whose tail extends along its orbit to wrap all the way around the sun. The surface of the Earth returns to the fiery magma sea of its birth, where no life can survive.

"When Venus, Earth, and Mars crash into the sun, it exacerbates the sun's ejection of solar matter into space. The single spiral flow of matter increases to four flows. Because the total mass of those three planets is forty times that of Mercury, and because their higher orbits mean they impact the sun at a much

higher speed, each new spiral is ejected with a ferocity tens of times greater than Mercury's. The existing spiral atmosphere rapidly expands until its edge approaches the orbit of Jupiter.

"Friction produces only a very small deceleration effect on the huge mass of Jupiter, so it is quite some time before the spiral has a noticeable effect on Jupiter's orbit. But Jupiter's satellites meet one of the following two fates: friction strips them away from Jupiter and they lose speed and fall into the sun, or they lose speed in Jovian orbit and fall into the liquid planet.

"As the chain reaction continues, the decrease in speed from the spiral atmosphere, though small, is still present, and Jupiter's orbit gradually decays. This causes it to pass through an increasingly dense atmosphere whose friction accelerates its loss in speed, thereby causing the orbit to decay even more quickly. . . . In this way, Jupiter eventually falls into the sun, too. Its mass is six hundred times that of the previous four planets, and the impact that such a massive body makes on the sun will, even according to the most conservative reasoning, produce an even more violent ejection of stellar matter, increasing the density of the spiral atmosphere and exacerbating the bitter cold of Uranus and Neptune. But another possibility is more likely: The fall of the Jovian giant pushes the edge of the spiral atmosphere out to the orbit of Uranus or even Neptune, and though the atmosphere is quite thin at the top, friction's decelerating effects pull these two planets and their satellites toward the sun, too. What state the sun will be in and how the Solar System will have been transformed after the chain reaction finishes and the four dense terrestrial planets and four gas giants are consumed is unknowable. But one thing is certain: For life and for civilization, this will be a hell even crueler than attack by Trisolaris.

"As for Trisolaris, the Solar System is their only hope before their planet is engulfed by their stars. There is no other world they can migrate to in time, and therefore, their civilization will follow humanity into total destruction.

"This is your strategy: death for both sides. Once everything

is prepared, with all of the stellar hydrogen bombs in place on Mercury, you will use it to coerce Trisolaris to surrender and gain the ultimate victory for humanity.

"What I've just presented is the outcome of the years of work that I, your Wallbreaker, have performed. I am not seeking your opinion or critique, because I know that all of this is true."

As the Wallbreaker spoke, Rey Diaz had been listening quietly. The cigar in his hand was more than halfway gone, and he now turned it about as if appreciating the glow of the tip.

The Wallbreaker sat down on the sofa, close beside him. Like a teacher evaluating a student's homework, he continued unfatigued: "Mr. Rey Diaz, I said you are a brilliant strategist, or at least you demonstrated many excellent qualities in the formulation and implementation of this plan.

"For one thing, you took advantage of your own background. Right now, people clearly remember the humiliations you and your country suffered when the Orinoco nuclear facility was forced to be taken down as you were developing nuclear energy. The whole world saw your gloomy face, and you took advantage of outside perceptions of your paranoia about nuclear weapons to reduce or even eliminate any possible suspicion.

"But every detail in the execution of your plan demonstrates your talent as well. I will mention but one example: During the Mercury test, you wanted the rock to be blasted into the sky, but you insisted on excavating an ultra-deep shaft in a farsighted gambit. You quite precisely understood the tolerance of the PDC's permanent member states for the cost of this enormous undertaking, and that is admirable.

"But you had one major slipup. Why did the first test have to be carried out on Mercury? There would have been plenty of time to bring the bombs there in a later phase, but maybe you got impatient and wanted to see the outcome of a stellar hydrogen bomb blast there. You saw it: lots of rock matter blasted to escape velocity, perhaps even exceeding your expectations. You were satisfied. But this provided the final confirmation of my hypothesis.

"Yes, Mr. Rey Diaz, even given all my previous work, without that final event I might never have been able to determine your true strategic intentions. The notion was too mad. But it was grand, and even beautiful. If the chain reaction triggered by Mercury's fall actually took place, then it would be the most magnificent movement of the entire symphony of the Solar System . . . although, unfortunately, humanity would only be able to enjoy the first section. Mr. Rey Diaz, you are a Wallfacer with the makings of a god. It is my honor to become your Wallbreaker."

The Wallbreaker stood up and offered Rey Diaz a genial bow.

Rey Diaz did not look at him. He took a puff of his cigar and blew out the smoke as he continued to examine it. "Fine. Then I'll ask the question that Tyler asked."

The Wallbreaker asked the question for him. "If what I say is true, then so what?"

Rey Diaz stared at the lit end of the cigar and nodded.

"My answer is the same as Tyler's Wallbreaker's: The Lord does not care."

Rey Diaz lifted his eyes from the cigar and looked questioningly at his Wallbreaker.

"You look crude, but your mind is sharp. Yet in the depths of your soul, you're still crude. Your nature is that of a crude man. And this crudeness is revealed in the basis of this strategic plan. It's greedy. Humanity doesn't have the ability to manufacture so many stellar hydrogen bombs. Even if all of Earth's industrial resources were exhausted, it wouldn't produce even one-tenth of that number. And a million stellar hydrogen bombs is far from enough to decelerate Mercury into the sun. With a soldier's recklessness, you formulated this impossible plan, and then stubbornly carried it forward step by step with the wily calculations of a superior strategist. Wallfacer Rey Diaz, this is truly a tragedy."

As Rey Diaz looked at the Wallbreaker, his expression gradually filled with an elusive softness, and hints of convulsions showed on his coarsely lined face, gradually taking shape, until at last his suppressed laughter erupted.

"Ha ha ha ha ha . . ." he laughed, pointing at the Wallbreaker. "Superman! Ha ha ha ha. I remember now. That . . . that old Superman. He could fly, and he could reverse the rotation of the Earth, but when he was riding a horse . . . ha ha ha ha . . . when he was riding a horse, he fell and broke his neck . . . ah ha ha ha . . ."

"It was Christopher Reeve, the actor who played Superman, who fell and broke his neck," the Wallbreaker corrected him, quietly.

"Do you imagine . . . imagine that your fate will be better than his? Ha ha ha ha . . ."

"Since coming here, I have no regard for my fate. I've lived a full life," the Wallbreaker said evenly. "But you, Mr. Rey Diaz, ought to think about your own fate."

"You'll die first," Rey Diaz said, smiling with his entire face as he pressed the cigar end directly between the Wallbreaker's eyes. Then, when the Wallbreaker was covering his face with his hands, Rey Diaz took up a military-issue belt from the sofa, wrapped it around the Wallbreaker's neck, and strangled him with every ounce of his strength. Although the Wallbreaker was young, he had no way to defend himself against Rey Diaz's agile strength, and was thrown to the floor by his neck. Rey Diaz bellowed, "I'll wring your neck! You bastard! Who sent you here to play smart? Who the hell are you? Bastard! I'll wring your neck!" He tightened the belt and slammed the Wallbreaker's head into the ground repeatedly, to the crunch of teeth smacking into the floor. When the guards burst in to separate them, the Wallbreaker's face was purple, he was foaming at the mouth, and his eyes were protruding like a goldfish's.

Rey Diaz, still in a fury, struggled with the guards as he continued to shout, "Wring his neck! String him up and hang him! Right now! This is part of the plan! Do you fucking hear me? Part of the plan!"

But the three guards did not carry out his order. One of them held Rey Diaz tightly while the other two lifted up the Wallbreaker, who had recovered his breath somewhat, and started to carry him out.

"Just wait, you bastard. You won't die easy," he said, abandoning his efforts to escape the guard and have another go at the Wallbreaker. He let out a long sigh.

The Wallbreaker looked back over the guard's shoulder, a smile on his bruised and swollen face. He opened up a mouth that was missing several teeth and said, "I've lived a full life."

PDC Wallfacer Hearing

As the meeting commenced, the United States, United Kingdom, France, and Germany put up another proposition, this one demanding the immediate suspension of Rey Diaz's position as Wallfacer and his trial before the International Court of Justice for crimes against humanity.

The US representative declared, "After substantial investigation, we believe that Rey Diaz's strategic intent as disclosed by the Wallbreaker is credible. What we are facing now is a person whose crime dwarfs all of the crimes ever committed in human history. We were unable to find a single law applicable to his crime, so we recommend that the crime of Extinction of Life on Earth be added to international law, and that Rey Diaz be tried under it."

Rey Diaz appeared quite relaxed at the hearing. Sneering, he said to the US representative, "You've been trying to get rid of me, haven't you? Ever since the Wallfacer Project began, you have all applied a double standard to the Wallfacers. I'm the one you like least."

The UK representative retorted, "Wallfacer Rey Diaz's claim is baseless. In fact, the countries he is accusing are the ones who invested the most money into his plan, far exceeding what they invested in the other three Wallfacers."

"Sure," Rey Diaz said with a nod, "but the real reason you invested so heavily in my plan is because you wanted to get your hands on the stellar hydrogen bombs."

"Ridiculous! What would we do with them?" the US representative shot back. "They're incredibly inefficient weapons in a space battle, and on the Earth, there's no practical significance even for those old twenty-megaton hydrogen bombs, much less a three-hundred-megaton monster."

Rey Diaz responded calmly, "But the bombs will be the most

313

effective weapon in battles on other planets, particularly in wars among humans. On the desolate surface of other planets, there's no need to be concerned with civilian casualties or environmental damage, so you're free to carry out wide-area destruction, or even a devastating sweep of the entire surface. Here's where the stellar hydrogen bombs will prove useful. You must have anticipated that, as humanity expands into the Solar System, Earth's conflicts will expand outward as well. This won't change even with Trisolaris as a common enemy, and you're preparing for it. Right now, it's politically indefensible to develop superweapons for use against humans, so you took advantage of me to make them."

The US representative said, "That's the preposterous logic of a terrorist and a dictator. Rey Diaz is the kind of man who, granted the status and power of a Wallfacer, turns the Wallfacer Project into as big a danger as the Trisolaran invasion. We must take decisive action to correct this mistake."

"They're as good as their word," Rey Diaz said, turning to Garanin, the incumbent rotating chair. "The CIA has men waiting outside to arrest me as soon as I go outside after this hearing."

The rotating chair glanced in the direction of the US representative, who was fiddling intently with his pen. Garanin had first taken office at the start of the Wallfacer Project, and even he had forgotten the number of short terms in office he had served during the ensuing two decades. But this was the last time. Now white-haired, he was about to retire.

"Wallfacer Rey Diaz, if what you say is true, then that is inappropriate. So long as the principles of the Wallfacer Project still hold, Wallfacers have legal immunity, and none of their words and actions can be used as evidence to charge them of a crime," he said.

"Additionally, please remember that this is international territory," the Japanese representative said.

"So does that mean," the US representative said, raising a pencil, "that even when Rey Diaz is about to detonate the million superbombs he's buried on Mercury, society still won't be able to charge him with a crime?"

"According to the relevant provisions in the Wallfacer Act, placing limitations and curbs on the strategic plans of Wallfacers who exhibit dangerous tendencies is an entirely separate matter from the Wallfacer's own legal immunity," Garanin said.

"Rey Diaz's crimes have crossed outside the boundary of legal immunity. He must be punished. This is a precondition for the continued existence of the Wallfacer Project," the UK representative said.

"May I remind the chair and the representatives," Rey Diaz said, rising from his seat, "that this is a PDC Wallfacer hearing, and that I'm not on trial."

"You'll stand in court soon," the US representative said, with a chilly smile.

"I agree with Wallfacer Rey Diaz. We should return to the discussion of his strategic plan," Garanin said, seizing the opportunity to temporarily bypass the thorny issue.

The Japanese representative broke his silence. "From the way it looks now, the representatives have reached a consensus on the following point: Rey Diaz's strategic plan exhibits dangerous tendencies toward clear violations of human rights, and according to the relevant principles in the Wallfacer Act, it should be stopped."

"Then Proposition P269, proposed at the previous Wallfacer hearing, regarding halting Rey Diaz's strategic plan, can now be put to a vote," Garanin said.

"Mr. Chair, wait one moment." Rey Diaz raised his hand. "Before the vote, I hope I might be able to offer a final explanation of some of the details of my plan."

"If they're just details, is this really necessary?" someone asked.

"Save it for court," the UK representative said sarcastically.

"No, these details are important," Rey Diaz persisted. "Right now, let us assume that what the Wallbreaker has disclosed about my strategic intentions is true. One representative spoke of the moment when the million hydrogen bombs deployed on Mercury are ready to be detonated, at which point I will face the omnipresent sophons and declare to Trisolaris humanity's intent to die with them. What will happen then?"

"The Trisolarans' reaction can't be predicted, but on Earth, it's certain that billions of people will want to wring your neck, just like you did to that Wallbreaker," the French representative said.

"Exactly. So I took certain measures to deal with such a situation. Take a look at this." Rey Diaz raised his left hand and displayed his wristwatch to the assembly. It was entirely black, and the dial was twice as large and thick as a normal men's watch, although it didn't appear large on his thick wrist. "This is a transmitter sending a signal through a space link directly to Mercury."

"You'll use it to send the detonation signal?" someone asked.

"Precisely the opposite. It sends a non-detonation signal."

His words focused the attention of the entire assembly. He went on: "The system is code-named 'cradle,' meaning that when the cradle stops rocking, the baby will wake. It sends a continuous signal, received continuously on Mercury. If the signal is interrupted, then the system will immediately detonate the hydrogen bomb."

"It's called a dead-man's switch," the US representative said stoically. "In the Cold War there was research into using anti-triggers and dead-man's switches on strategic nukes, but they were never implemented. Only a madman would actually do it."

Rey Diaz brought down his left hand and covered the cradle with his sleeve. "I was taught this wonderful idea not by an expert in nuclear strategy but by an American film. In it, a man has one of these gadgets that sends out a continuous signal, but if his heart stops beating, the signal is terminated. Another man has a bomb strapped to him that's impossible to remove, and if the bomb doesn't receive the signal, it'll explode. So even though this hapless fool doesn't like the first guy, he has to do everything he can to protect him. . . . I like watching American blockbusters. Even today I can still recognize the old version of Superman."

"Do you mean that this device is tied to your heartbeat?" the Japanese representative asked. He reached over to Rey Diaz, who was standing next to him, to touch the device under his sleeve, but Rey Diaz moved his arm and stood a bit farther away.

"Of course. But the cradle is more advanced and refined than

that. It monitors not just the heartbeat but lots of other physiological indicators such as blood pressure, body temperature, and so forth, and conducts a comprehensive analysis of these parameters. If they're not normal, then it immediately stops the anti-trigger signal in the dead-man's switch. It can also recognize many of my simple voice commands."

A nervous-looking man entered the auditorium and whispered something into Garanin's ear. Before he had finished whispering, Garanin glanced up at Rey Diaz with a peculiar look in his eyes, which did not escape the keen-eyed representatives.

"There's a way to disarm your cradle. Countermeasures for anti-triggers were studied during the Cold War, too," the US representative said.

"It's not my cradle. It's the cradle for those hydrogen bombs. If the cradle stops rocking, they'll wake up," Rey Diaz said.

"I've thought of the same technique," the German representative said. "When the signal is transmitted from your watch to Mercury, it must pass through a complicated communications link. Destroying or shielding any node, then using a false signal source to continue to transmit the anti-trigger signal farther down the chain, will render your cradle system useless."

"That is indeed a problem," Rey Diaz said, with a nod at the German representative. "Without the sophons, the problem is easily solved. All the nodes are loaded with an identical encryption algorithm that generates every signal sent. To the outside world, it looks as if the signal values are random and different every time, but the cradle's sender and recipient produce a sequence of values that are identical. Only when the recipient receives a signal corresponding to its own sequence is the signal considered valid. Without this encryption algorithm, the signal sent out by your false source won't match the recipient's sequence. But the damn sophons can detect the algorithm."

"You've perhaps come up with another approach?" someone asked.

"A crude approach. Me, all my approaches are clumsy and crude,"

Rey Diaz said, with a self-mocking laugh. "I have increased the sensitivity of each node's monitoring of its own state. Specifically, each communication node is composed of several units that may be separated by a large distance, but are connected into a whole by continuous communication. If any one unit fails, the entire node will issue a command terminating the anti-trigger, after which, even if the false signal source resumes sending a signal to the next node, it will not be acknowledged. The monitoring of every unit can achieve a microsecond level of accuracy, which means that—using the German representative's approach—every unit of a node must be simultaneously destroyed and the signal resumed from the false signal source within the space of a microsecond. Every node is composed of at least three units, but may have dozens of them. These units are separated by a distance of about three hundred kilometers. Each one is built to be extremely rugged, and it will issue its warning upon any outside touch. Causing these units to fail within the space of a microsecond might be possible for the Trisolarans, but it's not currently possible for humans."

His final sentence put everyone on alert.

"I have just received a report that the thing on Rey Diaz's wrist has been sending out an electromagnetic signal," Garanin said. The atmosphere of the assembly turned tense at the news. "I'd like to ask you, Wallfacer Rey Diaz: Is the signal from your wristwatch being sent to Mercury?"

Rey Diaz chuckled a few times, then said, "Why would I be sending it to Mercury? There's nothing there but a giant pit. Besides, the cradle's space communication link hasn't been set up yet. No, no, no. You don't need to worry. The signal isn't going to Mercury. It's going somewhere in New York City, very close to us."

The air froze, and everyone in the assembly, apart from Rey Diaz, stood as shocked as wooden chickens.

"If the signal sustaining the cradle is terminated, what will it trigger?" the UK representative asked sharply, no longer attempting to mask his tension.

"Oh, something will be triggered, all right," Rey Diaz said to

him with a broad laugh. "I've been a Wallfacer for more than twenty years, and I've always been able to get a few things of my own."

"Well then, Mr. Rey Diaz, would you be able to answer an even more direct question?" the French representative said. He looked entirely calm, but there was a tremble in his voice. "How many lives will you, or will we, be responsible for?"

Rey Diaz widened his eyes at the Frenchman, as if he thought the question bizarre. "What? The number of people makes a difference? I thought all of you here were respectable gentlemen who prize human rights above all. What's the difference between one life and 8.2 million? If it's the former, then you don't have to respect it?"

The US representative stood up and said, "More than twenty years ago when the Wallfacer Project began, we pointed out what he was." Pointing a finger at Rey Diaz and spraying saliva as he spoke, he strove to contain himself, but ended up losing control. "He's a terrorist. An evil, filthy terrorist! A devil! You unstopped the bottle and let him loose, and you must take responsibility! The UN must be held responsible!" he shouted hysterically, sending his papers flying.

"Calm down, Mr. Representative," Rey Diaz said with a slight smile. "The cradle is very sensitive to my physiological indices. If I were to go into hysterics like you, if my mood wavered, it would immediately stop sending the anti-trigger signal. So you, and all of you sitting here, shouldn't make me too upset. It would be better for all of us if you could try and keep me happy."

"What are your conditions?" Garanin asked softly.

A bit of sadness crept into the smile on Rey Diaz's face as he turned toward Garanin and shook his head. "Mr. Chair, what other conditions could I name? To leave here and return to my own country. A charter plane is waiting for me at Kennedy Airport."

The assembly was silent. Unconsciously, they had all gradually turned their attention from Rey Diaz to the US representative, who, unable to stand all the eyes on him, threw himself back into his chair and hissed, "Get the hell out."

Rey Diaz slowly nodded, then stood up and walked out.

"Mr. Rey Diaz, I'll take you home," Garanin said, leaving the rostrum.

Rey Diaz stood waiting for Garanin as he walked over, less nimbly than before. "Thank you, Mr. Chair. I thought you might like to get out of here too."

The two were at the door when Rey Diaz grabbed Garanin and turned with him back toward the auditorium. "Gentlemen, I won't miss this place. I've wasted these two decades, and no one here understands me. I want to go back to my homeland, back to my people. Yes, my homeland and my people. I miss them."

To everyone's surprise, the big man's eyes shone with tears. At last he said, "I want to go back to my homeland. This is not part of the plan."

When he walked out the door of the UN General Assembly building, Rey Diaz opened his arms wide to the sun and called out with relish, "Ah, my sun!" His two-decade-long heliophobia had vanished.

Rey Diaz's flight took off, and crossed the eastern coastline to fly over the vast Atlantic Ocean.

In the cabin, Garanin said to him, "With me here, this aircraft is safe. Please tell me the location of the device you have connected to the dead-man's switch."

"There's no device. There's nothing. It was just a trick to escape." Rey Diaz took off his watch and handed it to Garanin. "This is just a simple transmitter converted from a Motorola phone. It's not connected to my heartbeat, either. It's been turned off. Keep it as a souvenir."

For a long time neither of them spoke. Then Garanin sighed and said, "How did this happen? The Wallfacers' privilege of sealed-off strategic thinking was meant to be used against the sophons and Trisolaris. But you and Tyler both used it against humanity."

"There's nothing strange about that," Rey Diaz said. He sat next to the window, enjoying the sunlight shining in from the outside. "Right now, the greatest obstacle to humanity's survival comes from itself."

Six hours later, the plane touched down at Caracas International Airport on the Caribbean coast. Garanin did not get off. He would be taking the plane back to the UN.

When they parted, Rey Diaz said, "Don't abort the Wallfacer Project. It really is a hope amid this war. There are still two Wallfacers. Please wish them the best for me."

"I won't be seeing them, either," Garanin said, with emotion. By the time Rey Diaz walked off, leaving him alone in the cabin, he was in tears.

The sky over Caracas was as clear as in New York. Rey Diaz walked down the airstair and smelled the familiar tropical atmosphere, then bent down and gave a long kiss to the ground of his homeland. Then, guarded by a large detachment of military police, he took a motorcade to the city. After half an hour on a winding mountain road, they entered the capital and drove up to the city center and Plaza Bolívar. At the statue of Simón Bolívar, Rey Diaz got out of the car and stood on the statue's base. Above him on horseback was the great armor-clad hero who had defeated the Spanish and tried to establish a unified Republic of Gran Colombia in South America. In front of him, a crowd of frenetic people boiled under the sun, swelling forward, only to be met with the vigorous resistance of the military police. Shots were fired into the air, but the tide of people eventually surged past the police line and poured toward the living Bolívar at the foot of the statue.

Rey Diaz held up his hands, and, with tears in his eyes, called out to the crowd in a voice dripping with emotion, "Ah, my people!"

The first stone thrown by his people struck him on his outstretched left hand, the second hit him in the chest, and the third smashed into his forehead and nearly knocked him out. After that, the people's stones came like raindrops, and had practically buried his lifeless body by the end. The last stone that hit Wallfacer Rey Diaz was thrown by an old woman, who struggled to carry it up to his corpse, then said, in Spanish, "Evildoer! You would kill everyone. My grandson would have been there. You'd have killed my grandson!"

Then, using all the strength in her trembling hands, she slammed her stone against Rey Diaz's broken skull, where it lay exposed beneath the pile of rocks.

Time is the one thing that can't be stopped. Like a sharp blade, it silently cuts through hard and soft, constantly advancing. Nothing is capable of jolting it even the slightest bit, but it changes everything.

The same year as the Mercury test, Chang Weisi retired. In his final media appearance, he frankly acknowledged that he himself had no confidence in victory, but this did not affect history's high opinion of the work of the space force's first commander. Working for so many years in a state of anxiety had damaged his health, and he died at the age of sixty-eight. The general was lucid on his deathbed and mentioned Zhang Beihai's name many times.

After leaving her second term in office, Secretary General Say launched the Human Memorial Project, whose goal was the comprehensive collection of data and commemorative artifacts of human civilization that would ultimately be sent out into the cosmos on unmanned spacecraft. The project's most influential component was called the Human Diary, a Web site that was set up to allow as many people as possible to record their lifetimes in the form of text and images from their everyday lives, to become part of the data of civilization. The Human Diary Web site eventually grew to have more than two billion users and formed the largest-ever body of information on the Internet. Later, the PDC, believing that the Human Memorial Project contributed to defeatism, passed a resolution stopping its further development, and even equated it with Escapism. But Say continued to pour her individual efforts into the project until she passed away at the age of eighty-four.

After retirement, Garanin and Kent made the same choice: to seclude themselves in that Garden of Eden in northern Europe where Luo Ji had lived for five years. They were never again seen by the outside world, and no one even knew the exact date they

died. But one thing was certain: They lived a long time. Some said that the two of them reached the century mark before dying a natural death.

Just as Keiko Yamasuki had predicted, Wu Yue spent the remainder of his life in depression and confusion. He worked for more than a decade on the Human Memorial Project but was unable to find any solace in it, and he passed away in loneliness at the age of seventy-seven. Like Chang Weisi, Wu Yue had Zhang Beihai's name on his lips in his final moments. They pinned their shared hopes for the future on the stalwart warrior now hibernating through time.

Dr. Albert Ringier and General Fitzroy both lived into their eighties and saw the completion of the hundred-meter Hubble III Space Telescope, which they used to look at the planet Trisolaris. But they never again saw the Trisolaran Fleet or the probes now flying ahead of it. They did not live long enough for them to cross the third patch of snow.

The lives of ordinary people continued and ended as well. Out of the three old Beijing neighbors, Miao Fuquan was the first to depart, passing away at the age of seventy-five. He really did have his son bury him two hundred meters down an abandoned mine, and his son obeyed his last wishes to blow up the mine wall and erect a tombstone to remember him. According to his father's will, the last generation before the Doomsday Battle was supposed to clear out the tombstone, and if humanity won, then it could be restored to its original location. But, in fact, less than half a century after his death, the area over the mine shaft became a desert. The tombstone disappeared, the mine's location was lost, and the Miao family's descendants couldn't be bothered to look for it.

Zhang Yuanchao died of illness like an ordinary person at the age of eighty, and, like an ordinary person, he was cremated. His ashes were laid in an ordinary rectangular slot on a long rack in a public cemetery.

Yang Jinwen lived till ninety-two, and the alloy vessel containing his remains headed out of the Solar System and into the

vast cosmos at the third cosmic velocity. This consumed all of his savings.

But Ding Yi lived on. After the breakthrough in controlled fusion technology, he turned his attention to theoretical physics, looking for ways to escape sophon interference in high-energy particle physics experiments. He had no success. When he reached his seventies, he had, like other physicists, abandoned all hope of the possibility of a breakthrough. He entered hibernation and planned to wake at the Doomsday Battle. His sole desire was to be able to see with his own eyes the superior technology of Trisolaris.

In the century following the start of the Trisolar Crisis, everyone who had lived through the Golden Age passed away. It was an era that was constantly recalled, and the old folks who had lived through those grand times chewed over their memories of it like ruminants, savoring the flavors. They always closed with one line: "Ah, if only we knew how to cherish things back then." Young people would listen to their stories with a mixture of envy and skepticism. That fabled peace, prosperity, and happiness, that ideal utopia free from care: Did it ever really exist?

As the elderly passed away, the departed Golden Shore vanished into the smoke of history. The ship of human civilization floated alone in the vast ocean, surrounded on all sides by endless, sinister waves, and no one knew if there even was an opposite shore.

PART III

THE DARK FOREST

YEAR 205, CRISIS ERA

Darkness. Before the darkness there was nothing but nothingness, and the nothingness was without color. Nothing was in the nothingness. Darkness at least meant that there was space. Soon, disturbances appeared in the darkness of space, penetrating everything like a gentle breeze. It was the sensation of time passing, for the nothingness was without time, but now time took shape in a glacial thaw. Only much later was there light, at first as a shapeless blob of brightness, and then, after another long wait, the shape of the world gradually emerged. The newly resurrected consciousness struggled to make sense of it, at first managing to work out a few thin, transparent tubes, then a human face behind them, which quickly disappeared, exposing the creamy-white light of the ceiling.

Luo Ji awoke from hibernation.

The face reappeared. It belonged to a man with a gentle expression who looked at Luo Ji and said, "Welcome to our era." As he spoke, a field of vibrant roses flashed on his white lab coat, then gradually faded and disappeared. As he continued speaking, the coat displayed a continuous assortment of delightful images that matched his expressions and emotions: seas, sunsets, and woods in the drizzle. He told Luo Ji that his illness had been cured during hibernation, and that his reawakening had gone smoothly.

Recovery would take just three days or so, and then he would completely regain normal bodily functions. . . .

Luo Ji's mind, still sluggish and only partially awake, caught just one piece of information out of everything the doctor said: This was year 205 of the Crisis Era, and he had been in hibernation for 185 years.

He found the doctor's accent peculiar at first, but he soon discovered that although the sounds of standard Mandarin hadn't changed much, it had been stuffed with a large quantity of English words. As the doctor spoke, the text of what he said was displayed on the ceiling, apparently through voice recognition. Perhaps to help the newly awakened better understand, the English words were replaced with Chinese characters.

At last the doctor said that Luo Ji could be transferred from the revival room to the general ward. His coat showed an evening scene in which a setting sun rapidly turned into a starry sky to say farewell. As this was going on, Luo Ji felt his bed begin to move. Just out the door, he heard the doctor call out, "Next." Twisting his head back to look, he saw another bed enter the revival room bearing someone who had obviously just been taken out of the hibernation chamber. The bed was quickly wheeled to a bank of monitors, and the doctor, his coat now a pure white, tapped on the wall with a finger, causing one-third of it to display complex curves and data that he began to manipulate intensely.

Luo Ji realized that his own reawakening was probably not a major event at all, but rather just a part of day-to-day work here. The doctor was friendly, but in his eyes Luo Ji was nothing more than an ordinary hibernator.

Like the revival room, the hallway had no lamps. The walls themselves emitted light, and although it was soft, Luo Ji still had to squint. But as he did so, the walls in the section of corridor he was in dimmed, and the dimmed segment followed him as his bed moved. Once his eyes grew accustomed to the light, he opened them again, at which point the hallway brightened again, remaining in his comfort zone. Evidently the hallway's

brightness adjustment system was able to monitor the changes in his pupils.

Judging by that, he had to be in a personalized age.

This far exceeded his expectations.

As the walls passed slowly by, he saw lots of activated displays of different sizes randomly distributed on them. Some of them were moving images that he didn't have the time to look at clearly, and might have been left behind by users who forgot to turn them off.

Sometimes, his automatic bed crossed paths with people walking down the hallway. He noticed that both the soles of their feet and the bed's wheels made luminous, watery waves of pressure where they contacted the ground, like what used to happen when you pressed a finger onto an LCD in his own time. The long corridor gave him an intense sense of cleanliness, as clean as a 3-D computer animation, although he knew all of it was real. He moved through it with a sense of tranquility and comfort he had never known before.

But what impressed him most about the people he saw was that everyone—doctors, nurses, and nonstaff alike—appeared clean and elegant, and smiled warmly at him or waved when they approached. Their clothes displayed gorgeous images, a different style for each person, some abstract, others concrete. He was won over by their expressions, because he knew that the eyes of ordinary people were the best reflection of the level of civilization in a time and place. He had once seen a set of photos taken by European photographers in the late Qing Dynasty, and his deepest impression had been of the dull expressions of the people in the photographs. Officials and commoners alike had eyes that revealed only numbness and stupidity, lacking the slightest shred of vitality. When the people of this new era looked at Luo Ji's eyes, they might be having the same feeling about him. The gazes that crossed his own were full of a vigorous wisdom, and a sincerity, understanding, and love that he had rarely perceived in his own age. But what impressed him most was the confidence in their expressions. The sunny confidence that filled every pair of eyes had evidently become the spiritual backdrop for the people of this new era.

This did not seem to be an age of despair, and that was another unexpected surprise.

Luo Ji's bed moved soundlessly into the general ward, which held two more reawakened hibernators. One of them was lying on a bed. The other, next to the door, was packing his things with a nurse's help and seemed about ready to leave. From the look in their eyes, Luo Ji knew that both of them were from his own era. Their eyes were like the windows of time, and through them he had another glance of that gray era he had come from.

"How can they be that way? I'm their great-grandfather!" Luo Ji heard the hibernator who was about to leave complaining.

"You can't pull seniority in front of them. It's the law: Hibernation doesn't count as age, so in the presence of the elderly, you're the younger generation. . . . Let's go. They've waited in the reception room long enough," the nurse said. Although she tried to avoid English words, sometimes she stumbled over Chinese words, as if speaking an ancient tongue, and was forced to use the modern language. Then the wall would display a translation into Chinese.

"I can't even understand it when they talk. All that bird-speak mixed in!" the hibernator said, as he and the nurse each picked up a bag and went out the door.

"In this age, you've got to keep learning. Otherwise, you'll just have to go live up top," Luo Ji heard the nurse say. By now he could understand the modern language without difficulty, but he was still unclear what the nurse meant by her last sentence.

"Hello. Did you hibernate due to illness?" the hibernator in the bed beside Luo Ji asked. He was young, and looked to be in his early twenties.

Luo Ji opened his mouth but no sound came out. The young man smiled at him encouragingly. "You can speak. Try harder!"

"Hello," Luo Ji managed hoarsely.

The young man nodded. "The one who just left did. I didn't. I came here to escape from reality. Oh, and my name's Xiong Wen."

"Here . . . how is it?" Luo Ji asked, much more easily this time.

"I don't really know. I've only been here five days. Still, it's

330

definitely a good era. But for us, it's bound to be difficult to integrate into society. Mostly because we woke up too soon. A few years later would have been better."

"A few years later? Wouldn't that be even harder?"

"No. It's still a state of war now, so society can't take care of us. In a few decades, after the peace talks, there'll be peace and prosperity."

"Peace talks? With whom?!"

"Trisolaris, of course."

Shaken by Xiong Wen's final statement, Luo Ji strove to sit up. A nurse entered and helped him up to a half-sitting position in bed.

"They said they want peace talks?" he asked anxiously.

"Not yet. But they'll have no other choice," Xiong Wen said, nimbly getting out of his bed and coming over to sit down on Luo Ji's. He had clearly been anticipating the pleasure of introducing someone newly awakened to this era. "Don't you know? Humanity is amazing now. Simply amazing!"

"How?"

"Our spacecraft are incredibly powerful. Far more powerful than Trisolaran ships!"

"How is that possible?"

"Why wouldn't it be? Put the superweapons aside and look purely at speed. They can reach fifteen percent of the speed of light! Tons faster than the Trisolarans!"

When Luo Ji turned a skeptical eye toward the nurse, he noticed that she was exceptionally pretty. Everyone in this age seemed to be attractive. She nodded with a smile. "It's true."

Xiong Wen went on, "And do you know how many ships there are in the space fleet? I'll tell you: two thousand! Twice as many as the Trisolarans! And the number's still growing!"

Luo Ji glanced again at the nurse, who nodded.

"You know how badly off the Trisolaran Fleet is now? In two centuries they've passed through the, ah, the space dust they call the snow patch three times. I heard someone say that the most recent time was four years ago, and the telescope observed that

their formation has become sparser. They're not holding together. More than half of the ships stopped accelerating long ago, and they decelerated considerably when they crossed the dust. They're crawling now, and they won't reach the Solar System for more than eight hundred years. They might already be broken hulks. Projecting from their current speed, no more than three hundred ships will arrive on time two centuries from now. However, one Trisolaran probe will reach the Solar System soon. This year. The other nine are following afterward and will get here three years later."

"The probe . . . What's that?" Luo Ji asked in confusion.

The nurse said, "We don't encourage the exchange of practical information. When the previous reawakened hibernator learned about these things, it took him many days to calm down. It's not conducive to recovery."

"It makes me happy, so what's it to you?" Xiong Wen said with a shrug. Then he returned to his own bed to lie down. As he lay watching the soft light emitted by the ceiling, he sighed, "The kids are all right. They're really all right."

"Who's a kid?" the nurse sniffed. "Hibernation doesn't count as age. You're the kid." To Luo Ji's eyes, she actually looked younger than Xiong Wen, although he knew that his appearance-based judgment of age might not be accurate in this era.

The nurse said to him, "The people from your time are all pretty despairing. But things aren't really all that serious."

To Luo Ji, this was the voice of an angel. He felt like he had turned into a child who had just awakened from a nightmare, and all the frightening things he had experienced were taken care of by a smile from an adult. When she spoke, her nurse's uniform shone a fast-rising sun, and under its golden light, the dry yellow earth turned green, and flowers bloomed in wild abandon. . . .

When the nurse had gone, Luo Ji asked Xiong Wen, "What about the Wallfacer Project?"

Xiong Wen shook his head in confusion. "Wallfacer . . . ? Never heard of it."

Luo Ji asked when Xiong Wen had entered hibernation. It had been before the Wallfacer Project had started, when hibernation was very expensive. His family must have had money. But if he hadn't heard anything about the Wallfacer Project in the five days he had been awake, that meant that even if the program hadn't been forgotten in this era, it was no longer important.

Next, Luo Ji personally experienced the level of technology of this new age in two trivial areas.

Soon after he entered the ward, the nurse carried in his first meal after reawakening, a very small quantity of milk and bread and jam, because his stomach functions were still recovering. He took a bite of bread and felt like he was chewing sawdust.

"Your sense of taste is still recovering, too," the nurse said.

"It'll taste even worse once you've recovered," Xiong Wen said.

The nurse laughed. "Of course, it's not as good as the food grown on the surface in your era."

"Then where does this come from?" Luo Ji asked, through his full mouth.

"It's produced in a factory."

"You're able to synthesize grain?"

Xiong Wen answered for the nurse. "There's no other option but to synthesize it. The land won't grow any crops anymore."

Luo Ji felt sorry for Xiong Wen. There had been people in his era who had become immune to technology and were indifferent to any sort of technological wonder, and Xiong Wen was apparently one of them. He was unable to properly appreciate this new age.

The next discovery was an incredible shock to Luo Ji, although the thing itself was still quite plain. The nurse pointed to the cup of milk and told him that it had been put into a heating cup especially for hibernators, because the people of this era generally did not drink hot liquids. Even coffee was taken cold. If he wasn't used to drinking cold milk, he could heat it up simply by moving a slider near the bottom of the cup to the desired temperature. When he finished drinking, he inspected the cup. It looked like an ordinary glass cup apart from a thick, opaque base which must contain the

333

heat source. But no matter how hard he looked, he couldn't find any controls but the slider, and when he tried to twist the base, he found it was integrated with the rest of the cup.

"Don't mess around with the supplies. You don't understand them yet. It's dangerous," the nurse said after watching Luo Ji's efforts.

"I'd like to know where it gets recharged."

"Re . . . charged?" The nurse awkwardly repeated the word, evidently hearing it for the first time.

"*Charge. Recharge,*" Luo Ji said in English, but the nurse just shook her head in confusion.

"What happens when the batteries run out?"

"Batteries?"

"*Batteries,*" he said in English. "You don't have batteries anymore?" When the nurse shook her head again, he said, "Then where does the electricity in the cup come from?"

"Electricity? There's electricity everywhere," the nurse said disapprovingly.

"The electricity in the cup won't run out?"

"It won't run out."

"It's inexhaustible?!"

"Inexhaustible. How could electricity run out?"

When the nurse left, Luo Ji still was unable to let go of the cup. He ignored Xiong Wen's ridicule, for his surging emotions told him that he was holding a sacred object, the age-old dream of humanity: a perpetual motion machine. If humanity had really achieved inexhaustible energy, then they could achieve practically everything. Now he believed the words of the pretty nurse: Things might not be so serious.

When the doctor came into the ward for a routine checkup, Luo Ji asked him about the Wallfacer Project.

"I know of it. It's an ancient joke," the doctor replied offhandedly.

"What happened to the Wallfacers?"

"I think one of them committed suicide, and another was

stoned to death. . . . It all happened in the project's early days, and it's been nearly two centuries since then."

"And the other two?"

"I don't know. They're probably still in hibernation."

"One of them was Chinese. Do you remember him?" Luo Ji ventured, staring nervously at the doctor.

"You mean the one who cast a spell on a star? I think he was mentioned in premodern history class," the nurse interjected.

"Right. And now he's . . ." Luo Ji said.

"I don't know. I think he's still in hibernation. I don't pay much attention to that stuff," the doctor said absently.

"And the star? The one he cursed, the star with a planet? What happened to it?" he asked, his heart tensing up.

"What do you think happened? It's probably still there. That spell? What a joke!"

"So nothing at all happened to that star?"

"Nothing I've heard, at any rate. You?" he asked the nurse.

"Me neither," she said, shaking her head. "The world was scared to death back then and lots of silly things happened."

"And then?" Luo Ji said with a sigh.

"Then there was the Great Ravine," the doctor said.

"The Great Ravine? What was that?"

"You'll find out later. For now, rest up," the doctor said with a gentle sigh. "But it's probably better that you don't know about it." As he turned to leave, his white coat displayed billowing dark clouds, and the nurse's uniform displayed lots of pairs of eyes, some of them frightened, some brimming with tears.

When the doctor had left, Luo Ji sat motionless on his bed for a long while, mumbling to himself, "A joke. An ancient joke." Then he began laughing, silently at first, and then in great guffaws, trembling on his bed and frightening Xiong Wen, who wanted to call the doctor.

"I'm fine. Go to sleep," Luo Ji told him. Then he lay down and soon fell asleep for the first time since his reawakening.

He dreamed of Zhuang Yan and the child. As before, Zhuang Yan walked through the snow, the child asleep in her arms.

335

When he awoke, the nurse walked in and said good morning to him. Her voice was soft so as not to wake the still-sleeping Xiong Wen.

"Is it morning? Why aren't there any windows in this room?" Luo Ji asked, looking around.

"Any place on the wall can turn transparent. But the doctors feel that you aren't ready to look outside. It's too unfamiliar, and it will distract you and affect your rest."

"I've been revived for a while now, but I still don't know what the outside world is like. This affects my rest." Luo Ji pointed at Xiong Wen, and said, "I'm not that kind of person."

The nurse laughed. "That's okay. I'm about to go off shift. Shall I take you out for a look around? You can have breakfast after you get back."

Excitedly, Luo Ji followed the nurse to the on-call room. Looking it over, he could guess what about half of the furnishings were, but he had no idea what the rest were for. There was no computer or similar equipment, but because a display could be activated anywhere on the walls, this was to be expected. Three umbrellas lined up outside the door caught his attention. They were in different styles, but from their shape, they were definitely umbrellas. What surprised him was their bulk. Weren't there folding umbrellas in this age?

The nurse came out of the changing room dressed in her own clothes. Aside from the flashing movies on the fabric, changes to women's fashion in this age were well within the scope of Luo Ji's imagination. Compared to his own era, the major difference was their conspicuous asymmetry. He was pleased that after 185 years had passed, he could still find beauty in women's clothing. The nurse picked up one of the umbrellas, which must have been fairly heavy, because she had to carry it over her shoulder.

"Is it raining out?"

She shook her head. "You think I'm carrying an . . . umbrella?" she said, unfamiliar with the last word.

"If it's not an umbrella, then what is it?" Luo Ji pointed to the

device on her shoulder, imagining that she would say some peculiar name for it.

But she didn't. "It's my bicycle," she said.

When they arrived in the corridor, Luo Ji asked, "Is your home far from here?"

"If you're talking about where I live, it's not far. Ten or twenty minutes biking," she said. Then, standing still and fixing him with her charming eyes, she said something that shocked him: "There are no homes now. No one has them. Marriage, family, they went away after the Great Ravine. That will be the first thing you'll have to get used to."

"That first thing is something I won't be able to get used to."

"Oh, I don't know. In history class I learned that marriage and family had already begun to disintegrate in your own time. Lots of people didn't want to be tied down. They wanted free lives." This was the second time she had mentioned history class.

I was like that once, but then . . . Luo Ji said to himself. From the moment he'd reawakened, Zhuang Yan and the child had never really left his mind. They were the desktop wallpaper of his consciousness, perpetually on display. But no one here recognized him, and with the situation so uncertain, he couldn't just rashly ask about their whereabouts, even though he was tormented by longing.

They walked a ways down the corridor. Then, after they'd passed through an automatic door, Luo Ji's eyes lit up as he saw a narrow platform extending into the distance and felt fresh air blowing toward him. He sensed that he was now outside.

"What a blue sky!" was the first thing he shouted to the outside world.

"Really? It can't compare to the blue skies of your era."

Definitely bluer. Much bluer. Luo Ji didn't say that out loud, just reveled in the boundless blue embrace and let his soul melt. Then he had a flash of doubt: Was this heaven? In his memory, he had only ever seen such a pure blue sky during the five years he had spent apart from the world, secluded in his Garden of Eden. But this blue sky had fewer white clouds, just a couple of pale wisps in

the western sky, like someone had unintentionally left a smudge. The sun that had just risen in the east shone like crystal in the entirely transparent air, with its edge rimmed in dew.

Luo Ji turned his eyes downward and immediately became dizzy. From high up, it took him a long moment to realize that what he saw from here was the city. At first he thought he was looking at a giant forest, the slender tree trunks stretching straight up toward the sky, each one sprouting perpendicular branches of varying lengths. The city's buildings were the leaves hanging off these branches. The layout of the city looked random, and different trees had different densities of leaves. The Hibernation and Reawakening Center formed a part of one of those large trees, and the leaf that contained his bed hung from the narrow platform that now extended out in front of him.

Looking back, the tree trunk his branch was connected to extended so far upward that it disappeared out of view. The branch they were on was located in the middle to upper section of the tree, and above and below them he could see other branches, and the structural leaves that hung on them. On closer inspection, the branches formed an intricate network of bridges in space, bridges with one end left floating in midair.

"What is this place?" Luo Ji asked.

"Beijing."

He looked at the nurse, even prettier now in the morning sun. Looking back at the place she called Beijing, he asked, "Where's the city center?"

"In that direction. We're outside the West Fourth Ring, in Tree 179, Branch 23, Leaf 18, so you're almost able to see the entire city."

Luo Ji looked for a bit into the distance where she pointed, and then exclaimed, "Impossible! How is there nothing left?"

"What would be left? In your day, there was absolutely nothing here!"

"Nothing? The Imperial Palace? Jingshan Park? Tiananmen? The China World Trade Center? It hasn't even been two hundred years. It can't all have been torn down."

338

"All those things are still there."

"Where?"

"On the surface."

Seeing Luo Ji's terrified look, she burst out laughing so hard that she had to lean on the railing for support. "Ah, haha. I forgot. I'm really sorry. I've forgotten so many times. Look, we're underground here. A thousand meters beneath the surface . . . If I ever get to time travel to your time, you can get back at me and forget to tell me that the city's on the surface, and I'll be as terrified as you are now. Ha ha ha . . ."

"But . . . this . . ." He held up his hands.

"The sky is fake. The sun is fake, too," the woman said, trying to suppress a smile. "Of course, saying it's fake isn't right, either, because it's an image taken from an altitude of ten thousand meters and displayed down here, so maybe it counts as real, too."

"Why build the city below ground? And a thousand meters—that's really deep."

"For the war, of course. Think about it. When the Doomsday Battle comes, won't the surface be an ocean of fire? Yeah, that battle is another outdated idea now, but when the Great Ravine ended, all the world's cities developed underground."

"So all the cities in the world are underground now?"

"The majority of them."

Luo Ji took stock of the world again. Now he understood that the trunks of the great trees were the pillars supporting the vault of the underground world, and also served as the columns from which the city's buildings were suspended.

"You won't be claustrophobic. Look at how broad the sky is! Up on the surface, the sky's not nearly this wonderful."

Luo Ji looked again at the blue sky, or rather the projection of the blue sky. He now noticed a few small objects—just some scattered bits, at first, but once his eyes got used to looking, he saw that there were so many that they covered the entire sky. Strangely, the objects in the sky reminded him of someplace completely unrelated, the showcase of a jewelry store. Before he became a Wallfacer, back

339

when he had fallen in love with the Zhuang Yan of his imagination, he had once been so obsessed that he wanted to buy his imaginary angel a present. He went to the jewelry store and looked at all the platinum pendants in the showcase, every one of them exquisite, lying there on the black velvet and twinkling under the spotlights. If the black velvet had been blue, then it would have been just like the sky he saw today.

"Is that the space fleet?" he asked excitedly.

"No. The fleet isn't visible from here. It's beyond the asteroid belt. Those, well, they're everything. The ones with a visible shape are space cities, and the points of light are civilian spacecraft. But sometimes there are warships in orbit, too. Their engines are very bright, so you can't stare at them. . . . Okay, I've got to get going. You should head back soon. It gets windy here."

Luo Ji turned around to say good-bye, but was so surprised he couldn't speak. The woman had her umbrella—or, rather, her bicycle—positioned on her back like a backpack, and then it stood up in back of her and opened overhead to form two coaxial propellers that started up silently, turning in opposition to offset rotational torque. Then she lifted slowly up into the air and hopped over the railing beside her into the abyss that had so dazzled him.

Suspended there, she called to him: "You can see how this is a pretty decent age. Think of your past as a dream. See you tomorrow!"

She flew gracefully, the small propellers churning the sunlight, until she turned into a tiny dragonfly between two giant trees in the distance. Swarms of these dragonflies flew between the giant trees of the city. More notable still were the streams of flying cars like schools of fish navigating endlessly among the plants on the ocean floor. The rising sun shone onto the city and was cut into shafts of light by the trees, coating the traffic with a layer of gold.

Tears streamed down Luo Ji's face at the sight of this brave new world, and the sensation of newborn life permeated his every cell. The past really was a dream.

———

When he saw the European man in the reception room, Luo Ji got the feeling that there was something different about him. Later, he realized that it was because the formal suit he wore didn't flash or display any image, but resembled the clothing of a bygone era. Perhaps this was an expression of solemnity.

After Luo Ji shook his hand, the visitor introduced himself. "I'm Special Commissioner Ben Jonathan from the Solar Fleet Joint Conference. I arranged your reawakening at the committee's behest, and now, we're going to attend the final hearing of the Wallfacer Project. Oh, can you understand me? English has changed quite a bit."

Luo Ji *could* understand what Jonathan said, but listening to him speak, the sense of Western cultural invasion that Luo Ji had felt over the past few days because of the changes to modern Chinese disappeared, because Jonathan's English was peppered with Chinese vocabulary. He said "Wallfacer Project" in Chinese, for example. English, formerly the most widely used language, and Chinese, spoken by the largest population, had blended with each other without distinction to become the world's most powerful language. Luo Ji learned later that the other languages of the world were undergoing the same fusion.

The past isn't a dream, Luo Ji thought. *The past catches up with you.* Then he recalled that Jonathan had said the word "final" and wondered if there was hope of a quick resolution after all.

Jonathan looked back, as if to make sure the door had been closed, and then walked over to the wall and activated an interface. He gave a few simple taps on the surface, and then all four walls and the ceiling disappeared into a holographic display.

Now Luo Ji found himself in an auditorium. Although everything was greatly changed, and the walls and table glowed softly, the designers had clearly tried to replicate the style of the old era. Everything from the great circular table and the rostrum to the overall layout embodied a nostalgia that allowed him to know at once where he was. The auditorium was empty but for two staffers laying out documents on the tables. Luo Ji was astonished to see

that paper documents were still being used. Just like Jonathan's clothes, this seemed to be an expression of solemnity.

"Remote meetings are a common practice now. Taking part in this way won't affect the meeting's importance or seriousness," Jonathan said. "There's still some time before the hearing begins, and you look like you don't know much about the outside world. Do you need me to tell you a bit about the basics?"

Luo Ji nodded. "Of course. Thank you."

Jonathan pointed to the auditorium and said, "I'll be brief. First, the countries. Europe is a single country, called the European Commonwealth, and it includes both eastern and western Europe, but not Russia. Russia and Belarus unified into a country still called the Russian Federation. Canada's French-speaking and English-speaking areas split into two countries. There have been some changes in other regions, too, but these are the major ones."

Luo Ji was shocked. "Those are the only changes? It's been nearly two centuries. I'd have thought the changes would have made the world unrecognizable."

Jonathan turned back from the auditorium and nodded solemnly at Luo Ji. "Unrecognizable, Dr. Luo. The world is indeed unrecognizable."

"No, there were early signs of those changes in our era."

"But there's one thing you never anticipated: There are no longer any great powers. All countries have declined in political power."

"All the countries? Then who rose up?"

"A suprastate entity: the space fleet."

Luo Ji thought this over for a while before realizing what Jonathan meant. "You mean the space fleet is independent?"

"Yes. The fleets do not belong to any country. They form independent political and economic entities that, like countries, are members of the UN. Right now, there are three major fleets in the Solar System: the Asian Fleet, the European Fleet, and the North American Fleet. Their names refer only to their primary region of origin, but the fleets themselves are no longer subordinate to those

regions. They are entirely independent. Each one possesses the political and economic might of a superpower of your era."

"My god," Luo Ji exclaimed.

"But please don't misunderstand. Earth is not ruled by a military government. The territory and sovereignty of the space fleets is in space, and they rarely interfere with the internal affairs of terrestrial society. This is stipulated by the UN charter. So right now the human world is divided into two international spheres: the traditional Earth International, and the newly emerged Fleet International. The three fleets of Fleet International—the Asian, European, and North American—make up the Solar Fleet, and the former Planetary Defense Council evolved into the Solar Fleet Joint Conference, nominally the highest command body in the Solar Fleet. However, as with the UN, it has a coordinating function, but no real power. In fact, it's a Solar Fleet in name only. The actual power of humanity's space-based armed forces lies in the hands of the supreme command of the three major fleets.

"Well, then, you now know enough to take part in today's hearing. It was convened by the SFJC, which inherited the Wallfacer Project."

Then a window opened up on the holographic display, and an image of Bill Hines and Keiko Yamasuki appeared in it. They looked unchanged. Hines greeted Luo Ji with a smile, but Yamasuki sat impassively next to him, giving only a slight nod of acknowledgement at Luo Ji's greeting.

Hines said, "I just woke up, Dr. Luo. I was quite sorry to learn that that planet you cursed is still orbiting its star fifty light-years away."

"Heh. A joke. An ancient joke," Luo Ji said self-mockingly, with a wave of his hand.

"But compared to Tyler and Rey Diaz, you're pretty lucky."

"You appear to be the only successful Wallfacer. Perhaps your strategy really has elevated human intelligence."

Hines displayed the same self-mocking smile that Luo Ji had just exhibited, and he shook his head. "No, it really hasn't. I know

now that after we entered hibernation, research into the human mind quickly encountered an insurmountable obstacle. Going forward meant approaching the quantum level of the brain's thought mechanisms. But at that point, like all other science, they hit the impassible sophon barrier. We didn't elevate human intelligence. If I did anything at all, it was just to increase some people's confidence."

When Luo Ji entered hibernation, the mental seal had not yet been developed, so he didn't really understand the last thing Hines said. But he noticed that when he said it, a mysterious smile flashed across Keiko Yamasuki's frosty face.

The window vanished, and then Luo Ji realized that the auditorium was full of people. Most of them were dressed in military uniforms whose styles hadn't changed all that much. None of the attendees had pictures decorating their clothing, but their lapel pins and epaulets all glowed.

The SFJC still used a rotating chair system. It was currently held by a civilian officer. As Luo Ji looked at him, he was reminded of Garanin. The thought struck him that he was an ancient man from two centuries ago, but he was at least fortunate compared to those of his own age who had been annihilated by the river of time.

Once the meeting opened, the chair spoke. "Representatives, at this hearing, we will hold the final vote on Proposition 649, put forth by the North American Fleet and the European Fleet at the forty-seventh Joint Conference this year. First, let me read the proposition.

"In the second year of the Trisolar Crisis, the UN's Planetary Defense Council established the Wallfacer Project. It was adopted unanimously by the permanent members of the UN and was implemented the following year. At its core, the Wallfacer Project attempted to develop hidden strategies for resisting the Trisolaran invasion by tasking four Wallfacers nominated by permanent member states with formulating and executing strategic plans in the seclusion of their own minds, out of reach of the sophons' omnipresent surveillance. The UN promulgated the Wallfacer

Act to guarantee privileges to the Wallfacers for formulating and executing their plans.

"The Wallfacer Project has been going on for two hundred five years to date, a time frame that has included more than a century's hiatus. During this time, leadership of the project passed from the former PDC to the present SFJC.

"The Wallfacer Project arose out of a unique historical background. The Trisolar Crisis had just begun, and in the face of a devastating crisis unheard of in human history, the international community had descended to unprecedented levels of fear and despair. This was the climate into which the Wallfacer Project was born. It was not a rational choice, but a struggle of desperation.

"The facts of history have proven that, as a strategic plan, the Wallfacer Project was a complete and utter failure. It is no exaggeration to say that it was the most naïve and foolish action that human society as a whole has ever taken. The Wallfacers were granted unprecedented power without any legal oversight, and even possessed the freedom to deceive the international community. This violated the basic moral and legal norms of human society.

"During the execution of the Wallfacer Project, enormous quantities of strategic resources were exhausted for no reason. Wallfacer Frederick Tyler's mosquito swarm was proven to have no strategic significance, while Wallfacer Manuel Rey Diaz's Mercury-chain-reaction plan was unrealizable, even given humanity's present capabilities. Moreover, both of those plans were criminal. Tyler sought to attack and wipe out Earth's fleet, while Rey Diaz's even more sinister goal was to hold every life on the planet hostage.

"The other two Wallfacers were similarly disappointing. The true strategic intent of Wallfacer Hines's mental upgrade plan has not yet been revealed, but the use in the space forces of its preliminary result, the mental seal, is also a crime. It is a serious violation of freedom of thought, which is the foundation of the survival and further progress of human civilization. As for Wallfacer Luo Ji, he

first irresponsibly squandered public funds on his own hedonistic lifestyle and then played to the crowds with ridiculous mysticism.

"We believe that given the decisive growth in humanity's strength and its seizure of the initiative in the war, the Wallfacer Project no longer has any meaning. The time has come to bring the problem that history has passed down to us to an end. We propose that the SFJC immediately terminate the Wallfacer Project and abolish the UN Wallfacer Act.

"Here ends the proposition."

The chair slowly set down the proposal document, and, glancing around the auditorium, said, "We will commence the vote on SFJC Proposition 649. All in favor?"

All of the representatives raised their hands.

Voting in this era was still done by primitive methods. Staffers walked through the auditorium solemnly verifying the number of votes, and when they reported the result to the chair, he announced, "Proposition 649 has passed unanimously and is effective immediately." The chair raised his head. Luo Ji didn't know whether he was looking at Hines or himself, because, like at the first remote hearing he had attended 185 years before, he still didn't know where in the auditorium his and Hines's images were displayed. "Now that the Wallfacer Project is terminated, the Wallfacer Act is abolished as well. On behalf of the SFJC, I hereby notify Wallfacers Bill Hines and Luo Ji that your Wallfacer status has been revoked. All associated rights granted you by the Wallfacer Act, as well as the corresponding legal immunity, are no longer in effect. You have recovered your identity as ordinary citizens of your respective countries."

The chair declared the hearing adjourned. Jonathan stood up and switched off the holographic image, switching off Luo Ji's two-century-long nightmare in the process.

"Dr. Luo, as far as I am aware, this is the outcome you were hoping for," Jonathan said to him with a smile.

"Yes. It's just what I wanted. Thank you, Mr. Commissioner. And I thank the SFJC for restoring my ordinary status," Luo Ji said, from the depths of his heart.

"The hearing was simple. Just a vote on a proposition. I've been empowered to discuss matters with you in more detail. You may start with your biggest concern."

"What about my wife and child?" Luo Ji asked, unable to hold back the question that had been tormenting him since reawakening. It was a question he had wanted to ask when he first met Jonathan, before the start of the meeting.

"Don't worry. They're both fine. They're still in hibernation. I can give you their files, and you can apply to reawaken them whenever you'd like."

"Thank you. Thank you." Luo Ji's eyes grew moist, and once again he had that feeling of arriving in heaven.

"However, Dr. Luo, I have a small piece of advice," Jonathan said as he slid closer to Luo Ji on the couch. "It's not easy for a hibernator to get used to life in this age. I advise you to stabilize your own life first before you wake them up. The UN funds are enough to keep them in hibernation for another two hundred thirty years."

"Well, how am I supposed to live out there?"

The commissioner laughed off his question. "Don't worry about that. You might not be used to the times, but living won't be an issue. In this age, social welfare is excellent, and a person can enjoy a comfortable life even if they don't do anything at all. The university you used to work at is still there, right in this city. They said they would consider the question of your work, and they'll contact you later on."

A thought suddenly occurred to Luo Ji, and it nearly made him shudder. "What about my security when I go out? The ETO wants to kill me!"

"The ETO?!" Jonathan burst into laughter. "The Earth-Trisolaris Organization was completely wiped out a century ago. There's no social foundation for them to exist in the world anymore. Of course, there are still people who have those ideological tendencies, but they aren't able to organize. You'll be absolutely safe outside."

As he was about to leave, Jonathan dropped his official attitude, and his suit started shining with an exaggerated, distorted image of the sky. He smiled and said to Luo Ji, "Doctor, out of all the historical figures I've seen, you've got the greatest sense of humor. A spell. A spell on a star. Ha ha ha . . ."

Luo Ji stood alone in the reception room, ruminating in silence over the reality before him. After two centuries as a messiah, he was once again an ordinary person. A new life was waiting before him.

"You're a commoner, my boy," a gruff voice loudly intruded on Luo Ji's thoughts. When he looked back toward the door, he saw Shi Qiang coming in. "Heh. I heard it from the guy who just left."

It was a happy reunion. They traded experiences, and Luo Ji learned that Shi Qiang had reawakened two months before. His leukemia had been cured. The doctors had also discovered that he was at high risk of liver disease, probably due to drinking, so they had taken care of that, too. To the two of them, it didn't really feel like they had been apart for very long. No more than four or five years, since there was no sense of time in hibernation. But meeting in a new era two centuries in the future added a deeper level to their friendship.

"I've come to pick you up when you're discharged. There's no reason to stay here," Shi Qiang said as he took a set of clothes out of his backpack and had Luo Ji put them on.

"Isn't it . . . a little big?" Luo Ji asked, opening up the jacket.

"Look at you. Two months late waking up, and you're a yahoo next to me. Try it on."

Shi Qiang pointed out an object on the front of the shirt and told him that he could use it to adjust the sizing. When Luo Ji put on the clothes, he heard a hissing sound, and the clothing slowly shrank to fit the dimensions of his body. It was the same with the trousers.

"Hey, you're not wearing that same set of clothes you wore two centuries ago, are you?" Luo Ji asked, looking at Shi Qiang. He remembered quite clearly that the leather jacket Shi Qiang was wearing now was the same one he had on the last time he saw him.

"Most of my belongings got lost in the Great Ravine, but my family did keep that set of clothes for me. But it wasn't wearable. You've got some things left over from that era too, and when you're settled down you can go pick them up. I tell you, my boy, when you see how that stuff has changed, that's when you'll really know that nearly two hundred years isn't a short length of time." As he spoke, Shi Qiang pressed something somewhere on his jacket and his outfit turned entirely white. The leather texture had just been an image. "I like it like the past."

"Can mine do that too? Can it put up images like theirs?" Luo Ji asked, looking at his own clothes.

"They can, but it's a little hard to get it set up. Let's go."

Luo Ji and Shi Qiang took the elevator in the trunk down to the ground floor, passed through the tree's large foyer, and out into the new world.

When the commissioner shut off the holographic image of the hearing, the meeting had not actually concluded. Luo Ji had in fact noticed that when the chair declared the meeting adjourned, a sudden voice had rung out. It was a woman's voice, and while he hadn't been able to make it out clearly, everyone in the assembly had turned in a particular direction. Then Jonathan had turned off the image. He must have noticed it, too, but once the chair had adjourned the meeting, Luo Ji, now an ordinary citizen without Wallfacer status, was not eligible to participate even if it was still in progress.

The speaker was Keiko Yamasuki. She said, "Mr. Chair, I have something to say."

The chair said, "Dr. Yamasuki, you are not a Wallfacer. You are allowed to attend today's meeting due to your special status, but you do not have the right to speak."

None of the representatives seemed interested in her. They were getting up to leave. For them, the entire Wallfacer Project was nothing but a footnote in history that they had to spend energy

349

dealing with. But what she said next stopped them in their tracks. She turned to Hines and said, "Wallfacer Bill Hines, I am your Wallbreaker."

Hines, who was getting up to leave, felt his legs buckle at Yamasuki's words, and he sat down in his chair again. The people in the auditorium glanced at each other, and then began to whisper, as the blood gradually drained from Hines's face.

"I hope you have not all forgotten the significance of that title," Yamasuki said imperiously to the assembly.

The chair said, "Yes, we know what a Wallbreaker is. But your organization does not exist anymore."

"I know." She appeared totally calm. "But as the last member of the ETO, I will fulfill my duty for the Lord."

"I should have known it, Keiko. I should have known," Hines said, his voice trembling. He looked weak. He had known that his wife was a devotee of the ideas of Timothy Leary, and he had seen her fanatical desire to alter the human mind through technological means, but he had never connected it with a deeply hidden hatred of humanity.

"First off, I'd like to say that the true goal of your strategic plan was not the elevation of human intelligence. You more than anyone are aware that it is utterly impossible for human technology to accomplish this in the foreseeable future, because you were the one who discovered the quantum structure of the brain. You know that when the study of the mind reaches the quantum level, the sophon lockdown on fundamental physics means that scientific research will be like water with no source: It's got no grounding, and will never succeed. The mental seal was not just a chance by-product of your study of the mind. It was the thing you always wanted. That was the ultimate goal of your research." She turned to the assembly. "Now, what I'd like to know from all of you is this: In the years that we've been in hibernation, what happened to the mental seal?"

"It didn't have much of a history," the representative of the European Fleet said. "Nearly fifty thousand people from national space forces voluntarily accepted faith in victory through the mental

seal, and they formed a special class in the military known as the 'Imprinted.' Later on, about ten years after you went into hibernation, the use of the mental seal was found by the International Court of Justice to be a crime, an infringement on the freedom of thought, and the sole mental seal device—the one in the Faith Center—was put into storage. The manufacture and use of that type of equipment was placed under a worldwide ban nearly as strict as nuclear nonproliferation. And, in fact, the mental seal was even harder to obtain than nuclear weapons, primarily because of the computer it used. By the time you entered hibernation, computing technology had basically stopped moving forward. The computer used by the mental seal is still a supercomputer today and is inaccessible to ordinary individuals and organizations."

Then Keiko Yamasuki revealed her first piece of substantive information: "What you don't know is that there was more than one mental seal device. Five were made, each with its own accompanying supercomputer. The other four, Hines secretly handed over to people who had already accepted the seal, the ones you call the Imprinted. There were only around three thousand of them at that time, but they had already formed a tightly knit supranational organization within the militaries of individual countries. Hines did not tell me this. I learned it from the sophons. The Lord does not care about staunch triumphalism, so we didn't take action."

"And how is this significant?" the chair asked.

"Let's hypothesize, shall we? The mental seal device is not a continuously operating piece of equipment. It's only activated when necessary. Each device can be used for quite a long time, and if they're properly maintained, it would be no problem for them to be used for half a century. If the four devices were used in turn, one run into the ground before the next one is started up, they would have been able to last for two centuries. Which means that the Imprinted may not have died off, but might have endured from generation to generation up to the present day. It's a religion that believes in faith hardened by the mental seal, and its induction ceremony is the voluntary use of the mental seal on your own mind."

The representative of the North American Fleet said, "Dr. Hines, you have lost your Wallfacer status and no longer have the legal power to deceive the world. Would you please tell the Joint Conference the truth: Is your wife, or, rather, your Wallbreaker, telling the truth?"

"It's true," Hines said, with a heavy nod.

"That's a crime!" the representative of the Asian Fleet said.

"Perhaps it is," Hines said, and nodded again. "But just like all of you, I don't know whether the Imprinted have endured to the present day."

"That's not important," the representative of the European Fleet said. "I think the next step should be to find the mental seal devices that are still around and seal them up or destroy them. As for the Imprinted, if they voluntarily accepted the mental seal, then that doesn't appear to have violated the laws of the time. If they applied the mental seal to other volunteers, then they were under the dominance of the faith or belief that they had already received through technical means, so they should not be subjected to punishment. So the only thing we need to do is find the mental seals. The matter of the Imprinted might not need to be pursued at all."

"That's right. It's not a bad thing for there to be a few people in the Solar Fleet who have absolute faith in victory. At least, it won't cause any harm. It should remain a matter of personal privacy, and no one needs to know who they are. Although it's hard to understand why anyone would voluntarily undergo the mental seal today, because humanity's victory is so apparent," the representative of the European Fleet said.

Keiko Yamasuki smiled derisively, revealing a seldom-seen expression that conjured up for the assembly an ancient picture of moonlight reflecting off the scales of a snake in the grass.

"You're being naïve," she said.

"You're being naïve," Hines echoed his wife, and deeply bowed his head.

She turned once again to her husband. "Hines, you've always hidden your thoughts from me. Even before you became a Wallfacer."

"I was afraid you'd despise me," he said, head still down.

"How many times did we look silently into each other's eyes in the bamboo grove in the quiet of the Kyoto night? From your eyes I saw a Wallfacer's loneliness, and I saw your desire to speak. How many times did you almost tell me the truth? You wanted to bury your head in my arms, put everything into words through your tears, and obtain total release. But the duty of a Wallfacer prevented you. Deceit, even toward the one you loved the most, was one of your responsibilities. So I could only look into your eyes in the hope of finding some trace of your true thoughts. You don't know how many sleepless nights I spent waiting next to you as you slept soundly, waiting for you to talk in your sleep. . . . More often, I carefully observed you, studying your every move and capturing your every look, including the years you were first in hibernation. I recalled every detail about you, not out of longing but because I wanted to see your true thoughts. For a very long time, I failed. I knew you wore a mask, but I knew nothing of what was below the mask. The years passed, until finally, when you had just awakened and walked through the neural-network cloud to my side, and I looked into your eyes, I finally understood. I'd matured eight years, while you were still the you of eight years before. And so you were exposed.

"From that moment, I knew the real you: a deep-rooted defeatist and a staunch Escapist. Both before and after you became a Wallfacer, your sole goal was to achieve an exodus of humanity. Compared to the other Wallfacers, your genius lay not in strategic deception, but in concealing and disguising your true worldview.

"But I still didn't know how you would achieve this goal through your research into the brain and thoughts. I was confused even when the mental seal came out, all the way up until the moment I entered hibernation, when I remembered their eyes. The eyes of those people who had been given the mental stamp . . . they were like yours. And all of a sudden I understood an expression of yours that I'd never been able to read before. That was when I broke through to your real strategy, but it was too late to say anything."

The representative of the North American Fleet said, "Ms. Keiko Yamasuki, I don't think there's anything unusual here.

We know the history of the mental seal. In the first group of fifty thousand volunteers, the procedure was carried out under the strictest of supervision."

"That's right," she said. "But the supervision was only absolutely effective so far as the content of the faith proposition was concerned. The mental seal itself was much harder to supervise."

"But the literature indicates that the supervision of the technical details of the mental seal was very strict as well, and it underwent a large number of tests before it was put into operation," the chair said.

Yamasuki shook her head. "The mental seal is an incredibly complicated piece of equipment. Any supervision will have gaps. Specifically, one tiny minus sign out of hundreds of millions of lines of code. Even the sophons didn't detect it."

"A minus sign?"

"When the neural circuit model for judging a proposition to be true was discovered, Hines also discovered the model for judging a proposition to be false. That was what he needed. He concealed this discovery from everyone, including me. It wasn't difficult, because the two models were highly similar. It manifested as the direction of flow of a key signal in the neuron transmission model, and in the mathematical model of the mental seal, it was represented by a sign. Positive for true, negative for false. Working in extreme secrecy, Hines manipulated this sign in the mental seal's control software. In all five devices, the sign was negative."

A deathly silence fell over the auditorium, a silence that had manifested only once before during a PDC Wallfacer Hearing two centuries ago, when Rey Diaz had shown off the "cradle" on his wrist and had told the assembly that the device receiving the anti-trigger signal was nearby.

"Dr. Hines, what have you done?" The chair turned toward him in anger.

Hines raised his head, and everyone could see that his pallid face had returned to normal. His voice was calm and even. "I admit that I underestimated the power of humanity. The progress

that you've made is truly unbelievable. I have seen it, and I believe it, and I also believe that victory in the war belongs to humanity. This faith is as steadfast as if it had been imprinted by the mental stamp. The defeatism and Escapism of two centuries ago is truly ridiculous. However, Mr. Chair and representatives, I would like to say to the world that it is impossible to make me repent of what I have done."

"You still think you shouldn't repent?" the representative of the Asian Fleet demanded angrily.

Hines raised his head. "It's not a question of 'should.' It's an impossibility. I used the mental seal to imprint this proposition on myself: Everything about my Wallfacer plan is entirely correct."

The assembly exchanged amazed glances, and Yamasuki even turned to her husband with the same expression.

Hines flashed her a small smile and nodded. "Yes, dear, if you'll permit me to call you that. Only by doing that could I obtain the spiritual strength necessary to execute the plan. Yes, right now I believe all I've done is correct. I absolutely believe it, regardless of what reality says. I used the mental seal to turn myself into my own god, and God can't repent."

"In the not-too-distant future, when the Trisolaran invaders surrender to a more powerful human civilization, will you still think that?" the chair asked, with a look in his eyes that was more curious than amazed.

Hines nodded earnestly. "I'll still think that I'm right. Everything about my Wallfacer plan is entirely correct. Of course, in the face of the facts, I'll be put through a hell of a torture." He turned to his wife. "Dear, you know I've already suffered that torture once, when I believed that water was toxic."

"Let's come back to the present day," the representative of the North American Fleet said, interrupting everyone's whispered discussions. "It's just speculation that the Imprinted have endured. It's been over one hundred seventy years, after all. If a class or organization with such an absolute faith in defeatism exists, why haven't there been any signs of it?"

"There are two possibilities," the representative of the European Fleet said. "One is that the mental seal vanished long ago, and this is just a false alarm. . . ."

The representative of the Asian Fleet completed his thought. "But there's another possibility: The most frightening thing about the situation is the fact that there aren't any signs."

Luo Ji and Shi Qiang walked through the underground city shaded by the tree-shaped structures as streams of cars flew through the gaps in the sky above them. Because the buildings were "leaves" hanging in the air, the ground was wide open, and the widely spaced trunks of the giant trees meant there was no sense of streets, just a rolling plaza dotted with tree trunks. The environment was wonderful: The wide swaths of grasses, forests of actual trees, and fresh air all made it look at first glance like beautiful countryside. Pedestrians passed through in shining clothes like glowing ants. Luo Ji was impressed to no end by the urban design that elevated modern noise and crowdedness into the air and let the ground return to nature. Here, there was no shadow of the war, only human comforts and pleasures.

Before they had gotten far, he heard a woman's gentle voice. "Is that Mr. Luo Ji?" He looked around and found that the voice was coming from a billboard on the grass at the side of the road. An attractive woman dressed in a uniform was looking at him from the moving image.

"I am," he said with a nod.

"Hello. I am Financial Counselor 8065 of the General Banking System. Welcome to our era. I will now inform you of your current financial situation." As she spoke, a table of data appeared beside her. "These are your financial records for Year 9 of the Crisis Era, including deposits at the Industrial and Commercial Bank of China and the China Construction Bank. There are investments in quoted securities as well, but those items may have been partially lost during the Great Ravine."

"How does she know I'm here?" he whispered.

Shi Qiang said, "A chip's been implanted in your left arm. Don't worry, these days everyone's got one. It's like an ID card. All billboards can recognize you. Ads are all personalized now, so no matter where you go, everything on the billboards is showing just for you."

Apparently hearing Shi Qiang's words, the counselor said, "Sir, this isn't an advertisement. It's a service from the General Banking System."

"How much do I have on deposit?" Luo Ji asked.

A highly complicated chart appeared next to the counselor. "This is the status of all your interest-bearing accounts since Year 9 of the Crisis Era. It's fairly complicated, but you can access it in your personal information area from now on." Another, simpler chart popped up. "This is your current financial situation in all of the various subsystems of the General Banking System."

Luo Ji had no concept of what those figures meant, and asked blankly, "That's . . . how much?"

"My boy, you're a rich man!" Shi Qiang said, slapping him vigorously. "I may not have as much as you, but I've still got money. Heh, two centuries of interest—it's a real long-term investment. Pauper to tycoon. I only regret not saving a little more."

"Well . . . are you sure there's nothing wrong?" Luo Ji asked, skeptically.

"Hmm?" The big eyes of the counselor looked at Luo Ji quizzically.

"It's been more than one hundred eighty years. Wasn't there any inflation? Did the finance system really just continue on smoothly?"

"You're overthinking it," Shi Qiang said, taking a pack of cigarettes out of his pocket. Luo Ji knew then that tobacco was still around. But when Shi Qiang took one out, he was able to puff out clouds of smoke without lighting it.

The counselor replied, "There were many rounds of inflation during the Great Ravine, and the finance and credit systems came close to collapse. But according to current laws, interest on the

deposits of hibernators is calculated according to a special formula that excludes the Great Ravine, and instead transfers the deposit amount over to the financial level of the post-Ravine period and resumes calculating interest from there."

"Wow, that's some preferential treatment!" Luo Ji exclaimed.

"My boy, these are good times," Shi Qiang said, blowing out smoke. Then, raising his still-burning cigarette, he said, "Except the cigarettes are terrible."

"Mr. Luo Ji, this is just an opportunity for us to get acquainted. When it's convenient for you, we can discuss your personal financial arrangements and investment plan. If there's nothing else, then I'll say good-bye." The counselor smiled and waved good-bye.

"I've got one question," he said quickly. He didn't know what to call young women in this era, and didn't want to risk making a mistake by addressing her improperly. So he simply said, "I'm not too familiar with this era, so please forgive me if my question is offensive to you."

The counselor smiled, and said, "Not a problem. Our responsibility is to help you get acquainted with this era as quickly as possible."

"Are you a real person or a robot? Or are you a program?"

The question didn't faze the counselor. She replied, "Of course I'm a real person. Could a computer handle services as complicated as this?"

After the woman on the billboard disappeared, Luo Ji said to Shi Qiang, "Da Shi, there are some things I find hard to understand. This is an age that has invented perpetual motion and can synthesize grain, but computer technology doesn't seem to have advanced at all. Artificial intelligence can't even handle personal finance."

"What perpetual motion? You mean a perpetual motion machine?" Shi Qiang said.

"Yeah. It signifies unlimited energy."

Shi Qiang looked around him. "Where?"

Luo Ji pointed up to the stream of traffic. "Those flying cars. Do they consume oil or batteries?"

Shi Qiang shook his head. "Neither. Earth's oil was pumped dry. Those cars can fly forever without batteries and they'll never run out of power. They're pretty awesome. I'm thinking of getting one myself."

"How can you be so unmoved by a technological miracle? Unlimited power for humanity. This is as big an event as when Pangu created the heavens and the Earth! Don't you realize what a magnificent age this is?"

Shi Qiang tossed aside the cigarette butt; then, thinking better of it, reached down and retrieved it from the grass and threw it into a nearby garbage can. "I'm unmoved? You're an intellectual whose imagination has gotten away from him. The technology is something we actually had in our era."

"You've got to be kidding."

"I don't understand most tech, but I do know a bit about this one thing in particular because, as it happens, I once had occasion to use a police bug that had no batteries but never ran out of power. You know how it worked? It was powered remotely by microwaves. That's what electricity is today, although the methods are a little different from our day."

Luo Ji stopped and stared at Shi Qiang for a long while, then up at the flying cars in the air. He thought about the heating glass, and finally understood: It was just a wireless power supply. The power source emitted electricity in the form of microwaves or other EM radiation to form an electric field over a certain space, allowing any equipment within it to draw power through an antenna or resonant coil. Like Shi Qiang had said, even two centuries ago, this technology was entirely ordinary. The only reason it hadn't been commonplace was because the power loss was too great. Only a small portion of the power emitted into a space could be used, but the majority was lost. In this era, however, mature controlled fusion technology meant that energy sources had been greatly enriched, to the point that losses from wireless power supplies were acceptable.

"And the synthetic grain? Can't they synthesize grain?" Luo Ji asked.

"I'm not really sure about that. Grain is still grown from seed, it's just that it's grown in factories in those cultivation tank things. Crops are all genetically modified, and I've heard that wheat grows just an ear, with no stalk. And it grows pretty quickly because of the strong artificial sunlight, and other things like intense, growth-inducing radiation. A season of wheat and rice can be harvested in a week, so from the outside it looks just like it's produced on a production line."

"Oh—" Luo Ji punctuated his thought with an extended sigh as the gorgeous bubbles before his eyes burst to reveal the true face of the world, and he knew that in this great new era, sophons still floated everywhere and human science was still deadlocked. Existing technology could never cross the line set down by the sophons.

"And the spacecraft that can reach fifteen percent of light speed?"

"Well, that's true. When those warships mobilize, it's like a tiny sun in the sky. And their space weapons—the day before yesterday I saw a news report on TV about an Asian Fleet exercise. A laser cannon swept a target ship as big as a carrier. Half of that iron guy evaporated like a chunk of ice, and the other half exploded like fireworks in a shower of sparkling molten steel. And there are rail-guns that can fire a hundred iron spheres a second, each the size of a football, at tens of kilometers per second. In a few minutes they can flatten a mountain on Mars. . . . So even though there isn't any of your perpetual motion, with these technologies, humanity is more than capable of putting down the Trisolaran Fleet."

Shi Qiang handed Luo Ji a cigarette and taught him how to twist the filter tip to light it. They smoked and watched the snow-white swirls drift upward. "Anyway, my boy, these are good times."

"Yes. Good times."

Luo Ji had hardly finished speaking when Shi Qiang pounced on him and the two of them tumbled onto the grass a few meters away, hearing a loud noise at their heels as a flying car smashed into the spot where they had just been standing. Luo Ji felt the

impact of the blast, and metal debris whizzed overhead, taking out half the billboard and sending the transparent glass tubes of the display crashing to the ground. While he was still on the ground with a dizzy head and a black eye, Shi Qiang leapt up and ran over to the flying car. Its disc-shaped body was entirely broken and deformed, but due to the lack of onboard fuel, it hadn't caught fire. There was only the sound of sparks crackling in the twisted metal.

"There's no one in the car," Shi Qiang said to Luo Ji, who was limping over.

"Da Shi, you saved my life again," Luo Ji said, leaning on his shoulder and massaging his injured leg.

"I don't know how many times I'll have to. You really ought to grow some sense, and a few more eyes." He pointed to the totaled flying car. "Remind you of anything?"

Luo Ji thought about that occasion two centuries before and shivered involuntarily.

Lots of pedestrians crowded round, the scenes of terror on their clothing flashing as one. Two police cars landed, sirens blaring, and several officers got out to form a line around the broken car. Their uniforms flashed like the police light, drowning out the crowd's clothing with their brightness. The one officer who came over to Shi Qiang and Luo Ji had clothing so bright they had to shut their eyes.

"You were right here when the car fell. You aren't hurt, are you?" he said with concern. He evidently could see that the two of them were hibernators, because he made an effort to speak "ancient Chinese."

Before Luo Ji could answer, Shi Qiang pulled the officer who had asked the question across the tape and out of the crowd. Once they had gotten away, the officer's uniform stopped flashing.

"You need to check up on this. It might be an assassination attempt," he said.

The officer laughed. "Really? It's just a traffic accident."

"We want to report it."

"Are you sure?"

"Of course. We're reporting it."

"You're making a big deal out of it. You may have been startled, but it really was a traffic accident. However, according to the law, if you insist on reporting it . . ."

"We insist."

The officer pressed a display area on his sleeve. It popped up an information window, which he looked over, and then said, "It's been reported. For the next forty-eight hours, the police will track you, but this requires your agreement."

"We agree. We might still be in danger."

The officer laughed again. "It's really a common occurrence."

"A common occurrence? Let me ask you: On average, how many traffic accidents of this kind take place in this city every month?"

"There were six or seven all of last year!"

"I'll have you know, officer: In our time, this city had more than that every day."

"Cars all ran on the ground in your day. I can't even imagine how dangerous that was. Well, you're now in the police surveillance system. You'll be notified of any progress on your case, but, please believe me, this is an ordinary traffic accident. Whether or not you filed a report, you would still receive compensation."

After they left the police and the scene of the accident behind, Shi Qiang said to Luo Ji, "We'd better get back to my place. I don't feel at ease when I'm outside. It's not far. We probably should walk back. Taxis are unmanned, so it's not safe."

"But hasn't the ETO been destroyed?" Luo Ji asked, looking about him. Off in the distance, the fallen car had been lifted up by a larger flying car. The crowd had dispersed, and the police car had left. A municipal works vehicle had landed, and several workmen had gotten out to gather scattered debris and begin repairs to the ground, which had been damaged by the crash. Following the small commotion, the city had returned to its normal, pleasing calm.

"Perhaps it has. But you've got to trust my intuition, my boy."

"I'm no longer a Wallfacer."

"That car didn't seem to think so. . . . While we're walking, pay attention to the cars above you."

They kept to the "shade" of the treelike buildings as much as possible, and crossed any open spaces they reached at a run. Soon they arrived at a broad plaza, and Shi Qiang said, "My place is just opposite. It's too far to go around, so we'll have to make a run for it."

"Isn't that being a little paranoid? Maybe it was just a traffic accident."

"That's a 'maybe,' though. There's nothing wrong with being careful. . . . See that sculpture in the center of the plaza? If anything happens, we can hide there."

There was a square sandy area in the center of the plaza, like a miniature desert. The sculpture that Shi Qiang mentioned, located right in the center of the sand, was a group of black pillar-like objects, each two or three meters tall. From a distance, it looked like a grove of withered black trees.

Luo Ji ran across the plaza behind Shi Qiang. When they neared the sandy area, he heard Shi Qiang call, "Hurry. Get in there!" and he was dragged skidding across the sand and then headlong into the withered grove. Lying on the grove's warm sand, he looked up between the black pillars at the sky and saw a flying car zoom down and buzz the grove before pulling up and accelerating away. The gust of wind it left in its wake blew a burst of sand into the air, which hit the pillars with a whoosh.

"Maybe it wasn't headed for us."

"Hmm. Maybe," Shi Qiang said, as he sat up and dumped the sand out of his shoes.

"Will they laugh at us for this?"

"Don't be afraid of that crap. Who's going to recognize you? Besides, we're from two centuries ago, so even if we're entirely normal, people are still gonna laugh. My boy, nothing's lost by being careful. What if the thing really was headed for you?"

Only then did Luo Ji turn his attention to the sculpture they were inside. He noticed that the pillars weren't withered trees, but arms extending out of the desert. The skinny arms were just skin and bones, so at first glance they looked like dead tree trunks. The

hands atop them made a variety of distorted gestures to the sky and seemed to express a kind of endless pain.

"What kind of sculpture is this?" Within this group of struggling arms, Luo Ji felt a chill, even though he was still sweating from the run. At the sculpture's edge, he saw a solemn obelisk, on which was carved a line of large golden characters: MAKE TIME FOR CIVILIZATION, FOR CIVILIZATION WON'T MAKE TIME.

"The Great Ravine Memorial," Shi Qiang said. He did not seem interested in explaining further, but led Luo Ji out of the sculpture and across the other half of the plaza at a fast clip. "Okay, my boy. This tree's where I live," Shi Qiang said, pointing to the massive architectural tree in front of them.

Luo Ji looked around him as he walked. All of a sudden he heard the floor creak, and then the ground fell away under his feet and he plummeted downward. Shi Qiang grabbed hold of him when his chest was already at ground level and struggled to haul him up. After he had his footing, the two of them stared at the hole in the ground. It was the mouth of a sewer, and its cover had slid aside just as Luo Ji was about to step on it.

"My god! Are you all right, sir? That's really dangerous!" said a voice issuing from a small billboard next to them. The billboard was attached to a small pavilion containing a machine selling drinks and such, and the speaker was a young man dressed in a blue uniform. His face was pale, and he seemed even more frightened than Luo Ji. "I'm with the Office of Evacuation and Drainage at the Third Municipal Administration Company. That cover opened automatically. It might be a software failure."

"Does this happen often?" Shi Qiang asked.

"Oh, no, no. At least, this is the first time I've ever seen it."

Shi Qiang picked up a small round stone from the grass next to the road and tossed it down the hole. It was quite some time before they heard any sound. "Damn. How deep is it?" he asked the man in the billboard.

"Around thirty meters. So, like I said, it's really dangerous! I've inspected the surface drainage system. The sewers in your day were

all pretty shallow. This accident has been recorded. You . . ." He glanced at his sleeve as he spoke. "Ah, Mr. Luo. You can go to the TMAC to be compensated."

At last they reached the lobby leading to Shi Qiang's tree, #1863. He said that he lived on branch 106, near the top, and advised Luo Ji to eat down below before going up. They went into a restaurant on one side of the lobby. Aside from being as clean as a 3D rendering, one characteristic of this age was even more obvious here than when he first saw it in the reawakening center: Dynamic information windows were everywhere, on the walls, tabletops, chairs, the floor and ceiling, and even on small objects like the glasses and napkin holders on the table. Everything had an interface and display with scrolling text or moving images. It was as if the entire restaurant was a giant computer display showing off a diverse and glittering splendor.

Not many people were dining. They chose a table by the window and sat down. Shi Qiang tapped the tabletop to activate an interface and then ordered a few dishes. "I can't read the foreign writing, so I've only ordered Chinese ones."

"The world seems like it's built using bricks made from displays," Luo Ji sighed.

"That's right. Anything smooth can light up." As Shi Qiang spoke he took out a pack of cigarettes and passed it to Luo Ji. "Look at this. Just a pack of cheap cigarettes." As soon as Luo Ji held the pack in his hands, it started displaying an animated image of several miniature pictures that seemed like an options menu.

"This . . . it's just a film that can display images," Luo Ji said as he looked at the pack.

"A film? You can go online with this gadget!" Shi Qiang reached over and tapped the pack, and one of the miniature pictures sank in like a button. Then the advertisement he selected took over the entire pack.

In the picture, Luo Ji saw a family with one child sitting in a living room. The picture obviously came from the past, and a shrill voice sounded from the pack: "Mr. Luo, this is the era you used to live in. We know that in that age, owning a house in the capital was

365

the grand dream of every person. Now, the Greenleaf Group can help you achieve that dream. As you can see, this is a wonderful age. Houses have turned into leaves on a tree, and the Greenleaf Group can provide you with every kind of leaf." Here the picture showed a scene of leaves being added to a tree branch, and then a dazzling variety of hanging homes, one of which was even completely transparent, with furnishings inside that seemed suspended in midair. "Of course, we can also build you a traditional home on the surface to return you to the warmth of the Golden Age, and build you a warm . . . family . . ." A lawn and detached home, perhaps another old photo, appeared onscreen. The voice artist in the ad spoke in fluent "ancient Chinese," but paused momentarily before the word "family," then said it with particular emphasis. After all, it was something the speaker didn't have, something that belonged to the past.

Shi Qiang took the cigarette pack out of Luo Ji's hands, withdrew the last two cigarettes, passed one to him, and then crumpled the empty pack into a ball and tossed it onto the table. On the crumpled ball, the images still flashed, but the sound had disappeared. "Whenever I go anywhere, the first thing I do is to turn off every screen that's around me. They're so annoying," Shi Qiang said, turning off the tabletop and floor displays with his hands and feet. "But the people here can't be away from them." He pointed around them. "There aren't any computers anymore. Anyone who wants to go online or something can just tap any smooth surface. Clothing and shoes can be used as computers, too. Believe it or not, I've even seen toilet paper that you can go online with."

Luo Ji pulled out a napkin. It was just ordinary, non-wired paper, but the paper box activated, and the pretty woman on it hawked bandages to Luo Ji, evidently aware of today's experiences and guessing that his arms and legs might have gotten scraped up.

"God," Luo Ji sighed, and stuffed the napkin back in the box.

"This is the information age. Our times were pretty damn primitive," Shi Qiang said with a laugh.

While they waited for their food, Luo Ji asked Shi Qiang about

his life. He felt a little guilty for only asking now, but looking back on how the day had gone, he had been something of a clockwork machine ticking relentlessly forward. Only now did he have a bit of free time.

"They had me retire. It's not a bad deal," Shi Qiang said simply.

"Was it the Public Security Bureau, or the unit you were at later? Are they still around?"

"They're around. And the PSB is still the PSB. But even before hibernation I wasn't connected to it anymore. The unit I was with later now belongs to the Asian Fleet. You know, the fleet is like a big country, so I'm a foreigner now." Saying this, he exhaled a long cloud of smoke. He watched the cloud ascend, as if he was trying hard to unravel a mystery.

"Countries don't have the significance they used to. . . . The world's changed. It's confusing. Fortunately, Da Shi, you and I are the kind of indifferent people who can live, and live well, no matter what happens."

"Luo, my boy, to tell you the truth, I'm not as open-minded as you in certain things. I'm not as uninvolved. If I'd been through everything you have, I'd have fallen apart long ago."

Luo Ji picked up the crumpled cigarette pack from the table, opening it to reveal the image that was still showing, with only a little discoloration. It was playing the Greenleaf Group advert. He said, "Whether as messiah, or as refugee, I can always use what resources I have to try and live a happy life. You might think I'm selfish, but to be honest, this is the only thing I respect about myself. Da Shi, let me say something about you. You look like a careless person, but deep in your bones you're someone who prizes responsibility. Leave that responsibility completely behind now. Look at this age. Who needs us? Carpe diem is our most sacred duty."

"Sure, but if I gave up all responsibility, you wouldn't have much of an appetite at all right now." Shi Qiang tossed his cigarette into the ashtray, activating a cigarette advert.

Luo Ji realized he had misspoken. "Oh, no, Da Shi, you've still got to carry out your responsibility to me. I'll die if I leave you.

Already today you've saved me one, two, three times. Or at least two and a half!"

"I can't just leave someone to die, you mean? That's the life I've got, a life of saving yours," Shi Qiang said disapprovingly as he cast his eyes about him, probably looking for someplace selling cigarettes. Then he looked back, leaned in to Luo Ji, and whispered, "But you really were a messiah for a little while, my boy."

"It's impossible for anyone in that position to be of sound mind. Fortunately, I'm now back to normal."

"How did you come up with the idea of putting a spell on that star?"

"I was seriously paranoid back then. I don't want to think about it. Believe it or not, Da Shi, I'm certain that while I was asleep, they not only cured my illness, but also conducted psychiatric treatment. Really, I'm not the same person now that I was back then. How could I have been so stupid as to have that kind of idea? That sort of delusion?"

"What delusion? Let me hear it."

"It's difficult to explain briefly. Besides, there's no point. In your work, you must have run into delusional patients, people who were always thinking someone wanted to kill them. Is there any point to listening to those people talk?" Luo Ji methodically tore the cigarette pack into pieces. This time the display was destroyed, but the scraps still flashed in a grotesquely colored heap.

"Okay. We'll talk about something happy. My son is still alive."

"What?" Luo Ji asked, practically jumping up in his surprise.

"I just learned about it two days ago. He looked me up. We haven't met, just spoken by phone."

"He's not . . ."

"I don't know how long he spent in prison, but afterward he went into hibernation. He said it was to come to the future to see me. Who knows where the kid got the money. Now he's on the surface, and he's arranged to come over tomorrow."

Luo Ji stood up excitedly, sweeping flashing scraps of paper to the floor. "Oh, Da Shi, that's just . . . We've got to drink to that."

"A drink, then. The alcohol in this age tastes awful, but it's still the same strength."

Then the food came. Luo Ji didn't recognize anything, and Shi Qiang said, "Nothing's good. There are restaurants supplied by traditional farms, but those are all high-end places. We'll eat at one when Xiaoming comes."

But Luo Ji's attention had shifted to the server. Her face and body were unrealistically beautiful, and he saw that the other servers sliding between the tables had the same angelic appearance.

"Hey, don't stare like an idiot. They're fake," Shi Qiang said, without looking up.

"Robots?" Luo Ji asked. At last the future had something he had seen in one of his childhood science fiction stories.

"Sort of."

"What do you mean, 'sort of'?"

Shi Qiang pointed to a robot server and said, "This silly girl only knows how to serve food. They travel fixed paths. How stupid is that? Once I saw a table that had been temporarily moved, but they kept bringing dishes to the original location, so everything crashed to the ground."

When the robot server had laid out the food, it smiled sweetly and wished them a good meal. Its voice did not sound robotic, but was incredibly lovely. Then, it extended a slender hand and picked up the dinner knife in front of Shi Qiang. . . .

Like lightning, Shi Qiang's eyes shot from the knife in the server's hands to Luo Ji across the table from him. He leapt up, vaulted the table, and pulled Luo Ji violently off his chair to the floor. Almost simultaneously, the robot stabbed the knife right where Luo Ji's heart would have been. The knife went through the back of the chair, activating its information interface. The robot retracted the knife and stood beside the table with a serving tray in its other hand, still with the sweet smile on its unrealistically beautiful face. Panicked, Luo Ji struggled to stand up, then hid behind Shi Qiang. But Shi Qiang just waved his hand, saying, "Don't worry. It's not that agile."

The robot stood motionless, holding the knife and smiling, and once again wished them a good meal in its gentle voice.

The startled diners had clustered around them looking at the scene in amazement. Then the duty manager came rushing over. When she heard Shi Qiang accusing the restaurant's robot of attempted murder, she shook her head. "Sir, that's impossible! Their eyes don't see people. They only see the sensors on the tables and chairs!"

"I'll testify that it picked up a dinner knife and tried to kill that man. We saw it with our own eyes!" one man said in a loud voice. The other onlookers added their proof.

While the duty manager was considering how to rebut this, the robot stabbed the knife at the chair a second time, putting it precisely through the hole punctured the first time and eliciting a few screams.

"Have a pleasant meal," it said with a smile.

A number of other people arrived, including the restaurant's engineer. When he pressed the back of the robot's head, the smile left her face and she said, "Forced shutdown. Breakpoint data backed up." Then she froze in place.

"It's probably a software failure," the engineer said, wiping away cold sweat.

"Does this happen often?" Shi Qiang said with a sarcastic smile.

"No, no. I swear, I've never even heard of anything like this," the engineer said, then directed two assistants to haul the robot out.

The duty manager energetically explained to the customers that until the cause of the failure was identified, the restaurant would use real human servers, but about half of the customers left anyway.

"You both reacted pretty fast," one bystander said admiringly.

"Hibernators. In their era, people had experience with this kind of sudden incident," someone else said. His clothing displayed a swordsman.

The duty manager said to Luo Ji and Shi Qiang, "Sirs, this was truly . . . Anyway, I guarantee that you'll receive compensation."

"Good. Now let's eat." Shi Qiang beckoned Luo Ji to retake his seat, and a human server brought over new dishes to replace those that had spilled.

Sitting there, his shock not yet abated, Luo Ji felt the uncomfortable hole in the chair back. "Da Shi, it seems the whole world is against me. I used to have a favorable impression of it."

Shi Qiang considered one of the dishes in front of him, then said, "I've got some ideas about this." He looked up and poured Luo Ji a drink. "Ignore it for now. I'll tell you in detail later."

"Here: to carpe diem, to living one day at a time. One hour at a time, even," Luo Ji said as he raised his glass. "Here's to your still-living son."

"Are you really okay?" Shi Qiang said, shooting him a smile.

"I've been a messiah. Nothing scares me." He shrugged, then drained his glass. The taste of the alcohol made him wince. "This is like rocket fuel."

"You kill me, my boy. That attitude of yours has always killed me," Shi Qiang said, sticking up a thumb.

The leaf where Shi Qiang lived was at the top of the tree. It was a spacious house, and was fully equipped with facilities for comfortable living. It had a gym, and even an indoor garden with a fountain.

He said, "The fleet gave me these temporary living quarters. They said I can buy a better leaf with my retirement money."

"Does everyone have so much space to live in these days?"

"Probably. This kind of structure is the best use of space. A big leaf is equivalent to an entire building from our era. But mainly it's because there are fewer people. Far fewer, ever since the Great Ravine."

"But Da Shi, your country is in space."

"I won't be going there. I'm already retired, you know."

Luo Ji's eyes felt more comfortable here, largely because most of the information windows in Shi Qiang's house were closed, although there were scattered flashes in the walls and on the floor. Shi Qiang tapped an interface on the floor with his foot, turning one wall entirely transparent and unfurling the night city before

their eyes. It was a dazzling, giant forest of Christmas trees chained together by the lights of the traffic.

Luo Ji went over to the sofa, which was hard as marble to the touch. "Is this for sitting?" he asked. At Shi Qiang's affirmative, he sat gingerly down on it, only to feel like he was sinking into soft clay. The sofa's cushions and backrest adapted to a person's body, forming a mold completely in sync with their body shape, keeping pressure to a minimum.

His vision from the slab of iron ore in the Meditation Room of the UN Building two centuries ago had become reality.

"Do you have any sleeping pills?" he asked. Now that he was in a space that felt safe, exhaustion hit him.

"No, but you can buy them here," Shi Qiang said, and operated the wall again. "Here. Nonprescription sleeping pills. This one, River of Dreams."

Although Luo Ji thought he would witness some sort of high-tech hardware-over-the-network transmission, the reality was much simpler than he imagined. In a few minutes, a small, flying delivery van pulled up outside the transparent wall and delivered the medicine through the portal that had just opened up with a slender mechanical arm. Luo Ji took the medicine from Shi Qiang. It was a traditional box without any active display. The instructions said to take one pill, so he opened the pack, took one out, and reached out for the glass of water on the coffee table.

"Wait a moment," Shi Qiang said, taking the box out of Luo Ji's hands and reading it carefully before returning it to him. "What does this say? The one I asked for was called River of Dreams."

Luo Ji saw a long string of complicated English-language drug names. "I don't recognize it. But it's certainly not River of Dreams."

Shi Qiang activated a window on the coffee table and began looking for a medical consult. With Luo Ji's help, they found one, a white-clothed consulting physician who examined the box, then looked from the box to Shi Qiang with a peculiar expression.

"Where did this come from?" the doctor asked warily.

"I bought it. Right here."

"Impossible. This is a prescription drug. It's only for use in the hibernation center."

"What's it got to do with hibernation?"

"It's short-term hibernation medicine. It can make someone hibernate for ten days to a year."

"You just swallow it?"

"No. It requires a whole set of external systems to sustain internal bodily circulatory functions before short-term hibernation can be achieved."

"And if you take it without them?"

"Then you'd die for sure. But you'd die comfortably. So it's often used for suicide."

Shi Qiang closed the window and tossed the box onto the table. He looked straight at Luo Ji for a while, then said, "Damn it."

"Damn it," Luo Ji said, pitching back onto the sofa. Then he was subjected to the final attempt on his life that day.

When his head touched back against the sofa, the hard headrest quickly adapted to the back of his head and began to form an impression of its shape. But the process didn't stop there. His head and neck continued to sink, until the headrest on either side formed a pair of tentacles that squeezed tight around his neck. He had no time to cry out, but could only open his mouth and eyes and scramble with his hands.

Shi Qiang bounded into the kitchen and returned with a knife, which he used to hack at the tentacles a few times, then resorted to his own hands to pry them from Luo Ji's neck. When Luo Ji left the sofa and pitched forward onto the floor, the sofa's surface lit up and displayed a large string of error messages.

"How many times have I saved your life today, my boy?" Shi Qiang asked, rubbing his hands.

"This is . . . the . . . sixth," Luo Ji said, through gasps. He vomited onto the floor. When he finished, he leaned back weakly against the sofa, but then pulled back immediately, as if shocked. He didn't know where to put his hands. "How long will it be before I can be as agile as you and save my own life?"

"Probably never," Shi Qiang said. A vacuum cleaner–like machine glided over to clean up the vomit on the floor.

"Then I'm dead meat. This is a twisted world."

"It's not that bad. I've got an idea about the whole situation, at least. The first attempt on your life failed, and then there were five more attempts. This is stupidity, not professional behavior. Something somewhere must have gone wrong. . . . Let's contact the police immediately. We can't wait for them to crack the case."

"Who made a mistake, and where? Da Shi, it's been two centuries. Don't just apply your mind-set from our time."

"It's the same thing, my boy. Certain things are the same no matter the age. As for whose mistake it is, I really don't know. I even wonder whether such a 'who' actually exists. . . ."

The doorbell rang. Shi Qiang opened it to see several people standing outside. They wore civilian clothes, but Shi Qiang identified them before the leader had even flashed his ID.

"Wow. So there are actual footbeats in this society. Come on in, officers."

Three of them entered the house, leaving two others outside to guard the door. The officer in charge, who looked about thirty years old, surveyed the room. Like Shi Qiang and Luo Ji, he had all the displays on his clothes turned off, which put them at ease, and he spoke a pure, fluent "ancient Chinese" without any English words.

"I'm Officer Guo Zhengming with the PSB's Digital Reality Department. I apologize for our tardy arrival. That was negligent. The last time there was a case like this was half a century ago." He bowed to Shi Qiang. "I pay my respects to my senior officer. Aptitude like yours is very rare in the force these days."

As Officer Guo was speaking, Luo Ji and Shi Qiang noticed that all of the information windows in the house had switched off. The leaf had evidently been cut off from the external hyper-information world. The other two officers were hard at work. They were holding something he hadn't seen in ages: a notebook computer. But the computer was as thin as a sheet of paper.

"They're installing a firewall for this leaf," Officer Guo explained. "Rest assured, you're safe now. And I'll guarantee that you'll receive compensation from the municipal PSB system."

"Today," Shi Qiang said, counting off on his fingers, "we've been guaranteed compensation four times."

"I know. And lots of people in lots of departments have lost their jobs over this. I beg for your cooperation, so that I don't join them. Thanks in advance," he said, bowing to them.

Shi Qiang said, "I understand that. I've been in that position. Do you need us to brief you on the situation?"

"No. We've actually been tracking you all along. It's just negligence."

"Can you tell us what's happening?"

"Killer 5.2."

"What?"

"It's a network virus. The ETO first released it about a century into the Crisis Era, and then there were lots of subsequent variants and upgrades. It's a murder virus. First it establishes the identity of the target by a variety of methods including the chip everyone has implanted in their body. When it locates the target, the Killer virus manipulates every possible piece of external hardware to carry out the murder. Its concrete manifestation is what you experienced today. It seems like everything in the world wants to kill you. So, at the time, people called it a 'modern hex.' For a while, the Killer software was even commercialized and sold on the online black market. You entered the personal ID number of your target and uploaded the virus. Then, even if that person was able to evade death, they would still have a hard time living in society."

"The industry developed as far as that? Incredible!" Shi Qiang exclaimed.

"Software from a century ago can still run today?" Luo Ji asked incredulously.

"Sure it can. Computer technology stopped advancing long ago. When the Killer virus first appeared, it killed quite a few people, including a head of state, but eventually it was controlled

by firewalls and antivirus software and gradually faded away. This version of Killer is programmed specifically to attack Dr. Luo, but because the target was in hibernation, it never had the opportunity to take any concrete action. It stayed dormant and wasn't detected or recorded by the information security system. It was only when Dr. Luo emerged into the world today that Killer 5.2 activated itself and carried out its mission. It's just that its creators were wiped out a century ago."

"They were still trying to kill me a century ago?" Luo Ji said. A mood he thought was gone forever returned, and he struggled to dispel it again.

"Yes. The key thing about this version of the Killer virus is that it was programmed specifically for you. It was never activated, which is why it was still lurking in wait today."

"Then what are we supposed to do now?" Shi Qiang asked.

"The entire system will be cleaned of Killer 5.2, but that will take some time. Before it's completed, you have two choices. First, Dr. Luo can be given a temporary false identity, but this will not totally guarantee his safety and might lead to other more serious consequences. Due to the technological sophistication of the ETO software, Killer 5.2 might have already recorded other characteristics of its target. In one case that caused a sensation a century ago, when a protected individual was given a false identity, Killer used fuzzy recognition to simultaneously kill over a hundred people, target included. The other choice, and my personal recommendation, is for you to live up on the surface for a while. Killer 5.2 won't have any hardware to manipulate up there."

Shi Qiang said, "I agree. Even without this situation, I've been wanting to go up to the surface."

"What's on the surface?" Luo Ji asked.

Shi Qiang explained, "Most of the reawakened hibernators live on the surface. It's hard for them to adapt down here."

"That's right. So you ought to spend at least some time up there," Officer Guo said. "Many aspects of modern society—politics, economics, culture, lifestyle, and relations between the sexes—

have changed greatly in two centuries, so it takes some time for us to adapt."

"But you've adapted well enough," Shi Qiang said, looking him over. He and Luo Ji had both noticed that the officer had said "us."

"I went into hibernation because of leukemia, and I was quite young when I reawakened, just thirteen years old," Guo Zhengming said with a laugh. "But people still don't understand the difficulties I've had. I don't know how many times I've gone for psychological treatment."

"Are there many other hibernators like you who have totally adapted to modern life?" Luo Ji asked.

"Lots. But you can still live quite well on the surface."

"Special Contingent of Future Reinforcements commander Zhang Beihai reporting," Zhang Beihai said, and saluted.

Behind the commander of the Asian Fleet flowed the brilliant Milky Way. Fleet Command was in orbit around Jupiter and rotated continuously to produce artificial gravity. Zhang Beihai noticed that the room lights were relatively dim, and the wide windows seemed intended to integrate the interior environment with space outside as closely as possible.

The commander saluted back. "Greetings, predecessor." He looked quite young, his Asian features illuminated by the glow of his epaulets and cap insignia. When he was issued a uniform on the sixth day after he reawakened, Zhang Beihai had noticed the familiar emblem of the space force: a silver star shining rays in four directions, the rays in the shape of sword. Two centuries had passed, and while the insignia had not changed much, the fleet had become an independent country, with a president as its supreme leader. The commander was just in charge of the military.

Zhang Beihai said, "That's too much, Commander. We're all just new recruits now, who have to learn everything."

The commander smiled and shook his head. "You can't say

377

that. You've already learned everything there is to know here. And the knowledge you've got, we'll never be able to learn. That's why we awakened you now."

"Commander Chang Weisi of the Chinese Space Force asked me to convey his greetings."

Zhang Beihai's words touched something in the commander's heart. He turned and looked out through the window at the river of stars, like the upper reaches of a long river. "He was an exceptional general, one of the founders of the Asian Fleet. Today's space strategy still uses the framework he established two centuries ago. I wish that he could have seen this day."

"Today's achievements are far beyond anything he ever dreamed."

"But all of this began in his . . . in your time."

Then Jupiter appeared, at first as a sliver of an arc that quickly took over the entire field of view in the window, bathing the office in its orange light. The dreamlike patterns of hydrogen and helium in its vast gaseous ocean were on a breathtaking scale and fascinating in their detail. The Great Red Spot moved into view. The super-storm that could hold two Earths looked like the giant, pupilless eye of this blurry world. The three fleets had put their primary base on Jupiter because its hydrogen-helium ocean held an inexhaustible supply of fusion fuel.

Zhang Beihai was transfixed by the Jovian scene. Countless times he had dreamed of the new domain that now presented itself before his eyes. He waited until Jupiter had moved out of the window before speaking. "Commander, the great achievements of this age are what make our mission unnecessary."

The commander turned to him and said, "No, that's not right. The Future Reinforcement Plan was a farsighted initiative. During the Great Ravine, when the space armed forces were on the brink of collapse, the special reinforcement contingents played a major role in stabilizing the overall situation."

"But our contingent arrived too late to be of assistance."

"I'm sorry, but that's how things are," the commander said. The lines on his face turned gentle. "After you left, they sent more

special reinforcement contingents to the future, and the last to be sent out were the first to be reawakened."

"That's understandable, Commander, since their knowledge framework was closer to that era's."

"Right. Eventually your contingent was the only one left in hibernation. The Great Ravine ended and the world entered a period of rapid development. Defeatism had practically vanished, so there was no need to reawaken you. At the time, the fleet made the decision to keep you until the Doomsday Battle."

"Commander, this was actually what we all hoped for," Zhang Beihai said excitedly.

"And it's the highest honor of all space servicemen. They were well aware of this when they made that decision. But present circumstances are totally different, as you of course know." The commander pointed at the river of stars behind him. "The Doomsday Battle might never even take place."

"That's excellent, Commander. My small regret as a soldier counts for nothing compared with the great victory humanity is about to welcome. I just hope you'll be able to fulfill our one request: to let us join the fleet at the lowest level, as ordinary soldiers, to do whatever work we can."

The commander shook his head. "The length of service for all special contingent personnel will resume from the date of reawakening, and ranks will be elevated one or two levels."

"Commander, that shouldn't be. We don't want to spend our remaining years in an office. We want to go to the fleet's front lines. Two centuries ago, the space force was our dream. Without it, our lives have no meaning. But even at our present ranks, we are unqualified for work in the fleet."

"I never said I wanted you to leave the fleet. Precisely the opposite. You will all be working in the fleet to complete a highly important mission."

"Thank you, Commander. But what mission can there be for us today?"

The commander did not answer him. Instead, as if it had only just

occurred to him, he said, "Are you okay with talking while standing like this?" The commander's office had no chairs, and the table had been designed to be high enough to work at while standing. Fleet Command's rotation produced one-sixth of Earth's gravity, which meant there wasn't much difference between standing and sitting.

Zhang Beihai smiled and nodded. "Not a problem. I spent a year in space."

"And the language? Do you have any communication problems in the fleet?"

The commander was speaking standard Chinese, but the three fleets had formed a language of their own, similar to the modern Chinese and modern English on Earth, but with the two languages blended more closely. Chinese and English words each accounted for half of the vocabulary.

"At first—mostly because I couldn't distinguish between Chinese and English vocabulary—but I was able to understand it pretty quickly. Speaking is more difficult."

"That doesn't matter. If you just use English or Chinese when you speak, we'll be able to understand you. So that means that the General Staff Department has fully briefed you?"

"That's right. In the first few days on base, they gave us a comprehensive introduction to everything."

"Then you must be aware of the mental seal."

"That's right."

"Recent investigations still haven't discovered any signs of the Imprinted. What's your read?"

"I believe that one possibility is that the Imprinted have disappeared. Another possibility is that they've been deeply hidden. If a person has an ordinary defeatist mentality, they will speak of it to others. But a one-hundred-percent unshakeable technologically hardened faith will inevitably produce a corresponding sense of mission. Defeatism and Escapism are intimately related, and if the Imprinted really exist, then their ultimate mission is bound to be accomplishing an escape into the universe. But to achieve this goal, they have to deeply conceal their true thoughts."

The commander nodded with approval. "An excellent analysis. This is the opinion of General Staff."

"Commander, the second alternative is very dangerous."

"Yes, it is, particularly with the Trisolaran probe so close to the Solar System. The fleet is divided by command system classifications into two major groups. The first, a distributed command system, is a traditional structure akin to the naval craft you once commanded. The captain's orders are carried out by various operating personnel. The second is a centralized command system. The captain's orders are carried out automatically by the ship's computer. The most recently built advanced space warships, as well as those currently under construction, fall into this category. It is mainly against this category of warship that the mental seal poses a threat, because the captain wields enormous power in the command system. He can unilaterally control when the ship leaves and returns to port, its speed and course, and even a large portion of its weapons systems. Under this command system, you could call the ship an extension of the captain's body. Right now, 179 of the 695 stellar-class warships in the fleet have a centralized command system. The commanding officers on board these ships will be the focus of review. Originally, all the warships involved in the review process were supposed to be docked and sealed up, but present circumstances no longer permit this, because the three fleets are preparing to intercept the Trisolaran probe when it arrives. This will be the first actual engagement between the Space Fleet and the Trisolaran invaders, so all warships must be on standby."

"So, Commander, the command authority for centrally commanded warships must be turned over to reliable individuals," Zhang Beihai said. He had been speculating about his mission but had not guessed it yet.

"Who is reliable?" the commander asked. "We don't know the extent of the mental seal, and we have no information about the Imprinted. In these circumstances, no one can be trusted, not even me."

The sun appeared outside the window. Although its light was far weaker than on Earth from this distance, the commander's body

was hidden in a glare when the disc passed behind him, leaving only his voice: "But you are all reliable. When you entered hibernation, the mental seal didn't exist. And one of the most important factors for your selection two centuries ago was your loyalty and faith. You are the only trustworthy group available to us in the fleet right now. So the fleet has decided to put the authority of the centralized command system into your hands, to appoint you as acting captains, through whom every order issued by the former captains must pass before being issued to the command system."

Two tiny suns ignited in Zhang Beihai's eyes. He said, "Commander, I'm afraid that's not possible."

"Saying no to an order is not our tradition."

The commander's use of "our" and "tradition" warmed Zhang Beihai, letting him know that the bloodline of the military of two centuries ago still endured in the space fleet of today.

"Commander, we're from two centuries ago, after all. In the context of the navy of our time, it's like using an official in the Beiyang Fleet to command a twenty-first-century destroyer."

"Do you think that the Qing admirals Deng Shichang and Liu Buchan[20] would really be unable to command your destroyers? They were educated, and their English was good. They would have learned. Today, captaining a space warship doesn't involve technical details. Captains issue general commands, but the warship is a black box to them. Besides, the warships will be docked at base while you serve as acting captain. They won't be navigating. Your duty will be to convey the former captains' commands to the control system once you've determined whether or not the commands are normal. You'll be able to pick that up as you learn."

"We'll have too much power in our hands. You could let the former captains retain a portion of that power, and we could supervise their orders."

"If you think about it carefully, you'll realize that won't work. If the Imprinted really do occupy key battle positions, they'll take

20 *Translator's Note:* Liu Buchan commanded the Beiyang Fleet's flagship, the battleship *Dingyuan*, in the aforementioned Battle of Weihaiwei in February 1895.

any necessary measures to evade your supervision, including assassinating their supervisors. A centrally supervised ship on standby requires just three commands to take off, after which it's too late to do anything. The system must only acknowledge commands from the acting captain."

As the personnel craft flew past the Asian Fleet's Jupiter base, Zhang Beihai felt he was flying over a range of towering mountains, except each was a docked warship. The naval base had entered nightside orbit around Jupiter, and the steel mountain clusters slept silently under the surface phosphorescence and the silvery moonlight from Europa overhead. A moment later, a ball of white light rose from the edge of the mountain range, lighting the moored ships in perfect clarity in an instant. To Zhang Beihai, it looked like a sunrise over the mountains, casting a moving shadow of the fleet upon the turbulent Jovian atmosphere down below. When a second light rose over the other side of the fleet, he realized it wasn't the sun, but two warships that were entering the dock and turning their fusion engines toward the base to decelerate.

The fleet's chief of staff, who was delivering Zhang Beihai to his new post, told him that more than four hundred warships, representing two-thirds of the Asian Fleet, were now moored at the base. The remainder of the fleet's ships now cruising the Solar System and beyond were also expected to return to port.

Zhang Beihai had to tear himself away from the grand spectacle of the fleet and return to reality. "Sir, won't recalling all of the ships provoke any Imprinted there are to immediate action?"

"Hmm. No, the order recalling the ships was given for another reason—a real one, not an excuse, although it does sound a little ridiculous. You haven't been watching the news lately, I take it?"

"No. I've been reading materials on *Natural Selection*."

"Don't worry about that. You've got a good grasp of things, judging from the last phase of basic training. Your task now is to familiarize yourself with the systems to the point that everything

can proceed in an orderly manner once you go aboard. It's not as hard as you think. . . . Competition among the three fleets for the task of intercepting the Trisolaran probe has turned into bickering, but a preliminary agreement was hammered out by the Joint Conference yesterday: Each fleet's ships will assemble back at base. A special committee will supervise the execution of the maneuver to avoid any ships being dispatched without authorization to carry out the interception."

"Why has it come to that? Any technological information and intelligence obtained from a successful interception would be shared."

"Yes, but it's a question of honor. There's considerable political capital to be gained by the fleet that makes first contact with Trisolaris. Why did I call it ridiculous? Because it's cheap and absolutely risk-free. The worst thing that could happen is if the probe self-destructs during the interception process, so everyone's gunning for it. If it was a battle with the main Trisolaran Fleet, then all sides would try to preserve their strength. Politics today isn't all that different from your time. . . . Look, there's *Natural Selection*."

As the personnel craft approached *Natural Selection* and the sheer bulk of the iron mountain gradually became clear, the image of *Tang* floated up in Zhang Beihai's mind. *Natural Selection*, comprised of a disc-shaped body and a separate cylindrical engine, looked entirely different from that seagoing aircraft carrier of two centuries before. When *Tang* met its untimely end, it was like he had lost his spiritual home, even though he had never moved in. Now, this giant spaceship gave him a new feeling of home. On *Natural Selection*'s stalwart hull, his spirit found a place to live after two centuries of wandering, like a child enfolded in the embrace of some enormous power.

Natural Selection was the flagship of the third squadron of the Asian Fleet, and in gross tonnage and performance it was second to none. Possessing the latest non-media fusion propulsion system, at full thrust it could accelerate to 15 percent of the speed of light, and its impeccable internal ecological systems could sustain a long-term voyage. In fact, an experimental version of this system

was first put into use on the moon seventy-five years ago and had not yet exhibited any major defects or faults. *Natural Selection*'s weapons were the most powerful in the fleet, too. Its gamma-ray lasers, railguns, high-energy particle beams, and stellar torpedoes made up a four-way weapons system that could obliterate the surface of an Earth-sized planet.

Natural Selection now occupied Zhang Beihai's entire field of view so that only part of it was visible from the personnel craft. He noticed that the outer walls of the ship were mirror-smooth, a broad mirror that perfectly reflected the atmospheric ocean of Jupiter, as well as the gradual approach of the personnel craft.

An oval opening appeared in the outer wall of the ship. The craft flew straight inside and came to a halt. The chief of staff opened the cabin door and exited first. Although Zhang Beihai was slightly nervous because he hadn't seen the craft pass through an air lock, he immediately sensed the influx of fresh air from the outside. The technology to maintain a pressurized compartment opening directly into space without allowing air to leak out was not something he had seen before.

Zhang Beihai and the chief of staff were inside a giant sphere the diameter of a soccer field. Spaceship compartments typically adopted a spherical structure, because during acceleration, deceleration, or change of direction, any point on the sphere could serve as a floor or ceiling, and during weightlessness, the center of the sphere would be the crew's main activity space. In Zhang Beihai's time, cabins had been modeled on the structure of Earth buildings, so he was not at all used to this entirely new cabin structure. The chief of staff told him that this was the fighter hangar, but since there were no fighters right now, a formation of *Natural Selection*'s two thousand officers and soldiers was floating in the center of the sphere.

Before Zhang Beihai entered hibernation, national space forces had begun conducting drills in the weightlessness of space. They had developed specifications and drill books as a result, but implementation had been particularly difficult. Personnel could use their space

suits' microthrusters to move about outside the cabin, but since they lacked propulsion equipment inside, they had to maneuver by pushing against bulkheads and paddling the air. Under such conditions, it was very difficult to form neat lines. Now, he was astonished at the sight of more than two thousand people floating in space in such a neat formation without any supports. These days, personnel moved through weightless cabins primarily by using magnetic belts, fabricated from superconductors and containing a circuit that generated a magnetic field that interacted with the magnetic field that was always present in the cabins and corridors of the spacecraft. With a tiny controller in hand, they could move freely inside the ship. Zhang Beihai was now putting on such a belt, but it would require skill to master.

He watched the formation of space soldiers, a generation that had grown up in the fleet. Their tall, slender bodies had none of the clumsy sturdiness of people growing up under Earth's gravity, but possessed the light agility of spacers. Three officers were in front of the formation, and his gaze eventually rested on the young woman in the center with four glittering stars on her shoulder— *Natural Selection*'s captain, no doubt. A typical representative of new space humanity, taller even than Zhang Beihai, who was himself quite tall. She drifted easily over from the formation, her slender body floating through space like an elegant musical note. When she reached Zhang Beihai and the chief of staff she stopped, and the hair that had been floating behind her rippled around the fair skin of her neck. Her eyes were full of sunshine and vitality, and Zhang Beihai immediately trusted her, because the Imprinted would never wear such an expression.

"Dongfang Yanxu, captain of *Natural Selection*," she said, saluting him. A note of playful challenge appeared in her eyes. "On behalf of the entire crew, I offer a gift to my forbear." She extended her hand, and he saw that, although the object she held in it had changed quite a bit, it was still recognizably a pistol. "If you really find that I have defeatist thinking and Escapist goals, you may use this to kill me."

Getting to the surface was easy. The trunk of every giant tree building was a pillar supporting the dome of the underground city, and from the trunk you could take an elevator directly to the surface, passing through more than three hundred meters of rock. When Luo Ji and Shi Qiang exited the elevator, they felt nostalgic, a feeling prompted by one thing: The walls and floor of the exit hall did not have activated display windows. Information was displayed on actual display screens that hung from the ceiling. It looked like an old subway station, and most of the handful of people in it wore clothes that didn't flash.

When they passed through the hall air lock, they were met by a hot wind blowing dusty air.

"There's my boy!" Shi Qiang shouted, pointing at a man bounding up the steps. From this distance, Luo Ji could make out only that the man was in his forties, so he was a little surprised at Shi Qiang's certainty. As Shi Qiang hurried down the stairs to welcome his son, Luo Ji turned his eyes from the reunion to the surface world before him.

The sky was yellow. He now realized why the image of the sky showing in the underground city was shot from a height of ten thousand meters, because, from the ground, the sun was only visible as a hazy outline. Sand covered everything on the ground, and cars passed by on the streets dragging dusty tails. It was another sight from the past for Luo Ji: cars that traveled on the ground. They didn't seem to run on gasoline. They came in all kinds of weird shapes, and some were new and some old, but they all shared one feature: Every car had a flat sheet installed on the roof, like an awning. Across the street, he saw an old-era building with sand-covered windowsills and windows that were either boarded up or glassless black holes. However, people were evidently living in some of the rooms, because he saw clothing hanging outside to dry and even some potted flowers on the windowsills. Though the airborne sand and dust kept visibility low, he soon located a couple of familiar building outlines

farther away and knew for certain that he was in the same city where he had spent half his life two centuries ago. He walked down the steps to the two men who were hugging and pounding each other in their excitement. Seeing the middle-aged man up close, he knew that Shi Qiang hadn't made a mistake.

"Dad, when you figure it, I'm only five years younger than you," Shi Xiaoming said, wiping tears from the corners of his eyes.

"Not bad, kiddo. I was afraid some damn white-bearded old man would be calling me Dad," Shi Qiang said with a chuckle. Then he introduced Luo Ji to his son.

"Oh, Dr. Luo. You used to be world famous," Shi Xiaoming said, as he looked Luo Ji up and down.

The three of them headed toward Shi Xiaoming's car, which was parked at the side of the road. Before they got in, Luo Ji asked about the thing on the roof.

"It's an antenna. Up on the surface, we have to use whatever electricity leaks through from the underground city, so the antennas are a little larger, and the power is only enough to run the cars on the ground. They can't fly."

The car wasn't fast, due either to the power or the sand on the road. Luo Ji looked out the window at the sandy city. He had a belly full of questions, but Shi Xiaoming and his father kept talking and he couldn't get a word in.

"Mom passed away in Year 34 of the Crisis. Me and your granddaughter were with her then."

"Oh, good. . . . You didn't bring my granddaughter with you?"

"After the divorce, she went with her mom. I looked up her file. She lived into her eighties and died in Year 105."

"Too bad I never met her. . . . How old were you when your sentence ended?"

"Nineteen."

"What did you do then?"

"Everything. At first, with no other way out, I kept up the swindles, but then I did a bit of legitimate business. After I had the money, I saw the signs of the Great Ravine and went into

hibernation. I didn't know then that things would get better later on. I just wanted to see you."

"Is our house still there?"

"Land-use rights were extended past the original seventy-year period, but I only got to stay a short time before it was demolished. The one we bought later is still there, but I haven't been to see it." Shi Xiaoming pointed outside. "The city population isn't even one percent of what it was in our day. Do you know what the most worthless thing is? That house. You dedicated your entire life to it, Dad, but everything's empty now. You can live wherever you like."

Finally Luo Ji managed to seize a gap in their conversation to ask, "Do all reawakened hibernators live in the old city?"

"No way! They live outside. There's too much sand in the city. But mostly, it's because there's nothing to do. Of course, you can't go too far from the underground city, or you can't get electricity."

"What do all of you do?" Shi Qiang asked.

"Think: What can we do that the kids can't? Farming!" Shi Xiaoming, like other hibernators, no matter their age, had the habit of calling modern people "kids."

The car left the city and drove east. As the sand lessened to reveal the highway, Luo Ji recognized it as the old expressway between Beijing and Shijiazhuang, although both sides were piled high with sand now. The old buildings still stood there amid the sand, but what brought a spark of life to this desertified plain of northern China were the small oases ringed by sparse trees, which Shi Xiaoming said were hibernator settlements.

They drove into one oasis, a small residential community surrounded by a sand-break of trees that Shi Xiaoming called New Life Village #5. When he got out of the car, Luo Ji felt time flowing backward: rows of six-story apartments fronted by open space, old men playing chess on stone tables, mothers pushing baby carriages, and a few children playing soccer on the sparse lawn growing on the sand. . . .

Shi Xiaoming lived on the sixth floor with a wife nine years younger than him. She had entered hibernation in Year 21 due

to liver cancer, but was completely healthy now. They had a four-year-old son who called Shi Qiang "Grampa."

A sumptuous lunch had been laid out to welcome Luo Ji and Shi Qiang: local farm produce, chicken and pork produced at other nearby farms, and even home-brewed alcohol. They called three of their neighbors to join them, three men who—like Shi Xiaoming—had entered hibernation relatively early, back when it was expensive and available only to rich members of the upper class or their sons and daughters. Now, gathered here after a span of more than a century, they were all just ordinary people. Shi Xiaoming introduced one neighbor as Zhang Yan, the grandson of Zhang Yuanchao, the man he had cheated back in the day.

"Remember how you made me return the money I cheated him out of? I began the day I got out, and that's how I met Yan. He had just graduated from college. Taking inspiration from his two neighbors, we went into the funeral business and called our firm the High and Deep Company. 'High,' for space burials. We shot ashes into the Solar System, and later on we were able to launch entire bodies. For a price, of course. 'Deep,' for mine burials. At first we used abandoned shafts, and later on we dug new ones, since they would work equally well as anti-Trisolaris tombs too."

The man called Yan was a little older—he looked to be in his fifties or sixties. Shi Xiaoming explained that Yan had been reawakened once before and lived for more than thirty years before going back into hibernation.

"What's our legal status here?" Luo Ji asked.

Shi Xiaoming said, "Completely equivalent to modern residential areas. We count as the city's distant suburbs, and we have a proper district government. It's not just hibernators who live here. We also have modern people, and people from the city often come out here for fun."

Zhang Yan took over: "We call the modern people 'walltappers,' because when they first get here they're always touching the wall out of habit, trying to activate something."

"So life's okay?" Shi Qiang asked.

They all said it was pretty good.

"But along the road I saw the fields you plant. Can you really support yourselves by growing crops?"

"Why not? In the cities these days, agricultural products are luxury items. . . . The government's actually quite good to hibernators. Even if you don't do anything, you can still live comfortably off government subsidies. But you've got to have something to do. The idea that hibernators all know how to farm is nonsense. No one was a farmer at first, but this is all we can do."

The conversation quickly turned to the history of the past two centuries.

"So what was the deal with the Great Ravine?" Luo Ji brought up the question he had long been wanting to ask.

Instantly their faces grew serious. Seeing that the meal was almost over, Shi Xiaoming allowed the topic to continue. "You've probably learned a little about it over the past few days. It's a long story. For more than a decade after you went into hibernation, life was pretty good. But later on, when the pace of economic transformation picked up, the standard of living declined by the day and the political climate constricted. It really felt like wartime."

A neighbor said, "It wasn't just a few countries. The entire Earth was like that. Society was on edge, and if you said something wrong they would say you were ETO, or a traitor to humanity, so nobody felt safe. And film and television from the Golden Age began to be restricted, and then was banned worldwide. Of course, there was too much of it to ban effectively."

"Why?"

"They were afraid of eroding the fighting spirit," Shi Xiaoming said. "Still, so long as there was food to eat, you could make do. But later on, things got worse, and the world began to starve. This was about twenty years after Dr. Luo went into hibernation."

"Because of the economic transition?"

"Right. But environmental deterioration was also a major factor. The environmental laws were there, but in those pessimistic times, the general attitude was, 'What the hell is environmental

protection for? Even if Earth turns into a garden, isn't it all going to the Trisolarans anyway?' Eventually, environmental protection was seen as no less treasonous to humanity than the ETO. Organizations like Greenpeace were treated like ETO branches and suppressed. Work on the space forces accelerated the development of highly polluting heavy industry, which made environmental pollution unstoppable. The greenhouse effect, climate anomalies, desertification . . ." He sighed.

"When I entered hibernation, desertification was just starting," another neighbor said. "It's not what you imagine, like the desert advancing from the Great Wall. No! It was patchwork erosion. Perfectly fine plots of land in the interior began turning to desert simultaneously, and it spread from those points, like how a damp cloth dries in the sun."

"Then agricultural production plummeted, and grain reserves were exhausted. And then . . . and then came the Great Ravine."

"Did the prediction that the standard of living would go backward a hundred years come true?" Luo Ji asked.

Shi Xiaoming gave a few bitter chuckles. "Ah, Dr. Luo. A hundred years? In your dreams! A hundred years back from that time would have been . . . around the 1930s or so. A paradise compared to the Great Ravine! No way the two are the same. For one thing, there were so many more people than in the Great Depression— 8.3 billion!" He pointed at Zhang Yan. "He saw the Great Ravine when he reawakened for a while. You tell them."

Zhang Yan drained his glass. Eyes blank, he said, "I have seen the grand march of hunger. Millions of people fleeing famine on the great plains through sand that blocked out the sky. Hot sky, hot earth, and hot sun. When they died, they were divided up on the spot. . . . It was hell on Earth. There are tons of videos to watch if you want. You think of that time, and you feel lucky to be alive."

"The Great Ravine lasted for about half a century, and in those fifty-odd years, the world population dropped from 8.3 billion to 3.5 billion. Think about what that means!"

Luo Ji got up and went over to the window. From here he could

see the desert across the protective tree line, its yellow covering of sand extending silently to the horizon under the noonday sun. The hand of time had smoothed over everything.

"And then?" Shi Qiang asked.

Zhang Yan let out a long breath, as if no longer having to talk about that period of history had taken a burden off his shoulders. "After that, well, some people came to terms with it, and then more and more people did. They wondered whether it was worth it to pay so high a price, even if it was for victory in the Doomsday Battle. Think about what's more important: the child dying of starvation in your arms, or the continuation of human civilization? Right now you might think the latter choice is more important, but you wouldn't have in that day and age. No matter what the future might bring, the present is most important. Of course, that mind-set was outrageous at first, the classic thinking of a traitor to humanity, but you couldn't stop people from thinking it. And very soon the entire world thought so. There was a popular slogan back then, which soon became a famous historical quote."

" 'Make time for civilization, for civilization won't make time,' " Luo Ji contributed, without looking back from the window.

"Right, that one. Civilization is meant for us."

"And after that?" Shi Qiang asked.

"A second Enlightenment, a second Renaissance, a second French Revolution . . . You can find all that stuff in the history books."

Luo Ji turned back in surprise. The predictions he had made to Zhuang Yan two centuries before had come to pass. "A second French Revolution? In France?!"

"No, no. That's just a saying. It was the entire world! After the revolution, the new national governments terminated their space strategies and poured their attention into improving people's lives. And then critical technology emerged: Genetic engineering and fusion technology were harnessed for large-scale food production, ending the age of weather-dependent food. From then on, the world would no longer be hungry. Everything moved quickly after

that—there were fewer people, after all—and in the space of just two decades, life returned to pre-Great Ravine levels. Then Golden Age levels were restored. People had set their hearts on this road of comfort, and no one wanted to go back."

"There's another term you might find interesting, Dr. Luo," said the first neighbor, drawing closer to him. An economist before hibernation, he had a deeper understanding of the issues. "It's called civilization immunity. It means that when the world has suffered a serious illness, it triggers civilization's immune system, so that something like the early Crisis Era won't happen again. Humanism comes first, and perpetuating civilization comes second. These are the concepts that today's society is based on."

"And after that?" Luo Ji asked.

"After that came the freaky stuff." Shi Xiaoming grew excited. "Originally, the countries of the world had planned to live in peace and push the Trisolar Crisis onto the back burner, but what do you think happened? There was swift progress everywhere. Technology sped forward and broke through all the technical obstacles that had stood in the way of space strategy before the Great Ravine, one after the other!"

"That's not freaky," Luo Ji said. "Emancipation of human nature inevitably brings with it scientific and technological progress."

"After about half a century of peace following the Great Ravine, the world turned its thoughts back to the Trisolaran invasion and felt it ought to reconsider the war. With humanity's power now on a completely different plane than before the Great Ravine, a global state of war was again declared, and construction was begun on a space fleet. But unlike the first time, national constitutions were clear about one thing: Resource expenditure for the space strategy had to be kept within a specified range, and must not have a disastrous impact on the world economy and on community life. And that's when the space fleets became independent countries. . . ."

"You don't actually have to think about any of this, though," the economist said. "From now on, just think about how to live a good life. That old revolutionary slogan is just an adaptation of the

old saying from the Golden Age: 'Make time for life, or life won't make time.' To new life!"

When they had drained their last glass, Luo Ji praised the economist for putting things so well. Now his mind had space only for Zhuang Yan and the child. He wanted to get settled as soon as possible, and then go wake them.

Make time for civilization, make time for life.

After boarding *Natural Selection,* Zhang Beihai found that the modern command system had evolved far beyond what he had imagined. The giant spacecraft, equal in volume to three of the largest seagoing carriers of the twenty-first century, was practically a small city, but it had no bridge or command module, or even a captain's room or operations room. In fact, it had no specific functional compartments whatsoever. All of them were identical, regular spheres that differed only in size. At any location inside the ship, you could just use a data glove to activate a holographic display, which, due to the high cost, was a rarity even in Earth's super-wired society. And at any location, so long as you had the appropriate system permissions, you could pull up a complete command console, including a captain's interface, which effectively made the entire ship, even the passageways and bathrooms, a bridge, command module, captain's room, and operations room! To Zhang Beihai, it felt like the evolution from a client-server model to a browser-server model in late-twentieth-century computer networks. With the former, you could only access the server through specific software installed on a computer, but using the latter, you could access the server from any computer on the network so long as you had the right permissions.

Zhang Beihai and Dongfang Yanxu were situated in an ordinary cabin that, like every other one, had no special instruments or screens. It was just a spherical compartment whose bulkheads were white most of the time, making it feel like the inside of a giant Ping-Pong ball. When gravity was produced by ship acceleration,

any part of the spherical bulkhead could be transformed into a shape suitable for use as a chair.

For Zhang Beihai, this was another aspect of modern technology that few people had imagined: the elimination of single-purpose facilities. Only the first tendrils of this trend had appeared on Earth, but it was part of the fundamental structure of the far more advanced world of the fleet. This world was spare and simple. Devices were no longer permanently installed, but would appear when necessary at any location required. The world, made complex by technology, was becoming simple again, its technology hidden deeply behind the face of reality.

"Now we come to your first onboard lesson," Dongfang Yanxu said. "Of course, you really shouldn't be getting this lesson from a captain who's under review, but no one in the fleet is more trustworthy than I am. Today, we'll demonstrate how to launch *Natural Selection* and put it into navigation mode. And, in fact, so long as you remember what you see today, you'll have closed off the primary opening for the Imprinted." As she spoke, she used her data glove to call up a holographic star chart in the air. "This may be a little different from the spatial maps of your time, but it still uses the sun as the origin."

"I studied this in training, so I can read it fine," Zhang Beihai said, looking at the star chart. His memory of the ancient Solar System map he and Chang Weisi had stood in front of two centuries ago was still fresh. This chart, however, precisely marked out the positions of all celestial bodies within a radius of one hundred light-years of the sun, at a scale more than a hundred times greater than the older one.

"You don't really need to understand much. In the present state, navigation to any position on the map is prohibited. . . . If I were Imprinted, and wanted to hijack *Natural Selection* to flee into the cosmos, I'd first need to select a heading, like this." She activated a point on the map, turning it green. "Of course, we're just in simulation mode right now, because I no longer have permissions. When you obtain captain's permissions, I'll have to go through you

to perform the operations. But if I really submitted this operation request, it would be a dangerous act, and you should refuse it. You should also report me."

Once the heading was activated, an interface appeared in the air. Zhang Beihai was already quite familiar with the appearance and operations from his training, but he still listened patiently to Dongfang Yanxu's explanation and watched how she brought the huge ship from complete shutdown to hibernation, then to standby, and finally to Slow Ahead.

"If these were real operations, *Natural Selection* would now leave port. What do you think? Simpler than spaceship operations in your day?"

"Yes. Much simpler." When he and the other special contingent members first saw the interface, they were surprised at its simplicity, and the total lack of technical detail.

"The operation is totally automatic, leaving the technical process entirely hidden from the captain."

"This display only shows general parameters. How do you see the ship's operational status?"

"Operational status is monitored by officers and noncommissioned officers at lower levels. Their displays are more complex—the further down you go, the more complicated the interface becomes. As captain and vice-captain, we must focus our attention on more important matters. . . . Very well, let's continue. If I were Imprinted . . . There I go with that supposition again. What do you think?"

"Given my position, any response would be irresponsible."

"Fine. If I were Imprinted, then I'd set the throttle directly to Ahead Four. No other ship in the fleet can catch *Natural Selection* under Ahead Four acceleration."

"But you couldn't do that, even if you had the permissions, because the system will only proceed to Ahead Four if it detects that all passengers are in a deep-sea state."

Under maximum propulsion, the ship's acceleration could reach 120 gs, but this exerted a force more than ten times what a human could tolerate under normal conditions. To go to maximum,

they had to enter a "deep-sea state," which consisted of the cabins being filled with an oxygen-rich "deep-sea acceleration fluid" that trained personnel could breathe directly. As they breathed, it would fill their lungs and then the rest of their organs. First dreamed up in the first half of the twentieth century, the liquid was intended at the time to facilitate ultra-deep dives. Pressure was in equilibrium inside and outside of a human body filled with deep-sea acceleration fluid, meaning it could sustain high pressures like a deep-sea fish. The environment of a liquid-filled cabin in a rapidly accelerating spacecraft was like that of the deep sea, so the liquid was now being used to protect human bodies against the ultra-high acceleration of space travel. Hence the term "deep-sea state."

Dongfang Yanxu nodded. "But you should know that there's a way to get around that. If you set the spacecraft to remote control, then it will assume that no one is on board and won't perform the check. This setting is part of the captain's permissions."

"Let me try it and you tell me if I've got it right." Zhang Beihai activated an interface in front of him and began setting up remote control mode for the spacecraft, looking at a small notebook from time to time as he did so.

Dongfang Yanxu smiled at the notebook. "There are more efficient recording methods now."

"Oh, it's just habit. For particularly important things, it's always more reassuring to write them down like this. It's just that I can't find a pen now. I brought two with me into hibernation, but only the pencil was still usable."

"You've learned quickly."

"That's because the command system retains a lot of the navy's style. After all these years, the names of things haven't even changed. The engine orders, for example."

"The space fleet did have its origins in the navy. . . . Okay, you'll soon be receiving system permissions as the acting captain of *Natural Selection*. This warship is in class-A standby, or, as they called it in your time, 'fired up and ready to go.'" She extended her slender arms and turned a circle in the air.

Zhang Beihai had not been able to figure out how to perform that action using the superconducting belt. "We didn't 'fire up' in those days. But you evidently know quite a bit of naval history," he said, changing the subject from the sensitive issue that was liable to make her hostile to him.

"A grand old branch of the service."

"Doesn't the space fleet inherit that grandeur?"

"Yes. But I'm going to leave it. I plan on resigning."

"Because of the review?"

She turned to look at him, her thick black hair leaping again from the lack of gravity. "You encountered this sort of thing all the time back then, didn't you?"

"Not necessarily. But if we did, every comrade would understand, because undergoing review is one of the duties of a soldier."

"Two centuries have passed. This is no longer your time."

"Dongfang, don't deliberately widen the gap. There are similarities between the two of us. Soldiers in all ages have to bear up under humiliation."

"Are you advising me to stay?"

"No."

"Ideological work. That's the word, isn't it? Wasn't that your duty once?"

"Not anymore. I have a new duty."

She floated easily around him, as if carefully studying him. "Is it that we're children to you? Half a year ago I went to Earth, and in one hibernator district, a six- or seven-year-old boy called me a kid."

He laughed.

"Are we kids to you?"

"In our day, seniority was very important. In the countryside, there were adults who called children Aunt and Uncle because of family seniority."

"But your seniority is unimportant to me."

"I can see that in your eyes."

"Your daughter, and your wife—they didn't come with you?

399

Special Contingent family members were allowed to hibernate, too, as far as I'm aware."

"They didn't come, and they didn't want me to go. You know, trends at the time pointed toward a very bleak future. They criticized me for being irresponsible. She and her mother moved out, and in the dead of night the day after they left, the Special Contingent received the order. I didn't even have time to see them again. It was on a late winter's night, a cold one, that I left home carrying my bags. . . . Of course, I'm not expecting you to understand any of this."

"I understand. . . . What happened to them?"

"My wife died in Year 47. My daughter in Year 81."

"They saw the Great Ravine." She lowered her eyes and remained silent for a while. Then she activated a holographic window and switched to an external display mode.

The bulkheads of the white sphere melted like wax and *Natural Selection* vanished, leaving them suspended in infinite space, facing the misty starfield of the Milky Way. They were now two independent beings in the universe, unattached to any world, with nothing but the abyss surrounding them. They hung in the universe like the Earth, the sun, and the galaxy itself, with no origin and no destination. Simply existing . . .

Zhang Beihai had experienced this feeling before, 190 years ago, when he floated in space wearing nothing but a space suit, holding a pistol loaded with meteorite bullets.

"I like it this way, where you can ignore the spacecraft and the fleet and everything outside your own mind," she said.

"Dongfang," he called softly.

"Hmm?" The captain turned around, her eyes shining with the starlight of the Milky Way.

"If the day comes when I have to kill you, please forgive me," he said gently.

She met his words with a smile. "Do I look to you like I'm Imprinted?"

He looked at her in the sunlight coming from five AU away. She was a lithe feather floating against the backdrop of the starfield.

"We belong to the Earth and the sea, you belong to the stars."

"Is that bad?"

"No. It's very good."

"The probe's gone out!"

The report from the duty officer came as a shock to Dr. Kuhn and General Robinson. They knew that once the news got out it would make waves in both the Earth International and the Fleet International, particularly since the latest observations of the probe's speed meant that it would cross the orbit of Jupiter in just six days.

Kuhn and Robinson were on the Ringier-Fitzroy Station that orbited the sun along the outside rim of the asteroid belt. Floating in space five kilometers away from the station were the most peculiar objects in the Solar System: a set of six giant lenses, the top one 1,200 meters in diameter, and the five below it slightly smaller in size. This was the latest incarnation of the space telescope, but unlike the previous five generations of the Hubble, this space telescope had no barrel, or any connecting material at all between the six giant lenses. They floated independently, the rim of each lens equipped with multiple ion thrusters that could precisely adjust the distance between them or change the orientation of the entire group. Ringier-Fitzroy Station was the control center for the telescope, but even from this close, the transparent lenses were practically invisible. When technicians and engineers would fly between them during maintenance, the universe on either side would be grossly distorted, and if they were at the proper angle, the protective iris on the surface would reflect the sunlight and reveal the entire giant lens, whose curved surface would then resemble a planet covered in bewitching rainbows. The telescope broke with the Hubble series naming convention and was dubbed the Ringier-Fitzroy Telescope, to commemorate the two men who discovered the tracks of the Trisolaran Fleet. Although their discovery had no scholarly significance, the name was fitting, because the primary purpose of this

massive telescope, a joint project of the three major fleets, was the continued monitoring of the Trisolaran Fleet.

A team like Ringier and Fitzroy—a lead scientist from Earth and a head of military affairs from the fleet—had always been in charge of the telescope, and in every such team there were the same differences of opinion that Ringier and Fitzroy had. Right now, Kuhn wanted to squeeze in some observation time for his own study of the cosmos, while Robinson worked to stop him, so as to safeguard the fleet's interests. They argued about other things, too: For example, Kuhn reminisced over the wonderful way that Earth's superpowers, headed up by the United States, were leading the world, in contrast to the fleets' current inefficient bureaucracy; but every time he did so, Robinson would ruthlessly dismantle Kuhn's ridiculous historical fantasies. But the most heated argument was over the station's rotation speed. The general insisted on a slow rotation for minimal gravity, even to the point of keeping the station in an entirely weightless state with no rotation at all, while Kuhn stumped for a fast rotation and Earth standard gravity.

But what was happening now overwhelmed all of that. The probe having "gone out" meant that its engines had turned off. Two years before, far beyond the Oort Cloud, the probe had begun to decelerate, which meant that its engine had started up in a sun-facing direction, enabling the space telescope to track the probe by engine light. Now that the light had gone out, tracking was no longer possible, because the probe itself was far too small—probably no bigger than a truck, based on the wake it left crossing the interstellar dust. An object that small out on the periphery of the Kuiper Belt, no longer emitting its own light and reflecting the weak light of the distant sun even more weakly—even a telescope as powerful as Ringier-Fitzroy couldn't see such a tiny dark object so far off in the darkness of space.

"The three fleets don't know how to do anything but struggle over power. This is just perfect—the target's been lost. . . ." Kuhn grumbled, waving his arms for emphasis. He forgot the station

was now in a weightless state, and his movements caused him to perform a somersault.

For the first time, General Robinson did not defend the fleet. The Asian Fleet had originally dispatched three light, high-speed ships to track the probe at close range, but after the dispute erupted among the three fleets over the right to intercept, the Joint Conference had issued a resolution recalling all craft to base. The Asian Fleet repeatedly protested that the three fighter-class spaceships had been stripped of all weapons and external equipment and were carrying a crew of just two people each to achieve maximum acceleration for tracking the target, and even so, they could not possibly intercept the probe. However, the European and North American Fleets were unconvinced, and insisted that all spaceships in transit be recalled and replaced by three spaceships dispatched by Earth International as a fourth party. If not for that, the fleet ships would already have made close contact with the probe and begun tracking it. Earth's ships, dispatched by the European Commonwealth and China, had not even passed the orbit of Neptune.

"Perhaps. Its engines might start up again," the general said. "It's still traveling pretty fast, and if it doesn't decelerate it won't be able to rest in solar orbit. It'll pass right through the Solar System."

"Are you the Trisolaran commander? Maybe the probe wasn't ever planning on remaining in the Solar System, but was just going to pass through anyway!" Kuhn said. Then a thought suddenly struck him. "If the engines are off, then it can't change course! Can't you just figure out where it's headed and send the tracking spacecraft to wait for it?"

The general shook his head. "That's not precise enough. It's not like an air force search in Earth's atmosphere. One minuscule error, and you'll be hundreds of thousands or even millions of kilometers off course. In such a huge area, the tracking craft won't be able to find such a tiny, dark target. . . . But we've got to come up with a way somehow."

"What can we do? Let the fleet figure it out."

The general turned tough. "Doctor, you've got to realize the

403

nature of the situation. Even though this isn't our fault, the media won't care. The Ringier-Fitzroy system was, after all, responsible for tracking the probe in deep space, so a good portion of that dirty water is going to land on our heads."

Kuhn said nothing, but remained with his body perpendicular to the general's for a while. Then he asked, "Is there anything else outside Neptune's orbit that could be useful?"

"For the fleet, probably nothing. For Earth . . ." The general turned to ask the duty officer and soon learned that the UN Environmental Protection Organization had four large ships near Neptune, working on the early stages of the Fog Umbrella Project. The three small craft newly tasked with tracking the probe had been dispatched from those ships.

"And they're there to mine oil film?" Kuhn asked. The reply was affirmative. Oil film was a substance found in Neptune's rings. At high temperatures, it turned into a rapidly diffusing gas that then condensed into nanoparticles in space, forming space dust. It was so called because when it evaporated, it became highly diffusive, so a small quantity of the substance could form a large patch of dust, like a tiny droplet of oil spreading into an oil film of molecular thickness across a large area of water. Dust formed from this oil film had another property: Unlike other types of space dust, "oil-film dust" was not easily dispersed by the solar wind.

It was the discovery of oil film that made the Fog Umbrella Project possible. The plan was to use nuclear blasts in space to evaporate and spread the oil-film substance into a cloud of oil-film dust between the sun and Earth as a means of decreasing the sun's radiation on Earth and alleviating global warming.

"I remember there's supposed to be a stellar bomb near Neptune orbit from before the wars," Kuhn said.

"There is. And the Fog Umbrella spaceships brought along a few, too, for blasting Neptune and its satellites. I'm not sure of the precise number."

"I'd say one is enough," Kuhn said excitedly.

Like Wallfacer Rey Diaz had predicted two centuries prior when

he developed the stellar hydrogen bomb for his Wallfacer plan, although the weapon would be of limited use in the Doomsday Battle, the major powers wanted it to prepare for the possible outbreak of interplanetary war between humans. More than five thousand bombs had been manufactured, mostly during the Great Ravine, when international relations grew volatile due to lack of resources, and humanity was pushed to the brink of war. When the new era dawned, the horrifying weapons became dangerous nonessentials that were kept in storage in outer space, although they still belonged to countries on Earth. A few of them were blown up in planetary engineering projects, and another set was sent into orbit in the remote Solar System with the notion that the fusion materials could supplement the fuel of long-range space-craft. However, because of the difficulty involved in dismantling the bombs, this idea was never realized.

"Do you think it'll work?" Robinson asked, his eyes aglow. He was a little rueful that he hadn't thought up such a simple idea himself, and that Kuhn had snatched the opportunity to go down in history.

"Give it a try. It's the only thing we've got."

"If your idea works, Doctor, then the Ringier-Fitzroy Station will forever revolve fast enough to generate Earth gravity."

"It's the biggest thing humanity has ever made," the commander of *Blue Shadow* said, as he looked out the spacecraft's window into the pitch-black of space. Nothing was visible, but he tried to convince himself that he could see the dust cloud.

"Why isn't it lit by the sun, like the tail of a comet?" the pilot said. He and the commander were the only crew on *Blue Shadow*. He knew the density of the dust cloud was as thin as a comet's tail, or about the same as a vacuum created in an Earth-based laboratory.

"Maybe the sunlight is too weak." The commander looked back at the sun, which, in the lonely space between Neptune's orbit and the Kuiper Belt, looked like a large star, its disc shape

only barely distinguishable. Still, even the weak sunlight could still cast shadows on the bulkhead. "Besides, a comet tail is only visible from a certain distance away. We're just at the edge of the cloud."

The pilot tried to conjure up a mental image of the thin yet gigantic cloud. A few days ago, he and the commander had seen with their own eyes how small the cloud was when compressed into a solid. At the time, the giant spaceship *Pacific* had arrived from Neptune and left behind five things when it stopped in this section of space. The *Blue Shadow*'s mechanical arm first retrieved a stellar hydrogen bomb from the early days of the war, a cylinder five meters long and a meter and a half in diameter. Next it picked up four large spheres between thirty and fifty meters in diameter. The four spheres, the oil film harvested from Neptune's rings, were placed at points several hundred meters from the bomb. Once *Pacific* had departed the vicinity, the bomb exploded, forming a small sun whose light and heat surged into the cold abyss of space and instantly vaporized the surrounding spheres. The gaseous oil film diffused rapidly under the typhoon of H-bomb radiation, then cooled into countless tiny particles of dust, forming a cloud. The cloud had a diameter of two million kilometers, greater than that of the sun.

The dust cloud was located in the region that the Trisolaran probe was expected to pass through, according to path observations made prior to its engine shutting off. Dr. Kuhn and General Robinson hoped to precisely determine the probe's path and position by the tracks it left in the man-made dust cloud.

Following the formation of the cloud, *Pacific* returned to Neptune base, leaving behind three small spaceships that would track the probe closely once its wake showed. *Blue Shadow* was one of them. The small high-speed ship had been dubbed a "space racer." With a small capsule that could seat five as its only payload, its remaining volume was entirely occupied by a fusion engine, giving it high acceleration and maneuverability. Once the dust cloud took shape, *Blue Shadow* flew through the entire area to test whether wakes would be left, with quite satisfactory results. Of course, the wakes could only be observed by the space telescope

more than one hundred AU distant. From *Blue Shadow* itself, its own wake was invisible, and the surrounding space was as deserted as it always had been. Still, after passing through the cloud, the pilot insisted that the sun looked a little dimmer, that its formerly sharp circumference had gone a bit blurry. Instrument observations confirmed the sole visual impression they had of this giant creation.

"Less than three hours to go," the commander said, looking at his watch. The dust cloud was actually a giant, thin satellite in orbit around the sun, its position constantly changing. When it eventually moved out of the space where the probe might pass through, another dust cloud would have to be created behind it.

"Do you really hope we'll catch up to it?" the pilot asked.

"Why not? We're making history!"

"Won't the thing attack us? We're not soldiers. This really ought to be done by the fleet."

Then their spacecraft received a message from the Ringier-Fitzroy Station reporting that the Trisolaran probe had entered the dust cloud and left a wake, and that precise parameters had been calculated for its trajectory. *Blue Shadow* was ordered to move immediately to rendezvous with and closely track the target. The station was more than one hundred AU away from *Blue Shadow,* meaning the message was delayed more than ten hours in transit, but the key had made an impression in the mold. Orbital calculations had even taken into account the effect of the thin dust cloud, so a rendezvous was just a matter of time.

Blue Shadow set a course in accordance with the probe's path and once again entered the invisible dust cloud, this time heading in the direction of the Trisolaran probe. It was a long flight this time, and over the course of more than ten hours, both pilot and commander grew sleepy. But the continuously shrinking distance between them and the probe kept them on edge.

"I see it! I see it!" the pilot shouted.

"What are you talking about? There's still over fourteen thousand kilometers to go!" rebuked the commander. The naked eye could not possibly see a truck at a distance of fourteen thousand

kilometers, even given the transparency of space. But soon he saw it for himself: On the trajectory described by the parameters, against the silent backdrop of space, a point of light was in motion.

After a moment's thought, the commander understood: The cloud of dust larger than the sun had been unnecessary, since the Trisolaran probe had restarted its engines and was continuing to decelerate. It did not intend to skip through the Solar System. It would remain here.

Because it was only a temporary measure in the fleets, the ceremony for handing over captain's permissions on *Natural Selection* was a simple and low-key affair attended only by Captain Dongfang Yanxu, Acting Captain Zhang Beihai, First Vice-Captain Levine, and Second Vice-Captain Akira Inoue, as well as a special team from the General Staff Department.

Despite this era's technological development, they had still not managed to overcome the stagnation of fundamental theory, so *Natural Selection*'s permissions transfer was done via means Zhang Beihai was familiar with: three-factor retina, fingerprint, and pass-phrase authentication.

Once the General Staff team had finished resetting the pupil and fingerprint data that identified the captain in the system, Dongfang Yanxu surrendered her pass phrase to Zhang Beihai: "Men always remember love because of romance only."

"You don't smoke," he replied calmly.

"And the brand was lost during the Great Ravine," she said with a trace of disappointment, and lowered her eyes.

"But the password's a good one. Not many people knew it back then either."

The captain and vice-captains exited, leaving Zhang Beihai alone to update the password and obtain complete control over *Natural Selection*.

"He's clever," Akira Inoue said when the door to the spherical cabin vanished.

"Ancient wisdom," Dongfang Yanxu said, watching the spot where the door had disappeared, as if trying to see through it. "We'll never be able to learn the stuff he brought from two centuries ago, but he can learn what we know."

Then the three of them remained silent and waited. Five minutes passed, clearly too long for changing a password, especially since Captain-in-waiting Zhang Beihai had come through training as the most skilled command system operator out of all the members of his Special Contingent. Five more minutes passed. The two vice-captains began swimming impatiently in the corridor, but Dongfang Yanxu remained silent and motionless.

At last the door reappeared. To their surprise, the spherical cabin had turned black. Zhang Beihai had a holographic star map pulled up on which the labels had been blocked, leaving only the twinkling stars. From the doorway, he seemed to be suspended outside the spaceship, with his interface floating alongside him.

"I'm done," he said.

"Why did it take so long?" Levin grumbled.

"Were you relishing the thrill of gaining *Natural Selection*?" Akira Inoue asked.

Zhang Beihai said nothing. He didn't look at the interface, but gazed off instead at a star in a distant part of the map. Dongfang Yanxu noticed that a green light was flashing in the direction he was looking.

"That would be ridiculous," Levin said, picking up from Akira Inoue. "May I remind you that the captainship still belongs to Colonel Dongfang? The acting captain is just a firewall. I'm sorry to be rude about it, but that's pretty much the truth."

Akira Inoue said, "And this state won't last for very long. The investigation of the fleet is nearing an end, and it's basically been proven that the Imprinted don't exist."

He was about to go on, but was stopped by a low gasp of surprise from the captain. "Oh, god!" she said, and the two vice-captains, following her eyes, noticed *Natural Selection*'s current status on Zhang Beihai's interface.

The warship had been set into remote control mode, thereby bypassing the check for deep-sea state prior to Ahead Four. Outside communication had been severed. And, finally, most of the captain's settings for putting the ship into maximum propulsion were in place. With the push of just one more button, *Natural Selection* would head off at maximum speed to the target selected on the map.

"No, this can't be happening," Dongfang Yanxu said, her voice so low only she could hear it. It was for her own ears, in response to her earlier "god" exclamation. She had never believed in the existence of God, but now her prayers were real.

"Are you insane?" Levin shouted. He and Akira Inoue rushed toward the cabin, only to crash into the bulkhead. There was no door, just an oval-shaped section of wall that had turned transparent.

"*Natural Selection* is about to proceed to Ahead Four. All crew must enter deep-sea state immediately," Zhang Beihai said, every word in his solemn, calm voice lingering in the air like an ancient anchor standing in the chill wind.

"This is impossible!" Akira Inoue said.

"Are you Imprinted?" Dongfang Yanxu asked, quickly calming herself.

"You know that's not possible."

"ETO?"

"No."

"Then who are you?"

"A soldier carrying out his duty to fight for humanity's survival."

"Why are you doing this?"

"I'll explain after acceleration is complete. I repeat: All crew must enter deep-sea state immediately."

"This is impossible!" Akira Inoue repeated.

Zhang Beihai turned around and, without so much as looking at the two vice-captains, stared straight at Dongfang Yanxu. His eyes instantly reminded her of the emblem of the Chinese Space Force, bearing swords and stars alike.

"Dongfang, I said that I would be sorry if I had to kill you. There's not much time."

Then the deep-sea acceleration fluid appeared within Zhang Beihai's spherical compartment, forming into balls in the weightless environment. Each liquid globe, containing his distorted reflection along with the interface and the star map, began to combine into larger ones. The two vice-captains looked at Dongfang Yanxu.

"Do as he says. The whole ship will enter deep-sea state," the captain said.

The two vice-captains stared at her. They knew what the consequences were for proceeding to Ahead Four outside of the deep-sea protective state: The body would be plastered to the bulkhead by a force 120 times that of Earth gravity. First blood would burst out under the immense weight, spreading into a thin layer of impossibly huge, radially patterned blood stains, and then the organs would be squeezed out, forming another thin layer that would be pressed together with the body into an ugly Dali painting. . . .

As they left for their cabins, they issued orders to the entire ship to enter a deep-sea state.

"You're a well-qualified captain." Zhang Beihai nodded at Dongfang Yanxu. "This shows maturity."

"Where are we going?"

"Wherever we're going, it's a more responsible choice than staying here."

And then he was submerged in the deep-sea acceleration fluid, and Dongfang Yanxu could only make out a murky body through the liquid now filling the spherical compartment.

Floating in the translucent liquid, Zhang Beihai recalled his diving experience in the navy two centuries before. He had never imagined that the ocean would be so dark a few dozen meters down, but that undersea world gave him the same feeling he later found in space. The ocean was space in miniature on Earth. He tried breathing, but his reflexes made him violently cough up liquid and residual gas, and his body shifted with the recoil. Still, there wasn't the suffocation that he had anticipated, and as cool liquid

411

filled his lungs, the oxygen it contained was supplied to his blood. He could breathe freely, like a fish.

On the interface suspended in the liquid, he saw that the deep-sea acceleration fluid was filling each occupied compartment in the spaceship in turn. The process continued for more than ten minutes. His consciousness began to blur as the breathing liquid was injected with a hypnotic component that put everyone aboard ship into a state of sleep so as to avoid damage to the brain from the high pressure and relative hypoxia generated by acceleration at Ahead Four.

Zhang Beihai felt his father's spirit alight on the spaceship from the beyond, becoming one with it. He pressed the button on the interface, issuing in his mind the command that he had been working toward his entire life:

"*Natural Selection*, Ahead Four!"

A small sun appeared in Jovian orbit, its bright light washing out the phosphorescence of the planet's atmosphere. Dragging the sun behind it, the stellar-class warship *Natural Selection* eased out of the Asian Fleet base and accelerated rapidly, casting shadows of the other warships—each dark spot big enough to contain the Earth—onto the Jovian surface. Ten minutes later, a larger shadow was flung onto Jupiter like a curtain drawn across the giant planet. *Natural Selection* was passing Io.

It was at this point that the Asian Fleet High Command confirmed the incredible fact that *Natural Selection* had defected.

The European and North American Fleets issued protests and warnings to the Asian Fleet under the initial impression that it was an unauthorized move to intercept the Trisolaran probe, but they soon realized from *Natural Selection*'s heading that this was not the case. It was headed in the opposite direction from the Trisolaran invasion.

The various systems hailing *Natural Selection* gradually let up after receiving no response. The high commands began to deploy pursuit and intercept ships, although they soon realized that little could be done about the defector warship. Bases on four of

Jupiter's moons possessed sufficient firepower to destroy *Natural Selection,* but they would not take that path, because it was quite likely that only a small minority of those on board, or even a single individual, had actually defected, and the two thousand-odd soldiers in deep-sea state were merely hostages. Commanders at the gamma-ray laser base on Europa could only watch as the small sun flew across the sky and into outer space, sprinkling Europa's vast ice sheets with light like burning phosphorus.

Natural Selection crossed the orbits of sixteen Jovian moons, and achieved escape velocity by the time it reached Callisto. Seen from the Asian Fleet base, the small sun gradually shrank, turning into a bright star that remained faintly visible for a week, as a reminder from the stars of the lasting pain of the Asian Fleet.

Since the pursuing force had to enter deep-sea state, it took forty-five minutes after *Natural Selection* left for those ships to launch, lighting up Jupiter with another six suns.

At Asian Fleet Command, which had stopped rotating, the commander silently faced the giant dark side of Jupiter as lightning flashed in the atmosphere ten thousand kilometers below him. Powerful radiation from the fusion engines of *Natural Selection* and the pursuing force had caused atmospheric ionization and lightning. The fleeting lightning strikes illuminated the surrounding atmosphere, visible at this distance as halos in constantly changing locations, turning the surface of Jupiter into a pond spattered with fluorescent rain.

Natural Selection accelerated in silence to one-hundredth the speed of light, the point of no return for its fusion fuel consumption. Now unable to return to the Solar System under its own power, it had become a lonely boat bound to forever wander in outer space.

The commander of the Asian Fleet gazed at the stars trying unsuccessfully to find one in particular, for all there was in that direction was the faint light of the pursuers' fusion engines. A report soon came in: *Natural Selection* had stopped accelerating. A while later, *Natural Selection* restored communication with the fleet.

Then the following communication took place, with delays of more than ten seconds between transmissions due to the fact that the ship was now over five million kilometers away:

NATURAL SELECTION: *Natural Selection* calling Asian Fleet! *Natural Selection* calling Asian Fleet!

ASIAN FLEET: *Natural Selection*, Asian Fleet reads you. Report your status.

NATURAL SELECTION: This is acting captain Zhang Beihai. I'll speak directly to the fleet commander.

FLEET COMMANDER: I'm listening.

ZHANG BEIHAI: I take full responsibility for *Natural Selection*'s breakaway voyage.

FLEET COMMANDER: Is anyone else responsible?

ZHANG BEIHAI: No. Responsibility is mine alone. The situation has nothing at all to do with anyone else aboard *Natural Selection*.

FLEET COMMANDER: I want to talk to Captain Dongfang Yanxu.

ZHANG BEIHAI: Not now.

FLEET COMMANDER: What is the ship's current status?

ZHANG BEIHAI: All is good. Every crew member is still in deep-sea state, apart from me. Power systems and life support are operating normally.

FLEET COMMANDER: And your reasons for this treason?

ZHANG BEIHAI: I may have deserted, but I am no traitor.

FLEET COMMANDER: Your reasons?

ZHANG BEIHAI: Humanity is certain to lose on the battlefield. I only want to save one of Earth's stellar-class spaceships to preserve a seed of human civilization in the universe, a scrap of hope.

FLEET COMMANDER: That makes you an Escapist.

ZHANG BEIHAI: I'm just a soldier fulfilling his duty.

FLEET COMMANDER: Have you received the mental seal?

ZHANG BEIHAI: You know that's not possible. That technology wasn't around when I went into hibernation.

FLEET COMMANDER: Then your unusually resolute defeatist beliefs are baffling.

ZHANG BEIHAI: I don't need the mental seal. I am the master of my beliefs. My faith is resolute because it doesn't come from my own intelligence. At the beginning of the Trisolar Crisis, my father and I began to seriously consider the most basic questions about this war. Gradually, a group of deep-thinking scholars, including scientists, politicians, and military strategists, gathered around him. They called themselves the Future Historians.

FLEET COMMANDER: Was it a secret organization?

ZHANG BEIHAI: No. They studied very basic questions, and their discussions were always conducted in the open. The government and military even came forward and held several academic conferences on Future History. And it was from their research that I arrived at the mind-set that humanity is doomed.

FLEET COMMANDER: But the theories of Future History have since been proven incorrect.

ZHANG BEIHAI: Sir, you underestimate them. They not only predicted the Great Ravine but the Second Enlightenment and Second Renaissance as well. What they predicted for today's era of prosperity is virtually indistinguishable from the real thing. And, finally, they predicted that humanity would be totally defeated, wiped out in the Doomsday Battle.

FLEET COMMANDER: Have you forgotten that you're on a spaceship capable of traveling at fifteen percent of the speed of light?

ZHANG BEIHAI: Genghis Khan's cavalry attacked with the speed of twentieth-century armored units. The mounted crossbow of the Song Dynasty had a range of up to fifteen hundred meters, comparable to twentieth-century assault rifles. But it's impossible for ancient cavalry and crossbows to compete with modern forces. Fundamental theory determines everything. The Future Historians clearly saw this point. You, on the other hand, have been blinded by the dying radiance of low-level technology and are luxuriating in the nursery of modern civilization, without any mental preparation whatsoever for the coming ultimate battle that will determine the fate of humanity.

FLEET COMMANDER: You come from a great army, one that was

victorious over an enemy with far more advanced equipment. It won victory in one of the largest land wars in the world, relying solely on seized weapons. Your behavior is a disgrace to that army.

ZHANG BEIHAI: My dear commander, I'm more qualified than you to speak of that army. Three generations of my family served in it. During the Korean War, my grandfather attacked a Pershing tank armed with a grenade. The grenade hit the tank and slid off before exploding. The target was barely scratched, but my grandfather was hit by machine-gun fire from the tank, had both legs broken under its treads, and spent the rest of his life an invalid. But compared to two of his comrades, who were crushed to a pulp, he was lucky. . . . It's that army's history that so clearly taught us the significance of a technological gap during wartime. The glory you know is what you've read in the history books, but our trauma was cemented by the blood of our fathers and grandfathers. We know more than you do what war means.

FLEET COMMANDER: When did you conceive of your treasonous plan?

ZHANG BEIHAI: I repeat: I may have deserted, but I am not a traitor. I conceived of the plan the last time I saw my father. I saw in his eyes what I needed to do, and it took me two centuries to realize my plan.

FLEET COMMANDER: And to do this you disguised yourself as a triumphalist. A very successful disguise.

ZHANG BEIHAI: General Chang Weisi almost saw through me.

FLEET COMMANDER: Yes. He was keenly aware that he had never worked out the foundation of your triumphalist faith, and his suspicions were only aggravated by your unusual enthusiasm for radiation propulsion systems capable of interstellar travel. He had always been opposed to you joining the Special Contingent of Future Reinforcements, but he couldn't breach his superiors' orders. He warned us in the letter he sent, but did so in your era's subtle way, and we overlooked it.

ZHANG BEIHAI: In order to obtain a spacecraft capable of fleeing into space, I killed three people.

FLEET COMMANDER: We did not know that. Maybe no one did. But one thing is certain: The research direction chosen at that time was crucial for the subsequent development of spaceflight technology.

ZHANG BEIHAI: Thank you for saying so.

FLEET COMMANDER: I will also say that your plan will fail.

ZHANG BEIHAI: Perhaps. But it hasn't yet.

FLEET COMMANDER: *Natural Selection*'s fusion fuel is only at one-fifth capacity.

ZHANG BEIHAI: But I had to act immediately. There would be no other opportunity.

FLEET COMMANDER: What it means is that you're only able to accelerate to one percent of light speed now. You can't consume excess fuel, because the spaceship's life-support systems still need power to maintain operations for a timespan that could be as short as a few decades or as long as a few centuries. But at that speed, the pursuing force will catch up to you quite soon.

ZHANG BEIHAI: I still control *Natural Selection*.

FLEET COMMANDER: True. And of course you know our concern: that pursuit will drive you to continue accelerating, expending fuel until life support fails and *Natural Selection* becomes a dead ship at near-absolute zero. That's why the pursuit force won't draw near *Natural Selection* for the time being. We have confidence that the commander and soldiers aboard will solve their own warship's problems.

ZHANG BEIHAI: I'm also convinced that all problems will be resolved. I will shoulder my responsibility, but I still firmly believe that *Natural Selection* is headed in the right direction.

When Luo Ji jerked awake, he recognized something else that had endured from the past: firecrackers. It was dawn, and through the window the desert glowed white in the early light, illuminated by

bursts of firecrackers and fireworks. Then came an urgent knock at the door. Without waiting for it to be answered, Shi Xiaoming opened it up and charged in, his face red with excitement as he urged Luo Ji to watch the news.

Luo Ji watched television only rarely. Since arriving in New Life Village #5, he had returned to a life in the past. After the post-awakening impact of the new era, this was a precious feeling for him, and, for the time being, he didn't want to be disturbed by information about the present day. He spent most of his time immersed in memories of Zhuang Yan and Xia Xia. All of the paperwork had been filed for their reawakening, but government controls on hibernators meant that it would not happen for two months.

The television news broadcast the following: Five hours ago, the Ringier-Fitzroy Telescope observed the Trisolaran Fleet cross yet again into an interstellar dust cloud. This was the seventh time since its launch two centuries ago that the fleet had revealed itself by passing through a dust cloud. The fleet had lost its rigorous formation, so that the brush shape it had formed on passing through the first cloud was now altered beyond all recognition. But just as in its second crossing, a bristle was observed extending out in front. What was different this time, however, was that the shape of the track indicated that the bristle was not a probe, but a warship of the fleet. Having completed the acceleration and cruising legs of their journey to the Solar System, some of the ships in the Trisolaran Fleet had been observed decelerating as early as fifteen years ago. Ten years ago, the majority of them had begun to slow down. It was clear now that this particular ship had never reduced speed. In fact, judging from its path through the dust cloud, it was still accelerating. At its current rate of acceleration, it would arrive in the Solar System half a century before the rest of the fleet.

A lone ship charging into Solar System territory and in range of Earth's powerful fleet would be suicide, if it was an invasion. This left just one possible conclusion: It was coming to negotiate. Observations of the Trisolaran Fleet over the course of two centuries had determined the maximum acceleration of every ship,

418

and projections indicated that this advance ship would be unable to decelerate sufficiently, so it would pass right through the Solar System in 150 years. That meant just two possibilities. The first was that the Trisolarans wanted Earth to assist in deceleration. More likely was that, before the ship passed out of the Solar System, it would drop a smaller craft that could decelerate more easily, a ship that would be carrying the Trisolaran negotiation delegation.

"But if they desired to negotiate, wouldn't they notify humanity by sophon?" Luo Ji asked.

"That's easy to explain!" Shi Xiaoming said excitedly. "It's a different way of thinking. The Trisolarans have totally transparent minds, so they imagine that we already know what they're thinking!"

Even though the explanation was unconvincing, Luo Ji shared Shi Xiaoming's feeling, like the sun outside was rising early.

When the sun rose for real, the revelry reached a climax. This was just a small corner of the world, and the center of the activity was in the underground cities, where people left their trees and crowded into the streets and plazas, their clothing turned up to maximum brightness to form a glowing sea of light. Virtual fireworks blossomed in the vaults overhead, and at times a colorful burst covered the entire sky, its brilliant light a match for the sun.

News continued to arrive. The government was cautious at first, and its spokespersons stated repeatedly that there was no conclusive evidence to demonstrate that Trisolaris had the intent to negotiate. But, at the same time, the UN and the SFJC convened an emergency summit to formulate strategies for negotiation procedures and terms. . . .

In New Life Village #5, a short interlude paused the revelry: A city legislator came to make a speech. He was a fanatical supporter of what was called Project Sunshine and was taking this opportunity to win the support of the hibernator community.

Project Sunshine was a UN proposal whose main thrust was that, in the event of a human victory in the Doomsday Battle, defeated Trisolarans ought to be provided with space in the Solar System. There were various versions of the project. The Weak

Survival Plan set up Pluto, Charon, and the moons of Neptune as Trisolaran reservations that would grant admission only to those aboard the defeated Trisolaris ships. The living conditions on these reservations would be very poor, and they would rely on fusion energy and the support of human society to sustain themselves. The Strong Survival Plan would use Mars for the Trisolaran sojourn and would eventually admit all Trisolaran immigrants, in addition to members of the fleet. This plan would provide Trisolaran civilization with the Solar System's best living conditions apart from Earth. The other versions were more or less situated between these two, but there were also a few more extreme ideas, such as accepting Trisolarans into Earth society. Project Sunshine had won broad support from Earth International and Fleet International, and preliminary studies and planning had already begun, with many nongovernmental forces in both Internationals pushing for it. Yet it had encountered fierce resistance from the community of hibernators, who had even coined a name for supporters of the project: "Dongguo," after the soft-hearted scholar in the fable who saved a wolf's life.[21]

As soon as the legislator's speech began, he was met with strong pushback from the audience, which tossed tomatoes at him. Ducking, he said, "I'd like to remind you that we're in a humanitarian age following the Second Renaissance. The life and civilization of every race are accorded the greatest respect. You are bathed in the light of this age, are you not? Hibernators in modern society enjoy citizenship in complete equality and suffer no discrimination. This principle is recognized in the constitution and in the law, but more importantly, it exists in everyone's heart. I trust you can appreciate this. Trisolaris, too, is a great civilization. Human

21 Translator's Note: In the fable "The Wolf of Zhongshan," attributed to the Ming Dynasty writer Ma Zhongxi, the bookish scholar Master Dongguo takes pity on a hunted, starving wolf and hides it in a bag as hunters pass by. When he lets the wolf out, it threatens to eat him but is persuaded to put the issue to a third party. An old farmer, after hearing the situation, protests that the wolf could not possibly fit in the bag. The wolf climbs back in, whereupon the farmer ties up the bag and bashes the wolf to death with his hoe.

society must acknowledge its right to exist. Project Sunshine is not a charity. It is an acknowledgement and an expression of humanity's own value! If we . . . Hey, jerks. Focus on your work!"

The legislator's final line was addressed to his team, who were busily gathering up the tomatoes that had fallen to the ground—they were quite expensive underground, after all. When the hibernators saw this, they began tossing cucumbers and potatoes onto the stage as well, and thus the minor confrontation was resolved in mutual merriment.

At noon, every household feasted. On the grass, a sumptuous meal of unadulterated agricultural products was laid out for the city folk who had come to join in the fun, including Mr. Dongguo the legislator and his entourage. The festivities continued tipsily through the afternoon and until sunset, which was exceptionally beautiful that evening. The sandy plains outside the neighborhood looked creamily soft and delicate under the red-orange sun, and the rolling dunes looked like the bodies of sleeping women. . . .

By nighttime, one news item pushed their flagging spirits to new heights of excitement: the Fleet International had made the decision to combine the stellar-class warships of the Asian Fleet, the European Fleet, and the North American Fleet into a single fleet of 2,015 ships to sally forth in unison and intercept the Trisolaran probe as it crossed the orbit of Neptune!

The news propelled the revelry to a renewed climax, and fireworks filled the night sky. But it also elicited some disdain and mockery.

"Mobilizing two thousand warships for a tiny probe?"

"It's like using two thousand butcher knives to kill a chicken!"

"That's right! Two thousand cannons to hit a mosquito! It's not that tough!"

"Hey, everyone, we should be more understanding of the Fleet International. You know, it might be the only chance they'll get to fight Trisolaris."

"Right. If this can be called fighting."

"It's okay. Just think of it as a military parade for humanity. Let's see what this superfleet's got. It'll scare the Trisolarans to

death! They'll be so frightened they won't be able to pee. If they even have pee."

Laughter.

Close to midnight, more news came: The combined fleet had set off from Jupiter base! Viewers were informed that in the southern sky, the fleet could be seen with the naked eye. At this, the revelers quieted down for the first time and searched the sky for Jupiter. It wasn't easy, but under the guidance of the expert on the television, they soon located the planet in the southwest. At this point, the light of the combined fleet was moving in Earth's direction from a distance of five AU. Forty-five minutes later, the brightness of Jupiter suddenly increased, soon surpassing Sirius to become the brightest object in the night sky. Then a brilliant shining star separated from Jupiter, like a soul leaving a body. The planet returned to its original brightness as the star moved slowly away from it. That was the launch of the combined fleet.

At practically the same time, live images of Jupiter base reached Earth. On the television, people saw the sudden appearance of two thousand suns in the blackness of space. Standing out awesomely in the eternal night of space, their clean rectangular formation put one thought in everyone's mind: *God said, Let there be light, and there was light.* Under the light of those two thousand suns, Jupiter and its moons seemed to have caught fire. The planet's atmosphere, ionized by the radiation, produced lightning that filled the entire fleet-facing hemisphere and covered it in a giant blanket of electric light. The fleet accelerated with no disruption to its formation, its huge wall blocking out the sun, and then made a stately advance into space with the force of a thundercloud, declaring to the universe the dignity and invincibility of the human race. The human spirit that had been repressed since the first appearance of the Trisolaran Fleet two centuries ago had finally found total liberation. At this moment, all the stars in the galaxy silently held back their light, and Human and God stepped out proudly into the universe as one.

The people wept and cheered, and many of them were moved to loud wails. Never before in history had there been such a moment,

in which every single person felt fortunate and proud to be a member of the human race.

But there were some who kept their heads. Luo Ji was one of them. Surveying the crowd, he noticed that someone else was calm: Shi Qiang was off by himself, leaning against one side of the giant holographic television, smoking a cigarette and watching the revelers indifferently.

Luo Ji went over and asked, "What are you . . ."

"Ah, hello my boy. I've got a duty to fulfill." He indicated the ebullient crowd. "Extreme joy easily turns to grief, and now's the best time for something to happen. Like when Mr. Dongguo lectured this morning. If I hadn't come up with the tomatoes and such in a timely fashion, they would have used stones."

Shi Qiang had recently been appointed chief of police for New Life Village #5. To the hibernators, the fact that someone belonging to the Asian Fleet, someone who no longer was a Chinese citizen, had been given an official post in the national government was a little strange. However, his work had been universally acclaimed among the villagers.

"Besides, I'm not the type to get carried away," he continued, clapping Luo Ji across the shoulders. "Neither are you, my boy."

"No, I'm not." Luo Ji nodded. "I was always out for instant gratification. The future had nothing to do with me, even though for a while there I was forced to become a messiah. Maybe my present state is a sort of compensation for the harm from that. I'm going to bed. Believe it or not, Da Shi, I'll actually be able to get to sleep tonight."

"Go and see your colleague. He just arrived. Humanity's victory might not be a good thing for him."

Luo Ji was slightly taken aback by this remark. Looking at the man Shi Qiang pointed to, he realized with surprise that it was the old Wallfacer Bill Hines. His face was ashen and he seemed to be in a trance. He had been standing not far off from Shi Qiang and had only just now noticed Luo Ji. When they hugged each other in greeting, Luo Ji felt that Hines's body seemed to tremble with weakness.

"I came looking for you," he said to Luo Ji. "Only the two of us, history's rubbish, understand each other. But now, I'm afraid even you don't understand me."

"What about Keiko Yamasuki?"

"Remember the Meditation Room in the UN Assembly Building?" Hines said. "It was always deserted. Tourists only visited occasionally. . . . Do you remember the chunk of iron ore? She committed seppuku on top of it."

"Oh . . ."

"Before she died, she cursed me, saying that my life would be worse than death, since I'm marked with the mental seal of defeatism even as humanity is victorious. She was right. I'm in real pain right now. Of course I'm happy for the victory, but it's impossible for me to believe any of it. It's like there are two gladiators fighting in my mind. You know, it's far harder than trying to believe that water is drinkable."

After he and Shi Qiang had gotten Hines set up with a room, Luo Ji returned to his own room and soon fell asleep. Once again he dreamed of Zhuang Yan and the child. When he woke, the sun was shining through the window and the revelries were still going on outside.

Natural Selection flew at 1 percent of the speed of light on a course between Jupiter and the orbit of Saturn. Behind it, the sun was now small, although it was still the brightest of the stars, while up ahead, the Milky Way shone with an even greater brilliance. The ship's heading was more or less in the direction of Cygnus, but in the expanse of outer space, its speed was imperceptible. To a nearby observer, *Natural Selection* would have seemed suspended in deep space. From its own vantage point, in fact, all movement throughout the universe had been erased, leaving the ship seemingly in a static state, with the Milky Way ahead and the sun behind. Time seemed to have stopped.

"You have failed," Dongfang Yanxu said to Zhang Beihai. All personnel aboard the ship but the two of them were still in deep-sea sleep state. Zhang Beihai remained shut inside the spherical

compartment, and Dongfang Yanxu, unable to enter, had to talk with him through the communication system. Through the section of bulkhead that was still transparent, she could see the man who had hijacked humanity's most powerful warship floating quietly in the center of the compartment, head bent, intent on writing in a notebook. In front of him floated an interface that showed the ship on standby for Ahead Four, ready to go at the press of a button. Around him floated several globs of liquid deep-sea acceleration fluid that hadn't yet been evacuated. His uniform had dried, but its wrinkles made him look much older.

He ignored her and continued to write, head bent.

"The pursuing force is only 1.2 million kilometers away from *Natural Selection*," she said.

"I know," he said without looking up. "You were wise to keep the entire ship in deep-sea state."

"It had to be this way. Otherwise, agitated officers and soldiers would have attacked this cabin. And if you took *Natural Selection* to Ahead Four at will, you would have killed them all. That's also the reason why the pursuers haven't closed in."

He said nothing. Flipping a page in the notebook, he continued writing.

"You wouldn't do that, would you?" she asked softly.

"You never imagined I'd do what I'm doing now." He paused a few seconds, then added, "The people of my time have our own ways of thinking."

"But we're not enemies."

"There are no permanent enemies or comrades, only permanent duty."

"Then your pessimism about the war is totally unfounded. Trisolaris has just shown signs of wanting talks, and the combined Solar Fleet has set off to intercept the Trisolaran probe. The war will end with a victory for humanity."

"I've seen the news that came in . . ."

"And you still persist in your defeatism and Escapism?"

"I do."

She shook her head in frustration. "Your way of thinking really is different from ours. For instance, you knew from the start that your plan would be unsuccessful, because *Natural Selection* has only a fifth of its fuel and is certain to be caught."

He set down his pencil and looked out of the cabin at her. His eyes were calm as water. "We're all soldiers, but do you know what the biggest difference between soldiers from my time and soldiers now is? You determine your actions according to possible outcomes. But for us, we must carry out our duty regardless of the outcome. This was my only chance, so I took it."

"You're saying that to comfort yourself."

"No. It's my nature. I don't expect you to understand, Dongfang. We're separated by two centuries, after all."

"So you've carried out your duty, but there's no hope for your Escapist endeavor. Surrender."

He smiled at her, then looked back at his writing. "It's not time yet. I need to write down all that I've experienced. Everything across two centuries needs to be written down, so that it might be of assistance to a few sober-minded people in the next two centuries."

"You can dictate to the computer."

"No, I'm used to writing by hand. Paper lasts longer than a computer. Don't worry. I'll bear full responsibility."

Ding Yi looked out through *Quantum*'s broad porthole. Even though the holographic display in the spherical cabin provided a better view, he still liked seeing things with his own eyes. What he saw was that he was situated on a large plane consisting of two thousand small, dazzling suns whose light seemed to set his gray hair aflame. The sight had grown familiar to him in the days since the launch of the combined fleet, but its grandeur still shook him each time he looked. The fleet was not just in this configuration as a show of force or majesty. In a traditional naval configuration of staggered columns, the radiation produced by the engine of every warship would have an effect on the ships to the rear. In this

426

rectangular formation, the ships were separated by about twenty kilometers. Even though each of them was an average of three to four times the size of a naval aircraft carrier, from that distance they were practically dots, with only the glow of the fusion engines to prove their existence in space.

The combined fleet was in a dense formation, one that had only ever been used in fleet review. In a normal cruising formation, the ships ought to have been spaced at roughly three hundred to five hundred kilometers, so a twenty-kilometer spacing was basically like sailing hull-to-hull through the ocean. Many of the generals in the three fleets disagreed with this dense formation, but conventional formations presented a number of thorny problems. First of all, there was the principle of fairness in battle opportunity. If the probe were approached in a standard formation, then the ships at the edge would still be tens of thousands of kilometers away from the target when the formation reached minimum distance. If combat broke out during the capture, a fair number of the ships could not have been considered to have taken part, leaving them nothing in the history books but eternal regret. But the three fleets couldn't break off into their own subformations, because it was impossible to coordinate which of them would occupy the most advantageous position in the overall formation. So the formation had to be made as dense as possible, a review formation that placed all ships within combat distance of the probe. A second reason for selecting this formation was that the Fleet International and the United Nations both desired stunning visuals, not so much to show off for Trisolaris as to give the masses something to look at. The visual impact held enormous political significance for both groups. With the main enemy force still two light-years away, the dense formation was certainly not in danger.

Quantum was located in a corner of the formation, giving Ding Yi a view of the majority of the fleet. When they crossed the orbit of Saturn, all the fusion engines turned toward the forward direction and the fleet began to decelerate. Now, as the fleet closed in on the Trisolaran probe, its velocity was negative—it was traveling

back toward the sun as it closed the distance separating it from its target.

Ding Yi put a pipe to his lips. With no loose tobacco in this age, it was an empty pipe that dangled there, the lingering flavor of two-century-old tobacco faint and indistinct, like a memory of the past.

He had been reawakened seven years earlier and had been teaching in the Peking University physics department since then. Last year he had put in a request to the fleet asking to be one of the people who would examine the Trisolaran probe up close when it was intercepted. Although Ding Yi was held in high regard, his request had been refused until he declared that he would kill himself in front of the three fleet commanders if they did not comply. Then they said they would think about it. In fact, selection of the first person to contact the probe was a knotty problem, because first contact with the probe meant first contact with Trisolaris. According to the fairness principle to be observed during interception, none of the three fleets could be permitted to enjoy this honor alone, but sending someone from each of them presented operational problems and could complicate matters. So the mission had to be undertaken by someone outside Fleet International. Ding Yi was naturally the most suitable candidate, although another unstated reason lay at the core of his request's ultimate approval: Neither the Fleet International nor the Earth International had much confidence in obtaining the probe, because it was practically certain to self-destruct during or after intercept. Before it did so, close-range observation and contact were imperative if they wanted to obtain as much data as possible. As the discoverer of the macro-atom and the inventor of controlled fusion, the veteran physicist was completely qualified in this area. At any rate, Ding Yi's life was his own, and at eighty-three, his unparalleled qualifications naturally gave the old man the power to do anything he wanted.

At the final meeting of *Quantum* command before the intercept began, Ding Yi saw an image of the Trisolaran probe. Three tracking craft had been dispatched by the three fleets to replace Earth International's *Blue Shadow*. They had captured an image at a

distance of five hundred kilometers from the target, the closest that any human spacecraft had come to the probe. The probe was about as large as expected, 3.5 meters long, and when Ding Yi saw it, he had the same impression as everyone else: a droplet of mercury. The probe was a perfect teardrop shape, round at the head and pointy at the tail, with a surface so smooth it was a total reflector. The Milky Way was reflected on its surface as a smooth pattern of light that gave the mercury droplet a pure beauty. Its droplet shape was so natural that observers imagined it in a liquid state, one for which an internal structure was impossible.

Ding Yi remained silent after he saw the image of the probe. He did not speak at the meeting, and his expression was downcast.

"Master Ding, you seem to have something on your mind," the captain said.

"I don't feel good," he said softly, and pointed at the holographic probe with his pipe.

"Why? It looks like a harmless work of art," an officer said.

"And that's why I don't feel so good," Ding Yi said, shaking his gray head. "It looks like a work of art rather than an interstellar probe. It's not a good sign when something's so far removed from our own mental concept."

"It is peculiar. Its surface is entirely sealed. Where's the engine nozzle?"

"Yet its engine lights up. We've observed that. When it went out for a second time, *Blue Shadow* wasn't close enough to capture an image in time, so we don't know where the light came from."

"What is its mass?" Ding Yi asked.

"We don't have an exact value right now. A rough value, obtained through high-precision gravitational instruments, is less than ten tons."

"Then at least it's not made of matter from a neutron star."

The captain put an end to the officers' discussion and continued with the meeting. He said to Ding Yi, "Master Ding, this is how the fleet has planned out your visit: After the unmanned craft completes its capture of the target and carries out an observation

period, if nothing unusual is found, you will enter the capture craft on a shuttle and conduct a closeup observation of the target. You may not stay longer than fifteen minutes. This is Major Xizi. She will represent the Asian Fleet and accompany you as you carry out your examination."

A young officer saluted Ding Yi. Like the other women in the fleet, she was tall and slender, the very epitome of New Space Humanity.

With only a glance at the major, Ding Yi turned to the captain. "Why does there have to be someone else? Can't I go alone?"

"Of course not, sir. You're unfamiliar with the space environment, and you need assistance throughout the entire process."

"In that case, I'd better not go. Does someone really need to follow me . . ." He broke off without uttering "to death."

The captain said, "Master Ding, this trip is dangerous, to be sure, but not completely so. If the probe self-destructs, then it will most likely occur during the intercept. The likelihood of it self-destructing two hours after the intercept is very low, so long as the examination process does not use destructive instruments."

In point of fact, the primary reason the Earth and Fleet Internationals decided to send a human to the probe was not for an inspection. When the world saw the probe for the first time, everyone was captivated by its magnificent exterior. The mercury droplet was just so beautiful, so simple in shape yet masterfully styled, with each point on its surface in exactly the right place. It was imbued with a graceful dynamism, as if at every moment it was dripping endlessly in the cosmic night. It inspired the feeling that even if human artists tried out every possible smooth closed shape, they wouldn't come up with this one. It transcended every possibility. Not even in Plato's Republic was there such a perfect shape: straighter than the straightest line, more circular than a perfect circle, a mirrored dolphin leaping out of the sea of dreams, a crystallization of all the love in the universe. . . . Beauty is always paired with good, so if there really existed a demarcation between good and evil in the universe, this object would fall on the good side.

So a hypothesis was quickly worked out: The object might not even be a probe. Further observation confirmed this hypothesis, to an extent. People first noticed its exterior, the highly smooth finish that made it a total reflector. The fleet conducted an experiment on the probe using a large quantity of monitoring equipment: Its entire surface was irradiated with different wavelengths of high-frequency electromagnetic waves, and the reflectance was measured. To their shock, they discovered that at every frequency, including visible light, the reflection was practically 100 percent. No absorption was detected. This meant that the probe could not detect any high-frequency waves—or, in layman's terms, it was blind. There must be a particular significance to a blind design. The most reasonable guess was that it was a token of goodwill from Trisolaris to humanity, expressed through its nonfunctional design and beautiful form. A sincere desire for peace.

So the probe was given a new name inspired by its shape: "the droplet." On both Earth and Trisolaris, water was the source of life and a symbol of peace.

Public opinion maintained that a formal delegation ought to be sent to make contact with the droplet, rather than an expedition team made up of a physicist and three ordinary officers. But after careful consideration, Fleet International decided to keep its original plan unchanged.

"Can't you at least swap in someone else? Letting this young lady . . ." Ding Yi said, gesturing at Xizi.

Xizi smiled at him and said, "Master Ding, I am *Quantum*'s science officer. I'm in charge of off-ship scientific expeditions during our voyages. This is my duty."

"And women make up half the fleet," the captain said. "Three people will accompany you. The other two are science officers sent by the European and North American Fleets. They'll be reporting shortly. Master Ding, let me reiterate one point: According to the decision of the SFJC, you must be the first to make direct contact with the target. Only then are they permitted to make contact."

"Pointless." Ding Yi shook his head again. "Humanity hasn't

changed at all. So eager to chase after vanity. . . . But, rest assured, I'll do as you wish. I just want to have a look, is all. What I'm really interested in is the theory behind this super-technology. But I'm afraid that this life is . . . ah."

The captain floated over to him and said with concern, "Master Ding, you can go rest now. The intercept will be starting soon, and you need to preserve your energy before setting off on your expedition."

Ding Yi looked up at the captain. For a moment he didn't realize that the meeting was going to continue after he left. Then he looked back at the image of the droplet, noticing now how its round head reflected a regular row of lights that gradually deformed toward the rear, merging into the reflected pattern of the Milky Way. That was the fleet. He looked again at *Quantum*'s commanders floating before him, all of them so very young. Just children. They looked so noble and perfect, from the captain to the lieutenants, and their eyes shone with a godlike wisdom. The light of the fleet streaming in through the portholes was tinted like a golden sunset by the auto-darkening glass, enveloping them all in gold. Behind them floated the image of the droplet like a supernatural silver symbol, making the place otherworldly and transcendent, and turning them into a host of gods atop Mount Olympus. . . . Something stirred deep within him, and he grew excited.

"Master Ding, do you have something else to add?" the captain asked.

"Er, I'd like to say . . ." His hands moved aimlessly, and he let his pipe float in the air. "I'd like to say that you kids have been great to me over the past few days. . . ."

"You're the man we admire the most of all," a vice-captain said.

"Oh . . . so there are a few things I'd really like to say. Just . . . the nonsense of an old fool. You don't have to take it seriously. Still, children, as someone who's crossed two centuries, I've been through a bit more than you. . . . Of course, like I said, don't take it seriously. . . ."

"Master Ding, if you've got something to say, then just say it. You really have our highest respect."

432

Ding Yi slowly nodded. Then he pointed upward. "If this spaceship has to go to maximum acceleration, everyone here will need to . . . be immersed in a liquid."

"That's right. Deep-sea state."

"Yes, right. The deep-sea state." Ding Yi hesitated again, and ruminated for a moment before resolving to go on. "When we go out for our examination, could this ship, ah, *Quantum,* be put into a deep-sea state?"

The officers looked at each other in surprise, and the captain said, "Why?"

Ding Yi's hands began fluttering again. His hair glowed white under the fleet's light. Like someone had noticed when he first came aboard, he looked quite a bit like Einstein. "Um . . . well, at any rate there's no harm in doing it, right? You know, I don't have a good feeling."

After saying this, he remained silent, his eyes locked onto the infinite distance. At last he reached out, plucked the pipe out of the air, and put it into his pocket. Without saying good-bye, he awkwardly worked his superconductor belt to float toward the door as the officers watched him.

When he was halfway out, he slowly turned back around. "Children, do you know what I've been doing all these years? Teaching physics at a university and advising doctoral students." As he looked out at the galaxy, an inscrutable smile played on his face—tinted with, the officers noticed, a hint of sadness. "Children, a man from two centuries ago is still able to teach university physics today." With that, he turned and left.

The captain wanted to say something to him, but now that he was gone, the words didn't come out. He remained deep in thought. Some of the officers looked at the droplet, but more of them turned their attention to the captain.

"Captain, you're not going to take him seriously, are you?" one lieutenant asked.

"He's a wise scientist, but he's still an ancient man. Their thoughts about modern things are always . . ." someone else added.

"But in his field, humanity hasn't made any progress. It's still stuck at his era's level."

"He spoke of intuition. I think his intuition may have discovered something," an officer said, in a voice full of awe.

"Also . . ." Xizi blurted out. But looking at the surrounding officers who outranked her, she swallowed the rest of her words.

"Major, please continue," the captain said.

"Also, like he said, there's no harm in doing it," she said.

"Think about it this way," a vice-captain said. "According to present battle plans, if the capture fails and the droplet unexpectedly escapes, then the fleet can only deploy fighters as a tracking force. But long-range tracking needs to be stellar-class, so the fleet ought to have warships prepared. This is an oversight in the plan."

"Make a report to the fleet," the captain said.

The fleet's approval was swift: When the examination team had set off, *Quantum* and the neighboring stellar-class warship *Bronze Age* would enter a deep-sea state.

To capture the droplet, the fleet's formation maintained a distance of one thousand kilometers from the target, a figure decided after careful calculation. There were various hypotheses about the manner in which the droplet might self-destruct, but the maximum release of energy would come from self-destruction by antimatter annihilation. Since the droplet had a mass of less than ten tons, the largest energy burst that needed to be considered was that produced by the annihilation of five tons each of matter and antimatter. That annihilation, if it occurred on Earth, would be enough to destroy all life on the planet surface, but in space, the energy would be released entirely in the form of light radiation. For stellar-class warships, with their super anti-radiation capacity, one thousand kilometers was far enough to allow for a sufficient margin of safety.

The capture would be accomplished by *Mantis*, a small unmanned craft that had previously been used for collecting mineral specimens in the asteroid belt. Its key feature was an extra-long robotic arm.

At the start of the operation, *Mantis* crossed the five-hundred-kilometer line held by the previous monitoring craft and carefully approached the target, flying slowly and pausing for several minutes every fifty kilometers so that the dense omnidirectional surveillance system behind it could perform a complete scan of the target. Only after confirming that there were no abnormalities did it proceed.

At one thousand kilometers from the target, the combined fleet had matched speed with the droplet, and most of the warships had turned off their fusion engines to drift silently in the abyss of space, their giant metal hulls reflecting the weak sunlight. They were like abandoned space cities, the whole fleet array a silent, prehistoric Stonehenge. The 1.2 million people in the fleet held their breath as they watched *Mantis* on its brief voyage.

The images seen by the fleet traveled at the speed of light for three hours before reaching Earth, where they were transmitted to the eyes of three billion people similarly holding their breath. All activity in the human world had stopped. The flying cars had disappeared from among the giant trees, and a stillness had fallen over the underground metropolises. Even the global information network, busy since its birth three centuries before, emptied out. The majority of data transmissions were images from twenty AU away.

Mantis's stop-and-go advance took half an hour to cover a distance that was hardly even a step through space. Finally, it hung in place fifty meters from the target. Now the *Mantis*'s distorted reflection could be clearly seen in the droplet's mercury surface. The ship's many instruments began a close-range scan of the target, first confirming prior observations: The droplet's surface temperature was even lower than the surrounding space, close to absolute zero. Scientists had thought that there might be powerful cooling equipment inside the droplet, but *Mantis*'s instruments were still unable to detect anything about the target's internal structure.

Mantis extended its extra-long robot arm toward the target, starting and stopping over the fifty-meter distance. But the dense monitoring system did not pick up anything abnormal. The grueling

process lasted half an hour before the tip of the arm finally reached the target's position and touched it, an object that had come from four light-years away on a nearly two-century-long trek through space. When the robot arm's six digits grasped hold of the droplet at last, a million hearts in the fleet beat as one, echoed three hours later by three billion hearts on Earth.

Holding the droplet, the mechanical arm waited motionless. When the target still showed no response or abnormality after ten minutes, it began to pull it back.

It was at this point that people noticed a strange contrast: The mechanical arm was obviously designed purely as a functional object, with a rugged steel frame and exposed hydraulics that felt complicatedly technological and crudely industrial. But the droplet was perfect in shape, a smoothly gleaming, solid drop of liquid whose exquisite beauty erased all functional and technical meaning and expressed the lightness and detachment of philosophy and art. The steel claw of the robot arm clutched the droplet like the hairy hand of *Australopithecus* clutching a pearl. The droplet looked so fragile, like a glass thermos liner in space, that everyone was afraid it would shatter in the claw. But that did not occur, and the robot arm began to retract.

It took another half hour for the arm to retract and pull the droplet into *Mantis*'s main cabin, after which the two bulkheads gradually came together. If the target were to self-destruct, this would be the most likely time. The fleet and Earth behind it waited quietly, as if through the silence they could hear the sound of time flowing through space.

Two hours later, nothing had happened.

The fact that the droplet had not self-destructed was final proof of what people had guessed: If it was a military probe, it surely would have self-destructed after falling into enemy hands. It was now certain that this was a gift from Trisolaris to humanity, a sign of peace sent in that civilization's baffling mode of expression.

436

Once again the world erupted with joy. This time the revelry wasn't as wild and abandoned as the last, because humanity's victory and the end of the war were no longer anything unanticipated. Taking a thousand steps back, even if the coming negotiations broke down and the war continued, humanity would still ultimately be the victors, because the presence in space of the combined fleet had given the masses a visual impression of human power. Earth now had the calm confidence to face any sort of enemy.

With the arrival of the droplet, people's feelings toward Trisolaris slowly began to change. They increasingly began to recognize that the race marching toward the Solar System was a great civilization, one that had experienced two-hundred-odd cyclic catastrophes and had endured with unbelievable tenacity. Their arduous journey of four light-years across the vastness of space was all for the sake of finding a stable star, a home in which to live out their lives. . . . The public's feelings toward Trisolaris began to change from enmity and hatred to sympathy, compassion, and even admiration. People also realized another fact: Trisolaris had sent out the ten droplets two centuries ago, but humanity had only just realized their true significance. This was no doubt because the behavior of Trisolaris was overly subtle, as well as a reflection of the fact that humanity's state of mind had been distorted by its own bloody history. In a global online referendum, citizen support for Project Sunshine rose rapidly, increasingly inclined toward the Strong Survival Plan that offered Mars as a Trisolaran reservation.

The UN and the fleets accelerated their preparations for negotiations, and the two internationals began organizing delegations.

All of this took place in the day after the droplet was captured.

But what excited people most of all was not the facts before their eyes, but the rudimentary outline of a bright future: What sort of fantastic paradise would the Solar System become after the union of Trisolaran technology and human power?

At about the same distance on the other side of the sun, *Natural Selection* coasted silently at 1 percent the speed of light.

"Message just received: The droplet didn't self-destruct upon capture," Dongfang Yanxu said to Zhang Beihai.

"What's a droplet?" he asked. They faced each other through the transparent bulkhead. His face was haggard.

"The Trisolaran probe. Now we have confirmation that it's a gift to the human race, an expression of the Trisolaran wish for peace."

"Is that so? That's very good."

"You don't seem to care very much."

He didn't reply. Instead he lifted the notebook up in front of him with both hands. "I've finished." Then he put it into a close-fitting pocket.

"So can you hand over control of *Natural Selection* now?"

"I can, but first I'd like to know what you plan on doing once you've gained control."

"Decelerating."

"To rendezvous with the pursuing force?"

"Yes. *Natural Selection*'s fuel store is below return capacity, so it needs to refuel before being able to return to the Solar System. But the pursuing force doesn't have enough fuel for us. Those six ships are only half the tonnage of *Natural Selection,* and in their pursuit they've accelerated to five percent of light speed and decelerated a similar amount. They've got enough fuel for a return. So *Natural Selection*'s personnel will have to return aboard the pursuing force. Later, a ship carrying enough fuel will be sent after *Natural Selection* to take it back to the Solar System, but that will require time. We need to decelerate as much as possible before leaving to minimize that time."

"Don't decelerate, Dongfang."

"Why?"

"Deceleration will consume all of *Natural Selection*'s remaining fuel. We can't become a powerless ship. No one knows what will happen. As captain, you ought to keep that in mind."

"What can happen? The future is clear: The war will end and humanity will win, and you'll be proven totally wrong!"

He smiled at her excitement, as if trying to quell it. As he looked at her, there was a softness in his eyes that had never been there before. It rocked her emotions. She found his defeatism unbelievable, and suspected him of having other motivations for defecting. She had even wondered about his sanity. But for some reason she felt a certain attachment to him. She had left her father when she was very young, certainly not anything unusual for a child of that era. Fatherly love was something ancient. But in this ancient soldier from the twenty-first century, she had come to understand it.

He said, "Dongfang, I come from troubled times. I'm a realist. All I know is that the enemy is still there and it's still approaching the Solar System. As a soldier knowing this, I can't be happy until everyone is at peace. . . . Don't decelerate. This is the condition under which I'll relinquish control. Of course, the only guarantee I have is your character."

"I promise that *Natural Selection* will not decelerate."

Zhang Beihai turned and floated to the interface panel, where he called up the permissions-transfer interface and entered his password. After a series of taps, he turned it off.

"*Natural Selection*'s captain's privileges have been transferred to you. The password is still Marlboro," he said, without looking back at her.

Dongfang Yanxu called up an interface in the air and quickly confirmed this. "Thank you. But I ask you not to come out of that cabin for the time being, or open the door. The ship's personnel are awakening from deep-sea state and I'm afraid they might act aggressively toward you."

"Will they make me walk the plank?" At her mystified expression, he laughed. "It's a form of the death penalty on ancient ships. If it had really carried on through to today, you would have to shove a criminal like me right out into space. . . . Okay. I'd quite like to be alone."

The shuttle that sailed out of *Quantum* seemed as small as a car leaving a city compared to its mother ship. The light of its engine illuminated only a small part of the ship's hull, like a candle beneath a cliff. It eased out of *Quantum*'s shadow into the sunlight, its engine nozzle glowing like a firefly as it flew toward the droplet a thousand kilometers away.

The expedition team consisted of four people: a major and a lieutenant colonel from the European and North American Fleets, Ding Yi, and Xizi.

Through the porthole, Ding Yi looked back at the receding fleet formation. *Quantum,* situated in a corner, still appeared large, but its nearest neighbor, the warship *Cloud,* was so small that its shape could only barely be made out. Farther away, the ranks of warships were just rows of points across his field of view. Ding Yi knew that the rectangular array was a hundred ships in length by twenty in width, with an additional fifteen ships maneuvering outside of the formation. But when he counted along the length, by the time he reached thirty he couldn't see clearly, and that was just six hundred kilometers away. It was the same looking up, where the short side extended vertically. The warships that could be made out in the far distance were just fuzzy points of light under the weak sunlight, nearly indistinguishable from the starry background. Only when their engines started up would the fleet array be totally visible to the naked eye. The combined fleet was a one-hundred-by-twenty matrix in space. He imagined another matrix being multiplied with it, the horizontal elements from one multiplied in turn with vertical elements from the other to form an even larger matrix, although in reality the only important constant for the matrix was one tiny point: the droplet. He didn't like extreme asymmetry in mathematics, so this attempt to calm himself through mental gymnastics failed.

When the force of acceleration subsided, he struck up a conversation with Xizi, who was sitting next to him. "Child, are you from Hangzhou?"

Xizi was staring straight ahead, as if trying to locate *Mantis,* which was still hundreds of kilometers away. Then she recovered

and shook her head. "No, Master Ding. I was born in the Asian Fleet. I don't know whether my name has anything to do with Hangzhou.[22] I've been there, though. It's a nice place."

"It was a nice place back in our day. But West Lake has now turned into Crescent Lake, and it's in a desert. . . . Still, even though the desert's everywhere, today's world still reminds me of the south, and the age in which the women were as graceful as the water." As he said this, he looked at Xizi, whose enchanting silhouette was set off by the soft light of the distant sun that streamed in through the porthole. "Child, looking at you, I'm reminded of someone I once loved. Like you, she was a major, and although she wasn't as tall as you, she was just as beautiful. . . ."

"In the old days, lots of girls must have been in love with you," Xizi said to Ding Yi, turning back to him.

"I wouldn't usually bother the girls I liked. I believed in what Goethe said: 'If I love you, what business is it of yours?' "

Xizi laughed.

He went on, "Oh, if only I had the same attitude toward physics! My life's biggest regret is that we've been blinded by the sophons. But here's a more positive way of thinking about it: If we're exploring laws, what business is that of the laws? One day, perhaps, humanity—or maybe someone else—will explore the laws so thoroughly that they'll be able to alter not only their own reality, but perhaps the entire universe. They'll be able to turn every star system into whatever shape they require, like kneading a ball of dough. But so what? The laws still won't have changed. Yes, she'll still be there, the one unchanging presence, forever young, like how we remember a lover. . . ." As he spoke, he pointed out the porthole at the brilliant Milky Way. "And when I think about that, my worries go away."

Xizi said nothing, and they fell into a heavy silence. *Mantis* soon came into view, albeit as a point of light two hundred kilometers

22 *Translator's Note: Xīzǐ* is another name for Xi Shi, one of the Four Beauties of ancient China, who lived near Hangzhou. West Lake (Xīhú) in Hangzhou has a particular association with Xi Shi.

away. The shuttle rotated 180 degrees, and the engine nozzle, now pointing ahead of them, began their deceleration.

The fleet was now directly ahead of the shuttle, around eight hundred kilometers away, a trivial distance in space, but one that turned the massive warships into barely visible points. The fleet itself was distinguishable from the starry background only by its neatly arranged ranks. The entire rectangular array seemed like a grid covering the Milky Way, its regularity standing in stark contrast to the chaos of the starfield. With its great size made tiny by the distance, the power of the formation was made apparent. Many people in the fleet and the distant Earth behind it who were watching this image sensed that it was a visual display of what Ding Yi had just been talking about.

The shuttle reached *Mantis* and the force of deceleration cut off. To the shuttle's passengers, the speed of the process made it feel as if *Mantis* had suddenly popped up in space.

Docking was completed quickly. Since *Mantis* was unmanned, there was no air in the cabin, so the four members of the expedition team put on light space suits. Upon receiving final instructions from the fleet, they filed weightlessly through the docking hatch and into *Mantis*.

The droplet floated dead center in *Mantis*'s one spherical main cabin. Its colors were entirely different from the image seen aboard *Quantum*, paler and softer, evidently due to differences in the scene reflected on its surface—the droplet's total reflectance meant that it had no color of its own. Arranged in the main cabin of *Mantis* was the folded robotic arm, an assortment of equipment, and several piles of asteroid rock samples. Floating in a mechanical and stony environment, the droplet once again presented a contrast between exquisiteness and crudeness, aesthetics and technology.

"It's the tear of the blessed mother," Xizi said.

Her words were transmitted from *Mantis* at the speed of light, first to the fleet and then resonating three hours later throughout the entire human world. Xizi, the lieutenant colonel, and the major from the European Fleet—ordinary people on the expedition team

442

placed, by unexpected circumstance, in a central position at the pinnacle moment in the history of civilization—shared a common feeling now that they were so close to the droplet: All sense of the distant world's unfamiliarity vanished, replaced by an intense desire for recognition. Yes, in the cold expanse of the universe, all carbon-based life shared a common destiny, one that might take billions of years to cultivate, but a destiny that cultivated feelings of love that transcended time and space. And now, they sensed that love in the droplet, a love that could bridge the chasm of any enmity. Xizi's eyes were wet, and three hours later, the eyes of billions of people like her would fill with tears.

But Ding Yi watched all of this dispassionately from the rear. "I see something else," he said. "Something far more sublime. A realm where both self and other are forgotten, an effort to encompass everything by shutting out everything."

"That's too much philosophy for me to understand," Xizi laughed through her tears.

"Dr. Ding, we don't have much time." The lieutenant colonel motioned for Ding Yi to come forward to be the first to touch the droplet.

Ding Yi floated slowly toward the droplet and placed a hand on its surface. To avoid frostbite from the cold mirror surface, he had to touch it with a gloved hand. Then the three officers touched it, too.

"It looks so fragile. I'm afraid of breaking it," Xizi said softly.

"I can't feel any friction at all," the lieutenant colonel marveled. "It's so smooth."

"How smooth is it?" Ding Yi asked.

To answer that question, Xizi took out a cylindrical instrument, a microscope, from a pocket in her space suit. She touched the lens to the droplet, and they could see a magnified image of the surface on the instrument's small display. Displayed on the screen was a smooth mirror.

"What's the magnification?" Ding Yi asked.

"A hundred times." Xizi pointed to a number in the corner of the screen, then adjusted the magnification to one thousand.

The enlarged surface remained a smooth mirror.

"Your device is broken," the lieutenant colonel said.

Xizi removed the microscope from the droplet and placed it against her space suit visor. The other three drew closer to look at the screen, where the visor—a surface which, to the naked eye, looked as smooth as the droplet—was a rough and rocky beach on the screen under one-thousand-times magnification. Xizi returned the microscope to the surface of the droplet, and the screen once again displayed a smooth mirror, no different from the surrounding, unmagnified surface.

"Increase it by another factor of ten," Ding Yi said.

This was beyond the capabilities of optical magnification, so Xizi carried out a series of operations to switch the microscope from optical to electron tunneling mode. Now the magnification power stood at ten thousand.

The magnified surface remained a smooth mirror. The smoothest surface that human technology could produce revealed itself as rough at just one thousand times magnification, like Gulliver's impression of the face of the beautiful giantess.

"Adjust to a hundred thousand times," the lieutenant colonel said.

Still they saw a smooth mirror.

"A million times."

A smooth mirror.

"Ten million times."

Macromolecules would be visible at this magnification, but what they saw on the screen remained a smooth mirror without the slightest sign of roughness, no difference in smoothness from the surrounding unmagnified surface.

"Push it up again!"

Xizi shook her head. This was the electron microscope's highest level of magnification.

More than two centuries before, in his novel *2001: A Space Odyssey*, Arthur C. Clarke had described a black monolith left on the moon by an advanced alien civilization. Surveyors had measured its dimensions with ordinary rulers and had found a ratio of one to four

to nine. When these were rechecked using the most high-precision measurement technology on Earth, the ratio remained an exact one to four to nine, with no error at all. Clarke described it as a "passive yet almost arrogant display of geometrical perfection."

Now, humanity was facing a far more arrogant display of power.

"Can an absolutely smooth surface really exist?" Xizi gasped.

"Yes," Ding Yi said. "The surface of a neutron star is nearly absolutely smooth."

"But this has a normal mass!"

Ding Yi considered this, then looked about him. "Hook up to the spaceship computer and find the spot that the robot arm gripped during capture."

This was accomplished remotely by a fleet surveillance officer. The *Mantis* computer projected thin red laser beams to mark the position on the droplet surface that had been gripped by the steel claw. Xizi examined one of the spots with the microscope, and at a magnification of ten million times, she still saw a smooth, flawless mirror.

"How high was the pressure at the point of contact?" the lieutenant colonel asked, and soon received a reply from the fleet: approximately two hundred kilograms per square centimeter.

Smooth surfaces are easily scratched, but the strong metal clamp did not leave any scratches on the droplet's surface.

Ding Yi floated away in search of something within the cabin. He returned with a rock pick, perhaps dropped in the cabin by someone during collection of rock samples. Before anyone could stop him, he slammed it forcefully into the mirror surface. There was a clang, crisp and melodious, like the pick had smashed into jade-paved ground. The sound traveled through his body, but the other three didn't hear it because of the vacuum. With the handle of the pick, he pointed out the spot he had struck, and Xizi examined it with the microscope.

At ten million times magnification, it was still a smooth mirror.

Ding Yi tossed the pick aside dejectedly and looked away from

the droplet, deep in thought. The eyes of the three officers, and the eyes of the million people in the fleet, were all focused on him.

"All we can do is guess," he said, looking up. "The molecules in this thing are neatly arranged, like an honor guard, and they're mutually solidifying. Do you know how solid it is? It's as if the molecules are nailed into place. Even their own vibrations are gone."

"That's why it's at absolute zero!" Xizi said. She and the other two officers understood what Ding Yi was getting at: At normal densities of matter, the separation between atomic nuclei is quite large. It would be no easier to fix them all in place than it would be to join the sun to the eight planets with rods to form a stationary truss.

"What force would allow that?"

"There's only one option: strong interaction."[23] Through his visor, it was obvious that Ding Yi's forehead was covered in sweat.

"But . . . that's like shooting the moon with a bow and arrow!"

"Indeed, they've shot the moon with a bow and arrow. . . . The tear of the blessed mother?" He gave a chilly laugh, a mournful sound that made them shiver, and the three officers knew what it meant: The droplet wasn't fragile like a tear. Entirely the opposite: Its strength was a hundred times greater than the sturdiest material in the Solar System. All known substances were as fragile as paper by comparison. It could pass through the Earth like a bullet through cheese, without even the slightest harm to its surface.

"Then . . . what's it here for?" the lieutenant colonel blurted out.

"Who knows? Maybe it really is just a messenger. But it's here to give humanity a different message," Ding Yi said, turning his gaze away from the droplet.

"What?"

"If I destroy you, what business is it of yours?"

The words were followed by a momentary silence as the three other members of the expeditionary team and the million members

23 *Translator's Note:* Strong interaction is the strongest of the four fundamental interactions, and is responsible for the strong nuclear force that binds together subatomic particles. It is roughly 100 times more powerful than electromagnetism, but is only effective at distances of less than a femtometer.

of the combined fleet ruminated over their meaning. Then, all of a sudden, Ding Yi said, "Run." The word was uttered softly, but then he raised his hands and shouted hoarsely, "Stupid children. Run!"

"Run where?" Xizi asked in fright.

Just seconds after Ding Yi, the lieutenant colonel realized the truth. Like Ding Yi, he shouted desperately: "The fleet! Evacuate the fleet!"

But it was too late. Powerful interference had already wiped out their communication channels. The image being transmitted from *Mantis* vanished, and the fleet was unable to hear the lieutenant colonel's final call.

A blue halo emerged from the tip of the droplet's tail. It was small at first, but very bright, and cast a blue shroud over its surroundings. Then it dramatically expanded, turning from blue to yellow and finally to red. It almost seemed as if the droplet wasn't producing the halo, but had just drilled out from within it. The halo weakened in luminosity as it expanded, and when it had reached a diameter twice that of the largest part of the droplet, it vanished. The instant it vanished, a second small blue halo emerged from the tip. Like the first one, it expanded, changed color, weakened, and quickly disappeared. The halos continued to emerge from the droplet's tail at a rate of two or three a second, and under their propulsion, the droplet began to move forward, and then rapidly accelerated.

But the four members of the expedition team never saw the second halo emerge, because the first one was accompanied by ultra-high temperatures approaching that of the sun's core, which vaporized them instantly.

The hull of *Mantis* glowed red, resembling from the outside a paper lantern whose candle had just been lit. Its metal body melted like wax, but no sooner had the ship begun to melt than it exploded, dispersing into space as an incandescent liquid with hardly any solid fragments left behind.

From a thousand kilometers away, the fleet had a clear view of *Mantis*'s explosion, but the initial analysis was that the droplet had

self-destructed. Everyone felt sorrow for the sacrifice of the four expedition team members, followed by disappointment that the droplet was not a messenger of peace. But the human race did not have even the slightest bit of psychological preparation for what was about to happen.

The first anomaly was identified by the fleet's space surveillance computer, which discovered during the course of processing images of *Mantis*'s explosion that one of the fragments was abnormal. Most of the pieces were molten metal that flew uniformly through space following the explosion, but this one was accelerating. Of course, only a computer was able to find a tiny object among the massive quantity of flying fragments. From an immediate search of its database and knowledge bank, which included an enormous amount of information on *Mantis,* it arrived at several dozen possible explanations for the peculiar debris, but none was correct.

Neither computer nor human realized that the explosion had destroyed only *Mantis* and the four-member expedition team, but not the droplet.

As for the accelerating fragment, the fleet's space surveillance system issued only a level-three attack alarm, because the approaching object was not a warship and was headed toward one corner of the rectangular formation. On its current heading, it would pass outside the formation and would not strike any warship. Due to the large number of level-one alarms issued following the *Mantis* explosion, this level-three alarm was completely ignored. The computer had, however, also noted the fragment's high rate of acceleration. By three hundred kilometers it had already passed the third cosmic velocity and was continuing to gain speed. The alert was upgraded to level two, but was still ignored.

By the time the fragment had flown roughly 1,500 kilometers from the explosion site toward the corner of the formation, only fifty-one seconds had elapsed. By the time it reached the corner, it was traveling at a speed of 31.7 kilometers per second. Now it was on the periphery of the formation, 160 kilometers away from *Infinite Frontier,* the first warship in this corner of the array. The fragment

did not pass by the formation, but executed a thirty-degree turn, and, without slowing down, sped straight toward *Infinite Frontier*. In the roughly two seconds it took to cover that distance, the computer actually dropped its alert from level two back to level three, concluding that the fragment wasn't actually a physical object due to the fact that its motion was impossible under aerospace mechanics. At twice the third cosmic velocity, executing a sharp turn without a drop in speed was like slamming into an iron wall. If it was a vessel containing a metal block, the change in direction would have exerted such force as to flatten that metal block into a thin film. So the fragment had to be an illusion.

In that manner, the droplet struck *Infinite Frontier* at twice the third cosmic velocity, at a heading straight along the first row of the fleet rectangle.

The droplet struck *Infinite Frontier* in its rear third and passed through with no resistance, as if penetrating a shadow. The extreme speed of the impact meant that two highly regular entry and exit holes roughly the diameter of the droplet's thickest part appeared in its hull. But no sooner had they appeared than the holes deformed and vanished as the surrounding hull melted under the heat produced by the high-speed impact and the ultra-high temperature of the droplet's trailing halo. The part of the ship that had been hit turned red-hot, and the redness spread from the point of impact until it covered half the ship, like a chunk of iron that had just been taken out of the forge.

After passing through *Infinite Frontier,* the droplet continued onward at a speed of thirty kilometers per second. In the space of three seconds it had crossed ninety kilometers, passing first through *Yuanfang, Infinite Frontier*'s neighbor in the first row, and then through *Foghorn, Antarctica,* and *Ultimate,* leaving their hulls red-hot, as if the warships were giant lamps lined up.

Then *Infinite Frontier* exploded. It and the four warships after it were hit in the fusion fuel tanks. But unlike *Mantis*'s conventional, high-temperature explosion, this explosion was a fusion reaction triggered in *Infinite Frontier*'s fuel. No one ever figured out whether

the fusion reaction had been sparked by the droplet's ultra-high-temperature propulsive halo or some other factor. The fireball of the thermonuclear explosion appeared at the point of impact with the fuel tank and swiftly expanded until it illuminated the entire fleet against the velvety background of space, outshining the Milky Way.

Nuclear fireballs then took shape on *Yuanfang, Foghorn, Antarctica,* and *Ultimate* in succession.

In the next eight seconds, the droplet passed through ten more stellar-class warships.

By this point, the expanding nuclear fireball had engulfed the entirety of *Infinite Frontier* and had begun to shrink, while more fireballs were lighting up and expanding on other ships that had been struck.

The droplet continued to traverse the length of the array, penetrating one stellar-class warship after another at intervals of less than a second.

The fusion fireball on *Infinite Frontier* had gone out, leaving the ship's hull totally melted. Now it exploded, spewing a million tons of glowing, dark-red metallic liquid like a bud bursting into bloom, the molten metal scattering unimpeded in an omnidirectional storm of burning metallic magma.

The droplet continued its advance, following a straight line through more warships and leaving a line of ten nuclear fireballs behind it. The entire fleet shone in the flames of these burning small suns as if it had been set ablaze and turned into a sea of light. Behind the line of fireballs, the melted warships continued to fling waves of hot molten metal into space, as if massive rocks were being pitched into a magma sea.

In one minute and eighteen seconds, the droplet had completed a two-thousand-kilometer course, passing through each of the hundred ships in the first row of the combined fleet's rectangular formation.

By the time the last ship in the row, *Adam,* was swallowed up in a nuclear fireball, the bursts of metallic magma at the opposite end had scattered, cooled, and spread out, leaving the heart of the

explosion—the spot where *Infinite Frontier* had been a minute before—empty of practically everything. *Yuanfang, Foghorn, Antarctica, Ultimate* . . . all of them vanished one after another into metallic magma. When the last nuclear fireball in the line went out and darkness fell upon space once more, the gradually cooling magma that had barely been visible reappeared as dark red lights in the blackness of space, like a two-thousand-kilometer-long river of blood.

After punching through *Adam,* the droplet flew a short distance of about eighty kilometers through empty space, then executed another sharp turn unexplainable by humanity's aerospace mechanics. This time the angle it described was even smaller: just fifteen degrees off a total reversal, executed nearly instantaneously even as it maintained a constant speed. Then, after a small heading adjustment that brought it in line with the second row of warships in the fleet's array—or what was now the first row, in light of the recent destruction—it sped toward the first ship in that row, *Ganges,* at thirty kilometers per second.

Until this point, Fleet Command had not made any response.

The fleet's battle information system had faithfully carried out its mission and captured through its massive monitoring network a complete record of all battle information over the course of that one minute and eighteen seconds. The sheer amount of information was for the time being only analyzable by the computerized battlefield decision-making system, which had arrived at the following conclusion: A powerful enemy space force had appeared in the vicinity and had launched an attack on the fleet. However, the computer did not provide any information about that enemy force. Only two things were certain: 1. The enemy space force was located at the position occupied by the droplet, and 2. The force was invisible to every means of detection they possessed.

By this time, fleet commanders were in a state of numb shock. For nearly two centuries, research into space strategy and tactics had dreamed up every possible kind of extreme battle condition, but witnessing a hundred warships blowing up like a string of

firecrackers in under a minute was beyond what their minds could comprehend. The tide of information surging out of the battle information system meant that they were forced to rely on the analyses and judgments of the computer battlefield decision-making system and focus their attention on detecting an invisible enemy fleet that didn't even exist. All battle monitoring capacity was directed into the distant regions of space, ignoring the danger right in front of them. A fair number of people even believed that the powerful invisible enemy might be a third-party alien force distinct from humanity and Trisolaris, because in their subconscious minds, Trisolaris remained the weaker, losing side.

The fleet's battle monitoring system did not detect the droplet's presence any earlier primarily because it was invisible to radar at all wavelengths and could only be located through analysis of visible spectrum images, but visible images were treated with far less importance than radar data. Most of the fragments scattered through space in storms of exploded debris were liquid metal melted by the high-temperature nuclear blasts, upward of a million tons melted in the destruction of each ship. A fair proportion of this massive amount of molten debris was roughly the same size and shape as the droplet, which presented the computer image analysis system with the difficult task of distinguishing the droplet from the debris. Besides, practically all of the commanders believed that the droplet had self-destructed inside *Mantis,* so no one issued specific instructions to perform such an analysis.

Meanwhile, other circumstances were exacerbating the confusion of battle. Debris ejected from the explosions of the first row of warships soon reached the second row, prompting their battle defense systems to respond with high-energy lasers and railguns to intercept the debris. These flying fragments, consisting largely of metal melted by the nuclear fireballs, were irregular in size, and although they had been partially cooled in flight by the low temperatures of space, only their outer shells had solidified. Their insides were still in a fiery liquid state, and when struck, they scattered in a brilliant explosion of fireworks. It was not long before

the second row turned into a flaming barrier parallel to the dull "river of blood" left behind by the exploded warships in the first, roiling with explosions as if washed in a tide of fire surging from the direction of that invisible enemy. Debris flew thick as hail, more than defensive systems could block, and when fragments slipped through and struck the warships, the impact of these jets of solid-liquid metal possessed considerable destructive power. A number of the ships in the fleet's second row suffered major hull damage, and some were even punctured. Shrill decompression alarms blared. . . .

Although the dazzling battle with debris did receive notice, given the circumstances, it was hard for the computers and humans in the command system to avoid the misconception that the fleet was engaged in a fierce exchange of fire with an enemy space force. Neither person nor machine noticed the tiny figure of Death that had begun to destroy the second row of ships.

And so, when the droplet charged at *Ganges,* the hundred warships in the second row were still assembled in a straight line. A death formation.

The droplet surged like lightning, and in the space of just ten seconds, it passed through twelve warships: *Ganges, Columbia, Justice, Masada, Proton, Yandi, Atlantic, Sirius, Thanksgiving, Advance, Han, and Tempest.* As in the destruction of the first row, each warship turned red-hot after penetration, before being engulfed in a nuclear fireball that left a million tons of dark red, glowing, metallic magma that then exploded. In this brutal destruction, the lined-up warships were like a two-thousand-kilometer fuse that burned with such intensity that it left behind nothing but ash glowing a dull, dark red.

One minute and twenty-one seconds later, the hundred ships in the second row had been completely annihilated.

After passing through the last ship, *Meiji,* the droplet reached the end of the row and turned another acute angle to charge straight at the first ship in the third row, *Newton.* During the destruction of the second row, debris from the explosions had raged into the third.

The tide of debris included molten metal flung from explosions in the second row as well as mostly cooled metal fragments from the ships of the first. Most of the third-row ships had by now started up their engines and defensive systems and had begun maneuvering, which meant that this time, the ships were not situated along a perfectly straight line, as had been the case for the first and second rows. Nevertheless, the hundred ships were still roughly in line. After the droplet passed through *Newton,* it sharply adjusted direction and, in a twinkling, crossed the twenty kilometers separating *Newton* from *Enlightenment,* now at a three-kilometer offset from the line. From *Enlightenment,* it turned sharply again, raced toward *Cretaceous,* which was moving toward the other side, and penetrated it. Following this broken path, the droplet drilled through the ships in the third row one after the other, never dropping its speed below thirty kilometers per second.

When analysts subsequently observed the droplet's route, they were amazed to discover that its every turn was a sharp corner, not the smooth curve of a human spacecraft. The diabolical flight path demonstrated a space drive entirely beyond human comprehension, as if the droplet was a shadow without mass, unconcerned with the principles of dynamics, moving at will like the nib of God's pen. During the attack on the fleet's third row, the droplet's sharp changes of direction occurred at a rate of two or three per second, a deathly embroidery needle sewing a thread of destruction through the row's hundred ships.

The droplet took two minutes and thirty-five seconds to destroy the third row of ships.

By this time, all of the warships in the fleet had started their engines. Although the array had lost its shape entirely, the droplet continued to strike the evacuating ships. The pace of destruction slowed, but, at any given time, three to five nuclear fireballs were burning among the ships. Their deathly flames drowned out the glow of the engines, turning them into a cluster of terrified fireflies.

The fleet command system still had no clue about the true source of the attack and continued to focus its energies on searching for

the imaginary invisible enemy fleet. However, subsequent analysis of the massive clouds of vague information transmitted by the fleet revealed that it was at this point that the earliest analysis to come close to the truth was performed by two low-ranking officers in the Asian Fleet. One was Ensign Zhao Xin, an assistant targeting screener on *Beifang,* and the other was Captain Li Wei, an intermediate EM weapons system controller on *Wannian Kunpeng.* A transcript of their conversation follows:

ZHAO XIN: This is *Beifang TR317* calling *Wannian Kunpeng EM986!* This is *Beifang TR317* calling *Wannian Kunpeng EM986!*

LI WEI: This is *Wannian Kunpeng EM986.* Please be advised, transmitting ship-to-ship voice communication at this information level is a violation of wartime regulations.

ZHAO XIN: Is that Li Wei? This is Zhao Xin! You're who I'm trying to find!

LI WEI: Hi! I'm glad to know you're still alive.

ZHAO XIN: Captain, here's the thing. I've discovered something that I'd like to transmit to the shared command level, but my privileges are too low. Could you help me out?

LI WEI: My privileges are too low, too. But shared command has plenty of information right now. What do you want to transmit?

ZHAO XIN: I've analyzed a visual image of the battle—

LI WEI: Shouldn't you be analyzing radar information?

ZHAO XIN: That's a system fallacy. When I analyzed the visual image and extracted only the speed characteristic, do you know what I found? Do you know what's been going on?

LI WEI: You seem to know.

ZHAO XIN: Don't think I've gone crazy—you know me, we're friends.

LI WEI: You're a stone-cold beast. You'll be the last to go crazy. Go ahead.

ZHAO XIN: Listen, it's the fleet that's gone crazy. We're attacking ourselves!

LI WEI: . . .

ZHAO XIN: *Infinite Frontier* attacked *Yuanfang*, and *Yuanfang* attacked *Foghorn*, and *Foghorn* attacked *Antarctica*, and *Antarctica* . . .

LI WEI: You're out of your damn mind!

ZHAO XIN: That's what's happening. A attacks B; and after B is attacked, but before it explodes, it attacks C; and after C is attacked but before it explodes, it attacks D. . . . It's like every warship that was hit attacked the next warship in the row—like an infection, damn it, or a game of pass the parcel, but to the death. It's insane!

LI WEI: What weapons are they using?

ZHAO XIN: I don't know. I picked up a projectile in the image, so frickin' tiny and so frickin' fast, way the hell faster than your rail-guns. And incredibly precise. It hit the fuel tanks every single time!

LI WEI: Send me the analysis.

ZHAO XIN: I've sent it over, the original data and vector analysis both. Take a look, god damn it!

Ensign Zhao Xin's analysis, though unconventional, was pretty close to the truth. Li Wei took half a minute to study the information he sent over. In that time, another thirty-nine warships were destroyed.

LI WEI: I've noticed something about the speed.

ZHAO XIN: What speed?

LI WEI: The speed of the small projectile. Its speed when it's launched from each warship is slightly slower. Then it accelerates to thirty kilometers per second during flight. Then it strikes the next warship, and when it launches from that warship prior to the explosion, its speed is a little slower. Then it accelerates. . . .

ZHAO XIN: That doesn't mean anything. . . .

LI WEI: What I mean is . . . it's a little like drag.

ZHAO XIN: Drag? How so?

LI WEI: Every time this projectile passes through a target, the drag slows it down.

ZHAO XIN: I see what you're doing. I'm not stupid. You said "this projectile" and "passes through a target." . . . Is it a single object?

LI WEI: Take a look outside. Another hundred ships have exploded.

This conversation took place not in the modern language of the fleet but in twenty-first-century Mandarin. From the mode of speech, it was obvious that the two were hibernators. There were few hibernators serving in the fleet, and although most of them had awakened while still very young, they still lacked a modern person's capacity to absorb information, which meant that most of them carried out relatively low-level duties. It was later discovered that the vast majority of officers and soldiers who recovered their senses and good judgment the earliest during the grand destruction were hibernators. These two officers, for instance, despite being at a level that did not even permit them the use of the ship's advanced systems, were nonetheless able to perform a remarkable piece of analysis.

Zhao Xin and Li Wei's information was not passed up the fleet command system, but the system's analysis of the battle was headed in the right direction. Realizing that the invisible enemy force posited by the computer decision-making system didn't exist, attention was now focused on analyzing the aggregated battle information. After a search and match on massive amounts of data, the system finally discovered the continued existence of the droplet. The image of the droplet extracted from battle recordings was unchanged apart from the addition of a propulsion halo at the tail. It was still a perfect droplet shape, only this time what was reflected as it sped onward was the glow of nuclear fireballs and metal magma, glaring brightness alternating with dark red. It looked like a drop of burning blood. Further analysis arrived at a model of the droplet's attack path.

Various scenarios for the Doomsday Battle had been concocted during two centuries of the study of space strategy, but in the minds of strategists, the enemy had always been big. Humanity would meet the main part of the mighty Trisolaran force on a space battlefield, with every warship a fortress of death the size of

a small city. They had imagined every extreme form of weapons and tactics the enemy could possibly possess, the most terrifying of which involved the Trisolaran Fleet launching an attack using antimatter weapons, and obliterating a stellar-class battleship with antimatter the size of a rifle bullet.

But now the combined fleet had to face facts: Their only enemy was a tiny probe, one drop of water out of the enormous ocean of Trisolaran strength, and this probe attacked using one of the oldest and most primitive tactics known to human navies: ramming.

Roughly thirteen minutes passed from the moment the probe started its attack until the fleet command system arrived at the correct assessment. Given the complex and grim battlefield conditions, this was fairly quick, but the droplet was quicker. In twentieth-century naval battles, there might have been time for commanders to be summoned to the flagship for a conference once the enemy fleet appeared on the horizon. But space battles were measured in seconds, and in that thirteen-minute span, more than six hundred warships were destroyed by the probe. Only then did humanity realize that command of a space battle was beyond their reach. And due to the sophon block, it was beyond the reach of their artificial intelligence as well. Purely in terms of command, humanity might *never* have the capacity to engage in a space battle with Trisolaris.

The speed of the droplet's strikes and its invisibility to radar meant that defensive systems on the first ships hit never responded. But as the distance between the warships grew and the droplet's striking distance increased, defensive systems on all warships were recalibrated based on the droplet's target characteristics. This meant that *Nelson* was the first ship to attempt to intercept, using laser weapons to increase the accuracy of firing on the small, high-speed target. When struck by the multiple beams, the droplet emitted a powerful visible light, even though the *Nelson* had fired gamma-ray lasers that were invisible to the naked eye. The droplet's imperceptibility to radar had never been understood, since it had a completely reflective surface and a shape that was perfectly diffuse, but perhaps the ability to alter the frequency of

reflected electromagnetic waves was the secret to this invisibility. The light emitted from the droplet when it was struck was so bright it drowned out the nuclear fireballs going off all around it, forced the monitoring systems to dim their images to avoid damage to their optical components, and caused sustained blindness to anyone who looked directly at it. In other words, this superpowerful light was indistinguishable from darkness in its effect. The droplet, wrapped in this all-engulfing light, entered *Nelson* and was extinguished, plunging the battlefield into pitch darkness. Moments later, the nuclear fireballs reestablished their dominance and the droplet emerged from *Nelson* unscathed and sped straight for *Green,* eighty-odd kilometers away.

Green's defense system switched over to EM-based kinetic weapons to intercept the attacking droplet. The metal shells fired by the railgun possessed enormous destructive power, and the kinetic energy inherent in their high speed meant that every shell that struck the target hit with the force of a bomb. Against ground targets, they would flatten a mountain in no time at all. The droplet's relative velocity only added to the shells' energy, but when they struck, the droplet slowed only slightly before it adjusted its propulsion and recovered its speed. Under a dense hail of shells, it flew straight at *Green* and penetrated it. Under the ultra-high magnification microscope, the droplet's surface would still be mirror-smooth and totally scratch-free.

Strong-interaction material differs from ordinary matter like solid differs from liquid. The attacks on the droplet by human weapons were like waves striking a reef. Damaging it was impossible, which meant that nothing in the Solar System could destroy it. It was untouchable.

The fleet command system had just stabilized itself, only to be plunged once again into chaos. This time, its despair over the loss of every weapon available to it meant it would not recover from this collapse.

The merciless slaughter in space continued. As the distance between ships grew, the droplet accelerated and had soon doubled

its speed to sixty kilometers per second. Exhibiting a cool and precise intelligence in its continuous attacks, it solved the traveling salesman problem in local regions with perfect accuracy, hardly ever retracing its path. With its targets in constant motion, the droplet accomplished a huge range of accurate measurements and complex calculations effortlessly and at high speed. In the course of its intensely focused massacre, it would occasionally veer off to the edges of the group of ships to quickly dispatch a few outliers and arrest the fleet's inclination to flee in that direction.

The droplet usually made precise strikes on the ships' fuel tanks—whether it found them by real-time location detection or with the use of a stored database of every ship's structure provided by the sophons was unknown. However, in around 10 percent of the targets, the droplet did not strike the tanks. The destruction of those ships did not involve fusion in the nuclear material, so it took a comparatively long time for the red-hot ships to finally explode, a brutal situation in which the crew suffered under high temperatures before burning to death.

The evacuation of the ships did not go smoothly. It was too late to enter deep-sea state, so the warships could only evacuate at Ahead Three acceleration, which made scattering impossible. Like a sheepdog racing alongside a flock, the droplet executed occasional blocking strikes at different positions at the fleet's edges to keep it in shape.

Space was full of cooled or still-molten debris and large chunks of warships, so ship defense systems had to continually sweep their flight path with lasers or railguns. The fragments formed glittering, flaming arcs that wrapped each ship in a brilliant canopy. Yet some debris still slipped through the defenses and caused serious hull damage and even loss of navigational capability when they struck the ships directly. Collision with larger fragments was fatal.

Despite the collapse of the fleet command system, High Command remained in charge during evacuation, but the density of the initial formation meant collisions between ships were unavoidable. *Himalaya* and *Thor* collided headon at high speed

and were smashed to bits. *Messenger* rear-ended *Genesis,* and the air that leaked like a hurricane through the gashes tore into both ships and blew personnel and other objects out into space, forming tails that dragged along in the wake of the two giant wrecks.

Most horrifying of all was what happened to *Einstein* and *Xia,* whose captains bypassed system protections via remote control mode and entered Ahead Four acceleration. None of their personnel was protected by deep-sea state. Images transmitted from *Xia* showed a hangar emptied of fighters but occupied by over a hundred people who were flattened against the deck by the high gs once acceleration began. From this vantage point, observers saw crimson flowers of blood bloom on the white space the size of a football field, forming extremely thin layers that spread out and ultimately merged into one under the immense force. . . . Spherical cabins presented the ultimate horror: At the beginning of hypergravitation everyone inside slid to the bottom, and then the devil's weighty hand squished them all into a lump, as if balling up a pile of clay men, with no time for anyone to even scream. The only sound was of shattering bones and viscera squeezing out. Then the pile of flesh and bones was submerged in a bloody liquid that turned eerily clear once the solids were precipitated out by the high gs, its surface flat and motionless as a mirror under the intense force. It seemed solid, and the formless pile of flesh, bone, and organs lay within it like rubies sealed in crystal. . . .

Afterward, people initially thought that putting *Einstein* and *Xia* into Ahead Four had been a mistake made during the chaos, but further analysis repudiated this view. Using the remote control mode to bypass the stringent procedures required by the warship control system prior to executing Ahead Four acceleration, including the confirmation that all personnel were in deep-sea state, involved a complicated series of operations that were unlikely to have been made in error. In the information transmitted from the two ships, it was also found that, prior to entering Ahead Four, *Einstein* and *Xia* had been using fighters and smaller craft to transport personnel outside. They did not enter Ahead Four until the

droplet drew nearer and neighboring warships began to explode. This suggested that they intended to escape the droplet at top acceleration to preserve humanity's warships, but even *Einstein* and *Xia* were unable to evade the droplet's clutches. The keen-eyed death god noticed that two ships were accelerating far faster than the average rate of the group and swiftly caught up to them and destroyed the ships and their lifeless cargo.

But two other warships successfully accelerated at Ahead Four and escaped the droplet's attack: *Quantum* and *Bronze Age*, which had both entered deep-sea state prior to the battle, at Ding Yi's behest. As soon as the third row of ships had been destroyed, the two of them entered Ahead Four and made an emergency escape in the same direction. Their position in a corner of the array, with the entire fleet separating them from the droplet, gave them sufficient time to escape into the depths of space.

More than a thousand ships, over half the fleet, had been destroyed in a twenty-minute attack.

Space was chock-full of debris in a cluster ten thousand kilometers in diameter, a rapidly expanding metallic cloud whose edges were illuminated time and again by the nuclear fireballs of exploding warships, as if a giant, stony face were flickering in and out of the cosmic night. In between the fireballs, the glow of metallic magma turned the cloud into a blood-red sunset.

The remaining warships were scattered widely, but nearly all of them were still within the metallic cloud. The majority had exhausted their railguns and had to rely on lasers to open up a path through the cloud, but the energy drain made the lasers underpowered and left the ships to wend a slow, torturous path through the debris. Most of them moved at a speed practically the same as the cloud's rate of expansion, turning it into a death trap from which evacuation and flight were impossible.

The droplet's speed was now ten times the third cosmic velocity, or roughly 170 kilometers per second. Its course took it smashing through debris that liquefied under impact, splashing away at high speed to collide with other debris and giving the droplet a brilliant

tail. First it resembled a comet bristling with rage, but as the tail lengthened, it turned into a huge silver dragon that stretched ten thousand kilometers. The entire metallic cloud glowed with the dragon's light as it whipped to and fro in its mad dance. The warships penetrated by the dragon's head began to explode along its body, so that it was dotted with the nuclear explosions of four or five small suns at any given time. Further back, molten battleships became million-ton metallic magma explosions that dyed its tail a bewitching bloodred. . . .

The brilliant dragon was still flying thirty minutes later, but the nuclear fireballs on its body had disappeared, and its tail was no longer bloodred. Not a single warship remained in the metallic cloud.

When the dragon flew out of the cloud, its body vanished at the cloud's edge, its head followed by its tail. Then it began taking out the remnants of the fleet. Only twenty-one warships had cleared the cloud, most of them suffering enough damage in the process that they retained minimal acceleration or were even coasting unpowered. These were quickly caught and destroyed by the droplet. The metallic clouds formed from the newly exploded ships expanded and merged into the larger cloud.

The droplet had to spend a bit more time destroying the five mostly intact ships because they had already picked up speed and were headed in different directions. The final ship to be destroyed, *Ark*, had traveled a considerable distance from the cloud, so when the fireball of its explosion lit up space for a few seconds before going out, it was like a solitary lamp in the wind of the wilderness.

Humanity's space-based armed forces had been annihilated.

The droplet briefly accelerated in the direction *Quantum* and *Bronze Age* had fled, but soon abandoned the chase because the two targets were too far away and had picked up too much speed. And thus, *Quantum* and *Bronze Age* became the only survivors of the tremendous destruction.

The droplet left the field of slaughter and set its heading in the direction of the sun.

Apart from those two complete warships, a small number of

people in the fleet had survived the holocaust by boarding fighters or other small craft before the destruction of their ships. Although the droplet could have destroyed them effortlessly, it had no interest in small spacecraft. The biggest threat to these vessels, which lacked defensive systems and couldn't survive an impact, was from high-speed metal fragments, and some of them were destroyed by debris after leaving their mother ships. They had the greatest chance of survival at the beginning and the end of the attack, because at the start the metallic cloud had not yet formed, and by the end the cloud had grown far less dense as it expanded.

The surviving small craft and fighters drifted for a few days beyond the orbit of Uranus and were eventually rescued by civilian spacecraft plying that region of space. The survivors numbered around sixty thousand, and included the two hibernator officers who had made the first correct assessment of the droplet's attack: Ensign Zhao Xin and Captain Li Wei.

The region eventually became still, and the metallic cloud lost its luster in the coldness of the cosmos and disappeared into darkness. Over the years, under the pull of the sun's gravity, the cloud stopped its expansion and began to lengthen, ultimately forming a long strip that turned into an extremely thin metallic belt around the sun, as if a million restless souls were floating endlessly in the cold outer reaches of the Solar System.

The destruction of the entirety of humanity's space force was accomplished by just one Trisolaran probe, and nine like it were three years away from the Solar System. The ten of them together weren't even one ten-thousandth the size of a single warship, and Trisolaris had a thousand of those that even now were flying onward toward the Solar System.

"If I destroy you, what business is it of yours?"

Awakening from a long sleep, Zhang Beihai looked at the time: He had been asleep fifteen hours, perhaps the longest he had ever slept apart from his two centuries in hibernation. Now he felt a

464

new feeling. Examining his mind, he realized where this feeling came from.

He was on his own.

In the past, even when floating alone in the endlessness of space, he had never had the feeling of being on his own. His father's eyes were watching him from the beyond with a gaze that was present every moment of every day. Like the sunlight during daytime and the starlight at night, it had become a part of his world. Now his father's gaze had disappeared.

Time to go out, he said to himself as he adjusted his uniform. He had slept weightless, so no part of his hair or clothing was out of place. Taking a last look at the spherical cabin in which he had spent more than a month, he opened the door and drifted out, prepared to calmly face the fury of the crowd, to face the count- less expressions of disdain and condemnation, to face the final judgment . . . and to face, as a conscientious soldier, a life whose duration he did not know. Whatever happened, the rest of his life was sure to be calm.

The corridor was empty.

He advanced slowly, passing compartments on either side, all of them open. They were all identical to his own spherical cabin, their snow-white walls resembling pupilless eyes. The environment was clean, and he saw no open information windows. The ship's information system had probably been restarted and reformatted.

He recalled a movie he had seen in his youth, in which the char- acters lived in a Rubik's Cube world made up of countless identical cubic rooms, each of which contained a different sort of death mechanism. They passed from one room to the next, endlessly. . . .

The free rein of his thoughts surprised him. This used to be a luxury, but now that his nearly two-century-long mission was at an end, his mind could walk a leisurely path.

He turned a corner, and ahead of him was another, longer corridor that was just as empty. The bulkheads emitted an even, milky-soft light that was enough to make him lose his sense of depth. The world felt compact. Again, the doors to the spherical cabins on

either side were all open, and each one was an identical white space.

Natural Selection looked abandoned. To Zhang Beihai's eyes, the massive ship he occupied was one enormous yet concise symbol, a metaphor for some law hidden beneath reality. He had the illusion that these identical white spherical spaces extended endlessly into space around him, repeating infinitely through the universe.

An idea popped into his mind: holography.

Every spherical cabin could achieve total manipulation and control of *Natural Selection,* so, at least from an informatics perspective, every cabin was the totality of *Natural Selection.* That meant *Natural Selection* was holographic.

The ship itself was a metal seed carrying the total information of human civilization. If it germinated somewhere in the universe, then it might grow into a complete civilization. The part contained the whole, hence human civilization might be holographic as well.

He had failed. He had not managed to spread these seeds, and for this he felt regret. But not sadness, and not just because he'd done everything he could to carry out his duty. His mind, now freed, took flight, and he imagined the universe as holographic, every point containing the whole, so that the entire universe endured so long as one atom remained. Suddenly he had an all-encompassing sense of focus, the same feeling that Ding Yi had just over ten hours ago at the other end of the Solar System on the last stage of his approach toward the droplet, while Zhang Beihai was still asleep.

He reached the end of the corridor and opened the door to enter the warship's largest spherical hall, the one he had arrived at when he first entered *Natural Selection* three months ago. As before, a formation of fleet officers and soldiers was floating in the center of the sphere, but their numbers were several times greater and made up three layers in the formation. The two-thousand-strong crew of *Natural Selection* formed the center layer, which he realized was the only real layer. The other two were holograms.

Looking closer, he saw that the hologram formations were made up of the officers and soldiers from the four pursuing ships. Right in the center of the three-layer formation was a row of five

colonels: Dongfang Yanxu and the captains of the four other ships. All but Dongfang Yanxu were holograms that were evidently being transmitted from the pursuing ships. When he entered the hall, the eyes of five thousand people focused on him with an expression clearly not directed at a defector. The captains saluted in order.

"*Blue Space,* of the Asian Fleet!"

"*Enterprise,* of the North American Fleet!"

"*Deep Space,* of the Asian Fleet!"

"*Ultimate Law,* of the European Fleet!"

Dongfang Yanxu was the last to salute him. "*Natural Selection,* of the Asian Fleet! Sir, the five stellar-class warships you have preserved for humanity are all that is left of Earth's space fleet. Please accept your command!"

"It's a collapse. Everything's collapsed. It's a collective mental breakdown!" Shi Xiaoming sighed and shook his head. He had just returned from the underground city. "The whole city's out of control. It's chaos."

The administrative officials had all come to a meeting of the neighborhood government. Hibernators made up two-thirds, with modern people accounting for the rest. They were easily distinguishable now: Although they were in a state of extreme depression, the hibernator officials kept their composure despite their low spirits, while the moderns manifested signs of breakdown to varying degrees and lost control on multiple occasions during the course of the meeting. Shi Xiaoming's words plucked at their fragile nerves once again. The neighborhood chief executive's eyes were wet with tears, and when he covered his face to weep, it prompted several other modern officials to weep with him. The official in charge of education laughed hysterically, and several other moderns began to snarl, before tossing their cups on the ground. . . .

"Quiet down," Shi Qiang said. His voice wasn't loud, but it had a dignity that quieted the modern officials. The executive and the

others who were crying struggled to hold back their tears.

"They're just kids," Hines said, shaking his head. Attending the meeting as a people's representative, he was perhaps the only person who had benefited from the destruction of the combined fleet, because now that reality was in line with his mental seal, he had returned to normal. Previously, he had been tormented day and night by the mental seal in the face of what seemed like an all-but-certain victory, and he had nearly suffered a mental breakdown. He had been sent to the largest hospital in the city, where expert psychiatrists had been powerless to help him, although they had proposed a novel idea, which Luo Ji and the suburban officials helped carry out. As in Daudet's "The Siege of Berlin," or the old Golden-Age film *Good Bye, Lenin!*, why not fabricate a fictional environment in which humanity had failed? Fortunately, at the pinnacle of modern virtual technology, it wasn't at all hard to create such an environment. Every day at his residence, Hines watched news that was broadcast especially for him, accompanied by lifelike three-dimensional images. He saw a portion of the Trisolaran Fleet accelerate and arrive at the Solar System early, and humanity's combined fleet suffer heavy losses in a battle at the Kuiper Belt. Then the three fleets were unable to hold the line at Neptune's orbit, and they were forced to stage a difficult resistance at Jupiter's orbit. . . .

The neighborhood official in charge of manufacturing this false world got quite wrapped up in it, and when the crushing defeat actually took place, he was the first to suffer a mental breakdown. He had exhausted his imagination painting humanity's defeat in the most disastrous way possible, both for Hines's needs and for his own personal pleasure, but cruel reality far outstripped anything he had imagined.

When the images of the fleet's destruction twenty AU away reached Earth after a three-hour delay, the public behaved like a gang of desperate children, turning the world into a nightmare-plagued kindergarten. Mass mental breakdown spread rapidly, and everything went out of control.

In Shi Qiang's neighborhood, all the officials ranked higher than him either resigned or simply broke down and did nothing, so the higher-level authorities gave him an emergency appointment to take over the duties of the local chief executive. It may not have been all that important a post, but the fate of this hibernator neighborhood was in his hands during this crisis. Fortunately, compared to the underground city, the hibernator societies remained relatively stable.

"I would ask everyone to remember the situation we're in," Shi Qiang said. "If there's ever a problem with the artificial environmental system in the underground city, the place will turn to hell and everyone there will flood out to the surface. If that happens, this place won't be fit for survival. We had better consider migration."

"Migration where?" someone asked.

"To somewhere sparsely populated, like the northwest. Of course, we would have to send people to check it out first. Right now, no one can say what will happen to the world, or whether there will be another Great Ravine. We have to make preparations to survive totally on agriculture."

"Will the droplet attack Earth?" someone else asked.

"What's the point of fretting?" Shi Qiang shook his head. "No one can do anything about it, at any rate. And until it punches through the Earth, we've still got to live, right?"

"That's right. Worrying is pointless. I'm quite clear on that point," Luo Ji said, breaking his silence.

Humanity's seven remaining spaceships flew away from the Solar System, split into two groups: five ships comprised of *Natural Selection* and its pursuers and another group of two ships, *Quantum* and *Bronze Age*, which had survived the droplet's devastation. The two small fleets were at opposite ends of the Solar System, separated by the sun. They were on headings that took them in almost opposite directions, and gradually getting farther apart.

On *Natural Selection,* after Zhang Beihai heard the account of the combined fleet's annihilation, his expression didn't change. His eyes remained calm as water, and he said lightly, "A dense formation is an unforgivable error. Everything else was to be expected."

"Comrades," he said, sweeping his eyes over the five captains and the three layers of assembled officers and soldiers, "I call you by that ancient title because I want us all to share a common will from this day forward. Each of you must understand the reality we are facing, and must envision the future that we will face. Comrades, we can't go back."

Indeed, there was no going back. The droplet that had destroyed the combined fleet was still in the Solar System, and nine others would arrive in three years. For this small fleet, their former home was now a death trap. From the information they had received, human civilization would totally collapse even before the main Trisolaran Fleet arrived, so Earth's doomsday was not far off. The five ships had to accept the responsibility of carrying civilization forward, but all they could do was to fly onward, and fly far. The spaceships would be their home forever, and space would be their final resting place.

Together, the 5,500 crewmembers were like an infant who had been cut from its cord, then cruelly tossed into the abyss of space. Like that infant, there was nothing they could do but cry. Yet Zhang Beihai's calm eyes were a strong force field that upheld the stability of the formation and helped them maintain their military poise. Children cast aside into the endless night needed a father most of all, and now, like Dongfang Yanxu, they found the power of that father in the person of this ancient soldier.

Zhang Beihai went on. "We will be a part of humanity forever, but we are an independent society and must rid ourselves of our psychological dependence on Earth. Now we need to choose a new name for this world of ours."

"We come from Earth, and we may be the sole inheritors of Earth civilization, so let's call ourselves Starship Earth," Dongfang Yanxu said.

"Excellent." Zhang Beihai nodded approvingly, then turned to the formation. "From now on, we are each of us citizens of Starship Earth. This moment might be a second starting point for human civilization. There are many things we need to do, so I would ask all of you to return to your posts now."

The two hologram formations vanished, and *Natural Selection*'s formation began to disperse.

"Sir, should our four ships rendezvous?" the captain of *Deep Space* asked. The captains had not vanished.

Zhang Beihai shook his head firmly. "That's not necessary. You are currently around two hundred thousand kilometers from *Natural Selection,* and although that's close, a rendezvous would expend nuclear fuel. Energy is the foundation of our survival, and with what little we have, we must conserve as much as we can. We are the only humans in this part of space, so I understand your desire to gather together, but two hundred thousand kilometers is a short distance. From now on, we have to think about the long term."

"Yes, we have to think about the long term," Dongfang Yanxu repeated softly, her eyes still staring at the horizon as if surveying the long years ahead of them.

Zhang Beihai continued, "A citizens' assembly must be convened immediately to set down basic issues, then the majority of the people need to be put into hibernation as soon as possible so that the ecological systems can be operated at a minimum. . . . Whatever transpires, the history of Starship Earth has begun."

Zhang Beihai's father's eyes emerged from the beyond once again, like rays from the edge of the cosmos that penetrated everything. He felt the gaze, and in his heart he said, *No, Dad. You really can't rest. It's not over. It's started up again.*

The next day, still keeping Earth time, Starship Earth convened its first plenary Citizens' Assembly, held in a venue formed from the combination of five holographic subvenues. The citizens in attendance numbered around three thousand, and the remainder who were unable to leave their posts networked in.

First off, the assembly identified an urgent matter: the destination of Starship Earth's voyage. Maintaining the current heading unchanged was passed by unanimous vote. This target was the one Zhang Beihai had set for *Natural Selection,* a heading in the direction of Cygnus—or, more precisely, the star NH558J2, one of the planetary systems closest to the Solar System. It had two planets,

both of which were gaseous like Jupiter and not suitable for human life, but could provide supplemental nuclear fuel. It now appeared that the choice of destination had been made after considerable thought, because along a different heading, at a distance just 1.5 light-years farther than their present destination, there was another planetary system which, according to observations, contained a planet whose natural environment was similar to Earth's. But that system had just one planet, and if it turned out to be an inhospitable world—the conditions for a hospitable world were more exacting than the rough observations from light-years away could reveal— then Starship Earth would miss the chance to refuel. After reaching NH558J2 and refueling, they could fly at even higher speeds toward their next target.

NH558J2 was eighteen light-years away from the Solar System. At their present speed, taking into account various uncertainties in the voyage, Starship Earth would reach it in two thousand years.

Two millennia. The grim number presented another clear picture of the present and the future. Even taking hibernation into account, most of the citizens of Starship Earth would never live to see their destination. Their lives would last just a small part of the twenty-century-long voyage, and even for their descendants who would reach it, NH558J2 was just a way station. No one knew what their next destination would be, much less when Starship Earth would finally reach its true, hospitable home.

In fact, Zhang Beihai had been exceptionally rational in his thinking. He clearly knew that Earth's suitability for human life was no coincidence, much less an effect of the anthropic principle, but rather was an outcome of the long-term interaction between the biosphere and the natural environment, an outcome that would not likely be repeated on another planet around some far-flung star. His choice of NH558J2 implied another possibility: Perhaps a hospitable world would never be found, and the new human civilization would forever voyage on a starship.

But he did not make this idea explicit. It might take the next generation born on Starship Earth to truly be able to accept a starship

civilization. The present generation would have to live their lives sustained by the thought of a home on an Earth-like planet.

The assembly also determined Starship Earth's political status. It decided that the five ships would remain part of the human world forever, but under the present circumstances, it was impossible for Starship Earth to be politically subordinate to Earth or the three fleets, so it would become a totally independent country.

When this resolution was transmitted back to the Solar System, the UN and the SFJC were silent for quite some time before replying. Without taking a position, they merely sent their tacit blessing.

And thus the human world was divided into three internationals: the ancient Earth International, the Fleet International of the new era, and the Starship International that was voyaging into the depths of the cosmos. The last group had just over five thousand people, but it carried with it all the hope of human civilization.

At the second meeting of the Citizens' Assembly, they began discussing the issue of Starship Earth's leadership structure.

When the meeting began, Zhang Beihai said, "I think it's too early for this agenda item. We've got to determine the shape of society on Starship Earth before we can decide what sort of governing bodies we need."

"You mean, we need to draft a constitution first," Dongfang Yanxu said.

"At least the basic principles for a constitution."

So the meeting continued along those lines. The inclination of the majority was that because Starship Earth was a highly fragile ecosystem traveling through the harsh environment of space, a disciplined society had to be established to guarantee a unified will to survive under these conditions. Someone proposed maintaining the present military system, and the idea received majority support.

"You mean a totalitarian society," Zhang Beihai said.

"Sir, there ought to be a nicer name for it. We're military, after all," the captain of *Blue Space* said.

"I don't think it'll work." Zhang Beihai shook his head decisively. "Staying alive is not enough to guarantee survival. Development is the best way to ensure survival. During our voyage, we'll have to develop our own science and technology to expand the size of our fleet. The historical facts of the Middle Ages and the Great Ravine prove that a totalitarian system is the greatest barrier to human progress. Starship Earth requires vibrant new ideas and innovation, and this can only be accomplished through the establishment of a society that fully respects freedom and individuality."

"Are you talking about establishing a society like the modern Earth International, sir? Starship Earth has certain intrinsic conditions," a low-ranking officer said.

"That's right." Dongfang Yanxu nodded at the speaker. "Starship Earth may have few people, but it possesses a highly refined information system through which any problem can easily be put to discussion and vote by all citizens. We can establish the first truly democratic society in human history."

"That won't work either." Zhang Beihai shook his head again. "Like those citizens said before, Starship Earth is traveling through the harsh environment of space, where catastrophes that threaten the entire world might occur at any time. Earth's history during the Trisolar Crisis has demonstrated that, in the face of such disasters, particularly when our world needs to make sacrifices in order to preserve the whole, the humanitarian society you have in mind is especially fragile."

All of those in attendance at the meeting glanced at each other, their eyes holding the same question: *So what should we do?*

Smiling, Zhang Beihai said, "I'm thinking too simply. There's never been an answer to this question throughout human history, so how can we solve it in one meeting? It will, I think, require a long process of practice and exploration before we can find the social model most suitable for Starship Earth. After the meeting, discussions should be opened up on the issue. . . . Please forgive me for disrupting the meeting's agenda. We should continue with the original topic."

Dongfang Yanxu had never seen Zhang Beihai smile like that. He rarely smiled, and when he occasionally did, it was confident and forgiving. But this smile had shown an apologetic shyness that she had never seen before. Even though interrupting the meeting wasn't a big deal, he was a man with an especially discreet mind, and this was the first time he had put forth an opinion only to retract it. She noticed his distraction. He hadn't taken notes during this meeting, unlike the careful recording he had done at the previous one. He was the only one on board who still used an ancient pen and paper, and it had become an emblem for him.

So what was occupying his thoughts now?

The meeting turned toward the matter of governing bodies. The citizens tended to feel that conditions were not yet right for holding elections, so the ships' present chains of command should not be changed. Captains would lead their respective ships, and a Starship Earth Authority Committee formed from the five of them would discuss and decide upon major affairs. Zhang Beihai was unanimously elected as chair of the committee, to serve as supreme commander of Starship Earth. The resolution was put to the entire assembly, and passed with 100 percent of the votes.

But he refused the appointment.

"Sir, it's your responsibility," the captain of *Deep Space* said.

"On Starship Earth, you're the only one with the prestige to command all the ships," Dongfang Yanxu said.

"I feel I've fulfilled my responsibility. I'm tired, and I've reached retirement age," Zhang Beihai said softly.

When the meeting adjourned, Zhang Beihai called for Dongfang Yanxu to stay behind. Once everyone had left, he said, "Dongfang, I want to recover my position as acting captain of *Natural Selection*."

"Acting captain?" She eyed him in surprise.

"Yes. Give me operational permissions over the ship again."

"Sir, I can hand over the captain's chair of *Natural Selection* to you. I mean it. And the Authority Committee and the body of citizens certainly won't oppose it."

He shook his head with a smile. "No, you'll still be the captain,

with a captain's full power to command. Please trust me. I won't interfere with your work at all."

"Then why do you want an acting captain's privileges? Is there a need for them in your present position?"

"I just like the ship. It's been a dream of ours for two centuries. Do you know what I've done for this ship to be here for us today?"

When he looked at her, the stony hardness that had been in his eyes was gone, revealing a tired emptiness and a deep sorrow that made him look like a different person. He was no longer the calm, grim survivor who thought deeply and acted decisively, but rather a man bent with the weight of time. Looking at him, she felt a concern and compassion she had never felt before.

"Sir, don't think about those things. Historians have a fair evaluation of your actions in the twenty-first century: Choosing research in radiation propulsion was a key step in the right direction for humanity's space technology. Perhaps at the time, it . . . it was the only choice, just like escape was the only choice for *Natural Selection*. Besides, according to modern law, the statute of limitations ran out long ago."

"But I can't get rid of the cross I bear. You can't understand. . . . I have feelings for this ship, more feelings than you. I feel like it's a part of me. I can't leave it. Also, I've got to have something to do in the future. Having things to do puts my mind more at ease."

Then he turned and left, a tired figure floating away, turning into a small black dot within the huge white spherical space. Dongfang Yanxu watched until he disappeared into the whiteness, and a loneliness she had never felt before surged in from all sides and overcame her.

In future Citizens' Assembly meetings, the people of Starship Earth immersed themselves in the passion of creating a new world. They held lively debates on the constitution and social structure of the world, drafted various laws, and planned the first election. . . . There was a thorough exchange of views between officers and soldiers of different ranks, and among the different ships. People acknowledged their prospects and looked forward to Starship

Earth forming a core that would snowball into a future civilization, continually increasing in size as the fleet reached star system after star system. An increasing number of people began calling Starship Earth a "second Eden," a second point of origin for human civilization.

But this state of wonder did not last very long, because Starship Earth truly was a Garden of Eden.

As *Natural Selection*'s chief psychologist, Lieutenant Colonel Lan Xi headed the Second Civilian Service Department, an agency of military officers trained in psychology that was responsible for psychological health on the ship during long space voyages and in battle. When Spaceship Earth began its journey of no return, Lan Xi and his subordinates went on alert, like warriors facing an attack from a powerful enemy. The plans they had rehearsed on many previous occasions had prepared them for a wide range of possible psychological crises.

They agreed that the biggest enemy was none other than "Problem N": nostalgia, or homesickness. This was, after all, the first time that humankind had embarked on an endless voyage, so Problem N had the potential to cause a mass psychological disaster. Lan Xi commanded CSD2 to take every necessary precaution, including establishing dedicated channels for communicating with Earth and the three fleets. This enabled everyone on board to maintain constant contact with their family and friends on Earth and in the fleet, and allowed them to watch most of the news and other programming from the two Internationals. Although Starship Earth was seventy AU away from the sun, meaning that signals were delayed nine hours, the quality of communication with Earth and the fleets was excellent.

In addition to conducting active psychological counseling and adjustments when signs of Problem N cropped up, CSD2 psychological officers also prepared an extreme means of responding to a large-scale mass psychological disaster: quarantining an out-of-control crowd in hibernation.

Subsequent events demonstrated that these concerns were

superfluous. While Problem N was widespread on Starship Earth, it was far from out of control, and did not even reach the level of previous, ordinary long-range voyages. Lan Xi was confused by this at first, but he soon found a reason: After the destruction of humanity's main fleet, Earth had lost all hope. Even though the ultimate doomsday was still two centuries away (using the most optimistic estimate), the news from Earth informed them that the world, plunged into chaos by the heavy blow of the great defeat, was full of the stench of death. For Starship Earth, there was nothing on the Earth or in the Solar System to provide them with sustenance. Nostalgia for a home like that was limited.

However, an enemy nevertheless appeared, one that was more ominous than Problem N. By the time that Lan Xi and CSD2 realized it, their position had already been overcome.

Lan Xi knew from his experience that on long space voyages Problem N tended to crop up in soldiers and low-ranking officers first, because their jobs and responsibilities commanded less of their attention compared to high-ranking officers, and their mental conditioning was comparatively poor. So CSD2 turned its attention to the lower levels from the start, but the shadow first fell upon the upper levels.

Around that time, Lan Xi noticed something peculiar. The first election for Starship Earth's governing bodies was about to take place, an election that would be open to the entire population, meaning that most of the senior commanders were facing a transition from being military officers to being government officials. Their positions would be reshuffled, and many of them would be replaced by lower-ranking competitors. Lan Xi was surprised to learn that no one in *Natural Selection*'s senior command was overly concerned about the election that would determine the rest of their lives. He saw no senior officers engaging in even the least bit of campaigning, and when he mentioned the election, none of them was at all interested. He couldn't help but recall Zhang Beihai's absentmindedness during the second Citizens' Assembly meeting.

Then he began to see symptoms of psychological imbalance

among officers above the rank of lieutenant colonel. Most of them started to become increasingly introverted, spending long periods alone with their thoughts and sharply reducing their social interactions. They spoke less and less at meetings, sometimes choosing to become completely silent. Lan Xi noticed that the light had disappeared from their eyes, and their expressions had turned gloomy. They couldn't look anyone in the eye for fear that others would notice the fog in theirs. When they occasionally met someone's gaze, they would break away immediately like they had been shocked. . . . The higher the rank, the more serious the symptoms. And there were signs that it was spreading through the lower ranks, too.

There was no way for psychological counseling to proceed. Everyone stubbornly refused to talk to the psychological officers, so CSD2 was compelled to exercise its special power to conduct mandatory counseling. Still, most of their subjects remained silent.

Lan Xi decided that he needed to talk to the supreme commander, so he went to Dongfang Yanxu. Although Zhang Beihai had once held supreme prestige and status on *Natural Selection* and the whole of Starship Earth, he had rejected it all, withdrawing from the race and insisting he was an ordinary person. The only duties he had retained were those of acting captain: transmitting the captain's orders to the ship's control system. The remainder of his time he spent wandering *Natural Selection,* learning about the specifics of the ship from officers and soldiers at all ranks and showing a constant affection for the space ark. Apart from this, he remained calm and indifferent, practically unaffected by the ship's mass psychological shadow. He was no doubt trying to remain aloof, but Lan Xi knew of another important reason for his immunity: The ancients were not as sensitive as moderns, and in the present circumstances, numbness served an excellent self-protective function.

"Captain, you ought to give us some indication of what's happening," he said.

"Lieutenant Colonel, you ought to be the one giving us an indication."

"Do you mean that you don't know anything about your present state?"

An infinite sadness welled up in her dull eyes. "I only know that we're the first humans who have gone into space."

"What do you mean?"

"This is the first time humanity has really gone to space."

"Oh. I see what you mean. Before, no matter how far humans traveled into space, they were still just a kite sent aloft by Earth. They were connected to Earth by a spiritual line. Now that line has been severed."

"That's right. The line is severed. The essential change is not that the line has been let go, but that the hand has disappeared. The Earth is heading toward doomsday. In fact, she's already dead in our minds. Our five spacecraft are not connected to any world. There is nothing around us apart from the abyss of space."

"Indeed. Humanity has never faced a psychological environment like this before."

"Yes. In this environment, the human spirit will be fundamentally changed. People will become—" She suddenly broke off, and the sadness in her eyes vanished, leaving only gloom, like a cloud-covered sky after the rain has stopped.

"You mean that in this environment, people will become new people?"

"New people? No, Lieutenant Colonel. People will become . . . non-people."

At that last word, Lan Xi shuddered. He looked up at Dongfang Yanxu, and she met his gaze. In the blankness of her eyes, all he saw were tightly closed windows to her soul.

"What I mean is that we won't be people in the old sense. . . . Lieutenant Colonel, that's all I can say. Just do your best. And . . ." The words that followed seemed like she was talking in her sleep. "It'll be your turn soon."

The situation continued to deteriorate. The day after Lan Xi's talk with Dongfang Yanxu, there was a vicious injury on *Natural Selection*. A lieutenant colonel with the ship's navigational system

fired upon another officer bunking with him. According to the victim's recollection, the officer had awakened suddenly in the middle of the night and, noticing that the victim was also awake, had accused him of eavesdropping on him talking in his sleep. In the struggle, his emotions had gotten away from him and he had fired the gun.

Lan Xi went at once to see the detained lieutenant colonel. "What were you afraid of him hearing you say in your sleep?" he asked.

"You mean he really heard it?" the attacker asked in terror.

Lan Xi shook his head. "He said that you didn't say anything."

"So what if I did say something? You can't take sleep talk for the truth! My mind doesn't really think that. Surely I'm not going to go to hell for something I said in my sleep!"

In the end, Lan Xi was unable to draw out what the attacker imagined he said in his sleep, so he asked whether he minded going under hypnotherapy. Unexpectedly, the attacker once again blew up at this suggestion, lunging at Lan Xi and strangling him until the military police finally came in and pried him off. Leaving the brig, one MP who had overheard the conversation said to Lan Xi, "Lieutenant Colonel, don't mention hypnotherapy again unless CSD2 wants to become the most hated place on the ship. You wouldn't last very long."

So Lan Xi had to contact Colonel Scott, a psychologist aboard *Enterprise*. Scott also served as the ship's chaplain, a position most ships in the Asian Fleet did not have. *Enterprise* and the other three ships in the pursuing force were still two hundred thousand kilometers away.

"Why is it so dark over there?" Lan Xi asked as he looked at the video sent over from *Enterprise*. The curved walls of the cabin Scott was in had been adjusted to glow a faint yellow, and they displayed an image of the stars outside, making it look as if he was inside a fogged-over cosmos. His face was shrouded in shadow, but even so, Lan Xi could still sense Scott's eyes slipping quickly away from his gaze.

"The Garden of Eden is growing dark. Blackness will swallow everything," Scott said in a weary voice.

Lan Xi had consulted him because, as chaplain of *Enterprise,* he would likely have had people confide the truth in him during confession, and he might be able to pass on some advice. But at these words, and noticing how the colonel's eyes loomed in the shadows, Lan Xi knew that he would come up with nothing. So he suppressed the question he was about to ask and turned to another, one that surprised even him:

"Will what happened in the first Garden of Eden be repeated in the second?"

"I don't know. At any rate, the vipers have come out. The snakes of the second Garden of Eden are even now climbing up people's souls."

"You mean, you've eaten the fruit of knowledge?"

Scott slowly nodded. Then he bowed his head, but did not raise it again, as if he was trying to hide the eyes that would betray him. "You could say that."

"Who will be expelled from the Garden of Eden?" Lan Xi's voice quavered, and a cold sweat was on his palms.

"Many people. But unlike the first time, this time some people might remain."

"Who? Who will remain?"

Scott gave a long sigh. "Lieutenant Colonel Lan, I've said enough. Why don't you seek the fruit of knowledge for yourself? Everyone's got to take that step, after all. Isn't that right?"

"Where should I seek it?"

"Set down your work, and think about it. Feel more, and you'll find it."

After speaking with Scott, Lan Xi halted his busy work amid chaotic feelings, and stopped to think, as the colonel had advised. Faster than he had imagined, Eden's cold, slippery vipers crawled into his consciousness. He found the fruit of knowledge and ate it, and the last rays of sunshine in his soul disappeared forever as everything plunged into darkness.

On Starship Earth, an invisible, taut string was being pulled close to snapping.

Two days later, the captain of *Ultimate Law* committed suicide. He had been standing on the aft platform at the time, a platform enclosed in a transparent dome that made it seem exposed to space. The stern of the ship faced the Solar System, where the sun was by now no more than a yellow star just a bit brighter than the rest. The peripheral spiral arm of the Milky Way lay in this direction, its stars sparse. The depth and expanse of deep space exhibited an arrogance that left no support for the mind or the eyes.

"Dark. It's so fucking dark," the captain murmured, and then shot himself.

When Dongfang Yanxu learned that the captain of *Ultimate Law* had committed suicide, she had the premonition that time was up, so she convened an emergency meeting with the two vice-captains in the large spherical fighter hangar.

In the corridor on the way to the hangar, she heard someone behind her call her name. It was Zhang Beihai. In her gloomy state of mind, she had practically forgotten about him for the past couple of days. He looked her up and down, his eyes full of a fatherly concern that gave her an undreamed-of sense of comfort, for it was hard to find a pair of eyes without a shadow on Starship Earth these days.

"Dongfang, I don't think you've been right lately. I don't know the reason, but you seem to be hiding something. What's going on?"

She didn't answer his question, but instead asked, "Sir, how have you been lately?"

"Well. Very well. I've been touring all over the place and studying. I'm familiarizing myself with *Natural Selection*'s weapons system. Of course, I'm only scratching the surface, but it's fascinating. Imagine how Columbus would feel visiting an aircraft carrier. I'm the same way."

Seeing how calm and relaxed he was now, Dongfang Yanxu felt a little jealous. Yes, he had completed his great endeavor and had the right to enjoy tranquility. The history-making great man had turned back into an ignorant hibernator. All he needed now was protection.

With that in mind, she said, "Sir, don't ask anyone else about the question you just asked. Don't ask about any of this."

"Why? Why shouldn't I ask?"

"It's dangerous to ask. Besides, you really don't need to know. Believe me."

He nodded. "Very well. I won't ask. Thank you for treating me like an ordinary person. That's all I've been hoping for."

She said a hurried good-bye, but as she went her own way, she heard the voice of the founder of Starship Earth behind her: "Dongfang, no matter what happens, let things go as they will. Everything will be okay."

She saw the two vice-captains in the center of the spherical hall. She had chosen to meet them here because the size of the hall made it feel like they were in the wilderness. The three of them floated at the center of a world of pure white, as if the whole universe was empty except for them. It lent a sense of security to their conversation.

Each of them looked in a different direction.

"We have to make things clear," she said.

"Yes. Every second we delay is dangerous," Vice-Captain Levine said. Then he and Akira Inoue turned around to face Dongfang Yanxu. His meaning was clear: *You are the captain, you speak first.*

But she didn't have the courage.

Whatever happened now, at the second dawn of human civilization, might be the foundation of a new Homeric epic or a Bible. Judas became who he was because he was the first to kiss Jesus, and that made him fundamentally different from the second one to kiss him. It was the same now. The first to speak would mark a milestone in the history of the second civilization. Perhaps he or she would become Judas, or perhaps Jesus, but whatever the possibility, Dongfang Yanxu did not have that courage.

But she had to undertake her own mission, so she made a smart choice. She did not avoid the gaze of her vice-captains. Language was not necessary now. All communication could be accomplished through the eyes. As they stared at each other, their interlocking

gazes were like information conduits linking their three souls together and communicating everything at high speed.

Fuel.

Fuel.

Fuel.

The route is still unclear, but at least two clouds of interstellar dust have been found.

Drag.

Of course. After passing through them, the spaceships will drop to 0.03 percent of the speed of light due to drag from the dust.

We're still more than ten light-years away from NH558J2. We'll need sixty thousand years to get there.

Then we'll never arrive.

The ships may arrive, but the life on board won't. Even hibernation can't be sustained for that long.

Unless . . .

Unless speed is maintained through the dust clouds, or we accelerate afterward.

Fuel is insufficient.

Fusion fuel is the only source of energy aboard ship, and it needs to be used in other areas: environmental systems, possible course corrections. . . .

And for deceleration once the target system is reached. NH558J2 is much smaller than the sun. We can't achieve orbit relying solely on gravity for deceleration. We'll have to expend large quantities of fuel, or else we'll fly by the target star system.

All of the fuel on Starship Earth is basically enough for two spacecraft.

But, if we're careful, it's enough for just one.

Fuel.

Fuel.

Fuel.

"And then there's the issue of parts," Dongfang Yanxu said.

Parts.

Parts.

Parts.

Particularly parts for critical systems: fusion engines, information and control systems, environmental systems.

It may not be as urgent as fuel, but it's the foundation of long-term survival. NH55J82 doesn't have a hospitable planet for settlement or establishment of industry, or even the necessary resources to do so. It's just a place to refuel before heading to the next system, where industry can be established to produce parts.

Natural Selection *has only two levels of redundancy for key parts.*

Too few.

Too few.

Apart from the fusion engines, most of the key parts on Starship Earth are interoperable.

Engine parts can be used after modification.

"Can all personnel be gathered onto one or two ships?" Dongfang Yanxu said aloud, but her voice was only meant to guide the direction of their eye communication.

Impossible.

Impossible.

Impossible. There are too many people. Environmental and hibernation systems can't accommodate them all. If present capacity is boosted even a little, it will be disastrous.

"So, is it clear now?" Dongfang Yanxu's voice resounded in the empty white space like the mutterings of someone deeply asleep.

Clear.

Clear.

Some people must die, or everyone will die.

Then their eyes went silent. The three of them felt an intense desire to turn away, as if shaken by thunder from the depths of the universe that made their souls quake in terror. Dongfang Yanxu was the first to stabilize her own gaze.

"Stop it," she said.

Stop it.

Don't give up.

Don't give up?

Don't give up! Because no one else has given up. If we give up, then we'll be expelled from the Garden of Eden.

Why us?

Of course, it shouldn't be them, either.

But someone has to be expelled. The Garden of Eden has a limited capacity.

We don't want to leave the garden.

So we can't give up!

Three pairs of eyes, so close to breaking apart, locked together again.

Infrasonic H-bomb.

Infrasonic H-bomb.

Infrasonic H-bomb.

Every ship is equipped with them.

It's hard to defend against a stealth launch.

Their gazes separated temporarily as their minds were pushed to the brink of collapse. They needed rest. When the three pairs of eyes met once again, they were uncertain and erratic, like candles flickering in the wind.

Evil!

Evil!

Evil!

We'll become devils!

We'll become devils!

We'll become devils!

"But . . . what are *they* thinking?" Dongfang Yanxu asked softly. To the two vice-captains, her voice, while soft, seemed to linger uninterrupted in the white space, like the buzz of a mosquito.

Yes. We don't want to become devils, but who knows what they're thinking.

Then we're already devils, or how else could we think of them as devils unprovoked?

Very well, then we won't think of them as devils.

"That won't solve the problem," Dongfang Yanxu said with a gentle shake of her head.

Yes. Even if they aren't devils, the problem remains.

Because they don't know what we're thinking.

Suppose they know that we're not devils?

The problem still exists.

They don't know what we're thinking about them.

They don't know what we're thinking about what they're thinking about us.

That carries on in an endless chain of suspicion: They don't know what we're thinking about what they're thinking about what we're thinking about what they're thinking about what we're . . .

How can this chain of suspicion be broken?

Communication?

On Earth, perhaps. But not in space. Some people must die, or everyone will die. This is the unwinnable dead hand that space has dealt for the survival of Starship Earth. An insurmountable wall. In the face of it, communication has no meaning.

Only one choice is left. The question is who makes that choice.

Dark. It's so fucking dark.

"We can't delay any longer," Dongfang Yanxu said decisively.

No more delays. In this dark region of space, the duelists are holding their breath. The string is about to snap.

Every second, the danger grows exponentially.

Since it's all the same no matter who pulls it, why not pull it ourselves?

Then Akira Inoue suddenly broke the silence: "There's another choice!"

We sacrifice ourselves.

Why?

Why us?

The three of us could, but do we have the authority to make this choice on behalf of the two thousand people on Natural Selection?

The three of them were standing on a knife blade. Though its cuts

were painful, a jump off either side would be into a bottomless abyss. These were the labor pains for the birth of the new space humans.

"How about this?" Levine said. "First lock in the targets, and then think it over some more."

Dongfang Yanxu nodded. Levine called up a control interface for the weapons system in the air and opened up the window for the infrasonic H-bombs and carrier missiles. On a spherical coordinate system with *Natural Selection* at the origin, *Blue Space*, *Enterprise*, *Deep Space*, and *Ultimate Law* were displayed as four points of light two hundred thousand kilometers away. The distance masked the structure of the targets, for at the scale of space, everything was just a point.

But the four points of light were ringed with four red halos, four deathly nooses indicating that the weapons system had already locked on the targets.

Stunned, the three of them looked at each other and shook their heads to say that it wasn't their doing.

Apart from them, privileges to place a target lock in the weapons system were also held by the arms control and target screening officers, but their lock placement had to be authorized by the captain or vice-captain. That left just one other person with direct privileges to lock a target and launch an attack.

We're idiots. He's only someone who's changed history twice! He realized all of this first!

Who knows when he realized it? Maybe when Starship Earth was founded, or even earlier, when he learned that the combined fleet had been destroyed. He is the last to show worry. Like the parents of his era, always keeping their children in mind.

Dongfang Yanxu flew across the spherical hall as fast as she could, followed closely by the two vice-captains. They went out the door and down that long corridor until they arrived at the door to Zhang Beihai's cabin. Suspended in front of him was an interface identical to the one they had just seen. They rushed forward, but the scene from *Natural Selection*'s escape replayed itself: They crashed into the bulkhead. There was no door, just an

oval-shaped area where the bulkhead was transparent.

"What are you doing?" Levine shouted.

"Children," Zhang Beihai said, the first time he had addressed them this way. Even though his back was turned, they could imagine that his eyes were as calm as water. "Let me do this."

"You mean, 'If I don't go to hell, who will?'[24] Is that it?" Dongfang Yanxu said in a loud voice.

"From the moment I became a soldier, I was prepared to go there if necessary," he said, continuing with the weapons' prelaunch operations. From outside, the three of them saw that while he wasn't skilled at these operations, every step he took was correct.

Tears welled up in Dongfang Yanxu's eyes, and she cried, "Let's go together. Let me in. I'll go to hell with you!"

He made no answer, but continued his manipulations. He set the guided missiles for manual self-destruct so that they could be detonated by the mother ship while in flight. Only after finishing the last step did he say, "Dongfang, think. Could we have made this choice before? Absolutely not. But now we can make it, because space has turned us into new humans." He set the missiles' warheads to explode at a distance of fifty kilometers from each target. This would avoid causing the targets any internal damage, but an even greater distance would still be within the fatal range for any life aboard the targets. "The birth of a new civilization is the formation of a new morality." He removed the first safety lock on the H-bomb warheads. "When they look back in the future on everything we've done, it may seem entirely normal. So, we won't go to hell, children." The second safety lock was removed.

Suddenly, the alert sounded throughout the ship like the crying of ten thousand ghosts in the darkness of space. Display interfaces popped up in midair like snowflakes, showing a huge quantity of information that *Natural Selection*'s defense systems had received about the incoming missiles, but no one had time to read it.

24 *Translator's Note:* This popular quotation sums up the great vow of the bodhisattva Ksitigarbha (Dìzàng Púsà) not to achieve Buddhahood until all living beings are saved.

There was a space of just four seconds from the sounding of the alert to the detonation of the infrasonic H-bombs.

Images transmitted back to Earth from *Natural Selection* showed that Zhang Beihai may have understood all of this in just one second. He had imagined that his heart had grown as hard as iron through the arduous procession of more than two centuries, but he had overlooked something hidden in the deepest part of his soul, and had hesitated before making the final decision. He tried to restrain the trembling of his heart, and it was that last moment's softness that killed him and everyone on board *Natural Selection*. After the month-long face-off in the darkness, he was just a few seconds slower than the other ship was.

Three small suns lit up the blackness of space, forming an equilateral triangle with *Natural Selection* at the center, at an average distance of forty kilometers. The fusion fireball lasted for twenty seconds and sparkled with infrasonic frequencies that were invisible to the naked eye.

The returned images showed that in the three seconds that remained, Zhang Beihai turned to Dongfang Yanxu, flashed her a smile, and spoke: "It doesn't matter. It's all the same."

The exact words were only a guess, because he didn't have time to finish before a powerful electromagnetic pulse arrived from three directions, vibrating *Natural Selection*'s enormous hull like a cicada's wings. The energy in these vibrations was converted to infrasonic waves, which, in the image, looked like a fog of blood that enveloped everything.

The attack had come from *Ultimate Law,* which had fired twelve cloaked missiles armed with infrasonic H-bombs at the four other ships. The three missiles fired at *Natural Selection,* which was two hundred thousand kilometers away, had been launched before the others so that the ones fired at its three neighboring ships would reach their detonation points at the same time. A vice-captain had taken over after the suicide of *Ultimate Law*'s captain, but it was unknown who ultimately made the decision to launch the attack. And it would never be known.

Ultimate Law was not one of the lucky ones remaining in the Garden of Eden at the end.

Of the three other pursuing ships, *Blue Space* had been the best prepared against unexpected incidents. Before it was attacked, it had turned its interior into a vacuum and put all personnel in space suits. Because infrasonic waves were impossible in a vacuum, no personnel were injured, and the body of the ship suffered only minimal damage from the electromagnetic pulse.

Right after the nuclear fireballs exploded, *Blue Space* began its counterattack with lasers, the fastest response possible. It lit up *Ultimate Law* with five gamma-ray laser beams and burned five huge holes in its hull. Its insides quickly caught fire and there were minor explosions, causing the ship to lose all combat capability. Harsher attacks from *Blue Space* followed, and under continuous attack by nuclear missiles and a rain of railgun fire, *Ultimate Law* exploded violently, leaving no survivors.

At almost the same time as Starship Earth's Battle of Darkness was going on, a similar tragedy was taking place far on the other side of the Solar System. *Bronze Age* launched a sudden strike on *Quantum,* using the same infrasonic H-bombs to kill off all life inside its target, but preserving the target ship whole. Because the two ships had sent only minimal information back to Earth, no one knew exactly what had taken place between them. They had both gone into intense acceleration to escape from the probe attack, but they had not decelerated like *Natural Selection*'s pursuers had, so their remaining fuel ought to have been more than enough to return to Earth.

The boundlessness of space nurtured a dark new humanity in its dark embrace.

In the expanding metal cloud formed from the explosion of *Ultimate Law, Blue Space* rendezvoused with *Enterprise* and *Deep Space,* neither of which showed signs of life, and collected all of their fusion fuel. After stripping them of their hardware, *Blue Space* flew the two hundred thousand kilometers to *Natural Selection* and did the same to that ship. Starship Earth was like a

construction site in space now, the massive hulls of the three dead ships dotted with the sparks of laser welding. If Zhang Beihai had still been alive, the scene would certainly have reminded him of the aircraft carrier *Tang* two centuries before.

Blue Space took pieces of the three derelict warships and set them up in a Stonehenge formation, forming a tomb in outer space. There, they held a funeral for all the victims of the Battle of Darkness.

Wearing space suits, the 1,273 crew members of *Blue Space* assembled in a floating formation at the center of the tomb. These were the remaining citizens of Starship Earth. Around them, huge pieces of spaceships towered like a ring of mountains, the gashes cut into the wreckage like enormous mountain caves. The bodies of 4,247 victims remained within this debris, which cast its shadows over all of the living as if they were a mountain valley at midnight. The only light was the iciness of the Milky Way where it shone through the gaps between the wreckage.

Moods remained calm during the funeral. The new space humans had passed through their infancy.

A small votive lamp was lit. It was a fifty-watt bulb with a hundred spare bulbs next to it that would be automatically substituted in the lamp. Powered by a small nuclear battery, the votary lamp could remain continuously lit for tens of thousands of years. Its dim light was like a candle in the mountain valley, casting a small halo onto a high cliff of the wreckage and shining on a piece of titanium bulkhead engraved with the names of the victims. There was no epitaph.

One hour later, the space tomb was illuminated one final time by the light of *Blue Space*'s acceleration. The tomb was traveling at 1 percent of the speed of light. In several hundred years it would decelerate to 0.03 percent of light speed due to the drag from interstellar dust clouds. It would still reach NH558J2 in sixty thousand years, but *Blue Space* would already have headed off toward its next star system more than fifty thousand years before that.

Blue Space traveled deep into space carrying plenty of fusion fuel and an eight-fold redundant supply of critical parts. There was

so much material it was impossible to fit it all inside the craft, so several external storage compartments were attached to the hull, completely altering the ship's appearance and turning it into an enormous, ugly, irregular body. Indeed, it looked like a traveler on a long journey.

The previous year, on the opposite side of the Solar System, *Bronze Age* had accelerated away from the ruins of *Quantum* in the direction of Taurus.

Blue Space and *Quantum* had come from a world of light, but they had become two ships of darkness.

The universe had once been bright, too. For a short time after the big bang, all matter existed in the form of light, and only after the universe turned to burnt ash did heavier elements precipitate out of the darkness and form planets and life. Darkness was the mother of life and of civilization.

On Earth, an avalanche of curses and abuse rolled out into space toward *Blue Space* and *Bronze Age,* but the two ships made no reply. They cut off all contact with the Solar System, for to those two worlds, the Earth was already dead.

The two dark ships became one with the darkness, separated by the Solar System and drifting further apart. Carrying with them the entirety of human thoughts and memories, and embracing all of the Earth's glory and dreams, they quietly disappeared into the eternal night.

"I knew it!"

That was the first thing Luo Ji said upon learning about the Battle of Darkness that had taken place at the edges of the Solar System. Leaving behind a baffled Shi Qiang, he ran out of the room and raced through the neighborhood until he stood facing the northern China desert.

"I was right! I was right!" he shouted at the sky.

It was late at night, and, perhaps because of the rain that had just fallen, atmospheric visibility was excellent. The stars were visible,

although they weren't nearly as clear as in the twenty-first century, and they were far sparser than before, since only the brightest could be seen. Yet he still swelled with that feeling he had on that cold night on the frozen lake two centuries ago: Luo Ji the ordinary person had disappeared, and he became a Wallfacer once again.

"Da Shi, I have in my hands the key to human victory!" he said to Shi Qiang, who had followed after him.

Shi Qiang laughed. "Oh?"

Shi Qiang's slightly mocking laughter dashed Luo Ji's excitement. "I knew you wouldn't believe me."

"So what will you do now?" Shi Qiang asked.

Luo Ji sat down on the sand, and his mood crashed rapidly. "What should I do? It looks like there's nothing I *can* do."

"You could at least find a way to report it upstairs."

"I don't know if that would work, but I'll give it a try. Even if it's just to fulfill my responsibility."

"How high up will you go?"

"The highest. The UN secretary general. Or the chair of the SFJC."

"That won't be easy, I'm afraid. We're just ordinary people now. . . . Still, you've got to try. You can, uh, go to the city government first. Find the mayor."

"Very well. I'll go to the city, then." He stood up.

"I'll go with you."

"No, I'll go alone."

"Even at this rank, I'm still an official. I'll have an easier time meeting the mayor."

Luo Ji looked up at the sky and asked, "When does the droplet reach Earth?"

"The news said it'll arrive in ten or twenty hours."

"Do you know what it's coming to do? Its mission wasn't to destroy the combined fleet. Nor was it to attack the Earth. It's here to kill me. I don't want you to be with me when it does."

Shi Qiang laughed the same mocking laugh again. "There's still ten hours, right? By that time, I'll just stay farther away from you."

495

Luo Ji shook his head with a wry smile. "You're not taking me seriously at all. So why do you want to help me?"

"My boy, it's up to the top whether they believe you or not. I always play things safe. If you were selected from out of billions of people two centuries ago, there's got to be a reason, right? If I delay you here, then won't I be condemned by the ages? If the higher-ups don't take you seriously, I won't have lost anything. It's just a trip into the city. But there's one thing: You say that the thing that's flying toward Earth is coming to kill you. I don't believe that at all. I'm well acquainted with killing, and that's excessive, even for Trisolarans."

They reached the passage from the old city to the underground city in the early hours of morning and saw that the elevators going down were still functioning normally. Lots of people were coming out carrying large quantities of luggage. Few were going down, however, and on their elevator there were only two other people.

"Are you hibernators? They're all going up top. Why are you going down?"

"The city's in chaos," one of them, a young man, said. On his clothes, fireballs shone continually against a black background. A closer look revealed that it was an image of the destruction of the combined fleet.

"Then what are you going down for?" Shi Qiang asked.

"I've found a place to live on the surface, so I'm going down to get a few things," he said. Then he nodded at them. "You on the surface are going to get rich. We don't have any houses there, and the property rights to the surface houses are mostly in your hands. We'll have to buy them off you."

"If the underground city collapses and all those people rush to the surface, there's probably not going to be any actual buying or selling," Shi Qiang said.

A middle-aged man huddling in a corner of the elevator was listening to them, and he suddenly covered his face with his hands and let out a whine. "No. Oh . . ." Then he squatted down and started crying. His clothing showed a classical biblical scene: a naked Adam and Eve standing beneath a tree in the Garden of

Eden as a bewitching snake crawled between them. It may have been a symbol for the recent Battle of Darkness.

"There are lots of people like him," the young man said, pointing disdainfully at the weeping man. "Unsound of mind." His eyes lit up. "Actually, doomsday is a wonderful time. The most wonderful time, even. This is the only time in history where there's a chance for people to abandon all of their cares and burdens and belong entirely to themselves. It's stupid to be like him. The most responsible way of life right now is to enjoy ourselves while we can."

When the elevator reached the bottom, Luo Ji and Shi Qiang exited the hall and immediately smelled the strong, strange odor of something burning. The underground city was brighter than before, but it was an irritating white light. Looking around, what Luo Ji saw through the gaps in the huge trees wasn't the blue sky, but a total blank. The projection of the sky on the vault of the underground city had vanished. The blankness reminded him of spherical spaceship cabins he had seen on the news. The lawns were littered with a mess of debris that had fallen from the huge trees. Not far off was the wreckage of several crashed flying cars, one of which was in flames and surrounded by a crowd of people who were picking up other combustibles from the lawn and throwing them into the flames. Someone even threw in his own clothing while it was still flashing images. A ruptured underground pipe sprayed a high column of water, drenching a group of people who played around in it like children. From time to time they would scream excitedly in unison and scatter to avoid debris falling from the trees, then they would regroup and continue their revels. Luo Ji looked up again and saw fires in several places on the trees. The sirens of flying firefighting vehicles screamed as they flew through the air, dangling plucked tree leaves that had caught fire. . . .

He noticed that the people they met on the streets fell into two types, much like the two people they had encountered in the elevator. One type was depressed, walking with dull eyes or simply sitting on the lawns enduring the torment of despair, a despair whose cause had now shifted from humanity's defeat to the present

difficult living conditions. The other type was in a state of crazed excitement and grew intoxicated from indulgence.

Traffic in the city was in chaos. It took Luo Ji and Shi Qiang half an hour to hail a taxi, and when the driverless flying car that carried them passed through the huge trees, Luo Ji was reminded of his first horrific day in the city and felt the tension of riding a roller coaster. Fortunately, the car soon arrived at City Hall.

Shi Qiang had been here several times because of work, and was fairly familiar with the place. After a considerable number of steps, they finally received permission to meet the mayor, but they had to wait until the afternoon. Luo Ji had expected complications, so the mayor's acceptance of the meeting caught him by surprise, since this was an extraordinary time, and they were little people. At lunch, Shi Qiang told Luo Ji that the mayor had taken office the day before. He used to be the official in charge of hibernator affairs in the city government and was, in a way, Shi Qiang's superior, so he knew him fairly well.

"He's one of our countrymen," Shi Qiang said.

In this age, the meaning of the term "countryman" had shifted from geography to temporality. But it wasn't used between all hibernators. Only those who had entered hibernation at roughly the same time counted as countrymen. When they got together across the long years, temporally based countrymen shared an even closer affinity than geographically based countrymen used to.

They waited until half past four to see the mayor. High-ranking officials in this age typically possessed a star quality, with only the most attractive getting elected, but the current mayor was plain. He was about Shi Qiang's age, but far thinner, and he had one trait that made him identifiable as a hibernator at a glance: He wore glasses. They were definitely antiques from two centuries ago, because even contact lenses had long since disappeared. But people who used to wear glasses tended to feel that something was wrong with their appearance when they didn't wear them, so lots of hibernators wore them even after their vision was repaired.

The mayor looked utterly exhausted and seemed to have

difficulty rising from his chair. When Shi Qiang apologized for the interruption, and congratulated him on his promotion, he shook his head. "These are vulnerable times. Us rugged savages come in handy again."

"You're the highest-ranking hibernator on Earth, right?"

"Who knows? As the situation develops, we might have countrymen promoted to even higher positions."

"And the former mayor? Mental breakdown?"

"No, no. There are strong people in this age, too. He was very competent, but he was killed in a car crash in a riot area two days ago."

The mayor noticed Luo Ji behind Shi Qiang and immediately extended a hand. "Oh, Dr. Luo, hello. Of course I recognize you. I worshiped you two centuries ago, because out of those four people, you seemed most like a Wallfacer. I really couldn't figure out what you wanted to do." But their hearts sank at the next thing he said. "You're the fourth messiah I've received in the past two days. And there are dozens more waiting outside who I don't have the energy to see."

"Mayor, he's not like them. Two centuries ago—"

"Of course. Two centuries ago, he was selected from billions of people, and it's for that reason that I decided to see you." The mayor pointed at Shi Qiang. "There's something else I need you for, but we'll talk about that afterward. First, let's talk about what you've got. But I have a small request: Can you not talk about your plan to save the world? They're always so long. First just tell me what you need me to do."

After Luo Ji and Shi Qiang explained what they wanted, the mayor immediately shook his head. "Even if I wanted to help, I couldn't. I've got piles of stuff of my own I need to report to the senior leadership. But that level's lower than you imagine. It's just provincial and national leaders. It's hard for everyone. You ought to know that the senior leadership is handling even bigger problems right now."

Luo Ji and Shi Qiang had been paying attention to the news,

so naturally they knew about the bigger problems that the mayor referred to.

The annihilation of the combined fleet saw the swift resurrection of Escapism after two centuries of silence. The European Commonwealth had even drafted a plan to select one hundred thousand candidates for departure through a nationwide drawing, and the plan had been passed by a popular vote. But after the results of the drawing, the majority of those who had not been picked were furious, leading to widespread rioting. The public turned unanimously to Escapism as crime against humanity.

After the Battle of Darkness erupted between the surviving warships in outer space, accusations of Escapism gained new meaning: Recent events had proved that when the spiritual bonds with Earth were snapped, people in space suffered total spiritual alienation. So even if escape were successful, what survived would no longer be human civilization, but some other dark and evil thing. And like Trisolaris, that thing would be the antithesis of human civilization and an enemy of it. It had even been given a name: Negacivilization.

As the droplet came closer to Earth, the public's sensitivity to Escapism reached a peak. The media warned it was highly likely that someone would attempt to escape before the droplet's attack. Crowds flocked to the vicinity of the space ports and the base points of the space elevators with the intent of cutting off all channels into space. They did indeed possess that ability. In this age, the citizens of the world all had the freedom to own weapons, and most of them had small laser guns. Of course, a laser pistol posed no threat to the cabin of the space elevator or the launching spacecraft, but unlike a traditional gun, a large number of lasers could focus their light on a single point. If ten thousand laser pistols fired at one point at the same time, they were unstoppable. Crowds numbering in at least the tens of thousands, with up to a million people in places, gathered around the base points and launching sites, and at least a third were carrying weapons. When they saw a cabin ascend or a spacecraft launch, they would fire their weapons

simultaneously. The straight path of the laser beam made aiming incredibly precise, so most of the beams would focus on the target and destroy it. In this way, Earth's transport links with space were almost entirely severed.

The chaos grew worse. Over the past couple of days, the target of the attacks had shifted to space cities in synchronous orbit. Rumors flew thick online that certain cities had been converted into escape ships, so they too became subject to attack by the people of Earth. Owing to the vast distance, laser beams dissipated and were weakened by the time they reached targets in space, and given the additional factor of the space cities' rotation, no material injury was caused. But the activity became a kind of collective entertainment for humanity in those last days. That afternoon, the European Commonwealth's third space city, New Paris, had been subject to simultaneous irradiation by ten million laser beams from the northern hemisphere, causing the temperature in the city to rise sharply and prompting the evacuation of its residents. From the space city, the Earth had been brighter than the sun.

There was nothing more for Luo Ji and Shi Qiang to say.

"I was really impressed with your work at the Hibernation Immigration Bureau," the mayor said to Shi Qiang. "And Guo Zhengming. You know him, right? He was just promoted to director of the Public Security Bureau, and he recommended you to me. I hope you'll come work at the city government. We need people like you right now."

Shi Qiang thought for a moment, and then nodded. "Once I've settled things in my neighborhood. How's the situation in the city right now?"

"The situation is deteriorating, but it's still under control. Right now the focus is on maintaining the operation of the induction field power supply. Once that goes, the city will collapse completely."

"These riots are different from those in our day."

"Yeah, they are. First, their source is different. They're sparked by total despair for the future and are incredibly hard to handle. At the same time, we have fewer means at our disposal than in those

501

days." As the mayor was speaking, he pulled up an image on the wall. "This is the central plaza from a height of a hundred meters."

The central plaza was where Luo Ji and Shi Qiang had taken refuge from the flying car. From this vantage point, the Great Ravine Memorial and its surrounding patch of desert couldn't be seen. The entire plaza was white, with white dots crawling around like rice in a pot of porridge.

"Are those people?" Luo Ji asked in wonder.

"Naked people. It's a tremendous sex party, with more than a hundred thousand people, and it's still growing."

Acceptance of heterosexual and homosexual relations in this era was far beyond anything Luo Ji had imagined, and some things were no longer considered remarkable. Still, the sight before them came as a shock to both of them. Luo Ji was reminded of the dissolute scene in the Bible before humanity received the Ten Commandments. A classic doomsday scenario.

"Why doesn't the government put a stop to it?" Shi Qiang asked sharply.

"How would we stop it? They're completely within the law. If we take action, the government would be the one committing a crime."

Shi Qiang let out a long sigh. "Yes, I know. In this age, police and the military can't do much."

The mayor said, "We've been through the law, and we haven't found any provisions for coping with the present situation."

"With the city like this, it would be better if the droplet smashed it apart."

Shi Qiang's words jerked Luo Ji awake. He asked hurriedly, "How long until the droplet gets to Earth?"

The mayor replaced the image of spectacular promiscuity with a breaking news channel showing a simulation of the Solar System. The eye-catching red line that marked the path of the droplet looked like the orbit of a comet, except that it terminated close to the Earth. In the lower right was a countdown clock indicating that if the droplet didn't reduce speed, it would reach Earth in four

hours and fifty-four minutes. The news crawl was now displaying an expert analysis of the droplet. Despite the terror gripping the world, the scientific community had recovered its senses after the initial shock of defeat, so the analysis was calm and sober. Though humanity knew absolutely nothing about the droplet's energy source and drive mechanism, the analyst felt that it had run into a power consumption problem, because its acceleration toward the sun after destroying the combined fleet had been particularly sluggish. It had passed close by Jupiter but, ignoring the three warships at the base, used the planet's gravity to accelerate, a move that further demonstrated that the droplet's energy was limited to the point of exhaustion. Scientists believed that the notion that the droplet would crash into Earth was utter nonsense, but they had no idea what it had actually come to do.

Luo Ji said, "I have to leave, or else the city will really be destroyed."

"Why?" the mayor asked.

"Because he thinks the droplet wants to kill him," Shi Qiang said.

The mayor laughed, but his smile was stiff. Apparently he hadn't laughed in a long time. "Dr. Luo, you're the most self-absorbed person I've ever met."

Luo Ji and Shi Qiang drove off immediately after traveling back to the surface from the underground city. The city's inhabitants were pouring out in large numbers, which meant that ground traffic was so heavy that it took them half an hour to leave the old city and reach full speed on the highway to the west.

On the car's television, they saw that the droplet was approaching Earth at a speed of seventy-five kilometers per second and showed no sign of slowing. At that rate, it would arrive in three hours.

The weakening of the induction field power supply slowed the car, and Shi Qiang had to tap a storage battery to maintain speed. They reached the large hibernator residential area, but drove past New Life Village #5 and continued westward. They stayed silent along the way, speaking little and focusing their attention on the breaking news on the television.

The droplet passed lunar orbit without slowing. At this rate it

would reach Earth in just half an hour. No one knew how it would behave, so to avoid a panic, the news didn't predict a point of impact.

Luo Ji made a determined effort to welcome the moment he had long wanted to postpone, and said, "Da Shi, stop here."

Shi Qiang stopped the car and they got out. The sun, now nearing the horizon, cast long shadows of the two men on the desert. Luo Ji felt the earth beneath his feet turn as soft as his heart. He almost lacked the strength to stand.

He said, "I'll try my best to reach a sparsely populated area. There's a city ahead of us, so I'm going to turn this way. You find your own way back, and get as far as possible from the direction I'm going."

"My boy, I'll wait for you here. When it's over, we'll go back together." Shi Qiang took out a cigarette from his pocket and looked around for a lighter before remembering that the cigarette didn't need to be lit. Like the other things he had brought from that distant past, his personal habits had not changed at all.

Luo Ji smiled a little sadly. He hoped Shi Qiang actually believed that, because at least that would make their parting a little easier to take. "Wait if you'd like. When the time comes, you had better move to the other side of the embankment. I don't know how powerful the strike will be."

Shi Qiang smiled and shook his head. "You remind me of an intellectual I met two hundred years ago. He had the same hangdog look you've got. I remember him sitting out early in the morning in front of the Wangfujing church, crying. . . . But he got out okay. I checked after I woke up: He lived to be nearly a hundred."

"What about the first guy to touch the droplet, Ding Yi? I believe you knew each other, too."

"He had a death wish. Nothing you could do about that." Shi Qiang looked up at the sky clothed in sunset, as if reminding himself what the physicist looked like. "Still, he was a truly broad-minded man, the kind that could accept any situation. I never met anyone like him in my whole life. Seriously, a great mind. My boy, you ought to learn from him."

504

"And again I say to you: We're just ordinary people, you and I." He looked at his watch, knowing that there was no more time for delay. He extended a firm hand to Shi Qiang. "Da Shi, thank you for everything you've done for me the past two centuries. Good-bye. Maybe we'll meet again in some other place."

Shi Qiang did not take his hand, but gave him a wave. "Cut the crap! Believe me, my boy. Nothing's going to happen. Go, and when it's over, hurry back and get me. And don't blame me if I make fun of you tonight over drinks."

Luo Ji got into the car quickly, not wanting Shi Qiang to see the tears in his eyes. Sitting there, he strove to etch the rearview-mirror image of Shi Qiang onto his mind, then set off on his final journey.

Maybe they would meet again someplace. The last time it had taken two centuries, so what would the separation be this time? Like Zhang Beihai two centuries before, Luo Ji suddenly found himself hating that he was an atheist.

The sun had now entirely set, and the desert on either side of the road shone white in the twilight, like snow. It suddenly occurred to him that it was along this very stretch of road two centuries ago that he had driven in the Accord with his imaginary lover, when the northern China plain was covered with real snow. He felt her hair blowing in the wind, its strands teasing him with their strange tickles on his right cheek.

No, no. Don't say where we are! Once we know where we are, then the world becomes as narrow as a map. When we don't know, the world feels unlimited.

Okay. Then let's do our best to get lost.

Luo Ji had always had the feeling that Zhuang Yan and Xia Xia had been brought into the world by his imagination. He felt a stab in his heart when the thought entered his mind, because, at this moment, love and longing were the most excruciating things in the world. Tears blurred his vision as he strove to keep his mind blank. But Yan Yan's lovely eyes stubbornly surfaced through the blankness, accompanied by Xia Xia's intoxicating laughter. It was all he could do to focus his attention on the television news.

The droplet had passed the Lagrange point,[25] but it still sped toward Earth at constant speed.

Luo Ji parked the car at what he thought was the most fitting spot, the border between the plain and the mountains, where there were no people or buildings as far as he could see. The car stood in a valley surrounded by a U-shaped ring of mountains, which would dissipate some of the shock waves from the impact. He took the television from the car and carried it onto the open sand, where he sat down.

The droplet crossed the 34,000-kilometer geosynchronous orbit altitude and passed close by the space city New Shanghai, whose inhabitants all clearly saw the bright point of light pass rapidly across their sky. The news declared that the impact would occur in eight minutes.

The news finally predicted the latitude and longitude of impact: to the northwest of China's capital.

Luo Ji knew that already.

Twilight had fallen heavily now, and the colors of the sky had shrunk to a small space in the west, like a pupilless eyeball watching the world indifferently.

Perhaps as a way to pass the remaining time, Luo Ji began to look back on his life.

It had been divided into two entirely distinct parts. The part after he became a Wallfacer spanned two centuries, but it felt densely compacted. He passed quickly back through it as if it had been just yesterday. That part of his life didn't seem like his own, including the love that was engraved onto his bones. It all felt like a fleeting dream. He didn't dare think about his wife and child.

Contrary to his expectations, his memories of life before becoming a Wallfacer were a blank. All that he could fish out from the sea of memory were a few fragments, and the farther back he went, the fewer there were. Had he really been to high school? Had he really attended primary school? Had he really had a first love? Some of the fragments bore clear scratches, reminding him that those things had indeed

25 *Translator's Note:* Lagrange points are the five positions where a small object affected only by gravity can remain in equilibrium in relation to two larger bodies.

taken place. The details were vivid, but the feelings had vanished without a trace. The past was like a handful of sand you thought you were squeezing tightly, but which had already run out through the cracks between your fingers. Memory was a river that had run dry long ago, leaving only scattered gravel in a lifeless riverbed. He had lived life always looking out for the next thing, and whenever he had gained, he had also lost, leaving him with little in the end.

He looked around at the twilight mountains, recalling that one winter's night he spent here more than two hundred years ago, in the mountains that had grown tired of standing for hundreds of millions of years, and had lain down "like old villagers basking in the sun," as his imaginary lover had once said. The fields and cities of the northern China plain had long since turned to desert, but the mountains didn't seem to have changed. They were still plain and ordinary in shape, and withered grasses and vitex vines still grew stubbornly from the crevices in the gray rocks, no lusher and no sparser than two centuries ago. Two centuries was far too short for any visible change to come to these rocky mountains.

What was the human world like in the eyes of the mountains? Perhaps just something they saw on a leisurely afternoon. First, a few small living beings appeared on the plain. After a while, they multiplied, and after another while they erected structures like anthills that quickly filled the region. The structures shone from the inside, and some of them let off smoke. After another while, the lights and smoke disappeared, and the small things vanished as well, and then their structures toppled and were buried in the sand. That was all. Among the countless things the mountains had witnessed, these fleeting events were not necessarily the most interesting.

Finally, Luo Ji located his earliest memory. He was surprised to discover that the life he could remember also began on the sand. It was in his own prehistoric age, in a place he couldn't remember, and with people he couldn't recall, but he clearly remembered the sandy shore of a river. There was a round moon in the sky, and the river rippled under the moonlight. He was digging in the sand. When he had dug out a pit, water seeped through the bottom, and

in the water there was a small moon. He kept digging like that, digging lots of pits and bringing forth lots of small moons.

That was his earliest memory. Before that, everything was blank.

In the dark of night, only the light of the television illuminated the small patch of sand surrounding him.

As Luo Ji worked to maintain a blank state in his mind, his scalp tightened, and he felt like an enormous hand had covered the entire sky overhead and was pressing down on him.

But then the giant hand slowly withdrew.

At a distance of twenty thousand kilometers from the surface, the droplet changed direction and headed directly toward the sun.

The TV reporter shouted, "Attention northern hemisphere! Attention northern hemisphere! The droplet has grown brighter, and you can see it with the naked eye!"

Luo Ji looked up. He could actually see it: It wasn't too bright, but its high speed made it easily distinguishable as it crossed the sky like a meteor and vanished in the west.

At last the droplet reduced its velocity relative to the Earth to zero and rested at a point 1.5 million kilometers away. A Lagrange point. That meant that, in the days to come, it would remain motionless relative to both Earth and sun, squarely between the two.

Luo Ji had a hunch that something else might happen, so he sat on the sand and waited. The mountains, like old men beside and in back of him, waited quietly with him and gave him a sense of security. For the time being, there was no more important information in the news. A world uncertain whether or not it had escaped catastrophe waited nervously.

Ten minutes passed, but nothing happened. The monitoring system showed the droplet suspended motionless, the propulsion halo gone from its tail and its round head facing the sun. It reflected the bright sunlight, so that its front third appeared to be on fire. To Luo Ji, some sort of mysterious induction seemed to be taking place between the droplet and the sun.

The image on the television suddenly blurred, and the sound turned scratchy. Luo Ji sensed commotion in the surrounding

environment: A startled flock of birds took flight in the mountains, and a dog barked in the distance. It might have been a false impression, but he felt his skin begin to itch. The television's sound and picture jittered for a moment and then cleared up. Later it was learned that the interference was still present, but global telecommunications systems had quickly filtered out the sudden noise with their anti-interference capabilities. However, the news reacted slowly to this development because of the vast amounts of monitoring data that needed to be pooled and analyzed. It was another ten minutes or more before precise information became available.

The droplet was sending a continuous, powerful electromagnetic wave directly at the sun with an intensity far exceeding the sun's amplification threshold and a frequency that covered all the bands that the sun could amplify.

Luo Ji began to giggle, and then laughed until he choked. Yes, he really was self-absorbed. He should have thought of all of this long ago. Luo Ji wasn't important. The sun was important. From now on, humanity could no longer use the sun as a powerful antenna to transmit messages to the universe.

The droplet had sealed it off.

"Hah! My boy, nothing's happened! We really should have wagered on it." At some point, Shi Qiang had made his way over to Luo Ji. He had flagged down a car to get here.

Luo Ji felt like something had been drained out of him. He lay limply down on the sand, which was still warm from the sun. It was comfortable beneath him.

"Yes, Da Shi. We can go and live our lives now. Everything's finished."

"My boy, this is the last time I help you do Wallfacer stuff," Shi Qiang said on the road back. "That occupation must cause mental problems, and you've just had another episode."

"I hope that's the case," Luo Ji said. Outside, the stars that were visible yesterday had vanished, and the black desert and night

sky joined into one at the horizon. A section of road illuminated by the headlights stretched out ahead of them. The world was like the state of Luo Ji's mind: darkness everywhere, with one spot incredibly clear.

"You know, it'll be easy for you to get back to normal. It's time for Zhuang Yan and Xia Xia to reawaken. Although, with the recent chaos, I don't know if they've suspended reawakening. But even if they have, it won't be for very long. The situation will quickly stabilize, I think. After all, there's still time left for several generations. Didn't you say you can go and live your life?"

"I'll go inquire at the Hibernation Immigration Bureau tomorrow." Shi Qiang's words reminded Luo Ji of the bit of color that existed in his dull mind. Maybe a reunion with his wife and child was his only chance for redemption.

But humanity was beyond hope.

As they neared New Life Village #5, Shi Qiang suddenly slowed the car. "Something's not right," he said, looking ahead. Following his gaze, Luo Ji saw a glow in the sky cast by a light on the ground, but the high embankments on the roadway meant they couldn't see its source. The glow was in motion. It didn't seem like the lights of a residential area.

When the car turned off the highway, a strange and spectacular sight met them: The desert between New Life Village #2 and the highway had been turned into a shining blanket dense with lights, like an ocean of fireflies. It took Luo Ji a moment to realize that it was a crowd of people. All of them were from the city, and the light came from their clothes.

As the car slowly approached the crowd, everyone ahead of them raised their hands to block the glare of the headlights, so Shi Qiang turned them off, leaving them facing a bizarre, gaudy human wall.

"Looks like they're waiting for someone," Shi Qiang said, looking at Luo Ji, who tensed up at his expression. The car stopped, and Shi Qiang went on, "You stay here and don't move. I'll go have a look." He jumped out of the car and walked over to the crowd. Against the glowing human wall, Shi Qiang's stocky body stood

out as a black silhouette. Luo Ji watched him walk to the crowd, then exchange a few words with the people before turning and walking back.

"Turns out they're waiting for you. Go," he said, leaning on the door. Seeing Luo Ji's face, he reassured him, "Relax. It'll be okay."

Luo Ji got out of the car and went over to the crowd. He had grown familiar with the wired clothing of modern people, but in the desolate desert, he still had the feeling that he was walking toward the Other. But when he drew closer and could make out their expressions, his heart began to beat faster.

The first thing he had learned when he awakened from hibernation was that the crowds of every age have their own unique expression. The differences across time to this far-off age were remarkable—you could easily distinguish between moderns and hibernators who had only just reawakened. But the expressions Luo Ji saw now weren't modern, nor were they twenty-first century. He didn't know what era they belonged to. Fear nearly rooted him to the spot, but his trust in Shi Qiang propelled his steps mechanically forward.

When he had gotten closer to the crowd, he finally stopped, because he saw the images they had on their clothes.

Their clothing displayed pictures of Luo Ji—some still photographs, some videos.

Luo Ji had rarely appeared before the media since becoming a Wallfacer, so he hadn't left much of a visual record, but a fairly complete set of those videos and images was now on display on the people's clothing. On some people, he even saw photographs of his pre-Wallfacer self. The clothing took its images from the Internet, which meant that these images must be circulating worldwide. He also noticed that the images were in their original state and had not been subjected to the artistic deformation that the moderns liked to do, which meant that they had just appeared online.

When they saw him stop, the crowd moved toward him. When they got as close as two or three meters, the people in front held back the rest of the crowd, and then knelt down. Those behind

them knelt down successively in a wave of glowing people that receded along the sand.

"Lord, save us!" he heard someone say. The words buzzed in his ears.

"Oh god, save the world!"

"Great spokesman, uphold justice in the universe!"

"Angel of justice, save humankind!"

Two people came up to Luo Ji, and he recognized the one whose clothing wasn't glowing as Hines. The other man was a soldier with glowing badges and ribbons.

Hines said to him gravely, "Dr. Luo, I've just been appointed your liaison to the UN Wallfacer Project Commission. It is my duty to inform you that the Wallfacer Project has been revived, and you have been named the sole Wallfacer."

The soldier said, "I am special commissioner Ben Jonathan of the SFJC. We met when you had just been reawakened. I am also instructed to inform you that the Asian Fleet, the European Fleet, and the North American Fleet have agreed with the revalidation of the Wallfacer Act and have recognized your status as Wallfacer."

Hines pointed to the crowd kneeling on the sand, and said, "In the eyes of the public, you now have two identities. For theists, you are the angel of justice. To atheists, you are the spokesperson for a just, superior civilization in the Milky Way."

This was followed by silence, with all eyes focused on Luo Ji. He thought for a while, but came up with only one possibility: "The spell worked?" he ventured.

Hines and Jonathan nodded, and Hines said, "187J3X1 has been destroyed."

"When?"

"Fifty-one years ago. It was observed a year ago, but no one was paying much attention to that star, so the observations were only discovered this afternoon. A few desperate people in the SFJC wanted to find inspiration in history, and they remembered the Wallfacer Project and your spell. So they looked at 187J3X1 and found that it wasn't there anymore. In its place was a nebula of

debris. They scanned through all observational records of the star until its destruction a year ago, then pulled all of the observational data of 187J3X1 at the time it exploded."

"How do they know it was destroyed?"

"You're aware that 187J3X1 was in a stable period, like the sun, so it would be impossible for it to go nova. And its destruction was observed: A body traveling close to the speed of light struck 187J3X1. The tiny object—they're calling it a 'photoid'— was observed the instant it passed into the periphery of the stellar atmosphere by the tracks it made. Even though it was small in volume, its near-light velocity meant that its vastly amplified relativistic mass had reached one-eighth of 187J3X1's by the time it struck the target. It destroyed the star immediately. The star's four planets were also vaporized in the blast."

Luo Ji looked up at the night's dark sky, where the stars were practically invisible. He walked forward, and the people stood up and silently made a path for him, closing back together immediately behind him. They were all trying to push closer to him, as if yearning for sunlight amid the cold, but they respectfully left him a circle of space, a dark spot in a fluorescent ocean, like the eye of a storm. A man pushed forward and fell to the ground in front of Luo Ji, compelling him to stop, and then the man kissed his feet. A few others entered the ring to repeat that act. Just when the situation seemed about to go out of control, there were critical shouts from the crowd, prompting the people to scramble and retreat back into the group.

Luo Ji continued on ahead, but realized that he didn't know where he was going. He stopped, found Hines and Jonathan in the crowd, and walked over to them.

"So what should I do now?" he asked when he reached them.

"You're a Wallfacer, so of course you can do anything within the scope of the Wallfacer Act," Hines said to him with a bow. "Although the act still has restrictions, you can now mobilize practically all of the resources of Earth International."

"That includes the Fleet International's resources, too," Jonathan added.

Luo Ji thought for a moment, and said, "I don't need to tap any resources right now. But if I've really recovered the power granted by the Wallfacer Act . . ."

"There's no doubt about that," Hines said. Jonathan nodded.

"Then I'll make two requests. First, order will be restored in all cities, and normal life will resume. There's no mystery about this request. I'm sure you understand."

Everyone nodded. Someone said, "The world is listening, oh god."

"Yes, the world is listening," Hines said. "Restoring stability will require time, but because of you we have faith that it can be done." His words were echoed in the crowd.

"Second: Everyone, go home. Leave this place in peace. Thank you!"

The people were silent after hearing this, but soon began to buzz as his words were passed back through the crowd. The crowd began to disperse, slowly and unwillingly at first, but eventually the pace picked up and car after car headed off down the road in the direction of the city. The many people walking along the roadside looked like a long glowing colony of ants in the night.

Then the desert was empty once again. Only Luo Ji, Shi Qiang, Hines, and Jonathan were left on the sand littered with chaotic footprints.

"I am truly ashamed of my former self," Hines said. "Human civilization has a history of just five thousand years, yet we cherish life and freedom so highly. There must be civilizations in the universe with a history of billions of years. What sort of morality do they possess? Is there any point to that question?"

"I'm ashamed for myself, too. The past few days, I've even begun to doubt God," Jonathan said. When he saw Hines about to cut in, he raised his hand to stop him. "No, friend. We might be talking about the same thing."

They embraced, tears streaming down their faces.

"So, gentlemen," Luo Ji said as he patted them on the back. "You can go back. If I need you, I'll get in touch. Thank you."

He watched them go off, supporting each other like a happy

pair of lovers. Now he and Shi Qiang were the only ones left.

"Da Shi, anything you'd like to say now?" he said, turning to Shi Qiang with a smile.

Shi Qiang stood rooted to the spot, as stunned as if he had just witnessed a thrilling magic trick. "My boy, I'm damn confused."

"What? You don't believe I'm an angel of justice?"

"You'd have to beat me to death before I'd say that."

"And a spokesperson of a superior civilization?"

"A little better than an angel, but I don't believe that either, to tell you the truth. I've never thought that was the case."

"Don't you believe in fairness and justice in the universe?"

"I don't know."

"But you're in law enforcement."

"I said I don't know. I'm genuinely confused."

"Then you're the most sober one here."

"So can you tell me about the justice of the universe?"

"Very well. Come with me." Then Luo Ji walked straight out into the desert, with Shi Qiang following close behind him. They walked a long while in silence, then crossed the highway.

"Where are we going?" Shi Qiang asked.

"To the darkest place."

They crossed the highway to where the embankment blocked out the lights of the residential area. Groping about in the dark that surrounded them, Luo Ji and Shi Qiang sat down on the sandy ground.

"Let's begin," Luo Ji's voice sounded in the dark.

"Give me the easy version. At my level, I'm not going to understand anything complicated."

"Everyone can understand, Da Shi. The truth is simple. It's the kind of thing that, once you hear it, you'll wonder why you didn't come up with it yourself. Do you know about mathematical axioms?"

"I took geometry in high school. 'Only one straight line can be drawn between two points.' That kind of thing."

"Right. So now we're going to set out two axioms for cosmic civilization. First, survival is the primary need of civilization.

515

Second, civilization continuously grows and expands, but the total matter in the universe remains constant."

"And then?"

"That's it."

"What can you derive from those little things?"

"The same way you can figure out an entire case from a bullet or a drop of blood, cosmic sociology is able to describe a complete picture of galactic and cosmic civilization from those two axioms. That's what science is like, Da Shi. The cornerstone of every discipline is quite simple."

"So let's see you derive something."

"First, let's talk about the Battle of Darkness. Would you believe me if I said that Starship Earth was a microcosm of cosmic civilization?"

"No. Starship Earth lacked resources like parts and fuel, but the universe doesn't. It's too big."

"You're wrong. The universe is big, but life is bigger! That's what the second axiom means. The amount of matter in the universe remains constant, but life grows exponentially. Exponentials are the devils of mathematics. If there's a microscopic bacterium in the ocean that divides once every half hour, its descendants will fill the entire ocean in the space of a few days, so long as there are sufficient nutrients. Don't let humanity and Trisolaris give you a false impression. These two civilizations are tiny, but they are only in their infancy. Once a civilization passes a certain technological threshold, the expansion of life through the universe is frightening. For instance, take humanity's present navigation speed. In a million years, Earth civilization could fill the galaxy. And a million years is a short time measured against the universe."

"So you're saying that, taking the long view, the entire universe might have that kind of . . . what are they calling it, a 'dead hand'?"

"No need for the long view. Right now the entire universe has been dealt that dead hand. Like Hines said, civilization may have started in the universe billions of years ago. Looking at the signs, the universe might be packed full already. Who knows how much

empty space there is in the Milky Way or the universe, or how many resources are left?"

"But that's not right, is it? The universe looks empty. We haven't seen any other alien life apart from Trisolaris, right?"

"That's what we'll talk about next. Give me a cigarette." Luo Ji groped about in the dark for a while before taking the cigarette from Shi Qiang's hand. When Luo Ji next spoke, Shi Qiang realized he had moved to a spot three or four meters away. "We need to increase the distance to make it feel more like outer space," Luo Ji said. Then he lit the cigarette by twisting its filter, and Shi Qiang lit one of his own. In the dark, two tiny red planets stood in distant opposition.

"Okay. To illustrate the problem, we now need to establish the most elementary model of cosmic civilization. These two balls of flame represent two civilized planets. The universe is made up of only these two planets, and apart from them there's nothing else. Erase all of our surroundings. Can you locate that feeling?"

"Yeah. That's an easy feeling to find in a dark place like this."

"Let's call these two civilized worlds your civilization and my civilization. They're separated by a great distance, say, a hundred light-years. You can detect that I exist, but you don't know any details. However, I'm completely ignorant of your presence."

"Right."

"Now we need to define two concepts, 'benevolence' and 'malice' between civilizations. These words themselves aren't very rigorous in a scientific context, so we've got to restrict their meaning. 'Benevolence' means not taking the initiative to attack and eradicate other civilizations. 'Malice' is the opposite."

"That's a low bar for benevolence."

"Next, consider your options for dealing with me. Please remember that the axioms of cosmic civilization should be kept in mind throughout the process, as well as the distance scale and the environment of space."

"I could choose to communicate with you."

"If you do that, you should be aware of the price you'll pay: You'll have exposed your existence to me."

"Right. In the universe, that's no small thing."

"There are different degrees of exposure. The strongest form of exposure is when I know your precise interstellar coordinates. Next is when I know your general direction, and the weakest is when I only know of your existence. But even the weakest form of exposure makes it possible for me to search for you, because since you've detected my existence, I know that I'll be able to find you. It's only a matter of time, from the standpoint of technological development."

"But my boy, I could still take the risk to talk to you. If you're malicious, then it's my bad luck. But if you're benevolent, then we could have further exchanges and ultimately be united into a benevolent civilization."

"Okay, Da Shi. Now we've come to the crux of it. Let's return to the axioms of cosmic civilization: Even if I'm a benevolent civilization, can I determine at the start of our communication whether or not you are also benevolent?"

"Of course not. That would violate the first axiom."

"So once I've received your message, what should I do?"

"Naturally, you ought to determine whether I'm benevolent or malicious. Malicious, and you eradicate me. Benevolent, and we can continue communicating."

The flame on Luo Ji's side rose up and moved back and forth. Evidently he had gotten up and was pacing. "That's fine on Earth, but not out in the universe. So next we'll introduce an important new concept: the chain of suspicion."

"That's an odd term."

"The term is all I had at first. It wasn't explained to me. But, later, I was able to infer its meaning from the words themselves."

"Who didn't explain it?"

". . . I'll tell you later. Let's continue. If you think I'm benevolent, that's not a reason to feel safe, because according to the first axiom, a benevolent civilization can't predict that any other civilization is benevolent. You don't know whether I think you're benevolent or malicious. Next, even if you know that I think you're benevolent,

and I also know that you think *I'm* benevolent, I don't know what you think about what I think about what you're thinking about me. It's convoluted, isn't it? This is just the third level, but the logic goes on indefinitely."

"I get what you mean."

"That's the chain of suspicion. It's something that you don't see on Earth. Humanity's shared species, cultural similarities, interconnected ecosystem, and close distances means that, in this environment, the chain of suspicion will only extend a level or two before it's resolved through communication. But in space, the chain of suspicion can be very long. Something like the Battle of Darkness will already have taken place before communication can resolve it."

Shi Qiang took a drag on his cigarette, and his contemplative face emerged from the darkness for a moment. "It looks now like the Battle of Darkness has a lot to teach us."

"That's right. The five ships of Starship Earth formed a quasi-cosmic civilization, not a real one, because they consisted of a single species—humans—who were very close to each other. But even so, when they were dealt that dead hand, the chain of suspicion emerged. In actual cosmic civilization, the biological differences between different groups might be as high as the kingdom level, and cultural differences are even further beyond our imagining. Add to this the vast distances between them, and you have chains of suspicion that are practically indestructible."

"That means that the outcome is the same, regardless of whether we're benevolent civilizations or malicious civilizations?"

"That's right. That's the most important aspect of the chain of suspicion. It's unrelated to the civilization's own morality and social structure. It's enough to think of every civilization as the points at the end of a chain. Regardless of whether civilizations are internally benevolent or malicious, when they enter the web formed by chains of suspicion, they're all identical."

"But if you're much weaker than I am, you're not a threat to me. So I could always communicate with you, right?"

"That won't work, either. Here we need to introduce a second

important concept: the technological explosion. I didn't get a full explanation for this, either, but it was far easier to infer than the chain of suspicion. Human civilization has five thousand years of history, and life on Earth might be as much as a few billion years old. But modern technology was developed over the course of three hundred years. On the scale of the universe, that's not development. It's an explosion! The potential for technological leaps is the explosive buried within every civilization, and if it's lit by some internal or external factor, it goes off with a bang. On Earth it took three hundred years, but there's no reason why humanity should be the fastest of all cosmic civilizations. Maybe there are others whose technological explosions were even more sudden. I'm weaker than you, but once I've received your message and know of your existence, the chain of suspicion is established between us. If at any time I experience a technological explosion that suddenly puts me far ahead of you, then I'm stronger than you. On the scale of the universe, several hundred years is the snap of a finger. And it might be that my knowledge of your existence and the information I received from our communication was the perfect spark to set off that explosion. That means that even though I'm just a newborn or growing civilization, I'm still a big danger to you."

Shi Qiang watched Luo Ji's flame in the darkness as he thought for a few seconds, then looked at his own cigarette. "So I have to keep quiet."

"Do you think that will work?"

They smoked. The balls of flame brightened and their faces emerged from the darkness like the gods of this simple universe, deep in thought.

Shi Qiang said, "No, it won't. If you're stronger than me, then since I was able to find you, one day you'll be able to find me. And then there will be a chain of suspicion between us. If you're weaker than me, you could experience a technological explosion at any time, and that would take us back to the first case. To sum up: one, letting you know I exist, and two, letting you continue to exist, are both dangerous to me and violate the first axiom."

"Da Shi, you've really got a clear mind."

"My brain can keep up with yours so far, but we're only getting started."

Luo Ji was silent in the dark for a long time. His face emerged in the weak light of the ball of flame two or three times before he said, "Da Shi, this isn't a start. Our reasoning has already reached a conclusion."

"Conclusion? We haven't figured anything out! Where's the picture of cosmic civilization you promised?"

"If neither communication nor silence will work once you learn of my existence, you're left with just one option."

In the long silence that followed, the two flames went out. There was no wind, and the dark silence turned thick as asphalt, connecting sky and desert into a murky whole. At last Shi Qiang uttered one word in the darkness: "Fuck!"

"Extrapolate that option out to the billions upon billions of stars and hundreds of millions of civilizations, and there's your picture," Luo Ji said, nodding in the darkness.

"That's . . . that's really dark."

"The real universe is just that black." Luo Ji waved a hand, feeling the darkness as if stroking velvet. "The universe is a dark forest. Every civilization is an armed hunter stalking through the trees like a ghost, gently pushing aside branches that block the path and trying to tread without sound. Even breathing is done with care. The hunter has to be careful, because everywhere in the forest are stealthy hunters like him. If he finds other life—another hunter, an angel or a demon, a delicate infant or a tottering old man, a fairy or a demigod—there's only one thing he can do: open fire and eliminate them. In this forest, hell is other people. An eternal threat that any life that exposes its own existence will be swiftly wiped out. This is the picture of cosmic civilization. It's the explanation for the Fermi Paradox."

Shi Qiang lit another cigarette, if only to have a bit of light.

"But in this dark forest, there's a stupid child called humanity, who has built a bonfire and is standing beside it shouting, 'Here I

am! Here I am!'" Luo Ji said.

"Has anyone heard it?"

"That's guaranteed. But those shouts alone can't be used to determine the child's location. Humanity has not yet transmitted information about the exact position of Earth and the Solar System into the universe. From the information that has been sent out, all that can be learned is the distance between Earth and Trisolaris, and their general heading in the Milky Way. The precise location of the two worlds is still a mystery. Since we're located in the wilderness of the periphery of the galaxy, we're a little safer."

"So what's the deal with the spell?"

"Using the sun, I transmitted three images to the cosmos. Each one consisted of thirty points representing the planar projection of a three-dimensional coordinate system containing the position of thirty stars. Combining the three images into three-dimensional coordinates forms a cubic space populated by those thirty points. That represents the relative positions of 187J3X1 and its twenty-nine surrounding stars. There's also a label pointing out 187J3X1.

"Think about it carefully and you'll get it. A hunter in a dark forest, stalking with bated breath, suddenly notices that a piece of bark has been stripped from a tree in front of him. On the eye-catching bit of white wood that's been revealed is a position in the forest, written in characters all hunters can recognize. What will he think about that location? He's certainly not going to imagine that someone has laid out supplies for him there. Out of all the possibilities, the most likely one is that the blaze is informing everyone that there's live prey at that location that needs to be eliminated. It doesn't matter what motivated someone to leave the mark. What's important is that the dead hand has stretched the nerves of the dark forest to the breaking point, and it's the most sensitive nerve that's most liable to make a move. Suppose there are a million hunters in the forest—the number of civilizations on the billions upon billions of stars in the Milky Way could be thousands of times that. Perhaps nine hundred thousand of them will disregard the marking. Of the remaining one hundred thousand, maybe ninety thousand of them

will probe the location, and, after confirming that it has no life, disregard it. But one of the remaining ten thousand hunters will surely make a choice to fire on that position, because for civilizations at a certain level of technological development, attacking may be safer and less of a hassle than probing. If there's really nothing at that location, then it's no loss.

"Now," Luo Ji concluded, "that hunter has appeared."

"That spell of yours can't be sent anymore, right?"

"That's right, Da Shi. The spell needs to be broadcast to the entire galaxy, but the sun's been locked down, so it can't be sent anymore."

"Was humanity just a step late?" Shi Qiang flicked aside his cigarette end. The flame drew an arc through the darkness as it fell, momentarily illuminating a small circle of sandy ground.

"No, no. Think about it: If the sun hadn't been sealed off, and I had threatened Trisolaris with sending out a spell against them, what would have happened?"

"You would've been stoned to death like Rey Diaz. And then they would have enacted legislation to prohibit anyone else from thinking along those lines."

"That's right, Da Shi. Because we've already revealed the distance between the Solar System and Trisolaris as well as our general heading in the Milky Way, exposing the location of Trisolaris is tantamount to exposing the location of the Solar System. That's a death strategy. Maybe we're a step late, but it's a step that humanity would never be able to take."

"You should have threatened Trisolaris back then."

"Things were too weird. I wasn't certain about the idea at the time, so I needed to confirm it. After all, there was plenty of time. But the real reason was that, deep in my heart, I really didn't have the mental strength. I don't think anyone else would, either."

"Thinking about it now, we shouldn't have gone to see the mayor today. This situation—if the world learns about it, then it's even more hopeless. Think about how the first two Wallfacers ended up."

"You're right. The same thing would happen to me, so I hope

that neither of us says anything. But you still can, if you want. Like someone once told me: Either way, I've fulfilled my duty."

"Don't worry, my boy. I won't say anything."

"Regardless, there's no longer any hope."

They walked along the embankment and to the highway, where it was slightly less dark. The sparse lights of the residential area in the distance were enough to blind them.

"There's one more thing. That person you mentioned?"

Luo Ji hesitated. "Forget it. All you need to know is that the axioms of cosmic civilization and the theory of the dark forest were not my invention."

"Tomorrow I'm going into the city to work with the government. If you need any help in the future, just say the word."

"Da Shi, you've helped me more than enough. I'll head into the city tomorrow, too, to the Hibernation Immigration Bureau, to take care of waking up my family.".

Contrary to Luo Ji's expectations, the Hibernation Immigration Bureau said that reawakening Zhuang Yan and Xia Xia was still blocked, and the bureau's director made it clear to him that his Wallfacer powers were ineffective in this regard. He consulted Hines and Jonathan, who were unacquainted with the details of the situation, but they told him that the revised Wallfacer Act contained a provision stating that the UN and Wallfacer Project Commission could take all necessary steps to ensure that the Wallfacer remained focused on his work. Which meant that, after two centuries, the UN was once again using Luo Ji's situation as a tool to coerce and control him.

Luo Ji requested that his hibernator settlement remain in its current state and be kept free of outside harassment. This request was faithfully executed. The news media and the masses of pilgrims were kept at a distance, and after calm was restored throughout New Life Village #5, it was like nothing at all had happened.

Two days later, Luo Ji attended the first hearing of the revived Wallfacer Project. He didn't go to the underground UN headquarters in North America, but attended by video link from his spartan

residence in New Life Village #5, where scenes from the assembly appeared on the ordinary television in his room.

"Wallfacer Luo Ji, we were prepared to face your anger," the commission chair said.

"My heart has been burnt to ash. It no longer has the capacity for anger," Luo Ji said, reclining lazily on the sofa.

The chair nodded. "That's a wonderful attitude. However, the commission feels you ought to leave your village. That little place isn't a worthy command center for the defense of the Solar System."

"Do you know about Xibaipo? It's an even smaller village not far from here. Over two centuries ago, that's where our nation's founders commanded one of the largest offensives in history."[26]

The chair shook his head. "Clearly you haven't changed at all. Very well. The commission respects your habits and choices. You should get to work. It's not going to be like back then, with you claiming that you're always at work, is it?"

"I can't work. The conditions for my work no longer exist. Can you harness stellar power to broadcast my spell into the universe?"

The representative of the Asian Fleet said, "You know that's impossible. The droplet's radio suppression of the sun is continuous. And we don't anticipate that it will stop for the next two or three years, by which time the nine other droplets will have reached the Solar System."

"Then there's nothing I can do."

The chair said, "No, Wallfacer Luo Ji. There's one important thing you haven't done. You haven't disclosed the secret of the spell to the UN and SFJC. How did you use it to destroy a star?"

"I can't tell you that."

"And if it were a condition for reawakening your wife and child?"

"That's a despicable thing to say at a time like this."

26 *Translator's Note:* Driven out of Yan'an by a Nationalist offensive in 1947, Communist forces established a base in Xibaipo, a village in the foothills of the Taihang Mountains in southwestern Hebei province. From there they directed the Liaoshen, Huaihai, and Pingjin campaigns, the decisive offensive in 1948 and 1949 that pushed the Nationalists out of northern China.

"This is a secret hearing. Besides, the Wallfacer Project doesn't have any place in modern society. The revival of the Wallfacer Project means that all decisions made by the UN's Wallfacer Project Commission two centuries ago are still in effect. And according to those resolutions, Zhuang Yan and your child would reawaken at the Doomsday Battle."

"Didn't we just fight the Doomsday Battle?"

"The two Internationals don't think so, since the main Trisolaran Fleet has yet to arrive."

"Keeping the secret of the spell is my responsibility as a Wallfacer. Otherwise, humanity will lose its last hope, though that hope may already be gone."

In the days following the hearing, Luo Ji stayed inside, drinking heavily, and spent most of his time in a state of intoxication. People occasionally saw him emerge with his clothes disheveled and his beard long. He looked like a tramp.

When the next Wallfacer Project hearing was convened, Luo Ji again attended from home.

"Wallfacer Luo Ji, your condition has us worried," the chair said when he saw Luo Ji's unkempt appearance in the video. He directed the camera around Luo Ji's room, and the assembly could see that it was littered with bottles.

"You ought to get to work, if only to restore yourself to a normal state of mind," the representative of the European Commonwealth said.

"You know what will return me to normal."

"The reawakening of your wife and child really isn't all that important," the chair said. "We don't want to use that to control you. We know that we can't control you. But it's a resolution made by the previous commission, so addressing the issue presents some difficulties. Bottom line: There must be a condition."

"I reject your condition."

"No, no, Dr. Luo. The condition has changed."

At the chair's words, Luo Ji's eyes lit up, and he sat up straight on the sofa. "And now the condition is . . ."

"It's simple. Couldn't be simpler. You just have to do *something*."

"If I can't send a spell out into the universe, there's nothing I can do."

"You have to think of something to do."

"You mean, it could be something meaningless?"

"So long as it looks significant to the public. In their eyes, you're either the spokesman of the force of cosmic justice or a heaven-sent angel of justice. At the very least, these identities can be used to stabilize the situation. But if you do nothing, you'll lose the faith of the public after a while."

"Achieving stability that way is dangerous. It'll lead to no end of trouble."

"But what we need right now is to stabilize the global situation. The nine droplets are coming to the Solar System in three years, and we have to be prepared to deal with that."

"I really don't want to waste resources."

"In that case, the commission will provide you with a task. One that won't waste resources. I'll ask the chairman of the SFJC to explain it to you," the chair said as he gestured to the SFJC chairman, who was also attending via video. The SFJC chairman was evidently in some space-based structure, because the stars were shifting slowly across the broad window behind him.

He said, "Our estimate of the arrival of the nine droplets in the Solar System is based entirely on speed and acceleration estimates obtained when they crossed the final interstellar dust cloud four years ago. They differ from the one that's already here in that their engines operate without emitting light. They don't emit any other high-frequency electromagnetic radiation that could provide a position. This is likely a self-adjustment made after humanity successfully tracked the first droplet. Locating and tracking such small, dark bodies in outer space is incredibly difficult, and now that we've lost their tracks, we don't know when they'll reach the Solar System. We don't even know how to detect that they've arrived."

"So what can I do?" Luo Ji asked.

"We hope that you can lead the Snow Project."

"What's that?"

"Using stellar hydrogen bombs and Neptune's oil film, we will manufacture clouds of space dust that the droplets will leave tracks in when they pass through."

"You've got to be joking. You do realize that I'm not entirely ignorant about space."

"You were an astronomer once. That makes you even more qualified to lead this project."

"Making a dust cloud was successful last time because the approximate path of the target was known. But now we know nothing. If the nine droplets accelerate or change course while dark, then they might even enter the Solar System from another side altogether! Where are you going to spread the dust cloud?"

"In every direction."

"You mean to say that you're going to manufacture a ball of dust to envelop the entire Solar System? If that's the case, then you're the one who's been sent by God."

"A ball of dust is impossible, but we can make a ring of dust on the ecliptic plane, between the asteroid belt and Jupiter."

"But what if the droplets enter outside the ecliptic plane?"

"That can't be helped. But from an astrodynamics perspective, if the droplet group wants to encounter every planet in the Solar System, then the greatest likelihood is entry on the ecliptic plane. That's what the first droplet did. That way, the dust cloud will be able to capture their tracks, and, once captured, the Solar System's optical tracking system will be able to lock onto them."

"But what's the point of that?"

"We'll at least know that the droplet group has entered the Solar System. They might strike civilian targets in space, so all ships will need to be recalled, or at least those in the droplets' path. And the inhabitants of space cities will have to be evacuated to Earth, because those are weak targets."

"There's another matter that's even more critical," the Wallfacer Project Commission chair said. "Identifying safe routes for the possible withdrawal of spacecraft into deep space."

"Withdrawal into deep space? We're not talking about Escapism, are we?"

"If you must use that name."

"Why not begin the escape now?"

"Present political conditions do not permit it. But when the droplet group approaches Earth, a limited-scale flight might become acceptable to the international community. Of course, it's only a possibility. But the UN and the fleets must make preparations for it."

"I understand. But the Snow Project doesn't really require me."

"It does. Even inside the orbit of Jupiter, creating a dust cloud is an enormous undertaking and will require the deployment of almost ten thousand stellar hydrogen bombs, more than ten million tons of oil film, and the formation of an enormous space fleet. To accomplish that within three years requires taking advantage of your current status and prestige to organize and coordinate the resources of the two Internationals."

"If I agree to undertake this mission, when will you wake them?"

"Once the project is started. Like I said, it won't be a problem."

But the Snow Project never got fully off the ground.

The two Internationals were not interested in the project. What the public wanted was a strategy for global salvation, not a plan that would merely inform them of the enemy's arrival so they could escape. Besides, they knew that this wasn't the Wallfacer's idea. It was just a plan implemented by the UN and SFJC that exploited his authority. A full launch of the Snow Project would bring the entire space economy to a standstill and lead to a general economic recession on Earth and in the fleet. In addition, contrary to the UN's prediction, as the droplets drew nearer, Escapism turned even more repugnant in the eyes of the public, so the two Internationals were unwilling to pay such a high price for an unpopular plan. As a result, both the construction of a fleet to gather the oil-film material on Neptune and the manufacture of sufficient stellar hydrogen bombs to supplement the fewer than one thousand from the Great Ravine that were still usable made very slow progress.

But Luo Ji poured himself entirely into the project. At first, the UN and the SFJC had only wanted to exploit his prestige to mobilize the resources needed, but Luo Ji immersed himself in every detail of the project, spending sleepless nights shoulder-to-shoulder with the scientists and engineers of the Technical Committee and proposing many of his own ideas. For example, he suggested that a small interstellar ion engine be installed onto each bomb to allow them a certain degree of mobility in orbit, enabling timely adjustments to the density of the stellar cloud in different regions. More importantly, the hydrogen bombs could act as attack weapons. He called them "space mines," and argued that even though stellar hydrogen bombs had proven incapable of destroying droplets, they might in the long run be useful against Trisolaran ships, because they had no evidence that the ships were also constructed out of strong-interaction material. He personally determined the orbit for every bomb's deployment. From a modern technological perspective, his ideas may have been full of a twenty-first-century ignorance and naiveté, but his prestige and Wallfacer status meant that most of his suggestions were adopted.

Luo Ji treated the Snow Project as a means of escape. He knew that he wanted to escape reality, and the best way to do that at present was to involve himself deeply in the project. But the more he devoted himself to it, the more disappointed in him the world became. Everyone knew he had only attached himself to the largely insignificant project so that he could see his wife and child as soon as possible. The world waited for a plan for salvation that never materialized. Luo Ji declared over and over in the media that without the capability to use stellar power to send out a spell, he was powerless to do anything.

The Snow Project ground to a halt after a year and a half, at which time only 1.5 million tons of oil film had been collected from Neptune. Even adding the 600,000 tons collected for the Fog Umbrella, the figure was still far from what the project required. Ultimately, 3,614 stellar hydrogen bombs packed in oil film were deployed in an orbit two AU from the sun. This wasn't even a fifth

of the intended number. When detonated, they would form a large number of independent dust clouds orbiting the sun, rather than a continuous dust cloud belt, greatly reducing their effectiveness as a warning.

It was an age in which hope came as quickly as disappointment, and after anxiously waiting for a year and a half, the public lost faith and patience in Luo Ji the Wallfacer.

At the general meeting of the International Astronomical Union, a body that last attracted worldwide attention in 2006 when it revoked Pluto's eligibility as a planet, a large number of astronomers and astrophysicists were of the opinion that the explosion of 187J3X1 was a chance occurrence. Being an astronomer, Luo Ji may have discovered certain signs that the star would explode. The theory was full of holes, but more and more people came to believe it, accelerating Luo Ji's decline in prestige. In the eyes of the public, his image gradually transitioned from messiah to commoner, and then to fraud. He still enjoyed the Wallfacer status granted by the UN, and the Wallfacer Act was still in effect, but he no longer had real power.

YEAR 208, CRISIS ERA

Distance of the Trisolaran Fleet from the Solar System:
2.07 light-years

On a cold, drizzly autumn afternoon, a meeting of the New Life
Village #5 Residents' Council came to the following decision: Luo
Ji would be expelled from the neighborhood on the grounds that
he was affecting the normal life of the neighborhood's residents.
While the Snow Project was in progress, Luo Ji had frequently
gone out to attend meetings, but the majority of his time was still
spent in the area, and he kept in contact with various Snow Project
entities from home. Disruptions had only worsened as his position
declined, since from time to time crowds of people would gather at
the foot of his building to jeer at him or throw stones at his win-
dow. Media interest in the spectacle was enough to make reporters
as numerous as protestors. But the real reason for Luo Ji's expul-
sion was that he was an utter disappointment to the hibernators.

When the meeting adjourned that evening, the neighborhood
committee director went to Luo Ji's home to inform him of the
council's decision. After pressing the doorbell repeatedly, she
pushed open the unlatched door and practically choked on the mix
of alcohol, smoke, and sweat that filled the room. She noticed that
the walls had been converted into city-style information surfaces
that allowed information screens to be called up anywhere with
just a tap. A confusion of images filled the walls, most of them dis-
playing complex data and curves, but the largest showing a sphere

532

suspended in space: a stellar hydrogen bomb packed in oil film. The transparent film with the bomb clearly visible within it reminded the director of a marble, the sort of thing children liked to play with back in Luo Ji's day. It rotated slowly. There was a small protrusion at one pole—the ion engine—and in the sphere's smooth surface was the reflection of a tiny sun. All of those dazzling screens turned the room into a huge gaudy box. Since the lights were off, they were the only source of illumination, dissolving everything into blurry color so that it was hard at first to distinguish what was a physical presence and what was just an image.

Once the director's eyes had adapted, she saw that the place looked like the basement of a drug addict, the floor littered with bottles and cigarette ends, the piles of clothes covered in ash like a garbage heap. She eventually managed to locate Luo Ji among the garbage. He was curled up in a corner, black against the backdrop of the images like a withered branch that had been cast aside. She thought he was asleep at first, but then noticed that his sightless gaze was fixed on the piles of garbage on the ground. His eyes were bloodshot, his face haggard, his body gaunt, and he seemed unable to support his own weight. When he heard the director he greeted her and turned toward her slowly, then just as slowly nodded at her, so that she knew he was still alive. But the two centuries of torment that had accumulated in his body had now completely overwhelmed him.

The director didn't show the slightest bit of mercy toward this man who had been totally used up. Like other people of their era, she had always felt that, regardless of how dark the world seemed, ultimate justice was still present in some unseen place. Luo Ji had first validated that belief and then mercilessly shattered it, and her disappointment with him had turned to shame and then anger. Coldly, she announced the results of the meeting.

Luo Ji nodded slowly a second time, then forced a voice through his swollen throat. "I'll leave tomorrow. I ought to be going. If I've done anything wrong, I ask for your forgiveness."

It was only two days later that the director learned the true meaning of his final words.

In fact, Luo Ji had been planning on leaving that night. After seeing the neighborhood committee director off, he rose unsteadily to his feet and went into the bedroom in search of a travel bag, which he packed with a few items, including a short-handled shovel he had found in the storage room. The shovel's triangular handle poked out of the travel bag. Then he retrieved a filthy jacket from the floor, put it on, slung the bag across his back, and went out. Behind him, the room's information walls continued to flash.

The hallway was empty, but at the foot of the stairs he ran into a kid, probably just home from school, who stared at Luo Ji with a strange and unreadable expression as he left the building. Outside, he found that it was still raining, but he didn't want to go back for an umbrella.

He didn't go to his own car because that would attract the attention of the guards. Walking along the street, he left the neighborhood without running into anyone. Then he walked through the protective forest belt outside the neighborhood and he was in the desert, the drizzle sprinkling on his face like the light caress of a pair of cold hands. Desert and sky were hazy in the dusk, like the blank space of a traditional painting. He imagined himself added to that blank space, like the painting that Zhuang Yan had left behind.

He reached the highway, and after a few minutes was able to flag down a car carrying a family of three, who warmly welcomed him aboard. They were hibernators on their way back to the old city. The child was small and the mother young, and they were squeezed next to the father in the front seat, whispering to each other. Occasionally the child would burrow his head into his mother's bosom, and whenever this happened the three of them burst out laughing. Luo Ji watched, spellbound, but he couldn't hear what they were saying because music was playing in the car, old songs from the twentieth century. He listened as he rode, and after five or six songs, including "*Katyusha*" and "*Kalinka*," he was filled with a longing to hear "*Tonkaya Ryabina*." He had sung that song to his imaginary lover on that village stage two centuries ago, and later with Zhuang Yan in the Garden of Eden on the shore of the lake that reflected the snowy peaks.

Then the headlights of an oncoming car illuminated the backseat as the child was glancing backwards. He turned entirely around to stare at Luo Ji, then shouted, "Hey, he looks like the Wallfacer!" The child's parents turned to look at him, and Luo Ji had to admit that he was.

Just then, "*Tonkaya Ryabina*" started playing.

The car stopped. "Get out," the child's father said coldly, as mother and child watched him with expressions as chilly as the autumn rain outside.

Luo Ji didn't move. He wanted to listen to the song.

"Please get out," the man said, and Luo Ji could read the words in their eyes: *Not being able to save the world isn't your fault, but giving the world hope only to shatter it again is an unforgivable sin.*

So he had to get out of the car. His travel bag was tossed out after him. As the car drove off, he ran after it for a few steps in the hopes of being able to listen to a little more of "*Tonkaya Ryabina*," but the song disappeared into the cold, rainy night.

By now he was at the edge of the old city. The old high-rises of the past were visible in the distance, standing black in the rainy night, each building's few scattered lights looking like lonely eyes. He came across a bus stop and sat shielded from the rain for nearly an hour before a driverless public bus finally arrived that was headed in the direction he wanted to go. It was mostly empty, and the six or seven people who were seated there looked like hibernators from the old city. No one on the bus spoke, just sat silently in the gloom of this autumn night. The journey passed smoothly until a little over an hour later, when someone else recognized him, and then everyone on the bus unanimously asked him to leave. He argued that he had paid the credits to buy a ticket, so surely he had the right to a seat, but a gray-haired old man took out two cash coins—rarely seen these days—and tossed them at him. So in the end he was forced off the bus.

As the bus started up, someone stuck their head out the window to ask, "Wallfacer, what are you doing with that shovel?"

"I'm digging my own grave," Luo Ji said, to a burst of laughter from the bus.

No one knew that he was telling the truth.

The rain was still coming down. There wouldn't be any more cars now, but fortunately he wasn't too far from his destination. He shouldered his backpack and headed off. After walking for about half an hour, he turned off the highway and onto a path. It got much darker away from the road lamps, so he took a flashlight out of his bag to illuminate the ground under his feet. The path grew more difficult, and his sodden shoes squished on the ground. He slipped time and again into the mud, which covered his body, and he had to resort to using the shovel from his bag as a walking stick. All he could see ahead of him was fog and rain, but he knew that he was walking in the right general direction.

After walking another hour through the rainy night, he reached the cemetery. Half of it was buried beneath the sand, while the half on slightly higher ground was still exposed. He used the flashlight to search the rows of headstones, ignoring the imposing monuments and only looking at the inscriptions on the smaller stones. Rainwater on the stones reflected the light like flashing eyes. He noticed that all of the headstones had been erected in the late twentieth and early twenty-first centuries. Those people were fortunate—in their last moments, they must have believed that the world they lived in would exist forever.

He didn't have much hope that he would find the headstone he was looking for, but, as it turned out, he found it quickly. The odd thing was, despite the passage of two centuries, he recognized it without even looking at the inscription. Maybe it was the wash of the rain, but the headstone showed no traces of time. The inscription, GRAVE OF YANG DONG, seemed like it had been cut yesterday. Ye Wenjie's grave sat beside her daughter's, the two tombstones identical apart from the inscription. Ye Wenjie's bore only her name and the dates of her birth and death, reminding him of the small tablet at the ruins of Red Coast Base, a memorial for the forgotten. The two headstones stood silently in the night rain, as if they'd been waiting for Luo Ji's arrival.

He felt tired, so he sat down next to Ye Wenjie's grave, but he soon began to shiver from the rain's chill. Grasping the shovel, he stood up and, next to the graves of mother and daughter, began digging his own.

At first, digging into the wet ground required little effort, but as he got farther down, the earth turned hard and was littered with stones, which made him feel like he was digging into the mountain itself. He at once felt both the power and the powerlessness of time: Maybe only a thin layer of sand had been deposited over the course of two centuries, but the long geologic age when humans were not present had produced the mountain that now housed these graves. He dug with great effort, resting frequently, and the night slipped away unnoticed.

Sometime after midnight, the rain stopped, and then the clouds parted to reveal some of the starry sky. These were the brightest stars that Luo Ji had seen since arriving in this age. On that evening 210 years ago, he and Ye Wenjie had stood facing the same stars.

Now he saw only the stars and the headstones, the two greatest symbols of eternity.

Finally, he ran out of stamina and couldn't dig any more. Looking at the pit he had dug, he saw that it was a little shallow for a grave, but it would have to do. Doing this was nothing more than a reminder to others that he wished to be buried on this spot, anyway. His most likely resting place would be the crematorium, where he would be burnt to ashes and then discarded in some unknown place. But it didn't really matter. It was highly likely that shortly after his death, his remains would join the world in an even grander fire and be reduced to individual atoms.

Resting against Ye Wenjie's headstone, he quickly dropped off to sleep. Perhaps it was because of the cold, but he once again dreamed of the snowy field. On it he saw Zhuang Yan holding Xia Xia, her scarf like a flame. She and the child were calling soundlessly to him. He shouted back desperately for them to leave this place because the droplet would strike right here, but his vocal cords produced no sound. It was like the entire world had

gone mute, and everything stayed absolutely silent. But Zhuang Yan seemed to understand what he meant and walked far across the snowy field holding the child, leaving a string of footprints in the snow like a faint ink mark on a traditional painting. The snow was blank, and the ink mark was all that revealed the land, revealed the existence of the world. The impending destruction was all-encompassing, but it was a destruction that had nothing to do with the droplet. . . .

Once more, Luo Ji's heart tore painfully and his hands clutched at the air in vain, but in the blankness of the snowy field, there was only Zhuang Yan's distant form, now a small black dot. He looked about him, hoping to find anything else that was real in the blank world. As it turned out, he found it: two black tombstones standing side by side on the snowy ground. At first they were eye-catching in the snow, but then their surface began to change. They turned to mirrors that recalled the finish of the droplet, and their inscriptions disappeared. He bent down toward one of them, wanting to look at himself in the mirror, but what he saw in the mirror wasn't a reflection. The snowy field in the mirror did not have the figure of Zhuang Yan, just a line of faint footprints in the snow. He whipped his head around and saw that the snowy field outside the mirror was just a blank expanse—the footprints had disappeared. When he turned back to the mirrors, they reflected the blank world and were practically invisible themselves. But his hand could still feel their cold, smooth surface. . . .

He awoke when it was just daybreak. The graveyard was clearer in the first light of dawn, and from his prone vantage point, the surrounding headstones made him feel like he was in a prehistoric Stonehenge. He had a high fever, and his body's violent trembling sent his teeth chattering. His body seemed like a wick that had burnt dry and was consuming itself. He knew that the time had come.

Leaning against Ye Wenjie's headstone, he tried to stand up, but then a small, moving black dot caught his attention. Ants ought to be fairly rare during this season, but it was indeed an ant crawling on the stone. Like its fellow ant two centuries before, it was

538

attracted by the inscription and devoted itself to exploring the mysterious crisscrossing trenches. Luo Ji's heart experienced a last spasm of pain as he watched it, this time for all life on Earth.

"If I've done anything wrong, I'm sorry," he said to the ant.

He stood up with difficulty, trembling weakly. He had to support himself on the headstone to be able to stand. Reaching out a hand, he straightened his soaked, mud-covered clothing and wild hair, then groped in his jacket pocket for a metal tube: a fully charged pistol.

Then, facing the dawn in the east, he began a final showdown between the civilization of Earth and the civilization of Trisolaris.

"I am speaking to Trisolaris," Luo Ji said. His voice wasn't loud. He thought about repeating himself, but he knew that they could hear him.

Nothing changed. The headstones stood quietly in the stillness of the dawn. Puddles on the ground reflected the brightening sky like countless mirrors, giving the illusion that the Earth was a mirrored sphere with the ground and the world just a thin layer on top. The rain's erosion had exposed small pieces of the sphere's smooth surface.

It was a world that had not awakened yet, and didn't know that it was now a chip placed on a cosmic gambling table.

Luo Ji raised his left hand, revealing an object on his wrist the size of a watch. "This is a vital signs monitor linked through a transmitter to a cradle system. You remember Wallfacer Rey Diaz from two centuries ago, so you certainly know about cradle systems. The signal sent from this monitor travels the links of the cradle system to the Snow Project's 3,614 bombs deployed in solar orbit. The signal is sent once every second to maintain the bombs in a non-triggered state. If I die, the system's maintenance signal will vanish and all of the bombs will detonate, turning the oil film surrounding the bombs into 3,614 interstellar dust clouds ringing the sun. From a distance, the sun's visible light and other

high-frequency bands will appear to flicker through the dust cloud coverage. The position of every bomb has been precisely arranged in solar orbit so that this flickering will generate a signal transmitting three simple images of the sort I sent out two centuries ago: each image an arrangement of thirty points, with one labeled, for composition into a three-dimensional coordinate diagram. But, unlike last time, the position will contain the transmission of Trisolaris relative to its surrounding twenty-nine stars. The sun will be a galactic lighthouse casting that spell, in the process, of course, also exposing the position of the sun and Earth. To receive the entire transmission at any single point in the galaxy will take more than a year, but there ought to be more than a few civilizations that have the technology to observe the sun from multiple vantage points. If that's the case, they may only need a few days, or even a few hours, to obtain all the information they need."

As daylight brightened, the stars went out one by one like the gradual shutting of innumerable eyes, even as the morning sky slowly opened in the east like a single giant eye. The ant continued its climb, threading the maze of Ye Wenjie's name on her gravestone. Its species had been living on the Earth a hundred million years before the emergence of this gambler who now leaned on the stone. Even though it had no care for what was now happening, it held a stake in the world.

Luo Ji left the gravestones and stood beside the pit he had dug for himself. He placed the tip of the pistol to his heart and said, "Now, I'm going to stop the beating of my heart. By doing so, I will be committing the greatest crime in the history of our two worlds. I express my deepest apologies to our two civilizations for the crime that I commit, but I have no regrets, because this is the only option. I know the sophons are nearby, but you have ignored humanity's call. Silence is the greatest form of contempt, and we have put up with this contempt for two centuries. Now, if you wish, you can continue to remain silent. I will give you thirty seconds."

He marked time according to his pulse, counting two beats to a second since his heart was beating so rapidly, but in his

heightened anxiety he started off wrong and had to begin again. So he wasn't certain how much time had passed by the time the sophons appeared. Possibly less than ten seconds in objective time, but subjectively, it took a lifetime. He saw the world before his eyes split into four parts: one part made up of the real world that surrounded him; the other three, deformed images in three spheres that appeared suddenly overhead, whose mirror surfaces were exactly like the gravestones he had seen in his last dream. He didn't know which of the sophons' dimensional unfoldings this was, but the three spheres were big enough to cover half the sky above him, blocking out the brightening light in the east. In the spheres' reflection of the western sky, he could see a few lingering stars, and the bottom of the spheres reflected a deformed graveyard and his own image. What he most wanted to know was why there were three of them. His first thought was that they symbolized Trisolaris, just like the work of art that Ye Wenjie had seen at the final ETO gathering. But looking at what the spheres reflected—an uncommonly clear, albeit deformed, picture of reality—he had the sense that they were entrances to three parallel worlds, implying three possible choices.

But what he saw next negated this notion, because the three spheres flashed the same word:

Stop!

"Can I discuss terms?" Luo Ji asked, looking up at the three spheres.

First put down the gun, and then we can discuss terms.

The words displayed simultaneously on the spheres in letters that glowed a striking red. He saw no deformation in the line of text. It was straight, and seemed as if it was both on the surface of and within the spheres. He reminded himself that he was looking at a projection of higher-dimensional space into a three-dimensional world.

541

"This is not a negotiation. These are my demands, if I am to go on living. All I wish to know is whether or not you accept."

State your demands.

"Have the droplet, or rather the probe, cease its transmissions toward the sun."

It has been done as you ask.

The spheres' answer was faster than he anticipated. He had no way to verify it at the moment, but he sensed subtle changes in his surroundings, as if a background noise whose continued existence meant it had escaped notice, had disappeared. Of course, this could be an illusion, since humans don't sense electromagnetic radiation.

"Have the nine droplets en route to the Solar System change course immediately and fly away."

This time the answer from the three spheres was delayed by a few seconds.

It has been done as you ask.

"Please give humanity the means to verify this."

The nine probes will emit visible light. Your Ringier-Fitzroy Telescope will be able to detect them.

This was still impossible for him to verify, but he believed Trisolaris.

"The final condition: the Trisolaran Fleet may not cross the Oort Cloud."

The fleet is now under propulsion power for maximum deceleration. It is impossible for it to bring its speed relative to the sun to zero before reaching the Oort Cloud.

"Then, like the droplet group, set a course away from the Solar System."

Changing course in any direction is death. This will cause the fleet to fly by the Solar System and into the desolation of space. The fleet's life-support system will not last long enough to return to Trisolaris or search for another viable star system.

"Death isn't a certainty. Perhaps human or Trisolaran ships can catch up and rescue them."

This will require a command from the High Consul.

"If changing course is a lengthy process, get started on it now. That will give me and all the other lives a chance to live on." The period of silence lasted for three minutes. Then:

The fleet will begin to change course in ten Earth minutes. Two years from now, human space observation systems will be able to observe the change of heading.

"Good," Luo Ji said, as he removed the pistol from his chest. With his other hand he leaned on the gravestone, trying not to fall. "Were you already aware that the universe is a dark forest?"

Yes. We knew about it long ago. What's strange is that you only realized it so late. . . . Your state of health concerns us. This won't unintentionally interrupt the cradle system's maintenance signal, will it?

"No. This device is far more advanced than Rey Diaz's. So long as I am alive, the signal won't be interrupted."

You really should sit down. That will help with your situation.

"Thank you," Luo Ji said, and he sat down against the headstone. "Don't worry. I'm not going to die."

We are in contact with the highest levels of the two Internationals. Do you need us to call you an ambulance?

He smiled and shook his head. "No. I'm not a savior. I just want to leave here like an ordinary person and go home. I'll rest for a bit and then be on my way."

Two of the three spheres disappeared. The text on the one that remained, which no longer glowed, now seemed dim and dreary.

In the end, strategy was where we failed.

Luo Ji nodded. "Blocking the sun with dust clouds to send an interstellar message wasn't my invention. Twentieth-century astronomers had already proposed the idea. And you actually had multiple chances to see through me. During the duration of the Snow Project, for example, I was always concerned with the precise placement of the bombs in solar orbit."

You spent two whole months in the control room remotely controlling the ion engines to make fine adjustments to their positioning. We didn't care about that at the time because we thought you were just using the meaningless task as a way to escape reality. We never imagined what the distance between the bombs really meant.

"Another chance was when I consulted a group of physicists with questions about sophon unfoldings in space. If the ETO was still around, they would have already seen through me."

Yes. Abandoning them was a mistake.

"Also, I requested that the Snow Project build this peculiar cradle trigger system."

That did remind us of Rey Diaz, but we did not pursue those thoughts. Two centuries ago, Rey Diaz was not a threat to us, nor were the other two Wallfacers. We transferred our contempt for them onto you.

"Your contempt for them was unfair. Those three Wallfacers were great strategists. They saw clearly the inevitable fact of humanity's defeat in the Doomsday Battle."

Perhaps we can begin negotiations.

"That's not my affair," Luo Ji said, and let out a long sigh. He felt as relaxed and as comfortable as if he had just been born.

Yes, you've fulfilled the Wallfacer mission. But you've got to have some suggestions.

"Humanity's negotiators will no doubt first propose that you help us build a better signal transmission system, so that we'll have the ability to transmit a spell into space at any time. Even though the droplet has lifted its seal on the sun, the present system is too primitive."

We can help build a neutrino transmission system.

"They may, as far as I understand things, be more inclined toward gravitational waves. After the sophons arrived, this was the area in which human physics progressed furthest. Of course, they'll need a system whose principles they can understand."

The antennas for gravitational waves are immense.

"That's between you and them. It's strange. Right now I don't feel like a member of the human race. My greatest desire is to be rid of it all as soon as possible."

Next they'll ask us to lift the sophon block and teach science and technology across the board.

"This is important to you as well. The technology of Trisolaris has developed at a constant speed, and two centuries later, you still haven't sent a faster followup fleet. In order to rescue the diverted Trisolaran Fleet, you have to rely on the future of humanity."

I must go. Are you really able to go back on your own? The survival of two civilizations hinges on your life.

"No problem. I feel much better now. After I go back, I'll immediately hand over the cradle system, and then I'll have no more to do with all of this. Finally, I'd like to say thank you."

Why?

"Because you let me live. Or, if you think about it a different way: You let us both live."

The sphere vanished, returning to its eleven-dimensional microscopic state. A corner of the sun was peeking out in the east, casting gold across a world that had survived destruction.

Luo Ji slowly stood up. After taking a last look at the gravestones of Ye Wenjie and Yang Dong, he stumbled slowly back the way he came.

The ant had reached the summit of the headstone and proudly waved its feelers at the rising sun. Out of all life on Earth, it was the only witness to what had just taken place.

FIVE YEARS LATER

Luo Ji and his family could see the gravitational-wave antenna in the distance, but it was still another half-hour drive away. Only when they arrived did they get a real sense of its enormous size. The antenna, a horizontal cylinder a kilometer and a half long and fifty meters in diameter, was entirely suspended about two meters off the ground. Its surface was mirror-smooth, half of it reflecting the sky and half the northern China plain. It reminded people of a few things: the giant pendulums of the *Three Body* world, the sophons' lower-dimensional unfoldings, and the droplet. The mirrored object reflected a Trisolaran concept that humanity was still trying to figure out. In the words of a well-known Trisolaran saying, "Hiding the self through a faithful mapping of the universe is the only path into eternity."

The antenna was surrounded by a big green meadow that formed a small oasis in the desert of northern China, but this meadow had not been specially planted. Once the gravitational-wave system had been completed, it began sending continuous, unmodulated emissions that were indistinguishable from the gravitational waves emitted from supernovae, neutron stars, or black holes. The density of the gravitational beam had a peculiar effect in the atmosphere: Water vapor collected above it, so that it frequently rained in the antenna's vicinity. At times, the rain only fell within a radius of three or four kilometers, and a small, circular raincloud would hang in the air above the antenna like a giant flying saucer, leaving the brilliant sunshine in the surrounding area visible through the

rain. And so this area grew lush with wild vegetation. But today, Luo Ji and his family did not witness that spectacle. Instead, they saw white clouds gather over the antenna, only to dissipate when the wind blew them away from the beam. Yet new clouds were continually forming, making the round patch of sky seem like a time wormhole to some other cloud universe. Xia Xia said that it looked like the white hair of a giant old man.

As the child ran about on the grass, Luo Ji and Zhuang Yan followed behind, until they reached the antenna. The first two gravitational-wave systems were built in Europe and North America, and employed magnetic levitation that suspended them a few centimeters from the base. But this antenna used antigravity, and could have been raised up into space if so desired. The three of them stood on the grass beneath the antenna, looking up at the huge cylinder curling up over their heads like the sky. Its large radius gave the bottom a low curvature, which meant there was no distortion in the reflected image. The setting sun now shone beneath the antenna, and, in the reflection, Luo Ji could see Zhuang Yan's long hair and white dress fluttering in the golden sunlight like an angel looking down from the sky.

He lifted up the child and she touched the antenna's smooth surface, pressing hard in one direction. "Can I make it turn?"

"If you push long enough, you can," Zhuang Yan said—then, looking at Luo Ji with a smile, asked, "Right?"

He nodded at her. "With enough time, she could move the Earth."

As had occurred so many times before, their eyes met and intertwined, a continuation of that gaze they had held in front of the *Mona Lisa*'s smile two centuries before. They had discovered that the language of the eyes that Zhuang Yan had dreamed up was now a reality, or maybe loving humans had always possessed this language. When they looked at each other, a richness of meaning poured from their eyes just as the clouds poured from the cloud well created by the gravitational beam, endless and unceasing. But it wasn't a language of this world. It constructed a world that gave it meaning, and only in that rosy world did the words of the language

548

find their corresponding referents. Everyone in that world was god; all had the ability to instantaneously count and remember every grain of sand in the desert; all were able to string together stars into a crystal necklace to hang around a lover's neck. . . .

Is this love?

The lines were displayed on a lower-dimensional unfolding of a sophon that appeared abruptly beside them. The mirrored sphere seemed like a droplet that had fallen off of some melted area on the cylinder above them. Luo Ji knew few Trisolarans and didn't know who it was who was speaking to them, or whether this one was on Trisolaris or on the fleet that was growing increasingly distant from the Solar System.

"Probably." Luo Ji nodded with a smile.

Dr. Luo, I have come in protest.

"Why?"

Because in last night's speech, you said that humanity had been so late to realize the dark forest nature of the universe not because your immature state of cultural evolution caused a lack of awareness of the universe, but because humanity has love.

"Isn't that correct?"

It's correct, though the word "love" is a little vague in the context of scientific discourse. But what you said next was incorrect. You said that humanity is probably the only species in the universe to have love, and it's this notion that supported you through the most difficult period of your Wallfacer mission.

"That's only an expression, of course. Just a nonrigorous . . . analogy."

I know that at least Trisolaris has love. But because it was not conducive to the civilization's overall survival, it was suppressed when it had only just germinated. Yet the seed possesses a stubborn vitality, and will still grow in certain individuals.

"May I ask who you are?"

We've never met. I was the operator who transmitted the warning to Earth two and a half centuries ago.

"My god, and you're still alive?" Zhuang Yan exclaimed.

I won't be for much longer. I've been in a dehydrated state, but over the long years, even a dehydrated body will age. However, I have seen the future I hoped to see, and for this I am happy.

"Please accept our respects," Luo Ji said.

I only wish to discuss with you one possibility: Perhaps seeds of love are present in other places in the universe. We ought to encourage them to sprout and grow.

"That's a goal worth taking risks for."

Yes, we can take risks.

"I have a dream that one day brilliant sunlight will illuminate the dark forest."

The sun was setting. Now only its tip was exposed beyond the distant mountains, as if the mountaintop was inset with a dazzling gemstone. Like the grass, the child running in the distance was bathed in the golden sunset.

The sun will set soon. Isn't your child afraid?

"Of course she's not afraid. She knows that the sun will rise again tomorrow."

DEATH'S END

CIXIN 刘慈欣 LIU

TRANSLATED BY KEN LIU

May 1453, C.E.
The Death of the Magician

Pausing to collect himself, Constantine XI pushed away the pile of city-defense maps in front of him, pulled his purple robe tighter, and waited.

His sense of time was very accurate: The tremor came the moment he expected it, a powerful, violent quake that seemed to originate from deep within the earth. The vibrating silver candelabra hummed, and a wisp of dust that had sat on top of the Great Palace for perhaps a thousand years fell down and drifted into the candle flames, where the motes exploded in tiny sparks.

Every three hours—the time it took the Ottomans to reload one of the monstrous bombards designed by the engineer Orban—twelve-hundred-pound stone balls battered the walls of Constantinople. These were the world's strongest walls: first built by Theodosius II during the fifth century, they had been continually reinforced and expanded, and were the main reason that the Byzantine court had survived so many powerful enemies.

But the giant stone balls now gouged openings into the walls with each strike, like the bite of an invisible giant. The emperor could imagine the scene: While the debris from the explosion filled the air, countless soldiers and citizens rushed onto the fresh wound in the walls like a swarm of brave ants under a sky full of dust.

They filled in the break with whatever was at hand: bits and pieces taken from other buildings in the city, flaxen-cloth bags of earth, expensive Arabic carpets.... He could even imagine the cloud of dust, steeped in the light of the setting sun, drifting slowly toward Constantinople like a golden shroud.

During the five weeks the city had been under siege, these tremors had come seven times a day, spaced as regularly as the strokes of some colossal clock. This was the time and rhythm of another world, the time of heathens. Compared to these tremors, the ringing of the double-headed eagle copper clock in the corner that represented the time of Christendom seemed feeble.

The tremors subsided. After a while and with an effort, Emperor Constantine pulled his thoughts back to the reality before him. He gestured to let the guard know that he was ready for his visitor.

Phrantzes, one of the emperor's most-trusted ministers, came in with a slender, frail figure trailing close behind.

"This is Helena." Phrantzes stepped aside, revealing the woman.

The emperor looked at her. The noblewomen of Constantinople tended to favor clothes bedecked with elaborate decorative elements, while the commoners wore plain, shapeless white garments that draped to the ankles. But this Helena seemed a combination of both. Instead of a tunic embroidered with gold thread, she wore a commoner's white dress, but over it she draped a luxurious cloak; however, instead of the purple and red reserved for the nobility, the cloak was dyed yellow. Her face was enchanting and sensual, bringing to mind a flower that would rather rot in adoration than fade in solitude.

A prostitute, probably one who did rather well for herself.

Her body trembled. She kept her eyes lowered, but the emperor noticed that they held a feverish glow, hinting at an excitement and zeal rare for her class.

"You claim the powers of magic?" the emperor asked.

He wanted to conclude this audience as quickly as possible. Phrantzes was usually meticulous. Of the approximately eight

thousand soldiers defending Constantinople now, only a small number came from the standing army, and about two thousand were Genoese mercenaries. Phrantzes had been responsible for recruiting the rest, a few at a time, from the city's inhabitants. Though the emperor wasn't particularly interested in his latest idea, the capable minister's standing demanded that he at least be given a chance.

"Yes, I can kill the sultan." Helena's quiet voice quivered like silk strands in a breeze.

THE THREE-BODY PROBLEM

CIXIN LIU is China's leading Science Fiction writer.
He has won the China Galaxy Science Fiction Award
nine times, the Nebula (Xingyun) award twice, and
was the first translated author to win the Hugo award.
Before becoming a writer, he was a computer engineer
in a power plant in Yangquan.

Translator KEN LIU is the winner of the Nebula,
Hugo, Locus, World Fantasy, Sidewise, and Science
Fiction & Fantasy Translation Awards. He is the
author of the epic series The Dandelion Dynasty, as
well as short story collections *The Paper Menagerie*
and *The Hidden Girl*.

BY CIXIN LIU

THE THREE-BODY TRILOGY

The Three-Body Problem

The Dark Forest

Death's End

Ball Lightning

The Supernova Era

Of Ants and Dinosaurs

SHORT STORY COLLECTIONS

The Wandering Earth

Hold Up the Sky

THE THREE-BODY PROBLEM

CIXIN 刘慈欣 LIU

TRANSLATED BY KEN LIU

An Ad Astra Book

Originally published as 三体 in 2008 by Chongqing Publishing Group in Chongqing, China. First serialized in *Science Fiction World* (科幻世界) in 2006. First published in the United States of America in 2014 by Tom Doherty Associates LLC, a Tor book

First published in the UK in 2015 by Head of Zeus Ltd
This paperback edition published in 2016 by Head of Zeus Ltd

Translation by Ken Liu

46

A CIP catalogue record for this book is available from the British Library.

ISBN (PB): 9781784971571
ISBN (E): 9781784971540

Typeset by Adrian McLaughlin

Printed and bound in Great Britain by
CPI Group (UK) Ltd, Croydon CR0 4YY

Head of Zeus Ltd
5–8 Hardwick Street
London EC1R 4RG
WWW.HEADOFZEUS.COM

LIST OF CHARACTERS

Chinese names are written with surname first.

The Ye Family

Ye Zhetai	Physicist, professor at Tsinghua University
Shao Lin	Physicist, Ye Zhetai's wife
Ye Wenjie	Astrophysicist, daughter of Ye Zhetai
Ye Wenxue	Ye Wenjie's sister, a Red Guard

Red Coast Base

Lei Zhicheng	Political commissar at Red Coast Base
Yang Weining	Chief engineer at Red Coast Base, once a student of Ye Zhetai

The Present

Yang Dong	String theorist and daughter of Ye Wenjie and Yang Weining
Ding Yi	Theoretical physicist, Yang Dong's boyfriend
Wang Miao	Nanomaterials researcher
Shi Qiang	Police detective, nicknamed Da Shi
Chang Weisi	Major-general of the People's Liberation Army

Shen Yufei	Japanese physicist and member of the Frontiers of Science
Wei Cheng	Math prodigy and recluse, Shen Yufei's husband
Pan Han	Biologist, friend/acquaintance of Shen Yufei and Wei Cheng, and member of the Frontiers of Science
Sha Ruishan	Astronomer, one of Ye Wenjie's students
Mike Evans	Scion of an oil magnate
Colonel Stanton	U.S. Marine Corps, commander of Operation Guzheng

PART I

SILENT SPRING

1

THE MADNESS YEARS

China, 1967

The Red Union had been attacking the headquarters of the April Twenty-eighth Brigade for two days. Their red flags fluttered restlessly around the brigade building like flames yearning for firewood.

The Red Union commander was anxious, though not because of the defenders he faced. The more than two hundred Red Guards of the April Twenty-eighth Brigade were mere greenhorns compared with the veteran Red Guards of the Red Union, which was formed at the start of the Great Proletarian Cultural Revolution in early 1966. The Red Union had been tempered by the tumultuous experience of revolutionary tours around the country and seeing Chairman Mao in the great rallies in Tiananmen Square.

But the commander *was* afraid of the dozen or so iron stoves inside the building, filled with explosives and connected to each other by electric detonators. He couldn't see them, but he could feel their presence like iron sensing the pull of a nearby magnet. If a defender flipped the switch, revolutionaries and counter-revolutionaries alike would all die in one giant ball of fire.

And the young Red Guards of the April Twenty-eighth Brigade were indeed capable of such madness. Compared with the weathered men and women of the first generation of Red Guards, the new rebels were a pack of wolves on hot coals, crazier than crazy.

The slender figure of a beautiful young girl emerged at the top of the building, waving the giant red banner of the April Twenty-eighth Brigade. Her appearance was greeted immediately by a cacophony of gunshots. The weapons attacking her were a diverse mix: antiques such as American carbines, Czech-style machine guns, Japanese Type-38 rifles; newer weapons such as standard-issue People's Liberation Army rifles and submachine guns, stolen from the PLA after the publication of the "August Editorial"[1]; and even a few Chinese *dadao* swords and spears. Together, they formed a condensed version of modern history.

Numerous members of the April Twenty-eighth Brigade had engaged in similar displays before. They'd stand on top of the building, wave a flag, shout slogans through megaphones, and scatter flyers at the attackers below. Every time, the courageous man or woman had been able to retreat safely from the hailstorm of bullets and earn glory for their valor.

The new girl clearly thought she'd be just as lucky. She waved the battle banner as though brandishing her burning youth, trusting that the enemy would be burnt to ashes in the revolutionary flames, imagining that an ideal world would

1 *Translator's Note:* This refers to the August 1967 editorial in *Red Flag* magazine (an important source of propaganda during the Cultural Revolution), which advocated for "pulling out the handful [of counter-revolutionaries] within the army." Many read the editorial as tacitly encouraging Red Guards to attack military armories and seize weapons from the PLA, further inflaming the local civil wars waged by Red Guard factions.

be born tomorrow from the ardor and zeal coursing through her blood. . . . She was intoxicated by her brilliant, crimson dream until a bullet pierced her chest.

Her fifteen-year-old body was so soft that the bullet hardly slowed down as it passed through it and whistled in the air behind her. The young Red Guard tumbled down along with her flag, her light form descending even more slowly than the piece of red fabric, like a little bird unwilling to leave the sky.

The Red Union warriors shouted in joy. A few rushed to the foot of the building, tore away the battle banner of the April Twenty-eighth Brigade, and seized the slender, lifeless body. They raised their trophy overhead and flaunted it for a while before tossing it toward the top of the metal gate of the compound.

Most of the gate's metal bars, capped with sharp tips, had been pulled down at the beginning of the factional civil wars to be used as spears, but two still remained. As their sharp tips caught the girl, life seemed to return momentarily to her body.

The Red Guards backed up some distance and began to use the impaled body for target practice. For her, the dense storm of bullets was now no different from a gentle rain, as she could no longer feel anything. From time to time, her vinelike arms jerked across her body softly, as though she were flicking off drops of rain.

And then half of her young head was blown away, and only a single, beautiful eye remained to stare at the blue sky of 1967. There was no pain in that gaze, only solidified devotion and yearning.

And yet, compared to some others, she was fortunate. At least she died in the throes of passionately sacrificing herself

for an ideal.

———————

Battles like this one raged across Beijing like a multitude of CPUs working in parallel, their combined output, the Cultural Revolution. A flood of madness drowned the city and seeped into every nook and cranny.

At the edge of the city, on the exercise grounds of Tsinghua University, a mass "struggle session" attended by thousands had been going on for nearly two hours. This was a public rally intended to humiliate and break down the enemies of the revolution through verbal and physical abuse until they confessed to their crimes before the crowd.

As the revolutionaries had splintered into numerous factions, opposing forces everywhere engaged in complex maneuvers and contests. Within the university, intense conflicts erupted between the Red Guards, the Cultural Revolution Working Group, the Workers' Propaganda Team, and the Military Propaganda Team. And each faction divided into new rebel groups from time to time, each based on different backgrounds and agendas, leading to even more ruthless fighting.

But for *this* mass struggle session, the victims were the reactionary bourgeois academic authorities. These were the enemies of every faction, and they had no choice but to endure cruel attacks from every side.

Compared to other "Monsters and Demons,"[2] reactionary academic authorities were special: During the earliest struggle sessions, they had been both arrogant and stubborn.

2 *Translator's Note:* Originally a term from Buddhism, "Monsters and Demons" was used during the Cultural Revolution to refer to all the enemies of the revolution.

That was also the stage in which they had died in the largest numbers. Over a period of forty days, in Beijing alone, more than seventeen hundred victims of struggle sessions were beaten to death. Many others picked an easier path to avoid the madness: Lao She, Wu Han, Jian Bozan, Fu Lei, Zhao Jiuzhang, Yi Qun, Wen Jie, Hai Mo, and other once-respected intellectuals had all chosen to end their lives.[3]

Those who survived that initial period gradually became numb as the ruthless struggle sessions continued. The protective mental shell helped them avoid total breakdown. They often seemed to be half asleep during the sessions and would only startle awake when someone screamed in their faces to make them mechanically recite their confessions, already repeated countless times.

Then, some of them entered a third stage. The constant, unceasing struggle sessions injected vivid political images into their consciousness like mercury, until their minds, erected upon knowledge and rationality, collapsed under the assault. They began to really believe that they were guilty, to see how they had harmed the great cause of the revolution. They cried, and their repentance was far deeper and more sincere than that of those Monsters and Demons who were not intellectuals.

For the Red Guards, heaping abuse upon victims in those two latter mental stages was utterly boring. Only those Monsters and Demons who were still in the initial stage could give their overstimulated brains the thrill they craved, like the red cape of the matador. But such desirable victims

3 *Translator's Note:* These were some of the most famous intellectuals who committed suicide during the Cultural Revolution. Lao She: writer; Wu Han: historian; Jian Bozan: historian; Fu Lei: translator and critic; Zhao Jiuzhang: meteorologist and geophysicist; Yi Qun: writer; Wen Jie: poet; Hai Mo: screenwriter and novelist.

had grown scarce. In Tsinghua there was probably only one left. Because he was so rare, he was reserved for the very end of the struggle session.

Ye Zhetai had survived the Cultural Revolution so far, but he remained in the first mental stage. He refused to repent, to kill himself, or to become numb. When this physics professor walked onto the stage in front of the crowd, his expression clearly said: *Let the cross I bear be even heavier.*

The Red Guards did indeed have him carry a burden, but it wasn't a cross. Other victims wore tall hats made from bamboo frames, but his was welded from thick steel bars. And the plaque he wore around his neck wasn't wooden, like the others, but an iron door taken from a laboratory oven. His name was written on the door in striking black characters, and two red diagonals were drawn across them in a large X.

Twice the number of Red Guards used for other victims escorted Ye onto the stage: two men and four women. The two young men strode with confidence and purpose, the very image of mature Bolshevik youths. They were both fourth-year students[4] majoring in theoretical physics, and Ye was their professor. The women, really girls, were much younger, second-year students from the junior high school attached to the university.[5] Dressed in military uniforms and equipped

4 *Translator's Note:* Chinese colleges (and Tsinghua in particular) have a complicated history of shifting between four-year, five-year, and three-year systems up to the time of the Cultural Revolution. I've therefore avoided using American terms such as "freshman," "sophomore," "junior," and "senior" to translate the classes of these students.

5 *Translator's Note:* In the Chinese education system, six years in primary

school are typically followed by three years in junior high school and three years in high school. During the Cultural Revolution, this twelve-year system was shortened to a nine- or ten-year system, depending on the province or municipality. In this case, the girl Red Guards are fourteen.

with bandoliers, they exuded youthful vigor and surrounded Ye Zhetai like four green flames.

His appearance excited the crowd. The shouting of slogans, which had slackened a bit, now picked up with renewed force and drowned out everything else like a resurgent tide.

After waiting patiently for the noise to subside, one of the male Red Guards turned to the victim. "Ye Zhetai, you are an expert in mechanics. You should see how strong the great unified force you're resisting is. To remain so stubborn will lead only to your death! Today, we will continue the agenda from the last time. There's no need to waste words. Answer the following question without your typical deceit: Between the years of 1962 and 1965, did you not decide on your own to add relativity to the intro physics course?"

"Relativity is part of the fundamental theories of physics," Ye answered. "How can a basic survey course not teach it?"

"You lie!" a female Red Guard by his side shouted. "Einstein is a reactionary academic authority. He would serve any master who dangled money in front of him. He even went to the American Imperialists and helped them build the atom bomb! To develop a revolutionary science, we must overthrow the black banner of capitalism represented by the theory of relativity!"

Ye remained silent. Enduring the pain brought by the heavy iron hat and the iron plaque hanging from his neck, he had no energy to answer questions that were not worth answering. Behind him, one of his students also frowned. The girl who had spoken was the most intelligent of the four female Red Guards, and she was clearly prepared, as she had been seen memorizing the struggle session script before coming onstage.

But against someone like Ye Zhetai, a few slogans like that were insufficient. The Red Guards decided to bring out the new weapon they had prepared against their teacher. One of them waved to someone offstage. Ye's wife, physics professor Shao Lin, stood up from the crowd's front row. She walked onto the stage dressed in an ill-fitting green outfit, clearly intended to imitate the military uniform of the Red Guards. Those who knew her remembered that she had often taught class in an elegant *qipao,* and her current appearance felt forced and awkward.

"Ye Zhetai!" She was clearly unused to such theater, and though she tried to make her voice louder, the effort magnified the tremors in it. "You didn't think I would stand up and expose you, criticize you? Yes, in the past, I was fooled by you. You covered my eyes with your reactionary view of the world and science! But now I am awake and alert. With the help of the revolutionary youths, I want to stand on the side of the revolution, the side of the people!"

She turned to face the crowd. "Comrades, revolutionary youths, revolutionary faculty and staff, we must clearly understand the reactionary nature of Einstein's theory of relativity. This is most apparent in general relativity: Its static model of the universe negates the dynamic nature of matter. It is anti-dialectical! It treats the universe as limited, which is absolutely a form of reactionary idealism. . . ."

As he listened to his wife's lecture, Ye allowed himself a wry smile. *Lin, I fooled you? Indeed, in my heart you've always been a mystery. One time, I praised your genius to your father—he's lucky to have died early and escaped this catastrophe—and he shook his head, telling me that he did not think you would ever achieve much academically. What he said next turned out to be so important to the second half*

10

of my life: "Lin Lin is too smart. To work in fundamental theory, one must be stupid."

In later years, I began to understand his words more and more. Lin, you truly are too smart. Even a few years ago, you could feel the political winds shifting in academia and prepared yourself. For example, when you taught, you changed the names of many physical laws and constants: Ohm's law you called resistance law, Maxwell's equations you called electromagnetic equations, Planck's constant you called the quantum constant. . . . You explained to your students that all scientific accomplishments resulted from the wisdom of the working masses, and those capitalist academic authorities only stole these fruits and put their names on them.

But even so, you couldn't be accepted by the revolutionary mainstream. Look at you now: You're not allowed to wear the red armband of the "revolutionary faculty and staff"; you had to come up here empty-handed, without the status to carry a Little Red Book. . . . You can't overcome the fault of being born to a prominent family in pre-revolutionary China and of having such famous scholars as parents.

But you actually have more to confess about Einstein than I do. In the winter of 1922, Einstein visited Shanghai. Because your father spoke fluent German, he was asked to accompany Einstein on his tour. You told me many times that your father went into physics because of Einstein's encouragement, and you chose physics because of your father's influence. So, in a way, Einstein can be said to have indirectly been your teacher. And you once felt so proud and lucky to have such a connection.

Later, I found out that your father had told you a white lie. He and Einstein had only one very brief conversation. The

morning of November 13, 1922, he accompanied Einstein on a walk along Nanjing Road. Others who went on the walk included Yu Youren, president of Shanghai University, and Cao Gubing, general manager of the newspaper Ta Kung Pao. *When they passed a maintenance site in the road bed, Einstein stopped next to a worker who was smashing stones and silently observed this boy with torn clothes and dirty face and hands. He asked your father how much the boy earned each day. After asking the boy, he told Einstein: five cents.*

This was the only time he spoke with the great scientist who changed the world. There was no discussion of physics, of relativity, only cold, harsh reality. According to your father, Einstein stood there for a long time after hearing the answer, watching the boy's mechanical movements, not even bothering to smoke his pipe as the embers went out. After your father recounted this memory to me, he sighed and said, "In China, any idea that dared to take flight would only crash back to the ground. The gravity of reality is too strong."

"Lower your head!" one of the male Red Guards shouted. This may actually have been a gesture of mercy from his former student. All victims being struggled against were supposed to lower their heads. If Ye did lower his head, the tall, heavy iron hat would fall off, and if he kept his head lowered, there would be no reason to put it back on him. But Ye refused and held his head high, supporting the heavy weight with his thin neck.

"Lower your head, you stubborn reactionary!" One of the girl Red Guards took off her belt and swung it at Ye. The copper belt buckle struck his forehead and left a clear impression that was quickly blurred by oozing blood. He

swayed unsteadily for a few moments, then stood straight and firm again.

One of the male Red Guards said, "When you taught quantum mechanics, you also mixed in many reactionary ideas." Then he nodded at Shao Lin, indicating that she should continue.

Shao was happy to oblige. She had to keep on talking, otherwise her fragile mind, already hanging on only by a thin thread, would collapse completely. "Ye Zhetai, you cannot deny this charge! You have often lectured students on the reactionary Copenhagen interpretation of quantum mechanics."

"It is, after all, the explanation recognized to be most in line with experimental results." His tone, so calm and collected, surprised and frightened Shao Lin.

"This explanation posits that external observation leads to the collapse of the quantum wave function. This is another expression of reactionary idealism, and it's indeed the most brazen expression."

"Should philosophy guide experiments, or should experiments guide philosophy?" Ye's sudden counterattack shocked those leading the struggle session. For a moment they did not know what to do.

"Of course it should be the correct philosophy of Marxism that guides scientific experiments!" one of the male Red Guards finally said.

"Then that's equivalent to saying that the correct philosophy falls out of the sky. This is against the idea that the truth emerges from experience. It's counter to the principles of how Marxism seeks to understand nature."

Shao Lin and the two college student Red Guards had no answer for this. Unlike the Red Guards who were still in junior high school, they couldn't completely ignore logic.

But the four junior high girls had their own revolutionary methods that they believed were invincible. The girl who had hit Ye before took out her belt and whipped Ye again. The other three girls also took off their belts to strike at Ye. With their companion displaying such revolutionary fervor, they had to display even more, or at least the same amount. The two male Red Guards didn't interfere. If they tried to intervene now, they would be suspected of being insufficiently revolutionary.

"You also taught the big bang theory. This is the most reactionary of all scientific theories." One of the male Red Guards spoke up, trying to change the subject.

"Maybe in the future this theory will be disproven. But two great cosmological discoveries of this century—Hubble's law, and observation of the cosmic microwave background– show that the big bang theory is currently the most plausible explanation for the origin of the universe."

"Lies!" Shao Lin shouted. Then she began a long lecture about the big bang theory, remembering to splice in insightful critiques of the theory's extremely reactionary nature. But the freshness of the theory attracted the most intelligent of the four girls, who couldn't help but ask, "Time began with the singularity? So what was there before the singularity?"

"Nothing," Ye said, the way he would answer a question from any curious young person. He turned to look at the girl kindly. With his injuries and the tall iron hat, the motion was very difficult.

"No . . . nothing? That's reactionary! Completely reactionary!" the frightened girl shouted. She turned to Shao Lin, who gladly came to her aid.

"The theory leaves open a place to be filled by God." Shao nodded at the girl.

The young Red Guard, confused by these new thoughts, finally found her footing. She raised her hand, still holding the belt, and pointed at Ye. "You: you're trying to say that God exists?"

"I don't know."

"What?"

"I'm saying I don't know. If by 'God' you mean some kind of superconsciousness outside the universe, I don't know if it exists or not. Science has given no evidence either way." Actually, in this nightmarish moment, Ye was leaning toward believing that God did not exist.

This extremely reactionary statement caused a commotion in the crowd. Led by one of the Red Guards on stage, another tide of slogan-shouting exploded.

"Down with reactionary academic authority Ye Zhetai!"

"Down with all reactionary academic authorities!"

"Down with all reactionary doctrines!"

Once the slogans died down, the girl shouted, "God does not exist. All religions are tools concocted by the ruling class to paralyze the spirit of the people!"

"That is a very one-sided view," Ye said calmly.

The young Red Guard, embarrassed and angry, reached the conclusion that, against this dangerous enemy, all talk was useless. She picked up her belt and rushed at Ye, and her three companions followed. Ye was tall, and the four fourteen-year-olds had to swing their belts upward to reach his head, still held high. After a few strikes, the tall iron hat, which had protected him a little, fell off. The continuing barrage of strikes by the metal buckles finally made him fall down.

The young Red Guards, encouraged by their success, became even more devoted to this glorious struggle. They were fighting for faith, for ideals. They were intoxicated

15

by the bright light cast on them by history, proud of their own bravery. . . .

Ye's two students had finally had enough. "The chairman instructed us to 'rely on eloquence rather than violence'!" They rushed over and pulled the four semicrazed girls off Ye.

But it was already too late. The physicist lay quietly on the ground, his eyes still open as blood oozed from his head. The frenzied crowd sank into silence. The only thing that moved was a thin stream of blood. Like a red snake, it slowly meandered across the stage, reached the edge, and dripped onto a chest below. The rhythmic sound made by the blood drops was like the steps of someone walking away.

A cackling laugh broke the silence. The sound came from Shao Lin, whose mind had finally broken. The laughter frightened the attendees, who began to leave the struggle session, first in trickles, and then in a flood. The exercise grounds soon emptied, leaving only one young woman below the stage.

She was Ye Wenjie, Ye Zhetai's daughter.

As the four girls were taking her father's life, she had tried to rush onto the stage. But two old university janitors held her down and whispered into her ear that she would lose her own life if she went. The mass struggle session had turned into a scene of madness, and her appearance would only incite more violence. She had screamed and screamed, but she had been drowned out by the frenzied waves of slogans and cheers.

When it was finally quiet again, she was no longer capable of making any sound. She stared at her father's lifeless body, and the thoughts she could not voice dissolved into her blood, where they would stay with her for the rest of her life. After the crowd dispersed, she remained like a stone statue, her body and limbs in the positions they were in when the two old janitors had held her back.

After a long time, she finally let her arms down, walked slowly onto the stage, sat next to her father's body, and held one of his already-cold hands, her eyes staring emptily into the distance. When they finally came to carry away the body, she took something from her pocket and put it into her father's hand: his pipe.

Wenjie quietly left the exercise grounds, empty save for the trash left by the crowd, and headed home. When she reached the foot of the faculty housing apartment building, she heard peals of crazy laughter coming out of the second-floor window of her home. That was the woman she had once called mother.

Wenjie turned around, not caring where her feet would carry her.

Finally, she found herself at the door of Professor Ruan Wen. Throughout the four years of Wenjie's college life, Professor Ruan had been her advisor and her closest friend. During the two years after that, when Wenjie had been a graduate student in the Astrophysics Department, and through the subsequent chaos of the Cultural Revolution, Professor Ruan remained her closest confidante, other than her father.

Ruan had studied at Cambridge University, and her home had once fascinated Wenjie: refined books, paintings, and records brought back from Europe; a piano; a set of European-style pipes arranged on a delicate wooden stand, some made from Mediterranean briar, some from Turkish meerschaum. Each of them seemed suffused with the wisdom of the man who had once held the bowl in his hand or clamped the stem between his teeth, deep in thought, though Ruan had never mentioned the man's name. The pipe that had belonged to Wenjie's father had in fact been a gift from Ruan.

This elegant, warm home had once been a safe harbor

17

for Wenjie when she needed to escape the storms of the larger world, but that was before Ruan's home had been searched and her possessions seized by the Red Guards. Like Wenjie's father, Ruan had suffered greatly during the Cultural Revolution. During her struggle sessions, the Red Guards had hung a pair of high heels around her neck and streaked her face with lipstick to show how she had lived the corrupt lifestyle of a capitalist.

Wenjie pushed open the door to Ruan's home, and she saw that the chaos left by the Red Guards had been cleaned up: The torn oil paintings had been glued back together and rehung on the walls; the toppled piano had been set upright and wiped clean, though it was broken and could no longer be played; the few books left behind had been put back neatly on the shelf. . . .

Ruan was sitting on the chair before her desk, her eyes closed. Wenjie stood next to Ruan and gently caressed her professor's forehead, face, and hands—all cold. Wenjie had noticed the empty sleeping pill bottle on the desk as soon as she came in.

She stood there for a while, silent. Then she turned and walked away. She could no longer feel grief. She was now like a Geiger counter that had been subjected to too much radiation, no longer capable of giving any reaction, noiselessly displaying a reading of zero.

But as she was about to leave Ruan's home, Wenjie turned around for a final look. She noticed that Professor Ruan had put on makeup. She was wearing a light coat of lipstick and a pair of high heels.

2

SILENT SPRING

Two years later, the Greater Khingan Mountains

"Tim-ber . . ."

Following the loud chant, a large Dahurian larch, thick as the columns of the Parthenon, fell with a thump, and Ye Wenjie felt the earth quake.

She picked up her ax and saw and began to clear the branches from the trunk. Every time she did this, she felt as though she were cleaning the corpse of a giant. Sometimes she even imagined the giant was her father. The feelings from that terrible night two years ago when she cleaned her father's body in the mortuary would resurface, and the splits and cracks in the larch bark seemed to turn into the old scars and new wounds covering her father.

Over one hundred thousand people from the six divisions and forty-one regiments of the Inner Mongolia Production and Construction Corps were scattered among the vast forests and grasslands. When they first left the cities and arrived at this unfamiliar wilderness, many of the corps' "educated youths"—young college students who no longer had schools to go to—had cherished a romantic wish: When the tank clusters of the Soviet Revisionist Imperialists rolled

over the Sino-Mongolian border, they would arm themselves and make their own bodies the first barrier in the Republic's defense. Indeed, this expectation was one of the strategic considerations motivating the creation of the Production and Construction Corps.

But the war they craved was like a mountain at the other end of the grassland: clearly visible, but as far away as a mirage. So they had to content themselves with clearing fields, grazing animals, and chopping down trees.

Soon, the young men and women who had once expended their youthful energy on tours to the holy sites of the Chinese Revolution discovered that, compared to the huge sky and open air of Inner Mongolia, the biggest cities in China's interior were nothing more than sheep pens. Stuck in the middle of the cold, endless expanse of forests and grasslands, their burning ardor was meaningless. Even if they spilled all of their blood, it would cool faster than a pile of cow dung, and not be as useful. But burning was their fate; they were the generation meant to be consumed by fire. And so, under their chain saws, vast seas of forests turned into barren ridges and denuded hills. Under their tractors and combine harvesters, vast tracts of grasslands became grain fields, then deserts.

Ye Wenjie could only describe the deforestation that she witnessed as madness. The tall Dahurian larch, the evergreen Scots pine, the slim and straight white birch, the cloud-piercing Korean aspen, the aromatic Siberian fir, along with black birch, oak, mountain elm, *Chosenia arbutifolia*— whatever they laid eyes on, they cut down. Her company wielded hundreds of chain saws like a swarm of steel locusts, and after they passed, only stumps were left.

The fallen Dahurian larch, now bereft of branches, was ready to be taken away by tractor. Ye gently caressed the

freshly exposed cross section of the felled trunk. She did this often, as though such surfaces were giant wounds, as though she could feel the tree's pain. Suddenly, she saw another hand lightly stroking the matching surface of the stump a few feet away. The tremors in that hand revealed a heart that reson- ated with hers. Though the hand was pale, she could tell it belonged to a man.

She looked up. It was Bai Mulin. A slender, delicate man who wore glasses, he was a reporter for the *Great Production News,* the corps' newspaper. He had arrived the day before yesterday to gather news about her company. Ye remembered reading his articles, which were written in a beautiful style, sensitive and fine, ill suited to the rough-hewn environment.

"Ma Gang, come here," Bai called to a young man a little ways off. Ma was barrel-chested and muscular, like the Dahurian larch that he had just felled. He came over, and Bai asked him, "Do you know how old this tree was?"

"You can count the rings." Ma pointed to the stump.

"I did. More than three hundred and thirty years. Do you remember how long it took you to saw through it?"

"No more than ten minutes. Let me tell you, I'm the fast- est chain saw operator in the company. Whichever squad I'm with, the red flag for model workers follows me." Ma Gang's excitement was typical of most people Bai paid attention to. To be featured in the *Great Production News* would be a considerable honor.

"More than three hundred years! A dozen generations. When this tree was but a shrub, it was still the Ming Dynasty. During all these years, can you imagine how many storms it had weathered, how many events it had witnessed? But in a few minutes you cut it down. You really felt nothing?"

"What do you want me to feel?" Ma Gang gave a blank

look. "It's just a tree. The only things we don't lack around here are trees. There are plenty of other trees much older than this one."

"It's all right. Go back to work." Bai shook his head, sat down on the stump, and sighed.

Ma Gang shook his head as well, disappointed that the reporter wasn't interested in an interview. "Intellectuals always make a fuss about nothing," he muttered. As he spoke, he glanced at Ye Wenjie, apparently including her in his judgment.

The trunk was dragged away. Rocks and stumps in the ground broke the bark in more places, wounding the giant body further. In the spot where it once stood, the weight of the fallen tree being dragged left a deep channel in the layers of decomposing leaves that had accumulated over the years. Water quickly filled the ditch. The rotting leaves made the water appear crimson, like blood.

"Wenjie, come and take a rest." Bai pointed to the empty half of the stump on which he was sitting. Ye was indeed tired. She put down her tools, came over, and sat down with Bai, back to back.

After a long silence, Bai blurted out, "I can tell how you're feeling. The two of us are the only ones who feel this way."

Ye remained silent. Bai knew that she likely wouldn't answer. She was a woman of few words, and rarely conversed with anyone. Some new arrivals even mistook her for a mute.

Bai went on talking. "I visited this region a year ago. I remember arriving around noon, and my hosts told me that we'd have fish for lunch. I looked around the bark-lined hut and saw only a pot of water being boiled. No fish. Then, as soon as the water boiled, the cook went out with a rolling pin. He stood on the shore of the brook that passed before the hut, struck the water with the rolling pin a few times, and

was able to drag a few big fish out of the water. . . . What a fertile place! But now, if you go look at that brook, it's just dead, muddy water in a ditch. I really don't know if the Corps is engaged in construction or destruction."

"Where did you get thoughts like that?" Ye asked softly.

She did not express agreement or disagreement, but Bai was grateful that she had spoken at all. "I just read a book, and it really moved me. Can you read English?"

Ye nodded.

Bai took a book with a blue cover from his bag. He looked around to be sure no one was watching, and handed it to her. "This was published in 1962 and was very influential in the West."

Wenjie turned around on the stump to accept the book. *Silent Spring,* she read on the cover, *by Rachel Carson.* "Where did you get this?"

"The book attracted the attention of the higher-ups. They want to distribute it to select cadres[6] for internal reference. I'm responsible for translating the part that has to do with forests."

Wenjie opened the book and was pulled in. In a brief opening chapter, the author described a quiet town silently dying from the use of pesticides. Carson's deep concern suffused the simple, plain sentences.

"I want to write to the leadership in Beijing and let them know about the irresponsible behavior of the Construction Corps," Bai said.

Ye looked up from the book. It took a while for her to process his words. She said nothing and turned her eyes back to the page.

6 *Translator's Note:* "Cadre," when used in the context of Chinese Communism, does not refer to a group, but to an individual official of the Party or the state.

"Keep it for now, if you want to read it. But best be careful and don't let anyone see it. You know what they think of this kind of book . . ." Bai got up, looked around carefully once again, and left.

More than four decades later, in her last moments, Ye Wenjie would recall the influence *Silent Spring* had on her life.

The book dealt only with a limited subject: the negative environmental effects of excessive pesticide use. But the perspective taken by the author shook Ye to the core. The use of pesticides had seemed to Ye just a normal, proper—or, at least, neutral—act, but Carson's book allowed Ye to see that, from Nature's perspective, their use was indistinguishable from the Cultural Revolution, and equally destructive to our world. If this was so, then how many other acts of humankind that had seemed normal or even righteous were, in reality, evil?

As she continued to mull over these thoughts, a deduction made her shudder: *Is it possible that the relationship between humanity and evil is similar to the relationship between the ocean and an iceberg floating on its surface? Both the ocean and the iceberg are made of the same material. That the iceberg seems separate is only because it is in a different form. In reality, it is but a part of the vast ocean. . . .*

It was impossible to expect a moral awakening from humankind itself, just like it was impossible to expect humans to lift off the earth by pulling up on their own hair. To achieve moral awakening required a force outside the human race.

This thought determined the entire direction of Ye's life.

Four days after receiving the book, Ye went to the company's

guesthouse, where Bai was living, to return the book. Ye opened the door and saw that Bai was lying on the bed, exhausted and covered by wood shavings and mud. When Bai saw Ye, he struggled to get up.

"Did you work today?" Ye asked.

"I've been here with the company for so long. I can't just walk around all day doing nothing. Have to participate in labor. That's the spirit of the revolution, right? Oh, I worked near Radar Peak. The trees there were so dense. I sank into the rotting leaves all the way up to my knees. I'm afraid I'll get sick from the miasma."

"Radar Peak?" Ye was shocked.

"Yes. The regiment had an emergency assignment: clear out a warning zone all around the peak by cutting down trees."

Radar Peak was a mysterious place. The steep, once-nameless peak got its moniker from the large parabolic antenna dish at the top. In reality, everyone with a little common sense knew it wasn't a radar antenna: Even though its orientation changed every day, the antenna never moved in a continuous manner. As the wind blew past it, the dish emitted a howl that could be heard from far away.

People in Ye's company knew only that Radar Peak was a military base. According to the locals, when the base was built three years ago, the military mobilized a lot of people to construct a road leading to the top and to string a power line along it. Tons of supplies were transported up the mountain. But after the completion of the base, the road was destroyed, leaving behind only a difficult trail that snaked between the trees. Often helicopters could be seen landing on and lifting off the peak.

The antenna wasn't always visible. When the wind was too strong, it was retracted.

But when it was extended, many strange things occurred around the area: Animals in the forest became noisy and anxious, flocks of birds erupted from the woods, and people suffered nausea and dizziness. Also, those who lived near Radar Peak tended to lose their hair. According to the locals, these phenomena only began after the antenna was built.

There were many strange stories associated with Radar Peak. One time, when it was snowing, the antenna was extended, and the snow instantly turned to rain. Since the temperature near ground was still below freezing, the rain turned to ice on the trees. Gigantic icicles hung from the trees, and the forest turned into a crystal palace. From time to time, branches cracked under the weight of the ice, and the icicles crashed to the ground with loud thumps. Sometimes, when the antenna was extended, a clear day would turn to thunder and lightning, and strange lights would appear in the night sky.

After the arrival of the Construction Corps company, the commander told everyone right away to take care to avoid approaching the heavily guarded Radar Peak, because the patrols were allowed to shoot without warning.

Last week, two of the men had gone hunting and chased a deer to the foot of Radar Peak without realizing where they were, and the sentries stationed halfway up the peak shot at them. Luckily, the forest was so dense that the two escaped without injury, though one of the men peed in his pants. At the company meeting the next day, both men were reprimanded. Maybe it was because of this incident that the base had directed the Corps to create a warning zone in the forest around the peak. The fact that the base could issue labor assignments to the Construction Corps hinted at its political power.

Bai Mulin accepted the book from Ye and carefully hid it under his pillow. From the same place, he retrieved a few

sheets of paper filled with dense writing and handed them to her. "This is a draft of my letter. Would you read it?"

"Letter?"

"Like I was telling you, I want to write to the central leadership in Beijing."

The handwriting was very sloppy, and Ye had to read it slowly. But the content was informative and tightly argued. The letter began by describing how the Taihang Mountains had turned from a historically fertile place to the barren wasteland it was today as a result of deforestation. It then described the recent, rapid rise in the Yellow River's silt content. Finally, it concluded that the Inner Mongolia Production and Construction Corps' actions would lead to severe ecological consequences. Ye noticed that Bai's style was similar to that of *Silent Spring,* precise and plain, but also poetic. Though her background was in technical subjects, she enjoyed the literary prose.

"It's beautiful," she said sincerely.

Bai nodded. "Then I'll send it." He took out a few fresh sheets of paper to make a clean copy of the draft. But his hands shook so much that he couldn't form any characters. This was a common reaction after using a chain saw for the first time. Their trembling hands couldn't even hold a rice bowl steady, let alone write legibly.

"Why don't I copy it for you?" Ye said. She took the pen from him.

"You have such pretty handwriting," Bai said as he looked at her first line of characters on the page. He poured a glass of water for Ye. His hands shook so much that he spilled some of the water. Ye moved the letter out of the way.

"You studied physics?" Bai asked.

"Astrophysics. Useless now." Ye did not even lift her head.

"You study the stars. How can that be useless? Colleges have reopened recently, but they're not taking graduate students. For highly educated and skilled individuals like you to be sent to a place like this . . ."

Ye said nothing and kept on writing. She did not want to tell Bai that for someone like her to be able to join the Construction Corps was very fortunate. She didn't want to comment on the way things were—there was nothing worthwhile to say.

The hut became quiet, filled only with the sound of pen nib scratching against paper. Ye could smell the fragrance of the sawdust on Bai's body. For the first time since the death of her father, she experienced warmth in her heart and allowed herself to relax, momentarily letting down her guard against the world.

More than an hour later, she was done copying the letter. She wrote out the address on the envelope as Bai dictated it and got up to say good-bye.

At the door, she turned around. "Let me have your jacket. I'll wash it for you." She was surprised by her own boldness.

"No! How can I do that?" Bai shook his head. "The woman warriors of the Construction Corps work just as hard as the men every day. You should get back to have some rest. Tomorrow you have to get up at six to work in the mountains. Oh, Wenjie, I'll be heading back to division headquarters the day after tomorrow. I will explain your situation to my superiors. Maybe it will help."

"Thank you. But I like it here. It's quiet." Ye looked at the dim outline of the dark woods in the moonlight.

"Are you trying to run away from something?"

"I'm leaving," Ye said in a soft voice. And she did.

Bai watched her slender figure disappear in the moonlight.

Then he lifted his gaze to the dark woods that she had been looking at a moment earlier.

In the distance, the gigantic antenna on top of Radar Peak rose once again, giving off a cold, metallic glint.

One afternoon three weeks later, Ye Wenjie was summoned back to company headquarters from the logging camp. As soon as she entered the office, she sensed the mood was wrong. The company commander and the political instructor were both present, along with a stranger with a stern expression. On the desk in front of the stranger was a black briefcase, and an envelope and a book lay next to it. The envelope was open, and the book was the copy of *Silent Spring* that she had read.

During those years, everyone had a special sensitivity for their own political situation. The sense was especially acute in Ye Wenjie. She felt the world around her closing in like a sack being drawn shut, and everything pressing in on her.

"Ye Wenjie, this is Director Zhang of the Division Political Department. He's here to investigate." Her political instructor pointed at the stranger. "We hope you will cooperate fully and tell the truth."

"Did you write this letter?" Director Zhang asked. He pulled the letter out of the envelope. Ye reached for it, but Zhang held on to the letter and showed it to her page by page until he reached the very last page, the one she was most interested in.

There was no signature except "The Revolutionary Masses."

"No, I did not write this." Ye shook her head in fright.

"But this is your handwriting."

"Yes, but I just copied it for someone else."

"Who?"

29

Normally, whenever she suffered some injustice at the company, Ye refused to protest openly. She simply endured silently, and would never consider implicating others. But this time was different. She understood very well what this meant.

"I helped a reporter from the *Great Production News*. He was here a few weeks ago. His name is—"

"Ye Wenjie!" Director Zhang's two black eyes were trained on her like the barrels of two guns. "I am warning you: Framing others will only make your problem worse. We've already clarified the situation with Comrade Bai Mulin. His only involvement was posting the letter from Hohhot under your direction. He had no idea as to the letter's contents."

"He . . . he said that?" Ye felt everything go black before her eyes.

Instead of answering, Director Zhang picked up the book. "Your letter was clearly inspired by this book." He showed the book to the company director and the political instructor. "*Silent Spring* was published in America in 1962 and has been quite influential in the capitalist world."

He then took another book out of the briefcase. The cover was white with black characters. "This is the Chinese translation. The appropriate authorities distributed it to select cadres as internal reference so that it could be criticized. As of now, the appropriate authorities have already given their clear judgment: The book is a toxic piece of reactionary propaganda. It takes the stance of pure historical idealism and espouses a doomsday theory. Under the guise of discussing environmental problems, it seeks to justify the ultimate corruption of the capitalist world. The content is extremely reactionary."

"But this book . . . it doesn't belong to me."

"Comrade Bai was appointed as a translator by the appropriate authorities. So it was perfectly legitimate for him

to carry it. Of course, he *is* responsible for being careless and allowing you to steal it while he was participating in Construction Corps work assignments. From this book, you obtained intellectual weapons that could be used to attack socialism."

Ye Wenjie held her tongue. She knew that she had already fallen to the bottom of the pit. Any struggle was useless.

Contrary to certain historical records that later became publicized, Bai Mulin did not intend to frame Ye Wenjie at the start. The letter he wrote to the central leadership in Beijing was likely based on a real sense of responsibility. Back then, many people wrote to the central leadership with all kinds of personal agendas. Most of these letters were never answered, but a few of the letter writers did see their political fortunes rise meteorically overnight, while others invited catastrophe. The political currents of the time were extremely complex. As a reporter, Bai believed he could read the currents and avoid dangerous sensitivities, but he was overconfident, and his letter touched a minefield that he did not know existed. After he heard about its reception, fear overwhelmed everything else. In order to protect himself, he decided to sacrifice Ye Wenjie.

Half a century later, historians would all agree that this event in 1969 was a turning point in humankind's history.

Without intending to, Bai became a key historical figure. But he never learned of this fact. Historians recorded the rest of his uneventful life with disappointment. He continued to work at *Great Production News* until 1975, when the Inner Mongolia Production and Construction Corps was disbanded. He was then sent to a city in Northeast China to work for the Science Association until the beginning of

31

the eighties. Then he left the country for Canada, where he taught at a Chinese school in Ottawa until 1991, when he died from lung cancer. For the rest of his life, he never mentioned Ye Wenjie, and we do not know if he ever felt remorse or repented for his actions.

"Wenjie, the company has treated you extremely well." The company commander exhaled a thick cloud of smoke from his Mohe tobacco. He stared at the ground and continued. "By birth and family background, you're politically suspect. But we've always treated you as one of our own. Both the political instructor and I have spoken to you many times concerning your tendency to sequester yourself from the people, and your lack of self-motivation in seeking progress. We want to help you. But look at you! You've committed such a serious error!"

The political instructor picked up the theme. "I've always said that I thought she had a deep-rooted resentment of the Cultural Revolution."

"Have her escorted to division headquarters this afternoon, along with the evidence of her crime," Director Zhang said, his face impassive.

The three other women prisoners in the cell were taken away one by one until only Ye was left. The small pile of coal in the corner had been exhausted, and no one came to replenish it. The fire in the stove had gone out a while ago. It was so cold in the cell that Ye had to wrap herself in the blanket.

Two officials came to her before it got dark. The older one, a female cadre, was introduced by her associate as

the military representative from the Intermediate People's Court.[7]

"My name is Cheng Lihua," the cadre introduced herself. She was in her forties, dressed in a military coat, and wore thick-rimmed glasses. Her face was gentle, and it was clear that she had been very beautiful when she was young. She spoke with a smile and instantly made people like her. Ye Wenjie understood that it was unusual for such a high-grade cadre to visit a prisoner about to be tried. Cautiously, she nodded at Cheng and moved to make space on her narrow cot so she could sit down.

"It's really cold in here. What happened to your stove?" Cheng gave a reprimanding look to the head of the detention center standing at the door of the cell. She turned back to Ye. "Hmm, you're very young. Even younger than I imagined."

She sat down on the cot right next to Ye and rummaged in her briefcase, still muttering. "Wenjie, you're very confused. Young people are all the same. The more books you read, the more confused you become. Eh, what can I say. . . ."

She found what she was looking for and took out a small bundle of papers. Looking at Ye, her eyes were filled with kindness and affection. "But it's not a big deal. What young person hasn't made some mistakes? I made mistakes myself. When I was a young woman, as a member of the art troupe for the Fourth Field Army, I specialized in singing Soviet songs. One time, during a political study session, I announced that China should cease to be a separate country and join the USSR as a member republic. That way, international

7 *Author's Note:* During that phase of the Cultural Revolution, most intermediate and higher people's courts and procuratorial organs (responsible for investigating and prosecuting crimes) were under the control of military commissions. The military representative had the final vote on judicial matters.

communism would be further strengthened. How naïve I was! But who wasn't once naïve? What's done is done. When you make a mistake, what's important is to recognize it and correct it. Then you can continue the revolution."

Cheng's words seemed to draw Ye closer to her. But after having gone through so many troubles, Ye had learned to be cautious. She did not dare to believe in this kindness, which almost resembled a luxury.

Cheng placed the stack of papers on the bed in front of Ye and handed her a pen. "Come now, sign this. Then we can have a good heart-to-heart and resolve your ideological difficulties." Her tone was like that of a mother trying to encourage her daughter to eat.

Ye stared at the stack of papers silently and motionlessly. She did not pick up the pen.

Cheng gave her a forgiving smile. "You can trust me, Wenjie. I personally guarantee that this document has nothing to do with your case. Go ahead. Sign it."

Her associate, who stood to the side, added, "Ye Wenjie, Representative Cheng is trying to help you. She's been working hard on your behalf."

Cheng waved at him to stop. "It's understandable. Poor child! You've been so frightened. There are some comrades whose political awareness is not adequately high. Some members of the Construction Corps and some of the folks from the people's court employ such simplistic methods and behave so rudely. It's completely inappropriate! All right, Wenjie, why don't you read the document? Read it carefully."

Ye picked up the document and flipped through it in the dim yellow light of the detention cell. Representative Cheng hadn't lied to her. The document really had nothing to do with her case.

It was about her father. In it was a record of her father's interactions and conversations with certain individuals. The source was Wenjie's younger sister, Wenxue. As one of the most radical Red Guards, Wenxue had always been proactive in exposing their father, and had composed numerous reports detailing his supposed sins. Some of the material she provided had ultimately led to his death.

But Ye could tell that this report didn't come from the hand of her sister. Wenxue had an intense, impatient style. When you read her reports, each line would make an explosive impact, like a string of firecrackers. But this document was composed in a cool, experienced, meticulous style. Who spoke to whom, when, where, what was discussed—every detail was recorded, down to the exact date. For someone who wasn't experienced, the contents seemed like a boring diary, but the calculating, cold purpose hidden within was very different from the childish antics of Wenxue.

Ye couldn't really understand what the document was getting at, but she could sense that it had something to do with an important national defense project. As the daughter of a physicist, Ye guessed that it was a reference to the double-bomb project[8] that had shocked the world in 1964 and 1967.

During this period of the Cultural Revolution, in order to bring down a highly positioned individual, it was necessary to gather evidence of his deficiencies in the various areas he was in charge of. But for those plotting such political machinations, the double-bomb project posed great difficulties. People in the highest levels of the government placed the project under their protection to avoid disruption by the

8 *Translator's Note:* This is the Chinese term for the work behind "596" and "Test No. 6," the successful tests for China's first fission and fusion nuclear bombs, respectively.

Cultural Revolution. It was difficult for those with nefarious purposes to pry into its inner workings.

Due to her father's family background, he couldn't meet the political requirements and did not work on the double-bomb project. All he had done was some peripheral theoretical work for it. But it was easier to make use of him than those who had worked at the core of the project. Ye Wenjie couldn't tell if the contents of the document were true or false, but she was sure that every character and every punctuation mark had the potential to deliver a fatal political blow. In addition to those targeted directly, countless others might have their fates altered because of this document.

At the end of the document was her sister's signature in large characters, and Ye Wenjie was supposed to sign as a witness. She noticed that three other witnesses had already signed.

"I don't know anything about these conversations," Ye said softly. She put the document back down.

"How can you not know? Many of these conversations occurred right in your home. Your sister knew them. You must, too."

"I really don't."

"But these conversations really did occur. You must have faith in us."

"I didn't say they weren't true. But I really don't know about them. So I can't sign."

"Ye Wenjie!" Cheng's associate took a step closer. But Cheng stopped him again. She shifted to sit even closer to Ye and picked up one of her cold hands.

"Wenjie, let me put all my cards on the table. Your case has a lot of prosecutorial discretion. On the one hand, we could minimize it as a case of an educated youth being fooled by a reactionary book—it's not a big deal. We don't even need

to go through a judicial procedure. We'll have you attend a political class and write a few self-criticism reports, and then you can go back to the Construction Corps. On the other hand, we could also prosecute this case to its fullest extent. Wenjie, you must know that you could be declared an active counter-revolutionary.

"Now, faced with political cases like yours, all prosecutorial organs and courts would rather be too severe than too lax. This is because treating you too severely would just be a mistake in method, but treating you too laxly would be a mistake in political direction. Ultimately, however, the decision belongs to the military control commission. Of course, I'm telling you all this off the record."

Cheng's associate added, "Representative Cheng is trying to save you. Three witnesses have already signed. Your refusal to sign is pretty much meaningless. I must urge you not to be confused, Ye Wenjie."

"Right, Wenjie," Cheng continued. "It would break my heart to see an educated young person like you ruined by something like this. I really want to save you. Please cooperate. Look at me. Do you think I would hurt you?"

But Ye did not look at Representative Cheng. What she saw, instead, was her father's blood. "Representative Cheng, I have no knowledge of the events recorded in this document. I cannot sign it."

Cheng Lihua became quiet. She stared at Ye for a long while, and the cold air in the cell seemed to solidify. Then she slowly put the document back into her briefcase and stood up. Her kind expression did not disappear, but was set on her face like a plaster mask. Still appearing kind and affectionate, she walked to the corner of the cell, where there was a bucket for washing. She picked it up and poured half

37

the water onto Ye and the other half onto her blanket, her movements never straying from a methodical calmness. Then she dropped the bucket and left the cell, pausing only to mutter, "You stubborn little bitch!"

The head of the detention center was the last to leave. He stared coldly at Ye, soaked through and dripping, shut the cell door with a bang, and locked it.

Through her wet clothes, the chill of the Inner Mongolian winter seized Ye like a giant's fist. She heard her teeth chatter, but eventually even that sound disappeared. The coldness penetrated into her bones, and the world in her eyes turned milky white. She felt that the entire universe was a huge block of ice, and she was the only spark of life within it. She was the little girl about to freeze to death, and she didn't even have a handful of matches, only illusions. . . .

The block of ice holding her gradually became transparent. In front of her she could see a tall building. At the top, a young girl waved a bright red banner. Her slender figure contrasted vividly with the breadth of the flag: It was her sister, Wenxue. Ever since her little sister had made a clean break with her reactionary academic authority family, Wenjie had heard no news about her. She had only learned recently that Wenxue had died two years ago in one of the wars between Red Guard factions.

As Ye watched, the figure waving the flag became Bai Mulin, his glasses reflecting the flames raging below the building; then it turned into Representative Cheng; then her mother, Shao Lin; then her father. The flag-bearer kept on changing, but the flag waved ceaselessly, like a perpetual pendulum, counting down the remainder of her short life.

Gradually, the flag grew blurry; everything grew blurry. The ice that filled the universe once again sealed her at its center. Only this time, the ice was black.

3

RED COAST I

Ye Wenjie heard a loud, continuous roar. She didn't know how much time had passed.

The noise came from all around her. In her vague state of consciousness, it seemed as though some gigantic machine was drilling into or sawing through the block of ice that held her. The world was still only darkness, but the noise grew more and more real. Finally, she was certain that the source of the noise was neither heaven nor hell, and she remained in the land of the living.

She realized that her eyes were still closed. With an effort, she lifted her eyelids. The first thing she saw was a light embedded deeply in the ceiling. Covered by a wire mesh that seemed designed to protect it, it emitted a dim glow. The ceiling appeared to be made of metal.

She heard a male voice softly calling her name. "You have a high fever," the man said.

"Where am I?" Wenjie's voice was so weak that she couldn't be sure it was her own.

"On a helicopter."

Ye felt weak. She fell back to sleep. As she dozed, the roar kept her company. Before long, she woke again. Now the numbness had disappeared and the pain reasserted itself: Her

head and the joints of her limbs ached, and the breath coming out of her mouth felt scalding hot. Her throat hurt so much that swallowing spittle felt like it was a piece of burning coal.

She turned her head and saw two men wearing the same kind of military coat that Representative Cheng had worn. But unlike her, both of these men had on the cotton cap of the PLA, a red star sewn onto the front. Their coats were unbuttoned, and she could see the red-collar insignia on their army uniforms. One of the men wore glasses.

Ye discovered that she was covered by a military coat as well. The clothes she was wearing were dry and warm.

She struggled to sit up, and to her surprise, succeeded. She looked out the porthole on the other side. Rolling clouds slowly drifted by, reflecting the dazzling sunlight. She pulled her gaze back. The narrow cabin was filled with iron trunks painted military green. From another porthole she could see flickering shadows cast by the rotors. She was indeed on a helicopter.

"You'd better lie back down," the man with the glasses said. He helped her down and covered her with the coat again.

"Ye Wenjie, did you write this paper?" The other man extended an open English journal before her eyes. The title of the paper was "The Possible Existence of Phase Boundaries Within the Solar Radiation Zone and Their Reflective Characteristics." He showed her the cover of the journal: an issue of *The Journal of Astrophysics* from 1966.

"Of course she did. Why does that even need to be confirmed?" The man wearing glasses took the journal away and then made introductions. "This is Political Commissar Lei Zhicheng of Red Coast Base. I'm Yang Weining, base chief engineer. It will be an hour before we land. You might as well get some rest."

You're Yang Weining? Ye didn't say anything, but she was stunned. She saw that he kept his expression calm, apparently not wishing to let anyone else know that they knew each other. Yang had been one of Ye Zhetai's graduate students. By the time he had obtained his degree, Wenjie was still a first-year in college.

She could clearly remember the first time Yang came to her home. He had just begun his graduate studies and needed to discuss the direction of his research with Professor Ye. Yang said that he wanted to focus on experimental and applied problems, staying away from theory.

Ye Wenjie recalled her father saying, "I'm not opposed to your idea. But we are, after all, the department of theoretical physics. Why do you want to avoid theory?"

Yang replied, "I want to devote myself to the times, to make some real-world contributions."

Her father said, "Theory is the foundation of application. Isn't discovering fundamental laws the biggest contribution to our time?"

Yang hesitated and finally revealed his real concern: "It's easy to make ideological mistakes in theory."

Her father had nothing to say to that.

Yang was very talented, with a good mathematical foundation and a quick mind. But during his brief time as a graduate student, he always kept a respectable distance from his thesis advisor. Ye Wenjie had seen Yang several times, but, perhaps due to the influence of her father, she hadn't noticed him much. As for whether he had paid much attention to her, she had no idea. After Yang got his degree, he soon ceased all contact with her father.

Again feeling weak, Ye closed her eyes. The two men left her and crouched behind a row of trunks to converse in

41

lowered voices. But the cabin was so cramped that Ye could hear them even over the roar of the engine.

"I still think this isn't a good idea," Commissar Lei said.

"Can you find the personnel I need through normal channels?" Yang asked.

"Eh. I've done all I can. There's no one in the military with this specialization, and going outside the army raises many questions. You know very well that the security clearance needed for this project requires someone willing to join the army. But the bigger issue is the requirement in the security regulations that they be sequestered at the base for extended periods. What's to be done if they have families? Sequester them at the base too? No one would agree to that. I did find two possible candidates, but both would rather stay at the May Seventh Cadre Schools rather than come here.[9] Of course we could forcefully move them. But given the nature of this work, we can't have someone who doesn't want to be here."

"Then there's no choice but to use her."

"But it's so unconventional."

"This entire project is unconventional. If something goes wrong, I'll accept the responsibility."

"Chief Yang, do you really think you can take responsibility for this? You are a technical person, but Red Coast is not like other national defense projects. Its complexity goes far beyond the technical issues."

"You're right, but I only know how to solve the technical issues."

9 *Translator's Note:* The May Seventh Cadre Schools were labor camps during the Cultural Revolution where cadres and intellectuals were "re-educated."

By the time they landed, it was dusk.

Ye refused to be helped by Yang and Lei, and struggled out of the helicopter by herself. A strong gust of wind almost blew her over. The still-gyrating rotors sliced through the wind, making a loud whistling noise. The scent of the woods on the wind was familiar to her, and she was familiar to the wind. It was the wind of the Greater Khingan Mountains.

She soon heard another sound, a kind of low, forceful, bass howl that seemed to form the background of the world: the parabolic antenna dish in the wind. Only now, when she was so close to it, did she finally feel its immensity. Ye's life had made a big circle this month: She was now on top of Radar Peak.

She couldn't help but look in the direction of her Construction Corps company. But all she could see was a misty sea of trees in the twilight.

The helicopter was carrying more than just Ye. Several soldiers came over and began to unload military-green cargo trunks from the cabin. They walked by without glancing at her. As she followed Yang and Lei, Ye noticed that the top of Radar Peak was spacious. A cluster of white buildings, like delicate toy blocks, nestled under the giant antenna. The trio headed toward the base gate, flanked by two guards, and stopped in front of it.

Lei turned to her and spoke solemnly. "Ye Wenjie, the evidence of your counter-revolutionary crime is incontrovert-ible, and the court would have punished you as you deserve. But now you have an opportunity to redeem yourself through hard work. You can accept it or refuse it." He pointed at the antenna. "This is a defense research facility. The research conducted here needs your specialized scientific knowledge. Chief Engineer Yang can give you the details, which you should consider carefully."

He nodded at Yang and then entered the gate after the soldiers carrying the trunks.

Yang waited until the others were gone and indicated that Ye should follow him a little distance away from the gate, clearly trying to avoid the sentries listening in.

He no longer pretended that he didn't know her. "Wenjie, let me be clear. This is not some great opportunity. I learned from the military control commission at the court that although Cheng Lihua advocates sentencing you severely, the most that you'll get is ten years. Considering mitigating circumstances, you'll serve maybe six or seven years. But here"—he nodded in the direction of the base—"is a research project under the highest security classification. Given your status, if you enter the gate, it's possible—" He paused, as though wanting to let the bass howl of the antenna add to the weight of his words. "—you'll never leave for the rest of your life."

"I want to go in."

Yang was surprised by her quick answer. "Don't be hasty. Get back onto the helicopter. It will take off in three hours, and if you refuse our offer, it will take you back."

"I don't want to go back. Let's go in." Ye's voice remained soft, but there was a determination in her tone that was harder than steel. Other than the undiscovered country beyond death from which no one has ever returned, the place she wanted to be the most was this peak, separated from the rest of the world. Here, she felt a sense of security that had long eluded her.

"You should be cautious. Think through what this decision means."

"I can stay here for the rest of my life."

Yang lowered his head and said nothing. He stared into the distance, as though forcing Ye to sort through her thoughts.

Ye stayed silent as well. She pulled her coat tightly around herself and gazed into the distance. There, the Greater Khingan Mountains were fading into the darkening night. It was impossible to stay out here much longer in the cold.

Yang began to walk toward the gate. He moved fast, as though trying to leave Ye behind. But Ye stayed close. After they entered the gate of Red Coast Base, the two sentries shut the heavy iron doors.

A little ways on, Yang stopped and pointed at the antenna. "This is a large-scale weapons research project. If it succeeds, the result will be even more important than the atomic bomb and the hydrogen bomb."

They came to the largest building in the base, and Yang pushed the door open. Ye saw the words TRANSMISSION MAIN CONTROL ROOM over the door. Inside, warm air tinged with the smell of engine oil enveloped her. She saw that the spacious room was filled with all kinds of instruments and equipment. Signal lights and oscilloscope displays flickered together. A dozen or so operators dressed in military uniform were almost entombed by the rows of instruments, as though they were crouching inside battlefield trenches. The unceasing stream of operational orders and responses gave the whole scene a tense, confusing feel.

"It's warmer in here," Yang said. "Wait here a bit. I'll take care of your living arrangements and return for you." He pointed at a chair and desk next to the door.

Ye saw that someone was already sitting at the desk: a guard carrying a handgun.

"I'd rather wait outside," Ye said.

Yang smiled at her kindly. "From now on, you'll be a member of the base staff. Other than a few sensitive areas, you can go anywhere you want." His face suddenly looked

uncomfortable as he realized another layer of meaning to his words: *You can never leave here again*.

"I prefer to wait outside," Ye insisted.

"All right." Yang glanced at the guard at the desk, who paid no attention to them. He seemed to understand Ye's concern and brought her back out of the main control room. "Stand somewhere out of the wind, and I'll be back in a few minutes. I just need to get someone to start a fire in your room—conditions at the base are a bit rough, and we have no heating system."

Ye stood next to the main control room door. The huge antenna was directly behind her and it blotted out half the sky. From here, she could clearly hear the sounds inside the main control room. Suddenly, the chaotic orders and responses ceased, and the room became completely quiet. All she could hear was the occasional low buzzing noise from some instrument.

Then a loud male voice broke the silence. "The People's Liberation Army, Second Artillery Corps,[10] Red Coast Project, one hundred and forty-seventh transmission. Authorization confirmed. Begin thirty-second countdown."

"Target Classification: A-three. Coordinates' serial number: BN20197F. Position checked and confirmed. Twenty-five seconds."

"Transmission file number: twenty-two. Additions: none. Continuations: none. Transmission file final check completed. Twenty seconds."

"Energy Unit reporting: all systems go."

"Coding Unit reporting: all systems go."

"Amplifier Unit reporting: all systems go."

10 *Translator's Note:* The Second Artillery Corps controls China's nuclear missiles.

46

"Interference Monitoring Unit reporting: within acceptable range."

"We have reached the point of no return. Fifteen seconds."

Everything became quiet again. Fifteen seconds later, as a klaxon started to blare, a red light on top of the antenna began to blink rapidly.

"Begin transmission! All units continue to monitor!"

Ye felt a light itch on her face. She knew that an enormous electric field had appeared. She lifted her face and gazed in the direction the antenna was pointing and saw a cloud in the night sky glow with a dim blue light, so dim that at first she thought it an illusion. But as the cloud drifted away, the glow disappeared. Another cloud that drifted into position began to give off the same glow.

From the main control room, she heard more shouts.

"Malfunction with Energy Unit. Magnetron number three has burnt out."

"Backup Unit is in operation: all systems go."

"Checkpoint one reached. Resuming transmission."

Ye heard a fluttering noise. Through the mist, she could see shadows lift out of the woods below the peak and spiral into the dark sky. She hadn't realized so many birds could be roused from the woods in deep winter. Then she saw a terrifying scene: One flock of birds flew into the region of air the antenna pointed at, and against the background of the faintly glowing cloud, the birds dropped out of the sky.

The process continued for about fifteen minutes. Then the red light on the antenna went out, and the itch on her skin disappeared. From the main control room, the confusing murmur of orders and responses resumed even as the loud male voice continued.

"Transmission one hundred forty-seven of Red Coast

completed. Transmission systems shutting down. Red Coast now entering monitoring state. System control is hereby transferred to the Monitoring Department. Please upload checkpoint data."

"All units should fill out transmission diaries. All unit heads should attend the post-transmission meeting in the debriefing room. We're done."

All was silent except for the howl of the wind against the antenna. Ye watched as the remaining birds in the flock gradually settled back into the forest. She stared at the antenna and thought it looked like an enormous hand stretched open toward the sky, possessing an ethereal strength. As she surveyed the night sky, she did not see any target that she thought might be serial number BN20197F. Beyond the wisps of clouds, all she could see were the stars of a cold night in 1969.

PART II

THREE BODY

4

THE FRONTIERS OF SCIENCE

Forty-plus years later

Wang Miao thought the four people who came to find him made a rather odd combination: two cops and two men in military uniforms. If the latter two were armed police, that would be somewhat understandable, but they were actually PLA officers.

As soon as Wang saw the cops, he felt annoyed. The younger one was all right—at least he was polite. But the other one, in plainclothes, immediately grated on him. He was thickset and had a face full of bulging muscles. Wearing a dirty leather jacket, smelling of cigarettes, and speaking in a loud voice, he was exactly the sort of person Wang despised. "Wang Miao?"

The way the cop addressed him by name only, so direct and impolite, made Wang uncomfortable. Adding to the insult, the man lit a cigarette as he addressed him, without even lifting his head to show his face. Before Wang could answer, the man nodded at the younger cop, who showed Wang his badge.

Having lit the cigarette, the older cop moved to enter Wang's apartment.

"Please don't smoke in my home," Wang said, blocking him.

"Oh, sorry, Professor Wang." The young police officer smiled. "This is Captain Shi Qiang." He gave Shi a pleading look.

"Fine, we can talk in the hallway," Shi said. He took a deep drag. Almost half the cigarette had turned to ashes, and he didn't blow out much smoke. He inclined his head toward the younger police officer. "You ask him, then."

"Professor Wang, we want to know if you've had any recent contacts with members of the Frontiers of Science," the young cop said.

"The Frontiers of Science is full of famous scholars, and very influential. Why can't I have contact with a legal international academic group?"

"Look at the way you talk!" Shi said. "Did we say anything about it not being legal? Did we say anything about you not being allowed to contact them?" He finally blew out the lungful of smoke that he had sucked in earlier—right in Wang's face.

"All right then. Please respect my privacy. I don't need to answer your questions."

"Your *privacy*? You're a famous academic. You have a responsibility toward the public welfare." Shi threw away the butt and took out another cigarette from a flattened pack.

"I have the right to not answer. Please leave." Wang turned around to go back inside.

"Wait!" Shi shouted. He waved at the young cop next to him. "Give him the address and phone number. You can come by in the afternoon."

"What are you really after?" Wang said, his voice now tinged with anger. The argument brought the neighbors, curious about what was happening, out into the hallway.

"Captain Shi!" The young cop pulled Shi aside and

continued speaking to him in hushed, urgent tones. Apparently, Wang wasn't the only one annoyed by his rough manners.

"Professor Wang, please don't misunderstand." One of the army officers, a major, stepped forward. "There's an important meeting this afternoon, to which several scholars and specialists are invited. The general sent us to invite you."

"I'm busy this afternoon."

"We know. The general already spoke with the head of the Nanotechnology Research Center. We can't have this meeting without you. If you can't attend, we'll have to reschedule."

Shi and the young cop said nothing. Both turned and went down the stairs. The two army officers watched them leave and seemed to sigh with relief.

"What's wrong with that guy?" the major whispered to the other officer.

"He's got quite a record. During a hostage crisis a few years ago, he acted recklessly, without concern for the lives of the hostages. In the end, a family of three all died at the hands of the criminals. Rumor has it that he's also friendly with elements of organized crime, using one gang to fight another. Last year, he used torture to obtain confessions, and permanently disabled one of the suspects. That's why he was suspended from duty. . . ."

Wang Miao suspected that he was meant to overhear the conversation between the officers. Maybe they intended to show him that they were different from that rude cop; or maybe they wanted to make him curious about their mission.

"How can a man like that be part of the Battle Command Center?" the major asked.

"The general specifically requested him. I guess he must have some special skills. In any case, his duties are quite

restricted. Other than public safety matters, he's not allowed to know much."

Battle Command Center? Wang looked at the two officers, baffled.

The car they sent for Wang Miao took him to a large compound in the suburbs. Since the door had only a number and no sign, Wang deduced that this building belonged to the military, rather than the police.

Wang was surprised by the chaos as he entered the large meeting room. Around him were numerous computers in various states of disarray. They had run out of table space and put a few workstations directly on the floor, where power cords and networking wires formed a tangled mess. Instead of being installed in racks, a bunch of routers were left haphazardly on top of the servers. Printer paper was scattered everywhere. A few projector screens stood in various corners of the room, sticking out at odd angles like gypsy tents. A cloud of smoke hovered over the room. . . . Wang Miao wasn't sure if this was the Battle Command Center, but he was sure of one thing: Whatever they were dealing with was too important for them to care about keeping up appearances.

The meeting table, formed by pushing several smaller tables together, was piled with documents and odds and ends. The attendees, their clothes wrinkled, looked exhausted. Those wearing ties had all pulled them loose. It seemed as if they had been up all night.

A major general named Chang Weisi presided over the meeting, and half the attendees were military officers. After a few quick introductions, Wang found out that many of the others were police. The rest were academics like him,

with a few prominent scientists specializing in basic research in the mix.

He also found four foreigners in attendance. Their identities shocked him: a United States Air Force colonel and a British Army colonel, both NATO liaisons, as well as two CIA officers, apparently acting as observers.

On the faces of everyone around the table, Wang could read one sentiment: *We've done all we can. Let's fucking get it over with, already.*

Wang Miao saw Shi Qiang sitting at the table. In contrast to his rudeness yesterday, Shi greeted Wang as "Professor." But the smirk on Shi's face annoyed Wang. He didn't want to sit next to Shi, but he had no choice, as that was the only empty seat. The already thick cloud of cigarette smoke in the room became thicker.

As documents were distributed, Shi moved closer to Wang. "Professor Wang, I understand you're researching some kind of . . . new material?"

"Nanomaterial," Wang answered.

"I've heard of it. That stuff is really strong, right? Do you think it could be used to commit crimes?" As Shi's face was still half smirking, Wang couldn't tell if he was joking.

"What do you mean?"

"Heh. I heard that a strand of that stuff could be used to lift up a truck. If criminals steal some and make it into a knife, can't they slice a car in half with one stroke?"

"There's no need to even make it into a knife. That kind of material can be made into a line as thin as one-hundredth of a hair. If you string it across a road, a passing car would be sliced into two halves like cheese—but what can't be used for criminal purposes? Even a dull knife for descaling a fish can!"

Shi pulled a document halfway out of the envelope in front of him and shoved it back in again, suddenly losing interest. "You're right. Even a fish can be used to commit a crime. I handled a murder case once. Some bitch cut off her husband's family jewels. You know what she used? A frozen tilapia she got out of the freezer! The spines along the back were like razors—"

"I'm not interested. Did you ask me to the meeting just to talk about this?"

"Fish? Nanomaterials? No, no, nothing to do with those." Shi put his mouth next to Wang's ear. "Don't be nice to them. They're prejudiced against us. All they want is to get information out of us, but never tell us anything. Look at me. I've been here for a month, and I still don't know anything, just like you."

"Comrades," General Chang said, "let's get started. Of all the combat zones around the globe, this one has become the focal point. We need to update the current situation for all the attending comrades."

The unusual term "combat zone" gave Wang pause. He also noticed that the general did not seem to want to explain in detail the background of what they were dealing with to new people like him. This supported Shi's point. Also, in General Chang's short opening remarks, he used the word "comrades" twice. Wang looked at the NATO and CIA officers sitting across from him. The general had neglected to add "gentlemen."

"They're also comrades. Anyway, that's how everyone addresses each other here," Shi whispered to Wang, pointing at the four foreigners with his cigarette.

While he was baffled by how Shi knew what he was thinking, Wang was impressed with his powers of observation.

"Da Shi, put out your cigarette. There's enough smoke here," General Chang said as he flipped through some documents. He called Shi Qiang by a nickname, "Big Shi."

Shi looked around but couldn't find an ashtray. In the end, he dropped the cigarette into a teacup. He raised his hand, and before Chang could even acknowledge him, he spoke loudly. "General, I have a request which I've made before: I want information parity."

General Chang lifted his head. "There's never been a military operation in which there was information parity. I have to apologize to all the scholars, but we cannot give you any more background."

"We are *not* the same as the eggheads," Shi said. "The police have been part of the Battle Command Center from the start. But even now, we still don't know what this is all about. You continue to push the police out. You learn from us what you need about our techniques, and then you send us away one by one."

Several other police officers in attendance whispered to Shi to shut up. It surprised Wang that Shi dared to speak in this manner to a man of Chang's rank. But Chang's response surprised him even more.

"Da Shi, it seems that you still have the same problem you had back when you were in the army. You think you can speak for the police? Because of your poor record, you had already been suspended for several months, and you were about to be expelled from the force. I asked for you because I value your experience in city policing. You should treasure this opportunity."

Shi continued to speak roughly. "So I'm working in the hope of redeeming myself by good service? I thought you told me that all my techniques were dishonest and crooked."

"But useful." Chang nodded at Shi. "All we care about is if they're useful. In a time of war, we can't afford to be too scrupulous."

"We can't be too fastidious," a CIA officer said, in perfect Modern Standard Mandarin. "We can no longer rely on conventional thinking."

The British colonel apparently also understood Chinese. He nodded. "To be, or not to be . . ." he added in English. "It's a matter of life and death."

"What is he saying?" Shi asked Wang.

"Nothing," Wang replied mechanically. The people before him seemed to be speaking out of a dream. *Time of war? Where is this war?* He twisted to look out one of the floor-length windows. Through the window he could see Beijing in the distance: Under the spring sun, cars filled the streets like a dense river; on a lawn someone was walking a dog; a few children were playing. . . .

Which is more real? The world inside or outside these walls?

General Chang said, "Recently, the enemy has intensified the pattern of attacks. The targets remain elite scientists. Please begin by taking a look at the list of names in the document."

Wang took out the first page of the document, printed in large font. The list seemed to have been generated in a hurry, containing both Chinese and English names.

"Professor Wang, as you look through these names, does anything strike you?" General Chang asked.

"I know three of the names. All of them are famous scholars working at the forefront of physics research." Wang was a little distracted. His eyes locked onto the last name on the list. In his mind, the two characters took on a different tint

than the names above it. *How can her name appear here? What happened to her?*

"You know her?" Shi pointed to the name with a thick finger, stained yellow from smoking. Wang did not reply. "Ha. Don't know her. But *want* to know her?"

Now Wang Miao understood why it made sense for General Chang to have asked to have this man who was once a soldier under his command. Shi, who appeared so vulgar and careless, had eyes as sharp as knives. Maybe he wasn't a *good* cop, but he was certainly a fearsome one.

A year earlier, Wang Miao had been in charge of the nanoscale components for the "Sinotron II" high-energy particle accelerator project. One afternoon, during a brief break at the Liangxiang construction site, Wang was struck by the scene before him. As a landscape photography enthusiast, Wang often saw the sights around him as artistic compositions.

The main component of the composition was the solenoid of the superconducting magnet they were still installing. About three stories high and only half completed, the magnet loomed like a monster made of giant blocks of metal and a confusing mess of cryogenic coolant pipes. Like a junk heap from the Industrial Revolution, the structure exuded inhuman technological grimness and steel-bound barbarity.

In front of this metal monster stood the slim figure of a young woman. The composition's lighting was fantastic as well: The metal monster was buried in the shadow of a temporary construction shelter, further emphasizing its stern, rough quality. But a single ray of light from the westering sun coming through the central hole in the shelter fell right

on the woman. The soft glow lit up her supple hair and highlighted her white neck above the collar of her overalls, as though a single flower was blooming in a metal ruin after a violent thunderstorm. . . .

"What are you looking at? Get back to work!"

Wang was shocked out of his reverie, but then realized that the director of the Nanotechnology Research Center wasn't talking to him, but to a young engineer who had also been staring at the woman. Having returned from art to reality, Wang saw that the young woman wasn't an ordinary worker—the chief engineer stood next to her, explaining something respectfully.

"Who is she?" Wang asked the director.

"You should know her," the director said, waving his hand around in a large circle. "The first experiment on this twenty-billion-yuan accelerator will probably be to test her superstring model. Now, seniority matters in theoretical physics, and normally, she wouldn't have been senior enough to get the first shot. But those older academics didn't dare to show up first, afraid that they might fail and lose face, so that's why she got the chance."

"What? Yang Dong is . . . a woman?"

"Indeed," the director said. "We only found out when we finally met her two days ago."

The young engineer asked, "Does she have some psychological issue? Why else wouldn't she agree to be interviewed by the media? Maybe she's like Qian Zhongshu,[11] who died without ever appearing on TV."

11 *Translator's Note:* Qian Zhongshu (1910–1998) was one of the most famous Chinese literary scholars of the twentieth century. Erudite, witty, and aloof, he consistently refused media appearances. One might think of him as a Chinese Thomas Pynchon.

"But at least we knew Qian's gender. I bet Yang had some unusual experiences as a child. Maybe it made her somewhat autistic." Wang's words were tinged with a hint of self-mockery. He wasn't even famous enough for the media to be interested in him, let alone to turn down interview requests.

Yang walked over with the chief engineer. As they passed, she smiled at Wang and the others, nodding lightly without saying anything. Wang remembered her limpid eyes.

That night, Wang sat in his study and admired the few landscape photographs, his works he was the most proud of, hanging on the wall. His eyes fell on a frontier scene: a desolate valley terminating in a snowcapped mountain. On the nearer end of the valley, half of a dead tree, eroded by the vicissitudes of many years, took up one-third of the picture. In his imagination, Wang placed the figure that lingered in his mind at the far end of the valley. Surprisingly, it made the entire scene come alive, as though the world in the photograph recognized that tiny figure and responded to it, as though the whole scene existed for her.

He then imagined her figure in each of his other photographs, sometimes pasting her two eyes into the empty sky over the landscapes. Those images also came alive, achieving a beauty that Wang had never imagined.

Wang had always thought that his photographs lacked some kind of soul. Now he understood that they were missing *her*.

"All the physicists on this list have committed suicide in the last two months," General Chang said.

Wang was thunderstruck. Gradually, his black-and-white landscapes faded into blankness in his mind. The photographs

no longer had her figure in the foreground, and her eyes were wiped from the skies. Those worlds were all dead.

"When . . . did this happen?" Wang asked mechanically.

"The last two months," Chang repeated.

"You mean the last name, don't you?" Shi responded with satisfaction. "She was the last to commit suicide—two nights ago, overdosed on sleeping pills. She died very peacefully. No pain."

For a moment, Wang was grateful to Shi.

"Why?" Wang asked. The dead scenes in those landscape photographs continued to flicker through his mind.

General Chang replied, "The only thing we can be sure of is this: The same reason drove all of them to suicide. But it's hard to articulate. Maybe it's impossible for us nonspecialists to even understand the reason. The document contains excerpts from their suicide notes. Everyone can examine them after the meeting."

Wang flipped through the notes: All of them seemed to be long essays.

"Dr. Ding, would you please show Yang Dong's note to Professor Wang? Hers is the shortest and possibly the most representative."

The man in question, Ding Yi, had been silent until now. After another pause, he finally took out a white envelope and handed it across the table to Wang.

Shi whispered, "He was Yang's boyfriend." Wang recalled that he had seen Ding at the particle accelerator construction site in Liangxiang. He was a theoretician who had became famous for his discovery of the macroatom while studying ball lightning.[12] Wang took from the envelope a thin, irregularly

12 *Translator's Note:* For more on Ding Yi, see *Ball Lightning* by Cixin Liu.

shaped sheet exuding a faint fragrance—not paper, but birch bark. A single line of graceful characters was written on it:

All the evidence points to a single conclusion: Physics has never existed, and will never exist. I know what I'm doing is irresponsible. But I have no choice.

There wasn't even a signature. She was gone.

"Physics . . . does not exist?" Wang had no idea what to think.

General Chang closed the folder. "The file also contains some specific information related to the experimental results obtained after the completion of the world's three newest particle accelerators. It's very technical, and we won't be discussing it here. The first focus of our investigation is the Frontiers of Science. UNESCO designated 2005 the World Year of Physics, and that organization gradually developed out of the numerous academic conferences and exchanges that occurred among world physicists that year. Dr. Ding, since you're a theoretical physicist, can you give us more background on it?"

Ding nodded. "I have no direct connection with the Frontiers of Science, but it is famous in academia. Its core goal is a response to the following: Since the second half of the twentieth century, physics has gradually lost the concision and simplicity of its classical theories. Modern theoretical models have become more and more complex, vague, and uncertain. Experimental verification has become more difficult as well. This is a sign that the forefront of physics research seems to be hitting a wall.

"Members of the Frontiers of Science want to attempt a new way of thinking. To put it simply, they want to use the methods of science to discover the limits of science, to try to

find out if there is a limit to how deeply and precisely science can know nature—a boundary beyond which science cannot go. The development of modern physics seems to suggest that such a line has been touched."

"Very good," General Chang said. "According to our investigation, most of the scholars who committed suicide had some connection with the Frontiers of Science, and some were even members. But we've found no evidence of the use of illegal psychotropic drugs or techniques akin to the psychological manipulation of religious cults. In other words, even if the Frontiers of Science influenced them, it was only through legal academic exchanges. Professor Wang, since they recently contacted you, we'd like to ask you for some information."

Shi added gruffly, "Including the names of your contacts, the times and locations of meetings, the content of your conversations, and if you exchanged letters or e-mails—"

"Shut up, Da Shi!" General Chang said.

Another police officer leaned over and whispered to Shi, "Do you think we'll forget you have a mouth if you don't use it all the time?" Shi picked up his teacup, saw the drowned cigarette butt inside, and put it back down.

Shi's questions irritated Wang again, not unlike the feeling a man has upon finding out that he has swallowed a fly with his meal. The gratitude he had felt earlier was gone without a trace. But he restrained himself and answered, "My contact with the Frontiers of Science began with Shen Yufei. She's a Japanese physicist of Chinese descent who currently works for a Japanese company here in Beijing. She once worked at a Mitsubishi lab, researching nanotech. We met at a technical conference at the beginning of this year. Through her, I met a few other physicist friends, all members of the Frontiers of Science, some Chinese, some foreign. When I talked with

them, all the topics were . . . how do I put this? Very radical. They all involved the question that Dr. Ding just described: What is the limit of science?

"Initially, I didn't have much interest in these topics. I thought of them as only an idle pastime. My work is in applied research, and I don't know much about these theoretical matters. Mainly, I was interested in listening to their discussions and arguments. All of them were deep thinkers with novel points of view, and I felt that I was opening my mind through the exchanges. Gradually, I grew more interested. But all our talk was limited to pure theory and nothing else. They once invited me to join the Frontiers of Science. But if I had done so, attending the discussions would have turned into a duty. Since my time and energy were limited, I declined."

"Professor Wang," General Chang said, "we'd like you to accept the invitation and join the Frontiers of Science. This is the main reason we asked you here today. Through you, we'd like to learn more about the internal workings of the organization."

"You want me to be a mole?" Wang was uneasy.

"A mole!" Shi laughed.

Chang gave Shi a reprimanding look. He turned back to Wang. "We just want you to give us some information. We have no other way in."

Wang shook his head. "I'm sorry, General. I cannot do this."

"Professor Wang, the Frontiers of Science is made up of elite international scholars. Investigating it is an extremely complex and sensitive matter. For us, it's like walking across thin ice. Without someone from academia helping us, we cannot make any progress. This is why we're making this request. But we'll respect your wishes. If you won't agree, we understand."

"I am . . . very busy at work. I just don't have the time."

General Chang nodded. "All right, Professor Wang, we won't waste any more of your time. Thank you for coming to this meeting."

Wang waited a few more seconds before realizing that he had been dismissed.

General Chang politely accompanied Wang to the door. They could hear Shi's loud voice behind them. "It's better this way. I disagree with the plan anyway. So many bookworms have already killed themselves. If we send him, he'd be a meat dumpling thrown to the dogs."

Wang turned around and walked back to Shi. Forcing his anger down, Wang said, "The way you speak is not appropriate for a good police officer."

"Who said I'm a *good* cop?"

"We don't know why these researchers killed themselves, but you shouldn't speak of them so contemptuously. Their minds have made irreplaceable contributions to humanity."

"You're saying they're better than me?" Still seated, Shi lifted his eyes to meet Wang's. "At least I wouldn't kill myself just because someone told me some bullshit."

"You think I would?"

"I have to be concerned about your safety." That trademark smirk again.

"I think I would be much safer than you in such situations. You must know that a person's ability to discern the truth is directly proportional to his knowledge."

"I'm not sure about that. Take someone like you—"

"Be quiet, Da Shi!" General Chang said. "One more sentence and you're out of here!"

"It's okay," Wang said. "Let him speak." He turned to General Chang. "I've changed my mind. I will join the Frontiers of Science as you wish."

"Good!" Shi nodded vigorously. "Stay alert after you join. Gather intelligence whenever it's convenient. For example, glance at their computer screens, memorize e-mail or Web addresses—"

"That's enough! You misunderstand me. I don't want to be a spy. I just want to prove you're an idiot!"

"If you remain alive after you've joined them for a while, that would be the best proof. But I'm afraid for you . . ." Shi lifted his face, and the smirk turned into a wolfish grin.

"Of course I'll stay alive! But I never want to see you again."

They kept Wang out of the way while the others left so he wouldn't have to deal with Shi Qiang again. Then General Chang walked Wang all the way down the stairs and called for a car to take him back.

He said to Wang, "Don't worry about Shi Qiang. That's just his personality. He's actually a very experienced beat officer and antiterrorism expert. Twenty years ago, he was a soldier in my company."

As they approached the car, Chang added, "Professor Wang, you must have many questions."

"What did everything you talked about in there have to do with the military?"

"War has everything to do with the army."

Wang looked around in the spring sun, baffled. "But where is this war? This is probably the most peaceful period in history."

Chang gave him an inscrutable smile. "You will know more soon. Everyone will know. Professor Wang, have you ever had anything happen to you that changed your life

67

completely? Some event where afterward the world became a totally different place for you?"

"No."

"Then your life has been fortunate. The world is full of unpredictable factors, yet you have never faced a crisis."

Wang turned over the words in his mind, still not understanding. "I think that's true of most lives."

"Then most people have lived fortunately."

"But . . . many generations have lived in this plain manner."

"All fortunate."

Wang laughed, shaking his head. "I have to confess that I'm not feeling very sharp today. Are you suggesting that—"

"Yes, the entire history of humankind has been fortunate. From the Stone Age till now, no real crisis has occurred. We've been very lucky. But if it's all luck, then it has to end one day. Let me tell you: It's ended. Prepare for the worst."

Wang wanted to ask more, but Chang shook his head and said good-bye, preventing any more questions.

After Wang got into the car, the driver asked for his address. Wang gave it and asked, "Oh, were you the one who took me here? I thought it was the same type of car."

"No, it wasn't me. I took Dr. Ding here."

Wang had a new idea. He asked the driver to take him to Ding's address instead.

5

A GAME OF POOL

As soon as he opened the door to Ding Yi's brand-new three-bedroom apartment, Wang smelled alcohol. Ding was lying on the sofa with the TV on, staring at the ceiling. The apartment was unfinished, with only a few pieces of furniture and little decoration, and the huge living room seemed very empty. The most eye-catching object was the pool table in the corner.

Ding didn't seem annoyed by Wang's unannounced visit. He was clearly in the mood to talk to someone.

"I bought the apartment about three months ago," Ding said. "Why did I buy it? Did I really think she was going to become interested in starting a family?" His laugh sounded drunk.

"You two . . ." Wang wanted to know the details of Yang Dong's life, but didn't know how to ask the questions.

"She was like a star, always so distant. Even the light she shone on me was always cold." Ding walked to one of the windows and looked up at the night sky.

Wang said nothing. All he wanted now was to hear her voice. But a year ago, as the sun sank in the west, when she and he had locked eyes for a moment, they had not spoken to each other. He had never heard her voice.

Ding waved his hand as though trying to flick something

away. "Professor Wang, you were right. Don't get involved with the police or the military. They're all idiots. The deaths of those physicists had nothing to do with the Frontiers of Science. I've explained it to them many times, but I can't get them to understand."

"They seem to have conducted some independent investigation."

"Yes, and the investigation's scope was global. They should already know that two of the dead never had any contact with the Frontiers of Science, including . . . Yang Dong." Ding seemed to have trouble saying her name.

"Ding Yi, you know that I am already involved. So . . . as far as why Yang made the choice that . . . she did, I'd like to know. I think you must know some of it." Wang thought he must sound very foolish as he tried hard to disguise his real intent.

"If you know more, you'll only get pulled in deeper. Right now you're just superficially involved, but with more knowledge your spirit will be drawn in as well, and then it will mean real trouble."

"I work in applied research. I'm not as sensitive as you theoreticians."

"All right, then. Do you play pool?" Ding walked to the pool table.

"I used to play a little in college."

"She and I loved to play. It reminded us of particles colliding in the accelerator." Ding picked up two balls: one black and one white. He set the black ball next to one of the pockets, and placed the white ball about ten centimeters from the black ball. "Can you pocket the black ball?"

"This close? Anyone can do it."

"Try."

Wang picked up the cue, struck the white ball lightly, and drove the black ball into the pocket.

"Good. Come, now let's move the table to a different location." Ding directed the confused Wang to pick up the heavy table. Together they moved it to another corner of the living room, next to a window. Then Ding scooped out the black ball, set it next to the pocket, and again picked up the white ball and set it down about ten centimeters away. "Think you can do it again?"

"Of course."

"Go for it."

Again, Wang easily made the shot.

Ding waved his hands. "Let's move it again." They lifted the table and set it down in a third corner of the living room. Ding set up the two balls as before. "Go."

"Listen, we—"

"Go!"

Wang shrugged helplessly. He managed to pocket the black ball a third time.

They moved the table two more times: once next to the door of the living room, and finally back to the original location. Ding set up the two balls twice more, and Wang twice more made his shot. By now both were slightly winded.

"Good, that's the conclusion of the experiment. Let's analyze the results." Ding lit a cigarette before continuing, "We ran the same experiment five times. Four of the experiments differed in both location and time. Two of the experiments were at the same location but different times. Aren't you shocked by the results?" He opened his arms exaggeratedly. "Five times! Every colliding experiment yielded the exact same result!"

"What are you trying to say?" Wang asked, gasping.

"Can you explain this incredible result? Please use the language of physics."

"All right . . . During these five experiments, the mass of the two balls never changed. In terms of their locations, as long as we're using the frame of reference of the tabletop, there was also no change. The velocity of the white ball striking the black ball also remained basically the same throughout. Thus, the transfer of momentum between the two balls didn't change. Therefore, in all five experiments, the result was the black ball being driven into the pocket."

Ding picked up a bottle of brandy and two dirty glasses from the floor. He filled both and handed one to Wang. Wang declined.

"Come on, let's celebrate. We've discovered a great principle of nature: The laws of physics are invariant across space and time. All the physical laws of human history, from Archimedes' principle to string theory, and all the scientific discoveries and intellectual fruits of our species are the by-products of this great law. Compared to us two theoreticians, Einstein and Hawking are mere applied engineers."

"I still don't understand what you're getting at."

"Imagine another set of results. The first time, the white ball drove the black ball into the pocket. The second time, the black ball bounced away. The third time, the black ball flew onto the ceiling. The fourth time, the black ball shot around the room like a frightened sparrow, finally taking refuge in your jacket pocket. The fifth time, the black ball flew away at nearly the speed of light, breaking the edge of the pool table, shooting through the wall, and leaving the Earth and the Solar System, just like Asimov once described.[13] What would you think then?"

13 *Author's Note:* See Isaac Asimov's short story "The Billiard Ball."

Ding watched Wang. After a long silence, Wang finally said, "This actually happened. Am I right?"

Ding drained both glasses in his hands. He stared at the pool table as though looking at a demon. "Yes. It happened. In the last few years, we finally obtained the necessary equipment for experimentally testing fundamental theories. Three expensive 'pool tables' have been constructed: one in North America, another in Europe, and the third you are familiar with, in Liangxiang. Your Nanotechnology Research Center earned a lot of money from it.

"These high-energy particle accelerators raised the amount of energy available for colliding particles by an order of magnitude, to a level never before achieved by the human race. Yet, with the new equipment, the same particles, the same energy levels, and the same experimental parameters would yield different results. Not only would the results vary if different accelerators were used, but even with the same accelerator, experiments performed at different times would give different results. Physicists panicked. They repeated the ultra-high-energy collision experiments again and again using the same conditions, but every time the result was different, and there seemed to be no pattern."

"What does this mean?" Wang asked. When he saw Ding staring at him without speaking, he added, "Oh, I'm in nanotech, and I also work with microscale structures. But that's orders of magnitude larger than the scale at which you do your work. Please educate me."

"It means that the laws of physics are not invariant across time and space."

"What does *that* mean?"

"I think you can deduce the rest. Even General Chang figured it out. He's really a smart man."

Wang looked outside the window thoughtfully. The lights of the city were so bright that the stars of the night sky were drowned out.

"It means that laws of physics that could be applied anywhere in the universe do not exist, which means that physics... also does not exist." Wang turned back from the window.

"'I know what I'm doing is irresponsible. But I have no choice,'" Ding said. "That was the second half of her note. You just stumbled on the first half. Now can you understand her? At least a little?"

Wang picked up the white ball. He caressed it for a bit and put it back down. "For someone exploring the forefront of theory, that would indeed be a catastrophe."

"To accomplish something in theoretical physics requires one to have almost religious faith. It's easy to be led to the abyss."

As they said their farewells, Ding gave Wang an address. "If you have the time, please visit Yang Dong's mother. She and her mother always lived together, and she was the entirety of her mother's life. Now the old woman is all alone."

"Ding, you clearly know a lot more than I do. Can you tell me more? You really believe that the laws of physics are not invariant across time and space?"

"I don't know anything." Ding stared into Wang's eyes for a long time. Finally, he said, "But that is the question."

Wang knew that he was only finishing what the British colonel had begun to say: *To be, or not to be: that is the question.*

6

THE SHOOTER AND THE FARMER

The next day was the start of the weekend. Wang got up early and left on his bicycle. As a hobby photographer, his favorite subjects were wildernesses free of human presence. But now that he was middle-aged, he no longer had the energy to engage in such indulgent travel and only shot city scenes.

Consciously or subconsciously, he usually chose corners of the city that held some aspect of the wild: a dried lakebed in a park, the freshly turned soil of a construction site, a weed struggling out of cracks in cement. In order to eliminate the busy colors of the city in the background, he only used black-and-white film. Unexpectedly, he had developed his own style and had gained some notice. His works had been selected for two exhibitions, and he was a member of the Photographers Association. Every time he went out to take pictures, he would ride his bike and wander around the city in search of inspiration and compositions that caught his fancy. Often he would be out all day.

Today, Wang felt strange. His photography style tended toward the classical, calm and dignified. But today he could not seem to get in the mood necessary for such compositions. In his mind, the city, as it awoke from its slumber, seemed to be built on quicksand. The stability was illusory. All night

long, he had dreamt of those two billiard balls. They flew around a dark space without any pattern, the black one disappearing against the black background and only revealing its existence occasionally when it obscured the white ball.

Can the fundamental nature of matter really be lawlessness? Can the stability and order of the world be but a temporary dynamic equilibrium achieved in a corner of the universe, a short-lived eddy in a chaotic current?

Without realizing it, he found himself at the foot of the newly completed China Central Television building. He stopped at the side of the road and lifted his head to gaze up at this gigantic A-shaped tower, trying to recapture the feeling of stability. His gaze followed the sharp tip of the building, gleaming in the morning sunlight, pointing toward the blue, bottomless depths of the sky. Two words suddenly floated into his consciousness: "shooter" and "farmer."

When the members of the Frontiers of Science discussed physics, they often used the abbreviation "SF." They didn't mean "science fiction," but the two words "shooter" and "farmer." This was a reference to two hypotheses, both involving the fundamental nature of the laws of the universe.

In the shooter hypothesis, a good marksman shoots at a target, creating a hole every ten centimeters. Now suppose the surface of the target is inhabited by intelligent, two-dimensional creatures. Their scientists, after observing the universe, discover a great law: "There exists a hole in the universe every ten centimeters." They have mistaken the result of the marksman's momentary whim for an unalterable law of the universe.

The farmer hypothesis, on the other hand, has the flavor of a horror story: Every morning on a turkey farm, the farmer comes to feed the turkeys. A scientist turkey, having

76

observed this pattern to hold without change for almost a year, makes the following discovery: "Every morning at eleven, food arrives." On the morning of Thanksgiving, the scientist announces this law to the other turkeys. But that morning at eleven, food doesn't arrive; instead, the farmer comes and kills the entire flock.

Wang felt the road beneath his feet shift like quicksand. The A-shaped building seemed to wobble and sway. He quickly brought his gaze back to the street.

To get rid of the anxiety, Wang forced himself to finish a roll of film. He returned home before lunch. His wife had taken their son out and wouldn't be back for a while. Usually, Wang would rush to develop the film, but today he wasn't in the mood. After a quick and simple lunch, he went to take a nap. Because he hadn't slept well the night before, by the time he woke up it was almost five. Finally remembering the roll of film he had shot, he went into the cramped darkroom he had converted from a closet.

The film developed. Wang began to look through the negatives to see if any shots were worth printing, but he saw something strange in the very first image. The shot was of a small lawn outside a large shopping center. The center of the negative held a line of tiny white marks, which, upon closer examination, turned out to be numbers: *1200:00:00.*

The second picture also had numbers: *1199:49:33,* as did the third: *1199:40:18.*

In fact, every picture in the roll had such numbers, until the thirty-sixth (and last) image: *1194:16:37.*

Wang's first thought was that something was wrong with the film. The camera he had used was a 1988 Leica

M2—entirely mechanical, which made it impossible for it to add a date stamp. Given the excellent lens and refined mechanical operation, it was considered a great professional camera even in this digital age.

After reexamining the negatives, Wang discovered another strange thing about the numbers: They seemed to adapt to the background. If the background was black, the numbers were white, and vice versa. The shift seemed designed to maximize the numbers' contrast for visibility. By the time Wang saw the sixteenth negative, his heart was beating faster, and a chill crept up his spine.

This shot was of a dead tree against an old wall. The wall was mottled, showing a pattern of alternating black and white patches on the negative. Given this background, either white or black numbers would have been hard to read. But in the picture, the numbers arranged themselves vertically to fit along the curve of the tree trunk, allowing the white numbers to show up against the dark coloring of the dead tree like a crawling snake.

Wang began to analyze the mathematical pattern in the numbers. At first he thought it was some kind of assigned numbering, but the difference between the numbers wasn't constant. He then guessed that the numbers represented time in the form of hours, minutes, and seconds. He took out his shooting diary, in which he recorded the exact time he took each picture down to the minute, and discovered the difference between two successive numbers on the photographs corresponded to the difference in time between when they were taken.

A countdown.

The countdown began with 1,200 hours. And now there were about 1,194 hours left, just under 50 days.

Now? No, at the moment I took the last photograph. Is the countdown still proceeding?

Wang walked out of the darkroom, loaded a new roll of film in the Leica, and began to snap random shots. He even walked onto the balcony for a few outdoor shots. Afterward, he took out the film and went back into the darkroom. In the developed roll, the numbers again appeared on every negative like ghosts. The first one was marked *1187:27:39*. The difference matched the passage of time between the last shot of the last roll and the first shot of this roll. After that, the number decreased by three or four seconds in each image: *1187:27:35, 1187:27:31, 1187:27:27, 1187:27:24 . . .* just like the intervals between the quick shots he had taken.

The countdown continued.

Wang again loaded a new roll of film. He snapped off the shots rapidly, even taking a few with the lens cap on. As he took out the roll of film, his wife and son returned. Before he went into the darkroom to develop the film, he loaded another roll of film in the Leica and handed it to his wife. "Here, finish the roll for me."

"What am I supposed to shoot?" His wife looked at him, amazed. He never allowed anyone to touch his camera, though she and their son had no interest in doing so either. In their eyes, it was a boring antique that cost more than twenty thousand yuan.

"Doesn't matter. Just shoot whatever you want." Wang stuffed the camera into her hands and ducked into the darkroom.

"All right. Dou Dou, why don't I take some pictures of you?" His wife aimed the camera at their son.

Wang's mind suddenly filled with the imagined sight of the ghostlike figures appearing over his son's face like a

hangman's noose. He shuddered. "No, don't do that. Shoot something else."

The shutter clicked, and his wife had taken her first shot. "Why can't I press it again?" she asked. Wang taught her how to wind the film to advance it. "Like that. You have to do it after every shot." Then he ducked back into the darkroom.

"So complicated!" His wife, a doctor, couldn't understand why anyone would use such expensive but outdated equipment when ten- or even twenty-megapixel digital cameras were common. And he even used black-and-white film.

After the third roll of film developed, Wang held it up against the red light. He saw that the ghostlike countdown continued. The numbers showed up clearly on every randomly shot picture, including the few he had taken with the lens cap on: *1187:19:06, 1187:19:03, 1187:18:59, 1187:18:56* . . .

His wife knocked on the darkroom door and told him she was finished with the roll. Wang opened the door and took the camera from her. As he took out the roll, his hands trembled. Ignoring his wife's concerned look, he took the film back into the darkroom and shut the door. He worked fast and clumsily, spilling developer and fixer all over the ground. Soon the images were developed. He closed his eyes, silently praying, *Please don't appear. No matter what, please don't appear now. Don't make it my turn.* . . .

He examined the wet film with a magnifying glass. There was no countdown. The negatives held only the interior shots his wife had taken. She had used a slow shutter speed, and her amateurish operation left all the scenes blurry. But Wang thought these were the most enjoyable pictures he had ever seen.

Wang came out of the darkroom and let out a held breath.

He was covered in sweat. His wife was in the kitchen cooking, and his son was playing in his room. He sat on the sofa and thought the matter over more rationally.

First, the numbers, which precisely recorded the passage of time between shots and which showed signs of intelligence, could not possibly have been preprinted on the film. *Something* exposed them onto the film. But what? Did the camera have a malfunction? Had some mechanism been installed in the camera without his knowledge? He took off the lens and disassembled the camera. He examined the interior with a magnifying glass and checked every dustless component without discovering anything out of place. Then, considering that the numbers showed up even in the shots taken with the lens cap on, he realized the most likely light source was some kind of penetrating ray. But how was this technologically possible? Where was the source of the rays? How could they have been aimed?

At least given current technology, such power would be supernatural.

In order to see if the ghostly countdown had disappeared, Wang loaded another roll into the Leica, and again began to shoot randomly. When this roll was developed, Wang's short-lived calm was again shattered. He felt himself pushed to the precipice of madness. The countdown had returned. Based on the numbers, it had never stopped, just failed to display on the roll shot by his wife.

1186:34:13, 1186:34:02, 1186:33:46, 1186:33:35 . . .

Wang rushed out of the darkroom and continued through the door of the apartment. He knocked loudly on the door of his neighbor, retired Professor Zhang.

"Professor Zhang, do you have a camera? Not a digital one, but one that takes film!"

"A professional photographer like you wants to borrow my camera? What happened to your expensive one? I have only digital point-and-shoots. Are you okay? Your face looks so pale."

"Please, let me borrow it."

Zhang returned with a common Kodak digital camera. "Here you go. You can just delete the few pictures already on there."

"Thank you!" Wang seized the camera and rushed back home. He actually had three more film cameras and a digital one, but Wang thought it better to borrow a camera from someone else. He looked at his own camera lying on the sofa and the few rolls of film, paused in thought, and decided to reload the Leica with new film. He handed the borrowed digital camera to his wife, who was setting out dinner.

"Quick! Shoot another few pictures, like before."

"What are you doing? Look at your face! What's happening?"

"Don't worry about it. Shoot!"

She put down the dishes and came over to him, her eyes filled with both worry and fright.

Wang stuffed the Kodak into the hands of his six-year-old son, who was about to start eating dinner. "Dou Dou, come help Daddy. Push this button. Right, like that. That's one shot. Push it again. That's another shot. Keep on shooting like that. You can take pictures of anything you want."

The boy learned quickly. He was very interested and made rapid shots. Wang turned around and picked up the Leica from the couch, and began to shoot as well. The father and son kept on pressing the shutters as though they were mad. His wife, not knowing what to do as the flashes went off around her, began to cry.

"Wang Miao, I know that you've been under a lot of pressure lately, but please, I hope you haven't . . . ?"

Wang finished the roll in the Leica and grabbed the digital from his son. He thought for a moment, and then, in order to avoid his wife, went into the bedroom and took a few more shots with the digital. He used the optical finder instead of the LCD because he was afraid to see the results, though he was going to have to face them soon enough.

Wang took out the film from the Leica and went back into the darkroom. He shut the door and worked. After the film was developed, he examined the images carefully. Because his hands were shaking, he had to hold the magnifying glass with both hands. On the negatives, the countdown continued.

Wang rushed out of the darkroom and began to look through the digital images on the Kodak. On the LCD, he saw that the pictures his son had taken did not have the numbers, but in the pictures that he took, the countdown showed clearly and was synchronized with the numbers on the film.

By using different cameras, Wang was trying to eliminate problems with the camera or the film as possible explanations. But by allowing his son and his wife to take some pictures, he discovered an even stranger result: The countdown only appeared on the pictures he took!

Desperate, Wang picked up the pile of film rolls, like a tangled nest of snakes, like a bunch of ropes tied into an impossible knot.

He knew that he could not solve the mystery on his own. Who could he turn to? His old classmates from college and his colleagues at the Research Center were hopeless. Like him, they were all people with technical minds. Intuitively, he knew that this went beyond a technical problem. He thought

of Ding Yi, but that man was now in a spiritual crisis of his own. Finally, he thought of the Frontiers of Science. These were deep thinkers who remained open-minded. So he dialed Shen Yufei's number.

"Dr. Shen, I have a problem. I must see you."

"Come over," Shen said, and hung up.

Wang was surprised. Shen was a woman of few words. Some in the Frontiers of Science jokingly called her the Female Hemingway. But the fact that she didn't even ask him what was wrong made Wang uncertain whether he should be comforted or even more anxious.

He stuffed the mess of film into a bag, and, taking the digital camera, rushed out of the apartment as his wife watched him anxiously. He could have driven, but even with the city being full of lights, he wanted to be with people. He called for a cab.

Shen lived in a luxury housing development reachable by one of the newer commuter rails. Here, the lights were much dimmer. The houses were set around a small artificial lake stocked with fish for the residents, and at night the place felt like a village.

Shen was clearly well off, but Wang could never figure out the source of her wealth. Neither her old research position nor her current job with a private company could earn that much income. But her house didn't show signs of luxury on the inside. It was used as a gathering place for the Frontiers of Science, and Wang always thought it resembled a small library with a meeting room.

In the living room, Wang saw Wei Cheng, Shen's husband. Wei was about forty years old and had the look of a staid,

honest intellectual. Wang knew little about him other than his name. Shen hadn't said much when she introduced him. He didn't seem to have a job, since he stayed home all day. He never showed any interest in the Frontiers of Science discussions, but seemed used to the sight of so many scholars coming to their house.

But he wasn't idle. He appeared to be conducting some kind of research at home, always deep in thought. Whenever he met any visitor, he would greet them absentmindedly and then return to his room upstairs. Most of his day was spent there. One time, Wang glanced into his room through the half-open door and saw an astonishing sight: a powerful HP workstation. He was sure of what he saw because the workstation was the same model as the one he used at the Research Center: slate-gray chassis, model RX8620, four years old. It seemed very strange to own a machine costing more than a million yuan just for personal use. What was Wei Cheng doing with it all day?

"Yufei is a bit busy right now. Why don't you wait a while?" Wei Cheng walked upstairs. Wang tried to wait, but he found that he couldn't be still, so he followed Wei Cheng. Wei was about to enter his room with the workstation when he saw Wang behind him, but he didn't seem annoyed. He pointed to the room across from his. "She's in there."

Wang knocked on the door. It wasn't locked, and it opened a crack. Shen was seated in front of a computer, playing a game. He was surprised to see that she wore a V-suit.

The V-suit was a very popular piece of equipment among gamers, made up of a panoramic viewing helmet and a haptic feedback suit. The suit allowed the player to experience the sensations of the game: being struck by a fist, being stabbed by a knife, being burned by flames, and so on. It was also

capable of generating feelings of extreme heat and cold, even simulating the sensation of being exposed in a snowstorm.

Wang walked behind her. As the game was displayed only on the inside of the panoramic viewing helmet, there were no colorful images on the computer monitor. Wang suddenly remembered Shi Qiang's comment about memorizing Web and e-mail addresses. He glanced at the monitor. The game site's URL caught his attention: www.3body.net.

Shen took off the helmet and stripped off the haptic feedback suit. She put on her glasses, which appeared extra large against her thin face. Without any expression, she nodded at Wang and said nothing. Wang took out the mess of film rolls and began to explain his strange experience. Shen paid full attention to his story, picking up the rolls of film and only casually looking at them. This surprised Wang, but further confirmed for him that Shen wasn't completely ignorant about what he was going through. He almost stopped speaking, but Shen kept on nodding at him, indicating that he should continue.

When he finished, Shen spoke for the first time. "How's the nanomaterial project you're leading proceeding?"

This non sequitur disoriented Wang. "The nanomaterial project? What does that have to do with this?" He pointed at the rolls of film.

Shen didn't answer, but continued to stare at him, waiting for him to answer her question. This was always her style, never wasting a single word.

"Stop your research," she said.

"What?" Wang wasn't sure he heard right. "What are you talking about?"

Shen remained silent.

"Stop? That's a key national project!"

Shen still said nothing, only looking at him calmly.

"You have to give me a reason."

"Just stop. Try it."

"What do you know? Tell me!"

"I've told you all I can."

"I can't stop the project. It's impossible!"

"Just stop. Try it."

That was the end of the conversation about the countdown. After that, no matter how hard Wang tried, Shen only repeated, "Just stop. Try it."

"I understand now," Wang said. "The Frontiers of Science isn't just a discussion group about fundamental theory, like you claimed. Its connection to reality is far more complicated than I had imagined."

"No. It's the opposite. Your impression is due to the fact that the Frontiers of Science concerns matters far more fundamental than you imagine."

Desperate, Wang got up to leave without saying good-bye. Mutely, Shen accompanied him to the door and watched as he got into the taxi.

Just then, another car drove up and braked to a hard stop in front of the door. A man got out. By the faint light leaking from the house, Wang recognized him immediately.

The man was Pan Han, one of the most prominent members of the Frontiers of Science. A biologist, he had successfully predicted the birth defects associated with long-term consumption of genetically modified foods. He had also predicted the ecological disasters that would come with cultivation of genetically modified crops. Unlike the prophets of doom who regularly warned of catastrophes without any particulars, Pan made predictions that always gave many specific details that later turned out to be correct.

His accuracy was such that there were rumors that he came from the future.

The other cause for his fame was that he had created China's first experimental community. Unlike the "return to nature" utopian groups in the West, his "Pastoral China" wasn't located in the wilderness, but in the midst of one of its largest cities. The community had no property of its own. Everything needed for daily life, including food, came from urban trash. Contrary to the predictions of many, Pastoral China not only survived, but thrived. Currently, it had more than three thousand permanent members, and countless others had joined for short stints to experience the lifestyle.

Based on these two successes, Pan's opinions on social issues had grown more and more influential. He believed that technological progress was a disease in human society. The explosive development of technology was analogous to the growth of cancer cells, and the results would be identical: the exhaustion of all sources of nourishment, the destruction of organs, and the final death of the host body. He advocated abolishing crude technologies such as fossil fuels and nuclear energy and keeping gentler technologies such as solar power and small-scale hydroelectric power. He believed in the gradual de-urbanization of modern metropolises by distributing the population more evenly in self-sufficient small towns and villages. Relying on the gentler technologies, he would build a new agricultural society.

"Is he in?" Pan asked Shen, pointing to the house.

Shen didn't answer, but blocked his progress.

"I have to warn him and also warn you. Do not force our hand." Pan's voice was cold.

Shen called to the taxi driver, "You can go now." After the taxi started, Wang couldn't hear any more of the

conversation between Shen and Pan, but he glanced back and saw that Shen did not let Pan into the house.

By the time Wang arrived home, it was already after midnight. As Wang got out of the taxi, a black Volkswagen Santana braked to a stop next to him. The window rolled down and a cloud of smoke emerged. Shi Qiang's thick body filled the driver's seat.

"Professor Wang! Academician Wang![14] How've you been the last couple of days?"

"Are you following me? Don't you have anything better to do?"

"Now, don't misunderstand me. I could have just driven past you, but instead, I chose to be polite and stop to greet you. You're making being nice a thankless task." Shi revealed his trademark roguish smirk. "Well? Did you find out any useful information over there?"

"I've told you already, I don't want anything to do with you. Please leave me alone from now on."

"Fine." Shi started the car. "It's not like I'm going to starve without the overtime for doing this. I'd rather not have missed my soccer match."

Wang entered the apartment. His wife was already asleep. He could hear her tossing and turning in bed, mumbling anxiously. Her husband's strange behavior during the day was surely giving her bad dreams. Wang swallowed a few sleeping pills, lay down on the bed, and, after a long wait, fell asleep.

14 *Translator's Note:* This refers to Wang's status as a member of the Chinese Academy of Sciences.

His dreams were chaotic, but there was one constant: the ghostly countdown, suspended in midair. Even before he fell asleep, he had known he would dream of it. In his dreams, he attacked the countdown. Crazed, he tore at it, bit it, but every attempt failed to leave a mark. It continued to hang in the middle of his dream, steadily ticking away. Finally, just as the frustration became almost intolerable, he woke up.

Opening his eyes, he saw the ceiling, indistinct above him. The city lights outside the window cast a dim glow against it through the curtains. But one thing did follow him from dream into reality: the countdown. It was still hovering before his eyes. The numbers were thin, but very bright with a burning, white glow.

1180:05:00, 1180:04:59, 1180:04:58, 1180:04:57 . . .

Wang looked around, taking in the blurry shadows around the bedroom. He was now certain that he was awake, but the countdown did not disappear. He shut his eyes, and the countdown remained in the darkness of his vision, looking like mercury flowing against a black swan's feathers. He opened his eyes, rubbed them, and still the countdown did not go away. No matter how he moved his gaze, the numbers stayed at the center of it.

A nameless terror made Wang sit up. The countdown clung to him. He jumped off the bed, tore the curtains apart, and pushed the window open. The city, deep in sleep, was still brightly lit. The countdown hovered before this grand background like subtitles on a movie screen.

Wang felt he was suffocating. He let out a stifled scream. His wife, frightened awake, questioned him anxiously. He tried to force himself to be calm and comforted her, telling her that it was nothing. He lay back on the bed, closed his

eyes, and spent the rest of his difficult night under the constant glow of the countdown.

In the morning, he tried to act normal in front of his family, but he could not fool his wife. She asked him whether his eyes were all right, whether he could see clearly.

After breakfast, Wang called the Research Center and asked for the day off. He drove to the hospital. Along the way, the countdown mercilessly hovered in front of the real world. It was able to adjust its brightness so that, no matter what the background, it showed up distinctly. Wang even tried to temporarily overwhelm the display by staring into the rising sun. But it was useless. The infernal numbers turned black and showed up against the orb of the sun like projected shadows, which made them even more frightening.

Tongren Hospital was very busy, but Wang was able to see a famous ophthalmologist who had gone to school with his wife. He asked the doctor to test him, without describing the symptoms. After careful examination of both eyes, the doctor told him they were functioning normally with no signs of any disease.

"There's something stuck in my vision. No matter where I look, it's always there." As Wang said this, the numbers hovered in front of the doctor's face.

1175:11:34, 1175:11:33, 1175:11:32, 1175:11:31 . . .

"Oh, you're talking about floaters." The doctor took out a prescription pad and began to write. "They're common at our age, the result of clouding in the lens. They're not easy to cure, but they're also not a big deal. I'll give you some iodine drops and vitamin D—it's possible that they'll go away, but don't get your hopes up too much. Really, they're nothing to worry about, as they don't affect your vision. You just have to get used to ignoring them."

"Floaters . . . Can you tell me what they look like?"

"There's no real pattern. It differs by person. For some, they appear as tiny black dots; for others, like tadpoles."

"What if someone sees a series of numbers?"

The doctor's pen stopped. "You see numbers?"

"Yes, right in the middle of the visual field."

The doctor pushed his pen and paper away, and looked at him sympathetically. "As soon as you came in, I could tell you'd been working too much. At the last class reunion, Li Yao told me you were under a lot of pressure at work. We have to be careful at our age. Our health is no longer what it used to be."

"You are saying this is due to psychological factors?"

The doctor nodded. "If it was anyone else, I'd suggest you go see a psychiatrist. But it's nothing serious, just exhaustion. Why don't you rest for a few days? Take a vacation. Go be with Yao and your kid—what's his name . . . Dou Dou, right? No worries. They'll go away soon."

1175:10:02, 1175:10:01, 1175:10:00, 1175:09:59 . . .

"Let me tell you what I see. It's a countdown! One second after another, it keeps on ticking precisely. Are you saying this is all in my head?"

The doctor gave him a tolerant smile. "You know how much the mind can affect vision? Last month we had a patient—a girl, maybe fifteen, sixteen. She was in class when she suddenly lost the ability to see, went completely blind. But all the tests showed that there was nothing wrong with her eyes physiologically. Finally, someone from the Department of Psychiatry treated her with psychotherapy for a month. All of a sudden, her vision returned."

Wang knew that he was wasting his time here. He got up. "All right, let's not talk about my eyes anymore. I have

one last question: Do you know of any physical phenomenon that can operate from a distance and make people see visions?"

The doctor gave this some thought. "Yes, I do. A while ago I was part of the medical team for the Shenzhou 19 spacecraft. Some taikonauts engaged in extravehicular activities reported seeing flashes that didn't exist. The astronauts on the International Space Station reported similar experiences. It was because during periods of intense solar activity, high-energy particles struck against the retina, causing them to see flashes. But you're talking about numbers—a countdown, even. Solar activity can't possibly cause that."

Wang walked out of the hospital in a daze. The countdown continued to hover in his eyes, and he seemed to be following the numbers, following a ghost that would not leave him. He bought a pair of sunglasses and put them on so that others would not see his eyes wandering around as though he were sleepwalking.

Before entering the main lab at the Nanotechnology Research Center, Wang took off his sunglasses. Even so, his colleagues noticed his apparent mental state and gave him concerned looks.

Wang saw that the main reaction chamber in the middle of the lab was still in operation. The main compartment of the gigantic apparatus was a sphere with many pipes connected to it.

They had made small quantities of a new, ultrastrong nanomaterial that they'd given the code name "Flying Blade." But the samples so far were all made with molecular construction techniques—that is, using a nanoscale molecular probe to stack the molecules one by one, like laying out bricks for a wall. This method was very resource-intensive,

and the results might as well have been the world's most precious jewels. It was impractical to produce large quantities this way.

At the moment, the lab was attempting to develop a catalytic reaction as a substitute for molecular construction so that large numbers of molecules would stack themselves into the right arrangement. The main reaction chamber could rapidly run through a large number of reactions using different molecular combinations. There were so many combinations that normal manual testing methods would have taken more than a hundred years. In addition, the apparatus augmented actual reactions with mathematical simulations. When the reaction reached a certain stage, the computer would build a mathematical model of it based on intermediate products and finish the remainder of the reaction via simulation. This greatly boosted the experimental efficiency.

When the lab director saw Wang, he hurried over and began to report a series of malfunctions with the main reaction chamber—a recent ritual whenever Wang arrived at work. By now the main reaction chamber had been in continuous operation for more than a year, and many sensors had lost sensitivity, resulting in measurement errors that required shutting down the apparatus for maintenance. But as the lead scientist on the project, Wang insisted that the machine would not be shut down until the third set of molecular combinations was finished. The technicians had no choice but to jury-rig more and more kludges onto the main reaction chamber to compensate. And now those kludges required their own kludges, a state of affairs that exhausted the project staff.

But the lab director carefully avoided the topic of shutting down the machine and temporarily halting the experiment,

as he knew that such discussions tended to enrage Wang Miao. He just laid out the difficulties before Wang, though his unspoken desire was clear.

Engineers rushed around the main reaction chamber like doctors around a critical patient, trying to keep it going for a little longer. In front of the whole scene, the countdown appeared.

1174:21:11, 1174:21:10, 1174:21:09, 1174:21:08 . . .

Just stop. Try it. Shen's words came to Wang.

"How long would it take to completely overhaul the sensors?" Wang asked.

"Four or five days." Now that the lab director saw a ray of hope, he quickly added, "If we work fast, it will take only three days. I guarantee it, Chief Wang!"

I'm not giving in, Wang thought. *The equipment really needs maintenance, so the experiment must be temporarily stopped. This has nothing to do with anything else.* He turned to the lab director and focused on him through the hovering countdown. "Shut down the experiment and perform the maintenance. Follow the schedule you gave me."

"Absolutely, Chief Wang. I'll give you an updated schedule right away. We can stop the reaction this afternoon!"

"You can stop it right now."

The lab director stared at him in disbelief, but soon he was excited again, as if afraid to lose this opportunity. He picked up the phone and issued the order to stop the reaction. All the exhausted researchers and technicians grew excited, too. They immediately began the procedures to shut down the main reaction chamber, flipping a hundred complex switches. The various control screens became dark one after another, until finally, the main screen reflected the main reaction chamber's halted status.

Almost simultaneously, the countdown before Wang's eyes also stopped. The final number was *1174:10:07*. A few seconds later, the numbers flickered and disappeared.

As the world reemerged, free of the ghostly numbers, Wang let out a long breath, as though he had just struggled up from underwater. He sat down, drained, and realized that others were still watching him.

He turned to the lab director. "System maintenance is the responsibility of the Equipment Division. Why don't all of you in the research group take a break for a few days? I know everyone's been working hard."

"Chief Wang, you're tired, too. Chief Engineer Zhang can take care of things here. Why don't you go home and rest as well?"

"Yes, I *am* tired," Wang said.

After the lab director left, he picked up the phone and dialed Shen Yufei's number. She picked up after one ring.

"Who or what is behind this?" Wang asked. He tried to make his voice calm, but failed.

Silence.

"What will happen at the end of the countdown?"

More silence.

"Are you listening?"

"Yes."

"Why nanomaterials? This is not a particle accelerator. It's just applied research. Is it worth your attention?"

"Whether something is worth the attention is not for us to decide."

"That's enough!" Wang shouted into the phone. The terror and desperation of the last few days suddenly turned into uncontrollable rage. "Do you think these cheap tricks can fool me? Can stop technological progress? I admit that

I can't, for now, explain how you're doing it. But that's only because I haven't been able to peek behind the curtain of your shameful illusionist."

"You're saying you want to see the countdown on an even greater scale?"

Shen's question stunned Wang for a moment. He forced himself to be calm so he wouldn't fall into a trap. "Put away your set of tricks. So what if you show it at a bigger scale? It's still only an illusion. You can project a hologram into the sky, like what NATO did during the last war. With a powerful enough laser you can project an image onto the surface of the moon! The shooter and the farmer should be able to manipulate matters at a scale that humans cannot. For example, can you make the countdown appear on the surface of the sun?" Wang's mouth hung open. He had shocked himself with his own words. Unconsciously, he had named the two hypotheses that he ought to have avoided. He felt on the verge of falling into the same mental trap that had claimed the other victims.

Trying to seize the initiative, he continued, "I can't anticipate all your tricks, but even with the sun, perhaps your despicable illusionist can still somehow make the deception seem real. To give a demonstration that will really be convincing, you have to display it at an even larger scale."

"The question is whether you can take it," Shen said. "We're friends. I want to help you *avoid* Yang Dong's fate."

The mention of Yang's name made Wang shudder. But another surge of anger made him reckless. "Will you take up my challenge?"

"Of course."

"What are you going to do?"

"Do you have a computer connected to the Internet?

Okay, enter the following Web address: http://www.qsl.net/ bg3tt/zl/mesdm.htm. You got it open? Now, print it out and keep it with you."

Wang saw that the page was nothing more than a Morse code chart.

"I don't understand. This—"

"During the next two days, please find a place where you can observe the cosmic microwave background. For specifics, please check the e-mail I'll send you."

"What . . . are you going to do?"

"I know that your nanomaterial project has been stopped. Do you plan on restarting it?"

"Of course. Three days from now."

"Then the countdown will continue."

"At what scale will I see it?"

A long silence followed. This woman, who was acting as the spokesperson for some force beyond human understanding, blocked every exit Wang had.

"Three days from now—that's the fourteenth—between one and five in the morning, the entire universe will flicker for you."

THREE BODY: KING WEN OF ZHOU
AND THE LONG NIGHT

Wang dialed Ding Yi's number. Only when Ding picked up did he realize that it was already one in the morning.

"This is Wang Miao. I'm sorry to be calling so late."

"No problem. I can't sleep anyway."

"I have . . . seen something, and I'd like your help. Do you know if there are any facilities in China that are observing the cosmic microwave background?" Wang had the urge to talk to someone about what was going on, but he thought it best to not let too many people know about the countdown that only he could see.

"The cosmic microwave background? What made you interested in that? I guess you really have run into some problems. . . . Have you been to see Yang Dong's mother yet?"

"Ah—I'm sorry. I forgot."

"No worries. Right now, many scientists have . . . seen something, like you. Everyone's distracted. But I think it's still best if you go visit her. She's getting on in years, and she won't hire a caretaker. If there's some task around the home that she needs help with, please help her Oh, right, the cosmic microwave background. You can ask Yang's mother.

Before she retired, she was an astrophysicist. She's very familiar with such facilities in China."

"Good! I'll go after work today."

"Then I'll thank you in advance. I really can't face anything that reminds me of Yang Dong again."

After hanging up, Wang sat in front of his computer and printed out the simple Morse code chart. By now he was calm enough to turn his thoughts away from the countdown. He pondered the Frontiers of Science, Shen Yufei, and the computer game she had been playing. The only thing he knew for certain about Shen was that she wasn't the type to enjoy computer games. She spoke like a telegraph and gave him the impression that she was always extremely cold. It wasn't the kind of coldness that some people put on like a mask—hers suffused her all the way through.

Wang subconsciously thought of her as the long-obsolete DOS operating system: a blank, black screen, a bare "C:\>" prompt, a blinking cursor. Whatever you entered, it echoed back. Not one extra letter and not a single change. But now he knew that behind the "C:\>" was a bottomless abyss.

She's actually interested in a game? A game that requires a V-suit? She has no kids, which means she bought the V-suit for herself. The very idea is preposterous.

Wang entered the address for the game into the browser. It had been easy to memorize: www.3body.net. The site indicated that the game only supported access via V-suit. Wang remembered that the employee lounge at the Nanotechnology Research Center had a V-suit. He left the now-empty main lab and went to the security office to get the key. In the lounge, he passed the pool tables and the exercise machines

and found the V-suit next to a computer. He struggled into the haptic feedback suit, put on the panoramic viewing helmet, and turned on the computer.

After entering the game, Wang found himself in the middle of a desolate plain at dawn. The plain was dun-colored, blurry, its details hard to make out. In the distance, there was a sliver of white light on the horizon. Twinkling stars covered the rest of the sky.

There was a loud explosion, and two red-glowing mountains crashed against the earth in the distance. The whole plain was bathed in red light. When the dust finally cleared from the sky, Wang saw two giant words erected between the sky and the earth: THREE BODY.

Next came a registration screen. Wang created the ID "Hairen," and logged in.[15]

The plain remained desolate, but now the compressors in the V-suit whirred to life, and Wang could feel gusts of cold air against his body. Before him appeared two walking figures, forming dark silhouettes against the dawn light. Wang ran after them.

He saw that both figures were male. They were dressed in long robes full of holes, covered by dirty animal hides. Each carried a short, wide bronze sword. One of them carried a narrow wooden trunk that was as long as half his height. He turned around to look at Wang. The man's face was as dirty and wrinkled as the hide he wore, but his eyes were sharp and lively, the pupils glinting in the early-morning glow.

15 *Translator's Note: Hairen* (海人) means "Man of the Sea." This is a play on Wang Miao's name (汪淼), which can be read to mean "sea."

"It's cold," he said.

"Yes, very cold."

"This is the Warring States Period," the man with the trunk on his back said. "I am King Wen of Zhou."

"I don't think King Wen belongs to the Warring States Period," Wang said.[16]

"He's survived until now," the other man said. "King Zhou of Shang is alive, too. I am a follower of King Wen. Indeed, that's my log-in ID: 'Follower of King Wen of Zhou.' He's a genius, you know?"[17]

"My log-in ID is 'Hairen.' What are you carrying on your back?"

King Wen put down the rectangular trunk and stood it up vertically. He opened one of the sides like a door and revealed five compartments within. By the faint light, Wang could see that every layer held a small mound of sand. Every compartment seemed to have sand falling into it from the compartment above, through a small hole.

"A type of sandglass. Every eight hours all the sand flows to the bottom. Flip it three times and you can measure a day. But often I forget to flip it, and I need Follower here to remind me."

"You seem to be on a very long journey. Is it necessary to carry such a bulky clock?"

"How else would we measure time?"

"A portable sundial would be much more convenient. Or else you could just look at the sun and know the approximate time."

16 *Translator's Note:* The Warring States Period lasted from 475 BC to 221 BC. But King Wen of Zhou reigned much earlier, from 1099 BC to 1050 BC. He is considered the founder of the Zhou Dynasty, which overthrew the corrupt Shang Dynasty.

17 *Translator's Note:* King Zhou of Shang reigned from 1075 BC to 1046 BC. The last king of the Shang Dynasty, he was a notorious tyrant in Chinese history.

King Wen and Follower stared at each other, and then turned as one to gaze at Wang, as though he was an idiot. "The sun? How can the sun tell us the time? We're in the midst of a Chaotic Era."

Wang was about to ask for the meaning of the strange term when Follower cried out piteously, "It's so cold! I'm going to die of the cold!"

Wang felt very cold as well. But in most games, taking off his V-suit would immediately cause his ID to be deleted by the system. He couldn't do that. He said, "When the sun comes out it will be warmer."

"Are you pretending to be some kind of oracle? Even King Wen cannot predict the future." Follower shook his head contemptuously.

"What does what I said have to do with predicting the future? Everyone can see that the sun will rise in about another hour or two." Wang pointed to the sliver of light above the horizon.

"This is a Chaotic Era!"

"What is a Chaotic Era?"

"Other than Stable Eras, all times are Chaotic Eras." King Wen answered the way he would have spoken to an ignorant child.

Indeed, the light over the horizon dimmed and soon disappeared. Night covered everything. The stars overhead shone even more brightly.

"So that was dusk instead of dawn?" Wang asked.

"It is morning. But the sun doesn't always rise in the morning. That's what a Chaotic Era is like."

Wang found the cold hard to take. "It looks like the sun won't rise for a long time." He shivered and pointed to the blurry horizon.

"What makes you think that? There's no way to be certain. I told you, this is a Chaotic Era." Follower turned to King Wen. "May I have some dried fish?"

"Absolutely not." King Wen's tone brooked no disagreement. "I barely have enough for myself. We must guarantee that *I* make it to Zhao Ge, not you."[18]

As they spoke, Wang noticed the sky brightening over another part of the horizon. He couldn't be sure of the compass directions, but he was sure the direction this time was different from last time. The sky grew brighter, and soon, the sun of this world rose. It was small and bluish in color, like a very bright moon. Wang still felt a bit of warmth, and could now see the landscape around him more clearly. But the day didn't last long. The sun traversed a shallow arc over the horizon and soon set. Night and the bone-chilling cold once more settled over everything.

The three travelers stopped in front of a dead tree. King Wen and Follower took out their bronze swords to chop the tree into firewood, and Wang gathered the firewood into a pile. Follower took out a piece of flint and struck it against a blade until the sparks caught. The fire soon warmed the front of Wang's V-suit, but his back remained cold.

"We should burn some of the dehydrated bodies," Follower said. "Then we'll have a roaring fire!"

"Put that thought out of your mind. Only the tyrant King Zhou would engage in that kind of behavior."

"We've seen so many dehydrated bodies scattered along the road here. They've been torn, and won't be revivable even when rehydrated. If your theory really works, what does it matter if we burn a few of them? We can even eat

18 *Translator's Note:* Zhao Ge was the capital of Shang China, where King Zhou held court.

some. How can a few lives compare to the importance of your theory?"

"Stop with that nonsense! We're scholars!"

After the fire burnt out, the three continued their journey. Since they were not speaking to each other much, the system sped up the passage of in-game time. King Wen flipped the sandglass on his back six times rapidly, indicating the lapse of two days. The sun never rose once, not even a hint of dawn over the horizon.

"It seems that the sun will never rise again," Wang said. He brought up the game menu to take a look at his health bar. Due to the extreme cold, it was steadily decreasing.

"Again, you're pretending you're some kind of oracle," Follower said. But this time he and Wang finished the thought together. "This is a Chaotic Era!"

Soon after this, however, dawn did appear over the horizon. The sky brightened rapidly, and the sun rose. Wang noticed that this time, the sun was gigantic. After just half of it rose, it took up at least one-fifth of the visible horizon. Waves of heat bathed them, and Wang felt refreshed. But when he glanced over at King Wen and Follower, he saw that both had terror on their faces as though they had seen a demon.

"Quick! Find shade!" Follower shouted. Wang ran after them. They ducked behind a large rock. The shadow cast by the rock gradually grew shorter and shorter. The earth around them glowed as though on fire. The permafrost beneath them soon melted, the steel-like hard surface turning into a sea of mud, roiled by waves of heat. Wang sweated profusely.

When the sun was directly overhead, the three covered their heads with the animal hides, but the bright light still shot through the holes and gaps like arrows. The three shifted

around the rock until they were able to hide inside the new shadow that had just appeared on the other side.

After the sun set, the air remained hot and damp. The three sweat-drenched travelers sat on the rock. Follower spoke with dismay. "Traveling during a Chaotic Era is like walking through hell. I can't stand it anymore. Also, I haven't had anything to eat because you won't give me any dried fish and you won't let me eat the dehydrated bodies. What—"

"The only choice is to dehydrate you," King Wen said, fanning himself with a piece of hide.

"You won't abandon me afterwards, will you?"

"Of course not. I promise to bring you to Zhao Ge."

Follower stripped off his sweat-soaked robe and lay down nude on the muddy earth. In the last glow from the sun, already below the horizon, Wang saw water oozing out of Follower's body. He knew that it was no longer sweat. All the water in his body was being discharged and squeezed out. The water coalesced into a few small rivulets in the mud. His body turned soft and lost its shape like a melting candle.

Ten minutes later, all the water had been eliminated from his body. Follower was now a man-shaped piece of leather stretched out on the ground. His facial features had flattened and become indistinct.

"Is he dead?" Wang asked. He remembered seeing such man-shaped pieces of hide scattered along the road. Some were torn and incomplete. He supposed they were the dehydrated bodies Follower spoke of earlier as potential kindling.

"No," King Wen answered. He picked up Follower's skin, brushed the mud and dust off, laid him out on the rock, and rolled him up like a balloon with its air let out. "He'll recover soon enough, when we soak him in water. It's just like soaking dried mushrooms."

"Even his bones have turned soft?"

"Yes. His skeleton has turned into dried fibers. This makes him easy to carry."

"In this world, can everyone be dehydrated and rehydrated?"

"Of course. You can, too. Otherwise we could not survive the Chaotic Eras." King Wen handed the rolled-up Follower to Wang. "Carry him. If you abandon him on the road, he'll be burned or eaten."

Wang accepted the skin, a light roll. He held it under his arm, and it didn't feel too strange.

With Wang carrying the dehydrated Follower and King Wen carrying the sandglass, the two continued their arduous journey. Like the previous few days, the progress of the sun in this world followed no pattern. After a long, frigid night lasting several days' worth of time, a brief but scorching day might follow, and vice versa. The two relied on each other for survival. They lit fires to hold off the cold, and ducked into lakes to avoid the heat.

At least the game sped up the progress of time. A month in game time might pass in half an hour. This made the journey through the Chaotic Era at least tolerable for Wang.

One day, after a long night that lasted almost a week (as measured by the sandglass), King Wen suddenly shouted joyously as he pointed to the night sky.

"Flying stars! Two flying stars!"

Actually, Wang had already noticed the strange celestial bodies. They were bigger than stars, and showed up as disks about the size of ping-pong balls. They moved through the sky at a pace quick enough for the naked eye to detect the motion. But it was the first time two of them had appeared together.

King Wen explained, "When two flying stars appear, it means a Stable Era is about to begin."

"We've seen flying stars before."

"Yes, but only one at a time."

"Is two the most we'll see at once?"

"No. Sometimes three will appear, but no more than that."

"If three flying stars appear, does that herald an even better era?"

King Wen gave Wang a frightened look. "What are you talking about? Three flying stars . . . pray that such a thing never happens."

King Wen turned out to be right. The yearned-for Stable Era soon began. Sunrise and sunset began to follow a pattern. A day-night cycle began to stabilize around eighteen hours. The orderly alternation of day and night made the weather warm and mild.

"How long does a Stable Era last?" Wang asked.

"As short as a day or as long as a century. No one can predict how long one will last." King Wen sat on the sandglass, lifting his head to gaze at the noonday sun. "According to historical records, the Western Zhou Dynasty experienced a Stable Era lasting two centuries. How lucky to be born during such a time!"

"Then how long does a Chaotic Era last?"

"I already told you. Other than Stable Eras, all other times belong to Chaotic Eras. Each of them takes up the time not occupied by the other."

"So, this is a world in which there are no patterns?"

"Yes. Civilization can only develop in the mild climate of Stable Eras. Most of the time, humankind must collectively dehydrate and be stored. When a long Stable Era arrives, they collectively revive through rehydration. Then they proceed to build and produce."

"How can you predict the arrival and duration of each Stable Era?"

"Such a thing has never been done. When a Stable Era arrives, the king makes a decision based on intuition as to whether to engage in mass rehydration. Often, the people are revived, crops are planted, cities begin construction, life has just started—and then the Stable Era ends. Extreme cold and heat then destroy everything." King Wen now pointed at Wang, his eyes sparkling. "Now you know the goal of this game: to use our intellect and understanding to analyze all phenomena until we can know the pattern of the sun's movement. The survival of civilization depends on it."

"Based on my observations, there is no pattern to the sun's movement at all."

"That's because you do not understand the fundamental nature of the world."

"And you do?"

"Yes. This is why I'm going to Zhao Ge. I will present King Zhou with an accurate calendar."

"But I've seen no evidence on this trip that you can do such a thing."

"Predicting the sun's motion is only possible in Zhao Ge, for that is where yin and yang meet. Only the lots cast there are accurate."

The two continued on through the harsh conditions of another Chaotic Era, interrupted briefly by a short Stable Era, until they finally arrived in Zhao Ge.

Wang heard an unceasing roar that sounded like thunder. The sound was generated by the numerous giant pendulums that could be seen all over Zhao Ge, each tens of meters in height. The weight of each pendulum was a giant rock,

suspended from a thick rope tied to a bridge that stretched between the tops of two slender stone towers.

All the pendulums were swinging as groups of soldiers in armor kept them in motion. Chanting incomprehensibly, they rhythmically pulled ropes attached to the giant stone weights, adding to the pendulums' arcs as they slowed. Wang noticed that all the pendulums swung in step. From far away, the sight was awe-inducing: It was as though numerous giant clocks had been erected over the earth, or colossal, abstract symbols had fallen from the sky.

The giant pendulums surrounded an even more enormous pyramid, standing like a tall mountain in the dark night. This was King Zhou's palace. Wang followed King Wen into a low door at the base of the pyramid, before which a few soldiers patrolled in the darkness, noiseless as ghosts. The door led to a long, narrow, dark tunnel going deep into the pyramid, with a few torches along the way.

As they walked, King Wen spoke to Wang. "During a Chaotic Era, the entire country is dehydrated. But King Zhou remains awake, a companion to the lifeless land. In order to survive during a Chaotic Era, one must live in thick-walled buildings like this one, as though one were living underground. It's the only way to avoid the extreme heat and cold."

After a long time in the tunnel, they finally arrived at the Great Hall at the center of the pyramid. Actually, the hall was not that big and reminded Wang of a cave. The man sitting on a dais and draped with a particolored hide was undoubtedly King Zhou. But what drew Wang's attention was a man dressed all in black. The black robe blended with the thick shadows in the Great Hall, and the pale white face seemed to float in air.

"This is Fu Xi."[19] King Zhou introduced the man in black to Wang and King Wen. He spoke as though Wang and King Wen had always been there, while the man in black was the newcomer. "He thinks that the sun is a temperamental god. When the god is awake, his moods are unpredictable, and thus we have a Chaotic Era. But when he's asleep, his breathing evens out, and thus we have a Stable Era. Fu Xi suggested that I build those pendulums you see out there and keep them in constant motion. He claims that the pendulums can have a hypnotic effect on the sun god and cause him to sink into a long slumber. But we can all see that so far, the sun god remains awake, though from time to time he seems to nap briefly."

King Zhou waved his hands, and servants brought over a clay pot and set it down on the small stone table before Fu Xi. Later, Wang found out that it was a pot of seasoned broth. Fu Xi sighed, lifted the pot, and drank in great gulps, the sound of his swallows echoing like the beating of a giant heart in the darkness. After he was halfway done with the contents, he poured the rest over his body. Then he threw down the pot and walked toward a large bronze cauldron suspended over a fire in the corner of the Great Hall. He climbed onto the edge of the cauldron and jumped in, stirring up a cloud of vapor.

"Ji Chang, sit down,"[20] King Zhou said. "We'll eat in just a little while." He pointed to the cauldron.

"Foolish witchcraft," King Wen said, glancing contemptuously at the cauldron.

"What have you learned about the sun?" King Zhou asked. Firelight flickered in his eyes.

19 *Translator's Note:* Fu Xi is the first of the Three Sovereigns, a Chinese mythological figure. He was one of the progenitors of the human race along with the goddess Nüwa.

20 *Translator's Note:* Ji Chang is King Wen's given name.

"The sun is not a god. The sun is yang, and the night is yin. The world proceeds on the balance between yin and yang. Though we cannot control the process, we can predict it." King Wen took out his bronze sword and drew a yin-yang symbol on the floor, dimly lit by the fire. Then, he carved the sixty-four hexagrams of the *I Ching* around the symbol, the whole composition resembling a calendar wheel. "My king, this is the code of the universe. With it, I can present your dynasty with an accurate calendar."

"Ji Chang, I need to know when the next long Stable Era will come."

"I will forecast it for you right now," King Wen said. He sat down in the middle of the yin-yang symbol, his legs curled under him. He raised his head to look up at the ceiling of the Great Hall, his gaze seeming to penetrate the thick stones of the pyramid, until it reached the stars. The fingers of his two hands began a series of rapid, complex movements, like components of a calculating machine. In the silence, only the soup in the cauldron in the corner made any noise, boiling and bubbling as though the shaman being cooked within was dream-talking in his sleep.

King Wen stood up in the middle of the yin-yang symbol. With his face still lifted to the ceiling, he said, "Next will be a Chaotic Era lasting forty-one days. Then comes a five-day Stable Era. Thereafter, there will be a twenty-three-day Chaotic Era followed by an eighteen-day Stable Era. Then we'll have an eight-day Chaotic Era. But when this Chaotic Era is over, my king, the long Stable Era you've been waiting for will begin. That Stable Era will last three years and nine months. The climate will be so mild that it will be a golden age."

"We have to verify your initial predictions first," King Zhou said, his face expressionless.

Wang heard a loud rumbling from above. A stone slab in the ceiling of the Great Hall slid open, revealing a square opening. Wang shifted his position and saw that the opening led to another tunnel going up through the center of the pyramid. At the end of the tunnel he could see a few twinkling stars.

Game time sped up. Every few seconds in real time, two soldiers flipped over the sandglass brought by King Wen, indicating the passing of eight hours in game time. The opening through the ceiling flickered with random lights, and once in a while a ray of sunlight from the Chaotic Era shot into the Great Hall. Sometimes the light was weak, like moonlight. Sometimes the light was very strong, and the incandescent white square cast against the ground glowed so brightly that the torches in the Great Hall paled in comparison.

Wang continued to count the flipping of the sandglass. By the time it had been flipped 120 times or so, the appearance of the sunlight through the square opening became regular. The first of the predicted Stable Eras had arrived.

After fifteen more flips of the sandglass, the flickering light through the opening became patternless again, the start of another Chaotic Era. Another Stable Era followed, and another Chaotic Era. The starting times and durations of the various eras were not exactly as King Wen had predicted, but they were close. After the conclusion of yet another eight-day Chaotic Era, the long Stable Era he predicted began.

Wang kept counting the flips of the sandglass. Twenty days passed, and the sunlight falling into the Great Hall maintained the precise rhythm. Game time slowed down to normal.

King Zhou nodded at King Wen. "I shall erect a monument for you, one even greater than this palace."

King Wen bowed deeply. "My king, awaken your dynasty and let it prosper!"

King Zhou stood up on the dais and opened his arms, as though he wanted to embrace the whole world. In a strange, otherworldly voice, he began to chant, "Re-hy-drate . . ."

As soon as the order was given, everyone in the Great Hall rushed to the door. Wang followed King Wen closely, and they exited the pyramid through the long tunnel they'd entered by. When they emerged, Wang saw the noonday sun bathing the land in warmth. In a passing breeze he seemed to smell the fragrances of spring. Together, King Wen and Wang walked to a nearby lake. The ice over the lake had melted, and sunlight danced between the gentle waves.

A column of soldiers shouted, "Rehydrate! Rehydrate!" as they ran toward a large stone building, shaped like a granary, next to the lake. On the road to Zhao Ge, Wang had seen many buildings like it, and King Wen had told him that these buildings were called dehydratories, warehouses where the dehydrated bodies could be stored. The soldiers opened the heavy stone doors of the dehydratory and carried out rolls of dusty skins. Each soldier walked to the lakeshore, and tossed them into the water. As soon as the skins touched the water, they began to unfurl and stretch out. Soon, the lake was covered by a layer of man-shaped floating skins, each rapidly absorbing the water and expanding. Gradually, all the man-shaped skin cutouts became fleshy bodies that gradually began to display signs of life. One by one, they struggled up out of the waist-deep water and stood up. Looking around at the sunny world with wide-open eyes, they appeared to have just awoken from a dream.

"Rehydrate!" one man cried out.

"Rehydrate! Rehydrate!" Other voices joyously echoed his.

Everyone climbed out of the lake and ran naked toward the dehydratory. They carried out more skins and tossed

114

them into the water, and even more of the revived climbed out of the lake. The same scene repeated itself around every lake and pool. The entire world was coming back to life.

' "Oh, heavens! My finger!"

Wang saw a man who had just been revived standing in the middle of the lake, holding up one hand and crying. The hand was missing its middle finger, and blood flowed from the wound into the water. Others, who had also just been revived, passed by him as they happily waded ashore, ignoring him.

"Count yourself lucky," one of them said to the man. "Some lost a whole arm or leg. Others had their heads chewed through by rats. If we hadn't been rehydrated in time, maybe all of us would have been eaten by the Chaotic Era rats."

"How long have we been dehydrated?" one of the revived asked.

"You can tell by looking at the thickness of the dust covering the palace. I just heard that the king is no longer the king from before. But I don't know if he's the old king's son or grandson."

It took eight days to complete the work of rehydration. All of the stored dehydrated bodies had been revived, and the world was given a new life. During these eight days, everyone enjoyed regular cycles of sunset and sunrise, each cycle precisely twenty hours long. Enjoying the springlike climate, everyone gave heartfelt praise to the sun and the gods who guided the world.

On the night of the eighth day, the bonfires scattered over the ground seemed even more numerous and denser than the stars in the sky. The ruins of cities and towns abandoned during the Chaotic Eras once again filled with noise and light. Like every mass rehydration in the past, the people

were going to celebrate all night to welcome their new life after the next sunrise.

But the sun did not rise again.

Every kind of timepiece indicated that the time for sunrise had passed, but the horizon remained dark in every direction. Ten hours later, there was still no sign of the sun, not even the slightest hint of dawn. The endless night lasted through a whole day, then two days. Coldness now pressed toward the earth like a giant hand.

Inside the pyramid, King Wen knelt before King Zhou, pleading, "My king, please continue to have faith in me. This is but temporary. I have seen the yang of the universe gathering, and the sun will rise soon. The Stable Era and spring will continue!"

"Let's begin to heat the cauldron," King Zhou said, and sighed.

"Oh, King!" A minister stumbled through the cavelike entrance into the Great Hall. "There . . . there are three flying stars in the sky!"

Those in the Great Hall were stunned. The air seemed frozen. Only King Zhou remained impassive. He turned to Wang, to whom he had never deigned to speak before. "You still don't understand what the appearance of three flying stars means, do you? Ji Chang, why don't you tell him?"

"It indicates the arrival of a long period of extreme cold, cold enough to turn stone into dust." King Wen sighed.

"De-hy-drate . . ." King Zhou again chanted in that strange, otherworldly voice. Outside, people had already begun the process. They turned themselves back into dehydrated bodies to survive the long night that was coming. The lucky ones had time to be stacked in the dehydratories, but many were abandoned in the empty fields.

King Wen stood up slowly and walked toward the cauldron over the roaring fire in the corner of the Great Hall. He climbed up the side and paused for a few seconds before jumping in. Perhaps he had seen the thoroughly cooked face of Fu Xi laughing at him from the soup.

"Keep the fire low," King Zhou ordered, his voice weak. Then he turned to the others. "You may exit if you wish. The game is no longer fun after it gets to this point."

A red EXIT sign showed up above the Great Hall's cavelike entrance. Players in the Great Hall streamed toward it, and Wang followed the crowd. Through the long tunnel, they finally emerged outside the pyramid. Heavy snow falling through the night air greeted them. The bone-chilling cold caused Wang to shiver, and a display in a corner of the sky indicated that game time had sped up again.

The snow continued without pause for ten days. By now the snowflakes were large and heavy, like pieces of solidified darkness. Someone whispered next to Wang, "The snow is now composed of frozen carbon dioxide, dry ice." Wang turned around and saw that the speaker was Follower.

After another ten days, the snowflakes turned thin and translucent. By the weak light from a few torches within the entrance to the long tunnel, the snowflakes gave off a faint blue glow, like pieces of dancing mica.

"Those snowflakes are now composed of solidified oxygen and nitrogen. The atmosphere is disappearing through deposition, which means it's near absolute zero above."

Snow gradually buried the pyramid. The lowest layers were composed of water snow, then dry ice, and finally, on top, snow made of oxygen and nitrogen. The night sky became especially clear, and the stars glowed like a field of silver bonfires. A line of text appeared against the starry background:

117

The long night lasted forty-eight years. Civilization Number 137 was destroyed by the extreme cold. This civilization had advanced to the Warring States Period before succumbing.

The seed of civilization remains. It will germinate and again pro-gress through the unpredictable world of *Three Body*. We invite you to log on in the future.

Before exiting the game, Wang noticed the three flying stars in the sky. Revolving closely around each other, they seemed to perform a strange dance against the abyss of space.

8

YE WENJIE

Wang took off the V-suit and panoramic viewing helmet. His shirt was soaked with sweat, as if he had just awoken from a nightmare. He left the Research Center, got into his car, and drove to the address given to him by Ding Yi: the house of Yang Dong's mother.

Chaotic Era, Chaotic Era, Chaotic Era . . .

The thought turned and turned in Wang's head. *Why would the path of the sun through the world of* Three Body *be devoid of regularity and pattern? Whether a planet's orbit is more circular or more elliptical, its motion around its sun must be periodic. Total irregularity in planetary motion is impossible. . . .*

Wang grew angry with himself. He shook his head, trying to chase away these thoughts. *It's only a game!*

But I lost.

Chaotic Era, Chaotic Era, Chaotic Era . . .

Damn it! Stop! Why am I thinking about this? Why?

Soon, Wang found the answer. He had not played any computer games for years, and the hardware for gaming had clearly advanced greatly in the interim. The virtual reality and multisensory feedback were all effects he had not experienced as a young student. But Wang also knew that

the sense of realism in Three Body wasn't due to the inter-face technology.

He remembered taking a class in information theory as a third-year student in college. The professor had put up two pictures: One was the famous Song Dynasty painting *Along the River During the Qingming Festival,* full of fine, rich details; the other was a photograph of the sky on a sunny day, the deep blue expanse broken only by a wisp of cloud that one couldn't even be sure was there. The professor asked the class which picture contained more information. The answer was that the photograph's information content—its entropy—exceeded the painting's by one or two orders of magnitude.

Three Body was the same. Its enormous information content was hidden deep. Wang could feel it, but he could not articulate it. He suddenly understood that the makers of *Three Body* took the exact opposite of the approach taken by designers of other games. Normally, game designers tried to display as much information as possible to increase the sense of realism. But *Three Body*'s designers worked to compress the information content to disguise a more complex reality, just like that seemingly empty photograph of the sky.

Wang let his mind wander back to the world of *Three Body.*

Flying stars! The key must be in the flying stars. One flying star, two flying stars, three flying stars . . . what did they mean?

As he had that thought, he found himself at his destination.

At the foot of the apartment building, Wang saw a graying, thin woman, about sixty years old. She wore glasses and was struggling to go up the stairs with a basket of groceries. He guessed that this was the woman he had come to see.

A quick greeting confirmed his guess. She was Yang Dong's mother, Ye Wenjie. After hearing the purpose of Wang Miao's visit, she was grateful and appreciative. Wang was familiar with old intellectuals like her: The long years had ground away all the hardness and fierceness in their personalities, until all that was left was a gentleness like that of water.

Wang carried the grocery basket up the stairs for her. When they got to her apartment, it turned out to be not as quiet as he had expected: Three children were playing, the oldest about five, and the youngest barely walking. Ye told Wang that they were all the neighbors' kids.

"They like to play at my place. Today is Sunday, and their parents need to work overtime, so they left them to me. . . . Oh, Nan Nan, have you finished your picture? Oh, it looks great! Shall we give it a title? 'Ducklings in the Sun'? Sounds good. Let Granny write it for you. Then I'll put down the date: 'June 9th, by Nan Nan.' And what do you want to eat for lunch? Yang Yang, you want fried eggplant? Sure! Nan Nan, you want the snow peas like you had yesterday? No problem. How about you, Mi Mi? You want some meat-meat? Oh, no, your mom told me that you shouldn't eat so much meat-meat, not easy to digest. How about some fishie instead? Look at this big fishie Granny bought. . . ."

Wang observed Ye and the children, absorbed in their conversation. *She must want grandkids. But even if Yang Dong were alive, would she have had children?*

Ye took the groceries into the kitchen. When she reemerged, she said, "Xiao Wang, I'm going to soak the vegetables for a while." She had slipped effortlessly into addressing him by an affectionate diminutive. "These days, they use so much pesticide that when I feed the children, I have to soak the

121

vegetables for at least two hours— Why don't you take a look in Dong Dong's room first?"

Her suggestion, tagged on at the end as though it was the most natural thing in the world, made Wang anxious. Clearly, she had figured out the real purpose of his visit. She turned around and went back into the kitchen without giving Wang another glance, and so avoided seeing his embarrassment. Wang was grateful that she was so considerate of his feelings.

Wang walked past the three happily playing children and entered the room that Ye had indicated. He paused in front of the door, seized by a strange feeling. It was as if he had returned to his dream-filled youth. From the depths of his memory arose a tingling sadness, fragile and pure like morning dew, tinged with a rosy hue.

Gently, he pushed the door open. The faint fragrance that filled the room was unexpected, the smell of the forest. He seemed to have entered the hut of a ranger: The walls were covered by strips of bark; the three stools were unadorned tree stumps; the desk was made from three bigger tree stumps pushed together. And then there was the bed, apparently lined with ura sedge from Northeast China, which the locals stuffed into their shoes to stay warm in the cold climate. Everything was rough-hewn and seemingly careless, without signs of aesthetic design. Yang Dong's job had earned her a high income, and she could have bought a home in some luxury development, but she chose to live here with her mother instead.

Wang walked up to the tree-stump desk. It was plainly furnished, and nothing on it betrayed a hint of femininity or scholarly interest. Maybe all such objects had been taken away, or maybe they had never been there. He noticed a black-and-white photograph in a wooden frame, a portrait

of mother and daughter. In the picture, Yang Dong was just a little girl, and Ye Wenjie was crouching down so that they were the same height. A strong wind tangled the pair's long hair together.

The background of the photograph was unusual: The sky seemed to be seen through a large net held up by thick steel supporting structures. Wang deduced that it was some kind of parabolic antenna, so large that its edges were beyond the frame of the photograph.

In the picture, little Yang Dong's eyes gave off a fright that made Wang's heart ache. She seemed terrified by the world outside the picture.

Next, Wang noticed a thick notebook at the corner of the desk. He was baffled by the material the notebook was made of until he saw a line of childish writing scrawled across the cover: *Yang Dong's Birch-bark Notebook*. "Birch" was written in pinyin letters instead of using the character for it. The years had turned the silvery bark into a dull yellow. He reached out to touch the notebook, hesitated, and retracted his hand.

"It's okay," Ye said from the door. "Those are pictures Dong Dong drew when she was little."

Wang picked up the birch-bark notebook and gently flipped through it. Ye had dated each picture for her daughter, just like she had been doing for Nan Nan in the living room.

Wang saw that, based on the dates on the pictures, Yang Dong was three when she drew them. Normally, children of that age are able to draw humans and objects with clear shapes, but Yang Dong's pictures remained only messes of random lines. They seemed to express a kind of passionate anger and desperation born out of a frustrated desire to express something—not the sort of feeling one would expect in a child that young.

Ye slowly sat down on the edge of the bed, her eyes staring at the notebook, lost in thought. Her daughter had died here, ended her life while she slept. Wang sat next to her. He had never felt such a strong desire to share the burden of another's pain.

Ye took the birch-bark notebook from him and held it to her chest. In a low voice, she said, "I wasn't good at teaching Dong Dong in an age-appropriate manner. I exposed her too early to some very abstract, very extreme topics. When she first expressed an interest in abstract theory, I told her that field wasn't easy for women. She said, what about Madame Curie? I told her, Madame Curie was never really accepted as part of that field. Her success was seen as a matter of persistence and hard work, but without her, someone else would have completed her work. As a matter of fact, Wu Chien-Shiung went even further than Madame Curie.[21] But it really isn't a woman's field.

"Dong Dong didn't argue with me, but I later discovered that she really was different. For example, let's say I explained a formula to her. Other children might say, 'What a clever formula!' But she would say, 'This formula is so elegant, so beautiful.' The expression on her face was the same as when she saw a pretty wildflower.

"Her father left behind some records. She listened to all of them and finally picked something by Bach as her favorite, listening to it over and over. That was the kind of music that shouldn't have mesmerized a kid. At first I thought she picked

21 *Author's Note:* Chien-Shiung Wu was one of the most outstanding physicists of the modern era, with many accomplishments in experimental physics. She was the first to experimentally disprove the hypothetical "law of conservation of parity" and thereby lend support to the work of theoretical physicists Tsung-Dao Lee and Chen-Ning Yang.

it on a whim, but when I asked her how she felt about the music, she said that she could see in the music a giant building, a large, complex house. Bit by bit, the giant added to the structure, and when the music was over, the house was done. . . ."

"You were a great teacher for your daughter," Wang said.

"No. I failed. Her world was too simple, and all she had were ethereal theories. When they collapsed, she had nothing to lean on to keep on living."

"Professor Ye, I can't say that I agree with you. Right now, events are happening that are beyond our imagination. It's an unprecedented challenge to our theories about the world, and she's not the only scientist to have stumbled down that path."

"But she was a woman. A woman should be like water, able to flow over and around anything."

As Wang was about to leave, he remembered the other purpose for his visit. He mentioned to Ye his wish to observe the cosmic microwave background.

"Oh, that. There are two places in China that work on it. One is an observatory in Ürümqi—I think it's a project by the Chinese Academy of Sciences' Space Environment Observation Center. The other is very close by, a radio astronomy observatory located in the suburbs of Beijing, which is run by the Chinese Academy of Sciences and Peking University's Joint Center for Astrophysics. The one in Ürümqi does ground observation, and the one here just receives data from satellites, though the satellite data is more accurate and complete. I have a former student working there, and I can make a call for you." Ye found the phone number and dialed it. The ensuing conversation seemed to go smoothly.

"You're all set," Ye said as she hung up. "Let me give you the address. You can go over anytime. My student's name is Sha Ruishan, and he's going to be working the night shift tomorrow. . . . I don't think this is your field of research, right?"

"I work in nanotech. This is for . . . something else." Wang was afraid that Ye was going to ask more questions about why he sought this information, but she did not.

"Xiao Wang, you look a bit pale. How's your health?" she asked, her face full of concern.

"It's nothing. Please don't worry."

"Wait a moment." Ye took a small wooden box out of a cabinet. Wang saw from the label that it was ginseng. "An old friend from the base, a soldier, came to visit me a few days ago and brought this—take it, take it! It's cultivated, not very precious. I have high blood pressure and can't use it anyway. You can slice it thinly and make it into a tea. You look so pale that I'm sure you can use the enrichment. You're still young, but you have to watch your health."

Wang accepted the box, warmth filling his chest. His eyes moistened. It was as though his heart, stressed almost beyond the breaking point by the last few days, had been placed onto a pile of soft down feathers. "Professor Ye, I will come visit you often."

9

THE UNIVERSE FLICKERS

Wang Miao drove along Jingmi Road until he was in Miyun County. From there he headed to Heilongtan, climbed up the mountain along a winding road, and arrived at the radio astronomy observatory of the Chinese Academy of Sciences' National Astronomical Center. He saw a line of twenty-eight parabolic antenna dishes, each with a diameter of nine meters, like a row of spectacular steel plants. At the end were two tall radio telescopes with dishes fifty meters in diameter, built in 2006. As he drove closer, Wang could not help but think of the background in the picture of Ye and her daughter.

But the work of Sha Ruishan, Ye's student, had nothing to do with these radio telescopes. Dr. Sha's lab was mainly responsible for receiving the data transmitted from three satellites: the Cosmic Background Explorer, COBE, launched in November of 1989 and about to be retired; the Wilkinson Microwave Anisotropy Probe, WMAP, launched in 2003; and Planck, the space observatory launched by the European Space Agency in 2009.

Cosmic microwave background radiation very precisely matched the thermal black body spectrum at a temperature of 2.7255 K and was highly isotropic—meaning nearly

uniform in every direction—with only tiny temperature fluctuations at the parts per million range. Sha Ruishan's job was to create a more detailed map of the cosmic microwave background using observational data.

The lab wasn't very big. Equipment for receiving satellite data was squeezed into the main computer room, and three terminals displayed the information sent by the three satellites.

Sha was excited to see Wang. Clearly bored with his long isolation and happy to have a visitor, he asked Wang what kind of data he wanted to see.

"I want to see the overall fluctuation in the cosmic microwave background."

"Can you . . . be more specific?"

"What I mean is . . . I want to see the isotropic fluctuation in the overall cosmic microwave background, between one and five percent," he said, quoting from Shen's email.

Sha grinned. Starting at the turn of the century, the Miyun Radio Astronomy Observatory had opened itself to visitors. In order to earn some extra income, Sha often played the role of tour guide or gave lectures. This was the grin he reserved for tourists, as he had grown used to their astounding scientific illiteracy. "Mr. Wang, I take it you're not a specialist in the field?"

"I work in nanotech."

"Ah, makes sense. But you must have some basic understanding of the cosmic microwave background?"

"I don't know much. I know that as the universe cooled after the big bang, the leftover 'embers' became the cosmic microwave background. The radiation fills the entire universe and can be observed in the centimeter wavelength range. I think it was back in the sixties when two Americans

accidentally discovered the radiation when they were testing a supersensitive satellite reception antenna—"

"That's more than enough," Sha interrupted, waving his hands. "Then you must know that unlike the local variations we observe in different parts of the universe, the overall fluctuation in the cosmic microwave background is correlated with the expansion of the universe. It's a very slow change measured at the scale of the age of the universe. Even with the sensitivity of the Planck satellite, continuous observation for a million years might not detect *any* such shift. But you want to see a five percent fluctuation tonight? Do you realize what that would mean? The universe would flicker like a fluorescent tube that's about to burn out!"

And it will be flickering for me, Wang thought.

"This must be some joke from Professor Ye," Sha said.

"Nothing would please me more than to discover that it was a joke," Wang said. He was about to tell Sha that Ye didn't know the details of his request, but he was afraid that Sha would then refuse to help him.

"Well, since Professor Ye asked me to help you, let's do the observation. It's not a big deal. If you just need one percent precision, data from the antique COBE is sufficient." As he spoke, Sha typed quickly at the terminal. Soon a flat green line appeared on the screen. "This curve is the real-time measurement of the overall cosmic microwave background—oh, calling it a straight line would be more accurate. The temperature is 2.725 ± 0.002K. The error range is due to the Doppler effect from the motion of the Milky Way, which has already been filtered out. If the kind of fluctuation you anticipate—in excess of one percent—occurs, this line would turn red and become a waveform. I would bet that it's going to stay a flat green line until the end of the world, though.

If you want to see it show the kind of fluctuation observable by the naked eye, you might have to wait until long after the death of the sun."

"I'm not interfering in your work, am I?"

"No. Since you need such low precision, we can just use some basic data from COBE. Okay, it's all set. From now on, if such great fluctuations occur, the data will be automatically saved to disk."

"I think it might happen around one o'clock A.M."

"Wow, so precise! No problem, since I'm working the night shift, anyway. Have you had dinner yet? Good, then I'll take you on a tour."

The night was moonless. They walked along the row of antenna dishes, and Sha pointed to them. "Breathtaking, aren't they? It's too bad that they are all like the ears of a deaf man."

"Why?"

"Ever since construction was completed, interference has been unceasing in the observational bands. First, there were the paging stations during the eighties. Now, it's the scramble to develop mobile communications networks and cell towers. These telescopes are capable of many scientific tasks—surveying the sky, detecting variable radio sources, observing the remains of supernovae—but we can't perform most of them. We've complained to the State Regulatory Radio Commission many times, never with any results. How can we get more attention than China Mobile, China Unicom, China Netcom? Without money, the secrets of the universe are worth shit. At least my project only depends on satellite data and has nothing to do with these 'tourist attractions.'"

"In recent years, commercial operation of basic research has been fairly successful, like in high-energy physics. Maybe

it would be better if the observatories were built in places farther away from cities?"

"It all comes down to money. Right now, our only choice is to find technical means to shield against interference. Well, it would be much better if Professor Ye were here. She accomplished a lot in this field."

So the topic of conversation turned to Ye Wenjie. And from her student, Wang finally learned about her life. He listened as Sha told of how she witnessed the death of her father during the Cultural Revolution, how she was falsely accused at the Production and Construction Corps, how she then seemed to disappear until her return to Beijing at the beginning of the nineties, when she began teaching astrophysics at Tsinghua, where her father had also taught, until her retirement.

"It was only recently revealed that she had spent more than twenty years at Red Coast Base."

Wang was stunned. "You mean, those rumors—"

"Most turned out to be true. One of the researchers who developed the deciphering system for the Red Coast Project emigrated to Europe and wrote a book last year. Most of the rumors you hear came out of that book. Many who participated in Red Coast are still alive."

"That is . . . a fantastical legend."

"Especially for it to happen during those years—absolutely incredible."

They continued to speak for a while. Sha asked the purpose behind Wang's strange request. Wang avoided giving a straight answer, and Sha didn't press. The dignity of a specialist did not allow Sha to express too much interest in a request that clearly went against his professional knowledge.

Then they went to an all-night bar for tourists and sat for two hours. As Sha finished one beer after another, his

tongue loosened even more. But Wang became anxious, and his mind kept returning to that green line on the terminal in Sha's office. It was only at ten to one in the morning that Sha finally gave in to Wang's repeated pleas to go back to the lab.

The spotlights that had lit up the row of radio antennas had been turned off, and the antennas now formed a simple two-dimensional picture against the night sky like a series of abstract symbols. All of them gazed up at the sky at the same angle, as though waiting expectantly for something. The scene made Wang shudder despite the warmth of the spring evening. He was reminded of the giant pendulums in *Three Body*.

They arrived back at the lab at one. As they looked at the terminal, the fluctuation was just getting started. The flat line turned into a wave, the distance between one peak and the next inconstant. The line's color became red, like a snake awakening after hibernation, wriggling as its skin refilled with blood.

"It must be a malfunction in COBE!" Sha stared at the waveform, terrified.

"It's not a malfunction." Wang's tone was exceedingly calm. He had learned to control himself when faced with such sights.

"We'll know soon enough," Sha said. He went to the other two terminals and typed rapidly to bring up the data gathered by the other two satellites, WMAP and Planck.

Now three waveforms moved in sync across the three terminals, exactly alike.

Sha took out a notebook computer and rushed to turn it on. He plugged in a network cable and picked up the phone. Wang could tell from the one-sided conversation that he

was trying to get in touch with the Ürümqi radio astronomy observatory. He didn't explain to Wang what he was doing, his eyes locked onto the browser window on the notebook. Wang could hear his rapid breathing.

A few minutes later, a red waveform appeared in the browser window, moving in step with the other three.

The three satellites and the ground-based observatory confirmed one fact: The universe was flickering.

"Can you print out the waveform?" Wang asked.

Sha wiped away the cold sweat on his forehead and nodded. He moved his mouse and clicked "Print." Wang grabbed the first page as soon as it came out of the laser printer, and, with a pencil, began to match the distance between the peaks with the Morse code chart he took out of his pocket.

short-long-long-long-long, short-long-long-long-long, long-long-long-long-long, long-long-long-short-short, long-long-long-short-short-short, short-short-long-long-long, short-long-long-long-long, long-long-long-short-short-short, short-short-short-long-long, long-long-short-short-short.

That's 1108:21:37, Wang thought.

short-long-long-long-long, short-long-long-long-long, long-long-long-long-long, long-long-long-short-short, long-long-long-short-short-short, short-short-long-long-long, short-long-long-long-long, long-long-long-short-short-short, short-short-short-long-long, long-short-short-short-short—that's 1108:21:36.

The countdown continued at the scale of the universe. Ninety-two hours had already elapsed, and only 1,108 hours remained.

Sha paced back and forth anxiously, pausing from time to time to look at the sequence of numbers Wang was writing down. "Can't you tell me what's going on?" he shouted.

"I can't possibly explain this to you, Dr. Sha. Trust me." Wang pushed away the pile of papers filled with waveforms. As he stared at the sequence of numbers, he said, "Maybe the three satellites and the observatory are all malfunctioning."

"You know that's impossible!"

"What if it's sabotage?"

"Also impossible! To simultaneously alter the data from three satellites and an observatory on Earth? You're talking about a supernatural saboteur."

Wang nodded. Compared to the idea of the universe flickering, he would prefer a supernatural saboteur. But Sha then deprived him of this last glimmer of hope. "It's easy to confirm this. If the cosmic microwave background is fluctuating this much, we should be able to see it with our own eyes."

"What are you talking about? The wavelength of the cosmic microwave background is seven centimeters. That's five orders of magnitude longer than the wavelength of visible light. How can we possibly see it?"

"Using 3K glasses."

"Three-K glasses?"

"It's a sort of science toy we made for the Capital Planetarium. With our current level of technology, we could take the six-meter horn antenna used by Penzias and Wilson almost half a century ago to discover the cosmic microwave background and miniaturize it to the size of a pair of glasses. Then we added a converter in the glasses to compress the detected radiation by five orders of magnitude so that seven-centimeter waves are turned into visible red light. This way, visitors can put on the glasses at night and observe the cosmic microwave background on their own. And now, we can use it to see the universe flicker."

"Where can I find these glasses?"

"At the Capital Planetarium. We made more than twenty pairs."

"I must get my hands on a pair before five."

Sha picked up the phone. The other side picked up only after a long while. Sha had to expend a lot of energy to convince the person awakened in the middle of the night to go to the planetarium and wait for Wang's arrival in an hour.

As Wang left, Sha said, "I won't go with you. What I've seen is enough, and I don't need any more confirmation. But I hope that you will explain the truth to me when you feel the time is right. If this phenomenon should lead to some research result, I won't forget you."

Wang opened the car door and said, "The flickering will stop at five in the morning. I'd suggest you not pursue it after this. Believe me, you won't get anywhere."

Sha stared at Wang for a long time and then nodded. "I understand. Strange things have been happening to scientists lately. . . ."

"Yes." Wang ducked into the car. He didn't want to discuss the subject any further.

"Is it our turn?"

"It's my turn, at least." Wang started the engine.

An hour later, Wang arrived at the new planetarium and got out of the car. The bright lights of the city penetrated the translucent walls of the immense glass building and dimly revealed its internal structure. Wang thought that if the architect had intended to express a feeling about the universe, the design was a success: The more transparent something was, the more mysterious it seemed. The universe itself was transparent; as long as you were sufficiently sharp-eyed, you

could see as far as you liked. But the farther you looked, the more mysterious it became.

The sleepy-eyed planetarium staffer was waiting by the door for Wang. He handed him a small suitcase and said, "There are five pairs of 3K glasses in here, all fully charged. The left button switches it on. The right dial is for adjusting brightness. I have a dozen more pairs upstairs. You can look as much as you like, but I'm going to take a nap now in the room over there. This Dr. Sha must be mental." He went into the dim interior of the planetarium.

Wang opened the suitcase on the backseat of his car and took out a pair of 3K glasses. It resembled the display inside the panoramic viewing helmet of the V-suit. He put the glasses on and looked around. The city looked the same as before, only dimmer. Then he remembered that he had to switch them on.

The city turned into many hazy glowing halos. Most were fixed, but a few flickered or moved. He realized that these were sources of radiation in the centimeter range, all now converted to visible light. At the heart of each halo was a radiation source. Because the original wavelengths were so long, it was impossible to see their shapes clearly.

He lifted his head and saw a sky glowing with a faint red light. Just like that, he was seeing the cosmic microwave background.

The red light had come from more than ten billion years ago. It was the remnants of the big bang, the still-warm embers of Creation. He could not see any stars. Normally, since visible light would be compressed to invisible by the glasses, each star should appear as a black dot. But the diffraction of centimeter-wave radiation overwhelmed all other shapes and details.

Once his eyes had grown used to the sight, Wang could see that the faint red background was indeed pulsing. The entire sky flickered, as if the universe was but a quivering lamp in the wind.

Standing under the flashing dome of the night sky, Wang suddenly felt the universe shrink until it was so small that only he was imprisoned in it. The universe was a cramped heart, and the red light that suffused everything was the translucent blood that filled the organ. Suspended in the blood, he saw that the flickering of the red light was not periodic—the pulsing was irregular. He felt a strange, perverse, immense presence that could never be understood by human intellect.

Wang took off the 3K glasses and sat down weakly on the ground, leaning against the wheel of his car. The city at night gradually recovered the reality of visible light. But his eyes roamed, trying to capture other sights. By the entrance of the zoo across the street, there was a row of neon lights. One of the lights was about to burn out and flickered irregularly. Nearby, a small tree's leaves trembled in the night breeze, twinkling without pattern as they reflected streetlight. In the distance, the red star atop the Beijing Exhibition Center's Russian-style spire reflected the light from the cars passing below, also twinkling randomly. . . .

Wang tried to interpret the flickers as Morse code. He even felt that the wrinkles in the flags flapping next to him and the ripples in the puddle on the side of the road might be sending him messages. He struggled to understand all the messages, and felt the passing of the countdown, second by second.

He didn't know how long he stayed there. The planetarium staffer finally emerged and asked him whether he was done. But when he saw Wang's face, sleep disappeared from the staffer's eyes and was replaced by fear. He packed up the

3K glasses, stared at Wang for a few seconds, and quickly left with the suitcase.

Wang took out his mobile and dialed Shen Yufei's number. She picked up right away. Perhaps she was also suffering from insomnia.

"What happens at the end of the countdown?" Wang asked.

"I don't know." She hung up.

What can it be? Maybe my own death, like Yang Dong's.

Or maybe it will be a disaster like the great tsunami that swept through the Indian Ocean more than a decade ago. No one will connect it to my nanotech research. Could it be that every previous great disaster, including the two World Wars, was also the result of reaching the end of ghostly countdowns? Could it be that every time there was some-one like me, who no one thought of, who bore the ultimate responsibility?

Or maybe it signals the end of the whole world. In this perverse world, that would be a relief.

One thing was certain. No matter what was at the end of the countdown, in the remaining one thousand or so hours, the possibilities would torture him cruelly, like demons, until he suffered a complete mental breakdown.

Wang ducked back into the car and left the planetarium. Just before dawn, the roads were relatively empty. But he didn't dare to drive too fast, feeling that the faster the car moved, the faster the countdown would go. When a glimmer of light appeared in the eastern sky, he parked and walked around aimlessly. His mind was empty of thoughts: Only the countdown pulsed against the dim red background of

cosmic radiation. He seemed to have turned into nothing but a simple timer, a bell that tolled for he knew not whom.

The sky brightened. He was tired, so he sat down on a bench.

When he lifted his head to see where his subconscious had brought him, he shivered.

He sat in front of St. Joseph's Church at Wangfujing. In the pale white light of dawn, the church's Romanesque vaults appeared as three giant fingers pointing out something in space for him.

As Wang got up to leave, he was held back by a snippet of hymnal music. It wasn't Sunday, so it was likely a choir rehearsal. The song was "Come, Gracious Spirit, Heavenly Dove." As he listened to the solemn, sacred music, Wang Miao once again felt that the universe had shrunk until it was the size of an empty church. The domed ceiling was hidden by the flashing red light of the background radiation, and he was an ant crawling through the cracks in the floor. He felt a giant, invisible hand caressing his trembling heart, and he was once again a helpless babe. Something deep in his mind that had once held him up softened like wax and collapsed. He covered his eyes and began to cry.

Wang's cries were interrupted by laughter. "Hahaha, another one bites the dust!"

He turned around.

Captain Shi Qiang stood there, blowing out a mouthful of white smoke.

10

DA SHI

Shi sat down next to Wang and handed him his car keys. "You parked right at the intersection at Dongdan. If I had arrived just a minute later, the traffic cops would have had it towed."

Da Shi, if I had known you were following me, I would have been comforted, Wang thought, switching to Shi Qiang's familiar nickname in his mind, though self-respect made him hold back the words. He accepted a cigarette from Da Shi, lit it, and took his first drag since he quit several years ago.

"So how's it going, buddy? Finding it hard to bear? I said you couldn't handle it. And you insisted on playing the tough guy."

"You wouldn't understand." Wang took several more deep puffs.

"Your problem is, you understand too well. . . . Fine, let's go grab a bite."

"I'm not hungry."

"Then we'll go drinking! My treat."

Wang got into Da Shi's car and they drove to a small restaurant nearby. It was still early, and the place was deserted.

"Two orders of quick-fried tripe, and a bottle of *er guo*

tou!"[22] Da Shi shouted, without even looking up. He was obviously a regular here.

As he stared at the two plates filled with black slices of tripe, Wang's empty stomach began to churn, and he thought he was going to be sick. Da Shi ordered him some warm soymilk and fried pancakes, and Wang forced himself to eat some.

Then they drank shots of *er guo tou*. He began to feel lightheaded, and his tongue loosened. Gradually, he recounted the events of the last three days to Da Shi, even though he knew that Da Shi probably knew everything already—maybe Da Shi even knew more than he did.

"You're saying that the universe was . . . winking at you?" Da Shi asked, as he slurped down strips of tripe like noodles.

"That's a very appropriate metaphor."

"Bullshit."

"Your lack of fear is based on your ignorance."

"More bullshit. Come, drink!"

Wang finished another shot. Now the world was spinning around him, and only the tripe-chomping Shi Qiang across from him remained stable. He said, "Da Shi, have you ever . . . considered certain ultimate philosophical questions? For example, where does Man come from? Where does Man go? Where does the universe come from? Where does the universe go? Et cetera."

"Nope."

"Never?"

"Never."

"You must see the stars. Aren't you awed and curious?"

"I never look at the sky at night."

22 *Translator's Note: Er guo tou* is a distilled liquor made from sorghum, sometimes called "Chinese vodka."

"How is that possible? I thought you often worked the night shift?"

"Buddy, when I work at night, if I look up at the sky, the suspect is going to escape."

"We really have nothing to say to each other. All right. Drink!"

"To be honest, even if I were to look at the stars in the sky, I wouldn't be thinking about your philosophical questions. I have too much to worry about! I gotta pay the mortgage, save for the kid's college, and handle the endless stream of cases. . . . I'm a simple man without a lot of complicated twists and turns. Look down my throat and you can see out my ass. Naturally, I don't know how to make my bosses like me. Years after being discharged from the army, my career is going nowhere. If I weren't pretty good at my job, I would have been kicked out a long time ago. . . . You think that's not enough for me to worry about? You think I've got the energy to gaze at stars and philosophize?"

"You're right. All right, drink up!"

"But, I did indeed invent an ultimate rule."

"Tell me."

"Anything sufficiently weird must be fishy."

"What . . . what kind of crappy rule is that?"

"I'm saying that there's always someone behind things that don't seem to have an explanation."

"If you had even basic knowledge of science, you'd know it's impossible for any force to accomplish the things I experienced. Especially that last one. To manipulate things at the scale of the universe—not only can you not explain it with our current science, I couldn't even imagine how to explain it *outside* of science. It's more than supernatural. It's super-I-don't-know-what. . . ."

"I'm telling you, that's bullshit. I've seen plenty of weird things."

"Then tell me what I should do next."

"Keep on drinking. And then sleep."

"Fine."

Wang Miao had no idea how he got back into his car. He tumbled into the backseat and fell into a dreamless slumber. He didn't think that he was asleep for long, but when he opened his eyes, the sun was already near the horizon in the west.

He got out of the car. Even though the alcohol that morning had made him weak, he did feel better. He saw that he was at one corner of the Forbidden City. The setting sun shone on the ancient palace and turned into bright gold ripples in the moat. In his eyes, the world became once again classical and stable.

Wang sat until it got dark, enjoying the peace that had been missing from his life. The black Volkswagen Santana that he was now so familiar with pulled out of the traffic streaming through the street and braked to a stop right in front of him. Shi Qiang got out of the car.

"Slept well?" Da Shi growled.

"Yes. What next?"

"Who? You? Go have dinner. Then drink a little more. Then sleep again."

"Then what?"

"Then? Don't you have to go to work tomorrow?"

"But the countdown . . . there's only 1,091 hours left."

"Fuck the countdown. Your first priority right now is to make sure you can stand straight and not collapse into a heap. Then we can talk about other things."

"Da Shi, can you tell me something about what's really going on? I'm begging you."

Da Shi stared at Wang a while. Then he laughed. "I've said the very same thing to General Chang several times. We're in the same boat, you and I. I'll be honest: I know fucking shit. My pay grade is too low, and they tell me nothing. Sometimes I think this is a nightmare."

"But you must know more than I."

"Fine. I'll tell you what little I know." Da Shi pointed to the shore of the moat around the Forbidden City. The two found a spot and sat down.

It was now night, and traffic flowed ceaselessly behind them like a river. They watched their shadows lengthening and shortening over the moat.

"In my line of work, it's all about putting together many apparently unconnected things. When you piece them together the right way, you get the truth. For a while now, strange things have been happening.

"For example, there's been an unprecedented wave of crimes against academia and science research institutions. Of course you know about the explosion at the Liangxiang accelerator construction site. There was also the murder of that Nobel laureate . . . the crimes were all unusual: not for money, not for revenge. No political background, just pure destruction.

"Other strange things didn't involve crimes. For example, the Frontiers of Science and the suicides of those academics. Environmental activists have also become extra bold: protest mobs at construction sites to stop nuclear power plants and hydroelectric dams, experimental communities 'returning to nature,' and other apparently trivial matters Do you go to the movies?"

"No, not really."

"Recent big-budget films all have rustic themes. The setting is always green mountains and clear water, with handsome men and pretty women of some indeterminate era living in harmony with nature. To use the words of the directors, they 'represent the beautiful life before science spoiled nature.' Take *Peach Blossom Spring*: it's clearly the sort of film that no one wants to see. But they spent hundreds of millions to make it. There was also this science fiction contest with a top reward of five million for the person who imagined the most disgusting possible future. They spent another few hundred million to turn the winning stories into movies. And then you've got all these strange cults popping up everywhere, where every cult leader seems to have a lot of money. . . ."

"What does that last bit have to do with everything you mentioned before?"

"You have to connect all the dots. Of course I didn't need to busy myself with such concerns before, but after I was transferred from the crime unit to the Battle Command Center, it became part of my job. Even General Chang is impressed by my talent for connecting the dots."

"And your conclusion?"

"Everything that's happening is coordinated by someone behind the scenes with one goal: to completely ruin scientific research."

"Who?"

"I have no idea. But I can sense the plan, a very comprehensive, intricate plan: damage scientific research installations, kill scientists, drive scientists like you crazy and make you commit suicide—but the main goal is to misdirect your thoughts until you're even more foolish than ordinary people."

"Your last statement is really perceptive."

"At the same time, they want to ruin science's reputation in society. Of course some people have always engaged in anti-science activities, but now it's coordinated."

"I believe it."

"*Now* you believe me. So many of you scientific elites couldn't figure it out, and I, having gone only to vocational school, had the answer? Ha! After I explained my theory, the scholars and my bosses all ridiculed it."

"If you had told me your theory back then, I'm sure I wouldn't have laughed at you. Take those frauds who practice pseudoscience—do you know who they're most afraid of?"

"Scientists, of course."

"No. Many of the best scientists can be fooled by pseudoscience and sometimes devote their lives to it. But pseudoscience is afraid of one particular type of people who are very hard to fool: stage magicians. In fact, many pseudo-scientific hoaxes were exposed by stage magicians. Compared to the bookworms of the scientific world, your experience as a cop makes you far more likely to perceive such a large-scale conspiracy."

"Well, there're plenty of people smarter than me. People in positions of power are well aware of the plot. When they ridiculed me at first, it was only because I wasn't explaining my theory to the right people. Later on, my old company commander—General Chang—had me transferred. But I'm still not doing anything other than running errands. . . . That's it. Now you know as much as I do."

"Another question: What does this have to do with the military?"

"I was baffled, too. I asked them, and they said that now that there's a war, of course the military would be involved. I was like you, thinking that they were talking nonsense.

But no, they weren't joking. The army really is on high alert. There are twenty-some Battle Command Centers like ours around the globe. And above them there's another level of command structure. But no one knows the details."

"Who's the enemy?"

"No idea. NATO officers are now stationed in the war room of the PLA General Staff Department, and a bunch of PLA officers are working out of the Pentagon. Who the fuck knows who we're fighting?"

"This is all so bizarre. Are you sure it's all true?"

"A bunch of my old buddies from the army are now generals, so I know a few things."

"The media has no idea about any of this?"

"Ah, that's another thing. All the countries are keeping a tight lid on this, and they've been successful so far. I can guarantee you that the enemy is incredibly powerful. Those in charge are terrified! I know General Chang very well. He's the sort who's afraid of nothing, not even the sky falling, but I can tell that he's worried about something much worse right now. They're all scared out of their wits, and they have no confidence that we'll win."

"If what you say is true, then we should all be frightened."

"Everyone is afraid of something. The enemy must be, too. The more powerful they are, the more they have to lose to their fears."

"What do you think the enemy is afraid of?"

"You! Scientists! The odd thing is that the less practical your research is, the more they're afraid of you—like abstract theories, the kind of thing Yang Dong worked on. They are more frightened of such work than you are of the universe winking at you. That's why they're so ruthless. If killing you would solve the problem, you'd all be dead by now. But the

most effective technique remains disrupting your thoughts. When a scientist dies, another will take his place. But if his thoughts are confused, then science is over."

"You're saying they're afraid of fundamental science?"

"Yes, fundamental science."

"But my research is very different in nature from Yang Dong's. The nanomaterial I work on isn't fundamental science. It's just a very strong material. What's the threat to them?"

"You're a special case. Usually, they don't bother those engaged in applied research. Maybe the material you're developing really scares them."

"Then what should I do?"

"Go to work and keep up your research. That's the best way to strike back at them. Don't worry about that shitty countdown. If you want to relax a bit after work, play that game. If you can beat it, that might help."

"That game? *Three Body*? You think it's connected to all this?"

"Definitely connected. I know that several specialists at the Battle Command Center are playing it, too. It's no ordinary game. Someone like me, fearless out of ignorance, can't play it. It has to be someone knowledgeable like you."

"Anything else?"

"No. But if I find out more I'll let you know. Keep your phone on, buddy. Keep your head screwed on straight, and if you get scared again, just remember my ultimate rule."

Da Shi drove away before Wang had a chance to thank him.

11

THREE BODY:
MOZI AND FIERY FLAMES

Wang Miao returned home, stopping on the way to buy a V-suit. His wife told him that people from work had been trying to get ahold of him all day.

Wang turned on his phone, checked his messages, and returned a few calls. He promised he'd be at work tomorrow. At dinner, he followed Da Shi's advice and drank some more.

But he didn't feel sleepy. After his wife went to bed, he sat in front of the computer, put on his new V-suit, and logged into *Three Body*.

Desolate plain at dawn.

Wang stood in front of King Zhou's pyramid. The snow that had once covered it was gone, and the blocks of stone were pockmarked by erosion. The ground was now a different color. In the distance were a few massive buildings that Wang guessed were dehydratories, but they were of a different design than the ones he had seen last time.

Everything told him that eons had passed.

By the faint dawn light, Wang looked for the entrance. When he found it, he saw that the opening had been sealed

by blocks of stone. But next to it, there was now a staircase carved into the pyramid leading all the way to the apex. He looked up and saw that the top had been flattened into a platform. The pyramid, once Egyptian in style, now resembled an Aztec one.

Wang climbed up the stairs and reached the apex. The platform looked like an ancient astronomical observatory. In one corner was a telescope several meters high, and next to it were a few smaller telescopes. In another corner were a few strange instruments that reminded him of ancient Chinese armillary spheres, models of objects in the sky.

His attention was drawn to the large copper sphere in the center of the platform. Two meters in diameter, it was set on top of a complex machine. Propelled by countless gears, the sphere slowly rotated. Wang noticed that the direction and speed of its rotation constantly shifted. Below the machine was a large square cavity. By the faint torchlight within, Wang saw a few slavelike figures pushing a spoked, horizontal wheel, which provided the power to the machine above.

A man walked toward Wang. Like King Wen when Wang had first encountered him, the man had his back against the sliver of light on the horizon, and he appeared to Wang as a pair of bright eyes floating in the darkness. He was slender and tall, dressed in a flowing black robe, his hair carelessly knotted on top of his head with a few strands waving in the wind.

"Hello," the man said. "I'm Mozi."[23]

"Hello, I'm Hairen."

"Ah, I know you!" Mozi grew excited. "You were a follower of King Wen back in Civilization Number 137."

23 *Translator's Note:* Mozi was the founder of the Mohist school of philosophy during the Warring States Period. Mozi himself emphasized experience and logic, and was known as an accomplished engineer and geometer.

"I did follow him here. But I never believed his theories."

"You're right." Mozi nodded at Wang solemnly. Then he moved closer. "During the three hundred and sixty-two thousand years you've been away, civilization has been reborn four more times. These civilizations struggled to develop through the irregular alternation of Chaotic Eras and Stable Eras. The shortest-lived one got only halfway through the Stone Age, but Civilization Number 139 broke a record and developed all the way to the Steam Age."

"You're saying that people from that civilization found the laws governing the sun's motion?"

Mozi laughed and shook his head. "Not at all. They were just lucky."

"But the effort to do so has never ceased?"

"Of course not. Come, let us see the efforts of the last civilization." Mozi led Wang to a corner of the observatory platform. The ground spread out beneath them like an ancient piece of leather. Mozi aimed one of the smaller telescopes at a target on the ground and gestured for Wang to look. Wang looked through the eyepiece and saw a strange sight: a skeleton. In the dawn light it gave off a snow-white glint and appeared to be very refined.

Astonishingly, the skeleton stood on its own. Its posture was graceful and elegant. One hand was held below the chin, as though stroking a long-missing beard. Its head tilted slightly up, as though questioning sky and earth.

"That's Confucius," Mozi said. "He believed that everything had to fit *li,* the Confucian conception of order and propriety, and nothing in the universe could be exempt from it. He created a system of rites and hoped to predict the motion of the sun with it."

"I can imagine the result."

"Right you are. He calculated how the sun would follow the rites, and predicted a five-year Stable Era. And you know what? There was indeed a Stable Era . . . lasting a month."

"And then one day the sun just didn't come out?"

"No, the sun rose that day as well. It rose to the middle of the sky, and then went out."

"What? Went out?"

"Yes. It gradually dimmed, became smaller, and then went out all of a sudden. Night fell. Oh, the cold. Confucius stood there and froze into a column of ice. And there he remains."

"Was there anything remaining in the sky after the sun went out?"

"A flying star appeared in that location, like a soul left behind after the sun died."

"You're sure that the sun really disappeared suddenly, and the flying star appeared just as suddenly?"

"Yes, absolutely. You can check the historical annals. It was clearly recorded."

"Hmmm . . ." Wang thought hard about this information. He had already formed some vague ideas about the workings of the world of *Three Body*. But this bit of news from Mozi overturned all his theories. "How can it be . . . sudden?" he muttered in annoyance.

"We're now in the Han Dynasty—I'm not sure if it's the Western Han or the Eastern Han."

"You've stayed alive until now?"

"I have a mission: observing the precise movements of the sun. Those shamans, metaphysicians, and Daoists are all useless. Like those proverbial bookish men who could not even tell types of grains apart, they do not labor with their hands, and know nothing practical. They have no ability to

do experiments, and they're immersed in their mysticism all day long. But I'm different. I know how to make things." He pointed to the numerous instruments on the platform.

"Do you think these can lead you to your goal?" Wang nodded specifically at the giant copper sphere.

"I have theories, too, but they're not mystical. They're derived from a large number of observations. First, do you know what the universe is? It's a machine."

"That's not very insightful."

"Let me be more specific: The universe is a hollow sphere floating in the middle of a sea of fire. There are numerous tiny holes in the surface of the sphere, as well as a large one. The light from the sea of flames shines through these holes. The tiny ones are stars, and the large one is the sun."

"That's a very interesting model." Wang looked at the giant copper sphere again and guessed at its purpose. "But there's a problem with your theory. When the sun rises or sets, we can see its motion against the background of fixed stars. But in your hollow sphere, all the holes remain in fixed positions relative to each other."

"Correct! That's why I've modified my model. The universal sphere is made of two spheres, one inside the other. The sky we can see is the surface of the inner sphere. The outer sphere has one large hole while the inner sphere has many small holes. The light coming through the hole in the outer sphere is reflected and scattered many times in the space between the two spheres, filling it with light. Then the light comes in through the tiny holes in the inner sphere, and that's how we see the stars."

"What about the sun?"

"The sun is the result of the large hole in the outer sphere being projected onto the inner one. The projection is so

bright that it penetrates the inner sphere like the shell of an egg, and that is how we see the sun. Around the spot of light, the scattered light rays are also very bright, and can be seen through the inner shell. That is why we can see a clear sky during the day."

"What is the force that propels the two spheres in their irregular motion?"

"It's the force of the sea of fire outside the two spheres."

"But the sun's brightness and size change over time. In your double-shell model, the sun's size and brightness ought to be fixed. Even if the brightness of the flames in the sea of fire is inconstant, the size of the hole would not be."

"Your conception of this model is too simplistic. As conditions in the sea of fire shift and change, the two shells will expand and shrink. This leads to changes in the size and brightness of the sun."

"What about the flying stars?"

"Flying stars? Why do you care about them? They're not important. Maybe just some random dust flying about the inside of the universal spheres."

"No, I think the flying stars are extremely important. Otherwise, how does your model explain the sudden extinguishing of the sun during the time of Confucius?"

"That's a rare exception. Maybe it was because a dark spot or cloud in the sea of fire just happened to pass over the big hole in the outer shell."

Wang pointed to the large copper sphere. "This must be your model, then?"

"Yes. I built a machine to replicate the universe. The complex gears that move the sphere simulate the forces from the sea of fire. The laws governing such motion are based on the distribution of flames in the sea of fire and the

154

currents within it. I deduced them from hundreds of years of observations."

"Can this sphere contract and expand?"

"Of course. Right now it's slowly contracting."

Wang used the handrail at the edge of the platform as a fixed visual reference. He found Mozi's assertion to be true.

"And there's an inner shell inside this sphere?"

"Of course. The inner shell moves within the outer shell through another complex set of mechanisms."

"Truly a skillfully designed machine!" Wang's praise was heartfelt. "But I don't see a large hole in the outer shell to cast the sun's light onto the inner shell."

"There is no hole. On the inner surface of the outer shell I have installed a source of light to simulate the hole. The light source is made of the luminescent material gathered from hundreds of thousands of fireflies. I used a cool light because the inner shell is made of translucent plaster, which is not a good heat conductor. This way, I can avoid the problem of too much heat accumulating inside the sphere that we would have with a regular source of light. The observer can then stay inside for a long time."

"There's a person inside the sphere?"

"Yes. A clerk stands on top of a shelf with a wheeled base that is kept at the center of the sphere. After we set up the model universe to correspond to the current state of the real universe, the motion of the model thereafter should be an accurate simulation of the future, including the motion of the sun. After the clerk records the movements of the sun, we will have a precise calendar. This is the dream of hundreds of civilizations before us.

"And it looks like you have come at an opportune time. According to the model universe, a four-year-long Stable

Era is about to begin. Emperor Wu of Han has just issued the order to rehydrate based on my prediction. Let's wait for sunrise!"

Mozi brought up the game's interface and slightly increased the rate of passage of game time. A red sun rose above the horizon, and the numerous frozen lakes and ponds scattered over the plain began to melt. These lakes had been covered by dust and had merged into the dun ground, but now they turned into numerous mirrors, as though the earth had opened many eyes. From up so high, Wang couldn't see the details of rehydration, but he could see more and more people gathered on the shores of the lakes like swarms of ants coming out of their nests in spring. The world had once again been revived.

"Do you not want to join this wonderful life?" Mozi asked, pointing to the ground below. "When women are first revived, they crave love. There is no reason for you to stay here any longer. The game is over. I am the winner."

"As a piece of machinery, your model universe is indeed incomparable. But as for its predictions May I use your telescope to observe something?"

"Please." Mozi gestured at the large telescope.

Wang walked up to the instrument and paused. "How can I use it to observe the sun?"

Mozi retrieved a black, circular piece of glass. "Use this smoked glass filter." He inserted it in front of the eyepiece.

Wang aimed the telescope at the sun, now halfway up the sky. He was impressed by Mozi's imagination. The sun did indeed look like a hole through which a sea of fire could be seen, a small view into a much larger whole.

But as he examined the image in the telescope more closely, he realized that the sun was different from the sun

he was used to in real life. The sun here had a small core. He imagined the sun as an eye. The core was like the eye's pupil, and though it was small, it was bright and dense. The layers surrounding it, by contrast, appeared insubstantial, wispy, gaseous. The fact that he could see through the outside layers to the core indicated that those layers were transparent or translucent, and the light from those layers was likely just scattered light from the core.

The details in the image of the sun stunned Wang. He was once again assured that the game designers had hidden a vast amount of data within the superficially simple images, just waiting to be revealed by players.

As Wang pondered the meaning of the sun's structure, he became excited. Because time in the game was now passing quickly, the sun was already in the west. Wang stood, adjusted the telescope to aim at the sun again, and tracked it until it dipped below the horizon.

Night fell, and the bonfires across the plains mirrored the sky full of stars. Wang took off the smoked glass filter and continued to scan the skies. He was most interested in the flying stars, and shortly found two. He only had time to observe one of them briefly before it was dawn again. So he inserted the filter and continued to observe the sun. . . .

In this manner Wang performed astronomical observations for more than ten days, enjoying the thrill of discovery. Indeed, the fact that time within the game had been sped up helped with the observations, as the motion of celestial bodies became more apparent.

On the seventeenth day of the Stable Era, five hours after the predicted time for sunrise, the world was still under cover of dark night. Multitudes thronged at the foot of the pyramid, their innumerable torches flickering in the chill wind.

"The sun will probably not rise again. It is like at the end of Civilization Number 137," Wang said to Mozi.

Mozi stroked his beard and smiled confidently. "Do not fret. The sun will rise soon, and the Stable Era will continue. I've already learned the secret of the motion of the universal machine. My predictions cannot be wrong."

As though confirming Mozi's words, the sky over the horizon brightened with dawn's first light. The crowd around the pyramid shouted in joy.

The silvery light brightened far more rapidly than usual, as though the rising sun wanted to make up for lost time. Soon, the light covered half the sky, even though the sun was still below the horizon. The world was already as bright as midday.

Wang looked toward the horizon and saw it giving off a blinding glare. The glowing horizon arched upward and became a curve that spread from one edge of his visual field to the other. He soon realized that he wasn't seeing the horizon, but the edge of the rising sun, an incomparably immense sun.

After his eyes adjusted to the bright light, the horizon reappeared in its old place. Wang saw columns of black smoke rising in the distance, especially clear against the glowing background of the solar disk. A fast horse rushed toward the pyramid from the direction of the rising sun, the dust from its hooves forming a distinct line across the plains.

The crowd parted before the horse, and Wang heard the rider scream at the top of his lungs: "Dehydrate! Dehydrate!"

Following the rider was a herd of cattle, horses, and other animals. Their bodies were on fire and they moved across the ground like a burning carpet.

Half of the gigantic sun's disk was now above the horizon, taking up much of the sky. The earth seemed to slowly sink down against a brilliant wall. Wang could clearly make out

the fine structures on the surface of the sun: eddies and surging waves filling the sea of flames; sunspots floating along random paths like ghosts; the corona lazily spreading out like golden sleeves.

On the ground, both those who had already dehydrated and those who hadn't began to burn like countless logs thrown into the belly of a furnace. The flames that consumed them were even brighter than glowing charcoal in a furnace, but were quickly extinguished.

The giant sun continued to rise and soon filled most of the sky. Wang looked up and felt his perspective shift. Suddenly he was no longer looking up, but down. The surface of the giant sun became a fiery earth, and he felt himself falling toward this brilliant hell.

Lakes and ponds began to evaporate, and puffs of white steam rose up like mushroom clouds. They rose, spilled open, and dispersed, covering the ashes of the dead.

"The Stable Era will continue. The universe is a machine. I created this machine. The Stable Era will continue. The universe . . ."

Wang turned his head. The voice belonged to Mozi, who was already on fire. His body was encased within a column of tall, orange flame, and his skin crinkled and turned into charcoal. But his two eyes still shone with a light that was distinct from the fire consuming him. His two hands, already burning pieces of charcoal, held up the cloud of swirling ashes that had once been his calendar.

Wang was burning up as well. He lifted his two hands and saw two torches.

The sun briskly moved to the west, revealing the sky behind it. It soon fell below the horizon, and the ground seemed to rise against the brilliant wall this time. A dazzling

sunset swiftly turned to night, as though a pair of giant hands had pulled a black cloth over a world that had turned to ash.

The earth glowed with a dim red light like a piece of charcoal just retrieved from a furnace. For a brief moment, Wang saw the stars, but soon steam and smoke hid the sky and covered everything on the red-glowing earth. The world sank into a dark chaos. A red line of text appeared:

> Civilization Number 141 fell into ruin in flames. This civilization had advanced to the Eastern Han Period.
>
> The seed of civilization remains. It will germinate and again pro-gress through the unpredictable world of *Three Body*. We invite you to log on in the future.

Wang took off the V-suit. After his mind had calmed down a bit, he again had the thought that *Three Body* was deliberately pretending to be merely illusory, while in fact possessing some deep reality. The real world in front of him, on the other hand, had begun to seem like the superficially complex, but in truth rather simple, *Along the River During the Qingming Festival*.

The next day, Wang went to the Nanotechnology Research Center. Other than some minor confusion due to his absence the day before, everything was normal. He found work to be an effective tranquilizer. As long as he was absorbed by it, he was no longer bothered by his nightmarish worries. He deliberately kept himself constantly busy the whole day and left the lab only after it was dark.

As soon as Wang left the Research Center building, the nightmarelike feeling caught up to him. He felt like the starry

sky was a magnifying glass that covered the world, and he was a tiny insect below the lens with nowhere to hide.

He had to find something to occupy himself. Then he thought of Yang Dong's mother Ye Wenjie and drove to her home.

Ye was alone at home. When Wang entered, she was sitting on the sofa reading. Wang noticed that her eyes were both myopic and presbyopic, and she had to switch glasses both when she read and when she looked at something far away. She was very happy to see Wang, and said that he looked much better than the last time he had come to see her.

Wang chuckled. "It's all because of your ginseng."

Ye shook her head. "What I gave you wasn't very good. We used to be able to find really high-quality wild ginseng around the base. I once found one about this long. . . . I wonder what it's like there now. I heard that it's deserted. Well, I guess I'm really getting old. These days, I'm always thinking about the past."

"I heard that you suffered a lot during the Cultural Revolution."

"You heard it from Ruishan, didn't you?" Ye waved her hand, as though trying to wave away a strand of spider silk. "In the past, it's all in the past. . . . Last night, Ruishan called me. He was in such a hurry that I had a hard time understanding him. All I got was that something seemed to have happened to you. Xiao Wang, let me tell you: By the time you're my age, you'll realize that everything you once thought mattered so much turns out to mean very little."

"Thank you," Wang said. He once again felt the warmth that he had missed. In his current state, his mental stability depended on two pillars: this old woman, who had weathered so many storms and become as gentle as water,

and Shi Qiang, the man who feared nothing because he knew nothing.

Ye continued. "As far as the Cultural Revolution is concerned, I was pretty lucky. Just when I thought I had nowhere to go, I found a place where I could survive."

"You mean Red Coast Base?"

Ye nodded.

"That was truly an incredible project. I used to think it was just made-up rumors."

"Not rumors. If you want, I can tell you some of what I experienced."

The offer made Wang a little worried. "Professor Ye, I'm only curious. You don't need to tell me if it's not appropriate."

"It's no big deal. Let's just imagine that I'm looking for someone to hear me talk."

"You could go visit the senior center. You wouldn't be lonely if you went there occasionally."

"Many of those retirees were my colleagues back at the university, but somehow I just can't mix with them. Everyone likes to reminisce, but no one wants to listen, and everyone feels annoyed when someone else tells a story. You're the only one who's interested in Red Coast."

"But for you to tell me about those things . . . isn't that prohibited?"

"That's true—it's still classified. But after that book was published, many others who were there also began to tell their stories, so they're like open secrets. The person who wrote that book was very irresponsible. Even if we put aside his agenda, the content of that book was often inaccurate. I should at least correct those errors."

Then Ye Wenjie began to tell Wang about what happened to her during her years at Red Coast.

12

RED COAST II

Ye wasn't given a real job immediately after entering Red Coast Base. Under the watchful eyes of a security guard, she was only allowed to perform a few technical tasks.

Back when she was still a second-year in college, Ye had already known the professor who would end up being her thesis advisor. He had told Ye that to do astrophysics research, it was useless to excel at theory without knowledge of experimental methods and observational skills—at least, that was true in China. This was very different from her father's view, but Ye tended to agree with her professor. She had always felt that her father was too theoretical.

Her advisor was one of the pioneers of Chinese radio astronomy. Under his influence, Ye developed a great interest in radio astronomy as well. Thus, she taught herself electrical engineering and computer science, the foundation for experiments and observations in the field. During the two years when she was a graduate student, the two of them had tested China's first small-scale radio telescope and had accumulated a great deal of experience in the area.

She hadn't expected the knowledge would one day be useful at Red Coast Base.

Eventually, Ye was assigned to the Transmission

Department to maintain and repair equipment. She quickly became an indispensable part of their operations.

Initially, this confused her a bit. She was the only person at the base who wasn't in a military uniform. And given her political status, everyone kept their distance. She had no way to ward off the loneliness other than devoting herself to work. However, this wasn't enough to explain why they relied on her so much. This was, after all, a key defense project. How could the technical staff here be so mediocre that she, who had not majored in engineering and who had no real working experience, easily took over their jobs?

She learned the reason soon enough. Contrary to appearances, the base's staff was composed of the best technical officers from the Second Artillery Corps. She could study all her life and have no hope of catching up to those excellent electrical and computer engineers. But the base was remote, the conditions were poor, and the main research work of the Red Coast Project was already completed. All that was left was maintenance and operation, so there was little opportunity for achieving any interesting technical results. Most people did not want to be indispensable, because they understood that in highly classified projects like this, once someone was put into a core technical position, it would be very difficult for him to be transferred out. Thus, all of them tried to deliberately hide their technical competence as they went about their jobs.

Yet, they couldn't appear *too* incompetent. So if the supervisor said to go east, they would work hard to move west, purposely playing the fool. Their hope was to put the following thought into the supervisor's head: *This man is working hard, but he's limited in his skills. There's no point in keeping him, because he'll only get in the way.* Many really did successfully obtain transfers through this method.

Under such conditions, Ye gradually became a key technician at the base. But the other reason that she could achieve this position puzzled her, and for that she could find no explanation: Red Coast Base—at least the parts that she had contact with—had no real advanced technology at all.

Over time, as Ye continued to work at the Transmission Department, the restrictions on her were gradually relaxed, and even the security guard assigned to watch her was called off. She was allowed to touch most components of Red Coast's systems, and could read the relevant technical documents. Of course, there were still areas forbidden to her. For example, she wasn't allowed near the computer control systems. However, Ye discovered that the impact of those systems on Red Coast was far smaller than she had imagined. For instance, the Transmission Department's computers consisted of three machines even more primitive than DJS130.[24] They used cumbersome magnetic core memory and paper input tape, and their longest uptime did not exceed fifteen hours. She also saw that the precision of Red Coast's targeting system was very low, probably not even on par with that of an artillery cannon.

One day, Commissar Lei came to speak with Ye. By this time, Yang Weining and Lei Zhicheng had swapped places in her eyes. During those years, Yang, as the highest-ranked technical officer, did not enjoy a high political status, and outside of technical matters he had little authority. He had to be careful with his subordinates, and had to speak politely even to the sentries, lest he be deemed to have an intellectual's resistant attitude toward thought reform and collaboration

24 *Translator's Note:* This was a Chinese 16-bit minicomputer modeled on the American Data General Nova.

with the masses. Thus, whenever he encountered difficulties in his work, Ye became his punching bag. But as Ye gained importance as a technical staff member, Commissar Lei gradually shed his initial rudeness and coldness and became kind toward her.

Commissar Lei said, "Wenjie, by now you're pretty familiar with the transmission system. This is also Red Coast's offensive component, its principal part. Can you give me your views of the system as a whole?"

They were sitting at the lip of the steep cliff on Radar Peak, the most secluded spot on the base. The cliff seemed to drop straight off into a bottomless abyss. At first, the spot had frightened Ye, but now she liked to come here by herself.

Ye wasn't sure how to answer Commissar Lei's question. She was only responsible for maintaining and repairing equipment and knew nothing about Red Coast as a whole, including its operation, targets, and so on. Indeed, she wasn't allowed to know. She wasn't even permitted to be present at the transmission. She pondered the question, began to speak, and stopped herself.

"Go ahead, speak your mind," Commissar Lei said. He ripped out a blade of grass next to him and played with it absent-mindedly.

"It . . . is just a radio transmitter."

"That's right, just a radio transmitter." The commissar nodded, satisfied. "Do you know about microwave ovens?"

Ye shook her head.

"They are a luxury plaything of the capitalist West. Food is heated by the energy generated from absorbing microwave radiation. At my previous research station, in order to precisely test the high-temperature aging of certain components, we imported one. After work, we would use it to warm *mantou*

bread, bake a potato, that sort of thing. It's very interesting: The inside heats up first while the outside remains cold."

Commissar Lei stood up and paced back and forth. He was so close to the edge of the cliff that it made Ye nervous.

"Red Coast is a microwave oven, and its heating targets are the enemy's space vessels. If we can apply microwave radiation at a specific power level of one-tenth of a watt to one watt per square centimeter, we'll be able to disable or destroy many electronic components of satellite communications, radar, and navigation systems."

Ye finally understood. Even though Red Coast was only a radio transmitter, that didn't mean it was conventional. The most surprising aspect was its transmission power: as high as twenty-five megawatts! This wasn't just more powerful than all communication transmissions, but also all radar transmissions. Red Coast relied on a set of gigantic capacitors. Because the power requirements were so high, the transmission circuits were also different from conventional designs. Ye now understood the purpose of such ultrahigh power in the system, but something seemed wrong right away. "The emission from the system seems to be modulated."

"That's right. However, the modulation is unlike that used in conventional radio communications. The purpose isn't to add information, but to use shifting frequencies and amplitudes to penetrate possible shielding by the enemy. Of course, those are still experimental."

Ye nodded. Many of her questions had now been answered.

"Recently, two target satellites were launched from Jiuquan. The test attacks by Red Coast were completely successful. Temperature inside the satellites reached nearly a thousand degrees, and all instruments and photographic equipment onboard were destroyed. In future wars, Red

Coast can effectively strike at the enemy's communication and reconnaissance satellites, like the KH-8 spy satellites on which the American Imperialists rely, as well as the KH-9, which are about to be launched. The lower-orbit spy satellites of the Soviet Revisionists are even more vulnerable. If necessary, we even have the capacity to destroy the Salyut space station of the Soviet Revisionists and the Skylab station that American Imperialists plan on launching next year."

"Commissar! What are you telling her?" Someone spoke behind Ye. She turned and saw that it was Yang Weining, who stared at Commissar Lei severely.

"This is for work," Commissar Lei said, and then left. Yang glanced at Ye without saying anything and followed Lei. Ye was left all by herself.

He's the one who brought me here, but he still doesn't trust me, a disconsolate Ye thought. She was worried about Commissar Lei. At the base, Lei had more authority than Yang, since the commissar had the final vote on most important matters, but the way he rushed away with Yang seemed to indicate that he felt the chief engineer had caught him doing something wrong. This convinced Ye that Lei had made a personal decision to tell her about the true purpose of the Red Coast Project.

What will happen to him as a result of this decision? As she gazed at Commissar Lei's burly back, Ye felt a wave of gratitude. For her, trust was a luxury that she dared not wish for. Compared to Yang, Lei was closer to her image of a real military officer, possessing a soldier's frank and forthright manners. Yang, on the other hand, was nothing more than a typical intellectual of the period: cautious, timid, seeking only to protect himself. Even though Ye understood him, the wide gulf already between them grew wider.

The next day, Ye was transferred out of the Transmission Department and assigned to the Monitoring Department. At first, she thought this was related to the events of the day before, an attempt to move her away from the core of Red Coast. But after arriving at the Monitoring Department, she realized that *this* was more like the heart of Red Coast. Even though the two departments shared some resources, such as the antenna, the technology level of the Monitoring Department was far more advanced.

The Monitoring Department had a very sophisticated and sensitive radio receiver. A ruby-based traveling-wave maser[25] amplified the signals received by the gigantic antenna, and in order to minimize interference, the core of the reception system was immersed in liquid helium at -269 degrees Celsius. Periodically, a helicopter came to replenish the supply of liquid helium. The reception system was thus capable of picking up very faint signals. Ye couldn't help but imagine how wonderful it would be to use the equipment for radio astronomy research.

The Monitoring Department's computer system was also much bigger and more complex than the one at the Transmission Department. The first time she entered the main computer room, Ye saw a row of cathode ray tube displays. She was stunned to see programming code scrolling across each of them, and the operators were free to edit and test the code using the keyboard. When she learned programming in college, the source code was always written on the grids of special programming paper, then transferred to paper tape using a typewriter. She had heard of input using a keyboard and screen, but this was the first time she had seen it.

25 *Translator's Note:* A maser is like a laser, but for electromagnetic radiation, typically microwaves, not in the visible light range.

The software available astonished her even more. She learned about something called FORTRAN, which allowed you to program using a language close to natural language. You could even type mathematical equations directly into the code! Programming in it was several times more efficient than programming in machine code. And then there was something called a database, which allowed for easy storage and manipulation of vast amounts of data.

Two days later, Commissar Lei sought Ye out for another talk. This time, they were in the main computer room of the Monitoring Department, in front of the row of green-glowing screens. Yang Weining sat close by, not part of their conversation, but also not willing to leave, which made Ye very uncomfortable.

"Wenjie," Commissar Lei began, "let me explain the work of the Monitoring Department to you. Simply put, the goal is to keep an eye on enemy activities in space, including intercepting communications between enemy space vessels and the ground, and between the space vessels themselves; collaborating with our telemetry, tracking, and command centers to determine the orbits of enemy space vessels and provide data for Red Coast's combat systems. In other words, the eyes of Red Coast are here."

Yang interrupted, "Commissar Lei, I don't think what you're doing is a good idea. There's no need to tell her these things."

Ye glanced at Yang and anxiously said, "Commissar, if it's not appropriate for me to know, then—"

"No, no, Wenjie." The commissar held up a hand to stop Ye from speaking. He turned to Yang. "Chief Yang, I'm going to tell you the same thing I did before. This is for work. For Wenjie to perform her duties better, she must be told the purpose of her work."

Yang stood up. "I will report this to our superiors."

"That is your right, of course. But do not fret, Chief Yang. I will assume responsibility for all consequences."

Yang got up and left with a bitter expression.

"Don't mind him. That's just the way Chief Yang is." Commissar Lei chuckled and shook his head. Then he stared at Ye and his tone became solemn. "Wenjie, when we first brought you to the base, the goal was simple. Red Coast's monitoring systems often had interference caused by electromagnetic radiation from solar flares and sunspots. Fortuitously, we saw your paper and realized that you had researched solar activity. Among Chinese scholars, your predictive model turned out to be the most accurate, so we wanted to ask for your help in solving this problem.

"But after you came, you showed very strong abilities, so we decided to give you more responsibilities. My thought was this: assign you first to the Transmission Department, then the Monitoring Department. This way, you'd gain a comprehensive understanding of Red Coast as a whole and we could wait and see where to assign you after that.

"Of course, as you can see, this plan has met with some resistance. But I have trust in you, Wenjie. Let me be clear: Until now, the trust placed in you has been mine, personally. I hope that you can continue to work hard and earn the trust of the organization as a whole."

Commissar Lei placed a hand on Ye's shoulder. She felt the warmth and strength conveyed through it. "Wenjie, let me tell you my sincere hope: One day, I'd like to call you *Comrade Ye*."

Lei stood up and strode away in the confident manner of a soldier. Ye's eyes were filled with tears. Seen through them, the code on the screen became flickering flames. This was the first time she had cried since the death of her father.

As Ye familiarized herself with the work of the Monitoring Department, she discovered that she was far less successful here than at the Transmission Department. The computer science knowledge she had was outdated, and she had to learn the software techniques from scratch. Even though Commissar Lei trusted her, the restrictions on her were severe. She was allowed to view the software source code, for example, but was forbidden from touching the database.

On a day-to-day basis, Ye was mainly supervised by Yang. He became even ruder to her, and would get angry at her for the smallest things. Commissar Lei talked to him about it multiple times without effect. It seemed that Yang became filled with a nameless anxiety as soon as he saw Ye.

Gradually, as Ye encountered more and more unexplainable matters in her work, she came to realize that the Red Coast Project was far more complex than she had imagined.

One day, the monitoring system intercepted a transmission that, after being deciphered by the computer, turned out to be a few satellite photographs. The blurry images were sent to the General Staff Department's Surveying and Mapping Bureau for interpretation. They turned out to be images of important military targets in China, including the naval harbor at Qingdao and several key factories of the Third Front program.[26] Analysis confirmed that these images came from the KH-9 American reconnaissance system.

The first KH-9 satellite had just been launched. Although it mainly relied on recoverable film capsules for intelligence gathering, it was also being used to test out the more advanced technique of radio transmission of digital images. Due to the

26 *Translator's Note:* The Third Front program was a secret, military-led industrialization effort during the Cultural Revolution that built factories in China's interior, where they would be less vulnerable to American and Soviet attacks.

technology's immaturity, the satellite transmitted at a low frequency, which increased its range of reception sufficiently for it to be intercepted by Red Coast. And because it was only a test, the encryption was not very secure and could be broken.

The KH-9 was without a doubt an important monitoring target, as it presented a rare opportunity to gather more information about American satellite reconnaissance systems. Yet, after the third day, Yang Weining ordered a change in the frequency and direction of monitoring and abandoned the target. Ye found the decision incomprehensible.

Another event also shocked her. Even though she was now in the Monitoring Department, sometimes the Transmission Department still needed her. One time, she accidentally saw the frequency settings for a few upcoming transmissions. She discovered that the designated frequencies for transmissions 304, 318, and 325 were lower than microwave range and could not result in any heating effect in the target.

One day, an officer summoned Ye to the main base administrative office out of the blue. From the officer's tone and expression, Ye knew that something had gone wrong.

As she walked into the office, the scene before her seemed familiar: All the senior officers of the base were present, along with two officers she didn't know. However, she could tell at a glance that they were from higher up in the chain of command.

Everyone's icy stares focused on her, but the sensitivity she had developed over the stormy years informed her that she wasn't the one in big trouble today. She was at most a sideshow. She saw Commissar Lei sitting in a corner with a dejected look.

He's finally going to pay for trusting me, she thought. At once, she decided that she would do whatever she could to

save him. She would take responsibility for everything, even lie if necessary.

But Commissar Lei was the first to speak, and what he said was completely unexpected. "Ye Wenjie, I must make it clear at the start that I do not agree with what is about to be done. The decision was made by Chief Engineer Yang after requesting instructions from our superiors. He alone will be responsible for all consequences."

Commissar Lei turned to look at Yang, who nodded solemnly. Lei continued, "In order to better utilize your skills at Red Coast Base, Chief Engineer Yang repeatedly requested permission from our superiors to abandon the cover story we've been using with you. Our comrades from the Army Political Department"—he indicated the two officers Ye didn't know—"were sent to investigate your work situation. Finally, with the approval of our superiors, we've decided to inform you of the true nature of the Red Coast Project."

Only after a long pause did Ye finally understand Commissar Lei's meaning: He had been lying to her all along.

"I hope you will treasure this opportunity and work hard to redeem your sins. After this, you must behave with the utmost propriety. Any reactionary behavior will be severely punished!" Commissar Lei stared at Ye. He was a completely different person from the image Ye had formed of him. "Are we clear? Good. Now Chief Yang can explain."

The others left, leaving only Yang and Ye.

"If you don't want this, there's still time."

Ye discerned the weight behind these words. She now understood Yang's anxiety whenever he had seen her the last few weeks. To make full use of her skills, it was necessary for her to know the truth about Red Coast. However, this choice would extinguish the last ray of hope she had of ever leaving

Radar Peak. Once she said yes, she really would spend the rest of her life at Red Coast Base.

"I agree," Ye said, softly, but resolutely.

Thus, on this early summer evening, as the wind howled through the giant parabolic antenna, and as the forest rustled over the Greater Khingan Mountains in the distance, Yang Weining explained to Ye Wenjie the true nature of Red Coast.

It was a fairy tale for the ages, even more incredible than the commissar's lies.

13

RED COAST III

SELECTED DOCUMENTS FROM
THE RED COAST PROJECT

These documents were declassified three years after Ye
Wenjie told Wang Miao the inside story of Red Coast
and provide background information for what she
told him.

I.

A Question Largely Ignored by Trends in Fundamental
World Scientific Research

(Originally published in Internal Reference, XX/XX/196X)

[Abstract] Based on modern and contemporary
history, there are two ways in which the results of funda-
mental scientific research can be converted into practical
applications: gradualistic mode and saltatory mode.

Gradualistic mode: theoretical, fundamental results
are gradually applied to technology; advances accumu-
late until they reach a breakthrough. Recent examples
include the development of space technology.

Saltatory mode: theoretical, fundamental results
rapidly become applied technology, leading to a

technological leap. Recent examples include the appearance of atomic weapons. Until the forties, some of the foremost physicists still thought it would never be possible to release the energy of the atom. But atomic weapons then appeared within a very short period. We define a technology leap to occur when fundamental science is converted to applied technology across a great span in an extremely brief time interval.

Currently, both NATO and the Warsaw Pact are intensely active in fundamental research and investing heavily in it. One or more technological leaps can occur at any time. Such an occurrence will pose a major threat to our strategic planning.

This article argues that our focus is currently on the gradualistic mode of technology development and insufficient attention is paid to the possibility of technology leaps. Starting from a higher vantage point, we should develop a comprehensive strategy and set of principles so that we can respond appropriately when technological leaps occur.

Fields where technological leaps are most likely:

Physics: [omitted]

Biology: [omitted]

Computer Science: [omitted]

The Search for Extraterrestrial Intelligence (SETI): Of all fields, this is the one in which the possibility for a technology leap is greatest. If a leap occurs in this field, the impact will exceed the sum of technology leaps in the other three fields.

[Full Text][omitted]

[Instructions from Central Leadership] Distribute this article to appropriate personnel and organize discussion

groups. The article's views will not be to the liking of some, but let's not rush to label the author. The key is to appreciate the author's long-term thinking. Some comrades cannot see beyond the ends of their noses, possibly because of the greater political environment, possibly because of their arrogance. This is not good. Strategic blind spots are extremely dangerous.

In my view, of the four fields where technology leaps may occur, we have given the least thought to the last one. It's worth some attention, and we should systematically analyze the matter in depth.

Signed: XXX Date: XX/XX/196X

II.

Research Report on the Possibility of Technology Leap Due to the Search for Extraterrestrial Intelligence

1. Current International Research Trends [**Summary**]

(1) The United States and other NATO states: The scientific case and the necessity for SETI are generally accepted, and strong academic support exists.

Project Ozma: In 1960, the National Radio Astronomy Observatory at Green Bank, West Virginia, searched for extraterrestrial intelligence with a radio telescope 26 meters in diameter. The project examined the stars Tau Ceti and Epsilon Eridani for 200 hours using ranges near the 1.420 gigahertz frequency. Project Ozma II, which will involve more targets and a broader frequency range, is planned for 1972.

Probes: The Pioneer 10 and Pioneer 11 probes, each of which will carry a metal plaque containing information about civilization on Earth, are

scheduled for launch in 1972. The Voyager 1 and Voyager 2 probes, each of which will carry a metal audio record, are scheduled for launch in 1977.

The Arecibo Observatory in Puerto Rico: Constructed in 1963, this is an important instrument for SETI. Its effective energy collection area is about 20 acres, which is greater than the sum of the collecting areas of all other radio telescopes in the world. When combined with its computer system, it can simultaneously monitor 65,000 channels and is also capable of ultrahigh-energy transmissions.

(2) The Soviet Union: Few sources of intelligence are available, but there are indications that large investments have been made in the field. Compared to NATO countries, the research seems to be more systematic and long term. Based on certain isolated information channels, plans are currently under way to build a global-scale very-long-baseline interferometry (VLBI) aperture-synthesis radio telescope system. Once the system is completed, it will possess the world's most powerful deep-space exploration capabilities.

2. Preliminary Analysis of Social Patterns of Extraterrestrial Civilizations Using a Materialist Conception of History [omitted]

3. Preliminary Analysis of the Influence of Extraterrestrial Civilizations on Human Social and Political Trends [omitted]

4. Preliminary Analysis of the Influence on Current International Patterns Due to Possible Contact with Extraterrestrial Civilizations

(1) Unidirectional contact (only receiving messages sent by extraterrestrial intelligence): [omitted]

179

(2) Bidirectional contact (exchange of messages with extraterrestrial intelligence and direct contact): [omitted]

5. The Danger and Consequences of Superpowers Making Initial Contact with Extraterrestrial Intelligence and Monopolizing Such Contact

(1) Analysis of consequences of American Imperialists and NATO making initial contact with extraterrestrial intelligence and monopolizing such contact: [still classified]

(2) Analysis of consequences of Soviet Revisionists and Warsaw Pact making initial contact with extraterrestrial intelligence and monopolizing such contact: [still classified]

[Instructions from Central Leadership] Others have already sent their messages out into space. It's dangerous if extraterrestrials only hear their voices. We should speak up as well. Only then will they get a complete picture of human society. It's not possible to get the truth by only listening to one side. We must make this happen, and quickly.

Signed: XXX Date: XX/XX/196X

III.

Research Report on the Initial Phase of the Red Coast Project (XX/XX/196X)

TOP SECRET

Number of Copies: 2

Summary Document: Central Document Number XXXXXX, forwarded to the Commission for Science, Technology, and Industry for National Defense, the

Chinese Academy of Sciences, and the Central Planning Commission, Department of National Defense; disseminated at the XXXXXX Conference and the XXXXXX Conference; partially disseminated at the XXXXXX Conference.

Topic Serial Number: 3760
Code Name: "Red Coast"

1. Goal [**Summary**]

 To search for the possible existence of extraterrestrial intelligence and to attempt contact and exchange.

2. Theoretical Study of the Red Coast Project

 (1) Searching and Monitoring

 Monitoring frequency range: 1,000 MHz to 40,000 MHz

 Monitoring channels: 15,000

 Key frequencies to monitor:

 Hydrogen atom frequency at 1,420 MHz

 Hydroxyl radical radiation frequency at 1,667 MHz

 Water molecule radiation frequency at 22,000 MHz

 Monitoring target range: a sphere centered around Earth with a radius of 1,000 light-years, containing approximately 20 million stars. For a list of targets, please see Appendix 1.

 (2) Message Transmission

 Transmission frequencies: 2,800 MHz, 12,000 MHz, 22,000 MHz

 Transmission power: 10–25 megawatts

 Transmission targets: a sphere centered around Earth with a radius of 200 light-years, containing approximately 100,000 stars. For a list of targets, please see Appendix 2.

(3) Development of the Red Coast Self-Interpreting Code System

Guiding principle: using universal, basic mathematical and physical laws, construct an elemental linguistic code that can be understood by any civilization that has mastered basic algebra, Euclidean geometry, and the laws of classical mechanics (nonrelativistic physics).

Using the elemental code above and supplemented with low-resolution images, gradually build up to a full linguistic system. Languages supported: Chinese and Esperanto.

The entire system's information content should be 680 KB. Transmission times at the 2,800 MHz, 12,000 MHz, and 22,000 MHz channels are 1,183 minutes, 224 minutes, and 132 minutes respectively.

3. Implementation Plan for the Red Coast Project

(1) Preliminary Design for the Red Coast Monitoring and Searching System [**still classified**]

(2) Preliminary Design for the Red Coast Transmission System [**still classified**]

(3) Preliminary Site-Selection Plan for Red Coast Base [**omitted**]

(4) Preliminary Thoughts on the Formation of Red Coast Force from within the Second Artillery Corps [**still classified**]

4. Content of Message Transmitted by Red Coast [**Summary**]

Overview of Earth (3.1 KB), overview of life on Earth (4.4 KB), overview of human society (4.6 KB), basic world history (5.4 KB).

Total information content: 17.5 KB.

The entire message will be sent after transmitting

the self-interpreting code system. Transmission times of message at the 2,800 MHz, 12,000 MHz, and 22,000 MHz channels are 31 minutes, 7.5 minutes, and 3.5 minutes, respectively.

The message will be carefully vetted by a multidisciplinary review to ensure that it will not give away the Earth's coordinates relative to the Milky Way. Among the three channels, transmission at the higher-frequency 12,000 MHz and 22,000 MHz channels should be minimized to reduce the likelihood that the source of transmission may be precisely ascertained.

IV.
Message to Extraterrestrial Civilizations
First Draft [**Complete Text**]

Attention, you who have received this message! This message was sent out by a country that represents revolutionary justice on Earth! Before this, you may have already received other messages sent from the same direction. Those messages were sent by an imperialist superpower on this planet. That superpower is struggling against another superpower for world domination so that it can drag human history backwards. We hope you will not listen to their lies. Stand with justice, stand with the revolution!

[**Instructions from Central Leadership**] This is utter crap! It's enough to put up big-character posters[27]

27 *Translator's Note:* Hand-written posters using large Chinese characters have become associated with the Cultural Revolution in the popular imagination. However, they have a long history in China as tools of propaganda as well as protest both before and after the Cultural Revolution.

everywhere on the ground, but we should not send them into space. The Cultural Revolution leadership should no longer have any involvement with Red Coast. Such an important message must be composed carefully. It's probably best to have it drafted by a special committee and then discussed and approved by a meeting of the Politburo.

Signed: XXX Date: XX/XX/196X

Second Draft [**omitted**]

Third Draft [**omitted**]

Fourth Draft [**Complete Text**]

We extend our best wishes to you, inhabitants of another world.

After reading the following message, you should have a basic understanding of civilization on Earth. By dint of long toil and creativity, the human race has built a splendid civilization, blossoming with a multitude of diverse cultures. We have also begun to understand the laws governing the natural world and the development of human societies. We cherish all that we have accomplished.

But our world is still flawed. Hate exists, as does prejudice and war. Because of conflicts between the forces of production and the relations of production, wealth distribution is extremely uneven, and large portions of humanity live in poverty and misery.

Human societies are working hard to resolve the difficulties and problems they face, striving to create a better future for Earth civilization. The country that sent this message is engaged in this effort. We are dedicated to building an ideal society, where the labor and value of every member of the human race are fully respected, where everyone's material and spiritual needs

are fully met, so that civilization on Earth may become more perfect.

With the best of intentions, we look forward to establishing contact with other civilized societies in the universe. We look forward to working together with you to build a better life in this vast universe.

V.

Related Policies and Strategies

1. Consideration of Policies and Strategies After Reception of Message from Extraterrestrial Intelligence [omitted]

2. Consideration of Policies and Strategies After Establishing Contact with Extraterrestrial Intelligence [omitted]

[**Instructions from Central Leadership**] It's important to take the time out of our busy schedules to do something entirely unrelated to our immediate needs. This project has allowed us to give some thought to issues we have never had time for. Indeed, we can think through them only when we take a sufficiently high vantage point. This alone is enough to justify the Red Coast Project.

How wonderful it will be if the universe really contains other intelligences and other societies! Bystanders have the clearest view. Someone truly neutral will then be able to comment on whether we're the heroes or villains of history.

Signed: XXX Date: XX/XX/196X

RED COAST IV

"Professor Ye," Wang Miao said, "I have a question. Back then, SETI was marginalized research. Why did the Red Coast Project have such a high security rating?"

"That question was asked during the very first phases of the Red Coast Project, and continued to be asked until the end. But now you should know the answer. We can only be impressed by the foresight of the top decision-maker responsible for the Red Coast Project."

"Yes, he thought far ahead." Wang nodded gravely.

Wang knew that it was only within the last couple of years that serious and systematic consideration had been given to the question of how and to what degree human societies would be influenced by establishing contact with extraterrestrial intelligence, but the research had rapidly gained interest, and the conclusions were shocking.

Naïve, idealistic hopes had been shattered. Scholars found that, contrary to the happy wishes of most people, it was not a good idea for the human race as a whole to make contact with extraterrestrials. The impact of such contact on human society would be divisive rather than uniting, and would exacerbate rather than mitigate the conflicts between different cultures. In summary, if contact were to occur,

the internal divisions within Earth civilization would be magnified and likely lead to disaster. The most shocking conclusion of all was that the impact would have nothing at all to do with the degree and type of contact (unidirectional or bidirectional), or the form and degree of advancement of the alien civilization.

This was the theory of "contact as symbol" proposed by sociologist Bill Mathers of RAND Corporation in his book, *The 100,000-Light-Year Iron Curtain: SETI Sociology.* Mathers believed that contact with an alien civilization is only a symbol or a switch. Regardless of the content of the encounter, the results would be the same.

Suppose that the nature of the contact is such that only the existence of extraterrestrial intelligence is confirmed, with no other substantive information—what Mathers called elementary contact. The impact would be magnified by the lens of human mass psychology and culture until it resulted in huge, substantive influences on the progress of civilization. If such contact were monopolized by one country or political force, the significance would be comparable to an overwhelming advantage in economic and military power.

"How did Red Coast end?"

"You can probably guess."

Wang nodded again. Of course he understood that, had Red Coast succeeded, the world today would be very different. To comfort Ye, he said, "It's still too early to tell if it succeeded or not. The radio waves sent out by Red Coast haven't gone very far in the universe yet."

Ye shook her head. "The farther the signals travel, the weaker they become, and the less likely that any extraterrestrial civilization will receive them. Of course, if aliens have already detected the Earth's existence and its oxygen-rich

atmosphere and decided to focus powerful equipment specifically at us, the story would be different. But, in general, research shows that in order for extraterrestrials to detect our signals, we must broadcast at a power level equal to the energy output of a midsized star.

"Soviet astrophysicist Nicolai Kardashev once proposed that civilizations can be divided into three types based on the power they can command—for communication purposes, let's say. A Type I civilization can muster an amount of energy equivalent to the total energy output of the Earth. Based on his estimates, the energy output of the Earth is about 10^{15} to 10^{16} watts. A Type II civilization can marshal the energy equivalent to the output of a typical star—10^{26} watts. A Type III civilization's communication energy can reach 10^{36} watts, approximately equal to the energy output of a galaxy. Civilization on Earth is currently about a Type 0.7, not even a full Type I. And the transmissions from Red Coast used only about one ten-millionth of the amount of power the Earth could muster. Our call was like the buzzing of a mosquito in the sky. No one could hear it."

"But if Kardashev's Type II and Type III civilizations really exist, we should be able to hear *them*."

"We never heard anything during the twenty years that Red Coast was in operation."

"Indeed. Given Red Coast and SETI, could all our efforts ultimately have proven only one thing: In the entire universe, only the Earth has intelligent life?"

Ye gave a light sigh. "Theoretically, there may never be a definitive answer to that question. But my sense, and the sense of everyone who went through Red Coast, is that that is the case."

"It's too bad that Red Coast was decommissioned. Once

it was built, it should have been kept running. It was a truly great enterprise."

"Red Coast's decline was gradual. At the beginning of the eighties, there was a large-scale renovation. Mainly, the transmission and monitoring computer systems were partially upgraded. The transmission system was automated, and the monitoring system incorporated two IBM minicomputers. The data processing capability became far more advanced, and it was able to simultaneously monitor forty thousand channels.

"But later, as people gained perspective, they had a better appreciation of the difficulty of the search for extraterrestrial intelligence, and the leadership lost interest in Red Coast. The first change was reducing the base's security rating. The consensus was that the extreme secrecy around Red Coast was unnecessary, and the security detail at the base was reduced from a company to a squad, until eventually only a group of five security guards were left. Also, after that renovation, although Red Coast remained administratively within the Second Artillery Corps, management of its scientific activities was turned over to the Chinese Academy of Sciences' Astronomy Institute, and it took on some research projects that had nothing to do with the search for extraterrestrial intelligence or the military."

"I believe you achieved most of your scientific accomplishments during that time."

"Initially, Red Coast also took on some radio astronomy projects. At the time, it was the largest radio telescope in the country. Later, as other radio astronomy observatories were built, Red Coast's research turned to the observation and analysis of solar electromagnetic activity. For this, they added a solar telescope. The mathematical model we built for solar electromagnetic activity was at the forefront of the

field back then, and had many practical applications. With these later research results, the large amount invested in Red Coast had at least a little return.

"Actually, much of the credit should be given to Commissar Lei. Of course he had his own agenda. He realized that as a political officer in a technical unit, his future wasn't bright. Before joining the army, he had studied astrophysics as well, so he wanted to return to doing science. The research projects that Red Coast took on outside of the search for extraterrestrial intelligence were all due to his efforts."

"I doubt that he could have returned to technical work so easily after spending so much time as a political commissar. Back then, you still hadn't been politically rehabilitated. It looks to me like all he did was to put his name on your research results."

Ye smiled forgivingly. "Without Lei, Red Coast Base would have been finished even earlier. After Red Coast was designated for conversion to civilian use, the military basically abandoned it. Eventually, the Chinese Academy of Sciences couldn't maintain the funds necessary for Red Coast's operation, and it was shut down."

Ye didn't talk much about her daily life at Red Coast Base, and Wang didn't ask. Four years after entering the base, she married Yang Weining. Everything just happened naturally, without any drama. Later, an accident at the base killed both Yang and Lei, and Yang Dong was born after her father's death. The mother and daughter only left Radar Peak in the mid-eighties, when Red Coast Base was finally decommissioned. Ye later returned to Tsinghua, her alma mater, to teach astrophysics until retirement. All this Wang had heard from Sha Ruishan at the Miyun Radio Astronomy Observatory.

"The search for extraterrestrial intelligence is a unique

discipline. It has a profound influence on the researcher's perspective on life." Ye spoke in a drawn-out voice, as though telling stories to a child. "In the dead of the night, I could hear in my headphones the lifeless noise of the universe. The noise was faint but constant, more eternal than the stars. Sometimes I thought it sounded like the endless winter winds of the Greater Khingan Mountains. I felt so cold then, and the loneliness was indescribable.

"From time to time, I would gaze up at the stars after a night shift and think that they looked like a glowing desert, and I myself was a poor child abandoned in the desert. . . . I thought that life was truly an accident among accidents in the universe. The universe was an empty palace, and humankind the only ant in the entire palace. This kind of thinking infused the second half of my life with a conflicted mentality: Sometimes I thought life was precious, and everything was so important; but other times I thought humans were insignificant, and nothing was worthwhile. Anyway, my life passed day after day accompanied by this strange feeling, and before I knew it, I was old. . . ."

Wang wanted to comfort this old woman who had devoted her life to a lonely but great enterprise, but Ye's last speech caused him to sink into the same sorrowful mood. He found that he had nothing to say except, "Professor Ye, someday I'll go with you to visit the ruins of Red Coast Base."

Ye slowly shook her head. "Xiao Wang, I'm not like you. I'm getting on in years, and my health isn't what it used to be. It's hard to predict the future. I live my life day to day."

Looking at the silvery head of hair on Ye Wenjie, Wang knew she was thinking of her daughter again.

15

THREE BODY: COPERNICUS, UNIVERSAL FOOTBALL, AND TRI-SOLAR DAY

After leaving Ye's home, Wang Miao couldn't calm down. The events of the last two days and the history of Red Coast, two seemingly unconnected strands, now twisted together, made the world unfamiliar overnight.

Once he was home, in order to escape this mood, Wang turned on the computer, put on the V-suit, and logged on to *Three Body* for the third time.

The attempt to adjust his state of mind worked. By the time the log-in screen appeared, Wang seemed like a different person, one filled with an unexplainable excitement. Unlike the first two times, this time Wang came with a purpose: He was going to reveal the secret of the world of *Three Body*.

He created a new log-in ID appropriate for his new role: Copernicus.

Once logged in, Wang again stood on that broad, desolate plain, facing the strange dawn of the world of *Three Body*. A colossal pyramid appeared in the east, but right away Wang

knew it was no longer the pyramid of King Zhou of Shang or Mozi. It had a Gothic-style apex, stabbing straight into the morning sky, recalling St. Joseph's Church at Wangfujing. But if that church were placed next to this pyramid, it would be nothing more than an entrance booth. He saw many buildings in the distance that were apparently dehydratories, but also now built in the Gothic style, with tall, sharp steeples, as though the ground had grown numerous spikes.

Wang saw a door on the side of the pyramid, lit from within by flickering lights. He walked over. Inside the tunnel was a row of statues of the gods of Olympus holding up torches, their surfaces blackened by smoke. He entered the Great Hall and saw that it was even dimmer than the entrance tunnel. Two silver candelabra on top of a long marble table provided a drowsy light.

Several men were seated around the table. The dim light allowed Wang to see only the outlines of their faces. Their eyes were hidden in the shadows of their deep eye sockets, but Wang could still feel their gazes focusing on him. The men seemed to be dressed in medieval robes. On closer examination, one or two of them had simpler robes, more like Classical Greek chitons. At one end of the table was a thin, tall man. The golden crown on top of his head was the only thing that glittered in the Great Hall other than the candles. With some effort, Wang saw by the dim candlelight that his robe was different from the others': it was red.

Wang realized that the game displayed a distinct world for each player. This world, based on the European High Middle Ages, was chosen by the software based on his ID.

"You're late. The meeting has been going on for a while," the gold-crowned, red-robed man said. "I'm Pope Gregory."

Wang tried to recall what little he knew of European

history in the Middle Ages so that he could deduce the level of advancement of this civilization based on the name. But then he remembered how wildly anachronistic historical references could be in the world of *Three Body* and decided the effort wasn't worth it.

"I'm Aristotle. You changed your ID, but we all recognize you. In the previous two civilizations, you traveled to the East." The speaker was the man with the Greek chiton. He had a head of white curls.

"Yes." Wang nodded. "There, I witnessed the destruction of two civilizations, one by extreme cold, another by a blazing sun. I also saw the great efforts the scholars of the East expended in trying to master the laws governing the sun's motion."

"Ha!" The sound came from a man with a goatee that curled upward. He was even thinner than the pope. "Eastern scholars tried to understand the secrets of the sun's motion through meditation, epiphany, or even dreams. Utterly laughable!"

"This is Galileo," said Aristotle. "He advocates understanding the world through observation and experiment. He is an unimaginative thinker, but his results demand our attention."

"Mozi also conducted experiments and observation," Wang said.

Galileo snorted. "Mozi's way of thinking was still Eastern. He was nothing more than a mystic dressed as a scientist. He never took his own observation data seriously, and he constructed his model based on subjective speculation. Ridiculous! I feel sorry for his refined equipment. We're different. Based on large amounts of observational data and experiments, we make strict, logical deductions to build a

model of the universe. Then we go back to experimentation and observation to test it."

"That's correct." Wang nodded. "That's also my way of thinking."

"Have you brought a calendar as well, then?" The pope's tone was mocking.

"I don't have a calendar. I only brought a model built upon observation data. But I must make it clear that even if the model is correct, it's not certain that by using it one can master the precise details of the sun's motion and create a calendar. However, it's a necessary step."

A few lonely claps echoed throughout the Great Hall. The applause came from Galileo. "Excellent, Copernicus, excellent. Your pragmatic way of thinking, adapted to the experimental, scientific approach, is lacking in most scholars. Based on this alone, your theory is worth listening to."

The pope nodded at Wang. "Go ahead."

After calming himself and walking to the other end of the long table, Wang said, "It's actually pretty simple. The reason why the sun's motion seems patternless is because our world has three suns. Under the influence of their mutually perturbing gravitational attraction, their movements are unpredictable—the three-body problem. When our planet revolves around one of the suns in a stable orbit, that's a Stable Era. When one or more of the other suns move within a certain distance, their gravitational pull will snatch the planet away from the sun it's orbiting, causing it to wander unstably through the gravitational fields of the three suns. That's a Chaotic Era. After an uncertain amount of time, our planet is once again pulled into a temporary orbit and another Stable Era begins. This is a football game at the scale of the universe. The players are the three suns, and our planet is the football."

A few hollow laughs rang out in the Great Hall. "Burn him to death," the pope said impassively. The two soldiers standing at the door in rusty armor started toward Wang like two clumsy robots.

"Burn him." Galileo sighed. "I had hopes for you, but you're nothing more than another mystic or warlock."

"Such men are a public nuisance," Aristotle agreed.

"At least let me finish!" Wang shoved away the iron gauntlets of the two soldiers.

"Have you seen three suns? Or know anyone who has?" Galileo asked.

"Everyone has seen them."

"Then, other than the sun that appears during Chaotic Eras and Stable Eras, where are the other two?"

"The sun that we see at different times may not be the same: It's only one of the three suns. When the other two are far away, they look like flying stars."

"You lack basic scientific training," Galileo said, shaking his head. "The sun must move continuously to a distant spot. It cannot jump over the intervening space. According to your hypothesis, there should be another observable situation: The sun must get smaller than it usually appears but bigger than a flying star, and gradually shrink into a flying star as it moves farther away. But we've never seen the sun behave that way."

"Since you have scientific training, you ought to have some knowledge of the sun's structure."

"That's my proudest discovery. The sun is made of a sparse but expansive gaseous outer layer and a dense and hot inner core."

"Very true," said Wang. "But you apparently haven't discovered the special optical interaction between the sun's

196

gaseous outer layer and our planet's atmosphere. It's a phenomenon akin to polarization or destructive interference. As a result, when we view the sun from within our atmosphere and it gets a certain distance from us, the gaseous outer layer suddenly becomes completely transparent and invisible, and all we can see is its bright inner core. The sun then appears to be only the size of the inner core, a flying star.

"This phenomenon has confused every researcher in every civilization throughout history, and prevented them from discovering the existence of the three suns. Now you understand why the appearance of three flying stars heralds a long period of extreme cold: because all three suns are far away."

A brief silence followed as everyone pondered this. Aristotle was the first to speak. "You lack basic training in logic. It's true that we can sometimes see three flying stars, and that's always accompanied by destructive periods of extreme cold. But based on your theory, we should also sometimes see three normal-sized suns in the sky. This has never happened. In all the records of all the civilizations, this has never occurred!"

"Wait!" A man wearing a strangely shaped hat and a long beard stood up and spoke for the first time. "I'm Leonardo da Vinci. There may be such historical records. One civilization saw two suns and was immediately destroyed by their combined heat, but the record was very vague."

"We're talking about three suns, not two!" Galileo shouted. "According to his theory, three suns must appear sometime, just like three flying stars."

"Three suns *have* appeared," Wang said, utterly calm. "And people have seen them. But those who saw such a great sight could not leave behind any information about them because seeing three suns would mean that they had at most

a few seconds left to live. They had no chance to escape or survive. Tri-solar days are the most terrifying catastrophes for our world. On such days, the surface of the planet would turn into a smelting furnace in a second, and the heat would be enough to melt rocks. After the destruction caused by a tri-solar day, an eon would pass before the reappearance of life and civilization. This is yet another reason why there's no historical record of them."

Silence. Everyone stared at the pope.

"Burn him," the pope said, gently. The smile on his face was a little familiar to Wang: the smile of King Zhou of Shang.

The Great Hall came alive, and everyone seemed to be preparing for a celebration. Galileo and some others joyfully carried a stake out of a dark corner. They pulled off the charcoal-black body still tied to the stake and cast it aside before fastening it in an upright position. Another group happily piled firewood around the stake. Only Leonardo ignored the commotion. He sat at the table, pondering, and occasionally using a pen to calculate something on the table.

"Giordano Bruno," Aristotle said, pointing at the blackened body. "Like you, he came here and spewed nonsense."

"Use a low fire," the pope said, his voice weak.

Two soldiers started to tie Wang Miao to the stake using asbestos ropes. Wang used the hand that was still free to point at the pope. "You are nothing more than a program. As for the rest of you, you're either programs or idiots. I will log back on!"

"You cannot return. You will disappear forever from the world of *Three Body*." Galileo cackled.

"Then you *must* be a program. A normal person would certainly understand the basics of the Internet. The most the game can do is record my MAC address. I can just switch

computers and create a new ID. I'll announce myself when I'm back."

"The system has recorded your retinal scan through the V-suit," Leonardo said, looking up at Wang. Then he returned to his calculations.

Wang Miao was seized by a nameless terror. He shouted, "Don't do this! Let me go! I'm telling the truth!"

"If you're telling the truth, then you won't be burnt to death. The game rewards those who are on the right path." As Aristotle grinned, he took out a silver Zippo lighter, flipped it in his hand in a complicated fashion, and then flicked it on.

As he was about to light the firewood piled around Wang, a bright red light filled the entrance tunnel, followed by a wave of heat and smoke. A horse dashed out of the light and into the Great Hall. Its body was already on fire, and as it galloped, the wind whipped it into a ball of flames. The rider, a knight in heavy armor that glowed red from the heat, dragged a line of white smoke behind him.

"The world has ended! The world has ended! Dehydrate! Dehydrate!" As the knight shouted, the animal under him fell down and turned into a bonfire. The knight was thrown some distance and rolled all the way to the stake, where he stopped moving. White smoke continued to pour out of openings in the armor. The sizzling grease from the dead man inside oozed out on the ground and caught fire, giving the armor a pair of burning wings.

Everyone in the Great Hall streamed toward the entrance tunnel and squeezed into it, disappearing in the red light from outside. Wang Miao struggled with all his strength until he was freed from the ropes. He dodged the burning knight and horse, dashed through the empty Great Hall, and ran down the sweltering tunnel until he emerged outside.

The ground glowed red like a piece of iron in a black-smith's furnace. Bright rivulets of lava snaked across the dim red earth, forming a net of fire that stretched to the horizon. Countless thin pillars of flame erupted toward the sky: The dehydratories were burning. The dehydrated bodies inside gave the fire a strange bluish glow.

Not far from him, Wang saw a dozen or so small pillars of flame of the same color. These were the people who had just run out of the pyramid: the pope, Galileo, Aristotle, and Leonardo. The fiery pillars around them were translucent blue, and he could see their faces and bodies slowly deform-ing in the flame. They focused their gazes on Wang, who had just emerged. Holding the same pose and lifting their arms toward the sky, they chanted in unison, "Tri-solar day—"

Wang looked up and saw three gigantic suns slowly spinning around an invisible origin, like an immense three-bladed fan blowing a deadly wind toward the world below. The three suns took up almost the entire sky, and as they drifted toward the west, half of the formation sank below the horizon. The giant fan continued to spin, a bright blade occasionally shooting above the horizon to give the dying world another brief sunrise and sunset. After a sunset, the ground glowed dim red, and the sunrise a moment later flooded everything with its glaring, parallel rays.

Once the three suns had completely set, the thick clouds that had formed from all the evaporated water still reflected their glow. The sky burned, displaying a hellish, maddening beauty.

After the last light of destruction finally disappeared and the clouds only glowed with a faint red luminescence reflect-ed from the hellish fire on the ground, a few lines of giant text appeared:

Civilization Number 183 was destroyed by a tri-solar day. This civilization had advanced to the Middle Ages.

After a long time, life and civilization will begin again, and progress once more through the unpredictable world of *Three Body*.

But in this civilization, Copernicus successfully revealed the basic structure of the universe. The civilization of *Three Body* will take its first leap. The game has now entered the second level.

We invite you to log on to the second level of *Three Body*.

16

THE THREE-BODY PROBLEM

As soon as Wang logged out of the game, the phone rang.

It was Shi Qiang, who said it was urgent that he come down to Shi's office at the Criminal Division. Wang glanced at his watch: It was three in the morning.

Wang arrived at Da Shi's chaotic office and saw that it was already filled with a dense cloud of cigarette smoke. A young woman police officer who shared the office fanned the smoke away from her nose with a notebook. Da Shi introduced her as Xu Bingbing, a computer specialist from the Information Security Division.

The third person in the office surprised Wang. It was Wei Cheng, the reclusive, mysterious husband of Shen Yufei from the Frontiers of Science. Wei's hair was a mess. He looked up at Wang, but seemed to have forgotten they had met.

"I'm sorry to bother you, but at least it looks like you weren't asleep," Da Shi said. "I have to deal with something that I haven't told the Battle Command Center yet, and I need your advice." He turned to Wei Cheng. "Tell him what you told me."

"My life is in danger," Wei said, his face wooden.

"Why don't you start from the beginning?"

"Fine. I will. Don't complain about me being long-winded.

202

Actually, I've often thought about talking to someone lately. . . ." Wei turned to look at Xu Bingbing. "Don't you need to take notes or something?"

"Not right now," Da Shi said, not missing a beat. "You didn't have anyone to talk to before?"

"No, that's not it. I was too lazy to talk. I've always been lazy."

Wei Cheng's story

I've been lackadaisical since I was a kid. When I lived at boarding school, I never washed the dishes or made the bed. I never got excited about anything. Too lazy to study, too lazy to even play, I dawdled my way through the days without any clear goals.

But I knew that I had some special talents others lacked. For example, if you drew a line, I could always draw another line that would divide it into the golden ratio: 1.618. My classmates told me that I should be a carpenter, but I thought it was more than that, a kind of intuition about numbers and shapes. But my math grades were just as bad as my grades in other classes. I was too lazy to bother showing my work. On tests, I just wrote out my guesses as answers. I got them right about eighty to ninety percent of the time, but I still got mediocre scores.

When I was a second-year student in high school, a math teacher noticed me. Back then, many high school teachers had impressive academic credentials, because during the Cultural Revolution many talented scholars ended up teaching in high schools. My teacher was like that.

One day, he kept me after class. He wrote out a dozen or so numerical sequences on the blackboard and asked me to

write out the summation formula for each. I wrote out the formulas for some of them almost instantaneously and could tell at a glance that the rest of them were divergent.

My teacher took out a book, The Collected Cases of Sherlock Holmes. *He turned to one story— "A Study in Scarlet," I think. There's a scene in it where Watson sees a plainly dressed messenger downstairs and points him out to Holmes. Holmes says, "Oh, you mean the retired sergeant of marines?" Watson is amazed by how Holmes could deduce the man's history, but Holmes can't articulate his reasoning and has to think for a while to figure out his chain of deductions. It was based on the man's hand, his movements, and so on. He tells Watson that there is nothing strange about this: Most people would have difficulty explaining how they know two and two make four.*

My teacher closed the book and said to me, "You're just like that. Your derivation is so fast and instinctive that you can't even tell how you got the answer." Then he asked me, "When you see a string of numbers, what do you feel? I'm talking about feelings."

I said, "Any combination of numbers appears to me as a three-dimensional shape. Of course I can't describe the shapes of numbers, but they really do appear as shapes."

"Then what about when you see geometric figures?" The teacher asked.

I said, "It's just the opposite. In my mind there are no geometric figures. Everything turns into numbers. It's just like if you get really close to a picture in the newspaper and everything turns into little dots."

The teacher said, "You really have a natural gift for math, but . . . but . . ." He added a few more "but"s, pacing back and forth as though I was a difficult problem that he didn't

know how to handle. "But people like you don't cherish your gift." After thinking for a while, he seemed to give up, saying, "Why don't you sign up for the district math competition next month? I'm not going to tutor you. I'd just be wasting my time with your sort. But when you give your answers, make sure to write out your derivations."

So I went to the competition. From the district level up through the International Mathematics Olympiad in Budapest, I won first place each time. After I got back, I was accepted by a top college's math program without having to go through the entrance examination. . . .

You're not bored by my talking all this time? Ah, good. Well, to make sense of what happened later, I have to tell you all this. That high school math teacher was right. I didn't cherish my talent. Bachelor's, master's, Ph.D.—I never put much effort into any of them, but I did manage to get through them all. However, once I graduated and went back to the real world, I realized that I was completely useless. Other than math, I knew nothing. I was half asleep when it came to the complexities of relationships between people. The longer I worked, the worse my career. Eventually I became a lecturer at a college, but I couldn't survive there either. I just couldn't take teaching seriously. I'd write on the blackboard, "easy to prove," and my students would still struggle for a long while. Later, when they began to eliminate the worst teachers, I was fired.

By then I was sick of everything. I packed a bag and went to a Buddhist temple deep in the mountains somewhere in southern China.

Oh, I didn't go to become a monk. Too lazy for that. I just wanted to find a truly peaceful place to live for a while. The abbot there was my father's old friend—very intellectual, but became a monk in his old age. The way my father told it, at

his level, this was about the only way out. The abbot asked me to stay. I told him, "I want to find a peaceful, easy way to just muddle through the rest of my life." The abbot said, "This place isn't really peaceful. There are lots of tourists, and many pilgrims too. The truly peaceful can find peace in a bustling city. And to attain that state, you need to empty yourself." I said, "I'm empty enough. Fame and fortune are nothing to me. Many of the monks in this temple are worldlier than me." The abbot shook his head and said, "No, emptiness is not nothingness. Emptiness is a type of existence. You must use this existential emptiness to fill yourself."

His words were very enlightening to me. Later, after I thought about it a bit, I realized that it wasn't Buddhist philosophy at all, but was more akin to some modern physics theories. The abbot also told me he wasn't going to discuss Buddhism with me. His reason was the same as my high school teacher's: With my sort, he'd just be wasting his time.

That first night, I couldn't sleep in the tiny room in the temple. I didn't realize that this refuge from the world would be so uncomfortable. My blanket and sheet both became damp in the mountain fog, and the bed was so hard. In order to make myself sleep, I tried to follow the abbot's advice and fill myself with "emptiness."

In my mind, the first "emptiness" I created was the infinity of space. There was nothing in it, not even light. But soon I knew that this empty universe could not make me feel peace. Instead, it filled me with a nameless anxiety, like a drowning man wanting to grab on to anything at hand.

So I created a sphere in this infinite space for myself: not too big, though possessing mass. My mental state didn't improve, however. The sphere floated in the middle of "emptiness"— in infinite space, anywhere could be the middle. The universe

had nothing that could act on it, and it could act on nothing. It hung there, never moving, never changing, like a perfect interpretation for death.

I created a second sphere whose mass was equal to the first one's. Both had perfectly reflective surfaces. They reflected each other's images, displaying the only existence in the universe other than itself. But the situation didn't improve much. If the spheres had no initial movement—that is, if I didn't push them at first—they would be quickly pulled together by their own gravitational attraction. Then the two spheres would stay together and hang there without moving, a symbol for death. If they did have initial movement and didn't collide, then they would revolve around each other under the influence of gravity. No matter what the initial conditions, the revolutions would eventually stabilize and become unchanging: the dance of death.

I then introduced a third sphere, and to my astonishment, the situation changed completely. Like I said, any geometric figure turns into numbers in the depths of my mind. The sphereless, one-sphere, and two-sphere universes all showed up as a single equation or a few equations, like a few lonesome leaves in late fall. But this third sphere gave "emptiness" life. The three spheres, given initial movements, went through complex, seemingly never-repeating movements. The descriptive equations rained down in a thunderstorm without end.

Just like that, I fell asleep. The three spheres continued to dance in my dream, a patternless, never-repeating dance. Yet, in the depths of my mind, the dance did possess a rhythm; it was just that its period of repetition was infinitely long. This mesmerized me. I wanted to describe the whole period, or at least a part of it.

The next day I kept on thinking about the three spheres dancing in "emptiness." My attention had never been so completely engaged. It got to the point where one of the monks asked the abbot whether I was having mental health issues. The abbot laughed and said, "Don't worry. He has found emptiness." Yes, I had found emptiness. Now I could be at peace in a bustling city. Even in the midst of a noisy crowd, my heart would be completely tranquil. For the first time, I enjoyed math. I felt like a libertine who has always fluttered carelessly from one woman to another suddenly finding himself in love.

The physics principles behind the three-body problem[28] are very simple. It's mainly a math problem.

"Didn't you know about Henri Poincaré?" Wang Miao interrupted Wei to ask.[29]

At the time, I didn't. Yes, I know that someone studying math should know about a master like Poincaré, but I didn't worship masters and I didn't want to become one, so I didn't know his work. But even if I had, I would have continued to pursue the three-body problem.

28 *Author's Note:* How three bodies would move under the influence of their mutual gravitational attractions is a traditional problem in classical mechanics that arises naturally in the study of celestial mechanics. Many have worked on it since the sixteenth century. Euler, Lagrange, and more recent researchers (aided by computers) have all found solutions for special cases of the three-body problem. Karl F. Sundman later proved the existence of a general solution to the three-body problem in the form of a convergent infinite series, but the series converges so slowly that it is practically useless.

29 *Translator's Note:* Poincaré showed that the three-body problem exhibited sensitive dependence on initial conditions, which we would now understand as characteristic of chaotic behavior.

Everyone seems to believe that Poincaré proved that the three-body problem couldn't be solved, but I think they're mistaken. He only proved sensitive dependence on initial conditions, and that the three-body system couldn't be solved by integrals. But sensitivity is not the same as being completely indeterminable. It's just that the solution contains a greater number of different forms. What's needed is a new algorithm.

Back then, I thought of one thing: Have you heard of the Monte Carlo method? Ah, it's a computer algorithm often used for calculating the area of irregular shapes. Specifically, the software puts the figure of interest in a figure of known area, such as a circle, and randomly strikes it with many tiny balls, never targeting the same spot twice. After a large number of balls, the proportion of balls that fall within the irregular shape compared to the total number of balls used to hit the circle will yield the area of the shape. Of course, the smaller the balls used, the more accurate the result.

Although the method is simple, it shows how, mathematically, random brute force can overcome precise logic. It's a numerical approach that uses quantity to derive quality. This is my strategy for solving the three-body problem. I study the system moment by moment. At each moment, the spheres' motion vectors can combine in infinite ways. I treat each combination like a life form. The key is to set up some rules: which combinations of motion vectors are "healthy" and "beneficial," and which combinations are "detrimental" and "harmful." The former receive a survival advantage while the latter are disfavored. The computation proceeds by eliminating the disadvantaged and preserving the advantaged. The final combination that survives is the correct prediction for the system's next configuration, the next moment in time.

"It's an evolutionary algorithm," Wang said.

"It's a good thing I invited you along." Shi Qiang nodded at Wang.

Yes. Only much later did I learn that term. The distinguishing feature of this algorithm is that it requires ultralarge amounts of computing power. For the three-body problem, the computers we have now aren't enough.

Back then, in the temple, I didn't even have a calculator. I had to go to the accounting office to get a blank ledger and a pencil. I began to build the math model on paper. This required a lot of work, and in no time at all I went through more than a dozen ledgers. The monks in charge of accounts were angry with me, but because the abbot wished it, they found me more paper and pen. I hid the completed calculations under my pillow, and threw the scratch paper into the incense burner in the yard.

One evening, a young woman suddenly dashed into my room. This was the first time a woman had shown up at my place. She clutched a few pieces of paper with burnt edges, the scratch paper I had thrown out.

"They tell me these are yours. Are you studying the three-body problem?" Behind her wide glasses, her eyes seemed to be on fire.

The woman surprised me. The math I used was unconventional, and my derivations took large leaps. But the fact that she could tell the subject of my study from a few pieces of scratch paper showed that she had unusual math talent and that she, like me, was very devoted to the three-body problem.

I didn't have a good impression of the tourists and pilgrims.

The tourists had no idea what they were looking at, only running around to snap pictures. As for the pilgrims, they looked much poorer than the tourists, and all seemed to be in a state of numbness, their intellect inhibited. But this woman was different. She looked like an academic. Later I found out that she had come with a group of Japanese tourists.

Without waiting for my answer, she added, "Your approach is brilliant. We've been searching for a method like this that could turn the difficulty of the three-body problem into a matter of massive computation. Of course, it would require a very powerful computer."

I told her the truth. "Even if we were to use all the computers in the world, it wouldn't be enough."

"But you must have an adequate research environment, and there's nothing like that here. I can give you the use of a supercomputer. I can also give you a minicomputer. Let's leave together tomorrow morning."

The woman, of course, was Shen Yufei. Like now, she was concise and authoritarian, but she was more attractive then. I'm naturally a cold person. I had less interest in women than the monks around me. This woman who didn't adhere to conventional ideas about femininity was different, though. She attracted me. Since I had nothing to do anyway, I agreed right away.

That night, I couldn't sleep. I draped a shirt over my shoulders and walked out into the yard. In the distance, I saw Shen in the dim temple hall. She knelt before the Buddha with lit joss sticks, and all her movements seemed full of piety. I approached noiselessly, and as I came by the door to the temple hall, I heard her whisper a prayer: "Buddha, please help my Lord break away from the sea of misery."

I thought I must have heard wrong, but she chanted the prayer again.

"Buddha, please help my Lord break away from the sea of misery."

I didn't understand religion and had no interest in any of them, but I really couldn't think of any prayer odder than this one. "What are you saying?" I blurted.

Shen ignored me. She kept her eyes barely closed, her hands clasped together in front of her, as though watching her prayer rise with the incense smoke toward the Buddha. After a long while, she finally opened her eyes and turned toward me. "Go to sleep. We have to get up early." She didn't even look at me.

"This 'Lord' you mentioned, is he part of Buddhism?" I asked.

"No."

"Then . . . ?"

Shen said nothing, just hurried away. I didn't get a chance to ask anything else. I repeated the prayer to myself over and over, and it seemed to grow even stranger. Eventually, I became frightened. I rushed over to the abbot's room and knocked on his door.

"What does it mean if someone prays to the Buddha to help another Lord?" I then told him the details of what I saw.

The abbot silently looked at the book in his hand, but he was thinking about what I said, not reading. Then he said, "Please leave me for a bit. Let me think."

I turned and left, knowing that it was unusual. The abbot was very learned. Usually, he could answer any question about religion, history, and culture without having to think. I waited outside the door for about the time it took to smoke a cigarette, and the abbot called for me.

"I think there's only one possibility." His expression was grim.

"What? What could it be? Could there be some religion

212

whose god needs worshippers to pray to the gods of other religions to save it?"

"Her Lord really exists."

This response confused me. "Then . . . the Buddha doesn't exist?" As soon as I said it I realized how rude it sounded. I apologized.

The abbot slowly waved his hand at me. "I told you, the two of us can't talk about Buddhism. The existence of the Buddha is a kind of existence that you cannot comprehend. But the Lord she's talking about exists in a way that you can understand I can say no more concerning this matter. All I can do is counsel you against leaving with her."

"Why?"

"It's just a feeling. I feel that behind her are things that you and I cannot imagine."

I left the abbot's room and walked through the temple toward my room. The night had a full moon. I looked up at it and thought it a silvery, strange eye that gazed down at me, the light suffused with an eerie chill.

The next day, I did leave with Shen—I couldn't stay in the temple the rest of my life, after all. But I didn't think that over the next few years, I would live the life of my dreams. Shen fulfilled her promise. I had a minicomputer and a comfortable environment. I even left the country several times to use supercomputers—not time-sharing, but having the whole CPU to myself. She had a lot of money, though I didn't know where it came from.

Later, we got married. There wasn't much love or passion, just mutual convenience. We both had things we wanted to get done. As for me, the few years after that could be described as a single day. My time passed peacefully. In her house, I was taken care of and did not have to worry about food or cloth-

ing, so that I could devote myself to the study of the three-body problem. Shen never interfered with my life. The garage had a car that I could drive anywhere. I'm sure she wouldn't even have minded if I brought another woman home. She only paid attention to my research, and the only thing we talked about day to day was the three-body problem.

"Do you know what else Shen has been up to?" Shi Qiang asked.

"Just the Frontiers of Science. She's busy with it all the time. Lots of people show up every day."

"She didn't ask you to join?"

"Never. She never even talks to me about it. I don't care, either. That's just the way I am. I don't want to care about anything. She knows it, and says I'm an indolent man without any sense of purpose. The organization doesn't suit me and would interfere with my research."

"Have you made any progress with the three-body problem?" Wang asked.

Compared with the general state of the field, my progress could be said to be a breakthrough. Some years ago, Richard Montgomery of UCSC and Alain Chenciner of Université Paris Diderot discovered another stable, periodic solution to the three-body problem.[30] Under appropriate initial conditions, the three bodies will chase each other around a fixed figure-eight curve. After that, everyone was keen to find such special stable configurations, and every discovery was greeted with joy. Only three or four such configurations have been found so far.

30 *Translator's Note:* For details, please see Alain Chenciner and Richard Montgomery, "A remarkable periodic solution of the three-body problem in the case of equal masses," *Annals of Mathematics*, 152 (2000), 881–901.

But my evolutionary algorithm has already discovered more than a hundred stable configurations. Drawings of their orbits would fill a gallery with postmodern art, but that's not my goal. The real solution to the three-body problem is to build a mathematical model so that, given any initial configuration with known vectors, the model can predict all subsequent motion of the three-body system. This is also what Shen Yufei craves.

But my peaceful life ended yesterday.

"This is the crime you're reporting?" Shi Qiang asked.

"Yes. A man called yesterday and told me that if I didn't cease my research, I would be killed."

"Who was he?"

"I don't know."

"Phone number?"

"Don't know. Caller ID showed nothing."

"Anything related to report?"

"Don't know."

Da Shi laughed and tossed his cigarette butt into an ashtray. "You went on and on forever, and in the end all you have to report is one line and a few 'I don't know's?"

"If I hadn't gone on like that, would you have understood the import of that call? Also, if that were all, I wouldn't have come here. I'm lazy, remember? But there was another thing: It was the middle of the night—I don't know if it was today or yesterday—and I was in bed. As I was drifting halfway between sleep and wakefulness, I felt something cold moving on my face. I opened my eyes and saw Shen Yufei, and I almost died of fright."

"What's so frightening about seeing your wife in the middle of the night?"

215

"She stared at me in a way that I had never seen. The light from outside fell on her face, and she looked like a ghost. She held something in her hand: a gun! Moving the barrel over my face, she told me that I had to continue working on the three-body problem. Otherwise she'd kill me."

"Oh, now this is getting interesting." Da Shi gave a satisfied nod. He lit another cigarette.

"Interesting? Look, I've nowhere to go. That's why I came to you."

"Tell us exactly what she said."

"She said: 'If you succeed in solving the three-body problem, you will be the savior of the world. If you stop now, you'll be a sinner. If someone were to save or destroy the human race, then your possible contribution or sin would be exactly twice as much as his.'"

Da Shi blew out a thick cloud of smoke and stared at Wei Cheng until he squirmed. He pulled a notepad out of the mess on his desk and picked up a pen. "You wanted us to take notes, right? Repeat what you just said."

Wei did.

Wang said, "What she said is indeed strange. What does she mean by exactly twice as much?"

Wei blinked. "This seems pretty serious. When I came, the officer on duty immediately sent me to see you. It looks like you've already been paying attention to Shen and me."

Da Shi nodded. "Let me ask you something else: Do you think the gun your wife held was real?" He saw that Wei didn't know how to answer. "Could you smell gun oil?"

"Yes, there was definitely an oily smell."

"Good." Da Shi, who had been sitting on his desk, jumped off. "Finally we have an opening. Suspected illegal possession of firearms is enough to justify a search. I'll leave

the paperwork until tomorrow, because we have to move right away."

He turned to Wang. "No rest for the weary. I have to ask you to come and advise me some more." Then he turned to Xu Bingbing, who'd been silent the whole time. "Bingbing, right now I have only two men on duty, and that's not enough. I know the Information Security Division isn't used to fieldwork, but I need you to come along."

Xu nodded, glad to leave the smoke-filled office.

In addition to Da Shi and Xu, the team for conducting the search consisted of Wang Miao, Wei Cheng, and two other officers from the Criminal Division. The six of them rode through the predawn darkness in two police cars, heading toward Wei's neighborhood at the edge of the city.

Xu and Wang were in the backseat. As soon as the car started, she whispered to Wang, "Professor Wang, your reputation in *Three Body* is very high."

Somebody mentioned Three Body *in the real world!* Wang was excited, right away feeling close to this young woman in a police uniform. "Do you play?"

"I'm responsible for monitoring and tracking it. An unpleasant task."

Wang anxiously asked, "Can you tell me its background? I really want to know."

In the faint light coming through the car window, Wang saw Xu give a mysterious smile. "We want to know as well. But all its servers are outside the country. The system and firewall are very secure and hard to penetrate. We don't know much, but we can be sure it's not operated for profit. The software quality is uncommonly high, and the amount

217

of information contained in it even more unusual. It doesn't even seem like a game."

"Have there been any . . ." Wang carefully picked the right words. ". . . *supernatural* signs?" Wang's night had been filled with coincidences: He had been called in to discuss the three-body problem with Wei Cheng immediately after he solved the *Three Body* game. And now Xu was telling him she was monitoring the game. Something didn't seem right.

"We don't think so. Many from all around the world participate in the game's development. Their collaboration method seems similar to popular open-source practices, like the kind used to make the Linux operating system. But they're definitely using some very advanced development tools. As for the content of the game, who knows where they're getting it? It does seem a bit . . . supernatural, like you said. *However,* we still believe in Captain Shi's famous rule: All this must be the work of people. Our tracking efforts are effective, and we'll have results soon."

The young woman was not experienced in lying, and her last remark made Wang realize that she was hiding much of the truth from him. "His 'rule' is famous now?" Wang looked at Da Shi, who was in the driver's seat.

When they reached the house, the sun had not yet risen. It was about the same time of night that Wang had seen Shen playing *Three Body*. A second-story window was lit, but all the other windows were dark.

As soon as Wang got out of the car, he heard noises coming from upstairs. It sounded like something was slapping against the wall. Da Shi, who had just gotten out of the car himself, immediately became alert. He kicked open the yard gate and rushed into the house with an agility surprising for his burly frame, his three colleagues close behind.

Wang and Wei followed them into the house. They went upstairs and entered the room with a light on, their shoes splashing in a pool of blood. Shen lay in the middle of the room, blood still oozing from two bullet wounds in her chest. A third bullet had gone through her left brow, causing her whole face to be covered in red. Not far from her, a gun lay in a crimson pool.

As Wang entered, Da Shi and one of the other officers rushed out and entered the dark room across the hall. The window there was open, and Wang heard the sound of a car starting outside. A male police officer began to make a phone call. Xu Bingbing stood a little ways apart, watching anxiously. She, like Wang and the others, had probably never seen a scene like this.

A moment later, Da Shi returned. He put his gun back in its holster and said to the officer holding the phone, "A black Volkswagen Santana with only one man. I couldn't get the license plate number. Tell them to block all entrances to the fifth ring road. Shit. He might actually get away."

Da Shi looked around and saw the bullet holes in the wall. He glanced at the shell casings scattered on the ground and added, "The man got off five shots, and three hit her. She shot twice—both misses." Then he crouched down to examine the body with the other officer. Xu stood farther away, stealing a glance at Wei Cheng next to her. Da Shi also looked up at him.

On Wei's face was a trace of shock and a trace of sorrow, but only a trace. His usual wooden expression didn't break. He was far calmer than Wang.

"You don't seem bothered by this," Da Shi said to Wei. "They probably came to kill you."

Wei gave a ghastly grin. "What can I do? Even now, I still don't know anything about her. I've told her many times to

keep life simple. I'm thinking of the abbot's counsel to me that night. But . . . eh."

Da Shi stood up and walked over to stand in front of Wei. He took out a cigarette and lit it. "I think you still have some things you haven't told us."

"Some things I was too lazy to talk about."

"Then you'd better work harder now!"

Wei thought for a moment and said, "Today—no, yesterday afternoon—she argued with a man in the living room. It's that Pan Han, the famous environmentalist. They had argued a few times before, in Japanese, as though afraid to have me listen in. But yesterday they didn't care at all and argued in Chinese. I overheard a few snatches."

"Try to tell us exactly what you heard."

"Fine. Pan Han said, 'Although we seem like fellow travelers on the surface, in reality we're irreconcilable enemies.' Shen said, 'Yes, you're trying to use our Lord's power against the human race.' Pan said, 'Your understanding is not completely unreasonable. We want our Lord to come to this world, to punish those who have long deserved it. However, you're working to prevent our Lord's coming, and that's why we can't tolerate you. If you don't stop, we'll *make* you stop!' Shen said, 'The commander was blind to allow you to join the organization!' Pan said, 'Speaking of, can you tell whether the commander sides with the Adventists or the Redemptionists? Does the commander want humanity eliminated or saved?' Pan's words briefly silenced Shen, and the two didn't argue so loudly anymore. I couldn't hear anything else."

"What did the man who threatened you on the phone sound like?"

"You're asking if he sounded like Pan Han? I don't know. He was speaking very softly, and I couldn't tell."

Several more police cars arrived, sirens blaring. A group of white-gloved policemen came upstairs with cameras, and the house hummed with activity. Da Shi told Wang to go back and get some rest.

Instead, Wang walked into the room with the minicomputer to find Wei. "Can you give me an outline of your three-body evolutionary algorithm? I want to . . . introduce it to some people. I know my request is abrupt. If you can't, don't worry about it."

Wei took out a CD and handed it to Wang. "It's all on here: the whole model and additional documentation. Do me a favor and publish it under your own name. That would be a big help."

"No, no! How could I do that?"

Wei pointed at the disk in Wang's hand and said, "Professor Wang, I noticed you the first time you came here. You're a good man, a man with a sense of responsibility. That's why I'm counseling you to stay away from this. The world is about to change. Everyone should try to live out the rest of their lives in peace. That would be best. Don't worry too much about other matters. It's all useless anyway."

"You seem to know even more than you let on."

"I spent every day with her. It's impossible to have no inkling."

"Then why not tell the police?"

Wei smiled contemptuously. "The police are worthless. Even if God were here, it wouldn't do any good. The entire human race has reached the point where no one is listening to their prayers."

Wei was standing next to an east-facing window. Through the glass, beyond the distant cityscape, the sky was brightening with the first light of dawn. For some reason, the light

221

reminded Wang of the strange dawn he saw each time he logged on to *Three Body*.

"In reality, I'm not so detached. I haven't been able to sleep the last few nights. Every morning when I see the sunrise, it feels like sunset." He turned to Wang, and after a long pause, added, "And it's all because God, or the Lord she talked about, can't even protect Himself anymore."

THREE BODY: NEWTON, VON NEUMANN, THE FIRST EMPEROR, AND TRI-SOLAR SYZYGY

The start of the second level of *Three Body* wasn't too different than the first: still the strange, cold dawn, still that colossal pyramid. But this time, the pyramid was back in the Egyptian style.

Wang heard the crisp sound of metal striking against metal. The clashing only highlighted the silence of the chilly dawn. Searching for the source, he saw two dark shadows flickering at the foot of the pyramid. In the dim light, metallic glints flashed between the shadows: a swordfight.

Once his eyes had adjusted, Wang saw the figures more clearly. Based on the shape of the pyramid, this should be someplace in *Three Body*'s version of the East, but the two fighters were Europeans dressed in a sixteenth- or seventeenth-century style. The shorter one ducked below a swinging sword and his silvery wig fell to the ground. After a few more thrusts and parries, another man appeared around the corner of the pyramid and ran toward the fighters. He tried to get the two to stop, but the swinging blades whistling through the air prevented him from getting close.

He shouted, "Stop! Don't you two have anything better to do? Where's your sense of responsibility? If civilization has no future, what good is this supposed bit of glory you're fighting over?"

Both swordfighters ignored him, concentrating on the duel. The taller one suddenly cried out in pain, and his sword fell to the ground with a clang. He turned and ran, holding his wounded arm. The other gave chase for a few steps and spat in the direction of the loser.

"Shameless!" He bent down to pick up his wig. As he straightened up, he saw Wang. Pointing in the direction of the escapee, he said, "He dared to claim that he invented calculus!" He put on his wig, put a hand over his heart, and bowed courteously to Wang. "Isaac Newton, at your service."

"Then the one who ran away must be Leibniz?" Wang asked.

"Indeed, an unscrupulous man. I don't really care about this little claim to fame. Inventing the three laws of mechanics has already made me the greatest, God excepted. From planetary motion to cell division, everything follows the three great laws. Now, with the powerful mathematical tool that is calculus, it will only be a matter of time before we master the pattern of the motion of the three suns."

"It's not that simple," said the man who had tried to stop the fight. "Have you considered the amount of calculation that's needed? I saw the differential equations you listed, and I don't think an analytical solution is possible, only a numerical one. However, the calculating capacity required is such that even if all of the world's mathematicians worked without pause, they'd still not be able to complete them by the time the world ended. Of course, if we can't figure out the pattern of the suns' movements soon, the end of the

world will not be too far away." He bowed at Wang as well, a more modern bow. "Von Neumann."

"Didn't you bring us thousands of miles to the East specifically to solve the problem of calculating these equations?" Newton asked. Then he turned to Wang. "Norbert Wiener and that degenerate who just ran away also came with us. We encountered some pirates near Madagascar. Wiener fought the pirates by himself so that the rest of us could escape, and he died valiantly."

"Why did you have to come to the East to build a computer?" Wang asked Von Neumann.

Von Neumann and Newton looked at each other, puzzled. "A computer? A *computing machine*! Such a thing exists?"

"You don't know about computers? Then what did you have in mind for completing the vast amount of calculations?"

Von Neumann stared at Wang with wide-open eyes, as though his question made no sense. "Using people, of course. Other than people, what else in the world is capable of performing calculations?"

"But you just said that all the mathematicians in the world wouldn't be enough."

"Instead of mathematicians, we'll use common laborers. But we need many of them, at least thirty million. We'll do mathematics using human wave tactics."

"Common laborers? Thirty million?" Wang was amazed. "But if I recall correctly, this is an age when ninety percent of the population are illiterate. Yet you want to find thirty million people who understand calculus?"

"Have you heard the joke about the Army of Sichuan?" Von Neumann took out a thick cigar, bit off the end, and lit it. "Some soldiers were being drilled, but because they had no education, they couldn't even follow the drill instructor's

225

simple orders to march LEFT-RIGHT-LEFT. So the instructor came up with a solution: He had every soldier wear a straw shoe on the left foot and a cloth shoe on the right. When they marched, he shouted"—here he switched to a Sichuan accent—"STRAW-CLOTH-STRAW-CLOTH. . . . That's the kind of soldier we need. Except we need thirty million of them."

Hearing this modern joke, Wang knew that the man before him wasn't a program but a real person, and almost certainly Chinese.

"It's hard to imagine such a large army," Wang said, shaking his head.

"That's why we've come to see Qin Shi Huang, the First Emperor." Newton pointed at the pyramid.

"He's still in charge?" Wang looked around. He saw that the soldiers guarding the entrance to the pyramid really were equipped with the simple leather armor and *ji*-style halberds of the Qin Dynasty. The anachronistic mix of historical elements in *Three Body* no longer surprised him.

"The whole world is going to be under his rule because he has an army of more than thirty million preparing to conquer Europe. All right, let's go see him." Von Neumann turned to Newton. "Drop the sword." Newton obeyed.

The three of them entered the pyramid, and just as they were about to emerge from the tunnel into the Great Hall, a guard insisted that they strip off all their clothes. Newton objected. "We're famous scholars. No one of our stature would carry hidden weapons!"

As the two sides explored this stalemate, a deep, male voice came from the Great Hall. "Is it the foreigner who discovered the three laws of motion? Let him and his companions in."

They entered the Great Hall. The First Emperor was pacing back and forth, his robe and his famous long sword both dragging along the ground. As he turned to gaze at the three scholars, Wang realized that his eyes were the same as the eyes of King Zhou of Shang and Pope Gregory.

"I already know the purpose of your visit. You're Europeans. Why not go find Caesar? His empire is vast. Surely he can find you thirty million men."

"But my most honored Emperor, do you know what kind of army he has? Do you know what shape his empire is in? In the magnificent eternal city of Rome, even the river that flows through the city has been heavily polluted. Do you know the cause?"

"Military industrial production?"

"No, Great Emperor, it's the vomit from Romans after their binge and purge feasts. When the nobles attend the feasts, stretchers have already been prepared for them under the tables. When they've eaten so much that they can no longer move, the servants carry them home. The entire empire has sunk into a quagmire of extravagance from which they cannot extricate themselves. Even if Caesar could organize an army of thirty million, it would not have the quality and strength necessary to perform this great calculation."

"I am aware of that," Qin Shi Huang said. "But Caesar is waking up and reinvigorating his army. The wisdom of Westerners is terrifying. You are not more intelligent than the men of the East, but you can see the right path. For example, Copernicus could figure out that there are three suns, and *you* could come up with your three laws. These are very impressive accomplishments. We here in the East cannot, for now, match them. I don't possess the ability to conquer Europe. My ships are not good enough, and the

supply lines cannot be maintained for long enough to go over land."

"That's why your empire must continue to develop, Great Emperor!" Von Neumann seized the opportunity. "If you can master the pattern of the suns' movements, you will be able to make the most of each Stable Era, and also avoid the damage brought by each Chaotic Era. This way, your progress will be much faster than Europe's. Believe us, we're scholars. As long as we can use the three laws of motion and calculus to accurately forecast the movements of the suns, we do not care who conquers the world."

"Of course I need to predict the suns' movements. But if you want me to gather thirty million men, you must at least demonstrate for me how such calculations would be conducted."

"Your Imperial Majesty, please give me three soldiers. I will demonstrate." Von Neumann grew excited.

"Three? Only three? I can easily give you three thousand." Qin Shi Huang glanced at Von Neumann, distrustful.

"Your Imperial Majesty, you mentioned just now the defect in the Eastern mind when it comes to scientific thinking. This is because you have not realized that even the complicated objects of the universe are made from the simplest elements. I only need three."

Qin Shi Huang waved his hand and three soldiers came forward. They were all very young. Like other Qin soldiers, they moved like order-obeying machines.

"I don't know your names," Von Neumann said, tapping the shoulders of two of the soldiers. "The two of you will be responsible for signal input, so I'll call you 'Input 1' and 'Input 2.' " He pointed to the last soldier. "You will be responsible for signal output, so I'll call you 'Output.' " He

shoved the soldiers to where he wanted them to stand. "Form a triangle. Like this. Output is the apex. Input 1 and Input 2 form the base."

"You could have just told them to stand in the Wedge Attack Formation," Qin Shi Huang said, glancing at Von Neumann contemptuously.

Newton took out six small flags: three white, three black. Von Neumann handed them out to the three soldiers so that each held a black flag and a white flag. "White represents 0; black represents 1. Good. Now, listen to me. Output, you turn around and look at Input 1 and Input 2. If they both raise black flags, you raise a black flag as well. Under all other circumstances, you raise the white flag."

"I think you should use some other color," Qin Shi Huang said. "White means surrender."

The excited Von Neumann ignored him. He shouted orders at the three soldiers. "Begin operation! Input 1 and Input 2, you can raise whichever flag you want. Good. Raise! Good. Raise again! Raise!"

Input 1 and Input 2 raised their flags three times. The first time they were black-black, the second time white-black, and the third time black-white. Output reacted correctly each time, raising the black flag once and the white one twice.

"Very good. Your Imperial Majesty, your soldiers are very smart."

"Even an idiot would be capable of that. Tell me, what are they really doing?" Qin Shi Huang looked baffled.

"The three soldiers form a computing component. It's a type of gate, an AND gate." Von Neumann paused to let the emperor digest this information.

Qin Shi Huang said impassively, "I'm not impressed. Continue."

Von Neumann turned to the three soldiers again. "Let's form another component. You, Output: if you see either Input 1 or Input 2 raise a black flag, you raise the black flag. There are three situations where that will be true: black-black, white-black, black-white. When it's white-white, you raise the white flag. Understand? Good lad, you're really clever. You're the key to the correct functioning of the gate. Work hard, and the emperor will reward you! Let's begin operation. Raise! Good, raise again! Raise again! Perfect. Your Imperial Majesty, this component is called an OR gate."

Then, Von Neumann used the three soldiers to form a NAND gate, a NOR gate, an XOR-gate, an XNOR-gate, and a tristate gate. Finally, using only two soldiers, he made the simplest gate, a NOT gate, or an inverter: Output always raised the flag that was opposite in color from the one raised by Input.

Von Neumann bowed to the emperor. "Now, Your Imperial Majesty, all the gate components have been demonstrated. Aren't they simple? Any three soldiers can master the skills after one hour of training."

"Don't they need to learn more?" Qin Shi Huang asked.

"No. We can form ten million of these gates, and then put the components together into a system. This system will then be able to carry out the calculations we need and work out those differential equations for predicting the suns' movements. We could call the system . . . um . . ."

"A computer," Wang said.

"Ah, good!" Von Neumann gave Wang a thumbs-up. "Computer—that's a great name. The entire system is a large machine, the most complex machine in the history of the world."

The passage of in-game time sped up. Three months went by.

Qin Shi Huang, Newton, Von Neumann, and Wang all stood on the platform at the apex of the pyramid. This platform was similar to the one where Wang had met Mozi. It was filled with astronomical instruments, some of which were of recent European design. Below them, a magnificent phalanx of thirty million Qin soldiers was arrayed on the ground. The entire formation fit inside a square six kilometers on each side. As the sun rose, the phalanx remained still like a giant carpet made of thirty million terra-cotta warriors. But when a flock of birds wandered above the phalanx, the birds immediately felt the potential for death from below and scattered anxiously in chaos.

Wang performed some computations in his head and realized that even if the entire population of Earth were arranged into such a phalanx, the whole formation would fit inside the Huangpu District of Shanghai. Though it was powerful, the phalanx also revealed the fragility of civilization.

Von Neumann said, "Your Imperial Majesty, your army is truly matchless. In an extremely short time, we have completed such complex training."

Qin Shi Huang held on to the hilt of his long sword. "Even though the whole is complex, what each soldier must do is very simple. Compared to the training they went through to learn how to break the Macedonian Phalanx, this is nothing."

Newton added, "And God blessed us with two consecutive Stable Eras to get them trained and ready."

"Even in a Chaotic Era, my army continues to train. They will finish your calculations even if it's a Chaotic Era." Qin Shi Huang glanced over the phalanx with pride in his eyes.

231

"Then, Your Imperial Majesty, please give the great order!" Von Neumann's voice trembled with excitement.

Qin Shi Huang nodded. A guard ran over, grabbed the hilt of the emperor's sword, and stepped backwards. The bronze sword was so long that it was impossible for the emperor himself to pull it out of the scabbard. The guard knelt and handed the sword to the emperor. Qin Shi Huang lifted the sword to the sky, and shouted: "Computer Formation!"

Four giant bronze cauldrons at the corners of the platform came to life simultaneously with roaring flames. A group of soldiers standing on the sloping side of the pyramid facing the phalanx chanted in unison: "Computer Formation!"

On the ground below, colors in the phalanx began to shift and move. Complicated and detailed circuit patterns appeared and gradually filled the entire formation. Ten minutes later, the army had made a thirty-six kilometer square computer motherboard.

Von Neumann pointed to the gigantic human circuit below the pyramid and began to explain, "Your Imperial Majesty, we have named this computer Qin I. Look, there in the center is the CPU, the core computing component, formed from your five best divisions. By referencing this diagram, you can locate the adders, registers, and stack memory. The part around it that looks highly regular is the memory. When we built that part, we found that we didn't have enough soldiers. But luckily, the work done by the elements in this component is the simplest, so we trained each soldier to hold more colored flags. Each man can now complete the work that initially required twenty men. This allowed us to increase the memory capacity to meet the minimum requirements for running the Qin 1.0 operating system. Observe also the open passage that runs through the entire formation, and the light

232

cavalry waiting for orders in that passage: That's the system bus, responsible for transmitting information between the components of the whole system.

"The bus architecture is a great invention. New plug-in components, which can be made from up to ten divisions, can quickly be added to the main operation bus. This allows Qin I's hardware to be easily expanded and upgraded. Look further still—you might have to use the telescope for this—and there's the external storage, which we call the 'hard drive' at Copernicus's suggestion. It's formed by three million soldiers with more education than most. When you buried all those scholars alive after you unified China, it's a good thing you saved these ones! Each of them holds a pen and a notepad, and they're responsible for recording the results of the calculations. Of course, the bulk of their work is to act as virtual memory and store intermediate calculation results. They're the bottleneck for the speed of computation. And, finally, the part that's closest to us is the display. It's capable of showing us in real time the most important parameters of the computation."

Von Neumann and Newton carried over a large scroll, tall as a man, and spread it open before Qin Shi Huang. When they reached the scroll's end, Wang's chest tightened, remembering the legend of the assassin who hid a dagger in a map scroll that he then displayed to the emperor. But the imaginary dagger did not appear. Before them was only a large sheet of paper filled with symbols, each the size of a fly's head. Packed so densely, the symbols were as dazzling to behold as the computer formation on the ground below.

"Your Imperial Majesty, this is the Qin 1.0 operating system we developed. The software for doing the calculations will run on top of it. That below"—Von Neumann pointed to the human-formation computer—"is the hardware. What's

on this paper is the software. The relationship between hardware and software is like that between the *guqin* zither and sheet music."

He and Newton then spread open another scroll, just as large. "Your Imperial Majesty, this is the software for using numerical methods to solve those differential equations. After entering the motion vectors of the three suns at a particular moment obtained by astronomical observation, the software's operation will give us a prediction for the suns' subsequent motion at any moment in the future. Our first computation will calculate all the suns' positions for the next two years. Each set of output values will be one hundred and twenty hours apart."

Qin Shi Huang nodded. "Good. Begin."

Von Neumann lifted both hands above his head and solemnly chanted: "As ordered by the great emperor, turn on the computer! System self-test!"

A row of soldiers standing halfway down the face of the pyramid repeated the order using flag signals. In a moment, the motherboard made of thirty million men seemed to turn into a lake filled with sparkling lights. Tens of millions of tiny flags waved. In the display formation closest to the base of the pyramid, a progress bar made of numerous green flags slowly advanced, indicating the percentage of the self-test that had been completed. Ten minutes later, the progress bar reached its end.

"Self-test complete! Begin boot sequence! Load operating system!"

Below, the light cavalry on the main bus that passed through the entire human-formation computer began to move swiftly. The main bus soon turned into a turbulent river. Along the way, the river fed into numerous thin tributaries,

234

infiltrating all the modular subformations. Soon, the ripple of black and white flags coalesced into surging waves that filled the entire motherboard. The central CPU area was the most tumultuous, like gunpowder on fire.

But suddenly, as though the powder had been exhausted, the movements in the CPU slackened and eventually stopped. Starting with the CPU in the center, the stillness spread in every direction, like a sea being frozen over. Finally, the entire motherboard came to a stop, with only a few scattered components flashing lifelessly in infinite loops. The center of the display formation blinked red.

"System lockup!" a signal officer called out. Shortly after, the reason for the malfunction was determined: There was an error with the operation of one of the gates in the CPU status register.

"Restart system!" Von Neumann ordered confidently.

"Wait!" Newton stopped the signal officer. He turned with an insidious expression and said to Qin Shi Huang, "Your Imperial Majesty, in order to improve system stability, you should take certain maintenance measures with respect to faulty components."

Qin Shi Huang grasped his sword and said, "Replace the malfunctioning component and behead all the soldiers who made up that gate. In the future, any malfunctions will be dealt with the same way!"

Von Neumann glanced at Newton, disgusted. They watched as a few riders dashed into the motherboard with their swords unsheathed. After they "repaired" the faulty component, the order to restart was given. This time, the operation went very smoothly. Twenty minutes later, *Three Body*'s Von Neumann architecture human-formation computer had begun full operations under the Qin 1.0 operating system.

"Run solar orbit computation software 'Three Body 1.0'!" Newton screamed at the top of his lungs. "Start the master computing module! Load the differential calculus module! Load the finite element analysis module! Load the spectral method module! Enter initial condition parameters . . . and begin calculation!"

The motherboard sparkled as the display formation flashed with indicators in every color. The human-formation computer began the long computation.

"This is really interesting," Qin Shi Huang said, pointing to the spectacular sight. "Each individual's behavior is so simple, yet together, they can produce such a complex, great whole! Europeans criticize me for my tyrannical rule, claiming that I suppress creativity. But in reality, a large number of men yoked by severe discipline can also produce great wisdom when bound together as one."

"Great First Emperor, this is just the mechanical operation of a machine, not wisdom. Each of these lowly individuals is just a zero. Only when someone like you is added to the front as a one can the whole have any meaning." Newton's smile was ingratiating.

"Disgusting philosophy!" Von Neumann said as he glanced at Newton. "If, in the end, the results computed in accordance with your theory and mathematical model don't match reality, then you and I aren't even zeroes."

"Indeed. If that turns out to be the case, you will be nothing!" Qin Shi Huang turned and left the scene.

Time passed quickly. The human-formation computer operated for a year and four months. Subtracting out the time spent to adjust the programming, the actual processing time

was approximately a year and two months. During this time, processing had to be stopped twice due to extremely bad weather in Chaotic Eras. But the computer stored the data at the time of each shutdown, and was able to resume calculations successfully after the pauses. By the time Qin Shi Huang and the European scholars ascended the pyramid again, the first phase of the computation was complete. The results precisely described the orbits of the three suns for the next two years.

It was a chilly dawn. The torches that had kept the motherboard lit through the night were extinguished. After the final calculation, Qin I entered standby mode. The turbulent waves over the motherboard settled into light ripples.

Von Neumann and Newton presented the scroll with the results of the computation to Qin Shi Huang. Newton said, "Great First Emperor, the calculations were completed three days ago. We waited until now to present the results to you because they show that the long night is about to be over. We'll soon welcome the first sunrise of a long Stable Era, which will last more than a year. Judging by the orbital parameters, the climate will be extremely mild and comfortable. Please revive your empire and order everyone to be rehydrated."

"Ever since the start of this computation, my empire has never been dehydrated," Qin Shi Huang said in a huff, grabbing the scroll. "I've devoted all the resources of the Qin Empire to maintain the operation of the computer, and we've run out of stored supplies. For this computer, countless people have died of hunger, cold, and heat." Qin pointed into the distance with the scroll. By the dim dawn light, they could see tens of white lines radiating from the edges of the motherboard in every direction, disappearing over the

horizon. These were the supply routes from every corner of the empire.

"Your Imperial Majesty, you will find that the sacrifices are worth it," Von Neumann said. "After mastering the orbits of the suns, Qin will develop by leaps and bounds, and will grow many times more powerful than before."

"According to the calculations, the sun is about to rise. Great First Emperor, prepare to receive your glory!"

As if in response to Newton's words, a sliver of red sun peeked over the horizon, bathing the pyramid and the human-formation computer in a golden light. A wave of joyous cries rose from the motherboard.

A man hurried toward them. He was running so fast that, as he knelt down, he couldn't catch his breath. He was the emperor's astronomy minister.

"Sire, the calculations were in error. Disaster is about to befall us!"

"What are you babbling about?" Without even waiting for the emperor to speak, Newton kicked the man. "Don't you see that the sun is rising at the exact moment predicted by our precise calculations?"

"But . . ." The minister half straightened, one hand pointing at the sun. "How many suns do you see?"

Everyone gazed at the rising sun, confused. "Minister, you received a proper Western education and obtained a doctorate from the University of Cambridge," Von Neumann said. "You must at least know how to count. Of course there's only one sun in the sky. And the temperature is very comfortable."

"No. There are three!" The minister cried, tears flowing from his face. "The other two are behind that one!"

Everyone stared at the sun again, still confused.

"The Imperial Observatory has confirmed that right now we are experiencing the extremely rare phenomenon of a tri-solar syzygy. The three suns are in a straight line, moving around our planet at the same angular speed! Thus, our planet and the three suns are in a straight line with our world at the end!"

"You're certain that the observation is not in error?" Newton grabbed the collar of the astronomy minister.

"Absolutely certain. The observation was conducted by the Western astronomers of the Imperial Observatory, including Kepler and Herschel. They're using the largest telescope in the world, imported from Europe."

Newton let go of the minister and stood up. Wang saw that his face was pale, but his expression was one of pure joy. He clasped his two hands in front of his chest and said to Qin Shi Huang, "Oh Greatest, Most Honorable Emperor, this is the most propitious sign of them all! Now that the three suns are orbiting around our planet, your empire is the center of the universe. This is God's reward for our efforts. Let me check the calculations one more time. I will prove this!"

While the rest remained stunned, Newton slipped away. Later, others would report that Sir Isaac had stolen a horse and left for parts unknown.

An anxiety-filled moment of silence later, Wang suddenly said, "Your Imperial Majesty, please unsheathe your sword."

"What do you want?" Qin Shi Huang asked, baffled. But he gestured at the soldier by his side, and the soldier pulled the sword out of its scabbard.

Wang said, "Please try to swing it."

Qin Shi Huang held the sword and waved it around. His expression turned to one of surprise. "Oh, why is it so light?"

"The game's V-suit cannot simulate the feeling of

diminished gravity. Otherwise we'd feel that we're much lighter as well."

"Look! Down there! Look at the horses, and the men!" Someone cried out. Everyone looked down and saw a column of cavalry moving at the foot of the pyramid. All the horses seemed to be floating. Each horse drifted over a long distance before the four hooves struck ground again. They also saw several running men. With each step, the men leapt a dozen meters, falling slowly back to the ground. On top of the pyramid, a soldier tried to jump up, and easily reached the height of three meters.

"What is going on?" Qin Shi Huang looked at the soldier slowly falling back down.

"Sire, the three suns are over our planet in a straight line, so their gravitational forces are added together. . . ." The astronomy minister tried to explain, but discovered that his two feet had already left the ground and he was now horizontal. The others were also floating in the air, leaning at different angles. Like a bunch of men who had fallen into water without knowing how to swim, they clumsily waved their limbs, trying to stabilize themselves but colliding into each other instead.

The ground they had just left now cracked open like a spiderweb. The cracks grew fast, and, accompanied by thunderous crashes and sky-obscuring dust, the pyramid below them broke into its constituent blocks. Through the slowly drifting gigantic blocks, Wang saw the Great Hall below come apart. The large cauldron that had once cooked Fu Xi and the iron stake to which he had once been bound were both adrift.

The sun rose to the middle of the sky. Everything that floated—men, colossal blocks of stone, astronomical

instruments, bronze cauldrons—began to rise slowly, then accelerated. Wang glanced at the human-formation computer and saw a nightmarish sight: The thirty million men who had formed the motherboard were floating away from the earth and rising, like a swarm of ants sucked up by a vacuum cleaner. The ground they left behind clearly displayed the marks of the motherboard circuits. The set of intricate, complex markings that could only be taken in from a great height would become an archaeological site that would confuse the next *Three Body* civilization, in the distant future.

Wang looked up. The sky was obscured by a strangely mottled layer of clouds. The clouds were made of dust, stones, humans, and other odds and ends. The sun sparkled behind them. In the far distance, Wang saw a long range of transparent mountains also rising up. The mountains were crystal clear, and changed shapes as they sparkled—they were formed from the ocean, which was also being attracted into space.

Everything on the surface of the *Three Body* world rose toward the sun.

Wang looked around and saw Von Neumann and Qin Shi Huang. As he drifted, Von Neumann shouted at Qin Shi Huang, but there was no sound. A small set of subtitles appeared: *I figured it out! Electronic elements! We can use electronic elements to make gate circuits and combine them into computers! Such computers will be many times faster and take up much less space. I estimate that a small building will be sufficient. . . . Your Imperial Majesty, are you listening?*

Qin Shi Huang swung his long sword at Von Neumann. The latter kicked at a giant block of stone drifting nearby and dodged out of the way. The long sword struck the stone, causing sparks to fly, and broke itself into two pieces. Right

after, the giant block of stone collided with another, with Qin Shi Huang in the middle. Stone chips and flesh and blood scattered everywhere, an appalling sight.

But Wang did not hear the noise made by colliding stones. Around him it was completely silent. Because the atmosphere was gone, there was no more sound. As the bodies drifted, their blood boiled in the vacuum and their inner organs were vomited out, until they turned into strange blobs surrounded by crystalline clouds made from the liquid they exuded. Also, due to the lack of an atmosphere, the sky turned pitch black. Everything that had floated into space from the Three Body world reflected the sunlight and formed a brilliant, starry cloud in space. The cloud then turned into a giant vortex, spiraling toward its final resting place: the sun.

Wang now saw the sun changing shape. He understood that he was actually seeing the other two suns, both peeking out from behind the first sun. From this perspective, the three stacked suns formed a bright eye in the universe.

Against the background of the three suns in syzygy, text appeared:

> Civilization Number 184 was destroyed by the stacked gravitational attractions of a tri-solar syzygy. This civilization had advanced to the Scientific Revolution and the Industrial Revolution.
>
> In this civilization, Newton established nonrelativistic classical mechanics. At the same time, due to the invention of calculus and the Von Neumann architecture computer, the foundation was set for the quantitative mathematical analysis of the motion of three bodies.
>
> After a long time, life and civilization will begin once

more, and progress through the unpredictable world of
Three Body.

We invite you to log on again.

Just as Wang logged out of the game, a stranger called. The voice on the phone was that of a very charismatic man. "Hello! First, we thank you for giving us your real number. I'm a system administrator for the *Three Body* game."

Wang was both excited and anxious.

"Please tell us your age, education, employer, and position. You didn't fill those out when you registered."

"What do they have to do with the game?"

"When you've reached this level, you must provide these pieces of information. If you refuse, *Three Body* will be permanently closed to you."

Wang answered the administrator's questions truthfully.

"Very good, Professor Wang. You satisfy the conditions for continuing in *Three Body*."

"Thank you. Can I ask you a few questions?"

"You may not. But tomorrow night there will be a meet-up for *Three Body* players. We welcome you to attend." The administrator gave Wang an address.

MEET-UP

The location for the *Three Body* players' meet-up was a small, out-of-the-way coffee shop. Wang had always imagined game meet-ups would be lively events full of people, but this meet-up consisted of only seven players, including himself. Like Wang, the other six did not look like gaming enthusiasts. Only two were relatively young. Another three, including a woman, were middle-aged. There was also an old man who appeared to be in his sixties or seventies.

Wang had originally thought that as soon as they met they'd begin a lively discussion of *Three Body*, but he was wrong. The profound but strange content of *Three Body* had had a psychological impact on the participants. All the players, including Wang himself, couldn't bring it up easily. They only made simple self-introductions. The old man took out a refined pipe, filled it with tobacco, and smoked as he strolled around, admiring the paintings on the walls. The others sat silently, waiting for the meet-up organizer to show up. They had all come early.

Actually, of the six, Wang already knew two. The old man was a famous scholar who had made his name by imbuing Eastern philosophy with the content of modern science. The strangely dressed woman was a famous writer, one of those

rare novelists who wrote in an avant-garde style but still had many readers. You could start one of her books on any page.

Of the two middle-aged men, one was a vice president at China's largest software company, plainly and casually dressed so that his status wasn't obvious at all; and the other was a high-level executive at the State Power Corporation. Of the two young men, one was a reporter with a major media outlet, and the other was a doctoral student in the sciences. Wang now realized that a considerable number of *Three Body* players were probably social elites like them.

The meet-up organizer showed up not long after. Wang's heart began to beat faster as soon as he saw the man: it was Pan Han, prime suspect for the murder of Shen Yufei. He took out his phone when no one was looking and texted Shi Qiang.

"Haha, everyone got here early!" Pan greeted them in a relaxed manner, as though nothing was wrong. Appearing in the media, he usually looked disheveled, like a vagrant, but today, he was dressed sharply in a suit and dress shoes. "You're just like I imagined. *Three Body* is intended for people in your class because the common crowd cannot appreciate its meaning and mood. To play it well requires knowledge and understanding that ordinary people do not possess."

Wang sent out his text: *Spotted Pan Han. At Yunhe Coffee Shop in Xicheng District.*

Pan continued. "Everyone here is an excellent *Three Body* player. You have the best scores and are devoted to it. I believe that *Three Body* is already an important part of your lives."

"It's part of what keeps me alive," the young doctoral student said.

"I saw it by accident on my grandson's computer," the old philosopher said, lifting his pipe stem. "The young man abandoned it after a few tries, saying it was too abstruse.

245

But I was attracted to it. I find it strange, terrible, but also beautiful. So much information is hidden beneath a simple representation."

A few players nodded at this description, including Wang himself.

Wang received Da Shi's reply text: *We also see him. No worries. Carry on. Play the fanatic in front of them, but not so much that you can't pull it off.*

"Yes," the author agreed, and nodded. "I like the literary elements of *Three Body*. The rises and falls of two hundred and three civilizations evoke the qualities of epics in a new form."

She mentioned 203 civilizations, but Wang had only experienced 184. This told Wang that *Three Body* progressed independently for each player, possibly with different worlds.

"I'm a bit sick of the real world," the young reporter said. "*Three Body* is already my second reality."

"Really?" Pan asked, interested.

"Me too," the software company vice president said. "Compared to *Three Body*, reality is so vulgar and unexciting."

"It's too bad that it's only a game," said the power company executive.

"Very good," Pan said. Wang noticed his eyes sparkling with excitement.

"I have a question that I think everyone wants to know the answer to," Wang said.

"I know what it is. But you might as well ask."

"*Is Three Body* only a game?*"

The other players nodded. Clearly the question was also on their minds.

Pan stood up and said solemnly, "The world of *Three Body*, or Trisolaris, really does exist."

"Where is it?" several players asked in unison.

After looking at each of them in turn, Pan sat down and spoke. "Some questions I can answer. Others I cannot. But if you are meant to be with Trisolaris, all your questions will be answered someday."

"Then . . . does the game really portray Trisolaris accurately?" the reporter asked.

"First, the ability of Trisolarans to dehydrate through its many cycles of civilization is real. In order to adapt to the unpredictable natural environment and avoid extreme environmental conditions unsuitable for life, they can completely expel the water in their bodies and turn into dry, fibrous objects."

"What do Trisolarans look like?"

Pan shook his head. "I don't know. I really don't. In every cycle of civilization, the appearance of Trisolarans is different. However, the game does portray something else that really existed on Trisolaris: the Trisolaran-formation computer."

"Ha! I thought that was the most unrealistic aspect," the software company vice president said. "I conducted a test with more than a hundred employees at my company. Even if the idea worked, a computer made of people would probably operate at a speed slower than manual computation."

Pan gave a mysterious smile. "You're right. But suppose that of the thirty million soldiers forming the computer, each one is capable of raising and lowering the black and white flags a hundred thousand times per second, and suppose also that the light cavalry soldiers on the main bus can run at several times the speed of sound, or even faster. Then the result would be very different.

"You asked about the appearance of the Trisolarans just now. According to some signs, the bodies of the Trisolarans

who formed the computer were covered by a purely reflective surface, which probably evolved as a response to survival under extreme conditions of sunlight. The mirrorlike surface could be deformed into any shape, and they communicated with each other by focusing light with their bodies. This kind of light-speech could transmit information extremely rapidly and was the foundation of the Trisolaran-formation computer. Of course, this was still a very inefficient machine, but it was capable of completing calculations that were too difficult to be performed manually. The computer did in fact make its first appearance in Trisolaris as formations of people, before becoming mechanical and then electronic."

Pan stood up and paced behind the players. "As a game, *Three Body* only borrows the background of human society to simulate the development of Trisolaris. This is done to give players a familiar environment. The real Trisolaris is very different from the world of the game, but the existence of the three suns is real. They're the foundation of the Trisolaran environment."

"Developing this game must have cost an enormous amount of effort," the vice president said. "But the goal is clearly not profit."

"The goal of *Three Body* is very simple and pure: to gather those of us who have common ideals," Pan said.

"What ideals do we have in common, exactly?" Wang immediately regretted the question. He wondered whether asking it sounded hostile.

Pan studied everyone meaningfully, and then added in a soft voice, "How would you feel if Trisolaran civilization were to enter our world?"

"I would be happy." The young reporter was the first to break the silence. "I've lost hope in the human race after

what I've seen in recent years. Human society is incapable of self-improvement, and we need the intervention of an outside force."

"I agree!" the author shouted. She was very excited, as though finally finding an outlet for pent-up feelings. "The human race is hideous. I've spent the first half of my life unveiling this ugliness with the scalpel of literature, but now I'm even sick of the work of dissection. I yearn for Trisolaran civilization to bring real beauty to this world."

Pan said nothing. That glint of excitement appeared in his eyes again.

The old philosopher waved his pipe, which had gone out. He spoke with a serious mien. "Let's discuss this question with a bit more depth: What is your impression of the Aztecs?"

"Dark and bloody," the author said. "Blood-drenched pyramids lit by insidious fires seen through dark forests. Those are my impressions."

The philosopher nodded. "Very good. Then try to imagine: If the Spanish Conquistadors did not intervene, what would have been the influence of that civilization on human history?"

"You're calling black white and white black," the software company vice president said. "The Conquistadors who invaded the Americas were nothing more than murderers and robbers."

"Even so, at least they prevented the Aztecs from developing without bound, turning the Americas into a bloody, dark great empire. Then civilization as we know it wouldn't have appeared in the Americas, and democracy wouldn't have thrived until much later. Indeed, maybe they wouldn't have appeared at all. This is the key to the question: No matter what the Trisolarans are like, their arrival will be good news for the terminally ill human race."

"But have you thought through the fact that the Aztecs were completely destroyed by the Western invaders?" the power company executive asked. He looked around, as though seeing these people for the first time. "Your thoughts are very dangerous."

"You mean profound!" the doctoral student said, raising a finger. He nodded vigorously at the philosopher. "I had the same thought, but I didn't know how to express it. You said it so well!"

After a moment of silence, Pan turned to Wang. "The other six have all given their views. What about you?"

"I stand with them," Wang said, pointing to the reporter and the philosopher. He kept his answer simple. *The less said the better.*

"Very good," Pan said. He turned to the software company vice president and the power company executive. "The two of you are no longer welcome at this meet-up, and you are no longer appropriate players for *Three Body*. Your IDs will be deleted. Please leave now. Thank you."

The two stood up and looked at each other; then glanced around, confused, and left.

Pan held out his hand to the remaining five, shaking each person's hand in turn. Then he said, solemnly, "We are comrades now."

19

THREE BODY: EINSTEIN, THE PENDULUM MONUMENT, AND THE GREAT RIP

The fifth time Wang Miao logged on to *Three Body*, it was dawn as usual, but the world was unrecognizable.

The great pyramid that had appeared the first four times had been destroyed by the tri-solar syzygy. In its place was a tall, modern building, whose dark gray shape was familiar to Wang: the United Nations Headquarters.

In the distance were many more tall buildings, apparently dehydratories. All had completely reflective mirror surfaces. In the dawn light they appeared as giant crystal plants growing out of the ground.

Wang heard a violin playing something by Mozart. The playing wasn't very practiced, but there was a special charm to it, as though saying: *I play for myself.* The violinist was a homeless old man sitting on the steps in front of the UN Headquarters, his fluffy silver hair fluttering in the wind. Next to his feet was an old top hat containing some scattered change.

Wang suddenly noticed the sun. But it rose in the opposite direction from the dawn light, and the patch of the sky around it was still completely dark.

The sun was very large, its half-risen disk taking up a third of the horizon. Wang's heart beat faster: Such a large sun could only mean another great catastrophe. But when Wang turned around, the old man continued to play as though nothing odd was happening. His silver hair shone brilliantly in the sun, as though it was on fire.

The sun was silvery, just like the old man's hair. It cast a pale white light over the ground, but Wang couldn't feel any warmth from the light. He gazed at the sun, which had now completely risen. On the giant silver disk he could pick out lines like wood grains: mountain ranges.

Wang realized that the disk did not emit light. It only reflected the light from the real sun, which was on the other side of the sky, below the horizon. What had risen wasn't a sun at all, but a giant moon. The giant moon moved briskly up the sky at a pace that could be detected by the naked eye. In the process, it gradually waned from a full to a half moon, and then a crescent. The old man's soothing violin strains drifted on the cold morning breeze. The majestic sight of the universe was like the music made material. Wang was intoxicated.

The giant crescent now fell into the dawn light and grew much brighter. When only two glowing tips remained above the horizon, Wang imagined them as the tips of the horns of a titanic bull rushing toward the sun.

"Honored Copernicus, rest your busy feet here a while," the old man said, after the giant moon had set. "Then after you've appreciated some Mozart, perhaps I can have some lunch."

"If I'm not mistaken . . ." Wang looked at the face full of wrinkles. The wrinkles were long and their curves gentle, as though they were trying to create a kind of harmony.

"You're not. I'm Einstein, a pitiful man full of faith in God, though abandoned by Him."

"What is that giant moon? I've never seen it the previous times I was here."

"It's already cooled off."

"What?"

"The big moon. When I was little it was still hot. When it rose to the middle of the sky, I could see the red glow from the central plains. But now it's cold. . . . Haven't you heard about the great rip?"

"No. What's that?"

Einstein sighed and shook his head. "Let's not speak of it. Forget the past. My past, civilization's past, the universe's past—all of it too painful to recall."

"How did you get to be like this?" Wang searched in his pocket and found some change. He bent over and dropped the money into the hat.

"Thank you, Mr. Copernicus. Let's hope that God doesn't abandon you, though I don't have much faith in that. I feel that the model you and Newton and the others created in the East with the help of the human-formation computer was very close to being correct. But the little bit of error left was like an uncrossable chasm for Newton and the others.

"I've always believed that without me, others would have discovered special relativity eventually. But general relativity is different. The bit that Newton lacked was the effect on planetary orbit from the gravitationally induced curvature of space-time described by general relativity. Though the error caused by it was small, its impact on the results of the computation was fatal. Adding the correction factor for perturbation from space-time curvature to the classical equations would yield the right mathematical model. The amount of computational power required far exceeds what you accomplished in the East, but is easily provided by modern computers."

"Have the results of the computation been confirmed by astronomical observations?"

"If that had occurred, do you think I'd be here? But from the perspective of aesthetics, I must be right and the universe must be wrong. God abandoned me, then others abandoned me as well. I'm wanted nowhere. Princeton dismissed me as a professor. UNESCO wouldn't even have me as a science consultant. Before, even if they had begged on their knees, I wouldn't have wanted the position. I even thought of going to Israel to be president, but they changed their minds and said I was nothing but a fraud. . . ."

Einstein began playing again, picking up right where he had stopped. After listening to him for a while, Wang strode toward the UN building.

"There's no one in there," Einstein said, still playing. "All the members of the General Assembly session are behind the building attending the Pendulum Initiation Ceremony."

Wang walked around the building and was greeted by a breathtaking sight: a colossal pendulum that seemed to stretch between the sky and the earth. In fact, Wang had seen it peeking out from behind the building, but he didn't know what he was seeing.

The pendulum resembled those constructed by Fu Xi to hypnotize the sun god during the Warring States Period, back when Wang Miao first logged on to *Three Body*. But the pendulum before him had been completely modernized. The two pillars holding up the pendulum were made of metal, each as tall as the Eiffel Tower. The weight was also made of metal, streamlined, with a smooth, mirrorlike, electroplated surface. The pendulum line, made of some ultrastrong material, was so thin as to be almost invisible, and the weight seemed to float in the air between the two towers.

Below the pendulum was a crowd of people dressed in suits, probably the leaders of the various countries attending the General Assembly session. They gathered in small cliques and talked amongst themselves quietly, as though waiting for something.

"Ah, Copernicus, the man who crossed five eras!" someone shouted. The others welcomed him.

"You're one of those who saw the pendulums of the Warring States Period with your own eyes!" A friendly man shook and held Wang's hand. Someone introduced the man as the secretary general of the UN, from Africa.

"Yes, I did see them," Wang said. "But why are we building another one now?"

"It's a monument for Trisolaris, as well as a tombstone." The secretary general looked up at the pendulum. From down here, it appeared as big as a submarine.

"A tombstone? For who?"

"For an aspiration, a striving that lasted through almost two hundred civilizations: the effort to solve the three-body problem, to find the pattern in the suns' movements."

"Is the effort over?"

"Yes. As of now, it's completely over."

Wang hesitated for a moment before taking out a stack of papers, Wei Cheng's three-body mathematical model. "I . . . I came here for this. I brought a mathematical model that solves the three-body problem. I have reason to believe it will likely work."

As soon as Wang said this, the crowd around him lost interest. They returned to their cliques to continue their conversations. He noticed that a few even shook their heads and laughed as they left him. The secretary general took the document and, without even glancing at it, handed it to

a slender man wearing glasses standing next to him. "Out of respect for your famed reputation, I'll have my science advisor take a look. Indeed, everyone here has shown you respect. If anyone else had said what you said, they'd be laughing at him."

The science advisor flipped through the document. "Evolutionary algorithm? Copernicus, you're a genius. Anyone who can come up with such an algorithm is a genius. This requires not only superior math skills, but also imagination."

"You seem to be suggesting that someone has already created such a mathematical model?"

"Yes. There are dozens of other mathematical models. Of those, more than half are more advanced than yours. They've all been implemented and run on computers. During the past two centuries, such massive computation became the principal activity of this world. Everyone waited for the results as if waiting for Judgment Day."

"And?"

"We have definitively proven that the three-body problem has no solution."

Wang gazed up at the massive pendulum overhead. In the dawn light, it was crystal bright. Its deformed mirrorlike surface reflected everything around it like the eye of the world. In this place, in a distant age separated from the here and now by many civilizations, he and King Wen had passed through a forest of giant pendulums on their way to the palace of King Zhou. Just like that, history had made a long circuit and returned to its starting place.

The science advisor said, "It's just like we guessed long ago: The three-body system is a chaotic system. Tiny perturbations can be endlessly amplified. Its patterns of movement essentially cannot be mathematically predicted."

Wang felt his scientific knowledge and system of thought become a blur in a single moment. In their place was unprecedented confusion. "If even an extremely simple arrangement like the three-body system is unpredictable chaos, how can we have any faith in discovering the laws of the complicated universe?"

"God is a shameless old gambler. He has abandoned us!" The speaker was Einstein, waving his violin. Wang didn't know when he had shown up.

The secretary general slowly nodded. "Yes, God is a gambler. The only hope for Trisolaran civilization is to gamble as well."

By now, the giant moon was rising again from the dark side of the horizon. Its large, silvery image was reflected by the surface of the pendulum weight. The light wriggled strangely, as though the weight and the moon had developed a mysterious sympathy together.

"This civilization seems to have developed to a very advanced state," Wang said.

"Yes. We've mastered the energy of the atom and reached the Information Age." The secretary general didn't seem to be too impressed by his own words.

"Then there is hope: Even if it's impossible to know the pattern of the suns' movements, civilization can continue to develop until it reaches a stage where it can survive the Chaotic Eras by protecting itself against the devastating catastrophes of those eras."

"People once thought as you do. That was one of the motivating forces pushing Trisolaran civilization to tenaciously come back again and again. But the moon made us realize the naïveté of such an idea." The secretary general pointed to the rising giant moon. "This is probably the first time you've seen

this moon. Actually, since it's about a quarter of the size of our planet, it's no longer a moon, but a companion to our world in a double planet system. It resulted from the great rip."

"The great rip?"

"The disaster that destroyed the last civilization. Compared to the civilizations before it, they had ample warning of the disaster. Based on surviving records, the astronomers of Civilization 191 detected a frozen flying star early on."

Wang's heart clenched as he heard the last phrase. A frozen flying star was a terrible omen for Trisolaris. When a flying star, or a distant sun, seems to come to a complete stop against the background starfield, then the sun's and the planet's motion vectors are aligned. This has three possible interpretations: the sun and the planet are moving in the same direction at the same speed; the sun and the planet are moving apart from each other; and the sun and the planet are moving toward each other. Before Civilization 191, this last possibility was purely theoretical, a disaster that had never occurred. But the population's fear of it and their vigilance did not diminish, so much so that "frozen flying star" became an extremely unlucky phrase in many Trisolaran civilizations. A single flying star remaining still was sufficient to terrify everyone.

"And then three flying stars froze simultaneously. The people of Civilization 191 stood on the ground, gazing up helplessly at the three frozen flying stars, at the three suns falling directly toward their world. A few days later, one of the suns moved to a distance where its outer gaseous layer became visible. In the middle of a tranquil night, the star suddenly turned into a blazing sun. Separated by intervals of thirty hours or so, the other two suns also appeared in quick succession. This was not a normal kind of tri-solar day. By

the time the last flying star turned into a sun, the first sun had already swept past the planet at extremely close range. Right after that, the other two suns swept past Trisolaris at even closer ranges, well within the planet's Roche limit[31], such that the tidal forces imposed on Trisolaris by the three suns exceeded the force of the planet's gravitational self-attraction. The first sun shook the deepest geological structure of the planet; the second sun tore open a great rift in the planet that went straight to the core; and the third sun ripped the planet into two pieces."

The secretary general pointed at the giant moon overhead. "That's the smaller piece. There are still ruins from Civilization 191 on it, but it's a lifeless world. It was the most terrible disaster in the entire history of Trisolaris. After the planet was torn apart, the two irregularly shaped pieces each returned to spherical form under self-gravitation. The dense, searing planetary core material gushed to the surface, and the oceans boiled over the lava. The continents drifted over the magma like icebergs. As they collided, the ground became as soft as the ocean. Massive mountain ranges tens of thousands of meters high rose in an hour and disappeared just as quickly.

"For a while, the two ripped-apart pieces were still connected by streams of molten lava that coalesced into a space-spanning river. Then the lava cooled and turned into rings around the planets, but because of perturbations from the planets, the rings were unstable. The rocks that formed them fell back to the surface in a rain of giant stones that

31 *Author's Note:* Roche limit: Édouard Roche, French astronomer, was the first to calculate the theoretical distance between two celestial bodies such that the smaller body will be torn apart by tidal forces from the larger body. The Roche limit is usually expressed as a function of the densities of the bodies and the equatorial radius of the larger body.

lasted several centuries. . . . Can you imagine what kind of hell that was? The ecological destruction caused by this catastrophe was the most severe in all of history. All life on the companion planet went extinct, and the mother planet almost became a lifeless waste as well. But in the end, the seeds of life managed to germinate here, and as the geology of the mother planet settled down, evolution began its tottering steps in new oceans and on new continents, until civilization reappeared for the one hundred and ninety-second time. The entire process took ninety million years.

"Trisolaris's place in the universe is even more grim than we had imagined. What will happen the next time frozen flying stars occur? Very likely, our planet will not just skim past the edge of the sun, but will plunge into the fiery sea of the sun itself. Given enough time, this possibility will become certainty.

"This was originally just a frightening speculation, but a recent astronomical discovery has caused us to lose all hope for the fate of Trisolaris. The researchers had intended to recover the history of the formation of the stars and the planets based on signs in this stellar system. Instead, they discovered that, in the distant past, the Trisolaran stellar system had *twelve* planets. Yet, now only this one remains.

"There is only one explanation: The other eleven planets have all been consumed by the three suns! Our world is nothing more than the sole survivor of a Great Hunt. The fact that civilization has been reincarnated a hundred and ninety-two times is only a kind of luck. Also, after further study, we discovered the phenomenon of 'breathing' by the three stars."

"The stars breathe?"

"It's only a metaphor. You discovered the gaseous outer layer of the suns, but you didn't know that this gaseous layer expands and contracts over cycles lasting eons, like

breathing. When the gaseous layer expands, its thickness can grow by more than a dozen times. This greatly increases the diameter of the sun, like a giant mitt that can catch planets more easily. When a planet passes by a sun at close range, it will enter the sun's gaseous layer. Friction will cause it to lose speed, and finally, like a meteor, it will fall into the blazing sea of the sun, dragging a long, fiery tail.

"The study results show that in the long history of the Trisolaran stellar system, every time the suns' gaseous layers expanded, one or two planets were consumed. The other eleven planets all fell into a fiery sea during times when the gaseous layers were at their greatest. Right now, the gaseous layers of the three suns are in a contracted stage—otherwise our planet would have already fallen into one of them the last time they skimmed past. But scholars predict that the next expansion will occur in one thousand years."

"We can't stay in this terrible place anymore," Einstein said, crouched down on the ground like an old beggar.

The secretary general nodded. "We can't stay here any longer. The only path left for Trisolaran civilization is to gamble with the universe."

"How?" Wang asked.

"We must leave the Trisolaran stellar system and fly into the wide open sea of stars. We must find in the galaxy a new world to emigrate to."

Wang heard a grinding noise. He saw that the giant weight of the pendulum was being pulled up by a thin cable whose other end was attached to an elevated winch. As it rose to its highest point, a great waning crescent moon descended slowly in the sky behind it.

The secretary general solemnly announced, "Start the pendulum."

The elevated winch released the cable tied to the pendulum, and the weight noiselessly fell along a smooth arc. Initially, it fell slowly, but then it accelerated, reaching maximum speed at the bottom of the arc. As it sliced through the air, the sound of the wind was deep and resonant. By the time the noise disappeared, the pendulum had followed the arc to its highest point on the other side, and, after pausing for a moment, began its backward swing.

Wang felt the great force generated by the movement of the pendulum, as though the ground was shaken by its swings. Unlike a pendulum in the real world, this giant pendulum's period was not stable, but changed constantly. This was due to the continually shifting gravitational attraction of the giant moon. When the giant moon was on this side of the planet, its gravity partially canceled out the gravity of the planet, causing the pendulum to lose weight. When it was on the other side of the planet, its gravity was added to the gravity of the planet, causing the pendulum's weight to increase, almost to the level it would have had before the great rip.

As he gazed up at the awe-inspiring swings of the Trisolaran Pendulum Monument, Wang asked himself, *Does it represent the yearning for order, or the surrender to chaos?* Wang also thought of the pendulum as a gigantic metal fist, swinging eternally against the unfeeling universe, noiselessly shouting out Trisolaran civilization's indomitable battle cry. . . .

As Wang Miao's eyes blurred with tears, he saw a line of text appear against the background of the swinging pendulum:

Four hundred and fifty-one years later, Civilization 192 was destroyed by the fiery flames of twin suns appearing

together. It had reached the Atomic Age and the Information Age.

Civilization 192 was a milestone in Trisolaran civilization. It finally proved that the three-body problem had no solution. It gave up the useless effort that had already lasted through 191 cycles and set the course for future civilizations. Thus, the goal of *Three Body* has changed.

The new goal is: Head for the stars; find a new home.

We invite you to log on again.

After logging out of *Three Body*, Wang felt exhausted, the same way he did after each previous session. But this time, he only rested half an hour before logging in again.

This time, against the pitch-black background, an unexpected line of text appeared:

The situation is urgent. The *Three Body* servers are about to be shut down. Please log on freely during the remaining time. *Three Body* will now go directly to the final scene.

THREE BODY: EXPEDITION

The chilly dawn revealed a bare landscape. There was no pyramid, no United Nations Headquarters, no sign of the Pendulum Monument. Only a dark desert extended to the horizon, just as Wang had seen the first time he had logged in.

But Wang soon realized that he was wrong. What he thought were numerous stones arrayed across the desert were not stones at all, but human heads. The ground was filled with a densely packed crowd.

From where he stood on a small hill, Wang could see no end to the sea of people. He estimated the number of individuals within his view alone to be in the hundreds of millions. All the Trisolarans on the planet were probably gathered here.

The silence of hundreds of millions created a suffocating sense of strangeness. *What are they waiting for?* Wang looked around and noticed everyone was gazing up at the sky.

Wang lifted his face and found the starry sky had been transformed to an astonishing sight: The stars were arrayed in a square formation! However, Wang soon realized that the stars in the formation were in a synchronous orbit above the planet, moving together against the dimmer, more distant background of the Milky Way.

The stars in the formation closest to the direction of dawn were also the brightest, shining with a silver light that cast shadows on the ground. The brightness decreased as one moved away from that edge. Wang counted more than thirty stars along each edge of the formation, which meant a total of more than a thousand stars. The slow movement of the obviously artificial formation against the starry universe exuded a solemn power.

A man standing next to him nudged him lightly and spoke in a low voice, "Ah, Great Copernicus, why have you come so late? Three cycles of civilizations have passed, and you've missed many great enterprises."

"What is that?" Wang asked, pointing at the formation in the sky.

"The Trisolaran Interstellar Fleet. It's about to begin its expedition."

"Trisolaran civilization has already achieved the capacity for interstellar flight?"

"Yes. All those magnificent ships can reach one-tenth the speed of light."

"That is a great accomplishment, as far as I understand it, but it still seems too slow for interstellar flight."

"The journey of a thousand miles begins with the first step. The key is finding the right target."

"What's the fleet's destination?"

"A star with planets about four light-years away—the closest star to the Trisolaran system."

Wang was surprised. "The closest star to us is also about four light-years away."

"You?"

"The Earth."

"Oh, that's not very surprising. In most regions of the Milky

Way, the distribution of stars is fairly even. It's the result of star clusters acting under the influence of gravity. The distance between most stars is between three and six light-years."

A loud, joyous cry erupted from the crowd. Wang looked up and saw that every star in the square formation was rapidly growing brighter. This was due to the light emitted by the ships themselves. Their combined illumination soon overwhelmed the dawn, and one thousand stars became one thousand little suns. Trisolaris was bathed in glorious daylight, and the crowd raised their hands and formed an endless prairie of uplifted arms.

The Trisolaran Fleet began to accelerate, solemnly gliding across the dome of the sky, skimming past the giant, just-risen moon's tip, casting a dim blue glow against the moon's mountains and plains.

The joyous cry subsided. The people of Trisolaris mutely gazed as their hope gradually shrunk in the western sky. They would not know the outcome of the launch in their lifetimes, but four or five hundred years from now, their descendants would receive the news from a new world, the beginning of a new life for Trisolaran civilization. Wang stood with them, silently gazing, until the phalanx of a thousand stars shrank into a single star, and until that star disappeared in the western night sky. Then the following text appeared:

The Trisolaran Expedition to the new world has begun. The fleet is still in flight. . . .

Three Body is over. When you have returned to the real world, if you remain true to the promise you've made, please attend the meet-up of the Earth-Trisolaris Organization. The address will be in the follow-up e-mail you receive.

PART III

SUNSET FOR HUMANITY

21

REBELS OF EARTH

There were many more attendees this time than at the last *Three Body* meet-up. They met at the employee cafeteria of a chemical plant. The factory had already been moved elsewhere, and the interior of the building, which was about to be demolished, was worn out but spacious. About three hundred people were gathered here, and Wang Miao noticed many familiar faces: celebrities and elites of various fields; famous scientists, writers, politicians, and so on.

The first thing to attract Wang's attention was the strange device at the center of the cafeteria. Three silver spheres, each slightly smaller than a bowling ball, hovered and swirled over a metal base. Wang guessed the device was probably based on magnetic levitation. The orbits of the three spheres were completely random: a real-life version of the three-body problem.

The others didn't pay much mind to the artistic portrayal of the three-body problem. Instead, they focused on Pan Han, who was standing on top of a broken table in the middle of the cafeteria.

"Did you murder comrade Shen Yufei?" a man asked.

"Yes," Pan said, perfectly calm. "It's because the Adventists have traitors like her in our midst that the Organization faces the crisis it does today."

"Who gave you the right to kill?"

"I did it out of a sense of duty to the Organization."

"Duty? I think you've always had malice in your heart!"

"What do you mean by that?"

"What has the Environment Branch done under your leadership? Your charge is to exploit and create environmental problems to make the population loathe science and modern industry. But in reality, you've only used our Lord's technology and predictions to gain riches and fame for yourself!"

"Do you think I became famous for myself? To my eyes, the entire human race is a pile of garbage. Why would I care what they think? But if I'm not famous, how do I direct and channel their thinking?"

"You always pick the easy tasks. What you've done could have been better accomplished by regular environmentalists. They're more sincere and passionate than you, and with just a little guidance, we could easily take advantage of their actions. Your Environment Branch should be creating environmental disasters and then exploiting them. For example, disseminating poison in reservoirs, leaking toxic waste from chemical plants . . . have you done any of those? No, not a single one!"

"We had devised numerous programs and plans, but the commander vetoed them all. Anyway, such acts would have been stupid, at least until recently. The Biology and Medicine Branch once created a catastrophe from the overuse of antibiotics, but that was soon detected. And the rash actions of the European Detachment almost drew attention to us."

"Talk about drawing attention to us—you just murdered someone!"

"Listen to me, comrades! Sooner or later, it would have been unavoidable. You must already know that the governments

of the world are preparing for war. In Europe and North America, they're already cracking down on the Organization. Once the crackdown begins here, the Redemptionists will no doubt side with the government. So our first priority is to purge the Redemptionists from the Organization."

"That is not within your authority."

"Of course the commander must decide. But, comrades, I can tell you right now that the commander is an Adventist!"

"Now you're just making things up. Everyone knows the scope of the commander's power. If the commander really is an Adventist, then the Redemptionists would have been purged long ago."

"Maybe the commander knows something we don't. Perhaps that's what the meeting today is about."

After this, the crowd's attention turned away from Pan Han to the crisis before them. A famous scientist who had won the Turing Award jumped onto the table and began to speak. "The time for talk is over. Comrades, what should be our next step?"

"Start a global rebellion!"

"Then we're asking to be killed."

"Long live the spirit of Trisolaris! We shall persevere like the stubborn grass that resprouts after every wildfire!"

"A rebellion will finally reveal our existence to the world. As long as we have an appropriate plan of action, I'm sure many people will support us."

This last remark came from Pan Han, and many applauded.

Someone yelled, "The commander is here!" The crowd parted to form a path.

Wang looked up and felt dizzy. The world turned white and black in his eyes, and the only spot of color was the person who had just appeared.

Surrounded by a group of young bodyguards, the commander in chief of the Earth-Trisolaris rebels, Ye Wenjie, walked steadily into the crowd.

Ye stood in the middle of the space the crowd cleared for her, raised a bony fist, and—with a resolve and strength that Wang could not believe she possessed—said, "Eliminate human tyranny!"

The crowd responded in a way that had clearly been rehearsed countless times: "The world belongs to Trisolaris!"

"Hello, comrades," Ye said. Her voice returned to the gentleness that Wang knew. It was only now that he could be sure that it was really her. "I haven't been well lately, and haven't spent much time with all of you. But now the situation is urgent, and I know everyone is under a great deal of pressure, so I've come to see you."

"Commander, take care of yourself," someone in the crowd said. Wang could hear the heartfelt concern.

Ye said, "Before we move on to more important matters, let's take care of one small detail. Pan Han—" She kept her eyes on the crowd even as she called his name.

"Here, Commander." Pan emerged from the crowd. Earlier, he had tried to lose himself in the throng. He appeared calm, but the terror in his heart was obvious. The commander had not called him *comrade*, a bad sign.

"You committed a severe violation of the Organization's rules." Ye spoke without looking at Pan. Her voice remained kind, as though talking to a child who had been naughty.

"Commander, the Organization is facing a crisis of survival! If we don't take decisive measures and cleanse the traitors and enemies within, we will lose everything!"

Ye looked up at Pan, her eyes affectionate. But his breath stopped for a few seconds. "The ultimate goal and ideal of

272

the ETO *is* to lose everything. Everything that now belongs to the human race, including us."

"Then you must be an Adventist! Commander, please openly declare this to be true, because it's very important. Am I right, comrades? Very important!" he shouted, and waved an arm as he looked around. But the crowd remained mute.

"This request is not yours to make. You have seriously violated our code of conduct. If you want to make an appeal, now is the time. Otherwise, you must bear the responsibility." Ye spoke slowly, enunciating every word, as though afraid the child she was teaching had trouble understanding.

"I went intending to eliminate Wei Cheng, that math prodigy. The decision was made by Comrade Evans and ratified by the committee unanimously. If he really succeeds in creating a mathematical model of the three-body problem that gives a complete solution, our Lord will not come, and the great enterprise of Trisolaris on Earth will be ruined. I only shot at Shen Yufei since she shot at me first. I was acting in self-defense."

Ye nodded. "Let us believe you. This is, after all, not the most important issue. I hope we can continue to trust you. Now, please repeat the request you made to me just now."

Pan was stunned for a second. That she had moved on didn't seem to relax him. "I . . . asked that you openly declare yourself to be an Adventist. After all, the action plan of the Adventists is also your ideal."

"Then repeat the plan of action."

"Human society can no longer rely on its own power to solve its problems. It can also no longer rely on its own power to restrain its madness. Therefore, we ask our Lord to come to this world, and with Its power, forcefully watch over us and transform us, so as to create a brand-new, perfect human civilization."

"Are the Adventists loyal believers in this plan?"

"Of course! Commander, please do not believe false rumors."

"It's not a false rumor!" a man shouted. He made his way to the front. "I'm Rafael, from Israel. Three years ago, my fourteen-year-old son died in an accident. I had his kidney donated to a Palestinian girl suffering kidney failure as an expression of my hope that the two peoples could live together in peace. For this ideal, I was willing to give my life. Many, many Israelis and Palestinians sincerely strove toward the same goal by my side. But all this was useless. Our home remained trapped in the quagmire of cycles of vengeance.

"Eventually, I lost hope in the human race and joined the ETO. Desperation turned me from a pacifist into an extremist. Also, probably because I donated so much money to the Organization, I became a core member of the Adventists. Let me tell you now, the Adventists have their own secret agenda.

"And it is this: The human race is an evil species. Human civilization has committed unforgivable crimes against the Earth and must be punished. The ultimate goal of the Adventists is to ask our Lord to carry out this divine punishment: the destruction of all humankind."

"The real program of the Adventists is already an open secret," someone shouted.

"But what you don't know is that this was not a program they evolved into. It was the goal set out at the very beginning; it's been the life-long dream of Mike Evans, the mastermind behind the Adventists. He lied to the Organization and fooled everyone, including the commander! Evans has been working toward this goal from the very start. He turned the Adventists into a kingdom of terror populated by extreme environmentalists and madmen who hated the human race."

"I didn't know Evans's real thoughts until much later," Ye

said. "Still, I tried to patch over the differences to allow the ETO to remain whole. But some of the other acts committed by Adventists lately have made the effort impossible."

Pan said, "Commander, the Adventists are the core of ETO. Without us, there is no Earth-Trisolaris Movement."

"But this is no excuse for you to monopolize all communications between our Lord and the Organization."

"We built the Second Red Coast Base; of course we should operate it."

"The Adventists took advantage of this and committed an unforgivable betrayal of the Organization: You intercepted the messages from our Lord to the Organization and passed on only a small portion of them. Even those, you distorted. Also, through the Second Red Coast Base, you sent a large amount of information to our Lord without the Organization's approval."

Silence descended over the meeting like a monstrous thing. Wang's scalp began to tingle.

Pan did not answer. His expression became cold, as if to say, *Finally, it has happened.*

"There is much evidence of the Adventists' betrayal. Comrade Shen Yufei was one of the witnesses. Though she belonged to the core group of Adventists, in her heart, she remained a resolute Redemptionist. You only discovered this recently, and she already knew too much. When Evans sent you, he wanted you to kill two people, not one."

Pan looked around, apparently reassessing the situation. His gesture didn't go unnoticed by Ye.

"You can see that most people attending this meeting are comrades from the Redemptionist faction. I trust that the few Adventists who are here will stand on the side of the Organization. But men like Evans and you can no longer be

saved. To protect the program and ideals of the ETO, we must completely solve the problem of the Adventists."

Silence returned. A few moments later, one of the bodyguards near Ye, a young woman, smiled. She walked toward Pan Han casually.

Pan's face changed. He stuck a hand inside the lapel of his jacket, but the young woman dashed quicker than the eye could follow. Before anyone could react, she wrapped one of her slender arms around Pan's neck, placed her other hand on top of his head, and, by applying her unexpected strength at just the right angle, she twisted Pan's head 180 degrees with practiced ease. The cracks from his cervical vertebrae breaking stood out against the complete silence.

The young woman's hands immediately let go, as though Pan's head was too hot. Pan fell to the ground, and the gun that had killed Shen Yufei slid under the table. His body still spasmed, and his eyes remained open, his tongue sticking out. But his head no longer moved, as though it were never a part of the rest of his body. Several men came and dragged him away, the blood oozing from his mouth leaving a long trail.

"Ah, Xiao Wang, you're here too. How have you been?" Ye's gaze fell on Wang Miao. She smiled kindly at him and nodded. Then she turned to the others. "This is Professor Wang, a member of the Chinese Academy of Sciences and my friend. He researches nanomaterials. This is the first technology our Lord wishes to extinguish from the Earth."

No one looked at Wang, and Wang had no strength to express himself in any way. He had to pull at the sleeve of the man next to him so that he wouldn't fall, but the man lightly brushed his hand away.

"Xiao Wang, why don't I continue to tell you the story of Red Coast from last time? All the comrades here can listen

too. This is not a waste of time. In this extraordinary moment, it is a fine time to review the history of our Organization."

"Red Coast. . . . You weren't done?" Wang asked foolishly.

Ye slowly approached the three-body model, seemingly absorbed by the swirling silver spheres. Through the broken window, the setting sun's light fell on the model, and the flying spheres intermittently reflected the light onto the rebel commander, like sparks from a bonfire.

"No. I've only just started," Ye said softly.

22

RED COAST V

Since she entered Red Coast Base, Ye Wenjie had never thought of leaving. After she learned the real purpose of the Red Coast Project, top-secret information that even many mid-level cadres at the base didn't know, she cut off her spiritual connection to the outside world and devoted herself to her work. Thereafter, she became even more deeply embedded in the technical core of Red Coast, and began to take on more important research topics.

Commissar Lei never forgot that it was Chief Yang who first trusted Ye, but Lei was happy to assign important topics to her. Given Ye's status, she had no rights to the results of her research. And Lei, who had studied astrophysics, was a political officer who was also an intellectual, rare at the time. Thus he could take credit for all of Ye's research results and papers, and cast himself as an exemplary political officer with both technical acumen and revolutionary zeal.

The Red Coast Project had initially requisitioned Ye because of a paper on an attempted mathematical model of the sun she had published in the *Journal of Astrophysics* as a graduate student. Compared to the Earth, the sun was a far simpler physical system, made almost entirely of hydrogen and helium. Though its physical processes were violent, they

were relatively straightforward, only fusing hydrogen into helium. Thus, it was likely that a mathematical model of the sun could describe it rather precisely. The paper was basic, but Lei and Yang saw in it a hope for a solution to a technical difficulty faced by the Red Coast monitoring system.

Solar outages, a common problem in satellite communications, had always plagued the Red Coast monitoring operations.

When the Earth, an artificial satellite, and the sun are in a straight line, the line of sight from the ground-based antenna to the satellite will have the sun as its background. The sun is a giant source of electromagnetic radiation, and, as a result, satellite transmissions to the ground will be overwhelmed by interference from the solar radiation. This problem could not be completely solved, even in the twenty-first century.

The interference that Red Coast had to deal with was similar, but the source of interference (the sun) was between the source of the transmission (outer space) and the ground-based receiver. Compared to communication satellites, the solar outages suffered by Red Coast were more frequent and more severe. Red Coast Base as constructed was also much more modest than its original design, such that the transmission and monitoring systems shared the same antenna. This made the times available for monitoring even more precious, and solar outages even more of a problem.

Lei and Yang's idea for eliminating interference was very simple: ascertain the frequency spectrum and characteristics of solar radiation in the monitored range, and then filter it out digitally. Both of them were technical, and at that time, when the ignorant often led the knowledgeable, that was a rare bit of fortune. But Yang wasn't a specialist in astrophysics, and Lei had taken the path of becoming a political officer, which prevented him from accruing in-depth technical

know-how. In reality, electromagnetic radiation from the sun is only stable within the limited range from near-ultraviolet to mid-infrared (including visible light). In other ranges, the radiation is quite volatile and unpredictable.

To set the right expectations, Ye made it clear in her first research report that during periods of intense solar activity—sunspots, solar flares, coronal mass ejections, and so on—it was impossible to eliminate solar interference. Thus, her research target was limited to radiation within the frequency ranges monitored by Red Coast during periods of normal solar activity.

Research conditions at the base weren't too bad. The library could obtain foreign-language materials related to the topic, including timely European and American academic journals. In those years, this was no easy feat. Ye also could use the military phone line to connect to the two groups conducting solar science research within the Chinese Academy of Sciences and obtain their observation data by fax.

After half a year of study, Ye saw no glimpse of hope. She quickly discovered that within the frequency ranges monitored by Red Coast, solar radiation fluctuated unpredictably. By analyzing large amounts of observed data, Ye discovered a puzzling mystery. Sometimes, during one of the sudden fluctuations in solar radiation, the surface of the sun was calm. Since hundreds of thousands of kilometers of solar material would absorb any shortwave and microwave radiation originating from the core of the sun, the radiation must have come from activities on its surface, so there should have been observable surface activity when these fluctuations occurred. If there were no corresponding surface disturbances, what caused these sudden changes to the narrow frequency ranges? The more she thought about it, the more mysterious it seemed.

Eventually Ye ran out of ideas and decided to give up.

In her last report, she conceded that she could not solve the problem. This shouldn't have been a big deal. The military had asked several groups within universities and the Chinese Academy of Sciences to research the same issue, and all of those efforts had failed. But Yang wanted to try one more time, relying on Ye's extraordinary talent.

Lei's agenda was even simpler: He just wanted Ye's paper. The research topic was highly theoretical and would show off his expertise and skill. Now that the chaos in society was finally subsiding, the demands on cadres were also changing. There was an acute need for men like him, politically mature and academically accomplished. Of course he would have a bright future. As to whether the problem of interference from solar outages could be solved, he didn't really care.

But in the end, Ye didn't hand in her report. She thought that if the research project were terminated, the base library would stop receiving foreign language journals and other research materials, and she would no longer have access to such a rich trove of astrophysics references. So she nominally continued her research, while in reality she focused on refining her mathematical model of the sun.

One night, Ye was, as usual, the only person in the cold reading room of the base library. On the long table in front of her, a pile of documents and journals were spread open. After completing a set of tedious and cumbersome matrix calculations, she blew on her hands to warm them, and picked up the latest issue of the *Journal of Astrophysics* to take a break. As she flipped through it, a brief note about Jupiter caught her attention:

Last issue, in "A New, Powerful Radiation Source Within the Solar System," Dr. Harry Peterson of Mount Wilson

Observatory published a set of data accidentally obtained while observing Jupiter's precession on June 12 and July 2, during which strong electromagnetic radiation was detected, lasting 81 seconds and 76 seconds, respectively. The data included the frequency ranges of the radiation as well as other parameters. During the radio outbursts, Peterson also observed certain changes in the Great Red Spot. This discovery drew a lot of interest from planetary scientists. In this issue, G. McKenzie's article argues that it was a sign of fusion starting within Jupiter's core. In the next issue we will publish Inoue Kumoseki's article, which attributes the Jovian radio outbursts to a more complicated mechanism—the movements of internal metallic hydrogen plates—and gives a complete mathematical description.

Ye clearly remembered the two dates noted in the paper. During those windows, the Red Coast monitoring system had also received strong interference from solar outages. She checked the operations diary and confirmed her memory. The times were close, but the solar outages had occurred sixteen minutes and forty-two seconds after the arrival of the Jovian radio outbursts on Earth.

The sixteen minutes and forty-two seconds are critical! Ye tried to calm her wild heartbeat, and asked the librarian to contact the National Observatory to obtain the ephemeris of the Earth's and Jupiter's positions during those two time periods.

She drew a big triangle on the blackboard with the sun, the Earth, and Jupiter at the vertices. She marked the distances along the three edges, and wrote down the two arrival times next to the Earth. From the distance between the Earth and

Jupiter it was easy to figure out the time it took for the radio outbursts to travel between the two. Then she calculated the time it would take the radio outbursts to go from Jupiter to the sun, and then from the sun to the Earth. The difference between the two was exactly sixteen minutes and forty-two seconds.

Ye referred to her solar structure mathematical model and tried to find a theoretical explanation. Her eyes were drawn to her description of what she called "energy mirrors" within the solar radiation zone.

Energy produced by reaction within the solar core is initially in the form of high-energy gamma rays. The radiation zone, the region of the sun's interior that surrounds the core, absorbs these high-energy photons and re-emits them at a slightly lower energy level. After a long period of successive absorption and re-emission (a photon might take a thousand years to leave the sun), gamma rays become x-rays, extreme ultraviolet, ultraviolet, then eventually turn into visible light and other forms of radiation.

Such were the known facts about the sun. But Ye's model led to a new result: As solar radiation dropped through these different frequencies on its way through the radiation zone, there were boundaries between the subzones for each type of radiation. As energy crossed each boundary, the radiation frequency stepped down a grade sharply. This was different from the traditional view that the radiation frequency lowered gradually as energy passed from the core outwards. Her calculations showed that these boundaries would reflect radiation coming from the lower-frequency side, which was why she named the boundaries "energy mirrors."

Ye had carefully studied these membranelike boundary surfaces suspended in the high-energy plasma ocean of the

sun and discovered them to be full of wonderful properties. One of the most incredible characteristics she named "gain reflectivity." However, the characteristic was so bizarre that it was hard to confirm, and even Ye herself didn't quite believe it was real. It seemed more likely an artifact of some error in the dizzying, complex calculations.

But now, Ye made the first step in confirming her guess about the gain reflectivity of solar energy mirrors: The energy mirrors not only reflected radiation coming from the lower-frequency side, but amplified it. All the mysterious sudden fluctuations within narrow frequency bands that she had observed were in fact the result of other radiation coming from space being amplified after reflecting off an energy mirror in the sun. That was why there were no observable disturbances on the surface of the sun.

This time, after the Jovian radio outbursts reached the sun, they were re-emitted, as if by a mirror, after being amplified about a hundred million times. The Earth received both sets of emissions, before and after the amplification, separated by sixteen minutes and forty-two seconds.

The sun was an amplifier for radio waves.

However, there was a question: The sun must be receiving electromagnetic radiation from space every second, including radio waves emitted by the Earth. Why were only some of the waves amplified? The answer was simple: In addition to the selectivity of the energy mirrors for frequencies they would reflect, the main reason was the shielding effect of the solar convection zone. The endlessly boiling convection zone situated outside the radiation zone was the outermost liquid layer of the sun. The radio waves coming from space must first penetrate the convection zone to reach the energy mirrors in the radiation zone, where they would be amplified

and reflected back out. This meant that in order to reach the energy mirrors, the waves would have to be more powerful than a threshold value. The vast majority of Earth-based radio sources could not cross this threshold, but the Jovian radio outburst did—

And Red Coast's maximum transmission power also exceeded the threshold.

The problem with solar outages was not resolved, but another exciting possibility presented itself: Humans could use the sun as a superantenna, and, through it, broadcast radio waves to the universe. The radio waves would be sent with the power of the sun, hundreds of millions of times greater than the total usable transmission power on Earth.

Earth civilization had a way to transmit at the level of a Kardashev Type II civilization.

The next step was to compare the waveforms of the two Jovian radio outbursts with the waveforms of the solar outages received by Red Coast. If they matched, then her guess would receive further confirmation.

Ye made her request to the base leadership to contact Harry Peterson and obtain the waveform records of the two Jovian radio outbursts. This was not easy. It was difficult to find the right communication channels, and numerous bureaucracies required layers of formal paperwork. Any error could lead to her being suspected of acting as a foreign spy. So Ye had to wait.

But there was a more direct way to prove the hypothesis: Red Coast itself could transmit radio waves directly at the sun at a power level exceeding the threshold value.

Ye again made her request to the base leadership. But she didn't dare to give her real reason—it was too fantastic, and she would have been turned down for certain. Instead, she

explained that she wanted to do an experiment for her solar research: The Red Coast transmission system would be used as a solar exploration radar whose echoes could be analyzed to obtain some information about solar radiation. Lei and Yang both had deep technical backgrounds, and wouldn't have been easily fooled, but the experiment described by Ye did have real precedents in Western solar research. In fact, her suggestion was technically easier than the radar exploration of terrestrial planets already being conducted.

"Ye Wenjie, you're getting out of line," said Commissar Lei. "Your research should be focused on theory. Do we really need to go to so much trouble?"

Ye begged, "Commissar, it's possible that a big discovery will be made. Experiments are absolutely necessary. I just want to try it once, please?"

Chief Yang said, "Commissar Lei, maybe we should try once. It doesn't seem to be too difficult operationally. Receiving the echoes after transmission would take—"

"Ten, fifteen minutes," Lei said.

"Then Red Coast has just enough time to switch from transmission mode to monitoring mode."

Lei shook his head again. "I know that it's technically and operationally feasible. But you . . . eh, Chief Yang, you just lack the sensitivity for this kind of thing. You want to aim a superpowerful radio beam at the red sun. Have you thought about the political symbolism of such an experiment?"[32]

Yang and Ye were both utterly stunned, but they did not think Lei's objection ridiculous. Just the opposite: They were horrified that they themselves had not thought of it. During

32 *Translator's Note:* Chairman Mao was often compared to the "red sun," especially during the years of the Cultural Revolution.

those years, finding political symbolism in everything had reached absurd levels. The research reports Ye turned in had to be carefully reviewed by Lei so that even technical terms related to the sun could be repeatedly revised to remove political risk. Terms like "sunspots" were forbidden.[33] An experiment that sent a powerful radio transmission at the sun could of course be interpreted in a thousand positive ways, but a single negative interpretation would be enough to bring political disaster on everyone. Lei's reason for refusing to allow the experiment was truly unassailable.

Ye didn't give up, though. In fact, as long as she didn't take excessive risk, it wasn't difficult to accomplish her goal. The Red Coast transmitter was ultra-high-powered, but all of its components were domestically produced during the Cultural Revolution. As the quality of the components was not up to par, the fault rate was very high. After every fifteenth transmission, the entire system had to be overhauled, and after each overhaul, there would be a test transmission. Few people attended these tests, and the targets and other parameters were arbitrarily selected.

One time when she was on duty, Ye was assigned to work during one of the test transmissions after an overhaul. Because a test transmission omitted many operational steps, only Ye and five others were present. Three of them were low-level operators who knew little about the principles behind the equipment. The remaining two were a technician and an engineer, both exhausted and not paying much attention after two days of overhaul work. Ye first adjusted the test transmission power to exceed the threshold value for her

33 *Translator's Note:* The Chinese term for "sunspot" (太阳黑子) literally means "solar black spots." Black, of course, was the color of counter-revolutionaries.

gain-reflective solar energy mirror theory, using the maximum power of the Red Coast transmission system. Then she set the frequency to the value most likely to be amplified by the energy mirror. And under the guise of testing the antenna's mechanical components, she aimed it at the setting sun in the west. The content of the transmission remained the same as usual.

This was a clear afternoon in the autumn of 1971. Afterwards, Ye recalled the event many times but couldn't remember any special feelings except anxiety, a desire for the transmission to be completed quickly. First, she was afraid to be discovered by her colleagues. Even though she had thought of some excuses, it was still unusual to use maximum power for a test transmission, because doing so would wear down the components. In addition, the Red Coast transmission system's positioning equipment was never designed to be aimed at the sun. Ye could feel the eyepiece growing hot. If it burnt out she would be in real trouble.

As the sun set slowly in the west, Ye had to manually track it. The Red Coast antenna seemed like a giant sunflower at that moment, slowly turning to follow the descending sun. By the time the red light indicating transmission completion lit up, she was already soaked in sweat.

She glanced around. The three operators at the control panel were shutting down the equipment piece by piece in accordance with the instructions in the operating manual. The engineer was drinking a glass of water in a corner of the control room, and the technician was asleep in his chair. No matter how historians and writers later tried to portray the scene, the reality at the time was completely prosaic.

The transmission completed, Ye rushed out of the control room and dashed into Yang Weining's office. Catching her

breath, she said, "Tell the base station to begin monitoring the twelve thousand megahertz channel!"

"What are we receiving?" Chief Yang looked in surprise at Ye, strands of hair stuck to her sweaty face. Compared to the highly sensitive Red Coast monitoring system, the conventional military-grade radio—normally used by the base for communicating with the outside—was only a toy.

"Maybe we'll get something. There's no time to change the Red Coast systems to monitoring mode!" Normally, warming up and switching over to the monitoring system required a little more than ten minutes. But right now the monitoring system was also being overhauled. Many modules had been taken apart and remained unassembled, rendering them inoperable in the short term.

Yang stared at Ye for a few seconds, and then picked up the phone and ordered the communications office to follow Ye's direction.

"Given the low sensitivity of that radio, we can probably only receive signals from extraterrestrials on the moon."

"The signal comes from the sun," Ye said. Outside the window, the sun's edge was already approaching the mountains on the horizon, red as blood.

"You used Red Coast to send a signal to the sun?" Yang asked anxiously.

Ye nodded.

"Don't tell anyone else. This must never happen again. Never!" Yang looked behind him to be sure there was no one at the door.

Ye nodded again.

"What's the point? The echo wave must be extremely weak, far outside the sensitivity of a conventional radio."

"No. If my guess is right, we should get an extremely

strong echo. It will be more powerful than . . . I can hardly imagine. As long as the transmission power exceeds a certain threshold, the sun can amplify the signal a hundred million–fold."

Yang looked at Ye strangely. Ye said nothing. They both waited in silence. Yang could clearly hear Ye's breath and heartbeat. He hadn't paid much attention to what she had said, but the feelings he had buried in his heart for many years resurfaced. He could only restrain himself, waiting.

Twenty minutes later, Yang picked up the phone, called the communications office, and asked a few simple questions.

He put the phone down. "They received nothing."

Ye let out a long-held breath and eventually nodded.

"That American astronomer responded, though." Yang took out a thick envelope covered with customs stamps and handed it to Ye. She tore the envelope open and scanned Harry Peterson's letter. The letter said that he had not imagined that there would be colleagues in China studying planetary electromagnetism, and that he wished to collaborate and exchange more information in the future. He had also sent two stacks of paper: the complete record of the waveforms of the radio outbursts from Jupiter. They were clearly photocopied from the long signal recording tape, and would have to be pieced together.

Ye took the dozens of sheets of photocopier paper and started lining them up in two columns on the floor. Halfway through the effort she gave up any hope. She was very familiar with the waveforms of the interference from the two solar outages. They didn't match these two.

Ye slowly picked up the photocopies from the floor. Yang crouched down to help her. When he handed the stack of

paper to this woman he loved with all his heart, he saw her smile. The smile was so sad that his heart trembled.

"What's wrong?" he asked, not realizing that he had never spoken to her so softly.

"Nothing. I'm just waking up from a dream." Ye smiled again. She took the stack of photocopies and the envelope and left the office. She went back to her room, picked up her lunch box, and went to the cafeteria. Only *mantou* buns and pickles were left, and the cafeteria workers told her impatiently that they were closing. So she had no choice but to carry her lunch box outside and walk next to the lip of the cliff, where she sat down on the grass to chew the cold *mantou*.

The sun had already set. The Greater Khingan Mountains were gray and indistinct, just like Ye's life. In this gray life, a dream appeared especially colorful and bright. But one always awoke from a dream, just like the sun—which, though it would rise again, brought no fresh hope. In that moment Ye saw the rest of her life suffused with an endless grayness. With tears in her eyes, she smiled again, and continued to chew the cold *mantou*.

Ye didn't know that at that moment, the first cry that could be heard in space from civilization on Earth was already spreading out from the sun to the universe at the speed of light. A star-powered radio wave, like a majestic tide, had already crossed the orbit of Jupiter.

Right then, at the frequency of 12,000 MHz, the sun was the brightest star in the entire Milky Way.

291

RED COAST VI

The next eight years were among the most peaceful of Ye Wenjie's life. The horror experienced during the Cultural Revolution gradually subsided, and she was finally able to relax a little. The Red Coast Project completed its testing and breaking-in phases, settling down into routine operation. Fewer and fewer technical problems remained, and both work and life became regular.

In peace, what had been suppressed by anxiety and fear began to reawaken. Ye found that the real pain had just begun. Nightmarish memories, like embers coming back to life, burned more and more fiercely, searing her heart. For most people, perhaps time would have gradually healed these wounds. After all, during the Cultural Revolution, many people suffered fates similar to hers, and compared to many of them, Ye was relatively fortunate. But Ye had the mental habits of a scientist, and she refused to forget. Rather, she looked with a rational gaze on the madness and hatred that had harmed her.

Ye's rational consideration of humanity's evil side began the day she read *Silent Spring*. As she grew closer to Yang Weining, he was able to get her many classics of foreign-language philosophy and history under the guise of gathering

technical research materials. The bloody history of humanity shocked her, and the extraordinary insights of the philosophers also led her to understand the most fundamental and secret aspects of human nature.

Indeed, even on top of Radar Peak, a place the world almost forgot, the madness and irrationality of the human race were constantly on display. Ye saw that the forest below the peak continued to fall to the deranged logging by her former comrades. Patches of bare earth grew daily, as though those parts of the Greater Khingan Mountains had had their skin torn off. When those patches grew into regions and then into a connected whole, the few surviving trees seemed rather abnormal. To complete the slash-and-burn plan, fires were lit on the bare fields, and Radar Peak became the refuge for birds escaping the fiery inferno. As the fires raged, the sorrowful cries of birds with singed feathers at the base never ceased.

The insanity of the human race had reached its historical zenith. The Cold War was at its height. Nuclear missiles capable of destroying the Earth ten times over could be launched at a moment's notice, spread out among the countless missile silos dotting two continents and hidden within ghostlike nuclear-powered ballistic missile submarines patrolling deep under the sea. A single *Lafayette-* or Yankee-class submarine held enough warheads to destroy hundreds of cities and kill hundreds of millions, but most people continued their lives as if nothing was wrong.

As an astrophysicist, Ye was strongly against nuclear weapons. She knew this was a power that should belong only to the stars. She knew also that the universe had even more terrible forces: black holes, antimatter, and more. Compared to those forces, a thermonuclear bomb was nothing but a tiny candle. If humans obtained mastery over one of those

other forces, the world might be vaporized in a moment. In the face of madness, rationality was powerless.

Four years after entering Red Coast Base, Ye and Yang married. Yang truly loved her. For love, he gave up his future.

The fiercest stage of the Cultural Revolution was over, and the political climate had grown somewhat milder. Yang wasn't persecuted, exactly, for his marriage. However, because he married a woman who had been deemed to be a counter-revolutionary, he was viewed as politically immature and lost his position as chief engineer. The only reason that he and his wife were allowed to stay on the base as ordinary technicians was because the base could not do without their technical skills.

Ye accepted Yang's proposal mainly out of gratitude. If he hadn't brought her into this safe haven in her most perilous moment, she would probably no longer be alive. Yang was a talented man, cultured and with good taste. She didn't find him unpleasant, but her heart was like ashes from which the flame of love could no longer be lit.

As she pondered human nature, Ye was faced with an ultimate loss of purpose and sank into another spiritual crisis. She had once been an idealist who needed to give all her talent to a great goal, but now she realized that all that she had done was meaningless, and the future could not have any meaningful pursuits, either. As this mental state persisted, she gradually felt more and more alienated from the world. She didn't belong. The sense of wandering in the spiritual wilderness tormented her. After she made a home with Yang, her soul became homeless.

One night, Ye was working the night shift. This was the loneliest time. In the deep silence of midnight, the universe

revealed itself to its listeners as a vast desolation. What Ye disliked most was seeing the waves that slowly crawled across the display, a visual record of the meaningless noise Red Coast picked up from space. Ye felt this interminable wave was an abstract view of the universe: one end connected to the endless past, the other to the endless future, and in the middle only the ups and downs of random chance—without life, without pattern, the peaks and valleys at different heights like uneven grains of sand, the whole curve like a one-dimensional desert made of all the grains of sand lined up in a row, lonely, desolate, so long that it was intolerable. You could follow it and go forward or backward as long as you liked, but you'd never find the end.

On this day, however, Ye saw something odd when she glanced at the waveform display. Even experts had a hard time telling with the naked eye whether a waveform carried information. But Ye was so familiar with the noise of the universe that she could tell that the wave that now moved in front of her eyes had something extra. The thin curve, rising and falling, seemed to possess a soul. She was certain that the radio signal before her had been modulated by intelligence.

She rushed to another terminal and checked the computer's rating of the signal's recognizability: AAAAA. Before this, no radio signal received by Red Coast ever garnered a recognizability rating above C. An A rating meant the likelihood that the transmission contained intelligent information was greater than 90 percent. A rating of AAAAA was a special, extreme case: It meant the received transmission used the exact same coding language as Red Coast's own outbound transmission.

Ye turned on the Red Coast deciphering system. The software attempted to decipher any signal whose recognizability rating was above B. During the entire time that the Red Coast

Project had been running, it had never been invoked even once in real use. Based on test data, deciphering a transmission suspected of being a message might require a few days or even a few months of computing time, and the result would be failure more than half the time. But this time, as soon as the file containing the original transmission was submitted, the display showed that the deciphering was complete.

Ye opened the resulting document, and, for the first time, a human read a message from another world.

The content was not what anyone had imagined. It was a warning repeated three times.

Do not answer!
Do not answer!!
Do not answer!!!

Still caught up by the dizzying excitement and confusion, Ye deciphered a second message.

This world has received your message.

I am a pacifist in this world. It is the luck of your civilization that I am the first to receive your message. I am warning you: Do not answer! Do not answer!! Do not answer!!!

There are tens of millions of stars in your direction. As long as you do not answer, this world will not be able to ascertain the source of your transmission.

But if you do answer, the source will be located right away. Your planet will be invaded. Your world will be conquered!

Do not answer! Do not answer!! Do not answer!!!

As she read the flashing green text on the display, Ye was no longer capable of thinking clearly. Her mind, inhibited by shock and excitement, could only understand this: No more than nine years had passed since the time she had sent the message to the sun. Then the source of this transmission must be around four light-years away. It could only have come from the closest extra-solar stellar system: Alpha Centauri.[34]

The universe was not desolate. The universe was not empty. The universe was full of life! Humankind had cast their gaze to the end of the universe, but they had no idea that intelligent life already existed around the stars closest to them!

Ye stared at the waveform display: The signal continued to stream from the universe into the Red Coast antenna. She opened up another interface and began real-time deciphering. The messages began to show up immediately on the screen.

During the next four hours, Ye learned of the existence of Trisolaris, learned of the civilization that had been reborn again and again, and learned of their plan to migrate to the stars.

At four in the morning, the transmission from Alpha Centauri ended. The deciphering system continued to run uselessly and emitted an unceasing string of failure codes. The Red Coast monitoring system was once again only hearing the noise of the universe.

But Ye was certain that what she had just experienced was

34 *Translator's Note:* Alpha Centauri, though appearing to the naked eye as

a single star, is actually a double-star system (Alpha Centauri A and Alpha Centauri B). A third star, called Proxima Centauri and invisible to the naked eye, is probably gravitationally associated with the double-star system. The Chinese name for the objects (半人马座三星) makes it clear that the "star" is really a system of three stars.

not a dream.

The sun really was an amplifying antenna. But why had her experiment eight years ago not received any echoes? Why had the waveforms of Jupiter's radio outbursts not matched the later radiation from the sun? Later, Ye came up with many reasons. It was possible that the base communication office couldn't receive radio waves at that frequency, or maybe the office did receive the echo but it sounded like noise and so the operator thought it was nothing. As for the waveforms, it was possible that when the sun amplified the radio waves, it also added another wave to it. It would likely be a periodic wave that could be easily filtered out by the alien deciphering system, but to her unaided eye, the waveform from Jupiter and from the sun would appear very different. Years later, after Ye had left Red Coast, she would manage to confirm her last guess: The sun had added a sine wave.

She looked around alertly. There were three others in the main computer room. Two of the three were chatting in a corner, while the last was napping before a terminal. In the data analysis section of the monitoring system, only the two terminals in front of her could view the recognizability rating of a signal and access the deciphering system.

Maintaining her composure, she worked quickly and moved all of the received messages to a multiply-encrypted, invisible subdirectory. Then she copied over a segment of noise received a year ago as a substitute for the transmission received during the last five hours.

Finally, from the terminal, she placed a short message into the Red Coast transmission buffer.

Ye got up and left the monitoring main control room. A chilly wind blew against her feverish face. Dawn had just brightened the eastern sky, and she followed the dimly lit

pebble-paved path to the transmission main control room. Above her, the Red Coast antenna lay open, silently, like a giant palm toward the universe. The dawn turned the guard at the door into a silhouette, and as usual, he did not pay attention to Ye as she entered.

The transmission main control room was much dimmer than the monitoring main control room. Ye passed through rows of cabinets to stand in front of the control panel and flipped more than a dozen switches with practiced ease to warm up the transmission system. The two men on duty next to the control panel looked up at her with sleepy eyes, and one turned to glance at the clock. Then one of them went back to his nap while the other flipped through a well-thumbed newspaper. At the base, Ye had no political status, but she did have some freedom in technical matters. She often tested the equipment before a transmission. Although she was early today—the transmission wasn't scheduled to occur until three hours later—warming up a bit early wasn't that unusual.

What happened next was the longest half hour of her life. During this time, Ye adjusted the transmission frequency to the optimal frequency for amplification by the solar energy mirror, and increased the transmission power to maximum. Then, putting her eyes to the eyepiece of the optical positioning system, she watched the sun rise above the horizon, activated the positioning system for the antenna, and slowly aligned it with the sun. As the gigantic antenna turned, the rumbling noise shook the main control room. One of the men on duty looked at Ye again, but said nothing.

The sun was now completely above the horizon. The crosshair of the Red Coast positioning system was aimed at its upper edge to account for the time it would take for the radio wave to travel to the sun. The transmission system was ready.

The Transmit button was a long rectangle—very similar to the Space key on a computer keyboard, except that it was red.

Ye's hand hovered two centimeters above it.

The fate of the entire human race was now tied to these slender fingers.

Without hesitation, Ye pressed the button.

"What are you doing?" one of the men on duty asked, still sleepy.

Ye smiled at him and said nothing. She pressed a yellow button to stop the transmission. Then she moved the control stick until the antenna was pointed elsewhere. She left the control panel and walked away.

The man looked at his watch. It was time to get off work. He picked up the diary and thought about recording Ye's operation of the transmission system. It was, after all, out of the ordinary. But then he looked at the paper tape and saw that she had transmitted for no more than three seconds. He tossed the diary back, yawned, put on his army cap, and left.

The message that was winging its way to the sun said, *Come here! I will help you conquer this world. Our civilization is no longer capable of solving its own problems. We need your force to intervene.*

The newly risen sun dazzled Ye Wenjie. Not too far from the door of the main control room, she collapsed onto the lawn in a faint.

When she woke up, she found herself in the base clinic. Next to her bed sat Yang, watching her with concern, like that time many years ago on the helicopter. The doctor told Ye to be careful and get plenty of rest.

"You are pregnant," he said.

24

REBELLION

After Ye Wenjie finished recounting the history of her first contact with Trisolaris, the abandoned cafeteria remained silent. Many present were apparently just hearing the complete story for the first time. Wang was deeply absorbed by the narrative and temporarily forgot about the danger and terror he faced. Unable to stop himself, he asked, "How did the ETO then develop to its present scale?"

Ye replied, "I'd have to start with how I got to know Evans. . . . But every comrade here already knows that part of history, so we shouldn't waste time on it now. I can tell you later. However, whether we'll have such an opportunity depends on you. . . . Xiao Wang, let's talk about your nanomaterial."

"This . . . Lord that you talk about. Why is it so afraid of nanomaterial?"

"Because it can allow humans to escape gravity and engage in space construction at a much larger scale."

"The space elevator?" Wang suddenly understood.

"Yes. If ultrastrong nanomaterials could be mass produced, then that would lay the technical foundation for building a space elevator from the ground up to a geostationary point in space. For our Lord, this is but a tiny invention; but for humans on Earth, its meaning would be significant.

With this technology, humans could easily enter near-Earth space and build up large-scale defensive structures. Thus, this technology must be extinguished."

"What is at the end of the countdown?" Wang asked the question that frightened him the most.

Ye smiled. "I don't know."

"But trying to stop me is useless! This is not basic research. Based on what we've already found out, someone else can figure out the rest." Wang's voice was loud but anxious.

"Yes, it is rather useless. It's far more effective to confuse the researchers' minds. But, like you point out, we didn't stop the progress in time. After all, what you do is applied research. Our technique is far more effective against basic research. . . ."

"Speaking of basic research, how did your daughter die?"

The question silenced Ye for a few seconds. Wang noticed that her eyes dimmed almost imperceptibly. But she then resumed the conversation. "Indeed, compared to our Lord, who possesses peerless strength, everything we do is meaningless. We're just doing whatever we can."

Just as she finished speaking, several loud booms rang out and the doors to the cafeteria broke open. A team of soldiers holding submachine guns rushed in. Wang realized that they were not armed police, but the real army. Noiselessly they proceeded along the walls and soon surrounded the rebels of the ETO. Shi Qiang was the last to enter. His jacket was open, and he held the barrel of a pistol so that the grip was like the head of a hammer.

Da Shi looked around arrogantly, then suddenly dashed forward. His hand flashed and there was the dull thud of metal striking against a skull. An ETO rebel fell to the ground, and the gun that he was trying to draw tumbled to fall some distance away. Several soldiers began to shoot at

the ceiling, and dust and debris fell. Someone grabbed Wang Miao and pulled him away from the ETO ranks until he was safe behind a row of soldiers.

"Drop all your weapons onto the table! I swear I'm going to kill the next son of a bitch who tries anything." Da Shi pointed at the submachine guns arrayed behind him. "I know that none of you is afraid to die, but we're not afraid either. I'm going to say this up front: Normal police procedures and laws don't apply to you. Even the human laws of warfare no longer apply to you. Since you've decided to treat the entire human race as your enemy, there's no longer anything we wouldn't do to you."

There was some commotion among the ETO members, but no one panicked. Ye's face remained impassive. Three people suddenly rushed out of the crowd, including the young woman who had twisted Pan Han's neck. They ran toward the three-body sculpture, and each grabbed one of the spheres and held it in front of his or her chest.

The young woman raised the bright metal sphere before her with both hands, as though she were getting ready to start a gymnastics routine. Smiling, she said, "Officers, we hold in our hands three nuclear bombs, each with a yield of about one point five kilotons. Not too big, since we like small toys. This is the detonator."

Everyone in the cafeteria froze. The only one who moved was Shi Qiang. He put his gun back into the holster under his left arm and placed his hands together calmly.

"Our demand is simple: Let the commander go," the young woman said. "Then we can play whatever game you want." Her tone suggested that she wasn't afraid of Shi Qiang and the soldiers at all.

"I stay with my comrades," Ye said, calmly.

"Can you confirm her claim?" Da Shi asked an officer next to him, an explosives expert.

The officer threw a bag in front of the three ETO members holding the spheres. One of the ETO fighters picked up the bag and took out a spring scale, a bigger version of the ones some customers brought to street markets to verify the portions measured by vendors. He placed his metal sphere into the bag, attached it to the spring scale, and held it aloft. The gauge extended about halfway and stopped.

The young woman chuckled. The explosives expert also laughed, contemptuously.

The ETO member took out the sphere and tossed it on the ground. Another ETO fighter picked up the scale and the bag and repeated the procedure with his sphere, and ended up also tossing the sphere to the ground.

The young woman laughed once more and picked up the bag herself. She loaded her sphere into the bag, hung it on the hook of the scale, and the gauge immediately dropped to its bottom, the spring in the scale having been fully extended.

The smile on the explosives expert's face froze. He whispered to Da Shi, "Damn! They really do have one."

Da Shi remained impassive.

The explosives expert said, "We can at least confirm that there are heavy elements—fissile material—inside. We don't know if the detonation mechanism works."

The flashlights attached to the soldiers' guns focused on the young woman holding the nuclear bomb. While she held the destructive power of 1.5 kilotons of TNT in her hands, she smiled brightly, as though enjoying applause and praise on a spotlit stage.

"I have an idea: Shoot the sphere," the explosives expert whispered to Da Shi.

"Won't that set off the bomb?"

"The conventional explosives around the outside will go off, but the explosion will be scattered. It won't lead to the kind of precise compression of the fissile material in the center necessary for a nuclear explosion."

Da Shi stared at the nuclear woman, saying nothing.

"How about snipers?"

Almost imperceptibly, Da Shi shook his head. "There's no good position. She's sharp as a tack. As soon as she's targeted by a sniper scope, she'll know."

Da Shi strode forward. He pushed the crowd apart and stood in the middle of the empty space.

"Stop," the young woman warned Da Shi, staring at him intently. Her right thumb was poised over the detonator. Her face was no longer smiling in the flashlight beams.

"Calm down," Da Shi said, standing about seven or eight meters from her. He took an envelope from his pocket. "I have some information you'll definitely want to know. Your mother has been found."

The young woman's feverish eyes dimmed. At that moment her eyes were truly windows to her soul.

Da Shi took two steps forward. He was now no more than five meters from her. She raised the bomb and warned him with her eyes, but she was already distracted. One of the two ETO members who had tossed away fake bombs strode toward Da Shi to take the envelope from him. As the man blocked the woman's view of Da Shi, he drew his gun with a lightning-fast motion. The woman only saw a flash by the ear of the man trying to take the letter from Da Shi before the bomb in her hands exploded.

After hearing the muffled explosion, Wang saw nothing before his eyes but darkness. Someone dragged him out of

305

the cafeteria. Thick, yellow smoke poured out of the door, and a cacophony of shouting and gunshots came from inside. From time to time, people rushed through the smoke and out of the cafeteria.

Wang got up and tried to go back into the cafeteria, but the explosives expert grabbed him around the waist and stopped him.

"Careful. Radiation!"

The chaos eventually subsided. More than a dozen ETO fighters were killed in the gunfight. The rest—more than two hundred, including Ye Wenjie—were arrested. The explosion had turned the nuclear woman into a bloody mess, but she was the only casualty of the aborted bomb. The man who had tried to take the letter from Da Shi was severely injured, but since his body had shielded Da Shi, his wounds were light. However, like everyone else who remained in the cafeteria after the explosion, Shi suffered severe radiation contamination.

Through the small window of an ambulance, Wang stared at Da Shi, who was lying inside. A wound on Da Shi's head continued to ooze blood. The nurse who was dressing the wound wore transparent protective gear. Da Shi and Wang could only talk through their mobile phones.

"Who was that young woman's mother?" Wang asked.

Da Shi grinned. "Fucked if I know. Just a guess. A girl like that most likely has mother issues. After doing this for more than twenty years, I'm pretty good at reading people."

"I bet you're happy to be proven right. There really was someone behind all this." Wang forced himself to smile, hoping Da Shi could see it.

"Buddy, you're the one who was right!" Da Shi laughed, shaking his head. "I would never have thought that actual fucking aliens would be involved!"

THE DEATHS OF LEI ZHICHENG AND YANG WEINING

INTERROGATOR: Name?

YE WENJIE: Ye Wenjie.

INTERROGATOR: Birth date?

YE: June 1943.

INTERROGATOR: Employment?

YE: Professor of Astrophysics at Tsinghua University. Retired in 2004.

INTERROGATOR: In consideration of your health, you may stop the interrogation temporarily at any time.

YE: Thank you. I'm fine.

INTERROGATOR: We're only conducting a regular criminal investigation now and won't get into more sensitive matters. We would like to finish quickly. We hope you'll cooperate.

YE: I know what you're referring to. Yes, I'll cooperate.

INTERROGATOR: Our investigation revealed that while you were working at Red Coast Base, you were suspected of murder.

YE: I did kill two people.

INTERROGATOR: When?

YE: The afternoon of October 21, 1979.

INTERROGATOR: Names of the victims?

YE: Base Commissar Lei Zhicheng, and my husband, Base Engineer Yang Weining.

INTERROGATOR: Explain your motive for murder.

YE: Can I . . . assume that you understand the relevant background?

INTERROGATOR: I know the basics. If something is unclear I'll ask you.

YE: Good. On the day when I received the extraterrestrial communication and replied, I learned that I wasn't the only one to get the message. Lei did as well.

Lei was a typical political cadre of the time, so he possessed an extremely keen sense for politics and saw everything through an ideological lens. Unbeknownst to most of the technical staff at Red Coast Base, he ran a small program in the background on the main computer. This program constantly read from the transmission and reception buffers and stored the results in a hidden encrypted file. This way, there would be a copy of everything Red Coast sent and received that only he could read. It was from this copy that he discovered the extraterrestrial message.

On the afternoon after I sent my message toward the rising sun, and shortly after I learned that I was pregnant at the base clinic, Lei called me to his office, and I saw that his terminal displayed the message from Trisolaris that I had received the night before. . . .

"Eight hours have passed since you received the first message. Instead of making a report, you deleted the original message and maybe hid a copy. Isn't that right?"

I kept my head down and did not reply.

"I know your next move. You plan to reply. If I hadn't discovered this in time, you could have ruined all human civilization! Of course I'm not saying that we're afraid of an interstellar invasion. Even if we assumed the worst and that really did happen, the outer space invaders would surely drown in the ocean of the people's righteous war!"

I realized then that he didn't know that I'd already replied. When I placed the answer into the transmission buffer, I didn't use the regular file interface. Luckily, this got around his monitoring program.

"Ye Wenjie, I knew you were capable of something like this. You've always held a deep hatred toward the Party and the people. You would seize any opportunity for revenge. Do you know the consequences of your actions?"

Of course I knew, so I nodded. Lei was silent for a moment. But what he said next was unexpected. "Ye Wenjie, I have no pity for you at all. You've always been a class enemy who views the people as your adversaries. But I've served many years with Yang. I cannot bear to see him ruined along with you, and I certainly cannot allow his child to be ruined as well. You're pregnant, aren't you?"

What he said wasn't idle speculation. During that era, my deeds would certainly have implicated my husband if revealed, regardless of whether he had anything to do with them.

Lei kept his voice very low. "Right now, only you and I know what happened. What we must do is to minimize the impact of your actions. Pretend that it never happened and never mention it to anyone, including Yang. I'll take care of the rest. As long as you cooperate, you can avoid the disastrous consequences."

I immediately knew what Lei was after. He wanted to

become the first man to discover extraterrestrial intelligence. It really was a great opportunity to get his name into the history textbooks.

I assented. Then I left his office. I'd already decided everything.

I took a small wrench and went to the equipment closet for the processing module of the receiver. Because I often needed to inspect the equipment, no one paid attention. I opened the main cabinet and carefully loosened the bolt that secured the ground wire to the bottom. The interference on the receiver suddenly increased and the ground resistance went up from 0.6 ohms to 5 ohms. The technician on duty thought it was a problem with the ground wire, because that kind of malfunction happened a lot. It was an easy diagnosis. He would never have guessed that the problem was at this end, at the top of the ground wire, because this end was securely fastened, out of the way, and I told him that I had just inspected it.

The top of Radar Peak had an unusual geological feature: a layer of clay more than a dozen meters thick—poor conductivity—covered it. When the ground wire wasn't buried deeply, ground resistance was invariably too high. However, the ground wire couldn't be sunk too deep, either, because the clay layer had a strong corrosive effect, and after a while, it would corrode the middle section of the ground wire. In the end, the only solution was to drape the ground wire over the lip of the cliff until the tip was below the clay layer, and then bury the ground terminal into the cliff at that point. Even so, the grounding wasn't very stable, and the resistance was often excessive. Whenever such problems occurred, the trouble always involved the part of the wire going into the cliff. Whoever was assigned to repair it would have to go over the edge of the cliff, dangling on ropes.

The technician on duty informed the maintenance squad of the issue. One of the soldiers in the squad tied a rope to an iron post and then rappelled down the cliff. After half an hour down below, he climbed back up, soaked in sweat, saying that he couldn't find the malfunction. It seemed that the next monitoring session would have to be delayed. There was no choice but to inform the Base Command Center. I waited by the iron post at the top of the cliff. Very soon, just as I had planned, Lei Zhicheng came back with that soldier.

To be honest, Lei was very dedicated to his job and faithfully followed the demands placed on political officers during that era: Become a part of the masses and always be on the front line. Maybe it was all for show, but he really was a good performer. Whenever there was some difficult and perilous work at the base, he was sure to volunteer. One of the tasks that he performed more than anyone else was to repair the ground wire, a task both dangerous and tiring. Even though this job wasn't particularly demanding technically, it did benefit from experience. There were many causes of malfunction: a loose contact due to exposure to open air—difficult to detect—or possibly the location where the ground wire went into the cliff was too dry. The volunteer soldiers responsible for external maintenance were all new, and none had much experience. So I had guessed that Lei would most likely show up.

He put on the safety harness and went over the cliff edge on the rope, as though I didn't exist. I made some excuse to get rid of the soldier who brought him so that I was the only one left on the cliff. Then I took a short hacksaw out of my pocket. It was made from a longer saw blade broken into three pieces and then stacked together. With the stacked blades, any cut I made would be particularly ragged, and it would not be obvious later that the rope was cut through with a tool.

Just then, my husband, Yang Weining, showed up.

After I explained to him what had happened, he looked over the cliff edge. Then he said that to inspect the ground terminal in the cliff face required digging, and the work would be too much for just Lei. He wanted to go down to help, so he put on the safety harness left by that other soldier. I asked him to use another rope, but he said no—the rope that Lei was on was thick and sturdy and could easily bear the weight of two. I insisted, so he told me to go get the rope. By the time I rushed back to the cliff with the rope, he had already gone down over the side. I poked my head over the edge and saw that he and Lei had already finished their inspection and were climbing back up. Lei was in the front.

There would never be another chance. I took out my hacksaw and cut through the rope.

INTERROGATOR: I want to ask a question, but I won't record the answer. How did you feel at the time?

YE: Calm. I did it without feeling anything. I had finally found a goal to which I could devote myself. I didn't care what price had to be paid, either by me or by others. I also knew that the entire human race would pay an unprecedented price for this goal. This was a very insignificant beginning.

INTERROGATOR: All right. Continue.

YE: I heard two or three surprised cries, and then the sound of bodies slamming against the rocks at the cliff bottom. After a while, I saw that the stream at the foot of the cliff had turned red. . . . That's all I'll say about that.

INTERROGATOR: I understand. This is the record. Please check it over carefully. If there are no errors, please sign it.

26

NO ONE REPENTS

The deaths of Lei and Yang were treated as accidents. Everybody at the base knew that Ye and Yang were a happy couple, and no one suspected her.

A new commissar came to the base, and life returned to its habitual peace. The tiny life inside Ye grew bigger every day, and she also felt the world outside change.

One day, the security platoon commander asked Ye to come to the gatehouse at the entrance to the base. When she entered the gatehouse, she was surprised to see three children: two boys and a girl, about fifteen or sixteen. They all wore old coats and dog fur hats, obviously locals. The guard on duty told her that they came from the village of Qijiatun. They had heard that the people on Radar Peak were learned and had come to ask some questions related to their studies.

Ye wondered how they dared to come onto Radar Peak. This was a restricted military zone, and the guards were authorized to warn intruders only once before shooting. The guard saw that Ye was puzzled and explained that they had just received orders that Red Coast Base's security rating had been reduced. The locals were allowed onto Radar Peak as long as they stayed outside the base. Several local peasants had already come yesterday to bring vegetables.

One of the children took out a worn-out middle school physics textbook. His hands were dirty and cracked like tree bark. In a thick Northeastern accent, he asked a simple physics question: The textbook said that a body in free fall is under constant acceleration but will always reach a terminal velocity. They had been thinking about this for several nights and could not understand why.

"You walked all this way just to ask this?" Ye asked.

"Teacher Ye, don't you know that they've restarted the exam?" the girl said excitedly.

"The exam?"

"The National College Entrance Exam! Whoever studies hard and gets the best score gets to go to college! It began two years ago. Didn't you know?"

"There's no need for recommendations anymore?"

"No. Anyone can take the exam. Even the children of the Five Black Categories in the village can take it."[35]

Ye was stunned. This change left her with mixed feelings. Only after a while did she realize that the children were still waiting with their books held up. She hurriedly answered their question, explaining that it was due to air resistance reaching equilibrium against the force of gravity. Then she promised that if they encountered any difficulties in their studies in the future, they could always come to her for help.

Three days later, seven children came to seek Ye. In addition to the three who had come last time, there were four more from villages located even farther away. The third time, fifteen children came to find her, and even a teacher at a small-town high school came along.

35 *Translator's Note:* The Five Black Categories, the targets of the Cultural Revolution, were five political identities used during the revolution: landlords, rich farmers, counter-revolutionaries, "bad elements," and right-wingers.

Because there was a shortage of teachers, he had to teach physics, math, and chemistry, and he came to ask Ye for some help on teaching. The man was over fifty years old, and his face was already full of wrinkles. He was very nervous in front of Ye, and spilled books everywhere. After they left the gatehouse, Ye heard him say to the students: "Children, that was a *scientist*. A real, bona fide *scientist*!"

After that, children would come to her for tutoring every few days. Sometimes there were so many of them that the gatehouse couldn't accommodate them all. With the permission of the officers in charge of base security, the guards would escort them to the cafeteria. There, Ye put up a small blackboard and taught the children.

It was dark by the time Ye got off work on the eve of Chinese New Year, 1980. Most people at the base had already left Radar Peak for the three-day holiday, and it was quiet everywhere. Ye returned to her room. This was once the home of her and Yang Weining, but now it was empty, her only companion the unborn child within her. In the night outside, the cold wind of the Greater Khingan Mountains screamed, carrying with it the faint sound of firecrackers going off in the village of Qijiatun. Loneliness pressed down on Ye like a giant hand, and she felt herself being crushed; compressed until she was so small that she disappeared into an invisible corner of the universe. . . .

Just then, someone knocked on her door. When she opened it, Ye first saw the guard, and then, behind him, the fire of several pine branch torches flickering in the cold wind. The torches were held aloft by a crowd of children, their faces bright red from the cold, and icicles hung from their hats. When they came into her room, they seemed to bring the cold air in with them. Two of the boys, thinly dressed, had

suffered the most. They had taken off their thick coats and wrapped them around something that they carried in their arms. Unwrapping the coats revealed a large pot, the fermented cabbage and pork dumplings inside still steaming hot.

That year, eight months after she sent her signal toward the sun, Ye went into labor. Because the baby was malpositioned and her body was weak, the base clinic couldn't handle her case and had to send her to the nearest town hospital.

This became one of the hardest times in Ye's life. After enduring a great deal of pain and losing a large amount of blood, she sank into a coma. Through a blur she could only see three hot, blinding suns slowly orbiting around her, cruelly roasting her body. This state lasted for some time, and she hazily thought it was probably the end for her. It was her hell. The fire of the three suns would torment her and burn her forever. This was punishment for her betrayal, the betrayal that exceeded all others. She sank into terror: not for her, but for her unborn child—was the child still in her? Or had she already been born into this hell to suffer eternally with her?

She didn't know how much time had passed. Gradually the three suns moved farther away. After a certain distance, they suddenly shrank and turned into crystalline flying stars. The air around her cooled, and her pain lessened. She finally awoke.

Ye heard a cry next to her. Turning her head with great effort, she saw the baby's pink, wet, little face.

The doctor told Ye that she had lost more than 2,000 ml of blood. Dozens of peasants from Qijiatun had come to donate blood to her. Many of the peasants had children who Ye had tutored, but most had no connection to her at

all, having only heard her name from the children and their parents. Without them, she would certainly have died.

Ye's living situation became a problem after the birth of her child. The difficult birth had damaged her health. It was impossible for her to stay at the base with the baby all by herself, and she had no relatives who could help. Just then, an old couple living in Qijiatun came to talk to the base leaders and explained that they could take Ye and her baby home with them and take care of them. The old man used to be a hunter and also gathered some herbs for traditional medicine. Later, after the forest around the area was lost to logging, the couple had turned to farming, but people still called him Hunter Qi out of habit. They had two sons and two daughters. The daughters were married and had moved out. One of the sons was a soldier away from home, and the other was married and lived with them. The daughter-in-law had also just given birth.

Ye still hadn't been rehabilitated politically, and the base leadership was unsure about this suggested solution. But in the end, there was no other way, and so they allowed the couple to take Ye and the baby home from the hospital on a sled.

Ye lived for more than half a year with this peasant family in the Greater Khingan Mountains. She was so weak after giving birth that her milk did not come in. During this time, the baby girl, Yang Dong, was breastfed by all the women of the village. The one who nursed her the most was Hunter Qi's daughter-in-law, called Feng. Feng had the strong, solid frame of the women of the Northeast. She ate sorghum every day, and her large breasts were full of milk even though she was feeding two babies at the same time. Other nursing women in Qijiatun also came to feed Yang Dong. They liked her, saying that the baby had the same clever air as her mother.

Gradually, Hunter Qi's home became the gathering place for all the women of the village. Old and young, matrons and maidens, they all liked to stop by when they had nothing else going on. They admired Ye and were curious about her, and she found that she had many women's topics to discuss with them.

On countless days, Ye held Yang Dong and sat with the other women of the village in the yard, surrounded by birch posts. Next to her was a lazy black dog and the playing children, bathing in the warm sunlight. She paid attention especially to the women with the copper tobacco pipes. Leisurely, they blew smoke out of their mouths, and the smoke, filled with sunlight, gave off a silvery glow much like the fine hairs on their plump limbs. One time, one of them handed her the long-stemmed cupronickel pipe and told her it would make her feel better. She took only two hits before she became dizzy, and they laughed about it for several days.

As for the men, Ye had little to say to them. The matters that occupied them all day also seemed outside her understanding. She gathered that they were interested in planting some ginseng for cash while the government seemed to be relaxing policies a little, but they didn't quite have the courage to try. They all treated Ye with great respect and were very polite toward her. She didn't pay much attention to this at first. But after a while, after observing how those men roughly beat their wives and flirted outrageously with the widows in the village, saying things that made her blush, she finally realized how precious their respect was. Every few days, one of them would bring a hare or pheasant he had caught to Hunter Qi's home. They also gave Yang Dong strange and quaint toys that they'd made with their own hands.

In Ye's memory, these months seemed to belong to

someone else, like a segment of another life that had drifted into hers like a feather. This period condensed in her memory into a series of classical paintings—not Chinese brush paintings but European oil paintings. Chinese brush paintings are full of blank spaces, but life in Qijiatun had no blank spaces. Like classical oil paintings, it was filled with thick, rich, solid colors. Everything was warm and intense: the heated *kang* stove-beds lined with thick layers of ura sedge, the Guandong and Mohe tobacco stuffed in copper pipes, the thick and heavy sorghum meal, the sixty-five-proof *baijiu* distilled from sorghum—all of these blended into a quiet and peaceful life, like the creek at the edge of the village.

Most memorable to Ye were the evenings. Hunter Qi's son was away in the city selling mushrooms—the first to leave the village to earn money elsewhere, so she shared a room in his house with Feng. Back then, there was no electricity in the village, and every evening, the two huddled around a kerosene lamp. Ye would read while Feng did her needlework. Ye would lean closer and closer to the lamp without noticing, and her bangs would often get singed, at which point the two of them would glance up and smile at each other. Feng, of course, never had this happen to her. She had very sharp eyes, and could do detailed work even in the dim light from heating charcoal. The two babies, not even half a year old, would be sleeping together on the *kang* next to them. Ye loved to watch them sleep, their even breathing the only sound in the room.

At first, Ye did not like sleeping on the heated *kang,* and often got sick, but she gradually got used to it. As she slept, she would imagine herself becoming a baby sleeping in someone's warm lap. The person who held her wasn't her father or mother, or her dead husband. She didn't know who it was.

The feeling was so real that she would wake up with tears on her face.

One time, she put down her book and saw that Feng was holding the cloth shoe she was stitching over her knee and staring into the kerosene lamp without moving. When she realized that Ye was looking at her, Feng asked, "Sister, why do you think the stars in the sky don't fall down?"

Ye examined Feng. The kerosene lamp was a wonderful artist and created a classical painting with dignified colors and bright strokes: Feng had her coat draped over her shoulders, exposing her red belly-band, and a strong, graceful arm. The glow from the kerosene lamp painted her figure with vivid, warm colors, while the rest of the room dissolved into a gentle darkness. Close attention revealed a dim red glow, which didn't come from the kerosene lamp, but the heating charcoal on the ground. The cold air outside sculpted beautiful ice patterns on the windowpanes with the room's warm, humid air.

"You're afraid of the stars falling down?" Ye asked softly.

Feng laughed and shook her head. "What's there to be afraid of? They're so tiny."

Ye did not give her the answer of an astrophysicist. She only said, "They're very, very far away. They can't fall."

Feng was satisfied with this answer, and went back to her needlework. But Ye could no longer be at peace. She put down her book and lay down on the warm surface of the *kang,* closing her eyes. In her imagination, the rest of the universe around their tiny cottage disappeared, just the way the kerosene lamp hid most of the room in darkness. Then she substituted the universe in Feng's heart for the real one. The night sky was a black dome that was just large enough to cover the entirety of the world. The surface of the dome

was inlaid with countless stars shining with a crystalline silver light, none of which was bigger than the mirror on the old wooden table next to the bed. The world was flat and extended very far in each direction, but ultimately there was an edge where it met the sky. The flat surface was covered with mountain ranges like the Greater Khingan Mountains, and with forests dotted with tiny villages, just like Qijiatun. . . . This toy-box-like universe comforted Ye, and gradually it shifted from her imagination into her dreams.

In this tiny mountain hamlet deep in the Greater Khingan Mountains, something finally thawed in Ye Wenjie's heart. In the frozen tundra of her soul, a tiny, clear lake of melt-water appeared.

Ye eventually returned to Red Coast Base with Yang Dong. Another two years passed, divided between anxiety and peace. Ye then received a notice: Both she and her father had been politically rehabilitated. Soon after, a letter arrived for her from Tsinghua, stating that she could return to teach right away. Accompanying the letter was a sum of money: the back pay owed to her father after his rehabilitation. Finally, at base meetings, her supervisors could call her *comrade*.

Ye faced all these changes with equanimity, showing no sign of excitement or elation. She had no interest in the outside world, only wanting to stay at the quiet, out-of-the-way Red Coast Base. But for the sake of Yang Dong's education, she finally left the base that she had once thought would be her home for the rest of her life, and returned to her alma mater.

Leaving the mountains, Ye felt spring was everywhere. The cold winter of the Cultural Revolution really was over, and everything was springing back to life. Even though the

calamity had just ended, everything was in ruins, and countless men and women were licking their wounds. The dawn of a new life was already evident. Students with children of their own appeared on college campuses; bookstores sold out of famous literary works; technological innovation became the focus in factories; and scientific research now enjoyed a sacred halo. Science and technology were the only keys to opening the door to the future, and people approached science with the faith and sincerity of elementary school students. Though their efforts were naïve, they were also down-to-earth. At the first National Conference on Science, Guo Moruo, president of the Chinese Academy of Sciences, declared that it was the season of rebirth and renewal for China's battered science establishment.

Was this the end of the madness? Were science and rationality really coming back? Ye asked herself these questions repeatedly.

Ye never again received any communication from Trisolaris. She knew that she would have to wait at least eight years to hear that world's response to her message, and after leaving the base, she no longer had any way of receiving extraterrestrial replies.

It was such an important thing, and yet she had done it all by herself. This gave her a sense of unreality. As time passed, that sense grew ever stronger. What had happened resembled an illusion, a dream. Could the sun really amplify radio signals? Did she really use it as an antenna to send a message about human civilization into the universe? Did she really receive a message from the stars? Did that blood-hued morning, when she had betrayed the entire human race, really happen? And those murders . . .

Ye tried to numb herself with work so as to forget

the past—and almost succeeded. A strange kind of self-protective instinct caused her to stop recalling the past, to stop thinking about the communication she had once had with another civilization. Her life passed this way, day after day, in tranquility.

After she had been back at Tsinghua for a while, Ye took Dong Dong to see her grandmother, Shao Lin. After her husband's death, Shao had soon recovered from her mental breakdown and found ways to survive in the tiny cracks of politics. Her attempts to chase the political winds and shout the right slogans finally paid off, and later, during the "Return to Class, Continue the Revolution" phase, she went back to teaching.[36]

But then Shao did something that no one expected. She married a persecuted high-level cadre from the Education Ministry. At that time, the cadre still lived in a "cowshed" for reform through labor.[37] This was part of Shao's long-term plan. She knew that the chaos in society could not last long. The young rebels who were attacking everything in sight had no experience in managing a country. Sooner or later, the persecuted and sidelined old cadres would be back in power.

Her gamble paid off. Even before the end of the Cultural Revolution, her husband was partially restored to his old

36 *Translator's Note:* During the initial phase of the Cultural Revolution, all classes ceased at colleges and elementary, junior high, and high schools as older students became Red Guards. The resulting chaos finally caused the leadership in Beijing to ask students to return to class in late 1967 and continue the revolution in a more controlled manner.

37 *Translator's Note:* "Cowsheds" were locations set up by work units (factories, schools, towns, etc.) during the early phases of the Cultural Revolution to detain the counter-revolutionary "Monsters and Demons" (reactionary academic authorities, rightists, the Five Black Categories, etc.) at the work unit.

position. After the Third Plenary Session of the Eleventh CPC Central Committee,[38] he was soon promoted to the level of a deputy minister. Based on this background, Shao Lin also rose quickly as intellectuals became favored again. After becoming a member of the Chinese Academy of Sciences, she very wisely left her old school and was promoted to be the vice president of another famous university.

Ye Wenjie saw this new version of her mother as the very model of an educated woman who knew how to take care of herself. There was not a hint of the persecution that she went through. She enthusiastically welcomed Ye and Dong Dong, inquired after Ye's life during those years with concern, exclaimed that Dong Dong was so cute and smart, and meticulously directed the cook in preparing Ye's favorite dishes. Everything was done with skill, practice, and the appropriate level of care. But Ye could clearly detect an invisible wall between her mother and herself. They carefully avoided sensitive topics and never mentioned Ye's father.

After dinner, Shao Lin and her husband accompanied Ye and Dong Dong down to the street to say good-bye. Then Shao Lin returned home while the deputy minister asked to have a word with Ye. In a moment, the deputy minister's kind smile turned to frost, as though he had impatiently pulled off his mask.

"We're happy to have you and the child visit in the future under one condition: Do not try to pursue old historical debts. Your mother bears no responsibility for your father's death. She was a victim as well. Your father clung to his own faith in a manner that was not healthy and walked all the

38 *Translator's Note:* This meeting marked the beginning of the "Reform and Opening Up" policy and was seen as the moment when Deng Xiaoping became the leader of China.

way down a blind alley. He abandoned his responsibility to his family and caused you and your mother to suffer."

"You have no right to speak of my father," Ye said, anger suffusing her voice. "This is between my mother and me. It has nothing to do with you."

"You're right," Shao Lin's husband said coldly. "I'm only passing on a message from your mother."

Ye looked up at the residential apartment building reserved for high-level cadres. Shao Lin had lifted a corner of the curtain to peek down at them. Without a word, Ye bent down to pick up Dong Dong and left. She never returned.

Ye searched and searched for information about the four female Red Guards who had killed her father, and eventually managed to locate three of them. All three had been sent down to the countryside[39] and then returned, and all were unemployed. After Ye got their addresses, she wrote a brief letter to each of them, asking them to meet her at the exercise grounds where her father had died. Just to talk.

Ye had no desire for revenge. Back at Red Coast Base, on that morning of the transmission, she had gotten revenge against the entire human race, including those Red Guards. But she wanted to hear these murderers repent, wanted to see even a hint of the return of humanity.

That afternoon after class, Ye waited for them on the exercise grounds. She didn't have much hope, and was almost

39 *Translator's Note*: In the later years of the Cultural Revolution, privileged, educated urban youths were sent down to the poor, mountainous countryside to live with and learn from the farmers there. Many of these so-called "Rusticated Youths" were former Red Guards, and some commentators believe that the policy was instituted by Chairman Mao to restore order by removing the rebels, who had gotten out of control, from the cities.

certain that they wouldn't show up. But at the time of the appointment, the three old Red Guards came.

Ye recognized them from a distance because they were all dressed in now-rare green military uniforms. When they came closer, she realized that the uniforms were likely the same ones they had worn at that mass struggle session. The clothes had been laundered until their color had faded, and they had been conspicuously patched. Other than the uniforms, the three women in their thirties no longer resembled the three young Red Guards who had looked so valiant on that day. They had lost not only youth, but also something else.

The first impression Ye had was that, though the three had once seemed to be carved out of the same mold, they now looked very different from each other. One had become very thin and small, and her uniform hung loose on her. Already showing her age, her back was bent and her hair had a yellow tint. Another had become thick framed, so that the uniform jacket she wore could not even be buttoned. Her hair was messy and her face dark, as though the hardship of life had robbed her of any feminine refinement, leaving behind only numbness and rudeness. The third woman still had hints of her youthful appearance, but one of her sleeves was now empty and hung loose as she walked.

The three old Red Guards stood in front of Ye in a row— just like they had stood against Ye Zhetai—trying to recapture their long-forgotten dignity. But the demonic spiritual energy that had once propelled them was gone. The thin woman's face held a mouselike expression. The thickset woman's face showed only numbness. The one-armed woman gazed up at the sky.

"Did you think we wouldn't dare to show up?" the thickset woman asked, her tone trying to be provocative.

"I thought we should see each other. There should be some closure to the past," Ye said.

"The past is finished. You should know that." The thin woman's voice was sharp, as though she was always frightened of something.

"I meant spiritual closure."

"Then you want to hear us repent?" the thick woman asked.

"Don't you think you should?"

"Then who will repent to us?" the one-armed woman asked.

The thickset woman said, "Of the four of us, three had signed the big-character poster at the high school attached to Tsinghua. Revolutionary tours, the great rallies in Tiananmen, the Red Guard Civil Wars, First Red Headquarters, Second Red Headquarters, Third Red Headquarters, Joint Action Committee, Western Pickets, Eastern Pickets, New Peking University Commune, Red Flag Combat Team, The East is Red—we went through every single milestone in the history of the Red Guards from birth to death."

The one-armed woman took over. "During the Hundred-Day War at Tsinghua, two of us were with the Jinggang Mountain Corps, and the other two were with the April Fourteenth Faction. I held a grenade and attacked a home-made tank from the Jinggang Mountain faction. My arm was crushed by the treads on the tank. My blood and muscle and bones were ground into the mud. I was only fifteen years old."[40]

40 *Translator's Note:* The Hundred-Day War at Tsinghua University was one of the most violent Red Guard civil wars during the Cultural Revolution. Fought between two Red Guard factions, it lasted from April 23 to July 27 in 1968. Mêlée weapons, guns, grenades, mines, cannons, etc. were all used. In the end, eighteen people died, more than eleven hundred were wounded, and more than thirty were permanently disabled.

"Then, we were sent to the wilderness!" The thickset woman raised her arms. "Two of us were sent to Shaanxi, the other two to Henan, all to the most remote and poorest corners. When we first went, we were still idealistic, but that didn't last. After a day of laboring in the fields, we were so tired that we couldn't even wash our clothes. We lay in leaky straw huts and listened to wolves cry in the night, and gradually we woke from our dreams. We were stuck in those forgotten villages and no one cared about us at all."

The one-armed woman stared at the ground numbly. "While we were down in the countryside, sometimes, on a trail across the barren hill, I'd bump into another Red Guard comrade or an enemy. We'd look at each other: the same ragged clothes, the same dirt and cow shit covering us. We had nothing to say to each other."

The thickset woman stared at Ye. "Tang Hongjing was the girl who gave your father the fatal strike with her belt. She drowned in the Yellow River. There was a flood that carried off a few of the sheep kept by the production team. So the Party secretary called to the sent-down students, 'Revolutionary youths! It's time to test your mettle!' And so, Hongjing and three other students jumped into the river to save the sheep. It was early spring, and the surface of the river was still covered by a thin layer of ice. All four died, and no one knew if it was from drowning or freezing. When I saw their bodies . . . I . . . I . . . can't fucking talk about this anymore." She covered her eyes and sobbed.

The thin woman sighed, tears in her eyes. "Then, later, we returned to the city. But so what if we're back? We still have nothing. Rusticated youths who have returned don't lead very good lives. We can't even find the worst jobs. No job, no money, no future. We have nothing."

Ye had no words.

The one-armed woman said, "There was a movie called *Maple* recently. I don't know if you've seen it. At the end, an adult and a child stand in front of the grave of a Red Guard who had died during the faction civil wars. The child asks the adult, 'Are they heroes?' The adult says no. The child asks, 'Are they enemies?' The adult again says no. The child asks, 'Then who are they?' The adult says, 'History.' "

"Did you hear that?" The thickset woman waved an arm excitedly at Ye. "History! History! It's a new age now. Who will remember us? Who will think of us, including you? Everyone will forget all this completely!"

The three old Red Guards departed, leaving only Ye on the exercise grounds. More than a dozen years ago, on that rainy afternoon, she had stood alone here as well, gazing at her dead father. The old Red Guard's final remark echoed endlessly in her mind. . . .

The setting sun cast a long shadow from Ye's slender figure. The small sliver of hope for society that had emerged in her soul had evaporated like a drop of dew in the sun. Her tiny sense of doubt about her supreme act of betrayal had also disappeared without a trace.

Ye finally had her unshakable ideal: to bring superior civilization from elsewhere in the universe into the human world.

EVANS

Half a year after her return to Tsinghua, Ye took on an important task: the design of a large radio astronomy observatory. She and the task force traveled around the country to find the best site for the observatory. The initial considerations were purely technical. Unlike traditional astronomy, radio astronomy didn't have as many demands on atmospheric quality, but required minimal electromagnetic interference. They traveled to many places and finally picked a place with the cleanest electromagnetic environment: a remote, hilly area in the Northwest.

The loess hills here had little vegetation cover. Rifts from erosion made the slopes look like old faces full of wrinkles. After selecting a few possible sites, the task force stayed for a brief rest at a village where most of the inhabitants still lived in traditional cave dwellings. The village's production team leader recognized Ye as an educated person and asked her whether she knew how to speak a foreign language. She asked him which foreign language, and he said he didn't know. However, if she did know a foreign tongue, he would send someone up the hill to call down Bethune, because the

production team needed to discuss something with him.[41]

"Bethune?" Ye was amazed.

"We don't know the foreigner's real name, so we just call him that."

"Is he a doctor?"

"No. He's planting trees up in the hills. Has been at it for almost three years."

"Planting trees? What for?"

"He says it's for the birds. A kind of bird that he says is almost extinct."

Ye and her colleagues were curious and asked the production team leader to bring them for a visit. They followed a trail until they were on top of a small hillock. The team leader showed them a place among the barren loess hills. Ye felt it brighten before her eyes. There was a slope covered by green forests, as though an old, yellowing canvas had been accidentally blessed with a splash of green paint.

Ye and the others soon saw the foreigner. Other than his blond hair and green eyes and tattered jeans and a jacket that reminded her of a cowboy, he didn't look too different from the local peasants who had labored all their lives. Even his skin had the same dark hue from the sun as the locals. He didn't show much interest in the visitors. He introduced himself as Mike Evans without mentioning his nationality, but his English was clearly American-accented. He lived in a simple two-room adobe hut, which was filled with tools for planting trees: hoes, shovels, saws for pruning tree branches, and so on, all of which were locally made and crude.

41 *Translator's Note:* Norman Bethune (1890–1939) was a Canadian surgeon who served with the Chinese Communists in their fight against the Japanese invasion force during World War II. As one of the few Westerners who showed friendship to the Chinese Communists, Bethune became a Chinese hero known to the elderly and children alike.

The dust that permeated the Northwest lay in a thin layer over his simple and rough-hewn bed and kitchen implements. A pile of books, most of which dealt with biology, sat on his bed. Ye noticed a copy of Peter Singer's *Animal Liberation*. The only sign of modernity was a small radio set, hooked up to an external D battery. There was also an old telescope.

Evans apologized for not being able to offer them anything to drink. He hadn't had coffee for a while. There was water, but he only had one cup.

"May we ask what you're really doing here?" one of Ye's colleagues asked.

"I want to save lives."

"Save . . . save the locals? It's true that the ecological conditions here—"

"Why are you all like this?" Evans suddenly became furious. "Why does one have to save *people* to be considered a hero? Why is saving other species considered insignificant? Who gave humans such high honors? No, humans do not need saving. They're already living much better than they deserve."

"We heard that you are trying to save a type of bird."

"Yes, a swallow. It's a subspecies of the northwestern brown swallow. The Latin name is very long, so I won't bore you with it. Every spring, they follow ancient, established migratory paths to return from the south. They nest only here, but as the forest disappears year after year, they can no longer find the trees in which to build their nests. When I discovered them, the species had less than ten thousand individuals left. If the trend continues, within five years it will be extinct. The trees I've planted now provide a habitat for some of them, and the population is rising again. I must plant more trees and expand this Eden."

Evans allowed Ye and the others to look through his

telescope. With his help, they finally saw a few tiny black birds darting through the trees.

"Not very pretty, are they? Of course, they're not as crowd-pleasing as giant pandas. Every day on this planet some species that doesn't draw the attention of humans goes extinct."

"Did you plant all of these trees by yourself?"

"Most of them. Initially I hired some locals to help, but soon I ran out of money. Saplings and irrigation all cost a lot—but you know something? My father is a billionaire. He is the president of an international oil company, but he will not give me any more funding, and I don't want to use his money anymore."

Now that Evans had opened up, he seemed to want to pour his heart out. "When I was twelve, a thirty-thousand-ton oil tanker from my father's company ran aground along the Atlantic coast. More than twenty thousand tons of crude oil spilled into the ocean. At the time, my family was staying at a coastal vacation home not too far from the site of the accident. After my father heard the news, the first thing he thought of was how to avoid responsibility and minimize damage to the company.

"That afternoon, I went to see the hellish coast. The sea was black, and the waves, under the sticky, thick film of oil, were smooth and weak. The beach was also covered by a black layer of crude oil. Some volunteers and I searched for birds on the beach that were still alive. They struggled in the sticky oil, looking like black statues made out of asphalt, only their eyes proving that they were still alive. Those eyes staring out of the oil still haunt my dreams to this day. We soaked those birds in detergent, trying to get rid of the oil stuck to their bodies. But it was extremely difficult: crude oil was infused into their feathers, and if you brushed a little too

hard, the feathers would come off with the oil. . . . By that evening, most of the birds had died. As I sat on the black beach, exhausted and covered in oil, I stared at the sun setting over a black sea and felt like it was the end of the world.

"My father came up behind me without my noticing. He asked me if I still remembered the small dinosaur skeleton. Of course I remembered. The nearly complete skeleton had been discovered during oil exploration. My father spent a large sum to buy it, and installed it on the grounds of my grandfather's mansion.

"My father then said, 'Mike, I've told you how dinosaurs went extinct. An asteroid crashed into the Earth. The world first became a sea of fire, and then sank into a prolonged period of darkness and coldness. . . . One night, you woke from a nightmare, saying that you had dreamt that you were back in that terrifying age. Let me tell you now what I wanted to tell you that night: If you really lived during the Cretaceous Period, you'd be fortunate. The period we live in now is far more frightening. Right now, species on Earth are going extinct far faster than during the late Cretaceous. Now is truly the age of mass extinctions! So, my child, what you're seeing is nothing. This is only an insignificant episode in a much vaster process. We can have no sea birds, but we can't be without oil. Can you imagine life without oil? Your last birthday, I gave you that lovely Ferrari and promised you that you could drive it after you turned fifteen. But without oil, it would be a pile of junk metal and you'd never drive it. Right now, if you want to visit your grandfather, you can get there on my personal jet and cross the ocean in a dozen hours or so. But without oil, you'd have to tumble in a sailboat for more than a month. . . . These are the rules of the game of civilization: The first priority is to guarantee the existence of

the human race and their comfortable life. Everything else is secondary.'

"My father placed a great deal of hope in me, but in the end I didn't turn out the way he wanted. In the days after that, the eyes of those drowned birds always followed me and determined my life. When I was thirteen, my father asked me what I wanted to do when I grew up. I said I wanted to save lives. My dream wasn't that great. I only wanted to save a species near extinction. It could be a bird that wasn't very pretty, a drab butterfly, or a beetle that no one would even notice. Later, I studied biology, and became a specialist on birds and insects. The way I see it, my ideal is worthy. Saving a species of bird or insect is no different from saving humankind. 'All lives are equal' is the basic tenet of Pan-Species Communism."

"What?" Ye wasn't sure she had heard the last term correctly.

"Pan-Species Communism. It's an ideology I invented. Or maybe you can call it a faith. Its core belief is that all species on Earth are created equal."

"That is an impractical ideal. Our crops are also living species. If humans are to survive, that kind of equality is impossible."

"Slave owners must also have thought that about their slaves in the distant past. And don't forget technology— there will be a day when humanity can manufacture food. We should lay down the ideological and theoretical foundation long before that. Indeed, Pan-Species Communism is a natural continuation of the Universal Declaration of Human Rights. The French Revolution was two hundred years ago, and we haven't even taken a step beyond that. From this we can see the hypocrisy and selfishness of the human race."

"How long do you intend to stay here?"

"I don't know. I'm prepared to devote my life to the task. The feeling is beautiful. Of course, I don't expect you to understand."

Evans seemed to lose interest. He said that he had to go back to work, so he picked up a shovel and a saw and then left. When he said good-bye, he glanced at Ye again, as though there was something unusual about her.

On the way back, one of Ye's colleagues recited from Chairman Mao's essay "Remembering Bethune": " 'Noble-minded and pure, a man of moral integrity and above vulgar interests.' " He sighed. "There really are people who can live like that."

Others also expressed their admiration and conflicted feelings. Ye seemed to be speaking to herself as she said, "If there were more men like him, even just a few more, things would have turned out differently."

Of course, no one understood what she really meant.

The task force leader turned the conversation back to their work. "I think this site isn't going to work. Our superiors won't approve it."

"Why not? Of the four possible sites, this has the best electromagnetic environment."

"What about the human environment? Comrades, don't just focus on the technical side. Look at how poor this place is. The poorer a village, the craftier the people. Do you understand? If the observatory were located here, there would be trouble between the scientists and the locals. I can imagine the peasants thinking of the astronomy complex as a juicy piece of meat that they can take bites from."

This site was indeed not approved, and the reason was just what the task force leader had said.

———

Three years passed without Ye hearing anything more about Evans.

But one spring day, Ye received a postcard from Evans with only a single line: "Come here. Tell me how to go on."

Ye rode the train for a day and a night, and then switched to a bus for many hours until she arrived at the village nestled in the remote hills of the Northwest.

As soon as she climbed onto that small hillock, she saw the forest again. Because the trees had grown, it now seemed far denser, but Ye noticed that the forest had once been much bigger. Newer parts that had grown in the past few years had already been cut.

The logging was in full swing. In every direction, trees were falling. The entire forest seemed like a mulberry leaf being devoured by silkworms on all sides. At the current rate, it would disappear soon. The workers doing the logging came from two nearby villages. Using axes and saws, they cut down those barely grown trees one by one, and then dragged them off the hill using tractors and ox carts. There were many loggers, and fights frequently erupted among them.

The fall of each small tree didn't make much sound, and there was no loud buzzing from chain saws, but the almost-familiar scene made Ye's chest tighten.

Someone called out to her—that production team leader, now the village chief. He recognized Ye. When she asked him why they were cutting down the forest, he said, "This forest isn't protected by law."

"How can that be? The Forestry Law has just been promulgated."

"But who ever gave Bethune permission to plant trees here? A foreigner coming here to plant trees without approval would not be protected by any law."

"You can't think that way. He was planting on the barren hills and didn't take up any arable land. Also, back when he started, you didn't object."

"That's true. The county actually gave him an award for planting the trees. The villagers originally planned to cut down the forest in a few more years—it's best to wait until the pig is fat before slaughtering it, am I right? But those people from Nange Village can't wait any longer, and if my village doesn't join in, we won't get any."

"You must stop immediately. I will go to the government to report this!"

"There's no need." The village chief lit a cigarette and pointed to a truck loading the cut trees in the distance. "See that? That's from the deputy secretary of the County Forestry Bureau. And there are also people here from the town police department. They've carried off more trees than anyone else! I told you, these trees have no status and aren't protected. You'll never find anyone who cares. Also, comrade, aren't you a college professor? What does this have to do with you?"

The adobe hut looked the same, but Evans wasn't inside. Ye found him in the woods holding an ax and carefully pruning a tree. He had obviously been at it for a while, his posture full of exhaustion.

"I don't care if this is meaningless. I can't stop. If I stop I'll fall apart." Evans cut down a crooked branch with a practiced swing.

"Let's go together to the county government. If they won't do anything, we'll go up to the provincial government. Someone will stop them." Ye looked at Evans with concern.

Evans stopped and stared at Ye in surprise. Light from the setting sun slanted through the trees and made his eyes sparkle. "Ye, do you really think I'm doing this because of this

forest?" He laughed and shook his head, then dropped the ax. He sat down, his back against a tree. "If I want to stop them, it'd be easy. I just returned from America. My father died two months ago, and I inherited most of his money. My brother and sister only got five million each. This wasn't what I expected at all. Maybe in his heart, he still respected me. Or maybe he respected my ideals. Not including fixed assets, do you know how much money I have at my disposal? About four point five billion dollars. I could easily ask them to stop and get them to plant more trees. I could make all the loess hills within sight be covered by quick-growth forest. But what would be the point?

"Everything you see before you is the result of poverty. But how are things any better in the wealthy countries? They protect their own environments, but then shift the heavily polluting industries to the poorer nations. You probably know that the American government just refused to sign the Kyoto Protocol. . . . The entire human race is the same. As long as civilization continues to develop, the swallows I want to save and all the other swallows will go extinct. It's just a matter of time."

Ye sat silently, gazing at the rays of light cast among the trees by the setting sun, listening to the noise from the loggers. Her thoughts returned to twenty years ago, to the forests of the Greater Khingan Mountains, where she had once had a similar conversation with another man.

"Do you know why I came here?" Evans continued. "The seeds of Pan-Species Communism had sprouted long ago in the ancient East."

"You're thinking of Buddhism?"

"Yes. The focus of Christianity is Man. Even though all the species were placed into Noah's Ark, other species were never given the same status as humans. But Buddhism is

focused on saving all life. That was why I came to the East. But . . . it's obvious now that everywhere is the same."

"Yes, that's true. Everywhere, people are the same."

"What can I do now? What is the purpose of my life? I have four point five billion dollars and an international oil company. But what good is all that? Humans have surely invested more than forty-five billion dollars in saving species near extinction. And probably more than four hundred and fifty billion has already been spent on saving the environment from degradation. But what's the use? Civilization continues to follow its path of destruction of all life on Earth except humans. Four point five billion is enough to build an aircraft carrier, but even if we build a thousand aircraft carriers, it would be impossible to stop the madness of humanity."

"Mike, this is what I wanted to tell you. Human civilization is no longer capable of improving by its own strength."

"Can there be any source of power outside of humanity? Even if God once existed, He died long ago."

"Yes, there are other powers."

The sun had set and the loggers had left. The forest and the loess hills were silent. Ye now told Evans the whole story of Red Coast and Trisolaris. Evans listened quietly, and the loess hills and the forest in dusk seemed to listen as well. When Ye was finished, a bright moon rose from the east and cast speckled shadows on the forest floor.

Evans said, "I still can't believe what you just told me. It's too fantastic. But luckily, I have the resources to confirm this. If what you told me is true"—he extended his hand and spoke the words that every new member of the future ETO would have to say upon joining—"let us be comrades."

28

THE SECOND RED COAST BASE

Three more years passed. Evans seemed to have disappeared. Ye didn't know if he really was somewhere in the world working to confirm her story, and had no idea how he would confirm it. Even though, by the scale of the universe, a gap of four light-years was as close as touching, it was still a distance that was unimaginably far for fragile life. The two worlds were like the source and mouth of a river that crossed space. Any connections between them would be extremely attenuated.

One winter, Ye received an invitation from a not-very-prominent university in Western Europe to be a visiting scholar for half a year. After she landed at Heathrow for her interview, a young man came to meet her. They didn't leave the airport, but instead turned back to the landing strip. There, he escorted her onto a helicopter.

As the helicopter roared into the foggy air over England, time seemed to rewind and Ye experienced déjà vu. Many years ago, when she first rode in a helicopter, her life was transformed. Where would fate bring her now?

"We're going to the Second Red Coast Base."

The helicopter passed the coastline and continued toward the heart of the Atlantic. After half an hour, the helicopter descended toward a huge ship in the ocean. As soon as Ye

saw the ship, she thought of Radar Peak. Only now did she realize that the shape of the peak did resemble a giant ship. The Atlantic appeared like the forest of the Greater Khingan Mountains, but the thing that reminded her most of Red Coast Base was the huge parabolic antenna erected in the middle of the ship, which resembled a round sail. The ship was modified from a sixty-thousand-ton oil tanker, like a floating steel island. Evans had built his base on a ship—maybe it was so that it would always be at the best position for transmission and reception, or maybe it was to hide from detection. Later, she learned that the ship was called *Judgment Day*.

Ye stepped off the helicopter and heard a familiar howl. It was caused by the giant antenna slicing through the wind over the sea. The sound again drew her thoughts to the past. On the broad deck below the antenna, about two thousand people stood in a dense crowd.

Evans walked up to her and solemnly said, "Using the frequency and coordinates you provided, we received a message from Trisolaris. We've confirmed everything you told me."

Ye nodded calmly.

"The great Trisolaran Fleet has already set sail. Their target is this solar system, and they will arrive in four hundred and fifty years."

Ye remained calm. Nothing could surprise her anymore.

Evans pointed to the crowd behind him. "You're looking at the first members of the Earth-Trisolaris Organization. Our ideal is to invite Trisolaran civilization to reform human civilization, to curb human madness and evil, so that the Earth can once again become a harmonious, prosperous, sinless world. More and more people identify with our ideal, and our organization is growing rapidly. We have members all over the world."

"What can I do?" Ye asked in a soft voice.

"You will become the commander in chief of the Earth-Trisolaris Movement. This is the wish of all ETO fighters."

Ye remained silent for a few seconds. Then she nodded slowly. "I'll do my best."

Evans raised a fist and shouted at the crowd, "Eliminate human tyranny!"

Accompanied by the sound of crashing waves and the wind howling against the antenna, the ETO fighters shouted as one, "The world belongs to Trisolaris!"

This was the day that the Earth-Trisolaris Movement formally began.

29

THE EARTH-TRISOLARIS MOVEMENT

The most surprising aspect of the Earth-Trisolaris Movement was that so many people had abandoned all hope in human civilization, hated and were willing to betray their own species, and even cherished as their highest ideal the elimination of the entire human race, including themselves and their children.

The ETO was called an organization of spiritual nobles. Most members came from the highly educated classes, and many were elites of the political and financial spheres. The ETO had once tried to develop membership among the common people, but these efforts all failed. The ETO concluded that the common people did not seem to have the comprehensive and deep understanding of the highly educated about the dark side of humanity. More importantly, because their thoughts were not as deeply influenced by modern science and philosophy, they still felt an overwhelming, instinctual identification with their own species. To betray the human race as a whole was unimaginable for them. But intellectual elites were different: Most of them had already begun to consider issues from a perspective outside the human race. Human civilization had finally given birth to a strong force of alienation.

As astounding as the speed of the ETO's growth had been, the number of members did not tell the whole story of the ETO's strength. Because most of its members had high social status, they held a lot of power and influence.

As commander in chief of the ETO rebels, Ye was only their spiritual leader. She did not participate in the details of the organization's operation, didn't know how the ETO grew so large, and wasn't even aware of the exact number of members.

In order to grow fast, the organization operated semi-openly, but the governments of the world never paid much attention to the ETO. The ETO knew that they would be protected by the governments' conservatism and lack of imagination. In those organs wielding the powers of the state, no one took the ETO's proclamations seriously, thinking that they were like other extremists who spewed nonsense. And because of its members' social status, governments always treated it carefully. By the time it was recognized as a threat, the rebels were already everywhere. It was only when the ETO began to develop an armed force that some national security organs began to notice it and realized how unusual it was. Consequently, it was only within the last two years that they had begun to attack the ETO effectively.

The members of the ETO were not of a single mind. Within the organization were complicated factions and divisions of opinion. Mainly, they fell into two factions.

The Adventist group was the purest, most fundamentalist strand of the ETO, comprised mainly of believers in Evans's Pan-Species Communism. They had completely given up hope in human nature. This despair began with the mass extinctions of the Earth's species caused by modern civilization. Later, other Adventists based their hatred of the human

345

race on other foundations, not limited to issues such as the environment or warfare. Some raised their hatred to very abstract, philosophical levels. Unlike how they would be imagined later, most of them were realists, and did not place too much hope in the alien civilization they served either. Their betrayal was based only on their despair and hatred of the human race. Mike Evans gave the Adventists their motto: We don't know what extraterrestrial civilization is like, but we know humanity.

The Redemptionists didn't appear until long after the ETO's founding. This group's nature was a religious organization, and the members were believers in the Trisolaran faith.

A civilization outside the human race would doubtlessly greatly attract the highly educated classes, and it was easy for them to develop many beautiful fantasies about such a civilization. The human race was a naïve species, and the attraction posed by a more advanced alien civilization was almost irresistible. To make an imperfect analogy: Human civilization was like a young, unworldly person walking alone across the desert of the universe, who has found out about the existence of a potential lover. Though the person could not see the potential lover's face or figure, the knowledge that the other person existed somewhere in the distance created lovely fantasies about the potential lover that spread like wildfire. Gradually, as fantasies about that distant civilization grew more and more elaborate, the Redemptionists developed spiritual feelings toward Trisolaran civilization. Alpha Centauri became Mount Olympus in space, the dwelling place of the gods; and so the Trisolaran religion—which really had nothing to do with religion on Trisolaris—was born. Unlike other human religions, they worshipped something that truly existed. Also unlike other human religions,

it was the Lord who was in crisis, and the duty of salvation fell on the shoulders of the believer.

The main path of spreading Trisolaran culture to society was the *Three Body* game. The ETO invested enormous effort to develop this massive piece of software. The initial goals were twofold: one, to proselytize the Trisolaran religion; and two, to allow the tentacles of the ETO to spread from the highly educated intelligentsia to the lower social strata, and recruit younger ETO members from the middle and lower classes.

Using a shell that drew elements from human society and history, the game explained the culture and history of Trisolaris, thus avoiding alienating beginners. Once a player had advanced to a certain level and had begun to appreciate Trisolaran civilization, the ETO would establish contact, examine the player's sympathies, and finally recruit those who passed the tests to be members of the ETO. But *Three Body* didn't attract much notice, because the game required too much background knowledge and in-depth thinking, and most young players didn't have the patience or skill to discover the shocking truth beneath its apparently common surface. Those who were attracted by it were still mostly intellectuals.

Most of those who became Redemptionists got to know Trisolaran civilization through the *Three Body* game, and so *Three Body* could be said to be the cradle of the Redemptionists.

While the Redemptionists developed religious feelings toward Trisolaran civilization, they were also not as extreme as the Adventists in their attitude toward human civilization. Their ultimate ideal was to save the Lord. In order to allow the Lord to continue to exist, they were willing to sacrifice the human world to some degree. But most of them believed that the ideal solution would be to find a way to

allow the Lord to continue to live in the Trisolaris stellar system and avoid the invasion of the Earth. Naïvely, they believed that solving the three-body problem would achieve this goal, saving both Trisolaris and the Earth. Admittedly, perhaps this thought wasn't all that naïve. Trisolaran civilization itself had thought so through many eons. The effort to solve the three-body problem was a thread that ran through several hundreds of cycles of Trisolaran civilization. Most Redemptionists with some in-depth math and physics knowledge had attempted the three-body problem, and even after knowing that the problem was mathematically unsolvable as posed, the effort did not cease, because solving the three-body problem had become a religious ritual of their faith. Even though the Redemptionists had many first-class physicists and mathematicians, research in this area never yielded any important results. It took someone like Wei Cheng, a prodigy who had no connection to the ETO or the Trisolaran faith, to accidentally come up with a breakthrough in which the Redemptionists placed much hope.

The Adventists and the Redemptionists were always in sharp conflict. The Adventists believed that the Redemptionists were the greatest threat to the ETO. This view wasn't without reason: It was only through some Redemptionists who had a sense of duty that the governments of the world gradually came to understand the shocking background of the ETO rebels. The two factions were of approximately equal strength within the organization, and the armed forces of both had developed to the point of starting a civil war. Ye Wenjie used her authority and reputation to try to patch over the division between the two, but the result was never ideal.

As the ETO movement continued to develop, a third faction appeared: the Survivors. After confirming the existence

of the alien invasion fleet, surviving that war became a most natural human desire. Of course, that war wouldn't occur for another 450 years, and had nothing to do with those living today, but many people hoped that if humans *did* lose, at least their descendants who were alive in four and a half centuries could live on. Serving the Trisolaran invaders would clearly help with this goal. Compared to the other two factions, the Survivors tended to come from the lower social classes, and most were from the East, and especially from China. Their numbers were still small, but they were growing rapidly. As Trisolaran culture continued to spread, they would become a force that could not be ignored in the future.

The ETO members' alienation developed variously from the faults of human civilization itself, the yearning and adoration for a more advanced civilization, and the strong desire for one's descendants to survive that final war. These three powerful motives propelled the ETO movement to develop rapidly.

By then, the extraterrestrial civilization was still in the depths of space, more than four light-years away, separated from the human world by a long journey of four and a half centuries. The only thing they had sent to the Earth was a radio transmission.

Bill Mathers's "contact as symbol" theory thus received chillingly perfect confirmation.

30

TWO PROTONS

INTERROGATOR: We will now begin today's investigation. We hope you'll cooperate again as you did last time.

YE WENJIE: You already know everything I know. In fact, by now there are many things that I'd like to learn from you.

INTERROGATOR: I don't think you've told us everything. First, we want to know this: Among the messages that Trisolaris sent to Earth, what were the contents of those portions that the Adventists intercepted and withheld?

YE: I can't tell you. They have a tight organization. I only know that they did withhold some messages.

INTERROGATOR: Change of subject. After the Adventists monopolized communications with Trisolaris, did you build a third Red Coast Base?

YE: I did have such a plan. But we only built a receiver, and then construction stopped. The equipment and the base were all dismantled.

INTERROGATOR: Why?

YE: Because there were no more messages coming from Alpha Centauri. There was nothing on any frequency. I think you've already confirmed this.

INTERROGATOR: Yes. In other words—at least as of four years ago—Trisolaris decided to terminate all communications

with Earth. This makes the messages intercepted by the Adventists even more important.

YE: True. But there's really nothing more I can tell you about them.

INTERROGATOR: *(pausing a few seconds)* Then let's find some topic where you can tell me more. Mike Evans lied to you, is that right?

YE: You could put it that way. He never revealed to me the thoughts buried deep in his heart, and only expressed his sense of duty toward the other species on this planet. I never realized that this sense of duty had caused his hatred of human civilization to develop to such extremes that he could make the destruction of the human race his ultimate ideal.

INTERROGATOR: Let's look at the current composition of the ETO. The Adventists would like to destroy the human race by means of an alien power; the Redemptionists worship the alien civilization as a god; the Survivors wish to betray other humans to buy their own survival. None of these is in line with your original ideal of using the alien civilization as a way to reform humanity.

YE: I started the fire, but I couldn't control how it burnt.

INTERROGATOR: You had a plan to eliminate the Adventists from within the ETO, and you even began to implement this plan. But *Judgment Day* is the core base and command center for the Adventists, and Mike Evans and other Adventist leaders usually reside there. Why didn't you attack the ship first? Most of the armed forces of the Redemptionists are loyal to you, and you should have enough firepower to sink it or capture it.

YE: It's because of the messages from the Lord that they intercepted. All those messages are stored in the Second Red

Coast Base, on some computer on *Judgment Day*. If we attacked that ship, the Adventists could erase all the messages when they realized that loss was imminent. Those messages are too important for us to risk losing them. For Redemptionists, losing those messages would be as if Christians lost the Bible or Muslims lost the Koran. I think you are faced with the same problem. The Adventists are holding the Lord's messages hostage, and that is why *Judgment Day* has remained unmolested so far.

INTERROGATOR: Do you have any advice for us?

YE: No.

INTERROGATOR: You also call Trisolaris your "Lord." Does this mean that you've also developed religious feelings for Trisolaris like the Redemptionists? Are you already a follower of the Trisolaran faith?

YE: Not at all. It's just a habit. . . . I do not wish to discuss it further.

INTERROGATOR: Let's get back to those intercepted messages. Maybe you don't know the exact contents, but surely you must have heard rumors of some of the details?

YE: Probably only baseless rumors.

INTERROGATOR: Such as?

YE: . . .

INTERROGATOR: Did Trisolaris transfer certain technologies to the Adventists, technologies more advanced than current human technology?

YE: Not likely. Because such technology would risk falling into your hands.

INTERROGATOR: One last question, and also the most important: Until now, has Trisolaris sent only radio waves to the Earth?

YE: Almost true.

INTERROGATOR: Almost?

YE: The current Trisolaran civilization is capable of space travel at one-tenth the speed of light. This technology leap occurred a few decades ago in Earth years. Before that point, their maximum speed had hovered around one-thousandth the speed of light. The tiny probes that they sent to the Earth have not even completed one-hundredth of the journey between there and here.

INTERROGATOR: Then I have a question. If the Trisolaran Fleet that had been launched is capable of flight at one-tenth the speed of light, it should take only forty years to reach the solar system. So why do you say that it would take more than four hundred years?

YE: Here's the thing. The Trisolaran Interstellar Fleet is composed of incredibly massive spaceships. Accelerating them is a slow process. One-tenth the speed of light is only their maximum speed, but they cannot cruise at this speed for long before decelerating as they approach the Earth. Also, the source of propulsion for the Trisolaran ships is matter-antimatter annihilation. In front of each ship is a large magnetic field shaped like a funnel to collect antimatter particles from space. This collection process is slow, and only after a long wait can it gather enough antimatter to allow the ship to accelerate for a brief period. Thus, the fleet's acceleration occurs in spurts, interspersed by long periods of coasting to collect fuel. This is why the time it takes the Trisolaran Fleet to reach the solar system is ten times longer than the flight time of a small probe.

INTERROGATOR: Then what did you mean by "almost" just now?

YE: We're talking about the speed of space flight within a certain context. Outside this context, even backward human

beings are capable of accelerating certain objects to close to the speed of light.

INTERROGATOR: *(a pause)* By "context," do you mean at the macro scale? At a micro scale, humans can already use high-energy particle accelerators to speed up subatomic particles to near the speed of light. These particles are the "objects" you meant, correct?

YE: You're very clever.

INTERROGATOR: *(points to his earpiece)* I have the world's foremost scientists behind me.

YE: Yes, I meant subatomic particles. Six years ago, in the distant Trisolaran stellar system, Trisolaris accelerated two hydrogen nuclei to near the speed of light and shot them toward the solar system. These two hydrogen nuclei, or protons, arrived at the solar system two years ago, then reached the Earth.

INTERROGATOR: Two protons? They only sent two protons? That's almost nothing.

YE: *(laughs)* You also said "almost." That's the limit of Trisolaran power. They can only accelerate something as small as a proton to near the speed of light. So over a distance of four light-years, they can only send two protons.

INTERROGATOR: At the macroscopic level, two protons are nothing. Even a single cilium on a bacterium would include several billion protons. What's the point?

YE: They're a lock.

INTERROGATOR: A lock? What are they locking?

YE: They are sealing off the progress of human science. Because of the existence of these two protons, humanity will not be able to make any important scientific developments during the four and a half centuries until the arrival of the Trisolaran Fleet. Evans once said that the day of

arrival of the two protons was also the day that human science died.

INTERROGATOR: That's . . . too fantastic. How can that be?

YE: I don't know. I really don't know. In the eyes of Trisolaran civilization, we're probably not even primitive savages. We might be mere bugs.

It was near midnight by the time Wang Miao and Ding Yi walked out of the Battle Command Center. They had been invited to listen to Ye's interrogation due to Wang's involvement in the case and Ding Yi's connection to Ye's daughter.

"Do you believe what Ye Wenjie said?" Wang asked.

"Do you?"

"Many things that have happened recently are incredible. But for two protons to block all progress of human science? That seems . . ."

"Let's focus on one thing first. The Trisolarans were able to shoot two protons at the Earth from four light-years away and they both reached the target! That accuracy is incredible! There are numerous obstacles between there and here: interstellar dust, for example. And both the solar system and the Earth are moving. It would require more precision than shooting a mosquito here from Pluto. The shooter is beyond imagination."

Wang's heart clenched when he heard "shooter." "What do you think this means?"

"I don't know. In your impression, what do subatomic particles such as neutrons and protons look like?"

"They would just look like a point. Though the point has internal structure."

"Luckily, the image in my head is more realistic than

355

yours." As Ding spoke, he tossed his cigarette butt away. "What do you think that is?" He pointed at the butt.

"A cigarette filter."

"Good. Looking at that tiny thing from this distance, how would you describe it?"

"It's practically just a point."

"Right." Ding walked over and picked up the butt. In front of Wang's eyes he tore it open and revealed the yellowed spongy material inside. Wang smelled burnt tar. Ding continued, "Look, if you spread this little thing open, the adsorbent surface area can be as large as a living room." He tossed the filter away. "Do you smoke pipes?"

"I no longer smoke anything."

"Pipes use another type of more advanced filter. You can get one for three yuan. The diameter is about the same as a cigarette filter, but it's longer: a small paper tube filled with active charcoal. If you take out all the active charcoal, it will look like a little pile of black particles, like mouse droppings. But added together, the adsorbent surface formed by the tiny holes inside is as large as a tennis court. This is why active charcoal is so adsorbent."

"What are you trying to say?" Wang asked, listening intently.

"The sponge or active charcoal inside a filter is three-dimensional. Their adsorbent surfaces, however, are two-dimensional. Thus, you can see how a tiny high-dimensional structure can contain a huge low-dimensional structure. But at the macroscopic level, this is about the limit of the ability for high-dimensional space to contain low-dimensional space. Because God was stingy, during the big bang He only provided the macroscopic world with three spatial dimensions, plus the dimension of time. But this

doesn't mean that higher dimensions don't exist. Up to seven additional dimensions are locked within the micro scale, or, more precisely, within the quantum realm. And added to the four dimensions at the macro scale, fundamental particles exist within an eleven-dimensional space-time."

"So what?"

"I just want to point out this fact: In the universe, an important mark of a civilization's technological advancement is its ability to control and make use of micro dimensions. Making use of fundamental particles without taking advantage of the micro dimensions is something that our naked, hairy ancestors already began back when they lit bonfires within caves. Controlling chemical reactions is just manipulating micro particles without regard to the micro dimensions. Of course, this control also progressed from crude to advanced: from bonfires to steam engines, and then generators. Now, the ability for humans to manipulate micro particles at the macro level has reached a peak: We have computers and nanomaterials. But all of that is accomplished without unlocking the many micro dimensions. From the perspective of a more advanced civilization in the universe, bonfires and computers and nanomaterials are not fundamentally different. They all belong to the same level. That's also why they still think of humans as mere bugs. Unfortunately, I think they're right."

"Can you be more specific? What does all this have to do with those two protons? Ultimately, what can the two protons that have reached the Earth do? Like the interrogator said, a single cilium on a bacterium can contain several billion protons. Even if these two protons turned entirely into energy on the tip of my finger, at most it would feel like a pinprick."

"You wouldn't feel anything. Even if they turned into energy on a bacterium, the bacterium probably wouldn't feel anything."

"Then what were you trying to say?"

"Nothing. I don't know anything. What can a bug know?"

"But you're a physicist among bugs. You know more than I do. At least you aren't completely at a loss when faced with the knowledge of these protons. I beg you. Tell me. Otherwise I won't be able to sleep tonight."

"If I tell you more, you really won't be able to sleep. Forget it. What's the point of worrying? We should learn to be as philosophical as Wei Cheng and Shi Qiang. Just do the best within your responsibility. Let's go drinking and then go back to sleep like good bugs."

31

OPERATION GUZHENG

"Don't worry," Shi Qiang said to Wang, as he sat down next to him at the meeting table. "I'm not radioactive anymore. The last couple of days they've washed me inside and outside like a flour sack. They didn't originally think you needed to attend this meeting, but I insisted. Heh. I bet the two of us are going to be important this time."

As Da Shi spoke, he picked a cigar butt out of the ashtray, lit it, and took a long drag. He nodded, and, in a slow, relaxed manner, blew the smoke into the faces of the attendees sitting on the other side of the table. One of the people sitting opposite him was the original owner of the cigar, Colonel Stanton of the U.S. Marine Corps. He gave Da Shi a contemptuous look.

Many more foreign military officers were at this meeting than the last. They were all in uniform. For the first time in human history, the armed forces of the world's nations faced the same enemy.

General Chang said, "Comrades, everyone at this meeting now has the same basic understanding of the situation. Or, as Da Shi here would put it, we have information parity. The war between alien invaders and humanity has begun. Our descendants won't face the Trisolarans for another four and

a half centuries. For now, our opponents are still human. Yet, in essence, these traitors to the human race can also be seen as enemies from outside human civilization. We have never faced an enemy like this. The next war objective is very clear: We must capture the intercepted Trisolaran messages stored on *Judgment Day*. These messages may have great significance for our survival.

"We haven't yet done anything to draw the suspicion of *Judgment Day*. The ship still sails the Atlantic freely. It has already submitted plans to the Panama Canal Authority to pass through the canal in four days. This is a great opportunity for us. As the situation develops, such an opportunity may never arise again. Right now, all the Battle Command Centers around the globe are drafting up operation plans, and Central will select one within ten hours and begin implementation. The purpose of this meeting is to discuss possible plans of operation, and then report one to three of our best suggestions to Central. Time is of the essence, and we must work efficiently.

"Note that any plan must guarantee one thing: the secure capture of the Trisolaran messages. *Judgment Day* was rebuilt from an old tanker, and both the superstructure and the interior have been extensively renovated with complex structures to contain many new rooms and passageways. Supposedly even the crew relies on a map when entering unfamiliar areas. We, of course, know even less about the ship's layout. Right now, we cannot even be certain of the location of the computing center on *Judgment Day,* and we don't know whether the intercepted Trisolaran messages are stored in servers located in the computing center, or how many copies they have. The only way to achieve our objective is to completely capture and control *Judgment Day*.

"The most difficult part is preventing the enemy from erasing Trisolaran data during our attack. Destroying the data would be very easy. The enemy would not use conventional methods to erase the data during an attack, because it's easy to recover the data using known technology. But if they just emptied a cartridge clip at the server hard drive or other storage media, it would all be over, and doing so would take no more than ten seconds. So we must disable all enemies near the storage equipment within ten seconds of their detecting an attack. Since we don't know the exact location of the data storage or the number of copies, we must eliminate all enemies on *Judgment Day* within a very brief period of time, before the target has been alerted. At the same time, we can't heavily damage the facilities within, especially computer equipment. Thus, this is a very difficult task. Some think it's impossible."

A Japanese Self-Defense Forces officer said, "We believe that the only chance for success is to rely on spies on *Judgment Day*. If they're familiar with where the Trisolaran information is stored, they can control the area or move the storage equipment elsewhere right before our operation."

Someone asked, "Reconnaissance and monitoring of *Judgment Day* have always been the responsibility of NATO military intelligence and the CIA. Do we have such spies?"

"No," the NATO liaison said.

"Then we have nothing more to discuss except bullshit," said Da Shi. He was met with annoyed looks.

Colonel Stanton said, "Since the objective is eliminating all personnel within an enclosed structure without harming other equipment within, our first thought was to use a ball lightning weapon."

Ding Yi shook his head. "The existence of this kind of weapon is now public knowledge. We don't know if the ship

has been equipped with magnetic walls to shield against ball lightning. Even if it hasn't, a ball lightning weapon can indeed kill all personnel within the ship, but it cannot do so simultaneously. Also, after the ball lightning enters the ship, it may hover in the air for some time before releasing its energy. This wait time can last from a dozen seconds to a minute or longer. They will have enough time to realize they've been attacked and destroy the data."

Colonel Stanton asked, "What about a neutron bomb?"

"Colonel, you should know that's not going to work." The speaker was a Russian officer. "The radiation from a neutron bomb cannot kill right away. After a neutron bomb attack, the amount of time left to the enemy would be more than enough for them to have a meeting just like this one."

"Another thought was to use nerve gas," a NATO officer said. "But releasing it and having it spread throughout the ship would take time, so it still doesn't achieve General Chang's requirements."

"Then the only choices left are concussion bombs and infrasonic waves," Colonel Stanton said. Others waited for him to finish his thought, but he said nothing more.

Da Shi said, "I use concussion bombs in police work, but they're toys. They're indeed capable of stunning people inside a building into unconsciousness, but they're only good for a room or two. Do you have any concussion bombs big enough to stun a whole oil tanker full of people?"

Stanton shook his head. "No. Even if we did, such a large explosive device would certainly damage equipment inside the ship."

"So what about infrasonic weapons?" someone asked.

"They're still experimental and cannot be used in live combat. Also, the ship is very large. At the power level

available to current experimental prototypes, the most that a full assault on *Judgment Day* could do is to make the people inside feel dizzy and nauseous."

"Ha!" Da Shi extinguished the cigar butt, now as tiny as a peanut. "I told you all we have left to discuss is bullshit. We've been at it for a while now. Let's remember what the general said: 'Time is of the essence!' " He gave a sly grin to the translator, a female first lieutenant who looked unhappy with his language. "Not easy to translate, eh, comrade? Just get the approximate meaning across."

But Stanton seemed to understand what he was saying. He pointed at Shi Qiang with a fresh cigar that he had just taken out. "Who does this policeman think he is, that he can talk to us this way?"

"Who do you think *you* are?" Da Shi asked.

"Colonel Stanton is an expert in special ops," a NATO officer said. "He has been a part of every major military operation since the Vietnam War."

"Then let me tell you who I am. More than thirty years ago, my reconnaissance squad managed to sneak dozens of kilometers behind Vietnamese lines and capture a hydroelectric station under heavy guard. We prevented the Vietnamese plan to demolish the dam with explosives, which would have flooded the attack route for our army. That's who *I* am. I defeated an enemy who once defeated *you*."

"That's enough!" General Chang slammed the table. "Don't bring up irrelevant matters. If you have a plan, say what it is."

"I don't think we need to waste time on this policeman," Colonel Stanton said contemptuously, as he lit his cigar.

Without waiting for a translation, Da Shi jumped up. " '*Pao-Li-Si*'—I heard that word twice. What? You look down on the police? If you're talking about dropping some

bombs and turning that ship into smithereens, yeah, you military are the experts. But if you're talking about retrieving something out of it without damage, I don't care how many stars are on your shoulder, you aren't even as good as a thief. For this kind of thing, you have to think outside the box. OUT. OF. THE. BOX! You will never be as good at it as criminals, masters of out-of-the-box thinking.

"You know how good they are? I once handled a robbery where the criminals managed to steal one car out of a moving train. They reconnected the cars before and after the one they were interested in so that the train got all the way to its destination without anyone noticing. The only tools they used were a length of wire cable and a few steel hooks. Those are the real special ops experts. And someone like me, a criminal cop who has been playing cat and mouse with them for more than a decade, has received the best education and training from them."

"Tell us your plan, then," General Chang said. "Otherwise, shut up!"

"There are so many important people here that I didn't think it was my place to speak. And I was afraid that you, General, would say I was being rude again."

"You're already the definition of rudeness. Enough! Tell me what your out-of-the-box plan is."

Da Shi picked up a pen and drew two parallel curves on the table. "That's the canal." He put the ashtray between the two lines. "This is *Judgment Day*." Then he reached across the table and pulled Colonel Stanton's just-lit cigar out of his mouth.

"I can no longer tolerate this idiot!" the colonel shouted, standing up.

"Da Shi, get out of here!" General Chang said.

"Give me one minute. I'll be done soon." Da Shi extended a hand in front of Colonel Stanton.

"What do you want?" the colonel asked, puzzled.

"Give me another one."

Stanton hesitated for a second before taking another cigar out of a beautiful wooden box and handing it to Da Shi. Da Shi took the smoking end of the first cigar and pressed it against the table so that it stood on the shore of the Panama Canal that he'd drawn on the table. He flattened the end of the other cigar and erected it on the other shore of the canal.

"We set up two pillars on the shores of the canal, and then between them we string many parallel, thin filaments, about half a meter apart. The filaments should be made from the nanomaterial called 'Flying Blade,' developed by Professor Wang. A very appropriate name, in this case."

After Shi Qiang finished speaking, he stood and waited a few seconds. Then he raised his hands, said to the stunned crowd, "That's it," turned, and left.

The air seemed frozen. Everyone present stayed still like stone statues. Even the droning from the computers all around them seemed more careful.

After a long while, someone timidly broke the silence, "Professor Wang, is 'Flying Blade' really in the form of filaments?"

Wang nodded. "Given our current molecular construction technique, the only form we can make is a filament. The thickness is about one-hundredth the thickness of human hair. . . . Officer Shi got this information from me before the meeting."

"Do you have enough material?"

"How wide is the canal? And how tall is the ship?"

"The narrowest point of the canal is one hundred fifty meters wide. *Judgment Day* is thirty-one meters tall, with a draft of eight meters or so."

Wang stared at the cigars on the table and did some mental calculations. "I think I should have enough."

Another long silence. Everyone was trying to recover from their astonishment.

"What if the equipment storing Trisolaran data, such as hard drives and optical disks, is also sliced?"

"That doesn't seem likely."

"Even if they were sliced," a computer expert said, "it's not a big deal. The filaments are extremely sharp, and the cut surfaces would be very smooth. Given that premise, whether it's hard drives, optical disks, or integrated circuit storage, we could recover the vast majority of the data."

"Anyone got a better idea?" Chang looked around the table. No one spoke. "All right. Then let's focus on this and work out the details."

Colonel Stanton, who had been silent the whole time, stood up. "I will go and ask Officer Shi to come back."

General Chang indicated that he should remain seated. Then he called out, "Da Shi!"

Da Shi returned, grinning at everyone. He picked up the cigars on the table. The one that had been lit he put into his mouth, and the other he stuffed into his pocket.

Someone asked, "When *Judgment Day* passes, can those two pillars bear the force applied against the Flying Blade filaments? Maybe the pillars would be sliced apart first."

Wang said, "That's easy to solve. We have some small amounts of Flying Blade material that are flat sheets. We can use them to protect the parts of the column where the filaments are attached."

The discussion after that was mainly between the naval officers and navigation experts.

"*Judgment Day* is at the upper limit in terms of tonnage

that can pass through the Panama Canal. It has a deep draft, so we have to consider installing filaments below the waterline."

"That will be very difficult. If there's not enough time, I don't think we should worry about it. The parts of the ship below the waterline are used for engines, fuel, and ballast, causing a lot of noise, vibration, and interference. The conditions are too poor for computing centers and other similar facilities to be located there. But for the parts above water, a tighter nanofilament net will give better results."

"Then it's best to set the trap at one of the locks along the canal. *Judgment Day* is built to Panamax specifications, just enough to fill the thirty-two-meter locks. Then we would only need to make the Flying Blade filaments thirty-two meters long. This will also make it easier to erect the pillars and string the filaments between them, especially for the underwater parts."

"No. The situation around the locks is too unpredictable. Also, a ship inside the lock must be pulled forward by four 'mules,' electric locomotives on rails. They move slowly, and the time inside the locks will also be when the crew is most alert. An attempt to slice through the ship during that time would most likely be discovered."

"What about the Bridge of the Americas, right outside the Miraflores Locks? The abutments at the two ends of the bridge can serve as the pillars for stringing the filaments."

"No. The distance between the abutments is too great. We don't have enough Flying Blade material."

"Then it's decided: The site of operation should be the narrowest point of the Gaillard Cut, a hundred and fifty meters across. Add in some slack for the pillars . . . let's call it a hundred seventy meters."

Wang said, "If that's the plan, then the smallest distance between the filaments will be fifty centimeters. I don't have enough material for a tighter net."

"In other words, we have to make sure the ship crosses during the day," Da Shi said, blowing out another mouthful of smoke.

"Why?"

"At night the crew will be sleeping, which means they'll all be lying down. Fifty centimeters between filaments leaves too much of a gap. But during the day, even if they're sitting or crouching, the distance is sufficient."

A few scattered laughs. The attendees, all under heavy stress, felt a bit of release tinged with the smell of blood.

"You're truly a demon," a female UN official said to Da Shi.

"Will innocent bystanders be hurt?" Wang asked, his voice trembling.

A naval officer replied, "When the ship goes through the locks, more than a dozen cable workers will come onboard, but they'll all get off after the ship passes. The Panama Canal pilot will have to accompany the ship the entire eighty-two kilometers, so the pilot will have to be sacrificed."

A CIA officer said, "And some of the crew aboard *Judgment Day* probably don't know the real purpose of the ship."

"Professor," General Chang said, "do not concern yourself with these thoughts. The information we need to obtain has to do with the very survival of human civilization. Someone else will make the call."

As the meeting ended, Colonel Stanton pushed the beautiful cigar box in front of Shi Qiang. "Captain, the best Havana has to offer. They're yours."

Wang could not even tell that he was in a foreign country. He knew that to the west, not too far away, was beautiful Gatun Lake. To the east was the magnificent Bridge of the Americas and Panama City. But he had had no chance to see either of them.

Two days earlier, he had arrived by direct flight from China to Tocumen International Airport near Panama City and then rode a helicopter here. The sight before him was very common: The construction work under way to widen the canal caused the tropical forest on both slopes to be quite sparse, revealing large patches of yellow earth. The color felt familiar to Wang. The canal didn't seem very special, probably because it was so narrow here, but a hundred thousand people had dug out this part of the canal in the previous century, one hoe at a time.

Wang and Colonel Stanton sat on lounge chairs under an awning halfway up the slope. Both wore loose, colorful shirts, with their Panama hats tossed to the side, looking like two tourists.

Below, on each shore of the canal, a twenty-four-meter steel pillar lay flat against the ground, parallel to the shore. Fifty ultrastrong nanofilaments, each 160 meters long, were strung between the pillars. At the end on the eastern shore, every filament was connected to a length of regular steel wire. This was to give the filaments enough slack so that they could sink to the bottom of the canal, aided by attached weights. The setup permitted other ships safe passage. Luckily, traffic along the canal wasn't quite as busy as Wang had imagined. On average, only about forty large ships passed through each day.

The operation's code name was "Guzheng," based on the similarity between the structure and the ancient Chinese zither by that name. The slicing net of nanofilaments was thus called the "zither."

An hour earlier, *Judgment Day* had entered the Gaillard Cut from Gatun Lake.

Stanton asked Wang whether he had ever been to Panama before. Wang said no.

"I came here in 1989," the colonel said.

"Because of that war?"

"Yes, that was one of those wars that left me with no impression. I only remember being in front of the Vatican embassy as 'Nowhere to Run' by Martha and the Vandellas played for the holed-up Noriega. That was my idea, by the way."

In the canal below them, a pure white French cruise ship slowly sailed past. Several passengers in colorful clothing strolled leisurely on the green-carpeted deck.

"Second Observation Post reporting: There are no more ships in front of the target." Stanton's walkie-talkie squawked.

Stanton gave the order. "Raise the zither."

Several men wearing hard hats appeared on both shores, looking like maintenance workers. Wang stood up, but the colonel pulled him down. "Professor, don't worry. They know what to do." Wang watched as those on the eastern shore rapidly winched back the steel wires attached to the nanofilaments and secured the tightened nanofilaments to the pillar. Then, slowly, the two pillars were stood upright using their mechanical hinges. As a disguise, the pillars were decorated with some navigational markings and water depth indicators. The workers proceeded leisurely, as though they were simply carrying out their boring jobs. Wang gazed at

the space between the pillars. There seemed to be nothing there, but the deadly zither was already in place.

"Target is four kilometers from the zither," the voice in the walkie-talkie said.

Stanton put the walkie-talkie down. He continued the conversation with Wang. "The second time I came to Panama was in 1999, to attend the ceremony for the handover of the canal to Panama. Oddly, by the time we got to the Authority's building, the Stars and Stripes were already gone. Supposedly the U.S. government had requested that the flag be lowered a day early to avoid the embarrassment of lowering the flag in front of a crowd. . . . Back then, I thought I was witnessing history. But now that seems so insignificant."

"Target is three kilometers from the zither."

"Yes, insignificant," Wang mumbled. He wasn't listening to Stanton at all. The rest of the world had ceased to exist for him. All of his attention was focused on the spot where *Judgment Day* would appear. By now the sun that had risen over the Atlantic was falling toward the Pacific. The canal sparkled with golden light. Close by, the deadly zither stood quietly. The two steel pillars were dark and reflected no sunlight, looking even older than the canal that flowed between them.

"Target is two kilometers from the zither."

Stanton seemed to not have heard the voice from the walkie-talkie. He continued, "After learning that the alien fleet is coming toward the Earth, I've been suffering from amnesia. It's so strange. I can't recall many things from the past. I don't remember the details of the wars I experienced. Like I just said, those wars all seem so insignificant. After learning this truth, everyone becomes a new person spiritually, and sees the world anew. I've been thinking: Suppose

two thousand years ago, or even earlier, humanity learned that an alien invasion fleet would arrive a few thousand years later. What would human civilization be like now? Professor, can you imagine it?"

"Ah, no . . ." Wang answered perfunctorily, his mind elsewhere.

"Target is one point five kilometers from the zither."

"Professor, I think you will be the Gaillard of this new era. We're waiting for your new Panama Canal to be built. Indeed, the space elevator is a canal. Just as the Panama Canal connected two oceans, the space elevator will connect space with the Earth."

Wang knew that the colonel's babbling was meant to help him through this very difficult time. He was grateful, but it wasn't working.

"Target is one kilometer from the zither."

Judgment Day appeared. In the light from the setting sun coming over the hills to the side, it was a dark silhouette against the golden waves of the canal. The sixty-thousand-ton ship was much larger than Wang had imagined. Its appearance was like another peak abruptly inserted among the hills. Even though Wang knew that the canal was capable of accommodating ships as large as seventy thousand tons, witnessing such a large ship in such a narrow waterway was a strange feeling. Given its immensity, the canal below seemed to no longer exist. The ship was a mountain gliding across solid earth. After he grew used to the sunlight, Wang saw that *Judgment Day*'s hull was pitch black, and the super-structure was painted pure white. The giant antenna was gone. They heard the roar from the ship's engines, accompanied by the churning sound of waves that had been generated by the round prow slapping against the shores of the canal.

As the distance between *Judgment Day* and the deadly zither closed, Wang's heart began to beat faster, and his breath became short. He had a desire to run away, but he felt so weak that he could no longer control his body. All at once, he was overwhelmed by a deep hatred for Shi Qiang. *How could the bastard have come up with such an idea? Like that UN official said, he is a demon!* But the feeling passed. He thought that if Da Shi were by his side, he would probably feel better. Colonel Stanton had invited Shi Qiang to come, but General Chang refused to give permission because he said that Da Shi was needed where he was. Wang felt the colonel's hand on his back.

"Professor, all this will pass."

Judgment Day was below them now, passing through the deadly zither. When its prow first contacted the plane between the two steel pillars, the space that seemed empty, Wang's scalp tightened. But nothing happened. The immense hull of the ship continued to slowly sail past the two steel pillars. When half the ship had passed, Wang began to doubt whether the nanofilaments between the steel pillars really existed.

But a small sign soon negated his doubt. He noticed a thin antenna located at the very top of the superstructure breaking at its base, and the antenna tumbling down.

Soon, there was a second sign indicating the presence of the nanofilaments, a sign that almost made Wang break down. *Judgment Day*'s wide deck was empty save for one man standing near the stern hosing down the ship's bollards. From his vantage point, Wang saw everything clearly. The moment that that section of the ship passed between the pillars, the hose broke into two pieces not too far from the man, and water spilled out. The man's body stiffened, and the nozzle tumbled from his hand. He remained standing for

a few seconds, then fell. As his body contacted the deck, it came apart in two halves. The top half crawled through the expanding pool of blood, but had to use two arms that were bloody stumps. The hands had been cleanly sliced off.

After the stern of the ship went between the two pillars, *Judgment Day* continued to sail forward at the same speed, and everything seemed normal. But then Wang heard the sound of the engine shift into a strange whine, before turning into chaotic noise. It sounded like a wrench being thrown into the rotor of a large motor—no, many, many wrenches. He knew this was the result of the rotating parts of the engine having been cut. After a piercing, tearing sound, a hole appeared in the side of the stern of *Judgment Day*, made by a large metallic piece punching through the hull. A broken component flew out of the hole and fell into the water, causing a large column of water to shoot up. As it briefly flew past, Wang recognized it as a section of the engine crankshaft.

A thick column of smoke poured out of the hole. *Judgment Day*, which had been sailing along the right shore, now began to turn, dragging this smoky tail. Soon it crossed over the canal and smashed into the left shore. As Wang looked, the giant prow deformed as it collided into the slope, slicing open the hill like water, causing waves of earth to spill in all directions. At the same time, *Judgment Day* began to separate into more than forty slices, each slice half a meter thick. The slices near the top moved faster than the slices near the bottom, and the ship spread open like a deck of cards. As the forty-some metal slices moved past each other, the piercing noise was like countless giant fingernails scratching against glass.

By the time the intolerable noise ended, *Judgment Day* was spilled on the shore like a stack of plates carried by a

stumbling waiter, the plates near the top having traveled the farthest. The slices looked as soft as cloth, and rapidly deformed into complicated shapes impossible to imagine as having once belonged to a ship.

Soldiers rushed toward the shore from the slope. Wang was surprised to find so many men hidden nearby. A fleet of helicopters arrived along the canal with their engines roaring; crossed the canal surface, which was now covered by an iridescent oil slick; hovered over the wreckage of *Judgment Day*; and began to drop large quantities of fire suppression foam and powder. Shortly, the fire in the wreckage was under control, and three other helicopters began to drop searchers into the wreckage with cables.

Colonel Stanton had already left. Wang picked up the binoculars he'd left on top of his hat. Overcoming his trembling hands, he observed *Judgment Day*. By this time, the wreckage was mostly covered by fire-extinguishing foam and powder, but the edges of some of the slices were left exposed. Wang saw the cut surfaces, smooth as mirrors. They reflected the fiery red light of dusk perfectly. He also saw a deep red spot on the mirror surface. He wasn't sure if it was blood.

Three days later

INTERROGATOR: Do you understand Trisolaran civilization?

YE WENJIE: No. We received only very limited information. No one has real, detailed knowledge of Trisolaran civilization except Mike Evans and other core members of the Adventists who intercepted their messages.

INTERROGATOR: Then why do you have such hope for it, thinking that it can reform and perfect human society?

YE: If they can cross the distance between the stars to come to our world, their science must have developed to a very advanced stage. A society with such advanced science must also have more advanced moral standards.

INTERROGATOR: Do you think this conclusion you drew is scientific?

YE: . . .

INTERROGATOR: Let me presume to guess: Your father was deeply influenced by your grandfather's belief that only science could save China. And you were deeply influenced by your father.

YE: *(sighing quietly)* I don't know.

INTERROGATOR: We have already obtained all the Trisolaran messages intercepted by the Adventists.

YE: Oh . . . what happened to Evans?

INTERROGATOR: He died during the operation to capture *Judgment Day*. But the posture of his body pointed us to the computers holding copies of the Trisolaran messages. Thankfully, they were all encoded with the same self-interpreting code used by Red Coast.

YE: Was there a lot of data?

INTERROGATOR: Yes, about twenty-eight gigabytes.

YE: That's impossible. Interstellar communication is very inefficient. How can so much data have been transmitted?

INTERROGATOR: We thought so at first, too. But things were not at all as we had imagined—not even in our boldest, most fantastic imaginations. How about this? Please read this section of the preliminary analysis of the captured data, and you can see the reality of the Trisolaran civilization, compared with your beautiful fantasies.

32

TRISOLARIS: THE LISTENER

The Trisolaran data contained no descriptions of the biological appearance of Trisolarans. Since humans would not lay eyes on actual Trisolarans until more than four hundred years later, Ye could only envision the Trisolarans as humanoid as she read the messages. She filled in the blanks between the lines with her imagination.

Listening Post 1379 had already been in existence for more than a thousand years. There were several thousand posts like it on Trisolaris, all of them dedicating their efforts to detecting possible signs of intelligent life in the universe.

Initially, each listening post had several hundred listeners, but as technology advanced, there was only one person on duty. Being a listener was a humble career. Though they lived in listening posts that were kept at a constant temperature, with support systems that guaranteed their survival without requiring them to dehydrate during Chaotic Eras, they also had to live their lives within the narrow confines of these tiny spaces. The amount of joy they got from Stable Eras was far less than others got.

The listener at Post 1379 looked through the tiny window

at the world of Trisolaris outside. This was a Chaotic Era night. The giant moon had not yet risen, and most people remained in dehydrated hibernation. Even plants had instinctively dehydrated and turned into lifeless bundles of dry fiber lying against the ground. Under the starlight, the ground looked like a giant sheet of cold metal.

This was the loneliest time. In the deep silence of midnight, the universe revealed itself to its listeners as a vast desolation. What the listener of Post 1379 disliked the most was seeing the waves that slowly crawled across the display, a visual record of the meaningless noise the listening post picked up from space. He felt this interminable wave was an abstract view of the universe: one end connected to the endless past, the other to the endless future, and in the middle only the ups and downs of random chance—without life, without pattern, the peaks and valleys at different heights like uneven grains of sand, the whole curve like a one-dimensional desert made of all the grains of sand lined up in a row: lonely, desolate, so long that it was intolerable. You could follow it and go forward or backward as long as you liked, but you'd never find the end.

On this day, however, the listener saw something odd when he glanced at the waveform display. Even experts had a hard time telling with the naked eye whether a waveform carried information. But the listener was so familiar with the noise of the universe that he could tell that the wave that now moved in front of his eyes had something extra. The thin curve, rising and falling, seemed to possess a soul. He was certain that the radio signal before him had been modulated by intelligence.

He rushed in front of another terminal and checked the computer's rating of the signal's recognizability: a Red 10.

Before this, no radio signal received by the listening post had ever garnered a recognizability rating above a Blue 2. A Red rating meant the likelihood that the transmission contained intelligent information was greater than 90 percent. A rating of Red 10 meant the received transmission contained a self-interpreting coding system! The deciphering computer worked at full power.

Still caught up by the dizzying excitement and confusion, the listener stared at the waveform display. Information continued to stream from the universe into the antenna. Because of the self-interpreting code, the computer was able to perform real-time translation, and the message began to show up immediately.

The listener opened the resulting document, and, for the first time, a Trisolaran read a message from another world.

> With the best of intentions, we look forward to establishing contact with other civilized societies in the universe. We look forward to working together with you to build a better life in this vast universe.

During the next two Trisolaran hours, the listener learned of the existence of Earth, learned of the world that had only one sun and remained always in a Stable Era, learned of the human civilization that had been born in a paradise where the climate was eternally mild.

The transmission from the solar system ended. The deciphering computer now ran uselessly. The post was once again only hearing the noise of the universe.

But the listener was certain that what he had just experienced was not a dream. He knew as well that the several thousand listening posts spread across Trisolaris had also

received this message, which Trisolaran civilization had awaited for eons. Two hundred cycles of civilization had been crawling through a dark tunnel, and there was finally a glimmer of light before them.

The listener read over the message from the Earth again. His thoughts drifted over the blue ocean that never froze and the green forests and fields, enjoying the warm sunlight and the caress of a cool breeze. *What a beautiful world! The paradise we imagined really exists!*

The thrill and excitement cooled, and all that remained was a sense of loss and desolation. During the long loneliness of the past, the listener had asked himself more than once: *Even if one day a message from an extra-Trisolaran civilization were to arrive, what would that have to do with me?* His own lonely and humble life would not change one iota because of it.

But I can at least possess it in my dream. . . . And the listener drifted off to sleep. In their harsh environment, the Trisolarans had evolved the ability to switch sleep on and off. A Trisolaran could put himself to sleep in seconds.

But he did not get the dream that he wanted. The blue Earth did appear in his dream, but under the bombardment of an enormous interstellar fleet, the beautiful continents of Earth were burning, the deep blue oceans were boiling and evaporating. . . .

The listener woke up from his nightmare and saw the giant moon, just risen, casting a thin ray of cold light through the small window. He looked at the frozen ground outside the window and reviewed his lonely life. By now, he had lived six hundred thousand Trisolaran hours. The life expectancy of Trisolarans ranged between seven hundred to eight hundred thousand Trisolaran hours. Most people, of course, would have lost the ability to work productively long before then.

They would have been forcibly dehydrated, and the resulting dry fibers cast to the flames. Trisolaris did not keep the idle around.

But now the listener saw another possibility. It was inaccurate to say that the receipt of the extra-Trisolaran message had no influence on his life. After confirmation, Trisolaris would surely reduce the number of listening posts. And posts like this one, behind the times, would be among the first to be cut. Then he would be unemployed. A listener's skills were very specialized, consisting only of some routine operations and maintenance. It would be very difficult to find another job. If he couldn't find another job within five thousand Trisolaran hours, he would be forcibly dehydrated and then burnt.

The only way to escape this fate was to mate with a member of the opposite sex. When that happened, the organic material making up their bodies would meld into one. Two-thirds of the material would then become fuel to power the biochemical reaction that would completely renew the cells in the remaining one-third and create a new body. Then this body would divide into three to five tiny new lives: their children. They would inherit some of the memories of their parents, continue their lives, and begin the cycle of life anew. But given the listener's low social position, lonely and enclosed workspace, and advanced age, what member of the opposite sex would be interested in him?

In the last few years, the listener had asked himself millions of times: *Is this all there is to my life?* And millions of times he had answered himself: *Yes, this is all there is. All that you have in this life is the endless loneliness in the tiny space of this listening post.*

He couldn't lose that paradise, even if it was only in a dream.

The listener knew that at the scale of the universe, due to the lack of a sufficiently long measurement baseline, it was impossible to determine the *distance* of a source of low-frequency radio transmission from space, only the direction. The source could be high-powered but far away, or low-powered but close by. In that direction were billions of stars, each shining against a sea of other stars at different distances. Without knowing how far away the source was, it was impossible to ascertain its exact coordinates.

Distance, the key was distance.

Indeed, there was an easy way to ascertain the distance of the transmission source. Just respond to the message, and if the other party replies quickly to the response, the Trisolarans could determine the distance based on the round-trip time and the speed of light. Or maybe they would take a really long time to reply and cause the Trisolarans to be unable to determine how long the message was en route.

But the question was: Would the other party reply? Since this source had actively sent out a call into the universe, it was very likely that they *would* reply after getting a response from Trisolaris. And the listener was sure that the Trisolaran government had already given the order to send a message to that distant world to lure them to respond. Maybe the message had already been sent, but maybe not. If the latter was true, then the listener had a singular chance to make his own humble life glow.

The listener dashed in front of the operations screen and composed a short, simple message on the computer. He directed the computer to translate the message into the same language as the message received from the Earth. Then, he pointed the listening post's antenna in the direction the message from Earth had come from.

The Transmit button was a red rectangle. The listener's fingers hovered above it.

The fate of Trisolaran civilization was now tied to these slender fingers.

Without hesitation, the listener pressed the button. A high-powered radio wave carried that short message, a message that could save another civilization, into the darkness of space.

Do not answer! Do not answer!! Do not answer!!!

We don't know what the official residence of the princeps of Trisolaris looked like, but we can be sure that thick walls separated him from the outside so as to protect him against the extreme weather. The pyramid from the *Three Body* game was one guess about what it could look like. That they built the residence deep underground is another.

Five Trisolaran hours earlier, the princeps received the report of the extra-Trisolaran communication. Two Trisolaran hours earlier, he received another report: Listening Post 1379 had sent out a warning message in the direction of the transmission.

The first report did not cause him to leap up in ecstasy, and the second report did not cause him to sink into depression. He wasn't even angry or resentful. All of these emotions—and other emotions, such as fear, sorrow, happiness, and appreciation of beauty—were things that the Trisolaran civilization strove to avoid and eliminate. Such emotions caused the individual and society to be weak spiritually and did not help with survival in the harsh environment of this world. The mental states that Trisolarans needed were calmness and numbness. The history of the past two hundred-some cycles of civilization proved that civilizations that relied on these two states as their spiritual core were the most capable of survival.

"Why did you do this?" the princeps asked the listener from Post 1379.

"So that my life isn't wasted," the listener answered calmly.

"The warning you sent out may have cost Trisolaran civilization the chance at survival."

"But it gave Earth civilization such a chance. Princeps, Trisolaran civilization's desire to possess living space is like the desire of a man who has been starving for a long time for food, and it is similarly boundless. We cannot share the Earth with the people of that world. We could only destroy Earth civilization and completely take over that solar system. . . . Am I right?"

"Yes. But there is another reason for destroying Earth civilization. They're also a warlike race. Very dangerous. If we try to coexist with them on the same planet, they will shortly learn our technology. Continuing in that state would allow neither civilization to thrive. Let me ask you: You wish to be the savior of the Earth, but do you not feel any sense of responsibility for your own race?"

"I am tired of Trisolaris. We have nothing in our lives and spirit except the fight for survival."

"What's wrong with that?"

"There's nothing wrong, of course. Existence is the premise for everything else. But, Princeps, please examine our lives: Everything is devoted to survival. To permit the survival of the civilization as a whole, there is almost no respect for the individual. Someone who can no longer work is put to death. Trisolaran society exists under a state of extreme authoritarianism. The law has only two outcomes: The guilty are put to death, and the not guilty are released. For me, the most intolerable aspects are the spiritual monotony and desiccation. Anything that can lead to spiritual weakness is

declared evil. We have no literature, no art, no pursuit of beauty and enjoyment. We cannot even speak of love. . . . Princeps, is there meaning to such a life?"

"The kind of civilization you yearn for once existed on Trisolaris, too. They had free, democratic societies, and they left behind rich cultural legacies. You know barely anything about them. Most details have been sealed away and forbidden from view. But in all the cycles of Trisolaran civilization, this type of civilization was the weakest and most short-lived. A modest Chaotic Era disaster was enough to extinguish them. Look again at the Earth civilization that you wish to save. A society born and bred in the eternal spring of a beautiful hothouse would not be able to survive even a million Trisolaran hours if it were transplanted here."

"That flower may be delicate, but it possesses peerless splendor. She enjoys freedom and beauty in the ease of paradise."

"If Trisolaran civilization ultimately possesses that world, we can also create such lives for ourselves."

"Princeps, I'm doubtful. The metallic Trisolaran spirit has infiltrated each of our cells and solidified. You really believe it can melt again? I'm an ordinary man living at the bottom of society. No one would pay any attention to me. My life is spent alone, without wealth, without status, without love, and without hope. If I can save a distant, beautiful world that I have fallen in love with, then my life has not been wasted. Of course, Princeps, this also gave me a chance to see you. If I had not done this, a man like me could only ever hope to admire you on TV. So permit me to express myself as honored."

"You're guilty beyond doubt. You're the greatest criminal in all the cycles of Trisolaran civilization. But now we make an exception in Trisolaran law: You're free to go."

"Why?"

"For you, dehydration followed by burning is not even remotely adequate as punishment. You're old, and you will not live to see the final destruction of Earth civilization. But I will at least make sure that you know that you cannot save her. I want to let you live until the day she loses all hope.

"All right. You may leave."

After the listener from Post 1379 left, the princeps called in the consul responsible for the monitoring system. The princeps also avoided being angry at him. He dealt with it as a routine matter. "How could you allow such a weak and evil man into the monitoring system?"

"Princeps, the monitoring system employs hundreds of thousands. To screen them all strictly is very difficult. After all, the man managed to perform his duties at Listening Post 1379 without error for most of his life. Of course, this most serious mistake is my responsibility."

"How many others bear some responsibility for this failure in the Trisolaran Space Monitoring System?"

"My preliminary investigation shows about six thousand, accounting for all levels."

"They're all guilty."

"Yes."

"Dehydrate all six thousand and burn them together in the square in the middle of the capital. As for you, you can be the kindling."

"Thank you, Princeps. This will at least calm our consciences a little."

"Before carrying out this punishment, let me ask you: How far can that warning message travel?"

"Listening Post 1379 is a small facility without high

transmission power. The maximum range may be twelve million light-hours, about twelve hundred light-years."

"That's far enough. Do you have any suggestions for what Trisolaran civilization should do next?"

"How about transmitting a carefully composed message to that world to lure them to respond?"

"No. That might make matters worse. At least the warning message is very short. We can only hope that they ignore it, or misunderstand its contents . . . All right. You may leave."

After the consul left, the princeps summoned the commander of the Trisolaran Fleet.

"How long would it take to complete the preparations for the first wave of the fleet?"

"Princeps, the fleet is still in the last phase of construction. At least sixty thousand more hours are needed before the ships are spaceworthy."

"I will soon present my plan for approval by the Joint Session of Consuls. After construction is complete, the fleet should set sail in that direction at once."

"Princeps, given the frequency of the transmission, even the direction of the source cannot be ascertained with great accuracy. The fleet is only capable of cruising at one-hundredth the speed of light. Also, it only has enough power in reserve to perform one deceleration, making it impossible to conduct a wide-area search in that direction. If the distance to the target is unclear, the fleet will ultimately fall into the abyss of space."

"But look at the three suns around us. At any moment, the plasma outer layer of one of them may begin to expand and swallow its last planet, our world. We have no other choice. We must make this gamble."

33

TRISOLARIS: SOPHON

Eighty-five thousand Trisolaran hours (about 8.6 Earth years) later

The princeps had ordered an emergency meeting of all Triso-laran consuls. This was very unusual. Something important must have happened.

Twenty thousand Trisolaran hours ago, the Trisolaran Fleet had launched. The ships knew the approximate direc-tion of their target but not its distance. It was possible that the target was millions of light-hours away, or even at the other end of the galaxy. Faced with the endless sea of stars, the expedition had little hope.

The meeting of consuls occurred under the Pendulum Monument. [As Wang Miao read about this episode, he couldn't help but recall the session at the UN Building in the *Three Body* game. In reality, the Pendulum Monument was one of the few objects in the game that really did exist on Trisolaris.]

The princeps's choice of meeting site confused most of the attendees. The Chaotic Era wasn't over yet, and a small sun had just risen over the horizon, though it could also set at any moment. The temperature was cold, and all the

attendees were forced to wear fully enclosed electric-heating suits. The massive metal pendulum swung magnificently, pounding the frigid air. The small sun cast a long shadow against the ground, as if a giant whose head touched the sky were striding there. Under the watchful eyes of the crowd, the princeps ascended onto the base of the pendulum and flipped a red switch.

He turned to the consuls and said, "I have just shut off power to the pendulum. It will gradually stop under the influence of air resistance."

"Princeps, why?" a consul asked.

"We all understand the historical significance of the pendulum. It's intended to hypnotize God. But now we know it's better for Trisolaran civilization to have God awake, because God is now blessing us."

Everyone was silent, pondering the meaning of the princeps's words. After three more swings from the pendulum, someone asked, "Has the Earth responded?"

The princeps nodded. "Yes. Half an hour ago I received the report. It was a response to the warning that was sent."

"So soon! Only eighty thousand hours have passed since then, which means . . . which means . . ."

"Which means that the Earth is only forty thousand light-hours from us."

"Isn't that the closest star from here?"

"Yes. That is why I said God is blessing Trisolaran civilization."

The attendees grew ecstatic, but they couldn't express the feeling, so the crowd seemed like a pent-up volcano. The princeps knew that allowing such weak emotions to explode would be dangerous. So he poured cold water on their sentiments.

"I have already ordered the Trisolaran Fleet to turn toward this star. But things are not quite as optimistic as you think. Given what we know, right now the fleet is sailing toward certain death."

The consuls calmed down.

"Does anyone understand my conclusion?"

"I do," said the science consul. "We've all studied the first messages from Earth carefully. The section most worthy of attention is their history. Let's observe the facts: Humans took more than a hundred thousand Earth years to progress from the Hunter-Gatherer Age to the Agricultural Age. To get from the Agricultural Age to the Industrial Age took a few thousand Earth years. But to go from the Industrial Age to the Atomic Age took only two hundred Earth years. Thereafter, in only a few Earth decades, they entered the Information Age. This civilization possesses the terrifying ability to accelerate their progress.

"On Trisolaris, of the more than two hundred civilizations, including our own, none has ever experienced such accelerating development. The progress of science and technology in all Trisolaran civilizations has been at a constant or decelerating pace. In our world, each technology age requires approximately the same amount of time for steady, slow development."

The princeps nodded. "The fact is that four million and five hundred thousand hours from now, when the Trisolaran Fleet has reached the Earth, that civilization's technology level will have long surpassed ours, due to their accelerating development. The journey of the Trisolaran Fleet is long and arduous, and the fleet must pass through two interstellar dust belts. It's very likely that only half of the ships will reach the Earth's solar system, while the rest perish along the way.

And then, the Trisolaran Fleet will be at the mercy of a much more powerful Earth civilization. This is not an expedition, but a funeral procession!"

"But if this is true, Princeps, then there are even more frightening consequences . . ." the military consul said.

"Yes. It's easy to imagine. The location of Trisolaris has been exposed. To eliminate future threats, an interstellar fleet from Earth will launch a counterattack against us. It's very possible that long before an expanded sun swallows this planet, Trisolaran civilization will have already been extinguished by humans."

The bright future had suddenly turned impossibly grim. The attendees fell silent.

The princeps said, "What we must do next is contain the progress of science on Earth. Luckily, as soon as we received the first messages from Earth, we began to develop plans to do so. As of now, we've discovered a favorable condition for realizing these plans: The response we just received was sent by an Earth traitor. Thus, we have reason to believe that there are many alienated forces within Earth civilization, and we must exploit such forces to the fullest."

"Princeps, that is not at all easy. We have but a thin thread of communication with the Earth. It takes more than eighty thousand hours to complete an exchange."

"But remember that, like us, the knowledge that there are extraterrestrial civilizations will shock all of Earth society and leave profound marks. We have reason to believe that the alienated forces within Earth civilization will coalesce and grow."

"What can they do? Sabotage?"

"Given a time gap of forty thousand hours, the strategic value of any traditional tactics of war or terror is insignificant,

and they can recover from them. To effectively contain a civilization's development and disarm it across such a long span of time, there is only one way: kill its science."

The science consul said, "The plan focuses on emphasizing the negative environmental effects of scientific development and showing signs of supernatural power to the population of Earth. In addition to highlighting the negative effects of progress, we'll also attempt to use a series of 'miracles' to construct an illusory universe that cannot be explained by the logic of science. After these illusions have been maintained for some time, it's possible that Trisolaran civilization may become a target of religious worship there. Then, unscientific ways of thinking will dominate scientific thinking among human intellectuals, and lead to the collapse of the entire scientific system of thought."

"How do we create miracles?"

"The key to miracles is that they cannot be seen as tricks. This may require that we transfer certain technologies far above current human technology level to the alienated forces on Earth."

"That's too risky! Who knows who will ultimately control such technologies? That's playing with fire."

"Of course, which specific technologies should be transferred to produce miracles requires further study. . . ."

"Please hold on for a moment, Science Consul," said the military consul as he stood up. "Princeps, I am of the opinion that this plan will be almost useless in terms of stopping human science."

"But it's better than nothing," the science consul argued.

"Barely," the military consul said contemptuously.

"I agree with your view," the princeps said. "This plan will only interfere slightly with human scientific development.

We need a decisive act that will completely suffocate science on Earth and freeze it at its current level. Let's focus on the key here: Overall technological development depends on the advancement of basic science, and the foundation of basic science lies in the exploration of the deep structure of matter. If there's no progress in this field, there can be no major breakthrough in science and technology as a whole. Of course, this is not specific to civilization on Earth. It is applicable to all targets that Trisolaran civilization intends to conquer. We had begun work in this area even before receiving the first extra-Trisolaran communication. But we've recently stepped up the effort.

"Now, everyone, look up. What's that?"

The princeps pointed at the sky. The consuls lifted their heads to gaze in that direction. They saw a ring in space giving off a metallic glow in the sunlight.

"Is that the dock for building the second space fleet?"

"No. That's a large particle accelerator still under construction. The plans for building a second space fleet have been scrapped. All resources are now devoted to Project Sophon."

"Project Sophon?"

"Yes. We've kept this plan secret from most of you present. I now ask the science consul to give an introduction."

"I knew about this plan, but didn't know it had progressed so far." The speaker was the industry consul.

The culture and education consul said, "I knew about this plan as well, but thought it was like a fairy tale."

The science consul said, "Project Sophon, to put it simply, aims to transform a proton into a superintelligent computer."[42]

42 *Translator's Note:* There is a pun in Chinese between the word for a proton, *zhizi* (质子), and the word for a sophon, *zhizi* (智子).

"This is a science fantasy that most of us have heard about," the agricultural consul said. "But can it be realized? I know that physicists can already manipulate nine of the eleven dimensions of the micro-scale world, but we still can't imagine how they could stick a pair of tiny tweezers into a proton to build large-scale integrated circuits."

"Of course that's impossible. The etching of micro integrated circuits can only occur at the macro scale, and only on a macroscopic two-dimensional plane. Thus, we must unfold a proton into two dimensions."

"Unfold a nine-dimensional structure into two dimensions? How big would the area be?"

"Very big, as you will see." The science consul smiled.

———————

Another sixty thousand Trisolaran hours went by. Twenty thousand Trisolaran hours after the completion of the huge particle accelerator in space, the unfolding of the proton into two dimensions was about to begin in a synchronous orbit around Trisolaris.

It was a beautiful and mild Stable Era day. The sky was particularly clear. Like the day when the fleet had set sail eighty thousand Trisolaran hours ago, the entire population of Trisolaris looked up into the sky, gazing at that giant ring. The princeps and all the consuls again came and stood under the Pendulum Monument. The pendulum had long stopped, and the weight hung still like a solid rock between the tall pillars. Looking at it, it was hard to believe that it had once moved.

The science consul gave the order to unfold into two dimensions. In space, three cubes drifted around the ring— the fusion generators that powered the accelerator. Their winglike heat sinks gradually began to glow with a dim

reddish light. The crowd anxiously stared at the accelerator, but nothing seemed to happen.

A tenth of a Trisolaran hour later, the science consul held his earpiece to his ear and listened intently. Then he said, "Princeps, unfortunately, the unfolding failed. We reduced the dimensions by one too many, and the proton became one-dimensional."

"One-dimensional? A line?"

"Yes. An infinitely thin line. Theoretically, it should be about fifteen hundred light-hours long."

"We spent the resources intended for another space fleet," said the military consul, "just to obtain a result like this?"

"In scientific experiments, there has to be a process during which kinks are worked out. After all, this was the very first time the unfolding has been tried."

The crowd dispersed in disappointment, but the experiment wasn't over. Originally, it was thought that the one-dimensional proton would stay in synchronous orbit around Trisolaris forever, but due to friction from solar winds, pieces of the string fell back into the atmosphere. Six Trisolaran hours later, everyone outside noticed the strange lights in the air, gossamer threads that flickered in and out of existence. They soon learned from the news that this was the one-dimensional proton drifting to the ground under the influence of gravity. Even though the string was infinitely thin, it produced a field that could still reflect visible light. It was the first time people had ever seen matter not made out of atoms—the silky strands were merely small portions of a proton.

"These things are so annoying." The princeps brushed his hand against his face over and over. He and the science consul were standing on the wide steps in front of Government Center. "My face always feels itchy."

"Princeps, the feeling is purely psychological. All the strings added together have the mass of a single proton, so it's impossible for them to have any effect on the macroscopic world. They can't do any harm. It's as if they don't exist."

But the threads that fell from the sky grew more numerous and denser. Closer to ground, tiny sparkling lights filled the air. The sun and the stars all appeared inside silvery halos. The strings clung to those who went outside, and as they walked, they dragged the lights behind them. When people returned indoors, the lines glimmered under the lamps. As soon as they moved, the reflection from the strings revealed the patterns in the air currents they disturbed. Although the one-dimensional string could only be seen under light and couldn't be felt, people became upset.

The torrent of one-dimensional strings continued for more than twenty Trisolaran hours before finally ending, though not because the strings had all fallen to the ground. Although their mass was unimaginably minuscule, they still had some, and so their acceleration under gravity was the same as normal matter. However, once inside the atmosphere, they were completely dominated by the air currents and would never fall to the ground. After being unfolded into one dimension, the strong nuclear force within the proton became far more attenuated, weakening the string. Gradually, it broke into tiny pieces, and the light they reflected was no longer visible. People thought they had disappeared, but pieces of the one-dimensional string would drift in the air of Trisolaris forever.

Fifty Trisolaran hours later, the second attempt to unfold a proton into two dimensions began. Soon, the crowd on the ground saw something odd. After the heat sinks of the

fusion generators began to glow red, several colossal objects appeared near the accelerator. All of them were in the form of regular geometric solids: spheres, tetrahedrons, cubes, cones, and so on. Their surfaces had complex coloration, but close examination showed that they were, in fact, colorless. The surfaces of the geometric solids were completely reflective, and what the people saw were just distorted, reflected images of the surface of Trisolaris.

"Have we succeeded?" the princeps asked. "Is that the proton unfolded into two dimensions?"

The science consul replied, "Princeps, it's still a failure. I just received the report from the accelerator control center. The unfolding left one too many dimensions in, and the proton was unfolded into three dimensions."

The giant, reflective geometric solids continued to pop into existence in great numbers, and their forms became more various. There were tori, solid crosses, and even something that looked like a Möbius strip. All the geometric solids drifted away from the location of the accelerator. About half an hour later, the solids filled more than half the sky, as though a giant child had emptied a box of building blocks in the firmament. The light reflected from the mirror surfaces doubled the brilliance of the light hitting the ground, but the intensity continuously shifted. The shadow of the giant pendulum flickered in and out, and swayed from side to side.

Then, all the geometric solids began to deform. They gradually lost their regular shapes, as though they were melting in heat. The deformation accelerated and the resulting lumps became more and more complex. Now the objects in the sky no longer reminded people of building blocks, but of a giant's dismembered limbs and disemboweled viscera. Because their shapes were no longer so regular, the light they

reflected to the ground became softer, but their own surface coloration turned even more strange and unpredictable.

Out of the mess of three-dimensional objects, a few in particular drew special attention from observers on the ground. At first, it was only because the objects in question were very similar to each other. But upon closer examination, people recognized them, and a wave of terror swept Trisolaris.

They were all eyes! [Of course, we don't know what Trisolaran eyes look like, but we can be certain that any intelligent life would be very sensitive to representations of eyes.]

The princeps was one of the few who kept calm. He asked the science consul, "How complicated can the internal structure of a subatomic particle be?"

"It depends on the number of dimensions of your observation perspective. From a one-dimensional perspective, it's only a point—that's how ordinary people think of the particles. From a two- or three-dimensional perspective, the particle begins to show internal structure. From a four-dimensional perspective, a fundamental particle is an immense world."

The princeps said, "To use a word like 'immense' to describe a subatomic particle such as a proton seems incredible to me."

The science consul ignored the princeps and continued, "As we move to higher dimensions, the complexity and number of structures within a particle increase dramatically. The comparisons I'm about to make will not be precise, but should give you an idea of the scale. A particle seen from a seven-dimensional perspective has a complexity comparable to our Trisolaran stellar system in three dimensions. From an eight-dimensional perspective, a particle is a vast presence like the Milky Way. When the perspective has been raised to nine dimensions, a fundamental particle's internal

structures and complexity are equal to the whole universe. As for even higher dimensions, our physicists haven't been able to explore them, so we cannot yet imagine the degree of complexity."

The princeps pointed to the giant eyes in space. "Do these show that the microcosmos contained within the unfolded proton harbors intelligent life?"

"Our definition of 'life' is probably not appropriate for the high-dimensional microcosmos. More accurately, we can only say that universe contains intelligence or wisdom. Scientists have long predicted this possibility. It would have been odd for such a complex and vast world to not have evolved something akin to intelligence."

"Why have they transformed into eyes to look at us?" The princeps looked up at the eyes in space, beautiful, life-like sculptures, all of them gazing upon the planet below strangely.

"Maybe they just want to demonstrate their presence."

"Can they fall down here?"

"Not at all. You may rest easy, Princeps. Even if they were to fall, the mass of all these huge structures added together is only that of a proton. Just like the one-dimensional string from last time, they won't have any effect on our world. People just have to get used to the strange sight."

But this time, the science consul was wrong.

People noticed the eyes moved faster than the other solids filling the sky, and they were gathering into one spot. Soon, two eyes met and merged into one bigger eye. More and more eyes joined this big eye, and its volume grew. Finally, all the eyes melded into one. It was so large that it seemed to represent the gaze of the universe upon Trisolaris. The iris was clear and bright, and at the center was the image of

a sun. Over the broad surface of the eyeball, various colors cascaded in a flood. Soon, the details over the giant eye faded and gradually disappeared, until it became a pupil-less blind eye. Then it began to deform until it finally lost the shape of an eye and became a perfect circle. When the circle began to slowly rotate, people realized that it was not flat, but parabolic, like a slice cut from a giant sphere.

As the military consul stared at the slowly spinning colossal object in space, he suddenly understood and shouted, "Princeps and others, please go into the underground bunker right away." He pointed upward. "That is—"

"A parabolic mirror," the princeps said calmly. "Direct the space defense forces to destroy it. We will stay right here."

The parabolic mirror focused the sun's beams onto the surface of Trisolaris. Initially, the spot of light was very large, and the heat at the focal point wasn't yet lethal. This spot moved across the ground, searching for its target. The mirror discovered the capital, the largest city of Trisolaris, and the light spot began to move toward it. Soon, the beam was over the city.

Those standing under the Pendulum Monument only saw a great brightness in space. It overwhelmed everything else, accompanied by a wave of extreme heat. Then the light spot over the capital shrank as the parabolic mirror began to focus the light more tightly. The brightness from space grew stronger until no one could lift up his head, and those standing within the spot felt the temperature rise rapidly. Just as the heat became unbearable, the edge of the light spot swept past the Pendulum Monument and everything dimmed. It took a while before the crowd's sight readjusted to normal light.

When they looked up, the first sight that greeted them was a pillar of light between the sky and earth, shaped like an inverted cone. The mirror in space formed the base of the

400

cone, and the tip stabbed into the heart of the capital, turning everything there incandescent at once. Waves of smoke began to rise. Tornadoes caused by the uneven heat of the light cone formed several other pillars made of dust that connected to the sky, twisting and dancing around the light cone. . . .

Several brilliant fireballs appeared in different parts of the mirror, their blue color distinct from the light reflected from the mirror. These were the exploding nuclear warheads launched by the Trisolaran space defense corps. Because the explosions were happening outside the atmosphere, there was no sound. By the time the fireballs disappeared, several large holes appeared in the mirror, and then the entire surface of the mirror began to tear and crack, until it had broken into more than a dozen pieces.

The deadly light cone disappeared and the world returned to a normal level of illumination. For a moment, the sky was as dim as a moonlit night. Those broken pieces of the mirror, now devoid of intelligence, continued to deform and soon could not be distinguished from the other geometric solids in space.

"What will happen with the next experiment?" The princeps's expression was derisive as he spoke to the science consul. "Will you unfold a proton into four dimensions?"

"Princeps, even if that were to occur, it's nothing to worry about. A proton unfolded into four dimensions will be much smaller. If the space defense corps is prepared to attack its projection in three-dimensional space, it can be destroyed just the same."

"You're deceiving the princeps!" said a furious military consul. "You have not mentioned the real danger. What if the proton is unfolded into zero dimensions?"

"Zero dimensions?" The princeps was interested. "Wouldn't that be a point with no size?"

"Yes, a singularity! Even a proton would be infinitely big compared to it. The entire mass of the proton will be contained in this singularity, and its density will be infinite. Princeps, I'm sure you can imagine what that would be."

"A black hole?"

"Yes."

"Princeps, let me explain," the science consul broke in. "The reason we picked a proton instead of a neutron to unfold into two dimensions is precisely to avoid this kind of risk. If we really were to unfold into zero dimensions, the charge of a proton would also be carried over into the unfolded black hole. We can then capture and control it using electromagnetism."

"What if you can't find it or control it?" the military consul asked. "It can then land on the ground, suck in everything it encounters, and increase its mass. Then it will sink into the core of this planet and eventually suck down all of Trisolaris."

"That will never happen. I guarantee it! Why are you always making things difficult for me? Like I said, this is a scientific experiment—"

"That's enough!" the princeps said. "What is the probability of success next time?"

"Almost one hundred percent! Princeps, please believe in me. Through these two failures, we have already mastered the principles governing unfolding subatomic structures into low-dimensional macro space."

"All right. To ensure the survival of Trisolaran civilization, we must take this risk."

"Thank you!"

"But if you fail again, you and all the scientists working on Project Sophon will be guilty."

"Yes, of course, all guilty." If Trisolarans could perspire, the science consul must have been soaked in cold sweat.

It was much easier to clean up the three-dimensional remnants of the unfolded proton in synchronous orbit than it was to clean up the one-dimensional string. Small spaceships were able to drag the pieces of proton matter away from Trisolaris and prevent them from entering the atmosphere. Those objects, some as large as mountains, had almost no mass. They were like immense silver illusions; even a baby could have moved them easily.

Afterwards, the princeps asked the science consul, "Did we destroy a civilization in the microcosmos in this experiment?"

"It was at least an intelligent body. Also, Princeps, we destroyed the entire microcosmos. That miniature universe is immense in higher dimensions, and it probably contained more than one intelligence or civilization that never had a chance to express themselves in macro space. Of course, in higher dimensional space at such micro scales, the form that intelligence or civilization may take is beyond our imagination. They're something else entirely. And such destruction has probably occurred many times before."

"Oh?"

"In the long history of scientific progress, how many protons have been smashed apart in accelerators by physicists? How many neutrons and electrons? Probably no fewer than a hundred million. Every collision was probably the end of the civilizations and intelligences in a microcosmos. In fact, even in nature, the destruction of universes must be happening at every second—for example, through the decay of neutrons. Also, a high-energy cosmic ray entering the atmosphere may destroy thousands of such miniature universes. . . . You're not feeling sentimental because of this, are you?"

"You amuse me. I will immediately notify the propaganda consul and direct him to repeatedly publicize this scientific fact to the world. The people of Trisolaris must understand that the destruction of civilizations is a common occurrence that happens every second of every hour."

"Why? Do you wish to encourage the people to face the possible destruction of Trisolaran civilization with equanimity?"

"No. It's to encourage them to face the destruction of Earth civilization with equanimity. You know very well that after we publicized our policy toward the Earth civilization, there was a wave of extremely dangerous pacifism. We have only now discovered that there are many like the listener of Post 1379. We must control and eliminate these weak sentiments."

"Princeps, this is mainly the result of recent messages received from the Earth. Your prediction has come true: The alienated forces on Earth really are growing. They have built a new transmission site completely under their control, and have begun to send us large amounts of information about Earth civilization. I must admit that their civilization has great appeal on Trisolaris. For our people, it sounds like sacred music from Heaven. The humanism of Earth will lead many Trisolarans onto the wrong path. Just as Trisolaran civilization has already become a religion on Earth, Earth civilization has this potential on Trisolaris."

"You've pointed out a great danger. We must strictly control the flow of information from the Earth to the populace, especially cultural information."

The third attempt to unfold a proton into two dimensions began thirty Trisolaran hours later. This time, it was at night. From the ground, it was impossible to see the ring of the

accelerator in space. Only the red glow from the heat sinks of the fusion reactors around it marked its location. Shortly after the accelerator was started, the science consul announced success.

People gazed up at the night sky. Initially, there was nothing to see. But soon, they saw a miraculous sight: The heavens separated into two pieces. Between the two, the pattern of the stars did not match, as though two photographs of the sky had been stacked together, with the smaller one overlaid on top of the big one. The Milky Way broke at the border between the two. The smaller portion of the star-studded firmament was circular, and it rapidly expanded against the normal night sky.

"That constellation in there belongs to the southern hemisphere!" the culture and education consul said, pointing at the expanding, circular patch of the sky.

As people exercised their imaginations to understand how stars that could be seen only from the other side of the planet were now superimposed over the northern hemisphere's view, an even more astonishing sight appeared: At the edge of the expanding patch of the night sky from the southern hemisphere, a part of a giant globe appeared. The globe was brownish, and it was being revealed a stripe at a time, as though on a display with a very slow refresh rate. Everyone recognized the globe: On it were the clear outlines of familiar continents. By the time the entire globe came into view, it already occupied one-third of the sky. More details on the globe could be made out: the wrinkles of mountain ranges covering the brownish continents, the scattered cloud cover like patches of snow over the continents . . .

Someone finally blurted out, "That's our planet!"

Yes, another Trisolaris had appeared in the sky.

Next, the sky brightened. Next to the second Trisolaris in space, the expanding circle of the night sky from the southern hemisphere revealed another sun. This was clearly the same sun that currently was shining over the southern hemisphere, but it appeared at only half the size.

Finally, someone figured it out. "It's a mirror."

The immense mirror that appeared over Trisolaris was the proton being unfolded, a geometric plane without any meaningful depth.

By the time the unfolding was complete, the entire sky had been replaced by the reflection of the night sky of the southern hemisphere. Directly overhead, the sky was dominated by the reflection of Trisolaris and the sun. And then the sky began to deform just above the horizon all around, and the reflections of the stars stretched and twisted as though they were melting. The deformation began at the edges of the mirror, but climbed up toward the center.

"Princeps, the proton plane is being bent by our planet's gravity," the science consul said. He pointed to the numerous spots of light in the starry sky. They looked as though people were waving flashlights up at the domed vault. "Those are electromagnetic beams being sent up from the ground to adjust the curvature of the plane under gravity. The goal is to eventually wrap the unfolded proton completely around Trisolaris. Afterwards, the electromagnetic beams will continue to hold up and stabilize this enormous sphere, like so many spokes. Thus, Trisolaris will be the workbench to secure the two-dimensional proton, and the work to etch electronic circuits on the surface of the proton plane can begin."

The process of wrapping the two-dimensional proton plane around Trisolaris took a long time. By the time the deformation of the reflection reached the image of Trisolaris

at the plane's zenith, the stars had all disappeared because the proton plane, now curved around the other side of the planet, blocked them completely. Some sunlight continued to leak inside the curved proton plane, and the image of Trisolaris in this fun-house mirror in space was distorted beyond recognition. But, finally, after the last ray of sunlight was blocked, everything sank into the darkest night in the history of Trisolaris. As gravity and the electromagnetic beams balanced each other, the proton plane formed a gigantic shell in synchronous orbit around Trisolaris.

Bitter cold followed. The completely reflective proton plane deflected all sunlight back into space. The temperature on Trisolaris dropped precipitously, reaching levels comparable to the appearance of three flying stars, which had ruined many cycles of civilization in the past. Most of the population of Trisolaris dehydrated and were stored. A deathly silence fell over much of the darkness-enclosed surface. In the sky, only the faint light spots from the beams that held up the proton membrane flickered. Occasionally, a few other tiny, sharp lights could be seen in synchronous orbit: the spaceships etching circuits into the gigantic membrane.

The principles governing micro-scale integrated circuits were completely different from those of conventional circuits, as the base material wasn't made of atoms, but matter from a single proton. The "p-n junctions" of the circuits were formed by twisting the strong nuclear forces locally on the surface of the proton plane, and the conducting lines were made of mesons that could transmit the nuclear force. Because the surface area for the circuit was extremely large, the circuits were also very large. The circuit lines were as thick as hairs, and an observer close enough could see them with the naked eye. Flying close to the proton membrane,

it could be seen as a vast plane made of complex, elaborate integrated circuits. The total area covered by the circuits was dozens of times the area of the continents on Trisolaris.

Etching the proton circuits was a huge engineering feat, and thousands of spaceships worked for more than fifteen thousand Trisolaran hours to complete it. The software debugging process took another five thousand Trisolaran hours. But finally, it was time to test the sophon for the first time.

The big screen at the sophon control center deep underground showed the progress of the long self-test sequence. Next came the loading of the operating system. Finally, the blank blue screen showed a line of large-font text: *Micro-Intelligence 2.10 loaded. Sophon One ready to accept commands.*

The science consul said, "A sophon has been born. We have endowed a proton with wisdom. This is the smallest artificial intelligence that we can make."

"But right now, it appears as the largest artificial intelligence," said the princeps.

"As soon as we increase the dimensionality of this proton, it will become very small."

The science consul entered a query at the terminal:

> Sophon One, are the spatial dimensionality controls operational?

Affirmative. Sophon One is capable of initiating spatial dimensionality adjustments at any moment.

> Adjust dimensionality to three.

After this command was issued, the two-dimensional proton membrane that had wrapped itself around Trisolaris began to shrink rapidly, as though a giant's hand was pulling away

a curtain over the world. In a moment, sunlight bathed the ground. The proton folded from two dimensions into three and became a gargantuan sphere in synchronous orbit, about the size of the giant moon. The sophon was over the dark side of the planet, but the sunlight reflected from its mirror surface turned the night into day. The surface of Trisolaris was still extremely cold, so the crowd inside the control center could only observe these changes through a screen.

> Dimensionality adjustment successful. Sophon One is
> ready to accept commands.
> > Adjust dimensionality to four.

In space, the gargantuan sphere shrank until it eventually looked to be the size of a flying star. Night again descended over this side of the planet.

"Princeps, the sphere we see now is not the complete sophon. It's only the projection of the sophon's body into three-dimensional space. It is, in fact, a giant in four-space, and our world is like a thin, three-dimensional sheet of paper. The giant stands on this sheet of paper, and we can only see the trace where its feet touch the paper."

> Dimensionality adjustment successful. Sophon One is
> ready to accept commands.
> > Adjust dimensionality to six.

The sphere in the sky disappeared.

"How big is a six-dimensional proton?" the princeps asked.

"About fifty centimeters in radius," the science consul replied.

 Dimensionality adjustment successful. Sophon One is
 ready to accept commands.
 > Sophon One, can you see us?
 Yes. I can see the control center, everyone inside, and
 the organs inside everyone, even the organs inside
 your organs.

"What is it saying?" The princeps was stunned.

"A sophon observing three-space from six-space is akin
to us looking at a picture on a two-dimensional plane. Of
course it can see inside us."

 > Sophon One, enter the control center.

"Can it go through the ground?" the princeps asked.

"It's not exactly going 'through.' Rather, it's entering from
a higher dimension. It can enter any enclosed space within
our world. This is again similar to the relationship between
us, existing in three-space, and a two-dimensional plane. We
can easily enter any circle drawn on the plane by coming in
from above. But no two-dimensional creature on the plane
can do such a thing without breaking the circle."

Just as the science consul finished, a mirror-surfaced
sphere appeared in the middle of the control center, float-
ing in air. The princeps walked over and gazed at his own
distorted reflection. "This is a proton?" He was amazed.

"This is the six-dimensional body of the proton projected
into three-space."

The princeps extended a hand. When he saw that the sci-
ence consul did not object, he touched the surface of the
sophon. A very light touch pushed the sophon a considerable
distance.

"It's very smooth. Even though it has only the mass of a proton, I could feel some resistance against my hand." The princeps was puzzled.

"That's due to air resistance against the surface of the sphere."

"Can you increase its dimensionality to eleven, and make it as small as a regular proton?"

As soon as the princeps said this, the science consul shouted to the sophon, his voice tinged with fear, "Attention! This is *not* a command!"

Sophon One understands.

"Princeps, if we increased the dimensionality to eleven, we would lose it forever. When the sophon shrinks to the size of a regular subatomic particle, the internal sensors and I/O ports will be smaller than the wavelength of any electromagnetic radiation. That means it would not be able to sense the macro world, and would not be able to receive our commands."

"But we must eventually make it shrink back to a subatomic particle."

"Yes, but that must await the completion of Sophon Two, Sophon Three, and Sophon Four. Multiple sophons may be able to form a system to sense the macro world through quantum effects. For example, suppose a nucleus has two protons. The two of them will interact and follow certain patterns of motion. Take spin: Maybe the direction of spin of the two protons must be opposite from each other. When these two protons are taken out of the nucleus, no matter how far apart they are, this pattern will remain in effect. When both protons are made into sophons, they will, based on this effect, create a mutual-sensing system. More sophons can then form

411

a mutual-sensing formation. This formation's scale can be adjusted to any size, and can thus receive electromagnetic waves to sense the macro world at any frequency. Of course, the actual quantum effects necessary to create such a sophon formation are very complicated. My explanation is only an analogy."

The unfolding of the next three protons into two dimensions succeeded on the first try. The construction of each sophon also took only half as long as Sophon One. After the construction of Sophon Two, Sophon Three, and Sophon Four, the quantum sensing formation was also created successfully.

The princeps and all the consuls once again came to the Pendulum Monument. Above them hovered four sophons shrunk to six-space. In the crystalline mirrored surface of each was an image of the rising sun, recalling the three-dimensional eyes that had once appeared in space.

> Sophon formation, adjust dimensionality to eleven.

After the command was issued, the four mirrored spheres disappeared. The science consul said, "Princeps, now Sophon One and Sophon Two will be launched toward the Earth. Using the large knowledge base stored in the micro circuits, the sophons understand the nature of space. They can draw energy from the vacuum and become high-energy particles in a moment, and navigate through space at nearly the speed of light. This might appear to violate the law of conservation of energy, but in fact the sophons are only 'borrowing' energy from the structure of vacuum. However, the time for returning such energy is far in the future, when the proton decays.

By then, the end of the universe will not be far.

"After the two sophons arrive on Earth, their first mission is to locate the high-energy particle accelerators used by humans for physics research and hide within them. At the level of science development on the Earth, the basic method for exploring the deep structure of matter is to use accelerated high-energy particles to collide with target particles. After the target particles have been smashed, they analyze the results to try to find information reflecting the deep structure of matter. In actual experiments, they use the substance containing the target particles as the bull's-eye for the accelerated bullets.

"But the inside of the substance being struck is almost all vacuum. Suppose an atom is the size of a theater; the nucleus is like a walnut hovering in the center of the theater. Thus, successful collisions are very rare. Often large quantities of high-energy particles must be directed against the target substance for a sustained period of time before a collision occurs. This kind of experiment is akin to looking for a raindrop of a slightly different color in a summer thunderstorm.

"This gives the sophons an opening. A sophon can take the place of a target particle and accept the collision. Because they're highly intelligent, they can precisely determine through the quantum sensing formation the paths that the accelerated particles will follow within a very short period of time and move to the appropriate location. Thus, the likelihood that a sophon will be struck will be billions of times greater than the actual target particle. After a sophon is struck, it can deliberately give out wrong and chaotic results. Thus, even if the actual target particle is occasionally struck, Earth physicists will not be able to tell the correct result from the numerous erroneous results."

"Wouldn't this destroy the sophon as well?" asked the military consul.

"No. When a sophon is smashed into several pieces, several new sophons are born. And they continue to have secure quantum entanglements between them, just like how, if you break a magnet in half, you would get two magnets. Even though each partial sophon's capabilities will be much lower than the original, whole sophon, under the direction of the self-healing software, the pieces will move together and reassemble into the original sophon. This process only requires a microsecond and will occur after the collision in the accelerator, and after the pieces of the sophon have left the wrong results in the bubble chamber or on sensitive film."

Someone asked, "Would it be possible for Earth scientists to find a way to detect sophons and then use a strong magnetic field to imprison them? Protons have positive charge."

"That's impossible. To detect sophons requires humans to make breakthroughs in the study of the deep structure of matter. But their high-energy accelerators will all have been turned into heaps of junk. How can they make progress in such research? The hunter's eyes have already been blinded by the prey he intends to catch."

"Humans may still resort to a brute-force method," the industry consul said. "They can build a large number of accelerators, faster than the rate at which we can build sophons. Then, at least some accelerators on Earth will not be infiltrated by sophons and can yield the correct results."

"This is one of the most interesting aspects of Project Sophon!" The science consul was visibly excited by the question. "Mister Industry Consul, do not worry that creating large numbers of sophons will cause the collapse of the Trisolaran economy. We will not need to resort to that. We might build a

414

few more, but not too many. Indeed, just these two are more than enough, because each sophon is capable of multitasking."

"Multitasking?"

"This is a bit of jargon related to ancient serial computers. Back then, a computer's central processing unit could only carry out a single instruction at a time. But, because it was so fast, and aided by interrupt scheduling, from our low-speed perspective, the computer was carrying out multiple programs at the same time. As you know, the sophons move at close to the speed of light. The surface of the Earth is a tiny space for sophons. If sophons patrol around the accelerators on Earth at this speed, then, from the perspective of humans, it is as if they simultaneously exist in all the accelerators and can almost simultaneously create erroneous results in all the accelerators.

"By our calculations, each sophon is capable of controlling more than ten thousand high-energy accelerators. It takes about four to five years for humans to build each of these accelerators, and it seems unlikely that they can be mass produced based on their economy and available resources. Of course, they can increase the distance between the accelerators, for example, by building accelerators on the different planets in their planetary system. That would indeed destroy the multitasking operation of the sophons. But in the time it would take to do that, it would not be difficult for Trisolaris to build ten or more sophons.

"More and more sophons will wander in that planetary system. Added all together, they still won't add up to the mass of even one-billionth of a bacterium. But they will cause the physicists on Earth to never be able to glimpse the secrets hidden deep in the structure of matter. Humans will never be able to access the micro dimensions, and the ability

for them to manipulate matter will be limited to below five dimensions. From now on, whether it's four point five million hours or four hundred and fifty trillion hours, Earth civilization's technology will never achieve this fundamental breakthrough. They will remain forever in the primitive stage. The science of Earth has been completely locked down, and the lock is so secure that humans will never be able to escape from it by their own strength."

"That's wonderful! Please forgive my lack of respect for Project Sophon in the past." The military consul's tone was sincere.

"In fact, there are currently only three accelerators with sufficient power to produce results that can lead to possible breakthroughs. After Sophon One and Sophon Two arrive on Earth, they will have a lot of extra capacity. In order to fully utilize the sophons, we will assign them other tasks in addition to interfering with the three accelerators. For example, they will be the main means to carry out the Miracle Plan."

"Sophons can create miracles?"

"For humans, yes. Everyone knows that high-energy particles can expose film. This is one of the ways that primitive accelerators on Earth once showed individual particles. When a sophon passes through the film at high energy, it leaves behind a tiny exposed spot. If a sophon passes back and forth through the film many times, it can connect the dots to form letters or numbers or even pictures, like embroidery. The process is very fast, and far quicker than the speed at which humans expose film when taking a picture. Also, the human retina is similar to the Trisolaran one. Thus, a high-energy sophon can also use the same technique to show letters, numbers, or images on their retina. . . . And if these little miracles can confuse and terrify humans, then the next *great* miracle will be sufficient to frighten their scientists—no

better than bugs—to death: Sophons can cause background cosmic radiation to flash in their eyes."

"This would be very frightening for our scientists as well. How would this be accomplished?"

"Very simple. We have already written the software to allow a sophon to unfold itself into two dimensions. After the unfolding is complete, the huge plane can wrap itself around the Earth. This software can also adjust the membrane so that it's transparent, but the degree of transparency can be tuned in the frequencies of the cosmic microwave background. . . . Of course, as sophons fold and unfold into different dimensions, they can display even more amazing 'miracles.' The software for accomplishing these is still being developed, but these 'miracles' will create a mood sufficient to divert human scientific thought onto the wrong path. This way, we can use the Miracle Plan to effectively restrain scientific endeavors outside of physics on Earth."

"One last question: Why not send all four of the completed sophons to Earth?"

"Quantum entanglement can work at a distance. Even if four sophons were placed at opposite ends of the universe, they could still sense each other instantaneously, and the quantum formation between them would still exist. Keeping Sophon Three and Sophon Four here will enable them to receive the information sent back by Sophon One and Sophon Two instantaneously. This gives us a way to monitor the Earth in real time. Also, the sophon formation allows Trisolaris to communicate in real time with the alienated forces within Earth civilization."

Unnoticed, the sun that had just risen disappeared below the horizon and turned into a sunset. Another Chaotic Era had arrived on Trisolaris.

While Ye Wenjie was reading the messages from Trisolaris, the Battle Command Center was hosting another important meeting to perform further analysis of the captured data. Before the meeting, General Chang said, "Comrades, please be aware that our meeting is probably already being monitored by sophons. From now on, there will be no more secrets."

When he said this, the surroundings were still familiar. The shadows of summer trees swayed against the drawn curtains, but in the eyes of the attendees, the world was no longer the same. They felt the gaze of omnipresent eyes. Under these eyes, there was nowhere to hide in the world. This feeling would follow them all their lives, and their descendants would not be able to escape it. It would take many, many years before humans finally made the mental adjustment to this situation.

Three seconds after General Chang finished his remark, Trisolaris communicated with humanity outside the ETO for the first time. After this, they terminated all communications with the Adventists. For the remainder of the lives of all attendees, Trisolaris never sent another message.

Everyone in the Battle Command Center saw the message in their eyes, just like Wang Miao's countdown. The message flashed into existence for only two seconds and then disappeared, but everyone got it. It was only a single sentence:

You're bugs!

34

BUGS

By the time Shi Qiang entered the door of Ding Yi's home, Wang Miao and Ding Yi were already very drunk.

The two were excited to see Shi Qiang. Wang stood up and hugged the newcomer's shoulders. "Ah, Da Shi, Officer Shi . . ."

Ding, who couldn't even stand straight, found a glass and put it on the pool table. He poured some liquor into it, and said, "Your out-of-the-box thinking was not helpful. Whether we look at those messages or not, the result four hundred years from now will be the same."

Da Shi sat down in front of the pool table, glancing at the two with a crafty gaze. "Is it really like you say? Everything's over?"

"Of course. It's all over," Ding said.

"You can't use the accelerators and can't study the structure of matter. That means it's all over?" Da Shi asked.

"Um . . . what do you think?"

"Technology is still making progress. Academician Wang and his people just created the nanomaterial—"

"Imagine an ancient kingdom, if you will. Their technology is advancing. They can invent better swords, knives, spears, et cetera. Maybe they can even invent

419

auto-repeating crossbows that can shoot many arrows like a machine gun—"

Da Shi nodded, understanding. "But if they don't know that matter is made from molecules and atoms, they will never create missiles and satellites. They're limited by their level of science."

Ding patted Da Shi on the shoulder. "I always knew that our Officer Shi was smart. It's just that you—"

Wang took over. "The study of the deep structure of matter is the foundation of the foundations of all other sciences. If there's no progress here, everything else—I'll put it your way—is bullshit."

Ding pointed at Wang. "Academician Wang will be busy for the rest of his life, and continue to improve our swords and knives and spears. What the fuck am *I* going to do? Who the hell knows?" He threw an empty bottle onto the table and picked up a billiard ball to smash it.

"This is a good thing!" Wang lifted his glass. "We will be able to live out the rest of our lives one way or another. After this, decadence and depravity can be justified! We're bugs! Bugs that are about to go extinct! Haha . . ."

"Exactly!" Ding also lifted his glass. "They think so little of us that they don't even bother to disguise their plans for us, telling the Adventists everything. It's like how you don't need to hide the bottle of bug spray from the little critters. Let's toast the bugs! I never thought the end of the world would feel so good. Long live bugs! Long live sophons! Long live the end of the world!"

Da Shi shook his head and drained the glass. He shook his head again. "Bunch of pussies."

"What do you want?" Ding stared at Da Shi drunkenly. "You think you can cheer us up?"

Da Shi stood up. "Let's go."

"Where?"

"To find something to cheer you up."

"Whatever, buddy. Sit back down. Drink."

Da Shi took the two by their arms and dragged them up. "Let's go. Bring the liquor if you have to."

Downstairs, the three got into Da Shi's car. As the car started, Wang asked in slurred speech where they were going. Da Shi said, "My hometown. Not too far."

The car left the city and sped west along the Beijing-Shijiazhuang Highway. It exited the highway as soon as they were inside Hebei Province. Da Shi stopped the car and dragged his two passengers out.

As soon as Ding and Wang got out of the car, the bright afternoon sun made them squint. The wheat fields of the North China Plain spread out before them.

"What did you bring us here for?" Wang asked.

"To look at bugs." Da Shi lit one of the cigars Colonel Stanton had given him and pointed at the wheat fields with it.

Wang and Ding now noticed that the fields were covered by a layer of locusts. Every wheat stalk had a few crawling over it. On the ground, more locusts wriggled, like some thick liquid.

"They're plagued by locusts here?" Wang brushed away some locusts from a small area near the edge of the field and sat down.

"Like the dust storms, they started ten years ago. But this year is the worst."

"So what? Nothing matters now, Da Shi." Ding spoke, his voice still drunk.

"I just want to ask the two of you one question: Is the

technological gap between humans and Trisolarans greater than the one between locusts and humans?"

The question hit the two scientists like a bucket of cold water. As they stared at the clumps of locusts before them, their expressions grew solemn. They got Shi Qiang's point.

Look at them, the bugs. Humans have used everything in their power to extinguish them: every kind of poison, aerial sprays, introducing and cultivating their natural predators, searching for and destroying their eggs, using genetic modification to sterilize them, burning with fire, drowning with water. Every family has bug spray, every desk has a flyswatter under it . . . this long war has been going on for the entire history of human civilization. But the outcome is still in doubt. The bugs have not been eliminated. They still proudly live between the heavens and the earth, and their numbers have not diminished from the time before the appearance of the humans.

The Trisolarans who deemed the humans bugs seemed to have forgotten one fact: The bugs have never been truly defeated.

A small black cloud covered the sun and cast a moving shadow against the ground. This was not a common cloud, but a swarm of locusts that had just arrived. As the swarm landed in the fields nearby, the three men stood in the middle of a living shower, feeling the dignity of life on Earth. Ding Yi and Wang Miao poured the two bottles of wine they had with them on the ground beneath their feet, a toast for the bugs.

"Da Shi, thank you." Wang held out his hand.

"I thank you as well." Ding gripped Da Shi's other hand.

"Let's get back," Wang said. "There's so much to do."

35

THE RUINS

No one believed that Ye Wenjie could climb Radar Peak by herself, but she did it anyway. She didn't allow anyone to help her along the way, only resting a couple of times in the abandoned sentry posts. She consumed her own vitality, the vitality that could not be renewed, without pity.

After learning the truth of Trisolaran civilization, Ye had become silent. She rarely spoke, but did make one request: She wanted to visit the ruins of Red Coast Base.

When the group of visitors ascended Radar Peak, its tip had just emerged from the cloud cover. After walking a whole day in the foggy haze, seeing the bright sun in the west and the clear blue sky was like climbing into a new world. From the top of the peak, the clouds appeared as a silver-white sea, and the rise and fall of the waves seemed like abstractions of the Greater Khingan Mountains below.

The ruins that the visitors had imagined did not exist. The base had been dismantled thoroughly, and only a patch of tall grass was left at the top. The foundations and the roads were buried below, and the whole place appeared to be a desolate wilderness. Red Coast seemed to have never happened.

But Ye soon discovered something. She walked next to a tall rock and pulled away the vines covering it, revealing

the mottled, rusty surface below. Only now did the visitors understand that the rock was actually a large metallic base.

"This was the base for the antenna," Ye said. The first cry from Earth heard by an extraterrestrial world was sent from the antenna that had been here to the sun, and then, amplified, broadcast to the whole universe.

They discovered a small stone tablet next to the base, almost completely lost in the grass.

Site of Red Coast Base (1968–1987)
Chinese Academy of Sciences 1989.03.21

The tablet was so tiny. It didn't seem so much a memorial as an attempt to forget.

Ye walked to the lip of the cliff. Here, she had once ended the lives of two soldiers with her own hands. She did not look over the sea of clouds as the others were doing, but focused her gaze in one direction. Below the clouds, there was a small village called Qijiatun.

Ye's heart beat with effort, like a string on some musical instrument about to break. Black fog appeared before her eyes. She used the last bit of her strength to stay upright. Before everything sank into darkness, she wanted to see sunset at Red Coast Base one more time.

Over the western horizon, the sun that was slowly sinking into the sea of clouds seemed to melt. The ruddy sun dissolved into the clouds and spread over the sky, illuminating a large patch in magnificent, bloody red.

"My sunset," Ye whispered. "And sunset for humanity."

AUTHOR'S POSTSCRIPT

A night from my childhood remains crisply etched in my memory: I was standing by a pond before a village somewhere in Luoshan County, Henan Province, where generations of my ancestors had lived. Next to me stood many other people, both adults and children. Together, we gazed up at the clear night sky, where a tiny star slowly glided across the dark firmament.

It was the first artificial satellite China had ever launched: *Dongfanghong I ("The East is Red I")*. The date was April 25, 1970, and I was seven.

It had been thirteen years since *Sputnik* had been launched into space, and nine years since the first cosmonaut had left the Earth. Just a week earlier, *Apollo 13* had safely returned from a perilous journey to the moon.

But I didn't know any of that. As I gazed at that tiny, gliding star, my heart was filled with indescribable curiosity and yearning. And etched in my memory just as deeply as these feelings was the sensation of hunger. At that time, the region around my village was extremely poor. Hunger was the constant companion of every child. I was relatively fortunate because I had shoes on my feet. Most of the friends standing by my side were barefoot, and some of the tiny feet still had unhealed frostbite from the previous winter. Behind

me, faint light from kerosene lamps shone out of cracks in the walls of dilapidated thatched huts—the village wasn't wired for electricity until the eighties.

The adults standing nearby said that the satellite wasn't like an airplane because it flew outside of the Earth. Back then the dust and smoke of industry hadn't yet polluted the air, and the starry sky was especially clear, with the Milky Way clearly visible. In my mind, the stars that filled the heavens weren't much farther away than the tiny, gliding satellite, and so I thought it was flying among them. I even worried that it might collide with one as it passed through the dense stellar clusters.

My parents weren't with me because they were working at a coal mine more than a thousand kilometers away, in Shanxi Province. A few years earlier, when I had been even younger, the mine had been a combat zone for the factional civil wars of the Cultural Revolution. I remembered gunshots in the middle of the night, trucks passing in the street, filled with men clutching guns and wearing red armbands. . . . But I had been too young back then, and I can't be sure whether these images are real memories, or mirages constructed later. However, I know one thing for certain: Because the mine was too unsafe and my parents had been impacted by the Cultural Revolution, they had had no choice but to send me to my ancestral home village in Henan. By the time I saw *Dongfanghong I,* I had already lived there for more than three years.

A few more years passed before I understood the distance between that satellite and the stars. Back then I was reading a popular set of basic science books called *A Hundred Thousand Whys*. From the astronomy volume, I learned the concept of a light-year. Before then, I had already known

that light could traverse a distance equal to seven and a half trips around the Earth in a single second, but I had not contemplated what kind of terrifying distance could be crossed by flying at such a speed for a whole year. I imagined a ray of light passing through the cold silence of space at the speed of 300,000 kilometers per second. I struggled to grasp the bone-chilling vastness and profundity with my imagination, felt the weight of an immense terror and awe, and simultaneously enjoyed a druglike euphoria.

From that moment, I realized that I had a special talent: Scales and existences that far exceeded the bounds of human sensory perception—both macro and micro—and that seemed to be only abstract numbers to others, could take on concrete forms in my mind. I could touch them and feel them, much like others could touch and feel trees and rocks. Even today, when references to the 15-billion-light-year radius of the universe and "strings" many orders of magnitude smaller than quarks have numbed most people, the concepts of a light-year or a nanometer can still produce lively, grand pictures in my mind and arouse in me an ineffable, religious feeling of awe and shock. Compared to most of the population who do not experience such sensations, I don't know if I'm lucky or unlucky. But it is certain that such feelings made me first into a science fiction fan, and later a science fiction author.

In that same year when I was first awed by the concept of a light-year, a flood (known as the Great Flood of August '75) occurred near my home village. In a single day, a record-breaking 100.5 centimeters of rain fell in the Zhumadian region of Henan. Fifty-eight dams of various sizes collapsed, one after another, and 240,000 people died in the resulting deluge. Shortly after the floodwaters had receded, I returned

to the village and saw a landscape filled with refugees. I thought I was looking at the end of the world.

And so, satellite, hunger, stars, kerosene lamps, the Milky Way, the Cultural Revolution's factional civil wars, a light-year, the flood . . . these seemingly unconnected things melded together and formed the early part of my life, and also molded the science fiction I write today.

As a science fiction writer who began as a fan, I do not use my fiction as a disguised way to criticize the reality of the present. I feel that the greatest appeal of science fiction is the creation of numerous imaginary worlds outside of reality. I've always felt that the greatest and most beautiful stories in the history of humanity were not sung by wandering bards or written by playwrights and novelists, but told by science. The stories of science are far more magnificent, grand, involved, profound, thrilling, strange, terrifying, mysterious, and even emotional, compared to the stories told by literature. Only, these wonderful stories are locked in cold equations that most do not know how to read.

The creation myths of the various peoples and religions of the world pale when compared to the glory of the big bang. The three-billion-year history of life's evolution from self-reproducing molecules to civilization contains twists and romances that cannot be matched by any myth or epic. There is also the poetic vision of space and time in relativity, the weird subatomic world of quantum mechanics . . . these wondrous stories of science all possess an irresistible attraction. Through the medium of science fiction, I seek only to create my own worlds using the power of imagination, and to make known the poetry of Nature in those worlds, to tell the romantic legends that have unfolded between Man and Universe.

But I cannot escape and leave behind reality, just like I cannot leave behind my shadow. Reality brands each of us with its indelible mark. Every era puts invisible shackles on those who have lived through it, and I can only dance in my chains. In science fiction, humanity is often described as a collective. In this book, a man named "humanity" confronts a disaster, and everything he demonstrates in the face of existence and annihilation undoubtedly has sources in the reality that I experienced. The wonder of science fiction is that it can, when given certain hypothetical world settings, turn what in our reality is evil and dark into what is righteous and bright, and vice versa. This book and its two sequels try to do just that, but no matter how reality is twisted by imagination, it ultimately remains there.

I've always felt that extraterrestrial intelligence will be the greatest source of uncertainty for humanity's future. Other great shifts, such as climate change and ecological disasters, have a certain progression and built-in adjustment periods, but contact between humankind and aliens can occur at any time. Perhaps in ten thousand years, the starry sky that humankind gazes upon will remain empty and silent, but perhaps tomorrow we'll wake up and find an alien spaceship the size of the moon parked in orbit. The appearance of extraterrestrial intelligence will force humanity to confront an Other. Before then, humanity as a whole will never have had an external counterpart. The appearance of this Other, or mere knowledge of its existence, will impact our civilization in unpredictable ways.

There's a strange contradiction revealed by the naïveté and kindness demonstrated by humanity when faced with the universe: On Earth, humankind can step onto another continent, and without a thought, destroy the kindred

civilizations found there through warfare and disease. But when they gaze up at the stars, they turn sentimental and believe that if extraterrestrial intelligences exist, they must be civilizations bound by universal, noble, moral constraints, as if cherishing and loving different forms of life are parts of a self-evident universal code of conduct.

I think it should be precisely the opposite: Let's turn the kindness we show toward the stars to members of the human race on Earth and build up the trust and understanding between the different peoples and civilizations that make up humanity. But for the universe outside the solar system, we should be ever vigilant, and be ready to attribute the worst of intentions to any Others that might exist in space. For a fragile civilization like ours, this is without a doubt the most responsible path.

As a fan of science fiction, it has molded my life, and a considerable part of the science fiction I've read comes from the West. The fact that Western readers can now enjoy my book makes me both pleased and excited. Science fiction is a literature that belongs to all humankind. It portrays events of interest to all of humanity, and thus science fiction should be the literary genre most accessible to readers of different nations. Science fiction often describes a day when humanity will form a harmonious whole, and I believe the arrival of such a day need not wait for the appearance of extraterrestrials.

I express my heartfelt thanks to Ken Liu, the translator of this and the third volume, and to Joel Martinsen, the translator of the second volume. Their diligence and care created the English edition. I am grateful to China Educational

Publications Import & Export Corporation Ltd. (CEPIEC), *Science Fiction World* Publishing, Tor Books and Head of Zeus, whose trust and faith have made this publication possible.

Liu Cixin (刘慈欣),
December 28, 2012

TRANSLATOR'S POSTSCRIPT

When I was asked to translate *The Three-Body Problem*, I was incredibly honored, but also full of trepidation: Translating another writer's work is a heavy responsibility. It's almost like being asked to care for someone's child.

The act of translation involves breaking down one piece of work in one language and ferrying the pieces across a gulf to reconstitute them into a new work in another language. When the gulf separating the two is as wide as the Pacific Ocean that separates China from America, the task can be daunting.

The obvious difficulties, such as differences in linguistic structure and cultural references, are actually relatively easy to resolve. *The Three-Body Problem* begins with the Cultural Revolution, and there are numerous allusions to Chinese history. I've tried to keep the number of explanatory footnotes to a bare minimum by, wherever possible, filling in the necessary knowledge for non-Chinese readers by the judicious addition of a few informational phrases in the text (all approved by the author).

But there are more subtle issues involving literary devices and narrative techniques. The Chinese literary tradition shaped and was shaped by its readers, giving rise to different emphases and preferences in fiction compared to what American readers expect. In some cases, I tried to adjust the narrative techniques to ones that American readers are more

familiar with. In other cases, I've left them alone, believing that it's better to retain the flavor of the original.

I've also tried, wherever possible, to avoid shading Western interpretations into those passages dealing with Chinese history and politics.

Overly literal translations, far from being faithful, actually distort meaning by obscuring sense. But translations can also pay so little attention to the integrity of the source that almost nothing of the original's flavor or voice survives. Neither of these approaches is a responsible fulfillment of the translator's duty. In a sense, translating may be harder than writing original fiction because a translator must strive to satisfy the same aesthetic demands while being subjected to much more restrictive creative constraints.

In translating, my goal is to act as a faithful interpreter, preserving as much of the original's nuances of meaning as possible without embellishment or omission. Yet a translator must also balance fidelity to the source, aptness of expression, and beauty of style. The best translations into English do not, in fact, read as if they were originally written in English. The English words are arranged in such a way that the reader sees a glimpse of another culture's patterns of thinking, hears an echo of another language's rhythms and cadences, and feels a tremor of another people's gestures and movements.

I may not have succeeded, but these were the standards I had in mind as I set about my task.

In moving from one language, culture, and reading community to another language, culture, and reading community, some aspects of the original are inevitably lost. But if the translation is done well, some things are also gained— not the least of which is a bridge between the two readerships. I hope my fellow American readers enjoy this novel.

I am indebted to the following individuals, who gave me invaluable feedback on various drafts of this translation: Eric Abrahamsen, Anatoly Belilovsky, Aliette de Bodard, David Brin, Eric Choi, John Chu, Elías F. Combarro, Hui Geng, Michael Kwan, Derwin Mak, Joel Martinsen, Erica Naone, Alex Saltman, Alex Shvartsman, Marie Staver, Igor Teper, Bingen Yang, Bingwei Yang, and E. Lily Yu. I lack words to sufficiently express my gratitude for their help in making this translation better, and I wish every translator had such wonderful beta readers.

Others also deserve thanks. Joe Monti, my former agent (and current editor of my original fiction), dispensed much useful advice. Liz Gorinsky, my editor at Tor Books, helped me improve the translation in a thousand ways large and small, and I can't imagine a better editorial experience than working with her. My wife, Lisa, provided the support and encouragement to keep me going on many late nights. More than anyone else, she made this possible.

Finally, I thank Liu Cixin, who entrusted me with his work and, in this process, became my friend.

Ken Liu,
June 20, 2014

THE DARK FOREST

CIXIN 刘慈欣 LIU

TRANSLATED BY JOEL MARTINSEN

PROLOGUE

The brown ant had already forgotten its home. To the twilight Earth and the stars that were just coming out, the span of time may have been negligible, but, for the ant, it was eons. In days now forgotten, its world had been overturned. Soil had taken flight, leaving a broad and deep chasm, and then soil had come crashing down to fill it back in. At one end of the disturbed earth stood a lone black formation. Such things happened frequently throughout this vast domain, the soil flying away and returning, chasms opening up and being filled, and rock formations appearing like visible markers of each catastrophic change. Under the setting sun, the ant and hundreds of its brethren had carried off the surviving queen to establish a new empire. Its return visit was only a chance passing while searching for food.

The ant arrived at the foot of the formation, sensing its indomitable presence with its feelers. Noting that the surface was hard and slippery, yet still climbable, up it went, with no purpose in mind but the random turbulence of its simple neural network. Turbulence was everywhere, within every blade of grass, every drop of dew on a leaf, every cloud in the sky, and every star beyond. The turbulence was purposeless, but in huge quantities of purposeless turbulence, purpose took shape.

The ant sensed vibrations in the ground and knew from how they intensified that another giant presence was

approaching from somewhere on the ground. Paying it no mind, the ant continued its climb up the formation. At the right angle where the foot of the formation met the ground, there was a spider web. This, the ant knew. It carefully detoured around the sticky hanging strands, passing by the spider lying in wait, its legs extended to feel for vibrations in the threads. Each knew of the other's presence but—as it had been for eons—there was no communication.

The vibrations crescendoed and then stopped. The giant being had reached the formation. It was far taller than the ant and blotted out most of the sky. The ant was not unfamiliar with beings of this sort. It knew that they were alive, that they frequently appeared in this region, and that their appearances were closely related to the swiftly disappearing chasms and multiplying formations.

The ant continued its climb, knowing that the beings were not a threat, with a few exceptions. Down below, the spider encountered one such exception when the being, which had evidently noticed its web reaching between the formation and the ground, whisked away the spider and web with the stems of a bundle of flowers it held in one limb, causing them to land broken in a pile of weeds. Then the being gently placed the flowers in front of the formation.

Then another vibration, weak but intensifying, told the ant that a second living being of the same sort was moving toward the formation. At the same time, the ant encountered a long trough, a depression in the surface of the formation with a rougher texture and different color: off-white. It followed the trough, for its roughness made for a far easier climb. At each end was a short, thinner trough: a horizontal base from which the main trough rose, and an upper trough that extended at an angle. By the time the ant climbed back out

onto the slick black surface, it had gained an overall impression of the shape of the troughs: "1."

Then the height of the being in front of formation was cut in half, so it was roughly even with the formation. Evidently it had dropped to its knees, revealing a patch of dim blue sky where the stars had begun to come out behind it. The being's eyes gazed at the top of the formation, causing the ant to hesitate momentarily while deciding whether it ought to intrude into his line of sight. Instead, it changed direction and started crawling parallel with the ground, quickly reaching another trough and lingering in its rough depression as it savored the pleasant sensation of the crawl. The color was reminiscent of the eggs that surrounded its queen. With no hesitation, the ant followed the trough downward, and after a while, the layout become more complicated, a curve extended beneath a complete circle. It reminded the ant of the process of searching out scent information and eventually stumbling across the way home. A pattern was established in its neural network: "9."

Then the being kneeling before the formation made a sound, a series of sounds that far exceeded the ant's capacity to comprehend: "It's a wonder to be alive. If you don't understand that, how can you search for anything deeper?"

The being made a sound like a gust of wind blowing across the grass—a sigh—and then stood up.

The ant continued to crawl parallel to the ground and entered a third trough, one that was nearly vertical until it turned, like this: "7." The ant didn't like this shape. A sharp, sudden turn usually meant danger or battle.

The first being's voice had obscured the vibrations, so it was only now that the ant realized that the second being had reached the formation. Shorter and frailer, the second

being had white hair that stood out against the dark blue background of the sky, bobbing silver in the wind, connected somehow to the increasing number of stars.

The first being stood up to welcome her. "Dr. Ye, is it?"

"You're . . . Xiao Luo?"[1]

"Luo Ji. I went to high school with Yang Dong. Why are you . . . here?"

"It's a nice place, and easy to get to by bus. Lately, I've been coming here to take walks fairly often."

"My condolences, Dr. Ye."

"That's all in the past. . . ."

Down on the formation, the ant wanted to turn toward the sky, but then discovered another trough ahead of it, identical to the "9"-shaped trough it had crawled through before the "7." So it continued horizontally through the "9," which it found better than both the "7" and the "1." although it could not say exactly why. Its aesthetic sense was primitive and single-celled. The indistinct pleasure it had felt upon crawling through the "9" intensified. A primitive, single-celled state of happiness. These two spiritual monocells, aesthetics and pleasure had never evolved. They had been the same a billion years ago, and would be the same a billion years hence.

"Xiao Luo, Dong Dong often spoke of you. She said you're in . . . astronomy?"

"I used to be. I teach college sociology now. At your school, actually, although you had already retired when I got there."

"Sociology? That's a pretty big leap."

"Yeah. Yang Dong always said my mind wasn't focused."

"She wasn't kidding when she said you're smart."

[1] *Translator's Note: Xiǎo* is a diminutive meaning "little" or "young" and is used before a surname when addressing children or to show affection.

"Just clever. Nothing like your daughter's level. I just felt astronomy was an undrillable chunk of iron. Sociology is a plank of wood, and there's bound to be someplace thin enough to punch through. It's easier to get by."

In the hope of reaching another "9," the ant continued its horizontal advance, but the next thing it encountered was a perfectly straight horizontal like the first trough, except longer than the "1" and turned on its side. And no smaller troughs at the ends. A "–" shape.

"You shouldn't put it like that. It's a normal person's life. Not everyone can be Dong Dong."

"I really don't have that kind of ambition. I drift."

"I've got a suggestion. Why don't you study cosmic sociology?"

"Cosmic sociology?"

"A name chosen at random. Suppose a vast number of civilizations are distributed throughout the universe, on the order of the number of detectable stars. Lots and lots of them. Those civilizations make up the body of a cosmic society. Cosmic sociology is the study of the nature of this supersociety."

The ant had not crawled very much farther along the formation. It had hoped, after crawling out of the "–" depression, to find a pleasurable "9," but instead it encountered a "2," with a comfortable initial curve but a sharp turn at the end that was as fearsome as that of the "7." The premonition of an uncertain future. The ant continued onward to the next trough, a closed shape: "0." The path seemed like part of a "9," but it was a trap. Life needed smoothness, but it also needed direction. One could not always be returning to the point of origin. This, the ant understood. Although there were still two more troughs up ahead, it had lost interest. It turned

vertically again.

"But . . . ours is the only civilization we know of right now."

"Which is why no one's done it before. The opportunity is left to you."

"Fascinating, Dr. Ye. Please go on."

"My thinking is that this can link your two disciplines together. The mathematical structure of cosmic sociology is far clearer than that of human sociology."

"Why do you say that?"

Ye Wenjie pointed at the sky. Twilight still illuminated the west, and they could still count the stars that had come out, making it easy to remember how the firmament had looked a few moments ago: a vast expanse and a blue void, or a face without pupils, like a marble statue. Now, though the stars were few in number, the giant eyes had pupils. The void was filled. The universe had sight. The stars were tiny, just single twinkling points of silver that hinted at some unease on the part of its creator. The cosmic sculptor had felt compelled to dot pupils onto the universe, yet had a tremendous terror of granting it sight. This balance of fear and desire resulted in the tininess of the stars against the hugeness of space, a declaration of caution above all.